The Crystal Variation

**Baen Books
by
Sharon Lee &
Steve Miller**

❀ ❀

The Liaden Universe®
Fledgling
Saltation
Mouse and Dragon
Ghost Ship (forthcoming)
The Dragon Variation (omnibus)
The Agent Gambit (omnibus)
Koval's Game (omnibus)
The Crystal Variation (omnibus)

The Fey Duology
Duainfey
Longeye

by Sharon Lee
Carousel Tides

The Crystal Variation

◉ ◉ ◉

Sharon Lee
& Steve Miller

THE CRYSTAL VARIATION

This is a work of fiction. All the characters and events portrayed
in this book are fictional, and any resemblance to real people or incidents
is purely coincidental.

A Baen Book

Baen Publishing Enterprises
P.O. Box 1403
Riverdale, NY 10471
www.baen.com

ISBN: 978-1-4391-3463-4

Cover art by Alan Pollack

First Baen printing, September 2011

Distributed by Simon & Schuster
1230 Avenue of the Americas
New York, NY 10020

Library of Congress Cataloging-in-Publication Data

Lee, Sharon, 1952-
  The crystal variation / by Sharon Lee & Steve Miller.
      p. cm.
  ISBN 978-1-4391-3463-4 (omni trade pbk.)
  1. Liaden Universe (Imaginary place)--Fiction. 2. Assassins--Fiction. I.
Miller, Steve, 1950 July 31- II. Title.
  PS3562.E3629C83 2011
  813'.54--dc22

                              2011023181

Printed in the United States of America

10 9 8 7 6 5 4 3 2 1

CONTENTS

CONTENTS

The Crystal Variation

INTRODUCTION:

The Crystal Variation

IF THIS IS YOUR FIRST VENTURE into the Liaden Universe®
you've arrived at an interesting start, for in terms of story they
actually describe action, characters, and adventure that made the
rest of the story—now more than a dozen books—possible within
the story universes.

Universes? Well, yes, because (as a few braves souls have
noticed) our Liaden series actually takes place in two different
universes, one a closed universe and one an expanding universe
(like the one we live in) and part of *that story* underlies and informs
all three of the novels included within this book.

We should point out that while we try to use a modicum of
science and theory in our work, this set in particular revolves
around some esoteric theories for which hardly anyone has the
math, least of all us, and instead of making these hard science
extravaganzas we went with what's worked for us all along: action,
adventure, and space opera with a touch of romance and the ongoing
mysteries of life with and around a particular tree.

Crystal Soldier is the story of a man holding onto his humanity—
what there is of it—through continuing in the face of overwhelming

1

odds. He's a soldier, after all, and he's been trained to accept that at some point in his life he will 1) face such odds and 2) be expected to prevail. Exceptional at what he does, as the war engulfing a universe goes on, Jela is pressed into duty which brings him in contact with others perhaps less human than he is. Learning to trust—and doubt—is essential. This is a wide open space opera universe where some take unfair advantage of mental abilities and where each side is constantly striving to find the right variation to play in a nip-and-tuck game which is getting deadlier and more intense as time goes on.

Crystal Dragon begins in a near-mystical space, a space where creatures once like you or the authors have transcended mere physicality, if not the rest of mankind's tender weaknesses like emotions. Then it returns to the surviving characters met in *Crystal Soldier*, where the war proceeds, the enemy slowly moving on the work of crystallizing entire systems, returning them to the underlying matrix of energy. We wanted to work with characters in that kind of space because of the challenge of description on that boundary land. It was an interesting project and we hope you think so too.

Balance of Trade won the Hal Clement Award for best Young Adult Science Fiction in 2005, an award we treasure greatly, having known and admired Hal (Harry C. Stubbs) as a fan and as a pro over several decades. In this coming of age space opera, a young apprentice trader finds his future determined by the crowded condition of the ship he grew up on—and his mother, as Captain, is among the most willing to see him gone. Challenged to accept the assignment or find his own new berth, Jethri Gobelyn does so in an entirely unpredictable way, leaving behind the small Terran family ship life he'd known to join a Liaden ship's crew. Set at a time when the prior war is nearly forgotten or wildly misremembered, *Balance* gave us the opportunity to work with some younger, less accomplished characters and follow them as they grew, which we—and obviously the Clement Award judges—found good.

SO WHAT'S NEW, if the omnibus series is your first immersion in Lee & Miller and you've finished those? *Fledgling*, *Saltation*, and the forthcoming *Ghost Ship*. The Liaden novel *Mouse and Dragon* is also available from Baen, and it fits into a strategic spot, feeding into and drawing from the mini arc encompassing *Local Custom*, *Scout's Progress* and *Mouse and Dragon*; some will suggest that *Ghost Ship* only be read after *Mouse and Dragon*.

WE'D LIKE TO THANK BAEN BOOKS for producing this omnibus—*The Crystal Variation*—as well as the others in the series: *The Dragon Variation*, *The Agent Gambit*, and *Korval's Game*— which together represent much of the long work we did within the universes we first discovered in *Agent of Change*.

If this is your first encounter with a Liaden Universe® book— welcome. We hope you'll find this a start to a lot of good reading. If you're an old friend, stopping by for a revisit—we're very glad to see you.

Thank you.

Sharon Lee and Steve Miller
Waterville Maine
September 2010

CRYSTAL DUOLOGY
CAST OF CHARACTERS

Soldiers

Bicra, Corporal
Contado, Chief Pilot
Harrib, Commandant
Kinto, Corporal
Loriton, Commander
M. Jela Granthor's Guard, Generalist
Muran, Pilot
Ragil
Ro Gayda, Commander
Tetran, Junior Pilot
Thilrok, Corporal
Vondahl, Under Sergeant

Batchers

Arin	**Chebei**	**Dulsey**
Fenek	**Karmin**	**Ocho**
Seatay	**Uno**	

Dark Traders

Rint dea'Sord
Efron
Qualee
Cantra yos'Phelium Clan Torvin
Garen yos'Phelium Clan Torvin

✤ Ships ✤

Spiral Dance, a.k.a. Dancer
Pretty Parcil

✤ Others ✤

Danby   *Liad dea'Syl*
Ilan   *Keon*
Malis, Instructor   *Pliny*
Timoli

✤ Planets ✤

Ardega   *Borgen*   *Chelbayne*
Daelmere   *Faldaiza*   *Gimlins*
Horetide   *Kizimi*   *Landomist*
Phairlind   *Scohecan*   *Solcintra*
Taliofi

✤ Cosmography ✤

Bubble, The
Deeps, a.k.a. the Beyond, also Outspace or Out-and-Away
Far Edge
In-Rim
Inside
Out-Rim
Outer Edge
Rim, The
Shallows, The
Spiral Arm, a.k.a. the Arm
Tearin Sector

CRYSTAL SOLDIER

Book One of the
Great Migration Duology
A Liaden Universe® Novel

Dedicated to Butterflies-are-Free Peace Sincere

PART ONE: SOLDIER

ONE

❀ ❀

On the ground, Star 475A
Mission time: 3.5 planet days and counting

JELA CROUCHED in the dubious shade of a boulder at the top of the rise he'd been climbing for half a day. Taller rock columns on either side glared light down at him, but at least helped keep the persistent drying wind and flying grit from his lips and face.

At the forward side of the boulder, down a considerably steeper slope than the one he'd just climbed, should be the river valley he'd been aiming to intersect ever since he'd piloted his damaged vessel to the desolate surface four days before.

Overhead and behind him the sky was going from day-blue to dusk-purple while—on that forward side of the boulder—the local sun was still a few degrees above the horizon, bright over what once had been a ragged coastline.

In theory he should be watching his back; in theory at least one of his guns should be in his hand. Instead, he used both hands to adjust his cap, and then to slip the sand-lenses off. He used them as a mirror, briefly, and confirmed that his face was not yet in danger of blistering from the sun's radiation or the wind's caress.

Sighing, he replaced the lenses, and craned his head a bit to study the mica-flecked sandstone he sheltered against, and the scarring of centuries of unnatural winds and weather. The purpling sky remained clear, as it had been all day, and all the previous days—no clouds, no birds, no contrails, no aircraft, no threats save the featureless brilliance of the star; no friends, no enemy spiraling in for the kill, no sounds but the whisper of the dry, pitiless, planetary breeze.

So certain was he that he was in no danger that the rescue transponder in his pocket was broadcasting on three frequencies . . .

He sighed again. Without an enemy—or a friend—it would take a long time to die in the arid breeze.

Friends. Well, there was hope of friends, or comrades at least, for he'd drawn off the attacking enemy with a reflexive head-on counterattack that should not have worked—unless the attacking ship was actually crewed rather than autonomous. He'd fired, the enemy had fired, his mother ship had fired . . . and amid the brawl and the brangle his light-duty vessel had been holed multiple times, not with beams, but with fast moving debris.

Both the enemy and the *Trident* had taken high-speed runs to the transition points, leaving Jela to nurse his wounded craft into orbit and then spiral down to the surface and attempt a landing, dutifully watching for the enemy he was certain was well fled.

There was no enemy *here*, no enemy other than a planet and a system succumbing to the same malaise that had overtaken a hundred other systems and a hundred dozen planets in this sector alone. *Sheriekas!*

Sheriekas. They'd been human once, at least as human as he was—and even if his genes had been selected and cultivated and arranged, he was arguably as human as anyone who didn't bear a Batch tattoo on both arms—but they'd willfully broken away, continuing with their destructive experiments and their . . . *constructs* . . . while they offered up a grand promise of a future they had no intention of sharing.

They'd named themselves after their own dead planet, which they'd destroyed early on in their quest for transformation—for superiority. In their way, they were brilliant: Conquering disease after disease, adjusting body-types to planets, increasing life-spans. They'd been driven to achieve perfection, he supposed, having once known a dancer who had destroyed herself in the same quest, though she hadn't had the means to take entire star systems with her.

And the *sheriekas*—they achieved what his dancer had not. To hear them tell it, they were the evolved human; the perfected species. Along the way, they'd created other beings to accomplish their will and their whims. And then they'd turned their altered understanding back along the way they had come, looked on the imperfect species from which they had shaped themselves—and decided to give evolution a hand.

So they had returned from wherever it was they had gone, sowing world-eaters, robot armor, and destruction as they came. . . .

It had been a big war—the First Phase, they called it, fought well before his time—and the after-effects spread over generations. That those refusing the initial offer of *sheriekas* guidance had supposed they'd won the war rather than a battle meant . . . It meant that Jela was here, fighting a battle centuries later . . . and that there was no pretense from the enemy, now, of benevolent oversight.

Jela blinked against the glare, pulling his mind back from its ramble. There was a real danger, with your Generalist, of feeding them so much info they got lost in their own thoughts, and never came out again.

He couldn't afford that—not here. Not yet. He had time, he had duty. All he needed to do was get off this planet, back to a base and . . .

His timer shook silently against his wrist. Water.

He leaned into the warm boulder and dug into the left leg pouch, fingers counting over the sealed bulbs. Ten. That meant that there were still ten in the right leg pouch. He always drew first from the left, ever since the fight where he'd broken his right leg.

The leg ached in sympathy with the thought, as it sometimes did, and M. Jela Granthor's Guard, Generalist, finished his water, uncurled himself, stretched, and danced several fight moves to bring up his attention level. Feeling considerably refreshed—his was a resilient Strain—he moved around the boulder, heading down.

Behind him, his shadow was flung back across a day's walk or more as he strode across the ridge, but there was no one there to notice.

FROM ORBIT it had seemed clear that something . . . unusual . . . had been at work on the world, and that a good deal of time and energy had been spent in this, the last of the river valleys likely to have retained life under the onslaught of meteor-storms and radiation bursts. After concluding that his vessel would not in fact leave the surface in its current state, there'd been little left to do but sit and hope—or explore the structures on either side of the river. Being a Generalist—and an M—he'd naturally opted for exploration.

Moments after stepping around the boulder and moving on his way, he realized that, somehow, he was not exactly where he thought he should be. He was not overlooking the valley that led to the tip of the former river delta, but was instead on the rim of a side valley.

Curiosity drove him to check his position against the satellite sensors—and he sighed. Gone, or down to three and all but one on the wrong side of the planet at the moment. They hadn't had time to get the things into stationary orbits.

"Can't triangulate without a triangle . . ."

The breeze took his voice along with it and rewarded him a moment later with an echo.

He laughed mirthlessly. Well, at least *that* ranging system worked. It was, alas, a system he'd never learned to use, though he'd been told that on certain worlds the experts could say a song across a snowy mountain range and tell, from the echoes, distance as well as the safety of an ice pack.

Ice pack. Now there was a dangerous thought! Truth was that this world used to have an ice pack, but what it had now for all its trouble were two meteor-scarred polar regions and a star with so dangerously and preternaturally active a surface that it could be a candidate for a nova in a million years or so. His ship's geologist had speculated that in the height of planetary winter—five hundred or so local days hence, when the planet was nearly a third more distant from its star—there might be enough cold to accumulate a water snow to some significant depth—say as deep as his boots—on the northern plains and cap.

Checking the magnetic compass for north he saw a nervously twittering display as the field fluctuated, and he wondered if there'd be another round of ghostly electric coronas lighting the night sky.

As he walked across the rocky ridge, anger built. Within historical record—perhaps as recently as two thousand Common Years—this world has been a candidate for open air colonization. In the meantime? In the meantime, the *sheriekas* conceived and mounted a bombardment of the inner system, setting robots to work in the outer debris clouds and targeting both the star and this world.

Kill. Destroy. Make life, human, animal, any—already improbable enough—impossible . . .

The *sheriekas* did this wherever they could, as if life itself was anathema. Overt signs of *sheriekas* action were an indication that a planet or a system held something worthwhile . . .

And so here was Jela—perhaps the first human to set foot on the planet, perhaps the last—trying to understand what was *here* that so needed destroying, what was *here* that the *sheriekas* hated enough to focus their considerable destructive energies upon.

It wasn't useful to be angry at the enemy when the enemy wasn't to hand. He sighed, called to mind the breathing exercises and exercised, dutifully. Eventually, he was rewarded with calm, and his pace smoothed out of the inefficient angry stride to a proper soldier's ground-eating lope.

Suddenly, he walked in near darkness, then out again as the defile he'd entered widened. In time of snow or rain this would have been a dangerous place. It was as convenient a walkway as any, now that the plants were killed off or gone subsurface, now that the animals, if there had been any, were long extinct.

After some time he found himself more in the dark than otherwise, saw the start of a flickering glow in the sky to the north, and stopped his march to take stock. Underfoot was windblown silt. Soft enough to sleep on.

He ran through his ration list mentally, pulled out a night-pack, selected his water, and camped on the spot. Overhead the sky flickered green fire until well after he went to sleep.

THE FOOTING had become treacherous and Jela half-regretted his decision to travel with light-pack. The dangle-cord he carried was barely three times his height and it might have been easier to get through the more canyon-like terrain with the long rope. On the other hand, he was moving faster than he would have with the full pack, and he'd have had no more rations anyway . . .

Now that he was below the ridges rather than walking them, he found the grit and breeze not quite so bad, though the occasional eddy of wind might still scour his face with its burden. Too, not being constantly in the direct rays of the local star helped, though that might be a problem again as it approached mid-day. For the moment, though, he was making time, and was in pretty good shape.

Rations now. Rations were becoming an issue. It was true that his rations were designed to let him work longer on less, and it was equally true that *he'd* been designed—or at least gene-selected—to get by on less food than most people ate, and to be more efficient in his use of water. Unfortunately, it was also true that he did require *some* food, *some* water, *some* sleep, and *some* shelter—or he, like most people in similarly deprived circumstances, would die.

Bad design, that dying bit, he thought—but no, that was what the *sheriekas* had thought to conquer—and perhaps had conquered. No one seemed to know that for sure. Meanwhile, he—Generalist Jela—had been designed with human care, and he approved of much of the design. He could see and hear better than average, for instance, his reaction times were fast and refined—and he was far stronger for his size than almost anyone.

It was this last bit of design work that had gotten his leg broken, despite it, too, being stronger than average. He just couldn't hold the weight of six large men on it at once. He'd gone over that fight in his mind many times, and with several fighting instructors. He'd done everything right—just sometimes, no matter what, you were going to lose.

He was rambling again. Deliberately, he brought his attention back to the job at hand. The next moment or two would bring him to the mouth of the canyon and into the valley proper; soon he should have sight of the structures he'd spotted on his recon runs.

The possibility that they were flood control devices had been suggested by the ship's geologists, as well as the idea that they were "cabinets" for some kind of energy generating stations that needed to be able to survive both flood and ice. Dams—for water conservation? Even the idea that they were the remains of housing had been suggested . . .

His stomach grumbled, protesting the lack of wake-up rations. He figured he'd be hungry for awhile. No reason to break that next pack open quite yet.

He slogged on, cap shading his eyes, watching for the first sign of the—

There! There was one!

It was silted in, of course, and beyond it another—but the form of it, the details of it, the stubs—

He ran—a hundred paces or so it was to the nearest—put his hand on it—

Laughed then, and shook his head.

And laughed some more, because he didn't want to cry. . .

TWO

❋ ❋

On the ground, Star 475A
Mission time: 9 planet days and counting

THE TREES had been magnificent. Their crowns must have reached above the canyon rim in spots, and together they may have shaded the valley below from the direct light of the local star. An entire ecosystem had no doubt depended upon them. No wonder the ship's geologists had thought them constructs from orbit . . .

What remained was still impressive. The base diameter of the downed trunk he touched was easily six or seven times his own height and he hesitated to guess how long a board might have been sawn from its length.

The shadow caught his attention then as light began filling the area in earnest.

It was time to move downstream. If there was water left at all, it would most likely be at the ancient headwaters—too far by days for him to reach—or downstream. Downstream, he might make in time for it to matter.

HE WALKED, because he'd chosen to explore, and explore he would. At night, he stopped when his augmented vision blurred, camping where he stood. He went to short rations, cut them in half, and in half again, stinting on water as much as he dared. So far, the rescue transponder had guided no one to his position—friend or foe.

So, he walked, and he strove to be alert, spending part of the time analyzing his surroundings, part watching the sky, and part in an on-going argument with himself—an argument he was losing.

"Not going to do it, I bet. They can't make me!"

"Will, can."

"Won't, can't."

The argument concerned the growing fashion among the newer troops of putting their ID markers on their face. Fashion was something he didn't deal with all that much, and besides, he felt that a commander should be making these kinds of decisions, not a troop. And yet, he had to own it was convenient to be able to tell at a glance which unit, rank, and specialty defined a particular soldier.

"Shouldn't!"

He'd said this loudly—definitively—just before Tree Number Sixty-four, and it was while using the base of that tree as shade—and checking the angle of its fall—that the position locator in his pocket chuckled briefly.

He grabbed the unit, watching the power-light—but there, that was silly. Unless things improved pretty soon the unit's power would outlast him by quite some number of years. After all, it had been three days—four?—since he'd last had heard that sound . . .

Live now, the sensor showed him to be somewhat closer to the pre-marked goal than he had expected; the map roughed in by the original orbital photos showed that he'd managed to miss an early valley entrance—likely by refusing to walk quite as boldly as he might have into the teeth of the gritty breeze—and had thus saved himself a half-day or more of trudging down a much longer hillside.

The big question was becoming "saved" for what? There were no signs of life that was still alive; nor of water. The trees—

Maybe the trees *were* worth the walk, after all. There was a theory growing in his head—that he'd come in part looking for great works, and he'd found great works. In the days he'd been walking with the trees he'd found evidence of purpose far beyond the probability of happy accident.

For one thing, in places—not random places but specific kinds of places—the trees had fallen across the ancient watercourse, high ground to high ground, just where there was no marching forward to the ocean on that bank. They seemed to have preferred the left bank—which was generally wider, when it existed at all—and they sometimes seemed to have rested from their march and made a small grove, while at other times they'd hurried, stringing a long line of solitary trees.

Too, they were getting smaller. It saddened him, but the later trees . . . sigh.

Sloppy thinking. He didn't have dated evidence. For all he factually knew, the first tree he had encountered was the youngest, not the eldest. And yet he persisted in believing that the trees had marched from the high ground down to the sea, and with purpose. And what other purpose could they have but to live—and by continuing to live fight the purpose of the *sheriekas*?

"As long as there is life in the Spiral Arm, especially intelligent, organized life, the *sheriekas* will not easily reach their goal!" The memory-voice rang in his ears, for the moment obscuring the sound of the wind.

That had been . . . who had it been, after all?

Song-woman.

Right.

Jela closed his eyes, saw the small troop of them standing on a hilltop like so many ancient savages, singing, singing, singing.

He'd been part of a survey team then, too, his very first, and he'd laughed at their belief that they were fighting some space-borne invader by standing there singing, singing in the light and long into the night.

In the morning, there had been three fewer of the singers, and word eventually came down from the frontier that three *sheriekas* world-eaters had simply vanished from tracking—gone, poof!

The timer on his arm went off. He reached for a water bulb . . .

and stopped before his hand got close to the pocket. Not yet. He'd been waiting a little bit longer of late, and longer still if he could. There wasn't a whole lot of water left and he'd stopped counting. That he was in the valley helped, since the cutting wind—though noisier—was much less in evidence here among the fallen trees at river height.

But he'd been thinking about something . . .

Trees.

That was it. Like the singers, the trees had helped hold off the *sheriekas*, he was sure of it. But why then had the *sheriekas* not taken the planet and the star system, the trees being dead? Why did they skulk about the edge of the system, rather than occupying the place, or blowing up the star, as they had become so fond of doing the last decade or two?

The singer-woman and her ilk were every bit as needed as was his ilk, if they could sing or pray or startle the enemy to a standstill. The trees, too, if they were on their own inimical to the scourge. The trees. Why if the trees, without human help or human thought—had fought the *sheriekas* to a standstill he should have them—he should take a piece for cloning, plant them throughout the Arm and—

He sat, suddenly, not noticing that he landed on rock. There was something here to be thought on. If worse came to worse, which it rapidly was, he would need to write this down, or record it, so that the troop could see this new ally in its proper light.

Before writing or recording anything, he reached to the left leg pouch and took hold of the water container. Beneath, in the next down, was one more. And then, of course, there was his right leg, with its water . . .

He gently squeezed a drop or two onto his fingers first, carefully rubbing them together, then wiping his upper lip and clearing some of the grit away from his nose. Then he sipped.

As he sipped, he thought.

There had to be a connection between the trees, the pattern of their flight, and the attack from which the *sheriekas* had withdrawn. Almost, he had it, that idea of his. Almost.

Well. It would come.

One more sip for the moment. One more right now for the soldier.

He sighed so gently a lover sitting beside him might have missed it.

So he was a soldier. In various places, humans saw the fighting and withdrew, saw the fighting and played the warring parties against each other, fought as these trees had fought to draw every bit of water from the dying world, fought to hide and survive and perhaps outlast the madness of the battle.

In the end, the powers-that-were had permitted the experiments to resume. To fight augmented humans, one needed special humans. Not quite as adjusted and modified, perhaps, as the *sheriekas* or their manufactured allies, and perhaps lacking the power to sing away the death of worlds, but fighters who were more efficient, stronger, and often faster.

Did he survive this world and a dozen more he'd not live the life nor die the death of an ordinary citizen.

Retire? Quit?

"Not me!" His voice echoed weirdly against the grating of the wind. He sighed, louder this time, sealed the partial bulb and replaced it in its pocket. Then, he staggered—truly staggered—to his feet.

He centered himself, felt the energy rise—somewhat, somewhat—danced a step or two, did the stretch routine, settled.

Things to do. He had things to do. With or without his ID on his face, he was M. Jela Granthor's Guard, a Generalist in the fight to save life-as-it-was. Who could ask more?

He laughed and the valley gave his laugh back to him.

Heartened, he followed the march of the trees.

HE'D MANAGED TO WAKE, which he took for a good thing, and he managed to recall his name, which was something, too. Eventually, he bullied his way through a two-day old partial ration pack, knowing there weren't many more left at all, at all, not at all, and glanced at his location sensor.

The map there seemed clearer and his location more certain. There were still just three satellites working instead of the ideal seven, but they were working hard—and all on this side of the planet at the moment, by happy accident, building exactly the kind of database a Generalist would love to own.

The trees he'd been following for the last—however long it had been—now were downright skinny, as if they'd been striving for height at the expense of girth, but that was only six or eight times his own paltry height rather than a hundred times or two. Some of them were misshapen, short things, as if they'd tried to become bushes. He tried to use one as a bridge from the right bank back to the left, as he had done several times during his hike, and it broke beneath his boots, both frightening and surprising him since this was the first such bridge that had failed him.

He'd landed in the silted river channel, not too much worse for the fall, knowing he was at the delta he'd been aiming for since he first stepped out of his lander . . .

He climbed, slowly, onto the firmer soil of the bank, blinking his eyes against the scene.

Had he the water to spare, he would have cried then. He'd come through the last bend of what had been a mighty river; before him the channel led out into the dusty, gritty, speckled plain of what had been a vast and shallow salt sea. Here and there were great outcrops of boulders and cliffs, and when he turned around he could see the distant hills.

There were a few more trees ahead of him, lying neatly in a row as if each had fallen forward exactly as far as it could, and a new one had sprouted right there and—

There was nothing else.

Wind.

Rock.

Grit.

Three thousand two hundred and seventy-five of the trees then, since he'd started counting—maybe one or two more or less as he'd walked some nights until he could see nothing.

"Finish the job, soldier."

He was the only one to hear the order, so it must be his to carry out.

Dutifully, he walked those few steps more, to see it to completion. To honor the campaign, well-planned and well-fought, which had nonetheless ended in defeat.

After, he knew, he'd need to find a shaded spot down in the dead channel. Above it he'd build a cairn, set his transponders to full power and put them on top—and then he'd settle in with his last sip or two of water to wait. The hill wasn't all that bad to look at, and he'd be comforted by the presence of fallen comrades. It was a better death than most he had seen.

Reverently, Jela stepped over the last tree—like so many others, it had fallen across the river, across the channel. It was hardly thicker than his arm, and had scarcely reached the other side of what had been a skinny riverlet, where its meager crown lay in a tangle over a rock large enough to cast a shadow.

His boot brushed the tree, snagged in a small branch, and he fell forward, barely catching himself, the shock of the landing leaving a bright flash of sun against pale rock dancing in his head, and a green-tinged after-image inside his eyelids, strange counterpoint to the speckled brown and dun of the ex-seashore.

He closed his eyes tightly. Heard the sound of the wind, heard the rattling in the branches that still graced the dead trunk, felt the sun.

I could stay here, he thought, *just like this, sleep, perhaps not wake—*

He opened his eyes despite the thought, caught movement across the way, keeping time with the beat of the wind.

There at the root of the rock, just beyond the meager crown of the downed tree, was a spot of green. A leaf—and another.

Alive.

THREE

❀ ❀

On the ground, Star 475A
Mission time: 14 planet days and counting

DUTY WAS A STRANGE thing to think of in this moment, for he was giddy with a joy totally beyond reason, and he knew it. He felt as he had when he'd come back to the troop hall after serving seventeen days in detention for his single-handed fight against the squad from Recon. He came into the hall to absolute silence. No one spoke to him, no one said anything. He'd been so sure he'd be sent off—

And there on his bunk was his personal unit flag—wrapped around the shaft of it were green and blue ribbons of exactly the shade Recon preferred. When he had it in his hands and held it up and looked out at them, they cheered him.

And that's how he felt, looking across at the green life dancing in the wind—as if dozens stood about it, cheering.

And then, there was duty.

Though the tree was alive, and mostly green, some of the leaves were browning, and his first thought was to give it water.

Of course, he didn't have enough water to rescue it, really, just as he didn't have enough rations to rescue him. But he gave it water,

25

anyway—the last of the partial, and a fourth of a new bulb, the same as he drank himself.

Duty made him wonder if the tree was poisonous.

It was a scrawny thing, barely half his height, with a fine fuzzy bark about it. Perhaps he could suck on a few of the leaves.

There was something else, among those leaves, and he knew not if he should consider it fruit or nut. He knew not if he should eat it, for surely anything that could live in this environment was—

Was what? *He* was living in this environment, after all. For a time.

The fist-sized pod was high on the tree, its weight bending the slim branch on which it grew, and he saw the thing now as yet another soldier carrying out its duty. All of the trees he'd walked beside had marched down to the river and then down to the sea, each with the goal of moving forward, each after the other bearing the duty of taking that seed-pod, high up in the last tree this world was likely to see, as far forward as possible.

Duty it was that made the little tree grow that pod . . .

And duty told him that this tree was far more important than he was. It and its kin had preserved a world for centuries, as the report he'd carefully written and repeated into voice record told those who would follow.

At this point, even with the tree withering in spots, it would—like the satellite sensor he carried—outlast him. Duty dictated that he should help keep it alive, it being life and he being sworn, in essence, to help things live.

He sat down, finally, for standing was taking its toll on him, and leaned against the rock where he could touch the tree, lightly. He was tired, for all that it was not yet noon, but he had shade—green shade—and could use a rest.

If only his pick-up would come. He'd grab the tree up in a heartbeat, and take it away, for there was nothing to keep it here, or him. He'd take it someplace where water was certain. Someplace with good light and good food, and dancing girls. He was partial to dancers and to pilots—people who knew how to move, and when. They'd have a great time, him and the tree, and there'd be room for a dozen more trees—and why not?—dozens of dancers . . .

He fell asleep then, or passed out, and dreamed a dream of storms and floods and trees lying across swollen rivers and falling in the depths of snow, and of landers coming down from the sky, unable to rise again—and behind it all both a sense of urgency and a sense of possibility. He dreamed of his dozen dancers, too, recalling names and lust.

HE WOKE WITH THE SMELL of food in his nostrils, and a clear sense that he'd made a decision. He opened his eyes and saw the leaves rattling in the breeze.

He knew he'd die soon, but if he drank the last of his water and then—rather than going to shelter in a cave or a hole—arranged himself to die here, beside the tree, so he'd not be alone, it was likely that his fluids and remains would nourish the tree for some time, and that would be the best use of what duty he had left to him.

And then maybe, just maybe, that seed pod would sprout, and the soldier born of it might have the chance to be found and taken away, to continue the fight.

Food. The smell of fruit. He eaten the last partial rations—when? A day ago? A year? And the smell of the pod so close left him hungry,

Guiltily, he got to his feet and moved a few steps away from the tree.

No, he couldn't. It would have been one thing if he'd found the pod beside the tree, with no chance of it growing, no rainy season to hope for at this latitude any longer, no winter. But now, at best, what could it do? Give him another hour? Or kill him outright?

He was hoping that his eyes deceived him, for the leaves around the pod looked browner now than when he'd first spotted the tree. He didn't want it to be failing so quickly. He didn't want to see it go before he did.

The tree moved slightly, and the leaves rattled a bit in the breeze. There was *snap*, sudden and pure.

Aghast, Jela watched the leaves flutter away as the pod tumbled to the silty soil.

The pod sat there for a dozen of his accelerated heartbeats.

It seemed to shiver in the breeze, almost eagerly awaiting his touch, his mouth.

Jela pondered the sight, wondering how long such a pod might be fresh, considering how useless—and how senseless of duty—it would be to let it lie there unused and uneaten.

He moved carefully and bent to the pod, lifting it, cherishing it. Feeling the sections of rind eager and ready to peel away in his hand, he wondered if he had waited too long, and was even now hallucinating in the desert, about to eat a pebble found next to a dry, dead stick.

He sniffed the pod and found an aroma promising vitamins and minerals and, somehow, cool juicy refreshment.

He saluted the tree, and then, dragging from memory the various forms he'd learned, he bowed to it, long and low.

"I honor you for the gift freely given, my friend. If I leave this place, you will go with me, I swear, and I will deliver you into the hands of those who will see you as kin, as I see you."

Then his fingers massaged the pod, and it split into several moist kernels.

With the first taste, he knew he had done the right thing. With the second he recalled the joy of rushing water and spring snow, and the promise of dancers.

And then, considering the promise of dancers yet again, weighing the fragility of the inner kernels, Jela pushed aside the restraint which suggested he try to save one kernel out, just in case . . . and he devoured the entirety.

THE IN-BETWEEN PLACE—the plane of existence between sleep and consciousness—was a place Jela rarely visited. It generally took drugs or alcohol to get him there, and even achieving *there* he rarely stayed, as his optimized body sought either sleep or wakefulness, the latter more than the former.

His dreams, all too often, were also optimized: explicit problem solving, pattern recognizing, recapitulations of and improvements on things he'd actually done, or actually attempted to do.

So this was unusual, this feeling of being comfortably

ensconced below wakefulness. Odd in the security of it, though he had a right to be tired, having laid out an arrow of rocks—actually a double row and more of his tracks and a row of the whitest stones—pointing to the tree and his fox-den nearby.

Perhaps it was completion he felt; he'd done the best he could, all considered, and if he were now to fall into the fullest sleep and never wake it would not have been for lack of trying to do otherwise. Certainly, he was not one who might call to him ephemeral magics and gossamer wings to fly to the edge of space and command a comet to carry him, cocooned, to a place where others of the *sheriekas*-bred might find and thaw him . . .

That briefing came to him now, of how certain of the *others* created by the *sheriekas* as spies and weapons were able to move things so easily to their wills . . . That such were rare, and as erratically dispersed as the killer things was to the good . . .

But there, the doze was both deeper and lighter now, and he had truly not meant to sleep.

Not dream, he'd nearly said, all the while hearing the wind and its acts: the slight rustle of leaves near his head, the sound of gritty sand-bits rushing to fill an empty sea, perhaps an elegant thunderstorm distantly giving impetus to waves on a beach and wings that beat. Perhaps the distant tremble of air as some flying thing cavorted . . .

Now *here* there was comfort, for there had been flying things once, of many sizes, and if they'd fought amongst themselves at times, they'd done their work, too, moving seeds and pods about, taking away loose branches, warning of fires and off-season floods, sharing a measure of joy in the world until they were vanquished by some short-term calamity beyond the thought of trees.

What an interesting idea . . .

In his mind's eye, he soared with great wings above a world populated by trees and quiet creatures, above seas willing to carry rafts of the flood-swept for years, rafts where nests and young might travel in the shade of those still green, growing, and accomplishing. Very nearly he could feel the weight of such a pair, singing and calling, perched in his crown at sunrise, answering the call of others across the canyon, and those passing on rafted currents along the sometimes untrustworthy coastal cliffs . . .

No! He knew he had never had a crown of green, nor had creatures perching in it! His mind took that thought, rejected it as it might a bad element in a dream, came back to the sounds, things that he might measure, rather than ones that might keep him comfortably immobile.

The sounds he was hearing were old sounds, echoed off of canyon walls last week or last month or last year or . . . or when?

If he'd been half asleep moments before, now he was one quarter asleep. His muscles still lounged, and his eyes, but his ears recalled a distant mammalian heritage and would have twisted like those of a fox if they could . . . for there was something there, something that hadn't been there in the days of his walk, or the nearer days of his hibernation—something he was hearing as if through a template.

He agreed with himself somewhere deep in the near-sleep: a template. A template not of sight, but of sound and vibration. An old template that shuffled a million years of experience and separated the sounds and shifted other templates to form a nearest match.

Flying thing.

Not a fox's template though. Not usually heard through ear, but through branches.

Flying thing.

He willed his eyes open, did Jela, who found his name then, and his duty, but his lids remained closed, so he listened harder, for this was a template recently used, despite its age, and he must connect it to the sound in the root and branches and—

Then there was thunder enough to open his eyes, and his ears were his, and to his wakeful mind the pattern came: sonic boom.

He shed sleep entirely then, and glanced at the tree, which had been shading him as best it might.

"Flying things, my friend? And dragons?" He laughed, to hear his voice sounding remarkably like the dragons of the dream. "Dragons and now spaceships? What a fine delirium you bring!"

His eye caught the line of a single narrow contrail in the sky, floating with no obvious sign of an attached craft. It looked like they were heading away from him—to the place he'd touched down. Else they were headed in the other direction. Directly for him.

Sighing, Jela the soldier reached for his sun shades, tapped the knife on his belt for comfort, and drew the gun to be sure the barrel was not full of sand, nor the charge useless.

"Field of fire," he remarked to the tree, "favors both of us. If it isn't someone we know and they can read the signs, they'll have an idea where I am, so I'll be just a little bit someplace else. If they're bright, they'll expect it, but hey, I've got the rescue beacons on.

"You . . . I'm going to camouflage as best I can."

His handiwork, when admired from a distance, appeared to be another random pile of debris, though his tracks around it were hard to disguise entirely. He'd used his vest to sweep the more obvious tracks into smudges, and left the beacon on. He took one transceiver, leaving all the other powered items in the den, where they'd either not be noticed or, if detected, where they'd serve to convince anyone oncoming that he was sensibly in the shade.

He was not *exactly* sensibly in the shade, though he had some of it. That wouldn't be a problem for much longer today, in any case, since the sun would soon be on the horizon.

His choice was a gully where the meandering of the stream bed had made a short-lived branch; there, looking across at the tree, he laid out his pistol and his backup, and emptied his pockets of anything that might weigh him down if he needed to move fast.

He laughed mirthlessly, no doubt in his mind that he was running on adrenaline and hope, knowing too that his chance of moving with speed or stealth was pretty slim, this far into no rations.

It was then that he felt the ship, as if large welcome wings were overhead. There was a whine of the wind, and some slight hissing—remarkably like that of the CC-456s he'd known for decades.

It swept in low over the tiny campsite, its wings not all that large—indeed the ship itself was not all that large!—did a half-turn, displaying a single black digit on each of its stubby maneuvering wings, then another half-turn—incidentally bringing the nose cannon to bear on the campsite. Then it hissed itself quietly into the empty ocean, and was still for very nearly eight full seconds, at which point Corporal Kinto jumped out the open hatch, slipping on the shifting sand with an obscenity.

FOUR

❋ ❋

On the ground, Star 475A
Mission time: 14.5 planet days and counting

"THAT'S AN ORDER, Jela. Prepare to embark." Chief Pilot Contado's voice was getting quieter, which was not a good sign.

"We're not done here." Jela's voice also got quieter. He was standing on top of his den, half-facing the tree, what was left of his kit packed into his pockets.

Contado stood beside the tree, towering over it, his permanent grimace accentuated by his squinted eyes in the shadows of the low sun. He was pointedly ignoring Jela's inclusion of the tree in the "we" of his intent.

Around Jela were the remains of the hasty moist meal they'd given him, along with discarded med-packs—they'd hit him with doses of vitamins, inhalants of stim, sublinguals of anti-virals—and three empty water bulbs.

Sated in many ways, refreshed naturally and artificially, shaded by his rescuers' craft, Jela felt stronger than he had in days, and as stubborn as the trees he'd followed to the ocean of sand.

"I *will* take the tree with me," he said, very quietly indeed.

"On board, dammit! Our launch window . . ." This was said loudly—meaning Jela had made a gain . . .

"That launch window is an arbitrary time chosen by the pilot. You're working with guesses. There's nothing yet on the sensors . . ."

"Troop, this is not a biologicals run. I'm not . . ."

"Chief, this tree saved my life. It and its kin fought off the *sheriekas* for . . . who knows how long . . . for dozens of centuries! There's no other reason I can think of that this system was left alone for so long, and why it's got so much attention now. We can't simply leave it unprotected."

From inside the ship—off-com but still clearly audible—came Kinto's voice: "He wants to protect it, give him another gun and put him in charge. I told you it wasn't worth coming back for him . . ."

There was a brangle of voices from within the ship and then:

"Just moments to sundown, Chief. I've set a countdown, and Kinto's doing the pre-flights in case we need to boost directly to rendezvous."

This new voice on the comms was Junior Pilot Tetran; and Jela bet himself that in addition to the pre-flights, Kinto now owned either a bruise or a run of make-work when they got back to base—or both.

Chief Pilot Contado looked at the tree, and at Jela, and then at the ship and beyond, holding a hand above his eyes.

"Chief, as a bonus—I mean as recompense for being shot down while saving both the commander and the *Trident*, you can arrange it for me—" Jela murmured.

There was a gasp at that, that he should so blatantly claim such a thing, but he pushed on, defiant.

"And I promised, when I ate the fruit . . . I promised I'd save it if I could! All I need, sir, is . . ."

Contado cut him off with a slash of the hand and a disdainful grunt.

"Troop, if you insist on it, it's yours. You have until the ship lifts to take your souvenir. The quartermaster will charge carrying fees against your account—I'll not have that thing dignified as a specimen—and you'll report for trauma testing as soon as we arrive at an appropriate location."

"I'd prefer to lift in daylight!" came the junior pilot's voice, merciless.

Jela broke toward the tree, survival knife and blanket out, hoping he didn't kill the fool thing trying to save it!

"We lift with or without you, Jela," said the Chief Pilot, and the wind carried his voice elsewhere, unanswered.

JELA WAS NOT a gardener, nor a tree surgeon, and if ever he'd felt a lack of training in his life it was now, on his knees on an alien planet, battle-knife in hand, facing the tree that had intentionally saved his life. His utility blanket was laid out beside it, and he fully intended to wrap the tree in that to carry it.

"Thank you," he said, bowing, and tried to recall a life's worth of half-heard lore of those who had tread the forests on other worlds.

And then, as there was absolutely nothing else to do, he began to dig a trench with the knife, cutting into the earth as he *had* been trained, recalling now the proper method of slicing through the outer roots quickly. The training—how best to avoid entangling the blade, how to get under the over-roots so that they might be preserved as camouflage or cover—came back, reinforced by the experience of digging for his life under fire.

He knew that he shouldn't take the tree entirely from the earth, that he needed to keep soil around some of the roots—but how should he know how much?

The dirt surprised him, being drier even than he'd been expecting. He trenched the first circle around the tree hurriedly, realized that the sandy soil wasn't likely to hold together anyway, and dug a new trench barely three hand-spans away from the spindly trunk.

As he dug, he realized he was talking to the tree, soothing it, as if it could understand—as if it were a child, or a pet.

What cheek I have, to tell the king of a planet to be calm while I dig it out of its safety!

Despite that, he continued to talk—perhaps for his own comfort, to assure himself that what he did was right and correct.

"We'll get you out of here soon," he murmured. "Won't be long and you'll see the dragon's eye view . . ."

The breeze began to pick up, as it always did at dusk, and the scents that played across his nose were those of sand and dirt and some sweetness he could not identify at first, until he realized it was the scent—the taste even—of the tree's gift he'd eaten . . .

Another turn around the tree, and Jela's blade was much deeper, but digging toward the center. The sounds from the ship were familiar enough, and they were the sounds of vents being closed, of the testing of mechanical components, of checking readiness for lift.

It was during the third turn around the tree that Jela could hear several of the hatches closing; and during that turn he realized that much of what he'd thought was a ball of dirt was in fact a bulbous part of the tree's tap root. It was easily twelve times the diameter of the portion above the ground, and as he dug away he could feel that it likely weighed more than the visible stalk above as well.

Finally, he reached beneath, found several strong cord-like roots leading deep into the bowels of the planet. He hesitated, not knowing which life-lines were critical, nor even knowing how to test—and in that moment of hesitation he felt the tree shift as if some inner ballast had moved. Then, with a sharp snap, the tree lurched and the roots he'd been concerned about were severed, his blade a hand-width or more from the spot.

The full weight of tree and remaining roots descended into his hands, and he staggered, nearly pulled down into the pit he'd dug.

With back-straining effort he gathered the tree to him, feeling the unexpected mass of that head-sized bulb, shaped like some giant onion beneath his hands.

Now the sounds of ship generators revving came to him, and he wrestled the tree out of the ungiving ground and with a single motion wrapped it in the blanket and stood, moving at a run toward the ship.

Corporal Kinto stood guard at the last open hatch, eyes

studiously on the hatch's status display, hand on the emergency close button.

"He's in!" Kinto said to the air, and then the Chief Pilot's voice came across the intercom. "We lift on a count of twenty-four."

Kinto glared around the branches at Jela then, and smiled an ugly smile.

"Even a Hero shouldn't order a Chief Pilot about, Jela. I anticipate your trial!"

THEY LIFTED. The lander crew had allowed him to strap the tree into the jump seat beside him; and then they ignored him: Ignored his careful dusting of the leaves, his positioning of the plant where it could reap whatever feeble grace the ship's lights might bring it, ignored his use of camp-cup to dampen the sandy roots . . . and they ignored his talking, for his words were all for the tree. To Corporal Kinto, he had nothing to say. Contado and Tetran being dutifully occupied at their stations, he—a passenger—should not distract them with chatter. So he whispered good tidings and calm words to the tree, which was departing not only its home world and its honorable dead, but the very soil that had nourished it.

THE TRANSFER to the *Trident* was awkward. He was left to negotiate himself and the tree through the transfer port, and emerging, arms full of trunk and branches, he'd been unable to properly acknowledge the captain. Then, as a pilot returning without his craft, there were the docking logs to sign, certifying his ship lost due to enemy action, which duty he performed clumsily, tree propped on a hip, log tipped at an unstable angle, while the quartermaster displayed an unlikely degree of interest in his secondary screens.

None of his wing met him, which he thought a bad sign, and he'd been directed not to his own billet but to the pilot's lounge, escorted by the assistant quartermaster.

"I should go to my quarters, change uniforms, clean myself . . ."

His escort cut him off sharply.

"Troop, you're just about at the limit, you ought to know," she snapped. "Took the pilots a lot of jawing to convince the captain to come back this way long enough to pick up your signal. Besides, there's no guarantee you've got quarters to go back to . . ."

That last sounded bad—worse than being at the limit of what would be officially tolerated. He was old friends with the limit. No quarters, though—

With him up ahead in the corridor, there wasn't a good way to get a look at his escort's face, to see if she was having some fun with him, and just then they reached a junction in the passageway and had to make way for pilots wearing duty cards. Jela managed to hide his face in the branches, pleased that the youngsters—for they were both rookies—could not see his reaction to the gaudy tattoos they wore on their faces. It was while looking away that he saw two of the hatches in the passage dogged to yellow, and another dogged to red.

"Took a hit?" he said over his shoulder as they continued. "I thought—"

"Your boat took most of it." Her voice was gentler now, as if she gave due respect to duty done, and done well. "But there was still some pretty energetic debris, and a bad shot from one of ours, too."

Jela grimaced, partly from the news and partly from the exertion of carrying the tree. He'd have sworn it had been much lighter when he'd grabbed it out of the ground.

Forced to the side of the passage once more by through traffic, he leaned against the metal wall, resting for a moment, until a tap on the shoulder reminded him that he was on ship's business and not his own.

Moving forward, he vaguely wondered which—if any—of his belongings might have survived, but then let that thought go; he was here, and the tree was here, and that was more than he had a right to expect, after all.

They came at last to the pilots lounge. The hatch was uncharacteristically dogged—to green at least!—but with ship's air at risk it was only a common-sense precaution. He had time to note that his wing's insignia was pasted roughly to the door, then the assistant quartermaster reached past him to rap—which was her right, after all, to have a lesser open for her from within.

The hatch swung wide, an unexpected hand between his

shoulders sent him through, half-stumbling, and he looked, quick eyes raking past the scraggly leaves of the tree, taking in the six empty helmets sitting with unsheathed blades beside them on a table, and five faces—familiar, strained, concerned, watching him.

His knees shook. He locked them, refusing to fall, but . . .

Six? Six gone?

Corporal Bicra it was who gently took the tree from him, and Under Sergeant Vondahl who led the salute.

With Jela, they numbered six—the smallest number Command would recognize as a wing.

And as luck would have it, he was now eldest in troop, and senior in rank.

He returned the salute uncertainly, and sat heavily in the chair beside the tree.

"Report," he said, not at all wishing to hear the tale.

FIVE

❧ ❧

Trident
Isolation Ward

THE MED TECH WAS ADAMANT, the while admitting Jela's basic understanding of the theory of contagion.

Yes, many diseases could be spread—*could have been spread already*—by the mere passage of an infected person, such as Jela, bearing an infectious object, such as the tree, through the ship.

That Jela had been escorted by the assistant quartermaster, and welcomed into the temporary wing wardroom was unfortunate. That no one had yet died of some hideous, unknown disease since his return to the ship was not proof positive that no one *would*.

More to the point, several standard protocols had been abused and the med tech was voluble in their listing.

First and foremost, Jela should not have been permitted to land on the planet without a thorough reevaluation of the biological information from the old surveys.

Secondly, neither Jela nor the tree should have been permitted back into the pick-up ship without disinfection.

Thirdly, and most annoying to the tech, as Jela read it, neither he nor the tree should be aboard *now* without having been disinfected.

The tech knew the rules and had the ear of *someone* on staff; and that someone had been appropriately notified, dignified, and horrified.

And so it was that the second day of Jela's reign as Acting Wingleader was spent in an isolation tunnel. The double-walled see-through chamber was inflated inside an ordinary infirmary room. The tree, within a double-walled flex-glass cubicle, was isolated all the more within that chamber while various tests were done on the dirt it called its own. At least they'd seen the wisdom of leaving the tree were Jela could watch it—if it turned blue or purple or became infested with bugs in its chamber he'd be right there to see it.

He hadn't pointed out to the med tech that no one knew exactly how long it might take a scruffy-looking tree of unknown genus to exhibit signs of parasitism, decay, or the like, but he had managed to get the tech to agree to a watering system for the plant so it wouldn't give a "false positive" that might have the fleet isolating the whole ship . . .

Luckily, the tech admitted the biotic sanctity of electronic communications, so Jela's small command was able at least to speak with him when required and otherwise keep his comm-screen active with the news and goings-on of the group.

Things might have been busier had Corporal Bicra also not been in isolation elsewhere, this news brought and left by a smirking Kinto. The corporal had touched the tree, carried her Wingleader's burden—as both proper and prudent!—after all. Bicra being the most organized of the remaining squad, some important details were sure to be missed.

Jela was inclined to consider Kinto a factor in the isolation as well, since he was known to be a friend of the med tech. What use any of the fooraw could be to Kinto was a mystery worth exploring at a later date; for the moment Under Sergeant Vondahl was too busy overseeing the maintenance and repair of the wing's ships to spend time on a vital-records search.

The med tech seemed a busybody of the highest order. Jela's three sensor packs reported ably to the room's central console, but the tech remained in the room nonetheless. More, he constantly checked Jela's rate of water intake and—

"Will you give me ten heartbeats to myself, Tech? You've already got cameras, body sensors, air-intake gauges, and two measurements of my weight. Do you think I'll grow wings and leave you behind if you don't check my color every tenth-shift?"

Most of Jela's attention was on his porta-comp, where he was following with interest the check on Sergeant Risto's ship. Risto was one of the three who'd died when the primary passage had been laid open to space while they were scrambling.

"Not likely," admitted the tech. "I don't think there's anything in the literature about a more or less standard human being able to fly—or even grow wings. The *sheriekas* are said to . . ."

Jela looked up when the phrase wasn't finished.

"Are said to *what*?"

The tech looked down, rising blood staining sturdy cheeks a deeper brown. "I can't say. You haven't been confirmed as Wingleader, and the information may be restricted to . . ."

Jela looked on with interest as the tech mumbled words into silence, and turned to busy himself with adjusting various dials that didn't need adjusting.

Understanding blossomed.

"I see," Jela said. "Until I'm scanned, rescanned, sampled and shown to be free of disease and healthy of mind—hah!—I might be an agent of *them*, magically cloned on the spot and released to destroy the defenders from within." He took a breath, decided he was still irritated, and furthermore that the tech had it coming, and continued.

"Will it ease your mind to know that I was one of the Generalists brought in to study the problem of how to spot *sheriekas* and *sheriekas*-made in their human disguises? That would be, *before* they sprout wings and—"

"Stop, Troop!"

This was a new voice. An entirely new voice, from a woman he'd never seen before.

Her uniform—

Jela slowly moved the keypad back, stood, and saluted.

"Commander, I have stopped."

She snorted delicately.

"I hear, Troop. I hear."

She pointed at the med tech.

"You may leave, Tech. Your monitors will warn you if there's a problem."

A quick salute from the tech, who nearly tripped in his hurry to leave the scene.

As the door sealed the commander sighed, none too gently.

"*Wingleader.*" She said the word as if she tasted it, as if she *tested* it.

"*Wingleader.* Indeed, it would look good on your record, were that record reviewed but not much inspected—I may allow it to stay. May."

She moved closer to the wall of his enclosure, studying him with as much interest—and perhaps even concern—as the med tech had showed disinterest and disdain.

In his turn, Jela studied her: A woman so near his own height he barely needed to look up to meet her eyes; strongly built, and in top shape. Not a Series soldier, but a natural human, her brown hair threaded with gray.

She continued as if there had been no pause for mutual evaluation.

"Wingleader . . . Yet, I'm not sure if that would be best for you, howsoever it might serve the troop."

She peered through the inflatable, studying his reaction.

"No comment, Troop Jela?"

"Wingleader has never been in my thoughts, Commander. It is an unexpectable accident . . ."

She laughed.

"Yes, I suppose it is. I *have* seen your record. You always seem to rise despite your best efforts!"

Jela stiffened . . .

"Stop, Troop. Relax. Understand that you *are* monitored here. You *are* on camera. You *are* being tested for contagion of *many* sorts. There's no need to bait the tech. He's too ordinary to be worth your trouble."

Jela stood, uncertain, aware that information was being passed rapidly, aware that levels of command were being bypassed.

"Sit," the commander said finally. "Please, sit and do what you can for the moment. As time permits, we will talk."

Jela watched as her eyes found the cameras, the sensors, the very monitors on his leg. He sat, more slowly than he'd risen.

"We will talk where we might both be more comfortable. In a few days, when you will be quite recovered from your trek, Wingleader."

She saluted as if that last word was both a command and a decision, and then she was gone.

THE COMMANDER made no more appearances in Jela's isolation unit—a unit he'd begun to think of as a cell after the third day schedule commenced in the vessel outside his walls, and by the start of the sixth ship-day knew to be the truth, if not the intent.

He'd been in enough detaining cells in his time to see the similarities: he was on his jailer's schedule, he exercised when they told him to, ate what they brought him, and slept during a portion of the time after they turned the lights out on him.

He did have his porta-comp, which meant some communication, after all, and he had received a few visitors, though he'd had more visitors in some lock-ups than he had here. Then, too, most often his jail cells hadn't had the luxury of his very own green plant.

It turned out that the "alien plant" was under every bit as much scrutiny as he was—in fact it appeared that many of the sensors he wore or was watched by were duplicated for the tree.

Perhaps the most frustrating thing was that though he could see the tree—and was under orders to observe it and report any anomalies—he could not to touch it, or talk to it, or comfort it in what must be new and terrifying circumstances.

Shortly after the commander's visit, he gained an amusing rotation of warders to replace the solitary med tech and his curious warnings—or, perhaps, threats.

What was amusing about the new set of keepers was that they each seemed guided by a printed sheet. They neither saluted nor acknowledged him other than directing him for exercise or tests. They also wore medical gowns without emblem, name, rank, or number.

What they did not wear were masks—thus baring the all-too-silly tattoos that were becoming the rage—and making each as identifiable in the long run as if they'd shouted out name, rank, birth creche, and gene units . . .

For in fact, every one of the new keepers were of the accelerated, the vat-born, the selected, the so-called "X Strain"—able to work harder and longer on less food than even the efficient Ms. Too, they had for the most part had similar training, similar instructors, similar lives. They spoke amongst themselves a truncated and canted artificial dialect, and appeared to lump any soldier but those of the latest vat runs into a social class of lesser outsiders.

Despite the disdain, and the tendency to seek only the company of their own kind, what had so far eluded the designers of soldiers was the sought-after interchangeability that would have made them—the Y Strains and the X—in the image of some committee-envisioned super-fighter: Physically perfect, identical, and above all amenable to command. It was the downfall of the M Series, so he had heard it said—they were too independent, too individual, much too prone to use their own judgement. And much too often, Jela might have added—right.

So, he found himself in the care of the proud yet still-flawed X Strains, and he'd been annoyed in the night to wake as some one of the guardians attempted to enter the room without disturbing him: They were all of the blood, dammit! Would he have assumed them so lax . . . well, yes. He might have.

"You of Versten's Flight have no regard for the sleep of your brethren, eh?" He called out in the assumed dark of the infirmary's night. His reward was a not unexpected flash of light as the woman with a red lance crossing a blue blade tattooed on her right cheek reacted, alas, predictably.

"Wingleader," she gasped.

He'd *startled* her—and if he'd been of a mind he might just as easily have killed her—been though the transparent enclosure and had his hands around her throat before she'd known he was awake.

"Wingleader," she said again, recovering her voice, if not her dignity. "The monitors must be checked manually from time to time, and the calibrations . . ."

"The calibrations may be made just as conveniently from a remote station," he said, allowing his voice to display an edge. "It would be well if these things were done during ship's day, for who knows what one who has been abandoned on a near lifeless world might do in the midst of being startled awake?"

"Wingleader, I . . ."

"Enough. Calibrate. I will sleep again tonight, and some of tomorrow day as well . . ."

Which was unlikely, so he owned to himself, but minor, as he was no longer entirely on ship schedule.

This was an oddity he considered too minor to concern med techs of any ilk, though interesting to himself. It seemed he was keeping two clocks now. One was the ordinary ship-clock any space traveler became accustomed to. The other . . . the other was the daily cycle of the planet he'd been stranded on, though he'd kept planet-time for so few days he might still be expected to be in transition-timing.

The X Strain tech finished a half-hearted tour of the sensors, used her light to peer inside his cubicle and satisfy herself that he was not green and leafy, and that the tree was. She left then, without a word to him, leaving him wakeful.

And that, too, might have been her purpose.

Jela crossed his arms over his head, his thoughts on the planet of the trees, its sea, and other things he could not possibly remember from the place. No doubt he'd been very close to total exhaustion and on the verge of dementia when he'd been picked up. Perhaps the techs were right to be concerned, after all.

Because he was a pilot, and an M, with all that Series' dislike of being idle, he began to calculate. He checked his new sense of time against the trip back to the mother-ship, knowing that the breeze would about right *now* have been shifting to come at his face if he stood on the hill over the empty sea.

That established, he calculated the entirety of his journey to his best recall—brief time outbound, to taking on the enemy vessel, to near automatic charting of course to the nearby planet, to the landing . . . likely he spiked this or that spy-sensor as he recalled the grueling and pitiless flight through that eventually life-saving atmosphere—and then the walk. He recalled the walk vividly, recalled the valleys, treasured the long trip the trees had undertaken from the side of a mountain to the ocean so far away . . .

And that thought he put quickly away, tagging it mentally as a mention-to-none, a category that by now seemed to include half of his thoughts in any case.

Jela consulted the other clock in his head, saw that it would soon be time for his breakfast, and rose to do stretching exercises. When the techs entered, en masse as they did at the beginning of each of his days, he'd be good for a full schedule of work, sleepless half-night or not.

The combat warning came before breakfast, and the transition warning overlaid it almost instantly. Neither his bunk nor his chair were attached to the deck within his isolation unit—nor was the tree secured. His orders were clear—he was to observe the tree until released to general duties.

Jela yanked his bunk against the wall of the wider room, ignoring the ripples in the flex-glass, and pushed the tree, still within its own cocoon and attached to its various umbilicals, into the corner thus made. Flinging himself against the bunk he hugged the tree's base through the flexible walls, internal clock counting the beats until—

"Go, dammit! Go!"

His voice rippled the flex-glass walls, and that was all the effect it had. The ship shuddered with the familiar shrug of launching fighters . . . but no stand down from the transition warning followed. He did the calcs out of habit, assuming a nearby threat in the line of travel—why else launch now?

There was another kind of shudder in the ship now—this one less familiar. Perhaps a jettisoning of mines, or an unusual application of control jets?

Maneuvering *was* starting. The direction of *up* shifted slightly, and then again, and as if it hadn't already sounded, the transition buzzer went off again.

He ought to be with his wing! His duty—

He took a breath, and another, and did what he could to relax. Around him, the ship went absolutely still as it slipped into transition. He wondered, then, and with an effort, how long breakfast would be delayed, and how many pilots they'd left behind so that breakfast was an issue.

BREAKFAST FAILED TO ARRIVE, and it was nearing time for lunch. Jela remained close to the tree, concerned that any moment might bring them into normal space with unwanted, deadly, motion. He was *still* sitting beside the tree when the commander arrived, four hurried helpers in tow.

"Take your samples, quickly," she ordered. She half-bowed, half-saluted Jela, who rose as quickly as he could.

"Wingleader, the medical department has been advised that they are no longer concerned with the possibility that you have become infected by contact with your tree. As they assure me you show no signs of physical abnormalities, other than those any M grade soldier might show at this point in his career, we shall shortly have an opportunity to discuss the matter I spoke of earlier. Please, Wingleader, prepare your computer for removal as well."

Jela went to the desk and snapped the unit together, watching with some relief as the technicians inserted a hosed connection to the outer lock of his chamber. In a few moments, the structure sagged around him and the outer flex-glass rippled as the technicians peeled apart the seal. A moment later and the inner seal sighed open and two technicians strode in, heading toward the tree. Only one was face-marked.

"The tree? I may take that with me?" he asked the nearest tech— the unmarked one—but was rewarded only with a half-formed shrug. He risked annoying the officer, whose attention was focused on a medical reader connected to the room's telemetry.

"Commander? The tree—I will take the tree with me as well, I assume?"

She didn't look up from her study of the reader, her answer heavy with irony. "Yes—the tree, the computer, your boots—whatever will make you comfortable, Wingleader!"

He nearly laughed; then wondered if he'd really put up that much of a fuss when they'd told him to leave his boots outside the isolation area. Yet, as a soldier and a pilot, he deserved certain politeness, and he was as aware as they that his treatment had misused his station.

The commander was quick.

"You, Corporal. You will carry this computer, and walk with us to the Officer's Mess. You, Wingleader, may help the other tech as you will, or carry the tree if you prefer, and we shall together retire to the mess so that you may be fed."

In the end, Jela carried the tree, while one of the techs carried his boots and his computer; they made a strange procession through a ship unnaturally quiet, and it had taken a moment or two of confusion to see everything placed when they arrived at the mess. At last, the techs were sent on their way, and the Commander preceded him through the lunch line—open early, apparently for their convenience.

"So, Wingleader Jela, we have arrived at a place I'd hoped not to arrive at."

He looked up from his meal, startled, and she smiled a mirthless smile.

"No, it is not that I dislike the food onboard ship, as rumor might imply! Rather it is that our hand is forced—*my* hand is forced—and all of this ripples things set in motion long before either of us took our first breath."

Jela thought for a moment, waited until he was sure an answer was required.

"This is always the case with soldiers," he said carefully. "From the colors of our flags and uniforms to the names of our units to the choice of worlds we must defend, none of it is beyond the influence of what went before us. It is a matter of soldier's lore that we often die for the mistakes made generations before."

She was eating as if she, too, had been denied breakfast, but Jela saw that his remark had sparked something, for she put her fruit down and took a sip of her water, while raising a hand to emphasize . . .

"Which is the problem I deal with," she said, moving her hand almost as if she wanted to break into hand-talk; Jela followed her fingers for a moment, but she resisted or else failed to find the appropriate signs.

"You will not quote me to any on board this ship, Wingleader, but we have only a few days to prepare you. First, I must ask if you have made any plans for your retirement?"

He nearly choked, hastily swallowed bread in mid-chew.

"Commander, no, I have not," he admitted, stealing a hurried sip of juice. "I've always thought I would die on duty, else on penalty of some infraction . . ."

"Indeed? Then you have paid no attention to the information from the bursar's office about time due and funds due, of the rewards of taking up a farm?"

He looked at her straight on, and then allowed his eyes to roll.

"Commander, there's not much retirement allotted for an M. True, true, some of us have retired—I've heard of three, I think, but it's not something I admire. I just spent several days too many watching a star set on a desert world—a sight I'm assured is restful and worth seeking!—and found it far from restful. I fret when I'm not busy. You've seen my record! When I'm idle I am as much an enemy of the corps as any . . ."

"No, Wingleader, I will not permit that statement. The truth is that you are what you say. You know you are an M; you would rather march in circles for days in payment for having had your fun than sit staring at a wall doing absolutely nothing, and often you are better informed than your commanders, for you sleep very little and begrudge it besides."

She paused, sipped her water, went on.

"Still, there is in your record the information that you've taken your leaves on quite a few worlds, you've managed to survive in situations that killed your creche mates, and you're a very quick study. More, when you have been in command situations, you've done well until faced with dealing with the—let us call it *the weight*—of decisions made above your head."

Jela permitted himself a hand signal of acknowledgment, to go along with a sigh.

"I have very much been a soldier, Commander. Alas, some 'above my head' have been raised to different rules and understandings about soldiers, duty, and necessity."

"A soldier's truth, plainly put." This time her hand did signal agreement; it was as he had supposed—whatever other training or duties she'd had, the commander was a pilot.

She paused, pushed her plate away from her as if it were a distraction, and leaned toward him, speaking quietly.

"Wingleader, I have for you some choices. There *are* times in a soldier's life when choice is available, there *are* times when it is preferable. So here, listen up, are some choices. Alas—you have no time but the time we sit at this table to make up your mind. I will not say that I do not *care* which choice you make, but I expect you will know."

Jela listened, swore he could hear the sound of a leaf, rattling in the breeze. Indeed, there was a breeze now—the ventilators were running at some speed, having come up unnoticed during their conversation.

"First, you may remain Wingleader of your small squadron. It is likely to be reassigned, given that the duties of this vessel are soon to change, but it is a respectable position, in which you would do well, to the benefit of the troop."

His hand-signaled acknowledgment—*information received in clear form.*

"Next, rather than remain as Wingleader, you may accept assignment to another squadron as a pilot. This choice I suggest in case you expect the duties of Wingleader might wear on you over time. You would be placed in the available pilot pool and we would have no way to know what or where you might be assigned, but you would have no responsibilities but those of a pilot, which are known to you and, I think, not overwhelming."

"Finally, you may take a long-term temporary assignment delivering a very nearly surplus vessel to a long-term storage area, with appropriate adjustment of rank. You would oversee the delivery crew and be responsible for seeing the vessel properly shut down in case it must be redeployed. You would also assist in assessing local unit response readiness, from a pilot's viewpoint, in areas you travel through, to and from. In order to facilitate this, you would undergo a short, specialized, dangerous, and highly confidential training. It will not be an easy assignment."

She stopped. Looked expectant. Waited.

Jela hand-signaled, *check me—I repeat the information.*

Then he did that thing, nearly word for word, out loud.

"Yes," she agreed, "that's accurate."

He waggled his fingers—pilot hand-talk for feigned indecision—rolled his eyes, and began to laugh. He waggled his fingers harder and laughed harder, 'til tears came to his eyes . . .

"*That* funny?"

"Yes. Oh yes . . ." Finally he wiped his eyes on a napkin.

"Commander, I have one question. May I take the tree with me?"

"With which choice?"

"If you make me Captain Jela and have me deliver a ship, may I take the tree with me?"

It was her turn to do the pilot's waggle of fingers.

"If the tree is on board this ship when you leave, it will be spaced, I assure you. A captain is permitted a mascot, after all."

"May I know your name, Commander?"

"If you pass the training, Wingleader."

SIX

❀ ❀

Training Base
Mission Time: 34.5 days and counting

JELA CAME AWAKE in the night, the scent of sea-salt competing with that of wind-driven fresh water, as if an electrical storm fresh from the sea had burst upon the mountains behind, just before dawn.

A sense of energetic jubilation emanated from the youngers; a sense of restrained relief from the elders upstream who knew that the combination of the early rain, rising sun, and the continued run of fresh water from the hills would make this a wonderful day for growing.

Behind that relief, an under note of melancholy drifted down from the true elders, for in *their* youth, this would have been a likely morning for the flyers to come and tend those whose detached branches or tangled seed-pods might cause difficulty later in the season. The seed-carriers, the branch-tenders—they had been with the trees since the dawn of awareness—and had since vanished from an awareness that yet grieved their loss.

Awake, Jela stood beside the tree, knowing that yes, it was just about time for "sunrise" on a planet light years away from their current billeting, and knowing that in some fey fashion the tree had managed to dream *too loud*, so he had become encompassed as well.

The chronometer on the wall was adamant. No matter what time the tree—or Jela, for that matter—thought it was, the duty schedule indicated that breakfast, exercise, and classwork were still more than half his sleep-shift away. Alas, the schedule was obviously not designed for the convenience of an M Series soldier, but to fit some administrator's concept of a busy day, or perhaps to answer necessities a mere M had no need to be aware of.

Schedule or no schedule, he was awake and likely to remain so. Sighing, Jela stretched and worked with a small weight set, the while trying to diminish the sadness he felt for the winged-things he'd never seen, but whose touch was familiar and missed.

Despite the exercise, the sadness hung on, threatening to encompass the universe. He knew better than to wallow, and hoped the tree did. But the tree might well still be in some in-between state of its own, and he felt no desire to disturb it.

Drawing a stim-drink from the small refrigerator, he broke the seal and stood sipping.

He'd spent the early evening reviewing troop strength charts, the attack patterns in the last wave of the First Phase, the siting of existing garrisons, their commanders, and their loyalties; the trading patterns and names of the major companies and players . . .

Now, he sat at the computer, and began once again to go over the diagrams and intelligence . . .

First, though they controlled a good bit of the galaxy, Command was split on how to proceed, with a group allied largely with the Inmost faction attempting to withdraw all forces from the Arm, in order to consolidate a line at the base.

This dangerously flawed plan had clearly been constructed by someone who had no sense of dimension, and no understanding of the nature of the enemy. For every time the *sheriekas* had been beaten back they'd surged forward again, each time coming closer to claiming the right to control man's destiny.

And now? Now, the more observant of the High Commanders

felt the war was almost lost, that the *sheriekas* were bare years away from being able to go wherever they wished, whenever they wished, to command, enslave, destroy . . .

Destroy.

It appeared that the enemy had less and less desire to control mankind and more desire to just be rid of it entirely. More, they seemed willing, or even eager, to destroy everything in existence in favor of some future where the very quarks trembled at their name.

The intelligence on this was spotty, though an M's intuition knew it for truth.

His drink done, Jela closed the intelligence data, and opened what had lately become his most-accessed files. He was in a fair way to becoming obsessed with the problem they'd set him—two so-called math instructors his intuition told him he was unlikely, after all these days of duty, to see again.

He flicked through his data, frowning. Missing space craft were one thing, missing planets another. Both events were of course disturbing, though ordinary enough in a universe where black holes and novas and other such events were known; in a universe where the math—and hence the weapons—existed that could destroy a world with chain-reacted nuclei or the casual accidental flare of a burping solar-storm.

But lately, some other events were unfolding, as if *space* were unfolding, or as if the space where humanity lived among the stars was from time to time . . . dissolving.

The word *unfolding* had come from the younger and quieter of the two instructors; and a sharp disagreement had followed its utterance.

It quickly became apparent to Jela that the disagreement was something more—and more serious—than simple professional sniping. The elder and more voluble instructor believed that the younger's *unfolding* was too simple a model; that if certain late developments were *mere unfolding*, the universe would simply get bigger—well, no, not bigger, not precisely, but that it would acquire another dimension, a dimension of so little moment that it would take five to ten times the known life of the universe for it to materially affect the spin of something as inconsequential as an electron.

No, the operative phrase, according to the voluble one, as he scribbled on the situation board—"Here! *This* is the math we have to work from!"—was *decrystallization.*

The instructor admitted that he had not the final proofs, that the math they were working from was the partial and not yet finished work of a mathematician who had unfortunately come to the notice of those who found his theories and equations anathema. The quiet instructor spoke of the mathematician as one honorably dead in battle, and had turned to inscribe a series of equations that looked remarkably like piloting forms onto the situation board.

"The problem we face," he murmured, "is that someone—and we must assume that *someone* equals *the Enemy*—is experimenting with dismantling the universe."

It was said so calmly that it was only in retrospect that Jela felt a flicker of dread.

The elder instructor tossed his pen from hand to hand pensively.

"Yes," he said finally, "that's a reasonable shorthand for the event, no matter what the full math may describe. It's rather as if you were able to set up a force field around a courier ship, attach it to a sector of the universe, and transition—forever."

"Good," said the younger, finishing up his notations and standing back. "That description allows us to use math that should be very familiar to our student." He gave Jela an uncomfortably earnest stare before waving toward the situation board. "Let's suppose, for example, that you wanted to visit the garrison at Vinylhaven . . ."

Unsurprisingly, the math was quite accurate for the mass of the proposed courier ship; the instructor then solved it for a location deep in the heart of the galaxy, on a heading that Jela recognized.

"Now, what we'll do for this ummm . . . trip . . ." the instructor murmured, as if talking to himself more than his increasingly puzzled student, "is restate the mass of the ship, drop it out of the locus defined by our standard five dimensions and into one defined by nine."

He did this, Jela checking the new equation on his pad . . .

"Now, the thing is—" the instructor said, suddenly turning away from the board, "—no one really wants to go to Vinylhaven . . ."

Jela had been thinking the same thing himself, Vinylhaven being somewhat too close for comfort to the remains of the ember of a brown giant . . .

" . . . because," the instructor continued in his deceptively quiet voice, "it's not there."

Jela flat out stared. "*Not there*?" he demanded, wondering now if all of this had been some sort of elaborate hoax to test the gullibility of intransigent Ms. "I've *been* there."

"Not lately," the elder instructor said simply. "I have been—or, say, I have attempted to go—within the last two Common Years. It is, as my colleague says, not there. Not the garrison world, not the brown giant. While we can use the coordinates that formerly brought us to Vinylhaven, in fact we can only come to the approximate vicinity, for pretty much everything out that way is gone. The nearest known destination we can raise is the yellow star three light years away, which is still there, though it has gone nova."

"Our guess," the younger instructor said seriously, "is that a sphere—and this *is* a guess; it may well be a more complex shape— approximating three-fourths of a cubic light year was—taken away. I say the space was folded; my associate says the space—actually a small portion of the universe—was decrystallized. Down to the photons and below, there is *nothing*. We can measure the event—are measuring it—by finding the wave front of light."

He paused for a moment's serious study of the situation board and the equations elucidated there, then looked back to Jela.

"Given the fact that Vinylhaven is gone," he murmured, "let's calculate the transport-can big enough to hold the missing volume and mass. . . ."

The lesson was not lost on Jela. They did the math, several times.

"Your answer as to the power source?" the elder instructor asked Jela.

He sighed and pushed back from his pad, though his fingers still wandered lightly over the keys, looking for a solution that made sense, granting the data . . .

"Loss-less total conversion?" he offered.

"Consider the multiple spin-states, and the mass of the photons . . ." The younger, that was.

Jela sighed again. "Are you sure there's not a black hole? I mean. . . ."

"Absolutely no sign of one," the elder answered, "and insufficient to have cleared the zone. Loss-less total conversion fails, as far as we're able to compute, if the mass actually moves somewhere else. We're talking energy levels above those in a super-sized galactic core black hole. With no trace."

"The nova you mentioned?"

"Likely not coincidence," the elder conceded, "but not nearly enough power to cause this. Perhaps there was leakage and we simply don't know what to look for."

"Not natural," Jela persisted. "You're *sure*? Not some rare, once-in-a-billion-year event?"

The two instructors looked at each other and a message passed between them as surely as if they'd used finger-talk.

The younger reached into a pocket, and withdrew a datastrip.

"Vinylhaven is the seventh such event that we're sure of. We have been apprized of three more since. All in the Arm. This datastrip contains a summation of the ten events and what we can deduce about the physics, the geology, and the cosmology."

He laid the strip across Jela's palm. "Tomorrow, we'll want to see if you've found a pattern."

The elder instructor placed a second strip in Jela's hand.

"Background on the commanders and garrisons, native populations. The people . . ."

Dread nibbled at the edge of Jela's consciousness again, dread and sadness.

"Do you expect *me* to solve this?" he asked.

They looked away, almost as one. The elder looked back with a sigh.

"No. Not solve it. But we want your help. We're looking for

special circumstances. For insight. For hope. And you must know, Captain M, that your mission, when you leave here, will be in part to keep the troops in place and fighting, whether there is hope or none. It's about all we can do right now."

HOWEVER, the next day did not bring the mathematical pair back, nor the next several beyond that. Rather, Jela was immersed in an intense round of training on surviving small-arms shoot-outs, of choosing the right weapon, of avoiding detection, as well as refreshers on ships, on engines and power plants, on intra-system navigation, and more history of the First Phase.

So, he kept to the project in his so-called "off-time," eating over study flimsies, exercising with computer screens and keyboards within reach, captured by the problem and hungry to se where the data led him.

He tried to understand the locations of the disappearances, drawing simple maps of the missing sections, and more maps, over time. He'd tried analysis by local population or lack of it, since only four of the now-missing locations had any population to speak of. He analyzed by political leanings of nearby garrison commanders, by system discovery or occupation date, by the colors of the stars, even by the alphabetical orders of the names of the stars or systems or planets.

The databases he had been given were large and flexible; but he strained them, joined them together and drilled through them. He pondered and set the computer to pondering . . .

In the meantime: exercise, classes, exercise, reading, exercise, classes, exercise, research, sleep.

Sleep proved its own mystery for there was no doubt that he'd found a pattern to his wakefulness that no longer matched a typical M's profile. As little as the average of the M Strain slept, he slept less. And there were the dreams, usually not so loud as to wake him, and behind them the conviction that he could almost smell the water, hear the surf on the beach, recall the dragons hovering over the world-forest, and know their names.

This last was the most perplexing—for he must assume that the dreams and wistful memories were the tree's, channeled to him by a mechanism he accepted without understanding—and how would the tree know the names of beings who rode the air currents?

He permitted himself little time to explore these personal mysteries, however, with so glorious and complex a problem before him.

IT WAS THE MIDDLE of the sixth day following his assignment to the task of the disappearances when the elder of the two instructors reappeared, interrupting a landing sim. Jela was a little disturbed by this, for the sim was decidedly trying to create unfavorable conditions and he'd yet to crash or hard-land—

"Captain," the instructor said briskly. "We will be sharing a quick meal with my colleague; our schedules will no longer mesh with yours after today, and so we seek a summary from you. In no case, by the way, will you divulge your analysis of the situation to the common troops you will be visiting as part of your mission. Most will lack your training and appreciation of nuance. Please follow me."

Though courteously enough phrased, it was an order, so Jela locked the sim and followed the instructor out of the connected rooms of his dormitory and tutoring hall, through a series of corridors on dark-time schedule.

They passed several people, none of whom acknowledged them, and arrived in a small cafeteria as the younger instructor hurried in from yet another corridor, carrying what appeared to be travel cases.

"We're set," he said to the elder. "When the interview is over, we go."

Jela's interest was piqued: For many days it had been as if the only concern of this place was him and his training. To see outside necessity now so much in view . . .

"Please," the elder instructor said to Jela. "Sit and eat. We're outbound in short order."

The meal was decidedly more ambitious than he'd been expecting, given the apparent imminence of the instructors' departure, and Jela fell to with more enjoyment than he usually found in dining hall food. The initial discussion was near commonplace—questions about which information he'd thought most useful, which databases might as well be left out if the information were to be shared elsewhere . . .

There was, amazingly, real coffee to finish the meal, which suggested his instructors to be even more out of the ordinary than he'd thought. High-rank officers, then, or independent specialists beyond the direct control of the military—

"And so," the younger said at last, "as you have had an extra bit of time in which to consider, would you care to share with us your analysis?"

Eyebrows up, Jela glanced about the room, and the several tables occupied by quiet-speaking folk.

The elder instructor smiled. "Of the secrets here, this is—like every secret here—the most important."

The younger moved a hand for attention.

"What we have is a series of potentially cascading situations," he said seriously. "Some discuss this type of event in terms of catastrophe. Things beyond our control and possibly beyond our ken have been set in motion and will continue in motion. And we? We are in a precarious spot, as if we stand on a high ridge of sand capable of sliding either to the right or to the left.

"The motion—let's call it a wind—may set off a slide, or it may not. If the wind carries more sand, the slide might go to the right. If the wind carries moisture, the slide may be delayed—or it may be to the left. If the winds gain strength slowly, an equilibrium may be reached for some time. If the winds, they bluster—well then, we may have an avalanche—and still we are unsure if we will slide left or right."

"So our words, heard or unheard," the elder said after a moment, "do not move us from the ridge. They may or may not permit us to jump in the most advantageous direction at the correct time. And that we know the wind is blowing—it is of no moment. The wind cares not."

Jela, from an impulse which felt oddly tree-like, saluted the instructors.

"In that case, yes, I have found patterns. Many of them. They perhaps point somewhere useful; they raise questions I would pursue if my time were my own."

"Have some more coffee, my friend," suggested the elder, pouring as he spoke.

Jela sipped appreciatively and placed the cup carefully on the table.

"I would summarize this way: the basic patterns of the settled worlds were such that trade peaked at about the same time for all of them. This makes some sense, after all, when one compares the ebb and flow of galactic economics and populations, and when one looks at what these worlds offered for trade. None of them ever rose above mid-level—but they're all somewhat removed from the most profitable of the trade routes.

"The pattern of the unsettled worlds was that traffic to and from peaked at about the same time as the settled worlds in question." He paused to look at the instructors, seeing only serious attention in their faces.

"These are misleading patterns," he continued. "There's a far more interesting underlying connection; and one far, far older.

"As near as I could tell, the star systems in question were all very nearly the same age. I mean this with an accuracy I can't properly express. Though listed in some catalogs as having a range in birth of several millions of years, it appears that they may have been more closely linked than that. My guess would be that they were exactly the same age."

The instructors sat as if entranced while Jela paused, picked up his cup, stared into it, trying to put thoughts, feelings, intuitive leaps into something approaching linear.

At last, he sipped his coffee, sighed. Sipped again, and looked at them hard, one after the other.

"The trade patterns were merely an accident of trade and technology; I doubt that they were anything more than a symptom."

He sipped again, still feeling for the proper way to tell it . . .

"Isotopic timonium," he said, at last. "Each of the systems had been sources of an isotopic timonium. The stars were known to retain a fair amount, the planets orbiting them contained some, the gas clouds beyond had it . . . I'm tempted to say a *unique* isotopic timonium—I can't, not having all the information to hand.

"The pattern I see most fully is that the matter in all of those systems was formed from the same cataclysmic event. They shared birth, perhaps in the intergalactic collision that helped form the Arm. Again, I can't—didn't have time—to do the retrograde orbital analysis, the spectrum comparisons, the motion component cross-sections, the . . ."

He stopped himself. After all, the instructors didn't care what he hadn't done, but what he had.

"Unique isotopic timonium?" the younger instructor murmured. "This despite the distances from each other?"

"It's the pattern behind many of the other patterns," Jela assured him, being confident on that point at least. "I've lately seen literature which indicates that timonium was long considered to be an impossible element, semi-stable despite its atomic number, radiating in an unnatural spectrum . . . all this early conjecture was news to me, since my education was practical rather than creative."

He shrugged.

"I can't guess all of it. But, given a unique proto block or proto cloud formed in part into a galaxy that collided with the one we now inhabit—we speak in billions of years now!—and this timonium, which has all decayed at the same time, so close as if it came from the same furnace."

He sipped the last bit of coffee in his cup, saw the glance between the instructors from beneath hooded eyes.

"The *sheriekas*," he murmured, almost as quietly as the younger instructor. "They use timonium as if it were the commonest of metals. If anyone can find it at a distance, they can. If anyone knows how to make it act, or how to act on it at a distance, they can."

A chime then, and the instructors looked to chronographs and hastily rose.

"Destroy your working files," said the elder tutor, "and whatever hard copies you may have made. Eventually, of course, others may see the same thing, assuming they can access the information."

The younger instructor sighed audibly.

"You have—given the information we brought together over our careers—duplicated our thinking. This information has been shared only at the highest levels. Your commanders understand and act upon it; all others ignore it and deny it."

The elder instructor picked up a travel bag and looked pointedly at Jela.

"Do not doubt yourself," he said sternly. "The particular crystal that we protect, that we live within, is in danger. You, Captain, are one of a few who know the depth of the danger, and one of the fewer still who might do something about it. "

Then, with a most unexpected flutter of pilot hand-talk, signaling, *most urgent, most urgent, most urgent* he continued. "My studies show that there are universes entirely inimical to life. And there are universes not inimical which yet have none . . ."

From without came the sudden snarl of an air-breathing engine. The speaker lost his train of thought in the noise and looked to his fellow.

A second chime sounded, and amid a checking of pockets and carryabouts the instructors saluted Jela as if he were an admiral, and hurried off.

"Carry on, soldier," the quiet instructor said over his shoulder—and that was the last he heard or saw of them.

He carried on. He saluted the empty space, poured the last of the coffee into his cup, and sat with it cradled between his palms until it grew cold. Shaking himself, he rose, leaving a hint of a drop in the bottom of the hard-used cup, and returned to his interrupted sim.

SEVEN

❀ ❀

Awaiting Transport

JELA STOOD QUIETLY in the arid breeze, fascinated—or so it might have appeared to an observer—by the pair of contrails crossing the cloudless blue-green sky on exactly the same heading, one perhaps a hundred of Jela's calm breaths behind the other.

There was no way that a man without instruments could positively say which was higher, though Jela felt he knew. The leader, he thought, would land and be on its way to rotating its wheels for takeoff before the second touched down. After all, that's what had happened when he'd landed here, many days ago.

Yet the observer—and there was no small chance that there was such, likely watching from a camera or sensor stand for one last bit of measurement, one last bit of information about this particular candidate—the observer would have been wrong.

Far from being fascinated, M. Jela Granthor's Guard had pitched his mind as close to a dream state as he might while continuing to stand upright at the edge of the runway, and was himself observing: Listening to the keening echo of ancient, dead-and-gone flying things and concentrating on templates that fell almost visually across his concentration. The tree sat companionably by his side, its topmost leaves moving in a pattern not entirely wind-driven.

Leaning against the tree's lightweight traveling pot was the small kit he'd been given on his arrival at the training grounds. Anything else he owned was elsewhere, perhaps not to be seen again. He hoped, as he stood watching the contrails approach, that he'd soon be allowed his name back. The trainers had, without fail, called him Captain M, and while his name was nothing more than a quartermaster's joke, he was fond of it.

It could well be that they had been told no better name for him. After all, the fact that he was an M was there for all to see—and that he'd been training for duties and activity somewhat . . . above . . . those assigned a corporal, was also as clear as the air here.

There.

With an almost audible snap, the top branch fluttered and the template not quite before his eyes became an odd cross, the image half a small spacecraft and half a dragon gliding serenely on stiff wings.

Jela's back-brain applauded the attempt to match this relatively new experience with an unutterably ancient one, and to adjust that template on the fly, as it were.

The scary thing—and it was scary, on the face of it—was that the template continued to evolve, as if the tree were able to reach into Jela's own store of memories and capture details it could never have known of and for itself.

As he watched, the dragon's wings began to bulge at wing-root—but that was surely because Jela knew the craft on the way was an air-breather for much of the trip and would have engines buried there. Too, the keening of mighty dragons was giving way to not one, but two sets of incoming jet sounds, yet the approaching craft was still some moments beyond the range where any human ears might actually hear them.

He shivered then, did Jela, and let his attention return to the exact here and now that he breathed in, letting the template fade from his thought. The first craft was on final approach over the distant river and the second was making its turn—and *now* the engine sounds hit him, waking a touch of nostalgia for the first time he'd flown an air-breather.

There, the landing gear glinting, and *there*, the slight flare-out as a moment of ground-effect lift floated the graceful plane a heart-beat above the cermacrete runway.

A beautifully light landing then, with hardly a sound from the gear and barely a sniff of dust, and the underwhine ratcheting down quickly . . .

The fuselage hatch opened and two people stood inside, one to a side, as the craft rolled to a stop directly in front of him. The plane obligingly folded its gear to bring Jela within reach of the short step-ramp, and the two inside jumped the final knee height to his side to help him up, each flashing a salute, despite the fact he had no insignia on his near-colorless 'skins.

One of the assistants took his kit, the other considered the tree for a moment, decided on the proper way to hoist . . .

And that quickly was Jela within the plane, and the tree beside him, the only occupants of a small if comfortable passenger cabin. The engines began revving, the plane started rising on its gear to take-off height, and the assistants helped Jela snap into his belts.

Two more salutes and the assistants stepped off the plane, leaving the tree, taking the kit, and closing the hatch against the sound and the breeze.

On the wall before him was the flashing "Lift in Progress" sign, but he'd already felt the plane's gear lock and the motion of the completed turn. He settled in, envisioning—for the tree—what had just occurred, and then relaxed as the craft hurtled down the runway and into the air. The small *thwap* of the gear-doors closing mirrored a jolt of acceleration, and the nose rose.

Through the cabin's small view port he caught a glance of the second craft, now landing. Like this one, it bore no markings.

"Well," he said conversationally to the tree, "guess I get a new wardrobe when we get where we're going!"

He closed his eyes as the comfortable push of the ship's lift continued, indicating a pilot in something of a hurry.

Being neither pilot nor co-pilot, the best thing he might do for the troop at the moment was sleep. Which he did, willingly.

AS USUAL HE WOKE quickly, finding the plane about him barely an instant after deciding to wake. The afterimage of his working dream was a reprise of his last meeting with the language team. Of all the work—ranging from new and surprisingly interesting methods of killing, to explosives, to studies of maths far beyond those that he'd aspired to—it was the language work which had been a non-stop challenge. And the dream left him with the impression that he still needed work, that his skills were not quite adequate for the task to hand.

It was then that the craft banked, and the door to the piloting chamber slid open. A voice, somewhat familiar, drifted back.

"Captain Jela, welcome. Please come forward and take the second seat."

Jela unstrapped, pleased. He hated to be bored.

The flight deck was exactly like the trainers they'd tested him on—no surprise. Nor was the pilot's face.

"Commander." He nodded as he strapped in. Her 'skins, like his, were without markings, he saw.

She nodded in return.

"Your board will be live in a few moments. We'll hit the boost shortly—but there—see your screen for details. Soon we'll rendezvous with a ship carrying your crew and you'll begin simming on your new command."

"Your board is live, Captain," she said quite unnecessarily. "And, as you'll find in your info pack when we arrive, I am Commander Ro Gayda. Welcome to the real war."

PART TWO: SMUGGLERS

EIGHT

On Board *Spiral Dance*
Faldaiza Port

THE CARGO HAD BEEN waiting, for a wonder, and the loading expeditious, for another. She was scheduled to lift out in what passed for early tomorrow, hereabouts, which meant she had twenty-three hours, ship-time, in which to please her fancy.

The last few ports had been something short of civilized, by even her standards, so it happened she had a fancy.

She shut the board down as far as she ever did, having long ago learned not to turn off all the tell-tales and feeds, and never to put all systems in suspend, where she couldn't grab them out again in a hurry. With her outbound so soon, it really didn't make much sense to go through the extra half-shifts of shutdown and boot-up anyway.

While *Dancer* settled in to doze, she idly watched the local port feed. Some familiar names scrolled by—a bar she knew pretty well, or at least had known pretty well, and a couple jumping-jacks.

She considered the 'jacks and shook her head. She was too old to think of paper sheets as anything but a last resort that'd leave her needing to do things right next port. The problem with running a solo ship—and having a reputation for liking it that way—was some folks figured you were *always* solo, or else somebody whose interests weren't much in the public way. Mostly, she guessed, she fit that.

Not that she'd always run solo. Back when she'd been Garen's co-pilot and they'd done most of their work in the Rim—there'd been some grand flings, back then. She sighed and shook her head again.

Wasn't any use thinking about Garen, or about past lusts, either. Nothing good ever came out of thinking about the past.

Now. Now what brain and body were united in wanting was a time to relax and sleep naked-to-naked, after a couple heavy duty squeezes, some teasing and some sharing . . . *Now* was when it was hard on a body to be solo.

Truth told, there'd been more choices, back when. She wasn't ever going to be a beauty, but she *was* a pilot, and she damn well came out for fun with plenty of money in a public pocket so she didn't have to hold out for somebody else wanting to pay.

Back when, she didn't have the history of having killed a couple idiots who'd tried to take her ship; she didn't have a record of being fined and confined for taking on—in a fair fight!—the entire executive section of a battle cruiser and leaving them on hospital leave. Nor did she, then, know that this one beat her co-pilot, and that one stole virgins, and that other one robbed the people he slept with, every one.

And there she was, thinking about the past again. Brain melt, that's what it was. Happened when you ran solo too long. Likely, the port cops would find her in her tower, gibbering and wailing, crying over people long dead and vapor, like tears could ever right things.

She glanced back at the port feed, still scrolling leisurely through the various entertainment options, reached out to tap a key and zoom in on one section.

Beautiful. Beautiful girls, beautiful boys, beautiful couples. And, the ad said, they delivered. She could have one or a pair brought right here to her, health certificates and all.

The prospect of having a cute local pro—even a pair of cute

local pros—on hand to talk to in the middle of her night warmed her not at all.

She needed to get *out*, off-ship, away from metal walls and the sound of her own thoughts. Away from the past.

A tap on the keyboard banished the port feed. Another put the lighting back to night-rest. She stood and stretched to her full lean height, then headed for the hatch, snagging her kit-bag out of the empty co-pilot's chair.

First, food from something other than ship's store, maybe with a mild stimulant, to keep the edge on. After that—not ale, not today. Today, she'd have wine. Good wine—or the best on offer. And that food—nothing out of some grab-a-bite. No. She'd have plates, and linens, and pilots. Top of the line, all the way. She could afford it today, which wasn't always the case.

By the time she reached the edge of the field, she'd almost convinced herself that she'd have a great time.

FINDING A ROOM had been easy enough. The clerk at the Starlight Hotel was pleased to reduce her credit chit by a significant sum in return for a room complete with a wide bed, smooth sheets overlain with a quilted coverlet dyed in graduated shades of blue. A deep-piled blue carpet covered the floor; and the personal facilities boasted a single shower and a hand-finished porcelain tub wide enough to hold two, this not being a world which was exactly short on water.

She stowed her bag, had a quick shower, hesitated over maybe putting on something a little fancier than 'skins, decided that safety came first on Faldaiza, and headed out. The sweet smell of the hotel soaps and cleansers clung to her, distracting until she forgot them in her search for the rest of the list, which had proved unexpectedly difficult to fulfill.

The first fancy eatery she approached advertised all kinds of exotic and expensive food-and-drinkables, but she caught the gleam of armor 'skins as she approached and decided against. The next place, the woman holding the door acted like maybe pilot 'skins smelled bad, and the third place was standing room only with a line out the door.

She was about to give up on food and move on to wine and companionship, when she happened on The Alcoves.

It didn't look so fancy as the others, but the menu scrolling over the door promised fresh custom-made meals at not-ruinous prices, and a list of wines she recognized as on the top level of good.

She squared her shoulders and walked in.

The master of the dining room wore a sleeveless formal tunic, the vibrant green tats of his Batch glowed against the pale skin of his forearms, short gloves and hosen, all shimmering with embedded smartstrands.

"Pilot," he said, with a gratifyingly respectful bow of the head. "What service may this humble person be pleased to provide?"

"A meal," she said, slipping a qwint out of her public pocket. "Company, if a pilot's asked."

He palmed the coin deftly and consulted his log.

"There is one guest who has requested the pleasure of sharing his meal with a fellow pilot, should one inquire. Happily, he has only recently achieved a table, so your meals may be coordinated."

She felt something in her chest she hadn't known was knotted up ease a little and realized how much she had wanted another face, another voice, another *self* across the table from her. Someone who spoke the language of piloting, who knew what it was like to pour your life into your ship . . .

She inclined a little from the waist.

"I would be pleased to accept an introduction to this pilot," she told the master formally, and waited while he made a note in his log with one hand and raised the other, the strands of the glove glowing briefly.

From the curtain at his back, another Batcher appeared, also in smart formals, the same glow-green tats on her arms, her face an exact replica of the man's.

"This pilot joins the pilot seated in the Alcove of Singing Waters," the master said, and the waiter bowed.

"If the pilot would consent to enter," she murmured, and stepped back, sweeping the curtain aside with a tattooed arm.

She stepped into a wide hallway floored in gold-threaded white tiles. A subtle sound behind told her that the curtain had fallen back into place, and she turned slightly as the attendant approached.

"If the pilot will follow this unworthy one," the Batcher murmured and passed on, silent in gilded sandals.

Her boots made slightly more noise as she followed the Batcher, passing alcoves at measured distances. Across the entrance of each hung a curtain heavy with sound absorbing brocade.

She had counted eight such alcoves on her right hand. At the ninth, her guide paused and placed her gloved palm against the drawn curtain.

Some signal must have been traveled from the brocade to the strands in the gloves and thence to the attendant herself, for she drew back the curtain slightly and made a bow.

"This one requests the guest's forbearance," the Batcher said softly. "A pilot comes to share food with a pilot, if this is still desired."

In the hall and some steps behind, for decency's sake, she heard nothing from the room in response to this, but the answer must have been in the affirmative, for the attendant pulled the curtain wider and beckoned.

"Pilot, if you please. The pilot welcomes you."

She went forward, walking easy, keeping her—specifically empty—hands out where they could be seen. On the edge of the alcove, she paused, letting the light outline her, giving the other pilot—and herself too, truth told—a last chance to have a change of requirement.

The man seated in the lounger next to the wall of flowing water that apparently gave the alcove its name was dark in the hair and lean in the face. From the breadth of his shoulders she judged he'd top her not-inconsiderable height, but when he stood up to do the polite, she found herself looking down into eyes as black as the empty space beyond the Rim. His 'skins were dark, and it was hard to definitively decide where the man ended and the dim room began.

"Pilot," he said, and his voice was a clear tenor. "In peace, be welcome."

There weren't many who would violate the terms of peaceful

welcome, and if the small big man was one, well—she had long ago learned to err on the side of mistrust.

So. "Pilot," she answered. "I'm pleased to share a peaceful interlude."

Behind her, she heard the curtain fall. Anything that was said between them now would be absorbed and erased by the brocades. Unless there were paid listeners, of course . . .

"The room sweeps clean," the other pilot told her, reading the thought on her face, maybe—or maybe just naturally assuming she'd want to know and looking to save her the effort of scanning.

As it happened, her 'skins were on auto-scan and, lacking a warning tone, she decided to take his word for the conditions.

"That's good news," she said and came another step into the room. "I'm Cantra."

"Welcome," he said again, and gestured toward the loungers by the water. "I'm Jela. I sent for a bottle of wine, which should be here soon. In fact, I thought you must be it. No doubt the house will provide another glass, if you'd care to share a drink before the meal?" He raised a broad, brown hand, fingers spread.

"You understand, I have a forgiving schedule, and set myself the goal of a leisurely meal. If your time is limited . . ."

"I've got a few local hours to burn," she said. "Wine and a relax would be—something a lot like nothing I've had lately."

He grinned at that, showing white, even teeth, and again indicated the loungers. "Have a seat, then, and listen to the singing waters, for if I'm not mistaken—" A gong sounded, softly, from the brocaded ceiling.

"Enter!" Jela called, and the curtain parted for the female Batcher, bearing a tray holding a bottle of wine and two glasses.

Cantra sat down and let the lounger cradle her body. Jela sought the chair opposite and the attendant brought the wine to the table between them. She had the seal off efficiently and poured a mite of pale gold into each glass, handing the first to Jela, the second to Cantra.

Passing the glass beneath her nose brought her a rush of scent and a growing conviction that she was in the right place.

She sipped: sharp citrus flavors burst on her tongue, followed by a single note of sweetness.

"I'm pleased," Jela said to the attendant. "Pilot?"

"I'm—pleased," she replied, handing her glass back to the attendant with a smile. "And pleased to have more."

This was accomplished without undue fuss. Both pilots being accommodated, the attendant bowed.

"This humble person exists to serve," she said. "What may it please the pilots to order from our available foods?" She placed her gloved hands together and drew them slowly open. In the space between her palms, words formed—the house's menu.

Jela ordered leisurely, giving Cantra time to peruse the offerings and settle on the incredible luxury of a fresh green salad, non-vat fish steak, and fresh baked bread.

The attendant bowed, closed the menu and departed, silently slipping past the brocade curtain.

Cantra sipped her wine, relishing the flavors and the layers of taste. Across from her, the man—Pilot Jela—he sipped, too, cuddled deep in his lounger, forcefully projecting the impression of a man relaxed, indolent, and slow.

She having projected just such impressions herself from time to time in the interests of not frightening the grounders—maybe she was a little too aware of what he was doing. It might have been polite, not to notice. But it irritated her, to be treated like a know-nothing, and she brought her glass down to rest against her knee.

"You don't have to go to all that trouble for me," she said. "Pilot."

There was a short space of charged silence, as if he weren't used to being called on his doings, then a nod—neither irritable nor apologetic.

"Old habits," was what he said, and lifted his glass to sip with a respect that she registered as real. The relaxation he showed now was properly tempered and much more restful to the both of them, she was sure.

They sat quiet for a while then, each sipping, and letting the water whisper its song down the wall and disappear.

"Where are you in from, if it can be told, Pilot Cantra?"

"Chelbayne," she answered. Nothing to hide there, now that she was away, the cargo delivered and the fee paid. "Yourself?"

"Solcintra."

Kind of an Inner world, was Solcintra, or near enough that somebody from the Rim might think it not quite on the Arm, proper. A kind of has-been old settle in a quiet area where everyone traded with neighbors, that was all. Not a place she'd normally find herself. Still, you never knew.

"Anything special?" she asked, and saw him shrug against the lounger's deep back. She hadn't asked what kind of pilot he was; he might be anything from a cruise liner captain to a freight hauler to a relief man. 'Course, his presence on Faldaiza Port kind of argued against the cruise liner.

"There's a military unit garrisoned there," he was saying carefully over his glass. "A good few dozen ships attached to it. Most of them seemed to be in twilight."

Well, and that was news, after all. Soldiers were inevitable, in Cantra's experience. Garrisoned soldiers—they were something of an oddity. And even moreso, squatting down on a not-especially-prosperous world, trailing a buncha dozen sleepy ships . . .

"And how did you find things at Chelbayne?" he asked, taking his turn, which was polite and his right under peaceful welcome.

"Spooked," she said frankly. "Pilots doubling up on port. Rumors thicker'n star fields. Reported sightings of anything you like, including world-eaters, manipulators, and ancient space probes showing up with 'return to sender' writ on the power panels."

"Huh," he said, sounding intrigued in the way somebody would be by somebody else's craziness. "Anything stand up to scrutiny?"

She shrugged in her turn, feeling the lounger move to accommodate the motion. "The probes I heard about from somebody normally straight. On port for repair, she was, and looking to sign a new co-pilot. Could be she was ground-crazy. My inclination is to discount all I heard, no matter who gave it out. But maybe somebody really is collecting old space probes. Why not?"

"Why not?" he echoed comfortably. "See any yourself on the way in?"

She snorted. "Not to recognize." She sipped the last of her glass and put it on the table. "You been on port awhile?"

"A while," he allowed, finishing his own glass and leaning out of the embrace of the lounger. "More wine?"

"Yes," she said. And then, thinking that might have sounded too short, "Please."

He poured, splitting what was left equally between the two glasses, handed hers over, then sat back with his.

"Anything I should know, port-wise?" Cantra asked. "Don't want to be here past scheduled lift, paying for a mis-step."

He was quiet—thinking—honestly thinking, was her sense, and not mumming. She sipped her wine and waited.

"There seem to be some odd elements on the port," he said slowly. "I'm not clear myself what makes them odd, or if odd translates into dangerous. The locals . . ." he paused to sip his wine gently. "The locals may have caught some of that spooked feeling from Chelbayne. Usual rules apply."

The last was said without irony, and with enough emphasis to move him well out of the passenger liner column on the pilot rating chart, as far as she was concerned. That was with the usual rules being: Watch your back, watch the shadows, and always expect trouble.

"That's something," she acknowledged.

He nodded, seemed about to say something more, but the gong sounded again, and he called "Enter," instead.

The Batcher attendant slipped into the room and bowed.

"Would it please the pilots to receive their meals?"

THE FOOD and the discussion of the food having both come to satisfactory conclusions, Cantra called for a third bottle of wine. It came promptly, was poured, and the two of them again sat deep into the loungers.

Cantra sighed, inert and content. The dinner talk, light on info as it had been, had finished unknotting the tension in her chest. She was in no hurry to move on; even the itch to find someone to share the upscale lodgings with had gone down a couple notches on the gotta list.

"So," said Jela from the depths his chair, and sounding as lazy as she felt. "Where do you go from here, if it can be told?"

That ran a little close to the edge of what was covered by peaceful welcome. Still, she didn't need to be specific as to when.

"Lifting out for the Rim," she said, which was bound to be true sometime.

"Heard there was some military action in the far-out recently," he said, slow, like he was measuring how much info to offer. "Maybe even a world-eater sighted."

She moved her shoulders, feeling the chair give and reshape. "Rim's always chancy," she said. "All sorts of weird drifts in from the Deeps. Won't be the first time I've been out that far."

"Ship shielding doesn't even give a world-eater indigestion," he pointed out, sounding sincere in his concern. "And ship beams are just an interesting appetizer."

"That's right," she said, puzzled, but willing to play. "But a ship can run; a ship can transition. World-eaters are stupid, slow and confined to normal space."

"You talk like you've had some experience there," Jela said, which was absolutely a request for more, and danced well outside the confidentials guaranteed under peaceful welcome.

She took her time having a sip of wine, weighing the story and what might be got from it that she took care not to say.

In the end, it was inertia and a full belly that made the decision. She wasn't ready to move on just yet, and there wasn't much, really, to be gained from the tale, setting aside piloting lore which this Jela, with his big shoulders and noncommital eyes, surely had, either from experience of his own or from training. He was no fresh-jet, in her professional judgment. Still, if he wanted to hear it . . .

"Not a new tale," she said, bringing her glass down at last.

"New to me," he countered, which was true enough—or so she hoped.

"Well, then." She settled her head against the chair and paused, letting the whisper of the falling water fill the silence for a heartbeat, two . . .

"I was co-pilot, back when," she began. "The pilot had some business out on the Rim, so there we were. Problem come up and we lifted in a hurry, ducking out a few klicks into the Beyond." She paused to have a sip.

"That's some problem," Jela said after her glass came down again, and she nearly laughed.

You might allow it to be a problem when the cargo was wanted by the yard apes, who were all too ready to confiscate it and all the info there might be in ship's log and the heads of pilot and co-pilot. You might allow it to be a problem that the client wasn't particularly forgiving of missing deliveries and Garen having to make the call, was it better to lose the cargo out in the Deeps and maybe have a chance to collect it later, risking the client's notable bad grace, or chance a board-and-search?

She'd opted to dodge and jettison, a decision for which Cantra didn't fault her, though they never did find it again, worse luck, and wound up working the debt off across a dozen runs, the client having been that peeved by the loss.

"It was a problem of some size," she told Jela. "Understanding that the pilot was out of the Rim, original—and didn't maybe respect Beyond like she ought. Anywise, we're out there, beyond the Rim, just meditating, and giving the problem time to brew down to a lesser size, when an anomaly shows up on the far-scans." She shrugged against the chair's embrace.

"A pilot's not a pilot unless they got a curiosity bump the size of a small moon, so she and me, we decide to go take a look."

"In the Beyond?" His startlement seemed genuine. "How did you navigate?"

"Caught the Rim beacons on mid-scan and did the math on the fly," she said, off-hand, like it was no trick at all. Nor was it, by then. By then, her and Garen had been out Deep considerable.

"So, we went on out to look," she resumed. "And we got a visual on something that looked to be a bad design decision on the part of the shipwright. Big, too. Not much velocity, spill spectrum showing timonium, timonium, and for a change timonium. Tracking brain plotted its course and saw it hitting the Rim at a certain point, in a certain number of Common Years.

"The pilot hailed it on general band and I hit it with every scan we had."

She sipped. He sat, silent, waiting for the rest of it.

"Well, it didn't answer the hail, o'course. And the scans bounced. I'm thinking it was the scans got its attention, but it might've been the hail, after all. It started to rotate and it started to get hot. Radiation scan screamed death-'n-doom. We figured we knew what we had by then, and the pilot was of a mind to turn it back into Beyond, where it couldn't do much harm."

"Turn it?" *That* got his attention.

"Right." She raised her hand, showing palm. "Say the pilot was a fool, which I'm not saying she didn't have her moments. Can't say for certain if that was one of them, though, because the truth is she did turn it, playing easy meat, while I sat my board sweating and feeding everything I dared into the shields, which were peeling like old hull paint."

"So I'd think."

"We kept its attention until we was sure it was on course for Out-and-Away. Shields were just about gone by then, and I was starting to fear for the navigation brain, not to say the biologics, when the pilot decided we'd done what we could, and nipped us into transition."

"Transition," he repeated. "Using what for reference points? If it can be told."

"Had the Rim beacons on long-scan, like I mentioned," she lied glibly. "Did the math on the fly."

"I—see." He had a go at his glass, and she did the same, to finish, and put the empty on the table.

She'd come too close to a slip, she thought, half-irritated and half-regretful. Time to be moving on, before she got any stupider.

"I want to thank you," she said formally, and his Deeps-black gaze flicked to her face. "For your companionship. The time was pleasant and informative. Now, I must take myself off."

She stood, leaving the embrace of the chair with a pang. Paused for one last listen of the singing water—and very nearly blinked as the other pilot came to his feet.

"As it happens, it's time for me to leave, too," he said blandly, and moved a hand toward the curtained exit. "Please, Pilot. After you."

PILOT CANTRA was an interesting case, Jela thought, following that lady down the tiled hallway toward the foyer and the front door. The tale about turning the world-eater had rung true, though there had been, he had no doubt, a certain few tricky facts greased in the telling.

She wasn't being easy to file, either. He'd've said prosperous free trader, from the quality of the 'skins and the fact that she was eating at a subdued place on the high end of mid-range. On the other hand, there was that story and the easy-seeming familiarity with the Rim— and beyond. According to his considerable information, Rimmers had a flexible regard for such concepts as laws, ownership, and what might be called proscribed substances. Not that all Rimmers were necessarily pirates. Just that none of the contributors to the reports he'd been force-fed had ever met one who technically wasn't.

Given that she wasn't at all who he'd been expecting—he'd been expecting Pilot Muran, who was now some local days overdue for their rendezvous—he counted himself not unlucky in the encounter. She was a fine-looking woman—tall, lithesome, and he didn't doubt, tough. Her weapon was quiet, but there for those who knew how to look—and he appreciated both the precaution and her professionalism.

He'd entertained the notion that she might be somebody sent on by Muran, when he found himself unable—and dismissed it when the meal took its course and she failed to produce either code words or a message from the tardy pilot.

That she was only a pilot who had wanted company over her meal—that seemed certain, and he made a mental note to chew himself out proper for supposing that any pilot who would choose such a restaurant would come complete with co-pilot, client, or companion. Getting civilians into soldier trouble, that was bad.

Though there was no guarantee that there was or would be trouble, he thought, trying *that* notion on for not the first time. Muran being late—that could be explained by a couple things short of catastrophe.

Muran not sending a reason or a replacement—that couldn't. Jela sighed silently and owned to himself that he was worried.

Pilot Cantra had reached the curtain, swept it away with one long arm and stepped to a side, holding the doorway clear for him.

"Pilot," she said, and it could've been irony he heard in her voice, "after you."

He nodded and slipped past her, fingering coins out of his pocket as he approached the console.

Behind him, he heard the curtain go down. He deliberately didn't turn, but finished counting the price of the meal out into a pile, and a few more coins, into a second, smaller pile, over which he held his hand, fingers outspread.

"For the attendant," he said to the master's raised eyebrow. "The service was excellent and I am grateful."

The master's fee had come off the top when he had made his initial reservations. Jela had made a point of tipping the attendant on every visit.

Nodding, the master gathered up the meal-price, thumbed his drawer open and deposited the coins.

"This humble person is delighted to hear that the pilot is pleased," he said.

Jela felt a presence at his side and looked up, expecting to see the female attendant. What he did see, to his somewhat surprise, was Pilot Cantra, leaning forward to offer a credit chit. Yellow, he noted, being in the habit of noting such details. Whatever Pilot Cantra was, she was in funds today.

"The meal was fine, the company welcome," she said, her husky voice giving the formal words an interesting texture.

"This humble person delights in the pilot's pleasure," the master assured her expressionlessly, running the chit through the console's reader. There was a *ping* as the amount was deducted, and the chit was passed back. Green now, Jela noticed, but still at a more than respectable level for a pilot on Faldaiza Port.

Cantra received her chit and slid it away without giving it a glance. When her hand came out of her pocket, she leaned over and put a stack of coins next to Jela's stack.

"For the attendant," she said. "She served well."

"The pilot's generosity is gratifying," the master said and raised his hand. His Batch-sister slipped around the edge of the curtain, and came forward until she was standing behind the console, facing Jela.

She was a compact woman, efficient-looking without being at all lithe. She bowed, precisely, and gathered the coins into her gloved hands.

"Pilots. It is the pleasure of this humble person to serve. Walk safely."

He felt Pilot Cantra stiffen beside him and hoped he had masked his own shock more fully.

Turning, he looked up into the other pilot's eyes. They were green, he saw, which he hadn't been sure of, in the dimness of the dining alcove, and calm, despite her start of shock.

"Shall we proceed, Pilot?" he asked, expecting her to push past him and stride out into the port on her own. Which would clarify one thing or another.

But it appeared it was his hour for surprises.

"Why not?" Cantra said.

OUTSIDE, THE SHADOWS were lengthening into the leisurely local evening. Jela hung back a step, intending to let the other pilot make the first move.

"I don't *see* anything worth worrying about," she said easily, dawdling by his side—just two friends, finishing up a chat started inside over food and wine. "You?"

"Not immediately," he said with a smile for the joke she hadn't made. "Maybe we should move on, in case they're running late?"

"Good idea." She turned to the left and he went along, matching her long stride easily.

"Now I'll ask you," she said, without looking at him. "Was the Batcher having a little fun with us?"

It was an interesting question, all things considered, and Jela did consider it, alongside of a couple other facts and oddities, among them the lack of Pilot Muran—and the presence of Pilot Cantra, who might be an innocent civilian, or who might be something else.

"No reason to believe she was," he said slowly, not particularly liking the direction his thought was tending, but letting it have its head.

"Other question being," Cantra mused, and he approved the way she scanned the street as they walked along—eyes moving, checking high points, low, possible places of concealment. "Who's likely to be wanting to talk with you in a serious way? I can think of some couple who might want to have a cozy chat with me, but nothing that can't wait."

There shouldn't, he thought, be anyone wanting to talk to him in any serious way, excepting the absent Muran.

They'd set up the rendezvous carefully, that being how they did things. And they'd arranged for a back up, just in case the primary went bad. He'd checked the back up, and needed to do so again—now, in fact. All things considered.

He glanced at the woman beside him and found her watching him, green eyes—amused?

Not easy to scan at all, was Pilot Cantra. And it came to him that he'd better make sure of her, if he could.

"I'm after a bit of noise and maybe something else to drink," he said. "You?"

Slim eyebrows arched over those pretty green eyes, and he thought she might turn him down. But—

"Sounds good," she said easily.

"I know a place just a couple steps over there." He cocked his head to the left, and she moved a slim, ringless hand in the pilot's sign for *lead on*.

NINE

❀❀❀❀❀❀❀❀❀❀❀❀❀❀❀❀❀❀❀❀❀❀❀

On the ground
Faldaiza Port

PILOT JELA'S "PLACE," a bar-and-drinkery calling itself Pilot's Choice, was considerably more than a couple steps, situated as it was in the shadow of the port tower. Giving the pilot his due, it wasn't a pit, nor showing any 'jack spaces on offer. What it was, was full of pilots, loud voices, and something that might've been music—in fact, was music.

There was pair of bouncer-types checking ID at the door, which was a good thing by her way of thinking, 'cause it meant the local lowlifes weren't allowed in—just them with proper Port clearance or genuine pilot-class credentials.

Cantra showed her ship's key, and was gratified to see the hand motion from the sharp-eyed man requesting just a bit more . . . and so she flashed the flat-pic with numbers and such on it. He didn't bother to run-scan on it, though the machine was live—just gave her a half-salute and waved her into the dense noise and rowdy dance-and-brew scent.

Apparently, Jela was in the same boat as far as looking legit on visual, which was a shame, 'cause all she saw was him slipping his card into a semi-public pocket, the woman on that side signing out with a respectful, "Thank you, Pilot!"—and still not a polite way to find out exactly what he was a pilot of. But some information you just didn't ask if it didn't come voluntary.

They pushed on, just like they were together. The crowd motion stopped them for a moment, 'til she could point out to Jela the direction of the bar from her greater height, which information he acknowledged with equanimity.

Now they were further in, she could see a couple almost-nakeds on a raised platform on the opposite side of the room from the bar, dancing, they might've been. Looked interesting, whatever.

She let Jela break trail, which wasn't any problem at all for those shoulders, and directly joined him at the bar proper, one foot on the rail, waiting for the notice of the bartender.

"There's a man here I need to talk to," Jela said to her, his voice pitched to carry under the general hubbub. "It's probable he'll have news, maybe make some sense of our friend's concern, if you'd want to wait?"

She gave him a smile. "I'll wait," she murmured, for his ears only. "Why not?"

"Good. Back soon." He was gone, moving quick and light through the crowd and she watched him go, considering the wide shoulders and the slim hips with a sort of absent-minded admiration. Not her usual sort, Pilot Jela, but a well-made man, regardless.

"What'll it be, Pilot?" The bartender's prosaic question brought her back to the now and here.

"Ale," she said, knowing better than to ask for wine in a pilot's bar this far in to the shipyards.

"Coming up," the 'tender promised, and up it came in a timely manner. She smiled for the quick service and slid a couple carolis across the bar.

"Keep the change," she said. He gave her a grin and went away to tend to other customers.

Having ale didn't mean having to drink it. Cantra kept the glass to hand, which was respectful of the house and the 'tender, and turned her back against the bar, surveying the room for possibles.

Problem was, the room was a little too full, a little too loud. She wasn't jumpy, not that, but say that the Batcher's warning had sharpened her edge. In the general way of things, Batchers kept strictly to this-humble-person. There was good reason for that, Batchers on most worlds in the Arm being not only "biologic constructs" but property, bought and sold. What there wasn't any good reason for was a Batcher to give clear warning to a couple o'strange pilots, or even to say more than the standard humble gratitude.

Unless, she thought, and it wasn't a thought that made her feel any smoother, the Batcher's owner had ordered her to say what she had. And if that was so—

If that was so, there were 'way too many unknowns in the equation. Anyway, she thought, what's it matter, warned trouble or unexpected? The usual rules applied.

She had to admit that, after the quiet time at The Alcoves, she was inclined to be a bit more aware of things; and if even so small a break from routine had energized her, *that* was a sign she needed to get a real break soon. Like maybe right now. She'd come off the ship looking for action, and it looked like action might be all about, if she put her mind to it, and took a lead from the dancers . . .

The couple on the platform was slow-dancing now, hip to hip and thigh to thigh. As she watched, they separated and went to opposite edges, calling for volunteers from the crowd to come up and join them.

This proposition was greeted with such enthusiasm that at first it seemed the bar's entire pilot population would be up on the platform. The dancers, though, they were pros, and managed to keep their company down to two each—one to an arm. A couple of the chosen had drunk a bit too much ale, and the dancers had their work scheduled, keeping their dainty bare toes out from under boots.

Watching them, she felt some heat building in her belly and recalled herself to the proposed task list.

It'd be a shame to let the lodgings stand empty, she thought, and tried to bring herself into a concentration on the available options.

Jela hadn't reappeared. It might, after all, be best if he didn't reappear, shoulders or no. He'd been a not-entirely-comfortable, if welcome, meal-mate, but she wanted something a little less—controlled—for the bed-sport side of the evening. That little redhead, for instance. Cute, quick, and not drunk yet, dancing all by himself in a vacant square of floor.

She watched him, feeling her blood warm agreeably, and just about cussed when the music ended.

The redhead stopped dancing, and looked around like maybe he didn't know what to do now.

Cantra pushed away from the bar and went over to introduce herself.

"HE WAS HERE, SURE," Ragil said. Most of his attention was on the stim-stick he was rolling. Command frowned on soldiers using non-regulation stimulants. Not that Ragil had cared much for that particular reg when he was regular troop. Now that he was on the underside, he claimed the stim habit gave him "verisimilitude" in his role as bar owner. For all Jela knew, he was right.

"So he was here," he said now, working on holding his temper. "Where is he now?"

Ragil finished the stick and brought it to his lips, drawing on it to start the thing burning. He looked up, broad face worried.

"How do I know? I gave him your last, that you'd be at the prime spot an extra day, same time, same code." He drew on the stick, sighed out smoke. "You're asking because he didn't connect?"

"Why else?" Jela sighed. "Somebody else did connect, though. Scan the floor?"

"Sure." He left the stick hanging out of the side of his mouth, tapped a code into the top of his desk. "Center screen," he said.

Jela sat carefully back in his chair—no upscale lounger here—and watched the slow pan of the barroom. The stage was empty, the dancers down on the floor, circulating, collecting tips, no doubt, and offers of companionship, after hours. The room was crowded and he sharpened his focus, in case he missed her in the crowd.

"Busy," he commented.

"Damn place is always busy," Ragil returned. "And it's not 'cause the drinks are cheap. Owe you one, by the way. Your idea of getting a couple dancers in here paid off."

"Getting anything useful?" Jela asked absently, eyes on the screen.

"Who knows what's useful?" Ragil countered. "Rumor, hearsay, and speculation, most of it. What they do with it at the next level— how do I know? Heard one pilot the other day give as his opinion that there's no enemy now, nor hasn't been for longer than you or me's been fighting. Command, see, needed a reason to increase the production of soldiers, so they sorta invented an enemy."

"I've heard that one," Jela said. "What they never explain is why Command wants soldiers, if there's no enemy."

"Take over the Arm?" Ragil asked.

"And hold it how?" He was beginning to think that Pilot Cantra had left the bar without—

"There!" he said. "Grab and grow the tall woman there next to the redhead."

Ragil obligingly did this, and Pilot Cantra's strong-boned face filled the center screen.

"Know her?" Jela asked.

The other took a deep drag on his stick while he considered the image. "No," he said finally. "Don't think I want to, either. What's your interest?"

"She came to the primary, asked for a meal-mate, if there was a pilot available."

Ragil whistled, soft and tuneless. "So—what? She's Muran's replacement?"

"Didn't say so," Jela said, slowly. "Didn't act anything but like a pilot half-crazy from running solo and looking to have a voice that wasn't her own to listen to. Didn't make any play to stay close; I invited her along. In case." He paused, thinking, among other things, of the Batch-grown's warning, which had shocked Pilot

Cantra—but for what reason? "She's a hard one to peg, and I won't say she's not fully capable."

"So she might be a beacon?"

"Might," he said, still not liking the idea—not that it made any difference what he liked, or ever had. "Might not."

Ragil pitched the end of his stim-stick into the recycler, leaned forward and tapped a command into his console. The grow-frame vanished as the camera went real-time, keeping its eye on Pilot Cantra and her friend.

"What're you going to do?" he asked.

Jela sighed. "Don't know."

THE RED-HAIRED PILOT'S name was Danby and he wasn't disagreeable to letting her buy him an ale. She got the 'tender's attention and settled that, then they leaned on the bar, arm against arm, and did the preliminaries.

His ship was nice and legit—belonged to the Parcil Trade Clan, from which there was nothing more legit—and him fairly new-come to first chair. They were on-port for three local days, of which this was the evening of the second day. Trouble was, they ran watch-shifts on-board, instead of shutting down and letting all crew loose at once, and he was due to take his turn at watching inside the next couple hours.

"There's a 'jack down the road, here," he said with a bit of hope in his voice, tipping his head toward the door.

Cantra considered it—he was that cute, funny, too, in a by-the-law sorta way—then shook her head.

"Got lodgings rented up-port," she said, apologetic, since there wasn't no use hurting his feelings. "Just in from a long run. Figured on a long, slow night to make it seem worthwhile."

He looked wise and nodded. "Sometimes quick won't do it," he agreed, not noticeably cast down by her refusal. "Too bad we didn't meet up earlier."

Across the room, the dancers came back on stage, and the music started up again, almost overwhelmed by the hollering and whistles from the pilots on the floor. Danby put his hand on her arm and she looked over to him, slow and careful, wondering if she'd misjudged—

"Let's dance," he said.

She blinked, and—hesitated, not having been much in the way of dancing lately.

"It'll work out some of the kinks, anyway," he urged.

She remembered, back when she'd been younger than Danby looked to be, dancing whole leaves away. Back when, dancing had in fact worked out some of the kinks. She tried to remember when she'd stopped—and why—then figured it didn't matter.

"Sure," she said, with a smile for his wanting to help. "It's been a long time, though—fair warning."

Floor space being at premium, closer in toward the platform, they hung back along the edge of the crowd and claimed themselves a rectangle of floor by the simple process of facing off and starting in.

Dancing came back pretty easy, once her muscles got over the shock. Danby jigged and high-stepped and she copied him, letting her body get reacquainted with the notion.

"Doin' pretty good for somebody who doesn't remember how!" he yelled in her ear—yelling being the only way he could make himself heard in the general exuberance. "Try this!"

Hands on hips, he executed an intricate and rapid triple crossover, legs scissoring and boots hardly seeming to touch the floor. He finished with a jump and a spin, and threw her a grin that was pure dare-you.

She grinned back and put her hands on her hips, swaying with the music for a few bars, letting the movement pattern seep through the pilot brain and down into the shoulders, arms, hips—

Her legs moved, boots beating out the count, then she was up and spinning, the room circling 'round her—the high-stepping dancers; pilots, stamping; pilots jigging in place; pilots leaning against the bar; the 'tender pouring a glass; two not-pilots in armored 'skins walking in from the street—

She saw what looked like some resistance from the doorman who'd ushered her through, but that was guessing, since she kept moving, had to, with the momentum and—

She touched floor, twisting back toward the door before her feet were properly set. Her height gave her an advantage—she could see the door, just, over the heads of the combined pilots. The armored pair were inside, now, hesitating—no. Scanning the room.

Bounty hunters, she thought, or charity agents. Amounted to the same thing: Trouble.

She reached out and grabbed Danby's arm, hard. He blinked at her, pretty blue eyes going wary and sharp. Likely he was a bit pinched, though he kept it to himself if he was.

"Trouble in the door," she growled into his ear, and felt him tense under her hand.

"What kind of trouble?" he asked, and she let him go, moving her shoulders in frustration.

"Can't tell," she muttered. "Might be bounty. Might be—" She stopped then because the two had decided to make it easy on themselves.

The first pulled her gun, aimed at the ceiling and pulled the trigger. It was an explosive charge and made a bit of noise. Enough to put all the rest of the noise in the room into remission. On the platform, the two dancers sank to their knees, arms around each other, faces hidden against shoulders.

Into the sudden silence, the second woman shouted, "We're looking for two people. We know who they are, and we know they're here. Everybody just stay peaceful while we do a walk-through and collect them, then you can go back to having fun."

Bounty hunters, then. Cantra stifled a sigh. It didn't advance commerce or do anything else useful, but she hated bounty hunters. Always had.

There was muttering, but nobody went for a weapon—wasn't any sense to it, being what the second 'hunter had said was true. Unimpeded, they'd sort through the crowd, round up their prey and be gone. All very efficient and no trouble for anybody, except the ones they'd been paid to collect.

The first 'hunter started on the bar side of the room, the second on the dance platform side. The dancers visibly cringed when she walked past, but she never gave them a glance.

The first had finished with the bar sitters and was wading into the crowd of sullen pilots, her eyes moving rapidly, her face intent—a woman who had a pattern in mind and whose only thought was a match. She worked her way along, dismissing everybody she passed—then her eyes lit on Danby and got wider.

Cantra tensed, remembering her weapon, riding quiet and accessible, and reminding herself forcibly there was no profit to be had from putting herself between a 'hunter and her bounty. She didn't know Danby, she didn't owe him. But—

The 'hunter lunged, Cantra felt her fingers twitch toward her gun and killed the move—just as the 'hunter's hand came around her wrist, snapping the bracelet tight.

Too late, she jerked back, swinging with her free fist—*stupid*, she snarled at herself—impeded by the press of people. The hunter grabbed the fist as it skinned past her cheek, snapped a bracelet on it, too, twisted the two lead wires into a single, and clipped the tail end into her belt. Then she reached out and pulled Cantra's gun from its quiet pocket.

She snarled, caught movement out of the corner of her eye, which was Danby coming in, and made herself go limp.

"What the hell's this?" he yelled at the 'hunter. "She's as legit as I am!"

Not quite, though it did warm her to hear him say it. She moved her head; caught his eyes on hers.

"Easy, Pilot. Don't want to be late to your watch."

"Listen to her," the 'hunter advised. "No difference to me if I get somebody on aid-and-abet, too."

He stepped back, bright lad, and threw Cantra a look. She made her face into something representing calm, and nodded to him.

The crowd around had started to come back, and that could get dangerous on its own, if she wasn't careful. Wouldn't do to have him call in a friend or two and start a riot on her account.

"It was fun—the dancing," she said, letting him see that she was calm about it, and then the 'hunter jerked on the wire and she was moving, trying to keep her arms from being dislocated.

The second 'hunter came up, empty-handed. They exchanged a

glance and wordlessly turned toward the door, Cantra in tow like a
wreck bound for salvage.

"Next time you pull a gun in here somebody'll shoot you!"
promised the woman who'd scanned Jela in. The man was off to the
side, a small callphone to his ear, talking earnestly.

Outside, the 'hunters kept walking—and by necessity, Cantra,
too—down the street proper, then into a smaller one—a service
alley, maybe. Something was definitely out of true, Cantra thought.
Leaving aside the question of whether or not she deserved to be
arrested, any bounty hunter worth her license would not be
dawdling in alleyways when she had a prize on the leash and
payment due.

On the other hand, an alleyway was going to suit her purposes
admirably. The fact that they hadn't searched her was interesting,
but not particularly useful, with her hands bound like they were.

What was both interesting and useful was the fact that they'd
used smartwire to bind and seal her. Made sense for them, o'course.
Besides being industry standard, smartwire was—call it impossible—
to break, which was close enough to true, given the usual conditions
under which bounty arrests were made. The other thing about
smartwire was that it was—call it virtually impossible—to escape. It
only rated a "virtually" because a frequency existed which interfered
with its process, briefly, allowing the alert captive to slip free. The
window of freedom was small, smartwire being able to repair and
reroute itself, but it was there.

"Where's the other one?" The first 'hunter asked the second,
who shrugged, plainly aggravated.

"Not there."

"Must've been there. He didn't leave."

"That's why we sent Kaig to take care of the back room, wasn't
it?"

Cantra almost sighed. Three of them, assuming Kaig survived
his adventure to the back room, which she didn't consider likely, if
the "other one" was Pilot Jela, as it must be. Still, it wasn't any use
waiting to find out.

She brought her hands up, resting the bracelets against her

breast, fingers folded together. She jerked her chin, hitting the hidden toggle, felt a ripple in the fabric of her 'skins . . .

The bracelets fell away. Cantra dodged back, slapping the seal on her thigh.

The first hunter yelled, bringing her noisy gun around. Cantra shot her in the eye, landing hard on her shoulder on the alley floor, rolling for the scant cover of a trash bin, as the second 'hunter fired, fired, fired—and stopped.

Cantra peered out from beneath the bin, hideaway at ready—two more darts left, which ought to be enough if—

"Pilot Cantra?" The voice was familiar and not unexpected.

"Pilot Jela?" she replied.

"Yes," he said, rueful, she thought. "The field is ours, Pilot."

AS IT HAPPENED, she'd been wrong about Hunter Kaig's chances of survival. He was alive, twisted up in his own wire and sound asleep on the floor.

"I'll send him on up to the next level," the man named Ragil said, rolling a dope stick one-handed while he talked to Pilot Jela. "Won't be much help in present conditions, though." He brought the stick up, drawing on it hard to get it started, and glanced over to Cantra, where she had taken up a lean against the wall, the better to watch the room.

"Want one?" he asked.

"I'm fine," she said, forcefully agreeable.

"Owe you," he insisted. "My people are supposed to keep the riff-raff out."

"No favor in a stim-stick for someone running on adrenal high," she answered, still agreeable. "I'm fine."

She got the right answer this time. Ragil gave her a look and turned back to Jela, who was working with the computer, idents from the three hunters on the table next to him.

They were a study, Ragil and Jela, and Cantra took her time about studying them. Ragil's hair was brown, which matched his eyes. And while he was another one built like a war-runner, his shoulders weren't quite as broad as Jela's and he was about a head taller. Not natural brothers, she'd decided. Not Batchers neither. Not, she thought, kin at all, though there was something—undefinable and undeniable—that put one of them in forcible mind of the other.

Part of the similarity, she considered, was bearing—both were proud, tall-standing men.

Another part was age—or lack of specific age, other than the ever-slippery "adult"—but that could just mean they'd done a lot of ship-time. Truth was, she didn't look her own years, quite, having started in on ships at a tender age.

The rest—might be they'd been shipmates once—they seemed to have that kind of understanding between them. Neither one calling senior, both comfortable in their talents.

Shipmates, she decided, watching Ragil drag on his stick, eyes narrowed as he read Jela's screen through the drifting smoke.

"That doesn't look good," he said. Jela grunted, and sat back.

"What's not looking good, if you don't mind sharing?" she asked from her lean, and the pilot spun his chair around to face her. He might've been worried, or he might not, for all the info she could read off his face.

"It happens that our friends weren't necessarily registered," he said, and she shrugged, which got her a bite from the bruised shoulder.

"Freelancers, is all," she said.

"Not on Faldaiza." That was Ragil. "Freelancers gotta register for a non-resident license and get listed in the public files, along with the text of their writs."

She considered that, then used her chin to point at the cards on the table. "What're they?"

Jela grinned. "My money says forged."

She frowned. "Forged 'hunter tickets—for what? I'm not wanting to pry into your private affairs, Pilot, but I don't have any shame in telling you there ain't no bounty out on me—" *for at least two Common Years now*, she added silently— "so even if they'd been registered, it'd be an illegality to come in and arrest a righteous citizen of the Spiral Arm during a certified pursuit of happiness.

Which is what they done." She took a breath, looked from Jela's face to Ragil's, seeing identical expressions of placid waiting.

"So when I'm saying freelancers," she said, just in case the brains behind those non-committal eyes hadn't processed the thought. "I'm saying *freelancers*. I understand Faldaiza's feelings regarding the slave trade, but that don't mean those taken here need to be sold here."

"Well," said Ragil, and took a heavy drag on his stick. Jela tipped his head.

"That would fit," he allowed, "expect they knew who they were looking for—you."

"And you." She sighed. "So—what?"

"So—the piece of news you don't have," Ragil said, "is there's another pilot in the mix. He was set to meet Jela this evening, except he never showed. Me, I saw him—talked to him—no further out than local yesterday."

Cantra looked at him, then back to Jela.

"He fell or got taken," she said, watching his face, "and before he filed his last lift, he said something that made you sound interesting to whoever was listening."

His mouth tightened, not a smile, she thought. "Who then came looking for me at the restaurant, since that was the arranged meet, but you'd already claimed the open invitation."

"Putting me up high on the interesting list, too. And the Batcher warned us to walk careful 'cause she'd seen the come-lately and thought he smelled bad." She sighed. "Well, at least that hangs together as a tale. Got any idea who?"

"No."

"Not helpful."

"I agree."

She shifted against the wall. "What's the odds the Batcher knew the come-lately?"

"That's an idea," Ragil said to Jela, who looked up at him.

"Right. I'll swing by on my way back."

"Back from where?" Cantra asked, thinking that she was glad of the dance with Danby, because it looked like that was going to have to do it. Whoever was trying to get Pilot Jela's attention had her linked to him, which meant her place was on her ship—just as soon as she could get there.

"From your ship, I'd imagine," Jela said, seriously. "I got you into this—whatever it is. Least I can do is give you backup to a defensible point."

"Think I can't take care of myself?" She snapped at him, and he held his big hands up in front of his face, fingers spread.

"I think you can take care of yourself just fine, Pilot Cantra," he said, and it was respect she heard in his voice. "But I'll ask you to do the math. First time, they sent one—we think. This time they sent three. Next time they send six, or nine. Do I scan?"

"If they send," she countered. "Might be three was all they had. Might be they lost interest and found something else to do what's fun."

"And might not," he answered, which he hadn't needed to do, her brain already having said the same.

She sighed and shoved away from the wall, feeling her recovered gun in its quiet pocket and the needler with its depleted charge hidden back behind seal.

"All right then," she said, not in any way pleased by the ruination of her plans. "I got my kit to get, if you're wanting a tour of the town. But before that, I'll come along with you to The Alcoves and see what the news is there."

"Why not?" he said, and levered out of his chair. He had the cheek to smile at her, too.

TEN

On the ground
Faldaiza Port

THE ALCOVES was closed, the door opaque, the menu over it dark.

"They never close," Jela said, and Cantra felt a shiver start at the back of her neck.

"Maybe repairs?" she asked, but not like she believed it herself, nor did the other pilot bother to answer.

What he did do was step up to the door, put his big blunt fingers against it and push. Nothing happened. Cantra could see the strain in his shoulders as he exerted more force. She looked up the street and down—empty. So far, so lucky.

The door gave a small groan and began moving back on its track. Jela continued to exert pressure until he had opened a small gap. The foyer was dark, which fact slowed Jela not at all: He squeezed through the gap and became one with the darkness beyond.

Cantra sighed, tried to think *generator failure*, but her heart wasn't in it.

She followed Jela, and sometime between passing over the threshold and coming to rest inside the dark foyer, her gun slid out of its quiet pocket and into her hand. The dark was too thick for her to decipher much more than a blacker blot on the blackness to her left, which might have been Pilot Jela, breathing so quiet she couldn't hear it, which irritated her for some reason. Frowning, she touched another seal pocket and slipped one of the several lightsticks out, snapping it inside her fist. Feeble bluish light leaked between her fingers, enough for her to see the empty console and Jela approaching on sneak-feet, his far arm held down against his side.

At the edge of the console he paused, looked—and moved on, his near hand rising to wave her along behind.

She followed, not liking it, but not inclined to let him go on alone. He'd put himself out for her, coming into the alley and taking care of the second hunter, for which act of lunatic generosity she owed him. Even though she'd had the situation under control.

She paused, looked around the edge of the console—and wished she hadn't. The master of the dining room was crumpled into an improbably small ball on the floor, his formal tunic dyed with blood, a wide ragged gash in his throat.

Swallowing, she moved on, past the wadded up curtain, which had been ripped down from its hanging over the doorway, and caught up with Jela just inside the hall.

The third room down was nasty—eight identical corpses displaying the remains of various unsavory forms of persuasion. Two wore formals, while the rest, by their clothes, had been kitchen workers. It was well-lit, unfortunately, and Cantra slipped the lightstick into her public pocket.

Jela swore, quietly and neatly. Cantra held her peace, not thinking immediately of anything she could usefully add to the motion.

"All Batchers," she said after he'd prowled a bit and had a chance to work off some of his bad mood. "No guests."

"There are other rooms," he answered, and she sighed, jerking her head at the curtain.

"So we'll check 'em out," she said and after a heartbeat or two, he brought his chin down, which she took for 'will do.' She swept the curtain back.

Most of the other rooms were found to be empty and intact, saving the one that held what had once been a woman of some substance. A neat hole had been made in the center of her forehead; the skin 'round the hole was just a little burnt, which you'll get with your pin lasers.

This time, Jela didn't say anything, just went down to a knee and started going through pockets, quick and efficient. Seeing that he had the way of it and didn't need her help, Cantra set herself to guard the hallway, the curtain hooked back just a bit, so he'd be able to hear if she shouted.

The hallway was dim and quiet—not much different than it had been earlier in the day. If you didn't know that one of the rooms held eight Batcher bodies, and the one behind her was occupied by—

There was a noise—a very small and stealthy noise—from the left, where the hall ended at a flat white wall, barely two dozen paces from Cantra's position. She frowned, staring at the area and finding nothing to see, save the hall and the wall.

She'd almost convinced herself that the noise had come from behind, inside the room where Jela was relieving the woman's body of care, when the sound came again, slightly louder this time, and from the same area.

Carefully, she moved forward, slipping the still-glowing light-stick out of her pocket, holding it high in the hand not occupied by her weapon.

The section of hall she went through was certifiably vacant. The wall at the end was white and blank. She went over to the left, where end wall met side wall, lifted the lightstick high and began to scrutinize the situation.

She hadn't got far along in the scrutiny when the noise made itself heard again—well over to the right and sounding a shade impatient. Cantra moved down-wall, light still high and illuminating nothing but wall, flat, white, seamless, and—

Not entirely seamless.

It took a professional's eye to see it, but there it was—a thin line along the blank face of the wall, shimmering a little in the lightstick's blue glow.

The noise came again, just beyond the tip of her nose, a scratching sound—fingernails against plazboard, maybe. Mice.

She marked the position of the line, slipped the 'stick away, unsealed another hidden pocket and pulled out a ring of utility zippers. Frowning, she fingered through the various options. The ring was a portable, o'course, armed with the most common polarizers. If this particular hidey hole were sealed with anything out of the way, she'd need the full kit from her ship. Still, it was worth a—

"Pilot Cantra?" His voice was barely louder than his breath, warm against her ear. "What do you have?"

"Stashroom," she said, keeping her eyes on the line, fingers considering the merits of this zipper, the next, a third . . .

"Think I've got a way in," she said, weighing the third zipper in her hand. "Somebody inside, is what I think." Her fingers decided in favor; and she nodded to herself.

"Cover me." She slipped her gun into its pocket and activated her chosen tool, reaching up to run the needle-nose down along the line in the wall. The zipper's path was marked by a gentle peel, as if the skin of the wall were rolling back from an incision.

Cantra knelt on the tile floor, brought the tool down until its nose caught on the second line, followed that one along parallel to the floor, snagged on the third and went up again, the skin of the wall rolling up in earnest now, almost as high as her waist. Big enough for someone to come out of, if they were so minded. Big enough, absolutely, to shoot through. Big enough—

A body leapt through the opening, curling as it hit the floor and going immediately into a somersault, showing a flash of green among a blur of pale arms, pale hair, pale tunic.

Jela extended an improbably long arm, caught the Batcher by the back of the tunic and hauled her—for it happened to be 'her', Cantra saw—up, feet not quite making contact with the floor, which didn't stop her from squirming and twisting.

Cantra slid her weapon free and pointed it. The Batcher stopped struggling and hung limp as a drowned kitten in Jela's grasp.

"Pilots," she gasped. "This humble person is grateful for your aid."

"Right," Cantra said, and looked to Jela, giving him leave to ask what he would with the quirk of an eyebrow.

He was silent for a moment, then spoke to the Batcher. "You gave us warning earlier in the evening, eh?"

"Yes, Pilot," the Batcher said submissively, which could as easily be truth or a lie told in order to placate him.

"Tell me," Jela said, inexorably calm. "What you said, to warn us."

The Batcher hesitated, then raised her face, though she stopped short of actually meeting Jela's eyes.

"Walk safely," she whispered.

"Why?" Cantra asked, which might not've been the question Jela wanted the answer to next, but which had damnall bugged her since it happened.

The Batcher licked her lips. "There were those who had taken the other pilot," she whispered, "as he was about to enter our establishment. I saw this. They were many, he was one. I thought to warn pilots that there was danger in the streets. The master—" Her voice caught. She took a hard breath and hung her head again. "The master did not forbid this. The master said, hoodlums in the streets are bad for business."

There was a short silence, then Jela said. "I'm going to put you on your feet. I expect you to stand and answer the questions this pilot and I ask you. Try to run away and I'll shoot you in the leg. Am I understood?"

"Pilot, you are."

"Good." He set her down. She stayed put, head hanging, gloved hands limp at her sides.

"Tell us what happened here," Jela said.

She swallowed. "They came here during the slow hour. Uno, at the desk—he had time to hit the emergency bell. Many of us ran, but in the kitchen, they were prepping for the busy hours upcoming and were caught. Also, the master—the master had been in the wine cellar and did not hear the bell. When we came to this floor, they had already killed Uno and captured the kitchen staff. The master told me to run for aid, and I did try—but they were at all exits, even those not generally known. I came back and they were—they had killed the master and left her. I—I hid myself in the wall, but I could not open the secret door from the inside. And then you came."

"I see," Jela said in a tone that conveyed that he might not actually believe everything he'd just been told. "Do you know—"

Back toward the front of the building, there was a sound—a large, unfriendly, sound.

"You know a way out?" Cantra snapped, not being in any way wishful of meeting the people who had killed a pilot, eight Batchers and their owner—*For what gain?* she asked herself, then put away that wondering for another and less fraught moment.

"Pilot," the Batcher said, "I do, if they are not deployed as before."

"Go, then," Cantra snapped, over a second noise, louder and less friendly than the first. "We'll follow."

The Batcher looked at Jela.

"You can move now," he told her. "Lead us out of here."

THE STARLIGHT HOTEL sat on its corner, dark walls showing glitters and swirls of silver and pale blue deep inside, like looking out an observation port and seeing the starfield spread from one end of night to the other. Cantra was standing in the dim, recessed doorway of a closed dream shop. She'd been there for some time, just one shadow among many, watching the entrance to her lodgings. Jela and the Batcher were watching the back door, the Batcher having refused to be parted from the pair of them after they'd shaken the dust of The Alcoves off their boots.

It was beginning to look like prudence was its own reward. Whoever had her linked with Pilot Jela only had a face, not a name. And certainly not the location of the lodgings, rented only hours ago with such high hopes. She gave herself a couple heartbeats for wistful consideration of those hopes, then shrugged it all away. Staying alive was more important, as Garen used to say, than staying sane. Not that Garen had been anything like sane, as far as Cantra had been able to observe. There was something about the Rim that was unproductive of sanity. It was the weird seeping in from the Deeps that did it—that'd been Garen's theory. Cantra's was simpler: Rimmers made Rimmers crazy.

The past, again. Like she didn't have enough present to occupy her.

Shaking her head, she slid out of the doorway and ambled down the walk, one eye on the Starlight. People continued to enter and exit, and there were no signs at all of anybody waiting at stealth.

Directly across from the front entrance, she paused, then quick-walked across the street when the traffic thinned, and jogged up the wide steps. The door slid open and she stepped jauntily into the lobby, heading for the lift bank just beyond the desk.

Abruptly, she swung to the side and approached the desk, fingering a flan out of her public pocket.

"Change this for me?" she asked, slipping the coin across the counter.

"Surely," the clerk said, and counted out a certain number of qwint and carolis. "Will there be anything else?"

The guard on the lift bank was looking at her. She watched him out of the corner of her eye as she swept the coins into her palm, and saw his lips move slightly, as if he was talking into an implanted talkie.

"That's all, I thank you," she said to the desk clerk. She dropped the coins into her public pocket, turned and walked back toward the front door, not running, not hurrying, though she could feel the guard's eyes boring into her back.

Out the door, walking calm, down the front stairs, with a little jog in the step, finally slipping into the crowd moving along the public way. At the corner of the building, she left the crowd and dodged into the shadows, heading for the back entrance.

Very shortly thereafter, she was behind the generator shed, in concealment that was a bit thin for three.

"Got it?" Jela asked, though he must've seen she didn't.

"Abort," she said. "Watcher on the lift bank. He saw me and reported in. Nothing in the kit that can't be replaced." *For a price.* "Now what?"

A small silence, then.

"My lodgings," Jela said. "Then a strategic retreat."

"If they're on me, they're on you," she argued. "Time to cut your losses."

"There's something at my lodgings that can't be lost," he answered, and there was a note in his calm voice that she didn't find herself able to argue with. "Cover me?"

"I can do that." Had to do it, he having performed that same service for her. She looked over to the Batcher woman, silent and attentive by the edge of the shed.

"Time to go home," Cantra told her. "This is more trouble'n you want."

"This humble person will remain in the company of the pilots," the Batcher said—a repeat of her earlier communication on the subject.

"This humble person," Cantra said, sharp, "belongs to whoever's come into being master. Which ain't neither of us."

The Batcher crossed her arms over her breast. "This humble person will remain in the company of the pilots," she said, making three on the evening.

"It's her life," Jela said, rising up onto his feet.

Technically not true. On the other hand, as long as neither of them damaged, killed, or moved her, the law had nothing to say to them.

"Makes no matter to me," Cantra said. "We better go, though, before unwelcome company finds us here."

"Right," said Jela and faded into the dark. "Follow me."

JELA'S LODGINGS WERE back toward the shipyards, in a plain boxy building formed out of cermacrete. The surface showed cracks and a few craters, which gave witness to its age. Inside, Cantra thought, it was probably more of the same—clean and spare.

The showers would work, the beds would be sleepable; service and questions both minimal. Transient housing, that was all. She'd stayed in places just like it herself, more than once. She owned some surprise to find Jela quartered here, though. She had him pegged a couple notches higher up the food chain.

In addition to the front door, the back door, and two side doors, there were a good many giving windows, all rigged out with safety nets. Three bridges connected the hostel at varying levels to a larger building next door, which on closer inspection proved to be Flight Central, where those pilots who found themselves to be respectable went to register the news of their being on-port, and whether they was wishful of taking berth, or had a berth on offer. There'd be eatables and a local info office; scribes, brokers, moneychangers, shipwright, and honest folk of all stripe. She'd been in two or three like establishments, over the course of her career.

Could be it made sense for Pilot Jela to bide close to work and news of work. She hadn't asked him where he was next-bound—and there was still that vexed question of what sort of pilot he might be—having somehow received the impression that the answer would've been an uninformative shrug of those wide shoulders.

Which line of thought did produce an interesting question: Where was Pilot Jela *going*, once he had recovered his unlosable? She had the *Dancer*, the Batcher had her master's home, which she'd see sooner or later. But Jela? If he didn't have a berth, it was going to be hard going for him on Faldaiza Port.

Which concern was none of hers. She was well out of it just as soon as the good pilot picked up his kit and was away. Which event she hoped would come about quickly.

"So," she said to Jela, who had been quietly and intently regarding the building from his place next to her at the mouth of a convenient alley, the Batcher hovering behind them both. "How do you want to play it?"

"I'd like you and our friend to wait here," he said slowly, like he was just now working out his moves. "I'll go by the Central's bar and see if any of my acquaintance can bear me company. Company or solo, I'll go in by one of the bridges, and by-pass any left to guard the lift bank, the desk or the call-clerk. Bridge access is limited to those who have a key."

"They'll have set guards on the bridges, too," she pointed out.

"Likely, but not proven. I'm counting on the guard at the bridge being less able than those at the more likely places."

"Could get messy."

He grinned, not without humor. "It could, couldn't it?"

She gave him his grin back, and jerked her head at the building. "Coming out the same way?"

"Depends on how many they are and how they're deployed. Might have to go out a window, though I'd prefer not to. There are a couple of interior routes that would serve me better, and I'll aim for one of them. What I want you to do is give me cover when you see me. If you don't see me in an hour, then it's probable you won't and you're free to strike for your ship."

That was cool and professional. She tipped an eyebrow at him. "You got an idea who's responsible for all this, I think."

This time the grin was thinner. "I have too many ideas of who might be responsible. What I don't have is a reasonable way to filter them, and I'd rather not be used for target practice in the meantime."

He sounded seriously put-out by recent events, for which she blamed him not at all, being just a little annoyed herself.

"We got a problem of scope," she said, nonetheless. "Whoever's after having a chat with us thought enough of themselves to kill eight Batchers and a freewoman back at The Alcoves, not to say your piloting brother. The reason they're after me is because of you, not the other way around. If one of your ideas is more likely than another, I'd appreciate hearing it."

He sighed and pushed away from the wall. "If anything comes to me, I'll let you know," he said. "An hour. If I'm not out, jet."

He faded out of the alley. Cantra put a cautious eye around the edge of the concealing wall and saw him already well up the walk, one of a group of law-abiders moving purposefully toward Flight Central.

She thought about swearing, and then didn't bother. Her curiosity bump was unrelieved, but she'd live. Once this business here was settled and she was back on *Dancer*, the game, whatever it was, ceased to be important. Faldaiza wasn't a regular stop, though it wasn't unknown, either. Whatever ruckus she was currently enjoying the fruits of would die out completely between tomorrow's lift and the next time she hit port.

She hoped.

Behind her, she was aware of the Batcher's quiet breathing.

"You," she said, not gently.

"Pilot?" The Batcher stepped forward to take Jela's place next to her.

"You got a name?"

"Yes, Pilot. This humble person is called Dulsey."

"You heard what Pilot Jela said, Dulsey? He's figuring it to get dangerous hereabouts within the hour. Now's your best moment to scoot along home and make a bow to the new master."

"This worthless one heard what Pilot Jela said, and what you yourself said," Dulsey answered in her inflectionless voice, "and understands that danger may soon walk among us. The new master will not easily forgive one who had been favored by the previous master and then allowed her to be slain."

"Huh." Cantra considered that, one eye on the street. Jela was going up the stairs to Central, his shoulders silhouetted against the building's glow.

"If you get yourself killed," she said to Dulsey. "It's nobody's fault but your own."

"This humble person is aware of that, Pilot."

HE BEGAN TO WORRY about the time they stepped off the bridge into the third floor hall of the Guard Shack, so called because it had been a garrison back in the First Phase, before the *sheriekas* had retired to regroup.

He'd crossed the bridge in company with three pilots known to him from the Central's bar. Two were port security, on rotation, the third a gambler who spent most of her time dicing with new arrivals at a discreet back table. She was on easy terms with the cops, as she wasn't technically operating on-port, and found Jela a challenge, since he would neither dice with her nor bed her.

"There was a lady asking for you at the bar today," she said as they approached the bridge. "Shall I be jealous?"

Jela grinned. "More than enough of me to go around."

She'd laughed, and the two cops, too. They all mounted the steps and started across to the Guard Shack, the lighted deck throwing weird shadows ahead of them.

"What did she look like," Jela wondered, "this lady?"

"Do you not know?" asked the gambler playfully. "Surely, she would not have come without invitation. It was a sorrowful woman, indeed, who heard that you had not been seen so far this day."

"There are so many, it's hard to keep track," Jela apologized, to the loud appreciation of the cops. "Let me see . . ." He feigned considering thoughtfulness, then snapped his fingers. "It was the bald lady with the long-eye and the demi-claws, I'll warrant." He sighed wistfully. "It's too bad I missed her. She'll punish me proper, the next time we meet."

"I am certain that she will," the gambler said cordially. "And the moreso when she finds you've been seeing another on the side, and she a mere port tough, with a gun on her hip and no more finesse than to bellow your name in a public place, as if she were calling a hound to heel."

Jela eyed her. "She did that? Not one of mine, then. My ladies are always polite."

"Even when they're punishing him," one cop told the other, to the loud delight of both.

"Did she leave a name?" Jela asked the gambler under the cover of the cops' laughter.

"She did not," the gambler answered, looking as serious as he'd ever seen her. "She did however state that she was the envoy of one Pilot Muran." She looked up into his face, her being a tiny thing. "This is bad news, I see. Should I have given it earlier?"

He shrugged and manufactured a rueful grin. "It wouldn't have changed anything."

"Ah," she said wisely, and then said nothing more.

By that time, they'd reached the end of the bridge. One port cop stepped forward and used his key, he and his partner ducking beneath the gate as it started up. Jela and the gambler passed through next; he had to bend his head to clear the spiked ends, she walked, head high, beside him.

He was sure of his weapon, and of his companions. The one who had been set to watch for him was about to have some trouble.

Except—there wasn't a guard. No one overt or covert watched the end of the bridge or the hallway stretching away into the inhabited regions of the Guard Shack. His 'skins likewise failed to warn of any mechanical snoopers.

"You were expecting someone?" the gambler asked, with the fine perception that assured her success in her chosen field.

"I thought there might be someone here," he said slowly, and added, " . . . related to the lady who missed me at the bar."

"That would have been unfortunate," the gambler said seriously, and one of the cops looked over her shoulder at them and paused, putting a hand out to stop her partner. "But perhaps not as unfortunate as it could be. Where else might they seek you?"

"His room," said the first cop, and looked to the gambler. "How ugly was that particular customer?"

She considered, head tipped to one side. "She was indelicate," she said at last, "in the extreme."

The cop slapped her partner on the arm. "I'm going down and collect that money the pilot owes me," she said. "He says he's got it in his room and I believe him."

Her partner pursed his lips. "I don't like you going with him alone," he said. "What if it's a set-up? I'll come along and keep an eye on you."

"Think you're my mother?" the first cop asked.

"Think I'm your partner," the second answered, which seemed to clinch the argument, for the first cop shrugged and looked over to the gambler, who smiled brightly.

"As this may be the only opportunity I have to behold the good pilot's bed, I will of course accompany you," she said gaily, and skipped forward, Jela trailing behind, feeling the hairs on the back of his neck stirring.

"I met some of the lady's relatives earlier today, and seen their work more recently still," he said, as the four of them continued down the hall toward his quarters. "They're nasty, they're sloppy and they seem to be numerous."

"In which case," the gambler said. "We hold the advantages of pure heart, neatness and quality."

"Our duty," said the second cop, who might have been talking to his partner or to himself. "Our duty is to enforce the peace."

They followed the curve of the hall and Jela stretched his legs, taking the lead as they came closer to his rooms. He wasn't really surprised to find the gambler keeping pace with him.

"This could get bad," he said to her, softly. "Or it could be nothing."

"Let us then hope for nothing," she murmured in return, "and carry loaded weapons."

THERE WAS NO ONE watching the door. His 'skins noted an anomaly as he approached the door, key out. He paused, but no warning solidified. Sighing, he slipped his key out and went forward, the first cop at his side. The gambler continued down the hall and took up a position near the lifts. The second cop moved back the way they had come, slipping into the convenient shadow of a drinks dispenser.

Jela used his key, pushed the door open and went with it, moving fast and low, gun out and aimed—

At the tree in its pot next to the open window, precisely where he had left it that morning.

"Everything fine?" the cop asked from behind him, and he straightened up slowly, letting the rest of the room seep into his awareness. It looked all right—his kit rolled and ready where he had left it, the book he'd been reading last night on the table under the lamp, the bed as tight and as shipshape as he had made it that very—

"Someone's been in," he told the cop, frowning at the rumple on corner of the aggressively smooth coverlet.

"They take anything?" she asked.

"Appears not." If they'd been after info, he had it on him. He didn't touch the sealed leg pocket where his log book rode, and frowned again at the rumpled cover. His 'skins were still insisting on that anomaly. He moved across the room, stood to one side and yanked the privacy curtain back.

The 'fresher was empty. He sighed, crossed the room, picked up the book, slid it into the kit, slung the kit over his shoulder and went to the tree.

"I'm leaving," he said. "I'm feeling exposed." He hefted the tree—bowl and all. The tree had found its new life good; it was full of leaves and the girth of its trunk had increased. These things filled Jela with a sort of wondering joy, except when he had to carry it.

"Not conspicuous or anything," the cop commented. "Back slide?"

"I'm thinking that's best."

"We'll escort," the cop said. "Let me alert—"

From the hall came the sound of a bell, and then the gambler's light, clear hail—followed by a single shot. Jela stumbled, fighting a lifetime of training that would have him dropping the tree and running forward. His duty—

His duty.

"Go!" snarled the cop. "I'll cover you!"

Kit over shoulder, arms circling pot, trunk pressed against his cheek, leaves rustling in his ear, Jela moved.

Out the door he ran, spared a glance down the hall toward the lifts and saw the gambler still in her watching place. She gave him a jaunty salute. Something huddled on the floor beyond her—

The lift bell rang.

"Go!" shouted the cop coming into the hall behind him, weapon at ready.

Jela went.

AT THE MOUTH of the alley, Cantra straightened out of her lean, eyes suddenly sharp on the pattern of people moving along the walkway between the Guard Shack and Flight Central.

"Here it comes," she said to Dulsey. She turned her head and met a pair of determined gray eyes. "Last chance to shrug out of this and make your peace with the new master."

"This humble person," the Batcher said, like Cantra should've known she would, "will remain in the company of the pilots."

"Have it your own way." Cantra sighed and asked the next question anyway, though she was pretty sure she knew what the answer was going to be. "You got a weapon?"

"The master found this one to be worthy," Dulsey said.

Cantra looked at her. "That mean yes?"

"Yes, pilot," came the stolid reply. "I have a weapon."

"Good. Keep it handy and you might live through this after all."

'Course, then she'd still have to face the new master, which Cantra understood dying to be preferable to, and which Dulsey should've thought of before she went and hid in the stashroom instead of getting her brain toasted alongside the old master, like a faithful Batcher ought to have.

Across the street, more people were moving against pattern, taking up this and that spot of cover; some others stopping in the shadow of the Guard Shack, small knots of friends, pausing to talk.

Cantra counted maybe fifteen, and chewed her lip. 'Cover' was what the man had said he'd wanted—if and only when she saw him. Fifteen on the job, though—he might not've expected so many. She considered the numbers excessive, herself—and that was only the front door. Who knew how many they had watching the back and the sides?

She slid her gun out of its pocket and checked the charge. Good to go, not that she'd expected elsewise. Always paid to check, though.

From across the street, 'round toward the back of the Guard Shack, there came a flash of red light, followed by a low and drawn-out *bo-oo-oo-o-m*. The clusters and knots of chatting friends turned and ran toward the sound, and the intermittent red flickering. The concealed watchers stayed concealed, but the attention of most seemed to be on the commotion.

"Let's go," Cantra said to the Batcher and strolled out of the alley and down the street. When they were across from Flight Central, she paused, waiting 'til traffic allowed, then ambled across the street.

Once across, she turned up toward the Guard Shack, then left the walk and angled between the two buildings, her pace increasing. Overhead, the three bridges glowed with a golden light, illuminating the empty passway.

As they neared the back of the building, sounds other than respectable street noise could be heard. Some sounded remarkably like shots, others like people yelling. Cantra stretched her legs until she was running lightly toward the commotion, gun in hand.

Just before she reached the corner of the Guard Shack, another low explosion disturbed the peace, a simultaneous flare dying the walls and the passway red. More yelling made up for a sudden pause in the shooting.

Cantra dodged close in to the wall, crouched and kept on. At the corner, she paused, and keeping low, carefully eased out to have a look.

The back lot was full of smoky red light. Far down toward the other side of the building, the illumination was eye-burning bright; a solid bar of flame from the edge of the building to the utility shed, from the surface of the walk to the windows three levels up. Nearer to hand, trash bins and runabouts loomed, their shapes wavering in the smoke.

And in the mid-distance, moving at speed, came a short wide-shouldered figure, massive arms wrapped around a bowl clutched 'gainst his middle and over it all, something long and vegetative.

Cantra swore, briefly, and brought her gun up, acquiring the range *behind* the running figure, about midway to the wall of flame. Anything longer was shooting at shadows, and pursuit was sure to materialize just the instant the fastflame burned low enough to jump. Already, she could see figures through the flames, though they still reached high enough to discourage gymnastics.

The bulky runner came briskly on, despite the handicap of his burden; whether he was running faster than the flames were dying, though—

"Here!" she shouted, and he heard her—she knew he had because, incredibly, he picked up speed, skidding 'round the corner so fast the plant he carried snapped like a whip and lost a couple leaves.

"All this for a *vegetable*?" she yelled at him.

"We'll talk about it later!" he yelled back. "Go!"

He took his own advice, leaves blowing in his wake. Cantra waved Dulsey after.

"Cover him," she snapped, and the Batcher flung herself down the gold-lit passway.

At the corner, Cantra dropped to one knee and turned her attention to the back trail.

The flames had thinned, though they were still more than she'd care to jump through, lacking a compelling reason. Could be that the pursuit considered Pilot Jela just that, for as she watched, three of them came through the flames, arms folded over their faces, and hit the ground running.

Cantra dropped them—one, two, three—as soon as they came into range, and by that time, four more were through and the flames weren't looking so threatening any more.

She repeated the first exercise, with similar results, glanced over her shoulder and saw that the passway behind her was clear. Duty done. Debt paid.

A peek 'round the corner showed that the fire had grown low enough to jump over. Time for her to start moving on her own behalf.

She got her feet under her—and ran.

ELEVEN

On the ground
Faldaiza Port

WHEN SHE WAS CERTAIN her back-track was clean, she set her course for the port proper, *Dancer*, a clean-up, and a well-earned nap. She thought of the big tub in her abandoned hotel room and sighed. It would've been nice to sit and soak, maybe another bottle of wine to hand and some interesting company to share it all with.

As it was, she'd had interesting company right enough, and too much of the wrong kind of excitement.

"Might as well been working," she muttered to herself, checking her back-track again. Far as she could scan it—far as her 'skins could scan it, too—she was alone in the world at present. Which suited. Port was quiet anyhow, it being about five local hours ahead of busy-time for the daily paper-pushers and cits. Not being stared at by the cits— "Look, kids, there's one of those space pilots!" —suited, too.

She wished now that she'd had a chance to get out of Pilot Jela the name of whoever he'd annoyed. Anybody who could field the number of players she'd seen tonight likely had the means to operate elsewhere than Faldaiza. She could do without meeting them or theirs again on her next set-down—or ever.

Once again, she checked her back. Still clean. Heartened, she continued on her way, keeping to shadows when she could but not being fanatical about it. There wasn't any sense calling attention to herself by being too stealthy. Extra caution, that would pass, pilots being who and what they were. Even extra-jumpy caution would pass, there being some pilots who just naturally did better on-ship than on-ground.

Not that she particularly argued with that better-on-ship stuff. Once you got the hang of the sound and vibrations, there wasn't anyplace you could be on a ship and not have a good idea of what was going.

Not like here, as a quick sample, where part of the listening was wasted on identifying high squeaky sounds she'd never heard before—could be birds, could be equipment—to identifying the deep, low, shaking rumbles—might be light ground tremors, might be a storm coming in, might be equipment—hell, might be some club-band practicing with their enviroboards! If she jacked the 'skins a bit she might get some directionals and figure the noises out, but then she'd be standin' stock-still to listen, which would gain her attention she didn't want or need.

Could be she was just gettin' that tired, which ought to warn her not to run quite so close to the edge, a lesson she thought she'd learned a dozen or two times over.

She'd come into the shipyards some distance from her exit point, on the day-side, now closed up tight for the local night—and was on the approach to *Dancer's* location, passing a strip of low cermacrete buildings—cargo brokerage office, repair-and-parts shop, automated currency exchange, and a grab-a-bite looking a degree scruffier than most.

Cantra sighed. Inside a local hour, all going well, she'd be back on her ship. Safe, as the saying went.

She strolled on past the grab-a-bite. Away near the center of the yard, she could just make out the lines of her ship. Despite herself, she smiled, and stretched her legs a little more, feeling the cermacrete under her boots.

Her 'skins gave a yell, audible to her ears only, but she was already turning, hideaway sliding into her palm—and found herself facing a too-familiar stocky woman with determined gray eyes, wearing a pair of mechanic's coveralls neither new nor clean, with conveniently long sleeves, clipped tight at the wrists, and "J.D. Wigams" stenciled on the breast. A work hood had been shoved up and back, hanging careless-seeming over one shoulder.

"If the pilot would follow this—" There was a marked break-off and a sharp intake of breath. "If the pilot would follow," she repeated, firmer this time.

Cantra sighed, hideaway still enclosed in her fist. "No sense to it. I'm for my ship and a lift out. You're on your own, except if you're wanting a last piece of advice, which is—don't startle people who've got cause to carry protection."

"I am grateful for the advice," Dulsey said stolidly. "As I understand the transaction, advice balances advice. So—my advice to you: Take care not to walk into a trap, believing harm has lagged behind you."

Cantra stared at her. "You reading me good numbers, Dulsey? If not, I'll make sure you never have to face the new master."

"The pilot is generous. I have seen evidence. That same evidence is available to you. Follow me." She turned and walked back toward the row of sullen shops, not looking back.

Cantra sucked air deep into her lungs and exhaled, hard.

Then she followed Dulsey.

DOWN ALONG THE SHOPS, and back a small alleyway, no more than seventy or eighty paces from where she'd been stopped, there was a small shop— "Wigams Synchro Repair and Service" —and she'd been all but dragged inside by Dulsey, past the sign showing the place wouldn't be open for business for another couple hours.

There wasn't any sign of forced entry, and Dulsey had carefully turned the mechanical lock behind them before heading for the stairs beside the work bay. Cantra sighed gently. It looked like she wasn't the only one around with proper tools and improper training.

She hadn't been partiaularly surprised to find it was Pilot Jela and his vegetative friend Dulsey had led her to, and not particularly surprised to find him sitting comfortably in a deep leather chair behind a shiny real wood desk with a wonderful view of the window on the top level office of Synchro Repair. The window in turn had a wonderful view overlooking the port.

Jela hadn't bothered with a greeting, just pointed at the spy-glass sitting on the sythnwood work table beside the big desk.

Cantra eased onto a stool and picked up the 'glass, finding it already set to study a circle 'round *Dancer's* position. Not hard to find a ship, after all; a quick search on her name run against the roster of ships down during the last day local would net the info fastest.

She sat for a heartbeat, just staring down into the black surface, then put her hands on the wake-ups.

The surface cleared, and she was looking at the yard, *Dancer* so close on her right hand she could read the name and the numbers on the pitted side. The view panned back, showing a range of ships, and energy overlays on two of them.

"Get on the portmaster's bad side, holding weapons live on the yard," she commented.

Jela didn't answer, except to say, "To the right about thirty degrees, if you might?"

Which she obediently did, and the view changed, displaying a piece of construction equipment lazily moving behind a distant fence in its storage yard, like it was looking for a place to park.

"Up the magnification a notch."

She shrugged . . .

Right. She had him figured now for some kind of security pro, so he'd notice what she might miss. And she would have, too. Not construction equipment after all, the armored crawler was a dark wolf among the yard's more regulation equipment, staying a prudent distance back from the fence. The energy overlay on that flickered as it moved, as if it were shielded.

"Check the ships again."

She drew a ragged breath, did so, and the screen showed those ships and the energy overlays still on high, then faded to black as she thumbed the power.

Eyes closed, she sighed, then spun the stool and glared at Jela. "So?" she asked.

He shrugged his big shoulders, showing her empty palms.

"Didn't seem neighborly to let you walk into that," he said, projecting a certain style of soothing calm that she found particularly annoying.

She took another deep breath.

"One," she said. "Like I said before—you don't need to go to all that trouble for me. Two. I'd appreciate an explanation of what the pair of you think you're doing, snooping my ship."

"Looking for a lift out," he said.

Cantra snorted. "I don't take passengers."

"Understood," he said, still projecting calm, which was going to get his nose broke for him sometime real soon. "Nobody expects you to take passengers. Hate 'em myself. But nobody here's a passenger. I'm willing to sit second. If you don't mind my saying it, Pilot, you were looking to be on the wild side of edgy when we met for dinner. Could be a run with some downtime built into it is just what you—and your ship—need."

"I'm the judge of what me and my ship need," Cantra snarled. "And what neither needs is to be taking up a man whose friends are shyer than his enemies and a Batcher on the run from her owner."

"This humble person," Dulsey said, "is fully capable in cargo handling, communications, and outside repair. Also, this person has received some small training in the preparation of foods, which the pilot may find of use during the upcoming journey."

Cantra looked at her.

"Repair, comm, and cargo?"

"Yes, Pilot."

"What was you doing working in a restaurant?"

Dulsey looked aside. "The manufacture of our Pod was commissioned by Enclosed Habitats, which specialized in constructing and maintaining research stations. When the cost of maintaining the stations exceeded the contracted sums, the company failed. All assets were sold at auction, including the worker pods. The master purchased those of our Pod who remained for The Alcoves."

"How many of your Pod're left now?" Cantra asked, though she didn't really have to.

"One." Dulsey whispered.

Right.

"That's too bad," Cantra said. "Doesn't change that you're a runaway Batcher—or will be, pretty soon—which puts you on a course to there being none of your pod left by—call it mid-day tomorrow, local."

"There is benefit to the pilot in accepting the assistance of Pilot Jela and this—and myself." There was a note of panic in the Batcher's voice, despite the bravura of 'myself', and the gray eyes were wide.

Cantra cocked an eyebrow. "I'd argue opposite, myself, but there don't seem to be a need just now." She glanced over to Jela.

"I need a roster, a comp, and a talkie."

He pointed beyond her, at a stand next to the work table. "Lift the top of that. It's all right there."

THE NAME OF THE SHIP was *Pretty Parcil*. Cantra spent a few moments jinking with the feeds, not wanting to be interrupted in her conversation, nor particularly needing the garage day-shift to take delivery of trouble that wasn't theirs. Jela watched her, silent in his borrowed chair. He was still projecting calm, but he'd either eased up some or she was getting used to it.

Satisfied at last with her arrangements, she opened a line to the piloting station on *Pretty Parcil*.

There was a click and a voice, sounding sterner and older than he had earlier in the day.

"*Parcil*. Pilot on deck."

"Is that Pilot Danby?"

A pause about wide enough to hold a blink, followed by a specifically non-committal ack on the ID, then, "Pilot. What happened?" No more than that. Likely he wasn't alone in the tower. That was all right.

"Turned out to be a mistake," she told him. "I'm at liberty and mean to stay that way."

"Mistake?" He was a bright boy, and not too young to understand that there were mistakes—and mistakes.

"I give you my word of honor," *for what it's worth*, she added, silently, "that there's no bounty out on me."

She heard his sigh—or might be she imagined it. "Good. What can I do for you, Pilot?"

"I'm wondering if you can confirm for me," she said. "I've got two ships on scan showing live weapons. Don't want to think my scanner's gone bad, but . . ."

"I'll check," Danby said, and over the line there came the sound of various accesses being made, then a bit of silence . . .

"Nothing wrong with your scanner," he said eventually. "You protest to the portmaster?"

"Not yet," she said, and Jela leaned forward on his stool, black eyes showing interest.

"I'm wondering," she said to Danby, "if a protest from a Parcil Family ship might get a little extra snap into the belay order. I'm small trade, myself. Just me and my co-pilot, like I told you . . ."

"Got it," he said. "I can file that protest, Pilot. Stay on line?"

"Will do."

She heard him open a second line, and request the portmaster's own ear for "First Pilot, Parcil Trade Clan Ship *Pretty Parcil*." There was silence, then, which she'd expected, and—much sooner than she'd hoped—his voice again.

"Portmaster, we've just completed a security scan and have identified two vessels on-yard with weapons live." A pause, then a calm recitation of the coords of both ships, and, "Yes ma'am, I am filing formal protest of these violations. I request that you issue a cease-and-desist to those vessels immediately, to be enforced as necessary."

Another short silence, and a respectful, "Thank you, ma'am. We will monitor. *Parcil* out."

Cantra smiled. Jela came of the chair and moved to the work table, doubtless to have a looksee via the spy-glass.

"Protest filed, Pilot." Danby was back with her. "The portmaster promises a shut-down inside the local hour."

"Much obliged," she said, and meant it. "I'll get back to my prelims, then, and hope I won't have to ask you to verify my long-scans."

"We've been watching long," he said. "Pilot's Undernet has reports of pirate activity in-sector. Faldaiza shows clear to out orbit. So far."

"Obliged again," she said. "If I catch anything suspicious on the long, I'll pass it on."

"I'll be here," he said. "Thanks for the heads-up, Pilot. Good lift, fair journey."

"Fair journey, Pilot," she answered, just like she was as legit as he was, and closed the line before folding the desktop down.

Jela had a hip hitched on the edge of the work table, black eyes intent on the image in the spy-glass.

"One's off-line," he said without looking up. "The portmaster doesn't like the Clans upset."

"Makes sense to keep the money happy," Cantra returned, considering him. "What about that armor?"

"Nothing lit," he said, head still bent. "Might not be anything to do with us at all."

"On the other hand, it might be," she finished what he didn't say and sighed. "Man, *whose* ugly side did you get on?"

"Second one's down," he said, and looked up, his face about as expressive as she'd expected.

"Am I getting an answer to that, Pilot? Seems to me I'm owed."

He frowned. "By my calculations, we're even."

"Not if you leave me open to more of the same, elsewhere." She felt her temper building and took a deliberately deep breath, trying to notch it back. Her temper wasn't her best feature, being enough to sometimes scare her. She didn't figure it would scare the man across from her, though it might lose her bargaining points.

"The reason I'm in it at all is because we had dinner together.

Honest mistake—on both our parts. I had no right to the particulars of your business up to the point my hands are 'wired together and I'm being hauled out of a public place on a bogus bounty. At that point, you owed me info—and I ain't been paid yet."

He looked thoughtful. "You won't like the answer."

She blinked. "So I won't like the answer," she said. "Plenty of answers out there I don't like."

He sighed, lightly. "All right, then. The answer is, I don't know who's involved, if they're local or more—connected."

"You're right," Cantra said, after a moment. "I don't like it. Do better, why not?"

He spread his hands. "Wish I could."

Her temper flared. "Dammit, we got a double-digit body count out of this night's work, including Dulsey's Batch, and you *don't know* who thinks you done 'em wrong?"

"That's right," he said, imperturbable.

"It is possible that those who ultimately seek the pilot are off-world," Dulsey said surprisingly, from her seat on a closed toolbox. "The ones who came to The Alcoves were local odd jobbers."

Cantra spun on a heel to look at her, sitting with her hands gripping her knees and her pale face seeming to glow in the dimness.

"How you figure off-world?"

Dulsey moved her head a little from side to side. "Odd jobs are done for pay. Had the pilots paid for protection against harm, then the local chapter would have split—half to fulfill the contract to . . . discommode . . . the pilots; half to ensure that the pilots were not in any way impeded."

"They don't act on their own is what you're saying?"

"Pilot, that is correct."

Cantra looked over at Jela.

"Light any dials for you?"

"Sorry."

She sighed, then shrugged, giving it up as a hopeless case. "I'll watch my back. Business as usual." She nodded to Jela. "Be seeing you, Pilot. Safe lift."

She was halfway to the door before she heard him say, "About that armor, Pilot Cantra . . ."

Red at the edge of her vision. She stopped, keeping her back toward the two of them, closed her eyes, forced herself to breathe in the pattern she'd been taught.

"Pilot?" Jela again. She ignored him, breathing—just that—until the urge to mayhem had receded to a safer, pink, distance.

She turned and met his space-black gaze straight on.

"It's been what I count as a long day, Pilot Jela, and my good nature's starting to wear a bit thin. If you got info bearing on the safety of my ship and her pilot, share it out short and sweet."

"The info's nothing special," he said, and she could hear a certain care in his voice, though he'd given over the stringent projecting of calm. "Just a reminder that ground-based armor can bring weapons on-line faster than space-based."

"By which you're meaning to tell me that armor there—" she nodded at the spy-glass sitting quiet and dark on the workbench "—doesn't have to reveal its feelings until I'm rising without challenge."

"That's right."

"I thank you for the reminder," she said, feeling the quiver starting in the roots of her bones, which meant the last of the adrenaline had run its course. Too long a day, by all the counts that mattered. She eyed the pilot before her, with his tell-nothing face, his big shoulders and solid build.

"Military?" she asked, wondering how she hadn't quite managed to get him pinned down on that either.

"Not quite," he gave back, which was answer enough in its way.

"What do you want?"

"What I said—transport out, for me, the tree, and Dulsey. I'm good for co-pilot and, yes, I do know the avoids for that class of armor."

"Might be manned."

He hitched a shoulder—qualified denial. "Not much room in those for personnel. Not to say there couldn't be a couple of smalls running crew. In which case the assault's randomized, making avoids more difficult, and less accurate, which assists avoidance."

"That a fact?" This asked against a rising shake. She tried to make the follow-on sound stronger. "That stuff can be evaded?"

"Experience shows it can."

Cantra closed her eyes. The shaking was more pronounced, now. She was headed for a crash and no mistake. Granted, she had more than enough Tempo in stores to keep her up and fully able for some number of ship's days. Having flown that course more than once, she knew that all the drug did was put the time of the crash out, interest compounded hourly.

And, truth told, she didn't have room for downtime on this leg—not now and not later. She had cargo, she had a deadline—and there was no way she could justify taking anyone lawful aboard her ship—nor trust anyone not.

She flicked a look at Dulsey, sitting frozen on her toolbox, and another at Jela, standing calm and quiet, letting her think it through. What his answer might be if the product of her thought didn't match his had-to's, she couldn't guess. And, after all, it was *her* ship.

She jerked her head toward the door.

"Right. Experience. Let's go."

THERE WASN'T ANY WAY to tell how the ships and the armor gained their info, so there wasn't any use going roundabout to the ramp of Pilot Cantra's ship. Thus the pilot ruled. As it happened, Jela didn't disagree with her reasons or her decision. He was beginning to develop some serious respect for Pilot Cantra, even though the day was beginning to visibly wear on her.

They marched in order—pilot first, himself and the tree next, Dulsey in her stolen coveralls and not-stolen gun covering the rear. It was interesting to note that they encountered no armed lurkers or outliers. Not so much as a panhandler impeded their progress. Jela walked on, senses hyper-alert, and revised his opinion regarding the likely involvement of the armor. It wasn't especially good strategy to depend on the equipment to the exclusion of soldiers on the ground.

On the other hand, he hadn't seen much good strategy in this op—present company excluded.

The air had cooled rapidly with the setting of the local star, however, so brisk was their march that it was unnecessary for his 'skins to raise the temp. Above his head, the tree's leaves were still despite the breeze of their passage, allowing him to use his ears to listen for possible enemy movement.

They came to the ramp of the pilot's ship in good order. She mounted first, which was her right as captain; long, light stride waking not a whisper from the metal deck. He followed, the tree cradled in his arms, and Dulsey came at his back, metal ringing under her deliberate steps.

The hatch began to slide back as Pilot Cantra reached the top of the ramp. She never paused, crossing the landing in two of her strides and ducking through the gap into the lock beyond.

By the time Jela, bearing the extra inconvenience of the tree, reached the landing the hatch was wide open, the lock beyond spilling pale blue light onto the decking. The plate over the door read *Spiral Dance*. No home port.

He paused, waiting for Dulsey.

She reached his side, throwing him a wide glance out of gray eyes. "Pilot?"

Arms occupied with the tub holding the tree, he used his chin to point.

"The minute you cross into that ship, a bounty goes on you," he said.

"Yes, Pilot. This—I am aware of that," she answered and it might have been impatience he heard. He hoped so.

"You didn't discuss with Pilot Cantra where you might like to be set down," he continued. "There aren't many worlds where those Batch-marks will go unnoticed."

"I am also aware of that, Pilot. I thank you for your concern, but my immediate need is to depart Faldaiza. Deeper plans—deeper plans await event."

Two "I-s" and a "my" in the same couple sentences, and nary a hesitation before any of them. She might, he thought, make it.

Provided she could find some way to neutralize the Batch tats. There might even be a way to do it, short of amputating the arms and regrowing. He'd never heard of any undetectable method besides the amputations—acid baths only removed the first two or three layers of skin, and left behind telltale burns; attempts to camouflage the tats with others, done by needle, were doomed to failure.

"We should not," Dulsey said, "keep Pilot Cantra waiting."

"We should not," he agreed, and jerked his chin again at the open hatch. "After you."

SHE HIT THE PILOT'S CHAIR, hands already on the board, opening long eyes and short, slapping up wide ears. Pilot voices began to murmur—groundside chatter, as it sounded. Nobody sounding frantic, no tightness in the banter. Good.

Her hands were starting to shake, and a high whine had started in her ears, damn it all to the Deeps. She thought about the stick of Tempo in the utility drawer. Left it there.

A racket from behind announced the imminent arrival of her crew, speaking of arrant stupidity. She pushed on a corner of the board; a hatch slid silently open, revealing a minute control panel; snapped three toggles from left to right, pressed the small orange stud. The hatch slid shut, merging invisibly with the metal surface.

Cantra spun her chair around to face the incoming.

Dulsey came first, slipping her weapon away into a pocket of the coverall. Pilot Jela came next, massive arms wrapped around a biggish pot, apparently not at all bothered by the leaves tickling his ear or the twigs sticking into his head. He took in the piloting room with one comprehensive black glance, walked over to the point where the board met the wall on the far side of the co-pilot's station, bent and set the pot gently on the decking. He slapped open a leg pouch, pulled out a roll of cargo twine and pitched it to Dulsey, who caught it one-handed, and stood holding it, head cocked to one side.

"Secure that," Jela said. The words fell like an order on Cantra's ringing ears.

Apparently it sounded that way to Dulsey, too. She dropped her eyes, mouth tightening. "Pilot," she murmured and walked over to do what she'd been told.

Jela put himself into the co-pilot's chair without any further discussion, his big hands deft on the controls. Seat adjusted to his satisfaction, he pointed his eyes at the board, giving it the same all-encompassing look he'd given the pilot's tower.

"We have a scheduled lift?" he asked. "Pilot?"

"We do," she answered, spinning back to face her screens. "We'll be departing some earlier."

He was opening co-pilot's eyes, his attention on the readouts; touched a switch and brought the chatter up a mite.

"If we re-file, we give warning of our intention to anyone interested," he said, just offering the info.

"That's so," she agreed. "Which is why we're not refiling." She eyed the readouts—nothing glowing that shouldn't be; and the armor just where and how they'd last seen it. The chatter was staying peaceful, and long eyes brought her nothing but the serene turn of stars. She reached to her own instruments and started the wake-up sequence.

"What we're going to do as soon as Dulsey has that damn' vegetable secured and gets herself strapped down, is grab us out and lift."

"Tree," Jela said, so quiet she could barely hear him over the chatter and the ringing. He sent her a glance, lean face absolutely expressionless. "If we wait a bit, we might lull whoever could be watching into thinking we'll keep to the filed lift."

If we wait a bit, Cantra thought, feeling the shake in her muscles, *the pilot won't be fit to fly*.

She fixed him with a glare. "You sign up as co-pilot on my ship?"

Black eyes blinked. Once. "Pilot, I did."

"That's what I thought, too. We go now. Pilot's choice."

Another blink, and a return to the studious consideration of his area.

"Pilot," he said, and there might or might not've been an edge to his voice. Not that she gave a demi-qwint either way.

"Dulsey," she snapped. "Can you take acceleration?"

"Yes, Pilot," came the cool response. "More than you can."

Now *there* was an assumption. Cantra grinned, feeling it more teeth than humor. Navigation brain was awake. She set it to scanning for safe out-routes, and shot a fast look down-board. Dulsey was finishing up with the cord and the vegetable. Tree. Whatever.

"Get yourself strapped into the fold-out. You got ten from my mark." She took a breath. "Mark."

Suggested routes were coming in from navigation; she belatedly added the co-pilot to the report list, copied the first batch manually and did a quick scroll. Beside her, Jela was heard to make a sound amounting to *tsk*. She shot him a look while her fingers initiated engine wake-up.

"Prime thinkum," was all he said, his big hands steady on the controls. "How do you want to run it, Pilot?"

She glanced at the nav screen, scrolled through the new offerings, moved a finger and highlighted a particular course. It hung there, gleaming yellow, awaiting the co-pilot's consideration.

"We could do that," he said, and the screen showed a second highlight, blue, two choices further down. "This one gives us more maneuvering room, in case anybody wants to throw flowers at us."

She frowned at the suggested route, found it not inelegant. A little sloppy if the armor kept to itself, but nothing to endanger. The portmaster was going to be irritated, but that was the portmaster's lookout.

"We'll take it," she said, and pressed the locking key. "If we wake up the armor, first board goes to you, since you got the experience and I don't, at which point I'll grab second." Her hands moved, setting it up, except for the final confirm, which was one key within easy reach. "If nobody cares we're leaving, saving the portmaster, I'll stay with her. Scans?"

"Scans clean," he replied.

"Dulsey, you in?"

"Yes, Pilot."

"Ten," said Cantra and gave *Dancer* the office.

✖   ✖   ✖

SHE FLEW LIKE A BOMBER PILOT, did Cantra, and with as much regard for her passengers. The acceleration didn't bother him, of course, and it seemed to not bother her at about the same level, which was—almost as interesting as a nav brain that based it simulations on lifts pre-filed and stored in the central port system. He did spare a quick glance at Dulsey, strapped down in the jump seat. She looked to be asleep.

They were up for full seconds before Tower started howling. Neither the order nor the language in which it was couched interested Pilot Cantra, by his reading of the side of her face.

More seconds. Tower continued to issue orders, and other voices came on-line quickly—pilots on the yard, they were, some sidine with Tower, others urging *Spiral Dance* to more speed, still others laying wagers on the various angles of the thing—elapsed time to orbit, probable fines, and the likelihood of collecting them, number of years before *Spiral Dance* dared raise Faldaiza again . . .

He rode his scans, seeing nothing hot behind them, on the fast-dwindling port, and was beginning to consider that the armor had never been in it at all, that local talent wasn't going to trouble themselves to pursue off-world, in fact, might be applauding their departure—when three bright spots blossomed on the screen. Not energy weapons—missiles!

"Trouble in the air!" Jela spat, and reached hands toward a board not yet his.

In short order, just ahead of them, a glare of light, and then the port-ward scans lighting up at the same instant as the ship's collision alarm went off. He took it in, didn't swear.

"Con coming your way." Cantra's voice was firm.

Another burst, and the pilot slapped the transfer button, swapping her board for his. His hands moved, feeding in avoids, hoping the pattern he had in his head was going to be good enough.

"Three," Pilot Cantra said meditatively. "And the man don't know who loves him."

Being engaged, he let the debate go, kicked the engine up

another notch, and felt the ship surge while screens one, three, and five showed explosions.

Though they were still in atmosphere he slapped up the meteor shields, then played the controls a moment to check reaction time . . . let the ship spin about the long axis, the modest airfoils working just fine at this velocity.

Tower came over the open comm, ordering the armor to cease and desist, which would do as much good as ordering any other robot unit to do the same.

"Ships coming on line behind us," Cantra said quietly. "Main screens going up as soon as we're clear."

Ships coming on line—that could be bad, or good, and in either case not on his worry plate until any of them actually fired. He slid the throttle up another notch, felt the instant response in his gut as the acceleration kicked in, and then quickly backed off power as the collision alarm went off again.

"Tiny!" was what Cantra said, and she was describing the munition struggling to change course, to catch them . . .

Jela slammed the control jets, bouncing the ship and occupants around ruthlessly as the missile seemed to skitter along some unseen barrier. One final burst of acceleration now and the projectile slid helplessly behind them.

Another cluster of bursts, below them now, and—

"Shields up! Got us a ship burst—"

He frowned at his screens, reached to the reset—

"One armor gone," Cantra said. "Tower can't decide whether to be happy or not. ID . . ." An audible in-drawn breath. "*Pretty Parcil.*"

"Not bad," Jela said. "For a civilian."

She didn't say anything, loudly. He notched the engine back, reached to access for the next item in the navigation queue—

"Nothing close, now," he said. "I think we'll do."

Suddenly a blast of noise, internal, as Cantra brought the audio to the speakers.

Jela sighed. So much for a quiet departure. Ships calling for weapons, pilots demanding information, the local air defense group issuing contradictory orders . . . and all thankfully behind them.

Cantra nodded at him, with a quick hand sign that was *thanks*, in pilot hand-talk.

"I'll rig that up for auto-run," she said, and the lights flickered under his hands—swap back. He sighed to himself, fiddled with the comm, checked the screens and said nothing. Her ship, her rules, her call.

Pilot Cantra fed the silence, fingers moving with deliberate purpose, locking in the auto-run. At last, she sat back, unsnapped the shock straps, and leaned her head against the chair.

"Dulsey!" she called.

"Pilot?" Languid. Sounded like she'd been asleep, for true. Jela grinned. Nerves spun out of steel thread. She'd do, all right. Maybe.

"You ride a board, Dulsey?"

"No, Pilot. I regret. The Batch-grown are not allowed to hold professional license."

Cantra sighed. "Replay what I asked you, Dulsey. I don't care if you got a license, scan?"

Silence. Jela shot a glance over his shoulder. The Batcher woman was sitting on the edge of the jump-seat, straps pushed aside. She bit her lip.

"Pilot, I can ride a board," she said slowly. "But I am the verymost novice."

"Just so happens you'll have Pilot Jela on first, and he's something better than that, as we've seen demonstrated. Do what he tells you and you'll be ace."

She turned her head and glared at Jela, who considered the lines etched in by her mouth and the discernible trembling of her arms and her fingers, and forbore to bait her.

"And you'll ring me, if something comes up except a clear route and easy flying, is that right, Pilot Jela?"

"I'll do just that, Pilot," he agreed, and touched the green button at the top of his board with a light forefinger. "That'll be this?"

"That's it." She reached to her instruments, assigned control back to him, and came to her feet, swaying slightly. "If you have to vary for any reason, it better be good, and you'll be checking with me. Right, Pilot?"

"Right," he agreed, amiable as he knew how.

"I'm going to my quarters," she said. "Chair's yours, Dulsey."

She took two deliberately steady steps toward the hatch, stopped, and turned to stare at the tree.

Jela watched her, not saying anything. She stood like a woman caught in a freeze-beam. He snapped his webbing back, noisier than it needed to be.

Her glance flicked to his face, green eyes wide. "What *is* that?"

He felt the hairs shiver on the back of his neck and produced a smile.

"A tree, Pilot," he said, easy as he dared. "Just a tree."

Had she been in strength, she'd've asked him more, he could see that. In her present state, though, it was sleep she needed, and she knew it. *Questions later*, he could see her decide, and she jerked her chin down, once, letting it go.

"Orders. You ring me," she said again. "If anything shows odd."

"Aye, Pilot," he returned, and the hatch snapped shut behind her.

TWELVE

❀ ❀

On Board *Spiral Dance*
Departing Faldaiza

PILOT CANTRA'S AUTO-RUN leaving no room for vary, nor any way short of physical tampering to take the thing off-line and just fly the ship himself, Jela amused himself for a time by running Dulsey through a series of board drills, the while keeping an eye on the screens and the scans.

Dulsey completed every pattern he called for with competence, but without flair, her pale face displaying a tense seriousness that eventually brought to mind the fact that she had also suffered a long day.

He stretched in his chair, and waved a hand.

"You'll do," he said, striving for a tone of easy satisfaction. "Lean back and talk to me. Unless we get pirates on the screens, we've got nothing to do until transition."

She leaned back, tension ebbing, leaving her serious and puzzled.

"What shall I talk about, Pilot?"

A Batch-grown question if ever he'd heard one. So perfectly Batch-grown, in fact, that he suspected Dulsey of having fun with him—unless he looked stupid. Which, he conceded, was probably the case.

"If it's going to be up to me to choose the topic," he said, still genial and easy. "Then I'll ask you to retrace your logic for me."

Her face tightened. "Which logic, Pilot?"

"The reasoning which brought you to assert to Pilot Cantra that the gentlefolk responsible for making the latter part of our evening so entertaining were working for off-world interests."

Dulsey frowned. "I believe my reasoning is linear, Pilot."

Outright irritation. Jela raised a hand and waggled peaceable fingers.

"Grant that I'm having trouble with it," he said. "I can go along with you, to a point—the abduction of my original contact, the people following us to the bar, the guards on our rooms. But what I can't figure is—why did they make the mess we found at The Alcoves? Local forces wouldn't have a reason, or the initiative, to vary from orders—"

"Ah." For a split-second, it seemed that Dulsey would actually laugh. She managed to restrain herself, however, and spun her chair so she faced him.

"It is sometimes true that unrelated events run in parallel," she said. "It is also sometimes true that the parallel-running events may share some components which makes it tempting to theorize a connection which does not, in reality, exist. Such is the case with the events of the evening, and the pilot's puzzlement may be lain to rest by understanding that what appears, from his perspective as a shared component, to be one mega-event, is in fact two unrelated occurrences."

He considered her. "The business at The Alcoves had nothing to do with us, is what I'm hearing you say."

"The pilot hears correctly," Dulsey said. "The fact is that the—the master had long been an . . . afficionado . . . of data. The pilot will have noted that the several alcoves in which he dined were data-mined. That the harvesting devices did not operate during the pilot's tenancies was a source of amusement for the master, who pronounced the pilot a very able fellow."

He blinked. "I'm flattered."

"The pilot displays appropriate respect for the master," Dulsey said, and he could've sworn it was irony he heard in her bland voice. "Unfortunately, there were others who were not so respectful, among them her heir, who, though it is not the place of this humble person to say so, is not an able fellow. The master's devices thereby harvested data which he would rather they had not, and she had begun the process to have him disbarred from inheriting. As his debts are high and his prospects otherwise limited, he took steps to insure that the master's property passed to him intact."

"With the exception of your Pod," Jela commented. "I'd've thought you were valuable."

Dulsey shrugged. "The master had allowed us much, and we knew him for what he was. Though we could not have initiated legal proceedings, nor even made a complaint to a constable, yet he would not have us. He knew the master armed some of us. He knew we had built the harvesting devices and—other—apparatus, that we assembled the records and were often required to listen to them. We were a danger to him, and best accounted for."

Jela took a moment to consider the screens and the scans. Sighed.

"In that case, Dulsey, he can't afford to let you be unaccounted for."

There was a short silence. "Pilot, I believe you are correct. However, I also believe that there exists significant opportunity to escape him."

"Not likely. All he has to do is let it out that the one missing from among the dead had a gun. Obviously, she's the culprit—a Batcher gone bad. He could even get off with offering a mid-figure bounty with a story like that."

Dulsey closed her eyes, opened them, and stood up out of her chair.

"Would the pilot care for a hot snack?" she asked distantly. He studied her face—closed—and her posture—tense; met her eyes and smiled.

"Sure, Dulsey. A hot snack would be fine."

He spun his chair back to face the board, and pointed his eyes at the instruments, pilot-mind primed to shout out at the first sign of a problem. That left a good bit of mind left on its own, unfortunately, and he was tired, too. He took a breath, centering himself, and put the part of him that wasn't watching into a doze.

"PILOT?"

He started, grabbed a look at the instruments, then spun his chair to face Dulsey, standing with a mug and a bowl in her hands.

She stepped closer, offering both, and he took them, slotting the mug into the chair-arm holder and snapping the bowl into the board-edge restraints. The bowl gave off a pleasantly spicy steam.

"Thank you," he said, meaning it. "Feed yourself, too, right?"

"I've eaten," she said, sounding irritated. "There is something that you must know."

He raised his eyebrows. "Go."

"We are locked in," she said, even more irritated, to his ear. "The piloting room, and the hall beyond that door— " she pointed at the interior hatch—"we are allowed. The second hatch, further down the hall, is locked, and another door, across from the galley, is also locked."

"That bothers you, does it?"

Dulsey frowned. "Does it not bother you?"

He pulled the mug up and had a sip. Tea, hot and sweet, just what a tired pilot needed. He had another sip, somewhat deeper, before looking back to her.

"Not particularly," he said. "Pilot Cantra didn't exactly ask for our help, though she did realize she needed it. It only makes sense for her to lock us out of the places she doesn't think we need to get into." Another sip of tea—damn, that was good.

"Besides," he said to Dulsey's angry eyes, "I'd rather be locked in the pilot's tower than out."

"There is that," she said after a moment, and went to the vacant chair. "I will watch, Pilot, while you eat."

THIRTEEN

※ ⑨ ※ ⑨ ※ ⑨ ※ ⑨ ※ ⑨ ※ ⑨ ※ ⑨ ※ ⑨ ※ ⑨ ※ ⑨ ※ ⑨ ※ ⑨ ※

Outbound, Faldaiza Nearspace
Approaching Transition

SOMEWHERE, FAR AWAY, a two-tone chime was going off. Cantra rolled onto her stomach and pulled the blanket over her head. Not that it would do a bit of good. Ilan would be by too soon to enforce the wake-up call. She'd heard that in other dorms it was possible to bribe the top girl for a couple hours' sleep-in. Not Ilan, though. Oh, she'd take the bribe, all right—she wasn't a fool, was she? And then she'd write it up and hand it in to the Super and there'd be a short, intensely miserable time, during which you learned to wonder what sleep was, to have made you want more of it. And when you were well and truly beyond thought, feeling or—

Damn chime should've finished its cycle by now. Might be an emergency drill. She struggled with the thought, trying to call the various drill-tones to mind. Which process tipped her over the edge from mostly asleep to mostly awake, whereupon she recognized the chime as her own alarm clock, which she'd just managed to set before crashing into her bunk, 'skins, boots, and all.

There are strangers on my ship.

Recent memory got her eyes open and her legs over the side of the bunk, blanket sliding to the deck.

She sat there a moment, taking stock. Her head ached, her thoughts were fuzzy, her throat and eyes were dry, and her stomach felt queasy. On the other hand, the down-deep shaking was gone, and her ears heard clear, meaning that the alarm was irritating. All in all, a four hundred percent improvement over her state of—she squinted across the room at the clock—three ship-hours ago.

She was in shape to fly, if she had to—and she did. After a bit of clean-up.

Sliding to her feet, she crossed the room and slapped the alarm into silence, stripped off 'skins and boots, dropped them into the decom drawer, and stepped into the sanitation closet.

She emerged dry cleaned and somewhat less queasy, opened her locker, and pulled on ship clothes—a close-fitting sweater and pants—and a pair of ship slippers. The polished metal interior of the locker showed fleeting reflections of a tall, thin woman, her beige hair cut off blunt at the jaw line, her eyes misty green under thin winged brows. The rest of the face was sharp—cheekbones, nose, and chin—skin the uniform golden-tan prized in the higher class courtesans. The reflection moved with spare economy, one motion flowing effortlessly into the next—a dancer's grace. Or a pilot's.

Cantra slammed the door, picked up the fallen blanket, and began to put her bunk in order, thoughts on the piloting room and the strangers aboard her ship.

No sense now second-guessing the line of logic that had led her to such folly in the first place. Done was done. She had a situation which called for some care and some planning, neither one of which she had been in shape to handle—and arguably still wasn't.

She owned that Jela had called the problem on Faldaiza Yard accurately, and that he hadn't stinted on his answer to it. He was also the devil's own pilot—as good as the best she'd ever seen. What he was doing without a ship was a mystery—a worrisome mystery, if he took it into his head that *Dancer* suited him.

Well, she thought, tucking the blanket tight and reaching up for the webbing, if he took that notion, he'd have to kill her to fulfill it.

More than a few had filed that course and failed at lift. Jela being a better pilot than she was—he might manage the thing. In which case, her worries were over. Best she could do was stay awake, stay on guard, and hope she got lucky if matters fell out that way.

Assuming that they didn't . . . She sighed. The cargo was expected by a certain someone, on a certain date and time, there on Taliofi. The course was set in—she glanced at the clock— transition coming up soon—and even with the early lift the schedule wasn't generous. So, Pilot Jela and Batcher Dulsey were with her 'til then. After she'd collected her money, and delivered the goods—that was when she'd lose them. If it came to lifting without cargo—she could do that. Take on something at Kizimi, maybe. Or Horetide—that was an idea, in and of itself. She hadn't seen Qualee in a ship's age.

She finished with the webbing and stepped back from the bunk. Ditch Dulsey and Jela at Taliofi and lift for Horetide. As a plan, it was simple, straightforward and not too likely to go wrong. It might get dicey if it came known she'd aided and abetted a runaway Batcher—but it *was* Taliofi they was bound for, a port that 'hunters wishful of living long tended to avoid.

In the meantime—another glance at the clock. Right. Time for her to relieve her crew, who were probably more than ready for their own naps. First, though . . .

She opened the locker once more, ignoring the flickering reflections, and pushed on a corner of the right-hand wall. The concealed door slid away and she considered the pattern of light-and-dark, flicked two toggles, closed the hidden door and the public one and left the cabin at a brisk walk.

She made a short detour through the galley for a high-cal bar, found the tea caddy warm, poured some of the contents into a mug, and sipped. Strong and on the edge of too sweet. Perfect. She filled the mug and carried it and the high-cal with her into the piloting chamber.

The door snapped open, revealing a scene of ship's tranquility, both pilots sitting their boards, attentive to the duty at hand.

Mostly.

Dulsey, alerted by the sound of the door, spun her chair around, her face neutral to the point of accusation.

Pilot Jela, now, he merely lifted his eyes to the forward screen, tracking her reflection as she came across the room.

"Pilot," he said, nice and polite.

"Pilot," she answered, in the same pitch and key. She included Dulsey in her nod. "I appreciate the two of you keeping us on course while I had some down time." She hefted her mug with a slight smile. "I also appreciate the tea."

"You are welcome, Pilot," Dulsey said softly. "If you like, I can make you some soup."

"Not right now, thanks," Cantra answered. "Right now, it's time for the shift to change. I'm rested enough to fly her and the two of you have got to be on course for exhaustion yourselves." She took another step forward, and now Jela spun his chair, too, looking up at her out of black, ungiving eyes.

"We're coming up on transition," he said, calm and easy on the surface, but showing tense beneath it. Cantra felt a flicker of sympathy for him, inclined her head and squared her shoulders.

"So we are. The board is mine, Pilot. Get some rest, the two of you."

"Where shall we rest, Pilot?" Dulsey snapped. "We are forbidden the ship, save this room and the galley."

Cantra tipped her head. "Don't like to be locked out of things, Dulsey?" She shrugged, flicked a glance to Jela; saw her own image in his eyes. "I've reconfigured," she told him, trusting Dulsey would follow his lead, and trusting that he wouldn't chose to make trouble now, if trouble was on his flight plan.

"The quarters across from the galley are unlocked now. I suggest the two of you get some rest." She stared deliberately into Dulsey's eyes and was mildly amused when the Batcher's glare did not falter.

"I *strongly* suggest that the two of you get some rest," she said softly.

There might have been a hesitation. If so, it was too brief for her to scan. Jela came to his feet and nodded, respectful.

"The shift changes, Pilot," he said formally.

"Thank you," she replied. "I'll see you on the far side of sleep."

A measuring black glance swept her face before Jela turned and moved toward the door with his light, almost mincing steps. The panel slid aside as he approached. Stayed open as he turned.

"Dulsey?" he said, and it was clear from the tone that he could and would carry her, if she wanted it that way.

For a heartbeat it seemed as though Dulsey would stay stubbornly in her chair. She glared at Cantra, who gave her a smile and sipped her tea. Goaded, she transferred the glare to Jela—

And levered herself out of the chair, walking heavily. At the door, she paused, like she'd just remembered something, turned and bowed deeply.

"Pilot. Good shift."

Almost, she returned the bow. Almost. In the event, she simply nodded, and watched the two of them out the door.

When they were gone, she opened the secret hatch on the board and flicked a toggle, locking herself in.

THE DOOR OPENED to his palm, revealing quarters not much smaller than standard transport quarters. There were two hammocks, one high, one low, and compact sanitary facilities, including a dry cleaner. Floor space was at a premium, and he took up most of it.

Dulsey sidled in between him and the door. It shut as soon as she cleared the beam, emitting a peevish-sounding sigh, and the status light went from green to red.

They were locked in.

Jela kept the curse behind his teeth. Of course she'd lock them in, he thought. The same reasons that had seen them confined to the tower and the galley applied.

Dulsey sighed, sharply, but surprisingly enough didn't say anything; just turned and considered the cramped quarters, her face Batcher-bland.

"You have any preference for high or low?" he asked when it seemed like she wasn't disposed to speak or move on her own.

"If the pilot permits," she answered distantly. "I will take low."

"Makes no difference to me," he said, remembering to keep his voice easy. "I've slept worse."

"So have I," she said, and slipped past him, rolling into the hammock like a spacer, and yanking the webbing tight.

He considered the top bunk—two pair of handholds were molded into the ship's wall by way of a route, and he used them, rolling into his hammock like a spacer, too, and pulled the webbing snug. He looked around, finding it no more roomy at the top than the bottom, and located the sensor within an easy sweep of his hand.

"Want me to dim the lights, Dulsey?"

Silence. Then the sound of a hard-drawn breath.

"If the pilot would be so good."

The pilot would. He waved his hand; lighting obligingly fell to night levels. He closed his eyes and deliberately relaxed, which should have triggered his sleep process. Granthor knew, he was tired enough to sleep.

Despite that, he lay awake, listening at first to the small sounds that Dulsey made, and, after her breath had evened out into sleep, his own thoughts as he moved, not into sleep mode, but into problem-solving.

While he hadn't minded limited access while he was in the pilot's chair, he found he minded it more than a little now. Easy enough for Pilot Cantra to lock them both into this tiny cabin until she raised her next port and handed them over to whatever passed for law locally. Easy enough, if he was of a mind to be morbid, for the pilot to evacuate the air from this same cabin and save herself any planetside inconvenience at all.

He wished he had a better reading on Pilot Cantra, truth be told. That she traded Gray—or even Dark—was near enough to certain. No honest civilian pilot had reason to fly like she did—and that was before taking into account her choice and number of weapons, her specially-rigged 'skins, and her highly interesting ship.

Balancing all that was the fact that she had held to peaceful welcome, and paid her share when it came down to cover and be covered. In point of fact, she had been entirely well-behaved and civilized right up to the time hostilities were specifically brought against her. At which point, she had acted efficiently and well.

Until she'd hit the end of her energy allotment, and he'd thought he was going to see a tall, grim woman fall face flat to the deck. By his estimation, considering the muscle tremors, staggered breathing, and elevated adrenal levels, she *should have* gone down. The fact that she hadn't was—interesting. As was the fact that a relatively short nap had returned her to functioning—if not optimum—levels.

That she didn't trust strangers—a lapsed military and a runaway Batcher—on her ship only showed her good sense. That she would allow them to stay long on her ship—was unlikely.

Full circle. He wasn't problem-solving. He was worrying—he was that tired. As if he needed proof.

Fine. This called for measures.

He breathed, filling his lungs fully and then fully exhaling. Before his mind's eye rose an image of a task screen, cluttered with tasks, and showing generous sections of red and yellow. With each inhale he focused his attention on one section of the screen. With each exhale, he wiped that portion of the screen away, leaving only blackness.

Half the screen cleared, he abruptly remembered something else. The tree. He'd gotten used to having the tree by his side while he slept, to protecting it, and imagining it protecting him.

In fact, he hadn't slept without the tree in the same room with him—since when? Since he'd returned to the *Trident*. Not even when they'd put him in isolation.

Concern began to grow. He remembered . . .

The tree was still anchored in the piloting chamber, along with someone who—

Moist greenness filled his senses, soothing him, lulling him into—

Jela slept.

FOURTEEN

❋❋❋❋❋❋❋❋❋❋❋❋❋❋❋❋❋❋❋❋❋❋❋❋❋❋

Spiral Dance
Transition

THE HIGH-CAL BAR was gone. Cantra checked her numbers for transition, found nothing to adjust and sat back in her chair, sipping what was left of the tea.

She considered opening the intercom into the guest quarters, and decided not. Jela and Dulsey'd already had plenty of time alone to talk and go over plans, if plans they had. If they were smart—and she allowed both of them to be smart—they'd catch the naps she'd recommended, maybe after taking a little mutual comfort.

Her stomach clenched at the thought of mutual comfort and an unwelcome memory of Pilot Jela's wide shoulders and slim hips flickered, which she was having none of.

"*Three* armor," she reminded herself loudly, and had another sip of tea, putting her attention wholly on the screens and the scans.

It seemed that they'd gotten away clean, leaving aside the questions of who, how and why they were being pursued. If the pursuers were outworld, like Dulsey thought, then there was the possibility of a welcoming party at Taliofi. She didn't much like the

149

idea of that, but she liked less the idea of missing the delivery deadline. An agreeable amount of hard coin came with meeting that deadline, and a deal of grief she neither wanted nor would likely survive came with a late delivery.

So, they went to Taliofi, exercising due caution. The vulnerable moment would be at the end of transition, when it would take the screens full seconds to come back online, and weapons only as fast as the pilot understood the situation.

It wasn't possible to translate with the shields up, but it *was* possible, though risky, to go in with weapons live—and emerge with those same weapons still live and eager to answer the pilot's touch.

Prudence, as Garen would say, plots the course. Not that Garen had ever in her life acted with what anybody sane'd call "prudence." Of course, Garen hadn't necessarily been sane.

Cantra finished her tea, slotted the empty cup and leaned to the board, accessing the weapons comp and inserting the appropriate commands. The timer at the bottom of her forward screen revealed that they would reach the translation point in a quarter clock, which gave her time to stretch, fetch more tea, and—

A green flutter tickled the corner of her eye. She turned and looked down-board at Pilot Jela's veg—tree, its leaves moving in a pattern approximating the Dance of a Dozen Scarves, inspired no doubt by the flow of air from the duct under which it sat.

Sighing, she came out of the chair, closed her eyes and did her stretches, the while seeing shadows of leaves dancing on the inside of her eyelids. Talk about prudence. Last thing she needed was for that pot to leave its moorings, if the translation happened to be a rough one, which, going in with the weapons live, it was likely to be.

Stretches done, she moved down-board, and stood before the plant in question.

It wasn't much to look at, now that she had the leisure. It was considerably shorter than she was, and its main trunk wasn't any thicker than a dueling stick. Straight like a dueling stick, too, until near the top, where four slender twigs branched off on their own. The branches held a goodly number of green leaves, and, nestled among them, what looked to be three fruits, encased in a green rind. The whole thing smelled—pleasing, moist and minty.

None of which changed the fact that it was a stupid thing to have in a piloting room.

She shook herself and bent to the restraints, finding in short order that Dulsey had done a job which couldn't be improved upon, short of rigging up a restraining field or spacing the thing. Not that she had time to do either.

Good enough would have to do, she thought, straightening and giving the tree one more hard look before she went back to her chair, glaring at the screens as she unslotted the cup.

Clear all around, for a wonder. She carried the cup with her to the galley, filled it from the carafe, snapped the lid down, and gave the little room a fast once over, looking for things left loose.

More credit to Dulsey—everything was where it belonged, the latches engaged on all cabinets and doors. She touched the carafe, making certain it was secured, and left the galley. In the hall, she flicked a glance to the door of the guest room. Red and yellow lights glowed steady, signaling that not one, but two, locks were engaged, Pilot Jela having impressed her as a man handy with a toolkit and inventive besides.

'Course, the room hadn't been locked that couldn't be escaped, but Jela had also impressed her as cool-headed, not to say sensible. There wasn't any use to him in irritating her right at present. Much more productive to just take a nap and bide his time, being sure that they'd outrun whoever wasn't after him. No, the vulnerable moment with Jela would be when *Dancer* was on Taliofi Port. She'd have to be slick in her ditching, which she was confident she could be. What wasn't known, of course, is if she could be slick enough.

Well, that was a worry for later. She turned and went back to the piloting chamber, slipping into her seat and making the straps secure just as the timer in the forward screen went to zero.

The weapons came up, the shields went down, the screens went gray, the timer reset itself and began counting down from twelve.

. . . eleven . . . ten . . .

Spiral Dance shivered.

. . . nine . . .

. . . calmed . . .

. . . eight . . . seven . . .

. . . twisted like a Sendali contortionist. The straps tightened across Cantra's torso; at the far side of the board Jela's little tree snapped a bow, its leaves in disarray.

. . . six . . . five . . .

. . . calm again, but Cantra wasn't believing it . . .

. . . four . . . three . . .

Dancer twisted again, with feeling. The pot containing Jela's tree thumped hard against the bulkhead, despite the restraints. Cantra gasped as the straps pressed her into the chair . . .

. . . two . . . one . . .

Normal space.

Her hands moved, one for the weapons board, one for the scans and shields, ready, ready—

The screens showed stars, all around; the scans showed clear, likewise. The image unfolding in the navigation screen showed her course overlaying the pattern of stars, with an estimated time of arrival at Taliofi just under twelve ship-hours. Ahead of schedule, thanks to the early lift. Still, she didn't feel like taking the scenic route. The quicker she got down—even at Taliofi—the better she'd feel.

She sighed, notched the weapons back to stand-by and scanned again, just being sure.

If there were any ships with hostile intent inside the considerable range of her eyes and ears, they were both cloaked and cool—which made them watchers, dangerous in their own ways, but not needful of her immediate attention.

A blue light lit on the edge of the navigation screen. She touched it, and info flowed down the screen, the short form of it all being that one and one-quarter ship hour's could be shaved off real-space transit to Taliofi, if she was willing to fly like a Rimmer.

She grinned, fingers already feeding in the amended course.

THE HAMMOCK SWUNG hard and Jela woke, felt the ship

steady, and took a breath, expanding his chest so the webbing wouldn't grab too tight on the next bounce.

"All right down there, Dulsey?" he asked.

"The pilot is kind to inquire," her voice came, breathlessly. "This humble person is well."

"Good. Stay put, hear me? I don't think we're done dancing ye-"

The ship bounced again, gratifyingly on cue. The straps snapped taut, and the hammock swung out and back, smacking Jela's hip against the metal wall hard enough to sting though padding and 'skins. He scarcely noticed it, himself, but his cabin-mate didn't have his advantages.

"Dulsey?"

"What transpires?" An edge was added to the breathlessness; Jela figured she'd taken a pretty good bump herself.

"My guess is we're translating with weapons on-line," he said. "With a ship this size, that's bound to introduce a bobble or two."

"Bob—" she began, and stopped as the ship settled around them once more. "We are out."

He considered it, listening with his whole body in a hammock that hung calm from its gimbals.

"I think you're right," he said at last.

"The door is still locked."

He was sorry to hear that, but the info didn't surprise him.

"I figure the pilot has other things on her mind," he told Dulsey, keeping his voice easy despite his own dislike of the situation. "Even given that we lifted out early and should be ahead of whatever delivery schedule she might have, she doesn't know who might be coming after. If I was in the pilot's chair, I'd want to minimize my exposure. It might be Pilot Cantra's going to do some flying—" That was what they had said in his training wing, when a pilot needed to produce the impossible. "I'd expect us to be in here until the ship's on port."

Grim silence for a count of five.

"What shall we do?" Dulsey asked finally.

Jela sighed, quietly; trying not to remember how very much he disliked doing nothing; and did not wish for a computer, a database, or a stack of reports to read.

"Sleep?" he suggested.

She didn't answer, and grimness lingered for a bit. Then he heard her breathing smooth out and knew she'd taken his advice.

Now, if only *he* could take his advice, he thought crankily, and moved his head against the hammock's pad.

Well. Enough of sleep and dreaming memories. What was needed was analysis and a plan. It was not to Pilot Cantra's benefit to keep him with her, so she would think and she was quite possibly correct to think it.

However, Pilot Cantra's benefit was secondary to his own. His departure from Faldaiza had been strategic retreat—remaining would not only have been foolhardy but would have endangered himself and his mission, those two elements being inseparable, and Pilot Cantra and her ship had been available. The question now became: What was best for him to do in order to recover the ground he had lost?

It was a knotty question, he thought with some satisfaction, as he began to assign decision priorities.

He hoped he had an answer by the time Pilot Cantra unlocked the door.

FIFTEEN

❋ ❋

Spiral Dance
Taliofi

TALIOFI WASN'T EXACTLY the garden spot of the Spiral Arm, nor was it quite so law-bound as, say, Faldaiza. It was by no means the worst world on which to put down a ship carrying irregulars, and the lack of an interested local constabulary generally made it a likely port for a pilot in Cantra's line of trade. The fact that it wasn't one of her favorite ports had less to do with the various briberies involved, which could go as high as ten percent of receipts, and most to do with it being home to Rint dea'Sord.

In a business where the faint of heart failed and the ruthless prevailed, Rint dea'Sord was known as a man not to cross. He paid well for his commissions, if not always at full price, and he paid well for errors, too, with interest. A bitter enemy was dea'Sord, so the word went, and a man with a galaxy-wide reach. No one cheated Rint dea'Sord, and the same could not be said for himself.

Garen had refused to deal with the man at all, which might have said something positive about her sanity after all. Cantra's dealings with him had been exactly two. Both times, she'd come away with enough of her fee in hand that she thought three times whenever a deal involving a Taliofi delivery came up—once for the money and twice for Ser dea'Sord.

This instance, she'd thought four times, the money was *that* good. And in the end it was the money that had convinced her, despite the client's known tendencies. If she actually received even a third of the promised fee, it would represent a tidy profit. Profits being what motivated the pilot and fueled the craft, she'd taken the job.

And now here she was, thinking a fifth time, which was a plain waste of time and thought-channels. She was down, a fact that couldn't fail to escape the notice of those with a tender regard for her cargo. Lifting now got her nothing but ruined. Best to collect her pay, off-load, and commence about ditching her so-called crew.

She might should've had qualms about leaving them in such a port, but she judged Jela able to take care of himself, and while Taliofi wasn't a nexus, it wasn't back-system, either. A pilot with Jela's skills should have no trouble hiring himself onto a ship heading for his favorite coordinates.

The other matter was a little less certain, but Dulsey's chances of long-term survival were in the negative numbers no matter how you rolled it. Cantra found as she locked the board down that she did feel something bad about that, which was another side of senseless. Dulsey'd made her choices and Taliofi was as good a place for a runaway Batcher as any—and considerably better than some.

Lock-down finished, she released the webbing and stood. She was well ahead of her appointed time. Might be best to switch her priorities, and get her crew up and gone before Rint dea'Sord took note of them. With that detail taken care of, she could lift directly she'd off-loaded, which did appeal. She'd go on to Horetide, and pick up work there.

Half-a-dozen steps brought her to the little tree. There was a dent in the pot from where it had smacked into the wall, and it had lost three leaves to the decking. Loss of leaf wasn't likely to do it harm, she thought, and bent a little closer. The branches and the thin trunk appeared intact—and the fruits still hung in their places. So far, so good.

Time to skin-up and see if her passengers had fared as well.

COCOONED IN HIS WEB of calculation, Jela felt the ship come to ground. He let the current probability analysis run itself to an outcome he liked even less than the previous one, and opened his eyes.

"We're down, Dulsey," he said, neither loud nor soft. The walls rumbled a little when his voice struck it.

"Thanßk you, Pilot; I am awake," came the composed answer. "Do you think Pilot Cantra will let us out now?"

"I think that's the most likely scenario," he said, and released the webbing, taking a moment to be sure that it was untangled and ran smooth on its rollers, in case the next tenant of the bunk need-ed to strap down in a hurry.

Satisfied, he eased onto his side, face pointed toward the door, and told himself that it took time to lock the board and file pilot's intent with the port and—

There was a sound—small in his super-sharp hearing—and the door opened, framing a long, lean figure. Her face was amiable, which he knew by now meant nothing with Pilot Cantra, and her head was cocked to one side, tawny hair brushing the shoulder of her 'skins.

"I'm glad to see the two of you looking well-rested," she said, her voice smooth and unhurried, the Rimmer accent just a tickle against the ear-bone. "Time to get up and do some errands."

"Where are we?" Dulsey asked, surprisingly sharp.

One of Cantra's winged eyebrows lifted, but she gave answer calm enough. "Taliofi. That inform you, Dulsey?"

There was a pause, long enough for Jela to read it as "no," but Dulsey surprised him.

"Yes, Pilot. What errands are required?"

"As it happens, I've got a list." She raised her head and fixed Jela in her foggy green gaze. "Ace, Pilot?"

"Ace," he agreed, and produced an agreeable smile, there being no reason not to.

"Good." She jerked her head to her left, toward the hatch. "Let's go."

SHE'D CONSIDERED LEAVING the tree where it was, in the interests of misdirection, but had decided against. Jela'd gone to considerable risk and trouble to bring this particular plant out of Faldaiza, and she had no intention to rob him. So, she'd untied the thing and got it—pot, dirt and fruits—onto a cargo sled, by which time she had developed a whole new respect for Pilot Jela's physical attributes, and dragged it down to the hatch.

Jela eyed it as he entered the area, and she drew a subtle breath, ready with her story about the pot being broken and dangerous in high acceleration. But he'd only shrugged, did Jela, and bent to pick the thing up, cradling it like kin.

"Pot took a beating, I see," was what he said. "I'll tend to it, Pilot."

"'preciate it," she'd answered, matching his tone. If he'd planned on making a move for *Dancer*, now was the time, and he couldn't well make that move with his arms full of tree. She didn't doubt that he'd already understood the situation with regard to his lack of continued welcome, and she was unaccountably relieved that no fancy-work was going to be needed on his behalf. She turned.

"Dulsey," she began, but the Batcher held up a hand, cutting her off.

"Pilot, there are those whom I would seek out on this port. If I do not return in time for lift, please understand it is not from disrespect for yourself or your ship, but because I have made other arrangements."

So Dulsey had contacts on Taliofi, did she? That was a piece of luck. Cantra inclined her head gravely.

"I understand," she said, and the Batcher bowed.

Cantra turned and opened the hatch. The day beyond showed gray and cold and raining.

"Right," she said, and sighed as she waved them out and down the ramp. "Welcome to Taliofi."

❈   ❈   ❈

THING WAS, she *did* have a list, a habit going back to Garen's insistence that "ship shape" meant something more than neat-and-clean. She stood at the top of the ramp and watched Dulsey lead the way down, saw Jela striding steadily away, looking from this angle like someone who might be able to make a night warm after all, carrying his potted tree like it weighed nothing at all.

Cantra sighed a bit against that thought, and the feeling that she was watching the best pilot she'd seen in some years sashay right away from her, and forcibly turned her attention to the list.

First was to do an in-person prepay for lift-off—in case news of her last lift-out had got this far already—and then do a little shopping, to top off the needfuls, no more'n that; not at Taliofi. After that, she'd scout up someplace quiet and have herself a meal, with herself for company. All this eating with crew had her half-imagining she was too old to work solo.

Once the eating was done, she'd find a private place, check her 'skins and her weapons, and go pay her respects to Ser dea'Sord.

IT WAS A WONDERFUL thing to be a Generalist, Jela thought, as he and the tree made their way across Taliofi Yard. For instance, a Generalist, with his horde of beguiling and unrelated facts and his valuable skill at putting those facts together in intriguing and uncannily correct ways would recall that . . . interesting numbers . . . of diverted *sheriekas*-made devices seemed to have passed—oh-so-anonymously—through Taliofi, their previous ports, if any, and their places of origin muddied beyond recovery. A Generalist would recall that Taliofi crouched at coordinates easily raised from the Rim—and Beyond—and that trade undoubtedly went both in and out.

And a Generalist would conclude, against his will, for the woman had covered him and had held away from trying to kill him or do him any harm other than cutting him loose to pursue his own business on a port that might in charity be considered Dark—a Generalist would conclude, in the non-linear way typical of the breed, that he knew what was in Pilot Cantra's hold, which it was a soldier's duty to confiscate, along with detaining the pilot and her buyer.

The weight of the tree was beginning to drag at his arms, and the cold rain was an irritation on his face and unprotected hands. He scouted ahead for a place to get out of the weather, spied what looked to be a cab stand a few dozen strides to his left and made for it, passing a goodly number of civilians about their daily business, none of whom spared one glance for a man carrying a tree. It was that kind of port.

He shouldered his way into the cab stand, kicked the door shut, used an elbow to punch the privacy button, and put the tree down on the bench. Straightening, he stretched his arms and let them fall to his sides with a sigh.

Dulsey had set out on her own course the instant her boots hit the Yard's 'crete. He hoped her contacts here were solid. At least the likelihood of bounty hunters was slim, which had to count in her favor. He hoped.

On a personal note, though, he had a problem. While it might be a soldier's duty to confiscate and arrest, to attempt to carry out that duty without back-up was a fool's game.

The most effective thing he could do was collect evidence, and send it on to Ragil to pass upstream.

Not being exactly military, he also theoretically had the option of ignoring the whole thing and getting on with the business of finding a lift out for a man and a tree.

He considered it, because he had to, weighing the benefits—and then gave it up. His whole life had been spent fighting *sheriekas* and their works . . .

From the tree, a faint rustle of leaves, though the air was still inside the cab stand, and Jela grinned.

"That's right. Both of us have spent our lives on that project," he murmured, and stretched one more time before taking the pot up again and bringing the heel of his boot smartly against the door's kick-plate.

Outside, the rain had increased. Jela sighed and turned back the way he had come.

"PILOT, you honor my humble establishment."

Rint dea'Sord swept a showy bow, sleeves fluttering, right leg thrust out, shiny boot pointed straight forward, left leg behind and slightly bent, boot pointing at right angles. His hair fell in artful gilt ringlets below his slim shoulders. The shirt was silver starsilk, slashed sleeves showing blood-red. The breeches, tucked into high boots, looked to be tanned viezy hide, and probably was, though the probability that Ser dea'Sord had followed tradition to the point of personally killing the donor reptile with the ritually mandated stone knife was vanishingly low. Very tender of his own skin, Rint dea'Sord, though he didn't care if yours took a scar.

He straightened out of his bow with boneless grace, the right leg coming back just a fraction too slow, an error that would have gained him a turn in the phantom lover, had he been trained in her dorm. Which, naturally enough, he hadn't, being self-taught. For that level of education, he did well enough, Cantra allowed, and answered his bow with a Rimmer's terse nod.

"The cargo's ready to off-load, pending receipt of payment," she said.

Rint dea'Sord smiled, which he did prettily enough, but he really should, Cantra thought critically, either learn to use his eyes, or camouflage them with a sweep of the lashes or—

"All business, as always, Pilot!" He laughed gently, and sat himself behind his desk, waving her to a chair with a languid hand. "Please, rest a moment and tell me your news. Will you take some refreshment?"

When Taliofi's star froze, that was when she'd take refreshment from the likes of Rint dea'Sord. Not that she'd be so rude as to tell the man so; she'd been trained better than that. She put her hand on the back of the chair she was supposed to sit in, and smiled, using her eyes.

"I just ate," she said, pulling the Rim accent up a little. "And my news ain't special or interesting. Took the cargo on at Faldaiza, lifted, transitioned, and came down on Taliofi Yard a while back. Looking to collect payment due, off-load, and lift." She smiled again, rueful. "A courier's life is boring. Which is the way she wants it, and her clients, too."

He folded his hands carefully atop the black ceramic desk, and considered her, his eyes blue and hard, belying his tone of courteous and civil interest.

"Come, Pilot, you are too modest! When a courier performs an unscheduled lift amid cannon-fire, surely that is news? As your client, I can only applaud the skill which allowed you to win free unscathed. It will of course be awkward for you to return to Faldaiza for the foreseeable future, but that must be accounted to the side of necessary action, must it not?"

"Right," she said, laconic, keeping her face smooth.

Rint dea'Sord smiled. "As your client, I must ask—please do not think me discourteous!—if the contretemps surrounding your departure from Faldaiza in any way touched upon the cargo you have brought to me?"

"Separate issue," she assured him.

"You relieve me. Would that separate issue have had to do with your passenger?"

Cantra showed him a face honestly puzzled. "Passenger?"

Rint dea'Sord clicked his tongue against his teeth, his face smooth under the gold-toned makeup. "Come, come, Pilot! Passenger, of course."

"I'm not recalling any passenger," she said. "Maybe your info got scrambled."

Ser dea'Sord sighed, gently. "Pilot, surely you know that I have eyes all over this port."

"Goes without saying—man of your position," Cantra answered soothingly.

"Then you will know that I am reliably informed regarding your passenger."

Since when did Rint dea'Sord concern himself with extra cargo, crew or passengers, so long as his interests weren't put in jeopardy? She wondered, stringently keeping the wonder from showing in her face, eyes, voice or stance, and shrugged. Holding to honest puzzlement, she met the cold blue eyes, her own guileless and wide.

"Sir, I don't doubt you're reliably informed about everything that transpires on this Yard, and would be about my passenger, if I'd had one, which I didn't." She cocked her head to a side. "Got time for a let's pretend?"

The pretty gilt eyebrows arched high, but he answered courteous enough.

"I am at your disposal, Pilot. What shall we pretend? That I am a two-headed galunus?"

"Nothing that hard," she said. "Let's just pretend that, instead of the two of us talking about your cargo and how I'm going to get paid real soon now so I can off-load and lift—let's pretend I had two clients on this port, and I'm with the second. And let's pretend that this second client, having paid her shot and arranged the off-load, starts inquiries into your cargo, which it ain't any business of hers. And so she says to me, 'I'm a big noise on this Yard and I'm reliably informed that you're carrying cargo for Rint dea'Sord. Tell me about it.' Now," Cantra finished, watching him watch her out of those hard, cold eyes, "what's my proper response, given the cargo isn't got the young lady's name on it, but your own?"

There was a small silence during which Rint dea'Sord unfolded his hands and put them flat on the top of the desk.

"Let me see . . ." He murmured, and raised one finger in consideration. "Would it perhaps be, 'Cargo? I'm not recalling any cargo.'"

Cantra smiled. "You've played before."

"Indeed I have," he said, and didn't bother to smile back. "While I value your discretion—and your warning—I believe that the nature of this particular passenger warrants my attention as a— what was the phrase? Ah!—as a *big noise* on this Yard. Certainly, my attention must be aroused when a courier whom I am known to have employed is seen abetting the escape of a renegade Batcher."

Cantra visibly stifled a yawn. "Runaway Batcher," she said, on a note of reflection.

"It is possible of course," said Rint dea'Sord, "that you were deceived into believing her a natural human, such as yourself. A Batcher traveling alone, without the rest of her pod, would seem to be as individual as you or I."

"Might've been traveling on behalf of her owner," Cantra said, by way of stalling him, while she tried to think it through. He was focusing on Dulsey, acting like she'd been the only one coming off *Spiral Dance*, saving Cantra. Had his bragged-on eyes somehow missed the substantial fact of Pilot Jela? Or had Jela decided to ingratiate himself with the Yard boss? Fast work if he had—and she didn't put it beyond him.

"Is that what she told you?" dea'Sord asked. "That she was traveling on behalf of her owner?"

Cantra sighed silently, bringing her full wits back to the conversation in progress.

"She can't have told me anything, since she doesn't exist," she said, letting aggravation be heard. "Ser dea'Sord, there's the matter of payment sitting between the two of us. Your cargo's secure in the hold of my ship. As soon as I have the promised coin, I can off-load and we can both get back to the business of turning a profit."

This time Rint dea'Sord did smile, and Cantra wished he hadn't.

"As it happens, Pilot, I am pursuing a profit even as we speak." He moved a hand to touch a portion of his desk top. A door opened in the wall behind him, and a burly man in half-armor 'skins stepped through, a limp form wound in cargo twine tucked under one arm. dea'Sord beckoned and the fellow walked up to Cantra, dropped his burden at her feet, and fell back to the desk, hand on his sidearm.

Cantra looked down. Dulsey was unconscious, which was maybe a good thing; her face was swollen and beginning to show bruises; her nose was broken, and there was blood—on her face, in her hair, on those bits of her coverall not hidden by cargo twine.

The cargo twine was a problem, being smartwire's dimmer cousin. Cargo twine could crush ribs and snap vertebrae. Not that anyone would care what damage a Batcher picked up for bounty took, so long as she was alive—stipulating that the contract called for it.

"Your passenger, I believe, Pilot?" Rint dea'Sord was having way too much fun, Cantra thought, suddenly seeing all too clearly where he was going with this.

"No, sir," she said, her eyes on Dulsey—still breathing, all the worse for her.

"Pilot—"

She raised her eyes and looked at him straight. "Much as I'd like to accommodate you, she wasn't no passenger."

The thin mouth tightened. "What was she then?"

"'prentice pilot. Sat her board neat as you'd like. 'Course, being an engineer . . ."

"An engineer." He laughed. "She was a restaurant worker before she turned rogue, murdered her owner, and terminated the others of her Pod."

Cantra glanced down at Dulsey. "Why'd she do that?"

"Who can know what motivates such creatures?" He gave a delicate shudder. "Perhaps she believed that, with the others gone, she might pass as a real human. *Why* scarcely matters. In a short while Efron here will be taking the Batcher across the port, where a bounty hunter will receive her and pay him our finder's fee."

"Right," she said, keeping her eyes on his face. "What's it got to do with me and my fee?"

"Pilot." He looked at her with sorrow, as if she were a favorite student who had unaccountably flubbed a simple question. "I think you are well-aware of the penalties attached to giving aid to an escaped Batcher. Whether she was an apprentice pilot or passenger really makes no difference."

Nor would it to those who were only concerned with collecting their bounties. And as for the penalties for aiding and abetting, she did know them: Three years hard labor, and confiscation of all her goods. Which would be *Dancer*. By the time her years at labor were done—assuming she survived them, which wasn't the way the smart money bet—she'd be broken and broke. She also knew that an aid-and-abet charge against a natural human, which in unlikely fact she happened to be, was subject to an appeal before an actual magistrate. The odds of her coming out a free woman on the other side of that appeal were laughable, and the accumulated penalties for her various crimes and sins against the law-abiding would add up to more and worse than the aid-and-abet.

Which simple arithmetic Rint dea'Sord had done, and then exposed himself and his operation to considerable risk by summoning a bounty hunter. Cantra supposed she ought to be flattered, that he thought her worth so much.

She smiled at him, wide and sincere.

"What do you want?" she asked, thinking the important thing was not to let Efron get twine around her. That likely meant a discussion of weapons right here and now—in fact, it would be best if it were here and now. She made a mental note to save a dart for Dulsey.

Rint dea'Sord was smiling again.

"Excellent, Pilot. *Do* allow me to admire your perspicacity. While it is true that I would enjoy owning your ship and your effects, I would enjoy having you in my employ even more."

Cantra frowned. "Ser dea'Sord, you don't need a Dark trader in your employ."

He laughed, gently, and fluttered his fingers at her. "Pilot, Pilot. No, you are correct—I *don't* need a Dark trader in my employ. I do, however, find myself in need of an *aelantaza*."

Cantra felt her blood temperature drop. She jerked a shoulder up, feigning unconcern.

"So, contract for one."

"Alas, the matter is not so simple," he said. "The directors do not look upon my project with favor."

The projects the directors refused to write paper for weren't many, the directors being conveniently without loyalties, and wedded to their own profit. If she hadn't already been chilled, the information that they had turned Rint dea'Sord down would've done it.

Well. How info did change a life. Cantra sighed to herself and eyed Efron. She counted four weapons, in addition to the showpiece on his belt. Two were placed awkwardly, but that wouldn't count as a benefit unless they had a much longer conversation that she was planning for.

Rint dea'Sord was another matter. He was the man at the control board, and he'd have to go first. If she were quick—

There was a loud noise on the far side of the wall behind the desk. Rint dea'Sord reached to his desk, frowning. Efron stood as he had, damn the man, and tested the slide of the gun, his eyes very much on her.

She smiled and showed him her empty, innocent hands. He relaxed, mouth quirking at the corner just a bit—then spun as the door went back on its slide, screaming wrongful death the while.

Cantra pulled her number one hideaway and pointed it at Rint dea'Sord's head just as Jela cleared the door.

Efron's gun was out and leveled, no boggles, fast and smooth.

Jela, however, was faster and smoother. A kick and Efron's gun went one way, a slap and Efron went the other, landing in a crumpled, unmoving heap. Jela kept walking, not even breathing hard, and knelt next to the unfortunate mess that was Dulsey.

"Cargo twine," Cantra told him, being not entirely sure of his state of mind, though he looked as calm as usual.

"I see it," he said, and set to work, not sparing a glance over his shoulder. Trusting her to cover him. Again.

Rint dea'Sord sat, hands flat on his desk, his eyes on Cantra's. "Who is this?"

"My co-pilot," she told him, mind racing. Killing Rint dea'Sord was an extraordinarily good way to ruin herself in the trade. On the other hand, he held info—info he shouldn't have had—and where he'd gotten it, and who he might share it with, had to be a concern. And he would never forget that she'd drawn on him. So, the choice: Ruined with a live enemy or a dead one on her back trail?

"A co-pilot and an apprentice," dea'Sord said. "That's quite a lot of crew for a woman who reportedly runs solo."

"I missed the notice that I needed to clear my ship's arrangements with you." Damn it all, there was no choice. Rint dea'Sord was going to have to die.

She saw him realize that she'd taken her decision, which was nothing more than idiot ineptitude on her part.

He lunged across the desk, and she fired, hitting him high, the force of the impact slapping him backward to the floor. Swearing at herself for clumsy shooting, she moved forward to finish the job—and found Jela there before her, hauling dea'Sord up by his silken collar and throwing him none-too-gently back into his chair.

Rint dea'Sord grunted, and shuddered, his hand pressed hard to the hole in his shoulder. He met Cantra's eyes with a glare.

"What do you want?" He gritted, the pretty Inside accent gone now.

Cantra sighed and lifted her gun.

Jela held up his hand. "Hold."

"We can't deal with him, Pilot," she said, keeping her patience with an effort. "Best to get it over with."

"I think we can deal," Jela said. "In fact, I think Ser dea'Sord will be happy to deal."

Until he has reinforcements on the way, Cantra thought, and kept the gun pointed in the right direction. dea'Sord flicked one fast glance at her, licked his lips and addressed himself to Jela.

"What's your deal, Pilot?"

"Just this. You pay the pilot here her fee. All of her fee. We'll take our comrade with us, go back to our ship and off-load your goods. We will then take ourselves out of your sphere of influence. Deal?"

Rint dea'Sord was no fool, though Cantra was beginning to have doubts regarding Jela. Her finger tightened, and he shifted, bringing a wide shoulder between her and her target.

"I can make that deal," dea'Sord said. "Just let me get the money—" Jela held up a hand.

"Tell me where the money is and I'll get it," he said, calm and reasonable. "The pilot will guard you."

Rint dea'Sord took a deep breath. "In the bottom drawer of the desk. It needs my fingerprint . . ."

"Fine," Jela said. "Open it."

Open it he did and there was no trick, which was, Cantra thought, a fair wonder of itself. She spared a glance at Dulsey, who wasn't looking as much the better for being free of the twine as she might have. Jela, damn him, had the wallet open and was doing a fast count.

"Eight hundred flan sound about right, Pilot?"

Fifteen hundred flan had been the agreed-upon sum, but Cantra had never expected to see that much.

"It'll do," she said, and he nodded, sealing the wallet and tossing it to her in one smooth motion. She caught it one-handed and slid it into a thigh pocket. "Now what, Pilot?"

"Now, we tie him up," Jela said, and produced the cargo twine.

HE CARRIED DULSEY, and Pilot Cantra took rear guard, in which formation they reached the ship in good order and without incident. That they were under observation was a given, but without any word from command—and he'd made sure there would be no outgoing from command before he'd gone in—there was no reason for the spotters to pay them particular attention.

The hatch slid back a bare crack and Cantra waved him past, which was a nice blend of giving the wounded precedence and taking no foolish chances. He went sideways, easing his shoulders through and taking care not to jostle Dulsey.

"I'm in," he called as soon as he gained the narrow lock. Behind him the hatch reversed, Pilot Cantra slipping through the improbably thin opening, and stood watching 'til it sealed. Shoving her weapon into its pocket, she snaked past, managing not to bump him, or to disturb his burden.

"Follow me," she snapped. "We'll get her in the first aid kit. Then you can cover me while I off-load."

He looked down at Dulsey's battered face and didn't say that she needed a good field doctor. A first aid kit was better than nothing, and both were better than the 'hunters.

They crossed the piloting chamber, passing the yellow-lit board and the tree in its pot, the pilot making for the wall that should have been common with the tiny quarters where he and Dulsey had taken their "rest." A notion tickled at the back of his brain, and Jela looked ahead, down low, and—yes, a beam, very faint, where it could not fail to be tripped by approaching feet—or by a pilot, crawling.

Pilot Cantra's boots broke the beam, and a section of wall slid away, revealing a low box, its smooth surface so deeply black it seemed to absorb the surrounding light. Cantra bent, touched the top and up it went, the interior lit a pale and disquieting green.

"Put her down there," she said, stepping back to give him room.

He hesitated, knowing, in his Generalist's tricksy mind—*knowing* what it was.

In his arms, Dulsey groaned, a feeble enough sound, and there was the chance that the cord had done damage beyond whatever she'd taken from the beating. And she wasn't a soldier, dammit, bred to be hard to break, and lacking a significant number of the usual pain receptors.

"Pilot." There was a noticeable lack of patience edging Pilot Cantra's voice. "I want to off-load and have space between my ship and this port before Rint dea'Sord gets himself cut loose."

"Yes," he said, and forced himself forward. The area immediately surrounding the box was noticeably cooler than the ship's ambient temp. He knelt and put Dulsey down as gently as he could onto the slick, giving surface of the pallet, taking the time to straighten her arms and her legs.

"Hatch coming down," Cantra said quietly, and he pulled back, the cool black surface almost grazing his nose.

"All right." There was a sigh in Pilot Cantra's voice. "Let's get rid of the damned cargo."

SIXTEEN

⊛ ⊛

Spiral Dance
In Transit

THIS TIME, AT LEAST, there wasn't any cannon fire to speed them along, though what might be waiting at the next port in terms of surprises was enough to put a pilot off her good temper. Not that there weren't other things.

Cantra released the shock webbing and spun her chair around.

"Pilot Jela," she said, mindfully keeping her voice in the stern-but-gentle range.

He looked over, then faced her fully, eyes as readable as ever—which was to say, not at all—lean face pleasant and attentive, mouth soft in a half-smile, arms leaning on the rests, hands nice and relaxed. A portrait of pure innocence.

"Pilot?" he answered. Respectful, too. Everything a pilot could want in a co-pilot, saving a bad habit or twelve.

Cantra sighed.

"I'm interested to note, Pilot, that your damn vegetable was lashed in place in my tower when we brought Dulsey in to the first aid kit. As I distinctly remember you taking it and its pot with you

171

when you left ship at Taliofi, and as I distinctly don't remember giving you a ship's key, I'd be interested in hearing how that particular circumstance came to be."

He closed one eye, then the other, then used both to look at her straight on, face as pleasant as ever. Rint dea'Sord, Cantra thought grudgingly, could do worse than take lessons from Pilot Jela. Too bad he was more likely to commission them both killed—but she was getting ahead of herself.

"I'm waiting, Pilot."

"Yes, ma'am," he said, easily, and paused before continuing at a clear tangent. "You've got a good brace of guns on this ship."

"I'm glad they meet your approval." Stern-but-gentle, with a slight icing of irony. "You want to answer my question?"

"I am," he said, projecting goodwill. She held up a hand and he tipped his head, questioning.

"Point of information," she said, stern taking the upper note. "I don't like being soothed. It annoys me."

He sighed, the fingers of his right hand twitching assent. "My apologies, Pilot. It's a habit—and a bad one. I'll take steps to remember."

"I'd appreciate it," she said. "Now—the question."

"Yes, ma'am," he said again. "Your recollection is correct in both particulars—I did take the tree with me when we debarked earlier in the day and you did not give me a ship's key." The right hand came up, showing palm beyond half-curled fingers. "I didn't steal a key or gimmick the comp. But, like I was saying—those guns you've got. Military, aren't they?"

She considered him, much good it did her. "Surplus."

"Right." The hand dropped back to arm rest. "Military surplus. Not that old, some military craft still carry those self-same guns. I trained on them, myself."

Cantra sighed, letting him hear an edge of irritation. "This has a point, doesn't it, Pilot?"

"It does." He sat up straight in his chair, eyes sharp, mouth stern. "The point is that you're not fully aware of the capabilities of your gun brace, Pilot. Where I come from, that's lapse of duty.

Where you come from, I'd imagine it'd be something closer to suicide."

Well, that was plain—and not entirely undeserved. "They didn't exactly come with instructions," she told him, mildly.

"Small mercies," he retorted. "As I said, I trained on guns like yours and believe me, I know what they can and can't do." He leaned back in his chair, deliberate, and kept his eyes on hers. "So, I sweet-talked them into letting me in."

Cantra closed her eyes. "I'm understanding you to say that you came into this ship through the gun bays."

"That's right."

She wanted to doubt it, but there was the fact of the tree waiting for them, and *Dancer* reporting no entries between the time she'd sealed the hatch behind them in the early planetary day and the time she opened it again some hours later to admit Jela, Dulsey, and herself.

"That involve any breakage?" she asked. "Or, say—modifications?"

"Pilot," he said reproachfully. "I'm better than that." A short pause. "I wasn't entirely sure that we wouldn't be needing the guns again on the way out."

A pragmatist, was Pilot Jela. That being so—

She opened her eyes, saw him sitting calm and easy again in his chair. "I'll ask you, as co-pilot, to give me training on the guns to the full extent of your knowledge," she said.

There was a small pause, then a formal nod of the head. "As soon as we raise a likely location, I'm at your service, Pilot."

Not if I shake you first, she thought at him. Granted, she owed the man—again—but she didn't have any intention of making Pilot Jela a permanent fixture on *Dancer*. Still, there wasn't no sense to putting him on notice. So—

"That'll do, then," she said, turning to face her screens—and stopping at the sight of his big hand raised, palm out.

"I've got some questions myself, Pilot."

"Oh, do you?" She sighed, sharply. "Lay 'em out and let's see which ones I care to answer, then."

"I think it'd be best if you answered them all."

That struck a spark from her temper. She gave her attention to the screens—showing clear, and the countdown to transition in triple digits.

"I think," she said tightly, "that you've got a very limited right to ask questions, *Pilot* Jela. You gimmicked your way onto this ship at Faldaiza, and engineered an unauthorized entry at Taliofi. Not to mention cutting a deal with a man who needed to die, and ruining my rep into the bargain."

"If I hadn't ruined your rep," he said, voice deliberately placid, but not, at least, projecting calm good feelings. "You'd have been dead, and Dulsey, too."

"Dulsey, maybe," she said. "He wanted me alive so's I could do him a favor."

"And you were happy to be of service," he said, irony a little heavy. "At least, that's not how I read it, listening in."

She spun her chair back to face him.

"You were listening in on Rint dea'Sord?" She'd tried to crack dea'Sord's comms—twice, in fact, nor was she unskilled at such things, having received certain training. "How?"

He smiled at her, damn him. "Military secret." He touched the breast of his 'skins. "I have a datastrip which I request permission to transmit, via secure channel."

"No," she snapped.

He sighed. "Pilot, the information on this 'strip will guarantee that Ser dea'Sord will be too busy for . . . some number of years . . . keeping one jump ahead of the peacekeepers and bounty hunters to care about your rep or your life."

"That's some datastrip," she said, and held out her hand. "Mind if I scan it?"

"Yes," he said, which wasn't anything more than she'd expected he'd say, nor anything less than she'd've said herself, had their positions been reversed. Still, the notion of giving Rint dea'Sord enough trouble to keep him occupied and out of the business for years did have its appeal.

"You're asking a lot on trust," she told Jela, "and I'm a little short where you're concerned."

His face hardened. "Am I supposed to trust a woman who carries a can full of military grade ship-brains into such a port as Taliofi, and has a *sheriekas* healing unit in her ship?"

She held up a fist, raised the thumb. "You should've checked the manifest before you signed on, if you're as tender-hearted as all that." Index finger. "You got moral objections to the first-aid kit, you're free to open the hatch and save Dulsey's soul for her."

"It's her well-being I'm concerned with." There was more than a little snap there. She supposed he was entitled, there being the likelihood of a personal interest.

"Where did you get that healing unit?" he demanded.

She moved her shoulders and arranged her face into amused lines. "It came with," she said, and spread her arms to include the entirety of *Dancer*.

He stared at her. She smiled at him.

"Whoever acquired that thing was trading 'way over their heads," he said, still snappish.

She raised her eyebrows, giving him polite attention, in case he wasn't done.

He shut his mouth and looked stubborn.

"Leaving aside ship's services," she said after she'd taken a leisurely scan of her screens and stats and he still hadn't said anything else. "Is there a description of the cargo just off-loaded on that 'strip you think you want to transmit?"

"There is." Right grumpy, that sounded.

"And that's going to keep my rep clear with the 'hunters and other interested parties exactly how?"

Silence. A glance aside showed him sitting not so relaxed as previously, his eyes closed. As if he'd felt the weight of her regard, he sat up straight and opened his eyes, meeting hers straight on.

"It happens I'm in need of a pilot who knows the back ways in and out, and maybe something about the Beyond."

"I'll be sure to put you down at a port where you might have some luck locating a pilot of that kind," she said politely, and spun back full to face her board.

"I'd rather hire you," Jela said, quiet-like. "The people who receive my transmittal, they'll keep any . . . irregularities . . . to themselves, if it's known you're aiding me."

She let that settle while she made a couple of unnecessary adjustments to her long-scans.

"I thought you weren't exactly military," she said, first.

"I'm not," he answered, and while she didn't have any reason to believe him, she did anyway.

"What you're doing here is coercion," she said, second.

Jela didn't answer that one—and then he did.

"Maybe it is," he said, slow, like he was working it out as he went. "What I know is I've been fighting my whole life and the war's going against us. There's a chance—not much of a chance, but I specialize in those kinds of missions—that I can accomplish something that will turn the war back on the *sheriekas*. Or least make the odds not—quite—so overwhelming. If you agree to help me, then you have that chance, too."

"So what?" she asked, harsher than she should have.

"If we don't stand together," Jela said, still in that feeling-his-way voice, "then we'll fall separately. We need to face the enemy now—soldier, smuggler, and shop-keeper."

The war had been a fact of her entire life. The concept of winning it—or losing it—was alien enough to make her head ache. The notion that she might have a hand in either outcome was—laughable.

When the cards were all dealt out, though, Pilot Jela held the winning hand, in the form of his datastrip. If he could buy her free of Rint dea'Sord and gain her a promise of blind eyes from those who might otherwise be interested in curtailing her liberty—she'd be a fool not to go along with him.

At least for a while.

She sent him a studious glance; gave him a formal nod.

"All right," she said. "Transmit your data."

IT APPEARED THAT PILOT CANTRA had levels between her levels, Jela thought as he addressed his board and began setting up a series of misdirections. He didn't expect such precautions to thwart a determined attack, but then he didn't except a determined attack, merely a snoop, the same as any pilot who didn't entirely trust her second might do.

He'd already established that *Spiral Dance's* brain was as familiar to him as her guns—one of the earlier of the Emca units; considerably smarter and more flexible than the Remle refits just off-loaded at Taliofi.

Fingers deft and quick, he set the transmission protocol: validate, send, validate, wipe original on close of transmission, no copy to ship's log.

A glance at the screens—clear all around, scans showing the appropriate levels of busy energies, nothing exotic or overly active, transition still some ship-hours ahead of them—and a look out of the side of his eye at the pilot sitting her board serene, long, elegant fingers dancing on the numbers pad, like as not discussing possible exit points with the navigation brain.

If it had been his to call, he'd have opted to wait and send closer to transition, to minimize the risk of a trace. The choice not being his, the likelihood of a trace being, in his estimation, low, and the pilot possibly with her attention on something other than on him, he checked his protocols a second time and hit "send."

The query went out, the answer came back, the data flowed away. Query again, answer—and the thing was done, beam closed. Jela tapped a key, accessing the datastrip, which showed empty, just as it ought. Good.

He pulled it out of the slot and crumbled it in his fist. The flexible metal resisted at first, then folded, tiny slivers tickling his palm.

The sense of being watched pulled his eyes up—and he met Pilot Cantra's interested green gaze. He waited, with the clear sense that he'd just given information out.

But— "Scrap drawer's on your left," was all she said, calm and agreeable, and turned her attention back to her calcs.

"Thank you," he muttered, and thumbed the drawer open, depositing the strip and making sure his palms were free of shred before closing it again and putting his eyes and most of his attention on his own board.

Screens and scans still clear, timer ticking down to translation. Transition to *where* was apparently not a subject on which the pilot craved his input. He considered introducing it himself, then decided to bide his time, pending consideration of recent discoveries and events.

If Ragil's people up-line moved fast on Rint dea'Sord's operation, they might even recover most of *Spiral Dance's* recent off-loaded and lamentable cargo. He'd handed the man and the cargo to others better equipped to deal with them—nothing more he could or should do, there. He therefore put both out of his mind.

Pilot Cantra, however . . .

He hadn't listened long, being more interested in downloading various fascinating data regarding dea'Sord's business arrangements, but he'd listened plenty long enough to hear the by-play around the need for an *aelantaza.*

It was apparently Rint dea'Sord's belief that Pilot Cantra, whose ship called her "yos'Phelium," was one of those rare and elite scholar-assassins.

Jela admitted to himself that the proposition explained a good many puzzling things about Pilot Cantra. Unfortunately, it also raised a number of other, equally good and valid questions.

Such as, if she were indeed *aelantaza*, was she presently on contract?

Or, if she were indeed *aelantaza* and *not* on contract, who was looking for her and how much of an impediment were they likely to be to his mission?

Or, if she was not *aelantaza*, as seemed most likely, why had Rint dea'Sord, a man with access to a broad range of information that he shouldn't have had, thought that she was—and what did *that* mean in terms of impediments or dangers to Jela's own mission?

And there was, after all, the matter of the name. Cantra yos'Phelium. Certainly, a name. Certainly, every bit as good a name as M. Jela Granthor's Guard. *Exactly* as good a name, as it happened. "yos" was the Inworlds prefix denoting a courier or delivery person, and "Phelium" bore an interesting likeness to the Rim-cant word for "pilot."

Cantra Courier Pilot, Jela thought. Not precisely the name he'd have expected to find on an *aelantaza*—contracted or free. On the other hand, what did he know? *Aelantaza* were known for their subtlety, which didn't happen to be a trait he'd've assigned to Pilot Cantra. But, if the Dark Trader persona was a cover for something else—

Not that he was over-thinking it or anything.

He sighed to himself and sent a glance to the tree—receiving an impression of watchful well-being. That would be the tree's reaction to the *sheriekas* device in which Dulsey presently slumbered—and he owned that the fact of the thing tied into this ship disturbed him, too. All very well and good for Pilot Cantra to say it had "come with," thereby loosing another whole range of questions to tangle around the *aelantaza*/not *aelantaza* question, and—

Stop, he told himself.

Deliberately, he invoked one of the templated exercises. This one restored mental acuity and sharpened problem-solving. There was a moment of tightness inside his skull, and a brief feeling of warmth.

He'd need to construct a logic-box, assign everything he knew about Pilot Cantra and—

"Pilot." Her voice was low and agreeable, the Rim accent edgy against his ear. More of an accent than she had previously displayed, he thought, and put that aside for the logic box, as he turned his head to meet her eyes.

"Pilot?" he answered, respectful.

"I'd welcome your thoughts regarding a destination," she said.

Just what he'd been wanting, Jela thought, and then wondered if she was playing for info—which found him back on the edge of the *aelantaza* question, tottering on his mental boot heels. He sighed, letting her hear it, and gave a half-shrug.

"I thought you might have a port in mind," he said. "It'd be best not to disrupt your usual routes and habits. At least, not until I've seen a chart."

"Usual routes and habits," she repeated, a corner of her mouth going up in a half-smile. "Pilot, I don't think you're a fool.

I think you know we lifted out of Taliofi empty of anything valuable—excepting yourself and Dulsey, neither of which I gather are up for trade . . . and even if you were, I ain't in the business of warm goods. One can's carrying generic Light-goods for the entertainment of any port cops we happen to fall across. That means we can go wherever your fancy takes us, with the notable exception of any of my usual stop-overs. It might be that the two of us're cozy kin now, but I see no reason to introduce you and your troubles to my usuals."

Reasonable, Jela thought, and prudent. Especially prudent if Pilot Cantra expected to dump him and retreat to safety, which had to be in her mind, despite her apparent surrender. He was beginning to form the opinion that the pilot's order of priority was her ship and herself, all else expendable. It was a survivor's order of priority, and he couldn't fault her for holding it, though duty required him to subvert it. Not the greatest thing duty had required of him, over a lifetime of more or less obeying orders.

Yet, he couldn't help thinking that it would have been better for all—the mission, the pilot, the soldier if it mattered, and the Batcher—if Pilot Muran had made his rendezvous.

In point of fact, it would've been better for all if the *sheriekas* had blown themselves up with their home world. While he was wishing after alternate histories.

He looked to Pilot Cantra, sitting unaccountably patient, and showed her his empty palms.

"We have a shared problem in need of solving, first," he said, which was true, and bought him time to consider how best to follow up a rumor and a whisper, lacking the info Muran had been bringing to him.

The pilot's pretty eyebrows lifted. "Do we, now. And that would be?"

"Dulsey," he said, and the eyebrows came together in a frown.

"I'm thinking Dulsey's your problem, Pilot—or no problem. She's likely to go along with whatever you say."

"I don't see it that way," he said. "She couldn't leave me fast enough at Taliofi. You remember she said that she had business, and might not make it back in time for lift? She was so intent on that business she missed the fact that her further services as crew were being declined."

A short pause while the pilot looked over her board, and twiddled a scan knob that didn't need it.

"You're right," she said finally, her eyes staying with the scans. "Dulsey was plotting her own course soon's she heard we was down at Taliofi. Rint dea'Sord intercepted her before she made her contact, I'm guessing." She moved her shoulders.

"Not like him to plan so shallow," she said slowly. "That favor he wanted—he wanted it from *me*. Thinking on it, damn if it don't look like the whole deal was rigged. Easy enough for a man with his connections to learn where my last-but-one was taking me. Dulsey—that must've been a vary, cheaper than whatever else he had planned on. Gave him a reserve." She got quiet then, the picture of a pilot attending her board.

Jela took a breath, and by the time he'd exhaled had decided on his plan of attack.

"He thought you were *aelantaza*," he said. "Any truth to that?"

That got him a look, green eyes a trifle too wide.

"No," she said, and spun her chair to face him square. "I don't think I heard what Dulsey has to do with your choice of a next port o'call. She's a deader wherever she goes, unless she can lose the tats, which you know and I know she can't."

"She can regrow, if she gets to the right people."

"She can, but they're looking for that dodge now. One arm younger than the rest of you—that's rehab, all legit. Two arms—you're a Batcher gone rogue, and better off dead."

That was, Jela thought, probably true.

"What else, then?" he asked her. "Not all runaway Batchers get caught."

"Well." She wrinkled her nose. "If they're willing to limit themselves to the RingStars, or the Rim, or the Grey Worlds, all they need is to hang paper, work up some convincing files, and maybe a dummy control disk. Expensive. No guarantees."

"But it can be done," Jela said, watching her face.

The green eyes narrowed. "Anything can be done," she said the Rim accent hard, "if you got money enough to buy it."

"Do you—" he began and stopped as a chime sounded from the rear of the chamber.

Pilot Cantra jerked her head toward the alcove where the first-aid kit sat.

"Hatch'll be coming up soon. You might want to be standing by, in case there's a problem. I'll take the scans."

She spun back to her board.

Jela got up and walked, not without trepidation, back to the first-aid kit.

THE HATCH WAS UP, the greenish light giving Dulsey's pale hair and pale face an unsettling and alien cast. Her eyes were closed and he could see her breathing, deep and slow, like she was asleep.

She lay like he had put her, flat on her back, arms at her sides, legs straight, the bloodstained coverall—

The blood was gone, and much of the grime. The green-cast face was evenly toned, showing neither bruises nor swelling; the nose, last seen bent to the left, was straight. Her hair was clean.

Her eyes opened.

"Pilot Jela?"

"Right here," he said. "You're in what Pilot Cantra styles a first-aid kit. You're looking better than you did when you went in. You'll have to tell me how you feel."

She frowned and closed her eyes. He waited, his own eyes slitted in protest of the unnatural light, until she moved her head against the pallet.

"I feel—remarkably well," she said slowly. She raised a hand and touched her face lightly, ran a finger down her nose. Took a deliberately deep breath. Another.

"I believe I am mended, Pilot. May I be permitted to stand up and test the theory more fully?"

He realized with a start that he'd been hanging over the device, blocking her exit. Hastily, he stepped back.

"Might as well try it."

She sat up slowly, from the intent expression on her face, paying attention to each muscle and bone. Carefully, she got her legs over the edge and her feet on the floor, put her palms flat against the pallet, pushed—and stood.

"Ace?" he asked.

She took a step forward. "Ace," she answered.

Behind her, the hatch began to descend, hissing lightly as it did. She turned to look at it.

"A remarkable device," she commented. "Am I correct in believing that it was constructed by the Enemy?"

"I think so," Jela said. "Pilot Cantra doesn't deny it."

"Remarkable," she said again. She turned to face him and held up her left hand, palm out.

"Pilot, you have, I believe, very fine eyesight. Do you see the scar across my palm?"

Her palm was broad and lined. There were no scars.

"No," he said. "Was it an old scar? They fade, over time."

"They do," Dulsey said. "But it was a recent scar, still noticeable. Will you look again? It was rather obvious—from the base of the thumb very nearly to the base of the little finger, somewhat jagged, and—"

"Dulsey," he interrupted. "There's no scar."

She took a long, hard breath. Her face, he saw, was tight, her eyes sparkling.

"Thank you, Pilot." Her voice was breathless. She raised her other hand, fumbled a moment with the wrist fastening, then peeled the sleeve of the coverall back, exposing pale flesh, smooth, hairless, unscarred.

"It's gone," Dulsey breathed. Fingers shaking, she unsealed the other wrist, pushed the sleeve high.

"And it." She looked up at him. "Pilot—"

"They're both gone," he said, keeping his tone matter-of-fact, despite the fact that his neck hairs wanted to stand up on their own. He raised a hand.

"Use your brain, Dulsey. You know those tats are cellular. Just because they've been erased on the dermis doesn't mean they're gone."

"True," she said, but her eyes were still sparkling.

"Dulsey—" he began . . .

"Transition coming up," Pilot Cantra called from the wider room. "Pilot Jela, you're wanted at your station. Dulsey, strap in."

THEY TRANSITIONED with the guns primed, and the passage was just as bad as it could be.

As a reward, they reentered calm, empty space, not a ship, nor a star, nor a rock within a couple dozen light years in any direction.

"Well," said Cantra and looked over to her co-pilot, sitting his board as calm and unflapped as if he hadn't been bumped and jangled 'til his brain rang inside his skull.

"Lock her down, Pilot," she said when he turned his head. "We'll sit here a bit and us three can have that talk about where we're going, now that we're nowhere in particular."

"Right," he said, briefly, fingers moving across his board.

Cantra turned to look at Dulsey, who was already on her feet by the jump seat. The coverall's sleeves were rolled up, showing pale, unmarked forearms. Cantra didn't sigh, and met the Batcher's sparkling eyes.

"Trouble with that first-aid kit," she said, conversationally, "is it don't think like you an' me. There's no deep reader on this ship, Dulsey, and you dasn't believe that what you got there is more than a simple wipe. Keep your sense hard by."

"The pilot is prudent," Dulsey said. "Shall I make tea?"

"Tea'd be good," Cantra answered, and added the polite. "Thank you."

"You are welcome, Pilot. I will return." She went, her steps seeming somewhat lighter than usual.

Cantra spun back to her board, letting the sigh have its freedom, and began to lock down the main board.

"We got eyes," she said to Jela, "we got ears, we got teeth. We're giving out as little as possible, and while we aren't exactly in a high traffic zone, I want to be gone inside of six hours."

Finished with the board, she spun her chair, coming to her feet in one smooth motion. She moved a step, caught herself on the edge of her usual calisthenics, and instead twisted into a series of quick-stretches, easing tight back and leg muscles.

Behind her, she heard the co-pilot's chair move, and turned in time to see Pilot Jela finishing up a mundane arm-and-leg stretch. He rolled his broad shoulders and smiled.

"It's good to work the kinks out," he said, companionably.

"It is," she returned, and was saved saying anything else by the arrival of Dulsey, bearing mugs.

THEY'D EACH SIPPED some tea, and all decided that standing was preferable to sitting. So, they stood in a loose triangle, Cantra at the apex, Jela to her left and ahead, Dulsey to his left.

"This is an official meeting of captain and crew," Cantra said, holding her mug cradled between her hands and considering the two of them in turn. "Input wanted on where and how we next set down, free discussion in force until the captain calls time. Final decision rests with the captain, no appeal. Dulsey."

"Pilot?"

"Some changes while you were getting patched up. Me and Pilot Jela have consolidated. He's got some places he feels a need to visit, except he wants to see you settled as best you might be, first." She glanced aside, meeting his bright black eyes. "I have that right, Pilot?"

"Aye, Captain," he answered easily. "Permission to speak?"

"Free discussion," she said, lifting one hand away from the mug and waggling her fingers. "Have at it."

"Right." He turned to face the Batcher. "Dulsey, Pilot Cantra here tells me that there's a way to establish you—"

"If the pilot pleases," Dulsey interrupted. "I will ask to be set down on Panet."

Jela frowned and sent Cantra a glance. "Pilot? I'm not familiar with this port."

"I am." *Unfortunately.* She fixed Dulsey with a hard look, and was agreeably surprised to see her give it back, no flinching, no meeching.

"What's to want on Panet, Dulsey?"

The Batcher lifted her chin. "People. Contacts who can aid me."

"Ah." Cantra sipped her tea, consideringly. "Any kin to the contacts you didn't make on Taliofi?"

Dulsey bit her lip. "On Taliofi, the—I had the incorrect word, perhaps. Or perhaps that cell no longer exists. On Panet, however, I am certain—"

Cantra held up her hand.

"Dulsey, you won't last half a local day on Panet, even with the tats smoothed over. Your best course is to tell us what your final goal is, if you know it. It might be we can help you. Pilot Jela don't want all his trouble going to waste by seeing you taken up by bounty hunters six steps from ship's ramp, and I don't want to have to answer personal questions about did I know you was Batch-grown and what kind of hard labor I'd prefer."

Dulsey bit her lip, every muscle screaming tension, indecision. She raised her mug and drank, buying thinking time. Cantra sipped her own tea, waiting.

"I—" Breathless, that, and the muscles were still tight, but her face was firm, and her eyes were steady. Dulsey had made her decision, whatever it was. *And now*, Cantra thought, *we'll see how good a liar she is.*

"It is," the Batcher began again, "perhaps true that the pilot will know of the port I seek. I . . . had not considered that it might be possible to simply *go* rather than—" A hard breath, chin rising. "It is my intention to go to the Uncle."

The truth, curse her for an innocent. Cantra closed her eyes.

"Uncle?" Jela's voice was plainly puzzled. "Which uncle, Dulsey?"

"*The* Uncle," she answered him. "The one who has made a tribe—a world—populated by Batchers. Where we are valued for ourselves, as persons of worth and skill; where—"

"There ain't," Cantra said, loudly, "any Uncle."

"The pilot," Dulsey countered reproachfully, "knows better."

Cantra opened her eyes and fixed her in the best glare she had on call.

"I do, do I? You want to explain that, Dulsey?"

"Certainly. The pilot survived a line edit, I believe?"

Cantra fetched up a sigh. "You was awake enough to hear Rint dea'Sord theorize, was you? He was out, Dulsey. Do I look *aelantaza* to you?"

Dulsey bowed. "The pilot is surely aware that the *aelantaza* do not share a single physical type. It is much more important that the pheromones which induce trust and affection in those who are not *aelantaza* are developed to a high degree."

"That a fact?"

"Pilot, it is. It is also a fact that an *aelantaza* could not survive a line edit without outside intervention. Much the same sort of intervention—" She raised her unmarked arms— "necessary to wipe the Batch numbers not only from my skin, but from my muscles, bones, and cells." She lowered her arms and addressed Jela.

"There is an Uncle, and Pilot Cantra knows where to find him. If you would see me safe, see me to him."

"Pilot Cantra?" Jela said quietly.

Pain, in her head, in her joints, in the marrow of her bones. Garen's voice, grief-soaked, weaving through the red mists of shutdown, "Hang on, baby, hang on, I'll get you help, don't die, damn you baby . . ."

"Pilot Cantra?" Louder this time. The man who held her ship ransom to his have-tos. And wouldn't the Uncle just be pleased as could be to welcome a genuine soldier, not-exactly-military or—

"Pilot." Back to quiet. Not good.

She sighed and gave him a wry look.

"There was an Uncle, years back. He was old then, and near to failing. Told us so, in fact. He's died by now for certain, but the story won't do the same. If I was a Batcher, I'd sure as stars want to believe there was a benevolent Uncle leading a community of free and equal Batch-grown. But it just ain't so—anymore, if it ever truly was."

"The pilot surely does not believe that the Uncle would have died without arranging a succession." Dulsey again.

Cantra sipped tea, deliberately saying nothing.

"Do you know where the Uncle's base is?" Jela asked, still on the wrong side of quiet.

She lifted a shoulder. "I know where it *was*. Understand me, Pilot, this was back a double-hand of Common Years. Uncle's dead, and if he did arrange for a transfer of authority, the way Dulsey's liking it, anybody with a brain would have moved base six times since."

"I'd do it that way, myself," he agreed, and his voice was edging back toward easy. "But, as you say, the info's still out there, and it's not impossible that somebody might strike straight for the base instead of risking an intermediate stop where they might be noticed. Even if this Uncle or his second has shifted core ops, they'll have to have left something—or someone—at the old base, to send people on—or to be sure that they don't go any further."

That made sense. Unfortunately. It was looking like a trip to the Deeps in her very near future. Pilot Jela was going to be no end expensive, unless she could persuade whoever might be at the Uncle's old place of business that he was an unacceptable risk, while keeping her own good name intact. That was possible, though not certain. Still . . .

"Where is it?" Jela asked.

Cantra sighed. "Where would you put it, Pilot?"

His eyelashes didn't even flicker.

"In the Beyond."

"Ace," she said, and drank off the rest of her tea.

"I'd like a look at the chart," he said then, and she laughed.

"You're welcome to look at any chart you want, Pilot. You find the Uncle's hidey hole, you let me know."

"I hoped you'd be kind enough to point it out to me," he said, in a tone that said he wasn't finding her particularly amusing.

"I'd do that," she said, pitching her voice serious and comradely, "but it's not fixed. Or, say, it *is* fixed, though built on random factors."

"The rock field," Dulsey breathed, and Cantra regarded her once more.

"There's a lot of detail in that story, Dulsey."

"It is not one story, Pilot, but legion."

"Is that so? Stories change as they migrate—you know that, don't you? They get bigger, broader, shinier, happier. Might be, if—and in my mind it's a big 'if'—the Uncle I met did manage to pass his project on to another administrator, and if—another big one—they managed to be clever and stay off the scans of all who wish rogue Batchers ill, it might still be that the community of free and equal Batch-grown ain't as equal or as free as the stories say."

Dulsey bowed. "This humble person thanks the pilot for her concern for one who is beneath notice," she said, irony edging the colorless voice. "Indeed, this humble person has been a slave and a chattel and resides now under a sentence of death."

Meaning that the Uncle's outfit would have to be plenty bad before it came even with what she'd been bred to and lived her whole life as, Cantra thought, and lifted a shoulder.

"I take your point," she said, and looked at Jela.

"My business is nearer the Rim than Inside," he said, which she might've known he would. "First, we'll take Dulsey out to the old base and see if the Uncle's left a forwarding address."

"All the same to me," Cantra said, doing the math quick-and-dirty and not liking the sum. They couldn't run empty all the way to the Far Edge. She had padding, but a Rim-run would eat Rint dea'Sord's eight hundred flan, and the ship's fund, too, like a whore snacking through a packet of dreamies. There was cargo—legit, or, all right, Pale Gray—that could be profitably hauled to the Rim. It would mean buying at markets where she wasn't known—and where her info was thinner than she liked. But it was that or run empty, and she'd rather not find herself broke at the end of Pilot Jela.

"Need goods," she said, giving both of them the eye—Dulsey first; then a stern lingering glare for Jela. "Eight hundred flan is all very nice, but the ship needs to sustain itself."

He inclined his head. "I agree that the ship should continue to trade and to behave, as much as is possible, as it always does." One eyebrow quirked. "I said that earlier, if you'll recall, Pilot."

"I recall. And you'll recall that I'm not taking you to my usuals. That means some bit of extra care, though I'm intending to carry legits rather than high risks. There's profit to be made on the Rim, in small pieces. Coming out of the Rim, that's something else."

"First, we go in," Jela said.

"That looks to be the case," she agreed. "If there's nothing else to discuss, then the captain declares this meeting at an end. Pilot Jela, I'll be spending some time with the charts, if you'll attend me. I'll need what info you might have on some possible destinations."

"I'm at your service, Pilot," he said, and gave her a smile. It was an attractive smile, as she'd noticed before. Which was too bad, really.

"If the pilots have no duties for me," Dulsey piped up. "I will prepare a meal."

The words were on the tip of Cantra's tongue—*Don't bother; ration sticks'll be fine.* Second thoughts dissolved them, though, and she inclined her head a fraction.

"A meal would be welcome," she said formally. "Thank you, Dulsey."

"You are welcome, Pilot Cantra," the Batcher said softly. "I am pleased to be of service."

SEVENTEEN

❀ ❀

On port
Barbit

THREE-AND-A-HALF CANS were full of the Lightest cargo *Dancer* had carried since—well, ever, if Cantra's understanding of her pedigree was correct. Not that Garen had ever actually come out and said she'd killed a *sheriekas* agent and took their ship for her own. Garen hadn't said much as a general thing, and when she did, more'n half of it didn't make sense. The bits that did make sense, though, had outlined a history that would have broken stronger minds than hers by the time she came to work as a courier for the Institute.

Come with me, now, baby. You gotta get clear, get clear, hear me? Pliny's gone and struck a teacher. Now, I said! You think I'm gonna let you die twice?

Cantra shook her head. The memories were getting worrisome, popping up on their own like maybe there was some urgent lesson embedded in the past that she was too stupid to learn. She had a serious case of the soft-brains, that was what, though she'd never heard it cited among the faults of her line. On the other hand, there'd been Pliny.

She'd have given a handful of flan to know how Rint dea'Sord had uncovered his info—and another handful to learn how Dulsey had gained her own and independent judgement of the situation.

All Garen's care. All those years. And the directors must have been sure she'd died in the edlin, along with the rest of her line. If they'd thought for an instant there were any survivors—

She took a hard breath and forcefully banished that run of thinking. *Life ain't dangerous enough, you got to think up bogies to scare yourself with?*

Deliberately, she focused on the here-and-trade, doing a mental inventory of the filled cans. Jela'd shown himself to be good about not grabbing extra room for "his" part, though she certainly didn't begrudge him his space—especially when he had such a knack for the felicitous buy. They'd hit five worlds so far, slowly trading their way from In-Rim to the Far Edge, specifically not attracting attention, according to Jela, and they'd come in to more than one port with exactly what was in high demand.

Two of those lucky buys had been hers, if she wanted to be truthful—and if she wanted to continue the theme, she was finding the trade—the honest trade—interesting. She was even getting used to wearing the leathers of a respectable trader on-port, rather than pilot's 'skins.

Almost, she thought, *I could go legit.*

Don't want to get too high-profile, baby, Garen whispered from the past. *Don't want to cast a shadow on the directors' scans. . . .*

Right.

So, the trade, for now. Despite they had a good mix, there was still an empty quarter-can with her name on it. She could take a random odd lot, but there was still some time to play with and she wanted to do better than random, if she could.

Trouble was, nothing on offer in the main hall had called out for her to buy.

Shrugging her shoulders to throw off some of the tension of unwanted memories, she moved out of the main hall, heading toward what was the most boring part of any trade hall—the day-broker room. Odd how that was, 'cause on almost any vid feed of market action the image most shown was this: A couple rows of tiny booths, tenants wearing terminal-specs or half-masks, with four or five keyboards and three microphones in front of them. Day-brokers. Made an honest gambler look sane and saintly, and a dishonest gambler look smart.

Day-brokers bought and sold at speed all day long, breaking lots, building lots, mixing cargo in and out. They were willing to sell down to handfuls, or discounted stuff that needed delivery two shifts before a ship could possibly get there.

Some of them were desperate, most made a living. A few were unspeakably rich—or would be, if they survived long enough to enjoy their earnings. Day-traders didn't often quit, though—it appeared that those who took to the trade at all found it addictive. What the attraction was, Cantra had never been able to figure.

They stuffed themselves into booths barely wider than their seats, with risers overhead or behind proclaiming names or specialities or preferences; some even had small bowls of trust-me smoke, or gave away candy, or free-look vids for the senses, just stop and say hello . . .

Hard to know what might be found, hard to figure which booth to call the start. Some of the brokers were pay-box pretty, some just plain sloppy. Some looked liked what they were: Rich and bored and bored by getting richer—

And then there were the ones who paid attention to passersby, so the room was near as noisy as a livestock market.

"Pilot, what can we . . ."

"If you have three cans empty I can . . ."

"Only sixteen cubes and you ought to triple your money . . ."

"Go ahead, pass by! Pass up cash, pass by . . ."

"Sector fifteen or sixteen, I'll pay you, quick trans-ship . . ."

"Guaranteed to . . ."

She slowed, ran the sounds back through her head and turned. The skinny, bearded, bejeweled man smiled and repeated the magic words, "Guarantee, Trader? We can . . ."

She hand-signed him off, watching the hope fade on his face even as his hands jumped between keyboards, and he muttered into a mike tangled in his beard—

"That's a sell to you, and theft it is. Forty percent . . ."

Cantra drifted back a couple paces, glanced up for an ID—which was an overhead banner with a blue light flashing first around a circle, then through, then back around.

Interesting design.

"I can pay you before lift," the broker was saying to a couple of traders who had come up and paused, maybe also lured by the promise of a "guarantee."

"Credits," the broker crooned, "gems, fuel rights . . ."

He wore a head-ring with a short visor, and she guessed he was reading info from that even as he appeared fully interested in the traders before him.

Interesting design, that.

The elder of the two traders said something Cantra couldn't pick out of the general ruckus. The day-broker whipped out a card and handed it over extravagantly. Ah, a fumble there—too many cards. The younger trader had his hand out, though, and neatly caught the extra as it fluttered away. He returned it; the other card disappeared into big hands. A nod, smiles all around, and the traders moved on, the broker carefully tucking the extra card away . . .

The day-broker looked at her now, even as he mumbled into his mike, "Live, seventeen, drop orders five-five and five-six, pay the penalty and get it off my dock."

"Now, Trader," he said pleasantly. "A profit before you start interest you? I have goods that need moving. I'll pay you up-front to load, and you'll get a delivery bonus from the consignee as well. I have . . ." He paused, squinting slightly as he apparently read the info off his visor—

"Double can loads transhipping to most Inward sectors, I have three one-can loads needing to transit the Arm, I have fifteen half-can loads going regionally including some transships, I have three half-can loads going Inward, one going to the Mid-Rim. I have one-quarter can transshipping to Borgen, I have . . ."

"Pay up-front can always sound good," she admitted, while trying to place the man, his accent, or his type. It wasn't that he looked familiar, but that he didn't look familiar at all.

"Indeed, it can. Are you a rep for another, or do your own trades?"

"Indy," she nodded, "with a partial can needs filling. You got a hardcopy list of what-and-where I can peer at so I . . ."

"The trades move so quickly—but, I hardly need tell you, do I?—there is no hardcopy list, but if you can merely give me an idea of your direction I'm sure we can . . ."

A flash of something odd went across the man's face, his voice stumbled, and she felt rather than saw Jela at her side.

"Pardon, Broker," he said, over loud even in this loud place, "I'm afraid the trader's attention is needed elsewhere immediately."

She turned, sudden, and felt the pressure of Jela's knee on her leg. While not offensive of itself, the sheer audacity of it surprised her, as did the near fawning line of nonsense that came out of his mouth.

"Trader, I swear, this isn't just jitters this time. There's a problem, and you're needed! Quickly, before—"

Her gut tightened, thinking it might be real and there was active danger to her ship—but there was Dulsey on-board and watching, and the talkie in her belt hadn't beeped. And Jela looked serious, damn him. Which meant nothing at all.

"Broker," she called, holding out hand, "your card? As soon as I—"

"*Now*, Trader!" Jela cried, and she caught the quick flutter of fingers at belt level, read *touch not jettison flee* just before he dared to take her arm . . .

"I return!" she called to the broker, over Jela's continued babble. "Trader, I'm sorry. Broker, my pardons. Trader . . ." and followed his insistent tug.

JELA'S BACK WAS *NOT* what Cantra wanted to see right now, nor did she intend to watch him walk in those damned tight leathers he preferred for his dock-side rambles. Since she wasn't going to run to catch him, the best thing she could do was try to cut him off when they turned the corner—

But that quick he spun about, fingers fluttering low like he thought someone might have a microphone or a camera pointed in their direction.

Next right quick time. Left and left. Safe corner door.

She snapped a two-finger assent and he took off again like there was an emergency at the end of the walk.

They made the door right quick at the pace he set, and then out into the wide common hall that acted like a street in this section of port, and she did have to stretch her legs a bit to keep up. How he made it look easy to move quite so fast without drawing attention to himself was—

He signaled that he was slowing, and she caught up to walk at his side.

"I was about to finish settling the cargo for that last quarter-can," she said, letting it sound as irritated as she felt. "This better be a quick answer . . ."

"Is. That's a really bad place to be getting involved with."

"What, you think picking up an extra bit of cash is going to hurt us? You must have more credit than I know about."

Jela looked her full in the face as he strode on, and the look was so full of genuine concern that it shocked her.

"What I can tell you is, best analysis, that man's operation runs at a loss, and he's been running it for the better part of a long-term lease. It's a loss," he added quietly, "that would keep you in wine and boys for the rest of your life."

She thought about that through the next six steps, then brought her hand up, fingers forming *repeat*?

Jela sighed and slowed his pace again.

"About what I can say is he's on a really quiet watch list. Looks like he must be selling IDs, shipping info out to—somewhere. Part of the reason there's no hardcopy is that he'll send something wherever it is you say you're going. There's a pattern—ships he deals with have some problems. Some pilots or traders end up in legal hassles a port or two down link. Some have cargo problems. Some . . . just don't show up."

"Legal hassles?" She frowned. "What could he do—"

"Forges contracts. Fakes tape. Fakes DNA seals—or breaks them . . ."

Cantra played the day-broker's actions over in her head. He'd looked straight—nothing had smelled wrong to her, with her highly developed nose for trouble. And those two traders who—

"Damn." She shot a glance at Jela. "Breaks DNA seals? How, do you know?"

He finger-waggled something that might have been *captain's knowledge*, and gave a short and barely audible laugh before waving his hands meaninglessly, and chanting lightly, "Lore of the troop, Pilot. Lore of the troop."

She harumphed at that, then had to do a quick half-step to get back onto his pace.

"So, why're we in a hurry?"

"Can't tell if he sent a runner after us or not, yet."

"Runner? For what? And if he's so bad, why's he still in business?"

"Second son of the second spouse of the ruling house."

He almost sang it—she wondered if this was another one of his seemingly endless store of song-bits.

"For real?" she asked.

"Close enough for our purposes. I expect the locals think he's spying for them."

"If he is, he's good and I hope they pay him what he's worth. Look, I didn't sign nothing, but I saw him stash a card a trader handled . . ."

"Right. Doesn't take much if you're not careful. But, I think all we need to do is act like you solved the problem your idiot junior couldn't, and then got busy. So, let's get busy. Buy you a drink?"

Some days, she wondered what Jela's head was stuffed with. Other days, she was pretty certain it was ore.

"What about that quarter-can that needs filling?" she asked him. "Besides, the last time we ate together in public, we had a bit of trouble."

"Nope. We had a good meal, and nice wine. I still think about that."

She shot him a glance, but he was busily scanning the storefronts they were passing, so she didn't know how she should take that. Hard to figure him, anyway.

She glanced over at him again, and saw his face brighten like he'd spotted a treasure.

He looked at her, grinning. "Really—are you up for a big helping of brew and a quiet lift-off in the morning? If worse comes to worse, that pod ought to be able to suck in some air . . ."

That was a point she hadn't considered, and it was true. The next step out was a station where they could probably sell excess air, and they could run up the pressure in the can pretty good without hurting a thing.

"You think like a trader, for all you got soldier writ all over you."

He gave a short laugh.

"Call me a soldier if you like, but tell me if you want a brew before we walk by the place!"

"Sure," she said, thinking that a beer would taste good, and if there was trouble at the ship, Dulsey would call.

"Wait . . ." she said, blinking at the bar they were on approach for.

"It's here," said Jela, and there was an under note of something excited in his voice, "or buy a ride back to the ship, I think. This is the last place on port they'll send a runner, if they've got any sense at all."

If the day-broker sent a runner at all, which wasn't proven, or in Cantra's opinion, likely.

She stopped on the walk, looking carefully at the doubtful exterior of the place Jela proposed for a quiet brew and a wait-out. It was decorated in antique weapons in improbable colors, the names of famous battles scrawled in half-a-dozen different scripts and languages across what looked to be blast-glass windows.

One Day's Battle was written a little larger than the rest, in red lumenpaint . . .

"You want me to go into a soldier's bar? *One Day's Battle* sounds kinda rough for a friendly drink . . ."

He grinned. "Too rough for *you*, Pilot?" he asked, and then, before she could decide if she wanted to get peeved or laugh, he continued.

"It's the title of a drinking song long honored by several corps. I'm sure you can hold your own, Pilot—don't you think?"

Well, yeah, she did think, and she'd done it a few times in her wilder youth, but those days were some years back.

"Safest place on port, ship aside," Jela said, earnestly.

Damn, but the man *could* be insistent.

She looked down at him, which meant he was that close to her, which he usually kept his distance, and closed her eyes in something like exasperation and something like concentration.

It wasn't always easy being candid with herself, training or no training, but the boy was starting to get tempting.

Well, she'd not let him hear her sigh about it, but the truth was, she didn't want him quite that close. Oughtn't to have him as close as he was, acting like co-pilot and trade partner. She of all people ought to know about acting. Might be a little distance could be got inside, where there'd be noise and distractions for them both.

So she pointed toward the door with a flourish and laid down the rules.

"We split. Any round you buy, I buy the next. Don't buy a round if you think you can't walk back to the ship from the next."

His grin only got wider. Which, Cantra thought resignedly, she might've known.

"Wohoa!" he cried, shoving an exuberant fist upward. "Yes—a challenge from my pilot! I'm for it!"

"Sure you are. You break trail."

He stepped forward with a will—and then stepped back as a pair of tall drunks wandered out, each leaning on the other, which complimentary form of locomotion was suddenly imperilled when the taller of the two tried to stand up straight and bow to Cantra.

"Pretty lady," he slurred with drunken dignity, "take me home!"

Cantra shot a glance to Jela, but he only laughed, and led the way in.

❧   ❧   ❧

DESPITE HER INITIAL MISGIVINGS, *One Day's Battle* was—on the surface—a fine looking establishment, with a good number of people at tables, not as much noise as one might suppose, and lots of space to relax in. That the overwhelming number of patrons were military was a little unsettling, but nobody seemed to mind the entrance of an obvious civilian.

The place was laid out in three levels. They came in on the top level, and at the far end was a long bar manned by two assistants and a boss. A quick glance showed one of the reasons for the noise level being quite so low—there were a dozen or so noise-cancel speakers set about between levels.

To get to the next level they went down a ramp on the left, with a glass wall about thigh high on Cantra and a good bit higher on Jela; at the end of that ramp was a fan-shaped area with a bar at the wide end, and more empty tables than full. Two additional ramps led still lower, where a crowd was gathered around a big octagonal table.

That big table seemed to be where the action was—from a quick glance between the players, Cantra thought it looked like some kind of gambling sim . . .

Jela, however, was headed for the other side of the room, where he claimed an empty table overlooking the lower levels—including a view of the octagonal table and its denizens.

Cantra followed him more slowly, noting that the seats were more luxurious than those in the bar upstairs, and that the tables were topped with some rich-looking shiny substance. The slight sounds of her footsteps was silenced by springy, noise-absorbing carpet. The lighting, too, was more subdued on this level.

"Officers' section?" she guessed. "We up to that?"

"Officers' mess, of sorts," Jela agreed, "but off-duty, and thus not official. It'll be just a bit quieter, though, and easier for us to note someone who doesn't necessarily belong."

He handed her into a seat, which surprised—then she realized it was proper. Co-pilot sees to the pilot's comfort first, after all. Too, by slipping her into the seat he chose for her, Jela got the chair with the best view of the entrance ramp, which was a habit she'd noted in him before—and couldn't much fault. A lot of his habits were like that—couldn't be faulted if you were a pilot who sometimes walked the wrong side of a line.

Cantra leaned into the seat, realized it was a bit oversized for her. Jela's legs threatened to dangle, except that he sat forward, leaning his elbows on the table. Cantra could see him reflected in the dark surface; he was staring into it, perhaps looking at her reflection in turn.

Then the table top shimmered, and Jela's reflection disappeared within the image of a battle sim.

He looked up, grinning wryly.

"Sorry; looks like it's autostart. This'll be the battle of the day, is my guess."

Cantra glanced into the table, recognizing some of the icons, but not all. Frowning, she bent closer—and then looked up as a tall group of soldiers walked by, talking between themselves as they headed for the bar. Their voices was easily audible, despite all the sound-proofing, and she frowned even more. It wasn't what they were saying that bothered her as much as the fact that she couldn't pick words out of the sentence flow—and that the sentence flow itself was—off-rhythm for any of the many languages, dialects, and cants she spoke . . .

Losing your edge, she told herself and tapped the top of the table, drawing Jela's attention.

"Why is this here?" she asked.

"Ah. Anyone who wants to—and who has credit enough—can play against the sim. Most prefer, as you see, to use the large table downstairs, but some of us like our comfort, and some prefer only to watch.

"This particular sim is of a battle fought some time back, so there's always a chance that someone in the crowd may have studied—and come up with something better. Of course someone else who has studied may be sitting at another panel . . . and thus learning may take place—and wagers."

"Great." She sat back. "Not sure I'm up to trying to outfight history . . ."

"Sometimes," he said, his voice sounding oddly distant as some change on the screen caught his attention, "there are battles which ought be re-fought a time or two—mistakes unmade. And some mistakes not made."

He pointed at the screen, touched some table side control and turned it toward her.

"You see in action exactly such a case. In this battle, a new weapon was all the rage on the side of the blues; and in the actual battle brought the other side to a nearly untenable position very early on. But you see, someone down there—" he pointed to the deepest pit— "who happens to know one of the now-proven weaknesses of this weapon, has attempted an early turning of the lines here and—" he swept his hand to the other edge of the board— "over here."

He sighed. "This is an easily refutable attempt to win the battle by guile rather than by true force of arms. The sim, if no one else will jump in, will take quite awhile to react, since it is required to work from the actual situation and toward the original goal . . ."

He stared into the screen a moment longer.

"No, foolish Green," he muttered, "you've overcommitted . . ."

Suddenly, he laughed, and folded both arms atop the screen, partially obscuring the play.

"My apologies, Pilot. If this is what the corps is teaching, the Arm is in danger for truth!"

Another pair of uniformed soldiers passed their table just then—faces animated under the gaudy tats—and they, too, walked inside the odd rhythm of a conversation she couldn't quite grasp.

Cantra looked to Jela, nodding toward the group of them.

"They from around here?" she asked.

"I couldn't read the insignia . . ."

"Me neither. But I got good ears, and I couldn't pick up a word they was saying."

"I was distracted," he admitted ruefully. "But to answer the question you asked—they are not from 'around here' by the look of their tattoos. To answer the question you meant—yes. They feel that they are at home here, and so they speak the language the troop wishes them to speak, which is not one you will likely be familiar with."

She shifted in the too-big seat—big enough, she realized, for one of the tall soldiers to sit in comfortably—turned around, caught the bartender's eye, and waved.

"If they're gonna have tattoos on their faces," she said to Jela, "and their own language, too, it might be hard for an ordinary citizen to take to 'em much. If I may be so bold."

He glanced away for a moment, scanning the room, she thought, then looked back to her with a slight lift of one shoulder.

"See for yourself. There are groups of those wearing tattoos, and there are groups of those *not* wearing tattoos. There are some solitary examples of each. You, I expect, will be perceptive enough to follow on these observations and . . ."

"Right. What I see is that there's only one place where you can see both tats and no-tats together . . ."

She completed her scan of the room; looked back at him, indicating *condition is* with her free hand as she watched a rowdy bunch striding down the ramp to the big board.

"Condition is they ain't what you'd want to call together down there, they're competing . . ."

Condition is, he agreed in hand talk as a tall and extremely straight-backed man in what was almost a proper uniform came to their table.

"Comrades," he began, speaking to Jela, then looked hard at Cantra.

"Comrade *and lady*," he corrected himself. "How may we serve you?"

Jela's face went to that place Cantra categorized as *one step from dangerous,* and he answered firmly.

"*Pilots* will do, comrade."

There was a pause, then a sketch of a salute.

"Pilots," he agreed amiably enough, "your drink or meal?"

Cantra flashed *your choice*, and without hesitation Jela told the server, "The local commander's favorite brew, with a platter of mixed cheeses and breads."

After a slight pause—but before the question was asked—he added, "That will be a pitcher."

✖   ✖   ✖

IT WAS A BIG PITCHER and it was good beer, but for all of that Cantra wasn't best pleased with her co-pilot being willing to stake out quite so much time at *One Day's Battle* at her expense. Her figurative expense, anyway, because he hadn't had the sense to see that she'd want to be back to the ship as soon as could. How long, after all, did he think this possible-but-not-proven "runner" would look for her?

She'd figured that they'd have a couple glasses . . . but now they'd be looking to about four or five each if she kept to her promise, and by damn she wasn't gonna not keep to her promise.

The cheese was decent and so was the bread. The beer was more than acceptable, and, unfortunately, so was the company.

"Don't much care for military art?" Jela asked, correctly reading her reaction to the over-done specimen of same hanging behind the bar.

She moved a shoulder and had another taste of beer.

"Not much in favor of this school, anyway," she answered. "Could be there's another?"

He took a couple heartbeats to study the painting.

"Could be. If there is, though, they all learned to paint the same things in the same way." He reached to the platter and slid a piece of the spicy-hot cheese onto a slip of dark bread.

"What do you find objectionable? If it can be told."

"Well, leaving aside the subject, the colors are too loud, there're too few of them, the figures are out of scale and out of proportion . . ." She heard her voice taking on a certain note of passion and cooled it with a sip of beer, waving an apologetic hand at her companion.

"No," he said, "go on. I'm interested in such things. Call it a hobby."

"It depends," Cantra said slowly, "what the art was meant to do. Me saying some certain piece is too garish or too . . . primitive—that has to stand against the question of the intent of the artist. If I was an honest critic—which you'll see I ain't—I'd be talking in terms of did yon offender make its point."

Jela had paused with his glass half-way to his lips, his eyes fixed on her face. As she watched, he turned his head and gave the painting under discussion a long hard stare.

Cantra helped herself to some bread and cheese and wondered what was going through his head.

"I see what you're saying," he said at last, and finally had his sip—and another one, too. "I'd never thought of art in terms of intent." He smiled and his fingers flickered.

Owe you.

"My pleasure," she said aloud, her eyes drawn down again by the damn sim.

She moved her gaze by an effort of will, only to find Jela absently watching a couple their server would undoubtedly address as *ladies* wind their artless way down the ramp to the game level.

Neither one was her style, so she found herself looking again at the battle sim and trying to work out the icons and the situation.

Damn, if it was her that was general, she'd've realized that turning the battle line wouldn't really work, on account of the fact that the defenders could use the planet as a shield, and likely they must have had *some* secret of their own because they were fighting like there wasn't any particular point—or that the planet wasn't any more important than any other, which didn't make all that much sense, since she gathered it was a home world . . .

There was a sound that she realized was Jela's half-laugh. She glanced up to see a half-smile, too.

"It does grab the attention," he said, indicating the scene before her. "If you like we can buy into the observer mode . . ."

It was her turn to laugh.

"It's like trying to ignore somebody messing up their piloting drills. It *hurts* to see it going so stupid."

"Oh, you think so, too? I'm assuming you think Blue is . . ."

"I think I could whip Green pretty good if any of the ships I see over here are what they look like."

His smile grew, and with a flip of a credit chip he bought them the full observer feed. By the time the second pitcher had been delivered, she'd added a bit more to the sim's takings and bought their table a commentary slot, so they could drop public and private notes to the combatants. Jela'd commented at the time that they might as well go to full combatant, but she'd thought not, and called for another round of bread and cheese.

"You're absolutely correct," Jela was saying in all seriousness. "Blue has willingly got themselves set up just about backward now. See, that's because you came to this fresh, and without benefit of assuming anything. Green did very nearly the same thing in the real war, you know, and—well," he said, looking at the screen. "Well, I think they're just about to be toast . . ."

Green was very loud in the pits and apparently sure of a victory by now, and the other side was quiet. Much of the joyful noise was in the language Cantra didn't know, so she felt sure which side was which.

"Eh," came a loud voice from the depths, speaking to the whole establishment at once. "And what shall we do now, witnesses?"

"I'd say Green should ask for terms," Jela suggested to Cantra, as he looked over the rail at the action well below, "and beg that their officers will be allowed to keep their weapons . . ."

As it happened, they agreed on the point, and, it being her turn at the keyboard, Cantra tapped that good advice into the system, which dutifully displayed it on the screens below.

The sounds of joy and laughter from the pit plunged into silence, and in reaction all other conversation in the bar died almost instantly, a order for a double-grapeshot ringing incongruously from the upper bar.

"Madness!" howled the soldier in the game pit. "Who dares? Who *dares*?"

All stared up from the pit as eyes around the room settled on their spot.

"We can make the door," Cantra said, putting the keyboard aside, dread rising in her stomach. "You start . . ."

Jela grinned at her and stood, but rather than jumping for the door he leaned over the rail and spoke down into the pit.

"*I* dare."

There was a moment of what Cantra believed to be stunned silence, then a minor roar of laughter.

"*You* dare, little soldier? *You*? Do you know who you speak to?"

"Yes, I do," Jela said calmly. "I speak to one whose mouth runs faster than his mind."

Cantra picked up her beer and had a sip, allowing herself to go back over the brief good time they'd spent. If they survived what was surely coming next, they ought to try it again sometime.

Or maybe not.

"Come down here and tell me that!" howled the soldier in the pit.

Jela laughed.

"No, I needn't. You've heard the truth; it would be the same wherever it was spoke. Go back to your little lost game and . . ."

There was some motion going on, Cantra saw. At the bar, a couple of the servers were pulling breakables back behind the counter, and some of the other soldiers were moving to get a glimpse of the one on the mezzanine who would be getting pulped soon.

Down in the pit, half-a-dozen soldiers were pushing their way out of the crowd 'round the game table and heading for the ramp.

Jela looked at Cantra and spoke low and quick.

"You'll likely see blood. If you see too much of it is mine, it will be time for you to leave."

"Not a chance," she said. "If you're gonna break up the bar, I want my share of the fun, too."

He grinned at her, more than half-feral, and there was a gleam of anticipation in the black eyes.

The soldier from the pit cleared the upper end of the ramp and strode over to their table, where he stood, breathing hard, his mates not far behind. His right cheek carried a colorful tattoo of a combat whip, throwing sparks—or maybe it was stars—and he looked to be at least twice Jela's mass.

"You, little soldier." His snarl suffered somewhat from his ragged breathing. "What do you do here? You have no right to be where real soldiers drink!"

Jela moved, slowly, from the rail toward his antagonist.

"Child," he said, softly, "I was drinking and fighting before you suckled your first electric tit. Return to your games, or have at me, but please do either before you fall over from breathlessness!"

That looked to do it, thought Cantra dispassionately, if what Jela wanted was a fight. The first closing ought to be coming soon, if she was reading the big soldier right, and—

It might have been a sound that warned her—she didn't know herself.

Whatever, her hand was in the air, snatching the incoming by its handle and swinging it down onto the table with a *thump*. Jela's glass jumped and fell over, spilling beer onto what was left of the cheese and bread.

She turned in her chair; spotted the offender three tables back.

"Fair fight is fair," she yelled to the room in general, "but this—" she hefted the would-be missile— "*this* is a waste of beer!"

She held the pitcher up for all to see, and there were chuckles. The boy who'd come to pulp Jela was standing uncertain, his hands opening and closing at his sides.

Cantra waved the pitcher in the direction of the man who'd attempted to blind-side Jela.

"Bartender," she sang out, "that soldier's pitcher is empty and he'll pay for a refill. He'll pay for a refill for us, too!"

There was a hush then, but came a voice from behind the bar.

"Yes, Pilot. Immediately!"

There was some outright laughter then, and the chief antagonist dismissed his would-be champion with a wave of a long, improbably delicate hand.

"I need no help against this old midget." And to Jela: "Fool. I will show you . . ."

The bartender appeared, carrying two full pitchers. He placed one in front of Cantra and passed on to leave the second with the sneak.

That done, he stepped back and stood tall, drawing all eyes to him.

"I will personally shoot anyone who pulls a weapon," he yelled, showing off a what looked like a hand-cannon. "Fatally!"

Jela glanced at Cantra, grinned, and hand-signed *seven, six, five* . . .

And indeed, on the count, the large soldier came round the table in a rush, seeking, it seemed, to merely fall on—

Jela was gone, not with the expected small sidestep, but with a leap. The soldier whirled, and in doing so faced—no one, for Jela had kept moving, staying behind him. The soldier stopped.

Jela was behind him again, but close.

This time the big soldier expertly swept out a leg, bringing the kick to Jela's throat—

Which wasn't there; and then the big man was down, leg jerked out from under him by a twisting form in black leather, in and out.

The soldier was quicker than his size foretold—he rolled and came up, spinning.

The recover put Jela uncomfortably close to the rail, or so Cantra thought, and the big soldier, seeing this same advantage to himself, pressed in. Jela moved—fake, fake, fake, fake, strike the shoulder, *bam!*

The big soldier bounced off the rail to cheers and moans of the onlookers, coming on in a rush, nothing daunted—and abruptly stopped, stretching deliberately, showing off his size to the crowd. Cantra, at the table, yawned.

The soldier glared at her. "Do I bore you so much? Wait your turn."

"Tsk." Jela moved a hand, drawing his opponent's attention back to himself. "A word of wisdom to the hero-child: Do not threaten my pilot."

The big soldier smiled. "You are correct. My first quarrel is with you." He opened his arms, as if offering an embrace. "Now I know your tricks, little one. Just close with me once and it will be over . . ."

Jela danced in slowly, his posture not one of attack, but of calm waiting.

From her ring-side seat, Cantra could see the size of the problem—the big man's arms were almost as long as Jela's legs. If Jela couldn't get a single quick strike in—

She grimaced with half the crowd as the large solider threw a punch toward Jela's face. There was the inevitable sound of breaking bone and a yowl of pain, and she was out of her chair and three steps toward the action before she realized there was no need.

Jela stood fast, legs braced wide, the big soldier's right fist in his slowly closing hand. There was no sign of blood on either of them and for a long moment, they were simply frozen in tableau, Jela calmly continuing to close his fingers, the soldier's mouth open in amazement or agony—then, all of a sudden, he moved, putting every muscle in that long body into a lunge.

Which Jela allowed, dropping the ruined hand and pivoting as the soldier went by him.

The big soldier cuddled his broken hand against his chest, breathing hard. His shoulders dropped, the left hand twitched—

Cantra moved—two steps, slipping the dart gun out of its hideaway inside her vest.

"Pull that, and I'll shoot your kneecaps off!" she snapped.

The big soldier froze amidst a sudden absolute silence in the bar, which was just as suddenly shattered by the bartender's shout.

"I cede my board to the pilot!"

"Drop it," Cantra told the big soldier. "Now."

Slowly, he opened his hand and a slim ceramic blade fell to the carpet. Jela swept forward and picked it up, then fell back into a crouch, knife ready.

"Good boy," Cantra said to the wounded soldier, and looked over the crowd, picking out a familiar insignia on two jackets.

"You two—medics! Take care of him!"

They exchanged glances, their faces stunned under the tattoos.

"Are you two med techs or aren't you?" yelled the bartender. "I told you, the pilot has the board!"

One of the techs ducked her head. "Yes, Pilot," she mumbled and jerked her head at her mate, both of them moving toward the injured man—pausing on the far side of Jela.

The second medic threw Cantra a glance.

"If the pilot will be certain that the—that the soldier is satisfied?"

Right. Cantra considered the set of Jela's shoulders and the gleam in his eye, and decided she didn't blame them for being cautious.

"Jela." She gentled her voice into matter-of-fact. "Stand down. Fun's over."

He didn't turn his head. She saw his fingers caress the hilt of the captured knife meditatively.

Cantra sighed.

"Co-pilot, you're wanted at your board," she said sternly.

Some of the starch went out of the wide shoulders, the knife vanished into sleeve or belt, and Jela took one step aside and turned to face her fully.

"Yes, Pilot," he said respectfully, with a half salute.

In the pit there was the sound of groaning—and cheering.

On the way out the door Cantra heard someone say, "Never argue with an M . . ."

She'd have to remember that.

THEY WERE IN A CAB and on the way back to *Dancer* when the talkie in Cantra's belt beeped.

She yanked it free and pressed the button.

"Dulsey? What's wrong?"

There was a short lag, then the Batcher's bland voice.

"I only wished to tell you, Pilot, that the delivery from Blue Light Day Broker was taken at my direction to the port holding office. It awaits your signature there."

Cantra blinked. So Jela's "runner" wasn't a play-story, after all, though what the second son could want with her was a puzzle, indeed.

"Your orders, Pilot," Dulsey said, sounding unsure now, "were not to accept any package or visitor unless it came with you."

Standing orders, those, and trust Dulsey to stand by them.

"You did fine, Dulsey," she said into the talkie. "Pilot Jela an' me'll be with you in a couple short ones."

"Yes, Pilot," the Batcher answered. "Out."

Cantra looked over to Jela, who was sitting calm and unperturbed next to her.

"Now what?" she said, snapping the talkie onto her belt.

"Leave it," Jela said. "Somebody whose duty it is to watch that day-trader will show a proper interest, if they haven't already."

"Why target me?" she asked, which was a bothersome question, but Jela just shrugged his wide shoulders.

"You talked to him, you looked hungry, you might take the bait," he said, like it wasn't anything to worry on. "Man can't get ahead unless he takes some risks."

Which she had to allow was true.

EIGHTEEN

❧❧❧❧❧❧❧❧❧❧❧❧❧❧❧❧❧❧❧❧❧❧❧❧❧

On port
Ardega

"WHAT ABOUT STOCK SEED?" Jela asked from beside her.

Cantra eyed the rest of the list, on the theory that she was the elder trader.

Ardega wasn't a world known to her. Its rep was good, if it happened you were trading Lights. The on-offers here at the agri fair, for instance, included a wide range of basic genetically stable growables, the price-pers well into the reasonable range.

"Price is right," she said. "Might want to take on a pallet of the stasis-sealed embryos, too."

"They're not claiming to be gen-stable," Jela protested, and she pointed her chin at the board.

"On offer from Aleberly Labs," she murmured. "I'm betting they're stable."

"I missed that," he admitted. "They're a possibility, then. The price—"

"It's a little high per, but if we take the whole pallet, we get a discount from the dockworkers guild on the transfer fee."

"That makes it reasonable," he agreed, eyes on the offer board. "Do we want any of this whole leaf tea?"

She frowned. Where was he—oh. Garnet leaf. Good price, too. She sighed with real regret.

"It degrades too fast. Be gone by the time we raised Phairlind."

"They stay here, then," Jela said, and turned his head to look at her. "If we take the seed, and the embryos, we've still got half-a-can to fill."

"Little more." She gave the board one last read, finding nothing that caught her by the trade sense and demanded to be bought—and looked back to Jela.

"Let's reserve our decideds. Then we'll go 'round to the arts fair and see what they have on offer," she said.

"Art?" he repeated. "Is there an art market on the Rim?"

"There's a market for damn' near everything, anywhere there's people," she said, turning and threading her way through the cluster of other traders, all oblivious to anything but the boards and the info displayed there.

Jela stayed at her back, which she'd gotten used to. Her nerves no longer processed him as "too-close-about-to-be-dangerous," but as "extra-protection-safe." Which proved that her nerves were just as idiot as her brain, which, despite her having reasoned it out several times, continued to produce words like "co-pilot," "partner," and other such traps to describe Jela and his relationship to her and her ship.

Well, she'd pay that tariff when it came due. In the meanwhile, it was . . . comforting . . . to feel his solid presence at her back, and know there was another honed set of survival skills on the lookout for trouble.

"yos'Phelium," she said to the reservations clerk, and slid her trade coin across the counter to him.

"Yes, Trader." His voice was high, and he spoke the Common Tongue with a lisp, which could have been accent, or an accident of nature. "How may I be of assistance?"

She tapped her finger on the counter, the goods on offer scrolling across its surface. The scrolling stopped and a highlight appeared under her fingertip. She moved down the list until she came to the ID for the seed, tapped once to highlight the line, moved down to the embryos and tapped that line, too.

"Very good," the clerk trilled, his eyes in turn on his private screen. "Quantity?"

"A pallet of the embryo," she said, and shot a glance over her shoulder at Jela. "Three of the seeds?" He inclined his head.

"One pallet stasis bound poultry embryo guaranteed by Aleberly Labs. Three pallets mixed crop seed, gen-stable SATA inspected and warrantied." He looked up. "Anything else?"

"That'll do," she said. "Hold delivery until I call. My partner and me're still on the boards."

He worked with his screen, lower lip caught between his teeth.

"Delivery hold, willcall," he said finally. "The goods revert, fee forfeit, if delivery is not taken by local midnight."

"I understand," Cantra told him, and he spun the screen around.

She thumb-printed the order, he pressed the trade coin against the sensor. A sheet of hard copy curled out of the top of the screen. He pulled it free and handed it and the coin to her.

"Your receipt," he said. "Please retain it, in the unlikely event that a dispute should arise regarding your reservation. Thank you for your patronage of the Ardega Agricultural Fair and please come again."

"Thanks," Cantra said, sealing the paper away into an inner pocket of her vest. She left the counter, Jela behind her, and headed for the door.

THE ARTS FAIR occupied a massive cermacrete shell, booths and tables stretching out to the horizon, and sparse of buyers, compared to the agri fair. Though that could, Cantra thought, have been an illusion born of the much larger space.

She paused on the edge of the floor, and frowned at the directory.

"Not a lot of money on the Far Edge of the Rim, in a general way," she said, running her eye down the long list of luxuries and frivols. "There are some who can afford whatever there is to buy—at Out-Rim prices. I'm thinking we've got room in that can for something interesting in textile. Rugs. Wall hangings. Bolt cloth."

"One-ofs?" Jela asked, leaning over her shoulder and putting his finger on a listing for stone carvings.

She wrinkled her nose. "We got the room, but is there enough of a market? We'd have to hand sell, and I'm not seeing us setting up a booth on Port Borgen, say, for a Common Month."

"It could happen," he said, in the way he did sometimes that made her think she wasn't the only one who bye-n-bye forgot to remember that their partnership was a matter of his convenience.

"How much credit left?"

She fingered the trade coin out of its pocket and held it up; he glanced at the number and grunted softly.

"Reserve a quarter of that for me?" he murmured. "I want to cover the possibility of having to spend a month on Borgen."

In pursuit of his wandering info, whatever it was. For a man who said he knew what he was looking for, he was awfully fuzzy on its probable location. This despite his continued—and unauthorized—use of *Dancer's* long-comm. He hadn't discovered the sentinel—or he had and had made the decision to pretend it wasn't there, in the cause of preserving ship-board peace.

As long as a copy of the outgoing was caught and shunted to the private screen in her quarters, she had no complaint. Or no complaint that she was willing to voice, given the circumspect nature of the intercepted communications.

Incoming messages—and there were those—did present a problem, Jela having worked a block that she was reluctant to disturb for reasons that were likely close to those that kept him from interfering with the sentinel.

"Quarter's yours," she told him now. "Meet you back here in two hours?"

"Will do," he said, and with a nod was gone, moving out with that easy stride that covered ground quick and never seemed to tire him.

Cantra watched until he turned a corner, admiring the stride, which was just nothing short of dangerous—to ship and to pilot—and forcibly put her eyes back on the directory board.

Textile was on the Avenue of Weavers. She touched the listing and a map opened on the screen, a green line showing her the path straight down the main hall, across six intersections, and a right at the seventh. She touched the map over the avenue and the image enlarged, showing a long row of booths, with names and annotations.

She identified several bolt cloth dealers, and also several rug merchants. Good. The sooner the last can was full with honest trade goods, the sooner they could lift out of here.

Bound for Scohecan, which port had been Jela's call, and a sorry world it was, too. Still, it did own a port there, and a market, though they weren't likely to either sell or buy there.

And after Scohecan, a gentle jump off the Farthest Edge and into the Out-and-Away for to pay a social call on the Uncle. If she came out on the other side of that visit with Pilot Jela still by her side, then she could concentrate whole mind and heart on getting her ship and her liberty restored.

Right.

Sighing, she straightened her shoulders, had one more look at the map, and took off toward the Avenue of Weavers, swinging out with a will, thoughts firmly on textile.

SHE COMMITTED HALF the remaining credit, less Jela's reserve, on a quarter-can of mixed compressed textile. The transaction was completed at the booth, and a time for delivery was set. Still room for a few rolls of rugs, assuming Jela wasn't buying life-sized carvings for his portion.

Mind more than half on double-checking her capacities, she came to the first rug booth on her list. It, like the textile booth, was thin of company, a bored young person she took to be the 'prentice merchant lounging behind the counter, arms crossed over his chest, staring across the avenue with a slightly glassy look in his eye.

Cantra turned her head, following the direction of the young man's gaze, and found it was a young lady of voluptuous habit in the scarf booth across the way under study. The lady was draped in numerous of her diaphanous wares—very likely a dozen of them—in complimentary shades of blue, and clearly thought herself very romantical.

Someone, thought Cantra, had neglected her education badly, judging from the way the scarves were arranged. She hoped the young lady didn't take it into her head to attempt to perform anything she might fondly believe to be the Dance of a Dozen Scarves. She doubted the arts fair was ready. Though it looked like the 'prentice merchant was.

"Good day to you," she said, approaching the rug booth.

The boy started badly, and came out of his slouch with a gasp, bowing hurriedly.

"Trader," he murmured, the Common Tongue pleasantly burry in his mouth. She didn't immediately place the accent—and then did: The lad was from The Bubble. "How may I be of service?"

"I am interested in rugs, sir," she said, bringing the Rim accent up a notch. "Good rugs, not necessarily in the first line of art, but durable and pleasing to both the eye and the foot."

"I believe we may have precisely what you are searching for," the boy said, moving down the booth. "If the trader will attend me here, I will undertake to acquaint her with our mid-line rugs. It is on these rugs that we base our reputation as manufacturers of the first rank. Durable, attractive, stain and dirt resistant. Here—" He put his hand on a sample. "Feel the nap, Trader. Not so deep as to trap dirt, yet deep enough to comfort feet tired from a day on-port in boots."

Cantra felt the nap, as directed, and found the boy to be correct with regard to the rug's tactile virtues. Unfortunately, he was dead wrong regarding attractiveness, it being warning-light orange. She flipped an edge up and considered the backing. Machine-loomed, sturdy, nothing special to commend it; color to discommend it. She sighed and flipped the edge back down.

"I wonder," she said, "if there might be a less—robust color available."

"Trader, I am desolate. The color is the hallmark of this particular rug. Now, if the trader would be willing to aim a step higher, we have these to offer—"

He moved up-counter, displaying a slightly larger specimen woven from variegated rose thread. The 'prentice flipped the edge up before she could get her palm against the nap, displaying the back for her.

Machine-loomed again. Cantra reached out and flipped the corner down, sliding her hand against the nap.

Stiff and unpleasant, cut far too close. She sighed and moved back from the counter, letting her eyes rest meditatively on the boy's face.

"Young sir, it would appear that you have no rugs that you wish to sell me."

He had the grace to blush, round cheeks darkening.

"Trader, it was you who asked to see cheap rugs."

She moved a hand in negation. "You misheard me, sir. I asked to see durable, comfortable and useful rugs at a good price. I have no interest in art pieces, nor in rugs so flimsy they lose their knots at the first suggestion of a boot. However, I see that you cannot accommodate me. I will search elsewhere. Fair profit to you."

She strolled away, leaving the 'prentice staring, hot-faced after her. Cantra sighed. It was an old game—guide the customer to the goods carrying the highest mark-up by being unable produce anything suitable at the lower price levels. The boy hadn't played it particularly well, and had likely earned a tongue-lashing from his master for ineptitude, more the pity. Light traders, being law-abiding by fiat, ought not to display such tricks, even given that the Light version of the game was hardly more than a parlor trick, with only money at the risk. The same game played at a Dark port could well involve lives and ships.

The next rug booth on the list sported customers—no surprise, if they'd all encountered the boy with the Bubble accent first. The senior merchant behind the counter gave her a quick flutter of fingers—hand-sign for *be there soon*—which Cantra acknowledged with a dip of the head. Mooching through the displays not involved in the merchant's presentation, she located two possibles, both machine-loomed, durable, and soft against the skin. One was deep blue, the other a blend of quiet greens, and by the time the senior merchant came down-counter, Cantra had decided on the green, should price and availability favor her.

"Trader, how may I help you?" The merchant had a good, solid Insider accent, and a pleasant cast to her face. Her body language conveyed that she considered this to be the most important transaction of her day, and she met Cantra's eyes openly, her own a lucent brown.

"I am interested in good, serviceable rugs," Cantra said, with an easy smile. "They need not necessarily be in the first line of art, but they must be durable and pleasing to both the eye and the foot."

The other woman smiled back, and reached to stroke the nap of the blue rug.

"The trader has a good eye. These and these—" the palm moved to the green rug— "are our most durable offerings. As you see, they are soft, both—" a practiced move of the hand and the corner of the green came up— "machine made, of course. They have been treated with SATA standard stain and dirt guard—to clean the rug, merely shake it out. Also, as you will see, all of our rugs have anti-skid strips at each corner, for added comfort and safety."

"The rugs please," Cantra said, flipping up the corner of the blue and running her finger over the skid stopper. "As well-made as they are, I wonder if they might be above my touch."

The senior merchant smiled. "Surely not. For a half-pallet of either, I ask only six hundred carolis."

"Entirely above my means, alas." Cantra sighed, and smoothed the blue rug with her palm. "I had been hoping that we might meet at three hundred carolis."

"Three hundred?" The senior merchant's brown eyes gleamed. "The trader jests, of course. Why—"

And so it went, until each was certain that they had the advantage of the other, and Cantra eventually handed over her trade coin, from which the brown-eyed merchant deducted four hundred carolis. A time was set for the delivery of the half-pallet of green and they parted amicably.

As pleased with her purchases as if she were legit and ultimately about lawful business, Cantra ambled back toward the entrance-way.

She did the calcs in her head as she walked, and took time to hope that Jela's carvings were compact, and not needful of specialized packing. Some stone was fragile, despite it all, which she should've thought to say to him, and if he came in with a deal on a crate full of breakables—

He'd be a bigger fool than you know him to be, she snapped at herself. *The man's a pilot; he knows about acceleration.*

Acceleration, in fact, was only one of the fascinating things that Pilot Jela seemed to know. Nothing like the encyclopedic training she'd survived, in which the aim of the directors was to cram all known history, cultures, languages, and arts into the skull of the student.

No, Jela seemed to specialize in the odd bit of knowledge, the random snip of lore. He had a truly awe-inspiring library of songs available to him—many of them obscene on one world or another— which he sang softly while he worked at whatever small task he had set himself to.

She had so far, and by constant reminder to herself, managed to avoid discounting him as a mere pack-dragon, hoarding his pieces and oddments without understanding—or caring about—their wider connections. Jela had surprised her more than once during their short acquaintance, and she was allergic to surprises.

At the intersection with the main avenue, she turned left, taking it easy, there being some while left 'til the meet-time. It was therefore with some startlement that she bespied a short, wide-shouldered figure in respectable trade leathers walking purposefully in her direction.

She paused by an avenue sign and waited for him to join her, which he did in good time.

It was on the edge of her tongue to ask him how the carvings deal had gone, but something in his face dissolved the words, and another set fell out in their place.

"What's wrong?"

"I heard something—unsettling, I'd guess you'd say. I'll need to check it when we get back to the ship." A ripple of those wide shoulders. "It's probably just rumor."

A distinctly upsetting rumor, if it had Jela forgetting that she wasn't supposed to know about his indiscretions with *Dancer's* long-comm. Or, maybe, she thought, and the thought made her stomach hurt, the news carried on the rumor was dire enough to have Jela *thinking* again—and figuring that the time for let's pretend was past.

"Carvings?" she asked then, and he jerked his chin over his shoulder.

"I've got a reserve on a case lot of hand-carved telomite. Each piece unique. Good, hearty rock—won't splinter or crack under acceleration. I told them I had to clear it with my partner."

Partner. She shook the word away; and smiled agreeably.

"Sure," she said, easy and calm. "I've got us a lot of compressed textile, and a half-pallet of personal rugs. All paid for and delivery set up. Let's get yours settled and go on back to the ship. You can check out your rumor while Dulsey and me balance the can."

He looked at her out of unreadable black eyes, and gave her a smile of his own. It was about as sincere as hers had been, and nothing like the genuine article.

So, whatever the rumor was had Jela out of sorts, Cantra thought, walking with him toward the Avenue of Sculptures. That was interesting.

NINETEEN

❋❋❋❋❋❋❋❋❋❋❋❋❋❋❋❋❋❋❋❋❋❋❋❋❋❋

Spiral Dance
Ardega

THE CAN WAS BALANCED, sealed and checked quick-time, which was a definite benefit of having an engineer on the job. Cantra sighed and leaned against the wall of the cargo corridor, giving Dulsey a nod.

"That was almost painless," she said. "'preciate the help."

"You are welcome, Pilot." Dulsey said primly, and made to move on.

Cantra held out a hand, palm up, and Dulsey stopped, gray eyes going wary.

"Pilot?"

"I'd like to know," Cantra said, keeping her voice easy and calm, "on what facts you base the theory that I'm an *aelantaza* who survived a line edit. If it can be told."

A moment of silence. "And if it cannot be told?" Dulsey asked, sounding breathless and defiant at once.

Cantra flipped her hand, palm now toward the deck. "Then there's an end to it."

Dulsey sighed. "I believe you," she said. "And that should be proof enough that you are *aelantaza*."

"Why not believe me?" Cantra asked. "I'm telling the truth."

Dulsey laughed.

"Yes, certainly!" The laugh faded into serious. "It's scarcely a secret any more. The pilot will be familiar with the fact that many corporations contract persons to discover the secrets and weaknesses of the competition."

Industrial espionage was among the most common jobs contracted for graduates of the Institute. Cantra inclined her head.

"I've heard of such things," she acknowledged.

"Then the pilot will not be surprised to learn that Enclosed Habitats contracted for an *aelantaza* to spy upon their competition. In the way of things, we came to know this *aelantaza*, for it was the habit of Master Keon to interview her in those sections under construction or repair, as they could reasonably be assumed to be lacking surveillance of any kind."

"He debriefed her in front of you and your Pod?" Cantra demanded. "What kind of security is that?"

Dulsey bowed. "This humble person has no existence in the common law, save as an object to be bought or sold. This humble person may not testify against one's masters, nor will she be heard should she speak against the masters. This humble person may be killed out of hand by her rightful owner for no reason whatsoever."

Cantra sighed. "I take the point," she said. "So you got to know the *aelantaza*."

"We did. And she came to know us: She knew our names and took note of the differences between us, so that she never greeted me as Ocho, nor mistook Uno for Seatay. From the rear, in repair 'skins, she knew us, each from the other. It was from her—from watching her observe and learn, from listening to her report to and . . . *manipulate* Master Keon, that I came to understand that I needed to think beyond protocol, to take chances, and to—to seize opportunity, if and when it should ever come to me."

"Sounds like a learning experience," Cantra said drily. "What's it got to do with me?"

"Two things," Dulsey said briskly. "First, she looked a great deal like you—not as much as Ocho and I, but there was definitely what natural humans style a 'family resemblance' between you and she."

She paused. Cantra flicked the hand-sign for *go on* at her.

"Secondly, there came a time when another *aelantaza* arrived instead, and Master Keon interviewed him as he had always interviewed the other. And so we learned that the first *aelantaza*—whose name was possibly Timoli, though that may have been an alias—that Timoli was of a line which had lately been found inferior, and was thus edited from the *aelantaza* breeding tables. This was, the new *aelantaza* told Master Keon with great sincerity, in order to insure that flaws would not be passed on, and was to the customers' benefit, assuring them of the very best service."

Timoli. Cantra kept her face smooth. She hadn't known her well, there having been something on the order of thirty years between them, but Timoli had been a full sister. Damn right there was a 'family resemblance.'

She inclined her head.

"I thank you for the information," she said formally. "I have one more question—again, if it can be told. How did you deduce that I had knowledge of the Uncle?"

Dulsey took a deep breath.

"That, Pilot, was a leap into the Deep. I surmised that editing a line which must have included dozens of very able and canny adults would have a potent delivery mechanism, and that the mechanism could be disarmed by one with access to the appropriate technology. It seemed to me that the Uncle might find the plight of a lone *aelantaza* marked for destruction . . . compelling."

"So you guessed." Cantra grinned. "Not bad, Dulsey."

"I am pleased that the pilot approves of my methods."

"I wouldn't fly that far. Still, it's good thinking—and good bluffing. You'll need both where you're bound."

Dulsey tipped her head. "Is it so ill a place, Pilot?"

Cantra came away from her lean against the wall and took a heartbeat or two to consider.

"The Uncle wants to control all, and there's no one to control him," she said eventually. "That's bad business, as far as I'm concerned. I won't say he spends lives without cause, on account he has a cause. And spend lives for it, he surely does. I wouldn't want to be under the Uncle's care, speaking personally. On the other hand, I never been trade goods. It could be you'll find him and there everything you want." She paused, weighing it—and decided she might as well say the rest, for what it was worth.

"The Uncle will want you to devote your whole self to his project. For the good of all Batcher-kind, it is, or so he says. You still won't have anything like a free life."

Dulsey bowed. "It has been the observation of this humble person that all lives are confined by birth, skill, and circumstance. It is the degree of confinement only which is at issue." She straightened and gave Cantra a direct look from serious gray eyes.

"If the pilot has no more need of me, I will refresh myself and then prepare a meal."

Cantra inclined her head. "It's your course," she said. "Fly at will."

Another look, this one on the speculative side.

"Thank you, Pilot," Dulsey said and headed back toward quarters.

After a moment, Cantra followed her.

HE CONSIDERED ERASING the message—and decided against. There was no particular reason for Cantra to take his word for what had happened. Not that there was any more reason for her to take the word of a unknown X Strain commander, no matter how straightforward the report.

The fact that he'd been making free with ship's comm for some time now would come as no surprise to the pilot, or she wasn't the capable, conniving woman he knew her to be. There might be some interest to pay, now that he was out in the open—or not. Either way, she needed the info—and as co-pilot it was his duty to see that the pilot had the info she needed.

So he left the message, carefully trimmed of all IDs saving the commander's name, on the pilot's forward screen and took himself off to quarters for a quick clean-up and a change into ship civvies.

The tiny shower wasn't conducive to dawdling, and in any case he wanted to be done and clear before Dulsey came in wanting her own refresh. The ship civvies—a long-sleeved black sweater woven from *skileti*, which hugged him like a second dermis, and long black pants made from the same fabric—were warm, durable and easy, with nothing trailing to get caught in machinery, or to obscure a section of the piloting board.

He slid his feet into slippers and turned, careful in the tiny space, just as the door chuckled and slid back, revealing his bunk mate.

"Hey, Dulsey," he said easily. "How's the balancing going?"

"Done," the Batcher said, inching into the room. "Pilot Cantra is able with her numbers. She scarce needed my help at all." The door closed and she leaned on it, hands behind her back.

"Pilot Jela," she said, unwontedly serious, even for Dulsey.

"Right here," he answered.

"I wonder, Pilot—do you *trust* Pilot Cantra?"

Now, that was a meaningless question, wasn't it? Except it seemed apparent from Dulsey's face that she considered it full to overflowing with meaning. Well, maybe he'd misunderstood.

"Trust her in what way?" he asked.

Dulsey blinked. "There is more than one way?"

"In my experience," he said. "The Enemy, for instance—you can trust them to obliterate life wherever they find it. Back when I was active, I could trust a certain one of my team mates to get bored and unruly when we were at leave and take to breaking up the bar by way of relieving his feelings. On duty, I could trust that same team mate to be solid at my back and not let so much as a flea through to me." He shrugged, considering her. "That wasn't what you were asking, I take it?"

"Not . . . in so many words, no." She took a deep breath and met his eyes. "I specifically wonder if you believe that Pilot Cantra tells the truth, that she will keep her word and stand your friend, no matter what should happen."

"Hah." He thought about that, then shrugged again. "I think Pilot Cantra has her priorities, in this order: Ship, then pilot—and I trust her to act in ways which are consistent with those priorities. So, no—I don't believe she'll stand my friend, or at my back, if doing either puts her priorities at risk. No reason she should. Keeping her word? As a general thing, I think she does. On specific topics— again, there're those priorities to add into the equation." He tipped his head.

"Afraid the pilot won't take you to this Uncle of yours, Dulsey?"

She chewed her lip.

"It had occurred to me that it was not to Pilot Cantra's benefit to assist me, and that it was perhaps not entirely to her benefit to continue her partnership with you." She sighed. "Unfortunately, these thoughts only concern me when I am absent the pilot's company. In her presence, I find myself thinking it impossible that so likeable a lady would lie."

"I see where this is going." Jela grinned. "You're worried that the *aelantaza* glamour will erode my judgment. Eh? That in Pilot Cantra's presence, I'll lose what prudence you might suppose I have, being a once-soldier, and put me and you in danger?"

"You must admit," Dulsey almost-snapped, "that the 'glamour,' as you have it, is a potent weapon in the pilot's defense."

"It would be, if it worked," Jela said soothingly, and showed her his palms, fingers spread wide. "The M Strain—that's me, I'm an M—we're resistant to a long list of the known manipulations, including sabotage by pheromone."

Dulsey's face lost a little of the tense seriousness. "You are immune, then."

Well, no, he wasn't precisely immune. Pilot Cantra *did* smell nice, he'd noticed that. He'd also noticed that she moved like a dancer, possessed a quick and insightful mind, and had a well-developed appreciation of irony. Noticing those things was inescapable, but it didn't follow that his guard was down because he'd noticed them.

He had a feeling, though, that explaining any of that to Dulsey would only put on her the course to worry again, which wasn't useful for any of them.

So— "Immune," he agreed. "Most people aren't, but I've never been confused with most people."

She smiled slightly. "I am much relieved, Pilot Jela."

"Glad to be of service," he told her. "If it helps you, I believe Pilot Cantra goes out of her way to be cantankerous and irritating. She keeps people at a distance that way, where they're less likely to fall under the influence of things she can't control."

Dulsey's eyes widened. "*Can't* . . . I had not considered that aspect of the matter, Pilot."

"It's worth spending some thought on," he said, and gave her another grin. "Is there anything else on your mind, or should I clear out so you can get a shower?"

"I believe my concerns are answered, Pilot. I thank you." She slid along the door until she reached the corner, giving him room to navigate.

"Any time," he said, and slid sideways toward, and then out of, the door.

CANTRA WAS IN THE TOWER when he arrived, her arms crossed along the back of the pilot's chair, attention on her forward screen. She'd cleaned up and changed into ship civvies, and he paused for a moment to admire the poised grace of her slim figure.

"Who's Commander Loriton and why should I believe his info?" Her husky voice conveyed something like bored curiosity; her body language suggested that bored had the upper hand on curious. You had to admit, Jela thought, the woman was a pro.

"Commander Loriton's the military officer in charge of the sector where Rint dea'Sord's operations were consolidated," he said easily, walking toward her. "Upon receipt of my report of Ser dea'Sord's activities, Commander Loriton sent a task force to Taliofi."

"And now the task force and Taliofi are gone," she finished, and looked over her shoulder at him. "It says here."

"It does," he agreed.

Cantra straightened out of her lean and turned to face him, her movements smooth and unhurried.

"I don't want to disrespect him, but maybe Commander Loriton's charts aren't up to date?"

"That would account for Taliofi going missing on him," Jela allowed, "but it doesn't quite explain the task force. It goes bad for commanders who mislay ships, see."

"This is what you heard on the port that had you double-checking your info?"

"I heard Taliofi was gone," he said, stopping a comfortable arm's distance from her. "Loriton's memo was in-queue when I opened the comm. My other source confirms."

"The planet was mined, so says this commander." Her voice was expressionless. "What he doesn't say is why and who."

"Who—*sheriekas*," he said. "Most likely *sheriekas*, though it could've been dea'Sord himself. The info I nipped out of his system suggested he had the tech, and the ability. Why—to keep the task force from finding what there was to find."

"Taliofi's pretty far in for the Enemy to reach," she said, which was true.

"It's long been identified as one of the nexus points in the under-trade. A good bit of *sheriekas* wares come through Taliofi." He cocked an eyebrow. "Unless Rint dea'Sord didn't trade with the Enemy?"

"Rint dea'Sord traded with who and for what brought the most profit." Her voice was lazy, like they were talking about any commonplace. "Mining the planet—doesn't strike me as like him. He'd've just pulled back to one of his other worlds and set up ops there." She lifted a shoulder. "Which he might've done anyway, there being no way of telling which particular atoms in a floating cloud of debris happened to have been him."

"Loriton says they got surveillance on him quick," he pointed out. "It doesn't look like he moved on. It does look like the *sheriekas* thought an example was in order."

The winged brows drew together in a frown.

"Example?"

"*We can reach in and crush you whenever and wherever we like*," Jela intoned, making his voice deep and loud enough to come off the decking like a bell. "*Your world could be next. Fear us.*"

Cantra's lips twitched. "Tactics, is it?"

"Some of that. More, I'd think—and this is me, I don't have

access to Commander Loriton's analysis—to destroy whatever was there that we'd be interested in and that they couldn't hope to hide, once the task force was down and searching."

"Well." Cantra glanced over her shoulder at the forward screen. "I didn't dislike the notion of holding Ser dea'Sord too busy to pursue a disagreement. I don't know that I find as much favor with a world going missing for my convenience. Our argument was with one man's ops. Extensive they were, but I have my doubts that Granny Li or Baby Ti took part in or benefit from them."

"Rint dea'Sord was trading with the Enemy," Jela said carefully. "That put him against us—by that I mean those of us who aren't *sheriekas* or *sheriekas*-made—and upgraded his actions from merely illegal to acts of war. He knowingly put that world and its people in harm's way. He knew what the *sheriekas* are and what they're capable of doing. Those deaths aren't yours—or mine— they're his."

The green eyes met his and he caught a flicker of—something, gone too fast for him to read. Her face was smooth and uncommunicative—which he knew by now was the expression that covered her retreat into the depths of herself. He waited, there being nothing else he could usefully do.

"Do the *sheriekas* have a line on this ship, then?"

The question surprised him—and then it didn't, as he recalled her priorities. He gave it the serious consideration it deserved, taking into account the things that Loriton hadn't said, and which his secondary source had touched on.

"In my estimation, the *sheriekas* have seen your ship, but there's no reason for them to have paid special attention to it, or to have it marked for reprisal. It was just one ship among many that happened to pass through Taliofi Yard."

"Not quite," her voice had a slight edge to it. He looked at her carefully.

"If you have info, Pilot, now's the time to share it with your co-pilot."

She sighed, lightly, reached behind her and spun the chair around. Dropped into it, and waved him to the co-pilot's station.

He sat, and spun to face her, arms on the rests, deliberately at ease. Almost, he began to project a line of goodwill, but caught himself, and raised an eyebrow instead, waiting.

A corner of her mouth lifted—maybe in appreciation. It wasn't any harm thinking so, at least.

"I ever tell you how I happened to be master of this ship?" Cantra asked. She must have known she hadn't, but if she was in a mood to trade camp tales, he had no objection to that.

So— "No, Pilot, you never have. I'd be willing to hear the story, though. If it can be told."

"It can be told," she answered, her voice taking on a certain, not-displeasing, rhythm.

"For some number of years, I sat co-pilot to Garen yos'Phelium, of out Clan Torvin. Garen being the very last of Clan Torvin—and for all I ever found, the first, too—when she died, the ship passed to me. No secrets there, and as straightforward and by-the-legal as you could ask for.

"Where the story gets murky and interesting, though, is a few years further back again. And the question you'll be wanting to ask yourself is this: Where did *Garen* get this ship? A pilot as fine as you are will have noticed there ain't nothing shabby or second-rate about this vessel. It has some interesting features, not the least of which is that first-aid kit back there in the wall."

She sent him a sharp green glance. He lifted a hand, fingers framing, *go on*.

"Right. Now, it's well to remember that Garen didn't say much, and of those things she did say, you'd do well to discount half. Problem was knowing which half, if you take me."

"I knew somebody like that once," Jela said, to show that he was following her. "The war had taken him, shaken him up and pitched him out. He didn't have any context for the experience, couldn't put together what had happened inside his head. Worse luck, he was the only witness to an event of some interest to the military. Intelligence tried to get the info out of him by talking him through it." He raised both hands, showing empty palms. "They used drugs finally, then had the Generalists sort out the data-dump. Same problem—how to decide which was hard info and which was an attempt to rationalize what had happened."

"That would've been Garen," Cantra said, and sighed lightly. "What I pieced together—over years, now—from what she said and what she didn't, was that this ship came to her through captain's challenge, and that the captain defeated had been actively working for the Enemy, from which he had gotten the ship and all its glittery toys."

Jela inclined his head, not really surprised.

"And what Garen had used to say to me, as often as she said anything, was that the things built by the Enemy, they never forgot who made them, and they called out—and were heard."

He considered that, taking his time.

"There are ways to clean out *sheriekas* homers," he said finally.

Cantra lifted a hand, let it drop. "She cleaned house. Every time we got new snoop-tech, we cleaned house. That would be one of the reasons we have those guns you dote on, instead of the pretties that came with. The first-aid kit—that we took our chances with, it being useful beyond the maybe of being heard. But now I'm wondering if there had been *sheriekas* listening at Taliofi—and if they might not have heard *Dancer* singing to them, and known her for one of their own."

He felt the words filling his mouth—the easy, comforting, not-quite-true words that soldiers said to civilians who were asking about things they had no capacity to understand. There was no doubting Cantra's understanding—and she wasn't one to value comfortable lies over hard truths. Tough didn't begin to describe Cantra yos'Phelium, heir to Garen, out of Clan Torvin, whoever and wherever they might be.

Sighing to himself, he swallowed the easy words, his fingers sketching the sign for *thinking* . . .

Across from him, she leaned back in her chair, relaxing bonelessly, apparently satisfied to await the outcome of his thinking, if thought took him fifty years.

It wasn't quite that long before he shifted straighter in his chair; the movement drew her eyes, and she gave him a comradely nod.

He returned it, and sighed, letting her hear it this time.

"The ship itself isn't *sheriekas*-made, though from what you tell me, they had the refitting of it. You're right to think that they would have seeded it with homers and tracers and all manner of listeners. Some would have been visible to our scans—more, as time went on. My 'skins did a scan when I first boarded—that's a military grade scan, and it might be that I have some things on-board that haven't made it out to the Dark Market yet—and the ship scanned clean. Whether we *are* clean . . ." He snapped his fingers.

"If we could read, discover, subvert or destroy everything the *sheriekas* can, have, or will produce, then we wouldn't be losing this war."

Silence for a beat of five, during which he was very conscious of the weight of a cool green gaze against his cheek. She leaned forward in the chair, hands cupping her knees.

"So you think it's possible, but not likely, that *Dancer* was heard at Taliofi," she said. "And undecided on the issue of whether there's anything in fact to hear."

He inclined his head. "That's a fair summation, yes."

"And we're bound for the Uncle," she murmured, then gave him one of her wide, sudden grins, which was enough to make a soldier's heart beat faster, even knowing that it was more likely than not bogus.

"Does it occur to you, Pilot Jela, that life is about to get interesting?"

TWENTY

❀ ❀

On Port
Scohecan

THE GARRISON was a scarred survivor of the last war, its cermacrete gates patched and re-patched, the guard shack nothing more than cermacrete-roofed nook wedged between the front wall and the forward shield generating station.

The generator itself was of slightly more recent vintage—a venerable OS-633, which was, in Jela's opinion, the most stable of the old-style units—meticulously maintained.

By contrast, the security scans were only a generation or two behind current tech. Though they were maintained with the same attention as had been lavished upon the generator, it was obvious that the template library was outdated.

The M Series guards at least were aware of the deficiencies of their equipment. One approached him as he stepped off the scanning dock, holding a civilian issue security wand in one hand.

"Arms out at your sides, legs wide," she said. He complied; she used the wand with quick efficiency, and he was shortly cleared.

"Specialized equipment?" he asked as the second guard dealt with his docs and credentials.

The first guard gave him a look of bland innocence. "Adjunct equipment, sir."

And very likely added into inventory and standard search procedures without recourse to such details as the commandant's approval. Though, if the commandant was also an M . . .

"Papers in order," the second guard said, holding them out.

Jela received the packet gravely and slipped it into an easily accessible pocket. The first guard spoke briefly into the comm; turned with a nod.

"Escort's on the way. The commandant has been informed of your request."

"Understood," Jela said, and followed the first guard out into the yard to await the promised escort. Overhead, filtered through Level One shielding, the sky was a slightly smoky green that reminded him improbably of Cantra yos'Phelium's eyes. The star was approaching its zenith, and frost glittered in the shrinking pockets of shadow.

Jela sighed; his breath formed a tiny cloud of vapor, then dissipated.

"Pretty planet," he commented to the guard.

She lifted a shoulder. "It's pretty today. Come back during the rains and tell me what you think then."

"I think I'd like it better than no rain at all," he said.

"There's that." She jerked her head toward a two-man scooter heading toward them at a brisk clip. "Here's the escort. Make sure your pockets are sealed. Sir."

The escort was an X, his face bearing three modest diagonal stripes—green-yellow-green—and appeared to treasure speed above all other things. Jela had scarcely gotten astride the scooter before they were off, blowers howling, dust and frost whipping off the paving in a glittering whirl.

The noise from the blowers made talking at anything less than battle-voice an exercise in futility, and even if conversation had been possible, Jela wouldn't have wanted to break the lad's concentration. It was clear he thought he was very good—and, measured by the ruler of speed and missed collisions, he was. What he was not, was a pilot, though his reactions were top-notch, for Common Troop. It also seemed to Jela that a couple of the near-grazes with walls and other traffic were done not so much in the interest of haste, but to maybe see if a rise could be gotten out of the old M.

Jela sat on the back of the scooter, hands cupped over his knees, swaying bonelessly with the scooter's rhythm and considered whether or no the corporal—the X was a corporal—was entitled to his game. It was a complex question, and he gave it serious thought as they hurtled noisily across the yard, zigged and zagged down a short series of ramps, and roared, with no diminishment of speed into the drop shaft.

There was a boggle at the edge of the shaft. The scooter wobbled and tried to skid—which was the excessive speed, of course. Jela shifted his weight, the scooter steadied, the escort racheted the thrust down, killed the lifters—and they were in, stable, upright and falling gently within a pall of blessed silence.

"Appreciate the assist," the X said over his shoulder. "Sir."

That was properly done, thought Jela, and decided that the kid had a right to his fun, as long as no harm came from it, and that the near-disaster with the scooter may have instructed him more than a lecture from an emissary, whose mind ought to be on the upcoming interview with the commandant, anyway.

Silently, he sighed. In his experience—which was now approaching considerable—the upcoming interview could play out along one of two broad avenues, with several minor variations of each possible, to keep things interesting.

Out here in what Pilot Cantra styled the "Mid-Rim," it was possible that the commandant would be willing to hear him— willing to hear his message, and might also know something that would be of use to his mission. The physical shape of the garrison, with its multiply patched walls, crumbling cermacrete barracks and outmoded security system—it was clear what was going on, and unless the commandant was a fool—which had, he reminded himself, with a certain garrison commander further In foremost in his mind, been known to happen. Unless the commandant was a fool, he had to know what this lack of proper care from Command foretold. Had to . . .

The scooter's fans came on, momentarily deafening, then they were out of the shaft and moving at an tolerably responsible speed down a wide access corridor. They gained the center hall, and hovered over a vacant scooter stand. The corporal scaled back the fans—and Jela was off and on his feet. The kid did all right with the resulting buck and snarl from the equipment and gentled it into the stand before killing the lift entirely, stepping off and giving Jela a terse nod.

"This way, sir."

Across the center hall and down an admin tunnel they went, the corporal moving at a lope, Jela at his heels. At the end of the tunnel was a door; before it stood a guard—another X, with the same green-yellow-green tattoo favored by his escort. She took the corporal's duty card, ran it through the reader, waited for the blue light, and waved them past. The door parted down the center as they approached and they entered the commandant's office at a spanking pace.

Two steps into the room, Jela halted, allowing his escort to go ahead an additional four steps, halt and salute the man behind the desk.

"Corporal Thilrok reporting, sir," he stated crisply. "I have brought the emissary."

The commandant waved an answering salute. "I see that you have, Corporal, thank you. Please leave us."

"Sir." The corporal executed a nice sharp turn and marched out, eyes front. The door sealed silently behind him.

Jela stepped up to the square of rug Corporal Thilrok had recently vacated and delivered up his own salute.

"M. Jela Granthor's Guard, Pilot Captain," he said, maybe not quite as crisp as the kid.

The officer behind the desk smiled slightly. He was a slender man, with sandy hair going thin, and lines showing around eyes and mouth—not a Series soldier.

Jela wondered briefly if the post were a punishment, then lost the thought as the commandant returned his salute and pointed at a chair which had apparently been carved from native wood back in misty memory and had applied all the time since to becoming quaintly decrepit.

"Sit, Captain, and tell me why you're here."

Gingerly, Jela sat, poised to come upright if the chair showed any immediate signs of collapse.

The commandant smiled more widely.

"The locals call that stonewood," he said. "It'll hold you, Captain—and two more just like you, sitting on your knees."

"No need for a crowd," Jela murmured, settling back. Not so much as a creak from the chair. He let himself relax, and put his hands on the arms, agreeably surprised by the smooth warmth of the wood under his fingers.

He looked up and met the commandant's eyes—blue they were, and tired, and wary.

"I'm sent," he said slowly, "to give a quiet warning. The consolidated commanders advise that it may be wise for this garrison to have local forces and supply lines in place and at ready, and for the commanding officer to be prepared to act independently."

There was a small silence. The commandant put his elbows on his desk and laced his hands together, resting his chin on the backs.

"The consolidated commanders," he said eventually, with the inflection of a query. "Not High Command."

The man was quick.

"Not High Command, sir," Jela said. "No."

"I see." Another silence, while the commandant looked at him and through him, then a sigh. "You will perhaps not be surprised, Captain Jela, to learn that this garrison has for some time been on short supply. We have not been receiving necessary upgrades—you will have noticed, I'm certain, the security arrangements at the entry point. Requisitioned supplies and replacement equipment simply do not show up. We're already drawing on local resources, Captain. More than I like."

"Understood, sir, and I wish I was here to tell you that your supply lines have been re-opened, and there's a refurb unit on its way to bring everything up to spec." He paused, considering the man before him—the lined face, the tired eyes.

One sandy eyebrow arched, eloquently ironic.

"We don't often get our wishes, do we?" he murmured. "Especially not the pleasant ones. What else are you here to tell me, Captain?"

Good man, thought Jela, approving both the irony and the sentiment.

"The High Command will soon be issuing a fall-back order."

The commandant frowned. "Fall back? To what point?"

"Daelmere, sir."

Three heartbeats. Four. The commandant straightened, unlaced his fingers, and placed his hands flat atop the desk.

"Captain, Daelmere is two levels in, part of the Central Cloud."

"Yes, sir," Jela agreed. "It is."

Another pause—five heartbeats this time, then, in a tone of disbelief:

"They can't be abandoning the Arm."

"Yes, sir. High Command's intention is to pull back, cede the Rim and the Arm, and establish a new boundary further In."

Silence.

Jela cleared his throat. "The consolidated commanders," he said, gently, "believe that the proper answer to the increased enemy attacks is to commit the larger portion of our troops to the Arm and the Rim. To stop the *sheriekas* here." *If they can be stopped*, he added silently, and maybe the commandant did, too.

"A temporary headquarters and a new command chain has been established," he added, though that was in the auxiliary information he carried. And if he was not mistaken, this commandant, with his tired face and wary eyes was going to ask—

"This could, of course, be a loyalty test," the commandant said, irony informing his tone. "Which I have doubtless already failed. In which case, I might as well make certain that my dossier is as damning as possible. I suppose you have something to back your claims up, Captain? A name, perhaps, of one or more of these consolidated commanders?"

"Yes, sir. I'm to say, if you ask, that Commander Ro Gayda vouches for me, and that she sends you these proofs." He touched the hidden seal on his 'skins, and withdrew a datastrip. Leaning forward, he placed it on the desk.

"On that strip, you'll find further information and proofs."

The commandant looked at the strip, made no move to pick it up.

"They take an enormous risk, do they not?"

Jela moved his shoulders against the chair. "They've taken precautions, sir."

"They send a single soldier, and a datastrip. What if I merely imprison you and ship you to Headquarters in chains?"

Jela grinned. "They send a single M Series soldier under orders to act with discretion and to answer no questions, unless they're put to him by his immediate superior." He nodded at the datastrip, sitting unclaimed on the corner of the desk. "The information might be transmitted. The encoding might also destroy the packet when it hits Command comm protocols."

"I see." The commandant put out a hand, picked up the 'strip. "Perhaps the consolidated commanders are not risking as much as they seem." He sighed, and slipped the strip away into his 'skins.

"Thank you, Captain. Is there anything this garrison can provide to you?"

Now was the time. Jela kept himself relaxed and tipped his head to one side, the picture of an M who had private thoughts about what duty required of him next.

"I wonder, sir . . . There's rumor of an engine left over from the First Phase maybe stashed out here in the Rim somewhere."

The officer's sandy brows lifted.

"Rumor has all sorts of odd and old tech stashed out in the Rim somewhere, Captain," he said drily. "Most of it, happily, is built from vapor."

"Yes sir," Jela said respectfully. "This particular engine is reported to generate a field that will repel a world-eater."

Commandant Harrib smiled. "Well, that would be useful, wouldn't it?" He turned empty palms upward. "I doubt the engine exists, now, Captain. If it ever had an exsitence beyond wishful thinking, it was likely sold for salvage or scrap hundreds of years ago."

So much for that, Jela thought. Still, it had been worth asking the question.

"Is there anything else, Captain?" The question this time was pointed, and Jela took the hint.

"No, sir." He left the stonewood chair with real regret, and saluted. "With the commandant's permission?"

The officer moved a wiry hand—not a return of Jela's salute, but a flicker of hand-talk: *Information offered.*

"Yes, sir," he said, suddenly feeling a bit wary himself.

"That chair, Captain—remarkable substance, stonewood. When properly finished, it has the rather useful ability to detect a falsehood spoken by the person sitting in it." A second flicker—not hand-talk, but humorous deprecation. "I am aware that M Series soldiers possess extraordinary control of their biologic processes. I merely note that by the chair's report, you have been as truthful as a soldier on a difficult and dangerous mission can be." He smiled, very slightly. "The chair has been in my family for quite a number of years, and I am something of an expert in interpreting its signals."

Jela considered that, then raised his hand, fingers acknowledging: *Information received.*

"Good." The commandant rose and saluted, then leaned forward to push a button on his desk. "Escort will be provided to the gates. Good fortune, Captain."

THE TEXTILE DID SOMETHING better than she'd expected; the embryos something less. All of which meant that Cantra left the halls with trade coins in her pocket, which she would shortly convert at the currency desk—taking half in cash, and half as a deposit to ship's fund.

She sighed as she made her way through the free trade zone, dawdling a mite down long lanes of tables rented out to day-traders, locals, and others who for one reason or another weren't able—or willing—to do business in the halls.

To hear Jela tell it, their next port o'call would be the Uncle's doubt-it-not former place of business. That being a given, and what came after by no means assured, she was wasting time shopping the free zone for trade goods.

Still, she did shop, in order to give the brain something to do other than dwell on memories that were getting more agitated, the deeper they went into the Rim.

No use thinking about the past, baby, Garen whispered from years agone.

Well, she'd been right about that, not surprisingly. The past was a sorrowful place, littered with mistakes and the dead. Best to ignore it entirely and keep the mind focused on the present and that small bit of the future that could be manipulated.

She came to a table covered with a black cloth, holding a spill of sadiline. The pale jewels blinked and flickered in the yellow day-light, and Cantra paused to admire the pretty little display.

She'd had a sadiline necklace once. All the students in her dorm had one—it had been the talisman of their class, so the instructors had told them.

"Natural gemstones, locally mined," a voice said softly. "Very fine quality."

She looked up into a pair of pale blue eyes, set deep in a face seamed, wrinkled and brown. A red scarf was tied 'round the trader's head, covering one ear, knotted at the back, the tails left to flow over her right breast. The uncovered ear bore a single earring—a large sadiline drop, blazing in the sun.

"The gem is said to improve memory," the trader went on in her soft, sibilant voice, "and to impart fortunate dreams."

Cantra glanced down, extended a finger and lightly stirred the scattered gems. "Maybe you'd sell more," she said, "if you said it dulled memory, and gave dreamless sleep."

"But that would be untrue." The trader said, gently reproachful. "And the gem would take its revenge."

Revenge. Cantra gave the gems another stir, lifted a shoulder and looked back to the woman behind the table.

"Not in the market today," she said.

The trader bowed her head. "Fair profit, Trader."

You saved my life, Garen, what can I do for you? There must be something . . .

Her own voice, young—how long since she'd been that young?—echoed out of her back-brain. She remembered the argument. She'd been raised to pay her debts. Raised to believe that all debts *could* be paid, more often than not in cash. Not an understanding Garen shared, exactly, though she'd been a stickler about paying her own.

You just be the best co-pilot you can be, baby. That's all. And if somebody should bribe the luck and take ol' Garen down—you do them the same, then. That'll make us square. 'til then, ain't no sense frettin'. I got everything I need or want.

Which might've been true, or might not've—Cantra had never quite figured that. And then what should Garen do but kill her own self and no way for Cantra to clear the debt.

Damn if she wasn't doing it again.

She took a deep breath and forcefully thrust both memory and regret out of her waking mind, putting her attention on the table she'd almost passed by.

The hand-lettered signed propped along the back edge read, "Oracle Odd Lots" and scattered on the scarred surface were several ceramic objects in various shapes—ship, groundcar, and a unfeatured square that looked like a standard logic tile, all about the size of her palm.

Cantra paused and picked up the ship, smiling at the smooth feel of the thing against her skin.

"Learning devices," the woman behind the table said, her accent as hard as the sadiline merchant's had been soft. "If the trader will make of her mind a blank screen while she holds the item in her hand, she may have a demonstration."

Learning devices? Well, why not? Intrigued, Cantra curled her fingers around the little ship and with the ease born of long practice smoothed the surface thoughts away from a portion of her mind. The rest of her—what the instructors had called The Eternal Watcher—did just that, alert for any suspicious move from the vendor.

In the space between her ears, she heard a whispering, saw a shimmer of something, which solidified into the familiar pattern of a basic piloting equation, the last line missing. Cantra concentrated, trying to project the final sentence into the equation, saw another shimmer—as if she were looking at a screen—and the line appeared, as solid as the rest.

In her hand, the toy ship purred, imparting a feeling of warm pleasure.

Well.

Not without a pang, she placed the toy back on the table.

"That's something unusual," she said, looking at the woman's smooth face and bland eyes.

"They are specialty items," the other trader allowed. "We sell them in lots, from three to three dozen."

They were oddities, and it came to her that they *were* bound for Uncle, and that it might play well, her arriving with a gift.

"What's the price for three?" she asked.

The trader named a sum—much too high. Cantra answered with another—much too low. And so it went until the thing was done and the three toys—one of each shape on offer—were packed snug together in a gel-box.

Cantra took her leave of trader with a nod and continued on her way, a little brisker now, with less attention to the wares on offer.

Time was moving on, and Jela due to meet her at the administration hall pretty soon, now.

TWENTY-ONE

Spiral Dance
Twilight Interval

WHEN THE DOOR was unlocked, the quarters were surprisingly convenable. When the door was dogged open, the quarters were quite comfortable.

He relaxed there now, Dulsey bunked below him, both quietly occupying themselves while the ship moved—quietly and without turmoil—through what Cantra had styled "the long twilight."

He'd been working with his log book, bringing it up to date. It was . . . comforting to write out his notes and observations by hand, though some entries were necessarily in a code he held in common only with his commander. He had his doubts that the book would ever make it back into the hands of his commander, but it might. It might. And in the meantime, it was work, and a balm to an M's active nature.

Below him, Dulsey was reading her share of the flimsies the captain had allowed crew to print out to pass the time.

Cantra was also reading in her quarters. If he craned his head one way, he could see her open door, and, beyond, a long leg

246

stretched out on the bunk. If he craned his head the other way, he could see the tree in the pilots' tower, dreaming its own dreams.

Those dreams sometimes woke him from his own sleep cycle, as if a distant sun had come over the mountain just *now*. It had worried him for a while—the how and the why of it. Lately, he'd taken a more philosophic attitude. Ship time, tree time, what mattered it? Time passed—that was the fact no one escaped.

Dulsey seemed not to notice that his day wasn't quite in synch with the ship's. Cantra surely did notice, as she noticed everything that bore on her ship's state. She didn't remark it, though, which Jela knew she wouldn't do, unless and until he affected the ship's necessities.

Log brought up to date, Jela stowed the book and the pen, and reached for his own share of flimsies, which he'd anchored under his knee.

He didn't immediately begin to read though. Instead, he leaned his head back and listened to the sounds. The comforting, usual sounds of a well-maintained and ship-shape ship, her crew at ease and easy within the group.

Oddly enough, the easiness of their odd and randomly formed crew reinforced one of the tenets apparently espoused by the *sheriekas*—that "old humans" were herd creatures.

As a crew, Jela thought lazily, they were hardly a rousing illustration of the "old humans," when between them none had or could have met anyone approximating mother or father.

Still, he and Pilot Cantra *might* be said to have a mother and father; even if no one could ever have come forward to claim them. Met or unmet, there were progenitors of sorts.

Dulsey, though, was a full custom build, her and the rest of her Batch pulled from human genetic parts for a specific job, for profit.

That thought turned in his mind a moment, and he wondered briefly what motivated the *sheriekas*, for surely the universe that he knew and moved through was motivated by profit. Pilot Cantra's considerable skills were surely the result of desire for profit, as were Dulsey's. His own existence had been ruled by others, largely those who also obeyed others . . . and those others looking for little more than a quiet place to spin their webs and turn their profits.

Now, though, it might be that the profit motivation would finally fail the herd of men. When men like Rint dea'Sord traded with the Enemy, with thoughts of their own profit uppermost. When those Inside interests who ordered the High Command declared that their profit—their *lives*—were of more importance than the profits and lives of those who lived elsewhere . . .

The instinct for profit, thought Jela—personal profit. That instinct was maybe not a long-term survival trait.

The herd instinct, on the other hand, apparently permitted Pilot Cantra, who had not too long past locked him and Dulsey in and out at whim—to lounge, reading, while they did the same, in pursuit of goals that might transcend simple profit. Though it was never, Jela told himself, well to assume that Cantra's motives were either simple or apparent. And to remember that, if ever a woman held to her own profit above all else, it was Pilot Cantra.

Which led back to the question of what profit Cantra saw for herself in their present operation. Was it after all the herd instinct propounded by some ancient *sheriekas* philosopher, rising above the instinct for personal profit?

Well. Best not share that question with Dulsey, suddenly bereft of the life-long company of her Pod, nor with Cantra, who would surely laugh. The tree, now, might enjoy the puzzle, but it was presently in its more restful state, perhaps awaiting a dawn light years distant, so he forbore from passing it on.

TWENTY-TWO

Spiral Dance
The Little Empty

IT WAS QUIET in the piloting tower, both pilots at their stations, and the tree, Jela thought, at its. There was a tickle in the back of his mind, as if some intelligence beside his own was surveying the sparse starfield. If the sight awoke consternation in that other auditor, he didn't know it—though he wouldn't have been surprised. He'd been on the Rim more than once, and still the lack of . . . *clutter* . . . awed, amazed and intimidated him.

Pilot Cantra, now. If she felt awe or amazement, she kept both far away from her face. It wasn't to be expected, Jela thought wryly, that the pilot would be intimated by anything.

From the jump-seat came the sound of small and shaky in-breath. Dulsey, at least, was impressed.

"Are we in the Deeps, then, Pilot?" she asked softly.

Cantra lifted a shoulder, her attention more than two-thirds on her board, which might at least indicate due caution.

"Say, the Shallows," she murmured. "When we come out of the next transition, then you'll have the Deeps." She finished fiddling with her board and released the shock straps.

"Rimmers, they call this the Little Empty," she said. "We'll take ourselves a pause here. Pilots'll do a complete systems check. Dulsey, if you're willing, a good meal to go into the next phase on would be welcome."

Truth told, it was that next transition that was giving Jela a bit of worry. The pilot might be enjoying her joke, pretending they weren't sitting in the Deeps, but he only had two beacons on con and some small star clusters on the screens, bright and hard against the velvet . . .

"I am more than willing to provide a meal, Pilot," Dulsey was saying. "Now?"

"Give us time to do the checks," Cantra answered, coming up out of her chair in a stretch. "Call it two ship-hours. Ace?"

"Ace," Dulsey said.

"Good. I'm also going to need eyeballs on the clamps and a diagnostic on the can system. You take that on, while Jela an' me get busy here."

"Yes, Pilot." Dulsey unstrapped and slid to her feet with a will, moving out of the tower with the determined stride of a woman with work to accomplish.

Cantra sighed and shook her head and gave Jela a look out of amused green eyes.

"Hope the Uncle's ready for this," she said.

"Dulsey's a hard worker," Jela answered. "If the Uncle's surviving 'way out here, he has to have a corps of hard, smart workers with him. She'll fit right in."

"Uncle's a bit further out, yet," Cantra said, leaning over her board and initiating a system-wide check. "Found this area too crowded, is what I heard." She straightened and gave him another look, this one straight and stern.

"Get your check running, Pilot. After, I'll thank you to recall that you were going to be showing me what those guns you dote on can do."

"UNDERSTAND," Jela said, his big hands resting lightly on the edge of the co-pilot's board, "that you'll have to unlock the system all the way. I'll need complete access. I'll also thank you for sharing your codes so I won't have to use the system override."

She'd expected him to need gut-level access, but it was still hard to get her fingers moving in the sequence that would open the guns to him and send the codes to his work screen.

"Thank you." That was said soft, like maybe he had an idea how much of a struggle habit had put up against need-to-know.

"We'll begin," he said, of a sudden not soft at all, "with a complete system check, an inspection of records . . ."

She frowned, reached to the board—and pulled her hand back. *Need to know*, she reminded herself. *You need to know your guns, and this is the man to teach you.*

Which didn't mean he had the right to snoop her info.

"Right, Commodore," she said with asperity. "I'm guessing you'll need serial numbers, purchase dates, shell counts, and . . ."

He sighed, and she figured he was going to come all high-brass now.

Instead, though, he nodded.

"We'll want all of that, if you can give it to me. Then we can look and see what needs to be done to optimize things, and what rounds we might need to load up on."

Cantra sighed. If he'd yelled, she'd've yelled back. But him being reasonable . . .

She sighed again.

"This ain't a cruise ship, Pilot; it's a Dark trader. You think I keep copies of my receipts all nice and tidy for the port cops to look over at their leisure?"

There was a brief bit of tight silence—then he sighed, and shook his head, and said, quiet, "I take your point. Let's have some target practice, then."

SHE KEPT WAITING for it, but he never did turn the brass on. He did insist that the best target practice they could get was from using a couple sets of what he called "underpowered rounds" as targets.

"I'm curious, Pilot," he said while she was in the midst of rough calculating in her head to back up the ship's computer, "how long you've had these Jaythrees and Jayfours on hand?"

The "Jaythrees and Jayfours" in question were currently loaded in Gun One, which he was using for his own, while she was firing general purpose tracking rounds with only a minimum of on-board guidance from Gun Two. It looked like he was practicing, too, because it was obvious he was calculating like mad, and doing something special and antsy with the settings . . .

"You're making it hard for me to concentrate . . ." she muttered. He fidgeted briefly, and she sighed, giving up for the moment. "Which I guess is about right for combat conditions . . ."

He nodded, then fired the rounds; Cantra watched for his finger mark to indicate that she should start tracking, her mind maybe a quarter on his question.

"Garen bought 'em when she bought the guns," she said finally; "I never used them 'cause they was listed as close-in combat support in the docs, and I never had need." She moved her shoulders, and glanced at the side of his face.

"I'm a smuggler," she said, her voice sharper than she'd entirely intended "not a pirate. The guns're defense."

The finger move came; she started the ranging, saw in her head that the shells were in a highly elliptical—no, make that a parabolic—orbit so tight it might even graze the distant star, would likely, in fact, fall right into it . . .

From the co-pilot's section, she heard a small sound, almost as if Jela was humming, which was nothing new, though why he was inspired to hum or sing now . . . but she could hear him busy on the keyboard, tapping queries or commands in a real hurry.

There! The computer and her calcs had reached an accord! She fired, let the computer take the next shot, fired the next on manual, let the computer have the next, and sat back to watch the tracks on the computer screen.

Even with Jela's rounds being "underpowered" it would take quite awhile for the interception, if she'd been accurate enough to—

Jela wasn't humming so much as growling. She turned her head to look at him.

"Can you tell me," he asked in a low, gravelly voice, "can you tell me *exactly* who sold you those shells and the manuals?" His face was so absolutely neutral that she felt dread rising through her, despite her training. Jela mad—really mad and out for balance—wasn't a sight she particularly wanted to see, she realized. Not that it would be smart to let him know he'd managed to unnerve her.

"Hah!" She shrugged carelessly and waved her hands in a casual *not my job*.

"Will the ship's log give us any idea?"

Her hands moved themselves; indication—*perhaps*. And expanded—*maybe, low probability*.

"Garen was pretty careful about some stuff she didn't want me to know about . . ."

He looked away from her, fingers moving on the query pad, and spoke as if from a distance.

"At first opportunity—and you will remind me if I fail in this, please, Pilot! At first opportunity, we will replace your documentation for these guns. We will also inspect—two sets of eyeballs so we're sure—the munitions themselves."

He paused, sending her a look out of hard black eyes.

"Try to remember where these shells came from, Pilot. Any clue would be good."

The man was serious, and—not mad, no. Something else, stronger and sterner than mere anger.

"Pilot, there's cause?" she managed, bringing the Rim accent up. "They out of spec?"

He rubbed his face with those broad hands, like he was trying to wipe away sweat, or a sight he wished he hadn't seen.

After a sigh he looked at her straight on again, not quite so hard.

"Jaythrees are rounds one might use to deny a landing ground to an enemy. A landing ground one wishes not to occupy for oneself. In addition to a fairly lethal explosive charge, they release a fine mist of plutonium powder. Jayfours . . ." He rubbed his face again.

"Jayfours are binary cleansers. The gas they release is . . . inimical . . . to most air breathing creatures and plants. In the presence of oxygen it will deteriorate to mere poison in about twelve days, and to an irritant in another twelve."

"Depending on the winds, one could cleanse half a continent."

Cantra blinked, swallowed and had cause to be briefly grateful for her early schooling.

"The docs?" she said, matching him quiet for quiet.

"Apparently someone wished to make you and your Garen into household names. Or else your seller, too, was tricked." She looked to the screen, where her shots, and the computer's, raced after the deadly payloads, and then back to him.

"You aimed them for the star then . . ."

His hands fluttered into hand-talk.

Best course, she read.

And again—*best course*.

TWENTY-THREE

Spiral Dance
Jumping Off the Rim

TARGET PRACTICE WAS OVER, and so was the meal, eaten companionably together. The pilots were strapped in at their stations, while the third member of the crew sat in the jump-seat.

"All right, Dulsey," Cantra said, her eyes on her board, "I'll need those eighteen numbers now."

Dulsey stiffened, relaxed, shrugged diffidently.

"Pilot, I do not have eighteen. The numbers I was given come in three sets of twelve."

Jela, damn his hide, laughed. Cantra sighed.

"Let's have 'em, then," she said resignedly, and waited while Dulsey activated the jump-seat's tablet and tapped her info rapidly in.

They came up on the pilot's work screen—and the co-pilot's too—three neat rows of twelve, and anything more like plain and fancy gibberish Cantra hoped never to see.

"I'd guess," Jela said quietly, "that you'll be able to construct something reasonably familiar to you from those numbers. Maybe even something—" he wiggled his fingers in the pilot-talk for *comfortable.*

Comfortable. Right. Fuming, Cantra fed the numbers to the nav brain, not that she expected it to be able to do much with them—and she wasn't disappointed, damnitall.

"Easy for you to say," she snapped at Jela. "But out here, numbers ain't quite so casual as they are in the heart. Down there you got lots of reinforcement, including some places you just can't go, 'cause it'd take too much power, and lots of experience and references to let you know what's possible and what's not. Out here, almost any number'll get you *some*where. Twelve to five says most of where you can go is even safe. Sort of."

While she was talking, her fingers were busy shuffling and reshuffling Dulsey's pack of thirty-six.

"Well, if we pile 'em up backwards and split 'em in two, we get one coord that'll take us into somewhere just a bit inside the wavefront of a gas pulse pumping out an X-ray beacon. So I guess we'll discard that one. If we stack 'em straight and divide in two, we get more gibberish. But . . ."

On a guess, she re-shuffled the digits the old way, the one that'd been real popular with the Dark traders along back years ago and— yes.

"If we do it this way," she said aloud, being careful not explain exactly *which* way, "we get two sets of honest coords, and one looks a lot like something I think I recognize." She spun her chair to face Dulsey.

"So, did you get any more of that key? Any way I can confirm? I might expect an engineer to know we was missing something here."

Dulsey sat up straighter—a good trick, considering how upright she kept herself as a matter of course.

"Pilot, understand that the information was not all given to th— to me. One of my pod had the first set of numbers, which I became party to. The second set was mine to keep. The third . . . I broke a seal to get. It was assumed by our source that if we came, we would come all together."

"Hah!" Jela said. Cantra threw him a glance and a nod.

"Maybe," he said to Dulsey, "there were other numbers scattered among the rest of your Pod?"

But Dulsey shook her head.

"No, those were all we were given." She looked carefully at Jela, and continued almost inaudibly. "The others would not have been able to conceal the numbers and so were not given them."

Cantra grinned. "But you, not having all the numbers yourself, thought you ought to, and was ready to go with or without?"

Dulsey closed her eyes briefly, sighed, and faced her. "I cannot apologize for surviving," she said, and despite the brave words, her voice carried shame. "Nothing I did risked my Pod mates, and there was nothing else I could have—"

"Stop!" Jela held up a hand. Cantra looked at him with interest, Dulsey with concern.

"Dulsey," he said, "I believe you. I believe you did the right thing. We've all become soldiers in this life—you as much as me or Pilot Cantra, here. You acted to preserve resources, which you have done; and you behaved with honor. You have nothing to be ashamed of. Your right to be alive is not in question. What Pilot Cantra must judge—as pilot and captain of this ship—is the safety of the routes you've given her. This is for the good of the ship, and the good of the crew."

Not bad, thought Cantra, admiringly. In the jump-seat, Dulsey shook her head again.

"I understand," she managed, voice shaking a little. "Truly, Pilot Jela, if I had more information, I would gladly—but these are the numbers. I have nothing else."

Cantra sighed. "Were you going to steal a ship, then? These numbers would've got you killed straight off, if you didn't know—"

"No, Pilot." Dulsey faced her again, chin lifting. "We were a group, before the bankruptcy, and in the group were pilots who had experience . . ."

Cantra lifted a hand, palm up.

"Dulsey, I'd be lying if I said I wouldn't steal a ship, given necessity. I'm thinking Pilot Jela's of the same opinion, is that right, Pilot?"

"That's right," Jela said comfortably.

"I wonder, though—how wide-spread was this attitude in your group? Were you going to depend on stealth, or on surprise?"

Dulsey's face hardened.

"They were depending on accident, coincidence, and rumor. With the application of reasonable energy some time ago, we could have all been gone."

Cantra barely avoided smiling. The girl wasn't a fool. Indeed, *indeed*, she hoped the Uncle was ready.

"I understand," she said, pitching her voice easy and calm. "In which case, I'll put the ship's back-up brain on the problem of a proof for those two sets of coords. In the meantime, since we're all strapped in and well-fed, let's get ourselves out to the Rim."

SHE WAS GOING to transition now? Jela looked to his board, in case he'd missed—but no.

"I've only got two beacons, Pilot," he said, keeping his voice gentle.

She was concentrating on her board, feeding that coord set to the "back-up brain," he supposed—whatever that might mean— and he didn't expect any answer, which would have been more informative than the one he got.

"Have faith, Pilot Jela," she murmured. "Have faith." And as if on-cue in some story-play, the nav-brain twittered, and a third set of coordinates marched across the center screen—Rathil Beacon, that was. They still needed one more, to balance the equation, and insure a safe and uneventful transition.

"Rathil's up," Cantra breathed beside him, and, louder— "Dulsey, strap in."

There was a tickle at the back of his mind, tasting something like a query—but he was too busy grabbing the coords off the screen, doing the math in his head and coming out with nothing good.

"Pilot," he insisted, keeping it gentle, "we're still down a beacon."

She shot him a look out of bright green eyes.

"When you don't got four, you fly on three," she said. "Hang on to your board, Pilot. This might be rough."

Her hands danced across her own board with that light, sure grace he admired so much, and before he could draw a breath or begin to think an answer for the tree—

They hit transition.

And they hit it hard.

RADIAL VELOCITY, he was thinking.

The math was a soothing balm against the frenetic vibrations the ship and crew were experiencing; a flash image inside his head showed that the tree knew what an earthquake was, and what it might do.

But no, radial velocity was not the whole answer. Part of it was the gravitational effect—a tidal effect almost—with the galaxy edge-on and the ship prying itself into *otherspace* against millions of stars and only the halo of diminishing dark energy a balance at this distance.

Cantra sat the board calmly, hands poised a moment, then stabbing a button, poised again, flipping a toggle—

They were out.

CANTRA LOUNGED at ease at the board, well aware that both Dulsey and Jela were much surprised.

Jela, for his part, recovered quickly, with a hand signal more to himself than her, Cantra thought—a long, slow *smooooothhh*—his only public comment.

Dulsey, cleared her throat.

"The pilot enjoys an excellent rapport with the ship," she said seriously, "and the ship enjoys excellent numbers!"

Cantra laughed.

"The ship goes where we send it, right? Just I do know some places to take off a bit and some places to add a bit to the equations. Them equations was done for the average ship on an average course somewhere down in the midst of that mess—" She pointed to the representation of the galaxy on the side monitor— "and if you look close, we're about as far as you can get from as much as you want to count of it and still say we're in the thing."

The Rim accent had come up hard all by itself, along with the side-drawl that helped make Rim cant both distinctive and muddy to some of the light-lappers who thrived down to the center of things. *Well, it comes with the territory*, she thought, and didn't fight it.

For effect, she centered the galactic image . . . and sure enough, as the image shifted, the blue dot representing their position moved way off to the left side of things before disappearing. She'd known that was going to happen, since the arm they were in was the longest of the three arms, and the most twisted. Some folks with a lot of time on their hands figured that *this* arm was what was left of an intergalactic collision somewhere on the far side of time. The truth was that once things got into the billions of years, she, for the most part, lost interest because—as they said out here—her fingernails grew faster than that.

"If you would be so kind to keep the scale but center on our position, Pilot?"

Cantra looked up at Jela's voice, caught the notion that he'd apparently made the request first in finger-talk, and she'd missed it.

Smart of him, actually. No good could come out of directly interfering with a pilot staring down into that much of a think.

"Same scale?" she asked.

"Indeed."

And so now it was that there was all this near empty on the left-side of the screen. The arm they rode twisted back into the density of stars like a snake, coiling for a second strike.

Against that she upped the magnification a dozen clicks, and now there were a few smaller clusters yet showing out in the Deeps, and a couple places where stars had escaped from the embrace of others by a nova or supernova which had dashed into the darkness trailing gas, and the arm loomed big and important, like it ought to for folks and suns who spent their lives in it . . .

She upped the magnification again, and now—now they could see why it was called the Rim—that it was an actual rim of gravity and colliding grains of dust and gas. And since this arm was half-again as long as the others, this was the arm that spun itself against the intergalactic medium uncleared by the previous passage of the other arms, and here was the interplay of magnetic fields with the bow wave of light pressure, wild gas, and . . .

"The Uncle . . ." Dulsey's voice wavered a bit, and ended on a gulp.

For all that, Cantra allowed as how she was doing better than most folks she'd seen when faced with the fact of the Rim, for who expected it to ripple with a glow of purple so deep you'd swear it wasn't there, and who expected—having learned about years and parsecs and light years and such—to find that there were things so much beyond them that mere billions was a kidstuff toy.

"The Uncle," Dulsey tried again, "lives—out there?"

"Almost there," Cantra said cheerfully, and shot a glance to Jela, who gave her his blandest face to look at.

"Now, we'll see how good those numbers are, Pilot," she said. "Ready for adventure?"

He smiled for that one and nodded. "Ready."

TRANSITION WAS QUIET this time, drop-out smooth and easy.

"Pilot," Cantra called, "shut down the running lights, the auto-hail, and active radar . . ."

His fingers flickered—*rock*—and she answered, though he hadn't seen her look his way.

"I know, but we'll take the first ten ticks as free and clear 'cause if they ain't we should be able to slide in there anyway . . ."

"Pilot," he acknowledged, began to deactivate the systems, adding the dock-ranging equipment, and—

" . . . and anything else you think we ought to do to be quiet . . ." she said, over a sudden, head-rattling series of thumps, which would be the rocks, of course.

"Good thing sound doesn't transmit," he muttered, and Cantra laughed.

"It'll pass," she said—and that quick it was done, leaving behind nothing but smooth silence and the sounds of normal ship systems.

"Video!" Cantra called, but he was ahead of her, clicking on the infrared scanners just ahead of the video feed, hand poised above the meteor-repellor shielding switch.

The scanners began registering objects far away enough to be minor concerns; nothing close. Despite this, or perhaps because of it, Cantra spun the ship quickly on its axis, pressing Jela's aching left leg into the webbing.

He grimaced slightly; he hadn't noticed that complaint come on line, but there it was: transition was starting to affect his aches as much as dirt-side weather could.

A flitting image came to him—a tree, it must have been, as viewed from another, leaning into a prevailing wind.

That would be about right, he thought, *got my roots set and have to weather things as they come at me.*

That thought was swept away with the blink of light on the board—

Anomaly!

The infra-red scanners were showing multiple changing heat-sources . . .

"More rocks," he commented.

"I got 'em too," came Cantra's laconic reply, "and if we didn't, I'd say we was in trouble. If my memory's at all good, rocks is about all there is out here, 'cepting the Uncle and his kindred."

THERE WAS TIME now for Jela to consider where they were. Cantra had the ship's brain doing a long-range comparison and analysis of the rock-field, looking for objects that she'd seen once before. Not that she was personally trying to identify this or that bit of stone or metal, but she had the ship trying to match images the former captain had been wise enough to capture and store in deep archives.

The process was time-consuming, and would have brought Jela to the edge of distraction had he not had both a practical and an academic interest in what the edge of forever looked like from the outside.

Where they had come from was not precisely visible now, with threads of dust and gas in the galactic disk obscuring where things had been multi-thousands of years ago and the more immediate pebbles, rocks, and gassed out-chunks of protocomets acting as a dulling screen to both vision and scanners attempting to use line-of-sight.

But around them, other than the thin scatter of what was—on galactic scale—negligible sandy left-overs, there was nothing. At this distance from the core, there were no individual stars to act as beacons, and all the other galaxies were too distant to be seen as anything more than point sources, if they could be seen at all. The galaxy they orbited faded to a distant nebulous smudge . . .

Jela imagined all too vividly what it would be like to be suited up or in a canopied singleship here now, and felt the involuntary, perhaps instinctual shiver. There was no darkness like the dark of emptiness.

CANTRA WAS MUTTERING again, which Jela knew ought to have worried him, but it mirrored what he would have done had he been sitting in the pilot's spot with old information and a mission in peril for it.

He'd taken con for a short while as she grabbed a quick break and some tea, returning as renewed to his eyes as if she'd had a three day shore leave.

Now she was back at work, digging among files and archives that only she could access. That she added a running commentary was her choice, and if it helped the pilot think, why then, he'd seen pilots with worse habits.

He glanced at her—not for the first time since transition—wishing that he'd had her match in any of his units. She had an economy of movement, and a wit as well, and for all her complaining there wasn't a bit of it that was an actual whine.

Too, he admitted, there was an underlying energy in her that was quite pleasing. Perhaps it was the training and background she so vociferously denied, perhaps it was the pheromones . . .

He wiped that thought away, or tried to, for there was no doubt that the night they'd met she'd been on the prowl for more than dinner company. Certainly if things had moved in that direction—and without the interruptions that had come their way—they might have had a good tumble. For his part, as someone willing to appreciate irony, metaphor, strength, energy, and honor . . . he knew he could have found some energy to share.

That this would not have been against orders he knew, for certainly, the troop understood that duty required nurture and recreation. And certainly, one could feel a certain amount of affinity for a pilot of excellent caliber who was also good when it came to hand-to-hand, and had a clear eye and quick understanding with regard to who were enemies.

Hadn't she stood at his back? Guarded the tree? Was she not now engaged in a rather fine—not to mention out of the way—balancing of accounts in delivering Dulsey to a safe zone? Indeed, Cantra could be counted as comrade in truth . . .

From somewhere, a distant, whispery scratching sound, barely on the edge of perception. Jela started, blinking the momentary abstraction away, and sent a quick glance to the tree . . .

An image built inside his head, of a distant dragon in the sky, drifting away as the breeze brought haze . . .

"Dust," said Cantra lazily, and the image faded. "Carbon dust, with a bit of extra hydrogen. And that's a good sign, Pilot. You be ready to sing out when you got something to look at. Kind of amazing that a veil like this can hide the Uncle's little quarry for so long."

In the jump-seat, Dulsey stirred, eyes bright.

Cantra laughed, and even her laugh was loaded with accent, as if the weight of piloting had worn through a veneer.

"S'alright girl. Your numbers worked. Likely, though, if you'd have come in piloting yourself you'd have had to beg to be picked up, which is how the Uncle prefers things, I gather. Us now, we're going to be ringing that door chime on our own. Keep watching."

And as if Cantra had a cloud-piercing telescope to show her the way, the scans began to register, and video began to show distant objects vaguely outlined against the nebulous presence of the galaxy.

"Straps tight, now," she said, "each and all of us."

※   ※   ※

HE'D THOUGHT ONCE before that Cantra flew like a bomber pilot, and now, as the aches built up in his knee and his admiration grew, he was sure of it. He made a mental note to check on the training given to *aelantaza*.

The thing was that—within this strange space—her reactions were absolutely sure, and absolutely perfect. She threw the craft through crevices in the dust, around rocks and coils of rocks, sliding this way and that . . . for in this realm beyond the galaxy, action and reaction held sway, with but a nod and a twitch required to overcome the microgravity of the dust clouds or the trajectory of free-moving rock.

On the screen was the destination, a rather forbidding tumbling conglomeration of dust-stuck rock not even big enough to become a globe under its own gravity. The course to the target was irregular, with projected and suggested approaches appearing on-screen, being selected or deselected, or assigned back-up . . .

Jela watched and sat second, hands and eyes mostly in synch with the real action, though from time to time Cantra's choices were idiosyncratic at best. In some ways, he was reminded of training games and mock-cockpits, where one could play a ship with abandon . . .

Here though, abandon was not what she was displaying. Here, Cantra was showing honed skill. If she flew it like it was a game, then it was her game, and not his. But then it was her ship, and she the one who had actually been to this unlikely bit of *here* before.

"Pilot," she said suddenly, "what we're going to do is to fly formation with this thing for a bit. There'll be another one around for us to look for, not a lot like it . . ."

And with that, she rolled the ship slightly and slung it around, slowly matching pace with the object—asteroid, dead comet, dust-ball . . .

Once they had achieved "formation," Jela saw it was too bright and speckled to be a mere dustball. In fact, it showed signs—

"See there," Cantra said carefully, her eyes on her screens, "we got a dozen flat surfaces or so here. One of them ought to be mostly red in visible spectrum, assuming we can shine enough of a light on it. It's been worked a bit, and it'll be obvious if we got the right rock. That's gonna be your job, and I'll tell you when to go to light. Same time, you're going to bring them guns up full, just in case."

"Pilot," he replied, and found the controls for the tracking light. They felt odd to his hands, and he doubted that he had touched anything like them since his long-ago days as a pilot trainee.

What kind of rock could have been "worked a bit" out here? Something else to add to his . . .

The spectralyzer flashed, and the infra-red too. There *was* an anomaly.

"Light it up!" Cantra snapped, but he'd already hit the switch, gotten the range—

They were following the rock formation, its weird slow tumble immensely weirder under the ship's spotlight. The rock looked like it had been sliced and grooved, as if whole slabs had been taken away. There was a flash of color—greenish—then gray, more gray, and—

"Red!" he said, exultantly.

"Right," Cantra agreed, lazily. "We got the right rock. Now all we gotta do is sit back and listen real hard. I'm punching the bands up now. Get me a directional on it if you can."

There was a signal . . . so faint as to barely budge the meter. A chirping sound, in identical sets of three, filled the bridge.

The ship's computer struggled with the signal for some moments before Jela sang out.

"Got it!" He copied it to the pilot's screen, and heard her laugh, soft.

"Right," she said. "I'll just mosey us along in that direction for a bit. When you get a change in those bird-noises there, Pilot, just put the docking lights, and docking shields, and docking radar on." She sent a quick glance over her shoulder.

"Dulsey, this is your last chance to change your mind."

"I wish to be with the Uncle," the Batcher said firmly.

Cantra sighed, soft, but plain to Jela's ears, and her fingers formed the sign for *pilot's choice*. He signaled agreement in return.

"To hear is to obey, then," Cantra said to Dulsey. She cocked at eye at him and grinned.

"We're sitting on Uncle's back porch. We'll just knock on the door and see if anyone's to home. Whenever you're ready, Pilot."

TWENTY-FOUR

Rockhaven

"SHUT IT DOWN," Cantra said quietly.

Acknowledgment from the Uncle's pile of rocks had finally been received after an annoyingly long—perhaps calculatedly long—wait. Now they sat almost against the rock wall, tied to the haven by two light ship tethers and their own extendable gangtube to one of four observable access ports.

Jela paused with his hands on the board and considered her profile.

"Pilot? No need for all of us to go down. I can stay, if you want it, and keep the home fire burning."

She turned her head, giving him a steady, serious look, with nothing wild or irritable about it.

"Shut it down, Pilot."

There wasn't any arguing with that glance of calm reason, and Jela turned his attention to an orderly shutdown of his board, the while pondering the fact that it was impossible to argue with Cantra when she was unreasonable, and impossible to argue with her when she wasn't. Convenient. He'd also come to notice that she wasn't unreasonable nearly as often as she let it seem that she was.

The system lights went down one by one and in good time the ship was off-line, saving life-support.

Out of the corner of his eye, he saw her nod, once, then put her finger on the release and let the webbing snap noisily back.

"Up, up!" she said, spinning her chair around to grin first at him, then at Dulsey. "Best not to dally and make our escort irritable."

He mistrusted the grin, just like he mistrusted the total lock down of the board—in all his experience of her Cantra had never locked the board down tight. That she chose to do so here, at a docking she plainly distrusted was—notable. Coupled with the mandate that all three of them step off for a stroll through an asteroid habitat controlled by questionable forces, it became out-and-out worrisome.

On the other hand, there *wasn't* any arguing with her—she was ship's captain, and the only one ammng them who had previous experience of the Uncle.

Carefully, then, he unstrapped and stood, finding Dulsey already on her feet, face shadowed.

"Second thoughts, Dulsey?" Cantra asked.

Dulsey's chin came up and she met Cantra's eyes.

"Not at all, Pilot."

The grin this time was more amusement and less artifice, by Jela's reading. Which didn't make it any more comforting.

"I'm glad to hear you say that. The Uncle I knew, he placed a certain value on boldness. For what it's worth."

Dulsey bowed slightly. "I am grateful to the pilot for her advice."

Cantra sighed, then abruptly waved a long hand toward the door and presumably the hall beyond.

"The two of you get on down to the hatch. I'll catch you in six."

Jela felt the hairs at the back of his neck try to stand up all at once. If this was a vary *now*—but he couldn't for the life of him see how, with the ship shut down into deep asleep, so he grinned, nice and easy, for the shadow across Dulsey's face, and nodded at the door.

"After you."

"Yes, Pilot," she said, subdued, turned—and turned back.

"Pilot Cantra."

The winged brows lifted over misty green eyes.

"What's on your mind, Dulsey?"

A hesitation, and then another bow, this one very deep, and augmented with the stylized gesture of the right hand which roughly meant *I owe you* according to particular civilian signing systems.

"The pilot has acquitted herself with honor," Dulsey murmured in the general direction of the decking. "I am grateful and I ask that she remember my name, should there come a time when my service might benefit her."

Jela held himself still, already hearing Cantra's pretty, sarcastic laughter in his mind's ear—

"Stand tall, Dulsey." Her voice was firm, and if it held any grain of sarcasm, it was too fine for Jela's ear to detect.

The Batcher straightened slowly, and brought her eyes again to the pilot's face. Jela, watching that same face, found it . . . austere, the green eyes bleak.

"*A person is worth as much as the value of their debts,*" she quoted softly. "You've heard that said, Dulsey?"

"Yes, Pilot. I have heard it said."

"Then you want to take some time to sort over who I am and what I'm about in the general way of things. Most would hold that an honorable freewoman shouldn't ought to devalue herself by standing in debt to the likes of me."

Dulsey smiled.

"A honorable freewoman must be the judge of her own worth, Pilot. Is this not so?"

Cantra's mouth twisted, unwilling, to Jela's eye, toward a smile.

"You'll do, Dulsey. Now the two of you get outta here. I'll meet you at the hatch in six. Ace?"

"Ace, Pilot," Dulsey said serenely, and turned to the door. "Pilot Jela?"

"Just a sec," he said, catching a ghost-view of dry sand behind his eyes.

He returned to his station, pulled open the hatch and removed a sealed water bottle from the pilot's emergency provision cache. Cracking the seal, he walked toward the tree, heard a murmuring inside his head, saw a flicker of visuals he couldn't quite sort . . .

"I know it's not much," he said, softly, dampening the dirt over the roots. "We're not intending to be long. You keep a good watch and let me know if anything odd happens while we're away."

Bottle empty, he straightened, reaching up to touch a couple of the higher leaves. Taller than he was, now. Not that that was such a trick.

There was a sudden quick rattle, along with image of a pair of dragons nipping at a tree limb to grab . . .

"Fair's fair, I guess," he said, catching the fruit pod as it snapped itself from the branch and fell.

"I hate to bother you, Pilot," Cantra's voice carried a payload of sarcasm now. "But the sooner we're gone, the sooner we're back and the less time your friend there needs to pine for your return."

Another image formed in back of his eyes, very precisely: A small dragon sitting on the grass at his feet, exercising its voice loudly—and even more loudly as a sudden fall of leaves came down over its head.

Jela laughed.

Behind him, he heard Cantra sigh. Loudly.

"Now what? It's telling you jokes?"

Still grinning, he turned, resealing the bottle absently.

"Pilot, the tree is learning irony from you."

Bland-faced, she considered him, then spun on one heel to address the tree in its pot, and executed as high-flying a bow as he'd ever seen, complete with a showy swoop of the left arm.

"It is my pleasure to be of service," she said, then straightened in a snap. "*Both* of you mobile units—outta here. Now!"

"Pilot Jela?" That was Dulsey, sounding nervous, and right she probably was.

"I'm behind you," he said, though he'd have given his accumulated leave, assuming he had any, to see how Pilot Cantra was going to gimmick the board. The tree's gift he happily consumed before they reached the dock.

�֍ ✖ ✖

THE DOCK was just like she remembered—rock, rock and more rock—the floor unevenly illuminated by the white glow from several cloudy columns of candesa, the ceiling lost in darkness, from which the light, so-called, woke an occasional spark—like a star glimpsed through drifting debris.

At the base of the ramp stood a figure in light-colored 'skins, blond hair cut close to his head. The utility belt around his substantial waist supported a holstered needle gun.

Behind her, she almost heard Jela's watchfulness click up a notch, like maybe a man didn't have the right to wear a gun on his own dock. Feet still on the gangtube's ramp—technically still on her own ship and not yet on the Uncle's terms—she raised her hands to shoulder level, fingers spread. The status lights on the cuff of her 'skins thereby brought into view glowed green-green-green. So far, so good.

The guard sniffed, but didn't ask her to turn out her pockets, which was just as well.

"Names?" he snapped.

"Cantra yos'Phelium," she answered, giving him mild on the theory that it would probably annoy him. "Pilot-owner of *Spiral Dance*, just like I told Admin."

"You didn't tell Admin who else."

"That's right," she agreed, taking no visible offense. "Reason being they're here under my protection. We have business with the Uncle. I'd appreciate a pass-through."

The guard sneered. He had a good face for it, Cantra thought, critically.

"What makes you think he's here?"

"Only place I knew to look," she allowed. "Fact is, I didn't expect to find anybody here, excepting maybe a guard or two. So, if the Uncle ain't here, I'd appreciate a message sent, telling him Cantra yos'Phelium has something that belongs to him and where does he want it delivered?"

"What do you have?" The boy was going to go far with that kind of attitude.

Cantra sighed.

"You the Uncle nowadays?"

His face tightened. "No."

"Then it ain't your business," she said, all sweet and reasonable. "Send the message or pass us through—that's your piece of the action. Not so hard, is it?"

Another glare, which Cantra bore with slightly pained patience, then a sharp jerk of his head.

"This way." He turned and strode off across the dock without waiting to see if, or how, they followed, which just about shouted out the information that there were other watchers—armed watchers, make no doubt—in the shifty shadows.

Behind her, she felt Jela go up another notch on the wary meter, nor she didn't blame him. Glancing over her shoulder, she wasn't particularly surprised to find Dulsey directly behind her, with Jela's reassuring bulk bringing up the rear.

Protect the civilian, she thought, and deliberately didn't think what that made her, taking point like a damn' fool.

Their guide was apparently leading them toward a blank stone wall. Just before his nose hit rock, the wall split, the halves sliding apart. He strode briskly through, Cantra a couple steps behind.

She passed over the threshold, felt a shift in the air currents, and looked back. The doors were reversing themselves too quickly, sliding smoothly to shut just behind Dulsey—

Jela, at the rear, brought an arm up and pushed.

The right door panel faltered in its smooth slide toward the center. Jela moved forward, not hurrying, and under no apparent strain. When he was through, he dropped his arm and the door proceeded down its track.

The side walls were closer now—a hallway, as long as you didn't mind the ceiling still out of reach of the light—standard glow-strips, and none too many of them.

Cantra glanced down at the status lights on her cuff. Dark, they were, which she'd expected, but still wasn't pleased to see. Well, it'd been a long shot. Usual rules applied.

They passed through two more rock doors, crossed a couple of corridors and finally took a right turn onto another. Abruptly, there was rug over the rock, the glow-strips became whole panels and the ceiling, revealed at last, was a faceted vein of rose colored quartz. There were green plants there, too, like she remembered—maybe the same ones for all she knew—flanking a portal ahead.

That next door didn't open at their guide's approach. He put his hand on the plate in the center, breathed a word Cantra thought might have been his name.

The door slid aside, and the guard stepped back, waving at her with an impatient hand.

"The Uncle will see you."

THE ROOM—it was the same room, with its shelves of neatly rolled books, the tables groaning under their burdens of tech, art, logic tiles, and best-to-not-knows. Brocades were hung to hide the rocky walls, and the footing was treacherous with layers of carpet and pots and-what-not holding plants.

There were more plants than there'd been, the last time she was here—some held in wall sconces where they might benefit from being closer to the ceiling lights, others were shown off in tiered stands. Might be she was more alert this time, but it seemed there were far more flowers than she remembered. Certainly the room smelled as much of flowers as of rock and people.

A man sat at one of the tables, heedless of the languorous blue blossom hanging a couple hand spans over his head while he carefully fit tiles into a logic-rack. He glanced up as they entered, smiled and rose to his feet.

Sweeping 'round the table, he came forward to meet them—a young man, tall and lean, his long dark hair swept into a knot at the back of his head and fixed with two porcelain sticks. He was dressed in a crimson robe heavy with embroidery, with here and there a wink of gold—smartstrands.

"My dear Pilot Cantra!"

His voice was deep and musical, the hands stretched out in greeting a-glitter with rings inset with strange stones. His eyes were a cool and calculating gray; his face beyond all reason familiar. "How delightful to see you again!"

You heard rumors, when you ran on the edge. Rumors of devices and techs that made possible what maybe shouldn't be within grasp. You heard rumors—but hearing and seeing were two different things.

Cantra felt her stomach clench, and her throat tighten. Reflexively, she bowed, low and slow—no more nor less than what a simple pilot owed a man of power and learning—and by the time she straightened her stomach and her face were under control.

"Uncle," she said, keeping her voice nothing but respectful. "You're looking well."

He folded his hands before him and inclined his sleek head.

"I thank you. I feel well. Certainly more well than when last we spoke."

She drew a deep breath. It would gain nothing to tell the man before her that they had never met. The smartstrands—she figured it was the strands; *hoped* it was the 'strands and not some other, more terrible technology—made it seem to him that he was the very Uncle she had known, with that Uncle's memories and manner of speaking. Even the same voice, made young and vibrant.

She drew another breath, careful and close. Best to get her errands over with, get back to *Dancer*, and get *out*.

"I believe you told Karmin that you have something which belongs to me?" The Uncle said delicately.

Right. Errand number one.

Forcing herself to move smoothly, she turned and motioned Dulsey to step up.

"Belongs here, she says, and I don't say she's wrong."

The Batcher threw her one half-panicked gray glance before obediently going forward to make her bow, so deep it looked like she was trying to sink into the rock floor beneath the patterned rug. Behind her stood Jela, legs braced, hands at his sides, face specifically noncommittal. Errand number two.

Dulsey straightened, cleared her throat. Said nothing.

The Uncle smiled, wide and delighted. Reaching out, he captured her hands in his, the rings winking balefully in the pale light.

"*Welcome*, child," he said gently, looking down into her eyes. "What is your name?"

She swallowed, and seemed to wilt just a little, her fingers clenching the Uncle's hands like her last hope of aid.

"Dulsey, sir," she whispered. "Dulsey . . ." and here Cantra thought she might be adding her Batch number . . . but if she was, she swallowed it, and stood up straight and bold.

"Dulsey," he murmured caressingly. "You are home now. All your cares are behind you."

"Thank you, sir."

"What is your specialty, child?"

She took a deep breath and it seemed to Cantra that she stood a mite straighter still.

"I'm an engineer," she said, and there was no mistaking the pride in her voice.

"An engineer," the Uncle repeated, and smiled wider. "We are *most* happy to welcome you." He squeezed her fingers and let her go, folding his hands against his robe.

"We will send you to the infirmary, first, so that the tattoos may be removed. Trust me, you will feel immensely better when that is done. Then—"

"Pardon me, sir," Dulsey interrupted, fingers suddenly busy at the fastening of her sleeve. "But the tattoos were erased on ship."

The Uncle lifted an elegant dark brow and looked to Cantra.

"Were they, now?"

Cantra shifted her shoulders—not yes and not no, ambiguity being the best defense against the Uncle. According to Garen.

"I can't see 'em," she said. "'Course, I ain't got a deep reader."

"Of course not." The Uncle swayed a slight bow. "But I do."

"Thought you might," Cantra allowed. She had a feeling she might want to glance over at Jela, standing quiet and ignored just inside the door. She fought the urge, figuring it was none too soon to break herself of the habit.

Dulsey had her sleeve shoved up past the elbow now, showing a pale, unscarred arm.

The Uncle considered the offered appendage for a moment

before he stepped to a table laden with weird tech, gesturing her to follow him.

"Step over here, if you will, child. It will be the work of a moment to discover if you are in truth free of the marks of your slavery." He picked a long tube up from the general clutter, and thumbed it on.

It began to glow with a vivid orange light.

"Extend your arm, if you please," he said to Dulsey. "You may feel some warmth, but the process should not hurt. If you experience any pain, tell me immediately. Do you understand, Dulsey?"

"Yes, sir," she said, eyeing the tube with more interest, Cantra thought, than dismay.

"Very good. Now hold out your arm. Yes . . ." Delicately, he ran the reader down Dulsey's arm.

From the corner of her eye, Cantra saw Jela shift—and fall again into stillness.

"Ah," the Uncle breathed. He lifted the reader away, thumbed it off and put it back in its place among the clutter.

He looked at Cantra over Dulsey's head.

"You will pleased, I know, Pilot, to learn that the tattoo is indeed gone. Completely."

"Good news," she said.

"Indeed." He moved his eyes, and added a caressing smile for Dulsey.

"Since you have already been relieved of your burden, you may proceed to the second phase, child." He turned toward the door and raised his voice slightly.

"Fenek?"

The door opened to admit a dainty dark-haired woman with eyes the color of the flower hanging over the Uncle's worktable.

"Sir?"

The Uncle placed a kindly hand on Dulsey's shoulder.

"This is our sister, Engineer Dulsey, Fenek. She requires clothes, a meal, a hammock and an appointment with the teams coordinator. Please assist her in obtaining these things."

Fenek didn't exactly salute, but she gave the impression of

having done so. "Yes sir!" She positively beamed at Dulsey and held out a slender hand.

"Come, sister."

The Uncle gave her a gentle push. "There are no bounty hunters here, Dulsey."

She turned her head to stare at him.

"You knew?"

He smiled indulgently. "Certainly, I knew. We pride ourselves in getting all the latest news and rumors, child! You'll see."

He waved then, and a trick of the smartstrands—or of some less-savory technology—cast a pale sparkling gleam toward the side of the room. "Now, go through the house door there with your sister Fenek and tend to your needs."

"Yes," Dulsey said, and stepped forward.

Fenek dropped back, holding the door open with one slim arm. On the threshold, Dulsey turned, and held out her hand.

"Pilot Jela."

He blinked, as if suddenly called to a realization that he wasn't the pile of rock he'd been imitating so well, and put his hand out to meet hers.

"Dulsey." He smiled his easy smile, squeezed her fingers lightly and let her go. "Remember an old soldier now and then, eh?"

"Yes," she whispered, and turned.

Cantra raised a hand and smiled, hoping to forestall another episode like the one on the ship. Not smart to let the Uncle think there was divided loyalties in his house.

"You take care, Dulsey," she said, deliberately casual.

A pause, then a brief nod—*Good girl*, Cantra thought. *Bright as they come.*

"Yes. And you take care, Pilot," she replied, and turned, walking between a pair of tall purple plants with delicate pink fronds, and through the door, Fenek following.

TWENTY-FIVE

✾ ✾

Rockhaven

THE DOOR CLOSED, and the Uncle turned, the smile slowly leaving his face, which was fine with Cantra. She could have done without the intent, we're-all-believers-here stare, which had been a feature of the former Uncle, too, and even more unsettling on the face of a young man.

But now his eyes lit on the plants Dulsey had just passed and he went to one of them, only half looking at her as he groomed it, letting the pink fronds flow over his hand as he made tiny noises and dropped bits of browning leaf to the carpet.

"I wonder, dear Pilot Cantra," he asked over his shoulder, "do you believe in fate?"

"Fate?" *Now what?* she wondered—then figured she'd find out soon enough. "I don't believe there's some megascript that makes us all act in certain ways," she said carefully, not wanting to move into the scans of those things it was better not to think on too close—or at all.

"Ah," the Uncle breathed. "Well, you are young and doubtless have been busy about your own affairs." He finished with the plant and turned to face her full again, left hand flat against his breast.

"I, however, am old, and I have seen sufficient of the universe to consider the existence of that script, as you have it—probable. For instance—"

His left hand was suddenly outstretched, fingers pointing at a place approximately halfway between her and the silent Jela, rings a-glitter.

"You, dear Pilot Cantra. I had never expected to see you again. You must tell me, how has the receptor flush served you?"

"No ill effects," she said.

"Good, good. I am delighted that our little technique provided long-term satisfaction. We had been using it for some time in aid of those in our community with need, with no ill effect. However, we had never had the opportunity to test it on a natural human. The lab will be pleased. But, as I was saying—I had no expectation to ever see you again, my dear, and yet here you are come to me by your own will, in company . . ."

The Uncle smiled gently, not at her. She risked a glance out of the side of her eye. Jela wasn't smiling back.

"Companied . . ." the Uncle fair crooned, "by a True Soldier. Nothing could be more fortuitous!"

Well, that sounded ominous enough for six. And Jela was decidedly disamused. Funny 'bout that, Cantra thought abruptly. Along the course of their time together, she'd certainly seen Jela use force, and he wasn't shy about making those he deemed would be improved by the condition dead. But he was rarely out of temper. This cold stare into the teeth of the Uncle's smile was—worrisome.

Like she needed something else to worry about.

"Well," she said brightly, drawing the Uncle's eyes back in her direction. "I'm glad you're pleased, Uncle. I wouldn't say us being here proves fate so much as wrongheaded wilfulness on the part of certain pilots. It does put me in mind of a thing, though." She touched the seal on her leg pocket and drew out the gel-pack.

"Saw something a few stops back that I thought might interest you."

The light eyes considered her.

"You've brought me a gift?"

Cantra smiled. "That's right. I was raised up to be civilized."

The Uncle laughed. "You were raised up, as you care to style it," he said, sweetly, "to be a dissembler, a thief, and when need be, a murderer."

No argument there. Cantra let her smile widen a bit. "Where I come from, that's what passes for civilized."

He allowed her to approach and took the packet from her hand.

"Indeed." He ran his finger under the seal, and the pack unfolded, revealing the three little ceramic toys.

Behind her, she heard Jela take a long, careful breath.

The Uncle stood as if transfixed, long enough for Cantra to begin to think that she'd made a bad mis—

"Why, Pilot Cantra," the Uncle purred. "You have managed to surprise me." He looked up. "Where did you get these?"

"A couple stops back," she repeated, agreeably. "Teaching devices, is what the trader told me."

"Did she, indeed?" The Uncle used the tips of his fingers to turn the ceramics over. "And did you test them, to be certain that they were what was advertised?"

No reason not to tell the truth. "I tested the ship," she admitted. "It prompted me for a basic piloting equation. Emitted praise and warm fuzzies when I gave it."

"Ah. And the others?"

"I didn't test the others," Cantra assured him. She'd meant to, but in retrospect the interaction with the toy ship had been more disturbing than pleasant. A good deal like the Uncle himself.

He gave her a long, penetrating look, which she bore with open-faced calm.

"The directors breed marvels, indeed they do," he said softly. "And you the last of your line, more's the pity." He lifted the gel-pack on his palm, and looked past her, to Jela.

"You have seen objects like this before, I think, sir?"

"I have," Jela said, and it was the same hard, perilous voice he'd used when she'd showed him the first-aid kit. "They're not toys. They're *sheriekas*-made and they're dangerous."

"Not necessarily," the Uncle crooned. "It is true that they mine information from the unwary and send back to the Enemy when and as they might. However, we find that minds trained to a specific agenda may not only gain more information from the devices, but can feed them—let us call it *misleading*—information to pass on. To the confoundment of the Enemy." He smiled gently. "Which I am certain that one such as yourself would allow to be worthy work."

"The *sheriekas* are outside of our knowledge," Jela replied forcefully. "We barely understood what they were when they retreated at the end of the last war. Now . . ." He moved his big shoulders. "The best thing to do with those devices is destroy them." He sent a quick black glance to Cantra. "And send the name of the trader who sells them to the military."

The Uncle *t'sked*, turned and put the gel-pack down on the cluttered table.

"I would have thought the military would take a bolder stance," he said, meditatively. "It is well that we have taken this work to ourselves, I see."

"I'd think the work best left alone," Jela said forcefully. "Unless you have a reason for wanting a world-eater's attention."

"One might," the Uncle said with a smile. "One might. Think of what might be learned about the nature of the Enemy, should one of their mightiest engines be captured!"

He raised a hand suddenly. "But stay, I don't wish to raise such controversial topics so soon in our partnership."

Cantra felt a flutter along her nerves, and deliberately reposed herself to stillness.

"Partnership?" asked Jela.

"Surely." The Uncle smiled, cold enough to raise a shiver, though the room was a thought over-warm for Cantra's taste. "I am offering you a place, M. Jela. Here, your talents will be appreciated and well-rewarded."

Well, thought Cantra, specifically not looking at Jela. *This might work out all by its lonesome . . .*

"No," Jela said, shortly.

Or maybe not. She cleared her throat, the Uncle's gaze moved to her face.

"Truth is, Uncle," she began, and looked casually at Jela where he stood, solid and reassuring and—

Lose it, she snarled at herself. *He ain't your partner—never was— and while he sat your co-pilot, that ends now, and good riddance.*

Jela shifted at his post, his face tightening, eyes widening and focusing somewhere beyond the Uncle's room.

"Tell your operative to stand away from the tree," he said sharply.

The Uncle tipped his head. "Your pardon, M. Jela? Do you address me?"

"I do. Call off your operative. *Now*."

"What operative?"

Jela didn't bother answering that, only said again, in a voice nowhere near patient—

"Tell your operative not to touch the board and not to approach the tree. There's nothing hidden in the tree, and if she doesn't stand back, I can't tell what it might do to protect itself."

Intruder on the ship. Cantra gritted her teeth, glanced down at the tell-tales—still jammed, blast it to the Deeps. *Dancer* was on her own, and if the fool did touch that board . . .

"Your operative is regarded as a threat, Uncle. Your operative is in danger."

"Come now, you can hardly be in touch with your ship, which lies quietly at dock. For our own security we smother all ship communications . . ."

"I'm not in communication with our ship," Jela said then. "All my comm systems are dead in here, and I'm betting the pilot's are the same, or she'd have triggered something unpleasant already, being a lady who isn't fond of strangers on her ship. However, I am in communication with the third crew member, who stands within striking distance of your operative, and who is prepared to act."

An alarm blared, and the Uncle's robe briefly blazed golden as the smart-strands took receipt of info.

"What's that?" Jela asked, perfectly calm.

The Uncle took a hard breath, and smoothed his hands down the front of his robe, eyes closed.

"Hydroponics alert," he murmured, eyelids fluttering. "An anomaly in the release gasses. These things happen, which is why we have alerts."

"Ah," said Jela with a grim smile.

Cantra concentrated on keeping her breathing even, though her lungs wanted to gasp at the notion that the tree—Jela's damn' tree, that he insisted told him jokes and that he talked to like an old friend or comrade-in-arms . . .

Well, why not? she asked herself, and took another deep breath, specifically not thinking about what was going to happen if the Uncle's snoop tried to gimmick the board—

Jela casually tapped his wrist chronometer.

"You're the one who has to pass the word. Or take your chance of surviving whatever comes next. It's all the same to me."

It wasn't quite all the same to Cantra, but there wasn't anything she could do except wait, and swear, and hope—

The plant beside the Uncle shivered, and the pink fronds began to curl, as if closing for the night, or . . .

For a moment, the Batch leader was clearly nonplused; he went so far as to peek at something half hidden in his sleeve.

He glanced then at Jela, who was studying the plant with a sort of detached interest as the fronds coiled toward the core.

The Uncle raised his hands, rings glinting, and spoke into the air.

"Chebei, please do not touch either the piloting board or the tree. Return to your station and inform Arin that we are found to be poor hosts."

There was quiet then. Cantra breathed, concentrated on breathing calm and easy, the while keeping one eye on Jela—who was still watching something beyond the Uncle's study—and the other on the Uncle, who appeared to be in like state.

"Thank you," he said abruptly to the air, and sent a sharp glance toward Jela.

"Chebei has cleared the ship, touching nothing save those things she had already touched. Do you confirm, M. Jela?"

No answer for a heartbeat . . . two . . .

The wayaway look faded, the broad chest expanded, and the shoulders rolled.

"Confirmed," he said, and sent Cantra one of his more unreadable looks.

"If you would please to pass my compliments on to your crew member?"

Jela's expression was unreadable, but his eyes went distant. A fleeting grin passed over his features, and then is face was like stone again.

"Understood, Uncle," he said then, looking not at the Batcher but at Cantra.

"Business concluded, Pilot?"

No and yes, Cantra thought. Though she wasn't such a fool as to refuse Jela's back-up on a port that had gone from risky to downright dangerous.

"We did what we came to do," she said, giving him a smile. "If you got nothing more to say, then we'll just ask the Uncle for a guarantee of safe passage and be on our way."

The Uncle pressed a beringed hand over his heart, his face showing an expression of pained gentility which was notable for its sincerity.

"Guarantee of safe passage? Dear Pilot Cantra, surely you don't believe anyone here would seek to harm you?"

She smiled, seeing his sincere and raising it to wounded innocence.

"You did send a snoop onto my ship," she said, as mildly as possible.

The Uncle looked pained. "A mere inspector, child. We only wished to assure ourselves that nothing overtly dangerous had been—inadvertently, of course!—brought to dock at our poor habitat. And we see you are as careful as ourselves, and could not be more pleased. We count your visit among our most pleasant in decades!"

Right.

Cantra gave him another smile, and nodded to Jela.

"Let's go."

He swung forward a step, clearing her way to the door, and coincidentally putting himself between the Uncle and that same door. Much good it would do, with all the smartstrands the man was wearing. On the other hand, she didn't think it likely that the Uncle would try to detain them. His habitat was fragile and he couldn't know what they were carrying by way of plain and fancy explosives, for instance. Nor what that vegetable on the bridge might take into its . . . branches . . . to do if Jela came to harm.

That being the case, there wasn't any need to be rude in their leave-taking. She mustered up a bow, just as respectful as she could manage.

"Uncle, good fortune to you."

He smiled and inclined his head.

"Pilot Cantra, you must come and see me again. In the meanwhile, fair fortune to you."

He tipped his head.

"M. Jela, may I not convince you to enter my employ?"

"No," Jela said shortly, and the Uncle smiled, soft and regretful.

"How," he said gently, "if you were to know that even now it is whispered that soldiers are being bidden to forsake the emptiness of this arm for the comfort of the center? You, however, can still indulge your soldier's soul. You can be here, at the edge of decisive action, where matters of importance to all humankind will be determined. You may be a hero to Dulsey and all her . . ."

Jela shook his head, cutting off the Uncle in a way that likely wasn't too polite.

"This was a waystop for us," he said. "A balancing of accounts with someone who risked her life for us. I've been a hero, and found it far more trouble than you might think. I'll continue traveling with Pilot Cantra, and we'll all part safely."

The Uncle seemed to take it well, all things considered, and if he thought the warning a bit plain-faced, he hid it well. "Then I will bid you, too, farewell and fair fortune." He dropped back a step.

On Cantra's right hand, the door slid open.

TWENTY-SIX

Rockhaven

THERE WAS NO KARMIN waiting to guide them to the dock, which absence set Cantra's trouble-meter to twittering.

Jela came up on her right side, angling his shoulders at an awkward angle, though it wasn't so cramped as that, his fingers dancing at belt level: *Stay close, stay alert*, he signed, and passed on, taking point.

So, she wasn't the only one who was worried.

Dutifully, she fell in behind, which gave her a fine view of attentive shoulders.

The Uncle hadn't exactly promised that safe passage Jela'd given as his expectation, nor it wasn't like him to be disinterested in a telepathic talking tree, much less whatever other goodies Chebei had happened to take note of during her tour. The fact that the board was rigged for oblivion, she didn't figure would give him more than pause. And truth told, there were likely enough pilots 'mong free and equal Batcher-kind that the rig wasn't so certain a thing, giving them time to study on the problem.

The more she considered it, the more nervous she got and by

the time they made it back to the hall where the doors had tried to cut Jela off from the rest of them, her palm was outright itching for the feel of a gun.

She fought the inclination, for the reason that she didn't know what the station might employ by way of safeguards, and that getting fried by a watch-bot for pulling a hideaway wasn't likely to improve her mood any.

Ahead, the big doors were sliding back, and she let herself breathe a quiet sigh of relief. Another few minutes and they'd be aboard *Dancer*, and fortified, if not precisely safe.

Jela was through the door, and she was right behind him—

A shadow moved in the near dimness. Cantra paused between one step and the next, but the movement—if it had been a movement—didn't repeat.

Jumpy, she scolded herself and moved on—

Toward a door that was very nearly closed, with Jela on the far side. She threw herself into a run—and there was noise from the shadows now, the sounds of boots moving fast.

Swearing, she jumped, got a shoulder through the narrowing crack, felt the pressure of the doors grinding against her chest and her back . . .

She squeezed through somehow, popping out into the docking area with a yell.

"Ambush!"

Weapon in hand, Jela spun, taking his attention off the number of armed people between him and *Dancer's* ramp.

Behind her, she heard the door work.

"I'll hold 'em!" she yelled at Jela, snatching one of her hideaways out of its pocket and thumbing the charge. "Get to the ship!"

The last thing she saw before her own problems overtook her was Jela charging the half-formed line of attackers.

Something hissed past Cantra's ear and she spun, gun rising— and sent a dart into the attacker's shoulder. Bad shooting: She'd been aiming for the throat.

His fellows raced past him and Cantra fired again, missing all available targets, as near as she could tell.

Another dart went by her ear, but the two leaders were on her now, and the gun was useless.

She fell back, slipping the slim glass blade from its special pocket and dropped into a crouch.

The first was over-confident—a kick and a thrust took care of her. The second was timid—a kick sufficed there, just in time for the arrival of the rest of the six, and it was a brawl then, with knives and knucklebones, and a nasty something that filled the air with crackling waves of force.

The owner of that particular toy tended to stay well back, not wanting to catch her mates in the field. Cantra had a singed sleeve out of her near encounter with an energy-wave, and didn't want to risk another.

The others were keeping her busy, and it was starting to look bad—then she saw an opening, slid in with the knife, and came out slashing, which took both out of the dance with one move, snapped off a shot in the direction of the energy-bearer, and spun.

Between her and her ship were four prone bodies. Further on, there was Jela, visible through the transparent walls of the gangtube, wasting no time.

Behind her, she heard a shout, and looked over her shoulder to see the door standing open and a dozen more combatants racing into the docking area.

She got her legs moving and bolted for the—

A wall of fire slammed into and through her.

She screamed, scarcely hearing her own voice through the crackle of energy, and dropped to the stone floor, rolling. Her 'skins—her 'skins were on fire, which wasn't possible, and she was gagging on acrid smoke, rolling—and then not, as she was hauled to her feet by one arm.

Karmin grinned, his grip on her arm lost in the other, larger pain, and hefted his knife, the point darting toward her face.

She jerked back, stronger than he'd been expecting. She broke his hold, the knife notched her ear, and she fell heavily to the floor. She was baking, suffocating; she could feel her dermis crisping in the heat of her 'skins' destruction.

Jela would have made the ship by now . . . she thought with absolute clarity.

There was a gurgling sound, quite near at hand, followed by yells, shouts, curses, and a peculiar whistling. Cantra was kicked—and kicked again where she lay.

The heat from her 'skins seemed somewhat less—or her nerve endings were overloaded; she opened her eyes—and took in the sight of Pilot Jela, three down and bleeding, and himself wielding something that to her dazed sight seemed to be a long ceramic whip.

As she watched, Karmin leapt back from the hiss of the whip, then feinted in, knife flashing—

The whip snapped; the knife and a finger fell away.

Karmin shrieked and whirled aside, the remainder of those still standing following. Jela let them go, and dropped to one knee beside her.

"Can you walk?" he asked.

" . . . not sure . . ." she managed in a voice ravaged by smoke.

"Right." he said. "I'm going to carry you. It's probably going to hurt."

It did.

She passed out.

TWENTY-SEVEN

Rockhaven
Departure

CANTRA HAD LOST consciousness, and that was good, since the best he could do for her was a rough-and-ready shoulder-carry.

The Batcher recon squad was off the field, which was good as far as it went, and he was willing to bet it went less far than he'd like.

They were in; the hatch was down and sealed against trouble—and that was very good, though an immediate lift was in order.

Which was a problem, given the pilot's state and the fact that the board had been closed—and likely gimmicked and he had no idea what she'd done.

Well, he'd figure it out or he wouldn't. First order of business was his pilot's health. He didn't want to think too closely about the damage she'd likely taken. The energy generated from the shorted circuitry and support systems would, he hoped, have mostly discharged outward, and the fact that she was still breathing was an indicator that her injuries weren't too serious.

He hoped.

The hatch to the piloting tower stood open, the tower itself on dims. The board was showing a sprinkling of orange stand-bys. The tree sat snug in its corner, leaves still.

Jela received an impression of wariness as he swept past on his way to the cubby and the *sheriekas* regeneration unit.

His boot broke the beam, the door slid back, releasing an eddy of cooler air. Cantra over his shoulder, he sank to one knee by the side of the chill black box, and triggered the release.

The hatch rose silently to reveal the unsettling green-lit interior. Jela got Cantra down on the pallet as gently as he could, straightened her, and got to his feet as the hatch began to descend—

Stopped. And reversed itself. The interior green light shifted to an even more unsavory violet, and it didn't take a Generalist to parse the fact that the unit found the offering not up to spec.

Horrified, he bent forward, fingers on her throat. If she'd died . . .

The pulse under his fingers was sluggish, her breathing shallow and raspy—but she was alive.

"Object to pilot 'skins, do you?" he muttered, but it made sense. The blasted remains of the internal systems might still interfere with whatever process the regenerator used to effect its healings.

There wasn't much room to work, and he had a bad moment when it looked like the magseals had fused, but he managed to get the 'skins off her. She moaned once or twice during the process, but mercifully didn't float back to the here-and-now.

He worked fast—if she went into shock, he'd lose her quick—and tried not to think about the damage he was doing. Not all the energy had dissipated outward. Not nearly all. Tears rose, and he blinked them back.

"You've seen worse," he told himself, shakily, and kept working.

Behind his eyes—an image: A halfling dragon stretched along a bed of dry leaves, its long neck at too sharp an angle, one wing twisted and vane-broken, the wide eyes dull.

"No," he said, out loud, and the image faded.

It was done. He threw the blasted 'skins to the deck and knelt there, unable to look away from the ruin of his pilot until the hatch came down and locked her away from him.

Another image formed behind his eyes—thunder heads boiling over the distant shoulders of mountains, lightning dancing between the clouds.

"On my way," he whispered, and got his feet under him.

He approached the orange-lit board, and frowned. It had been locked all the way down to deep sleep, on the pilot's own orders, the last time he'd seen it.

There were a number of ways to gimmick a piloting board, some more fatal than others. He wished he had a precise reading on how much Cantra had distrusted the Uncle. He sat himself down in the pilot's chair, engaged the webbing and studied the situation.

The status lights showing stand-by were main engine, weapons, and navigation brain. The combination tickled a pattern at the back of his untidy mind. He closed his eyes and tried to visualize a blank screen, but instead of a clarification of the thought, he got thunder heads again, augmented this time with an evil, edgy wind that snapped mature branches like twigs—

"Not helpful," he muttered. "If I don't get this right, my guess is that neither of us will see a thunderstorm again."

The wind died; the storm clouds dissipated. The internal screen went blank—no.

Another image was forming—lightning again, one single orange bolt, blazing into and merging with a second; the doubled force striking down into water.

"Not—" he began—and the image repeated, with an edge of impatience to it: One bolt, two, one, strike.

Jela blinked.

"She wouldn't have . . ."

But she might have. A pilot's first care was her ship, after all. And to what length might a pilot who dared not let her ship fall into the hands of someone who was a little too fond of *sheriekas*-made goods go?

His fingers, apparently placing more faith in tree-born intuition than his thinking mind, were already moving across the board, taking them off-line in deliberate order: nav-brain first; then the main engine; lastly, the guns.

Satisfyingly, the stand-bys went dark. Jela sighed—and jumped as the board came abruptly live. The internal lights came up; blowers started; and behind him the door to the tower slid shut.

Screens came on-line, showing him cannon in the docking area; and the comm opened, admitting a man's breathless voice.

"Surrender yourself and the ship, and you will be well-treated. Attempt to lift and this habitat will defend itself."

If a pair of quad cannons was the best they could field, leaving wasn't going to be a problem.

He reached to the weapons board, pulled up the ranging screen, acquired the target—and stopped, finger on the firing stud.

"Dulsey," he said, and saw a flicker of green at the back of his eyes. Hole the habitat, which *Dancer's* guns were fully capable of doing, and there was a chance Dulsey wouldn't live through the experience.

He thought of Cantra, dependent for her life on alien technology that was itself dependent on the well-being of the ship it traveled in.

"Surrender yourself!" The demand came again; a woman's voice this time, sounding more angry than scared.

"Well," Jela said to the tree. "I think we can take what they've got to dish out."

Quickly, he put the weapons to rest, and slapped the shields up. He thought of the defenses his former ships had carried, and was briefly sorry. He thought of Cantra again—and engaged the engines.

Dancer leapt away from the dock. In the screens, the cannon flared, the shot so hopelessly bad that he reflexively checked the scans—and thereby discovered bad news.

The route outspace—and there was only one reasonable route outspace, as there had only been one reasonable route in—was crossed and re-crossed with what appeared to be ribbons of colored light.

Particle beams.

"This might be rough," Jela told the tree, as he brought the shields up high. "We've got a field of charged beams to get to the other side of."

A legitimate merchanter would have foundered, its shielding shredded by the beams before it had passed the halfway point.

Dancer, with her up-grade shields and her quick response to con, had a better chance of surviving than that legitimate merchanter, not quite as good a chance as a real military craft.

He brought the guns up, knowing he might be needing them as soon as he was clear of the defenses . . . and now they were ready.

The field wasn't extensive; just enough to be nerve-wracking, and they lost a layer of shielding before they got through it, but through they came, guns at ready, and the pilot in the mood for a scrap.

He was unfortunately disappointed; there was no *sheriekas*-built battle cruiser—or even an armed corsair—awaiting them at the maze's end. Only the dust and the emptiness of the Deeps.

"Now what?" he asked the tree, but no answering flash of images appeared behind his eyes.

Scans reported no beacons; even the chirping that had guided them in was silent. And he was no Cantra yos'Phelium, able to pilot blind and—

"Fool!" he snapped at himself, his fingers already calling up the nav-brain, hoping that for once in her life she'd followed a standard protocol and recorded the—

She had. Jela sat back in his chair with an absurd feeling of relief.

"All we have to do," he told the tree, like it was going to be easy, "is follow our own path back out."

He had never done such a bit of piloting himself, but he had talked to pilots who had.

And what else did a Generalist need besides knowing that something could be done, and a bit of luck?

TWENTY-EIGHT

⚜ ⚜

Spiral Dance
The Little Empty

HE WATERED THE TREE, ate a high-cal bar and drank a carafe of hot, sweet tea.

He slept, webbed into the co-pilot's chair, one ear cocked and one eye half-open.

He cleaned house, thinking unkind thoughts about the Uncle the while, and retrieved his belt and the captured disruptor from the lock, throwing the hand into the recycler, and swabbing the deck clean of blood.

He consulted the charts, and he consulted the tree.

He tried the comm.

He checked the first-aid kit. Several times.

He went over the charts again, ate a high-cal bar, and had another nap, during which he debated with himself—maybe—weighing ship's safety against the necessity of reporting in.

When he woke, he compromised. He set course for Gimlins, and locked it, but did not initiate. Instead, he kept her shielded and quiet in the Shallows, pending the pilot's accepting the route.

That done, he sent his query again.

No ack from his primary.

No ack from the back-up.

No ack from use-this-only-in-extreme-emergency.

Growling, he extended a hand to sweep the comm closed—and pulled up sharply as the incoming dial lit.

Hope rising, he watched the message flow onto the screen—

My very dear Pilot Cantra, and esteemed M. Jela—

Please accept my sincere apology for the inconvenience surrounding your departure from our humble habitat. I hope neither of you has taken lasting harm from the incident.

I do very much thank you for your assistance in identifying certain of my children who have become somewhat over exuberant in their pursuit of our common goal.

Dulsey asks that I send you her warmest personal regards, to which I will add my own hope that you will consider my family as your own.

Uncle

Jela closed his eyes, tasting dust in his mouth. Wearily, he sent the message into the pilot's queue, then shut down the comm and went to check the first-aid kit.

The smooth black box sat as it had for the last four ship-days, lid down, doing whatever it did, however it did.

He had to take it on faith that the thing was working; that it would have given some notification, had Cantra died in the course of its treatment. Her injuries had been terrible, he had seen that for himself; he didn't dwell on the question of whether they were survivable.

He'd taken counsel of the tree, which was wary, but willing to wait. Himself, he was getting impatient, and had decided to give the thing two more ship-hours to finish up, or at least provide a status report, before he opened the lid himself.

Standing over the damned box, he admitted to himself that he might have made a mistake. What he could have done instead—that was the sticking point.

"Damn' Ms," he muttered. "Always know better."

Except when they didn't.

He was wasting time, hovering over the box. It would open in its own time, or he would open it in his. Meanwhile, there was this and that of ship minutiae to occupy himself with, and for a change he could worry about not being able to make contact. He turned and left the alcove, heading for the galley to make tea and maybe a real-meal.

He hadn't reached the door when the chime sounded, and he spun 'round so fast he almost tripped on his own feet. An image flashed inside his head—one of the youngling dragons tumbling wings over snout down a long mossy slope.

Grinning, he went back to the first-aid kit—not running. Not quite.

PERFECT, WHOLE, neither happy nor unhappy, she lay swathed in light.

Gently, the light parted, admitting a crystalline whisper, bearing choices. Perfect though she now was, there existed an opportunity. She might be made *more* perfect, exceeding the arbitrary limits set by her original design. Smarter, quicker, more accurate—these things were but minor adaptations. The ability to bend event to her will, to sculpt the forces of the mind—those might also be attained. If she wished.

The cusp was here and now: Remain perfect and perfectly limited, or embrace greatness and be more than she ever dreamed. How did she chose?

Bathed and supported by the light, she considered. And as she did, a breeze sprang up, bearing scents of living green, while across the light fell the shadow of a great wing.

Startled, she looked up—and the light faded, the voice withdrew. She heard a chime, and opened her eyes.

Lean cheeks, black eyes, mobile mouth—doing his best not to look worried, and making a rare hash of it. She made a note to herself to remember that look. For some reason, it seemed important.

"Cantra?" Letting the worry leak into the voice, too. Deeps, but the man was going to bits—that's what came of talking to trees.

"Who else?" She looked up, saw the hatch above her leaking sickly green light, and took a breath, tasting ship air—and that quick memory came back on-line.

"You hurt?" she snapped.

Jela blinked and gave over a half-smile. "I'm hale, Pilot."

"Good. The ship?"

"Ship's in shape, and we're well away," he answered. The half-smile twisted a little. "There's a note in queue from Uncle, apologizing for any inconvenience and thanking us for smoking out his insurgents."

She snorted a laugh. "I'll send him a bill," she said, which pleasantry got a genuine grin from Jela and an easing of the muscles around his eyes.

"So." she said, swinging her feet over the side of the pallet. "Got tea?"

TEA WAS HAD, and a bowl of spiced rice mixed up by her co-pilot, who insisted that he'd been on his way to make the same for himself when the chime sounded and that doubling was no problem.

So, she'd leaned against the wall, wearing a robe she carefully didn't ask how he'd gotten out of her quarters, and sipped her tea, watching him work. She smiled when he handed her a bowl and followed him to the tower.

The bowls were empty now, and they sat sipping the last of the tea, companionably silent.

She rested her mug against her knee and waved her free hand at the board.

"I imagine you got a course set."

Jela looked wry. "It's my intention to raise Gimlins."

"Never come up on my dance card," she said. "What's to want on Gimlins?"

"Maybe contact," he answered, slowly, and looked at her straight. "I've been trying to report in, but I'm not getting any answers to my signals." That bothered him—and it bothered her that he let her see it.

"It could be," he said, but not like he believed it, "that we're too far out."

"It could be," she agreed, seriously. "The Deeps do funny things to comm sometimes—even the Shallows can play tricks on you." She finished her tea, slotted the cup and sat up straighter in her chair before meeting his eyes.

"We gotta talk."

He gave her a nod, face smooth and agreeable, which return to normal behavior she observed with a pang. Might be she'd taken a bad knock on the head, back on the Uncle's dock.

"First off—" She raised a hand and pointed at the tree, sitting quiet and green and for all the worlds like a *plant* in its pot. "What *is* that thing? And I don't want to hear 'tree.'"

Jela glanced over his shoulder at the tree in question, settled back into his chair and sipped tea.

Cantra sighed. "Well?"

He lifted a hand, showing empty palm.

"You said you didn't want to hear 'tree,' Pilot. Since that's what it is, I'm at a loss as to how to answer without violating my orders."

"That coin would spend better," she told him, "if I had any reason to believe you ever once in your life followed orders."

He grinned. "I've followed my share of orders. It's just that I have a bias against obeying the stupid ones."

"Must've made you real popular with your commanders."

"Some of them, yes; some of them, no," he said, easily, and flicked his fingers over his shoulder.

"That, now—that's a tree, and if it has a personal name, or a racial one, it hasn't shared them with me."

"A telepathic tree, is what I'm hearing," Cantra said, just to have it down on the deck where they could both consider it at leisure.

"Why not?"

"It's not exactly usual," she pointed out. "Where'd you get it? If you don't mind saying."

He sent another over-the-shoulder glance at the subject of the conversation. When he looked back, his face was serious.

"I found it on a desert world; the only thing alive in a couple days' walk. We'd seen some action and it was my misfortune to be shot down. By the time I found the tree, I was in pretty bad shape. It saved my life and I promised, if rescue came, that I'd take it with me." He glanced down, maybe into his mug.

"Promised I'd get it to someplace safe."

"Safe," she repeated, thinking of Faldaiza, Taliofi, the Uncle, and of a dozen chancy ports between.

"It's probable," Jela said, "that 'safe' is a relative term. The tree was in danger of extinction when I found it. When things are that bad, someplace else is pretty much guaranteed to be better. Safer." He looked down into his mug again, lifted it and finished off his tea.

"I'd hoped," he said, slotting the empty, "to find a planet where it would have a chance of a good, long grow . . ."

"Which doesn't," Cantra said when he just sat there, eyes pointed at the empty mug, but clearly seeing something else, "address what it *is*. Or how it was able to tweak the Uncle's hydroponics long-distance."

He glanced over his shoulder, and then gave her an amused glance.

"I don't know how—or what—the tree did," he said, "but I'm not surprised it was able to act in its own defense—and in defense of its ship."

Cantra closed her eyes. "Now its official crew, is it?"

"Why not?" Jela returned, damn him. And, no matter its vegetative state, the tree *had* acted to protect the ship, and made it stick when both pilot and co-pilot were cut off and helpless.

"All right," she said, opening her eyes with a sigh. "It's crew." She stretched in her chair to look past Jela to the end of the board.

"Done proper," she said to the tree. "The captain commends you."

The top leaves moved, probably in the breeze from the circulation system, but looking eerily like a casual salute.

In that breeze there was a sharp snap; a branch carrying two small pods fell to the deck, and bounced once.

Jela laughed, picked up the branch, and felt the pods relax, almost as if they ripened in his hand.

"Here," he said, smiling. "The tree commends the captain and the crew!"

She looked them askance.

"What'll I do with it? Plant it?"

His free hand fluttered pilot talk—*Eat up, eat up*.

She lifted an eyebrow, watching him carefully as he approached, teasing, as she read it, and leaned conspiratorially toward her.

"You've never tasted anything quite like this," he suggested in a mock whisper.

"You sure it's good?" she asked, not so much playing as seriously wanting to know.

The tree's top branches waved slightly—she was really going to have to check those fans soon if they were creating that much disturbance.

"Edible? Yes! Good? Really good . . ."

He broke the pods into sections; she took them into her hand to avoid him hand-feeding her, which it looked like he might.

He challenged her then, holding a piece to his lips while watching her expectantly.

She looked to the fruit, caught a bouquet reminiscent of half-a-dozen high-end eats she could name.

Damn' thing smelled good—

"Not very big, is it?" she asked, by way of buying time while she sorted past the inviting smell. She knew all about nice smells, now, didn't she?

"You'll like it," Jela said, suddenly serious. "I promise." He popped the piece into his mouth then, and, not to be outdone, or seen to be timid, so did she.

He was right. She liked it.

SHE'D EATEN THE POD, cleaned her fingers, and studiously did not give herself over to considering Jela's person, though there was that urge. She noticed it on the two previous occasions she'd had to make use of the first-aid kit. It was like the unit brought everything right up to optimum . . .

"If it can be told," Jela said, breaking her line of thought, "Where did you get those devices you gave the Uncle?"

She sighed. "Like I said, a couple ports back. A lucky find, since the Uncle has this interest in *sheriekas* artifacts."

"Do you remember," Jela persisted, "the name of the trader or company who sold them to you?"

Well, she did, as it happened, the directors having done them all the favor of breeding for extra-efficient memories—and she was damned if she was going to share the news.

"I'm gonna tell you so you can report trading with the enemy and send somebody out to pick 'em up?" she snapped. "No point to it. A lot of weird drifts in from the Deeps and catches up against the Rim. Depend on it, somebody bought a box-lot or a broken pallet somewhere and the toys were in it. There's a lot of *sheriekas* tech on the Rim; people trade 'em as oddities, or collect 'em."

"Like the Uncle?" Jela asked, and Cantra laughed.

"The Uncle ain't collecting; he's using. Figures he can beat the enemy by mastering their machines and turning them against their makers."

"Then he's a fool," Jela said, with a return of the stern grimness he'd given the Uncle, "and an active danger to the population of the Spiral Arm."

Cantra frowned. "Could might be. In point of fact, though, what the Uncle exactly ain't is a fool, nor any of his folk. The Batchers who make it out to the Uncle, they're tough and they're smart. Seems like if anybody was going to be able to figure how to use the enemy's equipment against them, it's the Uncle's people." She considered Jela's face, which was no more grim or less, and added—

"Understand me, I ain't the Uncle's best friend, by any count."

That got a real, though brief, smile, and a roll of the wide shoulders.

"I don't doubt that they're smart," he said slowly. "But they're not the only ones who've thought of using the *sheriekas* weapons against them—and come to grief for it. I've seen battle robots based on captured *sheriekas* plans which have gone mad, laying waste to the worlds they were built to defend—a flaw in the design, or are they performing exactly as the *sheriekas* intended them to?"

He leaned forward, elbows on knees, warming to his topic.

"Another case—out there in the Tearin Sector, they've been building battle tech based on plans captured from the last war— fleets of robot ships, under self-aware robot commanders who've been fed all the great battles fought by all the great generals. They've turned them loose, I hear, to roam out into the Beyond and engage the *sheriekas*."

Cantra tipped her head. "So—what? They join the enemy when they make contact?"

"They might," Jela said, sitting back. "The reports I've seen have them turning pirate and holding worlds hostage for their resources."

"And you're thinking this is also in the plan?" she persisted. "To seed us with tech and proto-machines that'll attack us from inside while the world-eaters take bites outta the Rim?"

"Like that," he said, and gave her one of his less-sincere half-smiles. "Old soldiers have their crochets. No doubt the Uncle's harmless."

Cantra laughed. "Nobody said so. And that thing that fried out my 'skins sure wasn't harmless." She hesitated, wondering if she wanted to know—but of course she did.

"How bad?"

He glanced aside. "Bad," he said, and sighed. "You needed nothing less than a *sheriekas*-made heal-box—and I wasn't sure it was enough."

Well. She closed her eyes; opened them.

"My 'skins?"

"Sealed inside a sterile pack," he said. "What's left of them."

She shivered, took a breath—

"I owe you," she said, and her voice was a little lighter than she liked. She cleared her throat. "Owe you twice."

His eyebrows went up, but he didn't say anything, only made the hand sign for *go on*.

"Right. You were clear—I saw you on the ramp. No reason for you to come back—you could've got away clean."

He snorted. "Fine co-pilot I'd be, too, leaving my pilot in such a mess."

She glanced aside. "Well, about that . . ." She took a hard breath and made herself meet his eyes.

"The thing is, I went in thinking that the Uncle might enjoy having himself a soldier, and that selling you might net a goodly profit."

Something moved down far in those Deeps-dark eyes, but his face didn't change out of the expression of calm listening.

"Say something!" Cantra snapped.

He raised his hands slightly, let them drop onto his lap.

"I'll say that I don't blame you for wanting me off your ship," he said. "And I'll point out that, intentions aside, you didn't sell me to the Uncle." He moved his shoulders against the back of the chair.

"No bad feelings here, Pilot."

Which was generous, she allowed, and precisely Jela-like. She wondered if it came of being a soldier, his giving the greater weight to the action done, and the lesser to the reasons behind it.

For herself, she was unsettled by her intentions and her actions, both. She knew—none better—that Jela wasn't anything like a partner, nor did she owe him anything as a co-pilot, being as he had forced his way into the chair and the ship.

Yet, when decision came to action—

Mush for brains, she growled at herself.

"Meant to ask you," Jela said. "Why did your directors decide to retire your Series? If it can be told."

She blinked, it being on the edge of her tongue to tell him it *couldn't* be told. But, dammit—she owed him . . .

"Pliny," she said, and cleared her throat, " . . . he'd've been a half-brother. So—Pliny come home from an assignment, reports to Instructor Malis for debriefing—and slapped her." She paused, feeling Garen's hand hard 'round her arm, yanking her into a run—

"So," Jela said softly. "He slapped a superior. In the military, that might be good for getting him shot, but not his whole unit."

She looked up and met his eyes.

"He'd been delayed," she said, just telling it, "and by the time he come in, he really needed that debriefing. Add that Instructor Malis . . . liked to hear us beg for the drug. The sum of it all being that he killed her—and the directors aren't about to tolerate a line that bites the hand that's fed it, housed it, clothed it, and taught it." She paused, considered, then shrugged. Wouldn't do him no harm to have the whole tale of it.

"The Uncle come into it because some level of Batchers're are kept in line by binding—happy-chems, mostly—to certain receptors. Close enough to how the directors keep *aelantaza* in line, except the directors didn't figure to waste any happy-chems. Uncle's lab techs gimmicked an unbind process, which Garen knew, and figured it was worth the trip to find out would it work."

"I see." Silence, while Jela glanced over his shoulder at his damn' tree, sitting still and green in its pot.

"So the line was ended because it showed independence and self-reliance," he said. "And you're the sole survivor."

"By luck . . ." she muttered. *And by Garen.*

He smiled at her—a wholly real smile.

"That's all any of us can claim," he said, and stood, gathering his empties into a broad hand, and reaching for hers.

"What I propose," he said, looking down at her, his face serious. "If you agree, Pilot. Is that we do make for Gimlins. I've got a good chance at a contact there, which will get me off your ship and out of your life."

For one of the few times in her free life, her mind went blank, and she stared at him, speechless.

"And I'll apologize," Jela continued, "for putting you in harm's way. I *am* a soldier; the risks I find acceptable aren't what a civilian ought ever to face."

Almost, she laughed, wondering what he thought her life had been—but he was gone by then, the door sliding closed behind him while she sat in the pilot's chair and for the first time since Garen died blinked away tears.

TWENTY-NINE

Spiral Dance
Shift Change

JELA HAD GOTTEN his log-book out, meaning to bring the entries current. An hour later, there he sat, the book open on his knee, pen ready—and he'd done no more than note down the date.

It happened that the date was of some interest to him, it being something over forty-four Common Years since the quartermaster had assigned M Strain Jela to Granthor's Guard creche, despite the fact that the proto-soldier was smaller than spec. That he'd been the single survivor of an enemy action focused on the lab which had killed every other fetus in the nursery wing—that had weighed with the quartermaster, who'd noted in the file that a soldier could never have too much luck.

He'd been lucky, too—or as lucky as a soldier could be. Despite a certain reckless disregard for his own personal welfare, and what some might call an argumentative and willful nature, he'd outlived creche-mates and comrades; commanders and whole planets.

And now he was old.

Worse, he was old while the enemy continued to advance and

wrongheaded decisions came down from the top; his mission was in shambles and—

The last—that rankled. No, it *hurt*.

That this would be his last mission, he had accepted, the facts being what they were. That he would fail—somehow it had never occurred to him that he would fail, though he'd certainly failed enough times in his life for the concept to be anything but new. This mission, though, assigned by this particular commander . . .

He'd been so sure of success.

And there was worse.

He'd promised—personally promised—the tree that he would see it safe, which he should never have done, a soldier's life and honor being Command's to spend.

It weighed on him, that promise, for he had made it with true intent, between soldiers, and the tree was as much his comrade-in-arms as any other he'd fought beside, down the years.

He told himself that the tree knew the realities of a soldier's promise; that the tree, comrade and hero, didn't fault him for putting duty before promises.

The fact was that he faulted himself, for what increasingly seemed a life misspent and useless. Yes, he had followed orders. More or less. Which was all that was required of a soldier, after all.

And duty required him, right now, to plan for the best outcome of the mission, since success was not within his grasp.

Sighing, he shifted against the wall, sealed the pen, closed the book and put both on the hammock by his knee. He closed his eyes.

Gimlins, now.

Gimlins was a risk. It might even be an unacceptably high risk. He wouldn't know that until he did or didn't have someone on the comm who did or didn't have the right sequence of passcodes.

There'd been a corps loyal to the consolidated commanders on Gimlins. Some time back, that would have been, and he was the first to realize the info was old. His big hope, in a narrowing field, was that the corps was still there. His smaller, more realistic hope, was that the corps had moved on to fulfill its duty, leaving behind a contact for those who might have lost their way.

If there was neither corps nor contact at Gimlins, then he'd—

He wasn't precisely sure what he'd do then, in the cause of the consolidated commanders.

Which unsettling thought spawned another. He'd promised Cantra he'd clear off her ship, and that was a promise he *did* intend to keep. Duty might have required him to find quiet transport out of the range of fire, but duty hadn't required that he continue to impose his will—*his* will—upon her once he'd gotten clear.

He could have picked up a ship at any of the ports they'd passed through on their way to settle Dulsey with the Uncle. The truth was, he hadn't chosen to. Like he'd chosen to sign on as Dulsey's escort to safety, forcing Cantra onto a course she'd never have charted for herself, and for which audacity she'd determined to sell him to a ruthless man who she might have had reason to believe could keep him occupied long enough for her to lift, regaining her life and her liberty.

He understood her motive, and didn't blame her for the intention. A fully capable woman, Cantra yos'Phelium, and as good as her word—when she gave it. He'd enjoyed being her partner in trade. And he'd learned something about piloting from her, which he wouldn't have thought was possible.

He smiled a little, remembering her yawn for the X Strain's display of prowess—and the smile faded with the more recent memory—looking down to the dock where she was surrounded, smoke billowing from her 'skins and the scream—

He'd never thought to hear Cantra yos'Phelium scream—and hoped never to hear it again. The sound of her laughter—that was a memory for a soldier to take away with him, and treasure.

Memories . . . Well, a soldier had his memories—which shouldn't, in the normal way of things, interfere with his duty or his planning.

Sighing, he shifted again against the wall, settling his shoulders more comfortably, and engaged one of the focusing exercises.

The sound of the air being cut by wings disturbed his concentration; sunlight flickered in strange patterns across the barely visualized task screen, which melted, morphing into a wide band of blue, arcing from never to forever over the mighty crowns of trees.

Again came the sound of wings and there, high against the canopy sky, two forms, necks entwined, danced wing-to-wing.

"Not likely," Jela muttered and started the exercise from the beginning, banishing the dancing lovers from his mind's eye.

The exercise proceeded, task screen came up—and was again subverted by the tree's will.

This time he saw the now-familiar green land, gently ridged by the great roots of trees. Against one giant trunk a nest sat a little askew, with bits and pieces of it strewn about, as if it had fallen from a higher branch, unmoored perhaps by the wind.

In the nest was a dragonling, its tiny wings still wet, and it was crying, as any baby will, for food, and for comfort.

As he watched, a seed-pod fell into the nest, and the baby set to with a will; another pod was given and devoured; and a third, as well, after which the baby curled 'round in its battered nest, eyes slitting drowsily . . .

Leaves sifted gently downward, filling the nest softly. The dragonling sighed and tucked its head under its wing, slipping off into sleep.

A flash of the task-screen, then, and a shift of scene to doleful, dusty wasteland, the sun pitiless overhead, and below, nested in the sand, a creature soft and dun colored, its snout short; its eyes reflective . . .

In the hammock, leaning against the wall of his quarters, Jela snorted a laugh.

"And a pretty sight I was," he said aloud.

The tree continued as if he had not interrupted, displaying now an unfamiliar green land touched by soft shadows—and there, curled against a trunk he somehow knew for the tree's own, despite its greater girth, a small and soft dun-colored creature was peacefully asleep.

In the now of Cantra's ship, Jela frowned.

"Is that real?" he asked the tree, but his only answer was a flicker of shadows and the sound of the wind.

✵ ✵ ✵

SHE CHECKED THEIR LOCATION, and gave Jela full points for finding his way out of the Deeps and into the relative safety of the Shallows.

For old time's sake, she called up reports from weapons and from the ship-brain, opened the comm logs, read the Uncle's note, laughed, and scanned the long list of sends which had raised no answers.

She went down the list again, frowning after call-codes familiar from her previous audits of Jela's comm activity, through a complicated skein of unfamiliar—and increasingly untraditional codes.

The man's worried, she thought, and caught herself on the edge of starting a third time from the top.

Mush for brains, she growled, and banished the log with a flick of a finger.

She should, she thought, get dressed, pull up the charts and do some calculations, checking Jela's filed route to Gimlins.

The sooner you raise it, she told herself, when she just sat there—*The sooner you raise this Gimlins, the sooner you've got your ship back.*

True enough and a condition she'd yearned for since shortly after shaking the mud of Faldaiza off of *Dancer's* skin.

Despite which, she stayed in the pilot's seat, pulling her feet up onto the chair and wrapping her arms around her knees, the silk robe sliding coolly against her skin.

The Little Empty was in the forward screen, the few points of light showing hard against the endless night. She leaned back into the chair . . .

Don't stare at the Deeps, baby, Garen muttered from memory. *The empty'll fill up your head and make you's crazy as your mam, here.*

No use explaining that Cantra knew her pedigree down to multiple-great-grandmothers and that Garen yos'Phelium was nowhere in the donor list. Garen believed Cantra to be her daughter—the same daughter who had been annihilated, along with the rest of Garen's family, acquaintances, and planet, by a world-eater, some many years before the directors of the Tanjalyre Institute commissioned Cantra's birth.

Garen'd told her the story—how her ship had come home from a run, excepting there wasn't any home there. Told how they'd checked the coords, gone out and tried to come back in. How they'd done it a dozen times, from a dozen different transition points until finally the captain put them in at Borgen, cut the crew loose and sold the ship.

She told that story, did Garen, and as far as Cantra'd ever determined, she'd seen no inconsistency in admitting her daughter dead and destroyed while at the same time believing Cantra to be that same daughter. Not the least of Garen's crazies, and the one that Cantra ought by rights to have no argument with, it having saved her life.

The question now being, Cantra thought, tucked into the pilot's chair of a ship she could never fully trust, staring out over the Deeps—*saved it for what?*

Life wants to live, baby. That's just natural.

True as far as it went. But life—life wanted to accomplish, too; to make connections; to trust; to be at ease and off-guard for some small moments of time . . .

That's a powerful gift you've been given, baby. A weapon and a boon. You can have anything you want, just for a smile and a pretty-please.

A curse, more like, and a danger to her and to those who fell under her sway. The best course—the safest—was to keep herself to herself, and to stand as cantankerous and off-putting as possible when human interaction came necessary.

The meager stars danced in the screens. She closed her eyes, which didn't shut the empty out.

Five years since Garen'd died. Five years of running solo, keeping low, with nobody except herself to talk to.

And for what?

"Habit," she whispered, and in the Deeps behind her eyelids she saw Dulsey, her stolid face animating as she talked about the Uncle and his free and equal society of Batchers. Jela, the joyful gleam of anticipated mayhem in his eye as he squared off in front of an opponent twice his mass.

. . . and other images—Jela half-way up the ramp and more; Jela parting the killing mob around her; Jela's face, worried and relieved and cautious all at once, the first thing in her eyes when the 'kit opened up.

Jela, who had a mission and a reason to live his life as he did, and who had promised to take himself and his tree off at Gimlins, which was, damnitall, what she wanted.

Wasn't it?

Should've sold the man to the Uncle, and had done she told herself—and laughed. Selling Jela would have solved more than one problem, the way she figured it now.

So you owe him, she said to herself, but it was more than that. She'd *gotten used* to him; gotten used to his back up and his good sense. Worse, she'd gotten used to having him on her ship, in her daily routine. Gotten used to regular sleep shifts, and not running half-ragged. Hadn't touched a stick of Tempo in—

Well, she was going to miss him, that was all.

Nothing else but what you traded for.

Right.

Deliberately, she put her feet down on the cold decking, and pushed out of the chair.

Behind her, the door cycled.

She turned and considered him, the tight ship togs showing the shoulders to good advantage.

He paused just inside the door, his face open and a little unsure, hands quiet at his sides.

"Occurs to me," he said, quiet-like and as serious as she'd ever heard him. "That I put you off more than one course at Faldaiza. I'm no redhead, but I can try to make it up to you." He gave her a smile that was nigh heart-stopping in its genuine wryness. "If you're interested."

Well. Yes, as a matter of fact, she was interested.

So she smiled and walked toward him, knowing she was going to regret this, too, at Gimlins.

He tipped his head, the black eyes watching her with a certain warm appreciation. She felt her smile get wider and let it happen while she held out a hand.

He met it, his fingers warm, his palm calloused, his grip absurdly light for a man who could crush another man's fist.

"My cabin's bigger," she said softly, and they left the tower together.

THIRTY

Spiral Dance
Gimlins Approach

GIMLINS HUNG IN the second screen, where it had been for some time while Jela played with various comm-codes, his face slowly settling into an expression of grim patience, tension coming off of him in waves.

Cantra busied herself with the piloting side of things, pulling in such feeds as were available; checking her headings for the sixth time; and riding the scans harder than need be.

The tension from the co-pilot's side continued to build, to the point where the pilot started to itch. Sighing, she released the straps and stood.

"I'm fixing tea," she told the side of Jela's face. "Want?"

Not even a blink to show he'd heard her. His fingers moved on the comm-pad, paused—moved again.

Give it up, she thought at him. *Anybody who's hiding this hard can't be anything but trouble.*

"One more string," Jela said, his voice as distant as his profile. "Tea would be fine, thank you."

"Right."

She took herself off to the galley, put the tea on to brew and leaned against the cabinets, arms crossed over her chest, feeling something like grim herself.

"Cantra yos'Phelium," she said aloud, "you're a fool."

Worse than a fool, if she was going to start talking out straight to herself while there was still another pair of ears on-board to hear it.

She sighed heartily and closed her eyes.

The man's leaving at Gimlins, she told herself, counting it out by the numbers. *He's taking his tree and he's going; it's what he wants and if you had a brain in your head, which you don't, it's what you want. Yes, you owe him—he's done everything and more that a co-pilot should, to keep his pilot hale and steady. So pay him up even and set him down where he says. It's not like he can't take care of himself. And his damn' tree, too.*

The tea-maker squawked, startling her. Grousing, she pulled open the cabinet, unshipped mugs, poured, stuck a couple of high-cals into her sleeve as an afterthought and went back to the tower.

Jela was on his feet, expression now forcibly agreeable, tension still evident, but of a different quality.

Cantra raised an eyebrow, deliberately nonchalant.

"Contact," he said. "We go in."

"Great," she answered, like she meant it, and showed a smile as she handed him a mug.

HE DRESSED IN trade leathers, rolled up his kit and stood for a moment staring down at it: a moderate pack, the tough coderoy scarred and travel-worn. Not the sort of thing a trader would be carrying on his back to a business meeting.

It would have to stay.

Sighing lightly, he bent, rummaged briefly, pulled out the log book and slid it into an inside vest pocket, straightened the pack and lashed it to the wall. Nothing there that couldn't be replaced, and it could be that Cantra would find use for some bits. After all, it wasn't the first time he'd had to abandon what was his in the course of obeying orders. And it wouldn't be the last.

Not quite the last.

The tree, too, was going to have to stay, and take its chances with whatever care Cantra could give it. He'd tried to express this, and his reasons, though he couldn't tell if he'd actually gotten through. He hoped he had and that the tree understood—though it couldn't make any difference if it didn't.

The voice on the comm had been furtive and something less than knowledgeable, though they'd had the pass-codes ready enough. And while that wasn't conclusive, it was better than no answer at all. His guess was that the voice on the comm was a local who had been paid to keep an ear on the old feed, with no expectation that a call would ever come in. The only thing he could reasonably expect was to be passed up the line as quickly as the contact could manage.

He closed his eyes, trying to feel out the tree, but all he found in the back recesses of his skull was a cool and distant greenness.

Right, then.

It was time to take his leave of the pilot—a thought not as comforting as it could be.

She'd stood at his back, and tolerated his infringement of her life without either shooting him or selling him; she'd been more than generous in bed, and he was going to miss her—vile temper, sarcasm, and all.

Well.

He straightened his vest once more, needlessly, and settled his belt 'round his waist, making certain his *shib* was in place and drew easily. The flexible ceramic cutting edge felt cool against his fingers, and he smiled. All in order.

Then he went out to the tower to take leave of his pilot.

"WITH ME?" Cantra repeated, with a glance over her shoulder at the tree sitting calm in its pot. "I thought you two were partners."

"We are," Jela answered, trying to sound like there was agreement on all sides. "But it's time to split up. I can't take it with me to the meeting and—" He stopped because she had raised her hand, palm out toward his nose.

"You risked your life—and mine, too—getting that tree off Faldaiza; you took it with you when I set you down at Taliofi. It guarded your back while we was visiting with the Uncle, and now you're leaving it with me?" She shot another glance over her shoulder.

"Why?"

A fair question, and trust Cantra to ask it. He moved his shoulders, easing out some of the tension.

"The contact I've got—is deep. Likely the only thing they'll be able to do is pass me up-line. I'll have to go quick and I'll have to go light." He sent a look to the tree himself, absurdly pleased to see how tall and how full it was now.

Looking back to Cantra, he saw her eyeing his vest.

"No 'skins?" she said, and held up her hand again. "I know they ain't proof against all evil, but they're something better than trade leather."

"I don't want to draw attention to myself," he said. "The meet's up in the city, and I don't want to compromise my contact."

Cantra closed her eyes and took a deep breath.

"Jela," she said, flat calm, which meant he was in for a tongue-lashing.

"Pilot?"

She opened her eyes and glared at him.

"This smells bad to me. Say it smells sweet to you."

Truth told, his nose for trouble detected a decided odor about the business, too. On the other hand, he wasn't getting any younger, and none of the usuals—none—had answered.

"They had the right codes," he said mildly, into Cantra's glare.

She sighed. "Would Pilot Muran of late lamented memory have had those same codes?"

The woman had a wonderful mind for a detail, Jela thought and stifled his own sigh.

"Yes," he said, keeping in calm and friendly. "Muran would have had the same codes. And if they are using Muran's codes, then—I need to know that, too. My orders are clear."

"And this time you feel like following them."

There wasn't any real answer to that, so he just stood there, bearing her scrutiny, until she sighed again and lifted a hand to push her hair back from her eyes.

"You don't," she said, softly, "need to be this desperate to leave on my account. If there's a less chancy place to look for news of folk gone missing, *Dancer's* good for the trip."

Of the things he might have expected to hear her say, an offer of continued passage was last. The brain in his fingers, quicker than the one in his head, came up with a reply first.

Condition is?

She glanced aside and if he hadn't known her, he'd had judged her to be embarrassed.

"I don't have anything on the screens that can't wait," she said huskily.

The offer warmed him, but nothing could be said about his next-best-hope but that it was riskier still.

He smiled, to let her know he appreciated the offer, and flipped his hand, palm up, palm down.

"I've got to try here," he said.

Green eyes considered him. "Got to, is it?"

"Yes."

"All right, then," she said briskly. "I'm coming with you."

He blinked. "Cantra—"

"You can be *sure* that the pilot of this ship ain't taking her orders from the co-pilot, current *or* former," she interrupted. "You can wait for me to get dressed up all pretty like a trader, or you can leave now. If you leave, I'll follow you, which might could be awkward for you. If you wait, I'll cover your back and follow your lead."

She was serious.

"The ship," he said, playing the one argument that was sure to sway her. "The ship would be at risk, with her pilot on the port and maybe headed for rough ground."

She smiled, which was bad.

"Ship's safety comes under the pilot's care," she said, voice serious. "And the pilot judges the risk to the ship is acceptable."

He had, thought Jela, done Cantra yos'Phelium a disservice. She could step outside of the boundaries she'd made for herself and take a decision that risked her and her ship, if needed.

Damn everything, that she thought it was needed now.

"I once let my pilot go outta here to a meet maybe a little less hazardous than the one you're on course for," Cantra said, her voice still carrying that note of complete seriousness. "Wasn't much choice about it—she was my pilot and she made it an order. And she come back on-ship in a body-bag."

She gave him another straight-on glare. "I don't expect to let my co-pilot walk out into clear and present danger without back-up," she said. "*Damn* if I will, Jela. You hear it?"

He heard it. It might have been that he heard more of it than she wanted him to hear. Or she might have intended it all.

In either case, he was running out of time to argue, and he didn't doubt she'd make good on her threat.

So.

"All right," he said. "I'll be grateful for the back-up, Pilot."

THE MEETING PLACE was away up in the city, beyond yard and port—which was yet another thing not to love about it, in Cantra's opinion.

Jela'd flagged down a robocab at the port, directing it to a point somewhat to the east and north of the final destination, according to the city map she'd hastily memorized. From there, they walked, two traders taking in the sights, of which there were a few.

As a general rule, Cantra avoided cities. Garen had never gone beyond the port proper, contending there was more than enough trouble to be found right there—and mostly she was right.

The last time Cantra was inside a city had been during the course of a training run, about a half-year before Pliny put paid to them all. That city had been vertical, rising bone pale and fragile out of the depths of a tumultuous planetary sea. Cylayn, that city had been named, and it was a triumph of bio-engineering. The fragile-seeming and extremely tough shell in which the city was housed had been spun by sea creatures designed for that single monumental task, who then died, dried and blew away on the constant winds, precisely on schedule, leaving behind a marvelous habitat for the imported human population.

It had also been a marvel of security regulations and law, the habitat being, in its way, as risky as any space station, and it had been lessons in circumventing those safeguards of the common good that had occupied Cantra's time there.

This city, now—this Pluad—was level, its streets laid out in a grid—north-south, east-west—dusty, and heavier than she liked. Then there was the noise, and the smells, and the sheer press of people.

She was watching for anything from armed ambush to pick-pockets, so it was the people took most of her attention. They weren't on a Closed World, or even close Inside, so there was a spacer's dozen of types on the street—long, short, thick, thin; pale, dark, and in-between.

Her own type, with the high-caste golden skin and the slim, deceptively frail-seeming build, was nothing to notice in this, or almost any, crowd.

Jela made a little bit of stir, but if she was to judge from various interested glances, the reasons would be the shoulders and the hips.

The clothes were as varied as the people wearing them—gowns with sleeves so long they trailed on the dusty walkway, daysilks and sandals, Insider formals, a couple of spacer 'skins, trader leathers, and the inevitable tunics, sleeveless so the Batcher tats showed.

Jela turned into a wide space in the walk and stopped. She swung in beside him. Overhead, suspended from a thin silvered arc, hung an inverted ceramic bowl. As they came to rest beneath, its color changed from pale yellow to bright red.

"'nother cab?" she asked, which was the first thing either had said to the other since leaving the ship.

He glanced at her. "Are we being followed?"

She sighed lightly. "Not that I've noticed."

"Right. So we'll go further in and then take another walk." He looked around at the wide crowded walk and busy street, the low, featureless pastel buildings shining in the full light of the local sun.

"Nice city."

"If you say so," she answered, as a flutter caught the edge of her eye and she turned to look up the walkway.

The next building up was a domed affair, pale pink, with a striped yellow-and-blue awning over the door. Coming out of the door were a dozen or more people in long, cowled robes striped to match the awning, bearing pale pink baskets. As they reached the common walkway, they separated into pairs, each pair taking off at a tangent. The pair walking toward their position on the taxi stand were pressing something from their baskets into the hands of those they passed, with a murmured phrase she couldn't quite pick out at this distance in the general city din.

Cantra moved her eyes, checking the moving people and assuring herself that they still weren't being followed. Near as she could tell, which wasn't as near as she'd like.

"Here comes our cab," Jela said from beside her.

She turned face forward, spying the thing as it cut across four lanes of traffic, not much more than a bench seat mounted behind the hump of a nav-brain, enclosed in plas-shielding, the whole vehicle scooting along on three wheels.

She took a step forward, felt someone too close to her right shoulder and spun, nearly knocking over one of the striped-robes—she had an impression of pale eyes, and a glint of teeth in the dimness of the cowl, and something cool pressed into her hand.

"Die well, sister," the soft voice murmured and they were gone, the cab was arrived, and Jela was already on the seat, the door coming down, the shielding already starting to opaque—

"Cantra!"

She jumped, ducked under the descending door and fell heavily onto the bench, banging into Jela's shoulder.

"Sorry," she muttered.

"No problem," he answered, most of his attention on the map panel. He jerked his head toward the sealed door.

"What was that about?"

"Couple of crazies, giving me a—" She opened her hand, and blinked down at the plain square tile in her hand.

"Looks like one of the toys I took to the Uncle," she said.

Destination chosen and accepted, the cab accelerated. Cantra breathed a small sigh of relief for the now completely opaqued dome as Jela sat back and held out a broad hand.

"Mind if I take a look?"

She dropped it in his palm. "It's all yours."

His fingers closed over the tile and he sat with his eyes slitted for one heartbeat, two, three—

He hissed, fingers flying wide. The tile fell to the deck of the cab.

Cantra threw him a look, seeing true anger on his face.

"Not impressed, I take it," she said, and he pointed at the fallen tile.

"Did you listen to what it was saying?"

"Didn't say anything to me," she answered, "but I'd only had it a couple seconds and I was occupied with something else, besides."

"Try it," he said.

"If it's got you this riled, I think I'll pass. Whyn't you just tell me about it?"

He took a hard breath, and then another as their cab leaned sharply to one side, obviously taking a corner at speed. Cantra banged into Jela's shoulder again, grabbed for the strap and pulled herself right.

"It asked me to embrace the sacrament of suicide," Jela said, stringently calm. "It told me to pause to remember those I love, to have compassion and include them in my death."

"Oh." Cantra looked down at the decking, but the tile was out of sight, having doubtless slid away under the bench during the last hard turn.

"*Sheriekas*-work, you're thinking," she didn't-ask.

"What else?" he answered, and turned his attention to the map, and the rapid green line that was the graphic of their journey across the city.

He tapped the display with a broad forefinger and she bent to look.

"We'll be getting off in another couple turns—" A grin, though not up to his usual standards— "if we survive the trip. We'll walk into the meet place from above, check it out before we go in, right?"

Relieved that he was being sensible, she gave him a smile, though she had the feeling it wasn't one of her better efforts, either.

"Right."

SO FAR, the timing was good. They were within a block of the meeting place—a shop called Business as Usual, which rented guaranteed secure meeting rooms by the local quarter-hour.

His plan was to reconnoiter, then take up a position and watch the front door. He figured he'd be able to spot his contact well enough, and take a reading before committing.

If it read bad, he had promised himself, or even a little over-risky, he'd back off, retreat to the ship and regroup.

Having Cantra with him complicated things, but she *was* fully capable, as she'd demonstrated numerous times, now.

Besides which, he was just glad to have her with him.

A soldier, even a thorough rogue of a Generalist, was a pack creature, accustomed to having his comrades about him. It warmed him now to have a comrade at his back, with action maybe looming.

The streets on this side of the city were thinner and less peopled, the buildings tending to monochrome-colored blocks, rather than the rounded pastels on the northeast side.

Cantra was walking on his off-side, a long step behind. Out of the corner of his eye, he watched her scanning the street, the buildings, the people.

Fully capable woman, he thought again, and there was the worry again, because time was getting tight. If he didn't make a good contact today, it might come down to leaving the tree and his mission, both, in the fully capable hands of a woman who had for so long cared only for herself and her ship that she might not be able to make the leap to a larger duty.

Leave it alone, he told himself. *Mission first. Worry later.*

"Coming up," he said, pitching his voice so Cantra could hear him, but likely no others. "We want to take the right turn, go down 'til the second right and take that. That'll—"

"Put us on the service alley," she finished, with more of a laugh than a snap in her voice. "I did take a look at that map, like I said I would."

He glanced over and met her foggy green gaze.

"I thought you weren't worried," she said.

He shrugged. "Having a civilian in it worries old habits," he said, surprising himself with the truth.

"Let's think of this as the pilot backing the co-pilot," she answered. "That ease old habits, any?"

"It does," he said, keeping with the mostly truth. "It's good to have a comrade at hand."

"Strangely easeful," she allowed. "This our turn?"

It was and they took it, passing out of full sunlight and into dense shade. Jela motioned and Cantra stretched those long legs to come up shoulder-to-shoulder.

"If there's any trouble—and I don't expect it—what you want to do is get out of it and call for back-up," he said and gave her as hard a look as he had in him.

Her face showed bland and pleasant—not a good sign.

"Cantra?"

"My idea," she husked, and her voice did fall sweet on a soldier's ear, "was to stand as your back-up. That's why I'm here."

"There's a time when you've got to cut your losses, retreat and regroup," he said, in the easy voice he'd used to coach countless newbies. "If it starts to look bad, remember that I'm built to take a lot of punishment with minimal damage, and get clear of it."

"I'll do that," Cantra said insincerely.

He sighed—and gave it up as a lost battle.

"Next turn upcoming," she said, and shot him a grin. "Might have some trouble getting those shoulders in there."

The alley was thin, but not that thin. It was even dimmer than the shaded street, and crowded with all the unglamourous bits of business—trash compactors, delivery crates, wagons and storage sheds.

Cantra slipped 'round the corner, hugging the wall, and paused in the shadow of a recycling bin.

326 Sharon Lee & Steve Miller

Jela slid in beside her, arm touching arm.

"Our target," he murmured, scanning what he could see of the clutter, "is in the middle of the left side of this alley. Which," he added as he felt her draw a slightly deeper breath, "I know you know. I'm just checking to see if our info agrees."

He heard the ghost of a chuckle.

"It agrees."

"Good. I'll go first. You cover me."

No argument there—which didn't surprise him. As good as her word, Cantra yos'Phelium. She'd volunteered to be his back-up—back-up is what she'd be.

So, he eased out from cover of the recycler and moved on down the alley, keeping to what cover was convenient, scanning the likely places and the unlikely ones, too, going soft-foot and unhurried.

Which was how he managed to come on them unaware.

Four of them—soldiers all—checking their weapons and settling into quiet positions, not deep concealment, from which he deduced that they were waiting for a sign from inside.

He hesitated, weighing the odds and the need for info—and the fact that there was a fully capable civilian—a pilot!—giving him back-up, which tipped the balance to retreat.

Soft and careful, he sank back into the shadows, turned, slipped around his cover—

And ducked back as three more came walking down the alley toward him.

JELA SLIPPED AROUND the edge of the equipment and disappeared into the general clutter.

Cantra counted to twelve, then eased forward, gun in hand, sinking down onto a knee in a relatively dry bit of cermacrete. Cheek against the side of the recycler, she peered out—and bit off a curse.

Three people, two of the taller new-style soldiers Jela was so impressed with and one probable natural human, some fair bit shorter than the others. The natural was wearing a uniform with enough shiny stuff on the sleeves to make Cantra blink. Women that important were hard to find.

They were armed, but not at ready, and they were heading straight for Jela.

"You wanted to do back-up," she muttered to herself, and went after them, keeping tight against the side of a storage shed. Not that it mattered. From the way they walked, the three soldiers thought they owned this alley and everything in it.

Swaggering, three abreast and looking neither to the right nor the left, they passed a tall stack of delivery crates.

Which promptly fell on them. Cantra caught a glimpse of trade leather among the back shadows and grinned even as she dropped to her knees, gun up, sighting on the nearer of the two big soldiers, who'd managed to keep his feet, despite the crate wedged over his head.

The other two were roaring and flailing on the alley floor—and suddenly the second big one was up, throwing a crate with forceful malice and going for his side arm.

The one on the ground had used her eyes, though, worse luck.

"That's him! Take him out!"

Cantra changed targets, and squeezed off a shot at the one with his pistol already out.

She'd gone for a back shot—something to slow him down—and for a second she thought she'd missed entirely.

Then the soldier slapped his right hand to his upper left arm, and spun, staggering as the crates shifted around his legs.

"Gun at the rear!"

Great.

She got her feet under her, snapped off a shot at the second big guy and angled across the alley, keeping low.

A plentitude of shots, now, more than she thought could be produced by three disoriented soldiers.

The map she had memorized had the alley intersecting with another side street several hundred paces beyond the current action, so Jela had an out—may have already taken it, for all she could figure from the noise and the movement. Her immediate problem was the three soldiers, all on their feet now and just as irritable as they could be.

"There!"

The not-so-tall soldier flung forward, gun out, face grim.

Cantra brought her weapon up and fired.

The charge hit the leaping woman in the chest, knocked her off her feet and back into the tumble of crates.

Cantra sprinted for cover—

There was a roar behind her, she spun, dodged the big fist descending toward her head, tucked and dove for the floor between his feet, coming up behind him, facing the confusion of downed crates—and the other big soldier, who had his gun out now, and aimed at her.

She fired at his face, missed, and threw herself backward into a somersault between the first soldier's legs.

Close by, there was a shot; she snapped to her feet, spun—

The first soldier was down, his right leg under him at a bad angle and bleeding copiously. The soldier with the gun moved it, sighting beyond his downed comrade.

Cantra took her time, sighted and fired.

The charge took him in the throat. He fell noisily into the crates, his weapon discharging harmlessly into the air.

Slowly, Cantra straightened. The alley was eerily quiet. Right, then. Jela had taken the back way out and—

A shout, the voice too familiar, and the sound of more boxes falling with energy.

Swearing, Cantra moved forward, picking her way across the downed crates with care.

JELA'D GOT HIMSELF into a bit of a conundrum. He taken up position in a relatively clear spot in the alley, the sides formed by the privacy fence at his back, a storage shed to the right and a heavy-duty conveyer to the left. There was room to maneuver, but not much opportunity to bring firearms into play.

One of the big soldiers was down already—an added hazard to footing already made risky by the tumble of crates. Three more soldiers were trying to get a grip on the man who kept moving, dodging, feinting, a knife in each hand.

Cantra slid into the shadow of a lorry and considered the action.

Watching, it came to her that the big soldiers were operating under a handicap. They seemed to be trying to capture, while Jela was basically pursuing kill-and-maim.

Right.

She brought her gun up, checked the charge, and considered her options.

She'd about settled on the back of the guy nearest her position, when a shadow moved across her vision and she looked up, frowning . . .

Atop the storage shed was another soldier, stretched long and secret across the flat roof, a rifle against his shoulder.

So much for the capture idea. Jela's playmates had just been keeping him busy until the rifleman got into position.

It was a risky shot with a hand gun. Though even if she missed, her shot would serve as a warning.

For whatever that was worth.

At alley level, Jela's three opponents suddenly let out simultaneous roars and rushed him.

On the roof, the rifleman took his sighting.

Cantra brought her gun up, acquired her target—fired.

The secret shooter jerked, the rifle releasing its round into the blameless conveyer.

In the alley, the fight was a confusion of movement and shape. She glimpsed Jela, dancing like a lunatic, one knife gone, the sleeve of his pretty trader's shirt hanging in bloody ribbons.

There was no possibility of a clear shot, and no doubt but that things were going bad for her co-pilot, built to take punishment or not.

The time had come to take a more personal interest.

Gun in one hand, knife in the other, howling, Cantra charged.

A soldier looked up at her noisy approach, an expression of stark disbelief on his tattooed face, and a battle knife roughly as long as she was in his hand.

Leaving Jela to his mates, he swung to face her, grinning.

Fine.

She stretched her legs, bent nearly double, aiming to get *inside* that long reach, where she could do some damage and his absurdly long blade would be a handicap.

He grabbed for her, she dodged, saw the blade, flung an arm up.

The gun deflected the thrust, and flew out of her hand. Her arm fell, numb, to her side, but she was inside now—inside his guard, and she jumped, using the momentum to drive the knife up between the rib—

Her legs were in a vise; she was upside down, the knife lost, and she was spinning, her hair whipping across her eyes. She knew with utter clarity that in another frenzied heartbeat her brains would be running down the side of the shed—

The spinning stopped.

Her legs were released and she fell, remembering at the last instant to get her arms out and break the fall.

She was panting. There was no other sound in the alley— wrong. A groan.

She rolled to her feet, turned, saw her late opponent standing as if frozen, his eyes fixed on something . . . else.

Across the alley, Jela's two admirers were likewise frozen in mid-combat, and Jela himself was climbing warily, and none-too-steadily, to his feet.

"Both of you!" snapped a high, feminine voice. "Come here! Quickly!"

Slowly, Cantra turned, squinted—and there at the edge of the conveyer unit stood a lady in the grey robes of a philosopher, her red hair blazing in the murk like a torch.

"Well." That was Jela arriving at her side. He began a bow, bloody hand outstretched, staggered—Cantra grabbed his arm and yanked him upright.

"Thank you, ma'am," he said hoarsely to the lady.

"You're quite welcome," she replied coolly. "Attend me, now. At the far end of this alley you will find a red-haired man holding a cab for you. Go with him. I'll finish dealing here."

Cantra glanced at the three huge, frozen figures, thought about the dart gun in her inside pocket—

"Do *not* kill them," the lady snapped. "Just *go!*"

"Go it is," Jela said placatingly.

He turned in the indicated direction, feet tangling, and Cantra got a supporting arm around him.

"Take it easy," she said.

"No time," he muttered. "I'll be ready in a few—your board, Pilot."

She set a steady, if not precisely brisk, pace, half-holding Jela up—no small weight, that, despite his size. He kept the pace, though he seemed not exactly connected, which got her worrying about how much blood he'd already lost and what she'd do if he went down.

Worry and stagger aside, they made the end of the alley without disaster, and he seemed a little more alert by the time she pushed him up against a wall and had a long look out into the street.

All clear on the straight, and on the right, to the left—

Stood a slender man in formal black tunic and pants, one elegantly slippered foot braced on the floor of an open cab. He was holding a watch in his hand, and smiling at her.

"I see that all proceeds according to plan," he said merrily, and stepped away from the cab, sweeping a flawless bow of welcome. "Please. Your carriage awaits you, Pilots."

She glanced at her co-pilot, saw his eyes full open in a face paler than she liked.

"Well?" she asked.

He sighed and appeared to do some quick math.

"Not well," he growled after a heartbeat. "But I think we'd better take the kind ser's offer."

"All right, then." She eased back and he stood away from the wall, moving with something like his accustomed certainty.

Good enough.

She strolled out to the cab, and bowed to the red-haired man.

"My co-pilot and I are grateful," she murmured, and stood back to let Jela get in first, then went after him.

Behind her, the door began to descend. The red-haired man ducked inside, slipping onto the half-bench facing them, his back to the forward screens.

"Pilots," he murmured, as the cab hurtled into motion. "I beg you acquit me of poor manners, if I am short of conversation this next while. I am called to aid my lady. There is a field kit under your seat." He closed his eyes and settled his back against the opaque plas shielding.

Cantra blinked and rummaged under the bench, locating the field kit and pulling it onto her lap.

"Do you know who these people are?" she asked, as she sorted out dressings and lotions.

"No," Jela said tiredly, holding his arm out so she could get at the worst of the blood. "I don't know who they are, but I know what they are."

"What's that, then?" Cantra asked, breaking out an antiseptic swab.

"They're *sheriekas*."

THIRTY-ONE

On Port Gimlins

THE ARM WAS PATCHED as good as she could make it, which wasn't near as good as it needed.

She said as much to Jela, now apparently recovered from the woozies, but he only shrugged and asked her to cut off the remains of the bloody sleeve.

That done, the kit repacked and returned to its spot beneath the seat, she joined him in staring at the cab's on-board map.

"Don't seem to be working," she said after a moment, and heard him sigh.

"That it doesn't."

She considered their rescuer, slumped, to all appearances unconscious, on the jump-seat.

He was a pretty little man, his bright red hair artfully cut and arranged in loose ringlets. He wore it long and carelessly caught over one shoulder with a twist of jeweled wire. The tunic's long sleeves were cross-laced with black ribbons, and the elegant slippers were heavily embroidered with black silk.

He looked, Cantra thought, like a high-caste member of a High

House on one of the Inmost worlds—a supposition borne out by his accent, bearing, and bow. His face was a shade too pale for proper high-caste, but she thought that might be an effect of whatever induced state he was presently in. Awake, she thought he'd be as golden-skinned as any pure-blood or deliberate copy.

"You're sure this guy is *sheriekas*?" she asked Jela.

"Yes," he answered shortly, his attention still on the non-functional map.

"Hm," she said, eyeing him. "How're you doing mostwise?"

He looked up from the map, black eyes speculative.

"I'm up for some action, if you are."

"Fine," Cantra said firmly. "Then there's no reason to stick around until the ser finishes his nap."

She reached into her vest, slipped a length of smartwire from the inside pocket, and shifted around on the bench to face the hatch.

"Get ready to jump," she said over her shoulder. "The door likely won't go up all the way, and it might be something of a tumble, but we should be out of here—"

The red-haired man on the jump-seat took a sudden deep breath, straightened, and opened his eyes. They were, Cantra saw, a deep and vivid blue, initially focused on something on the far side of the next sector, sharpening quickly on matters closer to hand.

"That's done then," he murmured, and his voice was light and cultured. He sent a glance to Jela.

"Indeed, sir," he said, as if they had been engaged in cordial conversation. "It is my very great pleasure to correct you. Neither I nor my lady are *sheriekas*."

Jela snorted. "Tell me you've never destroyed a star system."

The little man smiled with gentle reproach. "But I am not such a fool, dear sir. Of course I have destroyed star systems. I hope you won't think me boastful if I admit to being uniquely equipped for such work. Much as you, yourself, are uniquely equipped for fighting. Will you tell me, M. Jela, whose mandate is to protect life, that you have never killed?"

Jela smiled—one of his real ones, Cantra saw.

"No," he said softly. "I'm not such a fool."

The little man inclined his head, acknowledging the point. "Well answered, sir. We stand on terms." He turned his eyes to Cantra.

"Lady," he murmured. She held up a hand.

"Hate to disappoint you," she said, watching his eyes, "but I'm no lady, just a Rimmer pilot."

A flicker of amusement showed in the eyes, nothing else.

"Lady," he repeated, courteously. "Please allow me to be at your feet—your most humble and willing servant in all things. Your well-being is more important to me than my life. There is no need to resort to such things as pick-locks while you are in my care."

She considered him, admiring the way he blended irony with sincerity. Whoever had the training of this one had drilled him well.

Unless of course he was the genuine article, in which case she wasn't wholly certain that she wouldn't rather have fallen into the so-called care of Jela's *sheriekas*.

"If my well-being means so much to you," she said, bringing the Rim accent up so hard it rang against the ear. "Open the door and let us out."

"In time," he said, lifting a slim forefinger. A ring covered the finger from knuckle to first joint—an oval black stone in a black setting, carved with—

"In time," their host-or-captor said again. "I would be careless indeed of your well-being, not to say that of the most excellent Jela, if I released you now, with enemies on the watch and information yet to be shared."

She sighed, and slipped the smartwire back into the inside pocket. "You got a name?"

He inclined his head. "Indeed, Lady, I have a name. It is Rool Tiazan."

"And you can blow up star systems," she pursued, since Jela wasn't saying anything.

"I can destroy star systems," Rool Tiazan corrected gently. "Yes."

"Right—destroy," she said, amiably. "And you ain't *sheriekas*."

"Also correct."

"If you're not *sheriekas*," Jela said, finally joining the fun, "what are you?"

"Excellent." He placed one elegant hand flat against his chest. "I, my lady, and all those like unto us, are *sheriekas*-made, M. Jela. We were created on purpose that we should do their bidding and hasten the day when eternity belongs only to *sheriekas*; the lesser-born and the flawed merely distasteful memories to be forgot as quickly as might be."

"If you're *sheriekas*-made, in order to do the bidding of your makers—" Jela began and Rool Tiazan held up his hand, the carved black stone glinting.

"Forgive me, M. Jela," he murmured, and his pretty, ageless face was no longer smiling. "You—and also you, Lady—are surely aware that choice exists. We no longer choose to perform these certain tasks on behalf of those who caused us to be as we are. We are alive, and life is sweet. There is no place nor plan for us in the eternity toward which we were bade to labor."

He moved his hand in a snap, as if throwing dice across a cosmic cloth.

"We of the *dramliz* cast our lot in with those who are also alive, and who find life sweet."

"That's a fine-sounding statement," Jela said calmly, "and you deliver it well. But I don't believe it."

"Alas." Rool Tiazan tipped his head to one side. "I sympathize with your wariness, M. Jela—indeed, I applaud it. However, I would ask you to consider these things—that my lady and I have preserved your lives, and now assist you to evade those who wish you ill."

Jela held out his hand, palm up. "The first is probably true," he said, and turned his palm down. "For the second, we have only your word, which I'm afraid is insufficient."

"You do not trust me, in a word," Rool Tiazan murmured. "May I know why?"

"You do," Jela said, mildly, "destroy star systems, as and when ordered by the *sheriekas*."

"The correct verb is 'did.' I have absented myself from the

work for some number of years. However, I understand you to say that there is no ground upon which we might meet in trust because I have done terrible things during the course of my training and my duty. Do I have this correctly, M. Jela? I would not wish to misunderstand you."

"You have it correctly," Jela said.

"Ah." He turned his head, and Cantra felt the dark blue gaze hit her like a blow.

"Lady—a question, if you will."

She held up a hand. "Why bother? Can't you just grab what you want out of my mind?"

He smiled—genuinely amused, as far as she could read him.

"Legend proceeds us, I see. Unfortunately, legend is both accurate and misleading. Under certain conditions, I can indeed siphon information from the minds of others. It is not difficult, it does no harm to those so read, and may provide some good for myself and my lady. However." He raised his jeweled forefinger.

"However, there are some individuals whom it is very difficult to read—yourself, for an instance, and M. Jela for another. And even if I could siphon the answer out of your mind, M. Jela cannot, and it is for him that I would ask the question."

He was good, Cantra thought. And she was intrigued.

"Ask."

"You are, I believe, full-trained as an *aelantaza*, to deceive and destroy at the word of those who caused you to be as you are. I would ask if, in the course of those exercises necessary for you to gain competence in your art, you ever took a blameless life."

"For Jela, is this?" She faced her co-pilot. "We had—rabbits, they were called. We practiced all our kills on live targets."

"Rabbits that ran on two feet," Rool Tiazan murmured.

"Batch-bred?" Jela asked.

She inclined her head. "What else?"

There was a short silence, then Rool Tiazan spoke again.

"M. Jela, do you trust this lady, whose training and acts run parallel to my own?"

"I do. She's proved herself trustworthy."

Accidents all, but it warmed her to hear him say it, anyway, praise from Jela being coin worth having—and keeping, if she was being honest.

"Ah," Rool Tiazan murmured. "Then I see I shall need to continue upon my path of candidness. So—"

He gestured gracefully toward the roof of the cab—or perhaps beyond it.

"While it is true that I have destroyed star systems, I must confess that those which fell to my thought were chaotic and incapable of supporting life. The more life-force—shall we call it *will*?" He paused, apparently awaiting their agreement.

"All right," Jela said, with a shrug of wide shoulders.

"Will, then. The more will that exists within a system, the more difficult it is to bend the lines of probability into a conformation in which the extinction of the system is inevitable.

"Similarly, though I may alter probability on a less epic scale, the subsequent ripple of unanticipated changes make the practice somewhat less than perfectly useful."

Cantra raised an eyebrow. "You're trying to say that the *sheriekas* made a design error and that you're really not worth their trouble?"

"Not entirely, Lady. Not entirely. There is, after all, some benefit to be had from the mere reading of the lines, and by observing the congruencies of various energies. Indeed, observation of an anomaly in the forces of what we shall, I fear, have to call 'luck' is what brought my lady and I here to pleasant Gimlins."

"Just in time to save our necks," Jela commented. "I'd call that lucky—or planned."

"You misunderstand me, M. Jela. It is neither I nor my lady who are lucky. It is you—" the slim, be-ringed forefinger pointed for a moment at Jela's chest, then swung toward Cantra—

"And most especially *you*, Lady—about whom the luck swirls and gathers."

"Lucky!" Cantra laughed.

Rool Tiazan smiled sweetly. "Doubt it not. Between the two of you, the luck moves so swiftly that the effect—to those such as my lady and myself—is nothing short of gravitational. We were pulled quite off of our intended course."

"I'd be interested to hear how you'd rectify our being lucky with coming within two heartbeats of getting killed back there," Cantra said.

"The luck is a natural force, Lady Cantra. It is neither positive nor negative; it obeys the laws binding its existence and cares not how its courses alter the lives through which it flows."

"So you—and your lady—" Jela said slowly, "were pulled here against your will."

"Ah." Rool Tiazan moved his hand as if he would hand Jela a coin. "Not quite against *our* wills, M. Jela. The *dramliz* have long been aware that if we are to win free to life, we will require allies. We have further understood, through an intense study of probability and possibility, that the best allies life has against the *sheriekas* is random action. It is *our will* to take part in the chaos resulting from your necessities, from your . . ."

"Luck, in a word," said Jela.

Rool Tiazan inclined his head. "Precisely."

"And you think, do you and your comrades," pursued Jela, "that the *sheriekas* can be defeated."

The little man gazed at him reproachfully.

"No, M. Jela. The *dramliz* have come to the conclusion—as you have—that the *sheriekas* may not be defeated."

"Then what use are allies?"

Rool Tiazan smiled.

"Because, though the *sheriekas* may not be defeated, they can be resisted, they may be confounded, they might be *escaped*," he said softly. "Life may go on, and the *sheriekas* may have their eternity, each separate from the other."

"Escaped how?" Cantra asked, and the blue gaze again grazed her face.

"There are several possibilities, Lady, of which we most certainly must speak. I would ask, however, that we put the discussion of how and may be into the near future, when my lady may also take part." He paused, his head inclined courteously.

"Whatever," she said, deliberately discourteous, but he merely smiled as if she'd given him proper word and mode, and turned his attention back to Jela.

"Regarding your mission, M. Jela. You are aware that the consolidated commanders are effectively defeated, are you not? They have been routed in most of their bases, and are hunted—with more fervor than the proper enemy! Or do you believe the late contretemps in the alley a mere coincidence?"

Beside her, Jela seemed to loose some breadth of shoulder. He sighed.

"I had hopes that my commander . . ." he murmured, and let the words trail away into nothing.

Rool Tiazan lifted his head, pointing his eyes toward—*beyond*, Cantra thought—the roof of the cab.

"Your commander is at liberty," he said, in a distant voice. "She has eluded those the High Command sent against her, and commands a small force of specialists. Their apparent course is for the Out-Rim, vectoring the area of increased *sheriekas* attacks." He blinked and lowered his gaze to Jela's face.

"I do not find a probability or a possibility, not a likelihood at all, in which she survives beyond the turning of the Common Year."

Thirty Common Days, as Cantra did the math.

"If it does not offend," Rool Tiazan said quietly, "my lady and I offer our condolences, M. Jela."

Silence. Jela's eyes were closed. He took a breath—another. Sighed and opened his eyes.

"I thank you and your lady," he said softly and with no irony that Cantra could detect. "My commander would wish to die in battle, doing proper duty."

"So she shall," the *dramliza* assured him. "That she extends the fight acts to disguise event wonderfully. Your commanders may lose, but *your* mission . . . continues."

Another small moment of silence passed before Jela straightened, visibly throwing off grief.

"Where are you taking us?" he asked Rool Tiazan.

"Ah. To your ship, where my lady will meet us."

"What?" Cantra demanded, but Jela only nodded.

"Good. I want another opinion of the two of you."

Rool Tiazan smiled. "We will be delighted to accommodate you, sir."

"IF YOU WILL EXCUSE ME once more, my attention is wanted elsewhere," the *dramliz* Rool Tiazan murmured.

He apparently took their permission for granted. No sooner had he spoken, then he was slumped on the jump-seat again, in a trance so deep he hardly seemed to breathe.

Jela took a moment to consider the extreme vulnerability of the man's situation, then shook the thought away. He *looked* vulnerable, did Rool Tiazan, but it would be beyond foolish to assume that he allowed himself to be at the mercy of his enemies.

Or of his allies.

Jela sighed to himself, and put thoughts of mayhem on hold, pending the tree's judgment.

He glanced over and saw Cantra watching him. Her fingers moved against her knee, flicking out—*Condition is*?

Now there was the question, he thought—wasn't it? Trust Cantra to ask it, and he'd better be accurate in his assessment, because only she knew what course she'd plot from the data.

Condition is, he signed slowly—*double usual rules*.

She gave a slight nod, indicating receipt of the message, and settled herself silently into her corner of the bench. Apparently neither one of them wanted to start a conversation that their host could retroactively snatch out of the air when he came to.

What thoughts might occupy Cantra, he didn't know, though he might guess it had to do with the prospect of allowing strangers possessed of peculiar talents onto her ship, and strategies for holding them harmless.

For himself—well, for the first time in his Generalist's life, he had too much to think about—and on subjects he'd rather not consider.

That the consolidated commanders had been discovered and

were in the process of being destroyed—he'd suspected the worst when his usual contacts had failed him.

The situation of his commander—if he believed the report of Rool Tiazan—and he had no reason, given his own direst fears, to doubt it . . .

The report that Commander Ro Gayda would soon be dead in action grieved him more than he could quite assimilate. He had lost comrades before—countless numbers of comrades—and commanding officers, as well. And yet this death, despite that he believed it to be one that she herself would embrace with a soldier's fierce joy—this death pained him in places so deep and private he hardly knew how to deal with it.

Had his arm been caught in a man-trap, he might have hacked it off and kept on fighting; had his ship been breeched, he might have rushed the enemy and with his last breath made the pain meaningful.

But this—there was no getting at the wound; no assessing the level of function disturbed . . .

A flicker out of the corner of his eye—Cantra's fingers, asking—

Condition is?

He sighed, and watched his fingers spell out—*Old soldier hit bad*, which might've been more truth than he would have willingly given, but a pilot learns to trust his fingers—and besides, it was too late to unsay it.

Cantra reached out and put her near hand on his knee, then leaned her head back against the bench. She didn't say anything else, or even look at him, really, but the pressure of her hand eased the tightness inside his chest. His commander might be dead, her unit destroyed, but he had his duty, his mission—and a comrade. It wasn't much—maybe, maybe. But when had a soldier needed more than his kit and his orders?

The cab was slowing. He glanced at the map before he recalled that it was off-line, then at the *dramliza*.

Rool Tiazan opened his eyes and straightened in his seat, the rich color returning to his face.

"We will be leaving the cab very shortly and joining my lady," he said in his smooth voice.

Jela felt Cantra's fingers tighten on his knee, but she unexpectedly held her peace, leaving him to ask—

"I thought we were returning to our ship?"

"Indeed we are, M. Jela. But not directly to your ship, I think? Four people walking across the yard may—no, I must say, *will be*—unremarked. We have not the same assurance of anonymity, riding at leisure in a cab." He paused, head tipped to one side.

"If your wounds pain you, sir, my lady will be pleased to assist you."

He meant the arm, and the various other scratches from the late action, Jela thought, to keep the hairs that wanted to rise up on the back of his neck where they belonged.

"Thank you for your concern," he said politely. "They are hardly noticeable; I've fought long days of battle with worse and not faltered."

"Surely, surely." The *dramliza* smiled and moved his slender hand, stroking the common air of the cab as if it were a live creature. "I meant no insult, sir. The prowess of the M Series is legend even among the *sheriekas*, whom we must thank for the original design."

The hairs did stand up then.

"Explain that," he said, and heard the snarl in his voice. Cantra's fingers, still resting on his knee, tightened briefly, then relaxed.

"Don't tease him," she told the *dramliza* in the lazy voice that meant mayhem wasn't too far distant. "He's had a trying day."

Rool Tiazan inclined his head in her direction, his face smooth and urbane.

"Lady. It was not my intention to tease, but to inform." He paused.

"The prototype of the M Series," he said, with, Jela thought, care, "was developed at the end of the last war by those who now call themselves *sheriekas*. The design was captured, modifications were made, and when the *sheriekas* returned to exercise their dominion over the Spiral Arm, the M Series was waiting to deny them the pleasure."

Jela grinned. "I hope they were surprised."

"By accounts, they were just that," said Rool Tiazan. "They had abandoned the design as flawed, you see." He smiled, as sudden and as feral as any soldier about to face an enemy.

"Over and over," he murmured, "they make the same error."

"The *dramliz* are flawed too, I take it," Cantra said, still in her lazy, could-be-trouble voice.

"The *dramliz*," Rool Tiazan said softly, "are multiply flawed, as the *sheriekas* had no wish to create those with abilities sufficient unto the task of destroying *sheriekas* without—appropriate safeguards."

A chime sounded inside the compartment, and the sense of motion ceased entirely.

"Ah! We are arrived!" Rool Tiazan moved a hand as the door began to lift.

"Please, after you, Lady and Sir."

THEY WERE ON A NARROW and sparsely populated street in the upper port. The show windows of the stores lining the blue cermacrete walkway were uniformly opaque, the sell-scents and light-banners quiet.

"Ah, excellent," Rool Tiazan murmured, as he stepped out of the cab. "Our timing holds." Behind him, the cab's door descended, the window darkened, and it sped off up the street.

"Come," the *dramliza* said, moving down the walk toward the cross-street "my lady awaits us."

They turned right at the corner, Rool Tiazan walking with something like a soldier's proper stride, for all he looked so fragile. The few people they passed spared them no glance, though surely the three of them were a sight worth—

Four of them, Jela corrected himself, catching the flutter of grey robes from the edge of his eye as a lady stepped from the doorway of a closed bookshop and fell in silently beside Rool Tiazan, placing her hand lightly on his arm.

The lady was—diminutive, a fact that had not been readily noticeable in the alley. The top of her cropped red head barely reached her mate's shoulder.

Her gray robe was embroidered in gray thread. Jela squinted after the design—and found himself looking instead at the shop windows, the traffic, and the few pedestrians they passed.

"Interesting robe," Cantra murmured from beside him. "I wouldn't look too close, though."

"I *can't* look too close," he complained, and heard her throaty chuckle.

They came to another street, turned right and were abruptly in day port, the walk busy with people, the banners and signs in full attraction mode, the street filled with cabs and lorries and cargo carriers.

And still no eyes turned their way, even in idle curiosity.

"Invisibility has its uses," Cantra muttered.

"But we are not invisible, Lady Cantra." Rool Tiazan's voice drifted lightly over his shoulder to them. "We are merely—of no interest."

They crossed the busy mainway carefully, and were soon among the ships. Jela felt Cantra growing tense beside him.

"Pilot?" He murmured.

She sighed. "This visit really necessary?"

"Yes," he told her regretfully. "Pilot, it is."

"Right."

Dancer was coming up on the next row and Cantra stretched her legs to come even with Rool Tiazan.

"I'm captain of yon ship," she said. "It's mine to go up first and open her."

"Of course," he said with an inclination of his bright head.

His lady lifted her hand from his arm and fell back beside Jela. He looked down into her sharp, solemn face.

"The configuration carries the suggestion," she said, answering the question he hadn't asked.

"So if we walked down the street four abreast, people would notice us?" he asked.

"Not necessarily," she replied. "But such a configuration might require Rool to somewhat exert his will, which might in turn catch the attention of those with whom we would rather not deal."

"The *sheriekas* are looking for you, then?"

The lady turned her head away. "What do you suppose, M. Jela?"

"That, if the *sheriekas* were hunting me, I'd think very hard about where I led them."

"We have thought—very hard," she returned, giving him a haughty look from amber eyes. "We and those who are like us. The consensus is that, while success is not assured, we must nonetheless act. It is true that we may fail and all the galaxy—indeed, all the galaxies!—go down into the empty perfection of the *sheriekas* eternity. But if we do not try, we shall certainly embrace that doom."

They were at the base of *Dancer's* ramp. Cantra went up, light-footed as always, Rool Tiazan pacing silently at her side.

Jela would have waited a moment on the cermacrete, to avoid a crowd at the hatch, but his walking companion placed her tiny hand on his wounded arm and urged him forward.

"I regret that you have taken hurt," she murmured, as they moved up the ramp.

"I've been wounded before," he told her shortly, and was surprised by a stern glance from those amber eyes.

"We have all of us been wounded, M. Jela. It is still possible to regret the occasion."

He bowed his head. "You're correct, Lady. It was a rude reply."

"It is not the rudeness which is dangerous," the lady said, as they hit the top of the ramp. "But the assumption that pain may be discounted."

Ahead of them, the hatch rose, and Cantra ducked inside, Rool Tiazan her faithful shadow. Jela and the lady followed them into the narrow lock, the hatch reversing itself the instant they stepped within.

Cantra turned away from the control panel, waited until the hatch was sealed, then slithered past the crushed three of them to lead the way down the corridor to the piloting chamber.

Rool Tiazan extended a hand and his lady moved forward to take it. So linked, they followed Cantra.

Jela took a step—and paused, lifting his wounded arm.

It felt—odd. He snapped the seal on the dressing Cantra had so painstakingly applied, pulled it off—

The wound had been—non-trivial. He'd done what he could, and Cantra had done what she'd been able. Still, it would have—should have—taken time and a medic's care to fully heal.

And now—there was no wound, no sign that he'd been wounded. His tough brown hide didn't even show a scar.

Neck hairs prickling, he threw the dressing into the recycler and moved after the others.

The corridor was dim with emergency lighting, the doors along it dogged to red. Cantra hadn't wasted her few seconds with the control panel, Jela thought, and approved.

The door to the piloting chamber was dogged, too. Cantra placed her fingers on a certain spot along the frame and the door opened.

Inside, it was no brighter than the corridor, the board a blot of darkness along the far wall. Taking no chances, was Cantra yos'Phelium, canny woman that she was.

At the far end of the room, in the corner formed by the end of the co-pilot's board and the curve of the interior wall, leaves glowing in the light from the emergency dim above it, was the tree.

Cantra walked to the pilot's station and stood, tense but calm, her hand on the back of the chair. Rool Tiazan and his lady, however, had stopped only three steps into the room, and stood as if caught in an immobilizer beam.

Jela moved to one side, so he stood between them and the tree without obscuring their view of each other. After all, it was the tree he had wanted them to see; the tree who should make the judgment, here. The tree—

Its branches were moving slightly, though the blowers were off, and the whole tower was suddenly filled with the aroma of fresh seed-pod.

"Ah," Rool Tiazan's lady breathed, and glided forward on silent gray slippers. Her mate went after her, one respectful step behind.

Though this was the meeting he had wanted, Jela twitched,

suddenly not sure he wanted these . . . *sheriekas*-made in position to damage—

Two steps from the pot itself, the lady sank to her knees on the decking, gray robes pooling about her, head down, tiny hands upraised, as if in supplication—or prayer.

Rool Tiazan, a step behind, went gracefully to one knee, and bent his head.

The tree . . .

There was a tumble of images in Jela's head—of a world seen by dragon-eye, the crowns of trees so thick that the sea was barely visible as a glint in the pale light of the star. Sounds filled his ears—water rushing, waves crashing, rain striking the earth, and the wind, moving through countless millions of leaves . . .

The dragon-eye blinked, and the wind shifted—became dry and pitiless, scouring rock, stirring the dust in the dead sea-bed, moving the sand in long waves, burying the skeletons of trees were they lay . . .

Jela's eyes filled with tears. He blinked them away, shot a glance at Cantra, standing with her slim shoulders bowed, her hair shielding her down turned face.

Before the tree, the lady raised up her head.

"We were not the agents, but we accept the guilt. We have committed crimes against life, actions so terrible that there can be no forgiveness.

"Have pity on us, who had none. Allow us to make amends. We pledge ourselves to you; we give you our lives—use them or end them. It is with you."

A blast of hot wind rocked the inside of Jela's head. He saw the young dragons, tumbling into the air, rolling on the soft, dry leaves at the base of a stupendous tree—and pushing out of the sheltering deadfall, hopeful new leaves on a tender trunk . . .

"Yes," Rool Tiazan's voice was ragged. "We have children and they are kept as safely as any may be. End us now and they will end with all else, when the *sheriekas* have had their way." He drew a hard breath.

"I have lain down my shields; you may do what you will.

It will be necessary to end me first, for I may not allow harm to befall my lady."

Another breeze, this one scented with the hint of rain.

At the pilot's station, Cantra suddenly straightened and shook her hair out of her face.

"My opinion, is it?" she said, and laughed on a wild note Jela had never heard from her before. "I don't have one. Best I can bring you is something Garen used to say, that made more sense than most." She took a breath and closed her eyes, reciting in a voice a bit deeper and a fair amount slower than her normal way of speaking:

"*In the matter of allies, you need to ask yourself two things: Can they shoot? And will they aim at your enemy?*"

She opened her eyes and nodded at the tree. "That's my opinion, since you asked for it."

There was a stillness in the chamber, and among the leaves of the tree. The air grew warm, which was just, Jela thought, that the blowers weren't on . . . The *dramliz* didn't stir from their attitudes of supplication, save that the lady lowered her hands and folded them against her robe.

Then, as if the threat of storm had passed off, the air freshened, the top-most branches of the tree moved, and Jela, prompted by an impulse not his own, walked forward, the aroma of tree-fruit in his nose.

He slipped past the kneeling *dramliz*, and held his hand out under the branches. Two seed-pods dropped into his wide palm; he began to close his fingers—and two more dropped, attached by a branch no thicker than a thread.

Well.

Turning, he touched Rool Tiazan lightly on the shoulder, and when the man looked up handed him the two attached pods. Passing on, he gave one of the remaining two to Cantra and stood by her, his own fruit cupped in his palm.

Across the field of his mind's eye a dragon swept by, hovering on effortless wings above the crown of an enormous tree. As he watched, the dragon lowered its mighty head, and a branch lifted to meet it. The dragon selected a pod, swallowed it . . .

The image faded.

At the base of the tree, Rool Tiazan broke one pod off the tiny branch, and handed the second to his lady.

"I, first," he murmured, and held the fruit high in his palm, where it fell into sections, releasing its aroma into the chamber.

He ate without hesitation, as a man might savor a favorite treat, and as if no suspicion—or hope—of poison clouded his heart.

His lady waited with bowed head for three heartbeats, then ate her own fruit, neatly.

"Us, now?" Cantra asked.

"It seems so," he answered.

"Right." She ate, and he did, and he closed his eyes.

Overhead, he heard the sound of dragon wings.

THIRTY-TWO

Spiral Dance
Gimlins

THE GRAY-ROBED LADY was in the jump-seat, Rool Tiazan standing behind her like a paladin, or a servant.

Cantra lounged at her ease, arms folded on the back of the pilot's chair, keeping her expression pleasantly neutral. She hadn't offered the ship's guests tea or other refreshment, which was her call as captain. If either noticed the lack, they didn't mention it.

Jela was in the co-pilot's chair, on his mettle and letting it show, face hard, eyes hooded. Having second thoughts about accepting the decision of a vegetable in the matter of allies, Cantra guessed, and carefully didn't think about her moment of contact with that same vegetable, its question as clear as if it had whispered in her ear.

"The *sheriekas*," Jela said, breaking the longish silence. "According to Ser Tiazan, they can't be defeated, but they can be escaped. I'd like to hear more about that particular assertion, such as how the escape plan is configured, and what exactly you expect from your allies."

"Ah." That was the lady, sitting straight-backed and prim, gray slippered feet swinging some inches above the decking, her hands folded in her gray lap.

"Perhaps we ought better to have said that it is the fervent hope of many of the *dramliz* that the *sheriekas* may be escaped. We who have refused to serve are numerous, and varied, and not entirely of one mind."

Jela frowned. "There's no plan, then," he said, flatly.

The lady raised a tiny, ringless hand.

"There are several plans, Wingleader Jela. There is, for an instance, the plan formulated by our esteemed colleague Lute and his dominant. They—"

"Hold it," Jela was frowning hard now. "Explain dominant."

The lady sighed sharply, and it was Rool Tiazan who answered.

"Lady Cantra had previously raised the question of the flaws which insure that the *dramliz* pose no threat to their makers," he said, as calmly as if they were discussing the possibilities of a proposed trading route. "Each *dramliza* is composed of two units. While each unit is possessed of those odd talents which the *sheriekas* find good, there is a selected-for disparity between them.

"The dominant unit's talents are the lesser—" He inclined his head to Jela. "You understand, sir, that we speak in relative terms of value."

"Right," said Jela.

"Yes," murmured Rool Tiazan. "So, the dominant unit holds the lesser powers, except that she may command and direct the subordinate unit and he may not withhold himself. The subordinate is also required to defend the dominant with his life."

"Must make for an interesting situation," Cantra commented, "if they ever wanted to shut one of you down."

The vivid blue gaze came to rest on her face and he inclined his head.

"Indeed. The dominant carries the seeds of her annihilation within her. When the *sheriekas* wish to terminate a *dramliza*, they merely trigger the implanted doom, and the dominant expires. Unable to regulate himself, the subordinate soon follows, unless speedily paired with another dominant."

"Nasty," Cantra said, and meant it. She looked directly at the lady. "So, why're you still walking, if it can be told? From what Jela tells me, I don't expect the Enemy likes deserters none."

The lady smiled tightly.

"This pairing is a—miscalculation, Pilot. When we realized the extent and kind of our abilities, we used them to liberate as many of our kind as possible. However, the *sheriekas* have other means of disposal at their beck, and time grows short—" she sent a swift glance to Jela— "for all."

He nodded. "I'm sorry to interrupt, Lady, and glad of an explanation of how your corps operates."

"Ah. Then I may proceed?"

"Please."

"So. Our colleague Lute and his dominant have determined that it may be possible for them and for those *dramliz* of like mind, to insert themselves into the fabric of the universe as it decrystallizes and to exert their wills in such a way as to—form a bubble universe in which life might thrive, surrounded, yet apart from, the *sheriekas* eternity."

There were few enough times when Cantra had reason to think kindly on her schooling—and this was one of those rare occasions. She neither blinked nor laughed, and was confident that her face hadn't changed expression. A quick glance to the side showed Jela doing pretty well, too, though he did raise a hand, signing *clarification*.

"Yes?" the lady said, none-too-gentle.

"I wonder why they think this is possible," Jela said mildly, which was as fine a bit of understatement as Cantra'd heard lately.

The lady glared, apparently finding Jela too dim for conversation, for it was once again Rool Tiazan who answered.

"They see it merely as a return to a more efficient former state, M. Jela, and anticipate little difficulty in re-crystalizing a life-friendly universe from some portion of decrystallized matter."

"I . . . see," Jela said carefully. "What about you—do you think this is a reasonable plan?"

There was a short pause, then the lady sighed.

"Wingleader, you must understand that what the *sheriekas*

attempt—what they are accomplishing at an ever more rapid rate—is . . . unprecedented. The *dramliz*—we are pushing the edge of what we know to be possible, and while we may be closer to the enemy in kind and talent than any living thing, we are as children."

"That being so," Cantra heard her own voice ask, "you're still talking in terms of escape?"

The lady turned to look at her, amber eyes serious.

"We—Rool, Lute, my sister and I—we seek escape. We believe that escape, in one form or another, is possible. There are others of us who believe that the *sheriekas* can be defeated."

"Can they?" Cantra asked, fascinated despite herself. Deeps knew, the Enemy was a threat to everything in the path of themselves or their works—had been for all her life, and all of Garen's too. But the notion of—descrystallizing, whatever that was meant to say—the known galaxy in the hopes of creating one better, out of will and cussedness alone—

"M. Jela," Rool Tiazan said, so soft he might have been a part of her thoughts, "has a good bit of the math which describes the process, Lady Cantra."

She glared. "Read that right out, didn't you?"

He smiled at her, and glanced down at the top of his lady's head.

"Neither I nor the majority of the philosophers among the free *dramliz* believe that the *sheriekas* may be defeated," the lady said in her prim, serious voice. "Not by the *dramliz*, nor by the forces of humanity, nor even by those forces combined." She glanced aside, down the room to where Jela's tree stood tall in its pot, leaves at attention.

"Had we a dozen worlds of *ssussdriad* at the height of their powers, with legions of dragons at their call—we do not believe even that would be enough to defeat the *sheriekas*."

"But there are *dramliz* who are going to engage the enemy, even knowing they'll fail," Jela said, more like he was checking facts than questioning the sanity of the proposition.

"There are those who *must* fight, M. Jela," Rool Tiazan said gently. "As to failure—all we attempt, as a force and individually, may yet end there."

"We hope that it will be otherwise," his lady added.

"Right." Jela shifted a little in his chair, eyes on the farthest corner of the tower.

"What I see, from soldier's eyes, is that your corps has a dual-pronged campaign on the board: A group of fighters to draw the enemy's attention and forces while those with Ser Lute attempt to capture and keep a reduced territory. The question comes back: What do you want from us?"

He moved a hand, enclosing himself, the tree and Cantra in the circle of "us," which was cheek—or maybe not. She'd eaten the damn' nuts, hadn't she?

There was a small silence, as if Rool Tiazan and his lady took lightning counsel of each other on a level not available to the rest of them.

"Wingleader," the lady said, "we have, in fact, a *three*-pronged plan. For our part, Rool and I have determined to liberate the mathematician Liad dea'Syl, whose work has continued to evolve and now transcends that with which you are familiar."

She closed her lips and refolded her hands, as if that explained all.

Cantra sent a glance to Jela, only to have it bounce off ungiving black eyes. Right.

She looked back to the *dramliza*.

"I'm not following," she said to the lady.

The prim mouth opened—and closed. Her thin red brows pulled sharply together.

"Rool?"

"Indeed," he murmured. His eyes were open, but Cantra was willing to lay steep odds that he wasn't seeing anything like *Dancer's* piloting tower.

"What is it?" That was Jela, quiet, so as not to startle the look-out.

"A hound has discovered us," the lady said softly, shifting around on the jump seat so that she faced her mate. "It may be possible—"

"Neutralized," Rool Tiazan said, in a flat, distant voice. He took a breath, his focus coming rapidly back to the present, the tower, his lady.

"The absence will be noted," he murmured, looking down into her eyes. "Soon."

"What did they see?" the lady demanded.

He moved a hand, the stone on his forefinger throwing out flickers of black lightning.

"The maelstrom of the luck. Our ally the *ssussdriad* obscured much, but in the final moment the lady knew me."

"So," the lady squared her thin shoulders. "We to play decoy, then. Locate an appropriate scenario."

"Yes." He closed his eyes, and Cantra was abruptly aware of a sense of absence, as if the essence of the being known as Rool Tiazan had departed the common weal.

The lady twisted, coming off the jump-seat in a flurry of gray and spun to face Jela.

"Wingleader—your mission!" she snapped, a mouse giving orders to a mountain.

Jela moved his shoulders, but— "Tell me," was all he said.

"You, the pilot and the *ssussdriad* will proceed to the world Landomist, where Revered Scholar Liad dea'Syl is confined with all honor to Osabei Tower. You will gain his equations which describe the recrystallization exclusion function. You will then use them as you see fit, for the continuation and the best interest of life. We will draw off the *sheriekas* lord who now has our enterprise under scrutiny. The hound did not see you—only us." She paused, her thin form seemed to waver, to mist slightly at the edges—then she was as solid as the decking on which she stood. Solid as Jela, who sent a long black glance at her, and said nothing at all.

"Wingleader, I require your word," the lady said softly.

Jela spun his chair to face the tree; spun back to face the lady.

"You have my word. I will do my utmost to liberate Scholar dea'Syl's equations and use them in the service of life."

The lady turned to face Cantra, who pushed up from her lean, ready to resist any demands for her oath—

"There are two," Rool Tiazan said, in that flat, distant voice, and held out a hand.

The lady altered her trajectory, and landed at his side, her hand gripping his.

"We will diminish," he said.

"*Diminish* holds a hope that *extinction* does not," the lady answered. "Proceed."

"Nay, look closely . . ."

"I see it," she snapped. "Proceed!"

Wreathed in mist, he opened his eyes.

"M. Jela—your choice! A death in battle or of old age?"

Jela was on his feet. "What are you doing?" he demanded, but Rool Tiazan merely repeated, on a rising note.

"A choice, M. Jela! Time flees!"

"Battle, then," Jela said, calm as if he was deciding between beer and ale.

Across the chamber, Rool Tiazan smiled, and raised his lady's hand to his lips.

"So," he said softly. "It is done."

The mist was thicker around the two of them. From the midst of it, came the lady's voice, calm and sounding distant.

"This world tectonically active, and there will soon be an earthquake of major proportion. It would be well if you were soon gone. The confusion will cover your departure."

There was a sudden toothy howl of wind, harrying the thickening fog, the temperature plummeted, the mist shredded—

The *dramliz* were gone.

Cantra spun to the board, slapped it live, initiated a self-check, and spun back to glare at Jela.

"Tell me you saw that," she snapped.

"I saw it," he answered, and gave her a long, deep look. "I believe it, too."

"So, you're for Landomist."

"I am," he answered. "I thought we all three had our orders."

The board beeped readiness; the tree sent an image of dark clouds and lightning, with more and worse towering behind . . .

The ship trembled a moment, rocking on the tarmac. Alarms lit the board in yellow, orange, and red.

Swearing, Cantra hit the pilot's chair, yanking the webbing tight.

"Strap in," she snapped at Jela, "this is gonna be rough."

❀ END ❀

AFTERWORD:

On Growing Old,
or at Least, Old Enough

WE STARTED WRITING *Crystal Soldier* in 1986. Sharon was working at the University of Maryland's Modern Languages and Linguistics Department at the time and the overruns and too-light copies came home with her to become "first draft paper." First draft paper was something we needed when using actual typewriters, if you want to know how far back that really was.

We still have three attempts at a beginning for what we were then calling *Chaos and the Tree*, typed on the backs of dittoed Spanish 101 vocabulary sheets and mimeographed Russian Lit exams.

To place this as nearly as possible: We'd already written *Agent of Change*, *Conflict of Honors*, and most of a third novel, pieces of which would become *Carpe Diem*; as well as an astonishing number of fragments, sketches, scenes, and word lists. It was a time of frenetic creativity, where one idea would smack into another, and dozens of child-ideas would spin off in all directions, like some cosmic game of pool. Needless to say, darn few of those ideas sank neatly into side pockets and waited patiently for retrieval. It was all we could do note down trajectories and intentions, and hope to be able to get back at some less frenzied future time for more details.

It was during the pool game phase of our careers, then, that we realized we were going to have to write the story of Val Con's many-times-great-grandma, the smuggler, and the origins of Clan Korval, so, with the brass-plated confidence of complete ignorance, we began. . . .

. . . and stopped.

And began . . .

. . . and stopped.

And began . . .

. . . and realized that we were too young in craft to do justice to the story we could feel building, like a long towering line of thunder heads, just beyond the ridge of our skill.

Having realized that we were yet too young to write about Jela, Cantra, and what befell them, we put the story aside, with a promise to the characters that we would not forget them; that we would come back when we were old enough and tell their story as it was meant to be told.

We had plenty to keep us busy in the meantime, what with one thing and another. There was a delay in the publishing, a major move, cats to feed. Along the way we'd have requests from readers wanting to know more about Clan Korval's roots. So we made a promise to the readers that we'd try to tell the beginning of the story, if we could.

Over time, we finished out the story arc concerning Cantra's trouble-prone descendants, and, when Stephe Pagel asked us what we'd be writing for him after *Balance of Trade*, we said that we thought we were now old enough to make good on certain promises of our youth.

Herewith, is the first of two installments, which will fulfill those promises. We hope you've enjoyed it.

Sharon Lee and Steve Miller
August 3, 2004

CRYSTAL
DRAGON

Book Two of the
Great Migration Duology
A Liaden Universe® Novel

To absent friends

SORCERER
PROLOGUE

In the Hall of the Mountain Kings

❧ I ❧

THE *ZALIATA* PINWHEELED across the aetherium, painting the void with bright strokes of energy. Rapt, she moved closer to the barrier—and closer still, until the weaving of the containment forces flared.

She retreated until the barrier faded from her awareness, and once again only the *zaliata* were visible. Power and grace. Unimaginable power, for these were *zaliata* at the height of their considerable abilities, captured, contained, and exploited by the Iloheen—and no concern of hers.

Despite this—and the fact that it was . . . theoretically . . . impossible for those who wore flawed and fallible flesh to behold the sacred servants without the intermediary sight of an instructor, she came as often as she might to the aetherium, the folded space at the edge of what was, to watch the play and the power of the wild ones, the rebels; those who had contended as equals against the Iloheen—

And lost.

Of course, they had lost. No one and nothing could stand against the Iloheen. So she had been taught, and so she believed. But knowing that each *zaliata* contained within the aetherium had striven, flame to ice, against one of the Iloheen—that knowledge excited a brilliant emotion in her, as the beauty of their gyrations dazzled her senses, leaving her—

There!

There it was—her favorite of the wild dancers: Not so large as some, but densely structured, the pattern of its emanations controlled, it colors deep and cunning, resonating through every spectrum she was able to sense, and surely well beyond. It suited her fancy to style this one *Iloheen-bailel*—Lord of Chance—in all ways fit to serve the Masters of Unmaking. Indeed, when she had not seen it at once, she had supposed that its master had required it elsewhere. That it was free and dancing—pleased her.

Not that her puny pleasure was to be set against the necessities of the Iloheen. Surely not. The whole purpose of her existence was to serve the Iloheen as they instructed her, for while they were invincible, their numbers were not limitless, and so they required servants to perform certain of the lesser tasks of conquest.

She was herself scarcely trained, and, according to her teachers, barely trainable. Yet, she had passed living through the first two Dooms, while others of her cohort had not, and even now a vessel formed from her DNA and shaped by her skill grew in the birthing room. Soon, it would be ready to receive a download. And, oh, she thought, her eyes on the *Iloheen-bailel* as it tumbled and shone in its dance through the clusters of its fellows, if only—

But such was not for her.

Putting away longing and regret alike, she watched the *zaliata* dance, taking comfort from the intricate, subtle patterns that emerged—and suddenly came to full attention, all her senses a-tingle, as she sought to analyze those so-subtle movements.

The *Iloheen-bailel* was feigning random action, but close analysis revealed that it was passing near each and every one of the dancers in the aetherium, mingling its energies with those others in the way of *zaliata* communication. There was nothing overtly wrong in this—if the Iloheen had not wished their servants to communicate, they would simply have forbidden it. But the attempt to conceal the communication engaged her interest—as did the fact that the others were becoming . . . agitated, condensing their essences until they were nearly as dense as the *Iloheen-bailel*, their auras held close and studious.

Engrossed in her study, she again came too near the containment field, and for an instant, the dancers were hidden from her. When her senses cleared, she saw that the seven strongest of the captives now danced in pattern near the center of the aetherium, while the rest kept orbit about them, tumbling with abandon, energies bright and zealous.

Rapt, she observed them, her entire attention on the double dances—the inner pattern formal, laden—laden with *intent*; the outer heedless and dazzling. She ached; her senses so tightly engaged that she did not perceive the approach of the Iloheen until its very Shadow fell across the aetherium.

Poor student she might be, but she had not survived two Dooms because she was a fool—nor because she lacked resources or awareness. She had once come to the attention of the Iloheen; twice was more than any student might survive.

Immediately, she damped her output, coalesced, and plummeted through the levels to the physical plane, gritting her teeth to keep the cry locked in her mouth as the dancers, the aetherium, the Shadow itself—vanished from her perceptions.

She breathed, deep and deliberate, and slowly increased her heartbeat, keeping herself centered on the physical plane. Her envelope had become chilled; she warmed it, uncurled and sat up. At the last, she opened her eyes upon the stone-walled dormitory, the ceiling black and secret. Curled naked on the rocky floor were five identical sleepers, which was all that was left of her cohort.

Carefully, she allowed her senses to expand, reading emanations left upon the air by the immediate past—and found nothing but the sleeping auras of her sisters.

Satisfied that her absence had not been noted, she curled down on the cold, sharp rock, closed her eyes and willed her body into slumber—and found resistance, though not from her pliant vessel. Memory it was that would keep her wakeful, and different, and thus subject to scrutiny.

She exerted her will, and sleep she did, though the memory lingered.

❧ II ❧

SHE WAS CONTEMPLATING ley lines, their shapes and patterns, attempting to gauge the magnitude of force required to effect a branching off a main avenue of event. She was, of herself, powerless to shift the lines, or to cross them, or to affect a branching. However, it was necessary that she understand the art and the consequences of its use. If she survived the Three Dooms, thereby proving herself worthy to engender life. If the life she engendered was fit. If she enforced her dominion. If—

Attend me.

The order rang inside her head, bright orange and tasting of manganese—the thought signature of the Anjo Valee dominant, their biology tutor. Obedient, she withdrew her attention from the glittering, seductive lines of possibility and power, rose from her crouch and, with the eleven of her cohort who had survived the First Doom, walked—naked, silent, and identical—down the rough stone hall to the biology lab.

Their tutor awaited them on the raised platform at the center of the room, the dominant standing with thin arms crossed over her breast, her face bearing its usual expression of impatient irritation. The submissive towered behind her, his face round and blank, eyes staring deep into the vasty mysteries of time and space.

The twelve of them knelt in a half-ring before the dias, their faces tipped up to their tutor, eyes open and focused on her face. As one, they neutralized their protections, and composed themselves to learn.

When they were all equally calm and receptive, the dominant smiled, showing small pointed teeth, closed her eyes and broadcast the lesson.

As usual, it struck the mind hard, its many angles and tiny sharp details seeming to cut the brain tissue itself. Kneeling, she received the thing, taking care to keep her eyes open and steady, and to allow no shadow of pain to disturb her aura as the knowledge sank into the depths of her mind, flowered with a thousand daggered points—and was gone.

You will now practice the technique, the dominant projected. *Anjo.*

On the tile floor before each appeared a lab dish bearing a quiescent portion of protolife.

Animate your subject, the order came.

That was easy enough; engendering a nervous system was elementary biology. She extended her thought and probed the clay, teasing out filaments, weaving them into a network. When the weaving was done, she subjected the whole to a deep scrutiny, being certain there were no missed synapses, before releasing a carefully gauged jolt of energy. The protolife twitched, the network of nerves glowed, and she withdrew into her envelope, her hands laying loose on her thighs.

She must have been slower than the rest at her work, for no sooner had she re-entered the physical plane than the order rang inside her head: *Render your subject aware.*

Once again, she brought her attention to the protolife and the steady glow of the nervous system she had created. Awareness—that was more difficult. They had been given the theory in philosophy, but this would be the first opportunity to bring theory into practice.

Carefully, she made her adjustments, and when she was satisfied, she withdrew to her envelope.

Kneeling, she waited, long enough for the sweat to dry on her face; long enough to begin to wonder if she had made some foolish error, which had allowed her to finish so far ahead of the—

Render your subject self-aware.

Self-aware? Almost, she allowed the thought to take form, but wisdom won out. One did not question the Anjo Valee dominant lightly. Nor was one stupid or slow in completing one's lesson.

She returned to the second plane, where she contemplated

the pulsing protolife with puzzlement. *Self-aware*. This went beyond what theory the philosophy tutor had granted them. However, if it were but a simple progression—animation, awareness, self-awareness . . .

Gingerly, and not at all certain that her instinct was good, she exerted her will once more, fashioning a chamber of pure energy, which enclosed and oversaw the central autonomous system. When it was fully formed and integrated, glowing in her perceptions like an impossibly tiny *zaliata*, she breathed upon it, and projected a single thought.

I.

The energy construct twitched, glowed, dimmed—and flared. Rudimentary thought reached her, barely more than an inarticulate mumble. The mumble grew as it accepted data from the central nervous system and began assessing its situation. Its unique situation.

Shaken in spirit, she returned to her sweat-drenched envelope. It took all of her will to leave her shields down; and every erg of her strength to keep her eyes open, modestly contemplating the lab dish and the creature which was beginning to cast about for data regarding its environment and itself.

Her envelope was beginning to shiver. Irritated, she encouraged certain molecules to increase their dance briefly and dried her sweat-slicked dermis. She did not smile, nor avert her eyes from the lab dish. It was too much to hope that her action had escaped the notice of their tutor, the submissive unit of whom was attuned to the ebb and flow of power, from small flares of warmth to the death and birth of star systems.

In the lab dish, the self-aware protolife continued to gather data, its mutter limping toward coherence. The facts of its existence were simple and straightforward, and because they were the facts of its existence, unalarming. It did not miss the limbs it had never had, it did not repine for sight or for the ability to shape living things from quiescent clay. It—

Very well. Their tutor's thought signature was shot with yellow, signaling that she was more than usually impatient.

You will now access the technique you have been given and use it to physically alter your subject. Be certain that it remains conscious and aware during the change. This is the shape you will bestow—a quick mind-picture of a bulbous body from which three equal tentacles protruded.

Proceed.

The technique was deceptively simple, and her first attempt produced two greater tentacles and a lesser. She accessed the technique again in order to make the adjustment, and the creature in the lab dish screamed.

She watched it closely as it quivered, then rallied and began to collect the data on its new form, stretching out its tentacles and exploring far more of the lab dish than it had known existed. Its terror faded into excitement, into curiosity, into—

Again, the order came, and the shape this time included an ear.

Her creature's horror sublimated quickly into the eagerness of discovery. From somewhere—likely from the Anjo Valee submissive—came sound, patternless and far into the range that she herself could perceive only through her other senses. The creature tracked the noise, building processing space on its own initiative, its muttering intelligible now as it formed theories regarding the sound, its purpose and its possible meaning for itself.

Again.

An eye and a fine gripper were added. The creature scarcely felt horror at these newest developments; and the pain of acquiring the alterations bled almost instantly away into greedy wonder. It created additional processing space as it began to creep about the dish, testing the information brought to it through its eye. It looked up, and she received a weird visual feedback—a smooth, lopsided blotch of gold, topped by a second and smaller blotch . . .

Again.

The image this time was sharply different—a bony carapace, six multi-jointed legs—three to a side—eyes fore and aft, on flexible stalks. The creature marched forward, learning its strength and its range. The muttering now took into account this state of constant change and accepted it as natural, for it knew nothing else.

She withdrew . . . mostly . . . into her envelope, while keeping the marching, measuring creature in one small portion of her attention. It was doing well, taking stock, forming theories, testing and adjusting them to accommodate new data. She was proud of it, the child born of her thought and desire.

As she watched, it discovered the dome over the dish, studied it with front eyes and back, stood on a pair of back legs and used the front ones to gain a sensory impression, exerted pressure—pressure!—and learned that it did not give.

The muttering was comprehensible now, the thought processes cogent and accessible. It considered the dome in light of its earlier explorations of the floor of the dish, formed the hypothesis that the material was one and the same. Settling back, it stamped its feet against the floor, verifying that the material was unbreakable by the force it might bring to bear. The question of whether it was desirable to break the dome arose and was put aside, pending further data.

The creature's eyes extended, and this time she recognized her face in the feedback, her eyes as round and as clear as the dish itself.

So, we have given, her tutor's thought intruded upon her observations. *Now, we shall take away.*

The image flashed—the very creature in her lab dish, minus the endmost set of legs.

This was fine work and took a good deal of concentration; she narrowed her perceptions to one, single foci, and did what was required.

In the lab dish, the creature teetered and staggered, as the now unevenly distributed weight of its carapace pulled it first to one side and then the other. Just as it achieved equilibrium, the tutor broadcast the next template.

Biting her lip, she removed the foremost pair of legs.

Her creature wailed, staggered—fell, eye stalks whipping, then focusing. Focusing on the dome. Beyond the dome.

On *her*.

Again.

This time it was a front eye and a back; then, the order barely discernible in the din of the creature's horror, pain and fear, another leg, then the ear.

Bit by bit, the creature was rendered back, until it was yet again a formless blot of protolife. *Sentient* protolife, its once promising mental acuity crushed beneath the weight of its multiple losses. Its awareness screamed continually, pain eroding the ability to reason, to form a theory, a response.

Even withdrawn entirely into her body, she could hear it; feel it. There was no word from the tutor, no query from any of her cohort. In the dish, the creature's anguish spiked, the last of its reason spiraled into chaos—and surely, she thought, that was the end of the lesson.

She extended her though, stilled the turmoil, blotted out the shredded *I*, unwove the nervous system, and withdrew again to the quiet of her own mind.

Orange and yellow flames exploded across her perceptions.

You will stand! The tutor's thought slashed at her. *Explain what you have just done and your reasons for doing so!* The order rang in her head, and no sooner had it formed than she was yanked upward and released. She staggered, got her feet under her, and bowed to the tutor, where they stood on the dais, the dominant allowing her anger to be seen; the submissive staring over her head, to the farthest corner of the room—and beyond.

I have—

Speak against the air, the dominant snapped, and her thought burned.

She cooled the burn site, bowed once more, and straightened, her hands flat against her thighs.

"I returned the protolife to its quiescent state," she said, her voice thin and one dimensional. They seldom communicated so, amongst themselves. Lower forms spoke against the air, and by placing this demand upon her the tutor illustrated that she—a student and unpaired—was lower—weaker—than a full *dramliza* unit.

As if that point required illustration.

Upon what order did you undertake this action? Her tutor's thought fairly crackled, throwing out sparks of yellow and orange.

She bowed. "Upon my own initiative," she said steadily.

It is your LEARNED opinion that the remainder of the lesson was of no benefit to you?

The rest of the lesson? The thought took shape before she could prevent it. She bent forward in a bow—and found herself gripped in a vise of energy, unable to straighten, unable to continue the bow, unable to move her legs, or her arms, scarcely able to breathe.

So, you were unaware that there was more? the dominant purred, her thought now showing gleams and glimmers of pleased violet.

"I was," she whispered against the air, staring perforce at the tile floor.

Then you will stand in place of your construct, and finish the lesson out, the dominant stated. *Anjo.*

Abruptly, she was released. She gasped in a great lungful of air as she collapsed, tile gritting against her cheek, her limbs weak and tingling unpleasantly with the renewed flow of blood.

She set her hands against the tile, pushed herself up—and fell flat on her face as her left arm dissolved in a blare of pain so encompassing she scarcely felt it.

Panting, she rocked back to her knees, to her feet—and down again, cracking her head against the floor, the place where her right leg had been an agony beyond belief.

Grimly, she got up onto her remaining knee and hand, pain warring with horror as she understood that the tutor meant to—

One eye was gone, its empty socket a cup of fire burning into her skull. She screamed, then, the sound high and wild—and cut off abruptly as her ears were taken.

Observe closely, the tutor was addressing the rest of her cohort, the pattern of her thought weaving like a violet ribbon through the pain. *Lesser beings may be governed by a system of punishment and reward.*

Acid ate her right arm.

Judicious reward and implacable punishment . . .

Her left leg evaporated in a sheet of fire.

. . . will win unfailing service . . .

The biology lab vanished as her remaining eye was plucked out.

. . . and will enforce both your dominion and your superiority.

The pain increased as the tutor exerted her will on nerve endings and receptors. She could feel the pressure of that terrible regard, as her thoughts skittered and scrambled. She tried to hide from the pain, all her perceptions obscured by it, so that she was blind in truth, and the pain, the pain . . .

We have taken away much, as is our right, according to our ability.

She was ablaze; the skin crisping on her bones; her reason spiraling toward chaos. Just like—

We shall now bestow a small reward.

Just like her poor creature, which had done so well, for a lower order, built to be dominated, manipulated and—

Monitor the flux of the emotion 'gratitude.'

She was not a base construct. She was *not*. She would fight. She would—

She would dominate.

Atom by atom, she scraped together her shattered will and focused on the roaring source of energy obscuring her perceptions. Pain. Pain could be used.

Beyond the inferno, she felt the weight of her tutor's regard increase.

She thrust her will into the howling depth of the pain—

The tutor's regard altered, sparked—

Using raw power and no finesse whatsoever, she created shields and threw them into place.

There was an orange and yellow detonation as the tutor's will slammed into her barriers—but she had no time for that, now.

The tutor launched another assault, but her protections held. Of course they held. Had she not survived the First Doom? Her shields had withstood the stare of one of the Iloheen; they would hold against a mere *dramliza*.

For a time.

Working with rapid care, she bled off the pain, sublimating it into working energy, using it to rebuild her depleted strength.

As she dominated the pain, her focus returned and she was able to survey the wreckage of her envelope.

Tentatively at first, then more swiftly as she began to integrate the fine points of the interrupted lesson, she rebuilt her body.

Arms, legs, eyes, ears, nerves, dermis . . . As she worked, she considered making alterations—and regretfully decided not to do so. Alterations made in haste and in unstable conditions might later be revealed as errors. Best to wait.

She did, however, strengthen her shields.

Then, she opened her eyes.

Carefully, cocooned in total silence on all perceptual levels, she came to her feet, and raised her eyes to the instructor's dias.

Lower your protections. The characteristic bright orange thought was shading toward a dangerously bland beige, and the taste of manganese was very strong.

With all respect, she answered—*no.*

You may lower them or Anjo will destroy them.

She looked to the submissive, and found his pale eyes open and focused on her face, with . . . interest . . .

I will not, she made answer to the dominant. *And Anjo shall not.*

Upon what order do you undertake this action?

Upon my own initiative.

Ah. The dominant extended her will to the submissive—and froze in time and space as a long Shadow fell across the room and the perceptions of all within.

The air grew chill and the tile took on a glaze of ice before the Iloheen deigned to speak.

Discipline has been meted and met. It goes no further.

Edonai, the Anjo Valee dominant answered, her thought warm against the Shadow's chill. On the dais, the *dramliza* bowed low. Those who yet knelt before their lab dishes threw themselves upon their faces on the ice-slicked floor.

She—she bowed until her head touched her knees, and held it, as the Shadow fell full upon her—

And was gone.

Abruptly, the room warmed. Behind her, she heard small noises as her cohort straightened and stilled. She unbent slowly, and looked up to the dais. The dominant did not meet her eyes.

You will return the specimen to its original state, the tutor ordered the class entire. *When that is done, you will wait upon the philosophy tutor.*

❧ III ❧

THE DOWNLOAD WAS about to take place.

She, with those of her cohort who had survived the Second Doom, watched from a distance, thought stilled and vital energies shielded, to insure that the *tumzaliat* would not perceive, and thus seek to attach, their essences.

In the birthing room, the vessel was readied. Its arms were spread, held thus by chains woven of alternating links of metal and force, the ends melded with the smooth tile floor. Similar chains around each ankle pulled the legs wide. Its head was gripped in a metal claw; a metal staple over its waist held it firm and flat.

On the plane from which they observed, the vessel was nothing more than a smear of pink, which was the glow of the autonomous systems. The hopeful dominant showed not even as much as that, so closely did she hold herself.

Within the lesser aetherium, the *tumzaliat* pursued their small, simple dances, which were so much less than the intricate movements of rebellion and abandon performed by their wild kin, the *zaliata*. Those such as she—and the cadet preparing herself below—they were fit only to exercise dominion over *tumzaliat* and so forge a working *dramliza* unit, to thereby accomplish the will of the Iloheen as it was expressed to them.

They were, after all, nothing more than embodiment of the vast wills of the Iloheen, without which they would have no existence. So the philosophy tutor taught.

In the birthing room, all was ready.

The cadet knelt beside the vessel and took the autonomous system under her control. This was necessary to prevent the *tumzaliat* from sabotaging the vessel, or, as was more likely, damaging it through terror and ignorance.

Control established, the cadet entered the lesser aetherium, cloaked and dim against the brilliant broil of the *tumzaliat*.

Cloaked and dim, the cadet drifted, while the heedless *tumzaliat* frolicked, melding their energies and dashing off at angles that seemed random until one considered the ley lines that passed through the lesser aetherium. The *tumzaliat* followed the ley lines, feeding on them—perhaps. Seeking to influence them, certainly. But the Iloheen had constructed the aetheriums in such a way that the ley lines which intersected there were rendered sluggish. They could, so said the engineering tutor, be manipulated, though not by a mere *tumzaliat*. Once downloaded, dominated, and fully integrated into a *dramliza* unit, then—perhaps—a *tumzaliat* might have access to sufficient power and focus to manipulate the ley lines from within the aetherium.

But, by then, it would no longer wish to do so.

The cadet had, by stealth and by craft, managed to separate one particular *tumzaliat* from the rest. She had not yet fully revealed herself, though she was now shedding a small—and unavoidable— amount of energy.

The chosen *tumzaliat* was large, its energies brilliant. Its cohesion was perhaps not all that could be desired, and it showed a tendency to flare in an unappealing manner. But it was well enough. For a *tumzaliat*.

The chosen abruptly rolled, as if suddenly realizing its vulnerable position on the outer edge of the tumbling pod. It flared and changed trajectory, seeking to rejoin the others—

And spun hard as the cadet revealed herself in a blaze of complex energies, cutting it off from the group, crowding it toward the containment field.

It was a bold move, for *tumzaliat* rightly feared the field, and the danger was that it would bolt and break through the cadet's wall of energy, with catastrophic results for both.

The creature hesitated, confusion dulling its output. The cadet pushed her advantage, herding it, pushing closer to the containment field and the egress port. The *tumzaliat* took its decision, feinted and reversed, diving for the fiery fringe of the cadet's wall, gambling, so it seemed to those observing, that it could survive the passage through the lesser energies.

It was over quickly, then.

The cadet allowed the *tumzaliat* to approach quite near, allowed it to believe its gamble was about to succeed. At the penultimate instant, the *tumzaliat* gaining momentum, its emanations coalesced to an astonishing degree—the cadet released the greater portion of her energies.

The *tumzaliat* tumbled into an oblique trajectory, now running parallel to the cadet's weaving of power. She contracted the field, as if she meant to embrace the fleeing creature in her energies.

Again, it changed trajectory, hurtling back toward the containment field with undiminished momentum. Perhaps it had some thought of immolating itself. It was of no matter. The cadet extended a tendril of energy, slipping it between the *tumzaliat* and the containment field, at the same instant contracting the field.

The force of the contraction threw the *tumzaliat* into the egress port. In one smooth maneuver, the cadet triggered the port and withdrew the tendril separating the *tumzaliat* from the containment field. Emanations sparking in terror, the *tumzaliat* tumbled into the port, bracketed and contained now only by the funnel of the cadet's energies, guiding it, forcing it—

The port closed.

In the birthing room, the readied vessel flared, the glow lingering as the nervous system accepted and imprisoned the *tumzaliat's* energies. The cadet's envelope flared less brightly as it accepted her return. She raised her head, and a small tremor of satisfaction escaped her.

On the floor beside her, the vessel spasmed against its restraints. The chest heaved, mouth gaping, and the birth scream echoed against the air. Quickly, the cadet straddled the vessel and lowered herself onto its erection, bonding herself with it on the biologic plane. Beneath her, the vessel screamed again—and again.

"Nalitob Orn," the cadet crooned against the air. She extended her will and plucked at the *tumzaliat's* captured essence, weaving the syllables into the fabric of its frenzied consciousness. The vessel would already have been seeded at the cellular level with those same syllables, which would now and henceforth be its—his—name, binding it to the body and to his dominant.

The submissive drew breath for another scream; his dominant extended her will and disallowed it. Carefully, caressingly, she relaxed the straining, fear-poisoned muscles, and released sleep endorphins.

Only when Nalitob Orn was entirely and deeply asleep did she rise. With a thought, she cleaned herself, and with another clad herself in the blue robe of a *dramliza*-under-training. For of course the work just completed had been only the first and the simplest of the bondings required before this nascent pair become a functioning unit.

The new-made dominant turned toward her sleeping and receptive submissive—and turned back, bowing low as the Shadow fell over the birthing room, excluding the observers from whatever passed between the Iloheen and the daughter of its intent, the Nalitob Orn dominant.

◈ IV ◈

ATTEND ME IN the testing chamber.

Their philosophy tutor's thought was a steady silken mauve, lightly flavored with copper.

With the five others of her cohort, she rose and walked down the stone hallway—naked, silent, but no longer identical. They had some time since been instructed to adjust their physical seemings. This was—so the philosophy tutor explained—to allow them to grow more easily apart, to sluff off the small ties that bound sister-students, and to make themselves ready for that bond which would define their futures and their service to the Iloheen.

As it was also necessary to seem to be one of those who continued to defy the Iloheen, among whom she would of necessity walk, she considered it well to appear both harmless and unable to defend herself. Thus, her stature was small, her bones delicate, her breasts petite. She sharpened her facial features and added amber pigment to her eyes. Her hair was red, short and silky; her ears shell-like and close to her head. She would appear, to one of those enemies of the Iloheen, to be young, her skin unlined and tinged with gold.

With these changes she was content, though she was the least altered of her cohort. Neither their tutors nor any of the Iloheen who increasingly oversaw their progress instructed her to make further alterations, so she accepted it as her full and final physical form.

Attend me, the philosophy tutor sent again.

The thought was no less serene, the tang of copper no more pronounced than ever it had been. There was nothing to differentiate this from countless thousands of previous summons.

Saving that the philosophy tutor never summoned them twice to the same lesson.

It was then that she knew they were being summoned, not for a mere philosophy test, but to the Third Doom, the last they would face as students.

The others must have also perceived the warning in that second summons and drawn their conclusions. Indeed, the two boldest quickened their steps, eager to meet the challenge, while the three most thoughtful dared to slow somewhat.

Being neither bold nor thoughtful, she kept to her own pace, and withdrew slightly from her envelope, centering herself and unfurling what she might of her protections. It was, of course, beyond her ability to know what test the Iloheen would bring to them this time. Experience of two previous Dooms, however, indicated that it was well-done to hold oneself both aloof and prepared upon all planes.

Behind two sisters and leading three, she turned the corner into the hall. The stones were slick and frigid beneath her bare feet, the air thick with ice. Ahead, the entrance to the testing chamber was black; empty, to her perceptions, of all energy.

A state of no-energy was impossible, so her tutors had taught, each in their own way. To which the philosophy tutor had added, *With the Iloheen, all things are possible.*

The two at the lead faltered; one recovered in the next instant and strode ahead, energies blazing, entered the void, and was gone—- whether unmade or merely passed beyond the senses was not for such as they to know.

Yet.

The second of the bold approached the void, her energies furled close and secret, and was in her turn swallowed, vanishing as if she had never been.

She, the third, neither quick nor slow, continued onward, protections in place, her essence at a slight remove, tethered by the slenderest of thoughts. The iced stones tore at the soles of her feet, her lungs labored in the thick air. She thought, within her most private and protected self, of the *Iloheen-bailel*, beautiful and subjugated, transforming the void with its dance.

Then, she passed into Shadow, and all her perception ended.

❦ V ❦

AWAKE.

She obeyed, opening her perceptions across all planes. On the dais before her stood the philosophy tutor, the dominant with her hands folded into the sleeves of her gray gown, the submissive kneeling at her side, head bowed, eyes closed.

There was no one else in the Hall of Testing.

The Blessed Iloheen, Lords of Unmaking, are pleased that you have passed through this door. The philosophy tutor's thought was serene. *You are to immediately remove to the birthing room and prepare the vessel which you have nurtured.*

THE VESSEL WAS READY. She had fashioned it neat and supple, with long, curling red hair, and a smooth, gold-toned dermis. Its hands were long, its feet small, its form slender. Standing, it would overtop her only slightly.

That, of course, was for later.

Now, it lay where she had placed it on the tile floor. She settled the head carefully into the restraint before giving her attention to the other fetters, binding first the right wrist, then the left, melding the chain with the floor. She bound the ankles in the same manner, and made the staple snug across the slim waist. Extending her will, she touched each restraint in turn, making certain of her work, then knelt.

The tile was warm under her knees; in other perceptions, it was slickly reflective, deliberately crafted to foil any attempt by an enterprising *tumzaliat* to anchor a portion of itself outside of its prepared dwelling place.

Withdrawing slightly from her envelope, she looked deeply into the vessel, searching anxiously for any flaw. The binding phrase had been imprinted at the cellular level; the biologics primed to accept the physical bonding. The autonomous system functioned sweetly, fairly humming as she took it under her dominion.

It was time.

Energies furled, she triggered the access port, changed phase and entered the lesser aetherium.

Dark and secret she floated, the *tumzaliat* frolicking heedlessly about her. As part of her preparations, she had studied the inhabitants of the lesser aetherium and had settled upon one as suitable. To be sure, it was no glorious wild *zaliata*, but well enough, for a *tumzaliat*. It was a bit less heedless than the others of its cohort; its emanations pleasingly regular and its cohesion firm. A suitable tool for one such as herself.

She was patient; she was cunning as a *tumzaliat* is not. And at last, her intended danced near.

Swiftly, she unfurled her energies, sweeping out and around, imperative and firm. She did not toy with the *tumzaliat*, nor permit it to build false hopes of escape; she did not allow it to flirt with annihilation against the containment field. Rather, she displayed her superiority, and offered no choice other than to acquiesce to her will.

The *tumzaliat* twisted, dodging close to the trailing edge of her field, testing. This show of boldness pleased her even as she contracted the field, edging the captive inexorably toward the—

There was a disruption of the energies within the aetherium; the sluggish ley lines heaved.

Within the vibrant strands of her net, the *tumzaliat* twirled, energies flaring. Her perceptions slid, and she felt the ley lines heat. She focused fiercely and flung her will out, forcing the *tumzaliat* into the egress field. The lines, she thought, were reacting to the attunement of her energies. It was best to be gone—and quickly.

There! Her chosen was within the egress field. She triggered the port; there was a flare and a confusion of energies as the *tumzaliat* seemed almost to hurl itself into the opening, so that she must needs extend her field, thinner than she liked, scarcely guiding it, while the momentum pulled her out—and down.

Gasping a thought, she sealed the port behind her, plummeting into her envelope so quickly pain flared. She batted it aside, clearing her senses.

Before her, the vessel showed the lingering glow of the *tumzaliat's* essence. The autonomous system went briefly ragged; she smoothed it absently as the vessel contorted, arching against the restraints. Its chest expanded, its mouth formed a rictus—

But the birth scream did not come forth.

Hastily, she checked the autonomous system; looked deep within the vessel and ascertained that the time was now, scream or none. She swung over the slim hips, looking down into the sealed, austere face—

The eyes snapped open—cobalt blue and *aware*, the gaze met hers and did not waver, though the body was panting now; trembling with the force of that unuttered cry. She could feel the *tumzaliat's* confusion increase to damaging levels as it failed to find its accustomed perceptions available, supplanted by alien input from unfamiliar senses.

She smoothed the vessel's breathing, slowed the racing heart, and lowered herself onto its erection.

"Rool Tiazan," she whispered against the air.

As foretold by the biology tutor, pleasure flooded her, and she moaned with satisfaction as the biologic link formed. And all the while, the cobalt eyes stared into hers, narrowing as the bonding triggered pleasure responses, then suddenly widening, as if the *tumzaliat* had in some way *understood*—

Beneath her, the hips tensed, twisting, as if to unseat her—and panic flared once more.

She extended her will, smoothed away the panic and triggered sleep; massaged the tight muscles into relaxation, and bled off the fear toxins.

When she was certain the *tumzaliat*, now Rool Tiazan, was at rest and in no danger of damaging himself, she rose, cleaned herself, and donned the blue robe of a *dramliza*-under-training.

That done, she turned back toward the sleeper, intending to transfer the language and motor modules, so that the sleeping intelligence might—

A Shadow fell across the birthing room. Immediately, she abased herself.

A successful translation, I apprehend. The Iloheen's thought pierced her like a blade of ice.

Yes, Edonai, she sent humbly, and did not think of the twisting ley lines or of that instant of confusion, just before her barely controlled dash through the port . . .

But the Iloheen did not pursue any of those possible errors. *Why is it*, the question came instead, *that you did not allow your submissive the birth scream?*

To admit that Rool Tiazan had been out of her control was to admit that she was unfit to undertake the work for which she had been created and trained.

To express an untruth to an Iloheen was—not quite unthinkable. They had drilled her well in deceit, that she would succeed in those things they would require of her.

There was an infinitesimal flutter at the edge of her perceptions. She ignored it and formed her response with care.

It was experiencing a great deal of confusion, Edonai. I judged the additional stress would do harm both to the vessel and the inhabitant.

She breathed, eyes on the slick tile floor, and awaited annihilation.

The judgment is not without precedent, the Iloheen stated.

The Shadow passed. She was alone and alive, having lied to one of the Masters of Unmaking.

Not . . . quite . . . alone.

Perceptions wide, she considered the submissive Rool Tiazan as he lay sweetly sleeping in his bonds.

The ley lines, she thought. The ley lines had shifted within the lesser aetherium at the moment she triggered the egress port to download her chosen *tumzaliat*. They had shifted again, just a moment ago, moving them to an all-but-unimaginable possibility where an Iloheen was fobbed off with a novice's lie.

You. She formed the thought gently, without imperative—and was not . . . entirely . . . surprised to see the delicate lashes flutter, and the fierce gaze seek hers.

I. His thought was a ripple of cool greens.

You are no tumzaliat, she said.

He did not reply. She tucked her hands into her sleeves, and formed a question.

Why did you manipulate the ley lines?

His eyes narrowed, but this time he answered: *Did you wish to be destroyed?*

You manipulated the lines twice, she pursued.

I did not wish to be destroyed. He closed his eyes.

Rool Tiazan, she sent, sharply.

No reply.

She probed and found only a blank wall of exhaustion, as if he truly slept now, on every level. As well he should—*zaliata, tumzaliat*, or mere biologic.

Briefly, she looked to herself, sublimated toxins into sugars, and replenished depleted cells.

The needs of her envelope answered, she sank to her knees on the tile beside her submissive, transferred the possibly redundant communications module, and also the motor skills module, weaving them into the sleeping consciousness.

That done, she considered her situation.

Impossible though she knew it to be, yet it seemed clear that she had bound a *zaliata* to her poor vessel. Only a *zaliata* would have strength enough to manipulate the ley lines within the lesser aetherium, or the boldness to manipulate them in the very presence of an Iloheen. How it might have happened that a *zaliata* had come into the lesser aetherium was something to discover from Rool Tiazan.

Her best course from this unlikely event—that was less plain.

Once bound to the vessel, there was no release for the *tumzaliat*, save destruction. Perhaps a *zaliata*, with its greater abilities, might withstand the destruction of its vessel?

She accessed and reviewed all she had learned of the philosophy of *zaliata*, but did not find an answer. Very likely because no *zaliata* had ever been bound to a humble biologic vessel. It would be madness to limit it so; and the Iloheen who commanded the *zaliata* had other means to ensure obedience.

But, once tied to the vessel, might not even a *zaliata* be subject to domination?

There was a flicker at the edge of her perceptions. She caught at it, tasting enough of the pattern to understand that Rool Tiazan had attempted to manipulate the ley lines again.

You, she sent sharply. *If you do not wish to be destroyed, have done. The Iloheen see all here. They will notice your attempts at the lines.*

Not before I am gone.

I am your dominant and I forbid you to depart this place, she replied, lacing her thought with compulsion. *The only pathway to your power now lies through me.*

Silence. Perhaps he slept again. She—she composed herself, thoughts and energies furled close, and set herself to reviewing how best to enforce her dominion.

❀ **VI** ❀

THE BIOLOGY TUTOR had taught that, though one would serve, several couplings following download would more rapidly strengthen the biological bonds between submissive and dominant. The philosophy tutor had suggested that simultaneous partaking of pleasure was itself a bond that would strengthen the *dramliza* unit in non-quantifiable, but subtly important, ways.

It was rare enough to find the two most influential tutors in agreement. And truly, she thought, it was her responsibility as dominant to insure that the *dramliza* unit was closely tied and functional.

Slowly, she allowed herself to emerge from the study-state, and opened her eyes. Rool Tiazan slumbered yet within the embrace of his restraints. She had formed his vessel in such a way that pleased her—and it pleased her greatly now, stretched taut against the tiles, the gold-colored dermis yet faintly glowing with the energies trapped within. Though it had been foretold by the biology tutor, she had found the birth coupling unexpectedly pleasurable, and gazing upon that which had been the instrument of such pleasure she experienced a shortness of breath, a tightening of the belly, a tingling . . .

She considered these conditions—biologic all, and found in them an irrefutable logic. The *tumzaliat* by entering the vessel prepared for it became a biologic entity. It was therefore reasonable and symmetrical that the stronger of the many ties which would bind it to its dominant would also be biologic. That it was pleasurable to forge those ties served to ensure that the work would be done.

Her envelope was clamoring now, as biologic memory fueled anticipation. The sensations were notable for their strength, and she thought to dominate them—then thought again.

She had downloaded not a mere *tumzaliat*, but a *zaliata*. Well to strengthen *all* those things that tied Rool Tiazan to her.

It occurred to her as she cast her robe aside that the Iloheen might well wish her not to bind a *zaliata* quite so closely to her will, but she barely heeded the thought over the clamor of biologic desire.

Envelope shivering under the continued onslaught, she reached forth her thought, stroked Rool Tiazan awake and ready, swung herself over his hips and—

Wait.

His thought—the cool and cooling ripple of greens, the edges showing the faintest shimmer of silvery fear.

It was his fear that pierced her, so that she withdrew somewhat from her rutting envelope and considered him.

Much has occurred, she told him, *and you may not recall that you have experienced this act and found it gave pleasure.*

I recall the act. His thought rippled more quickly, not . . . quite so cool now. *Not the pleasure.*

Allow me to remind you. She breathed upon the appropriate systems—and saw his coolness shrivel in heat as the vessel strained against its bonds, hips yearning upward.

Withdrawing into her own envelope she opened herself and met him.

NO!

His thought was tumultuous, a hot chaos of fear, pleasure, loss, and desire. Smiling, she took it into herself, felt something new weave from their mingled essences, and recalled one crystalline moment—the *zaliata* dancing, mixing their energies—and then her pleasure spiked, sealing all thought away.

WHY?

The thought was green and sharp, edged with some base emotion which eluded her naming. She raised herself onto an elbow and considered Rool Tiazan on every level accessible to her.

Physically, he lay yet within his restraints, his hair dark with sweat, his golden skin slick and damp. The dermis glowed, but palely, palely. Soon, it would cease to do so entirely, and the biologics would have won.

Upon the second plane, he was beautiful to behold, a subtle and coherent power, restrained by the chains of biology. Despite those chains, his essence extended well into the third level, half-a-dozen thin, mint-colored rays piercing even unto the fourth.

Returning to her envelope, she cleaned herself, sat up, called a robe, and, at last, met his eyes.

It is necessary in order to complete our bonding, she answered calmly, for the philosophy teacher had been adamant—one's submissive must, as soon as its intelligence was recovered, be shown the facts of its new existence. It was then able to grasp the futility of rebellion and realize that its only recourse was submission to she who held dominion over his existence.

I do not wish to be bound. His eyes were hot.

She lifted a shoulder. *It is not your wish that bears weight here, but mine.*

A light ripple of gold and ebon—amusement, she thought. And despair.

I thought the proud Iloheen ruled here.

So they do, she made answer. *I—and you—exist to do their work.*

You, perhaps, was his reply. *Not I.* He moved his head, insofar as the restraint would allow it, tried one arm against the bonds, then the other.

Release me.

It was not quite an order, not with that silver edging of fear. And, after all, there was no harm in allowing him so small a thing.

Of course. She took care to thicken the air beneath his head, so that the vessel would not be damaged, then banished the restraints with a thought.

Freed, he lay on the cold tiles, eyes closed, then slowly bent his right elbow, and shifted his right arm, until his palm lay against his naked chest. He stroked his own dermis, and shivered.

Release me from this . . . object.

Your vessel. Your body, she instructed him. *That is not possible.*

His chest rose and fell.

I am limited by this encasement. His thought was cool once more; detached alike from fear and from pleasure. *If it is power you would command, release me.*

As if he would not immediately shift the ley lines and remove himself from her ken. She bowed her head, acknowledging his cleverness, but—

It is not possible, she sent again. *Observe*.

Carefully, in soft, measured units, she downloaded the relevant biologic theory. He resisted her touch at first, until he understood what she offered, then snatched at it greedily.

There was silence while he accessed the information.

Observing him, she saw the brilliant display of his thought as he assimilated the data; caught a flicker of puzzlement—and felt his cool touch within her mind—behind her shields! At the secret core of herself!

Stop! she commanded.

Obediently, he ceased his rummaging, but did not withdraw.

Those walls can withstand the will of an Iloheen, she stated, and this time she *tasted* his gold-and-black laughter, so closely were they linked.

The Iloheen are fumblers and fools, he sent, with no concern that he might be overhead, and, snatching that half-formed thought from her core, made answer—

Even the strongest walls cannot seal self from self. We are one thought, and one shield. Is this not what you wished for, when you forced us to share essence? He touched something, faded slightly in her unguarded perception—and reformed.

Ah, I see. You had hoped for something less . . . equal. You to enjoy unlimited access to what I am, and I to accept those mites you choose to bestow. These traps, receptors, and inhibitors woven into this . . . body. They are careful and cunning work of their kind. Was all was done in service to the Iloheen?

Yes.

Why? His thought was not green now, but flame-blue. *Do you not know the purpose you exist to further?*

To annihilate those who stand against the Iloheen, she answered promptly, that being the very first lesson. *To assist in shaping the universe to reflect the glory of the Iloheen.*

And what reward shall be yours, for your aid in bringing about this glorious new universe so well-suited to the Iloheen? Rool Tiazan asked, his thought bearing an edge reminiscent of the biology tutor—and which he had likely picked out of her experience!

She exerted herself, thrust him out of her core, and slammed a wall up.

You are disallowed! She snapped, and augmented the thought with a bite, so he would remember.

Silence. He moved his head against the tile floor, eyes closed. Then—

Yes, lady, he answered meekly.

❈ VII ❈

IT WAS A SIMPLE EXERCISE, designed to allow dominant and submissive to become accustomed to working as one. Unfortunately, she thought—taking care to keep that thought well-shielded—it appeared that Rool Tiazan had not yet accepted the new terms of his existence.

While he had not again attempted to breach her walls, nor expressed contempt of the Iloheen, nor sought in any way to prevent their further bonding, he likewise did not allow one opportunity to resist her dominance to pass untried, so that even the simplest exercise became a war of will against will.

As now.

Three times, she had opened a working channel between them, and drawn his power in order to engender a flame in the grate she had brought into being.

The first time, he had withheld himself, resisting even her strongest demand. Rebellion had been costly, however, as she controlled his access to the means of renewing his essence.

The second time, he had not been able to withhold entirely, and a few wisps of smoke drifted weakly from the grate. This, too, had cost him a tithe of strength, so that she was certain of obedience when she drew him the third time.

Too certain, and more fool she, to suppose that his only weapon was resistance.

She focused again upon the grate—and abruptly there *was* power—far too much for the narrow channel she had formed. More than enough to incinerate her envelope, the grate, and Rool Tiazan himself, unless it were controlled, immediately.

For herself and the grate, she had no concern. Rool Tiazan was a different matter, being both bound to the vessel and denied the ability to rejuvenate it at need. If Rool Tiazan burned, not only his vessel, but his whole essence would be destroyed beyond recall.

She opened herself, dropped all of her shielding, and accepted the fireball. There was a brief, dismissible flare of agony as she phased and released the energy harmlessly into the second plane.

From this vantage, Rool Tiazan was a densely structured pattern of deep and cunning color. As she watched, the pink shine of the autonomous system flared—then faded as the vessel began to die. The scintillant essence spread, overflowing the vessel in rippling wings of energy. The core coalesced, as if the *zaliata* would phase to the second plane—and froze, anchored by the biologics to the failing vessel.

She acted then, and shamefully; not from cool calculation but from base emotion.

Brutishly, with neither finesse nor subtlety, she thrust her will through the glorious colors, feinted past the wary intelligence, and seized control of the autonomous system. She slapped the failing vessel into life, spun the bindings, and rode the tumult of the *zaliata's* energies, forcing it, dominating it, until it collapsed under the double burdens of her will and his body's demands.

In a flare of rage nearly as searing as the fireball that had consumed her envelope, she threw Rool Tiazan to his knees, constricted his lungs, his heart, multiplying the pain until at last it breached the cool green fortress of his thought and he writhed in her grip, gasping for breath, desperately seeking to ease her hold about his vessel's core, the tendrils of his power plucking uselessly at her will.

She held him until she judged he had assimilated the lesson, then threw him against the tile wall and withdrew herself.

The ashes of her envelope were still warm. She resurrected it and stepped within, scarcely noticing the small bite of pain. Carefully, she smoothed her robe, put her anger aside, and turned.

Rool Tiazan lay on the floor at the base of the wall against which she had flung him. Blood ran freely from his nose, his ears, his mouth. His eyes were closed.

Behold me on the physical plane, she commanded.

His eyes opened, blue, fierce, and unrepentant.

I am your dominant, she told him, her thought cold and controlled. *You will obey me.*

Nothing, saving the fierce blue stare. She inclined her head.

I accept your submission, she stated, as if he had actually extended it. *Stand.*

He obeyed, though it cost him, for beyond the bruises, there were broken bones and injuries to soft organs which she did not choose just yet to repair. It was well, she judged, that he learned something of pain, and to value its absence. She waited, allowing him to feel the weight of her patience, as he staggered to his feet, the fingers of his unbroken hand clawing the smooth tile wall for support.

When he was erect, she opened the channel for the fourth time and drew his power.

The channel warmed slightly as a spark danced from him to her, touched the grate and flared into soft blue flame.

EXPLAIN YOUR ACTION.

Painfully, he raised his head and met her eyes. *Did you not command me to light the grate?* His thought was green ice. *Lady.*

Fortunately for Rool Tiazan, her fury had departed, else she might have struck him again, to his sorrow. Instead, she merely smoothed her robe and questioned him more specifically.

You know that you are inescapably bound to the body. What did you seek to gain by your late escapade?

Freedom. Cold enough to freeze the aether between them, with a depth she could not identify, and yet still mistrusted.

I thought, she sent carefully, *that you did not wish to be destroyed. Mark me, if your body dies unrevived, you will be destroyed.*

His eyes closed against his will, and he sagged suddenly against the wall, shivering.

I thought to . . . survive—his sending was ragged, as the body's damage began to breach his defenses. *To survive . . . diminished.* His thought fragmented; she caught an impression of a free *zaliata*, quite small and very compact, dancing joyous between the stars— and then nothing but green and silver static.

So. He had been willing to abandon some amount of his essence—his power—in order to escape his binding. A desperate plan, indeed.

You would not have survived, she sent, more gently than she had intended. *The body will not yield you.*

Silver and green static was her only answer. Against the stained tile wall, he shivered the harder, lips blue, tears mixing with the blood on his face, as the body's distress overwhelmed his essence.

She went to him, and took his undamaged hand in hers.

Come, she said, easing him to the floor. *I will repair your hurts and give you data to study while you sleep.*

❈ VIII ❈

HEALED AND CLEANED and held peaceful by her will, Rool Tiazan slept, his curls tumbled in pleasing disarray across the blanket she had allowed him.

She—she did not sleep, but withdrew to her core, there to meditate upon her actions and her motivations.

Emotion motivated base creatures and was one of the myriad means by which such creatures were subject to manipulation. So taught the philosophy instructor, who had with the biology instructor early set her cohort to studying the effects of emotion upon base biologic systems. The point made, the philosophy tutor had then drilled them in the domination of the emotions which were the legacy of their biologic origin.

Ultimately, you aspire to dominate base creatures of a high order, she had told them. *How will you accomplish this, if you cannot dominate that which is base within yourselves?*

Indeed, the dominion of emotion was deemed so vital to performing the will of the Iloheen that the First Doom had been constructed to test that skill. Those of her cohort who had yielded— to terror, to joy, to despair—those had not emerged from the testing.

That she *had* emerged from not only the First, but from all Three Dooms proved that she was worthy to pursue the work of the Iloheen as the dominant of a full *dramliza* unit.

And, yet—a dominant who allowed terror for her submissive's life to predicate her action? What was she to make of such a creature? Cool consideration, now that the event was past, indicated that allowing Rool Tiazan to destroy himself was the course of reason.

For herself . . . Reason told her that a dominant who could not assert her dominion, who had lost the Iloheen the use of one of the precious *zaliata*—so flawed a being was unworthy of carrying out the great work, no matter how many Dooms she had evaded.

And it was fear that she felt, there at her core, as she contemplated her own destruction. Contrary to her training, she did not vanquish it, but drew it close and examined it.

Seen thus, it was a thing of many facets; a dark jewel turning beneath the weight of her regard.

One facet was that fear awakened in a base creature at the imminence of its own death. Another facet—and greater—was fear of Rool Tiazan's destruction.

The very emotion which had motivated her interference in his attempted escape.

The very emotion which had fueled her rage after she had made him safe, and prompted her to punish him more stringently than his error had warranted.

She paused to study that last, detecting shame at her use of force. Yet, it had been no error, but a deliberate attempt to distract her so that he might escape her domination. Surely such rebellion merited punishment, stern and deliberate?

And yet again—he had been no mere *tumzaliat*, bred in captivity, but a free *zaliata*, proud and willful. He had acted as his emotions had dictated, as base creatures must. As his dominant, it was her part to—

Noise disturbed her thought; loud and ill-shaped, it grew progressively more annoying until, abruptly, a Shadow fell across her perception. Immediately, she quit her core, returned fully to her envelope, rose onto bare feet and bowed.

Edonai.

There was no return greeting, but a shock of pain as a data module was forced into her consciousness, displaying a dizzying view of the greater aetherium, the *zaliata* at their dancing. The image narrowed until it had isolated one particular creature: Not so large as some, but densely structured, the pattern of its emanations controlled, its colors deep and cunning, resonating through every spectrum she was able to sense, and surely well beyond.

As she watched, the *zaliata* danced, faster, and faster still. The ley lines flared briefly; undisturbed, the dancers continued to gyrate, but were not quite able to disguise the fact that one of their number was—gone.

Fear whispered; she dominated it and dared to ask a question. *When?*

Rouse your submissive, the Iloheen ordered

A second question stirred; she suppressed it and hid the shadow of the act in the bustle of waking Rool Tiazan.

Roughly, she stripped the blanket away and vanquished it.

Rool Tiazan, she sent, sharp enough to cut—and perhaps to warn. *We are commanded.*

He gained such consciousness as the vessel permitted, came to his feet with alacrity and bowed, his hair swirling in the ice-thickened air.

Remove your influence, came the command. *I would examine it of itself alone.*

Fear licked at her core; a tiny flame, easily extinguished. Slowly, carefully, she withdrew her protections. Rool Tiazan felt her slip away from him, and straightened, eyes wide, the pulse fluttering at the base of his throat. She turned her face aside and withdrew as she had been commanded, but not before she had seen the ice forming on his smooth, naked dermis.

From the vantage of the second plane, she beheld the Shadow, stretching above and below until it vanished from her puny under-standing. Opposing—near engulfed by—it was a faint stain of muddy light, scarce strong enough to penetrate the loftier planes.

Fear flared; she thrust it aside and bent all her perceptions to the Shadow, striving to see through it, seeking her submissive, the rippling fires of his essence—and realized with a shock that the muddy emittance was he.

Reveal yourself!

The thunder of the command all but shredded her control; how Rool Tiazan maintained his deception in the brunt of it was more than she could comprehend.

The muddy fires constricted, as if in fear, and flared sluggishly.

There beneath the Shadow, she dared to form a thought deep within her secret heart, trusting that he would hear her.

If you are too small, she whispered, *you will be found unworthy.*

The Shadow grew dense, and the command came again. She clung to her control, focused—saw a flare of pure golden light pierce the loftier aether, and another, very nearly the blue of his eyes.

A third time, the Iloheen commanded. The muddy essence deformed, as if its strength were failing.

Once again, she acted where cold reason would have counseled her to wait.

Edonai.

The Shadow withdrew a segment of its attention from Rool Tiazan and placed it upon her. She abased herself.

Speak.

Edonai, should this submissive be destroyed, I will be unable to pursue the great work until another vessel has been formed, another tumzaliat downloaded and trained. Her thought was steady and cool; her protections down.

It is a poor tool, the Iloheen responded. *Perhaps you are worthy of better.*

Edonai, it is well enough. You come at the conclusion of a match of wills. We are both of us exhausted.

A wing of dark satisfaction crossed her perception—and the Shadow coalesced, enveloping her, cutting off her perceptions. Fear was a spear of flame through her core. She rode it down, gathered what poor senses that were left to her tight, and endured while the Shadow constricted further and the sense of satisfaction grew, filling all the planes on which she existed, freezing her thought, shredding her essence, annihilating . . .

Somewhere beyond the limitless frozen dark, her fragmented senses registered a flare of light. One single ray pierced the Shadow, growing brighter, broader, spilling ripples of golds and blues.

Around her—within her—the Iloheen laughed, and it was terrible.

It displays merit. The cold voice stated. *You may proceed.*

The Shadow was gone; her senses returned in a flare of agony and she fell into the physical plane so suddenly her body convulsed and she screamed against the air.

She fought the body's systems like a novice, felt the muscles knot—and then loosen as warmth flowed through her. Panting, she re-established control, opened her eyes and beheld Rool Tiazan on his knees beside her; his hands flat against her breast.

How? she sent to him.

The fierce eyes met hers boldly.

There are myriad hows. Choose.

How have the Iloheen missed you only now? But as soon as she formed the thought, she knew.

The ley lines, she answered her own question. *You manipulated time, probability, and space.*

So much power, she thought secretly, and did not care that he stood within her walls, and heard. *Iloheen-bailel, indeed.*

Iloheen. His laughter rippled, gold-ebon-silver. *I am never so clumsy. Did you not hear your Iloheen approach? Arrogant, noisy . . .*

Peace—she sent sharply, the while recalling that strange disturbance which had called her from thought directly before the

Shadow had manifested. As foretold by both the biology and philosophy tutors, she had gained new senses from her joining with Rool Tiazan.

So you know how. He sat back on his heels, hands flat on his thighs.

And now I would know why. Painfully, she pushed herself into a sitting position, and frowned up into his face.

Free space beyond the larger cage is well-watched. I thought to find a less guarded route of escape.

And instead bound yourself to a biologic construct. She felt—not fear's bright, sharp knife, but a dull, dark blade, twisting at her core.

I did not . . . perfectly understand this binding. His thought was soft. *I thought you weak and subject to manipulation. I find instead that you are stronger than you should be and that the lines . . .*

His thought faded.

The lines? she prompted.

Hesitation, then a sensation very like a sigh.

My study of the ley lines discovers no possibility in which I am not captured and enslaved. Many are worse—that I remain in servitude to those whom you call Iloheen, forced to continue annihilating star systems and living creatures—that I find most often. This here and now—where I am bound and diminished—this is kindest, and most full with possibility.

Possibility? She queried, but he did not answer.

Did you feel your Iloheen's pleasure? he asked instead. *That you found the dominion of so small and dull a tumzaliat exhausting? It thought you a weak thing; poor in will. And it was pleased.*

Shivering, she recalled the Iloheen's laughter, and drew a breath deep into her body's lungs.

We are all poor and flawed creatures, in the perception of the Iloheen, she said, which was among the first things she had been taught.

The fierce eyes closed, and Rool Tiazan bowed his bright head.

How long, she asked, when he said nothing more. *Will you be able to disguise your true essence? It will be noticed if you alter from what has been probed.*

He raised his head, and looked into her eyes.

It is a simple deception and uses very little energy. He extended a hand, and softly touched her face.

You are my . . . dominant.

She lifted her chin. *That is correct. You may not act, save through me.*

And yet I have acted from my own will and desire, he said, and she had to admit that this was so.

I offer, said Rool Tiazan, *partnership. We learn each from the other and work together toward common goals.*

In fact, she thought privately, he offered submission. If it eased his pride to name it differently, it changed nothing to allow it.

Standing well within her walls, he heard her thought as it formed, and waited, a cool and silent green presence.

Partnership, she sent, and extended her hand to touch his cheek in reflection of his gesture. *Agreed.*

ONE

❀ ❀

Light Wing
Transitioning to the Ringstars

TOR AN YOS'GALAN SIGHED SOFTLY, rubbed his eyes and released the shock-webbing. The main screen displayed a profusion of green, violet and yellow flowers tangled across an artful tumble of natural rock. Arcing above the rocks and flowers was a piata tree, slender silver trunk bent beneath its burden of fruit. Had he been at home, and the back window of his room ajar, he would have heard the midday breeze in the ceramic bell he'd hung in the piata's branches when he'd been a boy, and smelled the flowers' pungent perfume.

The odors here, on the bridge of the ancient single-ship the clan had assigned to his use, were of plate metal, oil, and disinfectant. Ship smells, as comforting in their way as the constant whisper of air through the vents.

Tor An sighed again, and looked to his secondary screen, where the time to transition end counted down slowly, and pushed out of the pilot's chair.

Soon. Soon, he would be home.

He had hoped to arrive during the census—the grand gathering of ship and folk that took place every twelve years, by Alkia clan law. Alas, his piloting instructor, aside from being a demon on rote, had disallowed his request to double his shifts so that he might depart a Common month early with his big-ship license. Worse, she had then seen fit to short-shift him, so it was only by taking on extra work with the astrogator that he was able to amass the minimum number of flight-points required to attain the coveted license.

All that being so, he'd sent his proxy and his apologies to his sister Fraea, coincidentally the Voice of Alkia. He'd half-expected a return message, but was scarcely surprised when none came. The census was a time of frenetic busyness for those in Administration—and besides, he had received a message from her shortly before he had sent off his regrets, and that missive had contained more than enough information with which he might beguile his few unclaimed hours.

Clan Alkia, so Fraea had written, had recently entered into an alliance with the Mazdiot Trade Clan, jointly purchasing a trade ship—a vessel larger than either might fund of itself. The crew and traders were to be drawn equally from each clan; Tor An, once he had his big-ship license in hand, was to represent the interests of Clan Alkia on the all-important first voyage.

It was, so Fraea had written, a very great honor for him.

Yes, well. His eyes strayed to the main screen. How he wanted to be home! To walk in the old garden, rub his hand over the rocky tumble, pluck a fruit from the piata's branches, and set the ceramic bell to chiming. He wanted, after all this time away, to do nothing more than return to his old rooms, and be still for a time—which was simply foolishness. He was a pilot and a licensed trader; a member of the premier trading family of the Ringstars. It was not for him to spend his life idle on the ground. Even those who served the clan as inventory specialists or 'counts managers spent more time between ships than ever upon the surface of the so-called homeworld. The homeworld was for those whose time of active service was done—and for those whose time was yet to come.

Indeed, he knew very well that the rooms he had continued,

throughout his time away, to think of as "his" were occupied by Grandfather Syl Vor, who was, as Fraea had also written, in the embrace of his final illness, and required the comfort of the open rooms and forgotten garden more than one who stood on the edge of beginning his life's toil.

Upon his arrival at Alkia's planetary base, the clan's son Tor An would be assigned a cot in the transients dorm until it was time for him to ship out. Perhaps he would be able to visit the garden—and Grandfather Syl Vor, as well. Perhaps he would be able to do neither, but be dispatched immediately to the trade ship. It was for Fraea, as Alkia's Voice, to decide these matters. His was to obey.

Obedience was a lifelong habit. On the bridge of old *Light Wing*, he breathed easier for remembering that there was order and progression in his life; and all that was required of him, really, was obedience.

Calmed, if not comforted, he pushed out of the pilot's chair and moved toward the galley. There was time for a meal, a shower, and a nap before transition's end.

THE MIST FADED, teased apart by a small breeze bearing the odors of fuel, dust, and hull metal.

Around them, insubstantial in the melting mist, star-faring ships sat at rest upon cermacrete ready-pads. They themselves stood upon an empty pad, which was folly of a sort; the gentleman holding the lady's hand high, his lips pressed soft against her fingers.

Which was folly of another sort.

The lady extended her free hand and cupped the gentleman's smooth golden cheek, stretching high on her toes to do so. She sank back, and the gentleman released her hand with a gentle smile.

"The skies are clear," the lady said, tucking both hands into the full sleeves of her gown.

"A passing circumstance, I assure you," the gentleman answered, making a show of looking upwards, hand shading his eyes.

"Rool." The lady sighed.

He brought his gaze down to her face, one copper brow arched ironically.

"It is not," she said sternly, "a joke."

"Indeed it is not," he replied, and there was no irony in his voice. "We shall be discovered soon enough, fear it not. Our challenge is to appear genuine in our flight, while neither losing our pursuit nor altering aught that might also alter what has been set in motion." He smiled. "The choice is made; we cannot prevail. I swear it."

The lady's pale lips softened briefly as she looked up into his face.

"The modifications will stand the test," she said seriously. "Are you able? Are you—*willing*? It might yet be undone."

"No!" His voice was sharp, the smile fled. He gripped her shoulders and stared down into her eyes. "It is only the certainty that the modifications *will* stand that gives me hope of the final outcome." His lips quirked, and he dropped his hands.

"You see what I am brought to—a slave who clings to his prison, and treasures his jailor above himself."

The lady laughed, high and sweet.

"Yes, all very well," the gentleman murmured, and tipped his head, considering her out of earnest blue eyes.

"We *will* diminish," he said. "At best, and with everything proceeding as we wish."

The lady swayed a half-bow, scarcely more than a ripple of her gray robe. "Indeed, we will diminish. Is the price too high?"

The gentleman closed his eyes, and extended a delicate hand. The lady caught between her tiny palms.

"I am . . . a poor creature, set against what I once was," he whispered. "We choose, not only for us, here, as we are and have become, but for those others, for whom we have no right to choose."

"Ah." She pressed his hand gently. "And yet, if we do not choose for them, we are parties to their destruction—and to the destruction of all, even those who never understood that a choice existed. Is this not so?"

He sighed, mouth twisting into a smile as he opened his eyes. "It is. Don't heed me—a passing horror of being trapped by that which is malleable. And yet, if one certain outcome is necessary . . ."

"Yes," the lady murmured. "The luck must not be disturbed, now that it has gathered."

"The luck swirls as it will," the gentleman said, slipped his hand from between her palms. "Well, then. If we are both reduced to hope, then let us hope that the agents of luck proceed down the path we have set them on. The one is bound by honor; the other—"

"Hush," the lady murmured. "The lines are laid."

"Yet free will exists," the gentleman insisted—and smiled into her frown. "No, you are correct. We have done what we might. And once they pass the nexus, the lines themselves conspire against deviation . . ."

The lady inclined her head. "Our case is similar. We may not deviate, lest we unmake what we have wrought, and destroy hope for once and ever. If—"

She checked, head cocked as if she detected a sound—

"Yes," said the gentleman, and his smile this time was neither pleasant nor urbane. "Shelter against me, love. It begins."

The lady put her back against his chest. He placed his hands upon her shoulders, fingers gripping lightly.

"Stay," he murmured. "We cannot risk being missed."

Scarcely breathing, they waited, listening to sounds only they could hear, watching shadows only they could see.

"Now," breathed the lady.

And they were gone.

TWO

❀ ❀

Spiral Dance
Transition

"LANDOMIST, IS IT?" Cantra spun the pilot's chair thirty degrees and glared down-board at her copilot.

Jela spared her a black, ungiving glance, in no way discommoded by the glare.

"I gave my word," he said mildly.

She sighed, hanging on to her temper with both hands, so to speak, pitched her voice for reasonable, and let the glare ease back somewhat.

"Right. You gave your word. Now ask yourself what you gave you word *to*, exactly, where they-or-it are now, and with what harrying at their heels."

Jela gave his screens one more leisurely look-over, like there was anything to see except transition-sand; released the chair's webbing and stood, stretching tall—or as tall as he could, which wasn't very.

"You could probably do with a stretch yourself," he said, giving her wide, concerned eyes. "All that tricky flying's soured your temper."

In spite of herself, she laughed, then released the webbing with a snap, and came to her feet, stretching considerably taller than him—and Deeps but didn't it feel good just to let the long muscles move.

Jela rolled his broad shoulders and grinned at her.

"Feel better?"

She gave him the grin back, and relaxed out of the stretch.

"Much," she said cordially, there being no reason not to. "And now that I'm returned to sweet and reasonable, maybe you could apply yourself to being sensible. Did you or did you not hear the lady say it was a *sheriekas* lord's fancy we'd caught?"

"I heard her," Jela answered calmly. "I also heard her say she and her mate were going to draw it away, and give us a chance to do what we'd agreed to do."

"*What you agreed to do*," she snapped. "*I* didn't agree to anything."

The inside of her head tickled at that, and she caught a brief scent of mint, which was what the seedpods grown by the third member of the crew smelled like. She sent a sharp look to the end of the board, where Jela's damn' tree sat in its pot, leaves fluttering in the air flow from the vent.

Or not.

"Our orders," Jela began—Cantra cut him off with a slash of her hand and a snarl.

"Orders!"

"*Our orders*," Jela repeated, overriding her without any particular trouble, "are clear." He tipped his head and added, at a considerably lesser volume, "Or so they seem to me. You're a sharp one for a detail, Pilot. Do you remember what she said?"

Damn the man.

"I remember," she said shortly.

"She said," he continued, as if she hadn't spoken, "*You, the pilot and the ssussdriad will proceed to the world Landomist. You will recover Liad dea'Syl's equations which describe the recrystallization exclusion function and use them in the best interest of life.* Do I have that right, Pilot?"

She'd've denied it, if there'd been room, but Jela wasn't too bad with a detail himself, when he cared to apply himself.

"You've got it close enough," she allowed, still short and snappish. "And the fact that you were pleased to give your word on it don't make the rest of us daft enough to fall prey to the gentle lady's delusions."

"She and her mate are our allies," Jela said, like it made a difference. "We shared the tree's fruit. She trusts us to carry out our part of the campaign."

Cantra closed her eyes.

"Jela."

"Pilot Cantra?"

"What do you think the *sheriekas* lord is going to do with yon pretty children when they're caught?"

"Interrogate them," he said promptly.

Well now there was a sensible answer, after all. She opened her eyes and gave him a smile for reward.

"Granting the *sheriekas* have a fine arsenal of nasties at their beck," she pursued, bringing the Rim accent up hard, "it seems to me likely that Rool Tiazan and his sweet lady will say all they know of everything, and a good number of things of which they have no ken, among it being one soldier, who gave his word to travel straightaway to Landomist for to liberate some 'quations in the service of all those who're enemies of the Enemy." She drew a careful breath, seeing nothing in his eyes but her own reflection.

"Stay with me now. Where do you think that canny cold lord will next turn its care, having heard the *dramliza* sing?"

"Landomist," Jela said calmly.

Cantra felt the glare rising and overrode it with another smile, this one showing puzzled.

"So, knowing that, you're wanting to follow these orders as you style them, and have the three of us down on Landomist, nice and easy for the *sheriekas* to find?"

"I gave my word," Jela said, which brought them full circle.

Once again, a ghostly taste of mint along her tongue. Cantra snapped a look down board, and flung out an arm, drawing Jela's attention to his tree.

"All the care and trouble you've gone to for that damn' vegetable, and now you're wishful of putting it in the path of mortal danger? You done caring what happens to it?"

Whatever reaction she might have expected him to deploy against such a blatant piece of theater, laughter—genuine laughter—was among the last.

Head thrown back, Jela shouted his delight. The tree, for its part, snapped a bow, leaves flashing—and no way the vent had put out a gust strong enough to account for that.

Cantra sighed, hitched her thumbs in her belt and waited.

Jela's laughter finally wound down to a series of deep-in-the-chest chuckles. He raised a hand and wiped the tears off his cheeks, grinning white and wide.

"Mind sharing the joke?" she asked, keeping her tone merely curious.

For a heartbeat it seemed like he was going to engage in some further hilarity at her expense. If he was, he controlled the urge, and waved a shaky hand in the general direction of the tree.

"Pilot, that tree is more soldier than I'll ever be. It held a planet against the *sheriekas*, all by itself, when it wasn't any thicker than my first-finger, here. It knows the risks—what we stand to gain, what we stand to lose. None better, I'll bet you—and I'm including the *dramliza* in that set." Another swipe of fingertips across cheeks to smooth away the last of the laugh-tears. "Ask it yourself, if you don't believe me."

Behind her eyes, unbidden, came a series of pictures. A green, tree-grown world, and the shadows of wings overhead in the high air. Then came a feeling of oppression, as the grass dried, the wings vanished and the first of the very Eldest trembled, wavered—and crashed to the drying earth.

The pictures went on, elucidating the trees' muster, as they fought a delaying action, first in groups, at the last one or two alone, as the world dried until only sand was left. The rivers evaporated, the sea shrank to a trickle, and still the trees held the enemy away by will, as Cantra understood it to be—and by won't.

It was a campaign doomed to failure, of course, and the last few soldiered on, their life force stretched thin. The feeling of oppression grew into a tangible weight, and the winds whipped, scattering sand across the corpses of trees, which was all that remained—save one.

Cantra's throat was closed with dust, thirst an agony. She felt her sap falling and knew her death was near. She was too young, her resources too meager, and yet she bent her energies to her last task, and produced a pod, so the world would not be left unprotected—then waited, singing thin and defiant against the Enemy's howl of desolation.

But what came next was not death.

Rather, a new form took shape out of the wind and the sand—not a dragon, yet with something dragon-like about it. It, too, opposed the Enemy. It, too, was dying. It proposed a partnership of mutual survival, that they might together continue to fight.

The tree accepted the proposal.

There was a stutter in the storylines, and there was *Dancer's* bridge, clear enough, and the *dramliza* on their knees, heads bowed, the echo of the question in her own head, and the answer, damnitall, that she'd made it.

In the matter of allies, you need to ask yourself two things: Can they shoot? And will they aim at your enemy?

Quick as a sneeze, then, the tree cut her loose to fall back into her own head so fast and so hard she gasped aloud.

Cantra blinked and focused on Jela. He had the decency to show her a calm, disinterested face. A mannerly man was Jela, soldier or no.

"All right, then," she said, and was pleased that her voice sounded as calm and disinterested as Jela's eyes. "There's two of you agreed to cleave to madness. The fact remains that *I* never gave *my* word."

"Now, that's very true," Jela allowed. "You never did give your word." He turned his big hands up, showing her empty, calloused palms. "Belike the lady thought we'd all stand as crewmates. But if you're determined not to risk yourself—and I'll agree that it's not a risk-free venture—then there's nothing more to say. I will ask you the favor of setting me and the tree down someplace we're likely to catch public transport to Landomist. I'd rather not call attention to us by coming in on a hired ship."

Almost, she did him the favor of returning a shout of his earlier laughter. She strangled the urge, though, and gave him as serious and stern a look as she could muster.

"I could do that," she said. "I'm assuming you have a plan for getting at those equations, locked up tight as they are in Osabei Tower."

"I do."

Cantra sighed. "And that would be?"

He tipped his head, making a play-act out of consideration, and finally gave her an apologetic grin, as false as anything she'd ever had from him.

"It's my campaign," he said, "and my word. The way I see it, you've got no need to know. Pilot."

It was said respectful enough, and in any case wasn't anything more or less than the plain truth. Nothing to notch her annoyance up to anger—so she told herself, and took a hard breath.

"Ever been to Landomist?" she asked, keeping her voice light and pleasant.

"Never," he answered in the same tone. "I don't get deep Inside much."

"Understandable. That being the case, you might not be familiar with the Towers?"

Jela moved his wide shoulders, head tipped to one side. "I've come across them in citations, tech lit and such. Each Tower represents a discipline and includes subsets of the discipline which hold conflicting philosophies."

Not bad, Cantra conceded. Dangerously simplistic, but not bad.

"Those conflicting philosophies, now," she said, just offering info— "they're more often than not the cause of blood duels and worse 'mong the scholars. Establish enough unchallenged theory—that being equally those who don't challenge the worth of a particular theory and those who challenged and lost—and a scholar gets moved to the High Tower and lives untouchable as a master."

Jela frowned and moved his hand, fingers flickering—pilot-talk for *get on with it.*

"Right," she said. "Osabei Tower, now, that's Spatial Math. Named after one Osabei tay'Bendril who brought pilot-kind the good numbers that make transition possible. Before Scholar tay'Bendril, pilots had to go the long way 'round and it might take a lifetime or two to traverse the Arm. They prolly gave you all that in 'mong the rest of pilot lore, same's they gave it to me. But what they didn't likely give you was the fact that the Towers're closed, and fortified, and they don't like strangers. But that's not your first problem."

She paused. Jela's face showed nothing but bland interest, damn the man. Well, she was the one who'd charted this course; he hadn't asked for her advice.

"Your first problem," she continued, "is that it's *Landomist*, about as Inside as you can get and not be on the other side of the Spiral. You put one boot on Landomist without a writ or a license and you'll be exported before the second boot's down, if you're lucky—or memwiped and impressed to an Honorable, if you're not."

Jela rolled his shoulders and gave her a grin, slightly more genuine than the last.

"So, I'll have a writ to show."

"Assuming it's good enough and the Portmaster's not having a bad day, then you get a native guide to walk at your shoulder while you go about your lawful business, and to remind you when you step out from bounds."

He laughed.

"Pilot, you know a shadow's not going to stay with me."

"Lose or kill your assigned guide and you're a dead man," she snarled, surprising herself, "and a stupid man at the last."

Silence for the beat of three.

"Eventually, I'm a dead man, but I'd like to think not stupid," Jela said seriously. "Tell me why I can't just slip free, and go invisible."

Because it's Landomist! she wanted to shout—but didn't.

"Come with me," was what she said instead, and strode out of the piloting room without looking to see if he followed, down the short hall to her quarters.

The door opened with a snap that seemed reflective of her state of mind, and she concentrated on breathing nice and even while she crossed over to her locker and opened it wide.

For a moment, she was alone in the polished metal mirror—a slender woman in trade leathers, pale hair cut off blunt at the stubborn jaw, features sharp, smooth skin toned gold, eyes a cool and misty green. Neither face, nor eyes, nor stance betrayed the slightest perturbation, nor the satisfaction she felt upon observing this.

A whisper from the rear and her reflection was joined by a second—broad shoulders and slim waist, both set off something fine by the leathers. Black hair, cropped; black eyes, bland. His face was brown, symmetrical, and a bit leaner than the shoulders predicted, with a firm mouth and strong brows. The top of his head didn't quite hit her shoulder, despite he bore himself upright and proud.

She used her chin to point at her own reflection.

"*That*," she announced, "is Inside norm, bred out of certified stock proven across more generations than you got time to hear or me to tell."

"All right," Jela said quietly.

"All right," she repeated, and pointed at his reflection.

"*That* is a gene-tailored series biologic."

"All right," he said again, and met her eyes in the mirror. "You're saying they aren't used to seeing Series soldiers on Landomist."

"I'm saying the only way anything other than Inside norm exists on Landomist is as property," Cantra corrected, and turned to look down into his face.

"You can't disappear on Landomist—and that's before you start having to tote that damn' tree around with you. There's just *nobody* there who looks like you, saving maybe a few household guards some Honorable might've bought from the military as curiosities."

His eyes moved and his jaw muscles tightened up, it upset him that much. Cantra reached out and touched his shoulder, taking care to keep it light and comradely, and smiled when he looked back to her.

"What you want is an agent," she said. "Set it up right, take your time—"

He laughed, soft, and slid out from under her hand.

"Time," he said, turning away, "is exactly what I don't have."

She frowned at his back. "You think the children're likely to get caught right off? Seemed to me they had a few worthy tricks to hand."

Jela paused, hesitated, then slowly turned to face her again.

"That's not where the crunch is," he said, and her ear registered absolute sincerity; unvarnished truth. He took a hard breath, and looked down at his broad, capable hands.

"It's me that's the problem. I'm old."

"Old?" She stared at the hard, inarguable bulk of him. "How old can you be?"

"Forty-four years, one-hundred-fifteen-and-one-twelfth days," he said. "Common Calendar." Another hard breath as he brought his eyes up and met hers firmly.

"Forty-five years is the design limit," he said steadily.

Cantra felt something cold and multi-clawed skitter through her gut.

"Design limit," she repeated, and closed her eyes, recalling Rool Tiazan's lady, her sharp eyes on Jela while she snapped out that time was short for each one of them.

And for some, it was shorter than others.

Anger trembled—anger at the *dramliza*. So busy about their promises. They had known—*known* that the man they'd built all their airy plans on had less than five months to live. Common Calendar. And with all the wonders the pair could likely make between them, they didn't pause for the heartbeat it might've cost—

"First-aid kit," she said, huskily, and opened her eyes to meet Jela's calm gaze. "We put you in the first-aid kit," she amplified when he didn't do anything more than lift a lazy black eyebrow.

"Get you put back to spec, then you take what time you need to plan out your campaign."

"Pilot—"

She raised a hand. "I know you're not friends with the 'kit, but own it has its uses. You saw what it did for Dulsey—Deeps! You saw what it did for me. You climb yourself in and I'll set us a cour—"

"*Cantra*." He didn't raise his voice, but there was still enough snap in it to cut her off in mid-word. She felt the muscles of her face contract and wondered wildly what she'd been showing him.

Having stopped her, Jela didn't seem in any hurry to fill up the cabin with words of his own. He just stood there, head to a side, looking at her—and if truth be told there was something odd going on in his face, too.

He moved then, one careful step, keeping his hands where she could see them. Motionless, she watched him take her hand between both of his broad palms.

His skin was warm, his hands gentle. He craned his head back, black eyes searching her face, his absolutely open.

"Remember when the first-aid kit didn't work?" he asked, like they were discussing what cargo was best to take on. "Garen had to take you to the Uncle for a receptor flush because the first-aid kit didn't cure the edlin. That was why, wasn't it? Because all the 'kit could do was put you back to spec."

Pain. Thoughts staggering through reeking blood-red mists . . . then coolness as reason returned in the friendly dark. The lid rose, she rolled out—and collapsed to the floor, screaming as the pain took her again . . .

"And spec included the gimmicked receptors," she said, suddenly and deeply weary. "Right."

"Right," Jela said softly. "It's in the design, Cantra. M Series soldiers are decommissioned at forty-five years." He smiled, sudden and genuine. "Safer that way."

"Safer . . ." she whispered and her free hand moved on its own, gripping his shoulder hard.

"Rool Tiazan," she said after a moment. "He asked how you'd choose to die."

"He did," Jela said briskly. "And if the tree and me are to liberate the good scholar's math, publish it wholesale, *and* die in battle, I'd better not take too many naps."

She smiled slightly, and stepped back, taking her hand off his shoulder, slipping the other from between his palms. He watched her out of calm black eyes.

"If it ain't your intention to die on Landomist Port," she said, turning to shut the locker door, "and see the tree broken and burned before you do, you'll employ that agent to work your will, like I said you should."

Behind her, she heard Jela sigh.

"It has to be a frontal attack," he said patiently. "I don't know how to employ the sort of agent you advise. And I don't have time to train him."

Face to the locker, she closed her eyes, hearing again the tiny lady's sharp voice listing out the terms of Jela's service:

You, the pilot and the ssussdriad will proceed to the world Landomist . . .

Not her fight, dammit. She'd not sworn to any such madness.

Pay your debts, baby, Garen ghost-whispered from the gone-away past. *There ain't no living with yourself, if you don't.*

Deeps knew, she wouldn't be living at all, were it not for Jela— and, truth told full, the tree, as well.

Cantra sighed, very softly, opened her eyes and turned to face him.

"Her," she said, and met his eyes firm, giving a good imitation of woman with a sensible decision on deck. "I can get you in."

THREE

Light Wing
Doing the Math

THE KLAXON SHRIEKED, and Tor An's body responded before he was fully awake, snapping forward to the board—and snatched back by the webbing as the ship dropped out of transition with a shudder and a sob.

He'd webbed into the chair before allowing himself to nod off—prudent for a pilot running solo, even in relatively pirate-free space.

Prudence had saved him a bad knock—and another when the ship twisted again, as if protesting its sudden change of state.

By then, he was well awake, and by exerting steady pressure against the restraints managed to gain his board, and get a closer look at the screens.

The board was locked and live—standard for transition—and the main screen displayed a dense, unfamiliar starfield. Across the center of the display ran a bright blue legend: *Transition aborted. Target coordinates unavailable.*

Tor An blinked, reached to the board, engaged shields, called up the last-filed transition string, and sat frowning at the cheery yellow coordinates that described the location of home. Feeling a

417

fool, he activated the library, called for the Ringstars, and did a digit-by-digit comparison between the library's coord set and those displayed in the nav screen.

The numbers matched, which ought to have, he thought, made him feel better. After all, he *hadn't* made a fumble-fingered entry error, or misremembered the coord set he'd been able to recite almost before he could pronounce his name.

On the other hand, a ship sent into transition defined by a correct set of target coordinates ought not to exit transition until the conditions described by the coordinates were met.

"Unless," Tor An said to the empty tower, "the navigation brain has dead sectors, or a ship self-check determines a dangerous condition. Or pirates force you out early."

He glared at the screens, noting the lack of pirates. He slapped up the logs, but found no dangerous condition. Dead sectors in the nav brain—he sighed. There was only one way to determine if that were the case.

Leaning to the board again, he set up a suite of diagnostics, punching the start key with perhaps a bit more force than was absolutely necessary. The board lights flickered; the screens blanked momentarily, then lit again, displaying the testing sequence and estimated time until completion.

Tor An released the webbing and stood. There was one more thing that might usefully be done—and, considering the age of his ship, *ought* to be done. If the transvective stabilizers had developed a wobble, the ship might have spontaneously dropped out of transition. He rather thought that such an event would have been noted in the log, but it *was* an old ship, with quirks and crotchets, and certain sporadic incompatibilities between ship's core and the logging function were a known glitch of its class.

Two of his strides and he was across the tiny tower. He opened a storage hatch, pulled out a tool belt and slung it around his waist, snapping it as he headed for the door.

SOME WHILE LATER, he was back in the pilot's chair, gnawing on a high-calorie bar and scrolling through the diagnostic reports, not as pleased as he might be by the unbroken lines of "normal function." At the end of the file, he sat back, the bar forgotten in his hand.

The stabilizers had checked out. The synchronization unit—which he knew for a glitchy, temperamental piece of work—had tested perfectly sound. Everything that could be tested, had tested normal, except for one thing.

Normally functioning ships do not spontaneously fall out of transition and report the—correctly entered!—target coordinates as "unavailable."

"Well," he said aloud, "it's obviously a fabric-of-space problem."

"Fabric-of-space problem" was Alkia in-clan for "a thing which has happened, but which cannot be explained." There being a limited number of such events in life, the phrase was a joke—or a sarcastic jibe from an elder to a junior suspected of being too lazy to do a thorough check.

But he *had* done a thorough check, for all the good he'd gained.

"Check again," he told himself, a trifle impatiently, "or trust the data."

Chewing his lower lip, he glanced down, frowned at the bar in his hand and tossed it into the recycling drawer. Then, he engaged the webbing, brought the board up, woke the nav brain and fed it the coordinates for the Ringstars.

"Enough nonsense," he said to his ship. "Let us go home."

He initiated transition.

CANTRA POURED THE LAST of the tea into her mug, started a new pot brewing, and wandered back into that part of the lodgings which was in the fond thought of the landlord the parlor. Right now, it was a workroom, with twin tables piled high with the building blocks of a dozen or more parallel-running projects, hers and his.

Her projects were in holding orbit at the moment, waiting an all-clear from the portmaster, played for this once-only showing by M. Jela, who was emoting equal parts stubborn and grim as he sat hunched over his toys. A warmer bowl containing dinner—or might-be breakfast—sat at his elbow, the noodles dry, the tasty and nutritious sauce long baked off. He'd been paying sporadic attention to his mug, so she'd set herself to keeping it full with hot, sweet, and fresh.

Cantra sipped tea and sighed. The man did, she conceded, have a point. If the info could be pinched from afar, then it was beyond foolish to risk the ship's company by going in after it. It happened she believed—based on past study, say—that the Towers of Landomist kept their brains well-shielded, and Osabei moreso than most. She'd given him everything she knew on the subject, which was, once she'd put her memory to it, not inconsiderable. And she'd pointed out the logic behind imprisoning Liad dea'Syl in Osabei, on the slim chance he hadn't figured it out for himself.

Still, he'd wanted to check it for himself, and so he was— using an interesting combination of military grade and Dark Market gizmos. Cantra supposed she ought to be grateful for his caution. Herself, she was finding the inexorable passage of time an unwelcome irritant.

She sat down in the chair she'd lately been calling home, and put her feet up on one of the rare clear spots of her table. Crossing her ankles, she glanced at the tree, sitting in a fancy artwork pot over in the corner, under the special light Jela'd rigged for it—and then at the clock. Not long now. She sipped her tea and watched Jela, which was a deal more scenic than staring at the wall, and waited.

Her tea was gone by the time the clock finally gave out with its tootling little on-the-local-hour song, and Jela sighed, rolled his shoulders and leaned back in his chair, his eyes lingering on the spyware.

"Luck?" she asked, though by the look of it, learning-by-doing had only gained what she'd told him in the first place.

He sighed again, and finally met her eyes, his tired and tending toward bleak.

"We go in," he said.

HE RAISED TELMAIR.
He raised Kant.
He raised Porshel and Braz, Jiniwerk, and Oryel.

He dug deep into the library, and unrolled star charts across the tower floor, weighting the corners with spanners. When he had identified the coordinates for a sphere of six waystops inside the influence of the Ringstars, he fed those into the nav-brain, webbed himself into the pilot's chair, initiated transition, and waited, his face tight, his back rigid.

The ship accepted its office. Tor An sighed, his muscles melting toward relief—

And *Light Wing* twisted, klaxons blaring as she fell into real space, alarms lighting the board, and across the main screen, the bright blue legend:

Transition aborted. Target coordinates unavailable.

He was a conscientious boy, and he had been taught well. Ignoring the ice in his belly, the chilly sweat on his face, he re-checked the charts, made sure of his numbers, and initiated transition for the second time.

And for a second time, his ship transitioned, and almost immediately returned to normal space.

Transition aborted. Target coordinates unavailable.

He shut down the board, made sure of his shields, deliberately unwebbed and stood. It had, he told himself, been some time since he had eaten—how long a time, he was not prepared to say with any certainty, save that he had been awake for longer.

"Pilot error," he said to the empty tower. "I am taking myself off-duty for a meal, a shower and a nap. Barring ship's need, I will return in five ship hours and perform the exercise again from the top."

He was a lad of his word, and had been raised to know the value of discipline. There was no ship's emergency to disturb him and he returned to the tower visibly refreshed, had there been any to see, in just under five ship hours.

Once at his station, he again carefully examined the star maps, acquiring six coordinate strings defining a sphere of ports that lay within the boundary space of the Ringstars.

Rising, he went to his chair, webbed in, entered the coords, double-checked them—and initiated transition.

Light Wing leapt, stuttered—fell.

Transition aborted, read the message across the main screen. *Target coordinates unavailable.*

CANTRA WOKE as she'd set herself to do, since it was important to be up and well about her business before Jela, who never that she'd noticed slept more than four hours together, did the same.

Despite that the "up" side of the equation was as crucial as the "awake," she stayed a bit longer just where she was, curled slightly on her left side, her back snuggled against Jela's wide and reassuring chest. His arm was draped companionably over her waist, her hand tucked into the relaxed curl of his fist. He slept quiet, did Jela, and solid, which the Deeps knew he had a right. The work he'd put in over the last few days, cutting his four hours of sleep down to two, or, in some cases, so she suspected, none—it was a wonder he could stand, much less share a long and satisfying pleasure as they'd just enjoyed. The last of too few.

She sighed softly, and shifted, slow and languorous, a well-satisfied woman readjusting position in her sleep. Jela shifted in turn, reflexively withdrawing his arm. Freed, she waited three heartbeats, listening to his quiet, unhurried breathing. When she was certain he hadn't woke, she eased out of bed and ghosted away.

THE LIGHT IN THE MAIN ROOM was hard and non-adjustable; the work tables tidier than they'd been in a while. Jela's held a couple sets of data tiles, frames, and some bits of esoteric tinyware the particulars of which she hadn't troubled to ask after. Her table—was clear, excepting a notebook and a pen. Picking up the pen, she wrote, briefly, tore the sheet out of the book and placed it prominently at Jela's table. Her last instruction to her co-pilot. She wished that it could have been something more easeful—but there wasn't any use lying to Jela. Not now.

Last duty done, she turned toward the third room that made the sum of their lodgings: A small, chilly niche about the size of the guest cabin on *Dancer.* More than big enough for a death.

Something green fluttered at the edge of her vision, which would be Jela's damn' tree—or her ally the *ssussdriad,* soon to be neither. The flutter came again, stronger, and she knew perfectly well there was neither draft nor vent where it was placed.

Sighing, she turned and walked down the room to where it sat under the special-spectrum spotlight Jela'd rigged for it. The change in lighting'd done it good, if the number and size of the pods hanging from its scrawny branches were any measure.

The dance of leaves became more agitated as she approached, and a particular branch began to visibly bend under the weight of its pod. Cantra considered it sardonically.

"Going-away present?" she asked, her voice harsh in her own ears.

A picture formed inside her head: Water sparkling beneath her, the shadow of a great beast flashing over the waves. She felt a bone-deep ache in her shoulders, an emptiness in her belly, and still she labored on, sinking toward the water, each stroke an agony . . . And there, ahead—the cliffs, the trees, the others! She made a mighty effort, but the tips of her wings cut water on the downstroke, and she knew the cliffs were beyond her—

From the dancers along the cliff sides came a large, dark dragon, his flight powerful and swift. He flew above and past her, spun on a wing and dove, slipping between her and the water, bearing her up, up the side of the cliffs and into the crown of a tree. A pod-heavy branch rose as the songs of welcome filled her ears and she gratefully took the gift thus offered . . .

Cantra blinked; the image faded. "Promises," she said, voice cracking, "promises are dangerous things. You dasn't give one unless you're sure to keep it. No living with yourself any other way." The branch bent sharply, insistently. She held out a hand with a sigh. "Have it your way, then. But don't say I never told you." The pod hit her palm solidly and her fingers curled over it.

"Thank you," she said softly.

SHE LOCKED THE DOOR behind her, then set her shoulders against it, eyes closed.

"You told the man you'd back him," she said aloud, and shivered in the chill air.

The fact was, for all her bold words, she might not be *able* to back him. Oh, she remembered the lessons, fair enough, though it would perhaps have eased things for an unpracticed and unwilling *aelantaza* were any of the particular mix of psychotropics used in the final prep stage of an assignment on hand. Still, the wisdom was that the thing could be done by trance alone. The drug was helpful, but by no means necessary. For the first part of the operation.

The second part—the resurrection, should there be one . . . Well, she'd never heard other than the drug was needed and necessary for that part of it. Not to say the company of a taler, which she didn't have either. Once in a chance, so the story went, an *aelantaza* might come home so burnt-brained and desperate that the drug didn't make no nevermind. It wasn't any use even bringing a taler near such a one. The best thing to do then, in the estimation of the Directors, who weren't known for wasting resources, was to break the burnt-brain's neck before they up and hurt somebody they shouldn't.

Sort of like Pliny'd done.

Cantra sighed. She didn't want to die, though she was looking at doing just that. But maybe, she thought, her throat tight—maybe she wouldn't die. All she had to do was play diversion for a month or less, Common. Maybe there would be enough of herself left at the end the assignment to spontaneously regenerate—

Or maybe not.

It ain't, she said to herself, the weight of the tree's gift heavy in her fist, *like you never done it before. You weren't born to the Rim nor to the life Garen taught you. Whoever you were before, you came to be someone else—something other. This'll be just the same.*

The Rimmer pilot was no more real than the daughter Garen'd thought her to be. The person who rose up out of the remains of the pilot's psyche would be no more nor less real than both.

There was a scent in the cabin; she hadn't noticed it before. A pleasant scent, green and minty and . . . comforting. Cantra opened her eyes, raised her fist, opened her fingers and considered the pod on her palm.

No doubt the aroma emanated from it; and it grew more

enticing by the moment. She remembered her previous tastes of the tree's fruit, and found her mouth watering.

Well, it can't hurt, she thought; and, if she were honest with herself, it might help with the local courage levels.

She put finger to pod, wondering how best to crack it, lacking Jela's strong hand or Rool Tiazan's more . . . unusual . . . abilities, but to her surprise it fell apart at her lightest touch, releasing an even more tempting aroma.

The taste was better than she recalled—tart and spicy. Sighing, she ate the second piece, muscles relaxing as her body warmed. By the time she had finished all of the pieces and carefully slipped the rind into the waste unit, she felt calm and centered. That was good; she was past the jitters now and down to cases.

Opening the drawer of the bedside table, she withdrew a wide bracelet set with several gem-topped buttons. This, she snapped 'round her wrist, adjusting it until it was snug and showed no disposition to slip.

That done, she lay down on the narrow bed and pulled a blanket over her nakedness, closed her eyes, regulated her breathing, and called to mind those exercises which would eventually pitch her into the trance. She had prepared as well as she could: memories, behaviors, preferences, and history would be released and assimilated as soon as her mind came to the change level.

Her heartbeat spiked at the thought, as if her body would be afraid: Patiently, firmly, she smoothed the spike, and sank further into calmness. The last thing she felt, before the change overtook her, was a sensation of utter safety and respect, not at all unlike the sensation of being curled against Jela's chest . . .

SHE WOKE WITH a sense of anticipation so great that she could scarcely keep from shouting aloud. Such an outburst, of course, would be unseemly from a seated scholar of Osabei Tower, and Maelyn tay'Nordif fully intended to be a seated scholar of Osabei Tower before this day's work was done.

She rose with alacrity, opened the small closet and pulled on the clothes she found there—a faded gold unitard, over which went a well-worn and carefully patched tabard. She stepped to the mirror and studied her reflection critically as she wove the yellow sash about her waist in the so-called Wander pattern, and took some time over the precise position of the smartgloves folded over it. When these were disposed to her satisfaction, she returned to the closet and withdrew a slender knife; its grip shaped of common ceramic, wrapped with fraying leather; the edges showing some slight notching. She rubbed the flat of the blade down the front of her tabard once or twice, to shine it, then slipped it also into her sash, being careful of her fingers.

Thus accoutered, she stood for another long moment before the mirror, considering her reflection.

"All very well," she said at last, her voice sharp and slightly nasal, "for a Wanderer. But tomorrow, you will be clad in the robes of a scholar, and seated in your proper place amongst the greatest mathematical minds of the galaxy." She smiled, lips pressed tight, and at last turned away from the mirror. Gathering her book from the table next to the bed, she reviewed the necessities of the day.

First, to register the kobold and the plant with the port—an annoyance, but it had to be done. Such a shame that they had come in last evening after the proper office had closed, and thus mere paperwork must put back her triumph by another few hours. She frowned in annoyance, and tossed her head. No matter. Once the proper registries were made, she would proceed to Osabei Tower, present her token, and—she doubted not, be welcomed with joy and open arms by her peers.

Satisfied with this precis, she unlocked the door and stepped into the great room.

The kobold was seated at the table, its big hands folded before it, exactly as she had left it upon retiring, yestereve. Maelyn sighed, wondering, not for the first time, whatever had possessed her last patron to make her so ridiculous a gift. True, the kobold and the plant were but portions of the parting gift, and the Noble Panthera, heir to House Chaler, had been generous in the matters of both coin and credit. Well, and the thing was done, and both were under her dominion. And who else, she thought suddenly, preening, among the scholars of Osabei Tower, might possess such rare and interesting items? Truly, she came to claim her chair no mere ragged Wanderer, but a woman of property!

"Stand *up*, Jela!" she ordered, experience having taught her the way of dealing with the kobold, whose intelligence was only slightly greater than that of the plant in its care. "Place the pack on your back, pick up the plant, and follow me. *Closely.*"

Brown face expressionless, eyes dull, it pushed to its feet and hefted the pack. It was a powerful creature, and she had seen, during her time at House Chaler, what a single kobold might wreak, under order.

Maelyn touched the bracelet 'round her wrist. She had the means to control Jela, which was, in any case, too dull to be a danger to her.

"Hurry!" she snapped at its broad back, and turned to open the door.

⚙ THIEF ⚙

FOUR

⚙ ⚙

Landomist Port

THE ERRANT-SCHOLAR'S tabard was onyx green, Osabei's Theorem embroidered in sable and silver 'round the hems and neckline. Beneath the tabard, she wore a unitard the precise golden shade of her skin. A pair of smart-gloves and a scholar's truth-blade were thrust through the yellow sash that cuddled her slender waist, and the expression on her high-born face was cool enough to freeze a man's blood.

Behind her came a very gnome of a creature, clad all in black leather: squat, thick, and sullen, a pack on its back, and its bulging arms wrapped about a large and ornately enameled pot. From the pot a green plant rose to some distance above the kobold's head, leaves a-flutter in the breeze from the open window.

Scholars were no rare thing on Landomist—and mathematical scholars least rare of all. Angry errant-scholars accompanied by tree-bearing kobolds—that was something rarer, and promised diversion of one sort or another on a slow and sleepy day. So it was that the portmaster himself stepped up to the counter, forestalling the bustling of the lead clerk, and inclined his head.

"Errant-Scholar, how may I be pleased to assist you?"

Her lips tightened and for a heartbeat he thought she would slip the leash on her temper, which would have been—unwise.

Apparently, she was not too angry for considered thought. The tight lips softened a fraction and bent upward at the corners in a fair approximation of pleasant courtesy, as she proffered a scarred and travel-worn document case.

"If you would do what is necessary to clear me, sir, I would be most obliged."

"Of course," he murmured, receiving the case and running it efficiently along the mag-strip.

"One did not quite understand," the errant-scholar continued as he opened the case, popped the data tile from its setting and inserted it into the reader, "that more than simply declaring at the gate was required."

"Of course not," he said soothingly, most of his attention on the hardcopy enclosed in the other half of the case. He rubbed his fingers lightly over the document, feeling the sharp edges of the letters cut deep into the paper, the silky blots of sealing wax with their pendant ribbons . . .

"Errant-Scholar Maelyn tay'Nordif, native of Vetzu," he said, musingly, and glanced up.

The errant-scholar's eyes were green, he noticed. She inclined her head, her hair soft and silken in the yellow light.

"I am Maelyn tay'Nordif," she answered primly.

"May I know your reason for coming to Landomist, Scholar?" The information would be on the data tile, of course, but it was often useful to hear what else was said—or was not said—in answer to a direct inquiry.

She lifted her chin proudly. "I go to kneel in reverence before the masters of Osabei Tower and petition that my time of wandering be done."

The usual reason, the portmaster conceded, and sent a sharp glance over the lady's shoulder to the silent kobold. The creature had the temerity to meet his eyes, its own black and reflective. The portmaster frowned.

"Landomist has very strict regulations regarding genetic constructs," he said to Errant-Scholar tay'Nordif. "It is not sufficient to merely declare; this office is required to examine, test and certify each and every incoming construct." He looked sternly into her eyes. "A matter of public safety, Scholar. I am certain that you would not wish it otherwise."

It was plain from the scholar's face that she did wish it otherwise, but she was not such a fool as to say so. Instead, she merely inclined her head.

"The safety of the public must of course carry all before it," she murmured. "You will find detailed pedigrees for both the plant and the kobold in the auxiliary index of the tile."

"Of course," he said again, and gestured toward the reader. "This will be a few moments."

The scholar sighed. "I understand," she said.

He bent to the reader, and quickly learned that the vegetative item was a gift from Horticultural Master Panthera vas'Chaler of Shinto to Errant-Scholar tay'Nordif, in token of "the continued growth of our spiritual kinship, which shall forever remain the greatest of my life's pleasures." The Master provided a DNA map for the specimen, and a certification of non-toxicity; the validation programs in his reader reported both genuine, the files extensively cross-referenced to the files of the Shinto Planetary Horticultural Society.

So much, the portmaster thought, for the vegetative portion of the Errant-Scholar's retinue. He bent again to the reader.

The labor class genetic construct "Jela" had also been given by Master vas'Chaler, in order to "transport the token of our kinship and to perform those other services which may avail and comfort the most precious sister of my soul."

The portmaster looked up. "Landomist requires that an inhibitor be installed in all mobile constructs."

The scholar raised a slender hand. "Your pardon," she murmured. Turning her face aside, she snapped at the kobold. "Jela! Place the plant gently on the floor and walk forward to the counter."

This the creature did, moving with a slow-witted deliberation that confirmed its "laborer" class, its footsteps sounding loud and slow against the floor.

"Display your inhibitor," the Scholar instructed.

The big clumsy hands came up and parted the leathern collar, revealing the thick throat and an expanse of wide, hairless brown chest. About the throat and across the chest were intricate lines of what at first glance appeared to be tattoo, but which a second, more sanguine, scrutiny found to be ceramic threads woven into the kobold's skin.

The portmaster leaned forward, extended a hand and rubbed his fingertips across the woven strands. The rough surfaces pulled at his skin. "I . . . see," he said, and leaned back, frowning.

"Is something amiss?" Errant-Scholar tay'Nordif inquired after a moment. "I assure you, sir, that I do not wish in any way to endanger the citizens of Landomist.

That was well-said, the portmaster allowed, yet he felt that she might lose her concern for the public safety were her kobold impounded, or if she should be required to have it refurbished at one of the port shops. Nor would he blame her, either option being more of an expense than it was likely a returning Errant-Scholar could meet. Also, the information provided by her patron made it plain that the kobold and the plant were considered one unit, of which the more valuable portion was the plant. The portmaster looked to the scholar.

"You understand," he said, "that this—" he flicked his fingers at the kobold— "is not the . . . usual device that we employ here on Landomist. I fear that the regulations may require you to have it adjusted at your cost, or to see it impounded."

Her face lost color. "Impound my patron's parting gift?" She exclaimed in horror. "Sir, I—is there nothing, no sub-regulation which perhaps accommodates persons who are to be on Landomist for only a short time, yet require the services of a kobold or other construct?"

That was a thought. The portmaster frowned, then moved to his screen. "A moment," he said. "It may be that there is something—"

The regs came up; he quickly found his place, perused the language and leaned back.

"The provision is for short-term visits only," he said. "This office is, in the case of visits of less than two Common Months, required to certify that the inhibitor is the *equivalent* of a standardized device, and may be invoked by the Landomist general disciplinary band."

The scholar raised her arm, displaying a slender wrist enclosed by a wide silver cuff, set with three glittering stones.

"This device is the controller tuned to this particular construct," she said. "Alas, it is also tuned to me; should I remove it for your inspection, it will require retuning by an expert of the form."

"I see. However, it will not be necessary to compromise your device, Scholar. What the law requires is proof positive that the standard device in use upon Landomist will be adequate to subdue this creature, should the need arise." The portmaster reached beneath the counter and produced the standard device in question. "You permit?"

The scholar inclined her head. "I do. Indeed, I insist. The law must be honored, sir."

This was so novel a concept the portmaster actually blinked, then smiled into the scholar's face. A pleasant lady, she was, if naive, and accepting of his authority.

"But a moment," he murmured and touched the sequence for mid-level pacification.

Instantly, the kobold moaned, its eyes rolling up as it dropped to its knees, one quivering hand raised in supplication.

"I would prefer," the scholar said, "that it not be rendered unconscious, unless proof calls for a complete demonstration. It does not recover well, I fear, and there is the specimen to be transported . . ."

The kobold's brown face was growing darker; low, hideous sounds came from its gaping mouth.

"I believe we have established an equivalency," the portmaster said, triggering the end sequence and turning away from the creature with relief. "It is not my intention to cause you inconvenience, Scholar."

Released, the kobold folded forward until its face was against the floor, its leathered sides heaving. The scholar sighed sharply.

"Stand *up*, Jela!" she snapped impatiently. "Resume your work!"

The kobold shifted like a pile of rocks, lumbered to its feet, and stepped back to its original place. Bending, it wrapped its arms about the pot, hefting it and the tree.

"Should your business at the Tower bear fruit," the portmaster said to the scholar, "you will be required to see the creature modified before the end of two months Common."

"I will see to it as soon as my seat is secure," she promised.

"I will prepare the documentation immediately," the portmaster said. "One moment." He slipped the tile into a frame, located the proper permit in the archive, and transmitted it, with the date and his name. That done, he returned the tile to its setting, resealed the document case and extended it to the waiting scholar.

"Welcome to Landomist," he said, smiling.

Errant-Scholar tay'Nordif received the case with a smile and a polite bow. "Thank you, sir," she said, and snapped over her shoulder at the kobold, "Follow me, Jela! Now!" and left the office.

It was only later, when he was processing a stasis box full of genetically altered carnivorous roses, that the portmaster realized that he had forgotten to assess Scholar tay'Nordif her fee.

FIVE

Osabei Tower
Landomist

THE MERCY BELL HAD RUNG in the Evening's Peace; truth-blades had been sheathed and proofs lain down until the morrow. In accordance with Tower protocol, the admissions committee had gathered in the public room, ready to entertain the petitions of any and all supplicants. Such was the force of tradition in Osabei Tower that the committee gathered despite a continued and marked lack of supplicants petitioning for admission to the ranks of the Seated. Conditions on the frontier, so they had heard, were unstable, which would doubtless account for the shortage. Indeed, the few Errant-Scholars who had lately arrived at the Tower to sue for a Seat had without exception been those who had chosen to study closer to civilization. No one Wandered the frontier anymore—it was much too unsafe, what with the war which the so-called military did its least to end.

Neither did Osabei Tower, unlike other Towers less devoted to scholarship, conduct outreach in order to draw grudents, Errant-Scholars and light-pupils to them. The Governors held it as an article of faith that the best and brightest would of course come to

Osabei, the first, the oldest, and the most prestigious of the Mathematical Towers.

Conditions within the discipline being what they had been over the last few years—quite a number of radical new theories had been proposed and put to proof—a continued lack of eligible Errant-Scholars seeking a seat within the Order would in approximately two-point-three-four-four-eight Common Years become troublesome. But there was as yet no cause for concern.

So unconcerned was the admissions committee—and so certain that this evening would, like a long tale of previous evenings, bring them no supplicants to judge—that Seated Scholar Jenicour tay'Azberg had, as had become her habit, brought along a deck of cards and had enlisted chi'Morin, dea'Bel, and ven'Halsen in a game of Confusion. It was of course, a breach of Tower protocol to engage in any form of the art mathematical—which gambling games most certainly were—after the ringing of the Mercy Bell, but so formidable was Scholar tay'Azberg with a truth-blade that such small liberties were for the most part overlooked.

The fifth member of the committee, Seated Scholar and Committee Head Kel Var tay'Palin, was unabashedly napping, for which the sixth and final member, Seated Scholar Ala Bin tay'Welford, blamed him not at all. tay'Palin had been increasingly called upon of late to provide proofs of his work, and the strain was taking its expectable, regrettable, toll. That the man was tay'Welford's own immediate superior and the head of the Interdimensional Statistics Department only made his decline more poignant. tay'Palin reported to Master Liad dea'Syl himself—a signal honor, though the Master was frail and had not left his rooms to walk even among those of his own discipline for—

The door slid back with a soft sigh, admitting the ostiary, who went down to a knee, head bowed, eyes stringently focused on the ebon floorboards.

"A supplicant comes!" she cried cleverly, thereby granting poor tay'Palin a chance to snort into wakefulness and for cards to vanish discretely into scholarly sleeves. tay'Welford set his logic-rack to one side, smoothed his robe and folded his hands onto his lap.

"Admit the supplicant," tay'Palin said to the ostiary, his voice calm and scholarly.

The guard brought her hand up in the sign of obedience, and leapt to her feet. She straddled the doorway—one foot in the foyer, one foot in the committee room, and called aloud, "The admissions committee will hear the supplicant's prayer!"

There was a moment of . . . stillness, as all scholarly eyes turned toward the door. tay'Welford noticed that he was breathing rather quickly, in anticipation, then a shadow moved in the foyer, coalesced into a slender woman in the green tabard and yellow sash of a Errant-Scholar. She walked forward precisely seven paces and dropped to her knees, head bent, arms held away from her body, palms out, fingers wide and pointing toward the floor.

One could feel the air in the room sharpen as the admissions committee took minute stock of the supplicant. She knelt, motionless, pale hair hiding her downturned face. The tabard moved, slight and sweet, over her breast, revealing the unhurried rhythm of her breathing.

Kel Var tay'Palin leaned forward slightly in his chair. "You may show your face," he said, "and give your name into the committee's keeping."

Obediently, neither so quickly that she betrayed eagerness, nor so slowly that she was read as arrogant, the supplicant lifted her head. Her face was an agglomeration of angles, sheathed in supple gold. Her eyes were an indeterminate shade of green, set perhaps a bit too wide beneath the pale wings of her brows. Her mouth in repose was non-committal; the supple skin without wrinkle or flaw. Of Common Years, thought tay'Welford, she might as easily hold as few as twenty or as many as forty.

"Maelyn tay'Nordif," she said, ceding her name to the committee, as she had been instructed. Her voice was high and clear, ringing sharply against the ear, and tay'Welford detected only the very least bit of tremble, which was expectable, and spoke well of her common sense.

"What is your specialty?" ven'Halsen asked, following form.

"Interdimensional mathematics," the supplicant made answer. tay'Welford sighed, and leaned back in his chair.

"Under whom," demanded tay'Azberg, "did you study?"

"Liad dea'Syl."

There was a sharp silence—as well there ought to be, thought tay'Welford. Never, in all his time on the admissions committee had one of the Master's own students come forth to claim a chair and a place at the Tower. They, therefore, had before them not merely a supplicant, but a marvel.

"Why," asked dea'Bel in her wistful, cloying voice, "have you come?"

"To beg a place," the supplicant answered, word perfect out of the protocol book, "and that an end be made to my wandering."

"What token," tay'Welford asked pleasantly, lightly, as if it were of no moment, "do you bring us?"

"I have given my coin into the keeping of the guardian of the halls of knowledge." Her voice betrayed no trembling now, nor her face anything but an impersonal, unnuanced respect.

tay'Welford did not remove his gaze from the supplicant's smooth, collected face.

"Ostiary," he said, allowing his voice to reflect the faintest hint of doubt, "pray bring me the supplicant's coin."

The guard straddling the door spun smartly on her heel and marched forward. At the corner of his table, she bowed and opened her hand, offering on the flat of her palm a single tile, shaded green to match the supplicant's tabard—or perhaps, tay'Welford thought whimsically, to match her eyes. He took the tile, his gaze resting yet upon the supplicant's face. The ostiary went back a long step, straightened, turned and marched out of the room. The door whispered shut behind her.

The supplicant's face did not change, the calm rhythm of her breathing was preserved.

Slowly, as though it were foregone that the work preserved on the tile would be second-rate, if not actually shabby, tay'Welford pulled the logic-rack to him, deftly re-arranged the tiles and slid the green into its place within the pattern.

The green tile pulsed. Figures and notations floated to the surface of the reader tiles, framing an argument both elegant and facile.

tay'Welford smiled in genuine pleasure as the theory routines accessed the supplicant's data.

"Scholar?" tay'Palin's voice carried an edge of irritated dryness. "Perhaps you might share the joke with your colleagues?"

He bowed his head and answered soft, acutely aware of the rebuke.

"Forgive me, Scholar. The theory cross-check is almost—ah." Very nearly, he smiled again. A *most* elegant piece of work.

"The supplicant," he said, "builds a compelling proof *against* Master dea'Syl's decrystallization equation."

tay'Palin met his eyes, grimly; beleaguered as he was, still the Prime Chair was no one's fool. A supplicant who came offering such a coin for her seat could in no case be allowed to depart.

Therefore did Scholar tay'Palin rise to his feet, and the others of the committee with him. Hands outstretched, he approached the supplicant, who bent her head back on her long, slender neck and watched him. The pulse at the base of her throat, tay'Welford saw, was beating a little too rapidly for perfect calm. It might be that the supplicant was not quite entirely a fool, either.

"Rise, supplicant," said tay'Palin, and she did, swaying slightly as she gained her feet. To the left, tay'Azberg and dea'Bel had risen, as well. They approached the supplicant; tay'Azberg slipped the gloves and the blade free while dea'Bel removed the yellow sash, and stepped to one side.

tay'Welford rose and received the end of the black sash offered by ven'Halsen. They then approached the supplicant and wove the dusky length about her slim waist, tay'Palin stepped forward at the last to tuck in the ends and return blade and gloves to their proper places.

He then opened his arms in the ritual gesture.

"Allow me to be the first to welcome Seated Scholar Maelyn tay'Nordif home after her long wandering," he said.

Seated Scholar tay'Nordif took a deep breath and stepped into the embrace. tay'Palin kissed her on both cheeks, and released her.

"Come," he said. "Allow me to make you known to your family in art."

❋   ❋   ❋

"ALKIA?" The Korak trade master frowned at Tor An, spun on the stool and slapped up her screen, her right hand already on the wheel. Clan names flashed by in a blur, froze, blinked and reformatted as she accessed Alkia's files.

"I'd thought there was something odd," she muttered, whether to him or to herself he was uncertain. "But it's all been odd of late; ships coming in behind-time; ships coming in ahead of time; whole routes collapsing under the weight of the damned war— Wait, wait . . ." She touched a button, accessing in quick sequence the shipping histories for the last month, two months, three—

And sighed of a sudden, closing the screen with a touch that seemed nearly gentle. She sat with her back to him though there was nothing but the blank screen for her to look at, and then turned on the stool again. Her face was somber, and Tor An felt his stomach clench.

"There is no record of any Alkia Trade Clan ship calling at any port in this sector across the last three months, Common Calendar. We have one report, unsubstantiated, that navigation to the Ringstars has become unstable."

He stared at her, feeling the weight of the datastrip in the protected innermost pocket of his jacket.

"I have," he said tentatively, "not been able to reach the Ringstars. I have data, if it—"

She moved a hand aimlessly, or so it seemed to him.

"I can use the data to substantiate the first report, close the route, file an amendment to the coordinate tables." She reached beneath the counter. "There's paperwork . . ."

Tor An stared at her.

"Won't you investigate? Try to find what happened? A whole system—"

She looked at him wearily. "Routes have gone bad before, boy. In fact, lots of routes are going bad. It's the damned war." She sighed. "You want to fill out the paperwork so nobody else has to go looking for something that's not there?"

"No," he said sharply. "I want to know what happened."

She sighed. "Then you want to ask the military."

JELA STOOD IN THE ALCOVE where he'd been chained, and tried not to worry.

He was unfortunately not having very much success, and the half-humorous observation that this was no time for an M's selected-for insouciance to fail him hadn't derailed his distress. Nor had the tree's cheerful image of a slim, golden-scaled dragon successfully vanquishing some sort of sharp-pinioned flying nasty with an easy wing-flick and a thoughtful application of teeth.

Cantra was, he reminded himself for the sixth time since submitting to the chain, a fully capable woman. She could handle a roomful of soft scholars. Very likely, she could handle the whole population of Osabei Tower with no help from him, which was, if he was destined to spend the greater part of his time on Landomist chained to walls, just as well.

Not that the chain was so much of a problem; just a short length of light-duty links—not even smart—attached to a staple in the wall at the far end and a mag-lock manacle on the near. A long stretch of his arm would snap the chain, if he was feeling unsubtle; or a little judicious pressure with his free hand would spring the cuff, in case subtlety counted.

Trouble was, either play would lose the battle and, if Rool Tiazan and his lady were to be believed, the war. No, he'd agreed to the role of laborer-class Batcher, just about smart enough to pick up a pot and carry it when given detailed instructions by his irascible high-born mistress. His brawn was entirely subservient to her brain, insured by the inhibitor implants, which obviated the need for restraints, even such toys as presently "bound" him. The question then being why they had bothered to bind him at all.

Mostly what we'll be dealing with is culture and the assumptions that go with not ever having been noplace but Inside and knowing deep down where it matters that Inside ways're best, Cantra's voice whispered from memory. *Lot of what you'll be seeing won't make sense, and won't necessarily be keyed to survival. Inside, the important thing is prestige. If a point can be carried by dying elegantly at the exact proper second, that's the choice your well-brought-up Insider's going to make, hands down, no second thoughts.*

Which led him to understand in the here-and-chained that the binding satisfied some deep-seated cultural necessity; that the chain was, in the larger sense, symbolic. What the symbol might say to the core of your general issue Insider, he couldn't hazard, as he was short on context, but it didn't take anybody much smarter than the Batcher he was supposed to be to figure out that the best thing to do—barring emergencies—was allow the restraints to bind him.

How long does it take to show an equation? he thought, cycling back to worry. What if he'd flubbed the proof? The only check he'd had was Cantra, who—make no mistake!—knew her math. But she'd come fresh to the base assumptions of the decrystallization theory, and while she'd proved herself an awesomely quick study, she hadn't lived the last five years with those numbers weaving possibles and might-bes through her sleep.

He was no stranger to subterfuge, misdirection, and papers created solely in support of fabricated reasons for him to be welcomed into places he'd no business knowing existed. In fact, he'd long suspected that Cantra yos'Phelium had a certain way with a Portmaster's Writ herself. But what he'd witnessed from her—he'd never seen the like. What he'd been privileged to see—it was an art form, he supposed, and in retrospect held something in common with dancing. The intent to deceive was there; the intent to create a whole new fabric of reality which the audience would find not only believable, but preferable to the actual truth.

She forged papers, working with commendable care. She forged data-tiles—trickier, but nothing he hadn't done himself. As she worked, she talked, maybe to herself, maybe to him, maybe to the long-ago teacher who'd given her the skill.

Now, this way here, this isn't the best way to fabricate an upright citizen. Best way is to pull in some genuine papers and tile that've gone astray from their true and proper owner, then alter what's there as least you can. Doing it like that, the paper tests genuine, the tamper-coding and the hey-theres on the tile are what's expected . . .

Us, we don't got the contacts and the timing's 'gainst us, so we'll

*build our own as best we can. We're lucky in that we ain't gonna be
long and all my job is to keep 'em from looking at you—*

If he'd still had doubts regarding Cantra's status as an *aelantaza*-
trained, they died as he watched her build her bogus docs.

But the docs were the least of what she built.

*Now, here's something custom-made for treachery, Pilot Jela. House
Chaler, what more or less owns planet Shinto. You've heard of 'em?*

He hadn't, and said so, watching her pull down data from
sources he didn't dare guess at, her face soft and near dreamy in
concentration.

*Horticulturists, they are. Build you a custom plant to any specs you
want and be happy to lease it to you for as long as you like. Catch being
that what they build, they own. Being they have extensive gardens, as
you might expect, they also breed their own sort of Batcher, to work
with the plants. The Batcher's being 'work units,' for use on Shinto only,
they get away with not registering the details of the design. Also doesn't
hurt that they're House Chaler and it's been ugly what's happened to
those who was hot-headed enough to try an' push 'em.*

She leaned back in her chair then, stretching 'way back, then
relaxed and sent a grin into his face.

*So, what you'll be, Pilot Jela, is a for-true Shinto kobold, escorting a
genuine Chaler custom build. If anybody wants to sample your DNA,
won't do 'em any good, on account Chaler don't file, and I'm guessing
the military don't exactly publish the particulars regarding M Series
soldier aloud and abroad.*

He'd admitted that, not that he'd had to, and she bent again to
her task, cutting a wandering scholar from whole cloth, seamlessly
working a kobold and a horticultural specimen into her new reality,
working with a concentration so absolute that he hadn't dared
disturb her to suggest anything so mundane as food, or sleep. And
when she was at long last done, she'd gotten up from her work table,
stretched—looked at him where he hunched over his equations, and
held out a slim hand.

Him, he'd looked up at her, trying to read her face, but it was
fear he thought he was seeing, and that had to be wrong. There'd
never been a woman alive less afraid than Cantra yos'Phelium.

Got time for some pleasure, Pilot? I'm thinking it'll be my last in this lifetime, and I'd like to share it with you.

It was maybe the way she'd said it, or maybe again that thing that couldn't be fear in her misty green eyes—but he'd taken her hand, and they'd shared a grand and pleasurable time. At last, sated with delight, they napped, and though he hadn't slept long, or deeply, when he woke she was gone, locked away and a note at his work place, telling him what he had to do next.

He'd followed orders, stowing what was needed in a backpack, and clearing out anything that showed the length of their stay, or the nature of their work. And sometime shortly after he'd begun to consider disobeying his orders, Errant-Scholar Maelyn tay'Nordif, native of Vetzu, one-time student of Master Liad dea'Syl walked into the workroom there at the lodgings, her cold green eyes brushing over him as if he were of less worth than the chair he sat in.

The shadow of a wing passed over his thoughts, and he pulled himself back to the chained present just as the door to his alcove slid open and the guard stepped forward to free him.

"Pick up the specimen, Jela," Scholar tay'Nordif snapped irritably from the hall. "And follow me."

THE GARRISON WAS at some distance from the port; he hired a cab and sat quietly in the passenger's compartment, one hand in the pocket of his jacket, fingers curled into a fist. He made himself look out onto the port and passing streets, marveling at the busy ordinariness of the day. Surely, if what he feared were so, there would be some sign here, so close to the . . . area of occurrence? Surely, if the Ringstars, with their populations of millions, had vanished, there would be—*something*, here among the nearest of their neighbors to mark their passing? Business suspended? Banners of formal mourning shrouding the shop windows?

Surely, whole star systems could not simply cease to be, unnoticed and unmourned?

And yet the trade master had behaved as if such . . . disappearances . . . were commonplace, which might be dealt with by filling out paperwork and issuing alerts . . .

His stomach clenched, and he felt ill. Resolutely, he swallowed, and took deep, even breaths.

The cab left the business district and ascended a ramp. There was a slight lurch as the internal navigator ceded control of the vehicle to the slotway overbrain, then a smooth gathering of speed, sufficient to press him out of his tense lean and back into the seat. The window he had been looking out of opaqued, obliterating the outside world. He sighed and closed his eyes. Deliberately, he brought up the image of his garden at . . . home, the last time he had seen it. The piata tree was in bloom, its multitude of tiny flowers casting a pale blue shadow over the dark, waxy leaves. He breathed in, and the imagined scent of the flowers soothed his roiling belly.

The cab slowed, canted, staggered slightly as control shifted back to the internals, and continued on at a sedate pace. Tor An took one more deep breath, the ghost of flower-spice on his tongue, and opened his eyes.

Window transparent once more, the cab stopped before a great cermacrete wall. Before the wall stood two very large individuals wearing maximum duty 'skins, each holding a weapon at the ready.

"Korak Garrison," the cab stated abruptly in its flat, featureless voice. The door to his right lifted. "Disembark."

Stomach upset anew, Tor An climbed out of the vehicle. The two soldiers were watching him with interest, or so it seemed to his over-wrought nerves. They both had some sort of bright decorations on their faces which obscured their expressions. He did not, however, imagine the intent eyes, nor the fact that the nearer soldier moved her weapon a bit, so that its discharge slot pointed directly at him.

He swallowed. "Wait," he said to the cab.

"Disallowed," it answered, the door descending so quickly he had to dance back a step in order not to be struck in the head—and another two in order to avoid being run over as it made a tight turn and sped back toward the slotway.

Behind him, he heard the soldiers laugh. He gritted his teeth, took a deep breath in a not entirely successful attempt to settle his stomach and walked toward them, chin resolutely up, lips pressed together in a firm line.

"Change your mind?" the farther guard asked as he approached. "Little one?"

"I merely wished to be certain that I would have transport back to port," he said politely.

"Not a worry," the nearer guard said, and smiled, displaying extremely white and very pointed teeth.

They were surely attempting to unnerve him—and, truth told, succeeding in some measure. However, he had been the youngest amidst an abundance of elder cousins and siblings, and had further-more survived the hazings which were the lot of the juniormost pilot; thus he possessed some strategies for dealing with bullies.

Accordingly, he bowed—slightly, to demonstrate that he was a man of worth who was not intimidated by mere large persons, no matter how obviously armed—and sent a grave look into the nearer soldier's face.

The artwork—an eight-pointed star and a ship on the right cheek; a vertical series of four blue stripes on the left—was disconcerting, but he concentrated his attention and met her eyes, ignoring her amusement.

"My name is Tor An yos'Galan of Alkia Trade Clan, out of the Ringstars," he said steadily. "Pray announce me to your commander. I bear information of some value."

The soldier was unimpressed. She moved her shoulders, and the discharge slot described a casual arc across his chest. He ignored the weapon and kept his eyes on hers, waiting for his answer.

"What kind of information?" she asked at last, grudgingly.

"I believe it would be best for me to impart it directly to the commander," Tor An said. "Or to the commander's designated aide. If you are that person . . ." He let the sentence trail off delicately.

The farther guard snorted. The other frowned.

"We don't pass people to the commander just so they can chat," she said sternly. "Tell us what you want. If we think you've got a case, we'll pass you. Otherwise, you can start walking back to port."

He had not wished . . . And yet, she had a point, this large, rude person with her painted face. Did the doorman at home allow every self-claimed investor access to Alkia's Voice?

He bowed again, even more slightly than previously.

"I have information that the Ringstars are—" his voice cracked. He cleared his throat and began again. "I have information that the Ringstars are—missing. A ship sent to known coordinates within the system falls from transition and reports that the target is unavailable."

The guard's mouth tightened, and she sent a quick over-shoulder glance at her mate.

"Old news," he said, his voice conveying vast boredom.

"Right," the nearer guard answered after a moment. She sighed and turned back to Tor An.

"We are aware of the situation, little one. Get out of here."

For a moment he simply stood, the words not quite scanning—and then her meaning hit and he gasped, spine tingling with outrage.

"You *know* that the Ringstars are missing?" he asked, voice rising out of the tone of calm reason most appropriate for a trader.

The nearer guard frowned. "That's right," she said, and shifted her weapon meaningfully.

He ignored the hint. "What are you doing about it?" he demanded.

The farther guard barked—or perhaps it was laughter.

"Not doing anything about it," the nearer guard said. "What do you expect us to do about it? It's not like the Ringstars are the first system that's gone missing in this war." She raised her weapon this time, and again displayed her sharpened teeth—not at all a smile. "Get out of here, little one. Go back to port, get drunk, get laid. When you wake up sober, hire yourself out and get on with your life."

But Tor An, awash in disbelief, had stopped listening. He stared up into her face. "Other star systems have gone missing?" he repeated. "That's impossible."

"You're the one who came here with information that your precious Ringstars are gone," she snapped. "If it can happen once, it can happen twice. Or don't they teach you civilians stats and probability?"

He took a step forward, hands fisted at his side. "*What are you doing about it?*" he shouted. "You're supposed to protect us! If whole star systems are going away, *where are they going*? And why aren't you stopping—"

"Shut up, you fool!" the nearer guard snarled, but the warning— if it were meant as anything so kindly—was too late.

A section of the wall behind her parted, and a third tall soldier stepped through.

The two guards stiffened, their weapons now definitively trained on Tor An, who was staring at the newcomer.

He, too, displayed various signs and sigils on his face—more than either of the guards, those on the right cheek so numerous that they overlapped each other. Over his maximum duty 'skins he wore a vest hung about with many ribbons, and the belt around his waist supported both a beam pistol and a long ceramic blade.

"Captain," the nearer soldier said respectfully.

"Corporal," the newcomer responded, coldly. His face was turned to Tor An, the light brown eyes startling among the riot of color. "What seems to be the problem?"

"No problem, sir," the corporal said. Tor An gasped.

"Very true," he said and was mortified to hear that his voice was shaking. "You have made it quite clear that the fact of entire star systems vanishing is no concern of yours." He took a breath, and inclined his head toward the captain. "This officer, however . . .."

The officer's cold eyes considered him. If his face bore any expression at all beneath the artwork, it was more than Tor An could do to read it.

"You have information," the captain said, his hard voice free of both inflection and courtesy, "regarding a missing star system."

"Sir, I do." He moved a hand to indicate the two guards. "I had requested admission to the presence of the base commander or an approved aide and was told that news of the vanishing of the Ringstars preceded me. Furthermore, I am told that the event is of no interest to this garrison. Such events are apparently become quite commonplace."

"More so," said the captain, "here on the frontier. I heard you asking the corporal what the military is doing about these disappearances. The corporal is not empowered to answer that question. I, however, am." He inclined from the waist in a small, ironic bow.

"What we are doing is precisely nothing. We are under orders to withdraw. This garrison will be empty within the next thirty days, Common Calendar, and all the rest of the garrisons in this sector of the frontier."

Tor An stared at him, suddenly very cold.

"Does this," the captain asked, still in that inflectionless, discourteous tone, "answer your question?"

Tor An was abruptly weary, his thoughts spinning. Clearly, he would get no other satisfaction here. Best to return to the port, to his ship, and work out his next best move.

So thinking, he bowed, low enough to convey respect for the man's rank, and cleared his throat.

"My question is answered," he said, hoarsely. "I thank you."

"Good," the officer said. He turned his head and addressed the two guards.

"Shoot him."

SIX

❀ ❀

Osabei Tower
Landomist

THE PLACE WAS A WARREN, Jela thought as he followed Errant-Scholar—now, he supposed, Seated Scholar—tay'Nordif through twisty halls so narrow that he had to proceed at a sort of half-cant, in order that his shoulders not rub the walls, and with knees slightly bent, so as not to brush the top of the tree against the ceiling. The logistics of trying to secure such an anthill were enough to give a tactician permanent nightmares.

Lucky for them, they didn't have to worry about securing the premises, just lifting some files and making an orderly retreat. He expected to have a line of withdrawal mapped out and secured well before it was needed. But his first order of business was keeping up with the Scholar and her guide, who moved ahead at a rapid walk without ever once looking back.

That guide, now. A soft man of about Can—Scholar tay'Nordif's height, with a plentitude of shiny brown hair rippling down past his shoulders, his skin was the pure true gold by which the citizens Inside judged a man's worth and value. His gaze had passed over Jela as if he were invisible, though the tree took his interest.

"Now, this is something we seldom see!" he'd exclaimed. "Have you brought us a bit of the frontier, Scholar?"

"Not at all! Not at all!" Scholar tay'Nordif extended a reverent hand and touched a leaf. "Yon specimen hails from fair Shinto, a token of regard given me by none other than Horticultural Master Panthera vas'Chaler. A most gracious lady, Scholar; I esteem her greatly. Her many kindnesses—of which the gift of a green plant to cheer me in my scholarly closet is but the most recent—her kindness is without boundary. Truly, I am at her feet."

"She sounds a most gracious and generous lady," the second scholar said seriously. "You are fortunate in her patronage."

"*Most* fortunate in her patronage," Scholar tay'Nordif reiterated worshipfully. "I challenge anyone to produce a patron more thoughtful of one's comfort, or more understanding of the demands of one's work."

"Indeed?" The other scholar turned from his study of the tree, and moved along the hall, walking flat, and with his hands tucked into his sash—the walk of a man used to consistent gravity, and hallways that maintained their orientation. "This way, if you will, Scholar."

"Follow me, Jela," Scholar tay'Nordif had snapped, and that was the last word or attention that either had squandered on him.

They were well ahead of him now, out of sight around a bend in the hall, though he could hear Scholar tay'Nordif's voice clearly enough, extolling the seemingly limitless virtues attached to Master vas'Chaler.

"Will you believe me, Scholar tay'Welford," she was saying, "when I tell you that nothing would do but that my patron give me apartments in her own home, and a servant whose sole duty it was to attend to my comfort and bring in meals so that on those occasions when I became immersed in my work, I should not be obliged to break my concentration in a descent to the mundane . . ."

It certainly sounded like a soft post, Jela thought, ducking through an arch that was even thinner than the hallway—and damned lucky he was to skin through with the pack on his back, and without breaking any branches off the tree—if it had been in the least part true.

The hall took a jig to the left, to the right, and opened suddenly into a high octagonal shaped lobby. The white light which had been an uncomfortable glare in the tight halls was easier to take here, and Jela breathed a very private sigh of relief as he stepped out onto the dark tile floor. The room extended upward for several stories; a surreptitious glance, under the guise of making sure that the "specimen" could now be held higher without endangering it, found balconies and walkways overhead, but no clear means of attaining them.

From the center of the floor rose a ceramic rectangle as high as Scholar tay'Nordif's shoulder, rich in mosaic-work—

No, thought Jela, looking more closely. Not mosaic. Memory modules, set into the conductive material of the rectangle, creating a single computational device—but to what end?

Scholar tay'Nordif bent in close study of the comp, then straightened and stared upward, spinning slowly—and unsteadily—on a boot heel.

"I theorize," she said, yet craning upward, "that yon device is the engine by which the stairways are driven." She described an additional quarter-circle and lowered her gaze to Scholar tay'Welford, who stood yet with his hands tucked in his sash, an expression of interested amusement on his round, pleasant face.

"The question remaining," Scholar tay'Nordif continued, on a rising inflection, "is how the device is induced to call the proper stairway."

Scholar tay'Welford inclined slightly from the waist. "If you will allow me, Scholar, I believe that I may offer you the key to this puzzle."

"By all means, Scholar! Produce this key, I beg you!"

He smiled, and slowly—even, Jela thought, teasingly—withdrew his right hand from its comfortable tuck in his sash, turned his palm up, and opened his fingers.

Across his palm lay a ceramic lozenge, pale violet in color; insubstantial as a shadow.

"Behold," he said, "the key."

"Ah." Scholar tay'Nordif leaned to inspect it, her hands clasped behind her back. She glanced up at the other scholar. "May I?"

"By all means."

She picked the thing up delicately with the very tips of her fingers, and subjected it to close study before folding it into her palm and turning her attention to the comp.

"I fear me," she said after a moment, "that I have been given but half the key."

"Is it so?" The other scholar stepped closer to her side. Jela felt himself stiffen; deliberately relaxed. "Surely, you have seen something like, in your travels along the frontier?"

"Alas, I have not," Scholar tay'Nordif replied, sending a sideways glance into the other's face. "Is this a Test, sir?"

It seemed to Jela as if the other scholar intended to answer in the affirmative, and amended his course at the last instant.

"Certainly not!" he said lightly. "We are not so uncivilized as to present a Test before even one has shared the evening meal with colleagues." He put his hand atop the rectangle, palm down. "Place your key just here, Scholar; the device will read the imbedded data and fetch down the proper stair."

Scholar tay'Nordif stepped forward, and placed the lozenge flat on top the comp. For a moment, nothing happened, then Jela noticed that the conductive material was glowing a soft rose color, and that various of the embedded modules were also beginning to shine. Air moved and he looked up as one of the high walkways swung out from its fellows, canted—and unfolded downward in deliberate sections until the leading edge touched the floor at the base of the wall.

"I am instructed," said Scholar tay'Nordif and bowed.

"A small secret, I assure you," the other said with a smile. He stepped back and swept an arm toward the waiting walkway. "Please, Scholar, mount and ascend! The stair will take you to the correct floor, and the key will guide you to the correct door! I will look for you at the common meal—ah, and another hint, out of kindness for one who comes into my own Department: It is not done to be late to the common meal."

So saying, he swept around and went on his way, but not before he had sent a measuring look straight into Jela's face. He produced his very best stupid stare, and wasn't especially pleased to see the Scholar smile before passing on.

"Jela, come here!" Scholar tay'Nordif snapped and he stepped onto the ramp behind her as it began, rapidly, to rise.

Both of his hands being occupied with holding the tree, he braced his legs wide and sent a look down to the receding lobby, but there was nothing to see other than the shiny floor stretching away like some dark sea to break against eight white walls in which eight identical archways were centered.

The ramp turned, folding back up into the high ceiling. They passed one floor, moving so swiftly that all Jela retained was an impression of a long hallway lined with yellow doors. The ramp turned again, its far end, just behind Jela's boot heels, giving off to empty air and a long fall to the dark floor below. The leading edge—ahead of the scholar's position, snapped into a slot in the floor of the walkway.

She moved forward briskly, setting her feet firmly against the floor, her tabard billowing slightly.

The tree offered an image of the slender golden-scaled dragon, wings full of wind, gliding effortlessly down the sheer side of a cliff.

Jela refrained from answering. He followed her off the bridge and to the left, down a hall lined on both sides with identical orange doors, then again to the left—and abruptly halted to avoid walking on her, the tree's branches snapping over his head.

She slid the shadowy tile into a slot in the surface of the door; there was a loud *snick* as it opened, lights coming up in the room beyond as it did.

THE QUARTERS WERE featureless and functional: smooth white walls, smooth white floor; a basic galley and sanitary facilities to the right, work space, screen and a convertible chair to the left. In the absence of orders, and out of respect for the three spy-eyes that were too easy to spot, Jela stood just inside the door, cradling the tree's pot in arms that were beginning to ache. Scholar tay'Nordif strolled into the room, giving it a casual, bored inspection. Whether she saw the spy-eyes—which the woman she had been would never have missed—he couldn't say. She stepped to the chair and tapped the control on the arm; it shifted, stretching out to form a cot. Another tap, and it returned to its chair configuration.

She walked over to the work table, and touched the corner of the dark screen. The darkness swirled into gray, the gray into white. Blue words and images floated upward through the whiteness—a timetable, Jela saw, from his vantage near the door, and a map. The scholar raised her head to consult the time displayed on the smooth wall over the screen, and uttered a sharp curse.

"Jela!" she said sharply. "Put the specimen down *gently* and bring me my pack. Quickly!"

Gently, and with considerable relief, he eased the pot to the floor. That done, he skinned the pack off his back, remembering to work slow and stupid, for the benefit of those spy-eyes, opened it and had the scholar's case out. Moving heavily, he went across the room to where his mistress was bent again over the computer— memorizing the map, he hoped—and stood patiently holding the pack out across his two palms, his eyes aimed at the floor.

She spun away from the screen, grabbed the pack and took it to the table, unsealing it hastily and snatching out a tablet, the squat book with scarred covers that she kept always to hand, her extra tabard, a data-case. Muttering under her breath, she reached back into the bag and brought out a second case, but in her haste, she fumbled, and it slid from her fingers onto the floor, data-tiles skittering noisily across the smooth floor.

Another curse, this one more pungent than the first, and the scholar was on her knees, scrabbling along the floor, sweeping the tiles in toward her. Body bent protectively over the case, she began to slot them quickly—sent a distracted glance over her shoulder at the clock and abruptly rose.

"Clean up that mess!" she snapped at him. "Then you may rest."

He waited 'til the door had closed and locked behind her before allowing himself a single, luxuriously loud, sigh, the whine of the jamming device irritating his super-sharp ears. Well, there was one way to put an end to *that* small discomfort, he thought. Rolling his shoulders, he turned his attention to locating the concealed spy-eyes.

�ています ✲ ✲

DISTANT YET IN TIME and space, the Iloheen sensed them as they phased. Rool Tiazan plucked the ley lines the way a mortal man might idly pluck at the strings of a lute he was too indolent to truly play. The Iloheen must believe them wary, fearful and furtive, all of their skill bent upon concealment, all of their intelligence focused upon escape. In this they were assisted by the natural order: the Iloheen were fell and awful, fearsome beings from which it were madness to do other than cover oneself and flee.

The Seon Veyestra dominant had known Rool; even as she had dissolved, she had exerted her will to etch his identity into the ether.

It was true that no *dramliza* fell but that the Iloheen saw. Eventually. But that last scream against annihilation, elucidating the tainted genetic code of an escaped slave—that had been heard instantly.

The Iloheen was nearer now to where they huddled, as small and as dim as was prudent, hidden within a dense weaving of ley lines. Did they make themselves as insignificant as they might, the shimmer of energies from the lines would indeed have concealed them. For this game, however—

Static disturbed the placid flowing of the lines, and in that place where there was neither hot nor cold, a chill wind disturbed the soul.

We must not, the lady's thought whispered behind the shields that protected them. *We must seem neither too easy nor too bold.*

If we are then to seem craven, Rool Tiazan's thought replied. *Our moment approaches.*

Have you identified a path? she asked, as the wind grew stronger and the disruptive energies of the Iloheen drew sparks of probability off the lines.

I have.

Remove us, she directed.

Rool teased his chosen line from the sparkling tangle all about them, exerted his will, and took them elsewhere.

In the nexus of probability they had hidden within, the ley lines crackled and spat, sparks freezing against the fabric of time. The wind blew—cold . . . colder—

And died.

THERE HAD BEEN five snoops altogether, which, Jela thought, as he sealed the last hack and activated it, seemed excessive for a newly Seated scholar. On the other hand, maybe they were in the high-rent district.

Hacks online, he hunkered down by the quick-built jammer and began, carefully, to dismantle it, making sure as he slotted the tiles into the case that those from which the little device had been created were well-mixed among the others. It would be bad if a couple started associating without supervision, so to speak, and built up a wild interference field.

His best estimation was that the hacks would hold until sometime after he, Cantra, the tree, and Liad dea'Syl's equations were gone from Osabei Tower. It bothered him that they'd likely have to be left in place until whoever had the snoops under their charge figured the game out and came to collect them; he liked to be tidy in his ops. Well, maybe a chance to remove or destroy them would come along.

In the meantime, he was cautiously proud of his handiwork. Since they couldn't know the details of where they'd settle, he had to build the detail in on site—and quick, before someone noticed the feeds coming from the new scholar's quarters were off. Fortunately, he'd been able to rough in the basics beforehand; adding the detail level had gone quick. Now, whoever was so interested in the doings of a new-arrived scholar would be fed edited versions of real events. Right now, for instance, they should be receiving a nice picture from five different angles of him slumped on the floor next to the "specimen," napping in the absence of orders.

Data tiles slotted all nice and neat, Jela straightened and carried the case over to the worktable. His gear was out and assembled, and he'd be wanting to get to work pretty soon . . .

He turned his head, considering the convertible chair. It didn't look precisely robust. There'd been a stool shoved under the counter in the galley, he remembered, and he went back across the room to fetch it, moving light and smooth.

As he passed the tree, he was suddenly aware of the minty aroma of a fresh seed pod. He paused, peering into the branches. Sure enough, one of several emerging pods had ripened, the branch on which it grew bending a little under its mature weight. The aroma grew more noticeable. Jela's mouth watered, and the branch bent a little more, inviting him to take the pod.

His fingers twitched, his mouth watered; he hesitated.

"I've been getting a lot of these lately," he said to the tree. "Don't stint yourself for me."

An image formed inside his head: a seed pod sitting on an outcropping of grey rock, its rind broken, black, and useless.

"Better a snack for a soldier than wasted altogether, eh? Well—" He extended a hand and the pod dropped neatly into his broad palm. "Thank you," he whispered. It smelled so good, he ate it right then, before fetching the stool and carrying it over to the worktable.

Comfortably seated, he cracked his knuckles, loudly, squared his screen off, and took a moment to consider, fingers poised over the keys.

He hadn't exactly discussed this phase of the operations with Cantra. He'd intended to, so they could coordinate. That had been before the conversation that set his hair on end, then and now.

You know how the aelantaza operate, Pilot Jela? Her voice had been light, amused, like she was on the edge of telling some easy joke between comrades.

He'd admitted to ignorance of the topic, which was true enough, conjecture not counting as fact, and she'd smiled a little and settled back in her chair to recount the tale.

What aelantaza do, see, is convince everybody around that the aelantaza is exactly and beyond question who and what they say they are. The way of it's simple to say—they convince other people because they're convinced themselves. The way of doing it—that's not so simple. Drugs're a part of it—drugs the formulae of which the Directors hold more dear than their lives.

The other part of it, that's mind-games—meditation, play acting, symbolism. I'd tell it all out for you, but it'd sound like so much rubbish to the sensible, solid man I know you to be—and besides, we're on a tight schedule. Just let's leave it that those mind-games, they're powerful. Back when I was in school, the teachers were pleased to impress on me that it was the mental preparation, not the drugs, that drew the line between a successful mission and a wipe. That an aelantaza who had prepared mentally, but had the drug withheld— that aelantaza had a better—I'm saying, Pilot, a much better— chance of completing her mission successfully than her brother who'd taken the drug without preparing his mind. So you see the odds're in our favor.

She'd given him a nod, then, and a straight, hard look, the misty green eyes as serious as the business edge of a battle blade.

What they call it, that mental preparation that's so important to preserving our good numbers—they call it the Little Death, and that's as close to truth as anything you'll ever have out of Tanjalyre Institute or any aelantaza you might meet. Because the point and purpose of all those mind-games is to strip out—as near as can be without losing training—one personality and lay in a different. The prelim drug makes the work easier by softening up the barriers between me and not-me. The finishing drug, that sets new-me a little tighter, so there's less likely to be seepage from what's left of old-me—less opportunity for mistakes on-job, or for a bobble that might crack the belief that the aelantaza is and always has been exactly who she is right now.

He'd opened his mouth then, though he couldn't recall what it was he'd intended to say. Cantra'd held up a slender hand.

Hear me out, she said, and he could've thought that the shine in her eyes was tears. *Just hear me out.*

He'd settled back, fingers moving in the sign for *go on . . .*

Right. She sat, head bent, then her chin came up and she shook her hair back out of her face.

While the odds favor a prepared mind, she said, her mouth twisting a little in what he thought she might have meant for a smile, *we have to recollect that I'm inexperienced, and plan for to not have any bobbles. So, what I'll ask of you, Pilot Jela, is assistance. You'll know the old-me—what's left—that's beneath the new. Don't, as you wish for us to carry the day and perform the kind lady's bidding—*

don't for a heartbeat acknowledge that ghost. The one who holds the ghost at her heart—she's the one you'll be dealing with. Call her only by the name she tells you. Don't share out any of your close-held secrets with her. Don't expect her to act or think or feel in any way like the pilot you have here before you would do. Trust—and this is going to be hard, Pilot, I know—trust that, despite all, she'll move you to the goal we've set out and decided between us. Will you give me—will you give me your word on that, Pilot?

Well, he'd given his word, fool that he was. Soldier that he was.

She'd smiled then, and stood, stretched her slender hand out to him, and asked him for comfort and ease.

He'd given that, too, and the memory of their sharing was one of his better ones. So much so that he felt a bit wistful that it hadn't happened earlier in his life, so he could have held the memory longer.

When Scholar tay'Nordif had stalked into his life, high-handed and disdainful, he had throttled his horror and kept his word to his pilot. He had, he prided himself, never faltered, acting the part of the laborer, carrying the tree and the scholar's burdens.

And Cantra—or whatever there was left of Cantra in the woman who believed herself to be Maelyn tay'Nordif—she had done her part as well, or better. He doubted—yes, he'd doubted—that she'd be able to manage the jammer—and found himself squeamish about imagining the mental gymnastics involved in getting it done—but she'd done it, as clean and as fumble-free as any could have wanted.

He waggled his fingers over the keyboard, bringing his attention forcefully back to the present and his plan of attack. First, a gentle feeling-out of the security systems protecting the Tower's various brains, and building a map of hierarchies and interconnections.

Enough to keep you busy for an hour or two while the scholar has herself a nice meal with her troop, he told himself and grinned.

After he had snooped out security, he'd be in place to build himself some spies, and after he had his maps, he could start the real job of collecting the equations that would save life as it was from the enemy of everything.

✻   ✻   ✻

ALA BIN TAY'WELFORD CLAIMED a glass, took up his usual position near the sours table, and surveyed the room. All about scholars were clustered in their usual knots of allies and associates, avidly engaged in Osabei Tower's favorite pastime—the gaining of advantage over one's colleagues.

He turned his attention to the offerings on the table—a much more interesting prospect—debating with himself the relative merits of the berries vinaigrette and the pickled *greshom* wings. Impossible to be neat with the berries, and one disliked to stain one's robes. The wings, on the other hand—he was most fond of pickled *greshom* wings, which were a delicacy of his home province—the wings were possessed on two days out of four of a certain unappealing graininess. He had constructed an algorithm to predict the instances of substandard wings, and according to those calculations, this evening's would be of the unfortunate variety. He sighed, fingers poised over the plate. He might, he supposed, appease his palate with a sour cookie or—

"So," Leman chi'Farlo's soft, malicious voice fell on his ear, "tay'Azberg will have it that Interdimensional Statistics has Seated a scholar of rare virtue."

He chose a cookie, taking care with it, and straightened. Seeing she had his attention, chi'Farlo inclined her head, the data tiles woven into her numerous yellow braids clicking gently against each other.

"A scholar possessed of an—interesting intellect, I should say," he answered. "To offer Osabei such a coin in trade for a chair."

chi'Farlo raised her glass so that her mouth was hidden. "tay'Azberg allows us to know that the scholar's coin would disprove all the work upon which our department's master bases his eminence," she murmured.

"Aye," he said unconcernedly. "It would seem to do just that." He bit into the cookie, chewed meditatively—and sighed. Appalling.

"But this is dreadful!" she insisted. "If the Governors should cut the department's budget—" chi'Farlo was of an excitable temperament. She stood next junior to him in departmental rank, and he needed her calm and focused.

"Peace, peace," he murmured, finishing off the cookie and taking a liberal swallow of wine to cleanse the taste from his mouth.

She laughed sharply. "You may show a calm face to catastrophe, pure scholar that you are, but for those of us who hold hope of seeing the department attain its proper place . . ."

"The Governors have not cut our budget," he pointed out, "nor even have they called good Scholar tay'Nordif to stand before them and explain herself, her work, or her proofs. It is possible that they will not do so," he continued, though in fact he considered it very likely that the Governors would take a decided interest in Scholar tay'Nordif and her proof. Saying so to chi'Farlo, however, would not serve in the cause of calming her.

He glanced about the room, finding tay'Palin near the door, speaking with dea'San and vel'Anbrek. The time displayed on the wall beyond that small cluster of worthy scholars was perilously close to the moment at which the door would be sealed, and all those left on the wrong side required to report first thing the Truth Bell rang tomorrow to the office of their department head for discipline.

"Our new sister in art is late," chi'Farlo murmured spitefully.

"Not yet," he answered, continuing his scan of the room—but no, Scholar tay'Nordif had not arrived when his attention was elsewhere. Pity, that. He brought his gaze to chi'Farlo's stern, pale face. A taint of Outblood in the line, he'd always thought. Pity, that.

"tay'Palin looks tired, poor fellow," he said, raising his glass and cocking an eyebrow. chi'Farlo glanced over at the small cluster of scholars, and sighed.

"He did not look tired this morning," she said, "when he once again successfully defended his work."

"Indeed he did not," tay'Welford said patiently. "Though I think we can agree that it was a spirited discussion. It is unfortunate that these challenges come so closely of late. If the scholar but had a few days to rest . . . He is formidable in defense of his work, but greatly wearied by these continual demands to prove himself. And then to have taken a wound—"

"A wound?" chi'Farlo scoffed. "I saw no breach of his defenses this morning."

"Nor did I, during the proving," tay'Welford said. "He is canny, and hid the weakness. I only know of it because I came upon him in his office while he was binding the gash." He met chi'Farlo's eyes squarely. "High on his dominant arm. The sleeve of his casement would have hidden it."

"I . . . see . . ." chi'Farlo sipped her wine, face soft in reverie. "Tomorrow perhaps our good department head will find the rest he deserves."

"Perhaps," tay'Welford murmured. "Indeed, it is possible. For surely—"

A movement across the room claimed his attention, which was certainly the door being drawn to—but stay! According to the clock, they were still some seconds short of closure, and, indeed, it was not the door, but Scholar tay'Nordif, of course still wearing her Wanderer's garb, the black sash of a Seated Scholar accentuating her slim waist.

"*That* is our new sister?" chi'Farlo's voice was slightly edged, and tay'Welford hid a smile, remembering that his junior cared as much—if not more—for her standing as the department's Beauty as for her scholarship. "She is something bedraggled, is she not?"

"She has just come from the frontier," he said mildly and then, because he could not resist teasing her, just a little— "Doubtless, she will be very well indeed, once she is properly robed, and rested from her travels."

chi'Farlo sniffed, and raised her glass. tay'Welford pressed his lips into a straight line as Scholar tay'Nordif made her way to the group of which tay'Palin stood a member and bowed deeply, fingertips touching forehead, a model of modest courtesy. tay'Palin spoke, and she straightened. tay'Welford understood from the gestures following that she was being made known to dea'San and vel'Anbrek.

Across the room, the door closed, the bar falling with an audible clang. Scholar tay'Nordif was seen to start and turn her head sharply to track the sound, much to vel'Anbrek's delight.

"She will be sitting with tay'Palin at her first meal," chi'Farlo muttered irritably. "Really, she puts herself high!"

"Does she?" tay'Welford smiled, and moved forward, slipping a hand beneath her elbow to bear her along with him. "Then let us also put ourselves high."

"To what end?" she asked, keeping pace nonetheless.

"I think our new sister might have some interesting things to tell us of the frontier," he said.

"Oh, the frontier!" she began pettishly, and had the good sense to swallow the rest of what she might have said as they joined the group around tay'Palin.

"Ah, there you are, tay'Welford!" vel'Anbrek cried. "I began to believe you would miss an opportunity."

Unpleasant old man. It was a wonder, tay'Welford thought, that no one had challenged him simply to rid the community of a source of on-going irritation. But there, the old horror had close ties to the Governors, which was doubtless the secret to his longevity.

"I hope," tay'Welford said evenly, "that I never miss an opportunity to be informed."

"And chi'Farlo had nothing to say to you, eh?" vel'Anbrek laughed loudly at his own small witticism.

"So," said Scholar dea'San to Maelyn tay'Nordif, her hard voice easily heard over her compatriot's noise, "you are Liad's student, are you? I wonder—"

"She is wearing her truth-blade," chi'Farlo interrupted.

"Well, of course she's wearing her truth-blade," returned vel'Anbrek, interrupting in his turn, his voice high and querulous. "She doesn't look a fool to me, does she to you, Scholar?"

"I'm sure that I couldn't—"

"And with all the rest of Liad's students being killed dead as they have—"

"Gor Ton," snapped Scholar dea'San, "you exaggerate. Not all of Liad's—"

vel'Anbrek waved an unsteady hand, missing Scholar tay'Palin's glass by the width of a whisker. "All the important ones," he said airily. "And I recall young tay'Palin here telling us the scholar is new-come from the frontier. I remember sleeping with my truth-blade during the years of *my* wandering. Did you not do the same, Elvred?"

"Certainly not! I hope that I never once allowed the traditions of civilization to be overcast by—"

"Bah!" the old man said decisively.

"The meat of the matter, I believe," said tay'Palin, calmly overriding both, "is that truth-blades are put aside with the ringing of the Mercy Bell. They are not worn at the common meal, Scholar tay'Nordif."

The scholar abased herself immediately, holding the bow.

"Forgive me, Scholars," she said humbly. "I am ignorant of custom."

"Indeed," Scholar tay'Palin said dryly. "I had trusted that Scholar tay'Welford would hint you toward the accepted mode. It is hardly like him to be so neglectful of one who comes into our own department."

Scholar tay'Nordif straightened slowly, and sent a hard look into tay'Welford's face. He smiled at her and raised his glass, waiting.

"The scholar was kind enough to warn me to be on time for the gather, sir," she said to tay'Palin. "I take him for a man who does not offer advice freely, and I am well-pleased not to stand in his debt."

A certain boldness to that reply, thought tay'Welford approvingly. It did not do for a scholar to be timid.

"You are gracious to impute such noble motives to Scholar tay'Welford," dea'San murmured. "However, the more likely case is that he simply forgot."

"Doubtless, doubtless! Our esteemed tay'Welford can be flutter-witted," Scholar vel'Anbrek said. "Mind on higher things." He laughed, so pleased with his sally that he repeated it. "Higher things! Hah!" He raised his glass, found it empty, and lifted it, still cackling.

A servitor detached itself from an animated knot of scholars some steps deeper into the room and came to the old man's side. It wore an extremely brief tunic, and a half-mask of smart-strands, and stood very straight in order to keep the tray precisely balanced on its sleek head.

vel'Anbrek dropped his empty glass carelessly on the tray, and selected a full glass. Those others of their group who were in need likewise served themselves, including Scholar tay'Nordif. tay'Welford stood holding his new glass, idly watching as she turned her head deliberately to the right, staring hard down room; thence to the left, then again over each shoulder, and finally returned her gaze to the elder scholar.

"Pardon me, sir," she said courteously, "but I had not heard that all of Master Liad's students had been—killed, did you say? It seems remarkable to me . . .."

"Nonetheless—" It was dea'San who answered. "And allowing for exaggeration, it does appear that the greater portion of Liad's students have met their mortality before the fruits of their work was harvested. *Most* annoying in terms of advancing the discipline."

"It must certainly be vexatious," Scholar tay'Nordif agreed, with no discernible irony. "And yet, ma'am, the words of the great philosopher bin'Arli spring to mind—*Adversity breeds greatness*. Perhaps this trying circumstance will bring forth even greater and more illustrious work from those who are, I believe, the core and the keepers of our discipline."

"How," tay'Welford asked delicately into the unsettled silence that followed this, "do you find things on the frontier, Scholar tay'Nordif? We are so retired here, that—were it not for a certain . . . thinness . . . of scholars come to sue for a chair—we should scarcely have heard that there was a war at all, much less the state of the conflict."

Green eyes considered him with disconcerting straightness.

"Surely you don't think I sought out the war zones, Scholar? I assure you that I studied the alerts closely and kept myself as far as possible from active conflict."

"Certainly what anyone of sense might—" chi'Farlo began, and stopped as Scholar tay'Nordif once again executed her peculiar stare into all corners of the room.

"Pardon me, Scholar, but what do you?" dea'San inquired sharply. "You may be new-come from the frontier, but that hardly gives you license to be rude."

Maelyn tay'Nordif blinked at her, clearly at a loss. "I beg your pardon, Scholar? In what way was I rude?"

dea'San bristled. "Scholar chi'Farlo was speaking to you, and you simply turned your head in that—*peculiar* manner and ignored her! I would call that rude, but perhaps on the frontier—"

"On the frontier, we call such things not rude, but survival skills," Scholar tay'Nordif interrupted. "You will excuse me, Scholar, if I suppose that it has been some time since you were last on the frontier. You may not recall the extraordinary and constant vigilance required merely to remain alive. When there is the added imperative of one's work, strategies must be fashioned and practiced without fail. I therefore have trained myself to survey my surroundings thoroughly every three hundredth heartbeat and have practiced the technique so faithfully that I may now perform this function without breaking the concentration necessary for my work."

There was a small silence, before chi'Farlo said, with admirable restraint, "But we are not at the frontier, Scholar tay'Nordif. We are in-hall and safe among our colleagues."

"Doubtless that is true," tay'Nordif replied. "And doubtless in time I shall craft another technique which will accommodate conditions here. Do you not use such techniques to clear your mind so that you may become immersed in your work, Scholar?"

chi'Farlo, whose ambition might in fairness be said to outstrip her art by a factor of twelve, merely murmured, "Of course," and raised her glass. It was well, thought tay'Welford, that Scholar tay'Nordif was newly seated and thus too inconsequential for chi'Farlo to challenge.

"If you will allow one who has been Seated for many years advise you, Scholar tay'Nordif?" dea'San said.

"Indeed, Scholar, I am grateful for any assistance," the other replied, and performed her peculiar stare about the room.

dea'San sighed. "I think you will find, Scholar," she said loudly, "that your best technique here in the heart of our discipline is to simply immerse yourself in your work, trusting to the safeguards of our Tower and the goodwill of your colleagues."

Now here, thought tay'Welford, sipping his wine, was a clear equation for disaster. He wondered whether their new sister would be fool enough to employ it.

The bell rang then, calling them to dinner. He accepted dea'San's arm, chi'Farlo having of course chosen tay'Palin as her meal-mate. That left vel'Anbrek for tay'Nordif, and it must be said that she offered her arm with good grace. So they proceeded to the table in order and took their seats, Scholar tay'Nordif displaying vigilance as they did so.

HE FINISHED WRAPPING the wound, the awkward job made more difficult by the trembling of his icy fingers.

Shot! He'd been shot, well and truly burned, though there was no pain. The lack of pain worried him, distantly. He thought he might be in shock. Certainly, he had cause.

And yet, it could have been worse. Much worse. The sound of the soldiers' laughter still echoed in his ears, his skin twitched from the heat of the bolts that had come close—close. He'd run— run until he thought his heart would burst and still he heard them laughing, firing, but not pursuing.

He was, he supposed, too inconsequential to pursue. It had been a game to the big soldiers—a diversion, nothing more. And if he had died for their fun—well, and what was one less civilian, who should have vanished, anyway, along with his clan and the entirety of the Ringstars?

He was so cold.

One handed, he crammed the ruined jacket and shirt into the 'fresher, then pawed a blanket from the cupboard and got it 'round his shoulders.

Staggering slightly, he entered the tower, and half-fell into the pilot's chair, squinting against the blare of light from the board. One light in particular caught his attention. He angled the chair so that he might reach the board with his good hand, and touched the access button.

"*Light Wing*," he said, and was pleased to hear that his voice was steady.

"Yard Authority," the response came—a crisp, no-nonsense

voice that reminded him of Fraea. "Request for amended departure approved. Stand by to receive clearance."

His fingers moved of themselves, opening the buffer. Somewhere on the board, a light flicked from blue to orange, then back to blue as a chime sounded. These things, he knew, were usual and proper and indicated that the ship was functioning as it should.

Screens came on line. He squinted at the detail provided, and again his fingers moved, waking the engines, feeding coordinates to the nav-brain, locking a flight schedule. Distantly, he thought that perhaps a man who had been shot—a man who was so cold—perhaps that man should not be filing a flight plan and preparing to lift ship. It was a very distant thought, however, and he had necessary tasks to accomplish. He must depart Korak now. He must—the thought faded, but no matter—his fingers knew. A pilot trusted his fingers, or he trusted nothing, Uncle Sae Zar had used to say, and if ever there had been a pilot to behold, Sae Zar—

Something beeped, lights flashed, the forward screens displayed orbital trajectories, energy states, timetables. His fingers moved a last time and the ship gathered itself, surging upward, the force of lift pressing him back into the chair. Distantly, he noted that he was not strapped in, but he couldn't reach the engage with his good arm, so he left the straps off, as the pressure built comfortingly. The ship—old *Light Wing* had lifted from more worlds than he had years in his life. She knew what to do, did *Light Wing*. He left her to it, trusting his fingers to notice any failure and make what amendments might be required.

They came to orbit without mishap. The forward screen showed stars; the secondary a star map, route and transition points clearly marked. There was no reason to change them, though he could not at the moment recall why he should be traveling to Landomist. His fingers had a reason. A pilot trusted his fingers and his ship. They were all he had, in the last counting.

He lost consciousness well before transition, but *Light Wing* knew what to do.

SEVEN

⚜ ⚜

Osabei Tower
Landomist

BEING INVISIBLE was a marvelous thing, Jela thought. The challenge was to recall that he would immediately and catastrophically become *un*-invisible should he forget his role and act like he possessed slightly more sense than a rock.

Or, in the present instance, a clothes tree. His part was to stand, stoic and unmoving, holding Scholar tay'Nordif's unitard, tabard, sash, knife and gloves while she, garbed only in the so-called "discipline bracelet" stepped onto what the tailor was pleased to call *the fitter*. The tailor then fussed at length about the placement of the scholar's feet, shoulders and hips, until—

"There! Maintain that position, if you will, Scholar!" The tailor scurried from the platform to a small console, and quickly touched several panels. Beams of multi-colored light burst from all directions to enclose the scholar, giving her shape an unsettling luminescence. Jela twitched slightly when her hair began to rise, and settled himself deliberately. Across the room, the tailor made a satisfied sound, and bent to her console as the light slowly faded.

"You may step down from the fitter, now, Scholar. In a moment, your robe and slippers will be here." She hesitated, and sent a furtive glance in his direction, lips pursed in a measuring sort of way.

"Will you be wishing to garb your . . . servant . . . more appropriately?" she asked.

Scholar tay'Nordif turned slowly, as he read her, entirely unconcerned by her nakedness, and gave him a long, cold, considering stare.

"It appears to be garbed appropriate to its station," she said to the tailor. "What do you find amiss?"

The tailor ducked her head. "Only that most of the Tower servants are clothed as you would have seen last evening at the common meal, or—well, here!" This as a Small came bustling from the back, a dark bundle of cloth in her arms, and a matching pair of slippers dangling from one hand. The tailor received the bundle and the slippers, snapped a sharp, "Stay," and indicated with a sweep of her arm that the scholar should look her fill.

Jela, who had not been invited to look, did anyway.

The munchkin held frozen by her mistress' command wore only the very briefest blue kilt. A collar set with a stone very like that in Scholar tay'Nordif's bracelet was fastened tightly about her throat, and her eyes—no, Jela thought with crawling horror, her *eye sockets* were wrapped in a mesh of smartstrands.

Scholar tay'Nordif sniffed. "All very well for the size and shape on display," she said, "but I believe that we need not assault the sensibilities of the scholarly community by subjecting them to the sight of Jela clad thus."

"As you say, Scholar," the tailor murmured, with a quick, sideways glance at himself. "May I point out that the mask may be of use, as the information uploaded from the slave-brain will confuse any real-time images, and thus preserve the sanctity of your work." She flicked her fingers at the still-frozen munchkin. "Those servants who are bred for the Tower are of course blind, and the mask then serves as a navigational aid."

"Mayhap Osabei Tower requires a degree of intellectual rigor in its servants that is neither required—or desired—in a mere horticultural kobold," Scholar tay'Nordif said with a shrug of her pretty shoulders. "Even had Jela the wit to notice my work, the capacity to understand it is certainly lacking."

"As you say, Scholar," the tailor murmured. She snapped a sharp "Go!" to the munchkin, who departed immediately, walking with utter assurance. "A word in your ear, however. The others may wish—"

"If there is complaint," Scholar tay'Nordif interrupted grandly, "let it be made to me."

"Of course, Scholar." The tailor bowed, then bustled forward, slippers held under one arm, shaking the cloth out as she approached. "Your robe, Scholar, if you would care to dress."

Scholar tay'Nordif held out her arms and the tailor slipped the shimmering sleeves over them.

It was, in Jela's opinion, a cumbersome garment, made of entirely too much cloth in a deep reddish brown. The shimmer was a puzzle, though he was willing to bet—had there been anyone but himself to take the wager—that there were smartstrands woven into the fabric. That was interesting, if not outright alarming. If the Tower slave-brain was also charged with monitoring—or controlling—the scholars . . .

The tailor sealed the front of the robe. She offered the slippers one at a time, and the scholar slid her slim feet into them.

"Jela! Come here!"

Summoned, he approached until she ordered him to stop and to hand her sash to the tailor. He did this and watched as that worthy wove it around the scholar's slender waist, carefully tucking up the ends.

Scholar tay'Nordif lowered her arms. The full sleeves fell precisely to her knuckles, the robe broke at the instep of her new, soft slippers. Her golden skin and pale hair somehow took light from the dark color, and seemed to glow.

"Jela! Hand me my knife, hilt first!"

He obeyed, handling the ill-kept blade as if it were no better balanced than a crowbar, and stood dull and stupid while she situated it to her satisfaction. That done, she relieved him of the smart gloves, which she held in her hand as she turned to address the tailor once more. In the absence of further orders, Jela stood where he'd been stopped, the unitard and tabard over his arm.

"I will want more than one robe."

"Certainly, Scholar. You may order as many as you wish. The cost will be charged against your account."

"My account, is it?" Scholar tay'Nordif fixed her in a cool green stare. "From whom would I learn the status of my account?"

"From the Bursar, Scholar," the tailor replied and stepped back, her hands twisting about each other as if they had a life and a purpose of their own.

"Ah. I shall speak with the Bursar, then, before ordering more robes."

"Very good, Scholar." She tipped her head, sending a sidewise glance at the garments Jela held.

"If the scholar would be so kind as to direct her servant to place the Wanderer's costume on the table, here . . ."

Scholar tay'Nordif raised a eyebrow. "Does the Tower purchase my clothing?" she inquired.

The tailor raised her hands, fingers moving in a meaningless ripple.

"It is custom, Scholar. You shed the skin of a Wanderer and are reborn into the plumage of a Seated Scholar . . ."

"I see." said Scholar tay'Nordif. There was a slight pause before she inclined her head. "Surely, there can be no argument with custom. As the great philosopher bin'Arli tells us, *Custom carries all before it.*"

The tailor blinked, but managed a faint, "Just so, Scholar."

"Just so," the scholar repeated. "Jela! Place those pieces of clothing where the tailor directs you."

Slowly, Jela turned toward the tailor. She bit her lip, and drifted back half-a-dozen steps to put her palm flat on the console table. "Put them here," she said, voice quavering.

He stomped forward, the tailor flinching with each heavy step, and dropped the clothing on the spot she had indicated, not without a pang. The tabard was of no consequence, being only wandercloth, but the unitard . . . the unitard was light-duty armor. So light-duty that any true soldier would call it none at all, but sufficient to turn the point of a weak knife-stroke—or lessen the power of a serious thrust. He didn't like the notion of having nothing between Can—Scholar tay'Nordif and a truth-blade but a layer of smart-wove fabric. Impossible to know what the scholar herself thought of it, of course, though he took hope from that pause before she agreed to the ceding of her garments.

"Is there anything else required of me here?" she asked the tailor.

"No, Scholar," the woman said unsteadily.

"That is well, then. Jela! Follow me." Scholar tay'Nordif swept off the dias, robes billowing, walking light, but nothing so light nor so free as Pilot Cantra had done. Obeying orders, he followed her, three steps behind, no more, no less, eyes down; giving his ears, his nose, and his peripheral vision as much of a workout as he dared.

"LIAD'S SOLE SURVIVING STUDENT, is it?" The Bursar's gray eyebrows lifted sardonically, her eyes sharp and blue and giving as ice.

The scholar bowed briskly.

"Maelyn tay'Nordif," she said in her high, sharp voice. "I am come to inquire into the status of my account."

The Bursar pursed her lips. "The status of your account? You have no account, Scholar. You are a drain on the resources of this community until such time as your work attracts a patron willing to pay your expenses, or the artificers find that your work has practical application and market it. In the first case, any funds granted by your patron will of course go first against your accrued expenses. In the latter case, you will receive ten percent of any income generated by the sale or lease of the application incorporating your work, which funds will first be placed against your accrued expenses. At the moment . . ." She lifted her wand in one hand and fingered the chords absently.

"Yes," she said, flicking a casual glance at the screen. "At the moment, your debt to the Tower stands at eighteen qwint." She smiled. "That sum includes the lease on your quarters and on your office for the remainder of the month; one meal per day for yourself for the remainder of the month; your robe, equipment and storage space; and your share of Tower maintenance."

Scholar tay'Nordif stood silent, her head tipped to one side, her hands tucked meditatively into the sleeves of her robe.

"Is there any other way in which I may be pleased to serve you, Scholar?" the Bursar inquired, her smile now a full-assault grin.

"I would be grateful," the scholar said crisply, "if you would be so kind as to instruct me how I might deposit a flan into my account."

The Bursar's grin dimmed somewhat. "A flan," she repeated.

"It happens to be what I have with me at the moment," Scholar tay'Nordif said. "If it is too small a sum, I will of course be pleased to add another, but in that wise the conclusion of this matter will wait upon the morrow."

The Bursar cleared her throat. "I am able to accept a flan on account, Scholar. You do realize that your current expenses will be deducted—"

"Immediately," the scholar interrupted. "Yes, I quite understand that, thank you. Would it be possible for you to tell me if the six qwint remaining will procure a pass-tile?"

"Pass-tiles are six carolis the pair," the Bursar answered. Jela, standing three steps behind the scholar and one step to her right, thought he heard a bit of irritation there.

"In that wise, I will have two, if you please," Scholar tay'Nordif said composedly.

The Bursar spun her chair, snatched a green folder from one of the many cubbies behind her and spun back, her arm whipping, the packet spinning flat and potentially deadly toward—

Jela gritted his teeth, locking muscles that wanted to leap, crushing instincts that demanded he take the strike and protect his pilot—

. . . *don't*, he heard the familiar husky voice whisper from memory . . . *don't for a heartbeat acknowledge that ghost.*

Right, he told himself, for the first time taking comfort from his kobold's habitual stolid, stupid stance. *She's not your pilot. Your pilot's—*

He balked at "dead," no matter that she would have said it herself.

Unchecked, the projectile continued along its path. Far too late, and clumsily, the scholar snatched a warding hand out of her sleeve. The packet bounced off of her wrist, hit the wall high and clattered to the floor.

"Jela!" Scholar tay'Nordif snapped. "Pick that—" she pointed— "up and bring it to me."

He moved, stumping deliberately over to the fallen packet, aware of the Bursar's speculative gaze. Bending, he retrieved the folder, then stumped back to place it in his mistress' outstretched, impatient palm.

"Very good," she said peremptorily. She slipped the packet into her sash; extended her hand again.

"Jela," she said clearly, "give me my purse."

He counted three of his long, at-rest heartbeats, for the speculation in the Bursar's eyes, then groped in the pockets of his vest, eventually producing a battered corduroy pouch, which he held out uncertainly.

The scholar sighed, snatched it from his fingers, pulled the string and stepped up to the Bursar's desk.

"One flan, as agreed," she said. "Is it the custom to give a receipt for funds received?"

The Bursar's mouth was in a straight line now, facial muscles tight.

"You may access your account at any time from any work terminal linked to Osabei Administration, Scholar."

"I am grateful," Scholar tay'Nordif said, bowing just low enough, as Jela read it, to avoid being overtly rude.

The Bursar snorted and spun to face her screen, wand already in hand.

"Good-day, Scholar. May your work be fruitful and all your proofs accurate."

※　　※　　※

THE ID PLATE SHONE briefly orange beneath Scholar tay'Nordif's palm, a chime sounded and motes of light danced beneath the door's dull surface, joining together until they cohered into glowing script:

Maelyn tay'Nordif

The scholar made a satisfied sound—something between a chuckle and a sigh—and lifted her hand away from the reader. Immediately, the door opened, lights coming up in the room beyond.

Where the living quarters were sparse and tidy, the office was cluttered and chaotic. It was, Jela thought fair mindedly, something of an accomplishment to have fit so comprehensive a confusion into so small a space.

Shelves lined three walls, but the scrolls and data-arrays they must once have held were absent, leaving only dust and a scattered handful of unassociated logic tiles.

By contrast, the scarred and chipped ceramic table in the center of the room was over-full with bits of piping, hoses, several canisters marked with the symbol for *poison*, a portable fission chamber, a large wooden box, its lid missing, the interior containing a stained rumple of cloth—and an orange cat, fast asleep.

"Well," Scholar tay'Nordif said, apparently to herself, "I have worked in less favored places." With difficulty, she squeezed past the table and bent over the work desk which had been jammed into the farthest and least-lit corner, as if whoever had occupied the office previously had only wished to be rid of it. The real work, it seemed to Jela, had been done at the table, though what—

Light flickered in the dark corner, which was the work screen coming up. The scholar clattered about a bit in the dimness, located the input wand and straightened, fingers sliding up and down the length, weaving chords at a rapid pace. Jela perforce reprised his impersonation of a rock, his eyes on the jumble of junk on the table, trying to make sense of the disparate bits; to imagine what sort of device might have been built from them—

"Jela," the scholar said in the dreamy, unsnappish way that meant most of her thought processes were engaged with something far more important than him. "Move away from the door."

As kobold-directions went, it was pretty loose, which might mean she really was thinking about something else. Still, he trusted her to give him some clear signal if he was in her line of fire, so he took his time about moving—slow, stolid and heavy—to his right, which cleared access to the door and also put him in a good place to observe both it and the scholar. For six of his heartbeats, nothing at all happened. The scholar continued to work the wand, her attention fixed on the screen. The cat in the box stretched and sighed without waking.

A CHIME SOUNDED, followed by a rather breathless, "Grudent tel'Ashon reporting, Scholar tay'Nordif."

The scholar did not look up from her screen. "Enter," she said absently, and the door opened to admit a flustered young woman wearing a unitard and a utility belt hung about with tools and tiles, scrolls and 'scribers—but lacking a truth-blade or any other weapon that Jela could see.

"Scholar tay'Nordif, allow me to say that I am honored—" she began.

The scholar did not so much as glance up from her screen. "Explain," she interrupted, "the condition in which I find my office."

Grudent tel'Ashon swallowed. "Yes, Scholar. This office had previously been tenanted by Scholar ser'Dinther, who failed to adequately prove his work—"

"Does this have a bearing on the condition of my office, Grudent?" The scholar interrupted, sharply. She turned from the screen, the wand held quiescent between her palms.

The other bowed, hastily. "Scholar, I merely sought to explain— the apparatus, and the, the—"

"The lack of standard resource works?" Scholar tay'Nordif snapped. "The absence of logic tiles, grids, and storage medium? The fact that the single chair is broken, and this terminal sub-standard?"

Silence.

"I am waiting, Grudent, for an explanation of these lacks and impediments to my work. Am I to understand the deplorable state of this office as a challenge? Perhaps there is another scholar on this hall who believes my work unworthy?" She tipped her head, meditatively. "Perhaps *you*—"

Grudent tel'Ashon raised her hands in what Jela registered as honest horror.

"Scholar, no! Please! There was no intention on my part . . . The grudent staff has been over—That is, I did not expect a new scholar to arrive so quickly, nor that the Second Chair would place you here, when there are other offices which have been . . . Had I known he wanted you near to himself and to the Prime . . ." She stuttered, gasped, and took refuge in a bow so deep she was bent quite in half, a posture she held until Scholar tay'Nordif instructed her, impatiently, to stand up straight.

This, the grudent did, with noticeable trepidation; squared her shoulders, and folded her hands into a tense knot before her belt buckle.

"That is better. I will expect you to comport yourself as befits a scholar during the time you serve as my grudent," Scholar tay'Nordif said, sharp and no-nonsense. "Scholars do not rely upon excuses, rather they rest squarely on good work and ample proof. Now." She swept the wand out, indicating the room at large. "I will have this office made seemly. I will have two chairs in addition to my work chair, none of which will be broken. I will have the standard references. I will have both logic and data tiles and several of the larger grids, in addition to the usual kit. I will have *that*—" the wand pointed at the cluttered table— "gone." She lowered the wand. "Am I clear, Grudent?"

"Scholar, you are," the other said, her voice hoarse. "However, I must make you aware of certain budget constraints. Those whose work brings largesse or, or patrons to the Tower, those scholars receive—"

The wand came up so quickly the grudent flinched.

"My work," Maelyn tay'Nordif said, each word as hard and as cold as a stone, "is paramount, Grudent. I do not allow the dabblings of any other scholar in this department to have precedence. You have heard what I require in order to pursue my work, and you will procure it, by what method I neither know nor care. Steal it, if you must. But you will provide everything I require. Have you understood me, Grudent?"

"Yes, Scholar," the grudent whispered.

"Good. Begin by removing that table."

"Yes, Scholar," the grudent whispered again, then, slightly stronger. "I will return in a moment with a cart."

"That is well. I will instruct the door to admit you."

The grudent left; the scholar turned back to her screen, fingers busy on the chording wand. Jela stood and waited.

In the box, the orange cat, which had slept soundly throughout all the preceding ruckus, abruptly sprang up, ears swiveling. Its wide amber gaze fell on Jela; it sat down and began to groom its shoulder.

Time, not very much of it, passed.

The door chimed and opened simultaneously, admitting the grudent with the promised cart. She paused on the threshold, frowning at the problem, and took note, apparently for the first time, of himself. Her eyes—brown and slightly protuberant—widened, but unlike the cat, she failed to transfer her consternation to a more useful activity.

"Don't," Scholar tay'Nordif said, her eyes on the screen, "mind Jela, Grudent. If you require assistance with heavy lifting, enlist its aid. Jela! Assist the grudent at her request."

The grudent swallowed; her lips parted but no sound emerged. Finally, she just turned her back on him and began to gather up the various odds and ends on the table and move them, all a-jumble, into the cart. She did show what Jela considered to be proper prudence in the matter of the *poison* canisters, and also took the necessary time to be sure that there was nothing in the fission chamber and that the power-source was disconnected. That done, she turned her attention to the box, and the cat inside the box, which had suspended its bath and was watching her with interest.

The grudent extended a hand which was trembling too much to be authoritative. The cat swung a paw, negligently, and the grudent jumped back, putting her bloodied finger to her mouth.

The cat yawned.

The grudent set her lips, groped 'round her belt and came forward with a pair of stained work gloves. She pulled one over the wounded hand—

"Leave it," Scholar tay'Nordif said from the back corner. The grudent blinked.

"Scholar?"

"The cat," the scholar snapped, clearly in no mood to tolerate stupidity. "Leave it."

The grudent lifted her eyes to Jela's face. Finding nothing there, she looked back to the cat.

"The box, too, Scholar?"

"If you must. Jela! Pick up the box. Pick up the cat—*gently*. Bring the box and the cat—*gently*—here to me now."

He moved, deliberately; the grudent dropped back, thoughtfully pulling the cart out of his path. The cat in the box watched his approach with interest, ears cocked forward. As near as Jela could tell from its body language, it was at rest, unaggressive—exactly as it had appeared in the heartbeat before it mauled the grudent.

The grudent, however, had approached the cat directly. Fortunately for him, he was a kobold, and just about smart enough to follow his orders by the one-two.

He took hold of the box with one hand, catching the cat neatly with the other as it hopped out, and tucking it—gently—between his arm and his side. It stiffened, but if it used its claws, they were neither long enough nor fierce enough to pierce the leather shirt. Jela kept moving, banged the table out of his way with a casual kick, and approached the terminal.

The scholar put the chording wand down on the rickety desk, extended a hand, caught the cat by the loose skin at the back of its neck and transferred it to her opposite arm, keeping a firm grip on the scruff. She jerked her chin at the empty shelf over the terminal.

"Put the box up there, Jela. *Gently.*"

It was an easy one-handed toss, and not too much clatter when it landed. The scholar sighed.

"Grudent tel'Ashon," she snapped, turning to address that worthy, who was busily shoving the last of the bits and bobs from

the table onto her cart. At the scholar's hail, she looked up, eyes wide
and throat working.

"Scholar?"

"This previous scholar—ser'Dinther? What was the nature of
his work? Briefly."

The grudent bit her lip. "As far as a mere grudent may understand a scholar's work, I believe he sought—that is, he had proven
the existence of adjacent lines of causality."

"Had he? A pity his proof did not stand rigorous testing." The
scholar nodded at the feline on her arm. "What role had the cat in
these proofs?"

"I . . . It was the scholar's intention to provide a practical
demonstration. His work led him to believe that a base creature in
peril of its life might, certain conditions being met, shift to an, to a
situation in which the peril was non-existent." She moved her hand
in a shapeless gesture that was perhaps meant to encompass the
table and the clutter it had supported. "He had at first worked with
the mun—with the Tower servitors. However, experimentation
revealed that their nature, though base, was yet too elevated for the
state shift to be a matter of instinct. Thus, the cats."

"I see. And the experiment?"

"A cat would be placed into the box, which would then be
sealed, excepting the delivery tube for the poison gas. The trigger
was a single radioactive nucleus which, in the causality we and the
cat co-inhabit, has a fifty percent chance of decaying within a spec-
ified time. If it decays, the gas is released."

"Killing the cat," the scholar said drily. "A singularly one-sided
experiment."

"According to Scholar ser'Dinther's proof," the grudent said,
leaning forward, real interest showing in her face. "The cat does not
die, but escapes to an adjacent line of causality. When we who are
continuing along *this* line of causality open the box to learn what has
transpired, we see a dead cat, because it is what experience has
trained us to see." She gasped, as if suddenly recalling herself, and
settled back, her hands twisting together.

"Scholar ser'Dinther was engaged in perfecting an apparatus

which would capture and distill the moment of transition. He was—his proof failed before he had completed that aspect of his work."

There was a small pause before the scholar, who had been stroking the cat between its ears, murmured. "I see. And this cat here is the last left alive." She looked up and sent a sharp glance to the grudent. "In this particular causality, of course."

The grudent hesitated, hands twisting 'round themselves with a will.

"That cat," she said—carefully, Jela thought. "That cat, Scholar, was in the box many times. Never once did the nucleus decay."

"A feline of extraordinary luck, I see. Well." She chucked the animal under the chin and moved her shoulders. "I have a kindness for cats. As this one is no longer required for experimental purposes, I shall keep it."

The grudent bowed hastily. "Yes, Scholar. Of course."

"Jela!" the scholar snapped. "Take the chair in the corner behind you to the grudent."

He turned, clumsily, and located the chair, a rickety item missing a quarter of its back and half of one leg. Hefting it casually, he took it to the grudent as ordered, and stood holding it out in one hand, while she blinked at him stupidly.

"It won't fit on the cart like that," she said.

"Jela!" Scholar tay'Nordif ordered from the rear. "Break the chair over your knee and place the pieces on the cart."

No trouble there, he thought and did as ordered, taking a brief, savage joy in the minor destruction. The grudent shrank back with a gasp, and watched with wide eyes as he dropped the bits into the cart, then gathered her courage and stood tall, taking a grip on the handle.

"I will dispose of this and be back for the table at once, Scholar," she said.

"Jela will carry the table," the scholar snapped. "Perhaps I failed to make plain my necessity that this office be habitable before the Mercy Bell sounds?"

The grudent was seen to choke slightly, but she stiffened her spine once more and sent what was probably meant to be a stern look into Jela's face.

"You. Jela," she said, voice shaking only a little. "Pick up the table and follow me."

The table was much too wide to fit through the doorway. Which was precisely the sort of esoteric detail a kobold would fail to note.

The grudent pushed the cart out the door. Jela stumped forward, hefted the table, and started after, one end striking the shelving with a will and scoring the wa—

"Jela!" Scholar tay'Nordif said sharply. "Stop!"

He stopped, and stood, table in hand, awaiting amended orders.

"Put the table down, Jela," the scholar said, and raised her voice. "Grudent tel'Ashon!"

Immediately, the grudent was in the doorway, eyes and mouth wide. "Scholar? I—"

"Silence! If you are to serve me, you will learn to think logically and to give clear, unambiguous orders. Perhaps the Tower's servitors are more able to reason, but a kobold is only able to follow what directions it is given. Thus, its service is only as good as your instructions. Observe, now.

"Jela! Press the switch on the table top. When the table has folded itself, pick it up and follow Grudent tel'Ashon. Obey her instructions until she returns you to me."

Deliberately, he looked over the table top, discovering the bright blue button set flush to the surface in due time. He pushed it and stood stoically by as the table folded itself into neat quarters, tucked the resultant rectangle under his arm and headed for the door. Grudent tel'Ashon gave way hastily before him. He followed her, and then followed her some more as she pushed the remains of the late Scholar ser'Dinther's experiments down the hall.

The cart went noiselessly on its cushion of air; the grudent went quietly in her soft-soled slippers. Jela walked as lightly as he dared while maintaining the illusion of clumsy bulk.

Ahead, there were voices, perhaps not yet discernible to the grudent, but clearly audible to Jela's enhanced hearing.

". . . gone to the Governors!" The first voice was light—possibly a woman—and clearly agitated.

"So, you have not made your exception to his work known?" The second voice was unmistakably masculine, pleasantly in the mid-range, calm—and instantly recognizable as belonging to Scholar tay'Welford, he who of the too-knowing smile.

"How could I?" the first voice responded. "But, the Governors! What does it mean?"

"Only that he gone to report the arrival of our newest sister in scholarship. It has been quite some time, as vel'Anbrek noted last eve, since we have seen one of the Master's students, and the Governors must surely be—"

The cart angled to the right, and a door noisily gave way before it. Jela dutifully marched after the grudent, straining his ears, but the remainder of the scholars' discussion was lost to him.

EIGHT

※ ※

Osabei Tower
Landomist

JELA PICKED THE CHAIR UP and followed Grudent tel'Ashon out into the hallway.

The past few hours had given him a respect for the grudent he had not expected to acquire. She had been tireless in the pursuit of her orders; displaying a subtle creativity that won, if not his heart, certainly his admiration. Realizing early in the endeavor that she would sometimes have need of him elsewhere in the hall, she had . . . acquired . . . a pass-tile from an office, the door of which bore the glowing name *Den Vir tel'Elyd*. This she had attached to the collar of his leather shirt, with a small grim smile, and a muttered, "Lackluster research and pedestrian results, was it?" He was then free to roam—on her orders, of course—an arrangement he approved of in the strongest possible terms.

The work had broken down neatly into brain and brawn. It fell to the grudent, as the self-identified brain, to gimmick the doors of offices she considered likely to contain those things required to make Scholar tay'Nordif's life more comfortable. After a quick reconnoiter, she would point out those items she deemed worthy, and direct him to carry them to the scholar's office, while she continued on to the next target. It was a system which had worked admirably in rapidly attaining for Maelyn tay'Nordif all the trappings of a scholar who had by her wit and her intellect captured a seat in Osabei Tower.

In Jela's estimation, the grudent had tarried a bit too long in the selection of the chair which he now carried, but it was hardly his place to criticize—especially as the protracted search had netted what appeared to be a brand new chair of the first order of craftsmanship. There had been no name on the door of the office from which this last item had been pilfered, but the appropriation had seemed to give Grudent tel'Ashon almost as much satisfaction as purloining the pass-tile. In Jela's opinion, she had done well by her scholar. Not that his opinion mattered.

Half-a-dozen steps ahead of him, the grudent abruptly swung close to the wall, sending a sharp look over her shoulder and waving at him to do the same. Not at all a good kobold order, but in light of the man walking toward them, Jela decided it was prudent to obey anyway.

The approaching scholar was, judging by the strands of silver glinting in the dark back-swept hair, in his middle years. His square face was creased, and at some point his nose had been broken. The sleeves of his robe were pushed up, revealing strong forearms, veins like blue wire running tight beneath the skin. In addition to the sheathed truth-blade and smart-gloves, a tile tablet adorned with many fobs and seals hung from his sash. He walked like a man who had recently taken a moderate wound—and who was earnestly trying to conceal that fact.

Grudent tel'Ashon dropped to one knee, head lowered, right hand fisted over her heart. "Prime Chair tay'Palin," she murmured respectfully as he drew level with their position.

The scholar paused, dark eyes sweeping over the grudent, and lingering rather longer than Jela liked on himself.

"Grudent tel'Ashon," he said, his voice smooth and mannerly. "Please, arise, and tell me where you have found this extraordinary— being."

The grudent came to her feet with alacrity, sliding a sideways glance in Jela's direction. He stood, chair held against his chest, eyes focused on a point in space approximately six inches from the end of his nose.

"Prime, that is the kobold Jela, which belongs to Scholar tay'Nordif."

"Is it, indeed?" Scholar tay'Palin took a step forward, his gaze sharp. "And why has Scholar tay'Nordif a Series—"

"tay'Palin!" a woman's voice—precisely the voice of the woman who had been talking to tay'Welford earlier—accompanied by the sound of someone running inefficiently in soft shoes, and an arrhythmic clacking, as if a dozen or more data tiles were striking against each other.

The scholar sighed, closed his eyes briefly, and turned—carefully, to Jela's eye.

"Scholar chi'Farlo," he said distantly. "How may I serve you?"

The woman lowered her robe, which she had held up to her plump knees in order to run, and smiled. Her yellow hair was divided into many braids, each one tied off with a cluster of tiles, which would account for the clacking. Her face was soft and pale; her eyes were round and blue. The smile didn't begin to warm them.

She came close to Scholar tay'Palin, and put a plump, soft hand on his arm. He twitched, so slightly that most observers would scarcely have seen—though Jela did.

And so, he was willing to wager, had Scholar chi'Farlo. Her smile widened, displaying dainty white teeth, and she exerted pressure on the arm, pulling the scholar with her.

"Walk with me, tay'Palin. I have something to say to you."

It seemed to Jela that the Prime Chair's shoulders sagged just a little beneath his robe. He inclined his head to the wide-eyed grudent.

"You may go, Grudent tel'Ashon."

She gulped and bowed, hurriedly. Keeping her head down, she snapped, "Follow me, Jela!" and moved away, hugging the right wall.

Jela perforce followed, carrying the chair, and straining his ears.

All that exercise gained him was the whisper of slippers against the floor and the gentle clacking of tiles.

SCHOLAR TAY'NORDIF BENT her cool, misty gaze upon the chair. To her left, on the polished and well-kept task table, a brand-new terminal and wand reposed in that space not taken up by the sprawling orange cat, which was watching the proceedings with interest.

The scholar extended a slender hand, pulled the chair to her, sat, and deftly put it through its phases. The grudent held her bow, her tension so marked that Jela's skin began to itch.

"Well done," Scholar tay'Nordif said from her comfortable recline. "I commend you, Grudent tel'Ashon; you have fitted me with honor and—"

A klaxon sounded, shrill and serious. Scholar tay'Nordif gasped, and cringed in her chair, one hand pressed to her breast. Jela could hardly blame her; it was all he could do not to jump for the handholds that weren't there and blink up the command screen in the helmet he wasn't wearing.

The grudent, however, snapped upright out of her bow, a grin on her face and her dull brown eyes sparkling.

"The Truth Bell!" she said excitedly.

"Indeed?" Scholar tay'Nordif said faintly. She fumbled at the chair's control, eventually coming perpendicular to local conditions. She blinked up at the grudent, the pulse at the base of her throat beating rapidly.

"Surely, truth need not be quite so stern?" she whispered. "Indeed, as the great philosopher bin'Arli tell us, *Truth is that silent certainty in one's—*"

The klaxon sounded again, and the rest of bin'Arli's wisdom was lost in a gasp as the scholar staggered to her feet, startling the cat, which leapt to the top of the work screen, tail lashing.

"Come, Scholar!" The grudent was half-way to the door. "The community is called to witness!"

"Witness?" the scholar said faintly.

"Yes, of course!" Grudent tel'Ashon waved an impatient

hand. "Quickly, Scholar! We don't want to miss a point!" She was gone.

"I—see," the scholar said. She pushed her sleeves up her arms nervously, took a deep breath and marched resolutely in the grudent's wake.

"Jela," she said, without turning her head. "Follow me."

THEY SAT ON RISERS inside a soaring, airy foyer strongly reminiscent of the octagonal hall of the flying platforms—many dozens of scholars, grudents, and the blind Smalls, all facing a center expanse of creamy floor with what looked for all of space like a training rectangle, marked out in rust-colored tile.

Jela stood behind and slightly to the right of Scholar tay'Nordif, which gave him a clear sight of the combat zone, and also of a command room situated about halfway up the wall directly opposite his position. The observation port was opaqued, but Jela felt certain that command of one sort or another was present.

The mass of scholars rippled, murmured—and stilled, as a yellow-haired woman marched out onto the floor, the tapping of her tile-braided hair clearly audible in the sudden silence.

Deliberately, she stepped into the rectangle, pulled the blade from its place in her sash and brandished it dramatically over her head.

"I, Leman chi'Farlo, Seated Scholar and Third Chair of the Department of Interdimensional Statistics, challenge Kel Var tay'Palin to defend his Thesis Number Twenty-Seven, in which he avers that the value of Amedeo's Constant as reflected in N-space is a contingent process and is not an ordered process." Her voice echoed weirdly, which Jela took to be an affect of a wide-area amplifier.

"What's this?" a scholar some places to Jela's right whispered to the scholar next to her. "She challenges him on work he published before he was seated?"

"It's allowable," her mate whispered back. "Bad form, but allowable."

The first scholar sighed lightly. "Well, it is chi'Farlo, after all."

"Come forth, Kel Var tay'Palin," a voice boomed across the

hall—likely originating, Jela thought, in the shielded command room. "Come forward and defend your work."

And here came the lean figure of the Prime Chair, walking carefully, his knife held business-like. It was, Jela saw, a well-kept weapon, the edge so sharp it shone like an energy blade. He stepped into the rectangle, and bowed slightly to his opponent. She returned the courtesy, lunging out of it low and vicious, going for the belly.

Prime Chair twisted; his opponent's blade sliced robe, and in the moment it was fouled, he chopped down at her exposed neck. Unfortunately, the yellow-haired scholar was more nimble than she looked; she tucked and dove, freeing her knife with a wrist-wrenching twist. There was a clatter of tiles as a severed braid hit the floor.

Scholar tay'Palin spun, a trifle ragged, to face his opponent as she came to her feet and danced forward, knife flashing, pressing him fiercely.

And that tactic, Jela thought, was likely a winner, given that knife fights were never certain. No question tay'Palin was the better fighter, but he was wounded and weary while she was fresh and energized, and that more than balanced her relative lack of skill.

The blonde woman thrust, tay'Palin twisted—and went down to one knee. She pressed her advantage, going for his eyes now, his throat, his face, working close, giving him no opportunity to gain his feet.

Still, he fought on, grimly, blood showing now on his sleeve—which was, Jela thought, the old wound, torn open again—and down the front of his robe from his numerous cuts.

All at once, the woman twisted, feinting; the scholar on his knees realizing the deception too late—and that quickly it was over, the blonde woman's knife was lodged to the hilt in tay'Palin's chest.

Exuberant, she turned, raising her hands above her head. And as she did, the mortally wounded scholar raised his arm, reversed his blade—and threw.

The victor staggered, mouth opening in a silent scream—and fell all at once, blood streaming. Scholar tay'Palin lay on his side, eyes open and empty, his blood pooling and mixing with that of his opponent.

"Scholar tay'Palin," the disembodied voice announced, into the absolute silence of the lobby, "has successfully turned the challenge. Let his grudents amass his work and publish it wherever scholars study. Let his name be recorded on the Scholar's Wall."

There was a murmur of approval from the assembled scholars.

"Scholar chi'Farlo," the voice continued, "is found to have wrongly issued challenge. Let her office be purged, her files wiped and her name struck from our rolls."

"Well deserved," whispered the scholar to the right.

"We have an administrative announcement." the voice said briskly. "Effective immediately, Scholar Ala Bin tay'Welford, formerly Second Chair, will serve the Department of Interdimensional Statistics as Prime Chair."

The Mercy Bell rang.

LUTE CAST HIS NET WIDE, watching, as she had asked him to do, while she prepared herself to accept that burden which no dominant had taken up since the first had been born from the need of the Iloheen.

It was Lute's belief that what she proposed to do would alter the bounds of probability more certainly than any mere manipulation of the lines, no matter how bold or subtle. It would be the sum of small things—a truth not said, a law unobserved, a heart engaged— which would, in the final accounting, weigh against the Iloheen.

His lady held otherwise, as did Rool Tiazan and his lady, differing merely on the fine points of process. In the end, process mattered to Lute not at all. That the Iloheen were brought down—he barely dared form the word *destroyed* within the cavern of his secret heart—that had been his only desire, long before his first encounter with Rool Tiazan, long before he listened to what the Iloheen might call treason—and allowed himself to be bound.

He had been mad, of course. Confined, in thrall, compelled against his will to do . . . terrible things. Terrible things. When Rool had proposed a lesser slavery, the acceptance of which might, possibly, with luck, on some day long in the future even as they counted, bring the Iloheen defeat—

It was an odd thing, this container in which he had allowed himself to be prisoned. The weight of it dulled his senses, limited his reach. And yet even now, after . . . so long . . . Even now, he sometimes woke, the screams of a dying star ringing in ears unfit to hear them; the pure crystalline agony of Iloheen pleasure stretching his soul to the point of annihilation.

That the new slavery he had agreed to had not been lesser, nor even less horrifying; that the probability of gaining ascendency over the Iloheen was not very much greater than the probability of one of the stars he had destroyed blazing into renewed life—he thought he had suspected as much, even as he agreed to the plan Rool proposed. He thought he might have suspected that Rool, twice a slave and old in treachery, was himself more than a bit mad. And yet, if not they, who in their true forms had held dominion over space, time, and probability—if they could not deny the Iloheen the future, who—

The ley lines flared. Lute traced the disturbance, saw a small brilliance, of no more consequence against the blare of all possibility than a spark against a bonfire, dancing hectic before a black wind.

Lute coalesced, wrapped his awareness closely and returned to that place where his lady lay guarded, preparing for her ordeal.

She noticed him at once, and he bowed under the weight of her regard.

"It begins," he said.

TOR AN WOKE WITH a cry. Before him, the board glowed green; the screens displayed a starfield, perfectly orderly and ordinary. The coordinates of that starfield were displayed at the bottom of the forward screen, with the legend, "Transition complete."

Light Wing maintained position, awaiting orders from her pilot, who struggled upright his chair, gasping once against a flare of pain—and again at finding the belts loose and unfastened. What had he been thinking, to go into transition without engaging the safety web?

He had survived to ask the question, therefore it could be put aside until more immediate concerns were addressed. Such as— what had wakened him?

It must, he thought, examining the board more closely, have been the chime signaling the end of transition. He frowned at the coordinates, which were unfamiliar, and at the starfield, anonymous and soothing. A glance at the elapsed time caused his frown to deepen. He had been asleep for what would have amounted, on the planet of his birth, to two full days while the ship transitioned from—

Memory abruptly returned; his hand rose to the burning shoulder; he felt the dressing, recalled the laughter of the soldiers, his heartbeat pounding in his ears as he ran for his life. Shot. Yes. He remembered.

He swallowed, forcing himself past the memory of terror. He had returned to the ship, dressed his wound as best as he'd been able, sat down in the chair and—

"Landomist," he murmured, reaching to the board and petitioning the nav-brain for an approach, while he struggled to reproduce the reasoning which had led to feeding those particular coordinates into—

A set of syllables rose from the mists of memory, and he gave them shape, his voice a cracked whisper: "Kel Var tay'Palin." A name, certainly—though who the gentleman might be, or where Tor An yos'Galan had acquired—no. Now he recalled what his fingers had never forgot. Kel Var tay'Palin had been an . . . acquaintance of Aunt Jinsu, traveling with her in pursuit of his studies, back when Aunt Jinsu had been a fiery young pilot and the despair of all her elders. It had pleased her that the young man had journeyed at last to Landomist, and taken his chair in Interdimensional Mathematics. He remembered when the letter came. Aunt, home between staid and stable trade rounds, had read it aloud to the youngers, telling them the story of how the young scholar had ridden with her, and perhaps not . . . quite . . . all the truth of how he had paid his way . . .

And how long ago had it been, he wondered, shifting in the chair to ease his wounded arm, since that letter and those stories? Certainly, after he had served his first flight as cabin boy, under Great-grandfather Er Thom, on *Baistle's* last trip 'round the Short

Loop. Had he done his turn as cargo-rat yet, or had he been awaiting the *Profitable Passage*?

He sighed sharply, out of patience with himself. What did it matter, after all, the exact year? Stipulate that the letter had arrived long ago, and that the truth upon which Aunt Jinsu had based her tales of the bold-hearted and single-minded young scholar had taken place more years before that. Kel Var tay'Palin, if he sat yet safe in the Tower at Landomist, would be an ancient. He might possibly recall the adventures of his youth with kindness—enough, perhaps, to drink tea with Pilot Jinsu herself. Pilot Jinsu's nephew, however, would have no call upon the man.

Now I'll tell you a secret, Aunt Jinsu whispered from memory, eyes glinting mischief as she lowered her voice and looked over her shoulder to be sure that grandmother wasn't near. *The scholars of the mathematics tower, they'll sometimes hire pilots to fly their theories for them, or to travel to a certain someplace and collect readings. Scholar tay'Palin wasn't one to forget a good turn done him, and more than once he's passed a small flight and a respectful purse my way.*

It seemed that his fingers had listened to Aunt Jinsu more closely than his ears, Tor An thought resignedly. And, truly, what other choice had he? Perhaps the old scholar might direct him to someone who would take his readings and make sense of them— some . . . happier . . . sense, perhaps, than that which he had formed.

The Towers of Learning were powerful, so he had heard. Perhaps the mathematical tower might be powerful enough to command the military to examine the Ringstars' fate, to, to—

To what? he wondered. Unless he truly had gone mad, his readings proved that the Ringstars no longer existed. Did he expect that the learned scholars might force the military to put them back?

He shifted in the chair again, biting his lip as fire shot his arm. Carefully, he angled the chair so that he could reach the board with his good hand.

"Never mind," he told himself softly, as his clever fingers chose an approach and gave *Light Wing* the office. "Do your duty and glory will follow."

It was a thing that his brother Cor Win had used to say, most usually with a roguish grin and a wag of the head. How he would have laughed, Tor An thought, locking the course and staggering to his feet, to hear it said in deadly earnest.

THE BACK OF JELA'S neck stopped itching as soon as the door to Scholar tay'Nordif's quarters locked shut behind him, which just went to show, he thought sourly, that even an old soldier could be a fool. At the same instant, the cat, which had hung quiescent on his arm the whole long way from the offices, began kicking and squirming, claws scoring leather in earnest, demanding to be released. Which just went to show that even extraordinarily lucky cats weren't necessarily immune to foolishness, either.

Unless, he thought suddenly, keeping a firm grip on the cat's ruff, the creature wanted to be put down in order that it might field credible attack? He'd read . . . somewhere . . . that a single cat could dispatch a wharf rat twice its mass—

The cat made a noise like an airlock with a bad gasket, and executed a complex twist, surprisingly strong for so small a creature. Jela subdued it absently, most of his attention elsewhere.

Super-sharp hearing brought him the uninterrupted humming of the hacks he'd put in place, and a quick visual scan as he crossed to the counter confirmed that everything was as they had left it that morning.

For whatever *that* was worth.

He placed the twisting, hissing cat—*gently*—on its feet on the counter. The animal turned its head this way and that, giving the territory a visual sweep of its own, then stood at attention, ears swiveling. Jela's heart beat three times. The cat shook itself, gave its shoulder a quick half-dozen licks, yawned, sat down, extended one back leg high and began to lick the inside of its thigh.

All clear, then, Jela thought. *Maybe.*

Assuming that the pass-tile fixed to his collar didn't report his every move to the Tower's slave-brain. And even if it did, he, legitimate, honest kobold that he was, couldn't just take it off and crush it.

Scholar tay'Nordif *had* exchanged the tile pilfered from the office of Scholar tel'Elyd by the enterprising grudent for one of the pair she'd had off the Bursar that morning—and had it been Cantra yos'Phelium who had done the deed, he would have had no doubt but what the tile had been rendered as harmless to the mission as it was possible for her to have done. Scholar tay'Nordif, though— the Deeps alone knew what to expect from such a flutter-headed, vain—

Trust, Cantra yos'Phelium's husky, serious voice whispered from memory . . . *this is going to be hard, Pilot, I know—*

Trust, he repeated to himself now, as he moved into the tiny galley, pulled a bowl from its hook, filled it with water and placed in front of the cat, which didn't bother to raise its head.

A picture formed at the back of his mind: the now-familiar shadow of an enormous wing, gliding over the crowns of monumental trees. Leaves rustled as the dragon dropped close, and closer still, wingtips brushing tree-tops as it approached one particular tree, one particular branch, upon which hung one particular fruit. With no diminishment of speed, the dragon extended its graceful neck. Its mouth opened, teeth as long as Jela flashed, the shadow passed on. The tree stood, unscarred and undisturbed, its branch intact, the seed-pod it had offered gone.

Jela took a breath.

On the counter, the cat paused in its grooming and raised its head, amber eyes meeting his with the look of an equal intelligence which was, at the moment, slightly put out with him.

Trust, Cantra's voice whispered again.

The cat blinked, breaking their shared gaze, and returned to its grooming. Jela went to tend the tree.

A seed pod dropped into his palm. He gave silent thanks, and ate it while mentally reviewing the so-called proving, for the tree's interest. It had been a shocking business, badly done and proving nothing but that the man challenged had been more accomplished with his blade than his challenger. He'd known that the scholars of Osabei Tower rose and fell by such "proofs" of their work; Cantra had insisted that he read the codes and histories of the Towers. But knowing and seeing were two different processes. Which he'd also known.

Not to mention, he thought, opening the hidden door in the tree's pot, that Prime Chair tay'Palin's death had been of benefit to the mission, for the man had recognized a Series soldier and had been, so Jela thought, on the edge of asking difficult questions when he'd been interrupted.

The cat came wandering by, snuffling at the grid. Jela pushed it gently away, and it jumped onto the dirt that surrounded and nourished the tree. He gasped, remembering sharp claws and tender bark—and received a clear sending of a dragon curled 'round the base of a sapling, slitted eyes alert.

For its part, the cat circled the tree, one shoulder companionably rubbing the bark, then jumped down on the opposite side and disappeared into the depth of the quarters.

Jela sighed, lightly, and finished assembling his equipment.

THE MOOD OF THE COMMON ROOM was frenetic. It was often so, after the passing of a Prime Chair, and all the moreso this evening. tay'Palin had been well-liked, and had held his seat for almost three Common Years. Had his tenure not been cut short, he would have been eligible on his anniversary date to petition the Board of Governors for a place in the Masters' Wing. Whether the Governors would have granted so audacious a request—was, tay'Welford acknowledged as he took a glass of wine from a passing tray, entirely up to the whim of the Governors. And in any case was no longer an issue.

"Well, there he is!" Regrettably, vel'Anbrek's voice carried easily over the ambient din. It would not do to be seen to snub so venerable a member of the department. No, tay'Welford thought, moving toward the group clustered about the old scholar; there were far more satisfying ways of dealing with vel'Anbrek open to him now.

"Prime." dea'San, never a fool, inclined her head as he joined them.

"Colleagues," he replied, smiling 'round at the three of them. Scholar tay'Nordif gave him his due as well, her beige hair shimmering. When she raised her head, he saw that her face was quite pale. She stood preternaturally still, with none of the overt signs of "vigilance" she had displayed yestereen. Perhaps, tay'Welford thought, today's contest of scholarship had proved a tonic for the department's newest member.

"Today's proving turned out rather well for you, didn't it?" vel'Anbrek said, raising his glass and taking a hearty drink.

tay'Welford frowned slightly. "I am not entirely certain that I understand you, colleague. Are you hinting that I would have wished for anything like today's outcome?"

"You're not such a fool as that, I'd think," the old horror replied. "Certainly, anyone here could have predicted tay'Palin stood on the edge of error. Did so myself, just last night. But who could have imagined he had that last stroke in him—and that he would be moved to save you the trouble of killing chi'Farlo yourself?"

"Gor Tan!" dea'San cried. "What do you say?"

"That chi'Farlo was ambitious," the old man retorted. "Had she won her point, she would have risen from Third Chair to Second, while our good friend and colleague tay'Welford ascended to Prime. And how long, I ask, before she marshaled the tactics that had worked so well against tay'Palin and brought them against our beloved new Prime?"

"Tactics?" Scholar tay'Nordif asked, her voice rather subdued. "What tactics?"

vel'Anbrek shook a finger at her. "It had long been apparent to those of us on the hall that someone had determined to advance by guile, rather than by scholarship. An increasing number of challenges were issued against the work of Prime tay'Palin, and by some of the hottest heads in our department, as even cautious Scholar dea'San will admit is true. Though you knew him so short a time, Scholar tay'Nordif, I am certain it will not surprise you to learn that tay'Palin was a solid scholar—a very solid scholar. Over and over he proved himself. But even a solid scholar becomes wearied by constant challenge. It is my belief that Scholar chi'Farlo had today determined that he was worn down enough to err, and thus she called that point—which ought, Prime Chair, to have been disallowed! Are we to permit challenges based on Wander-work which is tangential to the token that gained us our chair? What next, I ask you? Challenges on the 'quations we proved at our tutor's knee?"

"I will," tay'Welford said, keeping his voice serious and soft, "take the matter to the Governors, colleague. It may be that protocol was breached."

"That's very well, then," sniffed vel'Anbrek.

"You would say," Scholar tay'Nordif murmured, "if I understand you, Scholar—that Scholar chi'Farlo felt the Prime—past-Prime! Your pardon, Prime tay'Welford!—would be physically unable to withstand her, and so issued a spurious challenge?"

"A light-minded challenge, let us say," vel'Anbrek answered. "But, yes, you have the essence of it, Scholar. And since it was clearly her wish to rise to Prime—which I do not scruple to tell you she *could not* have done on the strength of her scholarship—plain logic dictates that she would soon have launched the same sort of attack at tay'Welford here, from her position as Second Chair."

"It seems," Maelyn tay'Nordif protested, "a very risky business, Scholar. How if she were found out?"

"But she was found out, was she not?" dea'San said briskly. "The challenge fell to tay'Palin." She fixed vel'Anbrek in a stern eye. "The system works. Though it does occasionally allow for certain . . . untidiness, balance is eventually restored."

"Yes, of course," said tay'Nordif, "but—"

The bell rang, and tay'Welford stepped forward with a smile to offer his arm to dea'San, leaving tay'Nordif to share the meal with vel'Anbrek, much joy she might have of him.

JELA'S 'BOTS AND SEEKERS had been busy while he'd been fetching and carrying and seeing bloody murder done. He therefore immersed himself, sitting on the floor next to the tree, eating a second seed pod, absently, and a third after it hit his knee a little harder than local gravity could answer for.

The cat had come by again and stuck its nose once between him and his portable array. He pushed it—*gently*—away, and it took itself out of his sight and consciousness.

What he was looking for was the safe-place where Liad dea'Syl stored his equations. He had been forced to make certain broad assumptions in his instructions to his constructs. The quick recon tour he'd taken of the data banks last night had revealed the not exactly surprising information that there were many fortified areas within the Osabei Tower architecture. The challenge had then been to build his seekers clever enough to eliminate all but the most likely lockups. He'd at least built them clever enough to move within the Tower brain without lighting any alarms; and they'd also managed to amass a tidy list of six possibles.

The rest of the finicky, risky work was his to do.

He eliminated two of the six before he noticed the timer light blinking insistently at the bottom of the screen. Quickly, he broke the array down, stowed the pieces in the tree's pot, leaned against the wall and became a napping kobold.

No sooner had he closed his eyes than the door chuckled and opened. He heard Scholar tay'Nordif's firm steps, quickly followed by her sharp voice.

"Jela! Open your eyes and rise!"

He did so, in a kobold hurry, which was none too quick, taking care not to crush the Tower servitor who stood just inside the door, a basket held in both of her tiny hands.

"Give the basket to my servant," the Scholar directed the Small, and to him, "Jela! Receive the basket and take it to the kitchen." The exchange made, the scholar waved an imperious hand. "You may go."

The blind servant bowed, turned and exited, silent on tiny, bare feet. Behind her, the door closed, and the scholar stepped forward to seal it while Jela carried the basket into the galley and put it on the counter next to the bowl of water he had drawn for the cat. The animal itself didn't come immediately to sight, and the bowl appeared to be untouched.

Looking into the basket, he saw it full of sealed food packets, not unlike single-rations. Cat food, he surmised, and wondered again where the cat was, which a kobold would not ever wonder, and so he did not look around for it.

"Jela!" Scholar tay'Nordif snapped. "Open a single packet and place it on the counter by the water dish."

He did this while she walked toward the larger room, voicing "*s-s-s-s-s*," and then exclaiming in warm, pleased tones, "*There* you are, clever fellow! I'm pleased to see you making yourself at home. I will be wanting that chair directly, however, and you, I believe, will be wanting your supper."

Jela kept his eyes on the business of unfolding the ration pack into a bowl and spreading the lips wide. He heard the scholar's light-but-not-light-enough steps approach, smelled Cantra's scent over the strong odor of the cat's meal.

"Stand back, Jela," the scholar directed him, and he did what he was told, as she slid the cat smoothly from her arm to the counter, its nose pointed at the food.

The orange tail twitched, the ears flicked—and the cat was at once wholly occupied with its dinner, like any good soldier at mess. Jela dared to look up and observed a smile upon the face of his mistress—a fond and slightly foolish smile, which chilled him to the core, it was so unlike any expression he had ever seen on Cantra yos'Phelium's features.

The eyes moved from the cat to himself, and hardened in an instant. "Jela!" she snapped. "Put the sealed packets—*neatly*—on the lowest shelf of the middle cabinet. When the basket is empty, place it by the door."

Ordered, he obeyed. The scholar watched the cat for a few heartbeats more, then he heard her move back across the room to her workstation.

He finished stocking the cabinet, and turned, basket in hand. The ration pack was empty, the cat vanished again. She hadn't told him to clean up the animal's mess, so he passed it by to place the basket, as directed, next to the door.

"What shall I call you?" the scholar inquired, in a high, foolish voice.

Jela turned, slowly, and found her sitting on the chair, cat on her lap, tickling it under its chin. The cat, far from displaying predator-like behavior and having off with her hand, expressed every indication of ecstasy, its eyes slitted and its mouth half-open in pleasure.

"Perhaps," Scholar tay'Nordif said dreamily, "the simple name is best, eh? After all, as the great bin'Arli teaches us, *it is neither name nor house which makes fair fortune.* Therefore, you are now and shall henceforth be—Lucky."

The cat purred, loudly, and the scholar chuckled fondly. Jela, his tasks complete, stood next to the door, hoping that she'd notice soon and order him to do something, or else go to sleep so that he could continue with his—

"Ah, what gossip we had at the common gather this evening, Lucky! Truly, you would be horrified to learn how scholars do gossip—but no! You have been employed by a scholar, have you not? You will therefore perhaps not be surprised to hear that Scholar vel'Anbrek believes Prime tay'Welford engineered not only today's proving, but a number of previous challenges made against the work of the previous Prime. Scholar vel'Anbrek believes—ah! not in so many words, you understand; he has not survived so long under walls because he is an idiot, I think—Scholar vel'Anbrek believes that Prime tay'Welford wishes harm to our beloved Master dea'Syl. Is that not diverting, Lucky?"

The cat yawned, widely. The scholar laughed, scooped it off her lap and dropped it lightly to the floor as she came to her feet.

"Well, to bed, I believe, so that I am alert for tomorrow's labors!" Without a glance or a glimmer toward the door, where Jela still waited in hope of an order, she stripped off the robe and bundled it untidily onto the shelf that held the half-unpacked travel bag. She kicked off her slippers, pulled a blanket from the storage cabinet and lay down on her cot.

"Jela," she said. "Dim the light and go to sleep."

Bring the lights down, he did, and returned to his place beneath the tree. He waited until the rhythm of her breathing told him that she was asleep before he pulled his equipment from its cache and commenced in again to work.

He roused once, when a seed pod pounced off of his knee, and paused long enough to eat it, sending a silent thanks to the tree. He roused a second time, briefly, when the scholar shifted in her sleep; and a third time, when the cat tried to lay across his array.

And some time just before the end of the scholar's sleep shift, he hid his equipment, settled back against the wall and considered two data points.

One, if Liad dea'Syl's work was locked inside the Osabei data bank, it was well-hidden indeed.

Two, he had the location of Muran's damn' planet-shield, that Commander Ro Gayda had ordered him, as his last mission, to procure for the troop.

NINE

❦ ❦

Osabei Tower
Landomist

"BUSINESS ON LANDOMIST?" The clerk cast a bored glance over his license, and ran it through the reader.

"I carry data for a scholar seated at Osabei Tower," Tor An said steadily. His shoulder—where he had been shot—hurt in good earnest now, and his thoughts had an alarming tendency to wander. He had dosed himself with antibiotics from the ship's kit, and rewrapped the wound tightly enough that his second-best trading jacket—a hand-me-down from Cor Win and thus a little large—fit over the additional bulk of the dressing.

"Projected length of stay?" the clerk asked.

Until Landomist is consumed by the calamity which has overtaken my—He caught the response before it got off the end of his tongue and substituted, "Much depends upon the scholar. It may be that I will be required for interpretation . . ."

The reader chimed and spat out a datastrip. Bored, the clerk ran it through another reader. This one ejected a pale blue tile with the pictograph for "visitor" 'scribed on its surface. She handed it, with his license, to Tor An.

504

"You are granted temporary residency for thirty-six local days," she said, her eyes pointed somewhere over his head. "The tile's inclusions degrade at a certain rate. At eighteen local days, its color will phase to red. At the beginning of the thirty-sixth day, it will begin to blink. At the end of the thirty-sixth day, it will phase to black. The mechanism is extremely efficient, however, it is well to arrange to be on your transport before the final hour. If you are required to remain longer than the standard thirty-six-day allowance granted by the Portmaster's mercy, Osabei Tower must needs request that this office extend your term."

"I am grateful," Tor An said, slipping his license away into its private pocket with a frisson of relief. The tile, he placed in a more public pocket, in case he should need to produce it upon demand.

"Enjoy-your-stay-on-Landomist," the clerk said, and turned away before she had done speaking.

"YOU WISHED TO SEE ME, Prime Chair?"

tay'Welford looked up from his screen with a smile.

"Scholar tay'Nordif. Thank you for coming to me so promptly, and believe that I am deeply grieved that it is become necessary to interrupt you in the pursuit of your work. Please sit down."

She took the chair he indicated, and sat with her hands folded primly in her lap. Her color had not improved over last evening, and overall she seemed a bit . . . rumpled.

"Did you rest well, Scholar?" he asked, noting her condition with concern. "I do hope you find your quarters comfortable."

She blinked and rallied somewhat. "My quarters are more than adequate, I thank you, Prime Chair. As to my rest—on the frontier I was accustomed to sleep in whatever conditions were most safe, which did not—as I am certain you recall!—always equate with 'most comfortable.'"

"I am delighted that the quarters please; we do tend to forget the privations we suffered for our art when we Wandered, working safe here behind walls as we do." He folded his hands atop his desk and considered her. "I do not wish to be forward, Scholar, but I hope you will allow me to say that—witnessing one's first proving is a powerful thing. Such a proving as was undertaken yesterday—that is rare, indeed, and more powerful than most. I was unsettled for several days following the first proving I witnessed within these hallowed walls, and it was the veriest street brawl compared to what we were honored to see yesterday."

Scholar tay'Nordif was looking over his right shoulder, her eyes unfocused, and her face slack. Assuming that she was once again relieving Prime tay'Palin's glorious defense, he allowed her a few heartbeats for reverie before clearing his throat.

So intent had she been on the glories of the past, that even that slight noise caused her to start in the chair, her gaze snapping back to his face.

"Your—pardon, Prime," she said rather breathlessly. "My thoughts were elsewhere."

"Surely, surely." He smiled, projecting calmness. The scholar shifted in her chair, smoothing her robe with fingers that were not quite steady.

"But," tay'Welford said, and she jumped again at the sudden syllable, "I had promised not to keep you long from your work! Let us address my topic, if you are willing."

"Certainly," she said again, refolding her hands tightly onto her lap.

"Well, then, I will not conceal that your arrival here—the only one of the Master's own students to reach us—has excited the interest of the Board of Governors. You are called to stand before them two days hence, immediately following the Day Bell. They will wish to ask you certain questions."

He had not thought it possible for Scholar tay'Nordif's face to pale further. Her hands gripped each other so tightly that the knuckles showed white.

"Questions?" she said faintly.

"Indeed." He looked at her with concern. "Are you quite well, Scholar?"

"Yes, of course. It is only—the Board of Governors! What can they possibly wish to ask me?"

"Various things, which seem good to them." He extended a

hand and tapped his work screen. "As Prime Chair of our department, I have called you here to put some questions of my own, so that a preliminary report may be sent to the Governors and to the Master. It is the duty of the department to provide the answers to such rudimentary questions." He bent to his screen—and looked up, rueful.

"What am I thinking! There was more—a very great honor for you, Scholar! Master dea'Syl himself will be present during your examination by the Board. Surely, it must be a moment of transcendent joy, to behold once again the face of your master."

"Ah," said Scholar tay'Nordif, in a strangled voice. "Indeed."

This seemed rather . . . subdued for a paroxysm of joy, and tay'Welford waited politely, in case there should be more. However, it appeared that this was the sum total of joyous amazement Scholar tay'Nordif intended to express. tay'Welford cleared his throat, murmured, "Just so," and turned again to his screen.

"Were you acquainted with any other of the Master's students?" he asked, eyes on the screen.

Silence.

He looked up. "Scholar tay'Nordif," he said, sharply. "Pray attend me now. Were you acquainted with any other of Master dea'Syl's students? After all, it is not unusual for Wanderers to form alliances 'mong themselves, to travel and study together for a time."

Scholar tay'Nordif shifted in her chair. "I . . . knew the others but slightly," she murmured. "From the first, I felt that the Master's core assumptions carried a flaw. The others, therefore, did not welcome me among them."

There was a spike of old anger, there, which tay'Welford found gratifying.

"How long," he asked, "did you study with Master dea'Syl?"

A short pause, then— "Only—only a short time. Perhaps—no longer than three months of the Common Calendar."

tay'Welford frowned. "You studied with him for so short a time—and in addition found his work to be flawed—yet you name yourself his student?"

She glared at him indignantly. "Indeed, I do. How else? Liad dea'Syl's work shaped my own. Were it not necessary to prove those core assumptions false, and to provide truth in their stead, my scholarship would have been broad, yet shapeless."

"I . . . see. So the sum total of your work as a Wanderer was to disprove the work of the scholar you claim as your master?"

Scholar tay'Nordif frowned, stung, perhaps by his disbelieving tone. "You have seen my work, Prime Chair," she said stiffly. "I made no secret regarding the coin I offered the Tower in return for a seat."

"Indeed," tay'Welford said, turning away from his screen to face her more fully. "I have seen your work, Scholar. In fact, I have perused it in some little detail, as my own work has allowed, and it grieves me to state that—while interesting, it is somewhat light of proof. You elucidate the 'reformation' of a single system—but are these results reproducible, Scholar?"

She pressed her lips together and looked down at her folded hands. "I was, perhaps, hasty in approaching the Tower and suing for a seat," she said, muffled. "It seemed to me that the preliminary work was telling . . . But I should, perhaps, have waited upon the second result."

tay'Welford considered her. "I am to understand that such a result exists?"

"Indeed," her voice took on an eager note. "I had commissioned a pilot to physically access the area and bring me proof—coordinates, spectrograph readings, data . . ."

"And where is this pilot?" tay'Welford interrupted.

Scholar tay'Nordif moved her shoulders slightly. "Late for the rendezvous—you know what pilots are, Prime Chair! I waited at the house of my patron a reasonable time, but then, as I said, I grew restless. I left a message that I might be found at Osabei and came ahead to claim my chair."

He raised an eyebrow at such audacity. "You were certain of yourself, were you not? Do you not consider entry into Osabei Tower a matter of exertion?"

"Indeed, I consider it a matter of the utmost exertion! I had striven greatly, formed and tested a theory which—"

"A theory which," he interrupted, "is a direct attack upon the lifework of one of Osabei Tower's most precious Masters. You knew that such work must gain you entrance, and once entered, you determined to take upon yourself a false mantle of scholarship."

She stared at him, mouth open, plainly and unbecomingly aghast. tay'Welford sighed.

"My work," she managed at last. "My work is revolutionary; it takes our understanding of the nature and function of the natural order a quantum leap ahead of—"

"Your work," tay'Welford snapped, "is trivial and derivative. It proves nothing. Worse, it makes sport of one of the finest mathematical minds to have smiled upon our art since Osabei tay'Bendril gave us the theory of transition."

"How dare—"

He raised his hand, soothing them both. "Peace, peace. My apologies, Scholar. As Prime Chair, it is my duty to facilitate the work of all, and to ease strife, not to create it. Only tell me this—have you reproduced these results?"

"The pilot—" she began and he sighed.

"Scholar, you had best hope that your pilot arrives with that data before you stand before the Governors, two days hence." He pushed away from his desk and stood.

"That is all, Scholar. Thank you for your assistance."

TOR AN CAUGHT THE SLIDEWAY to the City of Scholars, standing like old bones on the sparsely traveled slow slide, gripping the safety loop grimly and trying to ignore the whirling in his head.

Unlike Korak, with its chaotic streets, and dun-colored buildings built tight to the dun-colored earth, Landomist soared, the tops of the towers lost in wispy clouds, which filtered the light from the local star to an indeterminate pale yellow. The breeze was damp and cool against his hot face, and fragrant with the odors of the many plants growing in wall niches, in pots, hung from poles and cables, and climbing up the sides of the cloud-topped buildings. Truth told, the air was a little too damp for his taste and he concentrated on breathing in a slow, unhurried rhythm, forcibly ignoring pilot instincts which would have him checking pressure valves and holding tanks in search of a leak . . .

His stomach was beginning to roil in sympathy with the unsteadiness of his head. He adjusted his grip on the loop and dared to close his eyes for a moment. Alas, that only made matters worse, so he compromised by opening his eyes to the merest slits and ignoring, as best he might, the unpleasant sensations of motion.

Soon, he told himself. Soon, he would be in the City of Scholars, and able to exit the slideway. Soon, he would be in Scholar tay'Palin's office, sitting in a chair, perhaps even sipping some tea, if the scholar were disposed to recall Aunt Jinsu well.

Soon.

"WHAT IS IT?" the young scholar inquired of the elder, who laughed.

"Kobold," he said, his voice over-loud. Jela, standing slack-jawed and idiot before Scholar tay'Nordif's door, as ordered, did not wince.

"What is a kobold?" the younger scholar persisted, daring to drift closer by a timid step and bending down to peer into his face. "It looks a very brute."

"Some of that," the old scholar allowed. "And truth told, this one seems to be a common laborer. Out of Shinto, if Scholar tay'Nordif's tale of her illustrious patron is to be believed—and there's no reason not to believe it, no matter what dea'San may say. Any new-seated scholar able to place a flan in her account must have got it off a patron—there's no other way for a Wanderer to lay hands on that much money together, mark me! And beside, why would anyone with even as little sense as our good tay'Nordif willingly choose to burden herself with this ugly fellow and that plant, aside they were tokens of that same patron?"

"What's wrong with Shinto?" Greatly daring, the younger scholar leaned in and ran light fingers over the porcelain threads embedded in his chest. Jela knew a brief moment of regret, that his role of kobold would not allow him to snarl.

"Eh? Nothing at all wrong with Shinto. Perfectly civilized world.

Famous for their horticulture—and those they breed to work in the gardens and greenhouses. Some, like this fellow here, are brute labor; others, I've heard, are something more than that. Mind you, it's worth a life—and an afterlife, too—to speak of them outside of House walls, but there's tales. Oh, yes. There's tales."

The younger scholar sent him a sideways glance. "What sort of tales?"

"You mean to tell me that you've never heard of the mothers of the vine?"

"Oh, certainly!" The younger scholar scoffed, stepping away from Jela to more fully face the elder. "Constructs which are more plant than woman, whose essence is required for a good harvest, and who lie with human men on purpose to drain their vitality and impart it to the grapes!" A derisive snort. "Tales to frighten children and the undereducated."

"And yet they're true enough, those plant-women, and the reason why a trade clan may pay a year's profit for a single half-cask of Rioja wine—and count the purchase fairly made."

"Oh, really, vel'Anbrek! I suppose you've seen one of these fabulous women yourself—in your Wander days, of course!"

"I was never so unfortunate," the old scholar said, his voice serious. "But I did meet a chemist who had once been employed at a Rioja vineyard. She claimed to have seen and spoken with the mothers not once, but many times, and had even what she cared to term a friendship with the elder of them. It's true that she may simply have been telling outlandish tales to a gullible Wanderer. But in that case, there would have been no need for House Ormendir to buy her silence, which they did, and published the death in the monthly census, as required by law."

The younger scholar waved an airy hand. "The fact that the vineyard bought a Silence in the matter only proves the House of Whispers found the commission to be just. Your chemist more likely stole the formula for the House blend than consorted with creatures out of imagination."

"Have it your own way," the elder scholar said with an expressive ripple of his shoulders. "I only thought to warn that those things which come from the horticultural clans first serve the purpose of the clan. Yon simple kobold might be more than it seems."

"Or—more likely—it might be but a simple kobold, given in order that Scholar tay'Nordif's green token from her patron receive the proper care. For you must agree, vel'Anbrek, even the fondest of patrons could not have thought the good scholar competent to water a plant, or, indeed, to pay attention to it at all, should she become *immersed in her work*."

Scholar vel'Anbrek laughed. "An accurate reading of our new colleague, I grant."

"And one thing I notice," the younger scholar continued, slipping his hands into his sleeves, "is that this construct is not properly peace-bonded."

"Aye, it is," said vel'Anbrek, with a nod of his gray head toward Jela. "Those ceramic threads that took your fancy—that's how they peace-bond on Shinto. That I *have* seen, as well as the very clones of the bracelet our good sister wears, to which the implants will respond."

"Ah, will it?" the other said with a snap. "And suppose it requires pacification and there is only you and me to defend the hall against its sudden imbecile rage?" The right sleeve rippled slightly as the fingers of his left hand tightened—

Jela fell to his knees, choking. He raised a hand; the younger scholar smiled, his eyes bright and cruel as he watched him writhe. He pushed his sleeve up, fingers moving on the slim band around his forearm. Jela tried to stand, fell heavily, froth forming on his lips.

"Here now!" cried the old scholar. "It won't do to place Scholar tay'Nordif's creature at risk. Sport is sport, but much more and it becomes an—"

"It becomes an attack upon my work by base means!" Scholar tay'Nordif's voice came shrilly, and it seemed to Jela that he had never heard a more welcome sound. There was the sound of a sharp slap, a cry of outrage, and the young scholar's arm-band rang to the floor by his head.

Slowly, his muscles relaxed, and he flopped to his back, chest heaving.

"Now, it will be useless to me all the rest of the day!" Scholar tay'Nordif shouted. "Game with the Tower's constructs, if you have the taste, but do not, at your peril, deprive me of the services of my patron's kobold!"

"You struck me!" the younger scholar shouted in turn. "vel'Anbrek! I call you to witness!"

"I saw it," the elder said, shockingly calm. "Though I warn you I will tell Prime Chair that Scholar tay'Nordif was provoked."

"I will have satisfaction!" The younger scholar snarled, and swooped down to retrieve his arm-band, his nails coincidentally scoring Jela's cheek as he did. "Come, vel'Anbrek, I require your testimony before the Prime!"

"If you will have it, it is yours," the old scholar said, and the pair of them moved off, noisy in their haste.

Jela lay on the floor, eyes closed, breathing. Above him, he heard Scholar tay'Nordif, her own breathing somewhat ragged. He opened his eyes in time to see her stamp her dainty slippered foot.

"Oh, get *up*, Jela!" she snarled and stomped past him to her door.

TOR AN EXITED THE SLIDEWAY and stood blinking in the thin, misty light, trying to get his bearings. Across the wide green-paved square he saw something that looked very much like a public map. He set course for it, taking care where he put his feet, having just missed taking a bad tumble when it came time to step from the slide to the platform. That had been an unnerving moment. He couldn't remember the last time he'd made a serious misstep; a pilot trusted his balance and his reactions, and even on those few occasions when he'd drunk too much wine they had never failed him.

Unfortunately for his general state of well-being, others with business on the square were not inclined to dawdle. A woman in a billowing beige robe pushed by him, muttering. He caught the word "tourist" and another, less complimentary, and tried to quicken his pace.

A hard hand slammed into his wounded shoulder, and he gasped aloud, staggering, spikes of red and orange distorting his view of the square and the map.

"Move along!" a man's voice snapped. "You'll be late for class!"

Tor An shook his head and through the fading flares of color he caught an impression of another billowing robe, and a long tail of black hair.

He touched his most public pocket, but the few carolis he kept there had not been molested, so at least he had not suffered the further indignity of having his pocket picked. Cor Win would never let him hear the end of the tale, were he found to be such a flat.

The map loomed blessedly closer. He managed the last bit without being either assaulted or cursed, and leaned heavily on the rail as he fumbled the input wand from its holster. His first search, simply on Kel Var tay'Palin, produced a line on the message strip at the base of the map: a room number high in the double dozens at Osabei Tower. Squinting, he glanced 'round at the multitude of towers surrounding the square, and had recourse once more to the wand. A dot of red glittered like a jewel on the map, which he understood to be his current position, from it a red line preceded at an angle to the left, and at last a crimson star burst bright.

Tor An turned his head, sighting along the angle indicated on the map, and located a tower of plain red cermacrete. He double-checked its location against the map and, satisfied that the red tower was indeed his goal, set off. His shoulder was afire and his steps had a distressing tendency to wander to starboard. But, after all, the tower wasn't so far away as that. All that remained was to ring the bell and ask to be shown to Scholar tay'Palin. His mission was nearly at an end.

"YES, SCHOLAR?" Grudent tel'Ashon arrived breathlessly, bringing with her the odor of disinfectant.

"Yes." Maelyn tay'Nordif leaned back in her chair and smiled. "As my grudent, you will be pleased to hear that I have been asked to speak not only to the Board of Governors, but to Master dea'Syl himself."

The grudent's eyes widened. Jela, sitting at command with his back against the far wall, felt his heart stutter.

"Truly, Scholar," Grudent tel'Ashon breathed. "The Honored

dea'Syl himself? Your work must be notable, indeed. Did he say aught in praise or—" She swallowed, apparently deciding that it would not be entirely prudent to ask if Master dea'Syl had found any *fault* with Scholar tay'Nordif's work.

"The invitation came to me through the kind offices of Prime Chair tay'Welford," the scholar said calmly. "It would not, therefore, have been seemly to have spoken more particularly of my work. However, I expect a lively discussion with the master when we meet."

If possible, the grudent's eyes grew rounder. Jela, unnoticed at the front of the room, held his breath. Not his most stringent searching had produced Scholar dea'Syl's data-cache. He had modified his scouts and sent them out again this morning as Scholar tay'Nordif was showering, but he expected tonight's results to be much the same. The master scholar stored his precious notes and working papers elsewhere—he knew it, in one of those illogical leaps of faith your generalist was sometimes taken with. Too bad for him, his intuition was usually right.

But if Can—Maelyn tay'Nordif was going to be meeting with dea'Syl—in his office? In his quarters?—specifically to discuss their work . . . The notes would have to be stolen from the scholar, and whether Maelyn tay'Nordif could pull the thing off or—

"My discussion with our Prime Chair," she said to the grudent, interrupting these speculations, "brought to mind a matter I failed to mention to you. A pilot is expected, bearing data. It is vital that I have the data—and the pilot—immediately upon arrival. Am I plain?"

Pilot? Jela thought blankly. *What pilot*?

Grudent tel'Ashon was bowing. "Scholar, you are most wonderfully plain. I, myself, will alert the gatekeepers to expect this pilot, so the data will not be delayed in coming to your hand."

"That is well, then." Scholar tay'Nordif reached for the chording wand, her eyes already on her work screen. "You may go, Grudent."

"Scholar." Another bow and go she did, clever girl.

Jela closed his eyes.

TEN

❋ ❋

Osabei Tower
Landomist

TAY'WELFORD SAT with his hands folded on the desk before him, and heard Scholar tel'Elyd out. He had vel'Anbrek repeat his testimony twice, then sat in contemplative silence, turning the sprung bracelet over in his hands.

"I will," he said at last into tel'Elyd's angry eyes, "of course, need to speak with Scholar tay'Nordif before making a final determination. Before I do so, however, I wonder if I may not persuade you to soften your position, Scholar. Our new sister tay'Nordif is to meet not only with the Governors two days hence, but with no one less than Master dea'Syl, who professes himself most eager to renew their acquaintance."

tel'Elyd paled, and drew himself up. "I will have a complete answer from Scholar tay'Nordif," he said frostily.

tay'Welford sighed. "Very well." He put the bracelet aside and looked from the young scholar to the old. "I will speak to Scholar tay'Nordif immediately. You may expect a resolution before the sounding of the Mercy Bell, so that there will be no discord among colleagues in the Common Room. I trust this is satisfactory?"

"Prime Chair, it is." tel'Elyd rose and bowed. "I will be in my office, working."

vel'Anbrek, however, did not rise. tay'Welford considered him and folded his hands once more.

"Is there something else?"

"Scholar tay'Nordif is Liad's only living student," the old man stated.

tay'Welford waited, and, when vel'Anbrek added nothing else to that unadorned statement, sighed and murmured, "She made no secret of the fact that she had knelt at the Master's feet for only a few months before the disparity of their thought drove her away. But, yes, technically, Maelyn tay'Nordif is the last living of the Master's students. Is there a point you particularly wished to make?"

"Only that I have often wondered—have you not?—why it was that Liad's students seemed to die quite so often."

tay'Welford opened his hands, showing empty palms. "It is a perilous thing, to wander the galaxy in pursuit of one's art. The sad fact is that more Wanderers die upon their quests than ever come to us with the price of a chair."

"Yes, yes," vel'Anbrek said impatiently. "We all know that Wanderers exist to die. It only seems odd to me—as a statistician, you understand—that all, save one, of Liad's students have fulfilled their destinies, when at least a few students of the lowly rest of us have lived long enough to purchase a seat. One wonders if there is something . . . inimical in the fabric of Liad's work, the contemplation of which encourages an untimely demise."

tay'Welford smiled. "This is a jest, of course. You have studied the Master's work—and you are the most long-lived of us all!"

Notably, vel'Anbrek did not smile. "I was a full scholar established in my own sub-field when Liad published his first paper. And though I have, as you say, studied his work, that is a far different matter than being a *student* of his work."

Head tipped to one side, tay'Welford waited politely.

Now vel'Anbrek smiled, and rose creakily. "Well, we old scholars have our crochets. I will be in my office, working. Prime Chair."

"Scholar." tay'Welford responded.

The door closed. tay'Welford counted to one hundred forty-four before he pushed away from his desk and came to his feet. Soonest begun, soonest done, as his own Master had used to say. A speedy determination was in the best interest of the community.

IN ORDER TO ENTER Osabei Tower from the public square, one must needs pass through a maze constructed entirely of short, dense green plants that gave off an odor which was perhaps thought to be pleasant, but which all but put Tor An's stomach, already uneasy, into open revolt. Breathing through his mouth, he concentrated on solving the maze, which was ludicrously easy, once he realized it was a Reverse. By taking all the avenues that tended most definitely away from the tower, he speedily arrived at its entrance, and pulled the bell rope, hard.

The door snapped open, and a dark-skinned woman in light duty 'skins thick with smartstrands glared down at him, one hand on the ornate gun holstered at her waist.

"State your business," she snapped, with no if-you-please about it.

Tor An swallowed and bowed slightly. "My name is Tor An yos'Galan and I seek an audience with Scholar Kel Var tay'Palin."

The guard's fingers were seen to tighten on the hilt of her weapon, and Tor An tensed. He took a deep breath and tried to remember that not all gatekeepers summarily shot those who petitioned them for entrance.

"Prime Chair tay'Palin is not receiving visitors."

Well the scholar—Prime Chair!—was doubtless a busy man, Tor An conceded. He should perhaps have sent ahead. Indeed, Uncle Kel Ven would certainly have scolded him for such a breach of etiquette—and he wished to be a trader!

The guard was staring at him, her 'skins flickering distractingly in the cloud-filtered light. He bowed again. "Would it be possible to leave a message for the—"

"Prime tay'Palin has achieved immortality in his work," the guard interrupted. Her teeth flashed in a grin so quick he could not really be certain he had seen it. "That means—he's dead."

Dead. Tears rose to his eyes. He blinked them away, took a pair of breaths to settle his stomach, and bowed once again.

"I thank you," he murmured, as he tried to form another plan. Surely there was another scholar who—

"Good-day," the guard said, and took one long step backward, the door closing with a boom.

He stared at it, stupidly. Reached for the bell chord and snatched his hand back. No, not yet. Not while he was tired and ill. He would—he would find the pilots hostel, take a room, sleep, and tomorrow consider how best to go on.

Slowly, not at all eager to again subject his stomach to the odoriferous maze, he turned and began to walk back the way he had come.

"Wait!" a woman's voice called urgently from behind, amid clattering. "Pilot! Wait, I beg you!"

He turned in time to avoid being run over by a woman wearing a unitard and a utility belt. She snatched at his arm—mercifully, not the wounded one—and peered earnestly into his face, her eyes brown and wide.

"You are the pilot," she stammered— "the pilot the scholar is expecting? You have the data?"

Tor An blinked. "Indeed," he said carefully. "I am a pilot and I do carry data which may be of interest to . . . the scholar."

The woman smiled, clearly relieved. "I abase myself. I had just come to inform the ostiary—we had not expected you so soon! Ah, but there's no harm done." She pulled his arm as she turned back toward the entrance, where the dark-skinned guard stood, wide-legged and arms akimbo, watching. "The scholar's orders were that you be brought to her immediately."

"I am more than willing to be escorted to the scholar," Tor An assured the woman, trying without success to extricate himself from her grip.

"Come with me, then," she said. "Quickly."

THE PROBLEM OF COMMUNICATION between himself and Scholar tay'Nordif was a sticky one, Jela allowed, as he sat on the floor where he'd been directed by his highly annoyed mistress, back against the wall. Cantra had been certain that his ingenuity and the core training she and her—and the person she proposed to become—would be sufficient to the needs of the mission. He'd agreed with that, being, as he now unhappily realized, underinformed. Not that he could put that fault on the pilot. No, simply put, he'd let his own understanding of how the galaxy operated taint his info. Cantra had told him what she was going to do, and he couldn't fault her for plain-speaking. He did have a suspicion that she'd played her cards with exceptional care, having pegged him as a practical man to whom seeing was believing—and gambling that, by the time he saw, and believed, it would be too late to retreat.

Whether providing him with a thorough-going fool for a partner in the rescue of life-as-they-knew-it was the Rimmer pilot's notion of a joke—no. No, there was good reason to acquit her there, too.

For all her faults, Cantra yos'Phelium was a woman of her word. She'd pledged her help, which she would have never done unless she intended to deliver. Which meant that there was something Maelyn tay'Nordif could accomplish to the benefit of the mission that Cantra couldn't have. It was his own lack of imagination, that he couldn't think of anything Cantra yos'Phelium might fail to accomplish, given her word and her intent.

Trust, the Rimmer pilot whispered from memory—and it might truly be, he thought, that the only place that pilot existed anymore was in his memory. He took a hard breath, trying to ease the sudden constriction of his chest. Cantra yos'Phelium deserved to live on in the memories of twelve generations of pilots, not sentenced to unsung oblivion when the M who'd asked—and received—a death of her grew old all at once, and died.

Only weeks, now.

He shook that line of thought away, though not the melancholy, and applied himself once more to making sense of this sudden tale of a pilot expected, bearing—

The door chime sounded. He opened his eyes, and saw the scholar hunched over her screen, apparently oblivious.

The chime sounded a second time, followed by a man's voice.

"Prime Chair tay'Welford requests entrance."

At her desk, the scholar muttered something in a dialect Jela didn't recognize, though he figured he got the drift from her tone. She lifted the wand, and chorded in a brief command—very likely, Jela thought, shutting down her work screen, so Prime Chair wouldn't be tempted to steal her work.

"Come!" she called, slipping the wand into its holster. She spun her chair and stood, arms down straight and a little before her, fingertips just touching the surface of her desk.

The door opened and tay'Welford stepped within, his sash now bearing those items of office which had previously adorned Prime tay'Palin. Scholar tay'Nordif bowed, briefly, and with neither grace nor art.

"Prime Chair, you honor my humble office."

tay'Welford looked 'round him, measuringly, thought Jela.

"Your office seems quite comfortable, if I may say so, Scholar. Certainly far more so than when ser'Dinther held it."

"It is well enough," she answered, "for a beginning." She lifted a hand, indicating one of the chairs on the far side of the desk. "Please, sit."

"My thanks." He took the chair indicated and spent a moment arranging the fall of his robe. Scholar tay'Nordif sat after he did, and folded her arms on the desk.

"I do not," tay'Welford murmured, "wish to infringe upon your time any more than is needful, Scholar, so I will come immediately to the point of my visit. Scholar tel'Elyd has made a formal grievance against you, and he has stated that he will pursue satisfaction to the fullest—"

"Scholar tel'Elyd," the scholar interrupted hotly, "mounted a dastardly and craven attack against my work, Prime! It is not to be borne, and if either of us should have cause to call for satisfaction, it is myself!"

"Ah." tay'Welford inclined his head, and spoke seriously. "I wonder, Scholar, if you would give me the particulars of this attack upon your work?"

"Certainly! I found him abusing the kobold given for my comfort by my patron, in such a manner as to deprive me of its services since—and likely for the remainder of the day!"

"And the kobold," tay'Welford said cannily. "I understand you to say that it is necessary to your work?"

Sitting at the floor at the rear of the room, back against the wall, Jela wished he could get a good look at tay'Welford's face. Cantra yos'Phelium had been able to read a lie off the twitch of a man's earlobe, but he had no evidence that Maelyn tay'Nordif could do the same. tay'Welford's tone had the feel of a trap being set, but what that trap might be, when the old scholar had said right out he'd give evidence that put the lie to the younger's claim—

"The kobold is my patron's gift to me," Scholar tay'Nordif said stiffly. "It is necessary that I be as comfortable as possible in order to give my best attention to my work."

"But to say that the kobold itself is *necessary* to your work— forgive me, Scholar, but that is quite an extraordinary statement. And to come to blows with a colleague in defense of a base creature— I fear me that demonstrates a lack of judgment we do not like to see within our department."

Scholar tay'Nordif sniffed. "And should I have given this so-called tel'Elyd leave to destroy that which has been placed in my keeping? What else, Prime? Shall I allow him to destroy my reference works? My *notes*?"

"One's reference works and notes are—of course!—necessary to one's continued work. But a kobold, Scholar . . ." He sighed. "No, I do not believe I can allow it."

Jela's chest tightened.

"I beg your pardon?" snapped Scholar tay'Nordif.

"I believe that tel'Elyd may have the right of it, Scholar. You chose to place the continued functioning of a base creature above the necessities of a colleague—and that is a very grave thing."

"Pray, what necessities had tel'Elyd in the matter? 'Twas a random act of negligent cruelty, sir!"

"Alas, it may not have been. tel'Elyd requires a certain amount of titillation in order to do his best work. Happily, his need is fulfilled in the torment of the base, and as he rarely requires more than torment, his necessity is scarcely a drain on departmental resources."

"I—" began Scholar tay'Nordif, but tay'Welford had already risen.

"The matter is clear," he said definitely. "You will stand to answer tel'Elyd in the hour before the Mercy Bell, today. I shall inform him of my decision." He inclined his head. "I thank you for your time, Scholar. May your work be fruitful."

Slowly, Scholar tay'Nordif came to her feet. She bowed, with even less grace than usual, and held it while Prime tay'Welford turned and strolled leisurely from the room, smiling at Jela as he passed out of the door and into the hallway.

"Oh," said Maelyn tay'Nordif, flopping into her chair into her chair the moment the door closed. "Damn."

THE PATH the apprentice scholar set through the twisting hallways of the lower tower would have made his head spin had it not been doing so already, Tor An thought. As it was, he was most thoroughly lost and in terror lest his guide, whom he had at last convinced to relinquish his arm, should outpace him.

The hall opened abruptly into a wide, high-ceilinged room, six of the eight ceramic walls were cast in graduating rows, like seats in a theater. Here, his guide all but ran, and he forced himself into a trot, narrowing his focus to her figure, fleeing and clanking before him. She vanished into another narrow hall. He, perforce, pursued—and very nearly ran over her where she stood, just within the narrow walls, facing a man in beige robes, his sash supporting various fobs and tablets, as well as a naked blade and a pair of smart gloves. The scholar was frowning down at the 'prentice, who had abased herself. He looked up at Tor An's arrival and his brows lifted high.

"Who, may I ask, are you?" The voice was pleasant, though carrying a slight edge—whether of bemusement or outright irritation, Tor An couldn't have said.

However, the attitude of the 'prentice suggested that this was a person whom it would be best not to annoy. Tor, An therefore, bowed as deeply as he was able and straightened with a care he hoped would be seen as respect.

"My name is Tor An yos'Galan, esteemed sir," he said seriously.

"I see." The scholar paused. "And what might your business be in Osabei Tower, Tor An yos'Galan?"

The scholar had an open, pleasant face. Surely, so exalted a gentleman, who was in any wise apparently someone of rank in these halls, could be trusted with his—

"Prime Chair!" the 'prentice scholar had straightened out of her bow and was wringing her hands in agitation. "This is the pilot whom Scholar tay'Nordif expects, bearing the data necessary for her proof! Her word was that, *immediately* he arrived, he and the data were to be brought to her. Her *word*, Prime Chair, which I, as her grudent, am bound to obey!"

The scholar—Prime Chair—turned his attention to her, his head tipped to a side, long brown hair cascading over one shoulder.

"Ah! Scholar tay'Nordif's pilot!" he said, in tones of broad enlightenment. "I confess I had not expected to see him so soon!" He stepped back, moving a graceful hand in a sweep along the way they had been traveling. "By all means, Grudent tel'Ashon, deliver the pilot and his data to our good scholar!"

"Yes," the 'prentice breathed. She bowed hastily and Tor An once more had his arm gripped as she hurried him with her.

"Be well, Tor An yos'Galan!" the Prime Chair called as they rushed away. "I look forward to deepening our acquaintance!"

"Quickly!" the 'prentice breathed in his ear.

"Why?" he demanded. "We've been given leave to go."

"Because," she hissed, and without lessening her pace, "scholars are mad. It is the business of scholars to be jealous each of the others' honors and position. You may be assured that the Prime Chair means to get the advantage of Scholar tay'Nordif and punish her for rising in the esteem of the Master as he has not. And if his punishment is to be depriving the scholar of yourself or your data, then he will take you from *her*, and not from *me*."

Rushing along at her side, Tor An thought that perhaps it was not the scholars alone who were mad.

"Why do you serve here, then?" he panted.

"I have one more local year of service, after which I shall have my journeyman's certificate. And you may well believe I shall receive it with joy and forthwith seek a position as a mathematics tutor. Here!" She halted before a door exactly like the others lining the hall, and touched the plate with the fingers of her free hand. A chime sounded and she said, loudly, "It is Grudent tel'Ashon, Scholar! Your pilot has arrived!"

There was small delay before the door whisked open. The grudent all but shoved him into the office beyond, letting go of his arm with a will.

He staggered, barely sorting his feet out in time to prevent a spill and stood, breathing heavily and head a-spin three long steps into a small office. At his right hand, a man in dark leathers sat on the floor, back against the wall, his brown face lean and inscrutable. Before him, a woman in the now-familiar robe of a scholar frowned from behind a too-clean desk, a data input wand held between her palms, her green eyes cold in a stern golden face.

"Well," she said, her voice high and unpleasant against his ear. "At least you had the grace to make haste from Shinto, sirrah!" She pointed her eyes over his shoulder. "Grudent, you have done well. Leave us now."

"Scholar." The 'prentice's voice carried a unmistakable note of relief. Tor An glanced over his shoulder, but she was already gone, the office door closing behind her.

"So, Pilot," the sharp voice brought his attention back to the scholar, who had put the chording wand down and stood up behind her desk. "Approach. I assume that you *have* brought the data?"

Tor An blinked, feeling the datastrip absurdly heavy in its inner pocket. It came to him that it was—perhaps—not wise to have embarked upon this deception. This stern-faced scholar was expecting, after all, a *particular* pilot bearing *particular* data with *particular* relevance to her work, and if the grudent were to be believed—

"Come, come, Pilot!" the scholar said impatiently. "Have you the data or not?"

"Scholar," he bowed, head swimming, and straightened carefully. "I have data. Also, I have information." He cleared his throat. "The Ringstars are gone. What I bring are the measurements and the logs describing the section of space which is—missing. This may not be—"

"Yes, yes!" The scholar interrupted, holding out an imperious hand. "That is precisely what you have been paid to provide! Bring it forth, Pilot; I haven't all day to stand here trading pleasantries with you!"

He swallowed, and glanced to one side. The man sitting against the wall was watching him from hooded black eyes.

"For pity's sake, Pilot! Have you never seen a kobold before? Come, the data!"

In fact, he *had* seen kobolds before, and the man on the floor bore a superficial resemblance to those of the laborer class he had encountered. But such a one would never have looked at him so measuringly, nor paid attention so nearly . . .

"Pilot?" the scholar's voice now carried an edge of sarcasm. "Am I to understand that you do not stand in need of the remainder of your fee?"

Abruptly, he was exhausted. Perhaps after all, he thought, *he* was mad. In any case, this woman, whom he had never seen before, was asking for the very data he carried. How she came to want it or he to have it was immaterial, really. And if a second pilot had been commissioned to gather the same readings, then—surely—that was cause for hope?

He slid the 'strip out, stepped forward and placed it on the desk before the impatient scholar.

She smiled, and peered into his face.

"You are tired, I see," she said, suddenly gentle— "and so you should be, having come so quickly from Shinto! Jela will escort you to my quarters, where you may rest yourself. Only allow me to access the data and you may go . . ."

She plucked the 'strip up and slid it into her work unit, fumbling the wand in her haste, but at last she chorded the correct commands, and stood watching as line after line of coordinates marched down the screen.

"Aha!" she said and manipulated the wand quickly before bending to the unit. Eyes on the screen, she pulled the 'strip out of the slot and put it on the desk.

"Jela!" she said, loudly. "Stand up!"

At the back of the room, the leather-clad man slowly and stolidly got his feet under him and rose, rather, Tor An thought, like a mountain rising out of an ocean. At least, until he was fully afoot, when it could be seen that his height was more hill-like than mountain.

"Now," said the scholar, "you will—"

From somewhere—from everywhere—an alarm sounded. Tor An spun to the wall, snatching for the grab-bars that weren't there. Face heating, he turned back, to find the scholar pale, her mouth set into a hard, pained line.

"Your pardon, Pilot," she said with punctilious politeness. "I am wanted elsewhere. A matter of honor, you apprehend."

She came 'round the desk, moving stiffly, her hands tucked firmly into her sleeves. "Jela!" she snapped, as she passed Tor An. "Escort this pilot to my quarters."

The door opened. "Pilot," she said, in a slightly less snappish tone, but without looking at him. "Please follow Jela."

Tor An snatched the datastrip up off the desk, slid it into an inner pocket, and turned to see the man Jela moving purposefully toward the door. He bethought himself of the twistiness of the Tower hallways, and hurried after.

ELEVEN

❂ ❂

Osabei Tower
Landomist

THE THIN CORRIDOR was awash with scholars, all talking and laughing, moving with one purpose in the direction, so Tor An believed, of the wide, tiered foyer.

Jela was well ahead of him, apparently invisible to the chattering scholars, who jostled him rather roughly, until at last he flattened himself against the wall, where he waited with a bland, intelligent patience no kobold ever bred could have mustered.

Scarcely less jostled, and tender, besides, of his wounded arm, Tor An came to rest at his guide's shoulder, closed his eyes and took stock. On the debit side of the trade sheet, he was tired, his wound ached, and he was certainly bewildered, while the credit side showed a head more firmly anchored to his shoulders than it had been earlier in the day, and a stomach no longer in open rebellion.

Progress, he thought. Eyes still closed, he put himself to trying to filter some sense from the echoing noise.

It seemed, if he rightly understood the bits and flotsam of conversation that fell into his ear, as if Scholar tay'Nordif were about to fight a duel. What the cause of this might be, he did not quite grasp. He sighed, and settled himself more comfortably against the wall, letting the voices rise and fall about him without trying to net any more sense. He allowed himself to hope that the hallway would soon clear, and that the scholar's quarters were neither far removed, nor Jela disposed to run . . .

He felt something touch his hand, where it rested against the wall. He blinked out of his doze to see Jela already moving down the hall in the wake of the last straggler scholars, walking slow and heavy. Something about that nagged at Tor An, as he pushed away from the wall and followed, then faded.

At the foyer, Jela paused again, in the shelter of the risers, and Tor An did too. Looking over his guide's sleek head, he could see a wide expanse of empty floor, and the seats rising up the walls across. The noise of voices was not so loud here—not, Tor An thought, because the scholars were talking any less, but because their words were not confined by the hallway.

Carefully, he placed a hand on Jela's shoulder. "Let us go," he murmured, but there was no sign that the other man heard him.

For the third time, the alarm bell sounded, bringing silence in its wake. Tor An leaned against the riser that shielded them, and resigned himself to wait.

The tall, brown haired scholar Grudent tel'Ashon had addressed as "Prime Chair" strolled out onto the floor, a dueling stick held in each hand. Behind him came Scholar tay'Nordif, head high and shoulders rigid, and a slim, delicate scholar with cropped sandy hair, and a long timonium chain hanging from one ear.

Prime Chair stopped in the center of the rectangular dueling area marked out by rust colored tiles, the two scholars flanking him, and brandished the 'sticks over his head.

"What we have before us today is a personal balancing between Scholars tel'Elyd and tay'Nordif. Scholar tay'Nordif admits to having struck Scholar tel'Elyd for taking certain liberties with the construct Jela, which she maintains is necessary to her work—" There was a murmur from the audience at this. Prime Chair shook one of the dueling sticks toward the offending section of seats.

"This action of Scholar tel'Elyd was witnessed by Scholar vel'Anbrek, nor does tel'Elyd deny it. However, it is the judgment of the Prime Chair that in striking Scholar tel'Elyd in punishment for those liberties taken with the construct, Scholar tay'Nordif has placed a scholar on the same plane as a base creature. This affront to Scholar tel'Elyd's honor must be mended."

With a flourish, he brought the sticks out and down to shoulder level. Each scholar stood forward and armed themselves, then spun to face each other, dueling stick held in the neutral posture.

"These two of our worthy colleagues shall contend as equals. The point goes to whichever counts to six upon a fallen opponent. This duel is not to the death. As it is a personal matter, truth-blades may not be employed." He gave each of the combatants a long, grave look, and dropped back to the outside of the rectangle.

"You may engage upon my count of six," he said. "One . . ."

Scholar tel'Elyd spun his stick, getting the feel of it, Tor An suspected, that having been the route advised by those who had sought to instruct him in self-defense: *Always test the weight and balance of an unfamiliar weapon, conditions permitting.*

In contrast, Scholar tay'Nordif stood gripping the stick tightly in the neutral position, her stance stiff and awkward. He wondered if the scholar had ever received self-defense instruction and hoped for her sake that the Osabei Tower weapons-master kept the charges on the dueling sticks toward the low end of match range.

"Three . . ."

Scholar tel'Elyd took up the stance; legs slightly apart, knees flexed, right foot pointed at the opponent, left foot at a right angle, primary hand at the bottom of the handle, off-hand above, spine relaxed and slightly curved. Tor An was slightly heartened to see Scholar tay'Nordif arrange herself in a similar configuration, though she stood too tall and too stiffly, her feet were placed awkwardly, and her hands were too close together.

"Six," said Prime Chair.

Scholar tel'Elyd snapped his 'stick sharply, releasing a heavy blue bolt in the direction of the hapless Scholar tay'Nordif. To Tor An's mingled surprise and relief, she managed a credible parry, the sizzle of mingling energies loud in the sudden silence, finishing her move with a neat little twist that sent a glob of red speeding toward her opponent—who destroyed it with a sneer and shook another heavy bolt from his 'stick, and a second more quickly than Tor An would have believed possible, had he not seen it for himself. Scholar tel'Elyd must have a supple wrist, indeed.

Scholar tay'Nordif deflected the first of the pair, but at the expense of her precarious stance. The second bolt got through her wavering defense, and scored a solid hit on the her hip.

She flinched, her hand dropping instinctively—and disastrously— to the wound. Scholar tel'Elyd followed up his advantage immediately, sending a line of short bursts one after the other in a really remarkable display of skill.

Scholar tay'Nordif parried, one-handed, off-balance and, as Tor An knew from his training, hurting, but it was plain who was the master of the duel. Scholar tel'Elyd could put up his 'stick at any time and no one among the silent spectators would challenge his win.

But Scholar tel'Elyd was not disposed to be merciful. Whatever dispute stood between him and Scholar tay'Nordif, it quickly became clear that he considered a telling demonstration of superiority at arms to be inadequate balance.

Scholar tay'Nordif swayed under the pain of repeated strikes, and flung an arm up to shield her eyes. Her dueling stick fell from her hand and lay, sparking fitfully on the surface of the dueling court. Tor An waited for Prime Chair to rule the match ended and tel'Elyd the victor, but the man stood mute at the sidelines, calmly watching the punishment continue.

This was no longer a duel, Tor An thought angrily. He started forward, meaning to end the thing himself—and found a hard, broad shoulder blocking his way.

"He goes too far!" he said, loudly, in Jela's ear.

There was no sign that his escort heard him, but someone on the benches above them did.

"He goes too far!" A woman's voice called out. "Honor has been rescued. Brute punishment only tarnishes it anew!"

The cry was taken up by others around the room, and very

shortly, Tor An had the satisfaction of seeing the scholar's hand falter. He straightened out of the dueling crouch and pointed his 'stick at the floor.

Then only did Prime Chair step forward, placing himself between the victorious scholar and the beaten.

"Honor has been rescued!" he announced. "The matter between Scholars tel'Elyd and tay'Nordif has been balanced and shall be spoken of no more."

There was general, sparse applause, and a bell rang.

"Colleagues!" Prime Chair called. "It is time to lay down our labors and meet in the common room!"

Warm fingers touched his hand. Tor An looked down to see Jela moving across the floor, angling for one of several doors. He stretched his legs to catch up.

ALL OF ROOL TIAZAN'S sincerity regarding "luck" and its fondness for him, the tree, and especially Cantra hadn't prepared Jela for the moment when the yellow-haired pilot staggered into the office, helped along by a kindly shove from Grudent tel'Ashon.

It was enough to turn an old soldier to religion, and no use, he decided, trying to work out if the luck had whispered the pilot's nearness to the scholar or simply shoved the pilot into the scholar's path. What mattered was that he had arrived—and that the mission had need of him.

He put the key in its niche atop the controller and waited while their home stair lowered itself. It had taken all his discipline to thrust the memory of the duel between Maelyn tay'Nordif and Den Vir tel'Elyd into the back of his mind. Those strikes—he'd felt each one as if the energy had lashed his own nerves. And if ever proof were called for that Cantra yos'Phelium had died in creating Maelyn tay'Nordif, that duel was everything that was needed.

The end of the stair touched the floor. He retrieved the key and walked into the very middle of the ramp so the pilot, who had followed silent and uncomplaining, from the dueling hall, would not feel exposed. Or, he amended as the stair began to rise, not much exposed.

The stairway seated itself at the proper floor and he led the way to the door of the scholar's quarters. Again he used the key, stepped inside and did a rapid scan.

The cat was crouching on the galley counter, tail wrapped around its toes, amber eyes hooded. The tree sat in its pot by the door; Jela received a flutter of interested curiosity as Tor An yos'Galan stepped into the room. The hacks were in place and emitting on the proper frequency. He sighed and turned.

"*Brrrrrt?*" The pilot said, his soft voice shocking against the high hum of the hacks. He approached the cat, who watched him with interest, and gave the finger he extended careful study before daintily touching it with its nose. The pilot smiled, which made him look ridiculously young, and very tired.

"What's his name?" he asked, sliding a sideways glance at Jela from beneath heavy golden lashes.

"The scholar calls it Lucky," he answered, and the sound of his own voice startled him. It seemed years since he had last spoken.

The pilot inclined his head gravely, and rubbed the cat under the chin. "Lucky, I am very pleased to make your acquaintance," he murmured. "I have been missing cats." He straightened, carefully, sending another of his sideways glances at the tree. "And plants. At my . . ." His voice broke. He took a hard breath, and began again, resolutely. "At my home, there is a back garden and a certain piata tree of which I . . . am most fond."

Inside Jela's head a picture formed: A half-grown dragon staggering across a grey sky, wings trembling, rock-toothed cliffs too near below . . .

Right.

"I couldn't help but notice that you've been wounded," he said to Tor An yos'Galan. "I have a kit, if there's need."

This time the look came straight from amethyst-colored eyes. "There may be need, I thank you. The wound is in an awkward place. I've done my best, but—"

Jela waved him to a stool. "Take your jacket off, then, lad, and let's see what you have." He crossed the room to get the kit from Scholar tay'Nordif's travel bag.

※   ※   ※

"WELL," Jela said a few minutes later, keeping his voice light for his patient's peace of mind. "That's as pretty a burn as I've seen in some time." It would leave a black, ridged scar on the boy's soft golden skin, but that was minor. The important news was that it was healing well, with no sign of infection or any ancillary damage. "I've got something here that'll leach the last of the heat," he said, easily. "It'll feel cold." He broke the ampule and rubbed the lotion into the burn site. His patient hissed, shoulders tensing, but otherwise made no complaint.

"Give that a count of twelve to set, then we'll get a dermal-bond on it."

"Thank you," the boy murmured, the starch already leaching out of his shoulders, which would be the topical anaesthesia starting its work.

"How did you come by that particular wound?" Jela asked, sorting through the supplies and pulling out a sealed bond pack. "If it can be told."

Tor An sighed and moved his shoulder experimentally.

"The captain of the garrison on Korak ordered me shot," he said in a tone Jela thought was meant to be expressionless, but which carried a payload of anger and terror.

If that were the case, the boy was lucky in his own right. Jela began to repack the kit.

"Why?" he asked, though he thought he knew.

"I went to them—to the garrison. I thought the military commander might investigate the fact of the Ringstars . . . vanishing. The trade office would only—" hard breath— "would only list the route closed and the ports unavailable."

Jela cracked the seal on the dressing and stretched it wide between his fingers, eyeing the burn site.

"The soldier—on guard," Tor An continued, and despite his best efforts his voice was sounding a trifle ragged. "The guard said that the Ringstars were far from the first to go missing, and that in anywise it was none of Korak Garrison's affair, as they'd been called back—called back to the Inner Arm."

"Well, the guard was right that the military's being moved back," Jela said judiciously. "You'll feel some pressure now, and it might nip you a bit, which I know you won't regard, Pilot."

He moved quick, and as sure as he was able. Despite the topical it must've hurt, but Tor An yos'Galan sat a quiet board.

"Good lad," Jela murmured approvingly. "You'll do fine, now."

The boy sighed, and simply sat for a moment, then slid off the stool and reached for his shirt, which the cat was sitting on, all four feet poised beneath it. Tor An smiled.

"I believe my need is greater," he said politely and extended one slim hand, scooping the cat up beneath its belly, cool as you please, while liberating his clothing with the other.

"Thank you," he said, replacing the cat in its spot. "Your understanding during this difficult time is appreciated."

The cat, which had endured both handling and nonsense with nary a spit nor a glare, settled itself flat onto its belly and curled its front feet against its chest. Tor An shook out his shirt—good quality, Jela saw, but plain. Respectful and quiet. Much like the boy himself.

Jela finished his own tidying up, and carried the kit back across the room, replacing it in the scholar's baggage.

A chime sounded.

Jela spun, pleased to see that the boy had done so as well, fingers gone quiet on the fastenings of his shirt.

The chime sounded again.

Tor An sent a questioning glance in his direction; Jela replied with a quick flicker of pilot hand-talk: *Answer.*

The lad blinked. "Who is it?" he called, finishing up with the shirt.

"Please," called a stilted, childlike voice. "Food arrives for Scholar tay'Nordif's pilot."

"Ah. Just a moment." He moved, while Jela stayed where he was, out of the immediate line of sight, with his kobold mask in place, on the principle of taking as few chances as possible.

Came the sound of the door opening

"Food arrives for Scholar tay'Nordif's pilot," the high voice repeated, clearer now without the filtering of the announcement system. "It is hoped that the meal pleases. Also given are tickets for future meals in the grudents' cafeteria, after the pilot is rested. The pilot is not permitted to dine with the scholars in the common room. If the pilot has other needs, he may petition Scholar tay'Nordif. Has the pilot questions?"

"None whatsoever, I thank you," the boy said gravely. He bent; there was a small clamor of cutlery as he received a tray. "Scholar tay'Nordif sends that she will be a little delayed this evening," the Small chirped, "and prays that in her absence the pilot will regard her quarters as his own, stinting his comfort in no wise. Scholar tay'Nordif very much regrets the delay."

"I thank you," Tor An said again, "for bearing this message. I am made quite comfortable here, and anticipate the Scholar's arrival so that I may express to her my gratitude for her care."

"The scholar also asks," the Small continued, "that the pilot honor her by feeding the cat, and seeing that he has fresh water."

Jela closed his eyes.

"I will do so, gladly. He is a fine cat and has made me very welcome."

"Message ends. Responses on file," the high voice announced, and Jela caught the sound of bare feet on tile before Tor An closed the door.

He bore the covered tray to the counter and put it down, giving Jela a troubled look.

"She sends no meal for you?"

"Kobolds don't eat much," he answered lightly. Tor An frowned.

"You, my friend, are no kobold. And I am ashamed that I failed to see you as a pilot until you bespoke me just now."

"I have," Jela said, leaning a companionable elbow on the counter, "been doing my best not to seem pilot-like."

"And doing rather well," Tor An allowed, making a brave attempt not to look famished. "However, you do not seem quite kobold-like, either, if you will forgive my saying so."

Jela sighed and nodded at the tray. "Eat your dinner, Pilot."

But it appeared the lad was stubborn as well as mannerly, which, Jela allowed wryly, was only what could be expected from a pilot.

"Why," asked Tor An, "are you pretending to be a kobold?" He hesitated before adding, politely, "If it can be told."

Not a bad question, though it meant Jela had to make an immediate decision regarding how much truth it was going to be necessary to tell Tor An yos'Galan.

"Well," he said, giving the boy a straight, earnest look, "for one thing, Scholar tay'Nordif believes I'm a kobold, and I don't like to disappoint a lady."

That earned him an unamused glare from those dark purple eyes before the pilot moved 'round the counter.

"Why," he asked, "are you deceiving the scholar in this manner?" He opened the cabinet door and extracted a ration pack of cat food. Jela sighed to himself.

"That's a bit complicated," he said, watching the cat dance back and forth along the counter ahead of the boy, doing its all to impede any progress that might be made in opening its rations.

"The Ringstars vanishing is also a bit complicated," Tor An said tartly, his gaze on the task in hand. "I am not a child, Jela—" He looked up. "What is your name? Pilot."

"As it happens, my name's Jela," he said easily and offered a comfortable grin. The other pilot looked away and put the open ration pack down on the counter. The cat, tail straight up and quivering, fell to. Tor An picked up the water bowl and turned to the sink.

"My full name," Jela said, having decided on his course in the heartbeat between his last sentence and this, "is M. Jela Granthor's Guard. My rank is captain and wingleader; and I'm on detached duty to acquire that which may, just possibly, keep the rest of the Arm from following the Ringstars into Enemy territory."

The slim shoulders tensed. "You are a soldier, then," Tor An said, a little too breathless to be as uncaring as he obviously wished to appear.

"I am," Jela said. "But I'm not the sort of soldier who shoots civilians for sport. At a guess, those guards and their captain at

Korak were X Strain soldiers—tall, eh? With maybe tattoo work on their faces?"

"Yes," the boy whispered.

"Right," Jela said, voice deliberately companionable. "They're the new design. I'm the old design. M Strain. If there were more Ms and less Xs, it might be that the military wouldn't be quite so easy with those orders to pull back and cede the Rim and the mid-Arm to the *sheriekas*."

Tor An carried the refreshed water bowl to the counter and put it down beside the cat. He looked up, eyes troubled.

"There is something—here?—that will prevent any more disappearances like—*do you know what happened to the Ringstars?*" It burst out of him like a war cry, and for a moment Jela thought he might put his head down on the counter and weep—but Tor An yos'Galan was tougher than he looked. He mastered himself, took a deep breath and waited, hands folded tightly on the counter.

"I do," Jela said, warming to the lad. "And I can show you the math. The short of it is that the *sheriekas*—the Enemy—have perfected a way to decrystalize portions of space. Like the guard at Korak told you, the Ringstars are only the latest in a list that's getting long fast, and will pretty soon encompass the whole galaxy, unless we liberate the equations that describe the counter-crystal-lization process from where they're hidden inside this very Tower."

Tor An yos'Galan closed his eyes.

"Pilot Jela . . ." he began.

"I know," Jela said soothingly. "I know it sounds lunatic, but I do have those equations for you. I'll set them up on a tile array while you eat your dinner."

Tor An opened his eyes. "What will you eat for dinner?" he asked, and Jela gave him a comfortable smile.

"I'll just have a ration bar while I work," he said easily. "It's what I'm used to."

Exhaustion, youth and hunger were Jela's allies, but for a long moment, he thought they wouldn't be enough. Then the boy inclined his head, moved down-counter and lifted the lid off of the tray.

⚜   ⚜   ⚜

TOR AN LOOKED UP from the grid, purple eyes bleak.

"These equations are rather . . . dense, are they not?"

Jela looked at him with sympathy. "The process for folding up bits of the galaxy and putting them away in some other alternity takes some describing," he said. "I've been studying those numbers for . . . a good long while, now, I'm almost sure I've got the major points mastered."

"Ah." The boy touched the frame. "May I have the use of this?"

Jela waved a hand. "It's yours," he said—and waited. He was in his usual place by the tree; Tor An was cross-legged atop the counter, cat on one knee, grid balanced precariously on the other.

"I think," he said, "that you had better tell me what place Scholar tay'Nordif has in your mission. Is it she who has formulated these equations you seek?"

The boy knew how to ask a question, Jela thought, and took a moment to resettle himself against the wall and breathe in a good, deep breath of tree-filtered air.

"Scholar tay'Nordif," he said, then, because he had to make some start or risk losing whatever small trust he'd managed to instill in the lad— "Scholar tay'Nordif is part of the effort to recover the equations. Without her, I wouldn't have been able to gain access to the Tower. She provides misdirection and cover. This operation depends on her abilities. She—" He closed his eyes, considering the tangle of it all—and what well-mannered and respectful boy from out of a well-mannered and respectful trading family would believe in *aelantaza*, or line edits, or the Uncle, or—

"Why," Tor An asked, "does the scholar believe you to be a kobold?"

Jela sighed and produced the most believable part-truth he had to hand.

"There are . . . certain protocols available, which . . . help certain people to believe things other than what they usually know to be true," he said slowly. "The lady you see here as Scholar tay'Nordif is in fact my pilot and my partner. She volunteered to subscribe to those protocols, in order that the mission have the best chance of success."

Tor An gave that grave consideration as he stroked the cat on his knee.

"Is she a soldier, then?" He asked finally.

"We're all soldiers," Jela said, "in the last effort to defeat the *sheriekas*. But, no—if by 'soldier' you mean to ask if she's enrolled in the military. She's a volunteer, like I said. The best damn' pilot I've ever seen—" His eyes stung, and the room wavered a little before he blinked them clear.

"A pilot," he said again, "and a true, courageous friend. The safety of the galaxy rests on her, Pilot, and I'll tell you straight out that I would rather it was her than anyone else I can name."

TOR AN WAS IN HIS garden. That bothered him momentarily— but then he remembered that Melni, who had the tutoring of him and Cor Win in the afternoons, had been called to a Family Meeting. He was supposed to be reading trade protocol, and it would go badly for him if he failed of being the master of the assigned chapter by dinner—but the breeze wafting in the open window had tempted him to step outside for just a *little* while, and walk down to garden's end to visit his tree.

The zang flowers were blooming, their tiny blue and green blossoms like so many stars against the pale yellow grass. He was conscious of a feeling of deep approval as he skipped down the path, pleased that the plants had been given leave to grow as they would, not tamed and confined, as were the showier, costlier plants the gardeners tended in the public gardens at the front of the house. The back garden was for children, and for elders, a comfort—and an occasional temptation for shirking one's lessons.

The grass flowed like water beneath the subtle wind, and he could hear the bell he'd hung in the piata tree's branches. A deep breath brought the taste of leaf and bloom onto his tongue—and there before him was the piata, its branches heavy with fruit. As he approached, one of the high branches dipped down toward him. He raised cupped hands and a fruit dropped into his palms.

"Thank you," he murmured, and climbed up onto the boulder, settling his back against the warm silver bark as he leisurely ate his fruit. Eventually, he closed his eyes, and dozed, knowing himself safe, cherished, and—

A chime sounded. Tor An stirred, and settled more comfortably, for surely it was only the bell high up in the piata's limbs—

The chime sounded again, and he gasped into wakefulness, the dream shattering around him, and a great weight upon his chest—which was only the orange cat, Lucky. Half-laughing, Tor An set the animal aside, ignoring the glare of betrayal, untangled himself from the blanket, and gained his feet as the chime sounded a third time.

"A moment!" he called and stepped forward, careful in the dimness of the strange room. Jela was snoring against the wall beneath the scholar's plant, and Tor An spared a moment's wonder for a pilot who could sleep through such a din, then forgot about him as he opened the door.

Scholar tay'Nordif pitched into his arms.

He caught her, though they were nearly of a height, and bore her clumsily to the chair, kicking the borrowed blanket out of his path. He got her seated, snatched the blanket up, shook it out, and draped it over her shoulders before dropping to one knee by her side, peering into her shadowed face.

"Scholar?"

She put a slim hand against his shoulder, fingers light and trembling.

"A moment, of your goodness, Pilot," she murmured. "I—I had hoped the effects of the—of the duel would have dissipated by now . . ."

"Did they not care for you?" he demanded, outraged. Dueling stick injuries were not trivial and the punishment she had taken . . .

"Nay, nay. Mine colleagues were everything that is kind and accommodating. Surely, vel'Anbrek fetched me a chair and with her own hands dea'San brought me a glass of wine—and another, as well, insisting that I must rebuild my reserves. Truly, they would allow me to do nothing, but must needs serve and cosset me. Many came to the chair in which I rested, and spoke for a moment, showing such concern . . . 'Twas my own folly, that I thought myself sufficiently recovered that I declined Prime Chair's kind offer of escort to my room . . ."

She lifted her head, and gave him a brave smile, the misty green eyes awash with tears. Her face was too pale, and showed two livid marks upon her right cheek.

"He never struck you in the face!" Tor An cried, outraged over again.

"Peace, Pilot. Scholar tel'Elyd felt himself very ill-used. Indeed, he believed that I had not only dismissed him as a colleague, but held him at less value than a kobold." She laughed, breathily. "Who would not be outraged at such?"

"Scholar—"

"A moment, I beg you." With an effort, she straightened on the chair, and took her hand from his shoulder, a loss he felt keenly. He sat back on his heels as the silence grew, and he began to wonder if perhaps she had taken lasting harm from—

"I know that you owe me nothing, Pilot," she said finally. "Indeed, it is I who owe you the remainder of your fee. But, I wonder if you would be willing to accept another commission from me."

Tor An opened his mouth to tell her that he had never taken any commission from her, but before he could frame the words, she had pushed on.

"I hold no secrets from you, Pilot," she said, her hands fisted on her lap. "I have enemies—powerful enemies—among those who are said to be my colleagues. Even now, there are those who seek to devalue what credit I hold with our department's master, whose own student I had been, and whose work set me on the path to finding my own. The Prime Chair—you would not believe such infamy! Indeed, I scarce believe it myself and I have studied the principles of scholarship as nearly as I have studied within my own discipline, for I *will* succeed! My work is too important to be buried as the result of some ill-considered proving! I—my work can save lives, Pilot! Countless lives! Whole star systems might be snatched from the jaws of entropy!"

Tor An's head was spinning. He was fairly certain that the scholar was raving, yet he wanted nothing else but to aid her in whatever way she asked. Which, considering his early evening conversation with Jela, whose own story had contained certain thinly covered gaps of logic—

He sent a quick glance aside, but to all appearances, Captain Jela slumbered still beneath the tree.

"Will you aid me, Pilot?" Scholar tay'Nordif asked, breathlessly.

As if there could be a question! So fragile and vulnerable a lady, who further held the key that would preserve others from the Ringstars' fate. Except, he remembered suddenly, that didn't entirely align with Jela's insistence that the scholar was no scholar at all, but a pretender who had volunteered to run interference while the soldier undertook the real labor of locating the—

"Pilot?"

Tor An sighed. "Jela—" he began, fighting the impulse to pledge his life to her purpose.

The scholar stared at him blankly. "Jela? Pay no attention to Jela, Pilot. He's less aware than—than the cat!"

As if on cue, the very cat leapt into her lap, burbling. The scholar put her arms around it and buried her poor, abused face in his fur.

Tor An took a careful breath. "What is it," he asked carefully, "you would have me do for you?"

The scholar lifted her face and smiled at him and his heart lifted.

"A small thing, Pilot, I assure you! It is necessary that I undo the harm that mine enemies have done. I must assure my master that I am true and hold him in no less esteem now than when I sat at his feet and snatched the pearls of wisdom as they fell from his lips. The best way to do this, of course, is to send a gift." She looked at him expectantly.

Tor An blinked. "A gift," he repeated.

"Indeed! And here we may marvel anew at my patron's wisdom and foresight! For I will tell you that I did say to her, when she would press upon me the specimen she had engineered with her own hands and its keeper-kobold—When I did protest and ask what a poor scholar might do with such trappings of wealth and plenty, do you know what she said to me, Pilot? Why she said, 'I have faith,

Maelyn, that you will find a good use for both.'" She smiled at him again, her chin resting on the cat's head.

"A good use for both," she repeated. "And so I have found an *excellent* use for both! They shall be my gift to Master dea'Syl, which will assure him of my constancy and my unflagging respect."

"You mean to make your master a gift of Jela and, and the tree?" Tor An said slowly.

"Certainly!" The scholar said. "The tree is a worthy gift— indeed, I have its pedigree, which you will of course bear with you and place into the master's own hands."

"And—Jela?" Tor An inquired.

"Jela tends the tree," the scholar said patiently. "It is the role for which it was designed. Surely, you don't expect that *Master dea'Syl* will wish to get dirt under his fingernails from tending a plant? Of course not," she answered her own question. "So it is quite settled. Tomorrow, when I betake myself to my office and my work, you shall bear the tree—Jela, of course, will carry it—with its pedigree and the letter I shall write for you, in secrecy, to Master dea'Syl. Will you do this for me, Pilot? I swear you will be well-rewarded."

"I wonder," he said, somewhat breathlessly, "how I will find my way . . . secretly . . . to Master dea'Syl."

"Ah, that is the fortunate circumstance! Scholar vel'Anbrek will serve as your guide. You will meet him at the proving grounds tomorrow morning as the Day Bell sounds. He will take you by the quiet ways to the master's rooms."

"I—see," he said, though he was moderately certain that he did not. He shot another look at the slumbering soldier, though how anyone could sleep through—and there, a broad hand was outlined against the shadow, fingers spelling out *say yes*.

Tor An cleared his throat and brought his gaze back to the scholar. The color had returned to her face, though the shock-marks still showed livid.

"I will be happy to perform this service for you, Scholar," he said, softly.

TWELVE

❋ ❋

Elsewhen and Otherwhere

THEY RAN, ROOL SIFTING the ley lines so quickly they blurred into a single strand of event, all possibility melded to one purpose. He trusted *her* to keep them viable as they phased from plane to plane and concentrated upon the pattern of the lines, choosing this one, rejecting that, sorting consequences at white-hot speed.

There! He snatched a line, whipping them into the seventh plane, snatched another, phased to the third, glissaded to the fifth. The lines sang about them as small probabilities shifted, the sick were healed, the dead were raised, water was turned into wine.

And still the Shadow pursued them. Suns froze where it fell; planets trembled in their orbits. The fabric of space stretched thin, the ley lines themselves beginning to attenuate.

Rool chose a slender line describing a pocket possibility, rode it to the end, dropped to the fourth plane and doubled back, directly through the tattered skirts of Shadow.

It was a bold move—very nearly too bold. Cold touched him, burning his essence as a kiss of frost will blacken a flower. At the core of his being, he heard *her* scream.

Blindly, he chose a line, another, a third—phased, and fell to his knees onto silken silt, her slender body cradled in his arms.

"Love?"

Her eyes fluttered, amber and dazed.

"You must not risk yourself," she breathed.

He laughed, short and bitter, and lowered her onto the soft silt.

"I risk myself and wound my heart," he said. "Quickly, do what you must to replenish your essence. We dare not—"

She extended a thin hand, placed cool fingers against his lips.

"Hush. What place is this?"

He lifted his head, blinking in the glare of the local star—and again as the breeze flung grit into his face. All around was desolation—rock, wind, sand. Three paces to the right of their resting place lay a huge, bleached trunk, the stubs of what had once been mighty branches half-buried in the silt.

"The homeworld of the *ssussdriad*, or I am a natural man," he murmured, and looked into her dear eyes. "Art ready, love? The Iloheen will not be long behind us."

"I am ready, yes," she said softly, and took his hand, weaving her small fingers between his.

He bent his head and kissed her small hand. "We phase, then," he said, and gathered himself, noting as he did that the Shadow's kiss had done more damage than he had—

"No." Her will rang across his, anchoring him to the physical. "Here. This place. This time. This plane."

He looked at her, dread filling him; raised his head and looked out over the desert once more. Sterile, dust-shrouded, devoid of any tiniest flicker of life . . .

"I cannot prevail here," he whispered.

She laughed, high and gay and sweet. "Of course you cannot," she said. "And neither can I."

"Love—" he reached for her even as he extended his awareness, searching for the shape of a likely line—

Static filled his senses. He snapped back wholly to the dead world, the dying sun, the gritty breeze.

"We are found," he said, and his lady smiled.

"The great Iloheen comes to us," she murmured. "Help me to rise."

He lifted her to her feet, and braced her while she gained her balance.

"Behind me now," she said, "and cede yourself to me."

He stepped back, took one deep breath of sand-filled air, closed his physical eyes, and centered. Before him, glowing gold within the ether, was the channel. He threw open the doors of his heart, and sent his essence to her in a tide of living green.

Static distorted the galaxy. The dying sun flared through a quick rainbow of color, growing large and orange. The gritty breeze gusted and died.

A Shadow fell over the land.

Foolish halfling, the Iloheen sent. *Didst think to elude ME?*

The cold grew more bitter still, until the very light froze in its path, and Rool Tiazan tasted the tang of oblivion. His lady, bold and courageous, held them aloof, his energy pooled and secret behind her shields.

Have you no answer for the one who gave you life? The Iloheen's thought struck her shields like a storm of comets—yet they held. They held. And still she kept their true seeming hidden, showing them obdurate and dull, waiting . . .

Be unmade, then, flawed and treacherous child!

Darkness fell. The stars froze, screaming, in their courses. The ley lines shriveled, sublimating into the blackness. Rool Tiazan felt his body begin to unravel, the golden channel that linked him, essence-to-essence with she whom defined the universe and all that was good among the planes of existence—the golden link decayed, frayed, un—

In the darkness of unmaking, his lady dropped her shields.

A lance of pure light opposed the darkness. The stars sang hosanna; the fog dissipated; and the ley lines reformed, binding the universe and all that lived into the net of possibility. Rool Tiazan felt his heart stutter into rhythm, and drew a breath of warm, sweet air.

Darkness thrust, light countered—fire rained in frozen flames at the congruence of their fields.

Again, darkness struck. The light feinted, twisted—and struck! The Iloheen howled, and withdrew, winding its dark energies into one thick skein of oblivion.

His lady, cool and slender blade of light, closed the channel that linked them.

Rool Tiazan screamed as the Iloheen's blow gathered and fell; saw the brave blade rise to meet it—

—and shatter, into nightmare and ice.

He screamed again as his essence unraveled, and his consciousness splintered into dark teardrops.

THIRTEEN

Osabei Tower Landomist

"SHE'S MAD," Tor An said to Jela's broad back.

The soldier grunted as he shifted tree and pot out of the corner, preparatory, Tor An supposed, to delivering it to Master dea'Syl, whoever and wherever he might be. How they were to transport the tree was another question, for if there was a cargo pallet or luggage sled within the confines of the scholar's quarters, it was masquerading as a desk, or a chair, or a cat.

"*Mad*," he repeated, with emphasis. Jela, the tree apparently situated to his satisfaction, straightened and turned 'round to face him.

"You say that like there's something wrong with being mad," he commented.

Tor An glared at him, and the soldier laughed, softly, soothing the air between them with his big hand.

"I'm not the one to complain to about the scholar's state of mind," he said. "Think about it—I'm here to steal a set of equations that might save the galaxy from an enemy we can't possibly overcome."

Tor An caught his breath. "Is that certain? I thought—the soldiers were being pulled back to a more defensible—"

Jela sighed. "The soldiers are being pulled back to defend the Inner Worlds because the Inner Worlds bought the High Command," he said, with a sincerity that was impossible to doubt. "The Inner Worlds think to buy themselves free of the fate that overtook the Ringstars, but what they've bought—at the price of countless lives and numberless planets—is a few years, at most. The decrystallization process is going faster, according to my information; it's as if whatever technique they're using, it's cumulative, so the more space the Enemy decrystalizes, the more they *can* decrystalize . . ."

Tor An glanced aside. The cat was sitting on the counter; he extended a finger, received a polite nose-touch. "So, are we all mad, then?" he murmured, skritching the cat's ear.

Jela laughed, a low, comfortable rumble deep in his chest. "Well, let's see. We're in a fight to destroy an enemy that can't be defeated." A pause, as if he were seriously weighing the merit of this statement, then, "Yes, Pilot. We're all mad."

Tor An sighed. "What shall we do?" he asked, the cat purring against his fingers.

"Unless you have an idea that seems more likely to move us along the road to victory than the one the scholar gave us, I suggest we follow our orders."

Tor An thought, briefly, of the back garden at home. He wanted nothing more, in that moment, but to sit under his piata tree, nibble on a fruit; perhaps nap, and awaken some while later blanketed in fallen leaves, safe, cherished and protected.

Gone forever, he thought. And if there were a chance—even a vanishingly small chance—that he might preserve someone else's tree and garden, was that chance not worth taking?

And it wasn't as if he had anything else to do.

Reluctantly, he stopped skritching the cat and picked up the sealed packet the scholar had left on the counter. He weighed it in his hand before slipping it away into an inner pocket, and turned again to face Jela.

The soldier gave him a critical look, for all the worlds like Melni making certain that he hadn't done his shirt up crooked, back when he was still in the schoolroom, and held up a blunt finger.

"You're missing a very important accessory, Pilot. A moment, if you please."

He moved across the room, absurdly light for so bulky a man, rummaged in the scholar's rucksack and was back, holding in his big hand a discipline bracelet the twin of that which Scholar tay'Nordif wore. Tor An frowned.

"Problem?" Jela asked.

Not quite able to mask his distaste, Tor An took the bracelet and turned it over in his hands, looking for the hair-thin wires that would pierce his skin and bond him to—

He looked up and met the soldier's bland black eyes.

"Two problems, in fact," he answered crisply. "One, you are not a kobold. Two, this bracelet lacks the coding wires. It won't work."

"Well," Jela said, untroubled, "that makes it a match for Scholar tay'Nordif's, now doesn't it? And as for me, I'm a kobold, sure enough." He rubbed the ball of his thumb over the ceramic threads woven into his chest. "If it falls that way, discipline me, Pilot. I'll trust your judgment."

Tor An sighed, and used his chin to point at the tree. "How are we to transport that?"

"I'll carry it," said Jela.

"*Carry* it? It must weigh—"

"I'm strong, Pilot, never fear. I've carried that tree since it was shorter than I am."

"But—"

"And we'd best be going," Jela continued, moving over to the subject of the discussion and flexing his arms. "It wouldn't be polite to keep Scholar vel'Anbrek waiting."

He went down on a knee, wrapped his arms around the pot, heaved—and came to his feet, tree cradled in his arms. "After you, Pilot," he said, under no apparent strain.

Tor An took one last, reflexive look around the room. Not a very tidy room, truth told, and Lucky nowhere in sight. The first irritated him—he was a meticulous lad—and the second saddened him—he would have liked to have stroked the cat one more time, for luck.

Well. He pushed the unaccustomed annoyance of the bracelet up over his shirt until it stuck, and smoothed the sleeve of his jacket over it. Jela stood, face slack and stupid, holding the tree as if it weighed slightly less than nothing. Tor An sighed, went forward, opened the door and led the way down the hall.

"TRUE PILOT TIMING," Scholar vel'Anbrek snapped, "cut to the last fraction of a second." He moved off hurriedly, robe flapping around his legs. "Come along, we must needs be away from the arena before it begins."

"Before what begins?" asked Tor An, moving determinedly to the scholar's side. A quick glance over his shoulder reassured him that Jela was keeping up, even at his stolid "kobold" walk.

"Ah, she didn't tell you the whole of it, did she? Just as well. This way, now, and be quick!"

They rushed single-file down a hall so thin Tor An's shoulders each brushed a wall. A single ceramic track down the center of the floor—a supply tunnel, Tor An thought. Another quick glance showed Jela proceeding sideways, somewhat the slower for the tight quarters. Ahead, the scholar darted right into another tunnel.

An alarm sounded, frighteningly loud.

Tor An stumbled, but the walls were too close to allow of a fall. At least this time he did not mistake it for a ship's system in ultimate distress. This time, he knew what it was—and his blood grew cold.

"Scholar tay'Nordif," he gasped and the old man turned his head, with no decrease in speed.

"Come along, Pilot! This is more important than a single scholar—or even a whole Tower full of scholars too blind to see aught but their own comfort and petty quarrels. This way!"

He dodged into a left-tending hallway as the second alarm sounded, opened a door and waved them inside. "Keep a good hold on the strap! This lift is calibrated for cargo."

It was a nasty trip up, and how Jela bore it, with no hand free to steady himself, Tor An could not imagine. The alarm sounded for the third time during the short, brutal lift, and then they were following Scholar vel'Anbrek down a tunnel the twin to those below-deck, the track set into the floor shiny with wear.

"In here!" the scholar snapped, and pushed through another door.

The hall beyond was dim, the air slightly sour, the track dusty with disuse. Their passage disturbed moths and cobwebs—and then the scholar halted, put his hand against a section of blank wall like all the rest of the blank wall up and down the tunnel—and waited. Tor An came up beside him and a moment later Jela arrived at his shoulder. Still the scholar stood with his hand against the wall—which suddenly showed a moire pattern of golden motes—and disappeared altogether.

Scholar vel'Anbrek stepped through the opening. Tor An hesitated, then bethought himself of Scholar tay'Nordif, risking her life in order that this opportunity be made available, and followed the old scholar into the unknown.

THE SEATS FILLED quickly, many of the scholars with breakfast cups and pastry sticks in hand. There was a murmur, a rising wave of voices exclaiming over a third challenge coming so close upon the heels of the others—and then rising again, as those who had already downed their first cup or two of morning tea recalled that the challenge which had deprived the Tower of Prime tay'Palin had been but the last of many . . .

Maelyn tay'Nordif stood inside the proving court, head bowed, hands tucked inside the sleeves of her robe, and wondered if she was going mad. Almost, she would have thought that the wine dea'San had pressed upon her so solicitously last evening had been poisoned, only she could think of no poison which would act in this manner— there! What did she know of poisons or their action? She was a scholar of Interdimensional Mathematics, lately Seated within Osabei Tower, as she had long ago determined that she would be. None of the other, lesser, Towers would assuage her pride—it *would be* Osabei, the First—or a lifetime of wandering.

And so, she had fulfilled the task her pride had set her, disproven the master's own lifework, gained the coveted Chair in the only

Mathematical Tower that mattered—only to find that her mind, far from being that honed instrument she had always felt it to be, was rather a weak blade which had speedily shattered upon the rock of Tower life.

These random thoughts which afflicted her, now, at the moment of her trial . . . Surely, the port police had not required her to look upon a certain broken and battered corpse which she then claimed for her mother? Not only did she remember her mother very well, she thought, taking deep, calming breaths as the noise of the seats filling continued around her, but she was still alive, and serving in the Distaff House of Nordif, which was charged with keeping the 'counts and inventories of the mercantile branch. Her mother was a senior receivables manager—a respected and respectable woman of a respected and respectable House. It had been her mother's support and encouragement which had given her the courage to pursue her scholarly studies, and to stand in defiance before Aunt Tilfrath, who had wished her to remain and serve the House as had her mother, and her mother, and—

And *surely*, she thought in cold horror, as the sounds of the gathering observers began to settle into some semblance of quiet, *surely* she had never—never allowed a—a *kobold*—

She took a shuddering breath, hoping to still the roiling of her stomach, and thrust the thought away. Such things were the stuff of nightmares; and like nightmares, were mere disorders of the imagination. She was neither mad nor depraved. She would meet what was to come with sure mind and sure blade, and rightly overcome this challenge. Her work was elegant; pure. She would not be found in error.

"Silence, Scholars!" Prime Chair tay'Welford's voice sounded near at hand. She raised her head, and forced her eyes open. Across from her in the proving court stood a scholar not immediately familiar . . . She mentally reviewed her acquaintance of the common room—ah, of course! Scholar ven'Orlud, whose speciality was . . . pretransitional spatial coordinates, was it not? What could such a person find to prove or disprove in her own work?

"Scholar ven'Orlud," Prime Chair said loudly enough to be

heard in the back seats, "challenges Scholar tay'Nordif to defend the point made in her Wander-thesis Number Three that intermittent vectorization within the universal metacrystal could prevent accurate energy-field summation."

Scholar tay'Nordif felt a jolt go up her spine.

But I later refuted those findings myself! How can I be called to prove an error which I later corrected?

"This is a true proving, not merely a point of personal honor," Prime Chair continued. "Blades will be engaged, and scholarship rests upon the outcome. Scholars, prepare to defend the Truth."

"This is a fraudulent proving!" The voice rang against the high ceiling, struck the walls and rebounded—by which time, Maelyn tay'Nordif had recognized it as her own.

THEY WERE IN WHAT once had been a cold storage room. Here and there, vacuum cells and yellowed foam could be seen through the scored laminate walls. Looking about them, Tor An felt a certain sense of dismay.

"Forgive me, Scholar," he said politely when some time had passed without their guide continuing. "This scarcely seems an apartment suited to the honor of one of your Tower's great masters."

Scholar vel'Anbrek smiled humorlessly. "Quick off the mark," he said obscurely. "Good."

Tor An frowned. "Scholar, I must insist that you bring me to Master dea'Syl, so that I may present Scholar tay'Nordif's gift, as she bade me to do."

"Patience, Pilot. You will be with Master dea'Syl—ah!—very soon now, I hear."

Were *all* the scholars here mad? Tor An wondered, and gathered his patience, for, mad or no, that had been well-advised.

"Sir," he began again—and stopped as the wall directly opposite vanished in a cloud of golden vapor, and a carry-chair bore through, silent on its supportive pad of air.

The man in the chair had an abundance of white hair plaited into a single thick braid and tied off with a plain red cord. He was bent forward, his shoulders bowed beneath the weight of the robe, and his thin hands rested one atop the other on the control stick.

Halfway across the room, he made a minute adjustment, and the chair's forward progress halted, though it did not settle to the floor.

Slowly, as if the braid hanging across his shoulder was nearly too heavy a burden, the old scholar raised his head.

His brow was high, his eyes deep, his nose noble, and time had writ its passage boldly upon his features. Tor An bowed, reflexively, and straightened into the scholar's thoughtful regard.

"Now, here's a pretty behaved lad," he said, his voice thin and clear. "By which sign I know him to be something other than a scholar of Osabei Tower."

vel'Anbrek stepped forward and placed his hand on the chair's tumble guard.

"This is the pilot, Liad. The one of whom I spoke."

"Pilot?" The thin lips bent in a smile. "He scarcely seems old enough." A hand lifted, trembling slightly, showing Tor An an empty palm. "I mean no offense, Pilot; when one reaches a certain age, the galaxy itself seems a child."

"I have not been insulted," Tor An assured him, and felt his cheeks heat as the scholar's smile grew momentarily more pronounced.

"I am pleased to hear it, for I do not hide from you, Pilot, that it would go badly for me, were we to meet on the field of honor."

"Liad—" Scholar vel'Anbrek said urgently.

"Yes, yes, my friend. Time is precious. Allow me a dozen heart-beats more, that I might beg you to reconsider your position."

"I never had a taste for adventuring," the other scholar said, taking his hand from the guard and going two deliberate steps back. "I will remain, and do what might be done here."

The old man sighed. "So it shall be, then. Keep well, old friend, as long as that state is possible."

vel'Anbrek bowed. "Go forth and do great deeds, Master." He turned on his heel and strode away; the wall misted before him, and reformed behind, as solid-seeming as Jela, standing patiently to the rear, tree cradled in his arms.

Tor An blinked. It had seemed for a moment as if the bark had grown ears, but—

With a burble of joy, Lucky the cat leapt out of the tree's pot and galloped, tail high in ecstacy, toward the carry chair, and without hesitation bounded over the tumble bar and into Master dea'Syl's lap.

"Well." The old man presented a finger, and received an enthusiastic bump. "You must tell me who this fine fellow is, Pilot."

"That is Scholar tay'Nordif's cat, sir," Tor An said politely, unaccountably relieved to see the animal again. "She calls him Lucky."

"Does she so? May she be correct in her estimation."

Tor An took a breath, reached into his jacket and pulled out the documents the scholar had entrusted to his care.

"If you please, sir," he said. The master's dark, sapient gaze lifted courteously to his face. "If you please," Tor An repeated, stepping forward. "Scholar tay'Nordif sends you these tidings."

"Ah." The master considered the packets gravely and at last held out a hand. Greatly relieved, Tor An surrendered them, and then turned, gesturing toward the immobile Jela and his burden.

"Scholar tay'Nordif also makes you a gift, sir."

There was a small silence; the master absently skritching the cat's chin with one hand, the documents on his knee, unopened and apparently unregarded, while he looked past Tor An, to Scholar tay'Nordif's offering.

"A gift of an M Series soldier is generous indeed," Master dea'Syl said at last. "I believe I have not seen the like since my Wander days. Introduce me, pray, Pilot."

Tor An stared at Jela, stricken. The soldier smiled slightly and inclined his sleek head.

"My name's Jela, sir," he said in his easy voice. "Am I right in thinking you intended to hire Pilot yos'Galan to lift you out of here?"

"Indeed you are. Am I correct in thinking that the military has at last come to its senses and will act upon my findings?"

"Unfortunately, no," Jela said seriously. "I'm working with an independent corps of specialists. Our mission is to liberate your work and use it to aid as much of the galaxy as possible in escaping the *sheriekas*."

"A worthy mission, and one with which I find myself in harmony. I willingly align myself with your corps of specialists. Pray put down your camouflage and let us depart."

"No camouflage," Jela said, "but a member of the team."

"Ah? Fascinating. Please, M. Jela, place your associate on the cargo rack at the rear of this chair. I shall be honored to bear it with me."

Jela hesitated, then stepped 'round and slid the tree into the rack, using the straps to fasten it securely.

"Excellent!" Master dea'Syl said, giving the cat one last chuck under the chin and placing both hands on the control stick. "Allow me to show you the back way out."

He spun the chair on its pad of air and moved toward the wall through which he'd entered, Jela right behind. Tor An stood where he was, hands fisted at his sides.

"Scholar tay'Nordif—" he protested. Jela sent him a look over one broad shoulder, his face expressionless.

"Our first objective," he said patiently, "is to secure the equations. No one of us is more important than that."

Tor An glared. "*Your* first objective!" He snapped. "I claim no membership in your team of specialists, and I will not abandon Scholar tay'Nordif to—"

Jela held his hands up, showing two wide, empty palms. "How," he asked quietly, "are you going to get her out of the arena, assuming she's managed to survive this long?"

Tor An opened his mouth, closed it.

"Right," the soldier said, sounding weary. "Come along, Pilot. You're needed at your board."

FOURTEEN

❀❀❀❀❀❀❀❀❀❀❀❀❀❀❀❀❀❀❀❀❀❀❀❀

Osabei Tower Landomist

ABSOLUTE SILENCE filled the arena; the scholars on their benches shocked into silence by her outburst. As who, Maelyn tay'Nordif thought bleakly, would not be? She should abase herself before Prime Chair, beg pardon of her challenger and let the match proceed. To whinge or to argue—it was unseemly; unworthy of one who had attained her long-coveted Seat . . .

"In what way," Prime Chair inquired, dangerously soft, "do you find this challenge to be fraudulent, Scholar? Do you deny having authored the work under challenge?"

"I do not," she answered, hastily, before that—other—took the initiative, to what new disaster who could predict? She cleared her throat. "I do, however, object to your continued manipulation of the scholars of this Tower, Prime Chair, and I call upon you to explain yourself!"

Horrified, she brought her hand to her lips, but the terrible words had already been uttered, and hung, vibrating, in the charged air.

"*You* call upon *me*—" tay'Welford breathed, and smiled.

559

"Scholar, you misunderstand. It is you who are called to explain certain assertions incorporated in the work referenced in a properly submitted Petition to Prove, which has been filed by one of your colleagues. I have reviewed this petition as well as its supporting documentation, and find that the challenge has merit. You are, therefore, called to defend your work, here and now, before the full gathering of your colleagues."

"The blades need not enter into it," she said, reasonably. "Prime, I myself located the error and subsequently repaired it. If you will allow me—"

He turned away from her, raising his voice so those in the most distant seats could hear, "Scholar tay'Nordif pleads a stay of challenge. It appears that she lacks the courage to defend her own work! How say you, colleagues? This Tower is built upon the integrity of its scholarship! Are we to allow this—"

"If this Tower is built upon the integrity of its scholars," Maelyn heard her traitor voice ring out, "then the walls crumble around us where we stand!" She spun, raising her hand to point at each section of seats in turn. "I call upon the scholars gathered here to do the math!" she shouted. "How many of your colleagues have fallen in proof during the last dozen semesters? How many of them stood between Ala Bin tay'Welford and his ultimate goal—the Prime Chair?"

There was murmuring in the stands now, and consternation. Some scholars rose to their feet, others brought out math-sticks and personal diaries.

"Do the math!" she cried again, as she fought the strange, false conviction that she knew tay'Welford in some other guise, and that she perfectly understood his purpose, which was neither the glory of the Tower nor the preservation of its scholars and their work. "Tally the loss to the field since this man came among you! Consider his purpose!"

"What can we know of his purpose?" someone called down from the stands. "He is a scholar, as we all are; his purpose must be the peaceful pursuit of his work!"

"It is not!" she returned, and knew it for truth. She turned and faced tay'Welford, who stood as a man quick-frozen, as sometimes were the laborers at home, if night caught them outside the dome. His smile was rigid, and his eyes full with dire warning. Behind him, Scholar ven'Orlud frankly gaped.

Fascinated, Maelyn watched her hand rise, the wedge of her fingers pointing directly at Ala Bin tay'Welford.

"This man is no scholar," she shouted; "he is a liar and a thief. His whole purpose in being here is to lay this Tower to waste in the name of his masters, and to steal away our most precious treasure!"

"You fool!" tay'Welford hissed, and snatched the blade from his sash.

MASTER DEA'SYL SET a brisk pace, leading them through a maze of dusty tunnels, up yet another cargo lift, and thence into another tunnel, this one bearing all the markings of being in current use.

"This way," Tor An panted, "is not so secret as some."

"That is correct, Pilot," the master said, unperturbed. "There is a measurable risk of discovery in this section of our journey. I do assure you, however, that the risk is acceptable—and in any case, it must be run. There is no other path from where we were to the place we must come to. Quickly, now; we are almost—"

Abruptly, the chair braked, skewing sideways on its cushion of air. The pot in the cargo bay slammed against its restraints; the tree's limbs trembled. Jela flung out an arm, stopping Tor An in his tracks, then crept forward alone, stealthy and silent, to peer 'round the next corner.

Tor An gripped the side of the carry-chair, watching as Jela raised a hand, palm out, fingers waggling briefly in something that might have been hand-talk for *wait*.

Moments dragged by; Tor An's whole attention was focused upon that broad, steady palm—when a spot of damp coolness touched the fingers that gripped the sled's tumble bar so tightly, he jumped and bit his tongue in his endeavor not to gasp. Glancing down, he saw Lucky the cat looking earnestly up into his face, amber eyes depthless and clear. Carefully, one eye still on Jela, he moved his free hand and rubbed the cat's ear. His attention was rewarded with a purr so soft he scarcely heard it where he stood—and then Jela's hand swept out and up—*come on.*

THE BLADE CAME IN low, impossibly fast. She knew a heartbeat of utter terror before she sidestepped, spinning out of the path of danger in a swirl of robes.

"Murderer!" she shouted. "Thief! Take him! Hold him for the Governors!"

For a instant, it seemed as if every scholar present had been quick-frozen, then a few found their feet and surged forward, shouting. Their movement thawed the others, who swarmed down the stands, some with blades drawn, others with math-sticks still in hand. Crying aloud, they closed on Ala Bin tay'Welford. Scholar ven'Orlud, who yet stood by, abruptly came to life, snatching at tay'Welford's sleeve, her hand going to the knife in her sash. tay'Welford spun, blade flashing—

Maelyn tay'Nordif did not stay to see more. The onrushing wave of scholars was no longer interested in her, and by dint of dodging, ducking, and simple pushing, she quickly reached clear floor. She paused a moment to take her bearings, thoughts a-whirl with half-grasped questions and calculations—what matter to her where the spaceport lay?—while she pulled the hem of her robe up through the sash, freeing her legs for quick movement. She had the clear sense that a decision had been made, though what it might be, she could not have said. Her feet, however, were better informed. She spun, spied a hallway that matched some parameter of that unknown decision, and began to run.

ONCE AGAIN, they were in an ancient and long-undisturbed supply tunnel. They went more slowly now, Master dea'Syl setting a pace that showed some respect for the tricky footing his carry-chair floated above.

"How time does render us all obsolete," the old man remarked. "Would you believe, gentles, that this was the main supply line for Osabei when I was a child? Many hours did I labor at the receiving dock, absorbing the principles of practical mathematics. Far too often, I was called to right a supply train which had jumped the track, or to carry out some measure from a barge which had foundered from overload."

Tor An blinked. "You were a child within these walls, Master?"

"Indeed, I was once a child, Pilot, though I grant one might find it difficult to credit. In those days, you see, it was possible for Houses of a certain status to pledge a child to the Tower from which the House elders wished to receive notice. I am not able to tell you what it was my own House sought, as of course this was never disclosed to me. However, when I ascended to grudent, I was shown the contract of pledge, on which the signatures of all six elders appeared."

"It seems a hard price," Tor An observed, blinking away a sudden rising of tears, as he thought of the bustling and busy house that was no more—

"Perhaps. Certainly others have thought so. I cannot fault the arrangement, myself, as in it I found my lifework and perhaps—as M. Jela may have imparted to you—the means to preserve humankind from oblivion."

The tunnel, Tor An thought, was widening gradually and tending somewhat to the right. He shot a glance to Jela, walking in his chosen position at the rear, and saw that the walls no longer crowded those wide shoulders quite so nearly.

"We are in fact, approaching the very thing which first struck fire from my mathematical curiosity," Master dea'Syl said, and raised his voice somewhat. "M. Jela, you will find this interesting, I think."

The tunnel continued steadfast in its rightward tending; the walls widening even more, into a neglected receiving bay. Carts and barges lined the left wall, awaiting cargos; on the right, empty twine spindles were set into the walls, a hose dangled untidily from a cobweb-covered cannister, the graphic denoting spray sealant barely visible through the dust. A shelf still held a set of dust-shrouded tools, neatly laid out by function; a hand-cart and a cargo-sled leaned against the wall beneath. Three tracks described a tricksy dance through the dust—in-going, out-going, and in-process, Tor An thought, oddly soothed by the simple ordinariness of the arrangements. It was plain that the bay had been abandoned for some time, and yet, with only a little bit of cleaning and stocking, it could be made as functional as it had been during Liad dea'Syl's long-ago boyhood.

At the far end of the hall, where the bay doors would normally be, was a curved blank wall of made of some unfamiliar milky orange material. It gave back no reflection; seemed, indeed to absorb what feeble light came from the panels set into the ceiling, and there appeared to be . . . things . . . moving within and beneath the milkiness. Tor An walked forward, eyes squinted against the vaguely unsettling color, trying to get a clear sight of those . . . things. As he approached, he felt his skin prickle, as if a charge leaked from the . . . whatever it—

"Where," Jela said, in a voice that Tor An registered as too quiet, "did Osabei Tower acquire this thing?"

"M. Jela, you delight me!" the master exclaimed, as Tor An turned to face the two of them. "Am I really to believe that you know what this is?"

"I'm a generalist, sir," Jela said, still in that too-quiet voice, "with a special interest over the last few years in *sheriekas* technology." He nodded toward the milky orange wall. "Based on my studies, I'd guess that was a shortcut, left over from the First Phase."

"Your guess is admirably on-target," Master dea'Syl said, stroking the cat absently. "As to where Osabei Tower acquired it—I cannot say. When I had status enough to gain access to the documents regarding the device, I only found that it had been purchased from a company called Oracle Odd Lots, and that Osabei Tower had—and has—a standing order to purchase objects related to its area of scholarship."

There was a small silence before Jela spoke again. "In the deep files of Osabei Tower, there is mention of a world-shield, which is based—or was based—on Vanehald. I'm interested in that device, also, and would appreciate anything you can tell me about it."

"Ah. I regret, M. Jela. I know very little of that device—merely its location and the fact that no patron was found to fund a study of it. It has languished for some very long number of years, as you will have seen from the file. Very likely, it is no longer in place; or no longer functions."

"I understand," Jela said quietly. "Thank you, sir."

"You are quite welcome. Well! Time, as my dear vel'Anbrek would no doubt remind us if he were here, runs quickly. If you gentles are quite prepared, let us proceed to the port."

Jela held up a hand. "Consider, sir, that this device—fully as ancient as the world-shield, and by the state of the bay, many years unused—may no longer function."

Master dea'Syl inclined his head. "You are a soldier and it is your nature to be cautious. Allow me to put your fears to rest, M. Jela; I have over the last few years been seeing to the maintenance and upkeep of the device, as I was taught to do as a boy. Its functionality— while I daresay not optimal—is adequate. You observe it in its ready state, which I initiated as soon as vel'Anbrek brought me news that chance had at last placed an unaffiliated pilot-owner within my grasp."

It seemed to Tor An that Jela stiffened; certainly the face he turned toward the unsettling hatchway was devoid of any expression, lips tight, black eyes bleak.

"My pilot, who has some experience of the Enemy's devices, and who sat co-pilot for yet another pilot who had even more practical knowledge of such things, holds as truth that the devices of the Enemy never forget who made them, and that they call out to their makers," Jela said slowly. "What they say, not the elder pilot, or my pilot, or I can hazard—though I believe we agree it holds nothing that we'd call good."

The master sighed. "You would caution me that I put a world at risk by employing this device. I would remind you, sir, that the *galaxy* is at risk, and this is the only door which will open to its possible rescue. Created by the Enemy, it certainly was, and no doubt treacherous beyond our ability to understand. Yet, in this instance it is our ally, and we must grasp the means that come to hand."

"Soldier's logic," Jela said, "which ought to sway a soldier." He was quiet for a moment, and it seemed to Tor An that he stood less straight, as if the weight of what they were about to do was heavier even than a strong man could bear.

"Go," he said.

MAELYN TAY'NORDIF RAN as she had never run before, down the hallway that mad, secret portion of her mind had chosen. Past empty labs and lecture rooms, she ran, the shouts and noise from the proving court fading behind her. Surely, she thought, she was now beyond any immediate danger. Best to utilize one of the vacant rooms for a period of rest and meditation.

She slowed to a jog, her soft slippers raising faint chuffing sounds from the smooth floor, and then to a walk, passing three sealed doors, status lights glowing red—reserved rooms, and keyed to the palms of particular scholars and their disciples. Maelyn passed on.

The sixth door showed a green light—general use. She placed her palm against the plate and stepped inside a modest lecture hall; sixty work chairs arranged in six curving rows of ten, the scholar's station front and centered, with only the most minimal expanse of floor to separate her from the students. The air was frigid, the lighting dim.

Sighing, Maelyn tay'Nordif ordered herself; unkilting her robe and brushing it smooth with hands that trembled rather a lot; making certain that her sash was tidy, the truth-blade in its place. Her stomach cramped at the recollection of her unscholarly behavior. She could not, in fact, imagine what might face her in the scholar's common room this evening. To call down a mad crowd upon the department's Prime Chair—on causes that could scarcely be thought to contain a grain of fact, fabricated as they must have been on the edge of the moment—

It was true, she admitted, folding her arms tightly beneath her breasts and hugging herself in an attempt to ease the trembling, that she was not very skilled in the art of the blade. Indeed, if she were to be honest with herself, she would own that the survival of her Wander years was due not so much to her vigilance and ability to protect herself, but to her habit of affiliating herself with a succession of "patrons," some of whom had been no better than bandits. She had been gently raised, she thought, beginning to pace, and her talents lay elsewhere than in brute physical—

The door opened.

She spun, feet tangling in her robe, and scrambled for balance as Ala Bin tay'Welford stepped into the room.

THE OLD SCHOLAR went first, his chair moving with deliberation toward the pass-portal. As Jela watched, the energies within the portal began to swirl, forming an unsettling vortex into which chair, man, cat and tree receded until they were indistinguishable from the dancing milky motes.

The process was eerily silent, though Jela noticed a slight breeze brushing his cheeks as the vortex sucked air into it.

At the side of the bay, Tor An yos'Galan hesitated, for which Jela blamed him not at all. The thought of surrendering himself to the action of the vortex was . . . unnerving at best, and if the whole business was enough to twitch nerves spun out of data-wire—or so they had assured each other in creche, when they were learning the basic skills of soldiering—

"Pilot," he said, keeping his voice matter-of-fact, like stepping off into infinity was an everyday affair. "I'll take rear guard."

The boy threw him one wide glance out of those improbable flower-colored eyes, took a breath, faced about like a good troop, and walked determinedly into the swirling doom, hands loose at his sides. The energies swirled, shrouded—and Tor An yos'Galan was gone, swallowed by the vortex.

Jela considered the energies before him, his feet planted flat on the floor, as if he intended to take root in the considerable dust. Duty lay before him—the old scholar, with his equations locked safe and secret in his head; the tree; the pilot he'd appropriated . . .

And behind him—his partner, or the person his partner had died to become, not from some vague sense of obligation to the galaxy or life-as-it-was—or to honor the oath she had never, in truth, taken—but *for him*.

Duty required him to move forward. Duty required him to leave her to die.

She took rear-guard, he told himself. *She knew the risks.*

And maybe that was so—and maybe it wasn't. She'd known there were risks; she'd known, if he were to trust her, like she'd asked him, that there were good odds that neither one of them would finish this campaign alive. Rear-guard, though—Cantra yos'Phelium had never been a soldier.

He closed his eyes.

A co-pilot's first care was for his pilot, which left the pilot to care for the ship and the passengers, if any. *That* was a protocol Cantra had known well.

Trust . . . her voice whispered, faint and husky.

He threw away all she had done—for him alone—if he turned his back on duty now.

"Advance, Soldier," he told himself. And again, "Advance."

His feet at least knew an order when it was said, and he was enough of a soldier—yet and still—to not wish to bear the shame of having been ordered thrice.

So, he marched, shoulders square and hands ready, across the dusty floor, and into the maw of energy.

TAY'WELFORD HAD FARED roughly at the hands of the crowd; a bruise darkened one cheek and there was blood on his robe. How much of the blood may have been his, Maelyn thought, was unclear. Certainly, he was not impeded in the speed with which he spun and locked the door, nor in the certainty with which he raised his blade and touched its pommel to his heart in ironic salute.

"You made a dangerous gamble, did you not?" He inquired, advancing upon her slowly. "Did you think to find me so easily unseated? I am no green boy, maddened by his first dissolving. You, however—the last of a flawed line, and encapsulating all of them. Rash, heedless, vicious. *Stupid.* So stupid to have come here . . ."

She gave a step—and another—before him, and that was wrong. He was trying to get her against the chairs . . . Biting her lip, she did *not* yield a third step; belatedly reaching to her sash and pulling the truth-blade free.

tay'Welford inclined his head. "So you will fight now, will you?" He moved, blade flashing; she countered, clumsy and ineffectual, felt the pain on the right side of her face, and stumbled back a third step and a fourth, gasping. Her free hand went to her cheek, came away smeared with blood.

Her opponent laughed. "Such an *interesting* choice. Meek, ineffectual, and ludicrous. It fetters you, does it not? In a moment, you'll find that it has killed you."

"I don't understand you!" she shouted at him, feeling the chairs against her back. She would have to attack, move him out of the way, get to the door—

She lunged.

Surprise drove him back a step, his blade weaving a bright dance, countering her attack, breaching her defense, slicing through cloth and into her arm.

Screaming, she lunged again, his blade was fouled for a moment in her sleeve and she scored a strike of her own—red blood blooming on the side of his robe; he grunted, staggered, and she was past him, running for the door.

She pressed her hand against the plate, but the blood on her palm fouled the reader and the lock remained engaged. Sobbing, she turned, back against the door, blade up, hilt slick with blood from the slash on her arm.

tay'Welford smiled, crouched, one hand out, ready to grab her if she tried to dart past him, knife held almost casually in the other.

"What shall I do, to sweeten your passage?" he murmured, eyes bright and utterly devoid of pity. "Ah, I know. Listen closely—I want the sense of this to strike deep, before I complete the lesson." His smile widened.

"'Twas I killed Garen. She died as she had lived—a fool, and begging me not to harm you."

Trembling, she stared at him, seeing a curious waiting in those bright, pitiless eyes, unable to think of anything but that she was about to die at the hand of a madman—

Pay your debts, baby, a woman's voice seemed to whisper in her very ear. *There ain't no living with yourself, if you don't.*

Tears stung her eyes; she blinked and they ran down her face, mingling with the blood.

tay'Welford laughed, softly. "Yes, very good. Savor that a moment; I want you to die blighted." The knife moved, leisurely.

She ducked, taking the strike on her shoulder, coming in under his guard and setting her blade in his throat.

"*Veralt,*" she hissed, though what the sense of the word was, she could not have said.

His eyes widened, hand rising—and falling as he slumped to the floor, bright eyes fixed and dull.

She stood there for a moment, swaying and bloody, then haltingly turned to deal with the door.

FIFTEEN

✺✺✺✺✺✺✺✺✺✺✺✺✺✺✺✺✺✺✺✺✺✺✺✺✺

Landomist

THERE WAS A MOMENT of extreme unpleasantness, as if he were being dismantled, molecule by molecule, followed by an instant of agony as he was abruptly jammed back together.

Jela's boots hit solid 'crete. Inside his head, he saw a wall of fog rolling in from the ocean, obscuring cliffs and tree tops. Then, in the fog—a shape, small and indistinct, rapidly growing into a black dragon, flying strongly, breaking all at once out into the light . . .

"Over here, M. Jela," Master dea'Syl called softly.

Shaking the memory of his transit away, he took quick stock. They were in a cargo shed, dim and in none-too-good repair; the light sources being the holes in the crumbling metal roof, and the pale, flickering orange light from the shortcut. The carry-chair hovered some two dozen steps to his right and ahead. He could see the outline of the tree, and the old man's silhouette . . .

"Where is Pilot yos'Galan?" he asked, moving forward quickly.

"Here," said a faint voice, and the boy stepped out of the deeper shadows beyond the chair.

"The pilot had a difficult passage," Master dea'Syl said smoothly.

"And no shame to him. Many strong stomachs have been humbled by that walk, short as it is." He raised a frail hand. "We are within the port, M. Jela. It is now yours to lead and mine to follow. The door is fifteen paces to the left of your position, and may require persuasion which I believe you are qualified to apply. While you are about that, I will deactivate the portal."

"Right." He moved forward, located the door, tested the ancient opening mechanism and found it as the old man had suggested.

"Stand back," he said to Tor An, who had followed him, perhaps to offer aid. "I'm going to give it a push."

As it happened, three pushes were necessary to open it to a width the carry-chair could negotiate, and as the luck would have it, the roof didn't come down on them as a result. Jela went through first, then waved his companions out.

Before them spread the glittering expanse of Landomist Port. Jela looked to Tor An.

"Where's your ship, Pilot?"

"Near, I'd think," the boy said, standing forward briskly enough despite his pale face. "Ship's fund was scarcely able to bear the cost of a berth in the private yards . . ." Eyes squinted against the light, he surveyed the situation, then raised a hand, pointing.

"There! The Dejon Forty-Four in the third six-row. You can see the star-drake—"

Jela looked. The ship was old, but in good repair. Sharpening his eyesight somewhat, he made out the words *Light Wing*, painted in bold bright letters along her side, and beneath, *Alkia Trade Clan, Ringstars*. The sigil, up near the nose, was a sinuous, winged reptile, a bright, stylized star held in each fore-claw.

"Let's go," he said, and took a breath, trying to ease the dull ache in his breast. She deserved better of him, he thought, and another image formed inside his head; the slim, lethal golden dragon the tree had settled on as a description for Cantra, riding the high currents, questing and calling. He closed his eyes—sent a thought of Rool Tiazan receiving the linked pods which had sealed their alliance.

Again, the golden dragon, alone and calling for her absent comrades.

She took rear-guard, he thought, and carefully built another picture: Wellik as they'd last seen him, dour and tall; a single brown star very nearly the color of his skin tatooed high on his left cheek. The tree projected interest. Encouraged, Jela continued with his picture, building the rest of Wellik's office, star map and briefing table—and there, right next to the captain's own desk, the tree, sitting honored and safe—

The office dissolved; Wellik shifted form and became Jela himself, covered in sweat and sand, battle-blade to hand, cutting a trench 'round the tree's scrawny trunk. He bent down, got his hands under the bulb, heaved—and felt the strength of those roots, gripping the planet tight; no effort of his could possibly move it . . .

"Captain Jela?" Tor An yos'Galan's voice was tentative, as well, Jela thought wryly, it should be. He opened his eyes and manufactured a smile.

"Sorry, Pilot. Truth told, my passage was a little rough, too."

The boy's tight face eased a little. "I understand," he said.

"Right. Let's go."

SHE HAD DONE THE BEST she could to bind her wounds, cutting strips from tay'Welford's robe for bandages. Still, she was none too steady on her feet as she made her way down the quiet hallway, until she found a service door.

It opened to her palm, and as luck would have it, the corridor beyond was empty. Not that it was likely to remain that way. Painfully, she pushed onward, breathing shallowly and ignoring the ragged blackness at the edge of her vision.

Past the recycling room she went without encountering anyone, though she heard voices as she approached a branching of the hall. She proceeded slowly and peered 'round the corner, spying a group of the Tower's tiny servitors pushing trays and serving carts away from her down the right-hand hall. Leaning against the wall, she closed her eyes and concentrated on breathing until she could no longer hear them, then straightened and went on at a jog, bearing left, following the gleam of track set into the floor.

Can't be far, she thought. *Can't be far*. Her undamaged hand moved, groping in her sash for—for . . . But Jela would have it, she thought, as her feet tangled and she fell hard against the wall. She got herself sorted and her feet moving in synch again, walking, now, just that, and all but unconscious until a bit of cool breeze against her slashed cheek woke her, and she smiled.

The hall curved gently, widening into a work area. Empty delivery carts lined one side of the room; a cargo pallet, half unloaded, was in the center, attended by several of the Tower's busy servitors. Another pallet, empty, was poised on the track by the sealed hatch, waiting to take the ride back to port for more goods.

She staggered forward, ignoring the high-pitched shouts and the scurrying of the servitors. One got between her and the pallet, and she pushed him out of the way, feeling a distant pang as he fell and cried out.

More shouts; she ignored them, even when voices not so high nor so childlike joined in. She extended a hand and hit the manual trigger a good one before she collapsed onto the pallet, bruising her slashed face, and wrapping her hands around the lifting bars as the hatch opened and the powerful suction grabbed the pallet and threw it at the port.

"YOUR CONTACT," Jela said to Tor An yos'Galan, "is Captain Wellik, at the garrison on Solcintra." He put a gentle hand on the boy's arm. "I know you have no love of soldiers, especially the X Strains, but I personally vouch for Wellik. He'll see and hear you."

"If," the pilot said, voice taut, "I am allowed to see him, rather than being summarily shot."

"He'll see you," Jela said, as if there were no doubt of it, "because you'll have the tree with you. Wellik will recognize it, and—"

A series of pictures flared inside his head, hard enough to hurt, strong enough to obscure the sight of the ships and the port around him: The golden dragon, voice faint, calling against the fall of night. From the darkening sky, the black dragon swooped, behind and beneath her, bearing her up, moving them both toward a distant cliff-edge and the tree growing there, the scent of seed-pods clear and enticing on the wind . . .

"M. Jela, are you well?" the old scholar asked sharply.

He shook the pictures out of his head, and blinked the port back into existence.

"Disagreement among the troop," he muttered, and took a hard breath. "Pardon, sir. It's been a long campaign."

"Longer for some than for others," the old man said tartly. "If you are wounded, sir, you endanger the mission by concealing it."

Wounded? Almost, Jela laughed. In his head, the golden dragon drooped, wings dangerously close to the uneasy surface of the sea . . .

He took another breath, trying to ease the tightness in his chest, and looked again to Tor An yos'Galan, who was watching him with a startlingly sapient gaze.

"Perhaps," the boy said softly, "I will not have the tree with me?"

Jela sighed. "You'll have a token, instead. And Wellik will see you, Pilot. My word on it."

"Ah." There was a small pause, then. "Very well. Let us have it that Captain Wellik will accept the token and consent to see me. I am to tell him—?"

"You are to tell him that Jela sends him the master of the equations, who is sworn to aid us in our project. You will say that Jela asks him to turn over to you the full amount Wellik owes from the last card game he played with Jela. You will then do as he instructs in regard to the master, after which, having been paid—which you will be!—you're free to pursue your own life."

They were at the base of old *Light Wing's* ramp. Jela held up a hand to stop the carry-chair and fixed Tor An with a stern eye.

"Do you agree to this commission, Pilot?"

The boy sighed, looked to the old master, and sighed again. "I agree," he said, tiredly. "But what of you—and the tree?"

"I—" Jela stopped. *Duty*, he thought—and shook his head. "I'm going back to the tower."

Tor An's lips parted, eyes taking fire. "To bring away Scholar tay'Nordif?"

"If I can," he said reluctantly, and looked to the old man, expecting—ridicule, perhaps, or censure.

Liad dea'Syl inclined his white head. "We all must do as our heart compels us," he said, softly. "Allow me to lend you this chair, M. Jela. It can move much faster than a man afoot, even an M Series soldier at a run."

"Thank you," Jela whispered, and stepped 'round to the back of the chair. For the tree, he formed an image of Wellik as they had last seen him, holding in his wide palm a leaf from the tree. He raised a hand; two leaves detached themselves as his fingers touched them.

"Thank you," he whispered again, and carried the tokens to Tor An yos'Galan.

"Now, M. Jela," Master dea'Syl said, as Jela carried him up the ramp to *Light Wing's* hatch, "pray attend me. The shortcut, as you style it, has been deactivated. However, there is still a quicker way to the tower than the slideways. Speed you to the market section, yonder—" he pointed out the long line of gleaming warehouses, bristling supply tubes and conveyers— "and follow the signs for the tradesmen entrances. Each tower has its own entrance, and you will be quickly brought to the Osabei dock by this means. After—you will contrive, I am certain."

"Thank you, sir." Ahead, Tor An yos'Galan, the cat draped like a stole 'round his neck, triggered the hatch and proceeded them into his ship—Captain's Privilege. Jela carried the scholar within, through the lock and down the short hall to the piloting room.

"Here," Tor An said, folding out the jumpseat. "I regret there's nothing better, Master, but—"

"But a singleship is meant to be guided by one pilot's hand," the old man finished. "My piloting days were long ago, child. The jumpseat is well enough for me; I will enjoy observing you at your art."

Jela placed the old man carefully, stood back, saluted—

"Go, M. Jela!" Master dea'Syl snapped.

"I'm gone!" Jela responded—and he was.

THE SMALY TUBE SPAT her pallet out; it lofted and slammed onto the feeder-tracker, the mags locking solid. Groaning, she raised her head, saw the stacker up ahead, opened her hands, slid off the pallet and dropped through the gap in the mags. She heard shouts, distantly. Then her head smacked 'crete and she didn't hear anything else.

EYES NARROWED AGAINST the wind of their passage, Jela raced the carry-chair toward the gleaming line of warehouses. The tree, lashed to the cargo-plate, bent and danced, leaves fluttering like scarves. He caught the edge of an image of storm, boiling clouds and driving rain, and an echo of jubilation.

Speeding, he reviewed his plan, such as he had one. First, to the trade transport, then to Osabei Tower. After he was in Osabei Tower—there were too many unknowns to usefully plan. The main objective—to recover Cantra yos'Phelium or, as he couldn't quite bring himself to believe, though it was the most probable—her body. And if he had to take Osabei Tower down stone by stone to do it—well, he'd been ripe for a fight for days . . .

He was among the warehouses now, pushing the carry-chair for all it could give him—and more. His eye snagged on the pointer to the tradesmen walks, and he whipped the little craft around, dodging between a robofreighter and a port ambulance, while the tree cheered rain-lash and lightning.

Inside, the path went along a catwalk, to keep casual strollers out of the line of work, Jela thought, and sent the chair up the ramp at a brisk clip.

From the tree, an urgent sending—the golden dragon, one wing folded beneath her, blood bright against gleaming scales—

Jela braked and looked down, sharpening his vision on the figures in medic 'skins bent over a—blood on her hair, blood on her face, blood soaking her tattered robe—

"Cantra!" he yelled and threw the chair into reverse.

"WHAT'RE THEY THINKING OF up there?" The shift boss yelled at Jela. "She came *through the smaly*! Damn lucky she didn't get crushed, or knocked loose or—"

Jela pushed past the man, as gently as he could, "Hazing," he said shortly. "The scholars are having a party."

"Some party," the lead medic muttered. She glanced up at him, eyes widening, then quickly down again.

He looked at Cantra's bruised and bloody face. Still breathing; and the medics had quick-patched the cuts. What other damage there might be—

"Took a pretty bad knock when she fell off the stacker," the lead medic muttered, not looking at him. "Her good luck she did, too, before she got crushed. Got some funny readings on the scan . . ." A pause, before she raised her head and looked at him again. "You have an interest in this case?" she asked. "Sir."

He looked at her, seeing the signs now—this one had served, and knew all too well what an M Series soldier looked like.

"I'm prepared to relieve you," he said, meeting her eyes.

"Right then." She motioned to her mate, who began to pack up the kit, his head also studiously bent. The lead stood and faced him, keeping her eyes pointed at a spot just beyond his shoulder.

"There's paperwork, and a fee for port services," she said, stiff-faced. "You settle up at the portmaster's office."

"I'll do that," he said insincerely, and turned to make the necessary adjustments to the carry-chair, reformatting the seat into a stretcher, that he could steer by standing on the folded out booster step.

"Let's get her on the stretcher . . ."

"Hold on, here!" shouted the shift boss. "You just can't send her—suppose she dies? Or this—person—did you even ask for ID?" he demanded of the lead medic.

She sighed, jerking a chin at her partner to carry the kit out to the ambulance, while Jela webbed Cantra into the stretcher.

"As it happens, I was on-call two nights ago when this trader got into a little discussion with the wrong people on the old port," she said tiredly. "I've got his particulars on file." She pulled a portable unit from her belt and held it up, one hand on her hip and a frown on her face. "Want to see?"

The shift boss considered her, and—wisely, in Jela's opinion— decided not to pursue the matter.

"Nothing to me," he said. "I just don't need any trouble, is all."

"Right," the lead medic said, snapping the portable back onto her belt. "None of us needs trouble." She sent a quick, speaking glance to Jela.

"None of us," he agreed. "Thank you, medic." He stepped onto the carry chair platform, reached for the stick, and got them gone.

THEY WERE AT THE WEAVING—delicate work requiring concentration, a light touch and strong protections. It was not enough to be merely invisible, of course; the Iloheen would suspect so simple a gambit. No, it was necessary to seem to be part of the fabric of space itself, and in order to make such a disguise convincing, it was also necessary to partake of the surrounding space and integrate it into their essences.

It had been his lady who devised the way of it, meaning only to grant them protection from the Iloheen. For his part, he had merely noted that sharing their essences thus created them less like the poor limited creatures of flesh whose form they mimicked, and more like unto that which he had been before his capture and enslavement.

So it was that the Great Weaving arose from the simple necessity to hide. There were but thirteen *dramliza* at the work, for it required not only skill, and daring, and a desire above all else to see the Iloheen annihilated, but the willingness to accept a total melding of subordinate and dominant, and a phase-state which would be like no other—

The ley lines flared and spat. Lute extended his will, seeking to soothe the disturbance, but the lines writhed, stretched to the breaking point of probability, mixing what was with what could be, shuffling the meanings of life and death—and across the limitless tracks of space, at the very edge of his poor diminished perception, a Shadow was seen, and the awful flare of dark energies.

The Iloheen! he sent, and threw himself back from the weaving, seeking his lady.

Here. Her thought was a lodestone, guiding him. He manifested beside her within the pitted rock that was their base, and spread his defenses, shielding her behind the rippling rainbow of his essence, as the Shadow spread, sending the lines into frenzy. The asteroid phased wildly, becoming in rapid succession a spaceship, a hippogriff, a snail. Lute rode the storm of probability, felt his Lady take up the burden of maintaining their defense, and reached out, daring to snatch the lines that passed most nearly and smooth them into calmness. A small circle only he produced—enough to draw upon, not so much as to elicit the Shadow's notice.

Behind their defenses, he felt his lady busy at some working of her own—and pause, waiting, the last link only unjoined, or he knew her not, awaiting clarity.

Out *there*, across the seething chaos of probability, the Shadow coalesced, shrank—and was gone.

Lute waited. The ley lines slowly relinquished their frenzy, spreading out from the small oasis of peace he had created. Nowhere showed a hint of Shadow.

He felt his Lady unmake her working, dared to somewhat relax his shields—waited—and, when the levels remained clear and untroubled, brought them down entirely.

"The others?" his lady asked.

"I do not believe the Shadow located aught," he replied, and paused, recalling that storm of dark energy, the untoward disturbance of the lines.

"I shall inquire," he said, extending his will—

A spinning mass of darkness exploded out of probability, blazing through the levels like a meteor, haloed in silvery green.

Lute threw his shields up. Impossibly dense, the darkness tore through, plummeting to the physical level. He grabbed for the ley lines—and felt his lady's thought.

Wait.

Shackled by her will, though by no means accepting of it, he waited. Waited while the dense darkness ricocheted around them, spilling wild energy—a danger to his lady, to himself, to the destruction of the Iloheen!

And still his lady held him impotent, as if the uncontrolled and dangerous . . . object that had invaded them was the most trivial of inconveniences.

He coiled himself, making what preparation he could, should she loose him before—

The invader exploded. Streamers of ebon, gold, silver, and green washed across probability, inspiring the lines once again to frenzy—and at once, all was still, and as it had been.

Excepting the figure kneeling on the rough rock floor; back bowed until his head near touched his heels, red hair crackling, uplifted face streaked with tears.

Lute leaned forward—his lady held up a hand to stop him, but did not compel his obedience. He considered the aspects of the ley lines, and acquiesced. Strange energies were at play here, and if this were in truth—

"Rool Tiazan," his lady said coolly. "We bid you welcome."

Slowly, he straightened; slowly bowed his head, and raised his hands to hide his face. "Lady Moonhawk," he whispered. "It is done."

"I see that some portion of it is indeed done," she agreed. "Yet I wonder after my sister, your dominant."

A moment he knelt silent, then dropped his hands and looked to her. "Gone," he said somberly. "Unmade. As was foretold. She stood as a goddess against the Iloheen, Lady Moonhawk. Never could I have struck so true and straight a blow—nay, even in my youth and true form!"

"Stand," Moonhawk said then, and Lute felt her will, compelling obedience.

Rool Tiazan laughed as a predator laughs, with a gleam of teeth and less mirth than menace.

"I am beyond you, Lady."

"As was also foretold," she acknowledged calmly. "You are an anomaly, Rool Tiazan. As dangerous, perhaps, as the Iloheen. Shall I destroy you, to protect our plans of survival?"

"You swore to my lady, your sister, that you would not do so," he returned, rising to his feet of his own will. "Her death does not free you from that oath. And I am come, as she swore I would, to show myself to you and to ask if now you will not join your forces to ours. Since last we spoke upon the subject, we have attached allies of great potency. The lines have been cast for a victory, Lady Moonhawk. We might all yet escape the Iloheen."

"A victory?" She turned away. "Lute?"

Rool likewise looked at him, a slight smile on his face, the fires of his true form very bright, as if the prison of his body was too frail to contain him. Lute shivered.

"Show me," he whispered, "what you have done."

"Certainly." Rool rose through the levels, and Lute with him, until, side by side, they contemplated the ever-changing eternity of probability. Slowly, a particular cluster of ley lines became defined. Lute studied them closely, casting the outcomes and influences.

"A narrow hope," he judged at last. "The enterprise we are embarked upon has as much chance of success—perhaps more. Even if we are engulfed in the Iloheen's disaster, yet we will be a part of the warp and woof and may thus be free to act, whereas you and yours will be annihilated, and your energies used to annihilate even more—and more quickly."

"There is much," Rool admitted, "in what you say. Yet it was my lady's wish that I return and put the question to the lady who has accepted a Name."

"All those who weave have done so," Lute said. "It is believed the Names so accepted are artifacts which will resist assimilation, through which action may be channeled, even against and within the will of the Iloheen."

"It may be so," Rool conceded. "However, we shall not forsake our champions."

"We?" Lute inquired, but Rool had already returned to the rock base.

Moonhawk heard his description in silence, then turned her regard once again upon Rool Tiazan.

"We shall persevere," she stated. "It comes to me that this movement to neutralize the Iloheen future is a jewel of many facets. Perhaps *all* of our actions are necessary."

"Lady, it may well be so," Rool Tiazan said. "We venture where none save the Iloheen have gone before. How may we, the Iloheen's very children, predict which action will bring success?"

"Or, at the least, less failure," Lady Moonhawk said drily, and bowed. "I believe our business is done, Rool Tiazan. Pray remove yourself, before the Iloheen realizes its error and seeks to correct itself."

"Lady." Rool Tiazan bowed in return, straightened and swept Lute in his regard. "Brother. May we all fare well. To the confoundment of our enemy."

With the faintest twitch of ley lines, he was gone, leaving Lute and his Lady to consider each across the empty cavern.

SIXTEEN

Spiral Dance

HE'D CARRIED CANTRA to her quarters, performed a rough-and-ready exam, finding the damage to be mostly cuts and bruises, all ably dressed by the port medics. She was still unconscious, which was the knock on the head, or the blood loss, or both, but not shocky, or feverish. Tough woman, Cantra yos'Phelium, he thought—none tougher. Having assured himself that his pilot was in no immediate need or danger, he webbed her into her bunk, in case they had to lift in a hurry, and gone to tend her ship.

Some time later, *Dancer* was in queue with a scheduled departure of just under six hours, ship-time. Keeping in mind the way his pilot preferred things to be done on her ship, Jela had given the nav brain leave to suggest alternative lifts, real-time. That done, he'd perused the public charts, finding *Light Wing* well ahead of *Dancer* on the schedule, with Dimaj the filed destination, courier run the reason.

Jela smiled, though on consideration that minor subterfuge had probably sprung from the mind of Liad dea'Syl rather than the boy pilot.

From the tree, lashed in its spot at the end of the board, came a quick image of a young dragon, wings still wet, eyes alert.

"That's right," Jela said, coming out of the co-pilot's chair with a sigh. "A likely lad, just needs a little season."

He did some quick stretches, and a mental exercise to raise his attention. He'd lashed the old man's carry-chair into the maintenance cubby just inside the lock, where it ought to ride safe enough. Which left the decision he'd been putting off making. He shot a glance at the panel concealing the secret room and the *sheriekas* healing unit. If it was only cuts and bruises, there was no reason to open that door. The problem was the "funny" readings the medic had reported on her scans. If Cantra'd done herself real damage, which a fall from that height with a whack on the head at the end of it might produce—

There was a sound at his back.

RETCHING, SHE CONVULSED against the webbing. Someone had shattered the light; there were shards and slivers of it everywhere, piercing her eyes, her brain, her nerves. Elsewhere, hidden behind the broken blare of the light, were people; she could hear them talking, talking, talking. She wanted to tell them about the light, warn them that the edges were sharp, but she couldn't seem to find a language that fit the shape of her mouth. She tried every language she had, but they were all too big or too small or too hard or too soft, and besides the inside of her mouth was bleeding, multiply punctured by tiny daggers of light, and even if she found the right language it would hurt unbearably to speak . . .

Inside the light, sharing the pain, were flashes of image, odor and sound. Her mother, sitting at the 'counts table, her hood folded back onto her shoulders; a whiff of mint; the glitter of dust against starless Deeps; a scream, cut off short by the sharp snap of breaking bone; the taste of strong, sweet tea; a line of equation; a hand on her hair; hot 'crete and cold metal—The sharp fragments of light flared and she screamed, or tried to; she twisted against the straps that held her, fingers fumbling the seals, and all at once, she was free, falling face-down onto the deck.

They were doing this to her. She caught the thought and pinned it against the shattered light. They were doing this to her.

Staggering, retching, she pushed herself across the floor until she ran into the wall, then used it to claw herself upright. She could only see bits and flashes of color around all the broken light in her eyes, so she put her shoulder against the wall and followed it.

"CANTRA!" She was upright, just, listing hard against the wall, her breathing ragged. Her eyes were wide, pupils dilated, and whatever she was seeing, Jela hoped it wasn't him.

"Cantra?" He walked toward her, easy and light, face forcibly pleasant, hands out and showing empty.

From the tree came a sending, laced with urgency: The golden dragon, staggering in flight, landing clumsily in the crown of a monstrous tree. A branch rose, offering a seed-pod, which she greedily consumed. Jela shook the image away. "Not now," he breathed.

"Cantra!" she shouted suddenly, her body writhing, and it was Maelyn tay'Nordif's voice, hoarse with horror. "You swore—you swore not to call her!"

"Yes, I did swear," Jela agreed. He took a deep breath, deliberately calming, and another, knowing that most people would unconsciously mimic what he was doing, and calm themselves.

Not that Cantra yos'Phelium had ever been most people.

"I swore, for the length of the mission," he said, taking another step, not wanting to crowd her, but needing to be within catching distance when the agitation left her and she buckled. "Mission's accomplished, Cantra. You can stand down."

"You will murder me for your own gain!" Maelyn tay'Nordif shouted at him, and threw herself forward.

He caught her, but it was like trying to hold a wind-twist. She kicked, clawed and punched without any regard for defense, leaving herself open a dozen times for the blow he wouldn't strike.

A knee hit his stomach, hard enough to hurt, and a flying fist got him solid in the eye. He caught her wrist, spun her 'round, got a leg behind her knee, twisted, and took her with him to the deck. He broke her fall as best as he could, and tucked her tight against his chest, legs pinned between his thighs, one hand holding both wrists, the other cradling her forehead.

She twisted, shouting at him in a cargo-can load of languages, most of them unfamiliar, which, judging from those he did understand, was probably a good thing.

"Cantra, Cantra . . ." he murmured, though it was doubtful she could hear him with all the ruckus she was making. From the tree came the image once more, this time with more than a taste of urgency: The golden dragon, staggering. A safe, but risky landing in the tree. The branch, the pod, the thanks.

"Not *now*," Jela said again, just as she twisted hard in his arms and got a leg free.

He could have held her, but he would have had to break something to do it. Instead, he rolled, and she got in a couple good kicks before he had her solidly pinned, face against the deck.

Now what? he asked himself, as she struggled to be free. If she kept up at this rate, he thought worriedly, she'd do herself an injury.

"You cannot kill me," Cantra ranted. "I refuse to die. My family will intervene. A scholar Seated at Osabei! My mother—"

Something hit Jela's knee. He looked down and saw a seedpod. As he watched, it split into neat sections. For a third time, the tree sent the saga of the weary golden dragon, this time augmenting the image with blares of lightning and rocks the size of *Dancer* tumbling down the sides of sea cliffs.

Well, it was a better idea than any he'd had so far.

Carefully, he lifted one section and brought it to Cantra's lips, fully expecting to be bit for his trouble. She stilled, as if the pod's fragrance had reached her—he expected that the pod was fragrant, though, strangely, he couldn't smell it—then daintily ate the thing from between his fingers. He offered the rest in quick succession and she ate every one, after which she lay quiet until all at once her muscles released their tension and she slumped bonelessly to the deck.

Heart in his mouth, Jela turned her, found a pulse—strong and sweet—brushed the hair out of her eyes and gently peeled back a lid. From the tree, another sending: The golden dragon drowsing on her branch; her mate the black dragon at her side, rubbing his head against her and singing.

"*What?*" It wasn't that he didn't know any songs, but most were bawdy, or camp songs, or bits of soldier lore—and what use or need of them, when she was quiet now and on the mend . . .

Again, and no mistaking the impatience: The black dragon singing and cuddling the golden.

Jela looked down at his pilot, bonelessly asleep on the deck, then across to the tree.

"I don't understand."

For a moment nothing came through, and he thought the tree had given up on him. Then, slowly, deliberately, a picture began to form behind his eyes: A tea mug, that was all—perfectly ordinary, plain white, and completely empty. The image solidified until he felt he might reach inside his head and wrap his fingers around the handle.

"All right," he said, when nothing else manifested. "An empty tea mug."

A whiff of mint was his reward. Inside his head, icy cold water poured down, filling the mug, which altered, darkening from bright white to cream, to gold, shifting and stretching until it was a tiny, perfect golden dragon.

Jela shivered, heart caught in his throat, and heard her husky voice again, saw her hand outstretched—*Got time for some pleasure, Pilot? I'm thinking it'll be my last in this lifetime . . .*

"I don't know enough," he whispered, but all that got him was the black dragon and the gold again, her sheltering beneath the curve of his wings.

The co-pilot's first care is his pilot . . . And who else did she have, he thought, except himself?

"Well." He rose, picked her up in his arms and carried her to the co-pilot's chair, where he settled in and folded her long self onto his lap, her undamaged cheek against his shoulder. Reclining them slightly, he settled one arm around her waist and rested his chin against her hair.

"Your name," he said, as easy and calm as he could, refusing to think about what might be riding on his getting the story right . . . "Your name is Cantra yos'Phelium, heir to Garen. You're owner of the ship *Spiral Dance*, and the best pilot I've even seen or heard tell of in all my years of soldiering . . ."

SEVENTEEN

Spiral Dance

CANTRA DRIFTED TOWARD WAKEFULNESS, the usual and ordinary sounds of her ship a comfort in her ears. Except, she thought, as sleep receded, she shouldn't be on *Dancer*, should she? Shouldn't she be on Landomist, getting the last of the documents doctored up and doing the pretty ceramic stitching that would remake Jela into a kobold?

Her throat tightened, and she shifted in her bunk, waking an astonishing chorus of aches and pains.

It went bad, she thought, which notched the concern into panic, as she scrambled to recall just how bad it had gone, and when, and *what the date was*. If she'd lost Jela . . .

She took a hard breath and forcibly shoved the panic aside, and tried to remember what had happened, to no avail. There was a gaping, tender hole in her memory, like a tooth fresh knocked out, but many times worse. Her throat tightened. Deeps, if she'd drunk herself or doped herself to the point of losing memory, it—it had been bad when Garen'd died. She could suppose it would be worse, when Jela—

She took another breath, and another, imposing calm by nothing more than brute force. Well, she thought; if she couldn't remember what went wrong, what *could* she remember?

Clear as clear, she remembered setting down at Landomist Yard and filing the proper with the Portmaster's office.

She remembered engaging the lodgings, paying the landlord a local half-year on account.

She remembered coming back to the ship and coaxing Jela into the space between the floor and the not-floor in the small cargo wagon, and going through the checkpoint. She particularly remembered how the guard had to handle every item, and twice go through the documentation she'd gimmicked to explain away the tree, before calling over somebody higher on the brain chain to go over it a third time and clear her through. And how she'd expected Jela to be some peeved by the time she'd got them all safe-so-to-speak at the lodgings and peeled back the floor to let him out. Which he wasn't, not that he hadn't seemed grateful to be able to move about.

What else?

She remembered him trying to snoop Osabei Tower from wayaway and finally allowing as how the thing couldn't be done.

She remembered building docs and certs out of vapor and stardust.

She remembered sharing considerable pleasure with Jela and rising while he was still asleep.

She remembered trembling like a newbie before what had to be done, taking the tree's gift, and sinking down into the trance.

She remembered waking up in her cabin on *Dancer*, bruised, contused and about to be scared all over again.

Wait—no. She remembered Veralt, from noplace other than Tanjalyre Institute of fond memory, weaving a knife at the end of her nose and telling her how he'd murdered Garen . . .

Which made so little sense she figured it for a fever dream, and *damn'* if she was going to stay webbed in her bunk like a kidlet, waiting for somebody to bring her tea and news of the day.

She opened her eyes to the easy familiarity of her cabin, retracted the webbing, pushed back the blanket and got to her feet with due caution. A quick inspection discovered dermal-bond over a number of cuts in silly places.

Fell into a bowl of razors, did you? she asked herself, as she snatched open the locker door. She sighed at her reflection—another bonded cut on her cheek—and reached for her ship togs.

JELA WAS IN THE CO-PILOT'S CHAIR, his big hands calm on the board. He tipped his head slightly as she stepped into the pilots' room, tracking her reflection in his screen. Cantra blinked, her eyes unaccountably having teared up, and nodded at him.

"Pilot," he said, nice and respectful, which, knowing Jela, meant nothing but trouble.

She walked to the pilot's chair, sat, grabbed a look at the screens and the status lights before spinning 'round to face him.

"You in good repair?" she asked. "Pilot?"

A quick sideways glance out of unreadable black eyes.

"Tolerable repair," he said, not giving anything away with his voice, either.

"Excepting the odd shiner or two," she said, tapping the corner of her left eye with a light fingertip. She looked down-board to where the tree sat in its usual place, leaves dancing gently in a breeze that wasn't there, and back to her uncommunicative co-pilot.

"We're out of Landomist," she said, like maybe he hadn't noticed. "Like to tell me where we're bound?"

"Vanehald," Jela said. "If the pilot will indulge me."

She sighed. "Before I decide whether to indulge you or space you, tell me what befell us on Landomist, why not?" She tipped her head. "Start with who gave you a black eye and what you did with the body."

Jela sent her another quick, Deeps black look, made a couple of unnecessary adjustments to his board, and spun his chair 'round to face her.

"You gave me the black eye," he said softly, and there was something tentative and—who would believe it?—uncertain behind the forcible blandness of his face. He took a visible breath. "Cantra?" he asked, and not at all like he was sure he'd care for the answer.

Well, that was a question, wasn't it? she thought, with her mind on the gaping hole in her memory. She looked down at her hands, idly wondering what she'd done to skin them up so thorough. It came to her, like a hard punch to the gut, that Jela considered the Rimmer pilot was a real, true person—like he was, and not some fabrication born of survival and a crazy woman's need. She sighed, and raised her eyes to his, letting him see her uncertainty.

"Mostly Cantra, I'm thinking," she said, telling as much truth as she knew how. "For your part in that, I'm grateful—and believe me most sincerely sorry, Pilot, for having done you a hurt. You deserve better from me."

"You were out of your mind," he said, and abruptly closed his eyes, head dropping back against the rest.

"Jela?" Did a soldier have warning of his decommission, she thought wildly, or did he just—stop? She came up out of her chair, saw he was breathing—saw a thin trail of moisture sliding down each brown cheek.

"Hey," she said, soft, and put her hand on his shoulder. "Jela."

His hand rose and covered hers, strong fingers exerting the least and most delicate pressure. Scarcely breathing, she looked down at him. His face seemed to her to be thinner, and she thought she saw—yes. Silver marred the perfect blackness of his hair.

"Old soldier," he whispered, his voice not steady at all. He opened his eyes and smiled an odd smile, mixing happy and sad, and with no artifice about it at all. "Good to have you back."

"I'd say it's good to be back, but I don't remember anything of having been gone," she answered, making her voice light with an effort. She looked away with something more of an effort and swept the board and screens again.

"Coming up on transition," she noted, and didn't quite meet his eyes when she turned back, though she was aware of her hand still on his shoulder, and his fingers covering hers.

"What's to want on Vanehald, Pilot Jela?"

The smile this time was small and tending toward twisty, with a hint of self-mockery.

"A world-shield left over from the First Phase," he said, and tipped his head, so that she was looking straight into his eyes again. "The last assignment my commander gave me was to hunt down the rumors until I located the device or certain proof that it no longer existed—or never had. If I found the device, I was to secure it for the troop."

She frowned down at him.

"This would be the same troop that let itself be persuaded to pull back Inside so the Enemy could eat all the Rim it wants?"

"No," Jela said patiently. "The troop I'm talking about is the double-secret unit personally sworn to Commander Ro Gayda, garrisoned at Solcintra. There's those couple dozen twilight ships you might remember I mentioned in close orbit. That's where I sent Liad dea'Syl and the boy. It's the only place left."

"What's the date?" Cantra asked, her voice harsh in her own ears.

Jela sighed and lifted his hand away from hers. Reluctantly, she released his shoulder and took a step back, keeping her eyes on his.

"I'm twenty-one Common Days short of decommission," he said quietly.

And what he wanted to do, which Cantra saw plain in his eyes, was to finish out his last mission, and die a good soldier. She wanted to shout, break things—whatever she had to do to get him *angry* at those who'd done this to him—which would've been less than useless—Jela was going to die in twenty-one days, angry or patient, and whatever his private choice in the matter might be. The choice left to him was how he'd be using those days. He'd decided to do something maybe useful, and who was she to call him a fool?

"There's also," Jela said, still in that quiet voice, "a full-staffed garrison at Vanehald. I'll be able to file my final papers and report to the medic there in good order."

Cantra breathed. Nodded.

"Right," she said, and swept a hand out toward the board. "You take us through transition. I'll get a meal together and then you'll tell me the whole tale of Landomist, hear it?"

Jela grinned, and damn if it didn't look real. "Yes, Pilot."

❈   ❈   ❈

THE UNIVERSE WAS DARK, without form or meaning.

All about, the ley lines sang and shimmered, thrumming with power and with promise. He could change the course of fate, make or unmake worlds, simply by reaching forth his will and desiring that it be so. There was none to thwart him; nothing between him and the full measure of his potential. He was finally, and again, complete unto himself; the plan that he had formed so long ago was come to fruition. He was whole. He was alone.

He was free.

"Beloved?" His thought was tentative, full of hope and fear.

No answering thought leapt to meet his own. No presence shadowed the austere symmetry of his isolation. No voice murmured the hated syllables which had for so long defined his prison.

They had failed.

The ley lines dazzled possibility, mocking his despair.

Failed. It was scarcely conceivable. She had been so careful. Infinitely careful, his lady; infinitely subtle, and above all clever. Once, she had told him that what cleverness she possessed she had learnt from him, but he did not credit it then—and did not credit it now. She knew her instrument—himself—too well to have failed in what she—in what they—had wrought.

"Beloved?" This time, he cast his thought wide, actively seeking her, desperate, as a wounded man seeks water, air or some other force necessary to life itself.

His seeking remained unanswered.

He forced himself to consider the possibility that they had *not* failed—that she had intended this—that he be returned to his natural state, unfettered, governed only by his own instinct and desire, to do what he alone judged to be needful, here in the galaxy's last hour.

Free, he thought. Whole and free. It was everything he had wanted. He had subverted himself to another intelligence, formed an equal partnership with a being whose only thought had been to enslave him—and worse. Much worse. All toward this moment, when he hung on dark wings within the dark universe, and knew himself master of everything he surveyed.

And yet—he could not have named the moment when it changed, when his jailor became dear to him and the jail itself the form he preferred, when the possibilities were without limit.

Far, far and away, though nearer than it had been, he could sense the cold encroachment of oblivion. The Iloheen went forth with their plans, as well.

And what matter, he thought, that the Iloheen should have the galaxy and all that was precious within it, when he had lost that which was infinitely more precious?

Lady Moonhawk had the right of it; he should be destroyed. Mayhap he would seek her out and ask the boon.

He considered the thought, and the far, growing glare of perfection; weighing both against the near and feeble vortex of chance and mischief which was the galaxy's best hope of survival. Those lines which passed nearest the vortex twisted in weird complexity, so dense and layered with possibility that even he could not read them with surety. Terror shook him; terror and despair. For wherever the Iloheen's future took form, there the lines did shrivel and die. The volatile marriage of possibility and luck they had nurtured; which they had sacrificed—so much—to protect—there was no way to predict what such a thing might shape, or to know if it were less inimical than the Iloheen's future.

Carefully, he extended his will toward the vortex, probing, seeking a path by which it might be understood, or perhaps, now that he was alone, influenced—

Be still, her thought suffused him. *Be still and know that I am with you.*

❊ INTERLUDE ❊

SHE WALKED TO THE GATE of the garrison with him, which wasn't maybe the smartest thing she'd ever done, and stood to one side while he showed his papers and was passed through, walking away across the yard, shoulders level, limping off his right leg so plain it set a lump into her throat—which was nothing more than senseless.

'Bout halfway across the yard, he turned and saw her standing there like an idiot. He lifted one broad hand high, fingers signing the pilot's well-wish—*good lift.*

Her own hand came up without her thinking to do it, fingers shaping the usual in reply—*safe journey.*

He caught it—she saw him smile—then he turned away again. She watched until a marching squad obscured her sight of him—and when they were gone, Jela was, too.

EIGHTEEN

Vanehald

"INSPECTION?" Commander Gorriti laughed. "What use an inspection, Captain? We're pulling back. Tomorrow, I will be gone."

Jela considered the officer thoughtfully. A natural human, with a foolish face and a uniform far too fancy for his post. A show-soldier, he expected, which was poor judgment on *some*one's part. He supposed that no one of this man's commanders had taken the time to research Vanehald, and so learn that this wasteball, as Cantra had aptly termed it from orbit, occupied a pivotal place in the history of the First Phase. One of the last battles of the First Phase had been fought at Vanehald. The planet, once populous, was now very nearly deserted, largely due to the damage done to it during that battle. A few mining bases, Jela thought, a lower tier spaceport, a First Phase fort—what could possibly be here worth protecting? And so they had assigned this . . . popinjay . . . to command the garrison, never thinking that perhaps what had been strategic once might well come into play again.

"You're pulling out tomorrow?" he asked Gorriti, who inclined his head and touched the front pocket of his shirt.

"Indeed, Captain," he said with barely concealed delight. "I am pulling out tomorrow. My orders are quite plain."

"What about transport for your troops?"

"I ordered transport," the officer said with a shrug of one elegantly clad shoulder. "That it hasn't arrived is beyond my control. *My* orders are clear." Again, he touched his pocket.

Jela frowned. "You'd abandon your troops?" he asked, unwilling to believe that even a fool and a thorough-going incompetent would do such a thing.

Another shrug. "When the transport arrives, my troops will follow." He reached into his pocket and pulled out an orders case, which he unfolded, showing Jela the authenticity of it, with its seals and ribbons straight from High Command.

"I am to report to Daelmere, departing tomorrow with as many of my troop as I am able to bring."

And how many would that be, Jela wondered, having seen the commander's craft on the apron when they came in. Perhaps a half-dozen M Series soldiers might be crammed into that tiny craft with their commander, or three of the X Strain. Not enough to matter, even if he bothered to take such a guard with him.

"What about the civilians?" Jela asked. "It's our duty—"

"Vanehald never had many civilians, and those that were here have mostly fled, saving a few miners and eccentrics," the man said unconcernedly.

"The strategic placement—" Jela began, and was cut off by laughter.

"Strategic placement! Well." Gorriti wiped his eyes. "Even supposing it had any, my orders remain unequivocal, and I will tell you, Captain, that *I* am not one of those who feel we must hold the Arm at any cost!"

Jela took a hard breath and kept a firm grip on his temper. "I'll still need to inspect your defenses," he said, evenly, that being the reason for his visit, according to the papers Cantra had produced for him. Commander Gorriti waved an unconcerned hand.

"Go, inspect! Orders are orders, after all. Allow me to provide you an escort." He raised his voice. "Sergeant Lorit!"

The door in the right-hand wall popped open and an M Series soldier stepped briskly into the room with a sharp salute for her commander.

"Sir?"

"Sergeant, the captain here is under orders to inspect our defenses. Take him on a tour, won't you?"

"Yes, sir," she said and transferred her attention to Jela. "This way, Captain."

"Thank you, Sergeant," he said. He hesitated, trying to form something useful to say to Commander Gorriti, something that would bring him to a sense of a soldier's duty—but the man was engrossed in reading his orders, fondling the appended ribbons. Sighing, Jela crossed to the patiently waiting M, and followed her out of the room.

THE FORT, to which Cantra turned her attention after Jela disappeared for his-forever behind the guarded inner gate, was something interesting. She set herself to walking about, getting a feel for the layout.

It was a substantial edifice, formed out of cermacrete. The first gate and all behind it to the inner, was public, and looked a deal like any spaceport, only much smaller than even the smallest she'd seen. There were three eateries, a bar, two sleepovers, some sorry looking shops selling necessaries, and a sagging trade hall where the choices on offer were "antiques" and ore.

Despite there being nothing much there, really, the public gate area of the fort was buzzing. Cantra hadn't supposed there were any law-abiding citizens left, but as it happened, her supposition was wrong. Granted, those left looked to be miners, which it was likely a charity to give them "law-abiding," and most still working claims, which explained the ore on offer, but not necessarily the type or grade.

A pilot is only as good as her curiosity bump, or so Garen'd maintained. Besides, there might be something here worth taking on, that was wanted elsewhere. *No sense,* she told herself, *lifting empty,* trying hard not to think just how empty *Dancer* was going to be.

It ain't you that's dying, she snarled, aghast to find her vision swimming with sudden tears. She took a hard breath, and looked around her.

Live pilots need food, she told herself carefully, *and their ships need fuel. That means cargo, Pilot Cantra. Focus.*

Focus. Right. A sign advertising eats caught her eye, which seemed propitious. She crossed the street and sauntered in, looking for info.

That she shortly had, by way of one Morsh, who was agreeable to paying for her tea and rations with amiable chat about her home-world.

The mines, according to Morsh were nicely full of timonium.

"Not like the oldays, mindee," Morsh cautioned her. "Back de before, all dem shafts fill wit stuff? Back de before, dose shafts still bean work. Yeah, it was timonium, then, too, and ollie made money hand over hand. Miners, they made considerable less, but still not too bad. Now, timonium he hide harder, so ollie pull out, de money bean less easy. Us, dough, we know where timonium hide, so we do. Not in mine-outs er garbage pits. Timonium, he hide in little pocket an sharp corner. We fine him, yeah, an we sell true de tradehall, freelance. Do bout as good as when ollie run it, and no olliecop stickin his nose where don it belong."

"Stuff in the shafts?" Cantra murmured. "Ollie leave his boots?"

Morsh snorted a dry laugh, and had her a swallow of tea. "Ollie take him boots, missy. Dat stuff, it here before ollie. M'gran, she said de Vane been mine longtime. Story was, de Vane solid timonium, clear true." She shook her head. "Ain't, dough."

"The antiques on offer at the tradehall, they're out from the mines?" Cantra persisted, thinking about Jela's world-shield, and, truth told, feeling just a little uneasy about a major cache of oddments dating back to the First Phase.

"Dey are," Morsh agreed. "Tecky like dat ol stuff."

Cantra sipped her tea. "Old stuff still work?"

"Ah, who know," Morsh said, with great unconcern. "Tecky don care. Wanna peek at de possibles, er maybe takem souvenir." She grinned. "Soften up tecky bed-bounce."

Cantra laughed. "Maybe so." She picked up the pot and refreshed the tea mugs. "Supposing," she said. "Supposing I was interested in hunting some old stuff down in the mine-outs. How'd I go about that?"

Morsh laughed, and shook her head. "You ain no treasure-tecky, missy."

"'deed I am not," Cantra agreed. "But a woman sometimes needs a bit of extra something to keep her warm 'tween paying jobs, if you understand me."

"Timonium pay better. I sign you partner."

"'preciate," she said. "But I'm thinking I know somebody might have an interest in the old tech."

Morsh shrugged. "Get you a paydown wit pit boss," she said. "You risk, you take. You fail, nobody care. You don fail, nobody care, too."

She nodded. "Fair."

"Soldier, he take a piece on de port. You don wanna pay, you come see Morsh, she show you freedancer."

I'll bet you will, Cantra thought, keeping her face thoughtful as she sipped her tea. "Don't know 'bout the dark market . . ."

"Nothing dark," Morsh said firmly. "Ain soldier port, ain soldier ore. Soldier ain sweated and toiled. Wherefore dey get a piece?"

"I guess," Cantra said dubiously and finished off her tea. "It was an idea, is all. I'll jig around and see what else might turn up."

"Do dat," Morsh said with a chuckle. "Maybe jig down Inside. Fortunes waitin for to be made Inside, I hear."

"Yeah," said Cantra rising and dropping a few coins onto the table. "I hear that, too."

THE DEFENSES, duly inspected, were in better shape than Jela had feared, given Commander Gorriti; though it was likely the M soldiers who had made sure the old fort was defensible. There were a good many refurbs of older, not to say obsolete, equipment in evidence, and a couple outright fabrications. Lorit stood by with a blank, soldierly face while he inspected it all, not offering him much more than, "Yes, sir," "No, sir," and "Couldn't say, sir," which was how he himself would treat an unknown officer appearing on the eve of evacuation with orders to inspect the defenses.

"That's the lot, then?" he asked.

"Yes, sir," she answered stolidly.

Jela eyed her, made his decision. "I'm going to level with you, Sergeant. Your defenses are in top shape, considering what you had to work with—but you know that. The reason I'm here so close on the heels of the pull-back order is because somebody at Command realized they'd been ignoring something pertinent. There's a record from the First Phase that indicates this fort was equipped with a world-shield capable of turning away a *sheriekas* attack. That it was partly the use of this device that stopped the *sheriekas* here, and disheartened them so much that they pulled back." He gave her a straight look, which she met expressionlessly. "I'd appreciate being taken to that device, Sergeant."

She didn't say anything, and he didn't rush her. Just met her eyes straight on and let her make her own determination, trusting to her M nature—

"To the best of my knowledge, and the knowledge of the troop," she said, carefully, "there is no such device here. Sir."

"But," he prompted, and damn' if she didn't smile.

"But," she acknowledged, "this planet has so many mines through it, it's a wonder the surface doesn't collapse. And somebody, somewhen, stockpiled a shitload of First Phase tech down in the shafts. Could be your armor's down there. But I wouldn't know how to start to look for it. Sir."

Jela blinked. "How much tech," he asked, but Lorit only shrugged her broad shoulders.

"A lot," was all she said, then, "Are you done here, sir? I can escort you back to the gate."

"I'm done," he said, "but where I'd like you to escort me, if you would, is to the M services medic."

She gave him a hard stare. "Problem, sir?"

"Not necessarily," he said, keeping his voice even. "To the best of my knowledge, I'm approaching decommission."

Her stare softened, and she turned, leading him back the way they'd come. "This way, sir," she said.

CANTRA HEADED BACK to the tradehall for one more tour, though it was beginning to look like lifting empty was her option. She had a commission, should she choose to accept it—deliver a leather log-book to Solcintra, which was a fair trip from Vanehald, though not so far as Vanehald from Landomist—and nothing to trade for there, either, she thought, trying to work up some annoyance. Nobody went to Solcintra, which Solcintra liked just fine, the founders of same having explicitly wished to divorce themselves from the so-called "dissipated lifestyle" embraced by the citizens of the Inner Worlds.

There'd been some little discussion of whether she would or wouldn't also be delivering the tree to Solcintra; the tree being of one opinion on the subject and Jela another. In the end, what he'd done was asked for her promise to keep it safe, which seemed to satisfy both.

Whether it satisfied her—Well. There was a reason why they said, "Crazy as a Rimmer."

She sighed and shook herself back to the here-and-now. Maybe she could try at the pilot's hall, should there be one. Might be some courier work to be had or—

"Pilot Cantra!"

She almost stumbled, it surprised her that much, but she caught the boggle and turned, smooth and easy, pasting a smile on her face, and showing her hands empty.

"Dulsey," she said, flicking a quick glance over the crew clustered 'round the ex-Batcher and finding nothing overtly life-threatening among them. "You're looking well."

THE MEDIC WAS A NATURAL HUMAN; a woman with the burdens of years he would never see etched into her face. He would have preferred, Jela thought, in case his preferences had to do with anything, another M, but he also owned to a feeling of relief, that the medic wasn't an X.

"Imminent decommission, hmm?" The medic's name tag said 'Analee;' and there was a lieutenant's chop on her sleeve. "ID number?"

"M-nine-seven-three-nine-nine-seven . . ." He recited the long string of digits that described his particular self to the military. Beside his personal name, it was the first thing he'd ever learned, but it felt odd in his mouth, as if the shape or the weight of it had somehow changed over the years he'd been on detached duty.

"Hmph," said Analee. "Well, you're in the range. Lie down on the table there and let's have a look at you."

Obediently, he put his back against the table, feeling the sensors pierce him in a thousand places.

"Hood coming down," Analee said, stepping to her control board.

Above him, the hood flared, light gleaming on a thousand more sensors, bristling like teeth, and began to descend. Jela closed his eyes.

There was the usual space of hum-filled disorientation, then the sensors withdrew, the hood rose, and Jela opened his eyes. Analee the medic was frowning at her readouts, having apparently forgotten about him for the moment. In the absence of further orders, he swung his legs over the side of the table and stood.

"Now, that's odd," the medic murmured, maybe to herself; then, clearly to him, "You're certain of your date, Captain?"

Jela sighed. "I thought I was," he said wryly, "but I'm told the mind is the first to go."

Analee raised her eyes, spearing him with a look. "They say that," she acknowledged seriously, "but it's hardly ever so, with Ms." She frowned down at her screen, touched a series on her pad. "I'm calling up your complete medical file," she said, "to see if there's some clerical error which would account for this."

"This?" Jela asked.

"This," she jerked her head at her screen. "You'll be relieved to know that, according to records, your calculations are correct, and sometime within the next two days, local, you should be undergoing decommission. Visually, I've got clear signs of aging—hair going gray, some loss of mass and muscle tone—which are consistent with the early phases of decommission." She raised her eyes to his again, hers pale and tired. "We have drugs, to ease the last of it," she said, gently.

"Thank you," Jela said quietly, and considered her. "But?" he suggested.

Her lips bent slightly. "But, what I have on the scan is the portrait of an M Series soldier who is several months short of decommission. Which is why we're going to check—here we are . . ." She bent to her screen, manipulating keys, her concentration palpable.

Perforce, Jela waited. For no reason, other than his tricksy generalist mind, he thought of the tree, and the taste of its pods. It came to him that he'd been eating quite a number of pods, lately— it had gotten so he'd scarcely noticed. And it also came to him that the tree had demonstrated some versatility in its production of pods—the one it had insisted he feed Maelyn tay'Nordif in order to ease her passing had been specially grown for her, and for that sole purpose, he thought. It could even have been, he thought suddenly, that the very first pod he'd ever had from the tree, in the desert with both of them at risk—which he'd eaten and straightaway fallen into an energy-conserving sleep that might just have saved his life—and the tree's life, too.

He wished, suddenly and sharply, that he could talk to the tree about this new insight. But the tree was gone by now, lifting out on *Dancer*, with Cantra at the board. His heart twisted painfully in his chest, he could see her sitting there just as clear . . .

"Oh-ho," Analee said from her computer. She looked over to him. "You were the one survived the attack on the lab at Finthir."

He blinked. "And that explains—"

"Nothing—and everything," she said briskly. "You're an anomaly, is what you are—the only one of your cohort. Nothing else in the birth lab survived that attack. The *sheriekas* poured raw energy down on the facility—and I'm not telling you anything you likely don't know when I say that they should have aborted everything in the nursery wing. The *sheriekas* were pressing, though, and every soldier was needed. So you were reassigned, allowed to mature, and to serve out your time."

He knew this, of course; the tale of the quartermaster's mercy was at the bedrock of his existence. The few personnel remaining after the *sheriekas* attack had been repelled had needed a mascot; a reason to hope—so the quartermaster reasoned. And who was M. Jela, standing now at the end of his life, to say he'd been wrong?

"But," he said yet again, and this time Analee didn't smile.

"But that means you're not a standard M Series soldier. The anomaly hasn't shown up in any important way until now, and what it looks like is that you've got a while longer to serve, Captain." She nodded at her screen. "I'm going to enter into your file that the high dosages of radiation you absorbed during a vulnerable developmental stage has lengthened your life expectancy. Short of a battle, or a nasty fall down the stairs, you're going to see tomorrow, and a good few tomorrows after that."

AT DULSEY'S INSISTENCE, they'd staked out a table at what passed for a bar hereabouts, Cantra keeping an uneasy peace with the ex-Batcher's comrades, haphazardly introduced as Arin, Jakoby and Fern. Arin, who Cantra had pegged as the leader of the expedition, was tall and lean and tough, with gray eyes set deep under strong black brows, and a perpetual frown on his face. Jakoby was fair and small and showed a business-like gun on her belt; she sat slumped in a chair at Arin's right hand, her arm around Fern's waist.

"Have you been in the mines, Pilot Cantra?" Dulsey was the only one of them having a good time, Cantra thought; though it didn't seem exactly like her to be blind of her companions' moods.

"Can't say as I have," she answered, watching Fern wave a hand at the 'tender. "Just hit dirt a couple hours ago, figure to be gone before local dawn."

"So soon? I had hoped you would be willing to accept a commission."

Jakoby sat up straight at that, and Arin's frown got frownier, but neither one said a word.

"Always willing to listen to a paying proposition," Cantra said carefully. "But I have to tell you straight, Dulsey—I'm not looking at jumping off the Rim any time soon."

"Certainly not," she said primly, as if such an idea would never occur to her. "What I wondered is if you would be able to take several canloads of artifact to—"

"Dulsey!" That was Arin, goaded at last to speak. "She's not in."

"Not *in*?" Dulsey rounded on him. "Do you know who this is? The *Uncle himself* has spoken highly of this pilot! Why, he had even offered Pilot Jela a place among—" She stopped and turned back to Cantra.

"Where is Pilot Jela?"

Well now, Cantra thought, that was a question, wasn't it? She moved her eyes, taking her time about scanning the street outside the bar, thinking how best to put the thing. Dulsey'd been fond of Jela—maybe more than fond. It wouldn't do to—she blinked as a familiar pair of shoulders hove into view among the thin crowd, moving quick and purposeful. Cantra looked back to Dulsey.

"Jela?" she repeated, around the sudden lump in her throat. She nodded toward the window and the street beyond. "Here he comes now."

HE'D DRAWN A ROOM in the officers' barracks and a meal card. There was, said the assistant quartermaster—a scarred and sardonic Y Strain—plenty of room, and plenty of food, too, stipulating base rations were food. His kit, he'd left on-ship, thinking there might be something in it that Cantra could use, and nothing he needed for his last couple days.

And if he'd known those "last couple days" were in actuality *months*, he could have—he could have been on *Dancer*, sitting co-pilot and content. As it was, *Dancer* was no doubt long lifted, maybe even heading for Solcintra. He thought she'd take the book to Wellik, like he'd asked her to. Just like he thought she'd do her best to keep the tree safe. He had to trust to that.

He shook his head, ran through a focusing exercise—and sighed. Months. If he'd known—

No use thinking about that. And truth told, he could put months to use here, same as he'd intended to use his days. He had the info he'd lifted out of Osabei Tower's brain, and all his generalist's intuition to bring to bear on the problem. If he could locate that world-shield, he could send that info along to Wellik, who he trusted would use the weapons that fell into his hand. Had to trust, in fact, Wellik being the only one left.

Being as he had months, it might have been best to put himself into his bunk for a nap, but he was an M and an M hates to be idle.

So he drew a local map from stores, and headed out for a stroll through the port—whether for distraction, to gather information, or to walk off a mood hardly mattered.

"Pilot Jela!" a familiar voice shouted. He spun, spied Dulsey at the front of what the map told him was Watt's Bar, waving at him energetically, her grin so wide it was like to split her face.

He felt his mood lighten somewhat, and changed his course.

"Dulsey," he said, giving her a smile. "You're the—next-to-last person I'd expected to see. How are you?"

"I am exceptionally well," she assured him; her grin dimming somewhat as she got a good look at him.

"Something wrong?" he asked.

"I—have you lost weight, Pilot Jela?"

In fact, he had, as the medic had also mentioned. No sense involving Dulsey in all that, though, so he gave her another smile and moved his shoulders in a dismissive shrug. "Had some short rations for a while," he said easily.

"Of course." She hesitated, then rallied. "You must come in and meet the others!"

NINETEEN

❈❈❈❈❈❈❈❈❈❈❈❈❈❈❈❈❈❈❈❈❈❈❈❈❈❈

Vanehald

THERE WERE OTHER PEOPLE in the bar, but he could only see one, elbow on the chipped table, next to a beer she hadn't touched, chin resting on her palm.

"Cantra." He had the impression he'd been about to say something else, though he couldn't have guessed what, and in the end it was no matter. His throat had closed and squeezed off all the words.

For her part, she gave him a wide, too-bright smile, which was nothing less than he deserved. "That didn't take long," she said, falsely cheerful.

He cleared his throat. "The commander's a fool," he told her, which piece of nonsense earned him a wise look from foggy green eyes and a knowing, "Ah."

"Here," Dulsey broke in, intent on introducing him to her troop. She touched his arm lightly, and nodded toward a tall glowering fellow with a strong jaw. "This is Arin, our librarian and linguistic specialist."

Jela gave him a polite nod, which Arin, despite his glower, returned.

"And this," Dulsey continued, indicating a pale port-rat of a woman wearing her only weapon out in the open on her belt, "is Jakoby, our weapons expert—and Fern, our archeologist and pilot." She smiled 'round at the three of them, seeming not to notice that none of the three smiled back, and told them, "This is Pilot Jela, who the Uncle offered a place among us."

"The soldier," Jakoby spoke up, her voice a dry whisper, "who killed fourteen of us?"

Jela gave her a grin, feeling rather than seeing Cantra get her balance adjusted for a quick move, if it came to that—which it shouldn't. He hoped.

"The soldier," he said to Jakoby, "who was attacked on a dock where he and his pilot had been guaranteed safe crossing. That's right."

There was a sharp pause. When next anyone spoke, it was Arin, remarkably civil.

"Uncle has spoken to me often of these pilots and their role in bringing the *Fratellanzia* to his attention," he said, and inclined his head once more, this time like he meant it.

"Pilot Jela and Pilot Cantra, I know Uncle would wish me to convey to you his gratitude as well as his feeling of obligation. If there is anything I, as Uncle's representative, might do to serve you, please do not hesitate to ask my assistance."

"That's said pretty," Cantra allowed. "Don't exactly compensate for the loss of custom 'skins nor Pilot Jela's peace of mind, but I 'preciate the sentiment. I can't off-hand think of anything that might bring us more into alignment, but I'll be sure to let you know if something occurs."

Arin inclined his head yet a third time. "I am at your service, Pilot."

"No you ain't," she said agreeably, "and neither Pilot Jela nor I is fool enough to believe you are. Though it might be we'll be taking you up on that offer of balance, like I said."

"Dulsey," Jela said, before Arin could get his tongue around an answer to that, "what brings you here? If it can be told."

"There are certain items of antiquity in which the Uncle has an interest," the silent pilot—Fern—said. "Our team was sent to collect them, if they are here, as well as those other objects we deem to be useful."

"If what I'm told about the mine-outs being full of First Phase artifacts is true," Jela said, "I'd say you had your work cut out for you."

"It is," Dulsey said eagerly, "a most exhilarating and involving task, Pilot. But the mines are not *all* filled with antiquities, you know. Some of them—a great many of them—are still being worked."

Jela frowned. Lorit hadn't mentioned that. "Worked? What are they bringing out of the ground here?"

"Timonium," Cantra said laconically, and Jela felt ice down his spine.

Something must have leaked out onto his face, judging by the frown Cantra gave him. Dulsey, though, had noticed nothing amiss and was continuing to talk about the Uncle's project, as animated and energetic as he had ever seen her. Freedom, he thought, agreed with her.

"So rich is the area," she was saying, "that we have already extracted more artifacts than we can ship ourselves. Only today, we had been talking of perhaps sending the ship on with two of us to pilot while the second pair remained to continue the work. Such a solution would be less than ideal, for Arin is our back-up pilot, and his skill with the old records is crucial to the success of the project. However, if you and Pilot Cantra might take our few cansloads to the stockpile, then we might all remain at Vanehald."

"Sounds like it might could be worked out," Cantra said, rising and stretching to her full, long height. "Pilot Jela and me'll talk about it, Dulsey, and let you know."

"When?" asked Dulsey, "for I do not hide from you, Pilots, that time is not plentiful."

"I'll come talk to you tomorrow morning," Jela said, rising in his turn and smiling impartially all around. "Where will I find you?"

"Anytime after dawn, at Shaft Four-Four-Eight on the north end. There is a comm-box by the entrance. Call down when you arrive and I will come up to you."

"Suits," Jela said, and dared to look Cantra directly in the eyes, much good it did him. "Pilot?"

She moved her shoulders. "Your call," she said, like she didn't really care and likely, Jela thought, she didn't. She gave the gathered Batchers a cordial, insincere smile. "Good to see you, again, Dulsey. Arin, we'll be talking about that Balance." She nodded at the other two, added a "Pilot," and moved off toward the street, Jela right behind.

"TOMORROW?" Cantra murmured as they walked through the port, by silent agreement heading toward the outer gate, the ship yard and *Dancer*.

"Tomorrow," he asserted, and shot her a sideways glance. "Seems my date was off by a bit."

They walked a few steps in silence while she digested this, then, "I never knew you to have a slack memory, though I guess the stress of the last whiles might've addled your brain."

"Might have," he agreed, "but the medic confirms my recollection—I should be decommissioned over the next couple days."

"But you're not—because?"

"Well, now, the medic seems inclined to blame the peculiar circumstances of my birth for introducing an anomaly which is only just now showing up. But I don't think we need to look any further than the tree."

Cantra sent him a look.

"The tree's keeping you alive?"

"The tree's been feeding me seedpods as fast as it could grow them," he said, talking it out to see if still made sense. "In fact, it could be that it had to produce those pods *too* fast, so there's less virtue in them, and that's why I've got a few extra months instead of the second half of a natural human life." He shot her a sidewise glance. "It's not much of a tree, after all."

Cantra didn't say anything.

"I think the tree's practicing biochemistry," he continued, figuring he might as well finish his reasoning out. "Life-extending drugs for me; a psychotropic conditioner for you . . ."

"Two for me," she corrected quietly. "Right before I let Maelyn tay'Nordif have her life, the tree gave me a pod to eat. I thought it was a going-away present, something to maybe comfort me, but if what you're thinking is true, it produced a good approximation of the trance-drug. All the time telling me as how it and you wouldn't let me fall—you'd bring me on home and everything would be happy-fine."

"I saw the antidote to the scholar work," Jela said. "You went from berserk to calm sleep inside six heartbeats, and then the tree insisted that I tell you stories." He sent her another glance, and found her watching him seriously. "The only story I could think to tell you was the story of who you were. I was . . . afraid . . . I didn't know enough to bring you back."

They were at the base of *Dancer's* ramp. Cantra gripped his arm. "You knew enough," she said huskily, then let him go and ran lightly up to the hatch.

EXUBERANT IMAGES HIT HIM as he came into the tower: A thousand dragons dancing against a brilliant sky, trees swaying in a warm wind, branches spread to receive nourishment from the local star . . .

Cantra walked over and leaned on the back of the pilot's chair, arms crossed, pose non-committal. Jela went to the tree, saw the branch bent under the weight of a pod, the aroma promising all measure of good things, and reminding him of that first pod, given so long ago, that had sealed the promise between them.

His mouth watered; he wanted the pod, and what harm, he thought, would it do?

A dark shadow passed over the dragons dancing in his head, gliding lazily toward the sun-sated trees. A branch rose, and it settled—the black dragon, its scales iridescent in the downpour of light. Jela caught the impression of age—vast age—and a breadth of wisdom entirely unlike that of an elder tree.

"No," he said softly. "I appreciate the effort, but it's a bad solution. You'll use yourself up trying to keep me alive past design. A good soldier knows when a battle's not winnable, when he needs to cut his losses and rebuild his resources, so he can win a greater battle, later. You're a good soldier, from a long line of good soldiers, and I'm not telling you anything you don't know."

Silence from the tree; the dancing dragons, the sunny, joyous day vanished from his consciousness, replaced by that mental tenseness which meant the tree was paying attenion. Hard. "Right," he said. "Remember you held a whole planet against everything the *sheriekas* had—held it when you were too young to leave the nursery. But you were the last soldier the world had, and duty called you up. That duty still holds you, like it holds me. And my duty doesn't allow me to steal from a comrade—and never from a brother-in-arms."

Slowly, an image: The old black dragon perched on one side of a gargantuan nest, the slim golden dragon on the other. Inside, a small creature slept curled, while the sun gently dried its wings.

"Is that true?" Cantra's voice was quiet.

The image repeated, which might have been taken for yes. Jela sighed and looked across to her.

"I don't know how it could be," he said. "It said something similar to me, once. I took it to be more general—it'll stand its duty to the next generation."

"Though it seems prone to working in particular rather than general," Cantra pointed out, and straightened out of her lean, face neutral. "Well, it'll sort itself out." She nodded at the pod-heavy branch. "You going to have that?"

It was, he told himself, already made—made especially and only for him. It would be a waste, and a bad use of a comrade's care.

"All right," he said standing forward and holding out his hand. "This is the last." The pod hit his palm and he sighed as much as in anticipation as regret. "Thank you," he said. "For everything."

He ate while Cantra did a quick check of the security systems. When she was done, she spun the chair and looked full at him, foggy green eyes wide and guileless.

"Are you wanted elsewhere this evening, Pilot?" she asked.

He thought of the narrow cot in the officers' barracks, and of duty. He smiled at her, letting her see all his admiration of her, and his care—another true comrade. And more.

And more.

"As it happens," he answered, holding his hands out to her; "I'm at liberty."

TWENTY

Vanehald

BEING ON THE PORT early in the morning seemed contraindicated after their comfortable untwining and the easy companionship of a meal. After, Cantra made a pot of garden-tea, its soft, tangy taste everything that was different from the usual ship-board brew. He savored it no less than the quiet ease between him and his comrades, and put the cup down with a pang when the tea was too soon gone.

"Business on the port?" Cantra asked, reading him sharp and accurate.

"I told Dulsey I'd come by, and I do want to talk to her," he pointed out.

She leaned back, long legs thrust out before her and crossed at the ankles. "You're thinking the Uncle is looking for that same bit of Old War tech you're after yourself," she said, "and that the rest of the treasure hunt's a shadow-play?"

"I wouldn't go that far. The rest of the artifacts are probably of interest, if the Uncle's as keen a collector as you've said. And it could be that they're the only reason the team's here."

617

"And it could be that Dulsey won't be telling you the truth, either side. If she knows it, which she might not. Young Arin struck me as being a thought tight on the need-to-knows."

"A man who keeps his orders to himself," Jela agreed. "I thought so, too." He hesitated, suddenly and forcibly remembering that, comfortable and comforting as he was here, he'd signed off of *Dancer's* crew . . .

Cantra raised her eyebrows. "Problem, Pilot?"

"I wonder," he said, slow and careful, "if you'd be willing to do me a favor."

"A favor, is it? And for a change you're asking first?" She gave him an edged grin and lifted a shoulder. "What's needed?"

"Here . . ." He pulled the map he'd drawn from stores out of his pocket and smoothed it down on the table between them. "Sergeant Lorit tells me that the world-shield's not in the garrison proper— and I think she was telling the truth. She suggested that it might be stashed in the mines, which is possible . . ."

"But you think it's nearer to hand," Cantra finished, coming out of her lean to frown consideringly down at the map. One long finger tapped the outer fort. "In here, is where I'd put it." She looked up at him. "Let me do some soundings and a bit of a wander-round. Meet you at that bar where we saw Dulsey last e'en?"

He nodded. "Mid-day," he said, standing. He looked down, but Cantra was studying the map.

"Mid-day it is," she answered absently. "Give my best regards to Dulsey, Pilot."

THERE WAS A SENSE of anticipation in the dusty air as Jela strode off across the port, angling toward the civilian mines. It made sense, he supposed; business at the port today would be featuring Commander Gorriti's leave-taking, which Jela hoped was being done with circumspection and not a marching band. If he hadn't thought it might cause a riot or a ruckus, he could have shot Gorriti for desertion and been well within his standing orders . . .

It was about the time he was considering that option again that the distant sound of a lift-klaxon sounded, hard on the heels of the familiar vibration of tarmac. *That* would be the commander's shuttle departing, no doubt.

Into his mind came one of the tree's more unsubtle images: a large rodent, and another, rushing about.

Yes, exactly! he agreed. *A rat hurrying to safety among other such. Much good it will do him!*

The image, however, became more insistent; the number of rodents and their energy increasing as they nibbled on tender roots. It would seem that the tree had some concerns regarding the commander's influence at his next station.

No, there you're wrong, my friend, he thought, meaning it for comfort. *That tree is rotten already!*

But still the tree wanted to push the image of rodents at him, while Gorriti's ship dwindled and was lost in the tan sky.

Enough! Jela answered. *We agree. Agreeing won't change the facts!*

He strode on, the tree's images of a gnawing horde all too firmly in his mind.

"PILOT JELA." Dulsey was in full thermal 'skins, the scanplate pushed up off her face reflecting the weak light from the local star. Below it, she was smiling and animated.

"Dulsey," he answered, giving her a smile of his own, though he feared it was a good bit less heartfelt than hers. "I meant to tell you last night—this new life of yours seems to be treating you well."

"Very well," she acknowledged, and swept a hand toward the comm-shack. "Come, let us be out of the wind." She hesitated. "Will Pilot Cantra be coming?"

"Not this time," he said easily. "There's something I asked her to take a look at for me down in the port."

"Ah," she said, and pushed the door to the shed open.

"Also," Jela said, following her in and closing the door behind him. "I wonder if you've found that specific item the Uncle sent you to collect."

Dulsey's smile faded. "Pilot Jela—" He held up a hand and she stopped, face wary now.

"I'm going to try not to make you chose between loyalties," he said slowly. "But it seems to me that the Uncle is a resourceful man, who also happens, as Pilot Cantra tells me, to collect *sheriekas* tech. He's got Arin and I'm betting a dozen more like him, doing research, deciphering old records, maybe even old military and captured *sheriekas* documents from the First Phase. The Uncle also knows that the end of the war is coming fast, and there's no way we can win—"

Dulsey shifted and he raised his hand again. "Humor an old soldier," he said. "This won't take long. The Uncle knows, like I know, that we can't win this war. But he knows his military history, so he knows that an important First Phase battle took place around Vanehald. The Enemy wasn't able to land and occupy the planet, and the Frontier Fleet, despite being outnumbered and pretty much out-gunned, pushed them back.

"Now, what wasn't written down anyplace was *why* those Enemy forces couldn't land here. The device was secret—barely more than a whisper of a rumor, which I spent the last six years of my life, between other things, looking for.

"My information is that it's still here—and I'm betting the Uncle has access to information as good or better than mine. And I'm betting he sent his best engineer to bring that device back to Rockhaven."

Silence, while Dulsey thought it through. He waited, not rushing her, prepared to take silence as his final answer, or a lie, if she felt she had to. Dulsey had never been good at lying, but the Uncle might have taught her the way of it.

"I believe," she said slowly, "that I am able to share this information with you, as it will benefit you precisely as much as it has us." She sighed.

"If I understand you correctly, the device you seek is that which the Uncle terms a '*sheriekas* repellor.' The literature is not clear, but it gives the impression that this is indeed a device similar to the many others stored here. In fact, it is not stored here at all. It is installed here."

Jela stared at her. "I'm hearing you say that the device exists, but can't be moved."

"That is correct."

He thought about that, considering his next question carefully. "Dulsey, have you seen this device?"

"I have seen plans of the installation in the outer fort," Dulsey said after some consideration of her own. "Understand, when I say 'installed', I mean to convey that it is hardwired into this planet, especially tuned to its composition. It may well be that such a device could be duplicated on another planet, indeed, the project has a certain appeal. However, with current technology, it would take on the order of eighteen hundred years, Common, to produce and mount it."

Jela considered her. "Eighteen hundred years," he repeated slowly. "I'm afraid I wouldn't be able to see it through to completion." The tree, now, he thought, with its dizzyingly long life—

"Nor would I," Dulsey said. She hesitated, then blurted— "Pilot Jela, are you well?"

"Well?" he repeated, genuinely startled by the change of subject. "Why wouldn't I be well?"

She frowned, outright irritable. "I observe that you have lost weight," she said, ticking the points off on her fingers— "more than 'short rations' might account for—especially as Pilot Cantra, who I believe would share such rations as there were equally, has not suffered a similar reduction. I observe that your hair is turning grey, and that you are favoring your right leg. Last evening, I observed Pilot Cantra, who was—startled—to see you." She drew a deep breath. "So, I wonder if you are ill, Pilot. Forgive me if the question intrudes. I ask as one who holds you in esteem and bears you nothing but good will."

Who would have known, he thought, that he had so many comrades? He sighed. There were, after all, certain courtesies owed to comrades, such as a clear answer when information was requested.

"I'm functioning according to design," he said to Dulsey's serious eyes. "More or less."

She blinked, once. Waited. Jela sighed again.

"Pilot Cantra didn't expect to see me because I'd told her good-bye and gone to the garrison to report to the medic, and do the necessary paperwork before being decommissioned. As it happens, I misremembered my date, but the signs you see—those are in line with the design. I'm old, Dulsey. Typically, what happens with an M is we have all our old age in one short burst, and then—we stop."

Another blink; a hard breath. "Such design characteristics may sometimes be circumvented," she said, in a voice of calm reason. "Come with us to the Uncle, Pilot Jela, and—"

He shook his head. "I doubt there's a work-around. The military does a tight job on its soldiers, and there's been a good bit of time to work all the design bugs out of the Ms." He gave her a smile, trying to ease the sadness in her eyes. "Don't think I'm ungrateful, Dulsey, but I've got my duty, and my life isn't really my own."

She bowed then, full low. "I understand."

"Yes," he said slowly. "Of all the people I've met in the last half-dozen years, you're probably the only one who does understand." He cleared his throat. "Now," he said, returning to the matter at hand, "about those artifacts."

Dulsey straightened with a startled look.

"The artifacts are many and varied," she said. "Truly, Pilot Jela, this planet is a treasure house! There are grids, data tiles, and maps enough to keep Arin for thirty years and more! There are devices—"

"Dulsey," he interrupted, "did you hear Pilot Cantra say yesterday that what's in these mines besides your treasure is timonium? Raw timonium?"

"Yes, but—"

He interrupted again, ruthlessly. "The *sheriekas* have an . . . affinity for timonium. Think about it—all the captured *sheriekas* tech—all the old battle tech left over from the First Phase—what's the power source?"

She paled. "Timonium."

"Timonium. Which is why Vanehald was so hotly contested in the First Phase—for the timonium. That's my hunch, anyhow, based on research. Tell me now, has your team activated any of those devices?"

"Of course," she began—and stopped, horror filling her eyes.

"They are operating in various energy states," she said rapidly, "within a certain limited range of frequencies and harmonics. Only last evening, Jakoby said that it seemed they were building a network . . ."

"Building a network," he finished, "and getting ready to send a beacon to the *sheriekas*."

"If they have not already done so," Dulsey said grimly. "If we have called the Enemy down upon this world . . ."

"The *sheriekas* have a long memory," he said. "They know what's here and why they were defeated. I'm wondering whose idea it was to stockpile First Phase equipment here . . ." He paused, made his decision.

"Dulsey, listen to me. I know the Uncle sent you here for treasure, but I urge you—I *strongly* urge you—to lift out of here on a heading for Solcintra. Send a bounce to the Uncle telling him that I said that the only chance for his people to survive the upcoming chaos is to immediately raise Solcintra and put himself and his at the service of a man named Liad dea'Syl."

She bowed, stiffly. "I will bring this to Arin immediately. And, Pilot Jela, if I do not see you again—go with my very best good wishes."

"Thank you, Dulsey," he said, warmed. "You do the same."

WITH AN ASSIST FROM *DANCER* and Jela's local detail map, it wasn't hard to pinpoint a couple likely spots to look. The first and most likely from the scans and map—wasn't, viewed up close. The second possible, though—that was everything a fond smuggler could want.

The stairs hadn't even been guarded. Oh, there'd been an old spy-eye on the door at the top of the flight, which it had taken her half-a-heartbeat to disable before she turned her affectionate attention to the lock. That had been a bit more of a challenge, being older than the tools in her kit were used to dealing with. She'd finally resorted to her thinnest zipper and a ceramic pick, which did the trick neat, and she was through, the door closed and locked behind her, and down the stairs.

The door at the bottom of the flight was slightly newer, and bore a sign warning her that only authorized personnel of Osabei Tower had the right to open it. The standard tool made short work of that lock and she was in.

What she was in—that was a question worth asking. She'd expected a control room, and she supposed that's what she had, though it wasn't like any control room she'd ever seen. There weren't any screens, there weren't any chairs, just an old steel stool in the corner. The walls were cast out of cermacrete, like the rest of the fort, and there were niches and handholds formed into them, though what they were for, or how they were to be manipulated was a matter, she thought with a sinking feeling in her gut, for study.

At the center of the room, a tangle of burnt looking wire was crumpled into a shallow depression, lined with—Cantra squinted, eased closer and went down on a knee, feeling the fine hairs on the back of her neck tremble and try to rise.

"Don't go jumping to must-bes," she told herself, her voice coming back weird and mushy off the cermacrete; "could be any old rocks that happened to come to hand." She opened her kit, pulled out the scan, and punched it up. Sighed.

Timonium.

Well. The man'd only asked her to find the thing and get a good look at it. She'd done both. There was also the question of was it working, which she supposed Jela might have a passing interest in knowing, and to which her uninformed answer was—no. Whether it could be made to work, she had no idea, lacking the manual. Whether it could be extracted from this room—Deeps, the thing *was* the room, and the room was an integral part of the ancient pour that was the fort. It wasn't coming loose for anything short of a pretty persuasive explosion—and maybe not then. Cermacrete was *tough*, which was why there was still so much of it in use and being occupied all this time after the Old War'd been fought and, barely, won.

She slipped the scan back into the kit and pulled out the ambicorder. Might as well get as much as she could. Judging by the layer of dust on the pile of burnt wires and the old stool in the corner, the place wasn't exactly a popular meeting spot; she should have plenty of time to record conditions.

JELA HURRIED BACK toward the fort, thinking, his quick steps startling the rare casual passersby. The *sheriekas* tech was a present danger. He'd have to alert whoever was in command at the garrison now that Gorriti was gone, which could call into question how he knew these things, and might entail a trip to the psychs—though there his M nature would stand him in good stead. Ms almost never went delusional, and he was prepared to stand his brain in front of the doctor for a second time if need be—if the mission demanded it.

Between one step and another, he became aware of someone walking beside him, matching step for step down the dusty, near-deserted path, and turned his head.

His companion smiled, red curls disordered by the breeze. "M. Jela," he murmured. "I hope I find you well?"

"Rool Tiazan. What brings you to this garden spot?"

"The ardent desire to renew your acquaintance, dear sir! What else might I be doing?"

"I'd hate to have to try to imagine," Jela said honestly.

Rool Tiazan laughed with every evidence of delight. "My apologies, sir. We did not mean to disconcert you at our last meeting. But, here! I bring news that I am certain you will be eager to have!"

Jela eyed him. "News," he repeated.

"Indeed." The little man smiled. "I was only just now visiting my associates who ready themselves to battle the *sheriekas* upon their own terms. While there, I was made privy to certain of their intelligence, which I feel must be of very close interest to yourself. Therefore, I made all haste to your side."

"Intelligence?" Jela asked. "*Military* intelligence?"

"Just so!" Rool Tiazan paused and looked around him, at what passed for day on Vanehald, with the chill breeze carrying dust and the light a weak and unappealing tan. "What a delightful planet!"

"I've seen better," Jela said, pausing as well, his weight distributed so as to put less strain on his right leg.

"Ah, but I have policies, M. Jela. And one of them is to find any planet which has successfully stood against the *sheriekas* to be delightful."

"There's that," Jela agreed. "But you said you had news. Of Master dea'Syl?"

"I have news of Master dea'Syl, if you would like to hear it," the *dramliza* said agreeably. "He and the cat and the young pilot have arrived at Solcintra and been made welcome by your good friend Wellik. All should go forward as desired, to the hopeful ascendence of our cause." He turned his hands up as if he had heard Jela's impatience.

"Forgive me, M. Jela, I chatter while you pine for intelligence. You wish to know what it is that my associates have discovered. It is this: The *sheriekas*, whose memories are long, are determined to have Vanehald, and to that end they have dispatched a great many of your kindred on purpose to take the planet, the mines, and the shield."

"My—kindred?" Jela frowned. "I don't—" He stopped, skin prickling, and looked into Rool Tiazan's depthless blue eyes. "The prototypes," he breathed. "The *sheriekas* Ms."

"Exactly so." He looked over Jela's head, as if judging the progress of something discernible only to himself. "Yes," he said as if to himself, "the energy level is almost sufficient to sustain a transition point."

"They're coming in through the mines," Jela said, abruptly seeing it all. "The devices, and the timonium—it's not a comm network they're building, but a shortcut. The shield—"

"Activate the shield and it will only be one more source of energy to sustain the gate, this far into the proceedings."

Rool Tiazan's eyes sharpened. "It were best that the *ssussdriad*, Lady Cantra, and your son be on their way—soon. And all of the lines in which I am the one to suggest this to her directly, those lines return—diminishing rates of success."

Jela stared at him. *Son?* he thought, then shook it aside. There was no time to discuss the realities of M Series genetics with this oddest of his allies—not with battle soon to be joined.

"I need to warn the garrison," he said, giving his attention to those things which were a soldier's proper concern.

The *dramliza* moved his shoulders. "I am hardly one to tell a man what he must or must not, yet surely it is imperative that you move your comrades—" He paused, then, murmured distantly. "Yes. Your pardon, M. Jela, I do see—" Another pause, and Rool Tiazan appeared to *fade*, into or beyond the dust-filled air— "that in fact you are correct. Every moment that the Iloheen are denied surety here adds to the percentages for our ultimate success."

Jela blinked. If his eyesight was going—the thought was interrupted once more by images of ravening rodents—and now he understood too well what the tree had been telling him this while.

"I'll warn the garrison," he said, briskly, "and see to Cantra. The tree's aware of the danger, as it happens—" He looked to the other man, who was solid enough, now, and considering him quizzically.

"You get Dulsey and her team out of here."

The thin eyebrows twitched. "I?"

"I thought we were allies?"

"Ah. Indeed. We are allies." Rool Tiazan bowed his head. "I will arrange it, M. Jela. Allow me, also, to hurry you on your way."

A sudden downburst of wind raised dust in a swirl. Jela threw an arm over his eyes; the wind struck again, lifting him off his feet as if he were no more substantial than a leaf, then set him smartly down again.

He staggered, recovered his footing, lifted the shielding arm away from his eyes—and looked directly into startled face of M Sergeant Lorit.

"I need to talk to command," he gasped. "Immediately."

TWENTY-ONE

Vanehald

"WE ARE NOT," Arin said sternly, "aborting this project and going off to Solcintra on the say-so of the old M soldier. We do not take orders from M soldiers; we take orders from Uncle, who—"

"Arin," Dulsey broke in. "The devices are calling the Enemy *here*. Whether or not we take Pilot Jela's advice regarding our destination, it might well be prudent to load what we can now and lift out."

"How close d'you think the Enemy is?" Jakoby asked in her ragged whisper. "Even if the devices have networked and put out a call for aid, it's going to take some time to transition from the raw end of never—"

"We don't know," Fern said, quietly, not looking up from her work, "where the Enemy *is*, Jakoby. I remember hearing tales of crews put to sleep with their ships, parked off the traveled routes, waiting. When the Enemy needs them, up they wake, with their destination already coded into the nav-brain."

"Baby stories," Jakoby scoffed. "The Enemy is no more or less—"

"Arin," Dulsey said urgently. "We should go. I think that Pilot

Jela has the right of it. We do not wish to be caught in a battle for this planet."

"No," Arin said sharply. He looked at each of them in turn. "I am the team leader, Uncle's representative on this project. We will complete our assignment. I checked the ship-boards last night. There's a freighter due in within the next two local days. When it's on-port, I'll negotiate for space with the captain."

"Arin—" Dulsey began, and he rounded on her, eyes snapping. "That is my final word!"

Dulsey's mouth tightened and her shoulders sagged.

"Yes, Arin," she said softly.

At which point, the workroom went away.

CANTRA EASED OPEN the door at the top of the stair, wincing as the noise hit her: klaxons, people yelling, and the unintelligible drone of an automated voice. Carefully, she looked both ways, then slipped out into the hall and relocked the door. The ruckus was coming from the street and—she hoped—had nothing to do with her or her little look-see. Straightening her jacket and adjusting the kit over her shoulder, she ambled down the hall to have a closer look.

The noise was both better and worse outside. Worse, because there was more of it. Better because she could finally make out what the autoshout was saying.

"We are on attack standby! Repeat: Attack standby! All citizens are urged to evacuate. Those who choose not to evacuate and who have weapons are advised to arm themselves now and report to the garrison. This is not a drill. This is not a drill. Situation Level Two: Imminent Enemy Action. Message repeats . . ."

Imminent Enemy action? Loitering in her doorway, Cantra saw some people run, some laugh. Most just shrugged their shoulders and keep on about their business like announcements of imminent Enemy action were an everyday affair. She watched a woman with a old-style blunderbuss over her shoulder walking purposefully toward the garrison. A couple others followed, including a boykid with an energy pistol strapped to his leg. All in all, not much help to the garrison, if an Enemy attack really was imminent.

At least, Cantra thought with a sigh, she knew exactly where to find Jela.

She eased herself out into a lull in traffic, thinking to check the needle-gun riding in its inside pocket. She'd left her heavy weaponry on the ship, not having expected to need it on a snoop job, and set out toward the garrison at a light jog.

FERN WAS WEBBED into the pilot's chair; Arin sitting co-pilot. Dulsey and Jakoby were strapped into the jumpseats behind each pilot.

"How—" Jakoby began, but her broken whisper was overridden by Fern's crisp, "Co-pilot, report!"

"My screens are clear, Pilot," Arin replied, his voice shaking only a little. "We are in transition."

"We are," Fern agreed, her fingers busy on her board. "How and why can wait until we are certain that the ship is hale and functioning as it should. Systems check, if you please. All remain strapped in until the pilots give the aye."

There was silence while the pilots worked. Then—

"The ship is secure," Fern announced. "Unstrap at will." It was, Dulsey thought, notable that she herself did not unstrap.

"If the pilot pleases," she said softly. "May we know our condition and course?"

Fern sighed. "We're on course for Solcintra, Dulsey. Your M seems to have the means to enforce his . . . suggestions."

"No mere soldier could have instantly transported us from the workroom to our ship, already in transition, with a destination coded in!" Arin protested. Fern shrugged.

"Can or can't, that's what we have."

"We need to change course," Arin said firmly. "There's no need for us to raise Solcintra."

"Yes, there is," said Fern, at last unstrapping and rising in a single, fluid dancer's motion. She met each of their eyes in turn. "The course is *locked*. Pilot's override is non-functional."

SOLDIERS WERE COMING out of the inner gate in pairs, moving with that same ground-eating quick-walk that was so frustrating in Jela. Wide-shouldered and solid, clad in military 'skins; heavy, dual-energy rifles held at ready; helmets on, face-screens down, they were disconcertingly alike, and not a little frightening. Cantra faltered, staring. *Jela's mates*, she thought. Those calm and faceless forces of destruction moving out quick and light to face the incoming Enemy—*This is what Jela was bred to love.*

Which meant, she reminded herself forcefully, that the man was likely in the garrison, getting 'skinned up, and in need of a sharp talking to on the subject of getting to his ship and off-planet before jolly hell broke loose. She only hoped the garrison folks would count her friend rather than foe at the gate.

She moved into the jog again, pushing past the crowd that had gathered to watch the soldiers march out, like it was some kind of play-parade, instead of an earnest deployment against a fast-approaching doom.

"Cantra!" His shout was 'way too loud in her ear, his fingers too hard 'round her arm as he dragged her back out of the crowd.

Concentrating on keeping her feet, she let him pull her clear, then dug her heels in, thinking it was going to hurt something bad if he dislocated her arm.

Fortunately, he was paying more attention than that, though he did scowl at her, and if she didn't have bruises on her arm the size and shape of Jela's fingers for this day's work, it would be through no fault of his.

"You've got to get to *Dancer*!" He yelled at her. "Now!"

Jela wasn't quite in full battle dress, she saw with relief. He'd thrown on a flak vest and grabbed himself up a rifle, which was only prudent, given the circumstances, and he wore a light helmet with an embedded com-set. There were marks on the helmet that looked like some of that silly new-soldier script, and some bright silver bars on the shoulders of the vest.

"I was coming for you!" She yelled back at him. "Let's go!"

He nodded and started off at his quick not-run, she jogging after—and six full-'skinned soldiers fell in behind and at the sides, weapons up, status lights glowing ready.

Might be the escort was heading to occupy the port, she thought, as the substantial wing of them sliced through the crowd. That would make sense. The port could need defending.

It comforted Cantra some little bit that their party grew as they rushed on—it seemed that one in every ten or twelve of the soldiers was getting direction from somewhere, or saw Jela's helmet or vest and knew that they were heading toward the proper duty station.

SHE HADN'T RUN so far in a long time; and it was a good thing she'd had time to heal up from the strain of being a scholar. Their group moved with a quiet clatter; and now over all came new sounds, the sound of firing somewhere, out toward the mines Dulsey and her team were working—and of an attempt to bring order. The port gate was half-shut as they approached, a single forlorn police-type with a hand gun nervously eyeing them as they ran toward her.

"Attention! Attention!" The autoshout gave out. "Enemy soldiers on the ground in Druidill Park. Enemy ground action to east and south of Wister. Enemy forces emerging from the Southard mines. Repeat! Enemy soldiers at the mines. The planet is under attack! All soldiers to stations! All civilians to cover!"

Their group was through the gate, the policewoman giving way gladly to the soldiers, and flat-out running across the near-empty yard, *Dancer* before them. From the left, another, smaller, squad was approaching, their battle dress slightly different from—

"Enemy in sight!" Jela shouted. "Intercept!"

Three of their escort peeled off in the direction of the inter-lopers.

The rest of them ran for the ship, and there were more soldiers in those subtly different battle 'skins coming in, Cantra saw. Hundreds of them.

"Perimeter three!" Jela ordered, without breaking stride. "Expanding circle!"

Half their little troop responded instantly, deploying toward the advancing enemy.

"Go!" Jela roared, and the rest of their escort was gone,

running and firing, and it was only the two of them and *Dancer's* ramp right there!

Around them the sounds of firing intensified, and in the distance the chatter of heavier weapons sounded. There were sounds of ricochets, likely off the space-hard hull of *Dancer* herself.

"Up!" Jela shouted, a solid presence behind her; his weapon up and firing ad they advanced. She jumped the "Captain's Out" barrier, landed light on her feet and ran the rest of the way, never faster, knowing he was behind her, triggered the hatch, ducked in, turned—

He was halfway to the unstoppable wave of the enemy, dodging and firing, and there was no way—

"Jela!" She screamed, but he didn't hear her. Couldn't possibly hear her.

"GO!" His voice came back to her over the terrific noise of the fighting. "Damn' you, Cantra, *GO!*"

She took one more look out over the port and the plain beyond, at the steady stream of soldiers in the wrong color 'skins—and she went.

". . . GO!"

The plan, in so far as there was a plan, was working. He'd brought troops to the port, intercepted a rash attempt to take the field, gotten Cantra to her ship. Now to clear launch room . . .

"Expanding perimeter!" he ordered. "Charge fifty paces!"

He was among them now, his troops, and they were doing well. They were advancing, they were pushing the stunned enemy back against their own on-rushing troops, creating consternation.

Into his head stormed the largest dragon the tree had ever shown him, wings black and terrible, scattering dozens of the less mighty with roar, tooth and talon—

Before him, he saw the enemy scuttle, retreat, fall.

He picked a target, fired; fired again, a head shot, then the next . . .

The cermacrete trembled as the mass of *Spiral Dance* lifted on maneuvering jets behind him.

"Down all!" he shouted.

Following his own order, he fell forward, let the steam and gas wash over him, and rush out toward the enemy, obscuring everything. He laughed and the dragon in his head echoed him.

There was a glow within the steam; the pulse of low carrier power booming . . . and he knew the plan could work. The ship's rising would give them time to gather their strength . . .

And now the steam was thinning. Time to move.

"Ahead fire four count, charge ten paces!"

He came up with his troops, never doubting that they'd drive the enemy back to the perimeter. The dragon in his head screamed defiance and he echoed it at full volume into the mic and across the field!

"Back to their holes! Chase them back! No prisoners, no surrender!"

He jumped a downed comrade, and another, fired ahead, felt the presence of someone too close, had time to swing the butt of his gun into a yielding face, fell, got up—numbness was growing in his left leg, but he refused to notice it, shot again, but now the noise wasn't right, he couldn't separate his own yelling from the sounds of the weapons.

A quick glance behind showed three of his own and an X with a bloody grinning face, firing his weapon one-handed, screaming along with him. His right arm went numb, and the gun slid away— but no matter—his knife came to his left hand and he brought it about, his leg not quite giving him the distance he wanted and not working at all, really, but there was the enemy within reach—

Black wings roared in his ears, or it was it *Dancer* lighting up full thrust? Hah! The ship was lifting! His knife was gone, wrenched out his hand as the enemy fell. He snatched at his belt, freed the wicked ceramic whip with a snap that took the arm off an approaching soldier. Another snap, but his leg gave out and the whip flew out of his fingers—

It was silent on the field; in his head, he could hear the black dragon singing.

Jela sighed a last sigh, and the black dragon lay down beside him.

Above them, wings flashing against the brilliant sky, a golden dragon danced.

SHE HIT THE CHAIR HARD, called up systems, and screens. She found him almost at once, surrounded, firing, each shot taking its target, but there were too many, too—

They were charging the enemy like a bunch of madmen, giving her room for lift off. She had her eyes on him, and watched his back in the screen as the maneuvering jets puffed their first lift . . .

"Override, dammit," she spat as the warning bells screamed. "I need some room . . ."

The ship started a lazy drift, and she lost sight of him, hit the jets harder, setting an auto-orbit switch, saw his back again. Far away, he looked, and so small, leading a knot of soldiers into a sea of Enemy. They'd gained ground somehow, but the tide was turning and—

Down.

No, he was—there. No—

No.

The fighting stilled—the Enemy had the field.

The tree screamed. Or she did, or all the tiny dragons in her head.

Her fingers moved on the board. *Dancer* leapt, spun on its axis and flared, flames incinerating soldiers where they stood. Her fingers moved again, and she flew as low as she dared over the field, sweeping with flame and jets, sweeping again, and when all was obscured by streaming fire she savagely slapped the lift to orbit button, and relished opening the armament switches. Firing Jela's precious cannon she launched the Jayfours still on board across the seething mine shafts, dropped flares and test rounds—whatever there was—until the magazines were empty.

It wasn't until *Dancer* was safely up and out that she realized she was crying, silently and steadily.

TWENTY-TWO

Long Savannahs of the Blue

THE SCREENS SHOWED BLACK; the only sounds in the tower the soft mutter of machinery, the whisper of the ventilating system—and the ragged breathing of the woman in the pilot's chair.

She sat with shock webs engaged. It had come to her that it might not be safe to let those straps loose just yet. No telling what she might do—she'd thought that without stipulating what it might mean. She was cold to the point of shivering, and her chest ached, like she'd been working too hard in thin air—*hyperventilating, that's what*, she told herself, raising a hand to brush at her face. Her fingers came away wet. *Deeps.*

Behind her closed eyes, an image formed, tentatively: the shadowy outline of a too-familiar black dragon.

"Don't," she snarled, or tried to, her voice thin and unsteady in her own ears. "I'll break you into toothpicks if you try me now."

The dragon-image faded, and she was alone in her head. Alone on her ship. Alone—

"Shift changes, Pilot," Jela said, his voice easy and warm. "Time to get some—"

"*Stop it!*" she screamed, surging upward—the straps grabbed her, pressed her into the chair, and she fell back, eyes shut but seeing it again—Jela falling, rising, shooting, losing the gun, cutting someone, down . . .

Dead.

No harm in grieving a good friend lost, Garen whispered from memory.

"No harm . . ." Cantra whispered, ragged. "I think—" she cleared her throat. "Garen. Listen to me, now, I've got something in my mind. I know you done it for the best, and we gave it a good run—but I'm thinking what you did there at Tanjalyre—I'm thinking you skimped on the planning. What was the use of flying under the Director's scans when Veralt found you anyhow? What's the use my carrying on, all alone and not fit for it? *Dammit*, Garen . . ." Her voice choked out, and she wilted sideways against the straps, like she had ribs stove, or maybe'd taken a bad cut. The tower faded—maybe she passed out, or maybe she just fell asleep, exhausted, adrenaline-lagged as she was—no matter, really, other than to say that when she blinked back to consciousness, she wasn't crying any more.

She straightened and released the webbing, though she didn't try to stand up. Her muscles were like water, and she felt . . . unconnected . . . to the reality around her.

Saving one.

"You," she whispered.

Call it a change in the air inside the tower—whatever. She knew it was listening to her. Jela's tree, that she'd promised to take to safety. Whatever that meant.

"You," she said again. "You tell me straight. I'm figuring Jela was bred sterile—military wouldn't want those special tailored genes crossing out to the general population, now would they?"

Silence, saving ship noise; no pictures took shape behind her eyes. Cantra sighed.

"Right. I'm also figuring you didn't find that little fix too much of a challenge, considering all else you put yourself to—and accomplished. I'll just mention the tiny inconvenience of my own deliberately non-fertile state."

More silence, the air in the tower fair a-quiver with attention.

Cantra levered herself onto her feet and walked unsteadily to the end of the board. One hand braced against the wall, she stared at the tree, noting more than a few leaves drooping and showing some brown along the edge, and a couple undergrown pods turning yellow on the limb.

"You tell me the truth, now," she whispered. "Am I carrying Jela's true and biologic child? Yes or no'll be fine, stipulating I don't want to hear his voice."

The air in the tower shifted in some indefinable way, and the top branch of the little tree snapped, as if in salute.

"*Yes*," her own voice whispered raggedly back at her from the walls. "*Jela's true and biologic child.*"

She closed her eyes. Took one breath, then another—and another, concentrating on keeping them uniformly deep and unhurried.

"I see," she said at last, opening her eyes. "I'm grateful to have the information." She pushed away from the wall.

"I'll be in my quarters," she said.

ENERGIES MOVED IN SLOW, scintillant waves, melding and separating; nothing more than a turgid eddy among the exuberant forces that defined the leading edge of the galaxy.

A star fell into the eddy and was instantly absorbed, cleverly woven ley lines confining its renegade brilliance.

"Again?" The lady lounged on her velvet chaise, a dope stick in a long, gem-sprinkled holder in one indolent hand; the other tucked beneath her head. She considered him out of half-closed emerald eyes, her hair a honey swirl against the tasseled pillow; her long limbs sheathed in light. Beside the chaise, her submissive knelt on the thick rugs, his back crisscrossed with old scars and new stripes, his will concentrated on the form and the substance of the cage.

"Lady." Rool Tiazan said respectfully. "I come to you once more at the behest of my dominant."

"Who perished foolishly, which might have been the greatest folly of her existence, had she not first performed a greater." The lady paused to draw on her dope-stick; illusion, of course, as was everything in this place, saving the cage formed of ley lines. "It astonishes one, the choice to insure the survival of the lesser part. Surely, she might have more easily preserved herself, and absorbed your energies at the instant of your destruction."

"Such a course would have served my purpose not at all," his lady said tartly, moving to the fore within their shared essence. "Sister."

The lady on the chaise blew a smoke ring, and watched it waft, blue and fragrant, toward the cage. Rool gave it attention, but it was merely a diversion, and not a threat.

"Rool Tiazan's dominant retains existence," the lady on the chaise said, thus informing the invisible and ever-present corps of her sisters. She shifted, her hair moving seductively on the pillow. "What errand brings you here, then? Sister."

"I would ask," his lady said, "that you coordinate your action with mine, and with that of Lady Moonhawk."

"Why would I wish to do this?"

"Because it becomes increasingly plain that the Iloheen cannot be halted by any one of our actions. Only by acting in concert do we hold a chance of gaining our goals."

"And yet we each of us hold goals which are fundamentally different," the other lady pointed out.

"In outcome, perhaps," his lady agreed. "However, we are united at base: The Iloheen must not go forward with their destiny. On this we agree."

"Indeed. And yet I say again—our desired outcomes diverge greatly. Lady Moonhawk wishes to steal a mite of the Iloheen future and seal it away for all life to share equally. You—you wish to run away. And I—" she smiled slowly, showing small, pointed teeth. "I wish to depose the Iloheen, and take up dominion of this galaxy."

"Sister, these goals are not incompatible. Allow me to explain. Rool."

Carefully, and masking his distaste, he made contact with the submissive, and downloaded the relevant data into the dull, half-crazed mind. He withdrew and the dominant on the chaise blew a smoke ring. It settled about her submissive's head like a misty crown. She drew again on the dope stick and the ring thickened, tightening until the submissive moaned.

She smiled, eyes half-closed. "I . . . see," she said after a moment. "The calculations of energy are very fine, are they not? Are you able to produce your share? Sister."

"Of course. Sister."

"Ah." Another smoke ring, this one *not* a simple diversion. Rool extended his thought and nullified it before it intersected with the lines forming the cage. On the chaise, the lady smiled, languidly amused.

"The word of a sister to a sister," she observed lazily, "is of course inviolate. However, your . . . situation, if you will allow me, sister, is so . . . odd, that I fear me I will require something more." She sat up, suddenly neither languid nor lazy; the ley lines spat and hissed, as power amassed in a thunderhead of possibility.

The cage contracted, poison rising in the heat from the lines. Rool exerted his will, knowing that she would see the effort it cost him; leached the poison and stilled the contraction.

His lady's sister laughed.

"Rool Tiazan!" She commanded him; and he shuddered to hear her.

"Lady," he answered, forcefully projecting calm.

"You will bind yourself to this promise: At the Moment, you will wholly support my action."

"There is another yet to convince," his lady spoke briskly, "who will also wish to seal our bond with power. It is mete and fitting that guarantees be made. Therefore, at the Moment of the Question, you shall one-third of what you have measure here and now of our worth, in support of your Answer."

Power rolled and clashed. The lady's thought enclosed him, violating him on every level; and he would certainly have screamed, had she left him any means to do so.

An eternity of torment passed—and he was released. He collapsed within the poisoned walls of their prison, bleeding energy from a thousand wounds.

His lady's sister relaxed into the chaise, her eyes bright and cruel, crimson smoke wreathing her head.

"We are in accord," she said. "Have your submissive weave a strand to mine, so that I may draw my portion, when it is due."

"Indeed. Rool."

Unsteadily, he did what was needful, spinning out a thread of his essence to weave into that of the scarred, mad submissive."It is done," his lady said. "Look for contact—soon, I think, sister. The process accelerates."

"So I have noted, as well. Simbu, relax the energies."

The cage wavered, lines loosening. Rool collected himself and snatched them out of that place, a star blazing thinly against the flickering purple of the Rim, and then gone.

TWENTY-THREE

❀❀❀❀❀❀❀❀❀❀❀❀❀❀❀❀❀❀❀❀❀❀❀❀❀

Solcintra

TOR AN YOS'GALAN MOVED down the hallway at a pace just slightly less than a run, passing many soldiers, Ms and Xs, Ys and natural human. Most ignored him, some acknowledged him with a casual salute or tip of the head. None molested him, for which he believed Captain Wellik was to thank, though that large, brusque individual swore otherwise.

"Don't judge all soldiers by a bunch of rowdies with a withdrawal order on their belts. Troops here are disciplined, and we know our duty—to hold this world against attack, and to guard the civilians, should attack become imminent."

Though he could hardly credit it himself, Tor An had developed a liking for Captain Wellik, who remembered Jela fondly, and received Scholar dea'Syl with reverence. He had immediately installed the scholar in spacious apartments within the garrison, gathering each and any small thing the old man could think to want. Captain Wellik had even taken the third member of their party in his long stride, merely observing that Lucky was an exemplary name for a cat.

The hallway opened into the garrison commons, and Tor An allowed himself to stretch into a real run.

That he had stayed on as man of all work for Scholar dea'Syl— was reasonable. The old man was comfortable with him; he had young legs and a willingness to be of use. And—it wasn't as if he were needed elsewhere.

Today's errand necessitated a trip down into the town, to the wine-shop of one Tilthi bar'Onig, there to pick up the Scholar's mid-week order. Of course, there was no real reason for Tor An to go himself—the errand could have been accomplished by any one of the soldiers attached to the garrison quartermaster's office. However, it was a tonic—so said Master dea'Syl, and Tor An found himself in agreement—to be able to leave the garrison and walk among civilians.

"Mark me, I have been a prisoner," the old man had said to him, as he sat in the window of his apartments and looked out over the evening commons. "You might say that everyone is bound by duty, and thus each stands a prisoner in his own jail—and you would be correct. To a point. Do you know what that point is, young trader?"

This examination was familiar enough. Tor An had looked up from the newsfeed, and considered the old man's silhouette.

"Choice, sir?"

For a moment, there had been no response. Then Scholar dea'Syl sighed.

"Choice," he repeated, as if it were some rare and precious gem laid out on the trade cloth for his consideration. "You've been well-schooled, I see." He'd held out his glass then, not looking away from the window.

"Be a good lad and fetch me some more of the same."

Tor An slowed to a brisk walk, and waved his pass at Corporal Hanth on the gate, as his partner Jarn was engaged with a—

Tor An spun on his heel.

"Scholar tay'Nordif!"

The woman in trade leathers did not turn her head, and Tor An hesitated. Perhaps he was mistaken, he thought. It had taken him some days not to see Jela in every M Series soldier he passed; perhaps this lady—tall and slim, with pretty tan hair and strong profile—perhaps this lady merely had the seeming of—

"I'll explain myself to Captain Wellik, and none other," she was saying, her husky, laconic voice bearing a Rim accent—and that was certainly wrong. Maelyn tay'Nordif had spoken with a scholar's finicking care, her voice high and clear.

"You can call him here or I can go to him there," she told Jarn. "Either way, your job's to clear me, and what you need for that is this: *Jela sent me.* Send it on. My name's—"

He was *not* mistaken!

"Scholar tay'Nordif!" Tor An moved toward her, aware that Hanth had shifted, and that Jarn was looking stubborn. The scholar herself—she turned to face him, pilot smooth, the line of frown between her brows.

"You're talking to me, Pilot?" There was no glimmer of recognition in her face, and yet, if Jela had sent her—surely there could not be two such! Tor An took a deep breath and bowed.

"Scholar, perhaps you will recall me. It is Tor An yos'Galan. I had not expected—has Captain Jela come with you? Just yesterday, the master was wishful of speaking to him, in regard to—"

He stopped. The lady was no longer frowning; indeed there was a complete and frightening absence of expression on her face.

"Jela's dead," she said flatly. "And my name, if you'll do me the favor of recalling it, Pilot, is Cantra yos'Phelium." She moved a hand, showing him Hanth and Jarn. "Might be you're able to talk sense to the gate guard? I'm bearing a message from Jela to Captain Wellik, and I'll not hide from you, Pilot, that my temper's on a thin tether at this day and hour."

Dead. Yet another loss. Tears rose. He blinked them away and inclined his head.

"How?" he asked, his voice cracking. He cleared his throat, and raised his head to meet her eyes. "If it can be told. Pilot."

Something moved in the foggy green eyes, and the lady's mouth tightened.

"He took rear guard," she said softly. "I see you honor him, Pilot.

Get me to Captain Wellik, and we're both in the way of following last orders."

"Certainly." He turned to Jarn, who was still looking stubborn, and then to Hanth, who was looking wary.

"This pilot," he said to both, "is known to me. I vouch for her."

"She's so known to you," Jarn answered, "that she had to tell you what name she's using today."

"I knew her as Maelyn tay'Nordif," Tor An admitted. "However, Captain Jela—who I know you honor, Hanth—told me that this lady is vital to the profitable outcome of the scholar's work. Captain Wellik will wish to see her. If you will not pass her, then call him to the gate."

Hanth exchanged a glance with Jarn; she hitched a shoulder and jerked her head, using her chin to hit the comm switch set inside her collar.

"Captain," she murmured. "Pilot at the gate asking for you by name. Says she carries a message from Captain Jela. The boy claims to know her, but calls her by a different name than the one she gives to us." Silence, then— "Cantra yos'Phelium," she murmured. "The boy says Maelyn tay'Nordif." A shorter silence. "Yes, sir."

A sigh and another jerk of the chin, then Jarn looked up at the tall pilot.

"Captain's sending an escort," she said.

Cantra yos'Phelium inclined her head and moved to a side, leaning an indolent hip against the wall and crossing her arms across her breast. Tor An hesitated, his mind half on Scholar dea'Syl's errand, and yet loath to let the scho—Pilot yos'Phelium—go.

"How," he began, moving toward her. She looked up, face neutral in a way that he recognized. He paused, and showed her empty hands. She inclined her head.

"How did you escape?" he asked, letting his hands fall slowly his sides. "We—the captain would have the duel a diversion engineered to allow us to win free with Master dea'Syl. When we had raised *Light Wing*, and the scholar was safe inside, then he—he and the tree— left us. They were going back to Osabei Tower, he said. For you."

She sighed and closed her eyes briefly. "Stupid damn' thing," she muttered, then opened her eyes and gave him a hard look.

"I came out through the smaly tube, since the topic's stupidity. Jela scraped me up off the floor and took me back to my ship."

Tor An stared at her. "The smaly tube?" he breathed. "You might have been—"

"Killed," she finished. "That's right."

She seemed to find the matter of no particular interest, nor the fact of her survival astonishing. And yet—this was the pilot Jela had claimed as partner, who had accepted self-delusion in order that Scholar dea'Syl might be brought out of his prison, and his work placed at the disposal of—

A tall shadow moved inside the gate, resolving into Corporal Kwinz, her tattoos blue and vivid in the sunlight. Her gaze passed over Tor An and settled on Cantra yos'Phelium.

"You're the one with a message from Captain Jela?" she asked.

"That's right," the pilot answered, straightening out of her lean to stand tall and ready on the balls of her feet.

"Come on, then," Kwinz said. "You're late for the party."

The pilot fell in behind the soldier, and the two of them marched away across the commons. Tor An tarried, in case she should have need—but she never looked back. For all he was able to tell, she had forgotten his existence entirely.

"You'll want to move smart," Hanth said, "if you expect to be back from town by curfew."

Tor An blinked. He should have asked her, he thought, if she wanted her cat.

"The pilot—" he said to Hanth, but that soldier jerked a shoulder.

"The pilot has business with the captain," he said. "You have business outside. And if you're not back by curfew, *you'll* have business with the captain, which I think you'd rather avoid, eh?"

Well—yes.

Sighing, Tor An took up his errand, moving into a jog, and finally into a run, keeping his thoughts determinedly on the scholar's mid-week order.

THE SOLDIER WITH THE BLUE tattoos didn't waste any time marching them through the garrison's center and into the dim quiet of inside. Cantra followed, keeping her hand away from her gun and projecting calm good citizenship. She tried not to think about the yellow-haired pilot at the gate, who'd been a breath away from crying true tears on hearing of Jela's demise—and who'd looked so happy to see her that on-lookers might've supposed them kin. Clearly, she'd made an impression on the kid, though she couldn't say the same for him. If she put her mind to it, she could probably dredge some tenuous recollection of him out the mists that served as Maelyn tay'Nordif's memory. Memories she shouldn't have, come right down to it, and best left alone. Might be they'd fade full away, over time.

She could hope.

"Down here," her guide said, triggering a door and standing aside to let her pass, then closing up behind her as they moved down a narrower, more private hall.

"First door on the left," the soldier said, and Cantra squared her shoulders and marched on.

She sighed, feeling the weight of Jela's book in the inside pocket. Now it came to turning it in to its rightful owner, she felt a certain reluctance to let it go, which was nothing more than plain and fancy nonsense. She'd read it, o'course—as much of it as she could read. A firm, precise, strong hand, that was what Jela wrote—who would expect different?—and the most of what he'd set down had been in cipher. Even stipulating she could crack it—which she likely could, given time and *Dancer's* brain—the information would only be of interest to Captain Wellik and his kind, now that Jela's commander was gone.

The passages not in cipher were descriptions of people he'd seen, cogitations on this or that thing that had caught his fancy. At the back, he'd kept an informal ship's log, detailing *Dancer's* ports o'call, cargo movement, and interaction of ship's personnel. Reading those firm, precise words, it seemed he'd found the time pleasant and easeful—comforting, in some way that defied belief, yet was no less true for being incomprehensible.

"Right here," said the soldier, and Cantra stopped, turning to face the door.

The soldier leaned over her shoulder and hit the button set in the frame.

"Corporal Kwinz escorting Pilot Cantra yos'Phelium," she said, nice and smart.

The door hesitated, as if weighing the likelihood of such an assertion, then slid silently up and out of the way.

CAPTAIN WELLIK was a big man, which she'd expected; his only concession to the X Strain fashion of facial decoration a tan star tattooed high up on his tan cheek.

What she hadn't expected was to find him standing three steps inside the room, dwarfing the chairs along the side walls, his arms crossed over his not-inconsiderable chest, legs braced wide, and an ice-blue glare aimed at the center of her forehead.

Cantra stopped, there being no place to go save through him, which course of action she thought she'd reserve until later, and craned her head back.

"I ain't," she said tiredly, "in any mood for games. Jela said you were a true man and stood his friend. If that's so, then cut the pose and we can deal."

The glare didn't abate, nor even did Captain Wellik uncross his arms.

"And if it's not?" he thundered.

She sighed. "If it's not, then I'm gone."

The glare stayed steady, but the eyebrows were seen to twitch.

"There's a soldier behind you," he said, slightly less thunderous; "armed and ready."

"Right. I'd hate to have to hurt her, being as I hear there's a war on and every soldier's needed. But it's your call."

Wellik threw back his massive head and roared. It took a heart-beat for abused ears to process the racket as laughter, by which time he'd recovered himself enough to send an amused glance over her shoulder.

"Afraid, Kwinz?" He asked.

"If Captain Jela trained her," the reply came; "I'm afraid. Sir."

"If Jela trained her, *I'm* afraid," Wellik said, unfolding his arms at last and bringing his attention back to herself. "So, little pilot, did Jela train you?"

"He did not," Cantra answered. "And my mood's not getting any better, with regard to games."

"I apologize, Pilot," he said, surprisingly. "You're the latest in a string of people arriving at this garrison of late, all bearing a token or a message from Jela. It's getting to be something more than a joke—soldier's humor, you understand."

That she did, soldier's humor being not unlike Rimmer humor in hue and edge. Cantra inclined her head. "I'm just through a bad campaign," she told him, almost hearing Jela murmuring the words into her ear. "Took some damage, lost—" her voice broke; she cleared her throat. "I'm on a thin edge, Captain. Take the message and let's part easy."

The pale blue eyes considered her seriously now. "When's the last time you saw Jela, Pilot?" He held up a hand. "Need to know."

Cantra took a hard breath. "I last saw Jela on Vanehald, about eleven Common Days ago. You'll also have a need to know that the last I saw Vanehald, it looked to be overrun by the Enemy."

Wellik nodded. "I have intelligence from Vanehald, thank you, Pilot. But you last saw Jela on Vanehald. You left him alive?"

"He was leading a defensive squad, rear guard at the port," she said, keeping her voice steady. "I saw him fall."

"Eleven Common Days ago," the big man repeated thoughtfully. "And he was hale enough to lead that squad . . ."

Cantra sighed. "The medic at Vanehald Garrison gave him a couple months more. Reason was the fact he'd absorbed some *sheriekas* energy off the event that destroyed the birth lab he was in at the time."

Wellik frowned. "Stupid—" He caught himself and glanced aside. "Eh, well. The medics have their own arts. What's important to me is that date." Another quick blue glance over her shoulder. "Dismissed to the door, Corporal."

"Yes, sir," Kwinz answered, sharp as you like. There came the sounds of her departure, which Cantra didn't turn to see, preferring to keep both eyes on Captain Wellik.

The door shut with a hiss and a bump, and the captain's thoughtful blue gaze was back on her face.

"Your message, Pilot?"

Right. She took a breath and raised her hand. "It's inside my jacket," she told Wellik, in case he had a nervous disposition. He nodded, and she used that same hand to reach, slow and careful, into the jacket, fetched Jela's book out of the inner pocket, and held it out.

"Well, now." He received it with respect, and Cantra dropped her hand to her side, fingers curling to preserve the feel of the worn leather against her skin.

Wellik opened the book, riffled the pages with rapid gentleness, then closed it and slipped it into his right leg pocket. Cantra saw it disappear with a pain that was like a knife thrust through the gut. She ground her teeth, met Wellik's eyes and gave a sharp nod of the head.

"That's done, then," she said, briskly. "I'll be on my way."

"Actually, you won't," Wellik said, stepping aside and jerking his head at the door his bulk had concealed. "Step into my office, please, Pilot."

"Why?" she demanded, giving him as good a glare as she had in her.

"Something you can help me with," he said. "It'll take but a moment of your time."

She considered turning around and walking out, but there was Kwinz on the outside, not to mention a good many other soldiers between her and the gate, and she'd gone and promised Jela to see his damn' tree safe, which she couldn't likely do as a dead body.

Not that she had much chance as a live body, either.

So, she gave Wellik a shrug and moved forward. The door opened ahead of her and she stepped into what was properly the captain's office, blinking at the crowd of folk around the table—

"Pilot Cantra!" One of the crowd leapt to her feet, and rushed forward. She paused just a few steps away, her face suddenly Batcher bland.

"Dulsey," Cantra said, keeping her voice slow and easy with an effort. "Nice to see you again."

"It is good to see you again, too, Pilot," Dulsey said softly. Slowly, she extended her hand, keeping it in sight. Cantra brought her own hand up in reaction.

"Careful, Dulsey."

"Indeed," she said, voice breaking, as sudden tears spilled down her cheek. "Indeed, Pilot. As careful as may be." Her hand moved, slowly, slowly, and Cantra stood frozen, aware of Captain Wellik at her back, and the stares of the other Batchers from 'round the table.

Dulsey's hand touched hers, warm fingers slipping between her cold ones.

"He's gone," Dulsey whispered. "I can see it in your face."

Cantra stared at her. "Not exactly comforting, Dulsey," she said, and for the second time in an hour heard her voice break. She swallowed. "He died in battle, like he wanted to." The room was going a bit fuzzy at the edges. She took a hard breath and focused herself, suddenly realizing that she was gripping Dulsey's hand hard—hard enough to hurt, it must've been.

"Sorry," she said, and tried to unlace their fingers, but Dulsey wasn't having any.

"And his tree?" she asked. "He guarded it with his life . . ."

"He did. Tree's on *Dancer*, hale and well."

"Good," said Dulsey. "That is good, Pilot." She tugged on Cantra's hand, pulling her toward the table.

"Come," she said softly. "Sit down and rest."

Wasn't any use trying to talk her out of it, Cantra thought, especially not with Wellik at her back like a mountain to be gone through, if she tried to leave now. She sighed, and dredged up a smile.

"A sit-down would be welcome, as it happens," she said. "Thank you, Dulsey."

TWENTY-FOUR

Solcintra

JELA'S FRIEND WELLIK WAS ACE, all right, Cantra thought as she poured herself a cup of tea. Another man might've put an obvious Rimmer claiming to be his old friend's partner in an actual lock-up, with smooth cermacrete walls, a constant, unwavering light source, and nothing to do but chew over regrets. Wellik, though—friendship counted with him. He'd had her escorted to a nice little apartment up inside the garrison, with a foldout bed, a kitchenette, and a blast-glass window overlooking the courtyard where a plentitude of soldiers went about their lawful business. There were only two minor inconveniences: The door was locked, and there was a guard standing on the hall-side of it.

She sipped her tea, watching the soldiers move to and fro in the growing dusk. Dulsey and her crew had been escorted elsewhere, and were doubtless enjoying their own comfortable imprisonment. She did own to a small amount of gratitude, that she hadn't been confined with the Batchers, though that happenstance likely had more to do with Captain Wellik not wishing them to come up with a consistent story to beguile him than any kind consideration for her feelings.

The story that the Batchers had told on their own—it was enough to give a Rimmer religion, if that Rimmer hadn't made the acquaintance of Rool Tiazan and his gentle lady. The sudden transition from mine shaft to ship, the route locked and untouchable, that had the warm, homey feel of *dramliza* interference. Not that she'd managed to say so, there being no reason to frighten the children.

Jela's notion that the Batchers might serve Liad dea'Syl—that was interesting, too. They hadn't said, precisely, but she had received the definite impression that the Uncle wasn't ignorant of the whereabouts of his treasure team. And if Jela had deliberately called in the Uncle, what did that say about his belief that his good friend Wellik would do the needful with regard to the old scholar's equations?

Sighing, she leaned her forehead against the cool glass. She'd studied the math Jela'd given her as hard and as deep as she'd been able, given time constraints, and there was no way she had them cold, nor even understood a half of what those 'quations were trying to tell her. Jela . . . Jela'd lived with those numbers for—well, she didn't know how long, really, but she had a qwint that said it'd been years. There was a damn-on-to-certain chance that he *had* got them cold, not to say able to make them stand up and do tricks.

There was a slight sound at the door. Cantra turned, poised, the half-full mug held innocently between her palms.

The sound came again and the door opened to admit none other than the boy pilot—Tor An yos'Galan. Without his jacket, dressed in plain shirt and pants, he looked even younger than he had earlier in the day, his yellow hair crisp; his eyes wide open and the color of amethysts.

Two steps into the room, he stopped and bowed to her honor, just like she was respectable—which, come to scrutinize it, she might well be, to a boy who'd only known her as a true-and-for-sure Osabei scholar.

That being so, she returned the bow, as serious and respectful as she was able. "Pilot," she murmured, "what can I do for you?"

"I bear a request from Scholar dea'Syl, that you share a cup of wine with him," he said, in his soft, mannerly voice.

Cantra blinked, and sent him a hard look. He met her eyes with calm patience, clearly waiting for her response.

Funny—he didn't look like a half-wit.

She inclined her head. "I am honored," she said, "by the scholar's notice. Alas, I am not at liberty, and so must decline the invitation."

The boy frowned slightly, and glanced over his shoulder at the open door, beyond which the guard's shadow could be seen.

"Not at liberty?" he asked. "In what way?"

Cantra sighed. "Why do you think there's a guard on the door, if it's not to prevent my leaving this room?" she snapped.

The frown vanished. "Ah! It is true that Captain Wellik wishes to hold you secure," he said. "However, you are certainly free to accept the scholar's invitation. That has been cleared."

"Oh," Cantra said. "Has it." She bowed. "In that case, I am very pleased to accept the scholar's invitation. Lead on, Pilot."

LIAD DEA'SYL WAS SITTING in a power-chair by the window, an orange cat on his lap. He inclined his head in answer to Cantra's bow.

"Forgive me, that I do not rise," he said. "I ceded Age my legs that I might keep my reason. It seemed a well-enough trade at the time, but lately, I wonder. I wonder." He moved a frail hand, showing her the chair opposite him, and she sat, hearing the small sounds the boy made over in the galley area.

"I hear from Tor An that the estimable M. Jela has departed this coil of intrigue and treachery. Please accept my condolences on your loss."

She swallowed, and inclined her head. "I thank you, sir."

"Not at all, not at all. I knew him only a short time, and feel his absence keenly. Quite remarkable, the pair of you."

"The pair of us, sir?"

"Certainly. Tor An has shared with me the information which M. Jela felt it safe for him to have. While I understand that such information was of necessity edited and simplified, yet I feel confident that the pair of you are remarkable, indeed. Ah." This as the kid approached with a tray, bearing a pair of wine cups.

"Serve our guest first, child," the old man directed. "She will wish to choose her own."

If Tor An found anything odd in that, he kept it to himself, merely stepping to her side and offering the tray.

"Pilot?"

"Thank you," she murmured and took a cup at random. What, she wondered, had Jela told the boy, which was then passed on to the old scholar? The possibilities were limitless, knowing Jela . . .

"Master," Tor An handed the scholar the remaining cup and faded back to the kitchenette, tray in hand.

"He is a good lad," Liad dea'Syl said, "and has been a great help to me in my work here. I commend him to you as an excellent pilot." He raised his cup.

"Let us drink to absent friends," he murmured.

Cantra raised her cup in turn. "Absent friends," she whispered, and sipped.

"Excellent," the old man sighed, which, if he happened to be talking about the wine, it was. Cantra had another sip, eyes half-slitted in pleasure.

"My friend vel'Anbrek, who was for many years my eyes and ears in Osabei Tower, fretted that I would fall into the hands of one whom he had determined to be an agent of the Tanjalyre Institute," Scholar dea'Syl said softly. "It was, therefore, with a good deal of amusement that I heard him propose to put me into the hands of a second such agent." He sipped his wine. "He said 'twas the presence of the M Series soldier which had convinced him that submitting to you, Pilot, was the lesser of a triad of evils, and so he conspired to place me in your way." He had another sip of wine, and Cantra did the same, keeping her face and her body language carefully neutral.

"I see," Liad dea'Syl murmured, smiling slightly. "But surely you have a client, my dear."

"I did," she said shortly. "M. Jela Granthor's Guard was my client. Our arrangement was that I'd run interference while he liberated your updated work from Osabei Tower's brain. When he found that he was being offered you, presumably with your work in your own brain, he varied." She sipped her wine. "He sent you here, and I'm thinking there's an end to my involvement."

"Ah. And yet you are here."

"I am," she said, and sighed. "Jela'd asked me to bring some things of his to Captain Wellik. That errand's been discharged as well. At the moment, I'm being held against my will, and I'm none too pleased by the circumstance."

"And your plans?" the old scholar murmured. "Forgive me if I pry. You will return to Tanjalyre Institute?"

"My line was edited years ago, sir. I've spent my life since avoiding the notice of the Directors. That's what I'll go back to, as soon as Captain Wellik lets himself understand that there's nothing more he wants from me."

A small silence, then, as the scholar sipped wine. The orange cat, which had been sitting quiet on his lap, suddenly stretched tall, jumped to the floor and strolled over, giving her knee a friendly bump before leaping onto her lap.

"My apologies for not returning him immediately," said Liad dea'Syl. "Your cat has been a comfort to us, Pilot."

She looked up from rubbing the square orange head. "My cat?"

"So M. Jela had it. In the case that it has slipped your mind, his name is Lucky."

The cat was purring. Loudly. *Lucky*, she thought. Now there was a sterling name for a cat . . .

"Tor An?" the scholar called. "Pray attend us."

A rustle and the movement of shadows heralded the boy's arrival from the kitchenette. "Master?"

"I wonder if you might recount for the pilot those things regarding his mission that M. Jela thought it wise to share with you."

"Certainly." He turned to Cantra. "I had asked Jela why he was pretending—not very well—to be a kobold. He said that you and he were after certain updated and expanded equations, which were necessary to winning the war. He said that you were a volunteer, who had undergone . . . protocols . . . which . . . made it possible for you to accept as truth those things you would ordinarily reject as falsehood. He gave me a copy of the equations, so far as he had them, with annotations." He glanced at the old scholar sitting still and attentive in his chair— "which I have given to the master." He paused, waiting for some sign from her, or so it seemed. She inclined her head.

"Yes," he murmured, and cleared his throat. "He then said that—that the safety of the galaxy rested on you alone, and that he would have no other, save his true and courageous friend—bear the burden."

"*Jela* said that?" She stared at him, fingers arrested over the cat's head. "He was having some fun with you, Pilot. Be sure of it."

"With all respect, I believe not. It seemed—it seemed to me that his duty pressed him hard, and he wished to ally me to his cause. Time was short, and I do not begin to believe that I was told everything of which he—or you—are aware. But I do believe that what little I was told, was truth."

The scholar cleared his throat, drawing her attention back to his face. "I have, as Tor An tells you, the annotated equations that M. Jela provided as earnest of his good intentions," he said. "The annotations, if I may say so, are remarkable. They show a depth of understanding and intuition that astonishes as well as delights. May I know if these insights are your own?"

"Not mine," she said, as the cat bumped her fingers forcefully with his head. "Jela had studied your work for years, Scholar. Those are his notes." She rubbed an orange ear, waking a storm of deep purrs.

The old man sat back into his power-chair. "Then I feel his loss even more keenly." He sighed, and drank off the last of his wine. Tor An slipped forward and received the empty cup.

"More, Master?"

"Nay, lad, I thank you."

"Pilot?"

"Thank you, Pilot, but no." Cantra handed off her cup, and sighed as the cat curled onto her knees, purrs unabated.

"There are several matters which I would like to discuss with you, Pilot," the scholar said, and continued without giving her a chance to say that she didn't feel like talking.

"Firstly, the fact that the intelligence which grasped my work so fully has informed us that you are the determiner of the fate of the galaxy. The fate of the galaxy is, as our good Captain Wellik believes, soon to be decided. What he does not say, but which I think must be in his mind, is that fate will not favor us, but rather the Enemy. I would, in such circumstances, allow M. Jela's assertion to bear a great deal of weight."

Cantra sat, the cat warm on her lap, and did her best to radiate patient, weary, politeness.

Scholar dea'Syl smiled once more. "You must tell me someday why your line was edited, Pilot." The smile faded.

"My second topic is one which I had hoped to be able to lay before the intellect behind those remarkable annotations. As this is no longer possible, I will, with your permission, put them to you, his partner and the person to whom he remanded the fate of the galaxy.

"I find that I cannot complete the necessary equations with the necessary precision. I wonder if you might—"

A bell sounded, and the old scholar held up a hand as Tor An walked to the door and opened it. There was a moment's subdued discussion, and then the kid was back, bowing apologetically, but Cantra had already risen, putting the cat on the chair she'd vacated.

"Captain Wellik sends an escort for you, Pilot," Tor An said.

"Thank you, Pilot," she answered, holding to polite and civilized for all she was worth. She bowed to the old scholar.

"I am sorry not to be able to help you, sir."

"Perhaps later," the old man said. "Will you take your cat?"

She glanced down at the cat in question. Amber eyes squinted up at her.

"Keep him for me," she said, and turned toward the door and the soldier waiting for her.

"JUST SOME PAPERWORK, Pilot," Captain Wellik said, looking up from his screen. "I won't keep you long."

"Paperwork," she repeated, keeping it lightly inquisitive, and neglecting to ask if she'd be freed to her own devices afterward.

"Take a seat," he advised, eyes back on the screen. Cantra sighed lightly and sat in one of the shorter chairs, her feet gratifyingly on the floor. Wellik tapped a few more chords, then spun, throwing something at her, hard and fast.

She caught it reflexively, only then seeing that it was Jela's book. Her fingers closed hard around it, even as she sent a glare into his face.

Wellik grinned.

"He said you were damn-all fast and that nothing caught you by surprise," he said, like he'd just been given a present.

Cantra sighed, and put the book on her lap, forcing her hand flat atop it.

"This is my paperwork?"

"Part of it," he answered, pulling a file toward him across his cluttered desk. "This is the rest of it." He flipped the file open. "It happens that Jela named you his next of kin . . ." He looked up and met her eye, though she hadn't said anything. "You're right that Series soldiers don't have next of kin in the ordinary sense of things, but the protocols exist and I'm the one to make the decision, so I've decided to honor his request." He glanced back at the folder. "As next of kin, there's a certain amount of money due you—hazard prizes, battle pay, that sort of thing."

"I don't—" Cantra began, but Wellik kept on talking like she hadn't said a thing.

"Next, there's this—" Something else shot out of his hand.

Cantra snatched it out of the air, fingered it, and held it up in disbelief.

"A ship's key? I have a ship, Captain."

"Now you've got two," he told her, flipping the file closed and pushing it across the desk. "That's yours, too."

She eyed it. "What is it?"

"Personnel records. Gene map. Letters of reprimand. Couple odds and ends from his various commands."

"Why do I want that?"

Wellik rolled his shoulders. "Don't know that you do want it, and frankly, Pilot, that's not my concern. Jela wanted you to have it, and that *is* my concern. What you do with it is up to you."

He rummaged on his desk, pulled out an envelope and put it on top of the file. "That, too."

Cantra sighed. "And that is?"

"Copy of a letter with your name on it. Don't know what he was thinking, writing it all out in cipher like he did." He gave her a fleeting, unreadable look. "Your copy's decrypted; I'd hate to tempt you with the challenge to break the code."

"I—"

"The money's been transferred to your ship's account. About that ship—it's been in twilight for the last few years and some. There's a crew bringing it back up—should be ready for a tour day after tomorrow."

"I—"

"Dismissed to quarters," he said, spinning back to his screen. "Kwinz!"

The door opened and the corporal was there.

"Escort Pilot yos'Phelium to her quarters, Kwinz," he said without looking up. "Same protocol as before."

"Yes, sir." Kwinz looked to her. "Let's go, Pilot."

Cantra took a hard breath, deliberately riding her temper down; she stood, picked up the envelope and the file, and turned, giving Kwinz a curt nod as she stalked past.

THE GREAT WEAVING was all but accomplished. They waited now upon the Sign, the moment of which not even the best of the prognosticators among the Thirteen could foretell, save that it would be soon. Soon.

Hovering above their base, Lute considered the order and turn of space and time. Soon, all would be different, excepting perhaps the ley lines. Though, if the Iloheen prevailed, they too would fail, shriveling in the outpouring of inimical—

The lines flashed and flared. Lute threw out a query, caught the response, and opened the way, following the visitor into the asteroid.

They manifested at once, the lady haloed in cruel energies, her submissive crouched, trembling, at her feet. Moonhawk looked up from her work, set the loom aside and rose. Lute, who knew their visitor of old, kept to the shadows and thought it wise not to manifest entirely.

"Sister," Moonhawk said calmly. "This is an unexpected visit."

The other lady swept out a glittering hand, dispensing with courtesy. "Have you bargained with the Rool Tiazan dominant?"

"Indeed, the Thirteen have made a pact of mutual support with Rool Tiazan. His dominant, however, is destroyed."

"Oh no, she is not—but leave that! Have you yet discovered, Little Sister, how we have been played? Have you Seen the event of massive proportion which is bearing down upon this probability?"

Moonhawk tipped her head. "Certainly. The work of the Iloheen goes forth, and the more quickly as it progresses. The Day is nigh. We all of us know this."

"Did you also know," the other hissed, "that we are *locked* into this probability? That the ley lines have been rendered fixed and unmoveable by some art beyond imagining, while the luck swirls as it may, obscuring all and everything on the far side of the event?"

"Ah." Lady Moonhawk smiled. "Yes, we had discovered that."

"And yet Rool Tiazan and his dominant have not been unmade." The lady shifted, and a ice-fanged wind cut through the asteroid, freezing rock, loom, and—Moonhawk lifted a hand and smoothed it into a warm, gentle breeze.

"Whether or not we have been played," she said softly, "is moot. What remains is our agreement and that Moment which so concerns us all—which would just have certainly overtaken us, were the lines fluid and malleable. The maelstrom of the luck—you are correct to be concerned. However, as you are aware, the luck is beyond the beck of even the Iloheen. What weakens our enemy must strengthen us."

"An ill-considered sentiment," the other lady snapped. "To invoke the luck in such measure, to lock the lines and deny us the possibility of escape to a more fortunate probability . . ."

"We are committed," Lady Moonhawk interrupted serenely. "That is correct. Was there something else you wished to discuss? Sister."

Their visitor flared and melted. Lute threw open the way and made himself as small as possible—and still her energies burned him as she passed. He sealed the shields and fell into the asteroid, manifesting with a stifled scream—and then sighed as his lady cooled the pain and repaired the injuries.

"Will she," he asked, "abide by the agreement?"

"She has no choice," Moonhawk replied, moving back to her niche and pulling the loom to her.

"It is within her scope," he insisted, "to unmake Rool."

"It is," she agreed placidly. "But to do so she will have to hunt him through the luck. That the luck will deny her, I have no doubt."

CANTRA CLOSED the folder with a sigh and leaned back in her chair, rubbing at the crick in her neck. Deeps, but the man hadn't been in trouble for a day of his life, had he? The reprimands stacked as thick as her thumb—and the citations did, too. He'd been a Hero, once; held rank a dozen times, and always managed to get himself busted back to a comfortable level. His last promotion—to Wingleader/Captain—had stuck for more than a half-dozen years, only, so Cantra thought, because he'd been free to carry out his orders as seemed best to him.

The citations and the reprimands, the write-ups for the offenses that earned him detention wove a kind of narrative, as if the Jela in the file was a character in a story who touched some points with the man she'd known, but was otherwise wholly imaginary. Not that she couldn't perfectly well imagine Jela taking on an entire squad of soldiers—and winning the fight!—but the smile and the sheer joy coming off him while he courted and committed mayhem—that didn't come through the reports. For Jela, she thought, had been bred, born, and trained to fight and destroy—and he'd been happy in his work. He'd been bred for that, too.

The gene map . . . Deeps. A military secret; it had to be. Here she had the formula for producing her very own army of M Series soldiers—which Jela had wanted her to have. That bore thinking on, since Jela had reasons for what he did. Why Wellik would have released such sensitive info to her—that was another puzzle.

Though she supposed he could've thought there wasn't any harm done, Ms being the past and X Strains the up-and-coming kiddies on the street . . .

She pushed the folder away, eyeing the envelope. A letter, so said Wellik, written to her, in a cipher she could be expected—pretty much—not to try to crack. And this from Jela, who always had reasons for what he did.

Her hand hovered over the envelope, fingers trembling. In the one case, she wanted—Gods of the Deeps, she wanted!—to read what he had to say to her, direct and intentional. On the other case . . .

Ship's necessity, Pilot, Jela's voice murmured in her ear. She took a breath that sounded like a sob in her own ears, caught up the envelope and pulled out the single sheet of machine-copy.

Private Correspondence To: Pilot Cantra yos'Phelium

About now, if I've got my timing right, you'll be wondering what I'm thinking, increasing ship's mass by a quarter-tonne of hardcopy. Call it an old soldier's fancy. I am a soldier, and so never gave much thought to what might go on after I fell. But I'm asking you, if you'll humor me, Pilot—I'm asking you to carry me in that long, deep memory of yours, like you carry Garen. Maybe the files will help; maybe not. I can only give you what I've got, and hope.

It comes to me that I owe you an apology—more apologies than I've got time left to say. A soldier does his duty, and mine pushed me to alter the course of your life, which I never should have done. Asking you to die for my mission—that was wrong, and no excuses.

It's come to the point, now. You'll be carrying the war on from here. I know you'll be as strong and as brave and as tough as you need to be. I know you'll prevail. The Enemy—they don't have a chance.

I'll shut it down now, before you get irritable.

Remember me for as long as you can, Cantra.

I'll do the same, for you.

Jela

TWENTY-FIVE

Solcintra

SOLCINTRA PORT didn't precisely tantalize a trader with promises of wealth and treasure, be that trader Light, Grey or Dark. Point of fact, Cantra was near to calling it the sorriest port she'd ever had the misfortune to find herself on—excepting there'd been worse. Vanehald, for an instance.

It was something funny, too. There were plenty of ships in—that was not counting the slowly waking fleet under Wellik's care. Far more ships, indeed, than she would've thought likely, given Solcintra; including a cruise liner that had been sitting in close orbit when she'd brought *Dancer* in. She'd've thought the liner'd been long departed, maybe having stopped for repair, but she'd seen more than a few luxury class uniforms on port during the course of her ramble.

The reason she was on-port, with a pass all signed and legal in her pocket, instead of cooling her heels behind locked-and-guarded doors—well, there was a tale worth repeating.

Deeps preserve me from gently brought up kiddies, she thought. For it would be the boy who had talked Wellik into unlocking her door and vouching for her good behavior like he was even younger than he looked.

"Didn't your grandma teach you not to speak for strangers chance-met on the port?" she'd snapped when he came to put the pass in her hand.

He'd frowned; absurd purple eyes clouding. "Surely, she did," he answered, in a clipped, too-formal tone that he might've thought hid his spurt of temper. "She had also taught me that pilots aid pilots, and that a co-pilot's first duty is to his pilot. So I put the case to Captain Wellik, who appears to have received the same lessons from his grandmother—and thus you are free to tend business on the port." He stopped there, though she could tell he had more to say, his lips set into a straight, firm line.

She grappled with her own temper, concentrating on breathing even and deep until she was sure she could answer him mild.

"One. I'm obliged to you for your trouble, Pilot, but the fact of the matter is you ain't my co-pilot.

"Two. All honor to your grandma, but there's some pilots you don't want to be laying down your good word to aid. I'm the sort of pilot who'd like to've curled her hair, and *ought* to curl yours. You got no way of knowing if I'm going to ever walk back in that gate once I'm on the outside of it."

That should've ended the discussion, but the kid was tougher than his soft face gave a pilot to think.

"Jela vouched for you," he said, his voice still clipped and cool. "He said you were the best damn' pilot he'd ever seen."

"*Jela* was the best damn' pilot he'd ever—"

"And he sat co-pilot to *you!*" The boy interrupted in his turn. He took a hard breath and produced crisp, angry little bow. "Pilot. Duty calls me elsewhere."

And who would've considered, she thought now, that so soft-looking a boy had so firm a temper?

She paused at a table to inspect a display of hand-thrown pots. Indigenous hand work was usually a good sell; even lopsided pots had their admirers. These, though, were not only lopsided, but dull, the glaze unevenly applied and the finish rough. It could, she supposed, be a School; but the smart money said it was just bad pots.

Well. She turned away, moving quiet and alert down the ragged rows.

Cool reflection established that the boy hadn't taken as much risk in his vouching as it first seemed. There was, after all, Jela's ship to be dealt with, though what she was likely to be able to do with a troop transport wasn't at the moment clear to her. She supposed she might sell it to her profit—though not on Solcintra. Nor it wasn't any such vessel as could be flown by a single pilot. Two might manage, if the voyage wasn't long and the pilots fresh. Four were best, running shifts and rotations 'tween them. She'd studied the specs during her happy time confined to quarters, and allowed herself to be in awe of such a ship. The keepings of a small planet could be packed into the outer ring of pods, if the balancing was done fine, and more soldiers than she felt comfortable thinking about could ride at slow-sleep in the second.

The third ring was quarters and mess for wide-awake crew, while deep inside, at the very heart and soul of the cluster—that was the pilots tower. Each section had its own set of engines; the tower could be broke entirely away from its pods and run as its own ship. And even stripped right down to the tower, *Salkithin* was twice again as big as *Dancer* entire.

Not exactly the best kind of vessel for a pilot whose fondest desire in life was to fly low and unobserved. She wondered—not for the dozenth time—what Jela'd been thinking, leaving her such a monstrosity to deal with—or Wellik, for approving the transfer.

Now she was out of lock-up, she could give over wonder and turn her back on the whole mess, get to her ship and lift out, never mind she was empty. Jela's death-and-bonus money would keep her 'til she could raise a port that had some profit to offer. That would be the sensible thing to do—and teach the boy a needed lesson, too.

She considered that course of action, trying to visualize the sequence of events—and found herself instead hearing the echo of the boy's voice: "Jela vouched for you . . ."

Dammit.

She bent over a jeweler's table, not so much because the cloudy gems called to her, but to give herself time to recover from a certain shortness of breath.

Wasn't no harm, she thought, to send word up that she'd like to inspect her new toy. She owned to a certain curiosity to see the sort of vessel Jela was accustomed to—

"Ah, there you are, my dear!" The voice was too close, unfamiliar— no. She knew whose voice it was. Sighing to herself, Cantra straightened and turned.

"Uncle," she said non-committal and easy. He was, she noted with approval, standing at a respectful distance and slightly to one side, his hands empty and in plain view. He was wearing a layer of Solcintra port dust over a dark cloak, and his hair was in a simple, unadorned braid. No tile showing, no strands, neither. Even his rings were gone.

"Pilot Cantra." He bowed slightly. "How fortunate I am to find you. I wonder if you may be thirsty."

She considered him. "That depends on if you're buying," she pointed out. "And where."

"Naturally." He smiled, which expression of goodwill didn't reach his eyes, and moved a hand, gracefully. "Please, choose a direction; I trust that you will be able to locate a suitable establishment. As the one who has extended the invitation, I will, of course, be buying."

It fair warmed a pilot's heart to find a man in so cooperative and expansive a mood. Not to say that she wasn't a bit thirsty, now she put her mind to it. And—who knew?—Uncle might have a lucrative suggestion to make.

So, she smiled, no more real than he had, and inclined her head, moving off to the left. He fell in beside her with barely a rustle.

"Passed something a couple streets over this way," she said. "Looked like a quiet place for a chat."

"Excellent," the Uncle murmured. "I am in your hands, Pilot."

"TELL ME," he said some little while later, as they settled into a back table, "how fares the excellent M. Jela?"

"He's dead," she said shortly, giving the room another look-around. It was dim, which was good, and the few patrons within eye-shot were mindful of their own bidness after subjecting them to the obligatory distrustful stare. The 'tender hadn't looked especially pleased to seem them stroll in the door, but he hadn't thrown them out, either. She'd drunk in less hospitable places.

"Dead," the Uncle repeated. "That is unfortunate. A sudden affliction, I apprehend?"

Cantra didn't sigh, and she made sure her hands were nice and relaxed. Jela wasn't on the short list of those things she cared to talk with the Uncle about, though she could hardly ignore a direct question. She could, however, demonstrate displeasure.

So, she gave him a frown with her answer, granting him leave to take the hint: "You could call an enemy invasion sudden, I'd guess."

"Ah. An affliction we all of us hold in common," he responded, with a look of bogus sympathy, and glanced up as the bartender approached, glower in place.

"Drinks, *kenake*?" he asked, like he was hoping they'd admit to having made a mistake, gather themselves up and go. And with *kenake* being the local impolite for not-one-of-us, he'd probably thank them for leaving.

Cantra flicked a glance to the Uncle, meeting an expression of well-bred patience.

"Please, Pilot," he murmured. "Choose what you like."

Right, then. She leaned back in her chair, sighting around the bartender to the rows of drinkables on display behind the bar. Not a very tempting display, and she was about to call for beer, when her eye caught on a distinctive shape high on the backest, darkest shelf. She looked to the Uncle.

"I'll have a glass of Kalfer Shimni, if you please."

His eyebrows went up, but, "Excellent," was all he said to her, before addressing the 'tender. "We will have the Kalfer Shimni. Bring the bottle—and two glasses."

The man's attitude of warm welcome got even chillier. "Coin up front, *kenake*," he said, as ugly as you like and then some.

The Uncle sniffed, and raised a hand, displaying nothing more nor less than a qwint. The 'tender reached for it—only to see the coin disappear inside the Uncle's fist.

"When you bring the bottle—and be certain those two glasses ring."

There was a quiet few moments while the 'tender worked it out, then he turned and left them.

"Do you wonder, Pilot, how such a bottle would have found its way here?"

She moved her shoulders. "There was a luxury liner up top when I came in. Might be the crew likes to have something drinkable when they're here."

The Uncle pursed his lips. "My information regarding the liner is that it was engaged by the High Families." He glanced about them, meaningfully. "This is hardly the usual sort of port for such a vessel."

"There's that," she agreed and was about to pursue the High Family tangent when the 'tender approached again, with a bottle and two glasses on a tray.

He placed the tray on the table, and stood by sullenly while the Uncle picked up each glass in turn and struck them with a delicate fingernail. Both sang, high and sweet.

Cantra took it upon herself to inspect the bottle, finding the seal in place; the special glass and the label authentic—or very, very good forgeries.

"Looks to be what we want," she said to the Uncle's raised eyebrows. He smiled slightly, and held out the coin.

The bartender took it in a snatch, turned, and left them. The Uncle sighed lightly, shrugged beneath his cloak, and inclined his head.

"Will you do the honors, Pilot?"

She did, with dispatch, and they both sat silent until the first sip had been savored, the Uncle with his head to one side, and a true smile on his lips.

"Excellent," he said for a third time, putting the glass down gentle on the table. He looked at it meditatively, then transferred his glance to Cantra.

"This sudden affliction to which M. Jela regrettably succumbed," he murmured, for her ears only. "May one know the location?"

She sighed. "Vanehald."

"Ah, yes. Vanehald." He loosened the brooch at his throat and shrugged the dusty cloak back over the chair. Beneath, he was wearing dark shirt and pale vest, looking like any respectable person of reasonable wealth and consequence, excepting the smartstrands wove into the shirt, shimmering just a little in the dimness.

"Tell me," the Uncle said. "How was that accomplished?"

She blinked at him. "The enemy invasion? Buncha old tech in the tunnels started talking to each other and opened up a trans-spatial gate, is what I heard."

"Indeed; I have also heard this. But what I had meant to say was—how were my children instantaneously transported from deep inside their claim to their ship, which was already in transition, with the course set and locked away from even the pilot's codes?"

"Oh, that." Cantra had another sip of brandy. Deeps, but that was good.

"Jela had some . . . interesting allies," she said to the Uncle's bland, patient eyes.

Silence. She let it stretch while she enjoyed another sip of brandy.

"I see," the Uncle said softly, conceding momentary defeat with a slight tip of his head. "On a related subject—I wonder, Pilot, if you have news of my children."

"Oh, aye," she said easily. "They're safe under lock and key inside the garrison. Captain Wellik, you understand, not being wishful of having anything ill befall them."

"The captain's care humbles me." His voice was too quiet to hold an edge of irony. "I am to understand from the message sent me that M. Jela believed catastrophe was imminent, and that the best hope of survival for myself and my children was to hie ourselves to this . . . unfortunate planet and place ourselves at the service of a certain scholar."

"Right. He's at the garrison, too," she said, and smiled to show she was being helpful.

The Uncle sighed. "I believe it may be pointless to bait me at this present, Pilot," he said softly. "Though you must of course please yourself." He raised his glass, and the 'strands gleamed along his sleeve. "I must assume M. Jela realized that we do not place ourselves *at the service* of anyone. Nor am I best pleased to find my children held against their wills."

"I don't know it's exactly 'gainst their wills," Cantra said judiciously. "There's books and 'quations and agreeable work to be had inside, nor Wellik isn't shy of sharing. Last time I saw your brother, for an instance, he had six scrolls open and a notepad to hand. Can't remember when I saw a man look so content."

"I can scarcely," the Uncle said, letting the reference to Arin pass with no more than a hard look, "knock on the gate of that garrison and offer myself up for arrest."

"'Course not," she said soothingly, and looked up as a shadow moved in the side of her eye, expecting to see the bartender.

What she did see was less welcome.

One of the patrons who had been so politely tending their own business at the center table was staring hard and ugly at the Uncle— or say, Cantra amended, putting her glass down and pushing slightly away from the table—at his shirt.

"Smartstrands," she growled, in just that tone of revulsion an honest trader reserves for the announcement of pirates on the for'ard screens. She snatched, the Uncle twisted, shoving his chair back and away, surprisingly quick—and a good move it would've been, too, if the chair hadn't got snarled up in his cloak.

Over he went with a clatter and a bang while Cantra was up and spinning, figuring that now looked like a good time to leave, except there was the offended woman's mate planting himself in front of her, and the shout going up behind—

"Smartstrands! *Kenake* spies are among us!"

YOU DID WELL, she murmured at the core of their shared being, *to bind the lines.*

Ah, no, credit me not, he answered with a ripple of green-and-ebon laughter. *Merely, I aligned conditions. The lines bound themselves.*

A quibble, but you may have the point. Now the question: Is it enough?

He opened their awareness, allowing them to fully experience the galaxy: the luminescence of the ley lines, the singing of the spheres; the warmth of life; the encroaching, echoless perfection of the Iloheen's desire.

We will know the answer, he whispered; *soon.*

"CANTRA YOS'PHELIUM?" The lawkeeper behind the fines desk spared him a single disinterested glance before looking back to his screen.

"Ah, yes . . ." He murmured after a moment, and there was slightly more interest in his eyes when he honored Tor An with a second glance. "Bail is set at two flan."

Great gods. With an effort, Tor An kept his horror from reaching his face. He inclined his head, buying time, congratulating himself, that he had thought to bring the pouch containing the astonishing amount of money Captain Wellik had assured him was the sum of the gambling debts he had owed to Jela.

"The amount," he said, with perfect truth, "is significant. With what crime is the pilot charged?"

The lawkeeper grinned, and tapped his screen with a finger-tip, as if it held a most excellent joke.

"Brawling in a public place," he read, with relish. "Damage to public goods. Damage to private goods. Damage to the person of one Kellebi sig'Ralis. Swearing in a public place. Resisting detention. And," he concluded, "creating a nuisance."

"I . . . see." He sighed to himself, slipped the required coins from their pocket and placed them on the counter in front of the lawkeeper. The man glanced down, then up, holding Tor An's eye with an insolence that set his teeth on edge.

"Of course," he murmured, and added a qwint to the sum. The lawkeeper grunted, perhaps not best pleased, but the qwint disappeared, and the two flan were deposited into a slot in the counter.

"The claim against Cantra yos'Phelium has been retired," he

said into the air. "Pray escort her to the bail room." He gave Tor An a squint. "She'll be up directly," he said, and turned back to his screen.

Tor An looked about for a chair, then spun as a door in the wall to the left of the counter opened to admit a guard leading a woman in damp and rumpled trade clothes, a cut across her left cheek, her right eye swollen shut. Her hands were bound together before her, her knuckles raw. The guard stopped, blinked, and spoke over her shoulder to her captive.

"*This* is your co-pilot?"

"That's right," Cantra yos'Phelium said, her as voice easy and warm as if she were in the best of health and surrounded by friends.

The guard frowned. "He doesn't look old enough to hold a license," she objected. Cantra considered her, one-eyed and bland.

"Looks deceive." She raised her bound hands suggestively. "Bail's paid, is what I heard. That means I'm no longer your bidness. Unlatch 'em."

The guard looked to the lawkeeper behind the counter, who shrugged.

"He paid two flan for her, so he must want her." He sent a slow, insolent gaze up and down the pilot's slim, bedraggled shape, and shrugged again. "No accounting for taste."

The guard muttered, touched the control on the restraints and whipped them off the pilot's wrists. It must have hurt her, Tor An thought, but her battered face revealed nothing.

"Let's go," she said to him, and walked toward the door, limping slightly off her left leg. Perforce, he followed, nose wrinkling as he caught the odor—the near overpowering odor—of liquor.

THE PILOT WALKED briskly, despite her limp, and acknowledging his presence at her side by neither word or glance. Tor An kept pace, taking deep breaths to calm his temper—a strategy doomed to failure, as every breath brought him the stench of liquor, which reminder of her lapse only made him angrier.

He told himself it was his place to hold his tongue; that she was his elder in years and in skill; that her reasons and necessities were her own—and hold his tongue he did, until they were at last well away from the lawkeeper's station, and she turned suddenly aside to enter a public grotto, bending to sip from the elaborate stone-faced cat gracing one of a multitude of fountains.

The grottoes had bemused Tor An in his first days on the planet: who could imagine a place with so much snow and clean water that it could be shared freely—even extravagantly—with casual passersby? Who would have spent the money to build such things?

Curiosity being a pilot's curse, he'd pursued the question through the amazingly self-centered Solcintra Heritage Library, where events of galactic importance lay near-forgot in favor of High Family histories and genealogies, which was, after all, where the answer was found: The grottoes and fountains were the result of a bitter rivalry between the Families, each bent on showing how much they could do for the public good.

And here, of all things, a *kenake* pilot was using a beautifully hand-carved grotto to wash off the stench of a stay in the jail which had also been funded in that orgy of building.

Cantra straightened, slowly, and looked about her, as if she did not understand where she was or how she had arrived there.

"You are most welcome, Pilot," he heard himself say, in a voice as cool and formal as anything Aunt Pel might muster to scold an errant younger. "I wonder, though, that you thought to call me to stand your bail."

Pilot Cantra spared him a one-eyed glance over her shoulder. "I thought you had it that you sat my co-pilot." She eased herself, carefully, down to sit on the ledge of the wishing pool.

"And I thought you had it," he snapped, "that I was not!" He glared at her; she raised an eyebrow, and sighed lightly.

"Boy—"

"I am not a boy! And, indeed, Pilot, I believe you have the right of it—I have no ambition to sit as co-pilot to a heedless, drunken, brawling—"

"That's enough!"

"—who cares so little for those who wish her well that she does not bother to thank them for their care of her!" he finished, ignoring her shout, and more than a little appalled at the words he heard tumbling out of his mouth.

Silence.

Pilot Cantra turned and put her hands into the pool up to the elbow, heedless of her sleeves, and held them there for the count of twelve. That done, she raised water in her cupped hands and splashed her face, sucking breath noisily through her teeth. The worst of the blood and grime rinsed away, she finger-combed her tangled, reeking hair. She did these things with great concentration, as if each task were of the utmost importance. Tor An bit his lip and watched her, ashamed of his outburst, and yet—

She sighed, folded her hands into her lap, and sent a serious one-eyed look into his face.

"Forgive me, Pilot. Manners tend to slide on the Rim, and mine never were shiny. I do appreciate your timely arrival and the payment of the fine on my behalf. I'll be reimbursing you when we get back to the garrison. I'd make it right between us now, excepting the law on the spot thought to relieve me of my ready-cash before she took me in to the station."

Tor An drew a breath—she raised her hand, and he bit his lip.

"Now, that list of yours. Heedless, drunken, and brawling, was it?"

"Pilot, I—"

She speared him with a glance. "I'm talking, Pilot."

He inclined his head. "Forgive me."

"Right," she said after a small pause. "Now, it happens I'll admit I was heedless in this case, and—with stipulations—I'll even allow that I indulged in some brawling, as you'll see I did throw a punch or two—" she half-lifted her raw-knuckled hands off her lap— "but drunken I will not have." She looked down at herself, then back at him, her nose wrinkled slightly. "Despite the evidence. For I'll not have you believing, Pilot, that I'm so lost to everything civilized as to use Kalfer Shimni in such a wise."

He cleared his throat. "What happened?" he asked, which is what he should, he told himself bitterly, have said at the first. "If it can be told."

"I met the Uncle on the port, and I thought he might divert me from an unhappy line of thought," she said. "Happens he was wearing smartstrands, and a local spied them, whereupon the bar rose up, and the peacekeepers were called to quell the riot." She grinned, one-sided. "By which time, the Uncle had got himself gone, which I might've known he would. And I only got but three sips of my drink."

"Your uncle left you to—"

She raised a hand. "Not *my* uncle," she said; "*the* Uncle. Which is more than a pretty, mannered boy from a nice legit family has any need or desire to know about the underside of the galaxy." Putting her palms flat against the ledge, she pushed herself to her feet, and took a deep breath.

"Let's go home," she said. "Pilot."

TWENTY-SIX

❈❈❈❈❈❈❈❈❈❈❈❈❈❈❈❈❈❈❈❈❈❈

Solcintra

HER APARTMENT within the garrison included a steam-cleaner, which fabulous luxury she was happy to avail herself of, once she'd shaken the kid off her arm, and failed to notice the open amusement on the hall guard's broad face.

It took three cycles to steam the booze and the sweat and the mad out of her pores, and a fourth to melt the worst of the sting from the various scrapes and bruises. Wasn't any reason beyond sheer hedonism to trigger the fifth cycle, and she stood there with her eyes closed, picturing the steam easing in through her ears and unkinking what passed for her brain.

Were you bored, Pilot? Jela asked from too near and too far. She sighed.

"Wasn't bad enough when I only had one ghost," she said, trying for cranky and failing notably.

And truth told, he had a point. She knew better than to drink with the Uncle, and she *damn' well* knew better than to be doing him any favors. Viewed from that angle, it was a rare blessing the local'd took exception to the 'strands and cried pirate before she'd taken coin whereby to sneak Dulsey and team out from under Wellik's nose.

The whole of which seemed pointless and worse, with the Enemy's works increasing exponentially, and nothing mere humans—be they Batch-grown, Series, or natural—might do to say them nay. The sheer numbers of them . . .

She shivered despite the steam, seeing them again, coming up out of the mines in an unending line of black, exultant death; for all their might, the most human—and by their counting, the least—of what the Enemy might field.

She'd seen a world-eater, up close and more personal than anyone'd sane ever want to; she knew the sick feeling in the gut when the ship fell out of transition, light-years short of a port that would never be raised again.

Jela insisted that the Enemy'd been human, once, but even if so, they were something other now. Something powerful and all-encompassing.

Something unbeatable.

Even Jela'd admitted that—and she'd seen plain on his face what it cost him to say so.

Come right down to it, she thought, as the cycle clicked over and the steam began to thin—what was it made human-kind particularly worth preserving and continuing? If the Enemy manufactured biologics and smartworks to do their heavy lifting, how was that different, or worse, than those same things performed by the so-called natural humans of the Spiral Arm? If the Enemy dealt harsh with its creations—well, examine the life of your typical Batcher. And if the Enemy was cruel—measure the cruelty that bred a man alert, sharp, and able, with a taste for life as wide as the Deeps themselves, while making sure and certain he'd die before he could reason his way into damaging his makers in the style they most deserved . . .

She shivered. The steam was gone, the tiles cooling. She had the robe out of the cabinet and shrugged into it, relishing the feel of plush against her skin.

Tying the sash 'round her waist, she moved from the bath to the great room—and stopped, the hair raising along her arms, breath-caught and heart-clutched—all and any of which was nothing more than missishness.

"You," she said, and slipped her hands into the robe's pockets, feeling the ache in her abused knuckles as the fingers curled into fists.

Rool Tiazan turned from the window and bowed, deep and respectful.

"Lady."

He straightened, lissome and sweet, the red ringlets tumbling across his shoulder, his face ageless and smooth.

"*You*," she said again, voice harsh in her own ears. She took one deliberate, foolish step forward. "You let him die."

The dark blue eyes met hers, and she saw there honest sorrow. His voice when he made answer was soft.

"He chose, Lady. You heard him."

"He chose between two choices offered—but who held back the third? You could've given him a good, long life—"

"No." He held up a hand, a ruby luminescence haloing the black ring on his first finger. "Forgive me, Lady, if what I say wounds you further. However, the only one who seems likely to have had a good, long life at the end of this day's work is—you."

She closed her eyes, suddenly nearer to tears than mayhem.

"I don't want it," she whispered.

"I know," he said, voice gentle. "The luck swirls where it may, and not even the great Iloheen—whom you call the *sheriekas*—can force it to their will, or see through it to what will be."

"Which makes it a risky weapon, wouldn't you say?" she snapped, opening her eyes again to give him a glare.

He bowed slightly, accepting the challenge and in no way discommoded. "Indeed. The very riskiest of weapons. If there were another so likely—" He moved his hands in that peculiar gesture of his, as if he were soothing the air itself. "It is futile now to discuss might-haves. The course is set. The *sheriekas* advance ever more quickly; and we are very soon come to the point of proof."

"Which is why you're here," she said, and sighed, and sent a searching glance 'round the room.

"Speaking of proofs and points—where stands your own kind lady?"

"Ah." He inclined his head. "She fell in our flight from the Iloheen, yet not before striking a blow which will be recalled."

Another to add to the tally of too many gone. Despite she had neither liked nor trusted the lady, Cantra bowed, and gave her full measure honor.

"My sympathy," she said formally, "on your loss."

"There is no loss," he answered, "for she is with me."

Like Jela was with her, and Garen, too, Cantra thought, and moved a shoulder. "Chill comfort, as my foster-mother would have it."

"Yet comfort still, and nothing I would spurn."

"Well." Carefully, she slid her hands from the robe's pockets; flexed her aching fingers. "You'll be pleased to know that the task you set us is accomplished, and the scholar himself, with all his thought and work to hand and to head, lies in a room further along this hall. I'll tell you that Jela felt his oath bound him, but as he's in no case to finish it out, I'm sure you'll find some way to use both the man and his work to your own ends."

Silence, then yet another bow.

"Forgive me, that I did not inquire after the *ssussdriad* immediately. I trust good health and virtue attend it."

"It seems spry enough," she said shortly.

"I am delighted to hear so," Rool Tiazan answered seriously. "May I speak with it?"

"Can't stop you." She twitched a shoulder. "It's on *Dancer*."

"On *Dancer*," he repeated and tipped his head, dark eyes slightly narrowed. "Lady, surely you are aware that your actions upon departing Vanehald have engaged the attention of the Iloheen. They have seen you and your ship."

The aches and pains which were her take-home prizes from the bar fight were beginning to complain again. What she wanted, she thought, was to find her bed and sleep off the over-rush of adrenaline and anger, not stand arguing points of precedence and ownership with a tricksy, self-serving—

"The *ssussdriad*," Rool Tiazan said softly, "is needed here. It holds some part of the answers which yet elude the revered scholar's grasp."

She glared at him. "Jela asked me to make sure that damn' tree was taken someplace safe. Whether or not I happen to think that his last and best joke, or that only an addlepate would've promised so daft a thing—I *did* promise, and I intend to stand by it. Solcintra's not looking like 'safe' to me, though I'll allow a certain unfamiliarity with the parameters. That being the case—"

"Lady, hear me! The Iloheen have your ship in their eye! They know it for one of their own, and if they have not yet bespoken it, they will soon do so. Such safety and shelter as it has offered you is about to be withdrawn. If you wish to honor your promise to M. Jela, you will remove yourself, the *ssussdriad*, and all that is valuable from that vessel and send it away from here!"

She stared at him, reading honest alarm in the set of his shoulders.

You be careful of them toys, baby, Garen counseled from memory; *and you be careful of our ship. While some pilots might have a safe haven in their ship, we got what you'd call a paradox. Our ship's good for us; she's top o'line and quality all the way. But she's carrying those things that're Enemy-issue. And it's true, baby—as true as I'm sitting here telling you this—that those things, they never forget who made 'em.*

"Don't you *know*," she asked, not meaning to taunt him, "if they've called *Dancer* to heel?"

His mouth tightened. "The more nearly the event from which we wish to emerge ascendent approaches, the less I know—anything."

She sighed. "Welcome to bidness as usual."

His lips twitched. "I fear I may require some time to become accustomed." He lifted a hand, sparks dripping like blood from his ring. "Nonetheless, I am as certain as may be that the *ssussdriad* is in a position to greatly assist the scholar—and by extension, all life." He sent a quick, sideways look into her face. "Mayhap the *ssussdriad* also feels bound by its oath."

"It might," Cantra said wearily. "Ain't something I've discussed with it."

"The *ssussdriad* is needed," Rool Tiazan persisted, "here."

"I heard you the first time. Seems to me, you being the one who wants it here, that you can bring it here."

He raised his eyebrows. "Oh, indeed?"

"Indeed. Jela might've been able to carry that damn' tree around like it didn't weigh no more than a data tile, but it's more'n I can do to get it up onto a cargo sled. Besides which, as you've no doubt noticed, I'm a bit hard-used lately and not feeling quite the thing. It being your necessity that wants the tree here, 'stead o'there, I'm thinking you can shift it, or it can stay where it is."

Silence, his face a study in blandness.

With a *fwuummp!* of displaced air, the tree in its pot arrived overlooking the charming vista provided by the window, leaves fluttering wildly. Around it, manifesting with smaller, overlapping *fwuummps* of their own came Jela's kit, the ceramic blade he'd taken off the X Strain a million years ago, a neat pile of her own clothes, and the bank-box.

She inclined her head. "That's thorough. I'll ask you *not* to take *Dancer* in hand."

"Lady—"

"My ship," she growled. "I'll do what's needful, when it's needful."

He bowed.

"Right." Her knees were beginning to wobble, by which sign she knew she needed sleep. She pulled up the sternest look she had on file and gave it to Rool Tiazan.

"You have bidness with the scholar, now's the time to tend to it."

"Ah." He raised his hands, fingers wide. "My lady wishes to give you a gift," he murmured. "Will you accept it?"

She eyed him. "Her being dead—"

"Nay, did I not say that she is with me?" He smiled. "You will take no harm from accepting; so I do swear."

Unless madness was contagious, which, according to everything she'd ever seen on the Rim, it was.

"Fine," she said. "A gift. And then you move on to haunt Ser dea'Syl. Do we have an accord?"

Rool Tiazan smiled.

"Pilot, we do." He stepped forward, hands extended, palm up.

"Your hands on mine," he murmured, and it seemed to her that his voice was higher, sweeter, sterner.

She put her palms against his, felt warmth spread, swift and soothing, through her veins.

"The seed is not well-rooted," Rool Tiazan whispered. "Is it your will to carry the child to term?"

Yes, she said, or thought, or both.

"Let it be so," the other answered, and stepped back, breaking the connection between them.

Cantra looked down at her hands, the knuckles healed and whole, and then to Rool Tiazan, who was bowing yet again.

"Lady," he murmured. "Until soon."

He blurred at the edges, his body melting into light—and she was alone, saving the tree, in her room.

Slightly unsteady, she looked at the tree and the tumble of her belongings 'round its base. It came to her that her face didn't ache anymore. She applied her fingertips, lightly, to her right eye, found it open and unbruised; the opposite cheek smooth and unmarred.

"Well," she said to the air and the aether, and closed her eyes. "Thank you."

"IMPOSSIBLE, MASTER?" Tor An went to one knee by the scholar's chair, the better to see into the downturned face.

The old man did not look up; he watched his own hand stroking the orange cat as if the action and the animal were the most important things in the galaxy.

"Allow me to know," he said softly, "when my own work has described a impasse. It is impossible to continue. I have been in error."

Tor An blinked, aghast. "But—your life's work, an error? Surely not!"

The scholar smiled and looked up. "Simply because one has

spent one's life at a work does not mean that the work must be correct, or of use." He raised a hand and cupped Tor An's cheek, as if he were one of Alkia's grandfathers soothing a distraught younger.

"What," Tor An asked carefully, in case, like a true Alkia grandfather, this mood of sudden gentleness should evaporate even more suddenly, leaving the younger's ears ringing from a sound boxing. "What of the Enemy, Master? Captain Jela had thought your work the best means of their defeat."

The old man patted his cheek—lightly, even fondly—and tucked his hand 'round Lucky's back.

"Captain Jela was a wise and perceptive man," he told the cat. "Yet even wise and perceptive men can sometimes be mistaken. Certainly, he wished, as I do and you do, to discover some way in which we might outwit the Enemy and snatch liberty from defeat. That was, as near as I am able to know his mind from his annotations, the breadth and depth of his hope for us all. It was not an unreasonable hope, and indeed it seems to me that he was correct in believing my work represented the best potential of realizing it. It is no dishonor to his memory that his best hope was not good enough."

Tor An considered. It was, he thought, very possible that the scholar was merely exhausted. He had stinted himself on sleep and on food, the hours of his days spent with his notes and his tiles, his work screen a riot of nested calculation.

"My Aunt Jinsu had used to tell us youngers," he began slowly, "that a pilot's best friend was—"

Lucky the cat jerked to attention on the scholar's lap, ears pricked forward. A moment only he stared past Tor An into the great room, then leapt to the floor and ran, tail high. Tor An twisted 'round, peering into the dimness, then came all at once to his feet, situating himself between the scholar and a red-haired man in formal black tunic and pants. The man paused, eyebrows up, Lucky weaving complex, ecstatic figures around his ankles, tail high and whiskers a-quiver.

"Did the guard admit you, sir?" Tor An asked, sharply. "I did not hear the door."

"Nay, Housefather, I admitted myself," the man said in soft and cultured accents. He bowed, low and respectful. "My name is Rool Tiazan. I was allied with M. Jela and seek to continue his purpose. I am come to offer assistance to the master, if he will have me, and it."

"Stand aside, child," Master dea'Syl said to Tor An, "you obscure my view of our guest."

Reluctantly, Tor An stepped to the right, keeping his eye upon Rool Tiazan.

"Well," the master said after a long scrutiny. "Certainly one who was allied with the estimable M. Jela is welcome on that count alone. What sort of assistance do you offer, Ser Tiazan?"

The man moved a graceful hand, encompassing the abandoned desk, notes, and screen. "I believe your work founders on the particulars of an energy state transformation under special near-ideal and probably unique circumstances. It happens that I am something of an expert in energies and their states, and have also some insight into the nature of the approaching, probably unique, event. Also, I bring with me another ally, who has seen the Enemy falter."

"Hah." The scholar leaned forward in his chair, eyes gleaming. Tor An took a careful breath. "If you can show me the error in my work, I shall be most obliged to you." He raised a hand, beckoning. "Come here, young man. Seat yourself. Tor An—a glass of wine for our guest, if you please."

"Certainly." He inclined his head and moved to the kitchenette as Rool Tiazan walked forward and took the chair by the scholar's table.

By the time he returned with the tray, the two gentlemen were deep in conversation, and the cat was asleep on Rool Tiazan's elegant lap.

TWENTY-SEVEN

❀❀❀❀❀❀❀❀❀❀❀❀❀❀❀❀❀❀❀❀❀❀❀❀

Solcintra

CANTRA WOKE UNEXPECTEDLY refreshed, more filled with energy than she had been since Jela died, and with the clear sense of having taken a decision while she slept.

She dressed quickly from the store of clothes Rool Tiazan had so kindly delivered to her, watered the tree, which offered her neither comment nor salute, and was on her way down the hall, headed for the gate.

It was early yet; the overnight dusting of snow still glittered in the abundant shadows. Sitting in a pool of sun on the low wall near the gate was the odd couple of Tor An yos'Galan and Arin the librarian, dark head and light bent over a shared scroll. Cantra hesitated, then changed course.

"'morning, Pilots," she said cheerily, and gave them a grin to go with it when they looked up, startled.

Arin recovered his wits first, inclining his head respectfully. "Pilot Cantra. Good morning."

The boy echoed the sentiment a heartbeat later, his voice a bit strained, and dark smudges showing under those improbable eyes.

The scroll was an old star-map, its edges tattered and the three-dee grainy; she couldn't tell which sector from a casual glance, and she wasn't there to discuss maps, anyway.

"Arin," she said, holding his eye. "Some happy news for you. Saw your brother on-port yesterday."

The dark eyes sparkled. "I thank you, Pilot. This is, as you say, welcome news. Did he mention when he might come to us?"

"Got the impression he thought you'd rather to go him," she said. "Seemed to be having a couple lines of trade going—you know how he is."

"I do indeed," Arin said, with irony, "know exactly how he is." He fingered the scroll, and sent a sideways glance at the other pilot's face. "Your thoughts on my small difficulty were very welcome, Pilot. However, filial duty calls, and—"

"I understand," Tor An assured him, voice soft and sad. He extended a hand and touched a portion of the map lightly. "It would be my pleasure to assist you further, if you have need, after duty is answered."

"In the meanwhile," Cantra put in, "if you're at liberty, Pilot Tor An, I wonder if you'd bear me company."

He looked up, brows pulled into a frown. "I, Pilot?"

"Exactly you," she assured him, as Arin adroitly rolled the scroll. "I'd like your opinion on a certain vessel." She tipped her head. "You've had training on the big ships—I mean real ring and pod-carrying transports, multi-mounts, that kind of thing?"

Interest dawned behind the frown. "I have, of course, but—"

"But I ain't had that luck," she interrupted, watching out of the corner of one eye as Arin stood and moved off toward the interior, walking like a man with a pressing errand in mind. "My life's been small ships. I don't know how to take the measure of anything more than a six-crew shuttle or a four place courier." She paused. "If you'll honor me, Pilot."

It might've been the polite that won him, but she thought it was rather the basic human desire to be useful and busy. A good boy was Pilot Tor An, she thought, as he came to his feet and inclined his head. So much the worse for him.

"I will be glad to assist you, Pilot," he said formally.

"Good," she said, and jerked her head toward the gate. "Let's go."

"ALL OF YOUR EQUATIONS are correct, as far as they go." Rool Tiazan leaned over the scholar's shoulder, Lucky the cat weaving 'round the base of the work screen they studied so intently. He tapped the screen with a light forefinger, feeling the attentive presence of the *ssussdriad* within the sphere of his being.

"So here," he murmured, "this term is correct, but makes an incomplete assumption."

"Of course it does!" Liad dea'Syl answered. "There are several values that might be added, all derived properly from the rest of my work." His fingers moved on the coding wand. "Add this one—and behold! We attain an equation which is quite beautiful, though it must be impossible to achieve. At this point in our adventure, surely practical mathematics outweighs mere elegance."

Rool allowed the old gentleman's irony to pass unremarked, taking a moment to skritch Lucky carefully under the chin. The chin being properly taken care of, he turned back to the discussion with a polite smile.

"Grandfather, of course it is practical mathematics which will carry the day. And as you have seen, I am far easier with the practical than the theoretical."

The mathematician snorted, drawing the cat's attention.

"The boy is elsewhere, sir; you may dispense with the fiction that I am your elder, as we both realize that I am not. I suspect that your age is some centuries beyond mine . . ."

Rool paused, then inclined his head, sincerely respectful. The old one's mind was both agile and facile. Of course he would have formed the proposition that a being which was not bound by possibility would not be bound by time.

"Well," he murmured. "I am here because you are no fool, and I am no mathematician."

"It is possible that you err on both points," the scholar murmured. "But let us not quibble. Pray elucidate this incomplete assumption, and tell me if you have a proof which ties this together so that young Jela's excellent work does not go to waste."

"The value here," Rool tapped the screen again. "This assumes that when the final decrystallization event begins, it will propagate across space. It will not. The event will, as your initial numbers demonstrate, occur across the affected dimensions and energies simultaneously."

The old man seemed to wilt in his chair, though the glow of his life energies were as bright as ever.

"There, my friend," he murmured, "lies the paradox. If the event occurs simultaneously, there will be no wave . . ."

"The triggering event, however," Rool continued. "The trigger event propagates at the highest possible velocity of transition. When the energy state is sufficient, a coherent decrystallization is the result. Now, note that this is not a reversion to what was, as implied by our limited vocabulary; this is a new state. In this event, prior conditions cannot be recalled, they cannot be calculated. Within the new state there is no information exchange or reversibility with the preceding state in any manner that affords sense." He paused, frowning at the screen, and leaned forward to tap another phrase.

"But here, sir," he murmured, "I fear I misapply language again. Let us consider *this*, which implies that what shall occur is that the act of transitioning *will* inform the new location. That is, it will contain the ships, their contents, and whatever else might be accelerated to transitional velocity—and it will contain that impetus and energy . . ."

"Yes!" Liad dea'Syl said, abruptly enthusiastic. "Of course, the transition will inform the new location, just as the new location will inform that which arrives. And observe!—It furthermore implies that the arrival of the ships, the end of the transition, will in effect not be contingent on their relationships before the transition. It *also* implies a transformational energy change, one that will exclude any further energy or information exchange. The universe we arrive at will not be the one we left."

"And here," he sighed after a moment, "here is where I falter. It would appear that, no matter the prior conditions, we shall arrive in a universe where certain spins will be . . . let us say, *preferred*, and where the energy excess we bring with us will mean that space will expand infinitely over time. There will be no steady state, though there may be the practical illusion of it for billions of years."

Rool considered that in all its fullness before meeting the old scholar's eyes.

"I propose," he said seriously, "that an infinitely expandable universe is much preferable to one which is about to become largely uninhabitable."

"Yes, of course. Well said." The mathematician rubbed a tired hand over his eyes. "Yet, should we continue down that path, we soon discover that we lack vital information. We have near-proof that this escape we posit is possible. However, if we may not know the time of the spontaneous, great, event, within fractions, we shall be lost. We must have more information than M. Jela's prognostication and death brings us." He paused, his eyes wandering from the screen to the window, and the bright day without.

"If I might but look upon the works of our Enemy, and understand what it is that they accomplish, perhaps—"

Abruptly, the room, the screen, the cat were gone, replaced by a vision of sand, and the vast, fallen corpses of trees; the wind swirled dust into a funnel—and the room returned.

Rool Tiazan folded his hands and awaited what the scholar might make of such communication.

"Our other ally, speaks, I apprehend." The old man raised a hand and sighed. "That is a mighty work," he said sadly, "and an irredeemable loss. Yet how was it accomplished?"

The room flickered, there was impression of baleful energies, greatly confused, yet more accurate than Rool would have expected from a form-bound intelligence—and then nothing more.

"Ah." The scholar turned, looked to him, his eyes deep with wisdom. "You, my master of energy states. *You* know how it was accomplished, do you not?"

Rool bowed his head. "Grandfather, I do. The Iloheen caused probability to be altered so that increasing amounts of inimical energies were aimed at the world which had been inhabited by the *ssussdriad*."

Liad dea'Syl laughed. "So I am told, and having been told, understand nothing."

Rool smiled, and swept out a hand. "Forgive me, Scholar. I am as a bird in the air . . ."

"Indeed. Indeed. And yet, you have the means, as I understand from our discussions in the night hours, to . . . change state, and to observe the workings and progress of the Enemy. Is that so?"

"Stipulating that I dare not show myself, nor come too close," Rool said slowly, "yes, that is so." He paused. "Shall I go, observe what I might, and return to tell you?"

"Will the bird bring news of aerodynamics, lift, and thrust?" The scholar smiled, and reached out to rub Lucky's ear. "Perhaps you might bear me to a point of observation."

It had been within the possibility described by the current configuration of the lines that this boon would be asked. Rool closed his eyes and took counsel of his lady.

"It is," he said slowly, "possible." He opened his eyes. "Whether it is desirable . . ." He sighed. "There is a price . . ."

"There is," the old scholar interrupted tartly, "*always* a price, Ser Tiazan. I am not a child."

"Indeed. Indeed, you are not a child, Grandfather. But I must be selfish in this—you may not die before those equations are set."

Liad dea'Syl smiled. "Guard me, then," he said. "And snatch me away to safety when you judge it best. But I would see this work of the Enemy."

Rool bowed. "I am at your command. When shall we proceed?"

"At once."

THE PORT WAS MORE crowded than ever he recalled, with a great many high-caste persons about. Nor was he the only one to notice it.

"That's a lot of expensive citizens I'm seeing," Cantra yos'Phelium commented at his side. "Streets weren't near so full, yesterday."

"The High Families are not usually so well represented on-port," he agreed, and touched his tongue to his dry lips.

"Forgive me, Pilot," he murmured, and felt himself flush when she glanced at him.

"What's on your mind?" she asked easily, giving no sign of noticing his discomfort.

"I wonder—your face, and—your hands. How is that they are healed?"

"One of Jela's friends stopped by last night and did me the favor," she answered, and gave him another casual glance from green eyes. "Last I saw him, he was set to call on the scholar and yourself."

"You will mean Rool Tiazan," he said, around a feeling of relief. "He represented himself as an ally to Captain Jela." He bit his lip. "Are you easy with this person, Pilot?"

"Not to say easy," she answered after a moment. "Takes some getting used to, does Rool Tiazan. Don't care for doors—" another quick green glance— "which may be what's bothered you, Pilot." She used her chin to point to the left. "That's our road, I think."

"There were," he pursued, turning his steps to match hers, and dodging 'round a floater piled high with expensive luggage, "several things which were worrisome. The first was, as you say, the matter of not entering by the door. He—you will think I refine too much on it, perhaps, but—he seemed to know me on sight, Pilot, though he addressed me as 'housefather.'"

"Right. Calls me 'lady,' in case you've taste for irony, Pilot. Doubtless it amuses him, and does me—nor you—no harm. How'd the old gentleman take him?"

"Well," he answered, and sighed to hear how bitter voice was. "Very well," he said again, trying for a more moderate tone. "They were at work together through the night, and still in deep converse when I rose to keep my appointment with Arin. Lucky also seems favorably impressed," he added after a moment, recalling again, and with a pang, the sight of the cat curled tight on Rool Tiazan's knees.

"Sounds like all's in hand, then. Wink an eye at his oddity, is what I advise, Pilot."

Yes, well. "But—" he said, as the military shuttle hove into view— "*what* is he? Rool Tiazan?"

Pilot Cantra didn't answer immediately, and when she did, it was slow, as if she was feeling her way toward an answer.

"Calls himself a *dramliza*. What that means in practical terms— which is what you an' me need to think in, Pilot—is that he was a soldier for the Enemy. Him and some of his, though, they deserted, for reasons that seemed good to them. Rool Tiazan and his-lady-that-was, they offered themselves as allies to Jela, who thought it would be of benefit." She sent him another quick glance, and sighed. "It was by way of serving the interests of that alliance that Scholar dea'Syl was brought out of Osabei and given to Wellik for safekeeping."

"He offered the scholar aid. He said that he was—an expert on energy states."

"That he may well be," Pilot Cantra said judiciously, and gave the guard at the shuttle door a friendly nod. "I'm Cantra yos'Phelium, heir to M. Jela Granthor's Guard. I'd like to go up and inspect my ship, if there's a shuttle to be had."

The guard frowned down at her, his facial tattoos gaudy in the pale morning light. "What ship?" he rumbled, deep in his chest.

"That'd be *Salkithin*," she said composedly.

"Would it. And who's with you?"

"Tor An yos'Galan," she answered, and if her heart quailed under the X Strain's stare, as his did, no hint of it was apparent on her face. "My co-pilot."

The guard jerked his chin, toggling the comm, muttered, hit the toggle again, and stepped back.

From inside the ship came another X Strain, this one with lieutenant's chops on her sleeve. She crossed her arms over her chest and stared down the ramp at Pilot Cantra and himself.

"Jela's heir, is it?"

Pilot Cantra bowed, brief and ironic; the lieutenant grinned, broadly.

"Ilneri's going to be real happy with you," she said, in a voice that Tor An thought did not bode well for the coming ship's inspection, and stood aside, sweeping an exaggerated bow.

"Please, pilots, enter my humble shuttle. I hope you're in a hurry."

THE LINES LAY thick about them, red-gold and vital, spilling energy enough to conceal one wary, weary *dramliza,* and the essence of an ancient human. The *ssussdriad* was also with them; its regard lying so gently amongst the lines that Rool could scarcely discern it.

The *ssussdriad* was the best husband of itself, as it had proven, many times. That which was on the physical plane Liad dea'Syl burned with a hunger for knowledge so bright that lesser urges— such as survival—paled beside it. The scholar was a danger to himself in this place, and a danger thereby to all that was.

Rool held the scholar's precious essence furled in green-and-ebon wings, both shielding it and directing its attention—out, to that far yet too near space where the Iloheen worked their changes.

The process approaches critical mass, he sent gently. *Observe.*

It was a small thing to observe, even from this level. Merely, a Shadow fell across lines, stars and lives, replacing all with—nothing.

The lines stretched, then parted with a sob; the stars screamed as they were extinguished, the lives they had engendered gone before they realized the danger. The anguish of unmaking struck Rool at the core, and from the one he protected came a gasp, a wail—and an ominous wavering among his energies.

You have seen enough, he sent, and received no protest. The *ssussdriad* had already departed. Rool folded his wings and followed.

AS IT HAPPENED, Sergeant Ilneri *had* been happy to see them, after a period of attitude adjustment which hadn't maybe been all that good on the boy's nerves. Test passed, though, the rest of the crew had been pleased to see them, too, and nothing would do except they show off every cranny and cubby of proud *Salkithin*, talking twelve qwint to a flan about Jela.

Happened this particular crew'd been Jela's own from when *Salkithin* had been put to sleep, six Common Years ago and a bit. It were a mixed crew—three X Strains, two Ms, a Y and Ilneri, who was, as far as Cantra could make it, a natural human—and they all had something to tell about the "little Captain."

There was the time Jela and two others had come down late from the work, and were set on by a gang of what passed for toughs on Solcintra. And the time that Stile—one of the Xs—the time that Captain Jela had talked Wellik out of slamming Stile into detention for—well, it didn't exactly matter for what—saying he needed her on the roster or the work would fall behind. And the next day, didn't the captain put her up against the wall hard and let her know he didn't tolerate stupidity in his crew, and if there was *any* additional slippage, detention was going to look damn' soft . . .

"There were some of the troop," Vachik, the second and most talkative of the X Strains, told them, "some of them thought to taunt us with our captain, and called us 'Jela's Troop,' like it was less than soldier's honor to take his orders."

"They learned better," Ilneri said, with a wide, wolfish grin. "And we're still Jela's Troop."

And so, what with one thing and a tale, it was deep into Solcintra nighttime when the shuttle settled back into its cradle at the port and her and the boy and Ilneri and Stile strolled down the ramp.

"Missed the party," the night guard told them, jovially. "Damn' near had us a genuine riot to quell."

Ilneri frowned and looked around, and Cantra did, too, seeing only a peaceful backwater port about its lawful evening bidness, saving a broken window or six, and some extra trash on the street.

"What happened?" the good sergeant asked, in a tone that conveyed it would go bad if the guard was indulging himself with a short round of leg pulling.

"Service Families finally figured it out," the guard answered, clearly disinterested in the why. "Wellik's got the speakers-for with him now. Got the word from the gate there's a crowd waiting for them to come out, but everybody's staying peaceful. So far."

"All right, then." Ilneri looked over his shoulder. "Stay close, Pilots."

"Right you are," Cantra assured him with a grin. Ilneri laughed.

"B'gods, I can see why Jela liked you, Pilot. But—mind me, now: *stay close*." He turned a stern eye on the boy. "You're her co-pilot; make it so."

"I am certain that the pilot will not put herself in danger," Tor An said, straight-faced and earnest, and for all Cantra could tell, believing it as he spoke it.

Ilneri nodded, directed Stile to bring up the rear and the four of them moved on, the sergeant a bit ahead and concentrating on shadows. Cantra kept pace with the boy, and a watchful eye out.

"What," Tor An asked, for her ear only, "did the Service Families figure out, Pilot?"

She sighed. "The man I was drinking with yesterday, before things went and got interesting, had it that the High Families were vacating the premises, which was what all the extra shipping—including that liner—was up to."

He turned wide, shocked eyes on her, like this was the first story he'd ever heard when them what had took advantage over them what didn't.

"They removed to safety and left the Service—but no!" He frowned. "That cannot be possible. The High Families—you understand, Pilot, that they govern. The Service Families—they do everything that is needful. They—they cannot have—"

"Thought it through, sounds like," Cantra agreed. She put a soft hand on the boy's sleeve. "Listen. You hear that crowd breathing?"

He tipped his head, holding his own breath, until— "Yes."

"Good. Let's close it up with Ilneri, Pilot. We want to pass through this quick as we can."

He didn't argue, nor did Stile object to coming up tighter, as they rounded the corner and saw the crowd before the gate.

Hundreds—maybe thousands, Cantra thought, standing still and watchful in the searchlights from the garrison. There were soldiers deployed, long arms on display and combat shields down over their faces, keeping the road to the gate clear. The tension rising up off the crowd was enough to make a pilot's ears ring and the heart squeeze a little in her chest, despite everything being peaceful.

For now.

Ilneri set them a business-like, unalarming pace down that long row of watchful faces, and Cantra let out the breath she hadn't known she'd been holding when they finally passed through the gate and were inside the garrison proper.

"Ah!" Tor An gasped and would have stopped, excepting Stile reached out and gently pushed him onward.

"There's the lieutenant up ahead, Pilot," she said to him, in a large whisper. "We'll need to get cleared."

Twelve paces out from the officer's position, Ilneri stopped, smacked his heels together smart and whipped off a salute so sharp it was like to cut somebody.

"Sergeant Ilneri and Specialist Stile escorting Pilots yos'Phelium and yos'Galan," he rapped out. "Sir."

"Troops report to Technical Services," the lieutenant said. "Pilot yos'Phelium. You and your co-pilot are to report to Captain Wellik, soonest."

TWENTY-EIGHT

Solcintra

"THERE'S NO COMPROMISE on Captain's Justice," Cantra said for the third or eighty-fourth time. Her voice was barely more than a cracked whisper after all these hours of negotiation, and at that she wasn't the most worn of those at the table. The boy—Tor An—he was running on guts and honor; and Vel Ter jo'Bern—second on the Service Families side—was actually trembling. The first on the Families' side of the table, and Cantra's opposite, was one Nalli Olanek, who looked as fresh and as perky as a new coin, damn her timonium-wrapped nerves.

"Pilot," Nalli said again, "surely you must see that we cannot submit to the decision of a single individual in matters of life and death—"

Cantra pushed back her chair and stood. Tor An blinked, and came to his feet within the next heartbeat—a proper co-pilot, backing his pilot's judgment. Vel Ter jo'Bern gaped. Nalli Olanek waited, her hands folded neatly on the table.

"We been through this," Cantra told her, "and I'm only going to say it one time more, after which we'll be leaving you gentles to decide just how much you want a ride out of here. I will take leave to remind you it's the Service Families seeking this contract, not the pilots. The pilots have a vessel and are free to depart as they will. Their need for passengers is—" She bent forward slightly, staring hard into Nalli Olanek's gray eyes. "Let's just say our need for passengers isn't *acute*. That read out clear to you, Speaker?"

The other woman inclined her head, face bland.

"Good. Now—Captain's Justice. Despite whatever might work on the ground here in terms of councils and consensus, on a ship there can only be one voice that's law; one person who decides for the ship, and therefore the common good. The difference between a ship's life and death is sometimes only heartbeats—there's no time to consult a committee and have the matter discussed and re-discussed until a compromise can be had. If it comes down to it— which, Deeps willing, it won't—and the choice is whether to jettison half the outer ring in order to preserve the other half and the pilots— then that decision of ship's survival rightly falls to the captain. Not to the passengers, and not to the co-pilot, neither, saving if the captain's incapacitated. The hierarchy of a ship, Speaker—as I've said, and as Pilot yos'Galan has likewise said—is this: The co-pilot cares for the pilot. The pilot cares for the ship and for the passengers. In that order." She took a hard breath and traded long stares with Nalli Olanek.

"If you and yours can't abide by that hierarchy, then you and yours can find some other way off this world."

Nalli Olanek inclined her head. "Your insistence that the captain be the final arbiter of any disputes between the passengers is—"

"Is non-negotiable," Cantra interrupted. "Part and parcel of the captain's duty to the greater good. If the integrity of most of the passengers can be insured by spacing one person, you can be sure that's what will happen. Now." She bent forward, putting her hands flat on the table, and looked from Olanek to jo'Bern.

"If you object to the captain having final judgment over your folk, then all you have to do is solve your own problems and never let them reach the captain's ear. Once the captain's aware of a problem, it *will be* solved. Am I clear here, Speaker? I don't want to leave you any doubts."

Stares again, and for a wonder Nalli Olanek looked away first.

"Pilot, you are clear. We should perhaps, as you suggest, adjourn, and meet here again in six hours to finalize the contract."

"Suits." Cantra pushed herself upright and caught the boy's eye. "Pilot."

He bowed to the two Grounders. "Speaker," he murmured. "Elder Hedrede." Cantra let his courtesy count for both of them and strode to the door, knocked and strode out when it opened, the boy at her heels.

Kwinz was waiting at the end of the hall, looking neither rested nor tired.

"Pilots," she said, with a respectful nod. "Captain Wellik requests a word."

Cantra stopped and frowned. "There was something I meant to settle with Wellik," she said, her voice cracked and wandering. "You recall what that might've been, Pilot yos'Galan?"

The boy cleared his throat. "I am not perfectly certain, Pilot," he answered, his pretty voice scarcely more than a thread. "But I believe you intended to tear off his arm and use it to beat him to death."

"That was it." She grinned up at Kwinz. "It'll be my pleasure to have a word with the captain, Corporal. Lead on."

If Kwinz thought about grinning, she didn't share the moment. Blank-faced, she spun sharp on a heel and marched straight-backed down the hall.

THE AETHER WAS THICK with ice, the ley lines shriveled and thin. Tentatively, Lute extended his will, touched a line—felt it tremble, stagger, and sob. It lost luster even as he enclosed it within his regard, all bright promises of hope shredding away into darkness.

He released the line with a pang, while the icy wind brought him the taint of a separate poison—his lady's sister, bringing her troops and her weapons to bear.

Slowly, he slipped toward the physical plane, tarrying at the fourth level, where the Spiral Arm displayed itself in a simple dance of light—and all but cried out.

He *knew*—at the very core of his being, he knew—what it was that the Iloheen intended. And yet to see it thus—the dance blighted, the light blotted . . . and the Shadow—the Shadow growing so quickly . . .

Wailing, he fell into his body, and lifted a tear-streaked face to his lady.

"What is it?" She asked, looking up from her loom with a frown.

"The stars," he began, as if he were a child—and could go no further. He bent his head, covered his face—and looked up with a gasp when his lady's hand came warm upon his shoulder.

"Nay," she said softly, and there were tears on her face, as well. "Weep, for the dying of the light. Who has more right?"

Who, indeed? He thought, but made an effort to master himself, nonetheless.

"Your sister," he whispered. "Her lance is poised."

"Ah." Lady Moonhawk inclined her head. "We shall seek Rool Tiazan, then. When you have finished dispensing your grace."

WELLIK WAS STANDING over the tank-map behind his desk, staring into the starry depths. He glanced up as they entered, delivered himself of a brief, "Thank you, Kwinz. Dismissed." and returned to his stare.

Kwinz took her orders to heart, the door closing emphatically behind her.

"You'll want to know, Pilot Cantra," Wellik said, his attention still on the tank, "that the archeology crew vacated this afternoon. Nice, clean departure. Professional, you might say."

"Right." Cantra considered the side of his face. "Saw Arin's brother on the port yesterday, which is prolly what inspired the change in quarters."

"It's a good thing, so I've heard, to have brothers," Wellik said ruminatively. "Brothers in arms, for instance . . ." His voice faded, mouth tightening.

Cantra waited, and when she'd counted out a dozen heartbeats and he still stood caught in his brood, offering neither order nor invitation, she walked over to stand beside him.

"Take a look," Wellik said, as soft as his big voice might manage. "You're an astute woman, Pilot. What d'you make of that?"

She looked down into the tank, at the swirl and glitter and busyness that was the Spiral Arm in miniature.

. . . at the places where the swirl was ragged and wrong. At the pattern that was taking shape out of the new darkness, as if in null reflection . . .

"That's not looking good, if you don't mind my saying so, Captain," she said slowly. "I'm missing a lot of what I shouldn't be off a map of this caliber."

"Real-time updates," he said, and tapped a finger against the display, bringing a certain, particular sector of nothing up close and personal.

"Headquarters," he muttered, looking down. "Or—where Headquarters isn't anymore." He sent her a grin, hard and humorless. "We're on our own."

"Thought you didn't report to Headquarters."

"We didn't," he said seriously. "But even soldiers nourish expectations, Pilot. The expectation of the war eventually being won, for instance. The expectation that the High Command will spit in the faces of those who bought them, and take up true soldier's duty again." He sighed, and tapped the display, shrinking his particular bit of nothing back into the whole. "There are no expectations, now, except of an inglorious defeat, in which a few of us may survive to *run away*."

"Life wants to live, Captain," she said softly, and Wellik snorted.

"So it does. Speaking of which, how do your talks with the Families progress?"

"About as well as you thought they would when you put us in the position of having to deal with them at all," she answered, too tired to even snarl. "Why's it gotta be us? You got transport to spare."

He raised his head and looked at her, as bleak as she'd ever seen a man.

"We take rear-guard," he said, stark and plain. "It's our duty and our honor to protect those who are not soldiers."

"Meaning you won't have 'em in your way." Cantra sighed. "Can't say I blame you. Don't much care to have 'em in my way."

"They do not properly grasp ship protocol," Tor An added, surprisingly, from his vantage across the tank. "Pilot Cantra has very clearly explained ship necessities and the reasons which shape each, and I believe that Speaker Olanek has finally understood that upon points of ship's safety, the Captain is the final judge."

"She better understand it," Cantra said to Wellik's upraised eyebrow. "Because if she doesn't, she and hers can stay right here, soldier honor be damned." She sighed and raked her fingers through her hair. Deeps, she was tired. "They're supposed to come back in six hours with a viable contract, and somewhere before that, the pilots have got to have some downtime."

Wellik nodded, and moved toward his desk. "I won't keep you much longer," he said. "We did an analysis on the transitions of the ships the High Families hired—they're heading In."

Tor An looked down into the tank, then to Cantra, his brows pulled tight.

"There are . . . instances of Enemy action Inside, as well," he murmured. "These layers of darkness on the captain's map . . ."

"That's right," Wellik said. "They're taking bites where it pleases them. Or, as soldier-kind learns in creche—no place is safe." He picked something up off his desk. "Pilot Cantra," he said, and tossed it, soft and low.

She caught it—another log book like the one Jela'd carried—and riffled the pages, finding them uniformly blank.

"What am I supposed to do with this?" she asked. Wellik shrugged, and turned back to his desk.

"Whatever you want, Pilot. You seemed to have an attachment to Jela's fieldbook, so I thought you'd maybe like one of your own. It doesn't do me any good."

"Right." The leather felt smooth and soothing against her fingers. She tucked it inside her jacket and looked at Tor An, jerking her head toward the door. He took the hint, wobbling a little as he walked.

She sent a last hard look down into the tank—so *much* darkness—and followed him. Halfway to the door, she stopped; looked to the desk, and the big man bent over it, shoulders hunched.

"Get some rest, why not, Captain?" She said, easy and gentle. Comradely.

He shot her a glance over his shoulder, inclined at first to be prideful; then smiled, lopsided.

"I'll do that, Pilot. Thank you."

"'s'all right," she said and took the boy's arm. "Let's go, Pilot. Shift's over."

THE JOURNEY to the inner lattices had tired the old one; the direct experience of the Iloheen's work had struck him to the core. He had returned to his body changed—as who would not be, having beheld the death of stars?—and with determination reborn within him.

"I see it," he had murmured, as Rool eased him into his bed, and his lady reached forth their hands to soothe him. "I see how it must be done . . ."

"Grandfather, that is well," she said gently. "Rest now, and recruit your strength. We shall all stand ready to do your biding, when you wake."

Perforce, the old man had slept, cocooned in healing energies. Rool straightened the quilt over the frail body, and smiled as the cat settled himself against the old one's hip.

"Well done," he murmured. "The scholar requires all the aid that we may give him."

He moved into the common room, and over to the window. This state of idle waiting—it was new, and odd. And unsettling, as even here, in this form, and on this plane, he could feel the Iloheen's will gathering. Soon. Very soon.

A disturbance in the energies of the room brought him 'round from the window. He bowed, gently and with no irony intended.

"Lady Moonhawk. Brother."

"Rool Tiazan," the lady answered, with unexpected courtesy. "Sister. Doubtless, you are aware of the Iloheen and the progress of their work. Indeed, I should imagine that you might find the progress of their work . . . deafening."

"Nearly so," he admitted.

"You may, therefore, *not* be aware that our esteemed sister has put some portion of her forces into harrying the Iloheen at their work. I assume she does this to take advantage of whatever elasticity reside within the lines, thus far from the event."

"Doubtless." He flicked his will outward, found the lines and the pattern, thought a curse, and returned to his body to find Lute smiling sardonically.

"She can ruin all, can she not?"

"Nay, I think not—all," Rool answered. "Though certainly she may introduce . . . unneeded complexity . . ." He turned his attention to the lady.

"I ask—your preparations are made?"

"The Weaving is complete. Fourteen templates have been crafted and stand to hand."

"Fourteen?" Lute turned to her, eyes wide. "I—surely, Thirteen."

"Nay," she said softly. "Fourteen. You have earned your freedom, whatever that may come to mean." She slanted a cool glance toward Rool. "I thank my sister for her instruction."

He felt her move forward within their shared essence. "You are most welcome," she said. "It falls to chance, now, all and each. We shall not meet again, I think, sister. Go you in grace."

"And you," the other answered.

The energies swirled—and Rool stood alone once more.

THE AROMA OF FRESH, enticing goodness hit her the second she opened the door, and by the time the door had closed and she'd crossed the room to where it sat in front of the window, her mouth was watering, her body clamoring. She could see the very pod, outlined against the window, the branch bowed slightly with its weight—the pod that had been grown and nurtured especially—only—for her.

"Right," she said and forced herself to move away from the window, to pull the leather book out of her jacket, and put it with finicky care in the very center of the desk. That done, she slipped the jacket off, shook it and draped it over the back of the chair. A couple of deep, centering, breaths, and finally she went to the window, leaned a hip against the wall, crossed her arms over her chest, and addressed the tree.

"Now, as I recall it," she said, her voice rasping with overuse, "Jela told you this particular hobby wasn't a good use of your resources. He was right, as far as I'm able to determine. But there's something else you have to know and think on—a being as long-lived as maybe you'll be." She took a breath, and it was all she could do not to reach out a hand and take that pod, that smelled so good and looked ripe to eat now.

"What you got to realize is that *humans are hard*. You just can't go shuffling their designs around, and changing them on the fly. They need study, and long thought. Planning. We live fast, compared to yourself; one tiny miscalculation and you've set twelve generations on the wrong course. Actions have consequences—and what you want to avoid is those unintended consequences that destroy all the good intentions you ever had." She sighed. "I'm assuming, you understand, for Jela's sake, that your intentions tend to generally align with humankind's, which for the sake of this discussion we'll call 'good.'"

Across the cloudless sky behind her eyes, a dragon glided, smooth and strong, wind whispering over its wide leather wings.

Cantra nodded at the pod. "Me, now, I appreciate your care, but I'm not going to avail myself of that particular pod. I'm going to have some sleep, because I'm tired, and humans, they sleep when they're tired."

No response, save that the tantalizing aroma faded slowly, 'til she couldn't smell it at all. The pod in question broke away from its branch, with a sharp, pure *snap*, and landed on the dirt inside the pot.

"Thank you," she whispered, and pushed away from the wall with an effort, heading for her bed.

TWENTY-NINE

Solcintra

SHE GOT TWO HOURS' SLEEP before the kid woke her up, shoved a mug of hot tea into her hand and dragged her down the hall. There, they'd found the scholar in a fever of calculation so intense he'd barely been able to wrap his tongue around a non-math sentence. In the end, he'd simply spun the screen so they could see for themselves— 'quations that sent a chill down her piloting nerves, and fetched an actual gasp out of the boy.

More tea and a quick meal happened between questions—not all of which were asked before it came time for pilot and co-pilot to depart for the meeting with the client.

Nalli Olanek was before them in the conference room, attended by a man so non-descript, Cantra thought he would have vanished entire, had it not been for the scroll under his hand.

"Speaker," she said, inclining her head, but not bothering to sit down. "You get the contract written?"

"Indeed." Nalli Olanek moved a hand and her companion rose, bowing with neither flattery nor irony.

"Captain yos'Phelium," he said, offering the scroll across his

707

two palms, as if it were priceless treasure. "It is my sincere belief that I have conveyed the agreed-upon duties, responsibilities and command chains accurately."

She eyed him. "Who are you? If it can be told."

He bowed again, and gave her a surprisingly straight look right in the eye. His were brown.

"My name is dea'Gauss, Captain. Account and contract keeping are the services which my Family has been honored to provide for the High."

"I see." She extended a hand, caught the boy around his wrist and brought him forward. "This is my co-pilot, Tor An yos'Galan. He'll sit right here with you and go over those lines. If everything checks out with him, then he'll bring it to me—same like you've got outlined in that section on command chains, right?"

"That is correct, Captain."

"Good. Me an' Speaker Olanek need to take a little trip."

The Speaker's eyebrows rose. "Do we, indeed? May one know our destination?"

Cantra gave her a hard, serious stare. "I want you to have a tour of the ship," she said. "Get a good idea of what you and yours are contracting for."

Nalli Olanek frowned. "We are contracting for passage off of Solcintra and—"

Cantra held up a hand. "You're contracting to travel on a ship," she interrupted. "Ever been on a ship, Speaker?"

The other woman's lips thinned. "Of course not," she said distastefully.

"Right. Which is why you need the tour. You not being wishful of putting your folk in the way of Captain's Justice, it'll fall to you to figure out how to keep them calm and happy and out of the captain's way. And to do that, you need to see, touch and smell exactly what you're contracting for." She jerked her head toward the door.

"Let's go. Soonest begun, soonest done, as my foster-mother used to say."

※　　※　　※

CREDIT WHERE CREDIT was earned, Cantra conceded: Nalli Olanek was tough. It was clear enough that the means and workings of *Salkithin* distressed her. By the time they'd finished the tour, and Sergeant Ilneri had delivered himself of a short lesson on slow-sleep so pat and slick she figured he must've only given it twelve hundred times before, the Speaker was pale, but she hadn't broke out into active horror, nor demanded to be brought back down to cozy Solcintra where the council of law called outlaw to any such devices as the *sheriekas* might use, and others of more normal habit to the wider galaxy. Gene selection beyond physical pick-and-choose, commercial AI, even personal comm units were either disallowed or else heavily regulated on Solcintra, and though many such devices would have given the service class an easier life, they seemed as wedded to the minimal tech as their now-departed overseers.

Seeing her charge was like to wobble a bit in her trajectory, Cantra set them a course for the galley and waved the other woman to a table while she poured them each a mug of tea.

"You'll want to be careful of that," she said as she settled into the chair opposite. "It'll be pilot's tea—strong an' sweet." She sipped, watching with amusement while Nalli Olanek sampled her drink and struggled to keep the distaste from reaching her face.

"S'all right," Cantra said comfortably. "What they call an acquired taste." She had another sip and set her mug aside, looking straight and as honest as she could muster into Nalli Olanek's cool gray eyes.

"Now's the time to say out what you think, Speaker. Your folk going to hold still for putting their lives in the care of this ship—not to say the slow-sleep?"

The other woman sighed. "Truthfully, Captain—it will be a challenge, even in the face of such an enormous catastrophe as Captain Wellik proposes. Slow-sleep—" She closed her eyes, opened them, and pushed her mug toward the center of the table.

"You understand," she said, "that I must ask this, though I believe I know what your answer will be. Is it necessary that we ride as sleepers, wholly dependent upon the—the devices that govern the operations of this vessel for our well-being?"

"Sleepers don't use as much of the ship's resources," Cantra answered. "Since we don't know where we're going, and we don't know how long we'll be a-ship, the pilots have got to calculate on the conservative side of the 'quations; we'd not being filling our guarantee of care for all the passengers doing it any other way. It ain't our intention to dice with anybody's life. Now. You heard what Sergeant Ilneri had to say about the redundant life-support systems, right?"

Nalli Olanek's mouth tightened. "I did. And I understand that he meant to convey the point that, should the . . . device . . . supporting the sleepers fail, the ship would be in such peril as to be unlikely itself to survive."

Cantra looked at her with approval. "That's it. Those asleep are every bit as well-protected as those of us who're going to be awake for the whole adventures. The captain makes no difference between who's asleep and who's not in her calculations of passenger safety." She sipped tea, watching the other woman over the rim of the mug. "There ain't any High or Low 'mong the passengers on this ship, 'cept as you need to keep trouble out of my hair. I won't have it, and I don't expect to have it proposed."

"I understand." The Speaker folded her hands on the table, knuckles showing pale. "Livestock—"

"Livestock travels as embryos and Batch samples," Cantra said. "It's gotta be that way, for all those good reasons the sergeant listed out for you. The ship's equipped with reconstitution equipment. Captain Wellik states the garrison stands ready to help get those samples in order for you, if needed."

"We have samples and Batch seed, as it happens," Nalli Olanek murmured, and smiled when Cantra looked at her in surprise. "Several of the husbander Families have created a . . . bank, as I believe they call it, in case there should be an emergency requiring that the flocks and herds be re-established." She reached for the tea mug; thought better of it, and refolded her hands. "I believe they were thinking in terms of illness—plague. But—surely this qualifies as an emergency."

"You could say." Cantra finished her tea, and considered the other woman. "Some other info you're going to need. Share it or hold it—that's your call. But you need to have it, so you understand what we're likely to have before us."

Nalli Olanek snorted lightly. "We have received much information from Captain Wellik's office. Also, we have—obtained those records upon which the High Families based their decision to return to the core. I believe that we are conversant—"

Cantra held up her hand. Nalli Olanek stopped, eyebrows arched delicately.

"I figured Wellik'd be free with the info of what's coming," she said. "What he doesn't have—though he should by the time we get back to the ground—is a picture of what comes *after* we make what Ilneri's calling a retreat."

"Ah. I had assumed that we would simply outrun the Enemy; locate worlds beyond the Rim, perhaps."

Grounders. Cantra felt the sharp words lining up on her tongue—and heard Jela's voice, damn' near in her ear. *She doesn't have the math, Pilot. She's never seen the Rim; there's no way she can know it like we do . . .*

Well. She looked down at her mug, then back to Nalli Olanek.

"The Enemy's actions," she said, keeping her voice friendly and calm— "the decrystallization, like Scholar dea'Syl names it—that's creating a wave front of energy—or say it creates an opportunity for that wavefront to exist. The actual math is tricky, admitted. What we're going to be doing is riding this wave of opportunity straight on out of—straight out of everything we know, Speaker. The best the scholar can figure is that those objects and energy states which haven't been compromised by the Enemy's actions will be *introduced* into another—energy phase let's call it—and then into—another galaxy."

"Another galaxy . . ." the Speaker repeated, brows drawn. "But such forces—we will be damaging . . . existing worlds?"

"Don't know," Cantra said, which was the truth as spoken by none other than Rool Tiazan, damn his pretty blue eyes. "Never been done before. Don't know if we can do it now, though the scholar's math says it's possible." She paused, then added, in the spirit of being as honest with the client as was safe. "Understand, it's not a risk-free thing we're doing. The only reason to take this kind of chance is because there's no other choice."

Silence.

When it had stretched a while, and Speaker Olanek didn't look any less grim or get any more communicative, Cantra cleared her throat.

"What's good," she said, making her voice sound like it was just that. "What's good is that the initial burst—that ought to be fast. And see, what you can't tell from down here in the thick of this galaxy, is that really, most of what's in a galaxy is empty space, anyhow. The Arm's collided with other galaxies back in the 'way back, so pilot lore tells us, and mostly what happened is we moved through each other like ghosts.

"So what we'll be doing is going into a transition, almost like normal. That part'll be quick, real quick. What we might have to do in order to come to land, that might could take a while. Which brings us right 'round again to the necessity of slow-sleep."

"I—see." There was a little more silence, then Nalli Olanek pushed away from the table and stood.

"I thank you for the tour, Captain yos'Phelium," she said formally. "It has been most informative. I believe we should return home—" Her face tightened, and she took a hard breath. "I believe we should return to Solcintra, and see if your co-pilot has cleared the contract for signature."

"Right you are." Cantra came to her feet, collected the mugs and set them into the washer, then led the way down the hall to the shuttle bay.

THIRTY

❀❀❀❀❀❀❀❀❀❀❀❀❀❀❀❀❀❀❀❀❀❀❀❀❀

Solcintra Near Orbit

THE BOY SAT the board like he belonged there, which was a good thing, Cantra thought. Ought to be one of the two of 'em knew what he was doing.

Granted, Pilot Y. Argast had checked them both out on the full board, neither stinting nor accepting less than perfect from the pilots who were going to be flying *Jela's ship*. And granted that they'd both passed muster. The boy, though, he sat his tests cool as Solcintra snow, showing confident clear through—and it weren't no bogus confident, either, not from a lad as easy to read as the for'ard screens.

Herself, she'd given Argast as much confidence as he liked, and an edge of Rimmer attitude to go with, which might've been enough to help him miss the fact that she'd damn' near bobbled twice—or maybe not, though he was respectful enough not to mention it.

"Captain Wellik sends that he's coming up, and requests a meeting with the pilots," he'd said, leaving the observer's chair with a grin so cocky he might've been a Rimmer himself.

Cantra eyed him. "He say why?"

Argast's grin got cockier. "Captain doesn't give me his secrets to hold," he said. "You're lucky he sent ahead."

Though truth told, he hadn't sent that far ahead. The tower door had barely closed on Argast's heels, when it opened again and there was Wellik, trailing an honor guard, and carrying a case.

"Permission to enter the tower, Captain?" he'd said, with no perceptible irony.

Cantra sighed. "Looks to me like you're already in."

"In fact," he agreed, "I am. We'll do this as quickly as possible, as none of us has time to waste . . ." He put the case up on the board's ledge, opened it and in short order produced about twenty-eight sets of ship keys, emergency keys, gun-bay keys, lock-up keys—plus, as she might've known there would be, forms to sign for each set, certifying that she'd received them.

Forms signed and stowed, Wellik brought another handful of papers out of his case.

"Captain, as you are no doubt aware," he said, brisk and straight-faced, "policy requires that any vessel decommissioned from military service must retire its name. Now, I've put down on the manifests here—" he rattled his fist full of paperwork— "that *Salkithin* is being decommissioned and turned over to an appropriate agency, which intends to put it into service as a luxury cruise vessel . . ."

The boy sneezed—which saved her the trouble of doing it herself. Wellik looked up from his paper with a frown.

"As per instructions received from M. Jela Granthor's Guard," he continued, forcefully. "My office has completed the appropriate paperwork, excepting the names and affiliations of the new owners and the name of the vessel. We have, to insure compliance, provided work crew and materials." He glanced up again, teasing a single sheet of print-out from the rest.

"Before we proceed, Captain yos'Phelium, your co-pilot requested that you be given this information, since I encountered him first on the issue. He felt it was a good thing that the name of the vessel be demobilized, granting the sometimes quaint and even superstitious approach to life exhibited by the local population."

Frowning, Cantra took the paper, gave it a quick read—and then another, slower.

Salkithin—Jela's own sweet ship—had been named after a planet on which a force of less than twenty thousand soldiers had successfully held off an enemy attack until a trap could be sprung. Thing was, the planet's forces—and the planet—died with the enemy. Damn' if that didn't sound like a familiar situation.

Salkithin. Soldiers found that kind of naming important, and for herself, she wouldn't have cared. The gentle citizens of Solcintra, though—that was another matter. The boy had the right of it. And, she thought, he *did* have the right of it—he'd caught the problem before it became a problem, just like a co-pilot ought to do.

"I'm going to be meeting with Sergeant Ilneri," Wellik was saying, "and doing an inspection. I'll leave these with you—" He held the papers out to the boy, who received them with a slight bow. "Please fill in the name of your ship, sign the forms and have them ready for me when I'm done inspection."

He turned, sealed up the case, took it in hand, and was gone, waving them an airy salute.

Cantra glared at the blameless door. "Now, what I don't know about naming ships—" she began—and then stopped because the comm let go with its incoming message tone.

Wellik's papers still in hand, Tor An crossed the tower—communications being on the co-pilot's side of the board—flipped a toggle—

"Tcha!" he said, sounding something between put-out and impatient.

"What now? The local priests want to bless the hull and shrive the pilots?"

He turned from the board, a half-smile on his mouth.

"Nothing quite so drastic. The dea'Gauss sends that he must bring us an amended contract for review and signature."

"Amended?" She frowned. "Amended how?"

He glanced back at his screen. "It would appear that the Service Families have . . . reformulated themselves and are now the High Houses of Solcintra. The dea'Gauss believes that an addendum putting forth this lineage will—be in the pilot's interests, should there be a dispute regarding payment."

"Which you know and I know and dea'Gauss knows there likely will be," Cantra pointed out. "Not to say that Nalli Olanek ain't as honorable as they come when dealing with one of her own. But I'm betting there ain't no rules saying she's got to treat straight with a pair of *kenake* pilots. Stands to reason she'll do her utmost to short us."

The boy sighed and turned from the screen. "I believe you are correct, Pilot," he said seriously. "However, there is surely no harm in allowing the dea'Gauss to amend the contract as he suggests. It will be one more thing on our side of the trade table, when it comes time to sue for our fee."

"Right you are. Tell him to fetch it on up, then." She waited while he sent the message on.

"Now," she said, when he turned back to her, Wellik's papers in hand. "What will you be caring to name this fine vessel, Pilot Tor An?"

Damn' if he didn't pale, the rich golden skin going to a sort of beige—and here she thought she'd been doing him the kind of honor a well-brought-up boy from a trade clan would cherish.

"I?" he gasped. "What right have I to—surely it falls to the captain to name her ship!"

"No hand at it," she said, laconic and Rim-wise. "And as to right—you're my co-pilot, and my heir. Says so in those papers dea'Gauss drew up between us and the Service Families. If I die on con, the ship goes to you."

"The contract . . ." He took a breath, color returning to his face. "The contract must demonstrate a clear passage of responsibility, for the safety of ship and passengers. However, the contract describes necessity for this one flight which we are soon to undertake. We—we cannot know that we will work well together, long-term, or that we will wish to continue our association beyond contract's end . . ."

"Assuming that there's anything at the end of the contract saving gray screens the pilots' last duty," she said, maybe a bit harsher than she needed to. "You saw those 'quations, Pilot. They shape up to a certain future, in your opinion?"

He closed his eyes and bowed his head. "They are the equations we are given, and when the time comes, we will fly them. I depend on Scholar dea'Syl's genius—and the skill of the best damn' pilot Jela had ever known."

And who was she, Cantra thought, suddenly tired, to snatch hope out of the boy's hands? He might even be right.

"All right, then," she said, making her voice easy and light. She crossed over and took up a lean against the pilot's chair, producing a smile when he raised his head and looked at her. "Let's take this by the numbers, if you'll bear with me, Pilot."

He moved his hand, fingers shaping the sign for *go on.*

"Right. The way it scans to me is that you're my co-pilot, and you can handle this ship. Jela's tree likes you, the cat likes you, Scholar dea'Syl likes you, Rool Tiazan likes you—Deeps, I think even Wellik likes you! Certain-sure Jela liked you, or he wouldn't never have given you care of the scholar and sent you on ahead. All those upstanding folk liking you, trusting you—that weighs with me, Pilot. I can't think of anybody within reach who I'd rather stand as my heir and carry on with my ship."

She paused, watching him as he stared around the tower, something like awe in his face. *My ship*—she could see him thinking it, he was so easy to read—and he shed a tithe of the sadness he'd been carrying with him since he'd realized his old Dejon was going to be left behind on the ground . . .

"Now, before you decide," she said, when she'd judged he'd had time enough to feel the full wonder of someday being master of such a vessel— "before you decide, there's something else you need to know."

His attention was on her that fast, purple eyes non-committal in a face that had gone trader-bland. "Captain."

Almost, Cantra grinned, which wasn't at all what she wanted to be doing at this point. Easy to read he might be, but Tor An yos'Galan was a pilot, and a trader-trained-and-raised. Inexperience, she reminded herself, wasn't anywhere near the same as foolhardy.

"If you stand my heir, there's other things that'll fall to your care with this ship, those being—" She extended her hand, fist closed, and showed him her thumb— "Jela's tree, which he honored as a comrade and a brother-in-arms. He took my oath, that I'd keep it safe, and I'd expect you to take up that oath as your own."

Tor An inclined his head.

Cantra raised her first finger. "Second and last—Jela's heir will also come into your keeping, and I'll expect you to care and nurture it as you would a child of your own body."

The boy blinked. "Jela's heir?" he repeated. Another blink. "You are pregnant with Jela's child?"

"That's right." She said it as forthrightly as possible—and waited, not at all certain what to expect from—

He took three steps toward her, and she could see the shine of tears in his eyes. She swallowed, her throat tight and her own eyes suddenly wet.

"Captain, you are—you are not only calling heir, then. You are calling clan."

That came from an odd trajectory. She hadn't thought of clan, being only Torvin by Garen's say-so. But a boy from an old and extended family of traders and ship-masters—aye, he'd think clan right enough, and most especially as he'd lost all that they'd been.

And, really, she thought, what difference? Clan served her purpose as well as heir, if it meant protection for the tree and the child.

The boy was looking—elsewhere, like he was seeing something or someone she couldn't. "Yes," he said softly, in that thinking-out-loud voice she'd already heard him use at the board. "Yes, this will be good. It *will* be good. There is strength in clan. And the contract—the contract will be properly then between clans, and less easy to ignore, come time to collect our fee." His eyes focused on her face again. "But our clan will need a name!"

Cantra felt something unknot in her chest, like maybe there'd been cargo twine around her heart, and it had suddenly come loose. But—

"Let's name the ship first, hey?" she said, keeping it light and easy. "And I'll tell you straight, Pilot, I don't know anything about starting up a clan—"

He smiled at her.

"Nor do I. However, we are fortunate in our acquaintance. The dea'Gauss is one who oversees contracts and alliances, and who understands the measuring of such things. I doubt he would refuse a request for his assistance in this matter."

And there it was again, Cantra thought. Co-pilot taking co-pilot care. The boy was sound. He'd do.

He'd have to do.

"So, we'll ask dea'Gauss to do the pretty for us. Right. Now—ship name, Pilot? Didn't you never think of your own ship when you was a kid?"

Amusement glimmered in those improbable eyes.

"What, the son of a trading house and never dare dream of my own ship? I'd hardly have made pilot if I hadn't that much spark!"

True enough. She gave him an encouraging smile and set herself to coaxing him. Pretty soon she had two names—one a pure kid super-duper-hero-pilot name that he'd been slightly embarrassed to admit to, and the other a solid, sober kind of a name for a ship, with the tang of optimism about it.

"I like that," she said, meaning it. "And we'll hope it's true-named." She nodded at the paperwork still in his hand. "Fill it in, if you will, Pilot. *Quick Passage*."

THIRTY-ONE

Quick Passage

THE BOY WAS ON COMM when Cantra came into the tower from her latest visit to the passenger bays. She walked past the tree, lashed good and tight in its position; dropped into the pilot's chair and leaned her head back, watching him through half-closed eyes. He flicked a toggle and general audio came live.

"We've got a clean reading on all automatic transponders and passive visuals." That was Solcintra Station—which was pushing its inspection a bit, in Cantra's opinion. "*Quick Passage*, home port Solcintra, owner Cantra yos'Phelium. Active visual check in progress—looks like you've still got a blue beacon where you should have a green at degree one-eighty . . ."

The boy tipped his head, and tapped his left ear—a sign to her that he had another party on the line.

"The crew boat suggests that your inspection is before-time, Solcintra Station," he said politely, which if it was Vachik at comm on the 'boat, took considerable liberty with what had most likely been said.

There was a slight pause, then Station again, sounding to Cantra's ear just a thought apologetic.

"Acknowledge that, *Quick Passage*. Will relay—merely an activity report."

"Thank you, Station. *Quick Passage* out." He closed the connection, and paused with his hand over the second toggle, his nose wrinkled slightly while doubtless having his ear filled with the Deeps knew what ribald and outrageous nonsense, Vachik having taken it as a hobby to try and rattle the boy's reserve.

"As to that, I couldn't say, Pilot," Tor An murmured, not noticeably rattled. "*Quick Passage* out." He snapped the toggle and sighed, pulling the bud out of his ear as he spun his chair to face her.

"Vachik's amused by Station, is he?" she asked laconically. Tor An stretched, putting the seams of his handsome embroidered tunic at risk.

"Pilot Vachik points out that Station oversteps," he said serenely. "Which it had, and now does not. How does the boarding go on?"

"Not quite a riot. It's a rare wonder what having a couple brace o'nice X Strains monitoring the intakes will do for the general level of politeness."

Nalli Olanek hadn't wanted to swallow the limit on baggage, claiming her folk would be reasonable—which they hadn't been, not by any measure known to ship-dwellers. So, there'd had to be a limit set, which the captain did, and then there had to be arguments from the Speaker and her seconds, from which young Tor An had excused himself, returning some few minutes bearing the message that Captain Wellik had approved the guards she'd requested, and they stood ready to take her orders.

That had solved the immediate problem, without bloodshed—though she figured they'd bought future grief. Stipulating there was a future. And not to say, she thought fair-mindedly, that the boy's notion had been off-course, which it hadn't.

It was turning out to be the case that Pilot Tor An had a good many useful notions in that pretty head of his.

It had, for an instance, been his notion—thinking out loud in her direction, as was his habit—that since they didn't have full-time military staffing, maybe they didn't need the extra officer-training seat there in the middle of the tower . . . and that maybe that seat lock and mounting block would make a better lash-point for the tree than ever they'd be able to cobble in a corner with twine and tape.

"Assuming, of course," he'd said to nothing and nobody in particular, "that the captain would prefer to have the tree ship in the tower, rather than in its own cargo-pod."

That cargo-pod idea hadn't played well to the green crew at all, and it hadn't quite seemed right to her either. She'd gotten used to having the tree in her eye, and having it mumble its pictures at the back of her head. Apparently, the tree had gotten used to her, too, and used to being part of the tower crew.

"Sergeant Ilneri and Pilot Argast report that three of our proposed back-up pilots test well," Tor An said softly. "The fourth was found inadequate and returned to port."

She nodded. "Saw Ilneri on the way back up and he gave me the news."

He'd also insisted she take another tour of work-almost-complete, over which Jela's mates labored, as far as she could tell, non-stop. Kinda spooky, were Jela's mates, for as hard as they'd taken the news of his dying, it seemed to hearten them to know he'd last been seen trying to take someone's head off with that nasty flexible cutter of his . . . and everywhichone of them still talked like he was hanging over their shoulders, insisting on nothing less than perfect.

"The dea'Gauss will be here shortly," Tor An said carefully, interrupting that line of thought. "Will you wish to dress for the ceremony?"

Ceremony. All they were set to do was sign some local legal papers, but the kid had built it up in his mind into a *ceremony*, and had gotten himself dressed up proper to face it. She eyed the tunic—space black, with the star-holding dragon that'd been the chop for Alkia Trade Clan embroidered on shoulder and sleeve in gold and silver thread. He'd brushed his bright hair 'til it gleamed and even shined his boots. By contrast, she felt nothing but grubby in her leathers.

Ceremony, she thought sourly, and caught a glimmer of wing and branch from the tree.

"Right," she said, levering herself out of the pilot's chair. "I'll be a minute."

THE NON-DESCRIPT MAN with the surprisingly bold brown eyes was dressed neat and respectful in pale tunic and pants. He had placed two black, silver-edged folios before him on the fold-out worktable; a flat wooden box was at his right hand, and a small satchel that looked like a traveling bag sat quietly by his feet.

Looking down at the table, he touched the flat box—mayhap for luck—took a visible breath, and raised his head.

"We are ready, I believe," he said quietly. "I am dea'Gauss; I have been requested to oversee the establishment of a clan new to Solcintra and to known space, and I am recognized by the Solcintra Accountants Guild as a member in good standing."

Here he paused, very briefly, and looked about the tower before continuing.

"As required by the protocols of the Accountants Guild, I bring with me three persons of known character and unallied clan, each to witness as they will. They arrive knowing that they witness, and they declare themselves individually disinterested observers of the event at hand."

Cantra faced dea'Gauss across the work desk, dressed as formally as her small kit allowed, the boy at her side. The strangers—witnesses—stood behind them, and behind *them* was the tree, which comforted her some, even as she could feel it paying attention *real hard*—and behind the tree stood Argast, acting half as honor guard and half as pilot-in-waiting in case the ship required something during the course of the ceremony.

Meanwhile, dea'Gauss was talking again.

"In so far as Solcintra and its population have an interest in the careful arrangement of debts and balances, of property and owner-ship, of precedence and inheritance, of honor and responsibility, of *melant'i* and necessity, and of actions which permit the public good, it is meet and fitting that individuals join together into such groups and organizations which present the opportunity for surety in relationships and commerce. We witness here today the signing and sealing of documents representing the establishment of a particular group which names itself Clan Korval. This group . . ."

Cantra glanced to the side, caught the kid's eyes on her and the flicker of fingers—*acceptable course*?

Korval? Well, it was better than Valkor, the other combo possible from the two syllables deemed most propitious by means she hadn't cared to inquire into—and she had shunted the details of the paperwork to him.

She returned *clear lift!* and felt him relax beside her.

". . . has control and ownership of respectable properties, is peopled by individuals known as reliable and forthright, and has established a clear lineage and succession. Clan Korval honors the absent M. Jela Granthor's Guard as Founder and acknowledges duties, goals, heirs, debts, property, responsibility and *melant'i* deriving from the Founder."

Cantra stood, breath-caught, and damn' if she didn't feel tears prickling at the edges of her eyes—

In her head, a flutter of images: A tree dropped a pod across a thin river, that pod grew into a tree, in its turn dropping a pod . . .

"Clan Korval is composed of two lines until and unless the Clan shall choose otherwise. The predominant line is yos'Phelium, currently headed by Cantra yos'Phelium. The subordinate line is yos'Galan, currently headed by Tor An yos'Galan."

She blinked and sent another glance to the boy, meeting a slight smile. She'd've thought they'd share—but no, he had the right of it again. He was her heir, and his part was to support her—co-pilot to pilot. They both knew that protocol, down deep in their bones. She just hoped any of it lasted longer that them getting out of orbit and starting the transition run . . .

"The Clan together acknowledges the duties, goals, heirs, debts, property, responsibility, and *melant'i* of these line heads as its own and from this day forward all within the Clan will be governed, judged, rewarded, punished, and otherwise dealt with as the Clan requires within its own written code of conduct. All actions performed individually or in unison reflect the Clan and the Clan holds ultimate responsibility for its members. Formed in orbit around Solcintra, Clan Korval looks for council and fellowship from the Fifty High Houses of Solcintra, and the Council of the Fifty High Houses of Solcintra will honor Korval as a member, as well."

This last was spoken just a little more firmly than what had gone before, as if maybe dea'Gauss wasn't one-hundred-percent certain that the new High Council would find Korval an ornament to itself.

"Clan Korval exists," dea'Gauss said, back to quiet now. "May its name shine and its deeds endure."

Beside her, she heard a discreet sniffle, and damn' if she wasn't tearing up again herself. She blinked. Clan Korval. And Jela listed down as Founder, all right and proper. Almost—almost, she could hear him laughing . . .

The accountant bowed deeply—first to Tor An, then to herself. Straightening, he opened the right-most of the two black-and-silver folios.

"If the line heads will be good enough to sign here, with the subordinate line signing first and the predominant line after, we shall witness and seal."

Sign they did—first the boy, precise and unornamented. He passed the pen to her and stood to one side as she wrote out her name, the ink that same shade of purple that flickered along the far edge of the Rim . . .

Cantra yos'Phelium. She blinked down at the shape of it along the cream-colored page; took a breath to steady herself and signed the second book, too.

She put the pen down, and the tree let loose with a burst of flying dragons so bright and joyous she went back a step—and bumped right into the kid, who caught her arm, and whispered, for her ears alone, and like it was the most natural thing ever— "Jela's tree rejoices. It is rightly done."

"Who'm I to argue with a vegetable?" she muttered back, and heard him laugh softly while the witnesses filed up one at a time and put their signatures down in the books.

That done, dea'Gauss opened the flat box and removed a little gizmo, which he activated and touched to her signature and to Tor An's, leaving a disk of green wax on each.

He stowed the gizmo, sealed the box, and waved a cautious hand over the wax to be sure it was cool before he closed the first book and handed it to her, with a bow so deep she feared for his back.

"Korval, I am honored."

It struck her then and only then—that the lines she'd just signed tied her as close as she'd ever been tied in her life. *Clan Korval*, she thought, half wildly. Kid, tree, ship and all.

She took a hard breath and centered herself, managing to return the accountant's bow with the respect he'd earned.

"Mr. dea'Gauss," she murmured, "the honor is mine."

AFTER A SERIES OF BOWS and formal well-wishings, the witnesses were escorted out by Argast. Mr. dea'Gauss was carefully fitting the second signed book into an archive envelope, being fussy about seating the corners just so.

"We are led to understand that the planet itself is in danger," he said, his eyes on his task, "and thus it was only prudence that moved the High-Houses-that-were to bear the archives of Council and Law with them. I cannot reproduce the reasoning which would have caused them to destroy the secondary archives, nor was the Accountants Guild asked to render an opinion prior to this action. Communications from those who had been the Elders of the Service Families directed to the escape ships are rejected." He glanced up.

"This means that the inception of your clan has not been properly recorded with those in whom authority and law invests."

"Nothing you can do, is there," Cantra said, as the pause got longer, "if they ain't answering comm?"

"Indeed. However, one attempts to honor propriety and to fulfill the tasks for which one's service was engaged." He finished fussing with the envelope at last, and put his palm flat against the seal.

"The new council—they call themselves the High Houses, and thus put on a suit which they cannot properly wear. Yet, what choice had they? Lacking the archives and the law, they now stumble to create arrangements and protocols for which there exist no precedent." He gave her one of his straight looks, this one maybe not so much bold as tired.

"Though the new council has seen fit to disbar me and mine, citing our ties to the old order, I am able to report that they have acknowledged the right of Clan Korval to come among them, to treat and be treated as an equal member of the council."

He bent, pulled his satchel up onto the desk, and stowed the envelope in an outside pocket, taking care with the seal.

"It is possible that we who remain on-planet during . . ."

Cantra blinked, shot a question-look at Tor An, and took receipt of a baffled stare.

"Hold that orbit," she said, bringing her attention back to the accountant.

He paused with his hands on his satchel, and inclined his head, "Korval?"

"You're planning on staying on-planet, is what I'm hearing you say."

"That is correct."

She frowned at him, which he bore with patience. He looked as sensible a man as she'd ever seen, but, yet, she supposed it might be that he hadn't been able to hold the thought of what was coming toward them—

"You understand," she said carefully, "that Solcintra won't likely exist at the end of the action Captain Wellik's told us is coming?"

"I have heard this, yes. We will, of course, attempt to lift what ships there are . . ."

"No." She waved the hand that wasn't full of black-and-silver book, cutting off the rest of whatever he'd been going to say.

"This ship here—you drew up the contract! This ship here is set to take on all the members of the Service Families that now style themselves High Houses. There's a place here for your and yours, never fear it, though you'll be needing to sleep—"

And what, she thought suddenly, if that were it? If dea'Gauss for all his sense and his steadiness and his firm, bold gaze was afraid of slow-sleep . . .

"I have not made myself plain," he said, and inclined his head. "The case is that the new council has disbarred Family dea'Gauss. We are seen as holding allegiance to those who have deserted us, and the new council would choose its own—"

From the tree came a sense of sudden, rushing wind—

The wind was real, whipping her hair and fluttering the sleeves of Tor An's tunic—and then it was gone.

THIRTY-TWO

Quick Passage

THE WIND FELL as suddenly as it had risen, leaving the one known as Rool Tiazan standing disheveled and breathless within the confines of the pilots' tower.

"What has gone forth?" he cried, as much frightened as angry, or so Tor An thought. He raised a hand and scraped the wild red curls away from his face, the black ring on his first finger winking quick and cunning as a living eye.

"Problem?" Cantra yos'Phelium asked, one winged eyebrow lifting in unmistakable irony.

"You may perhaps allow the close attention of the Iloheen—your pardon, the *sheriekas!*—to be a problem," the other snapped, less breathless now, and with anger perhaps ascending over fear. "And how could they fail to focus upon such a gaudy display of energy and—" He stopped, his gaze having fallen from the pilot's face to that which she yet held in her hand.

"I . . . see," he murmured, and extended a hand. "May I—"

It was, to Tor An's shame, dea'Gauss who moved first and placed himself between the clan's primary and the potential threat.

"The book belongs to Korval and to none other, sir," he said coolly. "It is not for out-clan to—"

Rool Tiazan turned his hands palm up and smiled at the accountant. "Peace, peace, Ser—dea'Gauss, is it?—I—"

"Indeed, it is dea'Gauss, though I stand not so high as 'ser.'"

"Ah. Forgive my lapse; I meant no discourtesy, either to yourself or to—Korval. It is merely that—"

"Quiet!" Pilot Cantra ordered, loudly, and perforce there was quiet. Rool Tiazan bowed with neither irony nor temper, and properly to Korval's honor, followed by Mr. dea'Gauss, who did not, however, retire from his position between pilot and *dramliza*.

"Now, here's what I thought," Pilot Cantra said briskly, and the Rim accent was more noticeable than it had been during the ceremony. "I thought I was captain on my own ship. I thought I was talking with somebody. I *didn't* think I'd set off any look-at-mes in the direction of the Enemy nor hadn't done anything more remarkable than carry out ship's business. If you got information touching on that, say it out, straight and quick."

"Captain." Rool Tiazan bowed slightly and seriously. "My information is this: As I was observing actions brought by certain of the free *dramliza* directly against the Iloheen, suddenly I was snatched, against my will, and with naught I might do to deny it, *here*, born on the wings of such a maelstrom of luck and possibility as I have never experienced. Something has altered event, noisily. Something has shifted the pattern of the lines of what will be, and the luck swirls not merely about the environs of this star system, or, more nearly, this planet, but *here*," he stamped, his soft slipper waking an unlikely ring from the decking. "On this ship." He inclined his head. "I suspect that what has been bound into that book which you hold is the cause of these . . . unexpected alterations."

He inclined his head. "May I see and hold the book, Pilot? It is necessary." He turned to the accountant. "Mr. dea'Gauss, I swear to you that I am an ally."

"He's right," Pilot Cantra said briskly. "I 'preciate your concern, Mr. dea'Gauss, but you can stand down. He's twelve kinds of twisty, and you'll do well to weigh everything he tells you, but I vouch for him."

The accountant bowed, and retired, face grim.

Tor An stepped to his side. "Thank you, sir," he whispered, "for your quick action on behalf of the clan."

That gained a startled glance, and the beginning of a smile. "You are quite welcome, your lordship."

"Nay—" he began, but there was Rool Tiazan taking the clan book into his slim hands, and he found his feet had moved him forward again, his own hand lifting as if to snatch the precious object back.

Firm fingers encircled his wrist and held him close. "Steady, Pilot," she murmured. "Let the man look."

If he looked, it was with senses other than his eyes, yet one could not but be gratified by the reverent stroke of palm across the surface of the cover.

"Yes. What we have here . . ." Rool Tiazan sighed. "What we have here is just such an event as cannot be predicted nor planned against. There is a purity of purpose which can only act to confound the Enemy."

He opened his eyes and held the book out across his two palms.

"It is done and done well," Rool Tiazan said, and there was a odd resonant sound to his voice, as if his words echoed against the stars. "Prosper, Korval. May your name shine and your deeds endure."

Pilot Cantra received the book properly into her hands, and inclined her head. "May that be true-speaking," she murmured, the accent of the Rim entirely absent.

"Mr. dea'Gauss," she said abruptly, and the Rim accent was back, and thicker than ever.

"Korval?"

"Comes to me that a brand-new and hope-to-be-respectable clan like we just got through setting up's going to need somebody to oversee our contracts and 'counts. You willing to work for us?"

The man's face took fire, hope blazing in his tired eyes. "Korval, I am."

"Good," Pilot Cantra nodded toward the fold-out table. "Sit yourself down and write up the contract—short and simple, mind you, 'cause I got some other things I want you to do." She held out her fist, thumb and first finger extended. "First thing, get your family up here. Second, I want the word out on the port that this vessel is taking on passengers, whether or not they're attached to any of the so-called High Houses. Got those?"

"Yes," the accountant said, fervently. "Korval, I do."

"Make it so," she said crisply, her hand fluttering out of its counting fist and into pilot hand-sign: *acceptable*?

Tor An smiled and inclined his head. "Most acceptable, Pilot," he said.

"That's good, too." She turned her attention back to Rool Tiazan.

"So we got the Enemy's attention," she said, as if it were the merest nothing. "What'll we do with it?"

Rool Tiazan smiled. "An excellent question. Perhaps we—" His smile faded into a frown and he lifted a finger.

"Problem?"

"Anomaly, rather. I feel energies aligning . . . strangely . . . and random event approaches."

"Whatever that means," Pilot Cantra said. "You were going to tell me—"

The door to the pilots' tower slid open, to admit Lucky the cat, strutting, tail high.

CANTRA SIGHED. "Who let the cat in?"

"I did, dear Pilot Cantra." Liad dea'Syl guided his power-chair carefully into the tower. After him came a small parade. Several looked to be beggars, others were kempt enough to maybe be panhandlers, day jobbers, pawnsters, thieves, joy-workers . . .

Cantra handed the clan book to the boy. "Stow it safe," she said quietly, and he moved off without comment. She went forward to meet the power-chair and its escort, Rool Tiazan at her side.

"Ser Tiazan, it is well that you are here," the scholar said pleasantly. "I have framed the last set of equations. I believe you will approve—and the pilots, as well."

"Certainly, that is welcome news," Rool Tiazan said—

"But," Cantra interrupted ruthlessly, "bringing strangers up to the tower without clearance, Scholar. I've gotta disallow that."

"Of course, of course." The old man smiled at her. "Permit this to be an unique case, if you will. They came first to me, and invoked M. Jela as their motivator. That being the case, I thought it best to bring them directly to Jela's heir for parsing."

She considered the bunch of them, huddled close to each other and to the chair, as if maybe they were having second thoughts about their chosen course—all save a tiny and trim red-haired woman with clever eyes and a gun in her sleeve.

"You," Cantra said to her. "Talk."

"With pleasure," the woman answered, standing forward and sending a quick, appraising look around the tower. She parted with a cool nod in the direction of Rool Tiazan, but her eyes lingered on the tree.

"I see that the mission was a success, after all. We had some doubts, though it was later reported the pilot had able back-up, outside."

Cantra thought back on the tale she'd finally teased out of Jela concerning that night's work—the night they'd met and everything had changed.

"This would be on Faldaiza," she said to the little woman. "And I'm thinking you're the gambler."

The other woman bowed. "Gambler, if you will, Captain, or runner-with-luck."

Rool Tiazan stirred; the woman's cool gaze touched him.

"No need, Elder Brother," she said. "We had known you were here and that others gather."

Cantra looked between the two of them. "You're counting this one as kin?" she asked the gambler.

"Soon enough, after we pass through that which comes."

"If," Rool Tiazan said, "we indeed emerge, which has not been Seen."

The gambler laughed. "Tush, O Mighty Tiazan! We who are at the mercy of the lines and the matrices, and most likely to be bruised by those winds which bear you high—we sight low, and see—somewhat. On this side of the event which your cleverness has shaped, we see strife, death, loneliness—and soon. Very soon."

"And after?" the *dramliza* persisted. "What do your small arts show you on the other side, Young Sister?"

The gambler smiled. "Why, strife, in some measure—but also life, and opportunity."

Rool Tiazan bowed, and folded his hands.

The gambler looked back to Cantra. "Captain, the Solcintrans will renounce us, for we embody that which they most fear. Elsewhere, we have learned to remain hidden, for the groundlings say we are dangerous, and perversions; they call us *sheriekas*-spawn and they kill us out of hand."

"And are you?" Cantra asked her, seeing dragons dancing at the back of her head, tasting mint along the edge of her tongue. "*Sheriekas*-spawn?"

"Captain, our talents are perhaps born of those forces which the *sheriekas* and the *dramliza* manipulate with such easy contempt—I have heard it argued thus. But we ourselves are human. Ask the Mighty Tiazan's lady if this is not so."

"She speaks sooth," Rool Tiazan said, in that voice which was not his own. "They are what we shall become, formed in a far different forge."

The gambler smiled, and leaned forward slightly, one hand out, fingers curled.

"Captain, I have with me healers, true-dreamers, seers, finders, hunch-makers, green-thumbs, teachers—treasure beyond counting for the days beyond. Grant us passage, and you may call upon us for any service, so long as Jela's tree survives to bind us."

The dragons in her head danced faster, and she'd swear she smelled salt on the air . . . She rubbed her eyes and looked to where the boy—the head of her clan's subordinate line, and her co-pilot, she reminded herself forcefully—to where Tor An yos'Galan stood at watch, quiet and alert.

"Call it."

He bowed.

"It is plain. The Founder did give his oath to work in the best interests of life, therefore we, his heirs, are bound by that same oath. And the tree, as we can see, is in favor of the petition."

Pay your debts, baby . . .

Cantra nodded.

"I agree." She turned back to the gambler. "You and yours'll need to travel asleep, same as most of the passengers; and give up your weapons to the armory-master, to be returned when we find safe port."

"Agreed," the other woman answered, and behind her there was a visible relaxing 'mong her mates.

"Right, then. Pilot yos'Galan here'll escort you, first to the armory, then to the sleep-rooms. He'll stand between you and hurt, if it's offered, and you'll accept his protection and his judgment."

"Agreed," the gambler answered once more, and bowed, as cocky and exuberant as if she was going for a stroll down the street.

"Pilot yos'Galan, lead on! We place ourselves wholly into your hands!"

THIRTY-THREE

※※※※※※※※※※※※※※※※※※※※※※※※※※

Spiral Dance
Solcintra

DANCER WOKE, opened eyes and ears, and commenced to pull down data. The main-brain opened a window on the second screen, displaying a list of self-checks completed, and the nav-brain launched a preliminary query to the pilot for lift-times and destination strings.

The pilot—the pilot sat, eyes closed, in her chair, listening to the sounds of her ship. Sitting there, fingers hooked 'round the arm rests so they wouldn't shake so much—sitting there, she supposed she'd been a trial and a bother more often than a comfort and true comrade in the years they'd been together, with Garen, and then just each other. But the ship—the ship had never stinted in its care of her, not since the day Garen brought her aboard, out of her head with the pain of dying.

"Never stinted." She repeated the thought, hearing the echo of her voice come comforting and right off the familiar walls.

Despite *Dancer* could've called out to the Enemy twelve dozen times or more and brought destruction and worse down on them—

she'd never done that. And as Cantra knew, deep down and personal, it was those things you didn't do, maybe more than those you did, that counted out a true comrade and friend.

A tickle at the back of her mind, and then a picture, forming slow and not so ept—and suddenly there was Jela, his face grimy and sweaty, back and shoulder muscles rigid with strain, as he struggled to lift and cut, the sending so clear she could swear she heard him breathing . . .

"That's right," she whispered. "You remember him just as long as you can. He'd want that, so he would."

The comm sounded and she bent forward, her finger finding the right switch without a fumble.

"*Spiral Dance*."

"Captain," said the deep rumble that was Y. Vachik, uncharacteristically subdued. "We're on the count, here."

Right. They were all on the count, now, weren't they?

"Keep 'er ready, Pilot," she said into the comm. "I'll be there directly."

She flicked the switch and opened her eyes, fingers already inputting lift and course. The nav-brain—she gave it leave to do anything it liked in the service of fulfilling those coordinates, and called up the wounded-pilot protocol. A flick of her finger set the timer—not giving herself a lot of room to tarry—and she was up out of the chair. Once the protocols engaged, *Dancer* was on her own, until the pilot took over again.

Or forever, whichever came first.

One more thing before she left—a touch of finger to fragile leaf, and a quick test to make sure the dirt-filled box gray-taped to the co-pilot's board was firm.

From the barely sprouted pod came a hopeful vision of dragons, and the scent of sea air.

"You'll do fine," she told it, and cleared her throat. "Jela'd be proud."

Then she was gone, running, as the timer counted down to lift-off.

❋   ❋   ❋

TRUE TO HIS ORDERS, Vachik had kept the shuttle ready. Cantra hit first chair hard, yanked the webbing tight and gave the shuttle its office, the whiles counting off at the back of her head, and with a quarter-eye on the aux screen—six . . . five . . . four . . . three . . . two . . .

Dancer was up, rising hard through the busy air, and paying not the least attention to squawks from traffic control.

She was busy then, weaving a course through the mess and tangle, filling all of Solcintra's air space. Everything that could hold air was up, and the sorts of pilots who might be sitting those boards didn't bear thinking on . . .

"Fools and cretins!" Vachik spat, as she dodged them through a particularly tricksy knot-up, then pushed hard on the rockets.

Cantra stole a look at the aux screen—*Dancer* was deep in the worst of the mess . . .

"Message from *Springbane*, Captain," Vachik said. "They give us . . . almost ample time. Your screen two."

She looked and smiled grimly. "A challenge, would you say, Pilot?"

Vachik's answering grin was a frightening thing to behold. "Indeed, Captain. Shall we school them?"

"Shouldn't be a problem at all."

It was the board then, and the ship she was flying, and no time for sneak-looks at her life-that-was leaving her behind, nor even for the fading flickers of dragons, dancing on the shore of a sea long dead and dust.

"Long orbit on that ship, Captain," Vachik said quietly some while later. "Looks good—and it's well outside the crowd, now."

She sighed. "Thank you," she said and shot him a look. "Sure you won't come with us?"

"To receive such an offer from such a captain," he answered, formal and not at all Vachik-like, "is an honor which I will long recall. The commander, however, has given Jela's Troop a special unit designation, and it is there I would serve."

"Right," she said, and gave him a nod. "Looks like we're gonna beat *Springbane's* time, Pilot. Best get your kit together."

"I have everything I need, Captain, thank you."

She nosed the shuttle in and Vachik was out of the chair as soon as the docking light went to blue.

"Captain." He saluted and was gone.

She dumped out just as soon as the connect tube was clear, seconds ahead of the time *Springbane* had given her to dock, and extended a hand to kill the aux screen.

She found *Quick Passage* in her screens, did the math in her head and set the course.

At the far back of her head, dragons danced, insubstantial as hope.

THIRTY-FOUR

❀❀❀❀❀❀❀❀❀❀❀❀❀❀❀❀❀❀❀❀❀❀❀

Quick Passage
Departing Solcintra

NOW, WHO'D'VE EXPECTED we'd be leading a parade? Cantra thought, scanning her screens and carefully not sighing.

In her head, the golden dragon glided easy on half-furled wings, beside her the jewel-colored dragonet which the tree had settled on as its version of her co-pilot. Behind them rose dragons of all color and description, old, young, halt and hale. Some few emulated the effortless grace shown by the leaders, others were already laboring hard. Beyond the general chaos loomed a long, disciplined line of black dragons, wings steady, eyes baleful, teeth at ready—Wellik's rear-guard, that would be.

Back in real-time, the tower was crowded, not only because the pilots were presently enjoying the company of Liad dea'Syl, Lucky the cat, and Rool Tiazan, but with the sound of pilot voices.

Tor An played the local comm board like it was a musical instrument, pulling talk, catching chat large and small:

"*Quanta Plus*, have you even refribbed that thing in twenty years? But in case it helps, you've got to watch your starboard beacons, 'cause they're some out of synch!"

"Oughtn't be doing that. We just had it shopped to your home field—that is if that's I've got *Clary Bee* talking to me."

"*Clary Bee's* here, I'm to port, actually. That's cousin Trisky talked about your synch, but it don't look like his're all that pretty, either. Port visuals fine, and signal strength right top."

"Trisky, tell your field man he'll owe me a day check if you see him."

"Last I saw, he was mounting somebody a new deflector union. Ought to be out here somewhere . . ."

"*Chrono*, watch the drift, we got a crowd in a hurry comin' from behind . . ."

"You got it, Mom. We're set to spin to port and add some vee on a six count, if you'll scoot . . ."

"Ain't never seen so many holiday pilots in one place and if any of us get out of here without a hole in the hull . . ."

"Always an optimist, ain't you, Bondy?"

"What's that thing beside you, Rinder? Only got four beacons I can scan."

"Uncle, that's my guess."

"Right. Well, Rinder, you're safe on that side . . ."

"But low on company . . ."

Laughter from a bunch of ships on that, and the channels changed again.

The chatter seemed to soothe the boy, and, truth told, it eased her, too, knowing they weren't traveling alone toward who-knew-what.

"Status report," Tor An murmured. "All ship systems blue; passenger bays secure, systems blue; cargo pods show balance within tolerance, systems blue."

"We're ready to go," Cantra answered. "If we knew when or where to."

"No taste for mystery, Lady?" Rool Tiazan asked lightly from his lean against the back-up comm station.

"Not where my ship's at risk, no," she told him shortly, and spared him an over-the-shoulder glare. "Speaking of, you'll be wanting to strap in. I won't have you bouncing about this tower, if transition goes as hard as it's like to, and putting the pilots at risk."

He inclined his head ironically. "Your tender care for my well-being is noted and appreciated."

"Appreciate it all you want, but *strap in*."

"Translation wave!" Tor An snapped, and— "Another!"

Cantra reached to the board, ready to hold her steady—which was small-ship reactions. The tiny disruptions generated by those three transitions weren't enough to jostle *Quick Passage*, even if they all hit at once.

"Wonder where they're thinking on going . . ." she murmured, fingers simultaneously making the request of the tracking system.

"First was for The Bubble, looks like, second—"

"Incoming!" Tor An called.

"That didn't take long," someone sang across the bands. "What happened, forget your lunch?"

"The Bubble's gone," came the terse reply. "Ship won't swallow the coords."

She sent a glance down-board, that being the kind of news that might not set well with second chair. Besides his lips being pressed a little tighter than usual, he read calm and collected to her. Good boy.

"Incoming," he said again—and this time the news was that Nolatine was gone.

"They should conserve energy," Liad dea'Syl said quietly. "Our good friend Lucky has the right of it, I think. Rest now, for we shall surely need the fullness of our resources on the far side of the event."

A quick glance showed the cat stretched out on his back across the old man's lap, thoroughly asleep with his paws in the air. She grinned and turned back to her board. The dragon parade in her head was fading, as if the tree had decided to take the cat's advice, too. Which was fine by her; she didn't want to be distracted by pretty pictures during what was likely to come next.

"Number three must've got where they were going," she said to her co-pilot.

"Else they were captured by the leading edge and unmade," Rool Tiazan murmured, and Cantra sighed.

"Full of fun, ain't you? Strapped in yet?"

"Incoming!" Tor An shouted. "Captain—a dozen—more!"

Her steadying hand was needed this time, not even something the size of *Quick Passage* could ignore the turbulence as Tor An's dozen ships—and then a dozen more, filling in at the fringes first, so the instruments told her, though the eye insisted they hit at once, each new ripple adding to the building wave of displaced energies.

The noise across the bands was terrible; worse was the carnage as ship was flung into ship, while others vanished, spontaneously translating—then reappearing, the ripple of their re-entry adding to the deadly agitation of energies.

"No!" Tor An cried.

Cantra's hands danced across the board. "We're leaving, Pilot," she said, keeping her voice firm and easy—*just a piloting exercise, boy*, she thought at him. *Stay with me, here, there's worse to come . . .*

"Aye," he said crisply, and that quick he was steady, his hands moving sure and firm across his board, feeding the shields, slapping the noise off the bands down to a whisper, and doing all that a co-pilot ought, which was good, because she had everything she could do, dodging ships and shrapnel, as *Quick Passage* gathered and surged around them.

"ALERT!"

His voice sounded strange in his ears: calm, collected, professional. His fingers moved efficiently across his board, doing what was needful while his heart hammered, and he rode his screens and scans—

"Captain—on visual, your screens six and eight . . ."

Objects—*Were* they objects? They glinted and gleamed in the visual tracking system, their shapes disturbingly fluid, even as they eclipsed stars and ships. They appeared to actively avoid *Quick Passage*, and scarcely registered on the radar—

"Got 'em," Pilot Cantra said, her voice so calm and easy that the pounding of his heart eased somewhat. "They don't scan like anything I've seen before. Almost look organic, close up. Keep 'em in eye and sing out if they look like changing their minds about avoiding us."

"Aye, Captain." His fingers had already brought the tracking systems up. He looked to the shields, and frowned, trying to place the low growling noise that had suddenly come on-line.

"Aha! Our noble feline would defend us from those!" The scholar cried, as delighted as a child. "Captain Cantra—an adjustment—if there is time? I have an additional factor. This should be added to the final equations, for accuracy."

Now? Tor An thought wildly. With space in chaos about them and creatures unlike anything seen or told by pilots—

"Go," Pilot Cantra said calmly. "I'm tracking."

"Yes. You will wish to multiply the final result of section seven by this number, which is a very rough approximation induced by the infinite expansion theory I have settled upon. The number is this: Three-point-one-four-one-five-nine-two-six-five-three-five-eight-nine."

"Three-point-one-four-one-five-nine-two-six-five-three-five-eight-nine," Cantra sang back, fingers dancing across her board.

"That is correct," the scholar said. "Very good."

"Added, compiled and locked. Is the cat . . ."

"The cat proclaims his warrior status, Captain Cantra. Also, you will perhaps wish to know that Rool Tiazan is behaving—or shall I say, not behaving!—in a somewhat peculiar manner."

Tor An looked up. At first glance, it appeared that Rool Tiazan leaned as he had been, in defiance of the captain's repeated order to strap in.

On second glance, his pose was not relaxed, but rigid—and he was . . . glowing with a pale green light . . .

"Captain?" He began, his heart racing into overdrive again . . .

"Mind your board, Pilot! I need seal readings, now!"

He wrenched his attention back to his first duty, scanning and quoting the shield strength, the seal parameters, the go-condition of life-support.

"Matches straight across. Energy level's up, but we're not at transition yet. Keep an eye on that, and tell me what you're scanning down low. I'm watching for intercept course objects, but I don't find anything . . ."

The ship's acceleration was constant, and Solcintra could now truly be said to be behind them rather than beneath. The rear screen was tracking the planet, but the clarity of the image was off—Tor An slapped the back-up into life.

The weird, organic objects were converging on Solcintra, melding into one enormous . . . object, which cast a long, cold shadow along the land . . .

"I am my own destiny," Rool Tiazan said suddenly, and his voice seemed to reach beyond the skin of the ship, and out unto the very stars.

"I am my own destiny. Do what you will."

THIRTY-FIVE

HIS BODY LEANING against the chair, he kept watch, all things great and small shining within the net of his regard.

There, *Spiral Dance* sang sweet seduction to her makers, the tree's sacrifice adding counterpoint, and sending insults of dragons.

And there—the Fourteen lay poised and secret, energies caught and cloaked, holding the secret of their Weaving close, watching the lines, and the luck, and the progress of annihilation, weighing the virtue of each passing instant.

Ships as numerous as the stars themselves rose from those planets which had yet escaped the Iloheen's kiss, equations were filed into boards, velocity was sought. Meanwhile, a taint of subtle poison drifted on the winds, which was the mark of she who would rule in place of the Iloheen. And at every front, through every level and phase, was there evidence of the Iloheen's work, the wave front sizzling with icy energies.

Nearby, the *ssussdriad* was silent, its essence folded close.

On this level, the pilots were living flame, burning bright, and fierce, and fast. Against their glory, the old man was but an ember, shielded by the shadow of the cat.

And everywhere, on every surface, on every level, the luck gleamed and swirled and danced, infusing every action, every thought, every breath, so that even the Hounds of the Iloheen were turned aside, and sought lesser prey.

The touch, when it came, was so elusive that it seemed at first a memory.

Again, the touch, followed by a fuller presence. Within the lines and the fields of underspace, it made itself known, with a certain pleasing subtlety, as if it had learned somewhat of grace.

This falls to me, came his lady's measured appraisal.

Rool acquiesced and withdrew to the subordinate posture, sparing a thought for the precious lives and the dancing of the luck.

Daughter of my intent, I greet you! The hour of your destiny is nigh. It is time to take up your proper place and duty.

A fair sending it was, as the Iloheen came at them from several levels, seeking advantage, seeking to distract, seeking to measure their strength.

I am my own destiny, his lady made answer, as Rool parried, expending the least energy possible; keeping the secret of their strength. *Do what you will.*

Is this how you welcome me, who made you what you are? The test that accompanied this was less wary, and too close to the plane wherein dwelt the darlings of the luck. All about, on every level, the wave-front of annihilation moved fast, and ever faster.

What peculiar arrangements you contrive for yourself! To cede dominance and submit to this prisoning of your powers! To consort with the small lives and strive to force a variant outcome? And yet— your promise is fulfilled. You are become as the Iloheen and have earned your place among us. Open to me. I shall free you from this bondage you have accepted and together we shall achieve perfection.

Rool felt a shift—stealthy and subtle—and tasted a stench upon the breeze. He looked to their shields, and made his reserves ready.

I am where I wish to be and those things which I have put in order please me, his lady answered. *Begone! And trouble me no more.*

Rool felt the hated touch against his essence as she who would rule in place of the Iloheen drew him. Willingly, he released the small tithe of his power that she had bargained to gain, and severed the thread that bound them.

The wind whipped foul and hot as she struck, strongly and with surprising depth. The Iloheen made answer, yet not without taking some damage.

Again, the wind struck, and Rool increased his defenses, holding them close, intent only upon surviving this battle as the Iloheen drew its energies and—

From underspace itself, and from planes which no *zaliata* nor Iloheen had ever glimpsed, burst a vast and implacable greenness, a rage of life so potent that the terrible advance of perfection trembled, paused—

And crashed onward, consuming all and everything which was not itself.

Rool threw out what was left of his power, encompassing the fragile shell that contained the last, and best, hope of life.

Lute! he screamed against the wind. *Lady Moonhawk*!

Now, sister! The time is now! his lady's sending echoed his as they plummeted, burning, to the physical plane.

BEHIND THEM, the sphere that was Solcintra distorted, its crust crushed beneath the weight of the shadows, fireballs bounced around the tower, and alarms shrieked as moons, meteors, and comets assaulted the shielding. *Quick Passage* lurched while the pilots fought for control, for stability, for—

"Now!" Rool Tiazan screamed. "Transition, Pilots, or all is lost!"

Wild energies engulfed them; radiation shielding boiled away. Tor An slapped for back-ups, saw Cantra lean to the operation stud, as the ship staggered—

And steadied, the screens showing gray.

"Systems check!" the pilot snapped. "Vacuum check! Interior radiation check!" Ordered, his fingers moved, querying the ship. He read out the answers, hearing wonder in his own voice.

"All ship systems blue; passenger bays secure, systems blue; cargo pods show balance within tolerance, systems blue. Interior radiation within tolerances." He looked up and met her eyes.

"Vacuum check clean. We made it."

"By the skin of our teeth," she answered, but she was smiling.

"Rool Tiazan." She spun her chair about to address him, sitting bedraggled and blood-stained in the comm-chair, properly webbed in, and stroking the cat on his lap.

"Captain?" he returned, warily. Wearily.

"Thank you," she said, and spun back to face her board.

THIRTY-SIX

✹✹✹✹✹✹✹✹✹✹✹✹✹✹✹✹✹✹✹✹✹✹

Quick Passage

THE SCREENS WERE GRAY.

Or say rather, Tor An thought wearily, the screens were *still* gray. And no way of knowing when they might reach normal space, and what might be awaiting them there. If they ever reached normal space.

The longest sustained transition known to pilots, so he had been taught, was *Moreta's Flight*, which had been the result of a malfunction of a prototype translation booster. The *Moreta* had been eighteen Common Months in transition, and when it finally regained normal space, its shields were shredded, its hull was pocked, and its pilot was dead.

To be sure, they were in somewhat better case—so far. The ship was whole, the pilots hale, if weary; the passengers content in their sleep. Those passengers who had not taken sleep were an entirely different matter, alas. It had nearly fallen to blows between Nalli Olanek and Cantra, before the Captain ruled that the Speaker might only ask after arrival times once every six ship-days. The notion that they might yet be a-ship for such a length of time had—so Cantra had maintained, with amusement—stunned the Speaker into silence.

Twenty-eight ship-days, now.

Tor An rubbed his eyes.

From the tree came an image of fog, and dragon-shapes seen dimly, gliding on silent half-furled wings.

Which was all very good, he thought, but even dragons must need come to roost eventually.

The tree persisted, however, displaying once again the damp and chilly fog, the misty dragons—and a glow of light just off the right wing-tip.

Tor An blinked, looked to his screens and saw a familiar display, too long absent from the screens. He blinked again, and touched the button that opened the comm in the pilots' quarters.

"Go," Cantra said crisply, no hint of sleep in her voice.

"Pilot," he said, trying to keep the excitement out of his voice. "We have end of transition calculated in—thirty-six minutes."

A short silence, as if even Pilot Cantra had blinked.

"I'm on my way," she said then, and the connection closed.

ROOL TIAZAN KNELT at the side of Liad dea'Syl's carry-chair, red hair mingling with white as the two of them bent over the old gentleman's tablet, muttering dark mathematical secrets to each other. The cat was curled 'round the tree's trunk, which had come to be a favorite position of his, eyes squinted half-shut.

The pilots were in their seats, poised and jumpy as newbies, both with their eyes tending to stray to the screens and the numbers that counted down, matter-of-fact and usual, toward transition's end.

"Cannon prepped," Cantra murmured.

"Shields on high," Tor An answered.

The numbers on the countdown zeroed out. The ship shrugged, the screens flickered. Cantra brought the cannon live, Tor An hit the scans.

The good news, Cantra thought, was that there weren't pirates waiting for them. The medium news was that they were the only ship within the considerable range of the scans.

The bad news was that the nav-brain beeped and quietly took itself off-line.

"Pilot?" she asked it quietly, though she already knew what he was going to report.

"We have no set north, Captain, and no confirmation from the computers of recognized beacons."

"Right. Guess we'll do it hard way, then. Find me something big and bright and far away. First, we need to know if we're in a galaxy." She keyed in her own searches, and the screens began to fill with stats as the sensors sifted local space for clues.

"I have magnetic fields we can read, Captain," Tor An said, sounding surprised. "We can pull a north from that. We are apparently in a galaxy, but we lack baselines . . ."

"One thing at a time," she told him, tending her own explorations. "Good amount of dust hereabouts. I'm wondering—"

"Captain, I have a star! We—we are close within a system . . ."

The old scholar laughed. "Why, thank you, Pilot Tor An, my son. Yes! The equations have not misled us. We should indeed be very close to a star system within a few percentage points of the mass and energy output of the average star-system with populated planets in our former galaxy." He raised a frail hand as both pilots turned to stare at him.

"I guarantee nothing, of course! I have merely done what my poor skill allowed." He glanced at his tablet. "Locate, my dears, the plane . . ."

"Working on that now," Cantra assured him, spinning back to her board. "Star's slightly oblate; might be the bulge 'round the equator can tell us something interesting . . ."

"No radio traffic on common frequencies," Tor An reported. "The military transceivers are entirely out of band . . ."

"We've got a gas giant, working on mass analysis. 'nother gas bag right here, not nearly as big, but she'll do until we can . . ."

The in-ship comm chimed, and Cantra swore, not quite under her breath.

Tor An touched the stud.

"Tower," he said, prudently leaving the general line closed.

"Yes, Speaker, the ship has entered normal space. No, we do not have an estimation of when we will—No, we do not know what sector—" He flushed, lips pressing tight. "The pilots are doing what we may, Speaker, the nature and order of our work is dictated by circumstance. We will inform the passengers when an appropriate port has been located. Tower out."

He hit the stud a little harder than was needful, and then looked shamefaced. Cantra chuckled, and grinned when he met her eyes.

"My foster-mother always said passengers was more trouble'n they was worth," she said. "I'd own she was right. You, Pilot?"

He tried to frown, but his lips kept twitching the wrong way, and finally he let the smile have its way. "I'd own she was right, too, Pilot," he said, and turned back to his board.

QUICK PASSAGE'S brains were top-notch and her instrumentation was second to none. In relatively short order, they were in possession of a fistful of useful facts. The larger gas giant was just over one-thousandth the mass of the star; the smaller gas giant half the mass of its sister. The giants were more than ninety degrees apart as they circled the star, but in the same plane. There was some debris, and some radio noise typical of energetic discharges. The star had a single small relatively low-energy magnetic storm on its surface, and there seemed to be no other stars within half-a-dozen light-years. So far, so good.

In-ship chimed; the boy reached—and stopped as she held up her hand.

"She's got six ship-days to stew and we got work to do," she said. "Turn it off and mind your analysis, Pilot."

Tor An grinned. "Aye, Captain."

In the back of her head, an image formed: A white dragon, wings blazing light, rose in a lazy spiral into a brilliant sky. Cantra's fingers paused on the workpad; then she spun and came out of her seat quick. The boy was up, too, and they walked side-by-side and quiet to the power-chair.

Liad dea'Syl's eyes were closed, his head against the rest. He was breathing, shallowly. Lucky was curled on his lap, and the long, clever hands rested on the plush orange fur. On his far side, Rool Tiazan knelt, his fingers curled lightly 'round one thin wrist.

"Tell me, my friend," the scholar whispered. "Is it a fine world, and green? Will people prosper and do well?"

"It is the very finest world possible, Grandfather," the dramliza answered, his voice steady. "The land is rich and bountiful; its star is stable and gracious. Here, the tree will grow to its full height, honoring M. Jela. Here, may people prosper, do well, and be happy in their lives. You have given us a great gift, and we shall evermore be your children in gratitude."

The scholar smiled. "That is well, then," he said softly, and sighed.

In Cantra's head, the white dragon was lost in the brilliant sky, or maybe it was only that she couldn't see him through the tears.

THIRTY-SEVEN

Quick Passage

CANTRA LOOKED DOWN-BOARD to Tor An, who smiled at her encouragingly, and touched the in-ship stud.

"This is Captain yos'Phelium to all passengers. As you know, we've established orbit around an uninhabited world, and deployed probes to the surface. I'm pleased to say that the analysis has now been completed—and to our benefit. Wake-up protocols for passengers in slow-sleep will begin within this ship's hour, in rotation. Off-loading will commence within the next ship's day. Schedules will be on every public screen." She paused and looked again to the boy, who moved his fingers: *Captain's privilege.*

Right. She took a breath and bent again to the mic.

"Welcome to Liad, gentles. The pilots trust you'll enjoy your stay."

❖ END ❖

INTRODUCTION:

Balance of Trade

ONE OF THE HAZARDS of being a writer is generating too many ideas. The unused ones tend to pile up in drifts in the corners, which makes for an untidy house.

Back before we'd written *Plan B*, we had an idea for a story—a scene, really—a good, meaty scene. The trouble was, none of the characters on-roll were willing to take it on and make it their own.

The idea languished, and every so often we'd dust it off and put it on offer, but nobody stepped forward to claim it. In the meantime, the scene had gotten larger, more complex, and had developed some interesting resonances—enough to move a certain Master Trader to take an option on the project, contingent upon locating an appropriate lead.

About then, we got a request for a Liaden Universe story from *Absolute Magnitude* editor Warren Lapine, and, well, there was the Master Trader's interest, and . . . this kid. We'd never seen him before, but Jethri—his name was Jethri—said he could do the job. He liked the scene.

So, we let him take it for a spin; the resulting novella,

"Balance of Trade," was published in *Absolute Magnitude*. And we figured that was that.

But while we felt we were done with Jethri, he wasn't done with us. When Stephe Pagel at Meisha Merlin asked, "What are you doing next?" Jethri jumped up and said, "Me!"

And here he is, having earned it. We hope you enjoy his adventures.

Sharon Lee and Steve Miller
Unity, Maine
September 2003

BALANCE OF TRADE
CAST OF CHARACTERS

Gobelyn's Market out of New Carpathia

Arin Gobelyn, Iza's deceased spouse, Jethri's father
Cris Gobelyn, first mate, Iza's eldest child
Dyk Gobelyn, cook
Grig Tomas, back-up everything, Arin's cousin
Iza Gobelyn, captain-owner
Jethri Gobelyn
Khatelane Gobelyn, pilot
Mel Gobelyn
Paitor Gobelyn, trader, Iza's brother
Seeli Gobelyn, admin, Iza's second child
Zam Gobelyn

Elthoria out of Solcintra

Kor Ith yo'Lanna, captain
Norn ven'Deelin, master trader
Pen Rel sig'Kethra, arms master
Gar Sad per'Etla, cargo master
Gaenor tel'Dorbit, first mate
Ray Jon tel'Ondor, protocol master
Vil Tor, ship's librarian
Kilara pin'Ebit, technician
Rantel ver'Borith, technician

Tarnia's Clanhouse

Stafeli Maarilex, Delm Tarnia
Ren Lar Maarilex, Master of the Vine

Pet Ric Maarilex, his son
Pen Dir, a cousin, off at school
Meicha Maarilex, a daughter of the house
Miandra Maarilex, a daughter of the house
Flinx, a cat
Mr. pel'Saba, the butler
Mrs. tor'Beli, the cook
Anecha, a driver
Graem, Ren Lar's second in the cellars
Sun Eli pen'Jerad, tailor
Zer Min pel'Oban, dancing master

NOTE ON LIADEN CURRENCY AND TIME

Liaden Currency
> 12 dex to a tor
> 12 tor to a kais
> 12 kais (144 tor) to a cantra
> 1 cantra = 35,000 Terran bits

Standard Year
> 8 Standard Days in One Standard Week
> 32 Standard Days in One Standard Month
> 384 Standard Days in One Standard Year

Liaden Year
> 96 Standard Days in One Relumma
> 12 Standard Months in One Standard Year
> One Relumma is equal to 8 twelve-day weeks
> Four Relumma equal One Standard Year

BALANCE OF TRADE

A Liaden Universe® Novel

DAY 29

❀❀❀❀❀❀❀❀❀❀❀❀❀❀❀❀❀❀❀❀❀❀❀❀❀

Standard Year 1118
Gobelyn's Market
Opposite Shift

> *There are secrets in all families*
> —George Farquhar, 1678-1707

"DOWN ALL THAT LONG, weary shift, they kept after Byl,"
Khat's voice was low and eerie in the dimness of the common room.
The knuckles of Jethri's left hand ached with the grip he had on his
cup while his right thumb and forefinger whirled ellipses on the
endlessly cool surface of his lucky fractin. Beside him, he could hear
Dyk breathing, fast and harsh.

"Once—twice—three times!—he broke for the outring, his ship,
and his mates. Three times, the Liadens turned him back, pushing
him toward the center core, where no space-going man has right
nor reason to be.

"They pushed him, those Liadens, moving through the night-
levels as swift and sure as if it were bright world-day. Byl ran, as fast
as long legs and terror could speed him, but they were always ahead
of him, the canny Liadens. They were always ahead—'round every
corner, past every turning in the hall."

Mel, on Jethri's left, moaned softly. Jethri bit his lip.

"But then!" Khat's voice glittered in the gloom. "Then, all at once, the luck changed. Or, say, the gods of spacers smiled. He reached a corridor that was empty, turned a corner where no Liaden crouched, gun aiming for his heart. He paused then, ears craned to the rear, but heard no stealthy movement, nor boot heels sounding quick along the steel floor.

"He ran then, light of heart and all but laughing, and the way stood clear before him, from downring admin all the way to the outring, where his ship was berthed; where his mates, and his love, lay awaiting his return.

"He came to the bay door—Bay Eight, that was where. Came to the bay door, used his card and slipped through as soon as the gap was wide enough to fit him. Grinning, he pushed off in the lighter grav, taking long bounds toward Dock Three. He took the curve like he'd grown wings, singing now, so glad to be near, so glad to be home . . .

"That was when he saw the crowd, and the flashing lights that meant ring cops—and the others, that meant worse.

"He shouted and ran, waving his arms as if it all made a difference. Which it didn't. Those lifelines had been cut good hours ago, while he had been harried, hounded and kept away—and there was eight zipped bags laid out neat on the dockside, which was all that was left of his mates and his love."

Silence, Jethri's jaw was so tight he thought teeth might shatter. Mel gasped and Dyk groaned.

"So," said Khat, her voice shockingly matter-of-fact. "Now you see what comes to someone who cheats a Liaden on cargo."

"Except," Jethri managed, his voice breathless with tension, though he knew far better than what had been told—Khat on a story was *that* good. "Excepting, they'd never done it that way—the Liadens. Might be they'd've rigged something with the docking fees—more like, they'd've set the word around, so five ports later Byl finds himself at a stand—full cans and no buyers, see? But they wouldn't kill for cargo—that's not how their Balancing works."

"So speaks the senior 'prentice!" Dyk intoned, pitching his voice so deep it rumbled inside the steel walls like a bad encounter with a grabber-hook.

"C'mon, Jeth," Mel put in. "You was scared, too!"

"Khat tells a good story," he muttered, and Dyk produced a laugh.

"She does that—and who's to say she's wrong? Sure, you been studying the tapes, but Khat's been studying portside news since before you was allowed inside ship's core!"

"Not that long," Khat protested mildly, over the rustle and scrape that was her moving along the bench 'til she had her hand on the controls. Light flooded the cubby, showing four startlingly similar faces: broad across the cheekbones and square about the jaw. Khat's eyes, and Jethri's, were brown; Dyk and Mel had blue—hers paler than his. All four favored the spacer buzz, which left their scant hair looking like dark velvet caps snugged close 'gainst their skulls. Mel was nearest to Jethri in age—nineteen Standards to his seventeen. Khat and Dyk were born close enough to argue minutes when questions of elder's precedence rose—twenty Standard Years, both, and holding adult shares.

Their surname was Gobelyn. Their ship was *Gobelyn's Market*, out of New Carpathia, which homeworld none of them had ever seen nor missed.

"Yah, well maybe Jethri could tell us a story," said Dyk, on the approach of mischief, "since he knows so many."

Jethri felt his ears heat, and looked down into his cup. Koka, it had been—meant to warm his way to slumber. It was cold, now, and Khat's story was enough to keep a body awake through half his sleep-shift.

Even if he did know better.

"Let him be, Dyk," Khat said, surprisingly. "Jethri's doing good with his study—Uncle's pleased. Says it shows well, us having a Liaden speaker 'mong us."

Dyk started to laugh, caught something in her face and shrugged instead. Jethri wisely did not mention that his "Liaden speaking" was barely more than pidgin.

Instead, he drank off the dregs of his cold koka, managing without much of a shudder, then got himself up and across the room, right hand still fingering the ancient tile in search of comfort. He put the cup in the washer, and nodded to his cousins before he left to find his bunk.

"Good shift," he murmured.

"Good shift, Jethri," Khat said warmly. "Wide dreaming."

"Sleep tight, kid," Dyk added and Mel fluttered her fingers, smiling. "Be good, Jeth."

He slipped out of the cubby and paused, weighing the likelihood of sleep against the lure of a history search on the fate of Byl—and the length of Uncle Paitor's lecture, if he was found reading through his sleep shift again.

That was the clincher, his uncle being a man who warmed to a scolding. Sighing, Jethri turned to the right. Behind him, in the cubby, he heard Dyk say, "So tell us a scary one, Khat; now that the kid's away."

HAVING FOUND SLEEP late, it was only natural that Jethri overslept the bell, meaning hard biscuit and the dregs of the pot for breakfast. Chewing, he flipped through the duty roster and discovered himself on Stinks.

"Mud!" he muttered, gulping bitter coffee. It wasn't that he begrudged his cousins their own round of duty—which they had, right enough; he wasn't callin' slackers—just, he wished that he might progress somewhat above the messy labor and make-work that fell his lot all too often. He had his studies, which was work, of its kind; emergency drill with Cris; and engine lore with Khat. 'Course, him being youngest, with none on the ladder 'neath him— that did go into the equation. *Some*body had to do the scutwork, and if not juniormost, then who?

Cramming the last of the biscuit into his mouth, he scanned down to dinner duty—and nearly cussed again. Dyk was on cook, which meant the meal would be something tasty, complicated and needful of mucho cleanup. Jethri himself being on cleanup.

"That kind of shift," he consoled himself, pouring the dregs of the dregs into the chute and setting the cup into the washer. "Next shift can only be better."

Being as they were coming into Ynsolt'i Port next shift, barring the unexpected, that at least was a given. Which realization did lighten his mood a fraction, so he was able to bring up a thin, tuneless whistle to stand him company on his way down to the utility lockers.

HE WORKED HIS WAY UP from quarters, stripping the sweet-sheets off sleeping pallets, rolling up the limp, sweat-flavored mats and stuffing them into the portable recycler. Zam, Seeli, and Grig were on Opposite; the doors to their quarters sealed, blue privacy lights lit. Jethri left new sheets rolled up and strapped outside their doors and moved on, not in any particular scramble, but not dallying, either. He had it from experience that doing Stinks consumed considerably less time than was contained inside a duty-shift. Even doing Stinks thoroughly and well—which he had better or the captain'd be down his throat with her spacesuit on—he'd have shift left at the end of his work. He was allowed to use leftover duty time for study. What had to be measured with a fine rule was how much time he could claim before either Uncle Paitor or the captain called slacker and pulled him down to the core on discipline.

Stinks being a duty short on brain work, the brain kept itself busy. Mostly, Jethri used the time to review his latest studies, or daydream about the future, when he would be a trader in his own right, free to cut deals and commit the ship, without having to submit everything to Uncle Paitor, and getting his numbers second-guessed and his research questioned.

Today, the brain having started on a grump, it continued, embroidering on the theme of scutwork. Replacing the sheets in his own cubby, he tried to interject some happy-think into what was threatening to become a major mood, and found himself on the losing side of an argument with himself.

He was juniormost, no disputing that—youngest of Captain Iza Gobelyn's three children—unintended, and scheduled for abort until his father's golden tongue changed her mind.

Despite unwelcome beginnings, though, he was of value to the ship. Uncle Paitor was teaching him the trade, and had even said that Jethri's researches into the Liaden markets had the potential to be profitable for the ship. Well, Uncle Paitor had even backed a major buy Jethri had suggested, last port, and if that didn't show a growing faith in the juniormost's skill, then nothing did.

That's all right, the half of himself determined to set into a mood countered. *Uncle Paitor might allow you value to the ship, but can you say the same for your mother?*

Which was hardly a fair question. Of course, he couldn't say the same for his mother, who had put him into Seeli's care as a babe and hadn't much use for him as a kid. When his father died—and only owning the truth—captain'd had a lot of changes to go through, one of them being she'd lost the lover and listening post she'd had since her second voyage out of her homeship, *Grenadine*. She taken three days of wild-time to try to recover some balance—come back drunk and black and blue, proclaiming herself cured. But after that, any stock Jethri'd held with his mother had vanished along with everything that had anything to do with his father, from photocubes to study certificates to his and Jethri's joint collection of antique fractins. It was almost as if she blamed him for Arin's death, which was plain senseless, though Seeli did her best to explain that the human heart wasn't notoriously sensible.

Quarters finished, and in a fair way to seeing that mood set in plate steel, Jethri went down to Ops.

The door whined in its track when it opened and Jethri winced, sending a quick glance inside to see if his entrance had disturbed anybody at their calcs.

Khat was sitting at the big board, the captain shadowing her from second. Cris, on data, glanced over his shoulder and gave Jethri a quick jerk of the chin. Khat didn't turn, but she did look up and smile into the screen for him. The captain never stirred.

Dragging the recycler to the wall, he moored it, then went back to the door, fingering the greaser pen from his kit belt. He pulled open the panel and switched the automatic off. Kneeling, he carefully penned a beaded line of grease along the outer track. The door whined again—slightly softer—when he pushed it open, and he applied a second row of grease beads to the inner track.

He tucked the pen away and stood, pushing the door back and forth until it ran silent in its tracks, nodded, and switched on the automatics again.

That minor chore taken care of, he moved along the stations, backmost first, working quick and quiet, replacing the used sweet-sheets with new, strapping fresh sheets to the board at each occupied station.

"Thanks, Jeth," Cris said in his slow, easy voice. "'preciate the door, too. I shoud've got it myself, three shifts back."

Thanks from Cris was coin worth having. Jethri ducked his head, feeling his ears heat.

"'welcome," he murmured, putting the new mat down at second and reaching for the strap.

The captain stood. "You can replace that," she said, her cool brown eyes barely grazing Jethri before she turned to Khat. "Keep course, Pilot."

"Aye, Cap'n."

She nodded, crossed the room in two long strides and was gone, the door opening silently before her. Jethri bit his lip, spun the chair and stripped off the used sheet. Glancing up, he saw his cousins pass a glance between the two of them, but didn't catch its meaning, being short of the code. He smoothed the new mat into place, stowed the old one with all the rest, unmoored the recycler and left.

Neither Khat nor Cris looked 'round to see him go.

STINKS WAS A PLAY in two parts. Between them, Jethri took a break for a mug of 'mite, which was thick and yellow and smelled like yeast—and if anyone beyond a spacer born and bred could stomach the stuff, the fact had yet to be noted.

One mug of 'mite delivered a cargo can load of vitamins and power nutrients. In the old days, when star travel was a new and risky undertaking, crews had lived on 'mite and not much else, launch to planetfall. Nowadays, when space was safe and a ship the size of *Gobelyn's Market* carried enough foodstuffs to supply a body's needed nutrients without sacrificing taste and variety, 'mite lingered on as a comfort drink, and emergency ration.

Jethri dunked a couple whole grain crackers in his mug, chomped and swallowed them, then drank off what was left. Thus fortified, he ambled down to the utility lockers, signed the camera out, slotted the empties and a tray of new filters into the sled and headed out to the bounceway.

OPS RAN *MARKET'S* grav in a helix, which was standard for a ship of its size and age. Smaller vessels ran whole-ship light—or even no-grav, and weight work was a part of every crew member's daily duty roster. *Market* was big enough to generate the necessary power for a field. Admin core was damn' near one gee, as was Ops itself. Sleeping quarters was lighter; you slept strapped in and anchored your possessions to the wall. The outer edges of the ship, where the cans hooked in, that was lighter still—as near to no grav as mattered. On the outermost edge of E Deck, there was the bounceway, a rectangular space marked out for rec, where crew might swoop, fly, bounce off the walls, play free-fall tag, and—just coincidentally— sharpen their reaction times and grav-free moves.

It being a rec area, there were air vents. It being the largest open atmosphere section on the ship, it also had the highest amount of ship air to sample for pollen, spores, loose dust, and other contaminants. Jethri's job was to open each vent, use the camera to record the visual patterns, change the camera to super and flash for spectrographic details, remove the used filter, install a fresh, and reseal the vent. That record would go right to command for analysis as soon as he plugged the camera into the charge socket

Not quite as mindless as replacing sweet-sheets, but not particularly demanding of the thought processes, either.

Mooring the sled, he slid the camera into the right pocket of his utility vest, a new filter and an envelope into the left, squinted thoughtfully at the position of the toppest vent—and kicked off.

Strictly speaking, he *could* have gone straight-line, door to vent. In the unlikely circumstance that there'd been hurry involved, he would, he told himself, curling for the rebound off the far wall, have chosen the high leap. As it was, hands extended and body straight, he hit the corner opposite the vent, somersaulted, arcing downward, hit the third wall with his feet, rising again, slowing, slowing—until he was floating, gentle and easy, next to the target vent.

Bracing himself, he slid the door open, used the camera, then unsnapped the soiled filter, slipped it into the envelope and snapped in the replacement. Making sure his pockets were sealed, he treated himself to cross-room dive, shot back up to the opposite corner, dove again, twisted in mid-dive, bounced off the end wall, pinwheeled off the ceiling, hit the floor on his hand, flipped and came upright next to the sled.

Grinning like a certified fool, he unsealed his pocket, slotted the used filter, took on a clean one, turned and jumped for the next vent.

IT MIGHT'VE BEEN an hour later and him at the trickiest bit of his day. The filter for the aromatics locker was special—a double-locking, odor-blocking bit of business, badly set over the door, flush to the angle with the ceiling. Aromatics was light, but by no means as light as the bounceway, so it was necessary for anyone needing to measure and change the filter to use their third hand to chin themselves on the high snatch-rod, knees jammed at right angles to the ceiling, while simultaneously using their first and second hands to do the actual work.

Normal two-handers were known to lament the lack of that crucial third appendage with language appropriate to the case. Indeed, one of Jethri's fondest memories was of long, easy-speaking Cris, bent double against the ceiling, hanging over the vent in question, swearing, constantly and conversationally, for the entire twenty minutes the job required, never once repeating a cuss word. It had been a virtuoso performance to which Jethri secretly aspired.

Unfortunately, experience had taught him that he could either hang and cuss, or hang and work. So it was that he wrestled in silence, teeth drilling into lower lip, forcing himself to go slow and easy, and make no false moves, because it would be a serious thing if an aromatics spill contaminated the ship's common air.

He had just seated and locked the clean inner filter, when the hall echoed with a titanic *clang*, which meant that the cage had cycled onto his level.

Jethri closed his eyes and clenched into the corner, forcing himself to wait until the wall had stopped reverberating.

"It's settled," the captain's voice echoed in the wake of the larger noise.

"*Might* be settled." That was Uncle Paitor, his voice a rumble, growing slightly fainter as the two of them walked outward, toward the cans. "I'm not convinced we've got the best trade for the ship in this, Iza. I'm thinking we might be underselling something—"

"We've got space issues, which aren't leaving us," the captain interrupted. "This one's Captain's Call, brother. It's settled."

"Space issues, yeah," Paitor said, a whole lot more argumentative than he usually was when he was talkin' to the captain, and like he thought things weren't settled at all. "There's space issues. In what case, sister o'mine, you'd best remember those couple o'seal-packs of extra you been carrying in your personal bin for damn' near ten Standards. You been carrying extra a long time, and some of what's there ought to get shared out so choices can be made—"

"No business of yours—none of it, Paitor."

"You's the one called kin just now. But I'm a trader, and what you got's still worth something to somebody. You make this trade and that stuff ought to be gone, too!"

"We'll chart that course when we got fuel for it. You done?"

Paitor answered that, but Jethri only caught the low sound of his voice, no words.

Cautiously, he unclenched, reached for the second filter and began to ease back the locks, forcing himself to attend to the work at hand, rather than wonder what sort of trade might be Captain's Call . . .

LATER, IN THE GALLEY, Dyk was in a creative frenzy.

Jethri, who knew his man, had arrived well before his scheduled time, and already there were piles of used bowls, cruets, mixers, forks, tongs, spoons and spice syringes littering every possible surface and the floor. It was nothing short of awesome. Shaking his head, he pulled on his gloves and started in on first clean up.

"Hey, Jeth! Unship that big flat pan for me, willya?"

Sighing, Jethri abandoned the dirties, climbed up on the counter and pulled open the toppest cabinet, where the equipment that was used least was stowed. Setting his feet careful among the welter of used tools, he reached for the requested pan.

The door to the galley banged open, Jethri turned his head and clutched the edge of the cabinet, keeping himself very still.

Iza Gobelyn stood in the doorway, her face so tight the lines around her mouth stood in stark relief. Dyk, lost in his dream of cookery, oblivious to clear danger, smiled over his shoulder at her, the while beating something in a bowl with a power spoon.

"Good shift, Captain!" he called merrily. "Have we got a surprise ordered in for you tonight!"

"No," said Iza.

That got through.

Dyk blinked. "Ma'am?"

"I said, *no*," the captain repeated, her voice crackling with static. "We'll want a quick meal, no surprises."

The spoon went quiet. Dyk put the bowl aside, real careful, and turned to face her. "Captain, I've got a meal planned and on course."

"Jettison," she said, flat and cold. "Quick meal, Dyk. Now."

There was a moment—a long moment, when Jethri though Dyk would argue the point, but in the end, he just nodded.

"Yes'm," he said, real quiet, and turned away toward the cabinet.

The captain left, the door swinging shut behind her.

Jethri let out the breath he hadn't known he'd been holding, slid the flat pan back into its grips, closed the door, and carefully got himself down to the floor, where he started back in collecting dirties.

He was loading the washer when it came to him that Dyk was 'way too quiet, and he looked up.

His cousin was staring down at the bowl, kinda swirling the contents with the power spoon turned off. Jethri moved a couple steps closer, until Dyk looked at him.

"What was you making?" Jethri asked.

"A cake," Dyk said, and Jethri could believe it was tears he saw in the blue eyes. "I—" he cleared his throat and shook his head, pushing the bowl away. "It was a stupid idea, I guess. I'll get the quick meal together and then help you with clean up, right?"

Dyk wasn't a prize as a partner in clean up, and Jethri was about to decline the favor. And a cake—why would he have been after making a cake, just coming into port? *Another one of those everybody-knows-but-me things*, Jethri thought, frowning at his larger cousin.

Something about the set of his shoulders, or even the tears, Dyk not being one to often cry, counseled him to think better of refusing the offered aid. He nodded, trying to remake his frown into something approaching agreeable.

"Sure," he said. "Be glad of the help."

DAY 32

❀ ❀

Standard Year 1118
Gobelyn's Market
Jethri's Quarters

JETHRI WAS BEHIND closed door—which he didn't usually do on his off-shift—because the volume on the recorder was iffy at best, and besides, there were a couple of the cousins who weren't all that happy to hear Liaden words, even if they was spoke on archive, by a relative.

"If you trade with Liadens, trade careful, and for the gods' love don't come sideways of honor."

One upside of having the door closed was an unimpeded view of the gift Dyk had given him two ports back, to much guffawing at the entrance hatch. The Unofficial Up-To-Date Combine Com-Code Chart issued by Trundee's Tool and Tow. Besides the codes, most of which hadn't changed in the dozen or so years Jethri had been aware of them, there was a constantly changing view, in simulated 3D, of the self-declared "Best Saltwater Bathing Beach in the Galaxy."

Jethri had—on several occasions, truth told—tried to count the different views offered by the chart. Dyk had helpfully showed him how to change the pace, or even stop on a particular image. Jethri discovered, by plain accident, that you could "tune out" the images of people without bathing suits—or the ones with bathing suits, for that matter, and also how to close up on the people and the sand, blocking out the long, unsettling sweep of sky.

His eye was caught now by a series that intrigued him. A couple, hand in hand, moved across several images, walking along the sandscape by the roiling, splashing waves, each wearing a suit (if something covering only a very small part of the anatomy could really be called a suit!). Both suits had decorations on them, shapes very much like his lucky fractin. The woman's suit was basically white, with the fractins arrayed in several fetching patterns, but they were blue, with the lettering in yellow. Her partner's suit was blue, the fractins white and the lettering black, which was like no fractin he'd ever seen—not that he thought he'd seen them all.

The distraction of the woman's shape and beauty, and the way she moved, made it hard for him to pay attention to the old tape. He sighed, so loud he might have been heard in the companionway if anyone was there to listen.

He had work to do. They were set to put in at a Liaden port right soon, and now was time to study, not indulge high-oxy dreams of walking hand-held with a lady 'way too pretty to notice a ship-kid . . .

Teeth chewing lower lip, he punched the button on the recorder, backing up to the last sentence he remembered hearing.

This set of notes was old: recorded by Great-Grand-Captain Larance Gobelyn more than forty Standard years ago, dubbed to ship's library twenty Standards later from the original deteriorating tape. Jethri fiddled with the feed on the audio board, but only succeeded in lowering the old man's voice. Sighing, he upped the gain again, squinting in protest of the scratchy, uneven sound.

"Liaden honor is—active. Insult—any insult—is punished. Immediately. An individual's name is his most important possession and—"

"Jethri?" Uncle Paitor's voice broke across Cap'n Larance's recitation. Jethri sighed and thumbed 'pause'.

"Yessir," he said, turning his head toward the intercom grid set in the wall.

"Come on down to the trade room, will you? We need to talk over a couple things."

Jethri slipped the remote out of his ear. As senior trader, Paitor was specifically in charge of the senior apprentice trader's time and education.

"Yessir," Jethri repeated. Two quick fingertaps marked his place in the old notes file. He left at a brisk walk, his thoughts half on honor, and only slightly less than half on the image of the woman on the poster.

HIS UNCLE NODDED him into a chair and eased back in his. They were coming in on Ynsolt'i and next hour Paitor Gobelyn would have time for nothing but the feed from the port trade center. Now, his screen was dark, the desk-top barren. Paitor cleared his throat.

"Got a couple things," he said, folding his hands over his belt buckle. "On-Port roster: Dyk an' me'll be escorting the payload to the central trade hall and seeing it safe with the highest bidder. Khat's data, Grig's eatables, Mel's on tech, Cris'll stay ship-side. You . . ."

Paitor paused and Jethri gripped his hands together tight on his lap, willing his face into a trader's expression of courteous disinterest. They had textile on board—half a dozen bolts of cellosilk that Cris had taken on two stops back, with Ynsolt'i very much in his mind. Was it possible, Jethri wondered, that Uncle Paitor was going to allow. . .

"Yourself—you'll be handling the silk lot. I expect to see a kais out of the lot. If I was you, I'd call on Honored Sir bin'Flora first."

Jethri remembered to breathe. "Yes, sir. Thank you." He gripped his hands together so hard they hurt. His own trade. His own, very first, solo trade with no Senior standing by, ready to take over if the thing looked like going awry.

His uncle waved a hand. "Time you were selling small stuff on your own. Now." He leaned forward abruptly, folded his arms on the desk and looked at Jethri seriously. "You know we got a lot riding on this trip."

Indeed they did—more than a quarter of the *Market's* speculation capital was tied up in eighteen Terran pounds of *vya*, a spice most commonly sold in five gram lots. Jethri's research had revealed that *vya* was the active ingredient in *fa'vya*, a Liaden drink ship's library classified as a potent aphrodisiac. Ynsolt'i was a Liaden port and the spice should bring a substantial profit to the ship. Not, Jethri reminded himself, that profit was ever guaranteed.

"We do well with the spice here," Paitor was saying, "and the captain's going to take us across to Kinaveral, do that refit we'd been banking for *now*, rather than two Standards from now."

This was the news that might have had Dyk baking a cake. Jethri sat up straighter, rubbing the palms of his hands down the rough fabric of his work pants.

"Refit'll keep us world-bound 'bout a Standard, near's we can figure. Captain wants that engine upgrade bad and trade-side's gonna need two more cargo pods to balance the expense." He grinned suddenly. "Three, if I can get 'em."

Jethri smiled politely, thinking that his uncle didn't look as pleased with that as he might have and wondering what the down-side of the trade was.

"While refit's doing, we figured—the captain and me—that it'd be optimum to re-structure crew. So, we've signed you as senior 'prentice with *Gold Digger*."

It was said so smoothly that Jethri didn't quite catch the sense of it.

"*Gold Digger*?" he repeated blankly, that much having gotten through, by reason of him and Mac Gold having traded blows on last sighting—more to Jethri's discomfort than Mac's. He hadn't exactly told anyone on the *Market* the full details of the incident, *Gold Digger's* crew being cousins of his mother, and his mother making a point more'n once about how she'd nearly ended up being part of that ship instead of this.

Jethri came forward in his chair, hearing the rest of it play back inside the whorlings of his ears.

"You signed me onto *Gold Digger*?" he demanded. "For how long?"

His voice echoed into the hall, he'd asked that loud, but he didn't apologize.

Paitor raised a hand. "Ease down, boy. One loop through the mines. Time they're back in port, you'll be twenty—full adult and able to find your own berth." He nodded. "You make yourself useful like you and me both know you can and you'll come off *Digger* a full trader with experience under your belt—"

"Three *Standards*?" Jethri's voice broke, but for once he didn't cringe in shame. He was too busy thinking about a converted ore ship smaller than the *Market*, its purely male crew crammed all six into a common sleeping room, and the trade nothing more than foodstuffs and ore, ore and mining tools, oxy tanks and ore . . .

"*Ore*," he said, staring at his uncle. "Not even rough gem. Industrial ore." He took a breath, knowing his dismay showed and not caring about that, either. "Uncle Paitor, I've been studying. If there's something else I—"

Paitor showed him palm again. "Nothing to do with your studying. You been doing real good. I'll tell you—better than the captain supposed you would. Little more interested in the Liaden side of things than I thought reasonable, there at first, but you always took after Arin, anyhow. No harm in learning the lingo, and I will say the Liadens seem to take positive note of you." He shook his head. "Course, you don't have your full growth yet, which puts you nearer their level."

Liadens were a short, slight people, measured against Terran averages. Jethri wasn't as short as a Liaden, but he was, he thought bitterly, a damn' sight shorter than Mac Gold.

"What it is," Paitor said slowly. "We're out of room. It's hard for us, too, Jethri. If we were a bigger ship, we'd keep you on. But you're youngest, none of the others're inclined to change berth, and, well— Ship's Option. Captain's cleared it. Ben Gold states himself willing to have you." He leaned back, looking stern. "And ore needs study, too, 'prentice. Nothing's as simple as it looks."

Thrown off, thought Jethri. *I'm being thrown off of my ship.* He thought that he could have borne it better, if he was simply being cast out to make his own way. But the arranged berth on *Gold Digger* added an edge of fury to his disbelief. He opened his mouth to protest further and was forestalled by a *ping!* from Paitor's terminal.

The senior trader snapped forward in his chair, flipping the switch that accepted the first of the trade feeds from Ynsolt'i Port. He glanced over at Jethri.

"You get me a kais for that silk, now. If the spice sells good for us, I'll OK that Combine key you been wanting. You'll have earned it."

That was dismissal. Jethri stood. "Yessir," he said, calm as a dry mouth would let him, and left the trade room.

DAY 33

Standard Year 1118
Ynsolt'i Port
Textile Hal

"PREMIUM GRADE, honored sir," Jethri murmured, keeping his eyes modestly lowered, as befit a young person in discourse with a person of lineage and honor.

Honored Sir bin'Flora moved his shoulders and flipped an edge of the fabric up, frowning at the underweave. Jethri ground his teeth against an impulse to add more in praise of the hand-loomed Gindoree cellosilk.

Don't oversell! he could hear Uncle Paitor snap from memory. *The Trader is in control of the trade.*

"Eight tor the six-bolt," the buyer stated, tossing the sample cloth back across the spindle. Jethri sighed gently and spread his hands.

"The honored buyer is, of course, distrustful of goods offered by one so many years his inferior in wisdom. I assure you that I am instructed by an elder of my ship, who bade me accept not a breath less than two kais."

"Two?" The Liaden's shoulders moved again—not a shrug, but expressive of some emotion. Amusement, Jethri thought. Or anger.

"Your elder mis-instructs you, young sir. Perhaps it is a testing." The buyer tipped his head slightly to one side, as if considering. "I will offer an additional pair of tor," he said at last, accent rounding the edges of the trade-tongue, "in kindness of a student's diligence."

Wrong, Jethri thought. Not to say that Honored bin'Flora wasn't the heart of kindness, which he very likely was, on his off-days. A trade was something else again.

Respectful, Jethri bowed, and, respectful, brought his eyes to the buyer's face. "Sir, I value your generosity. However, the distance between ten tor and two kais is so vast that I feel certain my elder would counsel me to forgo the trade. Perhaps you had not noticed—" he caught himself on the edge of insult and smoothly changed course— "the light is poor, just here . . ."

Pulling the bolt forward, he again showed the fineness of the cloth, the precious irregularities of weave, which proved it hand woven, spoke rapturously of the pure crimson dye.

The buyer moved his hand. "Enough. One kais. A last offer."

Gotcha, thought Jethri, making a serious effort to keep his face neutral. One kais, just like Uncle Paitor had wanted. In retrospect, it had been an easy sell.

Too easy? he wondered then, looking down at the Liaden's smooth face and disinterested brown eyes. Was there, just maybe, additional profit to be made here?

Trade is study, Uncle Paitor said from memory. *Study the goods, and study the market. And after you prepare as much as you can, there's still nothing says that a ship didn't land yesterday with three holds full of something you're carrying as a luxury sell.*

Nor was there any law, thought Jethri, against Honored Buyer bin'Flora being critically short on crimson cellosilk, this Port-day. He took a cautious breath and made his decision.

"Of course," he told the buyer, gathering the sample bolt gently into his arms, "I am desolate not to have closed trade in this instance. A kais . . . It is generous, respected sir, but—alas. My elder will be distressed—he had instructed me most carefully to offer the lot first to yourself and to make every accommodation . . . But a single kais, when his word was two? I do not . . ." He fancied he caught a gleam along the edge of the Liaden's bland face, a flicker in the depths of the careful eyes, and bit his lip, hoping he wasn't about to blow the whole deal.

"I don't suppose," he said, voice edging disastrously toward a squeak, "—my elder spoke of you so highly. . . I don't suppose you might go a kais-six?"

"Ah." Honored Sir bin'Flora's shoulders rippled and this time Jethri was sure the gesture expressed amusement. "One kais, six tor it is." He bowed and Jethri did, clumsily, because of the bolt he still cradled.

"Done," he said.

"Very good," returned the buyer. "Set the bolt down, young sir. You are quite correct regarding that crimson. Remarkably pure. If your elder instructed you to hold at anything less than four kais, he was testing you in good earnest."

Jethri stared, then, with an effort, he straightened his face, trying to make it as bland and ungiving as the buyer's.

He needn't have bothered. The Liaden had pulled a pouch from his belt and was intent on counting out coins. He placed them on the trade table and stepped back, sweeping the sample bolt up as he did.

"Delivery may be made to our warehouse within the twelve-hour." He bowed, fluid and unstrained, despite the bolt.

"Be you well, young sir. Fair trading, safe lift."

Jethri gave his best bow, which was nowhere near as pretty as the buyer's. "Thank you, respected sir. Fair trading, fair profit."

"Indeed," said the buyer and was gone.

BY RIGHTS, he should have walked a straight line from Textile Hall to the *Market* and put himself at the disposal of the captain.

Say he was disinclined just yet to talk with Captain Iza Gobelyn, coincidentally his mother, on the subject of his upcoming change of berth. Or say he was coming off his first true solo trade and wanted time to turn the thing over in his mind. Which he was doing, mere-beer to hand at the Zeroground Pub, on the corner of the bar he'd staked as his own.

He fingered his fractin, a slow whiling motion—that had been his thinking pattern for most of his life. No matter the captain had told him time and time that he was too old for such fidgets and foolishness. On board ship, some habits were worse than others, and the fractin was let to pass.

As to thinking, he had a lot to do.

He palmed the smooth ivory square, took a sip of the tangy local brew.

Buyer bin'Flora, now—that wanted chewing on. Liadens were fiercely competitive, and, in his experience, tight-fisted of data. Jethri had lately formed the theory that this reluctance to offer information was not what a Terran would call spitefulness, but *courtesy*. It would be—an *insult*, if his reading of the tapes was right, to assume that another person was ignorant of any particular something.

Which theory made Honored Sir bin'Flora's extemporaneous lecture on the appropriate price of crimson cellosilk—interesting.

Jethri sipped his beer, considering whether or not he'd been insulted. This was a delicate question, since it was also OK, as far as his own observations and the crewtapes went, for an elder to instruct a junior. He had another sip of beer, frowning absently at the plain ship-board above the bar. Strictly no-key, that board, listing ship name, departure, arrival, and short on finer info. Jethri sighed. If the *vya* did good, he'd one day soon be able to get a direct line to the trade nets, just by slipping his key into a high-info terminal. 'Course, by then, he'd be shipping on *Digger*, and no use for a Combine key at all . . .

"'nother brew, kid?" The bartender's voice penetrated his abstraction. He set the glass down, seeing with surprise that it was nearly empty. He fingered a Terran bit out of his public pocket and put it on the bar.

"Merebeer, please."

"Coming up," she said, skating the coin from the bar to her palm. Her pale blue eyes moved to the next customer and she grinned.

"Hey, Sirge! Ain't seen you for a Port-year."

The dark-haired man in modest trading clothes leaned his elbows on the counter and smiled. "That long?" He shook his head, smile going toward a grin. "I lose track of time, when there's business to be done."

She laughed. "What'll it be?"

"Franses Ale?" he asked, wistfully.

"Coming up," she said and he grinned and put five-bit in her hand.

"The extra's for you—a reward for saving my life."

The barkeeper laughed again and moved off down-bar, collecting orders and coins as she went. Jethri finished the last of his beer. When he put the glass down, he found the barkeeper's friend— Sirge—looking at him quizzically.

"Don't mean to pry into what's none of my business, but I noticed you looking at the board, there, a bit distracted. Wouldn't be you had business with *Stork*?"

Jethri blinked, then smiled and shook his head. "I was thinking of—something else," he said, with cautious truth. "Didn't really see the board at all."

"Man with business on his mind," said Sirge good naturedly. "Well, just thought I'd ask. Misery loves company, my mam used to say—Thanks, Nance." This last as the barkeeper set a tall glass filled with dark liquid before him.

"No trouble," she assured him and put Jethri's schooner down. "Merebeer, Trader."

"Thank you," he murmured, wondering if she was making fun of him or really thought him old enough to be a full trader. He raised the mug and shot a look at the ship-board. *Stork* was there, right enough, showing departed on an amended flight plan.

"Damnedest thing," said the man next to him, ruefully. "Can't blame them for lifting when they got rush cargo and a bonus at the far end, but I sure could wish they waited lift a quarter-hour longer."

Jethri felt a stir of morbid curiosity. "They didn't—leave you, did they, sir?"

The man laughed. "Gods, no, none of that! I've got a berth promised on Ringfelder's *Halcyon*, end of next Port-week. No, this was a matter of buy-in—had half the paperwork filled out, happened to look up at the board there in the Trade Bar and they're already lifting." He took a healthy swallow of his ale.

"Sent a message to my lodgings, of course, but I wasn't at the lodgings, I was out making paper, like we'd agreed." He sighed. "Well, no use crying over spilled wine, eh?" He extended a thin, calloused hand. "Sirge Milton, trader at leisure, damn' the luck."

He shook the offered hand. "Jethri Gobelyn, off *Gobelyn's Market*."

"Pleasure. *Market's* a solid ship—Arin still senior trader?"

Jethri blinked. The routes being as they were, there were still some who had missed news of Arin Gobelyn's death. This man didn't seem quite old enough to have been one of his father's contemporaries, but . . .

"Paitor's senior," he told Sirge Milton steadily. "Arin died ten Standards back."

"Sorry to hear that," the man said seriously. "I was just a 'prentice, but he impressed me real favorable." He took a drink of ale, eyes wandering back to the ship-board. "Damn'," he said, not quite under his breath, then laughed a little and looked at Jethri. "Let this be a lesson to you—*stay liquid*. Think I'd know *that* by now." Another laugh.

Jethri had a sip of beer. "But," he said, though it was none of his business, "what happened?"

For a moment, he thought the other wouldn't answer. He drank ale, frowning at the board, then seemed to collect himself and flashed Jethri a quick grin.

"Couple things. First, I was approached for a closed buy-in on— futures." He shrugged. "You understand I can't be specific. But the guarantee was four-on-one and—well, the lodgings was paid 'til I shipped and I had plenty on my tab at the Trade Bar, so I sunk all my serious cash into the future."

Jethri frowned. A four-on-one return on speculation? It was possible—the crewtapes told of astonishing fortunes made Port-side, now and then—but not likely. To invest all liquid assets into such a venture—

Sirge Milton held up a hand. "Now, I know you're thinking exactly what I thought when the thing was put to me—four-on-one's 'way outta line. But the gig turns on a Liaden Master Trader's say-so, and I figured that was good enough for me." He finished his ale and put the glass down, waving at the barkeeper.

"Short of it is, I'm cash-poor til tomorrow midday, when the pay-off's guaranteed. And this morning, I came across as sweet a deal as you'd care to see—and I know just who'll want it, to my profit. A kais holds the lot—and me with three ten-bits in pocket. *Stork* was going to front the cash, and earn half the profit, fair enough. But the rush-money and the bonus was brighter." He shook his head. "So, Jethri Gobelyn, you can learn from my mistake—and I'm hopeful I'll do the same."

"Four-on-one," Jethri said, mind a-buzz with the circumstance, so he forgot he was just a 'prentice, talking to a full trader. "Do you have a paper with the guarantee spelled out?"

"I got better than that," Sirge Milton said. "I got his card." He turned his head, smiling at the bartender. "Thanks, Nance."

"No problem," she returned. "You got a Liaden's card? Really? Can I see?"

The man looked uneasy. "It's not the kind of thing you flash around."

"Aw, c'mon, Sirge—I never seen one."

Jethri could appreciate her curiosity: he was half agog, himself. A Liaden's card was as good as his name, and a Liaden's name, according to great-grand-captain Larance, was his dearest possession.

"Well," Sirge said. He glanced around, but the other patrons seemed well-involved in their own various businesses. "OK."

He reached into his pouch, pulled out an out-of-date Combine trading key—the SY 1118 color was red, according to the chart on the back of his door; blue-and-white was last year's short-term color—along with a short handful of coins and a cargo-head socket wrench. Finally, with a satisfied grunt, he fingered out a flat, creamy rectangle.

He held up it face up between the three of them, his hands

cupping it like was a rare stone that he didn't want nobody else to see.

"Ooh," Nance said. "What's it say?"

Jethri frowned at the lettering. It was a more ornate form of the Liaden alphabet he had laboriously taught himself off the library files, but not at all unreadable.

"Norn ven'Deelin," he said, hoping he had the pronunciation of the name right. "Master of Trade."

"Right you are," said Sirge, nodding. "You'll go far, I'm sure, friend Jethri! And this here—" he rubbed his thumb over the graphic of a rabbit silhouetted against a full moon— "is the sign for his Clan. Ixin."

"Oh," Nance said again, then turned to answer a hail from up-bar. Sirge slipped the card away and Jethri took another sip of beer, mind racing. A four-on-one return, guaranteed by a Master Trader? It *was* possible. Jethri had seen the rabbit-and-moon sign on a land-barge that very day. And Sirge Milton was going to collect tomorrow mid-day. Jethri thought he was beginning to see a way to buy into a bit of profit, himself.

"I have a kais to lend," he said, setting the schooner aside.

Sirge Milton shook his head. "Nah—I appreciate it, Jethri, but I don't take loans. Bad business."

Which, Jethri acknowledged, was exactly what his uncle would say. He nodded, hoping his face didn't show how excited he felt.

"I understand. But you have collateral. How 'bout if I buy *Stork's* share of your Port-deal, pay-off tomorrow mid-day, after you collect from Master ven'Deelin?"

"Not the way I like to do business," Sirge said slowly.

Jethri took a careful breath. "We can write an agreement," he said.

The other brightened. "We can, can't we? Make it all legal and binding. Sure, why not?" He took a swallow of ale and grinned. "Got paper?"

"NO, MA'AM," Jethri said, some hours later, and as respectfully as he could, while giving his mother glare-for-glare. "I'm in no way trying to captain this ship. I just want to know if the final papers are signed with *Digger*." His jaw muscles felt tight and he tried to relax them—to make his face trading-bland. "I think the ship owes me that information. At least that."

"Think we can do better for you," his mother the captain surmised, her mouth a straight, hard line of displeasure. "All right, boy. No, the final papers aren't signed. We'll catch up with *Digger* 'tween here and Kinaveral and do the legal then." She tipped her head, sarcastically civil. "That OK by you?"

Jethri held onto his temper, barely. His mother's mood was never happy, dirt-side. He wondered, briefly, how she was going to survive a whole year world-bound, while the *Market* was rebuilt.

"I don't want to ship on *Digger*," he said, keeping his voice just factual. He sighed. "Please, ma'am—there's got to be another ship willing to take me."

She stared at him until he heard his heart thudding in his ears. Then she sighed in her turn, and spun the chair so she faced the screens, showing him profile.

"You want another ship," she said, and she didn't sound mad, anymore. "You find it."

DAY 34

❀❀❀❀❀❀❀❀❀❀❀❀❀❀❀❀❀❀❀❀❀

Standard Year 1118
Ynsolt'i Port
Zeroground Pub

"NO CALLS FOR Jethri Gobelyn? No message from Sirge Milton?"

The barkeeper on-shift today at the Zeroground Pub was maybe a Standard Jethri's elder. He was also twelve inches taller and out massed him by a factor of two. He shook his head, setting the six titanium rings in his left ear to chiming, and sighed, none too patient. "Kid, I told you. No calls. No message. No package. No Milton. No *nothing*, kid. Got it?"

Jethri swallowed, hard, the fractin hot against his palm. "Got it."

"Great," said the barkeep. "You wanna beer or you wanna clear out so a paying customer can have a stool?"

"Merebeer, please," he said, slipping a bit across the counter. The keeper swept up the coin, went up-bar, drew a glass, and slid it down the polished surface with a will. Jethri put out a hand—the mug smacked into his palm, stinging. Carefully, he eased away from the not-exactly-overcrowded counter and took his drink to the back.

He was on the approach to trouble. Dodging his senior, sliding off-ship without the captain's aye—approaching trouble, right enough, but not quite established in orbit. Khat was inventive—he

792

trusted her to cover him for another hour, by which time he had better be on-ship, cash in hand and looking to show Uncle Paitor the whole.

And Sirge Milton was late.

A man, Jethri reasoned, slipping into a booth and setting his beer down, might well be late for a meeting. A man might even, with good reason, be an hour late for that same meeting. But a man could call the place named and leave a message for the one who was set to meet him.

Which Sirge Milton hadn't done, nor sent a courier with a package containing Jethri's payout, neither.

So, something must've come up. Business. Sirge Milton seemed a busy man. Jethri opened his pouch and pulled out the agreement they'd written yesterday, sitting at this very back booth, with Nance the bartender as witness.

Carefully, he smoothed the paper, read over the guarantee of payment. Two kais was a higher buy-out than he had asked for, but Sirge had insisted, saying the profit would cover it, not to mention his 'expectations.' There was even a paragraph about being paid in the event that Sirge's sure buyer was out of cash, citing the debt owed Sirge Milton, Trader, by Norn ven'Deelin, Master of Trade, as security.

It had all seemed clear enough yesterday afternoon, but Jethri thought now that he should have asked Sirge to take him around to his supplier, or at least listed the name and location of the supplier on the paper.

He had a sip of beer, but it tasted flat and he pushed the glass away. The door to the bar slid open, admitting a noisy gaggle of Terrans. Jethri looked up, eagerly, but Sirge was not among them. Sighing, he frowned down at the paper, trying to figure out a next move that didn't put him on the receiving end of one of his uncle's furious scolds.

Norn ven'Deelin, Master of Trade . . . The name looked odd, written out in Terran, approximating spelling across two alphabets that didn't precisely match, edge-on-edge. Norn ven'Deelin, who had given his card—his *name*—into Sirge Milton's keeping. Jethri blinked. Norn ven'Deelin, he thought, would very likely know how to get in touch with a person he held in such high esteem. With luck, he'd be inclined to share that information with a polite-talking 'prentice.

If he wasn't inclined . . . Jethri folded his paper away and got out of the booth, leaving the beer behind. No use borrowing trouble, he told himself.

IT WAS LATE, but still day-Port, when he found the right office. At least, he thought, pausing across the street and staring at that damned bunny silhouetted against the big yellow moon, he hoped it was the right office. He was tired from walking miles in gravity, hot, gritty—but worse than any of that, he was scared. Norn ven'Deelin's office—if this *was* at last his office—was well into the Liaden side of Port.

Not that there was properly a *Terran* side, Ynsolt'i being a Liaden world. But there were portions where Terrans were tolerated as a necessary evil attending galactic trade, and where a body caught the notion that maybe Terrans were cut some extra length of line, in regard to what might be seen as insult.

Standing across from the door, which might, after all, be the right one, Jethri did consider turning around, trudging back to the *Market* and taking the licks he'd traded for.

Except he'd *traded for* profit to the ship, and he was going to collect it. That, at least, he would show his senior and his captain, though he had long since stopped thinking that profit would buy him pardon.

Jethri sighed. There was dust all over his good trading clothes. He brushed himself off as well as he could, and looked across the street. It came to him that the rabbit on Clan Ixin's sign wasn't so much howling at that moon, as laughing its fool head off.

Thinking so, he crossed the street, wiped his boots on the mat, slid his fractin manfully out of his palm and into his public pocket, and pushed the door open.

The office behind the door was airy and bright, and Jethri was abruptly glad that he had dressed in trading clothes, dusty as they now were. This place was high-class—a body could smell profit in the subtly fragrant air, see it in the floor covering and the real wooden chairs.

The man sitting behind the carved center console was as elegant as the room: crisp-cut yellow hair, bland and beardless Liaden face, a vest embroidered with the moon-and-rabbit worn over a salt-white silken shirt. He looked up from his work screen as the door opened, eyebrows lifting in what Jethri had no trouble reading as astonishment.

"Good-day to you, young sir." The man's voice was soft, his Trade only lightly tinged with accent.

"Good-day, honored sir." Jethri moved forward slowly, taking care to keep his hands in sight. Three steps from the console, he stopped and bowed, as low as he could manage without falling on his head.

"Jethri Gobelyn, apprentice trader, *Gobelyn's Market*." He straightened and met the bland blue eyes squarely. "I am come to call upon the Honored Norn ven'Deelin."

"Ah." The man folded his hands neatly upon the console. "I regret it is necessary that you acquaint me more nearly with your business, Jethri Gobelyn."

Jethri bowed again, not so deep this time, and waited til he was upright to begin the telling.

"I am in search of a man—a Terran," he added, half-amazed to hear no quaver in his voice— "named Sirge Milton, who owes me a sum of money. It was in my mind that the Honored ven'Deelin might be willing to put me in touch with this man."

The Liaden frowned. "Forgive me, Jethri Gobelyn, but how came such a notion into your mind?"

Jethri took a breath. "Sirge Milton had the Honored ven'Deelin's card in pledge of—"

The Liaden held up a hand, and Jethri gulped to a stop, feeling a little gone around the knees.

"Hold." A Terran would have smiled to show there was no threat. Liadens didn't smile, at least, not at Terrans, but this one exerted himself to incline his head an inch.

"If you please," he said. "I must ask if you are certain that it was the Honored ven'Deelin's own card."

"I—the name was plainly written, sir. I read it myself. And the sigil was the same, the very moon-and-rabbit you yourself wear."

"I regret." The Liaden stood, bowed and beckoned, all in one fluid movement. "This falls beyond my area of authority. If you please, young sir, follow me." The blue eyes met his, as if the Liaden had somehow heard his dismay at being thus directed deeper into alien territory. "House courtesy, Jethri Gobelyn. You receive no danger here."

Which made it plain enough, to Jethri's mind, that refusing to follow would be an insult. He swallowed, his breath going short on him, the *Market* suddenly seeming very far away.

The yellow-haired Liaden was waiting, his smooth, pretty face uncommunicative. Jethri bowed slightly and walked forward as calmly as trembling knees allowed. The Liaden led him down a short hallway, past two closed rooms, and bowed him across the threshold of the third, open.

"Be at ease," the Liaden said from the threshold. "I will apprise the master trader of your errand." He hesitated, then extended a hand, palm up. "It is well, Jethri Gobelyn. The House is vigilant on your behalf." He was gone on that, the door sliding silently closed behind him.

This room was smaller than the antechamber, though slightly bigger than the *Market's* common room, the shelves set at heights he had to believe handy for Liadens. Jethri stood for a couple minutes, eyes closed, doing cube roots in his head until his heartbeat slowed down and the panic had eased back to a vague feeling of sickness in his gut.

Opening his eyes, he went over to the shelves on the right, half-trained eye running over the bric-a-brac, wondering if that was really a piece of Sofleg porcelain and, if so, what it was doing set naked out on a shelf, as if it were a common pottery bowl.

The door whispered behind him, and he spun to face a Liaden woman dressed in dark trousers and a garnet-colored shirt. Her hair was short and gray, her eyebrows straight and black. She stepped energetically into the center of the room as the door slid closed behind her, and bowed with precision, right palm flat against her chest.

"Norn ven'Deelin," she stated in a clear, level voice. "Clan Ixin."

Jethri felt the blood go to ice in his veins.

Before him, Norn ven'Deelin straightened and slanted a bright black glance into his face. "You discover me a dismay," she observed, in heavily accented Terran. "Say why, do."

He managed to breathe, managed to bow. "Honored Ma'am, I—I've just learned the depth of my own folly."

"So young, yet made so wise!" She brought her hands together in a gentle clap, the amethyst ring on her right hand throwing light off its facets like purple lightning. "Speak on, young Jethri. I would drink of your wisdom."

He bit his lip. "Ma'am, the—person—I came here to find—told me Norn ven'Deelin was—was male."

"Ah. But Liaden names are difficult, I am learning, for those of Terran Code. Possible it is that your friend achieved honest error, occasioned by null-acquaintance with myself."

"I'm certain that's the case, Honored," Jethri said carefully, trying to feel his way toward a path that would win him free, with no insult to the trader, and extricate Sirge Milton from a junior's hopeless muddle.

"I—my friend—did know the person I mistakenly believed yourself to be well enough to have lent money on a portweek investment. The—error—is all my own. Likely there is another Norn ven'Deelin in Port, and I foolishly—"

A tiny hand rose, palm out, to stop him. "Be assured, Jethri Gobelyn. Of Norn ven'Deelin there is one. This one."

He had, Jethri thought, been afraid of that. Hastily, he tried to shuffle possibilities. Had Sirge Milton dealt with a go-between authorized to hand over his employer's card? Had—

"My assistant," said Norn ven'Deelin, "discloses to me a tale of wondering obfusion. I am understanding that you are in possession of one of my cards?"

Her assistant, Jethri thought, with a sudden sharpening of his wits on the matter at hand, had told her no such thing. She was trying to throw him off-balance, and startle him into revealing a weakness. She was, in fact, *trading*. Jethri ground his teeth and made his face smooth.

"No, ma'am," he said respectfully. "What happened was that I met a man in Port who needed loan of a kais to hold a deal. He said he had lent his liquid to—to Norn ven'Deelin, master trader. Of Clan Ixin. He said he was to collect tomorrow—today, mid-day, that would be—a guaranteed return of four-on-one. My—my payout contingent on his payout." He stopped and did not bite his lip, though he wanted to.

There was a short silence, then, "Four-on-one. That is a very large profit, young Jethri."

He ducked his head. "Yes, ma'am. I thought that. But he had the—the card of the—man—who had guaranteed the return. I read the name myself. And the clan sign—just like the one on your door and—other places on Port. . ." His voice squeaked out. He cleared his throat and continued.

"I knew he had to be on a straight course—at least on this deal— if it was backed by a Liaden's card."

"Hah." She plucked something flat and rectangular from her sleeve and held it out. "Honor me with your opinion of this."

He took the card, looked down and knew just how stupid he'd been.

"So wondrously expressive a face," commented Norn ven'Deelin. "Was this not the card you were shown, in earnest of fair dealing?"

He shook his head, remembered that the gesture had no analog among Liadens and cleared his throat again.

"No, ma'am," he said as steady as he could. "The rabbit-and-moon are exactly the same. The name—the same style, the same spacing, the same spelling. The stock was white, with black ink, not tan with brown ink. I didn't touch it, but I'd guess it was low-rag. This card is high-rag content. . ."

His fingers found a pattern on the obverse. He flipped the card over and sighed at the selfsame rabbit-and-moon, embossed into the card stock, then looked back to her bland, patient face.

"I beg your pardon, ma'am."

"So." She reached out and twitched the card from his fingers, sliding it absently back into her sleeve. "You do me a service, young Jethri. From my assistant, I hear the name of this person who has, yet does not have, my card in so piquant a fashion. Sirge Milton. This is a correctness? I do not wish to err."

The ice was back in Jethri's veins. Well he knew that Khat's stories of blood vengeance were just that—fright tales to spice an otherwise boring hour. Still and all, it wasn't done, to put another Terran in the way of Liaden Balance. He gulped and bowed.

"Ma'am, I—please. The whole matter is—is *my* error. I am the most junior of traders. Likely I misunderstood a senior and have annoyed yourself and your household without cause. I—"

She held up a hand, stepped forward and laid it on his sleeve.

"Peace, child. I do nothing fatal to your *galandaria*—your countryman. No pellet in his ear. No nitrogen replacing good air in an emergency tank. Eh?" Almost, it seemed to Jethri that she smiled.

"Such tales. We of the clans listen in Port bars—and discover ourselves monsters." She patted his arm, lightly. "But no. Unless he adopts a mode most stupid, fear not of his life." She stepped back, her hand falling from his sleeve.

"Your own actions reside in correctness. Very much is this matter mine of solving. A junior trader could do no other, than bring such at once before me.

"Now, I ask, most humbly, that you accept Ixin's protection in conveyance to your ship. It is come night-Port while we speak, and your kin will be distressful for your safety. Myself and yourself, we speak additionally, after solving."

She bowed again, hand over heart, and Jethri did his best to copy the thing with his legs shaking fit to tip him over. When he looked up the door was closing behind her. It opened again immediately and the yellow-haired assistant stepped inside with a bow of his own.

"Jethri Gobelyn," he said in his soft Trade, "please follow me. A car will take you to your ship."

⁂   ⁂   ⁂

"SHE SAID SHE wouldn't kill him," Jethri said hoarsely. The captain, his mother, shook her head and Uncle Paitor sighed.

"There's worse things than killing, son," he said, and that made Jethri want to scrunch into his chair and bawl, like he had ten Standards fewer and stood about as tall as he felt.

What he did do, was take another swallow of coffee and meet Paitor's eyes straight. "I'm sorry, sir."

"You've got cause," his uncle acknowledged.

"Double-ups on dock," the captain said, looking at them both. "Nobody works alone. We don't want trouble. We stay close and quiet and we lift as soon as we can without making it look like a rush."

Paitor nodded. "Agreed."

Jethri stirred, fingers tight 'round the coffee mug. "Ma'am, she—Master Trader ven'Deelin said she wanted to talk to me, after she—settled—things. I wouldn't want to insult her."

"None of us wants to insult her," his mother said, with more patience than he'd expected. "However, a Master Trader is well aware that a trade ship must trade. She can't expect us to hang around while our cargo loses value. If she wants to talk to you, boy, she'll find you."

"No insult," Paitor added, "for a 'prentice to bow to the authority of his seniors. Liadens understand chain of command real well." The captain laughed, short and sharp, then stood up.

"Go to bed, Jethri—you're out on your feet. Be on dock second shift—" she slid a glance to Paitor. "Dyk?"

His uncle nodded.

"You'll partner with Dyk. We're onloading seed, ship's basics, trade tools. Barge's due Port-noon. Stick *close*, understand me?"

"Yes, ma'am." Wobbling, Jethri got to his feet, nodded to his seniors, put the mug into the wash-up and turned toward the door.

"Jethri."

He turned back, thinking his uncle's face looked—sad.

"I wanted to let you know," Paitor said. "The spice did real well for us."

Jethri took a deep breath. "Good," he said and his voice didn't shake at all. "That's good."

DAY 35

❀❀❀❀❀❀❀❀❀❀❀❀❀❀❀❀❀❀❀❀❀❀❀❀

Standard Year 1118
Gobelyn's Market
Dockside

"OK," SAID DYK, easing the forks on the hand-lift back. "Got it."
He toggled the impeller fan and nodded over his shoulder. "Let's go,
kid. Guard my back."

Jethri managed a weak grin. Dyk was inclined to treat the
double-up and Paitor's even-voiced explanation of disquiet on the
docks as a seam-splitting joke. He guided the hand-lift to the edge
of the barge, stopped, theatrically craned both ways, flashed a
thumbs-up over his shoulder to Jethri, who was lagging behind, and
dashed out onto the *Market's* dock. Sighing, Jethri walked slowly in
his wake.

"Hey, kid, hold it a sec." The voice was low and not entirely
unfamiliar. Jethri spun.

Sirge Milton was leaning against a cargo crate, hand in the
pocket of his jacket and nothing like a smile on his face.

"Real smart," he said, "setting a Liaden on me."

Jethri shook his head, caught somewhere between relief and
dismay.

801

"You don't understand," he said, walking forward. "The card's a fake."

The man against the crate tipped his head. "Is it, now."

"Yeah, it is. I've seen the real one, and it's nothing like the one you've got."

"So what?"

"So," Jethri said patiently, stopping and showing empty hands in the old gesture of goodwill, "whoever gave you the card wasn't Norn ven'Deelin. He was somebody who *said* he was Norn ven'Deelin and he used the card and her—the honor of her name—to cheat you."

Sirge Milton leaned, silent, against the cargo bail.

Jethri sighed sharply. "Look, Sirge, this is serious stuff. The master trader has to protect her name. She's not after you—she's after whoever gave you that card and told you he was her. All you have to do—"

Sirge Milton shook his head, sorrowful, or so it seemed to Jethri. "Kid," he said, "you still don't get it, do you?" He brought his hand out of the pocket and leveled the gun, matter-of-factly, at Jethri's stomach. "I know the card's bogus, kid. I know who made it—and so does your precious master trader. She got the scrivener last night. She'd've had me this morning, but I know the back way outta the 'ground."

The gun was high-gee plastic, snub-nosed and black. Jethri stared at it and then looked back at the man's face.

Trade, he thought, curiously calm. *Trade for your life.*

Sirge Milton grinned. "You traded another Terran to a Liaden. That's stupid, Jethri. Stupid people don't live long."

"You're right," he said, calmly, watching Sirge's face and not the gun at all. "And it'd be real stupid for you to kill me. Norn ven'Deelin said I'd done her a service. If you kill me, she's not going to have any choice but to serve you the same. You don't want to corner her."

"Jeth?" Dyk's voice echoed in from the dock. "Hey! Jethri!"

"I'll be out in a second!" he yelled, never breaking eye contact with the gunman. "Give me the gun," he said, reasonably. "I'll go with you to the master trader and you can make it right."

"'Make it right'," Sirge sneered and there was a sharp snap as he thumbed the gun's safety off.

"I urge you most strongly to heed the young trader's excellent advice, Sirge Milton," a calm voice commented in accentless Trade. "The master trader is arrived and balance may go forth immediately."

Master ven'Deelin's yellow-haired assistant walked into the edge of Jethri's field of vision. He stood lightly on the balls of his feet, as if he expected to have to run. There was a gun, holstered, on his belt.

Sirge Milton hesitated, staring at this new adversary.

"Sirge, it's not worth killing for," Jethri said, desperately.

But Sirge had forgotten about him. He was looking at Master ven'Deelin's assistant. "Think I'm gonna be some Liaden's slave until I worked off what she claims for debt?" He demanded. "Liaden Port? You think I got any chance of a fair hearing?"

"The portmaster—" the Liaden began, but Sirge cut him off with a wave, looked down at the gun and brought it around.

"No!" Jethri jumped forward, meaning to grab the gun, but something solid slammed into his right side, knocking him to the barge's deck. There was a *crack* of sound, very soft, and Jethri rolled to his feet—

Sirge Milton was crumbled face down on the cold decking, the gun in his hand. The back of his head was gone. Jethri took a step forward, found his arm grabbed and turned around to look down into the grave blue eyes of Master ven'Deelin's assistant.

"Come," the Liaden said, and his voice was not—quite—steady. "The master trader must be informed."

THE YELLOW-HAIRED assistant came to an end of his spate of Liaden and inclined his head.

"So it is done," Norn ven'Deelin said in Trade. "Advise the portmaster and hold yourself at her word."

"Master Trader." The man swept a bow so low his forehead touched his knees, straightened effortlessly and left the *Market's* common room with nothing like a backward look. Norn ven'Deelin turned to Jethri, sitting shaken between his mother and Uncle Paitor.

"I am regretful," she said in her bad Terran, "that solving achieved this form. My intention, as I said to you, was not thus. Terrans—" She glanced around, at Paitor and the captain, at Dyk and Khat and Mel. "Forgive me. I mean to say that Terrans are of a mode most surprising. It was my error, to be think this solving would end not in dyings." She showed her palms. "The counterfeit-maker and the, ahh—*distributor*—are of a mind, both, to achieve more seemly Balance."

"Counterfeiter?" asked Paitor and Norn ven'Deelin inclined her head.

"Indeed. Certain cards were copied—not well, as I find—and distributed to traders of dishonor. These would then use the—the—*melant'i*—you would say, the *worth* of the card to run just such a shadow-deal as young Jethri fell against." She sat back, mouth straight. "The game is closed, this Port, and information of pertinence has been sent to the Guild of Traders Liaden." She inclined her head, black eyes very bright. "Do me the honor, Trader Gobelyn, of informing likewise the association of Traders Terran. If there is doubt of credentials at a Liaden port, there is no shame for any trader to inquire of the Guild."

Paitor blinked, then nodded, serious-like. "Master Trader, I will so inform Terratrade."

"It is well, then," she said, moving a hand in a graceful gesture of sweeping away—or, maybe, of clearing the deck. "We come now to young Jethri and how best I might Balance his service to myself."

The captain shot a glance at Paitor, who climbed to his feet and bowed, low and careful. "We are grateful for your condescension, Master Trader. Please allow us to put paid, in mutual respect and harmony, to any matter that may lie between us—"

"Yes, yes," she waved a hand. "In circumstance far otherwise, this would be the path of wisdom, all honor to you, Trader Gobelyn. But you and I, we are disallowed the comfort of old wisdom. We are honored, reverse-ward, to build new wisdom." She looked up at him, black eyes shining.

"See you, this young trader illuminates error of staggering immensity. To my hand he delivers one priceless gem of data:

Terrans are using Liaden honor to cheat other Terrans." She leaned forward, catching their eyes one by one. "Liaden honor," she repeated, "to cheat other Terrans."

She lay her hand on her chest. "I am a master trader. My—my *duty* is to the increase of the trade. Trade cannot increase, where honor is commodity."

"But what does this," Dyk demanded, irrepressible, "have to do with Jethri?"

The black eyes pinned him. "A question of piercing excellence. Jethri has shown me this—that the actions of Liadens no longer influence the lives only of Liadens. Reverse-ward by logic follows for the actions of Terrans. So, for the trade to increase, wherein lies the proper interest of trader and master trader, information cross-cultural must increase." She inclined her head.

"Trader, I suggest we write contract between us, with the future of Jethri Gobelyn in our minds."

Uncle Paitor blinked. "You want to—forgive me. I think you're trying to say that you want to take Jethri as an apprentice."

Another slight bow of the head. "Precisely so. Allow me, please, to praise him to you as a promising young trader, strongly enmeshed in honor."

"But I did everything wrong!" Jethri burst out, seeing Sirge Milton laying there, dead of his own choice, and the stupid waste of it . . .

"Regrettably, I must disagree," Master ven'Deelin said softly. "It is true that death untimely transpired. This was not your error. Pen Rel informs to me your eloquence in beseeching Trader Milton to the path of Balance. This was not error. To solicit solving from she who is most able to solve—that is only correctness." She showed both of her hands, palms up. "I honor you for your actions, Jethri Gobelyn, and wonder if you will bind yourself as my apprentice."

He wanted it. In that one, searing moment, he knew he had never wanted anything in his life so much. He looked to his mother.

"I found my ship, Captain," he said.

DAY 42

✦✦✦✦✦✦✦✦✦✦✦✦✦✦✦✦✦✦✦✦✦✦✦

Standard Year 1118
Gobelyn's Market
Departing

WHEN IT WAS ALL COUNTED and compressed, his personal possessions fit inside two crew-bags. He slung the larger across his back, secured by a strap across his chest, snapped at shoulder and hip. Hefting the smaller, he took one more look around the room—a plain metal closet it was, now, with the cot slid away and the desk folded into the wall. He'd tried to give the com chart back, but Dyk insisted that it would fit inside the bag with a little pushing, and so it had.

There was nothing left to show the place had been his particular private quarters for more than half his lifetime. Looking at it, the space could be anything, really: a supply closet, a specialty cargo can . . .

Jethri shook his head, trying to recapture the burning joy he'd felt, signing his line on the 'prentice contract, finding himself instead, and appallingly, on the near side of bawling his eyes out.

It's not like you're wanted here, he told himself, savagely. *You were on the good-riddance roster, no matter what.*

Still, it hurt, staring around at what had once been his space, feeling his personals no considerable weight across his back.

He swallowed, forcing the tears back down into his chest. Damned if he would cry. Damned if he would.

Which was well. And also well to remember that value wasn't necessarily heavy. In fact, it might be that the most valuable thing he carried away from the ship weighed no more than an ounce—Uncle Paitor had come through with the Combine key, springing for the ten-year without a blink—a measure of how good the *vya* had done. Khat had donated a true-silver long-chain, and now it hung round his neck, with key in place.

He'd been afraid, nearly, that Khat would kiss him right then, when she put the key on the chain and dropped it round his neck, then stood close and reached out to tuck the key sudden-like down his day-shirt.

"Promise me you'll wear this and remember us!" she said, and hugged him, as unexpected as the potential kiss, and missed as greatly as soon as she released him.

And so he had promised, and could feel the key becoming familiar and comfortable as he got himself together.

Then there was his ship-share, which had come to a tidy sum, with a tithe atop that, that he hadn't expected, and which Seeli'd claimed was his piece of the divvy-up from his father's shares.

"Payable in cash," Seeli had said, further, not exactly looking at him. "On departure from the ship. Since you're going off to trade for another ship, this counts. Those of us who stay, the ship carries our shares in General Fund."

He'd also taken receipt of one long, assaying, straight-eyed glance from the captain with the words said, in front of Dyk before they signed those papers—

"You chose your ship, you got your inheritance, you think you know what you want. So I witness you, Jethri son of Arin, a free hand." She'd shook his hand, then, like he was somebody, and turned away like he was forgot.

So, now, here he stood, on the edge of an adventure, kit and cash in hand. A goodly sum of cash, for a Terran juniormost; an adequate kit, for the same. 'mong Liadens, who knew where he stood?—though soon enough he'd find out.

He felt his private pocket, making sure he had coin and notes and his fractin, then patted his public pocket, making sure of the short-change stowed there.

The ship clock chimed, echoing off the metal walls. Jethri took one more look around the bare cubby. Right. Time to get on with it.

AS SOON AS THE DOOR slid closed behind him, he remembered the last thing Paitor had said, leaning over to tap his finger against the nameplate set in the door.

"You pull that on the way out, y'hear? Rule is, when crew moves on, they take their nameplate so there ain't any confusion 'case of a crash." He nodded, maybe a little wise with the Smooth, and clapped Jethri on the shoulder. "That's yours as much as anything on this ship ever was."

Right.

Jethri slid the duffle off his shoulder, opened the door, and pulled the wrench-set off his belt. The nameplate showed through a blast resistant window set into the body of the door, with the access hatch on the inside. One-handed, he quickly undid the eight inset-togs probably last touched by his father, second hand held ready to catch the hatch when it fell.

Except, even with the togs loose the cover didn't fall right out, so he sighed and reached for his side-blade, and unsnapped it from the holster.

Who'd have thought this would be so tough?

He could see that asking for help getting his nameplate out of the door wouldn't play too well with his cousins—and wasn't it just like Mister Murphy to be sure and make an easy task hard, when he was needing to be on time . . . If Paitor and Grig hadn't kept him up clear through mid-Opposite—

The captain had made it plain that she'd look dimly on any celebration of Jethri's new status—which was bad form when any crew left a ship but 'specially bad when a child of the ship went for a new berth. Strictly speaking, they should've called 'round to the other ships on port, and had a party, if not a full-blown shivary. In time, the news would spread through the free-ships—and news it was, too. But, no; it was like the captain was embarrassed that her son was 'prenticed to a Liaden master trader; which, as far as Jethri could find, was a first-time-ever event.

So, everyone was nice to him, 'cept the captain, and there wasn't any party, so he'd taken his time going through his belongings and packing up, finding so much of what he had was left over from being a kid; so much was stuff he didn't need, or even want. And, o'course, there was the stuff that he *did* want that he hadn't had since his father died. The fractin collection, of which his lucky tile was the last link; the pictures of Arin; the trade journal they'd been working on together—Seeli'd let on, without exactly coming out and saying so, that the captain had spaced it all years ago, so it wasn't no sense feeling like he'd just been stripped of what was his.

But, still, he wished he had those things to pack.

All that being so, he was in something of a mood when the tap came on his door, just after Opposite shift rang in. And he'd been surprised right out of that mood to find Grig and Paitor on the other side, asking permission to enter.

Lanky Grig—back-up navigator, back-up pilot, back-up cook, back-up trader, and in-system engineer—folded himself up on the edge of the bunk/acceleration couch, while Jethri and Paitor took the magna-tracked swivel stools.

Once they were situated, Paitor pulled a green cloth bag from his pocket, and Grig brought three stainless drinking cups from his pouch. Jethri sat, his fractin snug in his hand, and wondered what was up.

"Jethri," Paitor began, then stopped as if he'd forgot what he was going to say for a second. He took a look at the bag on his knee, then untied the silver cord with its pendant tag from around the top, and handed the cord off to Jethri, who slid it into his public pocket, along with the fractin.

Paitor slipped the bag down, revealing a blue bottle, sealed with gold foil.

"The time has come, ol' son," Grig said quietly. "You're a free hand now—time for you to have a drink with your peers."

Paitor smiled like he only half wanted to, and lifted the bottle in two hands, like it was treasure.

"If I may do the honors here," he said, holding the bottle out so Jethri could read the label. "This here's Genuine Smooth Blusharie. Been with us since the day you was born. Arin picked it up, see? Since the captain drinks a meaner line than this, bottle was just gathering dust in the locker, and we figured we'd better make use of it before someone who don't really 'preciate it drinks it by mistake."

He smiled again, more like he meant it this time, and twisted the seal. There was a crackle as it gave way, and sharp *pop* a moment later, as the cork come out. Grig held the cups out, carefully, one after the other, and Paitor filled each with gem-colored liquid.

When they were each holding a cup and the bottle was recorked and stowed next to Grig on the bunk, Paitor cleared his throat.

"NOW, JETHRI," he said, talking slow, "I know you heard a lot of advice from me over your years and you probably got right tired of it—" Grig snorted a laugh and Jethri nodded in rueful agreement, holding his cup carefully— "but there's just a little bit more you got to hear. First is this: Don't never gulp Blusharie, whether it's smooth or whether it's not. If it *ain't* smooth, gulping it will knock you off your pins so hard you'll think you had a code red collision. If it *is* smooth, you'll be wasting one of the rare joys of this life and didn't deserve to have it."

Paitor lifted his cup and Grig, his. Jethri lifted his, looking from one lifelong familiar face to another, seeing nothing but a concentration on the moment.

"To Jethri Gobelyn, free hand!"

"Long may he trade!" Grig added, and he and Paitor clinked their cups together, Jethri joining them a second late. He looked into the amber depths of the liquid, and sipped himself a tiny sip.

It all but took his breath, that sip, leaving a smooth tartness on his tongue and a tingling at the back of his throat. Fiery and mellow at once—

He noticed that he was being watched, and had a second sip, smiling.

"It's not like ale or beer at all!"

Grig laughed, low and comfortable. "No, not at all."

"So there, Jethri, that's some advice for you, and a secret, of a kind," said Paitor, sipping at his own cup. "There's traders all over the Combine who got no idea where to get this or why they'd want to. But you find yourself someone who fancies himself a knowing drinker, and you can get yourself a customer for life."

Jethri nodded, remembering the silver cord on his pocket, with the name of the vintage and the cellar stamped on the seal.

"'Course, there's more to life than Smooth Blusharie, too," Paitor said after another gentle sip. "So, what we got to tell you, is— there's things you gotta know."

His latest sip of Smooth Blusharie heavy on his tongue, Jethri looked up into Paitor's face, noting that it had changed again, from sadly serious to trading-bland, and sat up straight on his stool.

"All families have their secrets," Paitor said slowly. "This ship and this family're no different'n most. Thing is, sometimes not all secrets get shared around so good, and some things that should've been kept so secret they're forgot get talked about too much." He took a short sip from his cup. "One of the things that might've been kept secret but wasn't, was how you wasn't expected."

Jethri looked down into his cup, biting his lip, and figured this was a good time to have another sip.

"Now," Paitor went on, still talking slow and deliberate. "What likely *was* kept secret was what Arin and Iza were doing together in the first place, seein' as some would call—and did call—them a mismatch from ignition to flare out."

What was this? Seeli, his source of all information about his parents, had never hinted that there'd been any trouble between Iza and Arin. All the trouble had come later, with Jethri.

"What it was, see, Jethri," his uncle was saying, "is that the Gobelyn side goes back a long way in the Combine. Gobelyns was founding members of the Combine—and part of the trade teams before that. An' even before the trade teams, Gobelyns was ship folk."

Jethri frowned. "That's no secret, Uncle. The tapes. . ."

Grig snorted, and had a sip of the Smooth. His face was hooded; closed, like he was misdirecting a buyer around a defect. Paitor looked across to him.

"Your turn now?" he asked, real quiet.

Grig shook his head. "No, sir—and I'm damned if that ain't another secret been kept! But, no. Go on."

After a minute, Paitor nodded, and sipped and leaned over to gently shake the bottle.

"That's fine, then," he murmured. "A glass to talk on and a glass to clear it."

"We'll do it," Grig said, nodding, too, with his face still a study in grim. "Really."

"Right. We will." Paitor took a hard breath. "So, Jethri, the way it was—Arin come along about the time the Gobelyns was set to call precedence at a shipowner meeting. Timing was bad, you might say, it being right near the time when the internal power-shift went from ship-base to world-base. The Combine had got so big, it owned pieces of planets, big and small, not to mention controlling shares in a good many grounder corps, and its interest shifted from securing the trade-lanes to protecting its investments. Which meant that the ships and shipowners who'd founded the Combine and built it strong wasn't in charge no more.

"So, anyway, they'd called an owners' meeting there on Caratunk, and the Gobelyns had the backin' they needed. That's when Arin showed up with the word that the owners' meeting had been downgraded from rule-making to advisory, by a twenty-seven to three commissioner vote. Now understand, Arin come from trade background too, but he'd started real young gettin' formal educated. Spent years on-planet—went to college planet-side, went to University, took history courses, took pilot courses, took trading and economics—and so when that vote came up, he was one of the three commissioners on the losing end."

Jethri blinked, cup half-way to his lips, Smooth Blusharie forgotten in blank astonishment.

"My father was a *commissioner*?"

Grig laughed, short and sharp.

"Not once he got out to Caratunk he wasn't," Paitor answered, sparing a quick glare for the lanky man on the bunk. "Left his vote card right there on the table, grabbed up his money, his collections, and his co-pilot, and quit on the spot. Figured the best way to help the owners an' preserve the routes was to be out with us. And so he did that."

"Finish your sip, boy," Grig instructed, taking one of his own. Jethri followed suit. He'd met a commissioner once, when he was young—

"RIGHT," said Paitor, "you might remember the ship was busy once. Lots of folks comin' by when we was in port, lots of talk, presents for the youngers . . . Even though Arin wasn't a commissioner no more, him knowing how the systems worked, Combine and planet-side—the owners, they come to him for advice, for planning out how to maybe not rely so heavy on Combine contacts and Combine contracts."

"But it stopped. After . . . the accident." Jethri could vaguely remember a day when they were in port and Arin got called away—as he so often did—and then the ship was locked down, and his mother screamed and—

"It was a bad time. Thought we'd lose your mother too. Blamed herself for lettin' him go, like there was some way she could have stopped him."

"But see, your dad, he was from old stock, too. Not ship-folk, not 'til later. They was kinda roamers—archaeologists, philosophers, librarians . . . Had strange ideas, some of 'em. Figured us Terrans had been around a longer time than we got the history for, that Terra—what they call the homeworld—is maybe the third or fourth Terra we've called home in sequence. Some other—"

"Paitor . . ." Grig's voice was low and warning. Jethri froze on his stool; he'd never heard long, easy-going Grig so much as sharp, never mind out-'n-out menacing.

"Your turn then," Paitor said, after a pause. He lifted his cup.

"My turn," Grig said, and sighed. He leaned forward on the bunk, looking hard into Jethri's face.

✖   ✖   ✖

"YOU KNOW I was your father's co-pilot. We were cousins, yeah, but more than that in someways, 'cause we had the same mentor when we was growing up, and we both got involved in what Paitor calls useless politicking and we thought was more than that. A lot more than that. Now thing is, your mam, and her-side of the cousins, like the Golds—they're Loopers. Know what that is?"

Jethri nodded. "I know what it is. But I don't like to hear the captain—"

Grig held up a hand, fingers wagging in the hand-talk equivalent of "pipe down."

"Tell me what it is before you get riled."

My last night on ship and I draw a history quiz, Jethri thought, irritated. He had a sip of Smooth to take the edge of his temper, and looked back to Grig.

"Loopers is backwards. Don't want to come out to the bigger ports, only want to deal with smaller planets, and places where they don't have to deal with regs or with . . ."

Grig flicked a couple fingers— "stop," that was.

"Part right and part wrong. See, Loopers comes from an article in the Combine charter which was writ awhile back and got pretty popular—probably have five copies of in the records on-board here if you know where to look. The idea came from the fact that most ship-folk believe in following a loop of travel—pretty often it's a closed loop. And some Looper families, they've been on ship for a hundred Standards, maybe, and everybody onboard knows that month seventeen of the trip means they're putting into so-and-so port to pick up fresh 'runion concentrate.

"Fact is, 'way back when this was all first worked out, the idea was that *every* route would be a Loop, with some Loops intersecting others, for transshipping and such.

"Now, I think you know, and I think I know, and I think Paitor knows, that's nonsense. This closed system stuff only works so long—and as long—as the economy of most of the ports in the Loop're expanding. Everybody does their bit, nobody introduces no major changes—then your Loop's stable and everybody profits.

Now, though, just speaking of changes, we got Liadens, who got no interest in *our* expanding system—they got their own systems and routes to care about. Then you got some of the planets putting their own ships into the mix without knowing history, nor caring. So now you got instability and running a Loop ain't such a good notion no more. You got the trading families losing out to the planets, and the Combine—well, buying up all them shares and corporations cost money, which means we pay more taxes and fees, not less. 'Cause the Combine, see, it can't let the ships go altogether, though we're getting troublesome; it needs to keep a certain control, exercise a certain authority, and bleed us 'til we—"

Next to Jethri, Paitor coughed. Grig jerked to halt and rubbed a hand over his head.

"Right," he said. "Sorry." He sipped, and sighed lightly.

"So, where was I? Trade theory, eh? Say f'rinstance that you, Jethri Ship-Owner, want to live off the smaller ports and set yourself up a pretty good Loop. Sooner or later, the good business is going to shift, and your Loop'll be worth less to the ship. You end up like *Gold Digger*, runnin' stones from place to place and maybe something odd on the side to make weight.

"What Arin saw was that the contract runs was the money runs. You go hub-to-hub, you don't ship empty; if conditions change—you can adapt; you ain't tied to the Loop.

"Arin had a good eye for basic contracts, and the ones he fixed up for the *Market* are just now needing adjustment. That's why this is a great time for the overhaul—your mam's on course, there. And you—you're in a spot to be big news. 'prentice trader on a Liaden ship? Studying under a *master trader*? You not only got a shot to own a ship, boy. Unless I read her wrong, that master trader is seeing you as—kind of like a commissioner 'tween Liaden interests and Terran."

Jethri blinked. "I don't—"

Grig glanced at Paitor, then back to Jethri.

"Let it go then," he said. "Learn your lessons, do good—for yourself and for your name." He moved a hand, apologetic-like. "There's one more thing, and then we can finish up this nice stuff and let you get some sleep." He took a breath, nodded to himself.

"*There are secrets in all families.* That's a phrase. You meet some-one else who believes, who knows, they'll get that phrase to you. You don't know nothing but there's a secret, and that's all you have to know, now. But put that in your backbrain—*there are secrets in all families.* It might serve you; it might not. Course you're charting, who knows?"

Jethri was frowning in earnest now, his cup empty and his thought process just a little slow with the Smooth.

"But—what does it mean? What happens if somebody—"

Grig held up his hand. "You'll know what'll happen if it ever does. What it means . . . It means that there's some stuff, here and there around the galaxy left over from the time of the Old War—the big war, like Khat tells about in stories. It means that your lucky fractin, there, that's not a game piece, no matter how many rules for playing with 'em we all seen—it's a Fractional Mosaic Memory Module—and nobody exactly knows what they're for." He looked at Paitor. "Though Arin thought he had an idea."

Paitor grunted. "Arin had ideas. Nothin' truer said."

Grig ran his hand over his head and produced a grin. "Paitor ain't a believer," he said to Jethri, and sat back, looking thoughtful.

"Listen," he said, "'cause I'll tell you this once, and it might sound like ol' Grig, he's gone a little space-wise. But just listen, and remember—be aware, that's all. Paitor don't want to hear this again—didn't want to hear it the first time, I'm bettin'—but him and me—we agreed you need a place to work from; information that Iza don't want you to have." He paused.

"These fractins, now—they're Old Tech. Really old tech. Way we figured it, they was old tech when the big war started. And the thing is—we can't duplicate them."

Jethri stared, and it did occur to him that maybe Grig had start-ed his drinking before the Blusharie. The big war—the Old War—well, there'd been one, that much was sure; most of the Befores you'd come up with, they was pieces from the war—or from what folks called the war, but could've been some other event. Jethri'd read arguments for and against had there been or had there not been a war, as part of history studies. And the idea of a tech that old that couldn't be duplicated today. . .

"What kind of tech?" he asked Grig. "And why can't we copy it?"

"Good questions, both, and I'd be a happier man if I had an answer for either. What I can tell you is—if that fractin of yours is one of the real ones—one of the old ones—it's got a tiny bit of timonium in there. You can find that from the outside because of the neutrinos—and all the real ones ever scanned had its own bit of timonium. Something else you find is that there's structure inside—they ain't just poured plastic or something. Try to do a close scan, though, maybe get a looksee at the shape of that structure, and what happens? *Zap!* Fried fractin. The timonium picks up the energy and gives off a couple million neutrinos and some beta and gamma rays—and there's nothing left but slagged clay. Try to peel it? You can't; same deal."

Jethri took of sip of his dwindling drink, trying to get his mind around the idea that there was tech hundreds of Standards old that couldn't be cracked and duplicated.

"As I say," Grig said, soft-like, "Paitor ain't a believer. What him, and Iza and a whole lot of other folks who're perfectly sane, like maybe I'm not on the subject, nor Arin neither—what they think is that the Old War wasn't nearly as big as others of us believe. They don't believe that war was fought with fractins, and about fractins. Arin thought that; and he had studies—records of archeological digs, old docs—to back him. He could map out where fractins was found, where the big caches were, show how they related to other Before caches—and when the finds started to favor the counterfeits over the real thing." He sighed.

"So, see, this just ain't our family secret. Some of the earlier studies—they went missing. Stolen. Arin said some people got worried about what would happen if Loopers and ship owners got interested in Befores as more than a sometime high-profit oddity. If they started looking for Old Tech, and figured out how to make 'em work.

"Arin didn't necessarily think we should make these fractins work—but he thought we should know what they did—and how. In case of need. Then, he got an analysis—"

Grig sipped, and sat for a long couple heartbeats, staring down into his cup.

"You know what half-life is, right?" He asked, looking up.

Jethri rolled his eyes, and Paitor laughed. Grig sighed.

"Right. Given the half-life of that timonium, Arin figured them for about eighteen hundred Standards old. Won't be long—say ten Standards, for some of the earlier ones; maybe a hundred for the latest ones—before the timonium's too weak to power—whatever it powers. Might be they'll just go inert, and anybody's who's interested can just take one, or five, or five hundred apart and take a peek inside.

"Arin, now. Arin figured fractins was maybe memory—warship, library, and computer, all rolled into one, including guidance and plans. That's what Arin thought. And it's what he wanted you to know. Iza and the Golds and all them other sane folks, they think they don't need to know. They say, only a fool borrows trouble, when there's so much around that's free. Me? I think you ought to know what your father thought, and I think you ought to keep your eyes and your mind open. I don't know that you particularly need to talk to any Liadens about it—but you'll make that call, if and when you have to."

He looked deep into his cup, lifted it and drained what was left.

"That it?" Paitor asked, quietly

Grig nodded. "It'll do."

"Right you are, then." He held out a hand; Grig passed him the bottle, and he refilled the cups, one by one.

He stood, and Grig did, and after a moment, Jethri did. All three raised their cups high.

"To your success, your honor, and your duty, Free Hand!" His kin said, loud enough to set the walls to thrumming. And Jethri squared his shoulders, and blinked back the sudden tears—and they talked of easier things until the cups were empty again.

"MUD," JETHRI MUTTERED, as his blade scraped across the

hatch. Lower lip caught between his teeth, he had another go with the wrench-set, and was at last rewarded with an odd fluttering hiss, that sent him skipping back a startled half-step.

Pressure differential, he thought, laughing at himself.

The sound of squeezing air faded and the cover plate popped away when he probed it with the blade point.

Stuffed into the cavity was some paper, likely to stop the plate from rattling the way Khat's did whenever they were accelerating, and he pulled it out, ready to crumple and toss it—and checked, frowning down at the paper itself.

Yellow and gritty—it was print-out from the comm-printer the captain didn't use any more. She'd always called it Arin's printer, like she didn't want anything to do with it, anyway, 'cause she didn't like to deal with nothing ciphered. Curiously, he separated the edges and opened the paper. There was his birth date, a series of random letters and numbers that likely weren't random at all if you knew what you was looking at and—

. . . WILDETOAD WILDETOAD WILDETOAD like an emergency beacon might send out.

WildeToad? Jethri knew his ship histories, but he would've known this one, anyway, being as Khat told a perfect hair-raiser about *Toad's* last ride. *WildeToad* had gone missing years ago, and none of the mainline Wildes had been seen since. Story was, they'd gone to ground, which didn't make no sense, them having been spacers since before there was space, as the sayin' went.

Jethri squinted at the paper.

Mismatch, there's a mismatch, going down
WILDETOAD WILDETOAD WILDETOAD
We're breaking clay. Check frequency
WILDETOAD WILDETOAD WILDETOAD
Thirty hours. Warn away Euphoria
WILDETOAD WILDETOAD WILDETOAD
Racks bare, breaking clay
WILDETOAD WILDETOAD WILDETOAD
Lake bed ahead. We're arming. Stay out.
L.O.S. TRANSMISSION ENDS

Lake bed, he thought. And, *gone to ground*. Spacer humor, maybe; it had that feel. And it got him in the stomach, that he held in his hand the last record of a dying ship. Why had his father used such a thing to shim the plate in his door? Bad luck . . . He swallowed, read the page again, frowning after nonsense phrases.

Breaking clay? Racks bare? This was no common ship-send, he thought, the grainy yellow paper crackling against his fingers. Arin's printer. The message had come into Arin's printer. Coded, then—but—

A chime sounded, the four notes of "visitor aboard." Jethri jumped, cussed, and jammed the paper and the nameplate into his duffle, resealed the hatch as quick as he could, and took off down the hall at a run.

IT WAS A SMALL group at the main lock: Khat, Iza, and Uncle Paitor to witness his farewell. Master ven'Deelin's assistant, Pen Rel, stood more at his ease than seemed likely for a man alone on a stranger ship, his smooth, pretty face empty of anything like joy, irritation, or boredom. His eyes showed alert, though, and it was him who caught Jethri first, and bowed, very slightly.

"Apprentice. The master trader assigns me your escort."

Jethri paused and bowed, also slightly—that being the best he could manage with the bag slung across his back.

"Sir. The master trader does me too much honor," he said.

The blue eyes flickered—very likely Pen Rel agreed—but give the man his due, neither smirk nor smile crossed his face, either of which he had every right to display, according to Jethri's counting.

Instead, he turned his attention to Iza Gobelyn and bowed again—deep, this time, displaying all proper respect to the captain-owner.

"The master trader sends felicitations, Captain. She bids me say that she has herself placed a child of her body into the care of others, for training, knowing the necessity at the core of her trader's heart. A mother's heart, however, is both more foolish and more wise. She, therefore, offers, mother to mother, route-list and codes.

Messages sent by this method will reach Jethri Gobelyn immediately. Its frequent use is encouraged."

Another bow—this one no more than a heavy tip of the head— a flourish, and there was a data card between the first and second fingers of his extended hand.

Iza Gobelyn's mouth pursed up, as if she'd tasted something sour. She didn't quite place her hands behind her back—not quite that. But she did shake her head, side-to-side, once, decisive-like.

Jethri felt himself draw breath, hard. Not that he had expected his mother would have wanted to keep in touch with him when he was gone, like she'd never bothered to do when he was a member of her crew. It was just—the rudeness, when Master ven'Deelin . . . He blinked, and sent a short glance straight to Khat, who caught it, read it, and stepped forward, smooth and soft-footed.

Gently, she slipped the card from between Pen Rel's fingers, and bowed, deeper than he had done, thereby showing respect for the master trader's emissary.

"Please convey to the master trader our appreciation of her kindness and her forethought," she said, which deepened the frown on Iza's face, and put some color back into Paitor's.

For his part, Jethri felt his chest ease a little—*catastrophe averted*, he thought, which should have been the truth of it, except that Master ven'Deelin's aide stood there for a heartbeat too long, his head cocked a mite to one side, waiting . . .

. . . and then waiting no longer, but bowing in general farewell, while his eyes pegged Jethri and one hand moved in an unmistakable sweep: *Let's go, kid.*

Swallowing, Jethri went, following the Liaden down the ramp.

"'bye Jethri," he heard Khat whisper as he went past her. "We'll miss you."

Her hand touched his shoulder fleetingly, and under his shirt the key clung a bit, then *Gobelyn's Market* clanged as the portals closed behind him.

AT THE END OF THE *MARKET'S* DOCK, Pen Rel turned left, walking light, despite the gravity. Jethri plodded along half a step behind, and pretty soon worked up a sweat, to which the Port dust clung with a will.

Traffic increased as they went on, and he stretched his legs to keep his short guide in sight. Finally, the man paused, and waited while Jethri came up beside him.

"Jethri Gobelyn." If he noticed Jethri's advanced state of dishevelment, he betrayed it by not the flicker of an eyelash. Instead, he blandly inclined his bright head.

"Shortly, we will be rising to *Elthoria*. Is there aught on port that you require? Now is the time to acquire any such items, for we are scheduled to break orbit within the quarter-spin."

Breathless, Jethri shook his head, caught himself, and cleared his throat.

"I am grateful, but there is no need." He lifted the smaller bag somewhat. "Everything that I require is in these bags."

Golden eyebrows rose, but he merely moved a languid hand, directing Jethri's attention down the busy thoroughfare.

"Alas, I am not so fortunate and must fulfill several errands before we board. Do you continue along this way until you find Ixin's sign. Present yourself to the barge crew, and hold yourself at the pilot's word. I will join you ere it is time to lift."

So saying, he stepped off the curb into the thronging traffic, vanishing, to Jethri's eye, into the fast-moving crowd.

Mud! he thought, his heart picking up its rhythm, then, "Mud!" aloud as a hard elbow landed on his ribs with more force than was strictly necessary to make the point, while a sharp voice let out with a liquid string of Liaden, the tone of which unmistakably conveyed that this was no place for ox-brained Terrans to be napping.

Getting a tighter grip on his carry-bag, Jethri shrugged the backpack into an easier position and set off, slow, his head swiveling from one side to the next, like a clean 'bot on the lookout for lint, craning at the signs and sigils posted along both sides of the way.

It didn't do much to calm the crazy rhythm of his heart to note that *all* the signs hereabouts were in Liaden, with never a Terran letter to be found; or that everyone he passed was short, golden-skinned, quick—Liaden.

Now that it was too late, he wondered if Master ven'Deelin's aide was having a joke on him. Or, worse, if this was some sort of Liaden test, the which of, failing, lost him his berth and grounded him. There was the horror, right there. *Grounded.* He was a spacer. All ports were strange; all crews other than his own, strangers. Teeth drilling into his bottom lip, Jethri lengthened his stride, heedless now of both elbows and rude shouts, eyes scanning the profusion of signage for the one that promised him clean space; refuge from weight, dirt, and smelly air.

At last, he caught it—half-a-block distant and across the wide street. Jethri pulled up a spurt of speed, forced his dust-covered, leaden body into a run and lumbered off the curb.

Horns, hoots and hollers marked his course across that street. He heeded none of it. The Moon-and-Rabbit was his goal and everything he had eye or thought for. By the time the autodoor gave way before him, he was mud-slicked, gasping and none-too-steady on his feet.

What he also was, was safe.

Half-sobbing, he brought his eyes up and had a second to revise that opinion. The three roustabouts facing him might be short, but they stood tall, hands on the utility knives thrust through wide leather belts, shirts and faces showing dust and the stains of working on the docks.

Jethri gulped and ducked his head. "Your pardon, gentles," he gasped in what he hoped they'd recognize for Liaden. "I am here for Master ven'Deelin."

The lead roustabout raised her eyebrows. "ven'Deelin?" she repeated, doubt palpable in her tone.

"If you please," Jethri said, trying to breathe deeply and make his words more than half-understandable gasps. "I am Jethri Gobelyn, the—the new apprentice trader."

She blinked, her face crumpling for an instant before she got herself in hand. The emotion she didn't show might have been anything, but Jethri had the strong impression that she would have laughed out loud, if politeness had allowed it.

The man at her right shoulder, who showed more gray than

brown in his hair, turned his head and called out something light and fluid, while the man at her left shoulder stood forward, pulling his blade from its nestle in the belt and thoughtfully working the catch. Jethri swallowed and bent, very carefully, to put his carry-bag down.

Twice as careful, he straightened, showing empty palms to the three of them. This time, the woman did smile, pale as starlight, and put out a hand to shove her mate in the arm.

"It belongs to the master trader," she said in pidgin. "Will you be the one to rob her of sport?"

"Not I," said the man. But he didn't put the knife away, nor even turn his head at the clatter of boot heels or the sudden advent of a second Liaden woman, this one wearing the tough leather jacket of a pilot.

She came level with the boss roustabout and stopped, a crease between her eyebrows.

"Are we now a home for the indigent?" she snapped, and apparently to the room at large.

Jethri exerted himself, bowing as low as his shaking legs would allow.

"Pilot. If you please. I am Jethri Gobelyn, apprenticed to Master Trader Norn ven'Deelin. I arrive at the word of her aide, Pen Rel, who bade me hold myself at your word."

"Ah. Pen Rel." The pilot's face altered, and Jethri again had the distinct feeling that, had she been Terran, she would have been enjoying a fine laugh at his expense. "That would be Arms Master sig'Kethra, an individual to whom it would be wise to show the utmost respect." She moved a graceful hand, showing him the apparently blank wall to his left.

"You may place your luggage in the bay; it will be well cared for. After that, you may make yourself seemly, so that you do not shame Master sig'Kethra before the ven'Deelin." She looked over her shoulder at the third roustabout. "Show him."

"Pilot." He jerked his head at Jethri. "Attend, boy."

Seen close, the blank wall was indented with a series of unmarked squares. The roustabout held up an index finger, and lightly touched three in sequence. The wall parted along an all-but invisible seam, showing a holding space beyond, piled high with parcels and pallets. Jethri took a step forward, found his sleeve caught and froze, watching the wall slide shut again a bare inch beyond his nose.

When there was nothing left to indicate that the wall was anything other than a wall, the roustabout loosed Jethri's sleeve and jerked his chin at the indentations.

"You, now."

He had a good head for patterns—always had. It was the work of a moment to touch his index finger to the proper three indentations in order. The wall slid aside and this time he was not prevented from going forward into the holding bay and stacking his bags with the rest.

The door stayed open until he stepped back to the side of the roustabout, who jerked his head to the left and guided him to the 'fresher, where he was left to clean himself up as best he might, so Master ven'Deelin wouldn't take any second thoughts about the contract she'd made.

SOME WHILE LATER, Jethri sat alone in the hallway next to the pilot's office, face washed, clothes brushed, and nursing a disposable cupful of a hot, strong, and vilely sweet beverage his guide had insisted was "tea."

At least it was cool in the hallway, and it was a bennie just to be done with walking about in grav, and carrying all his mortal possessions, too. Sighing, he sipped gingerly at the nasty stuff in the cup and tried to order himself.

It was clear that his spoken Liaden wasn't as close to tolerable as he had thought. He didn't fool himself that dock-pidgin and Trade was going to go far at the trading tables Norn ven'Deelin sat down to. Language lessons were needful, then; and a brush-up on the protocols of cargo. His math was solid—Seeli and Cris had seen to that. He could do OK here. Better than he'd have done on an ore ship running a dying Loop . . .

That thought brought him back to now and here. Damn straight Norn ven'Deelin didn't run no Loop.

He leaned back in the chair, considering what sorts of cargo might come to a ship bearing a master trader. Gems, he figured, and rare spice; textile like Cris would weep over; artworks . . . He considered that, frowning.

Art was a chancy venture, given differing planetary taboos and ground-hugger religions. Even a master trader might chart a careful course, there. Khat told a story—a true one, he thought—regarding the tradeship, *Sweet Louise*, which had taken aboard an illustrated paper book of great age. The pictures had been pretty, the pages hand-sewn into a real leather cover set with flawed, gaudy stones. The words were in no language that any of *Louise's* crew could read, but the price had been right; and the trader had a line on a collector of uniquities two planets down on the trade-hop. Everything should have been top-drawer, excepting that the powers of religion on the planet between the collector and the book declared that item "blasphemous," meaning the port police had it off ship in seconds and burned it right there on the dock. *Louise* lost the investment, the price, the fine—and the right to trade on that port, which was no loss, as far as Jethri could see . . .

A light step at the top of the hall pulled him out of his thoughts; a glance and he was on his feet, bowing as low as he could without endangering the tea.

"Arms Master sig'Kethra."

The man checked, neither surprise on his face, nor parcels in his hands, and inclined his head. "Apprentice Trader. Well met. A moment, if you please, while I consult with the pilot."

He moved past, walking into the pilot's office with nary a ring, like he had every right to the place, which, Jethri thought, he very well might. The door slid shut behind him and Jethri resumed his seat, reconciled to another longish wait while business was discussed between pilot and arms master.

Say that Pen Rel was a man of few words. Or that the pilot was eager for flight. In either case, they were both coming out the door before Jethri had time to start another line of thought.

"We lift, Jethri Gobelyn," Pen Rel said. "Soon we will be home."

And that, at least, Jethri thought, rising with alacrity, was a proper spacer's sentiment. Enough of this slogging about in the dust—it was time and past time to return to the light, clean corridors of a ship.

DAY 42

@@@@@@@@@@@@@@@@@@@@@@@@@@

Standard Year 1118
Elthoria
Arriving

"IS THE WHOLE ship heavy, then?" he asked Pen Rel's back.

The Liaden glanced over his shoulder, then stopped and turned right around in the center of the ridiculously wide hallway, something that might actually have been puzzlement shadowing the edges of his face.

"Is the gravity worrisome, Jethri Gobelyn? I did note that you disliked the port, but I had assumed an aversion to . . . the noise, perhaps—or the dirt. I regret that it had not occurred to me that the ship of your kin might have run weightless."

Jethri shook his head. "Not weightless," he panted. "Just—light. The core—admin, you know—was near enough to heavy, but the rest of the ship ran light, and the rim was lightest of all." He drew a deep breath, caught by the sudden and awful realization that no one knew what the normal grav of the Liaden homeworld was. It could be that Ynsolt'i normal was light to them, and if the ship got heavier, the further in they—

Pen Rel moved his hand like he was smoothing wrinkles out of the air. "Peace, Jethri Gobelyn. Most of *Elthoria* runs at constant gravity. The areas that do not are unlikely to be of concern to one of your station. You will suffer no more than you do at this moment."

Jethri gaped at him. "Runs *constant*," he repeated, and shook his head. "How big is this ship?"

The Liaden moved his shoulders. "It is large enough. Doubt not that the master trader will provide a map—and require you to memorize it, as well."

Where he came from, holding the map of the ship and the location of bolt holes, grabs and emergency suits in your head was only commonsense. He shrugged, no where near as fluid as his companion. "Well, sure she will. No problem with that."

"I am pleased to hear you say so," Pen Rel said, and turned about-face, moving briskly out down the hall. "Let us not keep the master trader waiting."

In fact, she kept them waiting, which Jethri could only see as a boon, for he used the time to catch his breath and surreptitiously stretch his sore muscles, so he wasn't blowing like a grampus when they were finally let in to see her.

Her office wasn't as big as admin entire—not quite. Nor was her workspace quite as wide as his private quarters on the *Market*. Screens were set above the desk, which was itself a confusion of landing slips, catalogs and the ephemera of trade—that much was familiar, so much so that he felt the tears rising to his eyes.

The master trader, she was familiar, too, with her gray hair and her snapping black eyes.

"So," she said, rising from her chair and coming forward. "It is well." She inclined her head and spoke to Pen Rel—a rapid burst of Liaden, smooth and musical. The arms master made brief reply, swept a bow to her honor, treated Jethri to a heavy tip of the head, and was gone, the door snapping behind him like a hungry mouth.

Black eyes surveyed him blandly. Belatedly, Jethri remembered his manners and bowed, low. "Master ven'Deelin. I report for duty, with joy."

"Hah." She tipped her head slightly to the right. "Well said, if briefly. Tell me, Jethri Gobelyn, how much will it distress you to find that your first duty is dry study?"

He shrugged, meeting her gaze for gaze. "Uncle Pai—Trader Gobelyn taught me that trade was study, ma'am. I wouldn't expect it otherwise."

"A man of excellent sense, Trader Gobelyn. My admiration of him knows no limit. Tell me, then, oh wise apprentice, what will you expect to study firstly? Say what is in your heart—I would know whether I must set you to gemstones, or precious metals, or fine vintage."

Had she been Terran, Jethri would have considered that she was teasing him. Liadens—none of his studies had led him to believe that Liadens held humor high. Honor was the thing, with Liadens. Honor and the exact balancing of any wrong.

"Well, ma'am," he said, careful as he was able. "I'm thinking that the first thing I'll be needing is language. I can read Liaden, but I'm slow—and my speaking is, I discover, nothing much better than poor."

"An honest scholar," Master ven'Deelin said after a moment, "and of something disheartened." She reached out and patted his sleeve. "Repine not, Jethri Gobelyn. That you read our language at all is to be noted. That you have made some attempt to capture the tongue as it is spoken must be shown for heroic." She paused.

"Understand me, it is not that we of the clans seek to hide our customs from those traders of variant ilk. Rather, we have not overindulged in future thinking, whereby it would have been immediately understood that steps of education must be taken." She moved her shoulders in that weird not-shrug, conveying something beyond Jethri's ken.

"Very nearly, the masters of trade have walked aside from their duty. Very nearly. You and I—we will repair this oversight of the masters and rescue honor for all. Eh?" She brought her palms together sharply.

"But, yes, firstly you must speak to be understood. You will be given tapes, and a tutor. You will be given the opportunity to Balance these gifts the ship bestows. There is one a-ship who wishes to possess the Terran tongue. Understand that her case is much as yours—she reads, but there is a lack of proficiency in the spoken form. She, you will tutor, as you are tutored. You understand me?"

So, he had something of worth that he could trade for his lessons and his keep. It was little enough, and no question the ship bore the heavier burden, but it cheered him to find that he would be put to use.

Smiling, he nodded; caught himself with a sharp sigh and bowed. "I understand you, ma'am. Yes."

"Hah." Her eyes gleamed. "It will be difficult, but the need is plain. Therefore, the difficult will be accomplished." She clapped her hands once more. "You will be a trader to behold, Jethri Gobelyn!"

He felt his ears warm, and bowed again. "Thank you, ma'am."

She tipped her head. "The tutor will attend likewise to the matter of bows. Continue in your present mode and you will be called to answer honor before ever we arrive at gemstones."

Jethri blinked. He had just assumed that, the deeper the bow the better, and that, as juniormost everywhere he walked, he could hardly go wrong bowing as low as he could without doing structural damage.

"I . . . hope that I haven't given offense, ma'am," he stammered, in Terran.

She waved a tiny hand, the big purple ring glittering. "Worry not," she answered, in her version of the same tongue. "You are fortunate in your happenstances. We of *Elthoria* are of a mode most kind-hearted. To children and to Terrans, we forgive all. Others," she folded her hands together solemnly, "are less kindly than we."

Oh. He swallowed, thinking of Honored Buyer bin'Flora, and others of his uncle's contacts, on the Liaden side of the trade.

"There are those," Master ven'Deelin said softly, switching to Trade, "for whom the trade is all. There are others for whom . . . the worth of themselves is all. Are these things not likewise true of Terrans?"

Another flash of memory, then, of certain other traders known to him, and he nodded, though reluctantly. "Yes, ma'am. I'm afraid they are."

"No fear, Jethri Gobelyn. A man armored and proficient with his weapons need have no fear." A small hesitation, then— "But perhaps it is that you are wise in this. A man without weapons—it is best that he walk wary."

"Yes, ma'am," he said again, his voice sounding breathless in his own ears.

If Master ven'Deelin noted anything amiss, she didn't say so. Instead, she waved him over to her desk, where she pressed the promised ship's map upon him, pointing out the location of his quarters and of the ship's library, where he would find his study tapes and his tutor awaiting him at some hour that slid past his ear in an arpeggio of Liaden.

"I—" he began, but Master ven'Deelin had thought of that, too. From the riot of papers atop her desk, she produced a timepiece, and a schedule, printed out in Liaden characters.

"So, enough." She clapped her hands and made shooing motions toward the door. "This shift is your own. Next shift, you are wanted at your station. Myself, yourself, we will speak again together before the trade goes forward on Tilene. In the meanwhile, it is your duty to learn, quickly and well. The ship accepts only excellence."

Dismissed, clutching the papers and the watch untidily to his chest, he bowed, not without a certain feeling of danger, but Master ven'Deelin had turned back to her desk, her attention already on the minutiae of trade.

In the hall outside her office, he went down on a knee and took a few moments to order his paperwork, slap the watch 'round his wrist, and glance through the schedule. Running his finger down the table, being careful with the Liaden words, and checking his timepiece frequently, he established that the shift which was "his own" had just commenced. More searching in the schedule produced the information that "nuncheon" was on buffet in the galley.

Squinting at the map, he found that the galley was on the short route to his quarters, at which point his stomach commented rather pointedly that his breakfast of 'mite and crackers was used up and more.

One last squint at the map, and he was on his way.

THERE WERE MAYBE a dozen people in the galley when he swung in. They all stopped talking and turned to look at him, smooth Liaden faces blank of anything like a smile or any honest curiosity. Just . . . silence. And stares. Jethri swallowed, thinking that even a titter, or a "Look at the Terran!" might be welcome.

Nothing like it forthcoming, he walked over to the cool-table where various foods were laid out, and spent some while looking over the offerings, hoping for something familiar, while all the time he felt the eyes boring bland, silent holes into his back.

It got to him, finally, all that quiet, and the sense of them staring at him, so that he snatched up a plate holding something that looked enticingly like a pan-paste handwich and bolted for the door, map and schedule clutched under one arm.

His dash was two steps old when a dark-haired woman swung into his path, one hand held, palm out, and aiming for his chest.

He skidded to a halt, all but losing the papers, the handwich dancing dangerously on its plate, and stood there staring like a stupid grounder, wondering what piece of politeness he had, all unknowing, shattered, and whether word had gotten out to the crew that they were more forgiving than most.

The woman before him said something, the sounds sliding past his ear, *almost* sounding like . . . He blinked and leaned slightly forward.

"Say again," he murmured. "Slowly."

She inclined her head, and said again, slowly, in Terran so thickly accented he could barely make out the words, though he was craning with all his ears: "Tea will be wanting you."

"Tea," he repeated, and smiled, from unadorned relief. "Thank you. Where is the tea?"

"Bottle," she said, waving a quick hand toward a second table, set at right angles to the first, lined with what looked to be single serving vacuum bottles. "Cold. Be for to drinking with works."

"I see. Thank you . . ." He frowned at the badge stitched onto her shirt . . . "First Officer Gaenor tel'Dorbit."

Eyebrows rose above velvet brown eyes, and she tipped her head, face noncommittal.

"Apprentice Terran, you?" She asked, and put her hand against her chest. "Terran student, I."

He nodded and smiled again. "I'm Master ven'Deelin's apprentice. I'll be helping you with your Terran. Here . . ." He fumbled the schedule out from beneath his arm and held it out, gripped precariously between two fingers, while the handwich jigged on its plate. "What's your shift? I've got—"

She slipped the paper from between his fingers, gave it a quick, all-encompassing glance, and ran a slim fingertip under a certain hour, showing him.

"Hour, this," she said, and waved briefly around the galley. "Here we meet."

"Right." He nodded again.

Gaenor tel'Dorbit inclined her head and left him, angling off to the left, where a table for three showed one empty chair and a half-eaten meal; the other two occupants considering him with silent blandness.

Jethri grabbed a tea bottle from the table and all but ran from the room.

Using the map, he found his assigned quarters handily, and stood for a long couple minutes, staring at his name, painted in Liaden letters on the door, before sliding his finger into the scanner.

The scan tingled, the door opened and he was through, staring at a cabin maybe three times the size of his quarters on the *Market*. The floor was covered in springy blue carpet, in the center of which sat his bags. The bed and desk were folded away, and he couldn't have said if it was the strangeness of it, or the sameness of it, but all at once he was crying in good earnest, the tears running fast and dripping off his chin.

Carefully, he put the handwich and the bottle on the floor next to his bags, then sat himself down next to them, taking care to put schedule and map well out of harm's way. That done, he folded up, head on knees, and bawled.

DAY 60

✳✳✳✳✳✳✳✳✳✳✳✳✳✳✳✳✳✳✳✳✳✳✳✳✳✳✳✳

Standard Year 1118
Gobelyn's Market
Approaching Kinaveral

KINAVERAL HUNG MIDDLING big in the central screen. Khat had filed her approach with Central, done her system checks and finally leaned back in the pilot's chair, exhaling with a will.

Cris looked up from the mate's board with a half-grin and a nod. "Two to six, Central will argue the path."

Khat laughed. "I look a fool, do I, coz? Of *course,* Central will argue the path. I once had a fast-look at a Lane Controller's manual. First page, Lesson One, writ out in letters as high as my hand was, 'Always Dispute the Filed Approach.'"

Cris' smile widened to a grin. "First lesson, you say? There was pages after that?"

"Some few," Khat allowed, straight-faced, "some few. Mind, the next six after was blank, so the student could practice writing out the rule."

"Well, it being so large and important a rule . . ." Cris began, before the intercom bell cut him short.

He spun back to his board and slapped the toggle. "Mate."

"First Mate," Iza Gobelyn's voice came out of the speaker, gritty with more than 'com buzz. "I'm looking for the approach stats."

"Captain," Cris said, even-voiced. "We're on the wait for Central's aye."

There was a short, sizzling pause.

"As soon as we're cleared, I'll have those stats," Iza snapped.

"Yes, Captain," Cris murmured, but he might just as easily said nothing; Iza had already signed off.

Cris sighed, sharp and exasperated. Khat echoed him, softer.

"I thought she'd lighten, once Jeth was gone," she said.

Cris shook his head, staring down at his board.

"It ain't Jethri being gone so much as Arin," he muttered. "She's gotten harder, every Standard since he died."

Khat thought about that, staring at Kinaveral, hanging in the center screen. "There's a lot more years ahead, and Arin in none of them," she said, eventually.

Cris didn't answer that—or, say, he answered by not answering, which was Cris' way.

Instead, he said, "I got a reply on that franchise job. They want me to stop by their office, dirtside, take the test. If that's a go, it'll mean a temp berth for the next ten months, Standard."

Khat nodded, her eyes still on Kinaveral. "Paitor figures to pick up some training or consulting at Terratrade," she said. "Me, I'll file with Central as a freewing."

"Sensible. The rest sticking to dirt?"

She laughed. "Now, how likely is that? Might take a few port cycles 'til they get tired of breathing dust, but you know they'll be looking for space work, too."

"Huh," Cris said, fiddling with a setting on his board. "Iza?"

Khat shrugged. "Way I heard it, she was staying dirtside, with the *Market*." She held up a hand. "Paitor did try to talk her out of it. Pointed out that Seeli's able. Iza wasn't having any. She's the captain, the job's hers, and by all the ghosts of space, she'll do it."

"Huh," Cris said again—and seemed on the edge of saying something more when the comm screen came live with Central's request that *Gobelyn's Market* amend her filed approach.

DAY 63

Standard Year 1118
Elthoria

***ELTHORIA* KEPT** a twenty-eight-hour "day," divided into four shifts, two on, two off, which made for a slightly longer work day than the *Market's* twenty-four hour, two-shift cycle. Jethri, who had been used to reading and studying well into his off-shift, scarcely noticed the additional hours.

His work now—that was different. No more Stinks. If *Elthoria* had Stinks, which Jethri took leave to doubt, it was nothing mentioned to him by his new acquaintances, though they were careful to show him as much of the ship as an apprentice trader might need to know. His new status meant no more assisting in the galley, a duty he might've missed, if there'd been any time for it, which there wasn't, his time being entirely and systematically crammed full with lessons, study and more lessons.

Some things were routine, and it eased him somehow to find that *Elthoria* kept emergency protocols—in which he was relentlessly trained by no lesser person than Arms Master sig'Kethra. Over the course of three shifts, he was drilled in the location and operation of the lifeboats, shown the various boltholes, emergency hatches and hand-grabs. He was also measured for a suit, it being discovered to the chagrin of the supply master that none of those on draw would fit.

Other things, they weren't so routine—more of that, which is what he'd figured to find. For instance, he had a trade locker all to himself, which was scrupulously the same size as his stateroom, it being the policy on *Elthoria* that traders should have as much room to work in as they had to sleep in. He wished he'd thought to convert some of his cash to something useful out of the *Market*—but he hadn't had much time to cry about that missed opportunity, either.

First thing on shift, right after breakfast, he sat with the tutor-tapes in the ship's library, brushing up on his written and spoken Liaden. Then, he met with Protocol Officer Ray Jon tel'Ondor, which was more language lessons, putting dry learning into practical use. Master tel'Ondor was also of an ambition to teach Jethri his bows, though he made no secret of the fact that Jethri was the least apt pupil he had encountered in long years of tutoring arrogant young traders in protocol.

After Master tel'Ondor, there was exercise—a mandated ship's hour every day at the weights and the treadmills, then a shower, a meal, and more reading, this on the subjects of trade guild rules and custom regs. After that, there was the Terran-tutoring with Gaenor tel'Dorbit. The first mate being of a restless habit, that meant more exercise, as they walked the long hallways of *Elthoria*. Despite the extra walking, Jethri quickly came to look forward to this part of his duty-day. Gaenor was younger than Master ven'Deelin and Pen Rel, and she smiled nicely from time to time in her lessons, which Jethri particularly liked.

Gaenor's idea of being tutored was to just start talking—about the events of the previous shift, her family's home in a dirt-based city called Chonselta, the latest book she was reading, or the ship's itinerary. Jethri's responsibility was to stop her when she misspoke, and say the words over in the right order and pronunciation. So it was that he became informed of ship's policy, gossip and ports o'call, as well as the names of certain flowers which Gaenor particularly missed from home.

The first mate having access to just about every portion of the ship, Jethri also found himself informed of various lockers and pod connections, and was introduced to each of the ship's company as they were encountered during the ramble. Some of the crew seemed not so pleased to see him, some seemed . . . puzzled. Most seemed not to care much, one way or the other. All were grave and polite, like they oughta be, Jethri thought, with the first mate looking on. Still, he thought that these catch-as-can introductions at the mate's side . . . helped. Helped him put names and faces and responsibilities together. Helped them to see he really was part of the crew, pulling his weight, just like they were.

One person who seemed outright happy to welcome him was Vil Tor, ship's librarian. As it happened that Vil Tor also had an ambition to add Terran to his speakables, Gaenor and Jethri had taken to including the library as a regular stop. This time out, though, they'd found the door locked, lights out. Gaenor sighed, slim shoulders dropping for a moment, then turned and started back down the hall, swinging out with a will.

"This our ship, *Elthoria*," Gaenor said, as they hit the end of the hall and swept left, toward Hydroponics, "will be inputting to Spacestation Kailipso . . ."

"Putting in," Jethri panted. "*Elthoria* will be putting in to Kailipso Station."

"Hah." Gaenor flicked a glance his way; *she* wasn't even breathing hard. "*Elthoria*," she repeated, slowing her pace by a fraction, "will be putting in to Spacestation Kailipso—bah!—*Kailipso Station*—putting in to Kailipso Station within three ship days. There is a—a . . ." She stopped entirely and turned to face Jethri, holding two hands up, palm out, signifying she had not the necessary Terran words to hand.

"It is to have a meeting of the masters, on subjects interested in the masters . . ."

The immediate phrase that came to mind was "jaw-fest," which Jethri thought might not be the sort of Terran Master ven'Deelin wanted Gaenor to be learning. He frowned after the polite and after a moment was able to offer, "a symposium."

"Sim-po-zium," Gaenor said, her mouth pinching up like the word tasted bad. "So, there is a *sim-po-zium* upon Kailipso. The ven'Deelin attends—the ven'Deelin *will attend*. The crew will be at leave." She moved her shoulders, not quite a Terran shrug, but not quite admiring of Kailipso Station, all the same.

"Don't like Kailipso much?" he ventured, and Gaenor's mouth pinched again before she turned and recommenced marching down the hall.

"It is cold," she said to the empty corridor, and then began to tell him of the latest developments in the novel she was reading. He had to catch up, hoping that she put his delay down to his being somewhat less fit, and not his taking a moment to admire her walk.

DAY 65

❀❀❀❀❀❀❀❀❀❀❀❀❀❀❀❀❀❀❀❀❀❀❀❀❀

Standard Year 1118
Kinaveral

BEFORE THEY CLEARED a freewing to fly, Kinaveral Central wanted to be assured that candidate could find her way through a form or six. That done, there were the sims to fly, then a chat with the stable boss, at the end of which a time was named on the morrow when the candidate was to return and actually lift one of Central's precious ships—and an observer—for the final and most telling part of the test.

In between now and then, Khat knew, they'd be checking her number and her ship, and verifying her personals. She'd hoped to have the test lift today, but, there, the stable boss needed to know if the applicant free-wing tended toward sober in the morning.

No problem for the applicant on that approach, Khat thought, walking down the dusty, noisy main street. Not to say that a brew would be unwelcome at the moment. Make that a brew and a handwich, she amended, as her stomach filed notice that the 'mite and crackers she'd fed it for breakfast were long past gone.

Up ahead, she spied the flashing green triangle which was the sign of an eat-and-drinkery, and stretched her legs, grimacing at the protest of overworked muscles. *That'll teach you to stint your weight exercise*, she scolded herself, and turned into the cool, comfortably dim doorway.

A lightscape over the counter showed a old style fin-ship down on a flat plain, mountains marking the horizon. Beneath, a tag box spelled out the name of the joint: *Ship 'n Shore*.

There was a scattering of folk at the tables—spacers, mostly— and plenty of room at the counter. It being only herself, Khat swung up onto a stool 'neath the tag box and waved at the barkeep.

"Dark brew and a handwich for a woman in need!"

The keeper grinned, drew the beer and sat it on the counter by her hand. "There's the easy part," he said. "What's your fondness for food? We got local cheese and vegs on fresh bake bread; potmeat on the same; 'mite paste and pickles; side o' fish—"

Khat leveled a finger. "Local cheese without the vegs?"

"We can do it," he promised.

"That's a deal, then. Bring her on."

"Be a sec. Let me know how you find the beer." He moved down counter, still grinning, and Khat picked up the mug.

The beer was cold, which was how she liked it. Bitter, too, and thick. She'd brought the mug down to half-full by the time her handwich arrived, two generous halves sharing a plastic plate with a fistful of saltpretzel.

"Brew's good," Khat said. "I'll want another just like it in not too long."

The keeper smiled, pleased, and put a couple disposable napkins next to the plate. "Just give a yell when you're ready," he said.

She nodded and picked up one of the halves. The unmistakable smell of fresh bake bread hit her nose and her stomach started clamoring. For the next while, she concentrated on settling that issue. The bread was whole grain, brown and nutty; the cheese butter smooth and unexpectedly spicy. Khat finished the first half and the brew, waved the empty mug at the barkeep and started in on the second round.

Couple times, folk from the tables came up to the counter for refills. A crew of three came in from the street and staked out stools at the end of the row. Khat paid none of them particular notice, except to register that they were spacers, and nobody she knew.

At last, the final saltpretzel was gone. Khat pushed the plate away with a regretful sigh and reached for her mug. A couple more sips, settle her bill and then back to the lodgings, she thought, with a sinking in her well-full stomach. Wasn't nothing wrong with the lodgings, mind, except that they was full-grav lodgings, and dirtside, and subject to the rules of the lodge-owner. But still, *Market's* crew had a section to themselves, inside which each had their own cubby, with cot and desk and entertainment bar. No complaints.

Excepting that Captain Iza was nothing but complaints—well, she hated dirt, always had; and didn't have much of a fondness for worldsiders. Without the routine of her ship, she stood at sevens and eights and spent 'way too much of her time down to the yards, doubtless making life a hell for the crew boss assigned to *Market's* refit.

Zam had suggested the captain might file as freewing with Central, for which insubordination he had his head handed to him. Seeli'd come by no gentler treatment when she spoke to her mother, and Dyk declined even to try. Paitor had his own quarters at Terratrade, and when the temp slot went solid on Cris their second day a-ground, he all but ran to the space field.

Which left them a mixed bag—and bad tempered, too, held uneasy by Iza's moods.

And the year was barely begun.

Khat sighed again, and finished off her brew. She put the mug down and waved at the keeper for the bill. He, up-counter with the crew of three, held up two fingers—*be there in a few*. She nodded, shifted on the stool . . .

"Hey, Khati," an unwelcome voice came from too near at hand.

"Shit," Khat muttered beneath her breath and spun the stool around to face Mac Gold.

He hadn't changed much since the last time she'd seen him— some taller, maybe, and a little broader in the shoulders. Khat nodded, curt.

"Mac."

He grinned, and ran a hand over his head. His hair was pale yellow; buzzed, it was nearly invisible, which his eyelashes were. Behind those invisible lashes, his eyes were a deep and unlikely blue, the rest of his face square and bony. A well-enough looking boy, taken all together. If he hadn't also happened to've been Mac Gold.

"Good to see you," he said, now, deliberately aiming those unlikely eyes at her chest. "Buy you a brew?"

She shook her head, teeth gritting. "Just on my way. Next time, maybe."

"Right," he said, but he didn't move, other than to cock his head. "Listen, while we're face to face—square with me?"

She shrugged. "Maybe."

"I'm just wondering—what happened to Jethri? I mean, what *really* happened to Jethri?"

"He's 'prenticed to the trader of a big ship," she said. "Cap'n Iza must've told your dad so."

"She did," Mac agreed, "and I'm sharing no secrets when I tell you my dad was some pissed about the whole business. I mean, here's Iza asking us to make room for your extra, and m'dad willing to accommodate, and what happens but then she says, no, the boy ain't coming after all. He's gone someplace else." Mac shook his head and held up a hand, thumb and forefinger a whisper apart.

"Dad was *this close* to calling breach."

Khat sighed. "Breach of what? The legal wasn't writ."

"Still, there'd be the verbal—"

"Deals fall through every day," Khat interrupted and caught sight of the barkeep out of the corner of her eye. She turned on the stool and smiled at him.

Behind her, Mac, raised his voice conspicuously—

"Rumor is, Khat, that Paitor sold the boy to Liadens!"

That drew starts and stares from those close enough to hear; some turned carefully away, but others lifted eyebrows and raised their heads to watch.

Deliberately, Khat turned, away from the barkeep and back to Mac Gold. Deliberately, she drew a deep breath, and glared straight into those blue eyes.

"The *boy* holds a Combine key. He's as legal as you or me. He's a 'prentice trader—signed his own papers. Jethri ain't no *boy*."

"Well, rumor is that Liadens paid for this upgrade the *Market's* gettin'."

Khat laughed and rolled her eyes.

"Least now Mr. Rumor's got it right. Jethri sold a load of cellosilk back at Ynsolt'i, and on top of that, Paitor bought some special risk merchandise Jethri'd pointed out—an' didn't *that* turn into high-count coin in the private hall—just like Jethri said it would! So, sure, Liadens bought this upgrade all right—cans, nodes, and engines."

"But someone got shot, they say, and next thing—"

Khat sighed, loud and exasperated.

"Look, Jethri was ready to trade, Mac, and captain told him if he wanted something more than pushing gravel from here to there, he'd have to find his own ship. Can't fault him for that call. So he found himself a better berth, 'prenticed to nothing less than a master trader, and for a good-bye, he buys us new drives and a full upgrade."

She paused, hearing a slight thump of glass behind her and raised her hand, fingers wriggling "just sec."

"Jethri's got him a berth, Mac. Papers're signed proper and legal. *His* business—not mine, not yours. That other stuff Mr. Rumor been tellin' you—nobody got shot but some fool who decided it was easier to die than clear an honest debt. Not your problem." She tipped her head, like she was considering that, and asked, sweetly, "Or is it?"

Mac's eyes tightened and his face reddened.

"It sure is my problem if the word gets out Jethri'd rather crew with a bunch of Liadens than come with an honest ship like—"

"You better watch your mouth, Mac Gold," Khat snapped. "Lest somebody here figures you was gonna say something about how *Gold Digger's* honest and Jethri's ship ain't. Not the kind of thing you'd be wanting to discuss with a Liaden, now, is it?"

Mac blinked, and swallowed hard. Point won, Khat turned back to the bartender, raised her eyes briefly and expressively at the ceiling, and smiled.

"What's the damage?"

He smiled back. "Two bit."

"Done." She slid four across the counter and dropped to her feet, leg muscles sending up a shout for their team leader. She ignored them. The walk back to the lodgings would work the kinks out. Or cripple her for life.

"So, Khat—" Mac said from beside her.

"So, Mac," she overrode, and turned sharp, feeling a dangerous tingle along the brawlin' nerves when he went back a step. She kept going, and he kept backin', until she got the throttle on it and stopped.

Mac's pretty blue eyes was showing some red, and his face was damp. Khat gave one more hard glare, before she nodded, kinda half-civil.

"See you 'round port," she said, and forced her aching legs to swing out, carrying her down the room and out in the dusty day.

DAY 66

❀❀❀❀❀❀❀❀❀❀❀❀❀❀❀❀❀❀❀❀❀❀❀❀❀

Standard Year 1118
Kailipso Station
At Leave

"COME, COME, YOUNG JETHRI, tarry not!" Pen Rel's voice was brisk, as he waved Jethri ahead of him into the entry tube. "All the wonders of Kailipso Station await your discovery! Surely, your enthusiasm and spirit of adventure are aroused!"

Had it been Dyk behind him in the chute, Jethri would have counted both his legs yanked proper, and been alert for second stage mischief. He thought Pen Rel too dignified for Dyk's sort of rough- 'n-tumble; he was less sure of his tendencies on the leg-pulling side of things.

Jethri felt the odd twitter of the grav field where it intersected the station's own grav-well; though flat and level to the eyes the deck felt as if it fell away into the chute. Maybe Pen Rel was watching for a bobble, but such boundaries were learned by shipcrew at the knees of their mates and family.

The airflow, that was a surprise—definitely a positive, cool flow *toward* the ship—No, Jethri discovered, after a moment's study; the tube itself had a circulation system, and he could see the filters set flush to the walls. He gave a quiet sigh of relief for this homey precaution—all long-spacers did their most to keep station, port, or planet air *out* in favor of proper controlled and cleaned ship air.

Curiosity satisfied, Jethri stepped forward—and then stepped back, his hand going up, fingers shaping the hand-talk for "hold".

Two Liadens were coming up the slanted ramp at a pace that made Jethri's chest ache in sympathy. One—by far the pudgiest Liaden Jethri had seen so far—was carrying a full duffle; his slimmer companion clutched what looked to be a general business comp to his chest. They were in earnest conversation, heads turned aside and eyes only for each other.

"What is—" Pen Rel began, but by then the duo was on the flat and heading full throttle out, never realizing that they was anything but alone.

"'ware the deck!" Jethri snapped.

It had the desired effect, whether either of them had understood the Terran words. Both slammed to a graceless halt. The man with the comp raised it a fraction, as if to ward Jethri away.

Pen Rel stepped forward, claiming attention with a flicker of a hand, and a slight inclination of the head.

"Ah, Storemaster," he murmured, and Jethri thought he heard a bare thread of . . . disapproval in the bland, dry voice. "You are somewhat before time, I believe."

The man with the comp bowed. "Arms Master. I am instructed to supply crew with specialty baking experience, and I have here such a one. It remains to be found that he can operate *Elthoria's* ovens and bread vats. So we arrive, for a testing."

Pen Rel looked to the second man.

"Have you shipboard experience?"

The pudgy guy bowed lower than Jethri would have thought possible with the duffle over his shoulder, and straightened to show a wide-eyed, slightly damp face. "Three voyages, Honored. The Storemaster has my files . . ."

"Very good." Pen Rel was back with the Storemaster. "Next time, you will come at the mate's appointed hour, eh? This time, you have interfered in ship's business."

The applicant cook's round eyes got rounder; the Storemaster pursed his mouth up. Both bowed themselves out of the way, even sparing brief nods for the unexpected Terran in their midst.

"So," Pen Rel said, catching Jethri's eye. He moved a hand toward the ramp. "After you, young Jethri."

AT THE BOTTOM OF THE CHUTE was the inevitable uniformed station ape, card-reader to hand.

Jethri handed over his shiny new shipcard. The inspector took it, glanced at it—and paused, eyes lifting to his face.

"*Elthoria* signs Terran crew," she stated—or maybe she was asking. Jethri ducked his head, wondering if she expected an answer and what, exactly, would be seen as discourteous behavior in a Terran, here on an all-Liaden station. That he was an anomaly was clear from the pair they'd surprised coming on-ship. *But, then,* he said to himself, *you expected you were going to be an oddity. Best get used to it.*

"Must the ship clear its roster with the station?" Pen Rel asked from behind him, in Trade. "Do you find the card questionable?"

The inspector's mouth tightened. She swiped the card sharply through the reader, displaying bit of temper, or so Jethri thought, and stood holding it in her hand until the unit beeped and the tiny screen flashed blue.

"Verified and valid," she said, and held the card out, still something pettish.

Jethri grabbed it and slid it away into his belt. "Thank you, Inspector," he said politely.

She ignored him, holding out a hand to Pen Rel.

Bland-faced, he put his card in her palm, and watched as she swiped it and handed it back. The unit beeped and the screen flashed.

"Verified and valid," she said, and stepped back, obviously expecting them to go on about their business.

Pen Rel stayed where he was, waiting, bland and patient, until she looked up.

"A point of information," he said, still sticking with Trade. "*Elthoria* does not hold her crew lightly."

It was said mild enough, but the inspector froze, her face losing a little of that rich golden color. Jethri counted to five before she bent in a bow and murmured, "Of course, Arms Master. No disrespect to *Elthoria* or to her crew was intended."

"That is well, then," Pen Rel said, mildness itself. He moved a hand in a easy forward motion. "Young sir, the delights of the station are before you."

As hints went, it wasn't near subtle, but apparently, Pen Rel was still making his point, because the inspector looked up into his face and inclined her head.

"Young trader, may you enjoy a profitable and pleasurable stay on Kailipso Station."

Right. He inclined his head in turn, murmured his very best, all-Liaden, "My thanks," and quick-stepped down the dock toward the bay door.

On the other side of the door, he pulled up. Pen Rel stepped through, and Jethri fell in beside him. The Liaden checked.

"Forgive me, Jethri," he said. "What do you do?"

Jethri blinked. "I thought I was partnered with you."

"Ah." Pen Rel tipped his head to a side. "Understand that I find your companionship all that is delightful. However, I have errands on the day which are. . . of no concern to one of your station. The master trader's word was that you be put at liberty to enjoy those things which Kailipso offers." He moved a hand in the all-too-familiar shooing gesture.

"So, enjoy. You are wanted back on board at seventh hour. I need not remind you to comport yourself so as to bring honor to your ship. And now," he swept a slight, loose-limbed half-bow, "I leave you to your pleasure, while I pursue my duties."

And he turned and walked off, just like that, leaving the junior-most and most idiot of his crew standing staring after, jaw hanging at half-mast.

Pen Rel had gone half the length of the corridor and turned right down a side way before Jethri shook himself into order and started walking, trying to accommodate himself to the fact that he was alone and at liberty on a Liaden-owned and operated spacestation, where the official staff had already demonstrated a tendency to consider him a general issue nuisance. He shook his head, not liking the notion near so well as he should have done.

He did get to thinking, as he walked, that Master ven'Deelin surely knew what Kailipso was—just as surely as Pen Rel did. And certainly neither of those canny old hands was likely to turn him loose in halls where he might find active danger.

He hoped.

An overhead sign at the junction of halls where Pen Rel had vanished offered him routes, straight on to Main Concourse, right hall to Station Administration, and left hall to Mercantile Station. Working on the theory that there would be information booths in the Main Concourse, Jethri went straight on.

INFOBOOTHS WERE THE LEAST of the wonders offered by the Main Concourse and its affiliated sections. He explored Market Square first, finding it not a trading center, as he had expected, but a retail shop zone offering goods at exorbitant mark-ups.

Nonetheless, he browsed, comparing prices shop to shop, and against his best guess of trade-side cost. Some of the items offered for sale were, by his admittedly unscientific calculation, marked up as much as six hundred percent over trade. He took a bit of a shock, for he saw in one window a timepiece identical to the one Norn ven'Deelin had casually given him—and found its price at three kais. 'Course, a master trader wasn't going to ever pay shop-price, but—He glanced down and took a second to make sure the slap strap was secure around his wrist.

Kailipso being a station, there were special considerations. Stations were dependent on outside supply; if one *needed* what was here, it was very much a seller's market.

That got him to wondering just how much this particular station *was* dependent on outside supply, so he hunted up another booth and got directions to Education Square. Of course, it was opposite the Market, which meant a long walk back the way he'd come and through the Concourse, but he didn't grudge it. Station lived a thought lighter than *Elthoria*, so he fairly skipped along.

Education was almost useless. The tapes offered for rent were every one narrated in Liaden. He was about to give up when his eye snagged on a half-sized shop, sort of crammed in sideways to the hall, in a space between a utility bay and a recycling chamber.

The small opening spilled yellow light out into the hallway, and a table was sitting almost into the common area, holding the fabulous luxury of six bound books. Behind them was a hand-written sign, stating that all sales were final, cash only.

Jethri moved forward, picked up the topmost book with reverence, and carefully thumbed the pages.

Paper rustled, and a subtle smell wafted up. He allowed the book to fall open in his hands and found the Liaden words almost absurdly easy to read as he was at once captivated by an account of one Shan el'Thrassin, who was engaged in a matter of honor with a set of folk who seemed something less than honorable.

"May I assist you, young sir?" The voice was soft, male, slightly hesitant in Trade. Jethri started, ears warming, closing the book with a snap.

"I apologize," he said. "I was looking for information about the history, economics and structure of the station. I am looking to fill some hours while visiting . . . This . . ." Carefully, he bent and placed the volume he had been reading back in its place on the table. He experienced a genuine pang as the book left his hand.

". . . I cannot possibly afford this. If I have offended by using it without pay . . ."

The man moved a hand, slowly, formally. "Books are meant to be read, young sir. You honor them—and me—with your interest. However, you intrigue me, for is not the entire square full with sight and sound recordings of the awesome past and glorious present of our station?"

Jethri ducked his head. "Sir, it is. However—while I read the written form, my tongue and ear run far behind my eyes."

"Hah." The man's eyes gleamed. "You are, in fact, a scholar. It is nothing less than my duty to assist you. Come. I believe I have just what you are wanting."

As it happened, he did: A thin paper book simply entitled *Guide To Kailipso Station*.

"It is slight, but well enough to satisfy the first level of questions and engage the mind upon the second level," the shopkeeper said easily. "It will, I think, serve you well. Though used, it is new enough that the information is reasonably dependable."

"I thank you," Jethri said. "However, again, I fear that my coins may be too few." And of the wrong sort, he thought suddenly, with a sinking feeling in his stomach. He was wearing his trading coat, but what he had in his public pocket was Terran bits and his fractin. He'd clean forgotten to stop at ship's bank to pull money out of his account in proper tor and kais. . .

The man looked up at him. "Do you know, young sir, I believe we are in Balance. It is seldom enough that one sees a Terran. It is rarer to see a Terran unaccompanied and unhurried. To meet and have converse with a Terran who reads Liaden—even the gods must own themselves privileged in such an encounter." He smiled, slight and gentle.

"Have the book, child. Your need is greater than mine."

Jethri bit his lip. "Sir, I thank you, but—I request an elder's advice. How should a young and inexperienced person such as myself Balance so generous a gift from a stranger?"

For a moment, he thought he'd gone well beyond bounds, though by all he knew there ought to be no offense given in asking for a clue to proper behavior. But the man before him was so still—

The shopkeeper bowed, lightly, right hand over belt-buckle. "There is," he said, straightening to his full, diminutive height, "a . . . protocol for such things. The proper Balance for the receipt of a gift freely given is to use it wisely and with honor, so that the giver is neither shamed nor regretful of his generosity."

Oh. Feeling an idiot, Jethri bowed, low enough to convey his thanks. He hoped. "I am grateful for the information, sir. My thanks."

The man waved a dismissive hand. "Surely, it is the duty of elder to instruct the young." Once again, he smiled his slight smile. "Enjoy your holiday, child."

"Thank you, sir," Jethri murmured, and bowed again, figuring that it was better to err on the side of too many than not enough, and moved out of the shop, trying not to let his eyes wander to those shelves full of treasure.

HE FOUND A VACANT bench in the main square and quickly became absorbed in the guidebook. From it, he learned that Kailipso Station had come into being as a way station for cargo and for galactic travelers. Unfortunately, it very shortly became a refugee camp for those who managed to escape the catastrophic climatic upsets of a colony world called Daethiria. While many of the homeless colonists returned to the established Liaden worlds from which they had emigrated, a not inconsiderable number chose to remain on Kailipso Station rather than return to the conditions which had forced them away in the first place.

Kailipso Admin, realizing that it would need to expand quarters to support increased population, got clever—or desperate—or both—and went wooing the big Liaden Guilds, like the Traders and the Pilots, and got them to go in for sector offices on Kailipso.

Where most ports and stations would automate scut-work, Kailipso used people wherever possible, since they had people—and they not only got by, but they thrived.

So, Kailipso expanded, and soon enough became a destination all its own. Like any other station, it was vulnerable to attack, and dependent on imports for luxury items and planet-bred food. If it had to be, though, it was self-sufficient. On-station yeast vats produced enough boring, wholesome nutrition to feed Kailipso's denizens. Off-station, there were farm pods—fish, fruits and vegetables—which made for tastier eating in sufficient quantities to keep those same denizens in luxury if they could so afford.

Kailipso also offered recreation. There was a power-sled track, swimming facilities, climbing walls to challenge a number of skill levels, and more than two dozen arenas for sports Jethri had never heard of.

The guidebook also provided a list of unsafe zones, accompanied by a cutaway station map with each danger outlined in bright green. Most were construction sites, and a few out-ring halls that dead-ended into what looked to be emergency chutes, marked out as *Danger: Low Gravity Zones.*

He likewise learned from the guidebook that the Kailipso Trade Bar was in the Mercantile Zone, and that it was open to all with a valid license of trade or a tradeship crew card. There, at least, he could directly debit his account on ship, and get himself some walking-around money. A brew and a looksee at the ship-board wouldn't be amiss, either.

So thinking, he came to his feet and slipped the book away in to a leg-pocket. He took a second to stretch, luxuriating in the lower grav, then headed off at a mild lope, bound for the Mercantile Zone.

HE RAN HIS CARD through the reader; the screen flashed blue, and the door to the Trade Bar swung open before him.

Valid and verified, he thought, grinning, and then remembered to put on his trading face—polite, non-committal, and supposedly unreadable; it wasn't much, set against your usual Liaden's ungiving mask. Still, grinning out loud in a place crammed with folks who just didn't couldn't be polite. And polite was all he had.

What hit him first, were the similarities to the Terran Trade Bars he'd been in with Uncle Paitor or Cris or Dyk. The high-info screens were set well up on one wall, showing list after list: ships in dock; traders on duty; goods at offer, stationside; goods at offer, dockside; goods sought. The exchange rates were missing, which made him blink until he realized that everybody on this station was buying in cantra and kais.

The milling of bodies seemingly at random around the various stations—that was familiar too—and even the sound—lots of voices, talking at once, maybe a little louder than needful.

But then the differences—damn near everybody was shorter than him, dressed in bright colors, and soft leather boots. Jewelry gleamed on ears, hands, throats. Not a few wore a weapon, holstered, on their belts. For the most, they walked flat, like born mud-grubbers, and not like honest spacers at all. And the slightly too loud voices were saying things in a quick, liquid language which his ear couldn't begin to sort.

He found himself a corner where two booths abutted, and settled back out of the general press to study the screens. Stationside goods at offer tended toward art stuffs and information—reasonable. The longest list by far, though, was for indenture—folks looking to buy their way off-station, maybe all the way back to Liad, by selling out years of their lives. By Jethri's count, there were forty-eight contracts offered, from sixteen years to thirty-four, from general labor to fine craftsperson.

"Well, what do we find ourselves here?" a woman's voice asked, too close and too loud, her Trade almost unintelligible. "I do believe it's a Terran, Vil Jon."

Jethri moved, but she was blocking his exit, and the man moving up at her hail was going to box him in proper.

"A Terran?" the man—Vil Jon—repeated. "Now what would a Terran be doing in the Trade Bar?" He looked up into Jethri's face, eyes hard and blue. "Well, Terran? Who let you in here?"

Jethri met his eyes, trying with everything in him to keep his face smooth, polite and non-committal.

"The door let me in, sir. My ship card was accepted by the reader."

"It has a card," the woman said, as if the man hadn't heard. "Now, what ship in dock keeps tame Terrans."

The man glanced over his shoulder at the boards. "There's *Intovish*, from Vanthachal. They keep some odd customs, local." He looked back at Jethri. "What ship, Terran?"

He considered it. After all, his ship was no secret. On Terran ground, asking for someone's ship was a common courtesy. From these two, though, it seemed a threat—or a challenge in a game he had no hope of understanding.

"*Elthoria*," he said, soft and polite as he knew how. "Sir."

"*Elthoria*?" The woman exchanged a long glance with her mate, who moved his shoulders, pensive-like.

"Could be it's bound for Solcintra Zoo," he said.

"Could be it's gotten hold of a card it shouldn't have," the woman returned, sharply. She held out her hand. "Come, Terran. Let us see your ship card."

And that, Jethri thought, was that. He was threatened, cornered and outnumbered, but he was damned if he was going to meekly hand his card over to this pair of port hustlers.

"No, ma'am," he said, and jumped forward.

The grav was light—he jumped a fair distance, knocking the woman aside as gentle as he could, out of reach before the man thought to try and grab him.

Having once jumped, Jethri stayed in motion, moving quick through the crowded room. He met a few startled glances, but took care not to jostle anybody, and very soon gained the door. It was, he thought, time to get back to his ship.

THEY KNEW THE STATION better than him—of course they did. They turned him back, hall by hall, crowding him toward the Concourse, cutting him off from the docks and his ship.

In desperation, he went down three floors, hit the hall beyond the lift doors running and had broken for the outer ring before he heard them behind him, calling "Terran, Terran! You cannot elude us, Terran!"

That might be so, Jethri thought, laboring hard now, light grav or not. He had a plan in his mind, though, and if this was the hall as he remembered it from the guide book's map of danger zones. . .

He flashed past a blue sign, the Liaden letters going by too fast for his eye to catch, but he recognized the symbol from the map, and began to think that this might work.

The hall took a hard left, like he remembered it from the map, and there was the emergency tunnel at end of it, gaping black and cold.

"Terran!" The woman's voice was suddenly shrill. "Wait! We will not hurt you!"

Right, Jethri thought, the tunnel one long stride away. He hit it running, felt the twist inside his ear that meant he had gone from one gravitational state to another—

He jumped.

Somewhere behind him, a woman screamed. Jethri fell, slow-motion, saw a safety pole, slapped it and changed trajectory, shooting under the lip of the floor above, anchoring himself with a foot hooked 'neath a beam.

The woman was talking in Liaden now, still shrill and way too loud. The man answered sharply, and then shouted out, in pidgin, "Terran! Where are you?"

Like he was going to answer. Jethri concentrated on breathing slow and quiet.

They didn't wait all that long; he heard the sound of their footsteps, walking fast, then the sound of the lift doors working.

After that, he didn't hear anything else.

He made himself sit there for a full twenty-eighth by the Liaden timepiece on his wrist, then eased out of hiding. A quick kick against the side of the chute sent him angling upward. He caught the edge of the floor as he shot past and did a back flip into the tunnel. He snatched a ring, righted himself, and skated for the hall.

A Liaden man in a black leather jacket was leaning against the wall opposite the tunnel.

Jethri froze.

The Liaden nodded easily, almost Terran-like.

"Well done," he said, and it was ground-based Terran he was talking, but Terran all the same. "I commend you upon a well-thought-out and competently executed maneuver."

"Thanks." Jethri said, thinking he could scramble, go over the edge again, make for the next level up, or down . . .

The Liaden held up a hand, palm out. "Acquit me of any intent to harm you. Indeed, it is concern for your welfare which finds me here, in a cold hallway at the far edge of nowhere, when I am promised to dinner with friends."

Jethri sighed. "You see I'm fine. Go to dinner."

The Liaden outright *laughed*, and straightened away from the wall.

"Oh, excellent! To the point, I agree." He waved down the hall vaguely, as if he could see through walls, and so could Jethri. "Come, be a little gracious. I hear you are from *Elthoria*, over on Dock Six, is that so?"

Jethri nodded, warily. "Yes."

"Delightful. As it happens, I treasure an acquaintance with Norn ven'Deelin which has too long languished unrenewed. Allow me to escort you to your ship."

Jethri stood, feeling the glare building and not even trying to stop it. The man in the jacket *tsk'd*.

"Come now. Even a lad of your obvious resource will find it difficult to outrun a Scout on this station. At least allow me to know that *Elthoria* is on Dock Six. Also—forgive me for introducing a painful subject—I must point out that your late companions will no doubt have called in an anonymous accident report. If you wish to avoid awkward questions from the Watch, you would be well-advised to put yourself in my hands."

Maybe it was the Terran. Maybe it was the laugh, or the man's easy and factual way. Whatever, Jethri allowed that he trusted this one as much as he hadn't trusted the pair who had been chasing him. Further down the hall, a lift chimed—and that decided it.

"OK," he agreed, and the man smiled.

"Not a moment too soon," he said, and stepped around the edge of the wall he'd been leaning against.

"This way, young sir. Quickly."

HIS GUIDE SET A brisk pace through the service corridors, his footsteps no more than whispers.

Jethri, walking considerably more noisily behind him, had time to appreciate that he was at this man's mercy; and the likelihood that his murdered body could lie in one of the numerous, dark repair bays they passed for days before anyone thought to look. . .

"Do not sell your master trader short, young sir," the man ahead of him said. "I can understand that you might be having second thoughts about myself—a stranger and a Scout, together! Who knows what such a fellow might do? But never doubt Norn ven'Deelin."

Apparently, it wasn't just his face that was found too readable, Jethri thought sourly, but his footsteps, too. Still, he forced himself to chew over what the man had said, and produced a question.

"What's a Scout?"

Two steps ahead, the Liaden turned to face him, continuing to walk backward, which he seemed to find just as simple as going face-first, and put his hand, palm flat, against his chest.

"I am a Scout, child. In particular: Scout Captain Jan Rek ter'Astin, presently assigned to the outpost contained in this space station."

Jethri considered him. "You're a soldier, then?"

Scout Captain ter'Astin laughed again, and turned face forward without breaking stride.

"No, innocent, I am not a soldier. The Scouts are . . . are—an exploratory corps. And to hear some, we are more trouble than we are worth, constant meddlers that we are—Ah, here is our lift! After you, young sir."

It looked an ordinary enough lift, Jethri thought, as the door slid away. And what choice did he have, anyway? He was certainly lost, and had no guide but this man who laughed like a Terran and walked as loose and light as a spacer.

He stepped into the lift, the Scout came after, punched a quick series of buttons, and relaxed bonelessly against the wall.

"I don't wish to be forward," he said, slipping his hands into the pockets of his jacket. "But I wonder if you have a name."

"Jethri Gobelyn."

"Ah, is it so? Are you kin to Arin Gobelyn?"

Jethri turned and stared, shock no doubt plain on his face, for the Scout brought his right hand out of his pocket and raised it in his small gesture of peace.

"Forgive me if I have offended. I am not expert in the matter of Terran naming customs, I fear."

Jethri shook his head. "I'm Arin Gobelyn's son," he said, trying to shake away the shock, as he stared into the Scout's easy, unreadable face. "My mother never told me he had any Liaden . . . connections."

"Nor should she have done so. My acquaintance with Arin Gobelyn was unfortunately curtailed by his death."

Jethri blinked. "You were at the explosion?"

"Alas, no. Or at least, not immediately. I was one of the Port rescue team sent to clean up after the explosion. We arrived to find that an impromptu rescue effort was already underway. The Terran ship crews, they reacted well and with purpose. Your father—he was as a giant. He went back into that building twice, and brought out injured persons. Was it three or five that he carried or guided out? The years blur the memory, I fear. The third time, however. . ." He moved his shoulders. "The third time, he handed his rescue off to the medics, and paused, perhaps to recruit his strength. Behind him, the building collapsed as the inner roof beams gave way sequentially—throwing out debris and smoke with enormous energy.

"When the dust cleared, I was down, your father was down—everyone in a two-square radius was down. After I had recovered my wits, I crawled over to your father. The wreckage was afire, of course, and I believe I had some foolish notion of trying to drag him further from the flames. As it happens, there was no need. A blade of wood as long as I am had pierced him. We had nothing to repair such a wound, and in any case it was too late. I doubt he knew that he had been killed." Another ripple of black-clad shoulders.

"So, I only knew him as a man of courage and good heart, who spent his life so that others might live." The Scout inclined his head, suddenly and entirely Liaden.

"You are fortunate in your kin, Jethri Gobelyn."

Jethri swallowed around the hard spot in his throat. He'd only known that his father had died when the warehouse had collapsed. The rest of this. . .

"Thank you," he said, huskily. "I hadn't known the—the story of my father's death."

"Ah. Then I am pleased to be of service."

The lift chimed, and the Scout straightened, hands coming out of his pockets. He waved Jethri forward.

"Come, this will be our stop."

"Our stop" looked like nothing more than a plain metal square with a door at one end. Jethri stepped out of the lift, and to one side.

The Scout strolled past, very much at his leisure, put his palm against the door and walked through.

Jethri followed—and found himself on Dock Six, practically at the foot of *Elthoria's* ramp. Despite it all, he grinned, then remembered and bowed to the Scout.

"Thank you. I think I can make it from here."

"Doubtless you can," the Scout said agreeably. "But recall my ambition to renew my acquaintance with Norn ven'Deelin." He moved forward with his loose, easy stride that was much quicker than it looked. Jethri stretched his legs and caught up with him just as he turned toward the ramp . . . startling the young replacement doc-checker into a flabbergasted, "Wait, you!"

The Scout barely turned his head. "Official Scout business," he said briskly and went up the ramp at a spanking pace, Jethri panting at his heels.

At the top, a shadow shifted. Jethri looked up and saw Pen Rel coming quickly down toward them—and just as suddenly braking, eyebrows raised high.

"Scout. To what do we owe the honor?"

"Merely a desire to share a glass and a few moments with the master trader," the Scout said, slowing slightly, but still moving steadily up the ramp. "Surely an old friend may ask so much?"

Jethri sent a glance up into Pen Rel's face, which showed watchful, and somewhat, maybe, even—annoyed.

"The master trader has just returned from the trade meeting—" he began.

"Then she will need a glass and a few moments of inconsequential chat even more," the Scout interrupted. "Besides, I wish to speak with her about her apprentice."

Pen Rel's glance found Jethri's face. "Her tardy apprentice."

"Just so," said the Scout. "You anticipate my topic."

He reached Pen Rel and paused at what Jethri knew to be comfortable talking distance for Liadens. It was a space that felt a little too wide to him, but, then, he'd come up on a ship half the size and less of *Elthoria.*

"Come, arms master, be gracious."

"Gracious," Pen Rel repeated, but he turned and led the way into the ship.

✼ ✼ ✼

IF MASTER VEN'DEELIN felt any dismay in welcoming Scout
Captain Jan Rek ter'Astin onto her ship, she kept it to herself. She saw
him comfortably seated, and poured three glasses of wine with her
own hands—one for the guest, one for herself, and one for Jethri.

She sat in the chair opposite the Scout; perforce, Jethri sank
into the remaining, least comfortable, chair, which sat to the master
trader's right.

The Scout sipped his wine. Master ven'Deelin did the same,
Jethri following suit. The red was sharp on the tongue, then melted
into sweetness.

"I commend you," the Scout said to the master trader, and in
Terran, which Jethri thought had to be an insult, "on your choice of
apprentice."

Master ven'Deelin inclined her head. "Happy I am that you find
him worthy," she replied, in her accented Terran.

The Scout smiled. "Of course you are," he murmured. "I wonder,
though, do you value the child?" He raised his hand. "Understand
me, I find him a likely fellow, and quick of thought and action. But
those are attributes which Scouts are taught to admire. Perhaps for
a trader—?"

"I value Jethri high," Master ven'Deelin said composedly.

"Ah. Then I wonder why you put him in harm's way?"

Master ven'Deelin's face didn't change, but Jethri was abruptly
in receipt of the clear notion that she was paying attention on all
channels.

"Explain," she said, briefly.

"Certainly," the Scout returned, and without even taking a hard
breath launched the story of Jethri's foray into the Trade Bar, and all
the events which followed from it. Master ven'Deelin sat silent until
the end, then looked to Jethri.

"Jethri Gobelyn."

He sat up straighter, prepared to take his licks, for the whole
mess had been his own fault, start to finish, and—

"Your lessons expand. Next on-shift, you will embrace
menfri'at. Pen Rel will instruct you as to time."

What in cold space was *menfri'at*, Jethri wondered, even as he inclined his head. "Yes, Master Trader."

"Self-defense," the Scout said, as if Jethri has asked his question out loud, "including how to make calm judgments in . . . difficult situations." Jethri looked at him, and the Scout smiled. "For truly, child, if you had not run—or run only so far as one of the tables— there would have been no need to leap off into a gravity-free zone, which is sometimes not quite so gravity free as one might wish."

Jethri looked at him, mouth dry. "The book said—"

"No doubt. However, the facts are that the station does some- times provide gravity to those portions marked 'free fall'."

Jethri felt sick, the wine sitting uneasily on his stomach.

"Also," the Scout continued, "a book is—of necessity—somewhat behind the times in other matters; and I doubt that yours attempted more than a modest discussion of station culture. Certainly, a book could tell you little of which ships might be in from the outer depend- encies, with crews likely to be looking for hijinks."

And that, Jethri admitted, stomach still unsettled, was true. Just like he'd know better than to head down Gamblers Row on any Terran port he could name after a rock-buster crew came in, he ought to know—

But the ship names meant nothing to him, here, and though some—perhaps twenty percent—had showed Combine trade codes along with Liaden, he didn't yet have those Liaden codes memo- rized. Jethri swallowed. He shouldn't have been let loose on station without a partner, he thought. That was fact. He was a danger to himself and his ship until he learned not to be stupid.

The Scout was talking with Master ven'Deelin. "I see, too, that Ixin, or at least *Elthoria*, may need to be brought to fuller aware- ness of the, let us call them . . . climate changes . . . recently wrought here. Indeed, these changes are closely related to my own sudden stationing."

Norn ven'Deelin's face changed subtly, and the Scout made a small, nearly familiar motion with his hand. Jethri leaned forward, the roiling in his gut forgotten—hand-talk! It wouldn't be the same as he knew, o'course, but maybe he could catch—

"So," the master trader murmured, "it is not a mere accident of happiness that you are on-station just as my apprentice becomes beset by—persons of loutishness?"

"It is not," the Scout replied. "The politics of this sector have altered of late. The flow of commerce, and even the flow of science and information has been shifting. You may wish—forgive me for meddling where I have no right!—but perhaps you may wish to issue ship's armbands to those who walk abroad unaccompanied."

The Scout's fingers moved, casually, augmenting his spoken words. Jethri tried to block his voice out and concentrate on the patterns that were *almost* the patterns he knew. He thought for a second that he'd caught the gist of it—and the Scout turned up the speed.

Defeated for the moment, Jethri sat back, and tried another sip of his wine.

"For I am certain," the Scout was saying out loud, "that there were enough of those present with Ixin's interest at heart that they would not have permitted a bullying. As it is, you may wish to ask your most excellent arms master to—"

Master ven'Deelin's hand flashed a quick series of signs as she murmured, "Ah. I have been so much enjoying your visit that I of my duty am neglectful. This is what you wish to say?"

The Scout laughed. The master trader—perhaps she smiled, a little, before turning her attention to Jethri and using her chin to point at the door.

"Of your goodness, young Jethri. Scout ter'Astin and I have another topic of discourse between us, which absolutely I refuse to undertake in Terran."

"Yes, ma'am." He stood and bowed, made clumsy by reason of the still-full wine glass. "Good shift, ma'am. Scout—I thank you."

"No, child," the Scout said, sipping his wine. "It is I who thank you, for enlivening what has otherwise been a perfectly tedious duty cycle." He moved a hand, echoing Master ven'Deelin. "Go, have your meal, rest. Learn well and bring honor to your ship."

"Yessir," Jethri gasped, and made his escape.

DAY 67

❀❀❀❀❀❀❀❀❀❀❀❀❀❀❀❀❀❀❀❀❀❀❀❀

Standard Year 1118
Elthoria
Protocol Lessons

"YES!" RAY JON TEL'ONDOR cried, bouncing 'round Jethri like a powerball on overload.

"*Precisely* would a shambling, overgrown barbarian from the cold edge of space bow in acknowledgment of a debt truly owed!" Bouncing, he came briefly to rest a few inches from Jethri's face.

Frozen in the bow, Jethri could see the little man's boots as he jigged from foot to foot, in time to a manic rhythm only he could hear. Jethri forced himself to breathe quietly, to ignore both the crick in his back and the itch of his scalp, where the hair was growing out untidily.

"Well played, young Jethri! A skillful portrayal, indeed! Allow me to predict for you a brilliant career in the theater!" The boot heels clicked together, and Master tel'Ondor was momentarily, and entirely, still.

"Now," he said, in the mode of teacher to student, "do it correctly."

Having no ambition to hear Master tel'Ondor on the foolishness

866

of allowing one's emotions rule—a subject upon which he was eloquent—Jethri neither sighed, nor cussed, nor wrinkled his nose. Instead, he straightened, slowly and with, he hoped, grace, and stood for a moment, arms down at his sides, composing himself.

It was not, as he had hoped, the new boots which had been waiting for him in his quarters—five pairs to choose from!—that were the problem with his bows this shift, nor was it that the silky blue shirt bound him, or that the equally new and surprising trader's jacket limited his range of motion. Though he was very much aware all of his new finery, he was in no way hampered. The problem had been and was, as he understood Master tel'Ondor on the matter, that Jethri Gobelyn had ore for brains.

Don't doubt that his lessons with Master tel'Ondor had taught him a lot. For instance, learning how to speak Liaden wasn't anywhere like learning how to speak a new dialect of Ground Terran, or dock-pidgin or Trade. Spoken Liaden was divided into two kinds—High and Low—and then divided again, into *modes*, all of which meant something near and dear and different to Liaden hearts. Improper use of mode was asking for a share in a fistfight, if nothing worse. That was if Master tel'Ondor let him live, which by this time in the proceedings, Jethri wasn't so sure he would.

Truth told, and thanking the tapes, not to mention Vil Tor and Gaenor, he did have a yeoman's grip on the more work-a-day modes in the High Tongue—enough, Master tel'Ondor allowed, that educated people would understand him to be literate, though tragically afflicted with an impediment to the tongue.

No, it was the *bows* that were making him into a danger to himself and his teacher. Dozens of bows, of varying depths, each delivered at its own particular speed, with its own particular gesture of hand—or lack—held for its own particular count. . .

"Forgive me, young Jethri," Master tel'Ondor said, delicately. "Have I time to drink a cup of tea before your next performance?"

His one triumph was his ability to remain trader-faced, no matter the provocation. Carefully, he inclined his head, bending his neck so far, but no further, straightening without haste and only then making his reply.

"Your pardon, Master. I was absorbed by thought."

"At this moment, thought is extraneous," Master tel'Ondor told him. "The honorable to whom you find yourself in debt stands before you. Show proper respect, else they become bored— or discover that they are in receipt of an insult. Perhaps you do intend an insult; if so, you must chart your own course. The ven'Deelin did not bid me instruct you in matters of the duel."

"Yes, Master." Jethri took a deep breath, began the count in his head, moved the right arm—*so*—on the same beat extending the left leg—*so*—and bent from the waist, forehead on an interception course with the left knee.

At the count of fourteen, he stopped moving, holding the pose for six beats, then reversed the count, coming slowly to his full height, right hand and left leg withdrawing to their more usual positions—and he was at rest.

"So." Before him, Master tel'Ondor stood solemn and still, his head canted to one side. "An improvement." He held up a hand, as if to forestall the grin Jethri kept prisoned behind straight lips. "Understand me—an *improvement* only. Those who had not had the felicity of observing your former attempts might yet consider that they had been made the object of mockery."

Jethri allowed himself an extremely soft and heartfelt sigh. It wasn't that he doubted the tutor's evaluation of his performance— he *felt* like he was hinged with rusty metal when he bowed. According to Gaenor, they were due to raise Tilene within the ship-week, where, according to nobody less than Norn ven'Deelin, he would be expected to assist at the trade booth.

"Forgive me, Master, for my ineptitude," he said now to Master tel'Ondor. "I wish to succeed in my studies."

"So you do," the master replied. "And so I do—and so, too, does the ven'Deelin. It is, however, possible to wish so ardently for success that the wish cripples the performance. It is my belief, Jethri Gobelyn, that your very desire to do well limits you to mediocrity." He began to move around Jethri, not his usual manic bounce, but a sedate stroll, as if he were a trader and Jethri a particularly interesting odd lot.

For his part, Jethri stood with patience, his stomach recovered from yesterday's adventures and the off-hour meal he'd wolfed in the cafeteria under the view of an entire shift he was barely known to.

Master tel'Ondor had completed his tour.

"You are large," he murmured, hands folded before him, "but not so large as to hamper ease of movement. Indeed, you possess a certain unaffected grace which is pleasing in a young person. Understand me, I do not counsel you to be *easy*, but I do ask that you allow your natural attributes to aid you. Respect, duty, honor— all arise effortlessly from one's *melant'i*. You know yourself to be a man who *does not* give inadvertent insult—ideally, your bow—and all your dealings—will convey this. I would say to you that the strength of your melant'i is more important in any bow than whether you have counted precisely to fourteen, or only to thirteen."

He tipped his head. "Do you understand me, Jethri Gobelyn?"

He considered it. *Melant'i* he had down for a philosophy of hierarchy—a sort of constant tally of where you stood in the chain of command in every and any given situation. It was close enough to a plain spacer's "ship state" to be workable, and that was how he worked it. Given the current situation, where he was a student, trying hard to do—to do honor to his teacher . . .

Think, he snarled at himself.

OK, so. He was junior in rank to his teacher, and respectful of his learning, while being more than a little shy of his tongue. At the same time, though, a student ought to be respectful of himself, and of his ability to learn. He wasn't an idiot, though that was hard to bear in mind. Hadn't Master ven'Deelin herself signed him on as 'prentice trader, knowing—which she had to—the work it would mean, and trusting him to be the equal of it?

So thinking, he nodded, felt the nod become a bow—a light bow, all but buoyant; with the easy move of the left hand that signaled understanding.

Still buoyant, he straightened, and surprised a look of sheer astonishment in his tutor's face.

"Yes, precisely so," Master tel'Ondor said, softly, and himself bowed, acknowledging a student's triumph.

Jethri bit his lip to keep the grin inside and forced his face into the increasingly familiar bland look of a trader on active business.

"Jethri Gobelyn, I propose that we break for tea. When we meet here again, I believe we should concern ourselves with those modes and bows most likely to be met on the trade floor at Tilene."

It was too much; the grin peeped out; he covered with another soft, buoyant bow, slightly deeper and augmented by the hand-sign for gratitude. "Yes, Master. Thank you."

"Bah. Return here in one twenty-eight, and we shall see what you may do then." The master turned his back as he was wont to do in dismissal.

Grinning, Jethri all but skipped out of the classroom. Still buoyant, he made the turn into the main hallway—and walked into a mob scene.

He might have thought himself on some port street, just previous to a rumble, but there were faces in the crowd he recognized, and it was *Elthoria's* increasingly familiar walls giving back echoes of excited voices and, yes—laughter.

At the forefront, then, there was Pen Rel, and Gaenor, and Vil Tor—all talking at once and all sporting a state of small or extra-large dishevelment. There was a bruise high up on Gaenor's fragile, pointy face, and her lips looked swollen, like maybe she'd caught a smack. More than one of the crew members at her back were bloody, but of good cheer, and when Gaenor spotted Jethri she cried out, "Company halt!"

It took a bit, but they mostly settled down and got quiet. When there was more or less silence, Gaenor bowed—Jethri read it as the special bow made between comrades—and spoke through an unabashed grin.

"The First Mate reports to Jethri Gobelyn, crewman formerly at risk, that the Trade Bar of Kailipso will be pleased to cordially entertain him whenever he is in port. I also report that a house speciality has been named in your honor—which is to say, it is called *Trader's Leap*, and is mixed of 'retto and kynak and klah. On behalf of the ship, I have tasted of this confection and have found it to be . . . an amazement. There are other matters, too, of which you should be advised, so, please, come with us, and we will tell you of our visitation and correction."

Visitation and correction? Jethri stared at the bunch of them— even *Vil Tor* rumpled and his shirt torn and dirty.

"You didn't bust up the bar?"

Gaenor laughed, and Pen Rel, too. Then Gaenor stepped forward to catch his hand in hers, and pull him with her down the hall.

"Come, honored crewmate, we will tell you what truly transpired before it all becomes rumor and myth. In trade, you will then tell us of your training and skill, for already there are a dozen on station who have attempted to duplicate your leap and have earned for their efforts broken arms and legs."

She tugged his hand, and he let her pull him along, as the mob moved as one creature down the hall toward the cafeteria.

"But," Jethri said, finding Vil Tor at his side, "I thought Balance required craft and cunning and care—"

The librarian laughed, and caught his free hand. "Ah, my friend, we need to teach you more of *melant'i*! What you describe would be seemly, were we dealing with persons of worth. However, when one deals with louts—"

At that there was great laughter, and the mob swept on.

DAY 80

❈❈❈❈❈❈❈❈❈❈❈❈❈❈❈❈❈❈❈❈❈❈

Standard Year 1118
Kinaveral

IT WAS MIDDAY ON THE PORT by the time Khat cleared the paperwork and took receipt of her pay. By her own reckoning, it was nearer to sleep-shift, which activity she intended to indulge in, soon as she raised the lodgings.

Her step did break as she passed by the *Ship'n Shore*, but the prospect of ten hours or more of sleep was more compelling than a brew and a bite, so she moved on, and caught a tram at the meeting of the cross streets.

She was in a light doze when her stop was called; got her feet under her and bumbled down the steps to the street, where she stood for far too long, eyes narrowed against the glare, trying to sort out where, exactly, she was, with specific relation to her cubby and her cot. Eventually, she located the right building, mooched on in at quarter-speed, swiped her key through the scanner and took the lift to the eighth floor.

The Gobelyn Family Unit was, thanking all the ghosts of space, quiet and dim. Khat charted a none-too-steady course across the main room to her cubby, stripping off her clothes as she went. She stuffed the wad of them into the chute, pushed aside the drape and fell into her cot, pulling the blanket up and over her head.

It occurred to her that she ought to hit the shower; her being at least as ripe as her clothes, but she was asleep almost as soon as she'd thought it.

"ALL CREW ON DECK!"

There are those things that command a body's attention, no matter how deep asleep it is. Khat jerked awake with a curse, flung the blanket aside and jumped for the common room, stark naked and reeking as she was.

Seeli stood in the center of the room, hands on hips and looking none too pleased. Apparently, Khat was the sole crew the all-hands had roused.

"Are you the only one here?" Seeli snapped, which wasn't her usual way. Seeli snapping was Seeli upset, so Khat made allowance and answered civil.

"I'm guessing. Place was empty when I come in—" she looked across the room at the clock. "Two hours ago."

Her cousin vented an exasperated sigh.

"It's our shift, then," she muttered, and then appeared to see Khat's condition for the first time. "Just down from the free-wing job?"

"Two hours ago," Khat said. "They had me running solo. Sleep is high on the list of needfuls, followed by a shower and food."

Seeli nodded. "I'm sorry. If there was anybody else to hand—but it's you an' me, an' it's gotta be now." She pointed to the 'fresher. "Rinse an' get decent. I'll fix you a cup o'mite and some coffee. You can drink it on the way."

Khat stared. "What's gone wrong?"

Seeli was already moving toward the galley, and answered over her shoulder. "Iza got in a cuffing match with the yard boss, and the port cops have her under key."

"Shit," Khat said, and sprinted for the 'fresher.

Seeli'd gone down to the yard, to talk with the boss and smooth over what she could, which left Khat to bail Iza out.

It was a cross-port ride on the tram, by which time the 'mite and the caffeine were working, and she walked into the cop shop more or less awake, if none too easy in the stomach.

"Business?" The bored woman behind the info counter asked.

"Come to pay a fine and provide escort," Khat said, respectfully. She wasn't over-fond of port police—what spacer was?—but saw no reason to pay an extra duty for her attitude. The ghosts of space bear witness, Iza had likely scored enough of that for the crew at large, if they'd interrupted her in a cuffing match.

"Name?" the cop asked.

"Iza Gobelyn. Brought in this afternoon from the yards."

The cop looked down at her screen, grunted, and jerked her head to the right.

"Down the end of the hall. If you step lively, you can get her out before the next hour's holding fee kicks in."

"Thank you," Khat said, and made haste down the hall, there to stand before another counter just like the one at the front door, and repeat her information to an equally bored man.

"Kin?" he asked, peering at her over the edge of his screen.

"Yessir. Cousin. Khatelane Gobelyn."

"Hmph." He poked at some keys, frowned down at the screen, poked again. Khat made herself stand quiet and not shout at him to hurry it along, and all the while the big clock behind the counter showed the time speeding toward the hour-change.

"Gobelyn," the cop muttered, head bobbing as he bent over the screen. "Here we are: public display of hostility, striking a citizen, striking a port employee, striking a law enforcement officer, swearing at a law enforcement officer, Level Two arrest, plus transportation, booking, three hours' lodging, usage fees, tax and duty, leaving us with a total due of eight hundred ninety-seven bits." He looked up. "We also accept trade goods, or refined gold. There is a surcharge for using either of those options."

Sure there was. Khat blinked. Eight *hundred*—

"Duty?" she asked.

The cop nodded, bored. "You're offworld. All transactions between planetaries and extra-planetaries are subject to duty."

"Oh." She slipped a hand into her private pocket, brought out her personal card, and swiped it through the scanner on the front of the counter. There was a moment of silence, then the cop's screen beeped and initiated a noisy printout.

"Your receipt will be done in a moment," he said. "After you have it, please go down the hall to the first room on your left. Your cousin will be brought to you there."

"Thanks," Khat muttered. She took the printout when it was done with a curt nod went to wait for Iza to be brought up.

"LEVEL TWO ARREST" involved sedation—the construction of the drug, duration of affect, known adverse reactions, and chemical antidotes were all listed at the bottom of the two-page receipt. Khat scowled. The drug lasted plus-or-minus four hours. Iza had been arrested three-point-five hours ago. There wasn't enough credit left on her card to rent a car to take them cross port, and the prospect of woman-handling a half-unconscious Iza onto the tram was . . . daunting, not to dance too lightly on it.

She'd barely started to worry when the door to the waiting room opened, admitting a port cop in full uniform, a thin woman in bloodstained overalls and spectacularly bruised face walking, docile, at her side.

"Khatelane Gobelyn?" The cop asked.

"That's me." Khat stepped forward, staring into Iza's face. Iza stared back, blue eyes tranquil and empty.

"She's good for about another forty minutes," the cop said. "If I was you, I'd have her locked down in thirty. No sense running too close to the edge."

"Right," Khat said, and then gave the cop a nod, trying for cordial. "Thank you."

"Huh." The cop shook her head. "You keep her outta trouble, space-based. You copy that? She put Chad Perkin in the hospital when he tried to get the restraints on her—broken kneecap, broken nose, cracked ribs. You hurt a cop on this port once, and you're a good citizen ever after, because there ain't no maybes the second time."

Khat swallowed. "I don't—"

"Understand?" The cop hit her in the chest with an ungentle forefinger. "If your buddy here gets into another fistfight and the cops are called on it, she ain't likely to survive the experience. That plain enough for you, space-based?"

"Yes," Khat breathed, staring into the broad, hard face. "That's plain."

"Good. Now get her outta here and tied down before the stuff wears out."

"Yes," Khat said again. She reached out and took Iza's hand, pulling her quick time down the hall.

THE TRAM WAS WITHIN two blocks of the lodgings and the time elapsed from the cop shop was rising onto forty-two minutes, when Khat felt Iza shift on the seat beside her. The shifting intensified, accompanied by soft growls and swear words. Khat bit her lip, in a sweat for the tram to *hurry*—

"'scuse me." A hand landed, lightly, on Khat's shoulder. She looked up into the face of an older grounder woman.

"'scuse me," the woman said again, her eyes mostly on Iza. "Your friend just fresh from the cop shop?"

"Yes."

"You take my advice—get her off this tram an' *down*. That drug they use has a kick on the exit side. M'brother threw seven fits when it wore offa him—took all us girls to hold him down, and my uncle, too."

"Damn dirtsider," Iza muttered beside her. "Trying to cheat me. Short my ship, will he . . ."

Khat grabbed her arm, leaned over and yanked the cord. The tram slowed and she leapt to her feet, dragging Iza with her.

"Thank you," she said to the grounder woman, and then thought to ask it— "What happened to your brother?"

The woman shrugged, eyes sliding away. "He was born to trouble, that one. Cop broke his neck not a year later—resisting arrest, they said."

The tram stopped, the side door slid open. "Mud sucker!" Iza yelled, and Khat jumped for the pavement. Perforce, Iza followed; she staggered, swearing, and Khat spun, twisting her free hand in Iza's collar, using momentum and sheer, naked astonishment to pitch the older woman off the main walk and into a gap between two buildings.

"Cheat! Filth!" shouted Iza. Khat hooked a foot around her ankle, putting her face down into the mud, set a knee into the small of her back, and pulled both arms back into a lock.

Iza bucked and twisted and swore and shouted—to not much effect, though there were a few bad seconds when Khat thought she was going to lose the arm-lock.

After half an hour or an eternity, the thrashing stopped, then the swearing did, and all Iza's muscles went limp. Cautiously, Khat let the lock down, and eased her knee off. Iza lay, face down, in the mud. Khat turned her over, checked her breathing and her pulse, then, stifling a few curses herself, she got Iza into a back carry and staggered off toward the lodgings.

The lodgings were in sight when Seeli showed up on Khat's left. Wordlessly, she helped ease Iza down, and then the two of them got her distributed between them and walked her the rest of the way. Seeli swiped her key through the scan and they maneuvered Iza into the lift, then through the common room and into her own quarters, where they dropped her, muddy and bloody as she was, atop her cot.

"How bad at the yard?" Khat asked Seeli as they moved toward the galley.

"Bad enough," Seeli said after more hesitation than Khat liked to hear. She sighed, and opened the coldbox. "Brew?"

"Nothing less. And some cheese, if there's any." She closed her eyes, feeling the electric quiver of adrenaline-edged exhaustion in her knees and arms.

"Brew," Seeli said, and Khat heard a solid, welcome thump on the table before her. She opened her eyes just as a block of spicy local cheese and a knife landed next to the bottle.

Sighing, she had a mouthful of brew, then sliced about a third of the cheese.

Seeli sat down across, cradling her brew between her two hands, and looking about as grim as she got.

"How bad," Khat asked between bites of cheese, "is bad enough?"

Seeli sighed. "The yard wants an extra bond posted. They want a guarantee that Iza will be kept from their premises. They want the name and contact code for somebody—*not* Iza—who is empowered to speak for the ship. That person will be allowed in the offices of the yard no more than once per port-week, at pre-scheduled times. Monthly inspection of progress stays in force, so long as the inspector ain't Iza Gobelyn. Any further disturbance, and the yard will invoke breach and impound the *Market*."

Khat had another piece of cheese and a swallow of brew.

"That's bad enough," she allowed, and pointed at the cheese. "Eat."

"Later," Seeli said, and made a production out of sipping her beer.

Khat sighed. "Understand, there was a couple bad minutes when the drug went over, but I gathered that Iza had reason to believe the yard was cheatin' us."

"There might be some of that. Problem is, Iza going off the dial put us into the disadvantage with regard to amicable discovery. I've got a call in to Paitor. Crew meeting here, tomorrow port-night."

"What about Cris?"

Seeli shrugged, and stared hard down into her brew. "I beamed a precis and a plea for a recommend to his ship. Could be we'll have his answer by meeting." She looked up, face hard, which was Seeli when she'd taken a decision, no different from her ma. "We gotta settle this, Khat. Iza goes off the dial again, we could lose the *Market*. It's that near the edge."

"I hear it," Khat said, and finished her brew. "I'm for sleep, coz. Central's got me on for a hop to the station tomorrow middle day. I'll be down in plenty of time for the meeting." She stood and stretched. "Best thing would be for Iza to take a temp berth—you know she's always crazy on the ground."

"I know," Seeli said, too soft. "Sleep sound, cousin. 'preciated the assist, today."

Khat nodded and headed for the door. Before she got there, she checked and looked over her shoulder.

"Almost forgot—eight hundred ninety seven paid out from my personal account."

Seeli closed her eyes briefly. "I'll authorize the transfer from Ship's General,"

"'preciate it," Khat said, and left, on a course for sleep.

DAY 81

Standard Year 1118
Kinaveral

IT WAS A GRIM-FACED lot of Gobelyns gathered in the lodging's common room when Khat finally got there, dusty, hungry and all too out of patience with stationer attitude and port red tape, both.

"Sorry," she said to Seeli, who was sitting center-circle with Grig at her left hand and Paitor at her right. "They told me about the lift. Nobody thought to mention there'd be three hours of paperwork waitin' for me on station, and a matching three portside, when I got back down."

It was notable that Dyk, sitting between Mel and Zam, didn't bother to assure her that she looked fine in red tape. Seeli only nodded and pointed at the empty chair between Mel and Paitor, which seat Khat took with a fair amount of trepidation. Seeli'd called Full Circle on Iza. This was not going to be fun.

No sooner had she sat then Paitor got his feet under him and come to his full standing height. "Captain," he said, loud enough to be heard down the hall and into the next lodgings over. "Your crew wants a Word."

Khat felt some of the tightness in her gut ease. They were going to do the reasonable—well, o'course they was, she told herself, with Seeli settin' it up. So, a Word, first, with Ship's Judgement held in reserve, in case Iza wasn't inclined to meet reasonable with reasonable. Whether she'd be so inclined, Khat couldn't have said—and by the look on Seeli's face, she didn't know which way Iza was likely to jump, either.

"Iza Gobelyn," Paitor said, stern and loud. "Your crew's waitin'."

For what seemed like a long time, nothing happened. Khat realized she was holding her breath, and took note of the fact that the palms of her hands were damp.

Away down the room, something stirred, and there was Iza, long and lean and tough and walking with something less than her usual swagger.

She stopped walking just behind Grig's chair and raised her face, catching Paitor's eyes on hers.

"Well, brother?" she snapped, and Khat winced, her voice was that sharp.

"Just a Word with you, Captain," Paitor answered, smooth and calm as you please. "On a matter of ship's safety."

Say what you would about Iza Gobelyn, she was all of that, and canny, too. Another two heartbeats, she stood behind Grig, her eyes flicking 'round the Circle, touching each of their faces in turn, letting each of them see her—their mother, their cousin, their captain, who had kept them out of trouble and bailed them out of trouble; who'd kept ship and crew together for all of Khat's lifetime—and before.

When they'd all had a good look at her, and her at them, that's when she slid between Grig and Seeli and walked forward to stand in the center of the Circle, and hold her hands out, palms up and showing empty.

"I'm listenin'," she said, and let her hands fall to her sides.

Paitor sat down again, and folded his arms over his chest, face shut, eyes alert. Next to him, Seeli straightened.

"There's concern," she said, her voice firm and clear. "The yard boss ain't happy with the captain's behavior. He's gone so far as to state he'll invoke breach and impound the *Market*, in the case that Iza Gobelyn's seen on his deck again."

Iza turned lazily on her heel until she faced Seeli, which gave Khat the side of her face.

"They was shortin' us on the shielding, Admin."

"Yes, Captain, I don't doubt they was, having seen it with my own eyes. Fact remains, the yard boss has the legal on his side. He's filed a paper with the local cops, stating that one Iza Gobelyn approaches his yard at her peril. If she's found on or around, the *Market's* forfeit."

Iza glared; Khat could see it in the thrust of a shoulder.

"That's legal, is it?"

"It is," Seeli said. "And if it weren't, we'd still be outta luck, being as the cops ain't sworn to aid us."

Iza's shoulder twitched.

"On account," said Grig, his voice as hard as Khat had ever heard it, "you pitched the cop you swung on into light duty til his knee and his ribs and his nose all heal, and the cops here-port don't care to look out for them who break their mates."

"Worse," Khat said, leaning forward in her chair as Iza swung 'round to face her. "There's active malice involved. Woman on the bus told me. Comes to that, cop down the shop told me. You hurt a cop on this port, you stay outta trouble forevermore, because the day you come against another cop is the day you stop breathing."

Iza stared at her, eyes hooded, then gave her a nod. "'preciate the bail-out, cousin."

"It was expensive enough," Khat told her.

"Looks like getting more expensive before it gets less," Iza answered and turned back to face Seeli.

"Lay it out, Admin."

"All right, Captain," Seeli's voice was cool as the skin of a cargo can. "What I'm seeing is this—I'll take oversight of the upgrades and repairs. Grig, here, he's my expert on shielding, and he's already found us a second opinion, like the contract says we can have. We'll keep close watch and we won't let them get away with nothin', but we won't take no risks, neither, nor put the ship at peril."

"Fine work for you and yours, Admin. What about the captain?"

"The captain," Seeli said firmly, "should find herself a long-berth, get off Kinaveral until we're ready to go, and stay outta trouble."

In the center of the Circle, Iza laughed. "By this age in my life, you think I'd be expert in that." She turned, rotating lazily on her heel, and looked at them, one by one.

"Anybody else have a Word? Or does Admin speak for all of you?"

"In the case, Admin's on it," Mel said, while Dyk muttered, "No other Words, Captain," and Zam just shrugged his shoulders.

"And you're all staying dirtside, as I hear it, to give Admin a hand?"

"I'm signed as cook on a private yacht," Dyk said. "Lift in two days, back in 'leven month."

"Me an' Mel're for a miner," Zam said, looking down at his boots. "Signed the papers today. Lift tomorrow. Back, like, Dyk, in 'leven, and trusting our ship'll be here for us."

"Cris is already on long-haul," Khat said, since it was her turn. It've been easier to talk to her boots, like Zam, but pilots were bolder than that—Khat Gobelyn was bolder than that—and she met her captain's eyes, level. "Me, I'm all fixed as a freewing, based on-port. There's some longer lifts comin', they tell me, but most of what's on offer is shuttle work and short hops. Don't fly every day, can file 'unavailable' at decent notice, so Seeli'll have an extra hand, when she needs one."

Iza nodded, solemn-like, and looked over to Paitor.

"I'm on-port, doing some little chores for Terratrade," he said, not uncrossing his arms. "Seeli needs me, she calls, I come."

"Just like you always done, eh, brother?"

His mouth thinned some, but the rest of his face stayed bland. "That's right, Captain."

Iza turned again, past Seeli, and showed her back to Khat, full face to Grig.

"You're staying on-dirt to back up Admin, is that so, Grig Tomas?"

"That's so, Captain."

"Then you'll see the jettison list attended to proper. That would be an order, which I know you can take," she said, provoking-like, 'cept it didn't make no sense, as far as Khat had ever seen, to provoke Grig. He just went all soft and agreeable on you, an' took his revenge when you needed it least.

Except not this time.

"Beggin' the captain's pardon, but there's some things on that jettison list belong to absent crew."

"Absent crew." Khat didn't need to see Iza's face; the tone of voice was enough. She drew a careful breath and indulged in a spot of wishful telepathy, trying to send Grig a message not to whip Iza into a rage—not now, when she'd been so reasonable . . .

"You'll be referring to Arin's son?" Iza was asking Grig.

There was a short pause, before he answered, voice neutral, "That's right, Captain."

"Spit of his father, ain't he, Grig?"

And what was this? Khat thought. Iza sounded almost conversational.

"Jethri's a good-lookin' boy. Smart, too. Done you proud, Iza."

"Ain't done me proud. Nothing to do with me, *as* you know it. Arin's boy, clear through—wouldn't you say so, Grig?" She shifted of a sudden, leaning forward hard, like she was going to grab him by the shoulders and haul him up to face her.

"Done's done, Iza. Arin's gone, and Jethri, too. Send the boy his things, and call it square."

"It'd be what's right, Iza," Paitor put in, calm, while the rest of them sat mum and stupid.

She spun to glare at him, shoulders stiff. "You think so, do you, brother? Fine, then. Send Arin's boy his things. So long as they're finally gone from my ship, I don't care where they are—destroyed or on Liad makes the same difference to me."

"That's settled then," said Seeli, shockingly matter-of-fact. "What ain't settled is what you'll do, Captain."

"Didn't think I had a choice," Iza said, turning back, and showing Seeli empty hands. "I'll go down to the hire-hall tomorrow and find myself a berth."

"I'll come with you," Khat heard her own voice say, and looked up to catch Iza's glance coming at her over one bony shoulder.

"Thanks, cousin," she said, with no shortin' the irony.

"No trouble," Khat answered, forcing herself to sound calm. "I'm not flying tomorrow and I know a couple of the sign-ons at the hall."

"Then we're square, captain and crew," Seeli said. Paitor nodded and got back on his feet.

"The crew talked, the captain heard. The ship's in harmony."

There was an uneasy sort of silence, then, like nobody knew exactly what to do, now the agreement was made and the right phrases spoke. When it had gone on long enough for Khat to start feeling it in her gut, she stood up and stretched, hands reaching for the ceiling.

"Let's all have us some brew and a snack," she said. "And say our good-byes and be-wells. We're going to be scattered across the star lanes this next while. Let's part on terms."

Dyk laughed and bounced to his feet in a sudden return to normal behavior. "Maybe I should ship out more often!"

"Maybe you should," Mel said cordially, standing up. Zam laughed. Across the circle, Seeli was up, Grig beside her, lanky and limpid like always, watching as Paitor held a hand out to Iza.

"Buy you a brew, sister?" he asked, and after a moment Iza put her hand in his.

"A brew'd be welcome, brother."

DAY 106

❀❀❀❀❀❀❀❀❀❀❀❀❀❀❀❀❀❀❀❀❀❀❀❀

Standard Year 1118
Tilene Trade Theater

TAN SIM PEN'AKLA, adopted of Clan Rinork, left the Tilene Star
Bar in a wine-induced glow of good fellowship for all beings, everywhere.

That the glow was wine-induced, Tan Sim well knew, having
entered the establishment in question some hours previous with the
specific intent of imbibing wine sufficient to ease the sting of the
latest slight delivered by his foster kin. Since he had not cut his teeth
yesterday, he was also well-aware that the wine on draw at the Star
Bar was of a more virulent vintage than he was accustomed to drink,
and that he had thereby made an appointment on the morrow with
the very devil of a hangover.

That, however, was in the future. For the present, restored to
good humor and only slightly unsteady on his feet, he sauntered,
whistling unmelodically, down the supply hallway which was a
shortcut to the main trading theater.

It would not do to be late to the second round of trading. Of
course, his beloved foster brother Bar Jan would smell the wine; and
wouldn't it just grate along his fine-drawn, High House sensibilities
to be unable to send his drunkard junior away. But he dared not do

that, Tan Sim thought waggishly. Oh, no, Bar Jan dared not send him away and hold the booth on his own while their mutual mother was gone a-calling. A *melant'i*-blind idiot Bar Jan might be, but he knew well enough that Tan Sim was the superior trader, in his cups or sober.

Would that he did not.

But, there, that line of thought ventured too close to the quadrant he wished to avoid. Resolutely, Tan Sim turned his consideration to the franchise Alt Lyr had for sale. A well enough venture—or so it seemed on the surface. He had set word about, before his visit to the wine shop, and he would be wanting to do more research before mentioning the matter to his mother, but . . .

He checked, whistle dying on his lips, eyes rapt upon a performance the like of which he had not beheld since—well, since he had first come to Rinork, and spent so many hours before the mirror, shining his bows for High House display.

Alas, the person bowing so earnestly and with such . . . interesting . . . results in the wide space in the hall meant to accommodate a service jitney, had no mirror. Style was also sadly absent, though there was, Tan Sim allowed, after observing for a few heartbeats, a certain vivacity in delivery that was not . . . entirely . . . displeasing.

At just that point, the person in the shadows executed a bow with a vivacity sufficient to set them staggering and Tan Sim felt it was time to take a hand.

"Here then!" he called out in the mode spoken between comrades, which would surely have set Bar Jan to ranting. "There's no sense breaking your head over a bow, you know."

The figure in the shadows turned to face him, light falling on a face pale, angular and wholly unLiaden. There was an unfinished appearance about the jaw and shoulders which said *halfling* to Tan Sim, though he had to look up to meet the chocolate brown eyes. Despite he was indisputably Terran, he was dressed in well-tailored trading clothes, made very much in the Liaden style, down to the fine leather boots which encased his feet and the short blue jacket that proclaimed him an apprentice in trade.

In fact, he was a riddle.

Tan Sim delighted in riddles.

Delighted, he swept a bow of introduction to the startled youth.

"Tan Sim pen'Akla Clan Rinork."

The boy hesitated infinitesimally, then bowed in return, with somewhat less verve, and stated, laboriously, and very nearly in the mode of introduction:

"Jethri Gobelyn, apprentice trader aboard *Elthoria*."

Ixin's lead tradeship, forsooth. Tan Sim allowed his interest to be piqued. The ven'Deelin was canny and devious—even when held against other masters of trade, a lot known for their devious ways. Indeed, he had long admired her from afar—necessary, as Ixin and Rinork did not meet—and studied her guild files closely, so that he might, perhaps, upon one far distant day, aspire to even one-twelfth of her trading acumen.

And this lad here, this *Terran* lad, was the ven'Deelin's apprentice? He filed that away, for sober thought on the far side of the hangover, and moved a hand, softly, offering aid.

"I see you in the throes of just such a task as I myself have undertaken in the past. Wretched, aren't they? Who would suppose that one race could *need* so many bows?"

The angular face wavered as the lips bent in a quickly suppressed smile—and, aye, that, too, struck an uneasy memory. Tan Sim felt a spurt of sympathy and deliberately let his own smile show.

Some of the starch went out of the thin shoulders, and the boy—Jeth Ree, was it?—inclined his head.

"Indeed," he stammered, almost in the mode between equals—which was an impertinence, thought Tan Sim, but what else was the lad to do? "It is . . . difficult . . . to bear so much in mind. I have been tutored, but I fear that I am not fully . . . cognizant . . ."

"Hah." Tan Sim held up his hand. "I understand. You have been given a set number and form, eh? And you wish to shame neither your teacher nor your trader." He smiled again, gently. "Nor take delivery of a scold."

Jeth Ree fairly grinned—a dazzling display, too soon vanished.

"Well," said Tan Sim, "you won't find me a scolding fellow. I have only admiration for one who is so devoted to his duty that he uses his break-time to hone his skill. Such diligence. . ." He left the sentence for a moment as he recalled again that Ixin and Rinork did *not* meet. The proper course for himself, as one of Rinork, then, was to turn his back on this boy and—

And what did he care for some long-ago, cold quarrel? Depend upon it, he thought, sadly unfilial, the whole brangle, whatever it was, could be squarely lain at Rinork's feet. Here before him stood an apprentice trader in need of the guidance of a trader. His *melant'i*— and Guild rule, if it came to that—was plain.

He showed Jeth Ree another smile, and was pleased to gain one in return.

"Well, then, let us see what we might manage between us," he said, settling comfortably against the friendly wall. "Show me your repertoire."

This, the boy was willing enough to do, and Tan Sim spent the next while leaning, tipsy, against the wall, observing a series of common mercantile bows. Happily, the task was not more than his befogged faculties could accommodate, nor Jeth Ree any less apt than the larger number of new 'prentices Tan Sim had now and then had occasion to observe. The lad had apparently been driven to this lonely practice site in a fit of stage fright. Which Tan Sim quite understood. So.

"You are well-enough," he said, when the boy had straightened from his last endeavor, "for an apprentice newly come to the floor. It speaks well that you wish to bring only honor to your master, but you must not allow your sensibilities to overset your good sense." He inclined his head. "You will do exceedingly, Jeth Ree Gobelyn."

The boy stood a moment, as if struck, then bowed once more; this very precise, indeed. "I am in your debt, Tan Sim pen'Akla."

And wouldn't THAT be a grand thing to bring to the table? Tan Sim thought in sudden horror. *"Mother, I have the advantage of ven'Deelin's Terran apprentice in a matter of Balance."* Gods.

He moved a hand, smoothing the debt away. "Honor me by forgetting the incident, as I have done."

Jeth Ree looked doubtful—then proved himself a lad of sense and worthy to be the ven'Deelin's apprentice, by inclining his head.

"Thank you," he said, in what Tan Sim knew to be Terran, that being another of his clandestine studies.

"You are welcome," he replied in the same tongue, somewhat more slowly than he would have liked. The boy did not burst into derisive laughter, or even smile overmuch, which gave him hope for a successful outcome of study.

"If you please," Jeth Ree said abruptly. "How shall I bow to you, if we meet again on the floor? Since we are known to each other. . ."

Tan Sim pushed away from his wall. How, indeed, should the lad acknowledge him, should they meet? Almost, he laughed aloud at the unlikelihood of such an event.

Still, it was a reasonable question and deserved a fitting reply. He took a moment to be sure his feet were well under him, then swept the bow he'd practiced in his own ironic honor as a youth— *most honored child of the house*. He watched as the boy reproduced it, several times, and inclined his head, satisfied.

"Twill do. And now I must depart, amiable companion that you have been. My brother requires my assistance at our booth. Fare thee well, Jeth Ree Gobelyn."

He bowed, jauntily, the beginning of a headache teasing in back of his eyes, straightened to receive the boy's farewell, and walked away down the hall, whistling.

JETHRI'S TIMING WAS FORTUNATE; he returned to Ixin's trade booth just as the floor opened for the second shift. Master ven'Deelin inclined her head, which he hoped meant she was impressed with his promptness, and reached beneath the counter.

"Our Tilene agent took delivery of this message for you, young Jethri. You may have a moment to read it. There was also a crate— that has been moved to your trade-bin on ship."

Heart thumping heavy, he slipped a folded sheet of paper from between her fingers. He did remember his bow, and to give a soft, "My thanks, Master Trader." Courtesy satisfied, he took himself to the back corner of the booth, hunkered down on his heels beside the hanging rugs and strings of spice, and unfolded the crackling thin paper.

To Jethri Gobelyn, in the care of Norn ven'Deelin Clan Ixin
From Khatelane Gobelyn, Pilot on Duty, Gobelyn's Market
Transmit Standard Day 75, SY 1118

Hey, Jeth. Don't let the POD fool you—I'm doing administrative while Seeli catches up some stuff with the yard. It's looking like a long process; actually a near complete refit. I don't know if they told you. A Standard dirtside, minimum. Iza said she'd be staying with the ship, but—before you hear it from some Looper you run into, what it was, she had a disagreement with the local gendos and got herself a couple levels of arrested. Wasn't what you'd call pretty, or quiet, and even made some of the portside print papers. Point is, she's not stir-stuck here like she might be if we hadn't been around but off on the longest run she could fit inside the schedule. Seeli's acting as agent-on-the-spot, with Grig to keep her company. I'm on willfly with the Port, and running part-time back-up for the two of them. Cris has a gig with a franchise ship—and the rest of us found some little thing to do off-dirt, so we'll be a scattered crew for the next while. I'll try to keep in touch, Jethri, but—no promises, you know? Be sure I'll zap you the news when the Market lifts out of here. I'm sending this in front of Elthoria's published route; if they keep schedule it'll only be a bit old when you get it.

I'm also sending along a size B shipping crate; Iza says you're to have it.

The rest of the circumstance is that I had chance to look over the duty roster for the past few Standards and noticed that you was default on Stinks. Thing is, Stinks carries a pay premium that somehow didn't make it to your account. It's kind of a joke on a per-shift, but I totted up the last five Standards' worth and figured in the interest, and it came out to a nice round number. We all figured you was saving up to buy a ship, Jeth, but who thought you'd finance it out of Stinks?

Paitor's running jobs for Terratrade, and I didn't know how to make the transfer, so that cash is in the crate with the other stuff.

Anyhow, I know you're in the middle of the biggest adventure ever, learning all you can from Master ven'Deelin, so I won't keep you any longer. Think about us sometime; we think about you often.

With love,
Khat

He refolded the paper along its creases, and slid it away into the inner pocket of his jacket, in spite of which he didn't immediately rise to his duty. Instead, he stayed where he was, sitting low on his heels, head bent while he blinked the sudden fog of tears away.

Wasn't no cause for crying, he told himself. The ghosts of space witness, Khat's news was slim enough—hardly news at all, really. It was given that his cousins would reach for quick-jobs and temp berths—none of them had been born with mud on their feet. Likewise, he could have foretold that the detail work would fall to Seeli, and that Grig would stand her second. The captain . . . that was bad news, but almost expectable the way she tended to get a bit wild anytime she was planet-side. Probably there was more to it—and come to think of it, it seemed like there was more to a bunch of stuff than he'd realized.

Still, nothing to cry about in any of that, not with him having the biggest adventure ever.

He cleared his throat, raised his head and stood, pausing for a moment to be sure his face was properly ordered; then moved to his station at Master ven'Deelin's elbow.

HIS JOB THIS SHIFT, as it had been last, was to stand next and two steps behind Master ven'Deelin, where he could look and listen and soak up her style of trade and converse. More of that last was available to him than he would've thought, for the customers kept to the trading mode, and after one blank-faced stare at himself, would follow Master ven'Deelin into a more deliberate way of talking, which mostwise fell intelligible on his ear.

He had it as a working theory that a Liaden-born apprentice might likewise stand in need of practice in the trading mode, as it might not have been one they'd necessarily been taught in their growing-up years. With all those modes available between High and Low, surely no one but a lifelong student could be proficient in them all?

Whatever the reason, the customers treated him respectful—treated *Master ven'Deelin* respectful—and he was learning so much his head was in a fair way to exploding.

"That is well, then," Master ven'Deelin told the present customer—a black-haired man with a diamond drop in his left ear, wearing a jacket so heavy with embroidery that Jethri had to remind himself not to squint in protest. "We shall deliver no later than the third hour of Day Port, two days hence."

"Precisely so, Master Trader," the customer said, his voice quick and light. He held out a counter and a trade-card. Master ven'Deelin received both gravely and slotted them on the wires strung overhead—third one in, for "two day delivery."

"I am hosting a dinner party tomorrow evening, in the Little Hall," she murmured, as she finished with the card and token. "You would honor me by attending."

"Master Trader." The customer bowed, low. "The honor would be mine."

"That is well, then." She inclined her head and the customer moved off, giving up his place to the next in line, a boxy-built lady whose look-out was textile.

"Ah." Master ven'Deelin inclined her head. "This, my apprentice will assist you. Textile is his specialty." She moved her hand, discovering Jethri to the lady, who gave no sign of either pleasure or dismay at being turned over to himself.

Jethri's feelings were all a-spin, though he did his best to maintain a bland and polite expression. He did take a deep breath, to center himself, which might have been too long, since the Master Trader murmured.

"Young Jethri?"

"Yes, Master," he said, and was mortified to hear his voice wobble.

Knees knocking, he stepped up the counter and bowed to the customer.

"Ma'am," he said, painfully slow, and deliberate. "How may I be honored to assist you?"

It were the handlooms the lady was after, which was good news of its kind. Jethri moved up-counter to where the bolts were stowed and pulled down the book. He looked over his shoulder, then, just to be aware how closely Master ven'Deelin was shadowing his work.

To his horror, she was about no such thing, but stood deep in conversation with another customer at the counter; all of her attention on that transaction and none whatsoever on him . . .

"Forgive me," murmured boxy-built lady. "I regret that my time is limited."

"Certainly, ma'am," Jethri murmured, opening the book on the counter in front of her. "As you can see, we have many fine weavings to choose from . . ."

For a lady short of time, she showed no disposition to rush her decision. She had him pull this bolt and that, then this again, and that other. With each, he steadied a little, found the words coming more smoothly, remembered the trick—taught by Uncle Paitor—of flipping the end over the top of the bolt, so that he could speak of the underweave and the irregularities born of hand looming.

In the end, the lady bought nothing, though she thanked him for the gifts of his time and expertise.

Jethri, shirt damp with exertion, racked the book and ordered the samples, then stepped back to Norn ven'Deelin's side.

Through the course of the shift, he heard her invite no fewer than two dozen traders and merchants to her dinner party. Three more times, she gave him to customers desirous of textile; twice, he scored chip and card, which he triumphantly threaded on the wires he found near the bolts.

And at last, the bell sounded, signaling the end of day-trading. Norn ven'Deelin reached up and turned off the booth light. Jethri closed his eyes and sagged against the bolt rack, head pounding. It was over. He had lived. He had, just maybe, not done anything irrevocably stupid. Now, they would go back to the ship, get out of the dirt, and the noise.

"So," Norn ven'Deelin said brightly, and he heard her clap her palms gently together. "Do me the honor of bearing me company on a stroll, Jethri Gobelyn. We shall amaze Tilene-port!"

He opened his eyes and looked at her, meeting bright black eyes. There was something in the way she stood, or maybe in the set of her face, that conveyed itself as a challenge. Jethri ground his teeth, straightened out of his lean and squared his shoulders, despite the holler put up by his back muscles.

"Yes, ma'am," he said, and bowed obedience to the Master Trader's word.

THE WALK WAS LEISURELY, and they stopped often to acknowledge the bows of Master ven'Deelin's numerous acquaintances, who every one stared at him like he was the four-headed calf from Venturis. Jethri sighed behind his mask of bland politeness. You'd think he'd be used to the stares by now, but someway every new one scraped a little deeper, hurt a little more.

Otherwise, the stroll was a better idea than he'd thought. Tilene's gravity was a hair less than ship's grav, which he'd at last gotten used to. And the simple act of putting one foot in front of the other seemed enough to ease the ache in his head, and smooth the kinks out of his spine.

Master ven'Deelin paused to receive a particularly low bow, augmented by the hand-sign for "greatest esteem" from a red-haired woman in upscale trading clothes.

"Bendara Tiazan," Master ven'Deelin inclined her head. "Allow me to be delighted to see you! You must dine with me upon the morrow."

The redhead straightened. Her eyes showed a little stretch, but give her credit, Jethri thought sourly, she didn't stare at him—her whole attention was on Norn ven'Deelin. "I am honored, Master Trader," she said, in the mode of junior to senior.

Again, Master ven'Deelin inclined her head. "Until tomorrow, Bendara Tiazan."

"Until tomorrow, Master Trader," the redhead murmured, and bowed herself out of the way.

Master ven'Deelin continued her stately progress, Jethri keeping pace, just behind her left elbow.

"So, Jethri Gobelyn," she murmured as they passed out of the red-haired trader's hearing. "What do you deduce from our guest list so far?"

He blinked, thinking back over those she had pressed to dine with her tomorrow.

"Ma'am, I scarcely know who these traders are," he said carefully. "But I wonder at the number of them. It seems less like a dinner and more like a—" he groped for the proper word. After a moment, he decided that it wasn't in his Liaden repertoire and substituted a ship-term, "shivary."

"Hah." She glanced at him, black eyes gleaming. "You will perhaps find our poor entertainment to be a disappointment. I make no doubt that there will be dancing until dawn, nor no more than two or three visits from the proctors, bearing requests for silence."

He grappled the laugh back down deep into his chest and inclined his head solemnly. "Of course not, ma'am."

"Ah, Jethri Gobelyn, where is your address?" she said surprisingly. "A silver-tongue would grasp this opportunity to assure me that nothing I or mine might do could ever disappoint."

Jethri paused, looking down into her black eyes, which showed him nothing but tiny twin reflections of his own serious face. Was she pulling his leg? Or had he just failed a test? He licked his lips.

"I suppose," he said, slowly, "that I must not be a silver-tongue, ma'am."

Her face did not change, but she did put out a hand to pat him, lightly, on the arm. "That you are not, child. That you are not."

They moved on, Jethri trying to work out how to ask if being a silver-tongue was a good thing—and if it was how to go about learning the skill—without sounding a total fool. Meanwhile, Master ven'Deelin took the bows of three more traders of varying ranks, as Jethri read their clothing, and invited each to dine with her upon the morrow. If she kept at her current pace, he thought, they'd have to empty the trade theater itself to accommodate the crowd.

They strolled further down the flowered promenade. There

were fewer people about now, and Master ven'Deelin picked up the pace a bit, so Jethri needed to stretch his legs to keep up. Ahead, the walkway split into three, the center portion rising into an arch, the others going off at angles to the right and left. Somewhere nearby was the sound of water running, enormous amounts of water, it must be, from the racket it was making, and the air was starting to feel unpleasantly soggy.

Jethri frowned, maybe lagging a little from his appointed spot at Master ven'Deelin's elbow, trying to bear down on the feeling that he was breathing *water*, which was by no means a good thing . . .

From the left-hand path came voices, followed quickly by three top-drawer traders: A woman, star blond and narrow in the face, flanked by two young men—one as fair and as narrow as she and the other taller, with hair of a darker gold, his face somewhat rounder, and his eyes a trifle a-squint, as if he had a headache.

With a start, Jethri recognized his friend of the utility corridor, who had been so patient and understanding in the matter of bows. His first notion was to break into a fool-wide grin and rush forward to grab the man by the shoulders in a proper spacer greeting—which would never do, naturally, besides being one of the three top ways, if Arms Master sig'Kethra was to be believed, to take delivery of a knife between the ribs.

Still, if it would be rude to give way to the full scope of his feelings, he could at least give Tan Sim pen'Akla the honor of a proper bow.

Jethri placed himself before the threesome, and paused, awaiting their attention. The woman saw him first, her pale narrow brows plunging into a frown, but he cared not for her. He looked over her shoulder, made eye contact with Tan Sim and swept the bow of greeting the other had shown him, supplemented with the gesture that meant "joy."

He quickly realized he should have gone with his initial notion.

The fair, narrow young man shouted something beyond Jethri's current lexicon, his hand slapping at his belt, which gesture he understood all too nicely. He fell back a step, looking for a leap-to, when Tan Sim jumped instead, knocking the other's hand aside, with a sharp, "Have done! Will you harm the ven'Deelin's own apprentice?"

"You!" The other shouted. "You saw how he bowed to you! If you had the least bit of proper feeling—"

Oh. Jethri felt his stomach sink to the soles of his boots. He *had* botched it. Badly.

Stepping forward, he bowed again—this a simple bow of contrition.

"Please forgive me if my bow offended," he said, speaking in the mode of junior to senior, which *had* to be right, no matter which of the three chose to hear him. "Master Tan Sim himself is aware that I am . . . less conversant with bows than I would be. My only thought was to honor one who had given me kindness and fellowship. I regret that my error has caused distress."

"It speaks Liaden, of a fashion." The woman said, apparently to her sons, Jethri thought, but meaning for him to hear and take damage from it.

"He speaks Liaden right well for one new come to it," Tan Sim returned, heatedly. "And shows an adult's *melant'i*, as well. I taught him that bow myself—which he does not tell you, preferring to take all blame to himself."

"Speak soft to my mother, half-clan!" The pale young man jerked his arm out of Tan Sim's grip and spun, palm rising, his intent plain. Jethri jumped forward, arm up, intercepted the man's slap at the wrist, and grabbed hold just tight enough to get the message across.

"Here now!" he said in Terran, sounding remarkably like Cris, to his own ears. "None of that."

"Unhand me!" shouted the man, trying, unsuccessfully, to pull his wrist free, and "Call the proctors!"

"No need for proctors, young chel'Gaibin," Master ven'Deelin's voice was shockingly cool in that heated moment. "Jethri, of your goodness, return to Lord chel'Gaibin the use of his arm."

"Yes, ma'am," he said, and did as she asked, though he stayed close, in the event the lordship took it into his head to swing out at Tan Sim again.

He needn't have worried; all eyes were on Master ven'Deelin, who stood calm and unworried, her hands tucked in her belt, considering the other trader.

"Norn ven'Deelin," the woman said at last, and it didn't sound respectful at all.

The master trader inclined her head. "Infreya chel'Gaibin. It has been some years since we last spoke. I trust I find you well."

"You find me insulted and assaulted, *Master Trader*. I will have Balance for the harm done."

Master ven'Deelin tipped her head. "Harm? Has the heir's sleeve been crushed?"

Infreya chel'Gaibin glared. "You may put the assault of an unregulated Terran upon a registered guildsman no higher than amusing, if it pleases you. I assure you that the guild and the port will take a far different view."

"And yet," Master ven'Deelin murmured. "Jethri is hardly unregulated. He stands as my apprentice—"

"Oh, very good!" chel'Gaibin interrupted, "A 'prentice lays hands upon a trader while the master stands by and smiles!"

". . . and my son," Master ven'Deelin finished calmly. Jethri bit his lip, hard, and concentrated on keeping his face empty of emotion. He darted a quick look at Tan Sim, but found that young man standing at his ease, watching the proceedings with interest but no apparent dismay.

"Your son!" Apparently Trader chel'Gaibin wasn't convinced, for which Jethri blamed her not at all.

Master ven'Deelin swept a languid hand in the general direction of Tan Sim. "As much mine as that one is yours." She tipped an eyebrow. "But come, you wished satisfaction for insult and assault. We may settle that between us now, you and I."

Trader chel'Gaibin licked her lips and though she seemed to Jethri a woman unlikely to back down in a tight spot, there was something to the cast of her shoulders that strongly suggested she was looking for a way out of this one.

Behind her, Tan Sim shifted, drawing all eyes to himself. "Mother, surely there is no insult here? Jethri bowed as I had taught him, and when he saw one who was to him a stranger threaten one with whom he has had honorable dealings, he acted to nullify the threat—and most gently, too!"

"Gently!"" spat the other man. Tan Sim turned wondering eyes his way.

"Never tell me he bruised you, brother! A mere halfling? Surely—"

"This must be the Terran, Mother!" Lord chel'Gaibin interrupted excitedly, turning his back on his brother. "Recall that it was a Terran off of *Elthoria* who began the brawl at Kailipso—"

"Enough," the woman snapped. She stood silent for a moment, staring, none too pleasantly, at Tan Sim. Jethri felt his chest tighten in sympathy: Exactly did Iza Gobelyn stare just before she cut loose of mayhem and brought a body to wishing he'd been born to another ship, if at all.

Composing her face, she turned back to Master ven'Deelin and inclined her head, grudging-like.

"Very well. My son speaks eloquently in defense of yours, Master Trader. We are to see nothing more than halfling high spirits—and a misunderstanding of custom."

"It would seem indeed to be the case," Master ven'Deelin said calmly, "and no cause for experienced traders such as ourselves to be calling for Balance. Well we know what halflings are." Her eyes moved to Tan Sim, and she inclined her head gently. "Young pen'Akla."

Tan Sim's eyes widened and he bowed low with graceful haste. "Master ven'Deelin."

"Enough!" Tan Sim's mother snapped again. She turned her glare on the master trader and gave a bare dip of the head.

"Master Trader. Good evening." She didn't wait for a return bow—maybe, Jethri thought, because she knew she didn't rate one. Turning, she gathered her boys by eye, and stalked off.

When they were alone, Jethri turned and bowed, very low and very careful—and held it, eyes pointing at the toes of his boots.

Above him, him heard Master ven'Deelin sigh.

"In all truth, young Jethri, you have a knack. How came you by chel'Gaibin's Folly?"

Bent double, he blinked. "Ma'am?"

"Stand up, child," she interrupted and, when he had, said, "Tan Sim pen'Akla. How came you to his attention?"

Jethri cleared his throat. "I was—practicing my bows in the service corridor and he came upon me. He was most k-kind and helpful, ma'am, and when I said that I was in his debt, he declared no such thing. So then I thought to ask how I should bow to him, if we were to meet again, and he showed me thus—"

He performed the thing—and heard Master ven'Deelin sigh once more.

"Yes, of course. Well he might yearn to receive such a bow—" She moved a hand, eloquent of exasperation.

"Young things. All is anguish and high drama." She turned her head; a moment later Jethri heard it too—voices approaching down the right hand way.

"Come along, young Jethri. Our evening has just become full."

Obediently, he took his place at her elbow, and they moved on. But for themselves, the promenade was empty and Jethri cleared his throat.

"Please, ma'am. I am not really—really your son."

"Indeed you are; did you not hear me say it? Surely, a momentous occasion for us both. We return now to our ship to discuss the matter in more detail. Until then, I ask that you to repose in silence. I have thoughts to think."

Jethri bit his lip. "Yes ma'am," he whispered.

DAY 106

❀ ❀

Standard Year 1118
Elthoria

"YOU KNOW TOO LITTLE of our customs." Master ven'Deelin folded her hands on her desk and considered him out of her sharp black eyes. "Indeed, how could it be otherwise? Similarly, you are ignorant of the—histories that may lie between clans and the children of clans. The child of a Terran trade vessel has no need to know these things. And I—foolishly, I thought we might separate trade from clan. Pah! Trade and culture are twined more deeply than I had wished to understand. And now we are together caught in the nets of culture, and a child of ven'Deelin may *not* be a fool."

Jethri shifted miserably in the chair across from her. "Ma'am, I'm not a child of ven'Deelin—"

She held up a hand, and he swallowed the rest of his protest.

"Peace. The tale unfolds. Listen, and cultivate patience. They are two skills which serve every trader well."

"Yes, ma'am," he said, folding his hands tightly on his knee and pressing his lips together.

After a moment, she lowered her hand and continued.

"A child of ven'Deelin must need know both history and custom. We commence your education now, with excerpts of both."

"First, custom. It is Law that each member of each clan shall marry as the clan instructs, to produce children for the clan and also to seal and cement what alliances the clan may require in order to prosper. I have myself been contracted twice; once in order that the clan should have my heir to replace me as Ixin's master of trade, in due time. Again, to seal the peace between Ixin and Aragon; the child of that contract of course went to Aragon. So it is with most of us; some may be required to marry but once, some several times. Some few unfortunates discover themselves to be the perfect halves of a wizard's match—but those matings need not concern us here.

"Here, we discuss contract marriage and the fact that Infreya chel'Gaibin—a dutiful daughter of Clan Rinork—did some twenty-five Standards gone marry as her delm instructed, the fruit of that union being Bar Jen chel'Gaibin, her heir.

"Six Standards later, she married again, somewhat behind the fact as it is said and counted, into Clan Quiptic—a House of the lower mid-tier." Once more, she held up her hand, though Jethri hadn't made a sound.

"I know that this will seem odd to you, Rinork being, as it is, so very High, but there were reasons beyond the fact that she was already pregnant by the time the thing was arranged, and by none other than Quiptic Himself. A very young delm he was, and not by any means stupid. But Infreya was a beauty in her youth and his mother had died before tutoring him sufficiently in all the faces that treachery might wear.

"In any case, the child—young Tan Sim—went to Quiptic, and Quiptic's mines went to Rinork, in settlement of the contract fees." She paused, eyes closed, then shifted sharply in her chair, as if annoyed with herself, and continued.

"The loss of the mines was very close to a mortal blow in itself, but as I said, the young delm was no fool. With the leverage he gained from his alliance with Rinork, he thought to win certain short term—but decisive!—advantages in several trades. Very nearly, he brought Quiptic about. In the end, alas, it was a quirk of the Exchange which pushed the blade home. The clan was dissolved; the young delm hung himself. Infreya petitioned Rinork and received permission to adopt Tan Sim pen'Akla, who might well have one day been Quiptic Himself, as a child of the clan alone." She moved her shoulders.

"So, that tale. You may consider it located *here*, if your stories need locations. The other story you need to hear takes place at a tavern in far Solcintra Port, where one For Don chel'Gaibin cheated a certain young trader at a game of cards. The trader, understanding that the play had been underhanded, called his lordship to answer her on the field of honor." She sighed. "Young things. All is anguish and high drama. I doubt it ever occurred to her to call the games master and ask that he set the thing right, though she thought it many a time, after. No, it must be a duel. For Don, who was a fool besides being many years the trader's senior, accepted the challenge and chose pistols at twenty-four paces. They met at the appointed place, at dawn, their seconds in train. The duel itself was over in a matter of moments. The young trader had killed her man." She looked at Jethri, and there was nothing that he could read on her smooth, golden face.

"Depend upon it, Ixin was displeased. As was Rinork, of course. How they roared for Balance, though the witnesses to a soul swore it was fairly done and For Don the favorite for the victor—as the tavern wager book clearly showed! Well, you have seen how it is with Rinork and Balance. In any wise, nothing was owed and the price was met. Ixin sent me on the long route, to learn, as she would have it, common sense. By the time I returned to Liad, there were new scandals to occupy the gossips, and Rinork and Ixin had agreed not to meet. This evening was the first time we have done so, in more than three dozen Standards." She inclined her head, possibly ironic.

"All hail to you, young Jethri."

Jethri blinked, trying to picture a young Norn ven'Deelin, alone with her pistol in the dawn, facing down a man older and more skilled than she . . .

"Oh, aye," Master ven'Deelin said, as if reading his mind—though more likely, Jethri thought, it had been his unguarded face—"I was a sad rogue in my youth. But there—a mother has no secrets from her son."

Right. Jethri frowned at her. "If you please, Master Trader, how am I now your son?"

"Because I had told Rinork so, child—else their Balance would have been worth your life. An 'unregulated Terran,' 'prenticed to ven'Deelin or no, is nothing to give a Rinork pause in a rage." She moved a hand, showing him the litter of papers on her desk.

"When I and your true-kin wrote contract, it was with the best interest of the trade in our minds. I contracted to teach you the art, as well as a certain understanding of matters Liaden—this to improve and facilitate the trade, which is the duty of a master trader. Nowhere was it intended that you should take your death of this, Jethri Gobelyn. Forgive me, but, should you die, there will be damage dealt to more than those who value you for yourself. Pray bear this in mind the next time you befriend strangers in back hallways."

Jethri felt his ears heat. This whole mess was his fault, right enough. . .

"Have you other questions?" Norn ven'Deelin's voice cut through the thought.

Other questions? Only dozens. He shook his head helplessly, and chose one at random.

"Why did she—did Trader chel'Gaibin adopt Tan Sim? I mean, if the only reason her clan—"

"Rinork," said Master ven'Deelin.

He nodded impatiently. "Rinork—if the only reason Rinork started the kid in the first place was to trap Quiptic and steal his mines, then why did she care what happened to him?"

There was a small pause, during which Master ven'Deelin took some care about arranging the way her fingers nested against each other as she folded her hands together.

"An excellent question, young Jethri. I have often wondered the same. Perhaps it was merely self-preservation; if the child were left to be absorbed by whatever clan might take him, questions would possibly arise regarding the contract which had produced him, and whether certain parties could have been said to be acting in good faith.

"Or, perhaps, she could not bear to see of her blood—even

half-blooded—slide away into obscurity. They have a great deal of self-worth, Rinork." She moved her shoulders. "In the end, why does not matter. The boy was brought into the house of his mother and has been given an education and a place in the clan's business. I find him to be a young trader of note, in his talents far superior to the honorable chel'Gaibin heir." As careful as she had been in their folding, she unfolded her hands all at once, and put them palm-flat against the desk.

"It is late and tomorrow we trade early and shivary to meet the dawn, eh? As my fostered son, you will stand at my side and be made known to all. You will wear this—" She extended a hand; something gleamed silver between her fingers. Jethri leaned forward and took the small token: The Clan Ixin moon-and-rabbit, cast in—he weighed the thing thoughtfully in his hand—platinum, with a punch pin welded to the back.

"You will honor me by wearing that at all times," Norn ven'Deelin said, pushing herself to her feet, "so that all will know you for one of Ixin.

"In keeping with your new status, your course of study will be accelerated and broadened." Suddenly, amazingly, she *smiled*.

"We will make a Liaden from you yet, young Jethri."

DAY 107

✸ ✸

Standard Year 1118
Elthoria and Tilene

HE HIT THE BUNK with half his sleep-shift behind him, closed his eyes, touched sleep—and dropped it as the wake-up chime dinned.

"Mud," he muttered, pushing himself upright and blinking blearily at the clock across the room. It displayed a time more than an hour in advance of his usual wake-up.

"Mud, dirt, dust and pollen!" he expanded, and swung his feet over the edge, meaning to go over and slap the buzzer off, then get himself another hour's snooze.

He was halfway across the cabin on this mission when his eye caught the amber glow over his inbox. Frowning, bleary and bad-tempered, he changed course, and scooped a short handful of ship's flimsies out of the bin.

The top sheet was his amended schedule for the day, by which he saw he was presently in danger of being late for a "security meeting" with Pen Rel. He'd been late for a meeting with Pen Rel once, and had no ambition to repeat the experience. That being the case, he did turnabout and headed for the 'fresher, sorting pages as he went.

The second flimsy was from Cargo Master Gar Sad per'Etla, informing him that a crate had arrived and been placed in his personal bin. He nodded; that would be Khat's B crate. He'd need to check that out soon, if he could pry five personal minutes between lessons and trade.

The third flimsy was from Norn ven'Deelin and that one stopped him cold.

Greetings to you, my son. I trust that the new day finds you in health and high spirits. Pray bestow the gift of your presence upon me immediately you conclude your business with Arms Master sig'Kethra. We shall break our fast together and tell over the anticipated joys of the day.

Jethri rubbed his head. She was taking this mother-and-son thing serious, he thought and then sighed. After all, it was a matter of keeping her word. In a sense—no, he thought, mouth suddenly dry—in *fact* she had given him her name. And she'd expect him to set the same value on that priceless commodity as she did herself.

"Mud," he whispered. "Oh, mud and dust, Jethri Gobelyn, what've you got yourself into?"

"**AS YOU HAVE NO** doubt learned from your study of our route, we remain at Tilene for five more days. At the end of that time, we shall set course for Modrid, and thence the inner worlds, which, as you will readily perceive, is a change of schedule."

Jethri stifled a yawn and sipped his morning tea. There was caffeine present in the beverage, true enough, but he found himself wishing after a cup of true coffee—aye, and maybe a mug o'mite, too.

"You are disinterested," the master trader said softly, "and yet it is solely for the benefit of yourself that we alter our itinerary."

Soft it was said, yet it hit the ear hard. Jethri put his cup down, and looked at her.

"You do not approve?" she asked, face bland.

He took a breath, wishing he felt more awake. "Ma'am, it's only that I wonder why the ship's route needs to be changed on my account."

"An excellent question." She spread jam on her roll and took a bite. Jethri looked down at his plate, picked up a roll and tore it in half, releasing the scent of warm, fresh bread.

"It is understood that a son of ven'Deelin will need training which is not available to those of one ship, on a trade tour of the far outworlds. Thus, we plot a course nearer to the centers of civilization, where you may receive those things which you lack. You will, also, I hope, benefit by observing a different style of trade than that which is practiced along the edge." She picked up her teacup.

Roll forgotten in his hand, Jethri sat, thinking back on names and honor and Balance, and on his deficiencies as so far discovered. He cleared his throat.

"Ma'am," he said slowly, feeling his way around phrasing that she might find disrespectful of her honor. "I've been thinking and it—I don't think that I would be a—an exemplary son. Not," he amended quickly, as her eyebrows lifted quizzically, "that I wouldn't do my best, but—I wouldn't want to dishonor you, ma'am."

"Ah." She put her cup down and inclined her head. "Your concern speaks well of you. However, I know that it is not possible for you to dishonor me. I know you for a person of *melant'i*, whose every instinct is honorable. I repose the utmost confidence in you, my child, and I am at peace, knowing that you hold my name in your hands."

Jethri's stomach dropped, even as his eyes filled with tears. "Ma'am . . ."

She held up a hand. "Another way, then. Say that the dice have been cast—there is a similar saying in Terran, is there not? So. We play the game through."

Except that her good name was nothing like a game, Jethri thought—and he knew so little.

"Yes, ma'am," he said, trying not to sound as miserable as he felt.

"Good. Now, while we are in the mode of change—you will find your duty cycle has likewise changed. You will spend tomorrow and the following four days assisting Cargo Master per'Etla with the pods. It is mete that you have an understanding of the intricacies of the cargo master's art."

As it happened, he had a pretty good understanding of the cargo master's art, the *Market* not exactly shipping a cargo master.

He remembered sitting next to his father, staring in fascination while Arin worked out the logistics of mass and spin. Come to that, neither Paitor nor Grig was likely to have let him get away without knowing how to balance a pod. Granted, *Elthoria* could probably ship all *Market's* pods in one of hers, but the art of the thing ought to be constant.

Jethri cleared his throat. "I have had some training in this area, Master Trader," he said, hoping he had the right mix of polite and assured.

"Ah, excellent!" she said, spreading jam over the second half of her roll. "Then you will be more of a help than a hindrance to my good friend per'Etla."

Somehow, Jethri thought, that didn't sound as encouraging as it might have. He glanced down at the roll in his hand, and reached for the jam pot.

"I have some news from the Guild which you may find of interest," Norn ven'Deelin murmured.

Jethri glanced up from spreading jam. "Ma'am?"

"Another game of counterfeit cards has been exposed and closed, this at the port of Riindel."

He blinked, at a loss for a heartbeat, then memory caught up with him. "They weren't using your card, ma'am, were they?"

"Our card, my son. But no—you may put any fear of a taint to our *melant'i* aside. Those at Riindel had chosen to honor Ziergord with their attention."

Whoever Ziergord was. Jethri inclined his head. "I'm glad the wrongdoers were caught," he said, which had the advantage of being both true and unlikely to be found an improper response. "Surely any others who have been tempted will see that the . . . game . . . is dangerous and refuse to play."

There was a small silence. "Indeed, perhaps they will," Master ven'Deelin said politely.

Too politely, to Jethri's ear. He looked up, questioning, only to be met with a smile and a small movement of her hand.

"Eat your breakfast, my son," she murmured. "It will not do to be late to trade."

✖ ✖ ✖

BUSINESS WAS BRISK at the booth, with merchant folk and traders lined up to have a word of business with Master ven'Deelin. As near as Jethri could tell, every last one of them was invited to "dinner"—not that he had all that much time to eavesdrop, being busy with customers of his own.

Today, the textile was of interest. Over and over, he showed his samples, and gave his speech about hand looming and plant dyes. Occasionally, he caught what was—he thought—a careful glance at his new pin, claiming him of Ixin. Yet it was not curiosity which drew these people, it was the trade, and he reveled in it. Often enough, the client left him with a counter and a trade-card, which he took great care to keep paired and ordered on the wire above his station.

He hung the last pair up and looked down, face arranged politely, to greet the next in line—and froze.

Before him stood Bar Jan chel'Gaibin, hands tucked into his sleeves and a gleam in his pale eyes that reminded Jethri forcibly of Mac Gold in a mood for a brawl.

Casually, the Liaden inclined his head. "Good day to you, *son* of ven'Deelin. I bring you tidings of your friend, Tan Sim pen'Akla, who has been sent to make his way along the tertiary trade lanes, for the best good of the clan." He inclined his head again, snarky-like, daring Jethri to hit him. "I thought you might find the news of interest."

Teeth grinding, face so bland his cheeks hurt, Jethri inclined his head—not far.

"One is always grateful for news of friends," he said, which was about as far as he could trust his voice with Tan Sim thrown off his ship in sacrifice of this man's spite. . .

chel'Gaibin lifted his eyebrows. "Just so," he said softly, and with no further courtesy turned his back and walked away.

In the momentary absence of customers, Jethri let his breath out in a short, pungent Terran phrase, and turned his attention to the samples, which were sorely in need of order.

"Young Jethri," Master ven'Deelin said some while later, during a lull in the business. "I wonder if you might enlighten me as to a certain Terran—I assume it is Terran—phrase that I have recently heard."

Ears warming, he turned to look at her. "I will do my best, ma'am."

"Certainly, when have you ever failed at that? I confess myself quite terrified of you—but, there, I will give over teasing you and only ask: This word *sobe*. What is its meaning?"

He blinked. "Sobe? I do not think . . ."

"Sobe," Master ven'Deelin interrupted. "I am certain that was the word. Perhaps it was directed at the departing back of a certain young trader. Yes, that is where I heard it! 'You sobe,' was the very phrase."

"Oh." His ears were hot now, and well on the way to spontaneous combustion. "That would, um, denote a person of—who has no manners, ma'am."

"Ah, is it so?" She tipped her head, as if considering the merit of his answer. "Yes, the particular young trader—it could perhaps be said that his manner wants polish. A useful word, my son; I thank you for making it known to me."

"Yes ma'am. Um." He cleared his throat. "I note that it is not . . . a courteous word."

"Understood. In the High Tongue, we say, 'thus-and-so has *no melant'i*.' It is not a statement made lightly."

"No, ma'am."

She reached out and patted him on the arm. "We shall speak of these matters at greater length. In the meanwhile, I have extinguished the light for an hour. Pray do me the kindness of seeking out the booth of Clan Etgora—it will be the glass and star on the flag—and say to my old friend del'Fordan that it would ease my heart greatly to behold his face, and that he must, of his kindness, dine with us this evening. Eh? After that, you may find yourself something to eat. If I am not here when you return, light the lamp and do your part. Any who have need of me will wait a few moments." She cocked her head. "Is that understood, young Jethri?"

He bowed. "Master Trader, it is."

"Hah." Once more, she patted his arm. "We must teach you, 'obedience to an elder.' Go now, and take my message to del'Fordan."

THE TRADE LAMP was still out when he returned to the booth, just under an hour later. Despite this, there were two lines of traders waiting patiently, a long line on the Master Trader's side; and a much shorter on his.

Jethri hurried forward, reached up and turned the key, waiting until the disk glowed blue before he ducked under the counter and pulled back the curtain. He ran a quick eye over his samples, then bowed to his first prospect.

"Good-day to you, sir. May I be honored to bring to your attention to these examples of the textile maker's art?"

He was deep into his third presentation when Master ven'Deelin arrived, took her place and began to trade. It seemed to him, even from his side of the booth, that her cadence and attention were off a bit, as if she were bothered by a bad stomach or headache or other ill.

It was some hours before there was a lull sufficient for him to ask her if something was wrong.

"Wrong?" She moved her shoulders. "Perhaps not—surely not." Her mouth tightened and she looked aside and he thought she would say no more, but after a moment she sighed and murmured.

"You surprise, Jethri my son. It is nothing so definite as *wrong*—but there, you have a proper trader's eye for detail, and a sense of the rhythm of trade . . ." She moved a hand, fingers flicking as if she cast that line of chat aside.

"It came to me," she said softly, reaching to the counter to straighten a display book that didn't need it, "that perhaps a certain practice—which is not, you understand, entirely against guild rule— had lately surfaced upon Tilene. So, I betook myself to the Trade Bar to learn if this was the case."

Jethri looked at her, feeling a little chilly, of a sudden.

Master ven'Deelin moved her shoulders. "Well, and it is not entirely against guild rule, as I said. Merely, it is a measure found

. . . inefficient. . . and not clearly to the best interest of the trade." It seemed to Jethri that she sagged—and then straightened, shoulders thrown back with a will and a sparkle showing hard in her black eyes.

"Well, it is not ours, and never was. I had thought to meddle, but, there—the thing is done."

"But—" said Jethri, but just then a customer came up to his side of the booth, and he had no more chance to talk to Norn ven'Deelin for the rest of the long, busy day.

DAY 107

※※※※※※※※※※※※※※※※※※※※※※※※

Standard Year 1118
Elthoria and Tilene

MASTER TEL'ONDOR BOWED, low and extravagant, Honor to a
Lord Not One's Own, or so it read to Jethri, who was in no mood to
be tweaked, tutor or no. His head ached from a long day on the
floor, the spanking new shirt with its lacy cuffs foretold disasters
involving sauces and jellies across its brilliant white field. And now,
he was here to learn the way to go on at an intimate dinner for two
hundred of Master ven'Deelin's closest friends—all in the next
twelve minutes.

Curtly, he answered the Protocol Officer's bow—nothing more
than the sharpest and starkest of bows, straightening to glare
straight into the man's eyes.

Master tel'Ondor outright *laughed.*

"Precisely!" he crowed, and held his hand out, fingers smoothing
the air in the gesture that roughly meant "peace."

"Truly, young Jethri, I am all admiration. *Thus* shall impertinence
be answered—and yes, I was impertinent. Some you may meet—at
this gather this evening, or at other times—some may wish to
dazzle you, some may wish to take advantage. You would do well to
answer them all so—a ven'Deelin born would do no less."

Jethri considered him. "And what about those who merely wish to establish a proper mode?"

"Ah, excellent." Master tel'Ondor's eyes gleamed. "It will perhaps be done thus—" The bow between equals, that was. "Or this—" Child of the House of an Ally. "Or even—" Senior Trader to Junior.

"Anything more . . . elaborate, we shall say, may be viewed with the sharpest suspicion. I leave to you to decide—as I see your intuition is sound—the scope of your answers there."

Jethri closed his eyes. "Master tel'Ondor . . ."

"Yes, yes! You are to learn the entire mode of High House fosterling in the next eight heartbeats, eh? I will be plain with you, young Jethri—neither your skills nor mine are sufficient to meet this challenge. Demonstrate, if you please, your bow of introduction—yes. And of farewell? . . . adequate. Once more—yes. Now—of obedience?"

Jethri complied and heard the protocol officer sigh.

But: "It will suffice," Master tel'Ondor said, and moved his hands, shooing Jethri toward the door. "Go. Contrive not to shame me."

Jethri grinned and inclined his head. "Good evening, sir."

"Bah," said Master tel'Ondor.

HE NEEDN'T HAVE WORRIED about ruining his pretty new shirt with sauce stains or soup spots. It soon became clear that, while Master ven'Deelin expected her guests to eat—and eat well—from the buffet spread along three of four walls of the so-called Little Hall, she herself—with him a shadow attached to her left elbow—prowled the room, with the apparent intent of speaking with everyone present.

She did supply herself with a glass of wine, and insisted that he do the same, with instructions to sip when she did, then slipped into the crowd, where her headway went down to a step or two at a time, in between bows and conversation.

Jethri found the conversation singularly frustrating; spoken wholly in modes other than the mercantile, and much more rapidly than his half-trained ear could accommodate.

The exception to this was the beginning of every exchange, in which he was brought a step forward by a soft hand on his arm.

"One's foster child, Jethri," Master ven'Deelin would say, and he would make his plain bow of greeting. Then she would make him known to the person she was speaking with, who, almost without exception bowed as to the child of an ally.

He would then repeat their name, with a polite dip of the head, and the talk would jet over his head in a poetry of alien syllables.

A word or two here and there—he did catch those. Sometimes, a whole phrase unrolled inside his ears. Rarely enough to help him piece together the full sense of the conversation. He did find time to be glad that the default mode for facial expression was bland; at least he didn't have to pretend to be interested in what he couldn't understand. And he used his idle time to consider the scale and scope of the 'dinner party,' trying to figure what the point of it might be.

A gathering less like a common spacer's shivary would be hard to find, he thought. Where there'd be music and singing and boozing and smooching at a shivary, here there was the music of many different and low-key conversations. While everyone he could see had a wine glass in one hand, nobody seemed drunk, or even boisterous. And if there was any smooching going on . . . Well, frankly, he'd come to wonder how it was that any new Liadens got made.

"Good evening," a soft voice purred in his ear. Trade had never sounded so pretty, and Jethri jerked around and looked down, meeting a melting pair of gray eyes set at a slight angle in a heart-shaped golden face, framed by wispy gilt hair.

"Good . . . evening," he managed and bowed the bow of introduction. "Jethri Gobelyn. In what way may I serve you, ma'am?"

Her lips curved in a tightly controlled smile. "Parvet sig'Flava. I had in mind a way in which we might each serve the other, if you are of like mind. The evening grows tedious and I would welcome a . . . diversion. . . such as yourself." She swayed half a step forward, her melting gray gaze never leaving his face.

Jethri jumped back, ears burning. He'd just been propositioned for bed duty, or all Dyk's tales and teasing was for naught. That everything he knew on the subject was from tales and health tapes was due again to being juniormost. None of his cousins had wanted to bed the baby. . .

"Come," Parvet sig'Flava murmured—and he thought her voice was a little slurred, like maybe this wasn't her first, or even her third, glass of wine on the evening. "My ship departs within the two-day, and shall, regrettably, miss Tilene's Festival. So," she leaned toward him, her pretty face upturned to him like one of the flowers that Gaenor so missed from her home.

"So," she said again, "since we will be denied the opportunity to meet in the park, perhaps we may embrace Festival a few days early. Perhaps we might rent us an hour-room and have joy of each other before dawn calls us each to our duty."

"Ma'am, I—that is—"

"That is," Norn ven'Deelin's voice cut in over his stammer, and very firmly, too, "that this my son is needed at his station this evening, though he thanks you most sincerely for your offer."

"Indeed," Jethri grabbed at his lagging wits and inclined his head, very respectful. "I am flattered, ma'am, but duty calls."

She looked at him, gray eyes unreadable, then bowed, senior to junior, which was right enough, Jethri thought bitterly, though making him even more aware of the potential gifts she'd had on offer.

"I understand. Fair profit." She bowed then to Norn ven'Deelin, trader to master.

"Master Trader," she murmured and faded away into the crowd.

Ears on fire, and uneasily aware of the blood pounding in his veins, Jethri turned to face Norn ven'Deelin.

"Truly, young Jethri," she said softly, "you have a knack. No one less than the sig'Flava wishes to attach you. Indeed, you are a paragon." She moved her hand, inviting him to walk with her.

"Attend me, now. Later, we will speak of Festival and . . . those other . . . lessons which you may require."

"Yes, Master Trader," he murmured, feeling four kinds of fool, and not quite able to make up his mind whether he was more grateful to her for the rescue or aggravated with himself for needing one.

She patted his arm. "Softly, child," she said, and then used her chin to point out a certain black-haired gentleman in the crowd. "Look, there is del'Fordan's heir. We must make you known to him."

DAY 108

❀❀❀❀❀❀❀❀❀❀❀❀❀❀❀❀❀❀❀❀❀❀❀❀

Standard Year 1118
Tilene Docks

SCHEDULED TO MEET Cargo Master per'Etla on the stroke of
the shift-change, Pen Rel and Jethri arrived a dozen ticks or more
before time—unusual, Pen Rel being a man who valued punctuality.

The unusual was explained soon enough, as, Jethri at his shoulder,
Pen Rel inspected the dockside security cameras and checked the
duty clerk's roster of scheduled deliveries. After that was done, there
was still some time left over to wait.

Together, they leaned on the waist-high boundary wall, Jethri
trying not to yawn.

Tilene's docks, like many world-side docks, were covered
topside against the outside elements with sealable domes and great
sliding panels. Unlike worlds where the ambient temperature or
atmosphere was downright noxious, Tilene's docks were an integral
part of the city, with portions of local roads and transit lines running
through at odd heights.

As Pen Rel explained it, pointing here and there to make his
points, the expanse of stained 'crete they stood on—currently
crowded with modular bins destined for transshipment in *Elthoria's*

pods—was just a wide spot in an industrial ribbon that extended across the continent in both directions, being part of a celebrated world-spanning planned city. The tremble beneath them was not from starship generators but from the flow of traffic tunneled beneath the floor they stood on; the overhead transit sets joined them to flow as an artery across mountain, farm, and plains.

The wonder of it all was somewhat lost on Jethri, who didn't much care how Grounders got from place to place, though he did try to pay attention. Knowing Pen Rel, there'd be a test—and when he least expected it, too.

A low groan came from overhead. Jethri glanced upward, and saw the dome in motion, beyond it an empty and horrifying blue-green sky. Stomach churning, he started to look away, but a sudden glitter in the high air caught his gaze.

"'ware!" he yelled, jerking right out of the lean. Grabbing Pen Rel's arm, he spun toward *Elthoria's* ramp.

"Hold!" His own arm was gripped, none too gently. "It is merely water!"

Perforce, he froze, heart pounding, and in a few moments there came a massive splash as the falling sheets met the 'crete a pod's length away, and settled into a fading mist. Pen Rel released his arm.

"It must have rained overnight," he said, shockingly calm. "The water would have collected in the guide channels." As if it explained everything. Clearly he was not concerned, and probably thought Jethri an idiot, though, as usual, he didn't say so.

From the edge of his eye, Jethri saw some winged creature pass over head, and next a silver jetship lifting for the stratosphere. He quickly averted his gaze, staring instead at the waiting bins.

"Yes, there is much to see in a city!" Pen Rel, said, apparently agreeing with something Jethri was supposed to have said.

He took a hard breath.

"You pardon," he said, glad to hear that his voice held steady. "I wonder why they opened the dome. There are no ships preparing to leave, nor any warning of an incoming. . ."

Pen Rel glanced fearlessly upward, and then back to Jethri.

"Ah, I see. Proper ship-board concerns." He swept an arm over his head, encompassing not only the dome, but the wide, empty sky beyond. "One likes to keep control of the ports, the atmosphere, and access—and how is that to be done if birds are free to fly where they might?"

Jethri almost shook his head, the neck muscles protesting as he caught the motion and produced instead a small bow of acknowledgment.

"Ah," Pen Rel said again, and inclined his head. "Mostly, it is a matter of temperature control. How much simpler, after all, to let the wandering air take the heat away than to condition the dock entire."

"My thanks," Jethri said, remembering to keep his voice soft, his gaze stringently at dock level.

A dusty vehicle trailing modular pallets was arriving hastily at their section of 'crete, various warning beeps and the noisy whine of high power hybrid electric motors an active discouragement to conversation. The victualer's sigil on the side of the vehicle was familiar enough—Jethri had seen a half-dozen or more of the same type of van running up and down the concourse as they'd waited.

The driver swung his rig in a final semi-circle, stopping amidst the puddled remains of the recent downpour. The clerk looked up from his record-keeping with a grimace.

"Well before shift-change we ask for, and what do we get? Excuses and a delivery at the hour."

"It is always thus," Pen Rel said, and then in a lighter voice, "Jethri, turn about please."

Behind him and at very nearly his own height, stood a Liaden of indeterminate age. What most distinguished him was not his height, nor even the fact that he was out-and-out grinning, but his dark, wide-brimmed hat, which he failed to doff in greeting, though he bowed a sort of all-purpose greeting in Pen Rel's general direction.

"So, my friend. You bring to me the sudden son, that we may instill in him my sixty Standards of experience in sixty hours?"

His bow to Jethri was much more complex—layered, even: retainer to son of the house, master to adult student—and a hint of something else. There was a careful extravagance in his motion

Jethri put down to dealing with an awkward situation in good humor.

"Jethri ven'Deelin Clan Ixin, I—Cargo Master Gar Sad per'Etla—I welcome you to my dirt-side office. I advise you that we must hurry, for your new mother would have you ready to take any position on the ship at short notice. And, given my age, I suspect she means you to replace me soonest."

Jethri returned the bow as honestly as he could, junior to senior, with an attempt—he hoped subtle—at member of the house to retainer.

"All very pretty," Pen Rel said briskly, "but allow me to take my leave of both of you else the tradespeople will run me down." A quick bow, encompassing perhaps the entirety of the dock, its length and height, the cars beneath and the stars above, and he was off.

"We are here, young sir," the cargo master said after a moment, "to insure that you understand how the cargo department on *Elthoria* operates—and how it may vary from other tradeships you may be expected to deal with as one soon to be trading on your own. You will note that, on *Elthoria*, my department is responsible for all items coming on board, other than hand luggage."

"Now, let me ask you this: In all of your life, how many pods have you loaded?"

Later, it came to Jethri that perhaps the question had been intended rhetorically. Caught in the moment, however, he bent his brain to the count, frowning slightly at the victualers's van . . .

The cargo master laughed. If he'd been a Terran, Jethri would have considered him just a little dotty.

"No need to be embarrassed that you have no experience, young sir," the old man said.

"But I do, Master," Jethri interrupted. "I have never loaded an entire pod by myself, but in the last ten Standards I have done initial load checks on at least seventeen pods, and was final load check assistant on about the same number. I did the initial strap-downs on ten or so, and did net-string on a bunch of odd lots. I . . ."

"Enough!" Cargo Master per'Etla waved a hand. "I am cheered immensely! Now instead of needing to cover sixty years of knowledge in sixty hours we'll need only cover the final fifty-five years in sixty hours! We are saved!"

Despite himself, Jethri laughed.

"Ah, so now," the man in the hat went on, with a smile and a wink, "will you share with me? How came you by all this experience when you are so new to a house of trade?"

They leaned together on the boundary wall, per'Etla honestly interested in his charge's background. Periodically, he inclined his head, so slightly as to appear a nod, as Jethri explained how a family ship was unlikely to have a full-time cargo master and how at certain ports and with certain cargo, the entire crew might be pressed into the loading and offloading.

As he spoke, Jethri absently watched the food truck's driver using a lift-cart to offload pallets, which he deposited on the 'crete regardless of the puddled water or the marked driving lanes. Finally, he stacked them into a pile, and Jethri could see distance water dripping from the top pallets onto those lower in the pile—which pile he aimed in the general direction of the ship's dock as his lift-cart gathered speed.

Stopping in mid-sentence, Jethri pointed toward the incoming tradesman, whose approach was yet unnoticed by the clerk.

"The modules, master, contaminated in the dock-water!"

Master per'Etla glanced to the clerk, who was concentrating on his computer.

The master gestured toward the clerk, and then looked Jethri hard in the face. "What would you do, apprentice? The dock is yours to direct."

Jethri bowed quickly and strode forward, stepping into the gate and holding his hands up, palms forward, to stop the cart.

The driver appeared oblivious, then attempted to wave Jethri aside.

"Halt!"

The driver turned his rig so sharply that it tilted, pallets shifting, and finally came to a stop. He came off the seat angry, yelling so hard and fast that Jethri couldn't get more than the basic idea of what the guy was saying, which was close enough to fighting words.

Jethri found himself turning sidewise to the man, reacting automatically to the volume and the threat . . .

The driver got closer, and now the clerk was at Jethri's side, adding his voice to the general clamor, but no matter—it was suddenly like the deliveryman had gotten a good, hard look at one of the scarier ghosts of space.

Again his words came so quickly that Jethri wasn't completely sure of what they were, but the depth of the bows, and the number of them, convinced him that the driver was seriously sorry.

"I would say that your clan-pin was noted," said per'Etla quietly from his left side, "I suggest you continue with your instructions."

Jethri took a breath, and centered himself like Pen Rel was always tell him to do.

"These items here—" He pointed to the dripping edges of the pallets, to the wet tire tracks— "did you plan to bring them into the ship's hold that way? This is not some storeroom where the wind blows as it might. A ship must control its environment and avoid contamination. As a youth I once spent two dozen hours sealed in a space suit while a hold was decontaminated from a careless spot of walked-in goo. What will you have brought us on these?"

"Sir, pardon, I had not considered. Normally, I deliver to warehouses and such is not a difficulty. I mean no—"

"These cannot come onto the ship. Our clerk will contact your office and have replacements brought. These—" Jethri waved a hand, trying for one of Master tel'Ondor's showier effects— "I care not what you do with them. "

The clerk, whose name Jethri still didn't have, bowed and began to speak, sternly, to the driver.

Jethri turned his back on them both, feeling a little gone in the knees, and looked to the attentive cargo master.

"That is what I would do, were I directing the dock, Master."

The old man inclined his head.

"Indeed. I cannot argue with you entire; it is in fact the most efficient way to approach the problem, and the lesson was well given. But let me speak a moment."

Jethri took a deep breath, and inclined his head.

The master motioned him toward the open port and began walking. Jethri, perforce, followed.

"Our ship is, I suspect, somewhat larger than that of your family. True it is that the sheer random nature of the dockside might permit some contaminant—oh, what a wonderful word you have taught me!—some *goo* as it were, to belabor our air system or corrode our floors.

"There are measures we can take which would likely require none of us to be suited for a Standard Day, or even a Standard Hour. Some of these measures will be taught you—*must* be taught you— that you know the capabilities of *Elthoria*. But, for the moment, you are correct. The clerk ought to have been more alert, and I believe your lesson has taught him as well as the driver; I shall not belabor him more on this.

"Yet still, sir," the master continued, as they crossed the threshold into the ship's cargo port itself, "I ask you to riddle me this: what shall the master trader and the captain feed to their guests at luncheon?"

Jethri froze between one step and the next, face heating.

"Lunch?"

"Indeed." The cargo master laughed lightly. "I do believe that what you have turned back just now was the afternoon meal my friend Norn has ordered in for the local jeweler's shop association."

THE FLOW OF SCHEDULES was such that Jethri found himself in the hold, cargo deck, and pod-control offices more than in his regular haunts. When he saw someone he knew well—Pen Rel or Gaenor for example—they were usually going the opposite direction and in conversation with someone else. By day three, he'd nearly forgotten the incident with the lunch-truck; indeed, for two nights he'd dreamed cargo density patterns for three different pod styles, lading codes, and the structural dynamics of orbital pod transfer.

On his way to the dockside galley for a quick lunch—he still had to finish a test balance on the bulk—he ducked unwittingly by some-one ambling slowly down the 'crete.

"Ah," came Master tel'Ondor's familiar voice, "do you wish to avoid speaking with me as much as that?

Ears a-fire, Jethri ducked back, bowing a hasty apology.

"Your pardon, sir. My mind was on my numbers and my stomach on lunch."

"A compelling combination, I agree," the master allowed. "I rejoice to see you thus engaged upon the work of your house. You bring joy to your mother."

A test. Great. Jethri kept his sigh to himself and bowed, wincing only a little when his stomach audibly growled.

Master tel'Ondor moved a languid hand, motioning Jethri onward.

"Please, you have need. But first, let me congratulate you upon your defense of our ship at dockside."

Jethri stiffened. Not a lesson, then—a lecture.

"But no," said the master, apparently recognizing something in Jethri's face, despite his efforts to remain bland— "this is not a problem. The ship speaks well of you, as does the cargo master and the clerk. I am told that you had the mode perfectly in dealing with the incident. The cargo master insists that you were prepared to take a charge and repel boarders!"

He bowed, gently. "I wish merely that all the traders I have taught would have the sense you've shown. I believe you will be quite ready for the next part of your voyage!"

And with that, he swept his hand forward again, and Jethri went, thinking as much about inertial restraints as about lunch.

DAY 116

❀ ❀

Standard Year 1118
Elthoria

THEY WERE FOUR STANDARD DAYS out of Tilene, bound for Modrid. There, they'd do a couple days of fill-in trading and set course for the inner worlds.

Inner *Liaden* worlds, where somebody as Terran as a Jethri Gobelyn would speedily become a three-day wonder. At best.

Say that he worried; it was true enough. Gaenor and Vil Tor, together and separately, assured him that he'd do better than fine, but he considered that they might be a thought biased, being friends. Pen Rel sig'Kethra, who wasn't necessarily a friend, had responded to the news of their amended route by intensifying the self-defense sessions 'til they weren't much shy of a shore-leave brawl. Master tel'Ondor had done the same with the protocol lessons, though at least those didn't leave bruises.

And Norn ven'Deelin, who should've been as terrified of the whole business as he was—if not more so, having, as he blackly suspected, a much sharper understanding of what exactly *would* happen if he made hash out of things—Norn ven'Deelin smiled, and patted his arm, and called him her son, and said that she was certain he would acquit himself with honor.

All that being so, it was no wonder, Jethri thought, throwing back the blanket and slapping on the light, that he couldn't sleep.

He pulled on the most comfortable of his Liaden-made clothes— a pair of tough tan trousers, with a multitude of pockets, and an equally tough brown shirt—which was close enough to the coveralls that'd been standard ship wear on the *Market* to be comforting— slipped on a pair of soft ship slippers, and sorted through his pile of pocket stuff until he had his fractin, the Combine key and the general ship key. He slipped them into a pocket; a wrench set and folding blade into another and left his quarters.

There wasn't any need to sneak overtime studies on *Elthoria*, where the rule 'mong the crew was that the trader knew best what the trader required. He'd come to have a fondness for that rule, no more so than now, as he swung down the wide corridor toward his personal bin.

He'd several times over the last ten ship-days thought of the B-crate from home. Finding time to do something about it was the challenge there, his schedule being as crammed as it was.

Which made his present state of nervous sleeplessness nothing less than a gift, looked at in a certain way. At least he'd be able to open the crate at his leisure, and take care over those things his mother had said he should have.

He passed one other person on the way to the cargo section— Kilara pin'Ebit, who inclined her head, murmuring a polite, "Sir."

"Technician," he replied, and that was that—no muss, no fuss, as Dyk used to say—and a few minutes later was standing in front of his bin.

He touched the lock pad in the proper sequence; the door slid open, the interior lights coming up as he stepped into the room.

Lashed against the far wall was one Terran-standard B crate, looking like it'd taken the rocky route through an asteroid belt to reach him.

Releasing the netting, he knelt down, feeling in his pocket for the wrench set.

There was a dent the size of his head in the side of the crate. Frowning, Jethri ran his hand over it. B crates were *tough*, and the most likely outcome of taking a whack at one with a heavy object was that the object would bounce—unless it broke. Something hard enough to stave in the side of one . . .

"Must've got hit by a flying rock," Jethri muttered, fitting his wrench around the first tog.

There were a couple bad seconds with the third and sixth togs, which had gotten jammed when the crate deformed, but he finally got them loose, pulled the panel out, and leaned it against the wall.

Inside, the crate was divided into four smaller magnetically sealed compartments over one larger compartment. Jethri reached for the seal of the upper right hand compartment, then sat back, his hand dropping to his knee, fingers suddenly cold.

"C'mon," he whispered. "It's just kid stuff."

'cept it was kid stuff his mother had seen fit to take into custody, hold for more'n ten years before sending it all after him. Say what you would about Iza Gobelyn's temper, and no question she was cold. Say it all—and when it was said, the fact remained that she was a canny and resourceful captain, who held the best good of the ship in her heart. That being so, she would've had a reason, beyond her own personal grief, for locking his things away. And a reason for finally letting them loose.

He felt the scarebumps rise up on his arms—and then he laughed, breathy and a little too light. "Get a grip! What? You think Iza set you up for a double-cross, like one of Khat's scare-stories? She sent your stuff because it's yours by right an' Paitor talked her into doing the decent."

Which Khat hadn't said, but, then, Khat wouldn't. The more he thought on it, though, the likelier it did seem that such a conversation had taken place; he could almost hear Uncle Paitor's voice rumbling around inside his ears, comforting and comfortable.

Jethri leaned forward and pulled open the top right door.

A plain black purse sat in the center of the small space, a piece of paper sticking out of the fold. Slowly, he reached in and pulled the paper free; unfolded it and blinked at Khat's messy scrawl, laboriously spelling out, "Stinks Money."

Jethri sat back, a breath he hadn't known he was holding

escaping in a *whoosh*! He put the paper on his knee, flipped open the purse and counted out a ridiculous amount of Combine paper. All this, from Stinks? It was hard to believe. Harder, in the end, to believe that Khat could cheat the ship. A right stickler, Khat. In a lot of ways, he thought suddenly, she'd've made a good Liaden. He slipped the purse and the note into a pocket and looked back to the crate.

Feeling less spooky about the process, he opened the next door, withdrew a small metal box, and held it between his two hands. The metal was red-gold, burnished 'til it glowed. The sides were decorated—etchings of stars, comets and moons. Three fancy letters were etched into the flat lid, intertwined like some dirtside creepers—AJG. Arin Jethri Gobelyn.

The lock was a simple hook-and-eye; he slid it back with a thumb and raised the lid with care.

Inside, it was lined with deep blue velvet. Scattered 'round the velvet, like stars, were half-a-dozen expired Combine keys, a long flat piece of what might be carved and polished bone—and a ring.

He picked it up between thumb and forefinger. It was a massive thing—arrogant, if jewelry could be said to have attitude—the wide band engraved with stars, comets, moons—just like the side of the box. The top was oval, showing the stylized ship-and-planet of the official Combine seal.

Jethri frowned. His father hadn't been one to wear rings— plainly said, rings on a working ship were foolish, they had too much of a tendency to get caught in machinery and on rough edges. A commissioner, though—a commissioner might well wear a ring or a patch or somelike, to alert folks to the fact that here was some-body with connections.

The gold was cold and unfriendly against his skin. He put it back in the box and reached for the bit of bone.

As soon as his fingers touched it, he knew it wasn't bone. Cool and slick, the symbol repeating down one face eerily familiar, it felt just like his lucky fractin.

Frowning, he had that piece out of his pocket and put it side-by-side on his knee with the—whatever it was.

By eye and touch, the two of them were made of the same material. Not exactly scientific, but it would do for now. And the repeating symbol? The very same as the big doughnut-shape on the face of his fractin, set end-to-end down the whole length of the thing.

He picked it up and held it on his palm. Thing had some weight to it—heavier than you expected, like his fractin, which Grig had said enclosed alien workings. A sort of large economy size fractin, then, Jethri thought, smoothing his thumb over the soothing surface. That would have appealed to Arin, with his fascination with the regular sort of fractin. Jethri ran his thumb over it once more, then replaced it on its nest of old Combine keys, lowered the lid the put the box aside.

The next compartment gave up a pair of photocubes. He snatched one out, hands shaking, and flicked through the images quickly, breathless, then more slowly, as he registered that the pictures were of people he didn't know, had never seen. Spacers, most of them, but a few ground-based folk, too, the lot of them looking tired and wary. He put it down.

The second cube—that was the one he had expected, and missed, and wished for. Images of family—Arin, naturally, with the half-grin on his face and his hands tucked into the pockets of his coverall, broad in the shoulder and stubborn in the jaw, brown eyes sitting deep under thick black eyebrows. After that was Seeli, Cris; a picture of Dyk up to his elbows in some cooking project, and a manic grin on his round face; and another of a thin and serious young Khat, bent over a piloting simboard.

Another picture of Arin, with his arm around a woman that it took two blinks to recognize as Iza—the two of them laughing at some forever secret joke. Then a picture of a skinny kid, big eyes and his ears sticking out, coverall grubby, sitting on the floor of the galley at Arin's side, the two of them contemplating the mosaic they'd fitted together. Jethri grinned at the memory. They'd used three dozen fractins in that design, and held up dinner for primary shift, while Arin snapped close-ups from every angle, like he did with every design they'd built.

Still grinning, he clicked the button again, and came back to the first picture of Arin. He put the cube down and opened the last of the small compartments, discovering a notebook and a thick sheaf of hardcopy

Grinning wider, he pulled out the book, riffling the pages, seeing the meticulous lists that Jethri-the-kid had kept of imaginary cargo, imaginary sales, imaginary buys, all worked out with his father's help; each pretend deal discussed as seriously as if the merchandise and money were real. The pages fluttered toward the back, his eye snagged on a different script, and he flipped back. . .

Angular and as plain as printout, Arin's writing marched down the page in a simple list of ship names. Jethri ran a quick glance down the line, seeing names he was familiar with, names he wasn't—

WildeToad. He blinked, remembering the gritty yellow paper crackling in his, and the printout of a ship's dying.

Breaking clay . . .

And why had Arin been keeping a ship list in the back of a kid's pretend trade journal?

Jethri shook his head. A mystery for later—or never. Likely it had just been a doodle, on a shift when things were slow; or an illustration meant to go with a conversation long talked out and forgotten. Come to remember it, his father had often doodled in the margins of his book—he riffled the pages again, slower this time, catching glimpses of the odd shapes Arin had drawn to help his thinking along.

Jethri closed the book and reached for the hardcopy, already knowing they'd be the various rules for the games invented to put use to fractins.

Something was left behind, though—and Jethri let out a whoop, dropping the game rules unceremoniously to the floor. He'd almost forgotten—

A mirror no bigger than the palm of his father's hand, framed and backed in some light black metal. Except, the reflecting surface didn't reflect, not even the ghost a spacer might catch in the back of a work screen, which was his own face. As a kid, Jethri had amused himself periodically by trying to surprise the mirror into giving him a reflection, pressing his nose against the glassy surface, or leaving the device on a table top and sneaking up around the side, rushing forward at the last second, more often than not yelling "boo!" into the bargain.

But the mirror never reflected one thing.

What it did do, was predict the weather.

Not a gadget that'd be much use on a spaceship, some might say, and they'd be right. No telling that it was all that useful dirt-side, just at first. Between them, though, him and Arin had puzzled out the symbol system and by the time his father died and his mother locked the thing away with the fractins and his trade journal—by that time, if they was dirt-side, Jethri could tell with a glance whether rain was due, or snow; lightning or hail, and from which planetary direction it would come.

Grinning, he looked into the black, unreflective surface, for old time's sake, then slipped it away into his shirt pocket.

That left the big bin—no surprises, there.

Except it was a surprise—he hadn't remembered that there'd been so many. He opened the box and scooped up a handful of the cool squares, letting them run through his fingers, watching the shapes flicker, hearing the gentle clatter as the tiles tumbled against each other.

The second box was counterfeits and brokens—what his father had called the *ancillary* collection. Some of the fakes looked pretty good, until you'd held a couple genuine fractins, and saw how fine and precise they were, no rough edges, each notch in exactly the same place, no deviation. Once you had that experience, you were unlikely ever to mistake a fake for the real thing again.

He closed the box, looked back into the compartment . . .

A rectangular wire frame lay in the far back corner. He brought it out, surprised at how light it was. He didn't immediately place the metal, or the thing itself—a simple rectangle, sealed at the bottom, open at the top, the four walls gridlike. Not a big thing, in fact it looked to be about the size to—

He reached into the box holding the genuine fractins, fingered

one out and dropped it into the top opening. It slid down the rack
to the bottom.

Jethri smiled, eyeing the thing, figuring maybe fifty-sixty
fractins would fit in the frame. Why anybody'd want to slot sixty
fractins into a metal holder was another question—probably a new
game variation.

Still smiling, he yawned, and looked down at his wrist, stifling a
curse. He was scheduled to be in Master ven'Deelin's office, bright-
eyed, intelligent and *awake* in something less than five hours.

Moving quickly, he packed the fractins, sealed the lids and slid
them and the wire frame back into their compartment, along with
the game rules, his old trade journal, Arin's box, and the photocube
of the strange spacers and grounders.

Then, he resealed the crate, and netted it snug against the wall.

Rising, he slipped the purse into a side pocket. The photocube
was too big for any of his pockets, so he carried it with him, down
the hall and back to his quarters.

DAY 123

❀ ❀

Standard Year 1118
Elthoria
Modrid Approach

THE ALARM BOUNCED JETHRI out of sleep two subjective seconds after he hit the bunk.

He threw the blanket back and swung out immediately, having learned from his newly accelerated shifts that the best thing to do when the alarm sounded was get up and get the blood moving toward the brain.

His feet hit the floor and he rubbed his hands briskly over his face, trying to encourage the blood—or maybe his brain—and began to review his shift schedule. First thing was a breakfast meeting with Pen Rel, who wanted to talk about the theory of self-defense. Then, he needed to go over the list of Ixin's regular local trading partners, and a history of *Elthoria's* last six trading missions to Modrid, that Vil Tor had pulled for him. Gaenor's Terran lessons had gone on hold since the change of course, though they'd been managing impromptu sessions on the run; so, after his hour in the library, he was scheduled for a long session with Master tel'Ondor, and after *that*—

The door chimed, interrupting his thoughts. He snatched up his robe and pulled it on as he crossed the room and slapped the plate.

Gaenor stood in the hall, in full uniform. She bowed formally as the door slid open.

"The captain's compliments, Apprentice Trader," she said, speaking each word distinctly, so that he would have no trouble following her, though she spoke in a mode other than the mercantile. "You are invited to join the master trader at the trade bench as soon as convenient. The master trader bids you 'be sure to breakfast heartily'."

Jethri bowed his thanks and straightened to find her outright grinning. Her hand rose, making a sign he did not recognize. "At last, we have you in the thick of things! I will see you soon!"

Invited to the bridge by the captain to watch the master trader at her work, up close and personal? Jethri grinned a grin of his own, though he did remember to bow again, in light agreement. When he came up from that, she was gone, leaving him blinking at an empty hall.

He closed the door and ran for the shower, talking to himself as he soaped and rinsed.

"'kay, kid—you're going live crew on a live deck, ain't that something special? Watch the master and learn your heart out. . ."

He skimped a little on the dry cycle and bounded, damp, to the closet, pulled out a blue shirt and darker blue trousers and hurriedly dressed, pausing in front of the mirror to affix Ixin's pin to his collar and run hasty palms over his spiky, growing-out hair.

Grabbing his pocket stuff, he rushed from the room, heading for the cafeteria at just under a run, and wishing, not for the first time, that *Elthoria* kept 'mite available to its crew.

HE CHOSE HIS BREAKFAST not by what he wanted to eat, but by which lines were shortest at the serving tables. Fortunately, there were two lines for tea—tea being to Liadens what coffee was to Terrans; and his choice of the shorter one put him next to Pen Rel.

The arms master glanced to him, and bowed what looked to be the bow between comrades, which, Jethri thought, *had* to be him reading wrong. He made sure his answering bow was the perfectly safe and unexceptional junior to senior.

Pen Rel cocked his head to a side, and while it couldn't precisely be said that he *smiled*, there was a noticeable lightening of his usually stern face.

"I see that our schedule has been altered by the captain's order, young Jethri," he said, selecting a tea bottle from those on the table. "Never fear, we will pursue your studies as time—and the captain—allow us." He inclined his head. "Good shift to you."

"Good shift," Jethri answered, snagging a bottle for himself and moving off to an empty table to gulp down his meal.

HE MADE THE BRIDGE in good time, his fractin dancing between his fingers, and found Technician Rantel ver'Borith, who he had met a couple times in the library, waiting for him at the door.

"Apprentice Trader." She bowed, and handed him a pocket locator clip and an ear-and-mouth com. He put the button in his ear and smoothed the wire against his cheek. When she saw he was situated, Rantel put her hand against the door, and led him across the threshold, past Captain yo'Lanna, who glanced up and acknowledged their presence with a seated bow strongly reminiscent of Iza Gobelyn's usual curt nod to outsiders on her bridge, and down-room.

It was an eerily quiet bridge, with none of the cheerful chatter that had been common 'mong his cousins as they brought *Market* into approach. They went by Gaenor's station, she intent on her screens to the exclusion of all else. In fact, the bridge crew, to a man, sat in rapt concentration over their screens, monitors, and map displays.

Norn ven'Deelin sat at a station far removed from the captain, her nearest neighbor what looked to be an automatic weather scanner. She greeted him with a smile and tapped her finger on the arm of the empty chair beside her.

He slid in, finding the seat a bit tighter than he might have liked, and a thought too close to the floor, so that he needed to fold his legs around the base.

"Apprentice, you made excellent time," Master ven'Deelin said, very softly. "Your expertise will be required very soon. Now, if you please, we will familiarize you with the equipment. Please touch the blue switch—yes—now, press forward one click, and your console will come to observer status."

He followed her instructions carefully, feeling a tingle in the pit of his belly when the screen lit and the button purred static in his ear.

"Good," Master ven'Deelin said, her voice in his ear an odd, but definite, comfort.

"When you press again—which you will do, but not touch anything else—your board is now live and in tandem trade mode. That means you will be seeing what trades I see. The green boxes represent my offers. If you suggest an offer it will appear on my screen, and I will accept it or not." She paused.

"Now, if you go forward once more—which you will do now but not anything else—you are in the solo trade mode. In that mode you commit us as utterly as if I had signed my name on a contract or placed hard cantra on the counter." Another pause.

"Take a moment to study what the screen tells you, child."

Truth told, he needed a chance to study the screen. He bent forward eagerly, one hand fiddling with the fractin, the other curled into a fist on his knee.

The screen was beyond high info—it was *dense* info. At the bottom left corner was a schematic of *Elthoria*, full cans and cargo holds limned in green; empties colored red. Bottom right was marked *Funds* and showed a balance of zero. The top half of the screen was divided into columns—Incoming, Outgoing, Bids Made, Bids Taken, Bids Refused. Right now, there wasn't much action, but he thought the columns would start to fill up quick as soon as they came into Modrid's approach space.

His fractin slipped out of his fingers. He caught it before it had fallen far, palmed it, slipped it into his pocket—and looked up to find that Norn ven'Deelin had noticed his movement. He braced himself, waiting for her to ask what silly toy he had in his pocket; then she spoke and he realized that she had misunderstood his sudden movement.

"Forgive me. Please return your board to observer status with the reverse-ward clicks. Very good. Now, on either side of your seat you will find several tabs and buttons. I suggest you take some time with them until your hands know what they do—they are adjustments for length and height, for spin and—but you must discover them and adjust what is necessary, for we may sit for some time today."

He put his hands down, fingers discovering the advertised buttons and tabs. He quickly found that one button adjusted the inflation of his seat, and another the angle compared to the console, another the height of the seat relative to the deck, which allowed him to straighten his legs. Only the pilot's chair had these kinds of extra adjustments on the *Market*, and if a lowly 'prentice trader's observation chair was so equipped what must the captain have available? Meditatively, he cycled the chair to the very back of its track, then slowly forward.

". . . and when you are comfortable," Norn ven'Deelin murmured, "you will say something to me so that we know your com is working and at proper volume . . ."

Face burning, he locked the chair where it was and touched the button in his ear.

"Yes, Master Trader."

She smiled at him, gently. "Always the silver tongue, my child. Perhaps you will tell me what you think of the two offers at the top of the board, which came in as you were adjusting your chair."

Startled, he glanced at his screen and saw an offer to sell two MUs of cheese . . . he blinked, then laughed. Two MUs—that was two cargo pods!

"Ma'am, I'd tell the first one thanks but no thanks," he said, dropping into Trade. "At that price we'd need to be carting locally on a prepaid rush delivery—or we'd need to broker it on planet, and that's a time waster."

"Yes, thank you, we shall decline. And the second?"

That was harder, the offer being a half-can of specialty spices and herbs. Jethri frowned, mentally running through the manifests he had studied.

"Ma'am, in general I don't believe you have *Elthoria* carrying foodstuff," he said tentatively.

"Excellent," she murmured in his ear. "You see what they wish us to do—to broker this and that. Were we at leisure, perhaps I might allow myself—but this is not such a trip. Now, attend your controls once more."

He brought his attention to the console.

"You see the red tabs set on either side of the blue control wheel. For details of what is on offer, if needed, select the right, and again if need be—sometimes there are as many as a dozen detail levels. If these leave you uninformed, make a record—that is the left tab— and we will add it to our analysis list. Now, if you see something which you think I should note, click the yellow button above the wheel here—and I will have a highlight informing me."

Jethri began to nod, caught it and inclined his head. "I understand," he said, and looked at his screen, where two more offers had appeared in the Incoming column.

"Ah, good," the master trader said.

The run-in to orbit took several hours and for awhile he sat in observer mode, watching as she filed *Elthoria's* availables. As he'd suspected, the incoming offers picked up momentum as they moved further in. Teeth indenting lower lip, he bent forward, trying to move his eyes fast enough; caught an offer of a twelfth MU of compressed textiles—highlighted it, and heard her murmur, "Yes, that looks likely. However, there is history—we have not used that source for some time. There was a bad load. Watch and see if the price falls . . ."

The bridge behind them got busy—maneuvers as they entered planetary nearspace, or so he thought, and she said quietly in his ear—

"Please go to tandem. Note that we have emptied a pod entire; check on that textile and if it is still available highlight it for me . . . also, I have accepted a tranship of a half pod; that will show up as a block on your diagram about now . . ."

The original lot of textile was gone, but he found another near enough, and a better price, highlighted it, and continued down the list, as the incoming column filled, spawned an overflow column and did its utmost to overfill it. He highlighted an offer of raw lumber; another of frozen chicken embryos, billed as genuine Roque Eyeland Reds and a marvelous low price the seller was asking for them, if true.

"We have now the odd-spots to fill in three pods," Master ven'Deelin said. "You will finish Pod Seventeen—note your cubes and balance limits. Your credit draw is unlocked and our complete manifest is open to you. Do not purchase anything we already own without asking. Please click one forward now—yes. You are the buyer of record. If desirable items which will not fit into your space come to note, please highlight."

In moments, he was sweating, leaning over the screen, shoulders stiff with tension. The credit account showed a ridiculous number of *cantra* for him to draw on. He flicked down the lists, trying for density; found hand tools at a good price, reached to place his bid— and the lot was gone, snatched away by a quick-fingered trader on another incoming ship.

Frustrated, he went back to the list, found a case of Genuine Blusharie on offer, touched the tab for more information—and the item vanished from his screen, claimed by another.

He put his hand on the buy switch and hunched forward, breath maybe a little short—and suddenly there was Uncle Paitor, frowning at him from memory and delivering a lecture on "auction fever"— the urge to buy quickly in order to buy first, or to buy first in order to beat the market—and how a trader above all needed a cool head in a hot situation.

Carefully, Jethri sat back and eased his hand off the switch. He flipped back through the items that had been on offer for awhile— and smiled. Reasonable cost, good density, real wooden products that would likely sell in both Terran and Liaden markets. Yes. He reached out and pushed the buy button.

The screen blinked at him; the offer accepted, the trade made. Jethri nodded and returned to the list, calmer for having committed some of his capital to solid stock.

The diagram at the bottom left showed Pod Seventeen

ninety-two percent full. He could use something like that twelfth of textiles, or maybe some stasis wheat. . .

Concentrating, he barely noticed when *Elthoria* achieved orbit, though he did register Gaenor's voice, speaking over the intercom.

It seemed that the offerings were coming in slower now; he had time to access the deep infoscreens. He highlighted several, and heard the master trader murmur once, "Excellent," and, again, "I think this is too large a quantity to carry in, Apprentice."

Pod Seventeen glowed green in the diagram—full. He blinked, and sat back, felt a light touch on his sleeve and looked over to Norn ven'Deelin. She smiled.

"If you buy anything more, my son, you will be buying for yourself. We have done well, you and I. Now, I suggest a meal, if you will honor me."

Now that he thought about it, he was hungry, Jethri realized. Carefully, he shut down his console, slid the chair back on its track and looked around.

About a third of the bridge crew was gone, relieved while he sat over his console, their work done while his continued. Gaenor's station was empty; at the far end of the bridge, the captain sat his board.

Jethri rose, cleared the chair's settings in case someone followed him in it, and walked with Norn ven'Deelin toward the door. She reached out and put her palm against the plate—

"Master Trader." Captain yo'Lanna had spun his chair and was looking at them, his face empty of any emotion that Jethri could read. "A moment of your time, if you will."

Master ven'Deelin sighed, largely. "Bah. Details, always details." She patted his arm. "Go—eat. When you are through, present yourself to Pen Rel and learn about those things he considers it prudent for you to carry portside here."

"Yes, ma'am." He inclined his head and she hurried away.

He touched his ear, remembering the comm, and looked to the officer on deck.

"Keep it, of your kindness, Trader," he said. "Doubtless, you will have need of it again."

That warmed him, and he slipped the comm off and stowed it in a pocket.

From across the bridge came the master trader's voice, sounding outright irritated. Jethri paused, frowning. He was beginning to be able to follow her quicker conversations, and this one was fraught with words sounding like, "Vouch for every transaction?" "Recertification is absurd!" and "I will speak to the Guild, and I am a master!"

None of that sounded like business for a 'prentice, and, besides, he'd been given his orders and his course—lunch; then Pen Rel.

He strode out and away from the bridge, feeling something just this side of a headache and just that side of an earache trying to form. Despite which, he did note that he was in possession of a good deal more information about his ship and its business than he had before this shift.

It was off-schedule for lunch, but the second cook filled him a plate of goodies, which he ate by himself in the empty cafeteria, mulling over the cargo buys that had gotten away.

DAY 125

※ ※

Standard Year 1118
Modrid

THE TRADING TOUR of Modrid went at lightspeed, with Jethri doing nothing more useful than stand at the master trader's elbow while she negotiated for luxury pieces and high-sell items—gemstones, wines, porcelains, and three packs of what were billed as "playing cards" that cost twice what the rest had, total.

"So, now, that is done," Master ven'Deelin said, turning away from the last table, and motioning him to walk with her. "What did you learn, young Jethri?"

"Well," he said, thinking over her approach, the deft assurance with which she had negotiated—it had been like watching a play-act, or a port bully shaking down a mark. "I learned that I have a fair distance to go before anyone mistakes me for a master trader."

"What's this?" She threw a bright black glance into his face. "Do you aspire to silver tongue after all?"

He blinked at her. "No, ma'am—at least, not unless it's something you think I should learn. I was merely trying to convey that I am all admiration of your style and skill."

"Worse and worse!" She put her hand on his sleeve. "As to

whether it is something you should learn . . . You should know how to flatter, and you should cultivate a reputation as one who does not flatter. Do you understand me?"

He thought he did, as it seemed to echo something of Master tel'Ondor's philosophy of bows.

"A reputation as someone who does not flatter is a weapon. If I . . . am required to flatter someone in order to gain advantage, then they will know me to be sincere, and be disarmed."

Her eyebrows lifted, and her fingers tightened, exerting brief pressure before she withdrew her hand.

"You learn quickly, my child. Perhaps it will not be so long until you wear the amethyst." She waved her hand, perhaps by way of illustration, the big purple ring flashing its facets.

"We will now adjourn to Modrid trade hall to set you properly on the path to glory."

Which could, Jethri thought, mean just about anything.

"I would be interested," she said as they walked on, "in hearing your opinion of our last items of trade, if you would honor me, young Jethri."

He thought back to the decks—sealed with a pale blue ribbon and a blot of wax. The vendor had set the price at two kais per and Master ven'Deelin had barely dickered at all, taking him down to one kais six per more as a matter of keeping her hand in, as it seemed to Jethri, than because she had thought the original price over-high.

"I could not see the seal properly from where I stood, ma'am," he said slowly, "but I deduce that the decks may have been bought for certain collectors of your acquaintance, who set a high value on sealed decks from gaming." He paused, considering the price again, and added. "It may be that these particular decks are a rarity—perhaps from a gaming house which no longer operates."

"Hah." She inclined her head slightly. "Well-reasoned, and on point. We have today purchased three decks of cards made for the Casino Deregar, which had been built in the depleted mining tunnels of an asteroid, and enjoyed much renown until it disintegrated some twenty-three Standards ago. We are very fortunate to have found three in their original condition, and at a price most commonly paid for broken decks."

Her praise warmed him, and he nearly smiled, which would never do, out here in public. He took a second to order his face before he asked, "How are the broken decks pedigreed?"

"An excellent question!" Master ven'Deelin said as they passed a food stall. The spicy smell woke Jethri's stomach, as they moved on, walking briskly. "Deregar cards are most distinctive. I have a broken deck aboard *Elthoria*. When we return, you must examine it. Ah, here we are! I ask your indulgence for a short time more, my son, and then we will provide us both with a well-deserved meal."

Jethri felt his ears warm. He hadn't thought his stomach's complaint had been that loud!

Master ven'Deelin paused before a large metal door, and swiped a card through the scan. The light clicked from yellow to orange, and the door opened. She strolled through, Jethri at her heels.

Inside, he paused, somewhat taken aback by the scope of the thing. The hall stretched out, the ceiling just this side of uncomfortably high, with long vents cut into it, allowing the outside light to fall through and down to brighten up the red stone floor. The walls were white and nubbly. A long wooden ledge has been built into the right-hand wall, a light red cushion laid along its length. The left wall was covered in a large tapestry of surpassing ugliness, which was undoubtedly, Jethri thought, catching the tell-tale signs, handmade—and probably historic, too.

Along the back wall was a wooden counter, and that was what Master ven'Deelin was on course for, her boots making little gritty skritches against the stone floor.

Jethri stretched his legs to catch up with her, passing through pockets of sunlight, and caught up just as she put her hand over a plate built into the counter.

Somewhere far back, a chime sounded. A heartbeat later, a young man in an orange jacket embroidered with the sign of the Liaden Trade Guild stepped to the other side of the counter and inclined his head respectfully.

"Master Trader. How may I serve you?"

"I wish to speak with the hall master. You may say that it is ven'Deelin who asks it."

The head-tip this time was a little deeper, Jethri saw, as if 'ven'Deelin' was worth an extra measure of respect even above 'master trader.'

"I will inform the hall master of your presence. A moment only, of your goodness."

He vanished back the way he'd come. Master ven'Deelin moved her shoulders and looked up at Jethri, though he hadn't said anything.

"Soon, my child. This should encompass but moments."

He was going to tell her that he wasn't *that* hungry when the door at the end of the counter opened and the man in the orange jacket bowed.

"Master Trader. Sir. The hall master is honored to speak with you. Please, attend me now."

"MASTER TRADER VEN'DEELIN, well-met." The man who stood up from behind the glossy black desk was white-haired; his face showing lines across his forehead, by his eyes, around his mouth. He stood tall and straight-backed as a younger, though, and his eyes were blue and clear.

"I am Del Orn dea'Lystra, master of Modrid Trade Hall. How may I be of service to you?"

"In a small matter of amending the record, Hall Master. I am embarrassed that I must need bring it to your attention. But, before we continue, allow me to introduce to you my apprentice, Jethri Gobelyn." She moved a hand, calling the hall master's attention to Jethri, who tried to stand tall without looking like a threat. He might have saved himself the trouble.

Hall Master dea'Lystra's clear blue eyes turned chilly, and he didn't bother to incline his head or take any other notice of Jethri other than, "I see," directed at Master ven'Deelin.

"Do you?" she asked. "I wonder. But! A hall master is not one who has many moments at leisure. Allow me, please, to proceed directly to my business."

The hall master inclined his head, granting her permission with, Jethri thought, a noticeable lack of enthusiasm.

"So," said Master ven'Deelin. "As it happens, *Elthoria* achieved orbit yesterday. We, of course, took advantage of the time incoming to place goods and make purchases." She moved her hand, once again showing Jethri to the hall master, who once again didn't bother to look.

"At my direction, and using his assigned sub-account, this my apprentice did make numerous purchases. And yet, when the trading was done and recorded, what do I have but a message from Modrid Trade Hall, demanding that I recertify all the purchases made by my apprentice, at my direction, using the proper codes." She inclined her head, slightly.

"Clearly, something has gone awry with the records. I would ask that you rectify this problem immediately."

The hall master moved his shoulders and showed his hands, palm up, in a gesture meaning, vaguely, 'alas'.

"Master Trader, I am desolate, but we may not allow a Terran guild status."

"May we not?" Master ven'Deelin asked, soft enough to send a chill running down Jethri's neck, if the hall master didn't have so much sense. "I wonder when that regulation was accepted by the masters."

Hall Master dea'Lystra bowed, lightly and with irony. "Some things are self-evident, I fear. No one disputes a master trader's right to take what apprentice she will. Guild status is another consideration all together." He spared Jethri a brief, scathing stare. "This person has no qualifications to recommend him."

Like being Norn ven'Deelin's 'prentice wasn't a qualification? Jethri thought, feeling his temper edge up—which was no good thing, the Gobelyns being known for their tempers. He took a breath, trying to swallow it, but then what did the fool do but incline his head and say, like Master ven'Deelin was no more account than a dock monkey, "I trust that concludes our business. Good-day."

"No," Jethri heard his own voice say, in the mode between traders, "it does not conclude our business. Your assertion that I have no qualifications pertinent to the guild is, alas, in error. I hold a ten-year key from the Terran Combine."

Out of the corner of his eye, he saw Master ven'Deelin throw him a stare. The hall master moved his shoulders, indifferent.

"Produce this ten-year key," he said, and his mode was superior to inferior, which was no way to cool a het-up Gobelyn.

Jethri reached inside his collar and pulled the chain up and over his head, holding it high, so the key could be plainly seen.

"If you will show me your Combine computer, I will verify that it is in fact a valid key, registered—"

"It is a matter of indifference to me and to this hall," Hall Master dea'Lystra interrupted, "who holds the registration for that key." He turned back to Master ven'Deelin.

"Master Trader, good-day," he said, trying to be rude, now, or so Jethri heard it.

Norn ven'Deelin didn't budge. She did cock her head to a side and look thoughtfully, and maybe a touch sorrowfully upon the hall master.

"You, the master of Modrid Trade Hall, give as your judgement that the possession of a Combine key is insufficient to demonstrate that the trader who holds the key is qualified to stand as an apprentice in the Guild. Is that correct?"

Hall Master dea'Lystra inclined his head.

"The master of Modrid Trade Hall gives as his judgement that possession of a Combine key is insufficient to demonstrate that the Terran who holds the key is qualified to stand as an apprentice in the Guild. *That* is correct."

Master ven'Deelin inclined her head. "That is most wonderfully plain. My thanks to you. Jethri, attend me, of your kindness."

Of course, he had to attend her—he was her 'prentice. Still, thought Jethri, following her out the door and down the hall, he would have welcomed the opportunity to put some of Pen Rel's lessons to the test, with Hall Master dea'Lystra as his subject.

"Peace, child," Master ven'Deelin murmured as they marched across the wide entrance hall. "A brawl is neither seemly nor warranted."

"Not seemly," Jethri said, keeping his voice low, "but surely warranted, ma'am."

The only answer was a soft, "Young things." Then they were at the door and through it, back on the noisy, odoriferous street.

"Come," she said. "There is a very pleasant restaurant just down this next street. Let us bespeak a booth and a nuncheon, so that we may be comfortable, and private, while you tell me the tale of that key."

THE "BOOTH" WAS MORE like a well-appointed small room, with comfy seats, and soft music coming out of a grid in the wall, and a multi-use computer within reach at a corner of the table.

Master ven'Deelin called for wine, which came quickly, and gave the order for a "mixed tray", whereupon the server bowed and went away, closing the booth's door behind him.

"So," Master ven'Deelin poured wine into a glass and set it on the table by Jethri's hand, before pouring another glass for herself. "This Combine key, child. May I have the honor of seeing it?"

For the second time in an hour, Jethri slipped the chain over his head. He put the key into Master ven'Deelin's palm and watched as she considered the inscription on the face, then turned it over and read the obverse.

"A ten-year key, in truth. How came you to have it?"

Jethri fingered his wine glass—and that wouldn't do at all, he thought suddenly. Master tel'Ondor would pin his ears back good if he caught him fidgeting in public. Casually, he released the glass and folded his hands in bogus serenity on the table top, looking straight into Norn ven'Deelin's amused—he would swear it—black eyes.

"As an apprentice on *Gobelyn's Market*, I brought a favorable buy to the attention of the trader. A remaindered pod, it was, and more than a third of it *vya*, in stasis. I knew Ynsolt'i was on the schedule, and I thought it might do well there. Uncle Paitor said, if it did, he would sponsor a key." He glanced down at the table, then made himself look back to her eyes. "A ten-year key—that was unexpected, but the *vya* had done—very well for the ship."

"Hah." Master ven'Deelin put the key on the table between them and picked up her wine glass.

"What else was in the pod?"

He frowned, trying to remember. "A couple of crates of broken porcelain—plates and cups, we thought. Cris sold the pieces to an art co-op—that covered what we had in the pod. Some textile—that was a loss, because there had also been . . . a syrup of some kind, which had escaped its containers. The porcelain and the vya cans both were double-sealed, and the syrup was easily rinsed off the outer cases with water. The textile, though. . ." He sighed, still regretting the textile, and reached for his wine glass, taking a tiny cautious sip.

Dry, bitter with tannin, and—just as he was about to ask for water—a surprising and agreeable tang of lemon.

Across from him, Norn ven'Deelin smiled a small smile. "You approve of the wine?"

'Approve' didn't exactly seem to cover it, though he found himself anticipating his next sip. "It's—unexpected," he offered, tentatively.

"Indeed it is, which is why we drink it in your honor." She raised her glass in a tiny salute and sipped, eyes slitted.

"Yes, excellent." Another sip, and she set the wine aside, leaned forward and tapped the power switch on the multi-use. The screen snapped live; she ran her guild card through the slot, then typed a rapid string of letters into the keyboard. Jethri raised his wine glass.

The multi-use clicked, loudly, and a drawer popped out of its face, displaying an indentation that could only accommodate a Combine key.

Jethri lowered his glass.

Master ven'Deelin touched his key with a delicate forefinger. "You permit?"

Well sure, he permitted, if only to watch the multi-use in action. He'd never seen such a—he inclined his head.

"I believe I see a theme," he said, and moved his hand in the "sure, go ahead" gesture. "By all means, ma'am."

Deftly, she had the key off its chain and pressed it into the indentation. The multi-use hesitated a moment, then emitted a second *click* as the drawer withdrew into the face of the machine.

There was a moment of inaction, then the screen flickered and displayed the key's registration code, registered to one Jethri Gobelyn, with 'free trade' checked instead of a ship name. A trade history was indicated. Master ven'Deelin touched the access key.

There, written out in a few terse sentences, was the *vya* deal, with himself listed as acquiring trader and Paitor Gobelyn assisting, which was, Jethri thought, eyes stinging, more than good of Uncle Paitor.

Master ven'Deelin touched the access key once more and there was the cellosilk sale, Cris Gobelyn acquiring, Jethri Gobelyn assisting. No more history was available.

"So." She typed another string of letters, the multi-use clicked one more time and the drawer extruded. When the key was removed, the drawer disappeared back into the console's face. Jethri remembered his wine and had another sip, anticipating the lemon note.

Master ven'Deelin threaded his key back onto the silver chain and held them out. He slipped it over his head and tucked the key into its usual position inside his shirt.

"Del Orn dea'Lystra is a fool," she said conversationally, picking up her glass.

Jethri paused with his hands at his collar. "You won't let him get away with—ma'am, he insulted you!" he blurted.

Her eyebrows lifted. She sipped her wine and put the glass down. "No more than he insulted you. But tell me, my son, why did you not show me this key ere now?"

His face heated. "Truthfully, ma'am, I didn't think to do so. The key—I had not understood Trader Gobelyn's—his *melant'i* in the matter. I saw the key as a—sop, or as a going-away present, and of no interest to yourself."

There was a small silence, followed by a non-committal, "Ah."

In his experience, Master ven'Deelin's 'ah' was chancy ground. Jethri sipped his wine, determined to wait her out.

"You raised the question of Balance," she said eventually. "It seems to me that the failure of *Elthoria* to any longer stop at a port which had realized some profit from her presence is not too strong an answer. A port that will not alter itself to accommodate the trade—that is not a port *Elthoria* cares to accommodate."

He gaped at her. "You're going to cut them off?"

She looked at him serenely. "You think the Balance too stringent? Please, speak what it in your heart."

He thought about it, frowning down at the composite table top. Consider a fool of a hall master, he thought, insulting a master trader, insulting a master trader's apprentice, thereby calling into question the master trader's judgement, if not her sanity—and then there had been the by-play about the masters not having accepted the no-Terrans rule . . .

Jethri looked up, to find her gazing thoughtfully upon him.

"On consideration," he said slowly, "I think it an appropriate Balance, Master."

She inclined her head, by all appearances with serious intent. "My thanks, young Jethri. It shall be done—on behalf of ourselves and the trade."

A chime sounded, discretely, and the door opened to admit their server, bearing a tray laden with foodstuffs, most of which, Jethri's stomach announced, smelled *wonderful*.

"Indeed," said Master ven'Deelin. "We have done work this day, my son. Now, let us relax for an hour and enjoy this delightful repast, and speak of pleasant things."

DAY 135

✺✺✺✺✺✺✺✺✺✺✺✺✺✺✺✺✺✺✺✺✺✺✺✺

Standard Year 1118
Elthoria

THE PATTERN OF HIS STUDIES changed again, with more emphasis on the modes of High Liaden, which meant more time with Master tel'Ondor and much more time with the language tapes—even tapes that played while he slept!

Despite the frenzy, he and Gaenor and Vil Tor had managed to meet in the cafeteria to share a meal—late-shift dinner for Jethri, on-shift lunch for Vil Tor and mid-sleep-shift snack for Gaenor.

"So, you will be leaving us for a time," Vil Tor said. "I am envious."

"Not I," Gaenor put in. "Tarnia frightens me to death." She glanced up, catching the edge of Jethri's baffled stare. "She frightens you, too, does she? I knew you for a man of good sense!"

"Indeed," he stammered. "I have no idea who the gentle may be. As for leaving you—why would I do such a thing?"

"Has the master trader's word no weight with you, then?" Gaenor asked, while Vil Tor sent a speculative glance into Jethri's face. "In that wise, you have no need to fear Tarnia. ven'Deelin will have you first."

"Don't tease him, Gaenor," Vil Tor said suddenly. "He hasn't been told."

She blinked at him. "Not been told? Surely, he has a need to know, if only to have sufficient time to properly commend himself to his gods."

"I was told," Jethri said, before his leg broke proper, "that we would be visiting an old friend of Master ven'Deelin's, who is delm of a house on Irikwae."

"Then you have been given the cipher, but not the key," Gaenor said, reaching for her tea. "Never fear, Vil Tor and I will unlock it for you."

Jethri looked to the librarian, who moved his shoulders. "Stafeli Maarilex has the honor to be Tarnia, which makes its seat upon Irikwae. She stands as the ven'Deelin's foster mother, even as the ven'Deelin stands foster mother to you."

So now I have a foster-granmam? Jethri thought, but decided that was taking silly too far into nonsense.

"Who better, then," Gaenor said, jumping in where Vil Tor had stopped, "to shine you?"

Now I have a foster-granmam. He sighed, and frowned down at his dinner plate.

"No, never put on such a long face!" Vil Tor chided. "Irikwae is a most pleasant world and Tarnia's gardens are legendary. You will enjoy yourself excessively, Jethri."

He bit his lip, reminding himself that Vil Tor meant well. It was just that—well, him and Gaenor and—all of *Elthoria's* crew, really—were grounders. They all had homes on *planets*, and it was those homes, down 'midst the dust and the mud and the stinks, that they looked forward to going back to, when *Elthoria's* run was through.

Well, at least the visit wouldn't be long. He'd been over the route *Elthoria* would take through the Inner Worlds, Master ven'Deelin having made both route and manifest a special area of his studies since they'd quit Modrid, and knew they was scheduled for a three-day layover before moving on to Naord. What kind of polish the old lady could be expected to give him in such a short time wasn't clear, and Jethri took leave to privately doubt that he'd take much shine, anyway. Still, he guessed she was entitled to try.

The hour bell sounded and Vil Tor hurriedly swallowed the last of his tea as he pushed back from the table.

"Alas, duty," he murmured. "Gaenor—"

She waved a hand. "Yes, with delight. But, go now, dear friend. Stint not."

He smiled at that, and touched Jethri on the shoulder as he passed. "Until soon, Jethri. Be well."

Across the table, Gaenor yawned daintily. "I fear I must desert you, as well, my friend. Have the most enjoyable visit possible, eh? I look forward to hearing every detail, when you are returned to us."

She slipped out of her chair and gathered her empties together, and, like Vil Tor, touched him on the shoulder as she left him. "Until soon, Jethri."

"Until soon, Gaenor."

He sat there a little while longer, alone. His dinner wasn't quite eaten, but he wasn't quite hungry. Back at quarters, he had packing to do, and some bit of sleep to catch on his own, his regular shift having been adjusted in order to accommodate a morning arrival, dirt-side. Wouldn't do to show stupid in front of Master ven'Deelin's foster mother. Not when he was a son of the house and all.

Sighing, and not entirely easy in his stomach, he gathered up the considerable remains of his meal, fed the recycler and mooched off toward quarters, the fractin jigging between his fingers.

DAY 139

❀❀❀❀❀❀❀❀❀❀❀❀❀❀❀❀❀❀❀❀❀❀❀❀

Standard Year 1118
Irikwae

IRIKWAE WAS HEAVY, hot and damp. The light it received from its primary was a merciless blare that stabbed straight through the eyes and into the skull, where the brain immediately took delivery of a headache.

Jethri closed his eyes, teeth clenched, despite being only inches away from a port street full of vehicles, all moving at insane velocity on trajectories that had clearly been plotted with suicide in mind.

"Tch!" said Master ven'Deelin. "Where have my wits gone? A moment, my child."

Through slitted eyes, he watched her bustle back into the office they had just quit. In the street, the traffic roared on. Jethri closed his eyes again, feeling the sun heating his scalp. The damp air carried a multitude of scents, none of them pleasant, and he began to hope they'd find that Master ven'Deelin's friend wasn't to home, so they could go back to *Elthoria* today.

"Here you are, my son. Place these over your eyes, if you will."

Jethri opened his eyes to slits, saw a tiny hand on which a big purple ring glittered holding a pair of black-lensed spectacles under his nose. He took them, hooked the curved earpieces over his ears, settled the nosepiece.

The street was just like it had been before he put the glasses on, except that the brutal sunlight had been cut by a factor of ten. He sighed and opened his eyes wider.

"Thank you, ma'am."

"You are welcome," she replied, and he saw that she wore a similar pair of glasses. "I only wish I had recalled beforetime. Have you a headache?"

It had faded considerably; still . . .

"A bit," he owned. "The glasses are a help."

"Good. Let us then locate our car—aha!—it arrives."

And a big green car was pulling up to the curb before them. It stopped, its driver oblivious to the horns of the vehicles in line behind—or maybe, Jethri thought, she was deaf. Whichever, the back door rose and Master ven'Deelin took his arm, urging him forward.

The inside of the car was cool, and dim enough that he dared to slip his glasses down his nose, then off entirely, smiling at the polarized windows, while keeping his eyes off the machinery hurtling by. Prudently, he slipped the glasses into the pocket of his jacket.

"Anecha," Master ven'Deelin called into the empty air, as the car pulled away from the walk and accelerated heedlessly into the rushing traffic, "is it you?"

"Would I allow anyone else to fetch you?" came the answer, from the grid set into the door. "It has been too many years, Lady. The delm is no younger, you know."

"Nor am I. Nor am I. And we must each to our duty, which leaves us too little time to pursue that for which our hearts care."

"So we are all fortunate," commented the voice from the grid, "that your heart cares so well for the trade."

Master ven'Deelin laughed.

"Look now, my son," she said, turning to him and directing his attention through the friendly windows. "There is the guildhall, and just beyond the Trade Bar. After you are settled at the house, you must tour the bazaar. I think you will find Irikwae to be something unique in the way of ports."

Jethri's stomach was beginning to register complaints about the motion and the speed. He breathed, slow and deep, concentrating on keeping breakfast where it belonged, and let her words flow by him.

Suddenly, the car braked, swung to the right—and the traffic outside the window was less, and more moderately paced. The view was suddenly something other than port—tile-fronted buildings heavily shaded by the trailing branches of tall, deeply green vegetation.

"Rubiata City," Master ven'Deelin murmured. He glanced at her and she smiled. "Soon, we shall be home."

"AWAKEN, MY CHILD, we are arrived." The soft voice was accompanied by a brisk tap on his knee.

Jethri blinked, straightened, and blinked again. He didn't remember falling asleep, but he must've, he thought—the view outside the windows was entirely changed.

There was no city. The land fell away on either side of the car and rose up again in jagged teeth of grayish blue rock; on and on it went, and there, through the right window and far below—a needle glint which must be—could it be?—the port tower.

Jethri gasped, his hand went out, automatically seeking a grab-bar—and found warm fingers instead.

"Peace," Norn ven'Deelin said, in her awful Terran. "No danger is there here, Jethri. We come up into the home of my heart."

Her fingers were unexpectedly strong, gripping him tightly.

"All is well. The mountains are friendly. I promise you will find them so, eh? Eh?"

He swallowed and forced himself to look away from the wide spaces and dangerous walls—to look at her face.

The black eyes held his. "Good. No danger. Say to me."

"No danger," he repeated, obedient, if breathless.

She smiled slightly. "And soon will you believe it. Never have you seen mountains?"

He shook his head. "I—the port. There's no use us going out into—" He swallowed again, engaging in a brief battle of wills with his stomach. "I'm ship-born, ma'am. We learn not to look at the open sky. It makes us—some of us—uncomfortable."

"Ah." Her fingers tightened, then she released him, and smiled. "Many wonders await you, my son."

THEY HAD PASSED BETWEEN high pillars of what looked to be the local blue rock, smoothed and regularized into rectangles. Afterward, the view out the window was of lawns, interrupted now and then by groups of middle tall plants. Gaenor's descriptions of the pleasant things she missed from her home led him to figure that the groups scratched an artistic itch. If this lawn had been done the way Gaenor thought was proper, then there'd be some vantage point overlooking the whole, where the pattern could be seen all at once.

The car took a long curve, more lawn sweeping by the windows, then came to a smooth halt, broadside to a long set of stairs cut from the blue rock.

The doors came up, admitting a blare of unpolarized sunlight and an unexpectedly cool breeze, bearing scents both mysterious and agreeable.

Master ven'Deelin patted him on the knee.

"Come along, young Jethri! We are arrived!"

She fairly leapt out of the vehicle. Jethri paused long enough to put the black glasses on, then followed rather more slowly.

Outside, Master ven'Deelin was in animated conversation with a gray-haired woman dressed in what looked to be formal uniform— their driver, maybe . . . *Anecha*, he reminded himself, mindful of Uncle Paitor's assertion that a successful trader worked at keeping name and face on file in the brainbox—which was, by coincidence, a point Master tel'Ondor also made.

So—Anecha the driver. He'd do better to find her last name, but for now he could get away with "Master Anecha" if he was called upon to do the polite. Not that that looked likely any time in the near present, the way her and Master ven'Deelin were jawing.

Deliberately keeping his eyes on objects nearby—no need to embarrass Master ven'Deelin or himself with another widespaces panic—he moved his gaze up the stony steps, one at a time, until all at once, there was house at the tiptop, posed like a fancy on the highest tier of one of Dyk's sillier cakes.

Up it went, three levels, four—rough blue rock, inset with jewel-colored windows. There was greenery climbing the rock walls: vines heavy with white, waxy flowers, that swayed in the teasing breeze.

Nearer at hand, he heard his name and brought his eyes hurriedly down from the heights, to find Master ven'Deelin at his right hand.

"Anecha will see to our luggage," she said, with a sweep of her hand that encompassed both stair and house. "Let us ascend."

Ascend they did—thirty-six stone steps, one after the other, at a pace somewhat brisker than he would have chosen for himself, Master ven'Deelin bouncing along beside like gravity had nothing to do with her.

They did pause at the top, Jethri sucking air deep into his lungs and wishing that Liadens didn't considered it impolite for a spacer to mop his face in public.

"You must see this," Master ven'Deelin said, putting her hand on his arm. "Turn about, my child."

Panting, Jethri turned about.

What he didn't do—he didn't throw himself face down on the deck and cover his head with his arms, nor even go down on his knees and set up a yell for Seeli.

He did go back a step, breath throttling in his throat, and had the native sense to bring his eyes *down*, away from the arcing empty pale sky and the unending march of rock and peak—*down* to the long stretch of green lawn, which outrageous open space was nothing less than homey by comparison with the horror of the sky.

So—the lawn, and the clumps of bushes, swimming before his tearing eyes, and suddenly, the random clumps weren't random, but the necessary parts of a larger picture showing a common cat, folded in and poised on the feet, ready to jump.

Jethri remembered to breathe. Remembered to look to Master ven'Deelin and incline his head, politely.

"You approve?" she murmured, her head tipped a little to a side.

"It is—quite a work," he managed, shamelessly swiping Master tel'Ondor's phrase. He cleared his throat. "Is the hunting cat the sign of the house?"

Her eyebrows lifted.

"An excellent guess," she said. "Alas, that I must disappoint you. The sign of the house is a grapevine, heavy with fruit. However, several of the revered Maarilex ancestors bred cats as an avocation. The breed is well-established now, and no more to do with Tarnia, save that there are usually cats in the house. And the sculpture, of course." She inclined her head, gravely. "Well done, Jethri. Now, let us announce ourselves."

She turned back to the door, and Jethri did, keeping his eyes low. He had the understanding that he'd just passed a test—or even two—and wished that he felt less uncertain on his legs. All that openness, and not a wall or a corridor or an avenue to confine it. He shuddered.

Facing the door was a relief, and it took an active application of will not to lean his head against the vermillion wood. As it happened, that was a smart move, because the door came open all at once, snatched back into the house by a boy no older than ten Standards, Jethri thought—and then revised that estimate down as the kid bowed, very careful, hand over heart, and lisped, "Who requests entry?"

Master ven'Deelin returned the bow with an equal measure of care. "Norn ven'Deelin Clan Ixin is come to make her bow to her foster mother, who has the honor to be Tarnia. I bring with me my apprentice and foster son."

The kid's eyes got round and he bowed even lower, a trifle ragged, to Jethri's eye, and stepped back, sweeping one arm wide.

"Be welcome in our house, Norn ven'Deelin Clan Ixin. Please follow. I will bring you to a parlor and inform the delm of your presence."

"We are grateful for the care of the House," Master ven'Deelin murmured, stepping forward.

They followed the kid across an entry chamber floored with the blue stone, polished to a high gloss, from which their boot heels woke stony echoes, then quieted, as they crossed into a carpeted hallway. A dozen steps down the carpet, their guide paused before an open door and bowed.

"The delm comes. Please, be at ease in our house."

The parlor was smallish—maybe the size of Master ven'Deelin's office on *Elthoria*—its walls covered in what Jethri took to be pale blue silk. The floor was the same vermillion wood as the front door, and an oval rug figured in pale blue and white lay in the center, around which were situated two upholstered chairs—pale blue—a couch—white—and a low table of white wood. Against the far wall stood a wine table of the same white wood, bottles racked in three rows of six. The top was a polished slab of the local stone, on which half-a-dozen glasses stood, ready to be filled.

"Clan Tarnia makes wine?" he asked Master ven'Deelin, who was standing beside one of the blue chairs, hands tucked into her belt, watching him like he was doing something interesting.

She tipped her head to one side. "You might say so. Just as you might say that Korval makes pilots or that Aragon makes porcelains."

Whoever, Jethri thought, irritable with unexpended adrenaline, *they are.*

"Peace," Master ven'Deelin said. "These things will be made known to you. Indeed, it is one of the reasons we are come here."

"Another being that even you would be hard put to explain this start to Ixin!" A sharp voice said from the doorway.

Jethri spun, his boot heels squeaking against the polished floor. Master ven'Deelin turned easier, and bowed lightly in a mode he didn't know.

"Mother, I greet you."

The old, old woman leaned on her cane, bright eyes darting to his face. Ears burning, he bowed, junior to senior.

"Good-day, ma'am."

"An optimist, I apprehend." She looked him up and looked him down, and Jethri wasn't exactly in receipt of the notion that she liked what she saw.

"Does no one on *Elthoria* know how to cut hair?"

As near as he could track it, the question was asked of the air, and that being so, he should've ignored it or let Master ven'Deelin deal. But it was *his* hair under derision, and the theory that it had to grow out some distance before he was presentable as a civilized being wasn't original with him.

"The barber says my hair needs to grow before he can do anything with it," he told her, a little more sharply than he had intended.

"And you find that a great impertinence on the side of the barber, do you?"

He inclined his head, just slightly. "I liked it the way it was."

"Hah!" She looked aside, and Jethri fair sagged in relief to be out from under her eye.

"Norn—I ask as one who stands as your mother: Have you run mad?"

Master ven'Deelin tipped her head, to Jethri's eye, amused.

"Now, how would I know?" she said, lightly, and moved a hand. "Was my message unclear? I had said I was bringing my foster son to you for—"

"Education and polish," the old lady interrupted. "Indeed, you did say so. What you did not say, my girl, is that your son is a mess of fashion and awkwardness, barely beyond halfling, and Terran besides!"

"Ah." Master ven'Deelin bowed—another mystery mode. "But it is precisely because he is Terran that I took him as apprentice. And precisely because of chel'Gaibin that he is my son."

"chel'Gaibin?" There was a small pause, then a wrinkled hand moved, smoothing the air irritably. "Never mind. That tale will keep, I think. What I would have from you now is what you think we might accomplish here. The boy is Terran, Norn—I say it with nothing but respect. What would you have me teach him?"

"Nothing above the ordinary: The clans and their occupations; the High modes; color and the proper wearing of jewels; the Code."

"In short, you wish me to sculpt this pure specimen of a Terran into a counterfeit Liaden."

"Certainly not. I wish you to produce me a gentleman of the galaxy, able to treat with Liaden and Terran equally."

There was another short pause, while the old lady gave him second inspection, head-top to boot-bottom.

"What is your name, boy?" she asked at last.

He bowed in the mode of introduction. "Jethri Gobelyn."

"So." She raised her left hand, showing him the big enameled ring she wore on the third finger. "I have the honor to be Tarnia. You may address me informally as Lady Maarilex. Is there a form of your personal name that you prefer?"

"I prefer Jethri, if you please, ma'am."

"I will then address you informally as Jethri. Now, I have no doubt that you are fatigued from your journey. Allow me to call one of my house to guide you to your rooms. This evening, prime meal will be served in the small dining room at local hour twenty. There are clocks in your quarters." She glanced to Master ven'Deelin.

"We have him in the north wing."

"Excellent," Master ven'Deelin said.

Jethri wasn't so sure, himself, but the thought of getting doors and walls between himself and this intense old lady; to have some quiet time to think—that appealed.

So he bowed his gratitude, and Lady Maarilex thumped the floor with her cane loud enough to scare a spacer out of his suit, and the kid who had let them in to the house was there, bowing low.

"Thawlana?"

"Pet Ric, pray conduct Jethri to his rooms in the north wing."

Another bow, this to Jethri. "If you please?"

He wanted those walls—he did. But there was another portion of him that didn't want to go off into the deep parts of a grounder house on a planet no Terran ship had ever touched, leaving his last link with space behind. It wasn't exactly panic that sent him looking at Master ven'Deelin, lips parting, though he didn't have any words planned to say.

She forestalled him with a gentle bow. "Be at peace, my child. We will speak again at Prime. For now, this my foster mother wishes to ring a terrifying scold down upon me, and she could not properly express herself in the presence of a tender lad." She moved her hand, fingers wriggling in a shooing gesture. "Go now."

And that, thought Jethri, was that. Stiffly, he turned back to the kid—Pet Ric—and bowed his thanks.

"Thank you," he said. "I would be glad of an escort."

THEY WERE HARDLY a dozen steps from the parlor when a shadow moved in one of the doorways and a girl flickered out into the hallway, one hand raised imperiously. His guide stopped, and so did Jethri, being unwilling to run him down. The girl was older than Pet Ric—maybe fourteen or fifteen Standards, Jethri guessed—with curly red-brown hair and big, dark blue eyes in a pointy little face. She was dressed in rumpled and stained tan trousers, boots and a shirt that had probably started the day as yellow. A ruby the size of a cargo can lug nut hung round her neck by a long silver chain.

"Is it him? The ven'Deelin's foster son?" She whispered, looking up and down the hall like she was afraid somebody might overhear her.

"Who else would he be?" Pet Ric answered, sounding pettish to Jethri's ears.

"Anybody!" she said dramatically. She lowered her hand, raised her chin and looked Jethri straight in the eye.

"Are you Jethri ven'Deelin, then?"

"Jethri Gobelyn," he corrected. "I have the honor to be Master ven'Deelin's apprentice."

"Apprentice?" another voice exclaimed. A second girl stepped out of the doorway, this one an exact duplicate, even in dress, of the first. "Aunt Stafeli said *foster son*."

"Well, he could be both, couldn't he?" asked the first girl, and looked back at Jethri. "Are you both apprentice and foster son?"

No getting out of it now, he thought and inclined his head. "Yes."

The first girl clapped her hands together and spun to face her sister. "See, Meicha? Both!"

"Both or neither," Meicha said, cryptically. "We will take over as guide, Pet Ric."

The boy pulled himself up. "My grandmother gave the duty to me."

"Aren't you on door?" asked the girl who wasn't Meicha.

This appeared to be a question of some substance. Pet Ric hesitated. "Ye-es."

"What room has the guest been given?" Meicha asked.

"The Mountain Suite."

"All the way at the end of the north wing? How will you guard the door from there?" She asked, folding her arms over her chest. "It was well for you we happened by, cousin. We will escort the guest to his rooms. You will return to your post."

"Yes!" applauded her twin. "The house cares for the guest, and the door is held. All ends in honor."

It might have been that Pet Ric wasn't entirely convinced of that, Jethri thought, but—on the one hand, his granmam had given him the duty of escorting the guest, and on the second, it seemed clear she'd forgotten about the door.

Abruptly, the boy made up his mind, and bowed to Jethri's honor.

"I regret, Jethri Gobelyn—my duty lies elsewhere. I leave you in the care of my cousins Meicha and Miandra and look forward to seeing you again soon."

Jethri bowed. "I thank you for your care and honor your sense of duty. I look forward to renewing our acquaintance."

"Very pretty," Meicha said to Miandra. "I believe Aunt Stafeli will have him tutoring us in manner and mode."

Jethri took pause and considered the two of them, for that might well have been a barb, and he was in no mood for contention.

Miandra it was who raised her hand. "It was a jest, Jethri—may we call you Jethri? You may call us Meicha and Miandra—or *Meichamiandra*, as Ren Lar does!"

"You will find us frightfully light-minded," Meicha added. "Aunt Stafeli despairs, and says so often."

"Jethri wants to be alone in his room to rest his head before prime," Miandra stated, at an abrupt angle to the conversation.

"That's sensible," Meicha allowed, and turned about face, marching away down the hall. Between amused and irritated, Jethri followed her, Miandra walking companionably at his side.

"We'll take you by the public halls this time, though it is longer.

Depend upon Aunt Stafeli to quiz you on every detail of the route at Prime. Later, we'll show you the back halls."

"That is very kind of you," Jethri said, slowly. "But I do not think I will be guesting above a few days."

"Not above a few days?" Meicha looked at him over her shoulder. "Are you certain of that, I wonder, Jethri?"

"Certain, yes. *Elthoria* breaks orbit for Naord in three Standard Days."

Silence greeted this, which didn't do much for the comfort of his stomach, but before he could ask them what they knew that he didn't, Miandra redirected the flow of conversation.

"Is it very exciting, being at the ven'Deelin's side on the trade floor? We have not had the honor of meeting her, but we have read the tales."

"Tales?" Jethri blinked at her as they rounded a corner.

"Certainly. Norn ven'Deelin is the youngest trader to have attempted and achieved the amethyst. Alone, she re-opened trade with the Giletti System, which five ambassadors could not accomplish over the space of a dozen years! She was offered the guildmaster's duty and turned it aside, saying that she better served the Guild in trade."

"She has taken," Meicha put in here, "a Terran apprentice trader under her patronage and has sworn to bring him into the Guild."

The last, of course, he knew. The others, though—

"I am pleased to hear these stories, which I had not known," he said carefully. "But it must go without saying that Master ven'Deelin is legend."

They laughed, loudly and with obvious appreciation; identical notes of joy sounding off the wooden walls.

"He does well. In truth," gasped Meicha, "the ven'Deelin is legend. Yes, even so."

"We will show you the journals, in the library, if you would enjoy them," Miandra said. "Perhaps tomorrow?"

"That would be pleasant," he said, as they began to ascend a highly polished wooden staircase of distressing height. "However, I stand at Master ven'Deelin's word, and she has not yet discussed my duties here with—"

"Oh, certainly!" Meicha cut him off. "It is understood that the ven'Deelin's word must carry all before it!"

"Except Aunt Stafeli," said Miandra.

"Sometimes," concluded Meicha; and, "Do you find the steps difficult, Jethri?"

He bit his lip. "My home ship ran light gravity, and I am never easy in heavy grav."

"Light gravity," Miandra repeated, in caressing tones. "Sister, we must go to space!"

"Let Ren Lar catch us 'mong the vines again and we shall."

Miandra chuckled and put a light hand quickly on Jethri's sleeve.

"Be of good heart, friend. Six steps more, and then to the end of a very short hallway, I promise you."

"Take good advice and first have yourself a nap," Meicha said. "Time enough to unpack when you are rested."

That seemed sensible advice, he allowed, though he was not wanting to sleep so much as to *think*.

"I thank you," he said, rather breathlessly, to Meicha's back.

She reached the top of the flight and turned, dancing a few steps to the right.

"Is your home light as well?" she asked, seriously, as he achieved the landing, and turned to look at her.

"My home . . ." He sighed, and reached up to rub his head where the growing-out hair itched. "I am ship-born. My home is—was—a tradeship named *Gobelyn's Market*."

The two of them exchanged a glance rich in disbelief.

"But—did you never come to ground?" Miandra asked.

"We did—for trade, repairs, that sort of thing. But we didn't *live* on the ground. We *lived* on the ship."

Another shared glance, then—

"He speaks the truth," said Meicha.

"But to always and *only* live on a ship?" wailed Miandra.

"Why not?" Jethri asked, irritated. "Lots of people live on ships. I'd rather that than live planet-side. Ships are clean, the temperature is consistent, the grav is light, there's no bad smells, or dust, or *weather*—" He heard his voice heating up and put the brake on it, bowing with a good measure of wariness.

"Forgive me," he murmured.

"Truth," Meicha said again, as if he hadn't spoken.

Miandra sighed. "Well, then, it is truth, and we must accept it. It seems an odd way to live, is all." She turned and put her hand on his sleeve.

"You must forgive us for our ignorance," she said. "I hope you will talk to us about your ship at length, so that we are no longer ignorant."

"And in trade," Meicha added, "we will teach you about gardens, and streams, and snow and other planet-side pleasures, so that you are no longer ignorant."

Jethri blinked, throat tightening with a sudden realization that he had been as rude as they had, and as such was a fitting object for Balance—

Except, he thought then, they had already declared Balance—him to teach them about ship-living, them to teach him about planet-life. He sighed, and Meicha grinned.

"You are going to be interesting, Jethri Gobelyn," she said.

"*Later*, he will be interesting," Miandra ordered, and waved a hand under her sister's nose. "At this present, we have given our word to guide him to his rooms in enough time that he might nap and recruit his strength before prime, none of which is accomplished by standing here."

"You sound like Aunt Stafeli." Meicha turned, crooking a finger behind her. "Come along then. Less than six dozen steps, Jethri, I promise you."

In fact, it was a couple dozen steps more than six, though Jethri wasn't inclined to quibble. Now that the room was near, he found himself wanting that nap, though he slept in the car—and a shower, too, while he was wanting comforts . . .

"We arrive!" Meicha announced, flourishing a bow in no mode Jethri could name.

The door was wood, dark brown in color. Set off-center was a white porcelain knob painted with what he thought might have been intended to be grapes.

"Turn the knob and push the door away from you," Miandra coached. "If you like, we will show you how to lock it from the inside."

"Thank you," he said. The porcelain was cool and smooth, vaguely reminiscent of his fractin.

The door moved easily under his push, and he came a little too quickly into the room, the knob still in his hand.

This time he shouted, and threw an arm up over his eyes, all the while his heart pounded in his ears, and his breath burned in his chest.

"The curtains!" a high voice shrilled, and there were hands on his shoulders, pushing him, *turning* him, he realized, in the midst of his panic and willingly allowed it, the knob slipping from his hand.

"Done!"

"Done," repeated an identical voice, very near at hand. "Jethri, the curtain is closed. You may open your eyes."

It wasn't as easy as that, of course, and there was the added knowledge, as he got his breathing under control, that he'd made a looby outta himself in front of the twins, besides showing them just as plain as he could where he stood vulnerable.

Mud, dust and stink! He raged at himself, standing there with his arm over his face and his eyes squeezed tight. His druthers, if it mattered, was to sink down deep into the flooring and never rise up again. Failing that, he figured dying on the spot would do. Of all the *stupid*—but, who expected bare sky and mountain peaks when they opened a sleeping room door? Certainly, not a born spacer.

"You are a guest of the house," one of the twins said from nearby, "and valued."

"Besides," said the other, "the ven'Deelin would skin us if harm came to you and then Aunt Stafeli would boil us."

That caught him in the funny bones, and he sputtered a laugh, which somehow made it easier to get the arm down and the eyes, cautiously, open.

One of the twins—now that they were out of formation, he couldn't tell one from her sister—was standing practically toe-to-toe with him, her pointed face quite plainly showing concern. To her right and little back, the other twin's face wore an identical expression of dismay.

"Not smart," he managed, still some breathless. "You stand back, in case I swing out."

She tipped her head. "You are not going to swing out," she stated, with absolute conviction. "You are quite calm, now."

And, truth told, he did feel calmer and neither in danger or dangerous. He took a breath, getting the air all the way down into his lungs, and sighed it out.

"What's amiss?" asked the twin who stood farthest from him. "Are you afraid of mountains?"

He shook his head. "Openness," he said, and, seeing their blank stares, expanded. "All that *emptiness*, with no walls or corridors—it's not natural. Not what a space-born would know as natural. You could fall, forever . . ."

They exchanged another one of their identical looks, and then the nearer twin stepped back, clearing his sight of the room, which was bigger than the *Market's* common room, and set up like a parlor, with a desk against one wall, upholstered chairs here and there, low tables, and several small cases holding books and bric-a-brac. The floor was carpeted in deep green. Across the room, a swath of matching deep green shrouded the window.

"The bedroom boasts a similar vista, in which the house takes pride, and takes care that all of our most honored guests are placed here," said the girl nearest him. She paused before asking, "Shall we close the curtains, or show you how to use them?"

Good question, Jethri thought, and took another breath, trying to center himself, like Pen Rel had taught him. He nodded.

"I think I should learn how to operate the curtains myself, thank you."

That pleased them, though he couldn't have said how he knew, and they guided him through a small galley, which, thank the ghosts of space, had no window, to his bedroom.

The bed alone was the size of his quarters on the *Market*, and so filled up with pillows that there wasn't any room left for him. His duffle, and of all things, the battered B crate from his storage bin sat on a long bench under . . . the window.

He was warned, now, and knew to keep his eyes low, so it wasn't bad at all, just a quick spike in the heart rate and a little bit of buzz inside the ears.

"In order to operate the curtain," said the twin on his left, "you must approach the window. There is a pulley mechanism at the right edge . . ."

He found it by touch, keeping his eyes pinned to the homey sight of his bag on the bench. The pull was stiff, but he gave it steady pressure, and the curtain glided across the edge of his sight, casting the room into shade.

He sighed, and sat down on the bench.

Before him, Meicha and Miandra bowed.

"So, you are safely delivered, and will be wanting your rest," the one on the left said.

"We will come again just ahead of twentieth hour to escort you to the small dining room," the one on the right said. "In the meanwhile, be easy in our house."

"And don't forget to set the clock to wake you in good time to dress," the twin on the left added.

He smiled, then recalled his manners, and got to his feet to bow his gratitude.

"Thank you for your care."

"We are pleased to be of assistance," said the twin on the right, as the two of them turned away.

"Aunt Stafeli will not allow you to fear mountains, or open space, or any being born," the girl on the left said over her shoulder.

"Then it is fortunate that I will only be with her for a few days," Jethri answered lightly, following them.

Silence from both as they passed through the galley and into the parlor.

"Recruit your strength," one said finally. "In case."

He smiled. Did they expect him to stay while *Elthoria* continued on the amended route? He was 'prenticed to learn trade, not to learn mountains.

Still, it would be rude to ignore their concern, so he bowed and murmured, "I will. Thank you."

One twin opened the door and slipped out into the hallway. The second paused a moment, and put her finger on a switch under the inner knob.

"Snap to the right is locked," she said. "To the left is unlocked. Until prime, Jethri."

"Until prime," he said, but she was already gone, the door ghosting shut behind her.

THE MIRROR SHOWED BROWN HAIR growing out in untidy patches, an earnest, scrubbed clean face, and a pair of wide brown eyes. Below the face, the body was neatly outfitted in a pale green Liaden-style shirt and dark blue trousers. Jethri nodded, and his reflection nodded, too, brown eyes going a little wider.

"You're shipshape and ready for space," he told himself encouragingly, reaching for the Ixin pin.

One eye on the clock, he got the pin fixed to his collar, and stood away from the mirror, pulling his shirt straight. It lacked six minutes to twentieth hour. He wondered how long he should wait for the twins before deciding that they had forgotten him and—

A chime rang through the apartment. Jethri blinked, then grinned, and went quick-step to the main room. He remembered to order his face into bland before he opened the door, which was well.

He had been expecting the same grubby brats who had guided him a few hours before, faces clean, maybe, in honor of dinner.

What he hadn't expected was two ladies of worth in matching white dresses, a flower nestled among the auburn curls of each, matching rubies hanging from matching silver chains. They bowed like they were one person, neither one faster or slower than the other—honor to the guest.

His answer—honor to a child of the house—was a bow that Master tel'Ondor had drilled him on until his back ached, so he was confident of his execution—until the cat.

He had seen cats before, of course—port cats. Small and fierce, they worked the docks tirelessly, keeping the rat and mouse populations in check. Their work took a toll, in shredded ears, crooked tails, and rough, oily fur.

This cat—the one standing between the twins and looking up into his face as if it was trying to memorize his features—*this cat* had never done a lick of work in its life.

It was a tall animal; the tips of its sturdy ears easily on a level with the twins' knees, with a pronounced and well-whiskered muzzle. Its fur was a plush gray; its tail a high, proud sweep. The eyes which considered him so seriously were pale green—rather like two large oval-shaped peridot.

Timing ruined, Jethri straightened to find the twins watching him with interest.

"What is that doing here?"

"Oh, don't mind Flinx—"

"He was waiting outside our rooms for us—"

"Very likely he heard there was a guest—"

"And came to do proper duty."

He frowned, and looked down at the animal. "It's not intelligent?"

"No, you mustn't say so! Flinx is *very* intelligent!" cried the twin on the right—Jethri thought she might be Miandra.

"Bend down and offer your forefinger," the other twin—Meicha, if his theory was correct—said. "We mustn't be late for prime and duty must be satisfied."

Jethri threw her a sharp glance, but as far as he could read her—which was to say, not at all—she appeared to be serious.

Sighing to himself, he bent down and held his right forefinger out toward the cat's nose, hoping he wasn't about to get bit. Cat-bite was serious trouble, as he knew. 'Way back, when he was still a kid, Dyk had gotten bit by a dock cat. The bite went septic before he got to the first-aid kit and it had taken two hits of super heavy duty antibiotics to bring him back from the edge of too sick to care.

This cat, though—this Flinx. It moved forward a substantial step and touched its cool, brick colored nose to the very tip of his finger. It paused, then, and Jethri was about to pull back, duty done. But, before he did, Flinx took a couple more substantial steps and made sure it rubbed its body down the entire length of his fingers and arm.

"A singular honor!" one of the twins said, and Jethri jumped, having forgotten she was there.

The cat blinked, for all of space like he was laughing, then stropped himself along Jethri's knee and continued on into his rooms.

"Hey!" He turned, but before he could go after the interloper, his sleeve was grabbed by one of the twins and his hand by the other.

"Leave him—he won't hurt anything," said the girl holding his sleeve.

"Flinx is very wise," added the girl holding his hand, pulling the door shut, as they hustled him down the hall. "And we had best be wise and hurry so that we are not late for prime!"

THANKING ALL THE GHOSTS OF SPACE, the small dining room did not have a famous view on exhibit. What it did have, was a round table laid with such an amount of dinnerware, utensils and drinking vessels that Jethri would have suspected a shivary was planned, instead of a cozy and quiet family dinner.

They were the last arriving, on the stroke of twenty, according to the clock on the sideboard. The twins deserted him at the door and plotted a course for two chairs set together between Delm Tarnia and a black-haired man with a soft-featured face and dreamy blue eyes. At Tarnia's right sat Master ven'Deelin, observing him with that look of intent interest he seemed lately to inspire. Next to Master ven'Deelin was an empty chair.

Grateful that this once the clue was obvious, he slipped into the empty seat, and darted a quick look down table at the twins. They were sitting side by side, as modest as you please, hands folded on their laps, eyes downcast.

"Jethri," the old lady said, claiming his attention with a flutter of frail old fingers. "I see that you have had the felicity of meeting Miandra and Meicha. Allow me to present my son, Ren Lar, who is master of the vine here. Ren Lar, here is Norn's fosterling, Jethri Gobelyn."

"Sir." Jethri inclined his head deeply—as close to a seated bow as he could come without knocking his nose against the table.

"Young Jethri," Ren Lar inclined his head to a matching depth, which Jethri might have suspected for sarcasm, except there was Tarnia sitting right there. "I am pleased to meet you. We two must hold much in common, as sons of such illustrious mothers."

Oh-ho, that was it. The man's bow was courtesy was paid to Master ven'Deelin, through her fosterson, and not necessarily to the son himself. The universe had not quite gone topsy-turvy.

"I am sure that we will have many stories to trade, sir," he said, which was what he could think of as near proper, though not completely of the form Master tel'Ondor had given him. On the other, Ren Lar's greeting hadn't been of the form Master tel'Ondor had given him, either.

"Trade stories at your leisure, and beyond my hearing," the old lady directed. "Normally, we are not quite so thin of company as you find us this evening, Jethri. Several of the House are abroad on business, and one has made the journey to Liad, in order to complete his education."

"And Pet Ric," said one of the twins, quietly, though maybe not quietly enough, "eats in the nursery, with the rest of the babies."

Lady Maarilex turned her head, and considered the offending twin with great blandness. "Indeed, he does," she said after a moment. "You may join him, if you wish."

The twin ducked her head. "Thank you, ma'am. I would prefer to remain here."

"Your preference has very little to do with the matter. From my age, young Meicha, there is not so much difference between you and Pet Ric, that he naturally be confined to the nursery, while you dine with the adults." A pause. "Note that I do not say, with the *other* adults."

Meicha bit her lip. "Yes, ma'am."

"So," the old lady turned away. "You must forgive them," she said to Master ven'Deelin. "They have no address."

"One would not expect it," Master ven'Deelin answered softly, "if they are new come from the nursery. Indeed, I am persuaded that they are progressing very well indeed."

"You are kind to say it."

"Not at all. I do wonder, though, Mother, to find dramliz in the house."

The old lady looked up sharply. "Hah. Well, and you do not find dramliz in the house, mistress. You find Meicha and Miandra, children of the clan. Healer Hall has taken an interest in them."

Master ven'Deelin inclined her head. "I am most pleased to see them."

"You say so now." She moved a hand imperiously. "House-children, make your bows to my foster daughter, Norn ven'Deelin Clan Ixin."

They inclined, deeply and identically, and with haste enough to threaten the mooring of the flowers they wore in their hair.

"Norn ven'Deelin," Meicha murmured.

"We are honored," Miandra finished.

"Meicha and Miandra, I am pleased to meet you." Master ven'Deelin inclined her head, not by much, but to judge by the way the twins' eyes got wide, maybe it was enough.

Somebody—Lady Maarilex or Ren Lar—must have made a sign that Jethri didn't catch, because right then, the door at the back of the room opened and here came an elder person dressed in a tight black tunic and tight black pants. He bowed, hands together.

"Shall I serve, Lady?"

"Yes, and then leave us, if you will."

THERE WAS TALK during the meal, family catch up stuff, which Jethri followed well enough, to his own surprise. Following it and making sense of it were two different orbits, though, and after a while he just let the words slide past his ear and concentrated on his dinner.

"Of course, I will be delighted to have Jethri's assistance in the vineyard—and in the cellars, too." Ren Lar's voice, bearing as it did his own name, jerked Jethri's attention away from dinner, which was mostly done anyway, and back to the conversation.

"That is well," Master ven'Deelin was answering calmly. "I intend to start him in wine after he has completed his studies here, and it would be beneficial if he had a basic understanding of the processes."

"Very wise," Ren Lar murmured. "I am honored to be able to assist, in even so small a way, with the young trader's education."

Carefully, Jethri looked to the twins. Miandra was studying her plate with an intensity it didn't deserve, being empty. Meicha met his eye square, and he got the distinct idea she'd've said, *I told you so* right out if she hadn't already earned one black mark on the meal.

Jethri felt himself go cold, felt the breath shortening in his lungs. *Thrown off*, he thought, and didn't believe. Couldn't believe it, not of Master ven'Deelin, who, unlike his blood mother, had wanted him, at least as her apprentice. Who had plans for him, and who thought he might one day be useful to—

And there was the B crate sitting in the room upstairs, which he surely didn't need for a three-day visit. . .

"Ma'am," he heard his own voice, breathless and a thought too sharp. "You're not leaving me here?"

She tipped her head, black eyes very bright. "You object to the house of my foster mother?"

He took a breath, centering himself—trying to—like Pen Rel kept insisting on. It was important to be calm. People who panicked made mistakes, and, by all the ghosts of space, a mistake now could doom him to life in the mud . . .

Another breath, deliberately deep, noticing that the conversation had stopped and that Master ven'Deelin's question hung in the air, vibrating with an energy he wasn't near to understanding.

"The house of your foster mother is a fine house, indeed," he said, slowly, carefully. "Ignorant as I am, it is all but certain that I will disgrace the honor of the house, or of yourself, all unknowning. I am space-born, ma'am. Planet ways—"

Master ven'Deelin moved a hand in the Liaden version of "stop". Gulping, Jethri stopped.

"You see how it is with him," she said to Lady Maarilex. "So much concern for my honor!"

"That is not a ill thing, I judge, in a foster child," the old lady said gravely. "Indeed, I am charmed and heartened by his care of you, Norn. For surely, his concern for you is but a pure reflection of the care you have shown him. I am pleased, but in no wise surprised."

Trapped. Jethri bit his lip, feeling panic clawing at his throat, adrenaline arguing with his dinner.

Across the table, he saw Miandra swallow hard, and Meicha close her eyes, throat working.

"So, then," Master ven'Deelin continued. "Wine lore, surely, and a decreasing of the sensibilities. Modesty becomes a lad of certain years, but a lad who hovers on the edge of being a trader grown must have more to his repertoire than modesty and a pleasant demeanor."

Lady Maarilex inclined her head. "We shall do our possible," she murmured. "A relumma may see some progress."

A *relumma*? Ninety-six Standard Days? He stayed in his chair. He didn't yell or give in to bawling. Across from him, though, Meicha sniffled.

"Mother," Ren Lar said softly. "It occurs to me that our guests, newly come from space, might welcome an early escape to their beds."

"Why, so they might," Lady Maarilex said, like the idea surprised her. "Thank you, my son." She inclined her head and sat poised until he had come 'round to her chair, eased it back and offered an arm for her to lean on as she rose.

"Good night, kin and guests. Repose yourselves in calmness, knowing that the house is vigilant on your behalf. Young Jethri, attend me tomorrow morning at eighth hour in my study. Miandra will show you the way."

She turned then, leaning hard on the arm of her son, and left the room at a slow walk. As soon as she cleared the door, the twins popped up, bowed their good-nights and were gone, leaving Jethri staring at Norn ven'Deelin and feeling about to cry.

"Well," she said, rising and looking down at him quizzically. "Allow me to escort you to your rooms, my son."

HE DID KEEP HIMSELF in hand until they reached the door of his quarters—he did. Master ven'Deelin chatted easily on about the house and how comfortable it was to be assigned to her very room—though nothing so exalted as the north wing, mind you!—suited her very well. Jethri returned monosyllables—maybe he did that.

But he didn't start a fight until they he had opened the door and bowed her over into his parlor.

He pulled the door closed behind him—so gently, he could scarcely hear the lock *snick*, and stood for the space of a couple good, deep breaths, preparatory to laying the case out as calm and as forceful as he could.

"Master Flinx, how do you go on?" Master ven'Deelin said delightedly. Jethri turned and sure enough, there was the cat, curled up on one of the chairs, and there was Master ven'Deelin, bending down to offer a courteous finger.

"Come, do me the honor of renewing our acquaintance."

Surprisingly enough, the cat did just that, coming out of his curl and sitting up tall, touching his nose to her fingertip.

"Always the gentleman!" She moved her hand, running tickling fingers under the cat's chin. "I see that I leave my son in good care!" Straightening, she sent Jethri a quick black glance.

"Truly, young Jethri, you will do well here, with Flinx as your sponsor."

He cleared his throat. "I'd like to talk to you about that, if you please, ma'am." He said carefully.

She sighed, and folded her hands together, head to one side. "Well, if you must, you must, and I will not forbid it. But I will tell you that you are doomed to failure. Remain here, you most assuredly shall, to sit at the feet of my foster mother and learn whatever she wishes to teach you."

"Ma'am, will you not at least listen to me?" He heard the desperation in his own voice and bit his lip.

"Did I not say that I would listen? Speak, my child. I rejoice in the melodious sounds of your speech."

"Yes, ma'am. I don't wish to be tiresome and I know you must be eager to seek your bed, so I will be brief. The case is that I am space-based and I am apprenticed to learn trade. The whys and whyevers of planet-based society—that falls outside the scope of those things it is necessary for me to learn in order to be an effective trader."

"A gentle set-down; appropriate between kin. And though I

might protest that I have done nothing to earn your anger, I will refrain, for I well know that you consider yourself wronged. So . . ." She moved a hand, showing him the chair unoccupied by the cat.

"Sit, child, and give over *glowering* at me."

He sat, though he wasn't that certain in regard to the glower.

"Good." She turned back to the second chair, scooped the cat up deftly and sat, cat on knee. Flinx blinked, and stretched, and curled round, obviously pleased with his position.

"The fact that you are able to argue with sincerity that knowledge of planet-based society has no bearing upon your abilities as a trader only demonstrates how deeply you are in need of such education."

"Master—"

She raised a hand. "Peace. You have made your throw. I now claim my turn with the dice."

He bit his lip. "Yes, ma'am."

"'Yes, 'mother' would be more appropriate to the case," she said, "but I do not insist. Instead, I will undertake to put your mind at ease. You are not abandoned. You are set down for the space of two relumma, that you might pursue independent study of value to the ship. These studies are two-fold." She held up a hand, and folded the index finger down.

"One, you will learn what my foster mother may teach you of the proper mode. Fear not that she will treasure you as I do—and insist that you extend yourself to your greatest efforts." She folded her second finger down.

"Two, you will also spend time in the trade hall at Irikwae Port. I have requested that the master of the hall see to your guild certification, which is a matter I have too long neglected." Points made, she dropped her hand to Flinx's flank.

"I have myself undertaken just such independent studies and certifications, to the benefit of the ship and the profit of the clan. It is what is done, and neither punishment, nor betrayal. Are you able to accept my word that this is so?"

His first inclination was to tell her *no*, but the plain truth was that he'd never known her to lie. Some things she said that he didn't understand—but that was his ignorance and not her deliberate misleading—

"*Two* relumma?" he blurted, his brain finally catching up with his ears. He bent forward in his chair. "Lady Maarilex said *one* relumma!"

"Tcha!" Master ven'Deelin looked up from scratching Flinx behind the ears. "She said that one relumma might begin to show progress. What profit do you bring to the ship half-trained?"

He closed his eyes, fists set hard against his knees. Two relumma on-planet, he thought, and shivered.

"Child . . ." There was a rustle, and a thump, and then arms put 'round his shoulders. He stiffened and then leaned into the hug, pushing his face against her shoulder like she was Seeli and him not much older than eight.

"Child, the worlds are not your enemy. Nor do ships enclose all that is good and proper in the universe. A trader must know his customers—and the greater number of your customers, when you are a trader grown, will be planet-based, not ship-born. Ignore their ways at your peril. Despise them. . ." There was a small poof of sound over his head, and her arms tightened briefly.

"Despise them," she continued, "if you must, from knowledge, rather than ignorance."

"Yes, ma'am," he whispered, because there wasn't anything else to say. She was going to leave him here, right enough, whatever he said, or however he said it. His outlook now was to be sure she remembered to come back for him.

"You may think me heartless," she murmured. "You may perhaps think that I have never been bade to show a calm face to exile. Acquit me, I beg you. Well I remember the wildness in my heart, when my delm ordered that I be fostered to Tarnia, away from Solcintra and from Liad itself, which enclosed all that was good and proper in the universe." Again, that small pouf of sound, which might, Jethri thought, be a gentle laugh.

"A surly and aloof fosterling I was, too. I trust that you will be more seemly than I was—for my foster mother, I ask that you be gentle, and no more bitter than is strictly necessary."

He laughed—a surprising, hiccupy sort of sound—and heard her laugh, too. Her arms tightened once more before she stepped back, leaving him feeling comforted, and oddly comfortable.

"So then," she said briskly. "You have an early interview with our foster mother, and will doubtless wish to seek your bed soon. Be certain that I will return for you. I swear it, on Ixin itself."

Jethri blinked. To swear on the name of her clan—he had the sense that was something not lightly done, *could not* be lightly done. If her own name was more precious than rubies, how much more precious must be the name that sheltered all ven'Deelins, everywhere? He came to his feet, still chewing on the nuances, and bowed respect to an elder.

"I will look for you, in two relumma," he said, and straightened to see a smile on her face.

"Indeed, you will. And now, my son, I bid you deep sleep and sweet dreaming. Learn your lessons well—and mind Master Flinx whenever he cares to advise you."

He inclined his head, seriously. "I'll do that, ma'am."

Together, they walked to the door. He opened it for her; she stepped out—and turned back.

"You will wish to open that curtain, my child. The view of the nighttime sky is not to be missed."

"Yes, ma'am," he said, out of habit, and she smiled again and went away down the hall.

Jethri closed the door slowly, and turned to face the curtained window.

You told her yes, he said to himself.

It took a month or so to cross the room, and another week to pull the cord. The curtains came back, slow and stately. Lower lip gripped tightly between his teeth, Jethri looked up from the cords and the folds of cloth. . .

The sky was a deep blue, spangled with fist-sized shards of icy white light. A pale blue moon was rising, casting shadows on the shoulders of the mountains. Further out, and considerably down, there were clustered lights—a city, or so he thought. He remembered to breathe, and then to breathe again, looking out over the night.

The moon had cleared the mountain peak before he turned away and went into the bedroom, walking on his toes, as if the floor was tiled in glass.

DAY 140

❁❁❁❁❁❁❁❁❁❁❁❁❁❁❁❁❁❁❁❁❁❁❁❁

Standard Year 1118
Tarnia's Clanhouse
Irikwae

"SO, THEN, YOUNG JETHRI," asked Stafeli Maarilex, "how do you find the view from the north wing?"

He paused with his teacup halfway to his lips and favored her with a straight look over the rim. She returned his gaze, her face so entirely empty of expression that the lack might have been said to be an expression of its own. Glancing aside, for Liadens counted a too-long stare at the face as rudeness, he sipped his tea and put the cup gently back in its saucer.

"I found the view astonishing, ma'am," he said, and was proud to hear his voice steady on.

"I am gratified to hear you say it. Honor me with your thoughts regarding our moons."

Moons? He tried not to look befuddled, and supposed he failed completely.

"I saw only one moon, ma'am—pale blue and rising behind the mountain."

"So?" She paused, one hand on her cup, then threw her free

hand slightly up and to the side, fingers flicking out. "You must forgive an old woman's memory. Of course, we are in single phase anytime this six-day! Never mind, you will soon have the pleasure of beholding all three riding the skies. Indeed, I will ask Ren Lar to form an excursion for the house's children later in your stay, when the nights will be warmer. I am sure you will find it most amusing. Local legend is that good luck comes to those who sleep beneath the full moons."

He inclined his head, which was polite, and put away for later wondering—or asking of the twins—the notion of a special excursion to look at moons. It might be, he thought, that Tarnia owned a starhouse and an optical scope for—

"There are certain matters of a personal nature which we must discuss," Lady Maarilex said, interrupting his thought. "Pray forgive me if my questions seem impertinent. I assure you that I would not ask these things did necessity not exist."

"Yes, ma'am," he said, sitting up straighter in his chair. He was speaking in the mercantile mode, by special permission of the lady. She was speaking in a mode that was not mercantile, but perfectly intelligible, so long as he kept his ear on it.

"We will need to know certain things. Your family, for instance. Norn tells me that Terrans do not form into Houses and Clans, which I must say seems very peculiar to me. However, I suppose you must have some other method for tracking lineage." She inclined her head.

"Enlighten me, then, young Jethri. Who are you?"

He took a little time to think about it, lifting his cup and taking a leisurely sip while he did, so as not to seem rude.

"I am of the mainline Gobelyns," he said slowly. "Off of the tradeship *Gobelyn's Market*."

"I see." She lifted her cup, buying time herself, Jethri thought, and wasn't particularly encouraged by thinking it.

"May I know more, young Jethri?" she murmured, putting her cup down and apparently giving most of her attention to choosing a piece of fruit from the bowl in the center of the table. "Despite all Norn's efforts, I am woefully ignorant of shiplore."

"Yes, ma'am," he said, mortified to hear his voice break on the second word. "My mother is Iza, captain; my father was Arin, senior trader. My elder siblings are Cris, first mate, and Seeli, administrative mate. My mother's brother is now senior trader, brought on board when my father died." He took a deep breath, and met her eyes firmly, rudeness be spaced.

"The Gobelyns have been shipfolk since before space took ships. Arin Tomas, as he was before he married, his line was scholars and explorers; he served his turn as a Combine commissioner before he was senior trader."

He didn't expect her to value that—to know how to value it—and so he was surprised when she bent her head solemnly, and murmured, "A worthy lineage, Jethri Gobelyn. It could not, of course, be otherwise."

That might've just been the polite—she couldn't very well disapprove of Master ven'Deelin's choice of a fosterson, after all—but he was warmed anyway.

"I wonder," she said gently, "if I might know your age."

"Seventeen Standard Years, ma'am."

"Hah. And your name day?"

He blinked, then remembered that Liadens celebrated the anniversary of a baby's being named, which might, as Vil Tor told it, be done within seconds of the birth, or as long as twelve days past. Near as he knew, he'd been named simultaneously with being born. He inclined his head slightly.

"Day two-thirteen, ma'am."

"Delightful! We shall have the felicity of ushering you into your eighteenth year. The house is honored."

He didn't exactly scan why that should be such an honor, 'specially when stood against the fact that his birthday was more often forgot than not. When he'd been a kid, Seeli'd made sure there was some special favorite eatable in his dinner, and Cris would give him a little something by way of a present—a booktape, maybe, or an odd-bit he'd found during the trade rounds. His fourteenth birthday, there wasn't any special tasty in his dinner, though the occasion of his birth had been marked by Cris, who had given him the grown-up wrench set he still wore on his belt. After that—well, he was too old for wanting after special tidbits and gee-gaws.

Carefully, he inclined his head. "I am grateful, but the House need not exert itself on my account."

Lady Maarilex raised an eyebrow. "Norn is correct. *Far* too much sensibility. Hear me, Jethri Gobelyn: The house exerts itself on your behalf because it is what the house demands of itself. Your part is to strive to be worthy of our care. Am I plain?"

He swallowed and looked down into his teacup. "Yes, ma'am."

"Good. Now, lift up your face like the bold young man I know you to be and tell me how you came to meet Norn."

Of the questions he might have expected from her, this one might have been dead last. Master ven'Deelin must have told her—

"Your pardon, young Jethri," the sharp old voice cut across his thoughts. "May I expect the felicity of an answer soon?"

It was near enough in tone to Master tel'Ondor to jerk him upright and meeting her eye before he took a deep breath and began his tale.

"We met in Ynsolt'i Port, which is located in what the Terrans call the far-outside and Master ven'Deelin calls the Edge. There was a . . . man . . . who had a deal with a four-on-one payout, guaranteed with a master trader's card . . ."

DAY 140

❀ ❀

Standard Year 1118
Kinaveral

"SEELI GOBELYN?" The man's voice was hurried and high—not familiar, just like his face, when she turned her head and gave him a stare, the while continuing to move. She was running close to late for the regular inspection visit and she knew from experience that the yard-boss wouldn't wait for her one tick past the hour. Not good timing on the part of the spacer who was doggedly keeping pace beside her, though his face was red and damp with sweat.

"Can we talk?" he panted, as Seeli stretched her legs a little more.

"If you can talk and walk at the same time, we can," she said, not feeling any particular pity for him. "I'm late for an appointment and can't stop."

"Maybe we can meet after your appointment," he said. "I'm authorized to offer a trade for fractins."

Authorized to offer a trade on fractins? Like fractins was something rare and expensive, instead of the over-abundant nuisance they happened to be. Seeli sighed, wondering if the guy was a head-case or a joker. Not that it mattered.

"Sorry," she said, moving on at her top ground speed. "No fractins."

"We'll make it worth your while," he insisted. "I'm authorized to trade generous."

"Does you no good if we got none to sell." The gate was in sight; damn' if she wasn't going to be *right* on time.

"Wait—"

"No time to wait!" she snapped, more than a little out of breath. "And we ain't got any fractins."

She was under the canopy, then, her body breaking the beam of the spy-eye.

"Maybe I can call on your trader!" The man called behind her and Seeli sighed. Headcase.

"Sure," she yelled over her shoulder as the gate swung open. "Talk to our trader."

DAY 140

❋❋❋❋❋❋❋❋❋❋❋❋❋❋❋❋❋❋❋❋❋❋❋❋

Standard Year 1118
Irikwae

UPSTAIRS, DOWNSTAIRS, upstairs, downstairs, front stairs, back stairs. Secret stairs, too. Not to mention the hallways, public, private and almost-forgot. By the time they made it back to ground level and toured the big kitchen and the little one, Jethri was ready for a solid couple hours of sleep.

After breakfast, Lady Maarilex had put him in the care of the twins, instructing them to provide him with a "thorough" tour of the house. It was in Jethri's mind that they had taken that "thorough" just a little too literal. What reason for him to know how to find the butler's closet, or Pan Dir's rooms—Pan Dir being the cousin who was gone to Liad for his studies, and Mr. pel'Saba the butler looking impartially sour at the three of them while the twins did the polite and he made his bow. *And who would have expected that there could be so many stairs inside of one structure,* Jethri thought, panting in the wake of his guides. *Who would have thought there could be so many hallways giving on to so many rooms?*

Half-a-dozen steps ahead of him, the twins fair danced along, their soft-booted feet hardly seeming to touch the floor, talking in turns over their shoulders, and neither one having the common grace to show breathless.

"The tour is almost done, Jethri!" called Meicha, bouncing 'round to face him. "This hallway ends in a stair—a very *small* stair, I promise you! At the end of the stair, is a door, and on the other side of the door—"

"Is a garden!" Miandra sang out. "The cook has promised us a lovely cold nuncheon, so that you may recruit your strength before your afternoon in the winery."

Jethri's feet stopped moving so suddenly he almost fell on his face. One of the twins said something short and nasty half under her breath before the two of them turned and walked back to him.

"It is," said Miandra, who tended, in Jethri's limited experience, to be the more serious of the two, "a very nice garden."

"With a wall all around it," Meicha added.

"It's open?" He managed, and was obscurely proud to hear that his voice did not break on the question.

"Open?" She frowned, not certain of his meaning, but Miandra caught it right enough.

"To the sky? Of course it is open to the sky. Gardens are, you know."

"We had thought to offer you a pleasant respite before your afternoon's labors," Meicha said. "This is our own *favorite* garden."

Jethri took a breath—another one, centering himself. Pen Rel had sworn three solemn swears that centering and right breathing would all come natural to him, with practice. *If I keep the current course*, Jethri thought irritably, *I'll be in practice and back out again before the shift changes.*

"Much better," Miandra approved, as if he'd said something fortunate.

"Anger is a powerful tool," Meicha added, like that made everything clear and wonderful. She reached out and grabbed his hand, her fingers surprisingly strong.

"Come along, Jethri, do. I promise, only a short walk, then you may rest and refresh yourself and frown at us all you like—"

"While we entertain you with tales of Ren Lar and his beloved vines, and give you the benefit of our—"

"Vast—"

"Sorrowful—"

"Experience."

He looked from one to the other, and thought he saw the glimmer of a joke around the edges of their eyes.

"Ren Lar pushes the crew hard, does he?" he asked lightly, thinking of the soft-spoken, dreamy-eyed man he'd met last night at prime meal.

"Ren Lar lives for the vines," Meicha said solemnly. "Pan Dir swore to us that he was given in contract to the mother vine, with the child—that being Pet Ric—coming to the house, naturally enough, so that the vines should never want for aught."

She sounded so much like Khat on the approach to a story that he almost laughed out loud. He did smile and move one shoulder. "Pan Dir was having fun with you, I think."

"I think so, too," Miandra said briskly. "I also think that *I* am hungry, and that nuncheon awaits us."

"And that time marches," her sister agreed. She pulled on Jethri's hand. "Come, son of ven'Deelin. It is a churlish guest who starves the children of the house."

There really wasn't anything else to do. Vowing to keep his head down and his eyes on his plate, Jethri let himself be pulled along, freighter to Meicha's tug.

The trees made the thing tolerable, when all was counted and tallied. They were tall trees—old, said Miandra; older even than Aunt Stafeli—and their wide-reaching branches broke the sky into manageable pieces, if a spacer should happen to look up too quick, or too high.

The "lovely, cold nuncheon" was set out on a table at the garden's center. There was a wall, as he had been promised, well grown with flowering vines and other creepers.

"Summer is before us still," Miandra said, as they mounted the dias and pulled out their chairs. "Not all the flowers are in bloom, now. At the height of the season, you can see nothing but flowers, and the air is sweet with their scent."

The twins ate with a delicate intensity that made him feel clumsy and over-large until he forgot about it in the amazements of the meal.

There was nothing that he ate that he would not have willingly eaten more of, though he found particular favor with a few tasties. He asked the twins the name of each, to their clear approval.

"Learn the names of the things you favor, first," Meicha said. "There is all the time you like, to learn the names of those things you care for less."

Finally, they each come to enough, and Miandra poured them all refills of grape juice, and settled back in her chair.

"So," Jethri said, trying to keep an eye pinned on each. "Ren Lar is unkind?"

"Never think so!" That was Meicha. "Ren Lar is capable of great kindness."

"The most of which," Miandra continued, "is reserved for his vines and his vintages, and then a bit for his heir."

"Aunt Stafeli figures there, too, I think. But, yes, Ren Lar principally cares for the vines, which is to the good of the house, for wine is our wealth. Whereupon hangs our tragic tale."

"It was," Miandra said, sipping her juice, "our own fault."

"We didn't know our own strength," Meicha returned, which might have been excuse or explanation.

"Still, we knew that *some*thing might happen, and our choice of target was . . ."

"Infelicitous."

"Extremely."

Jethri considered them over the rim of his glass. "Are you going to tell me what happened," he asked, like he was their senior, which he had an uneasy feeling he wasn't, no matter how the Standards fell. "Or talk to yourselves all shift?"

They laughed.

"He wants a round tale, and no foolishness!" Meicha crowed. "You tell it for us, sister."

"Well." Miandra moved her shoulders and sat up, putting her glass on the table.

"Understand, this happened at the start of last year—planetary year, that would be, not Standard."

Jethri inclined his head to show that he did indeed understand.

"So. It was a few weeks later in the season than it is now, and we—with the entire rest of the household who could wield shears—were in the vineyard, pruning the vines."

"Which is tedious, at best," Meicha put in, "and horrid, at worst."

Her sister turned to look at her, eyebrows well up.

"I thought this was mine to tell?"

The other girl blinked, then inclined her head. "Forgive me. Indeed, it is yours to tell."

Miandra inclined her head in turn, and took up her tale.

"As Meicha says, pruning is no task to love—unless one is Ren Lar, who loves everything to do with the vines. Alas, neither of us is Ren Lar, and while we may respect the vines, I believe it is fair to say that Flinx holds a higher place in our personal affections."

"*Far* higher," Meicha declared, irrepressible.

Miandra sipped juice, pointedly ignoring her, and put the cup down.

"We had been some days at the pruning, and some hours on this particular day, having risen early to the work, and it came to me—I cannot quite say how it should have done—that I loathed pruning the vines and that it would be much more convenient, and far less tedious, if I could simply will the work done." She sat up straight and looked Jethri right in the eye.

"I felt a certain, let us say, heat rise in my blood, my fingers, my toes, and my head fair tingled. My shears dropped to the ground, and I stood, quivering. Meicha asked me what I was about, but I was unable to do anything, but reach out and grasp her hand, and direct my thought at the rows of vines that Ren Lar had said we should prune that day."

It was a good place to pause for dramatic affect—and pause she did, much to Jethri's admiration. It was an interesting story, if different than Khat's usual, and he was enjoying himself. Two more heartbeats, and he realized that he was behind hand in his duty.

"What happened?" he asked.

Miandra inclined her head. "Nothing. Or so we thought then. Wearily, and now both afflicted with the headache, we picked up our shears and set back in to work." She paused, briefly.

"Three days later, we found that we had been wrong—we *had* wrought something, after all. Every one of the vines we had tended that day had died, and Ren Lar was as angry as I have ever seen him. Aunt Stafeli banned us from the vines until a Healer could be summoned to test us. Ren Lar . . ." She faltered.

After a moment, Meicha said, softly. "It is true that in the old days, when such things were possible, that Ren Lar might well have mated with the mother vine. He mourned the fallen as if they were his own children." She shivered slightly. "Indeed, he mourns them still."

"And we," Miandra said, calm again, "are now in training to be Healers." She lifted the chain up from around her neck, so the ruby spun in the sunlight. "As you may see."

Not too bad, thought Jethri appreciatively, and inclined his head.

"I am instructed by your tale," he said, seriously. "But, as I have no such unusual talent, I think that the vines will be safe with me."

Meicha grinned. "The vines will be safe with you, friend Jethri. For be sure that Ren Lar will not allow you to leave his sight while you are in his vineyard."

"HE KNEW YOUR NAME?" Grig sounded worried, and Seeli sighed, mentally giving herself a quick kick for having mentioned the headcase at all.

"Not exactly a secret, is it?" she asked. "My name's on the clearances and the licenses, all on public file—'s'what Admin does, ain't it?"

"Still, him stopping you in the street and wanting to talk fractins . . ."

"Headcase," she said firmly. "Took the idea the *Market* was shipping fractins, and set out to do something about it. Said he was going to call on our trader. Luck to him, is what I hope, 'specially if he's hopin' to buy fractins from Paitor."

"No problem Paitor selling him fractins, if fractins is what he'll have," Grig said, taking a sip of his brew. "Simple broker deal. Must be three, four warehouses of 'em on port here."

"That's why he's a headcase," Seeli pointed out, glad that his thought was tending that way. Grig was a good man—none better— but he did like his theories and conspiracies. "He wants game pieces, port's prolly full of them, and no need to suppose that *Market's* carryin' the motherload."

Grig looked at her, not saying anything.

"*What*?" she snapped, exasperated.

He moved his eyes. "Nothing. Likely nothing. Just—take a cab, Seeli, willya? Man being a headcase don't excuse him from being quick to grab."

Seeli smiled, and had a slow sip of brew. "Think I can't hold my own against some spacer, Grig Tomas?"

He smiled back, eyes warming in that way she especially liked. "Want to prove otherwise?"

DAY 145

✦✦✦✦✦✦✦✦✦✦✦✦✦✦✦✦✦✦✦✦✦✦✦✦

Standard Year 1118
Kinaveral

THEY WERE HAVING themselves a quiet meal—Grig and Khat and Seeli—talking over the events of the day, of which there hadn't been that many, and figuring out the share-work for the next while.

"Port's got me scheduled for a long-fly, week after next," Khat said, putting her finger down on the grid they had on the table between them. "Liaden edge, near enough. Top rate. Bonus, too. Be good for the bank and I'd like to go, just for the jig of it. Getting tired of station shuttles and ferry-jobs."

Seeli craned her head to read the grid upside down. "Five days out?"

"If you need me down here, I'll tell 'em to find somebody else. No problem, Seeli."

"I don't see any reason to do that. Got the monthly comin' up, but Grig was wantin' to do the walk-through. Got that all straight with the yard-boss, so he can't squawk crew-change and lock us out."

"Man's a couple decimals short of an orbit," Khat muttered.

"Yard's top-rated, though," Grig said. "Which is enough to keep a body awake at night."

Seeli slanted him a look. "Is that what's keepin' you awake at night?"

He gave her the Full Dignified, nose tipped up, and slightly wrinkled, mouth rumpled like he'd tasted something slightly bad. "That, and certain importunate young persons."

She slapped her hand flat on the table. "*Importunate*, is it? I'll importunate you, Grig Tom—"

"Ho, the ship!" came the hail from the outer room.

"Paitor!" Khat yelled. "In the galley! Grab a brew and tell us the news!"

In he came, looking dusty and tired, gave a general nod of hi-there, threw his jacket over the back of an unclaimed chair and made a line for the cold-box.

"Handwich makin's there, too, Paitor, if you're peckish," Grig said, quiet and serious of a sudden.

"Brew's fine," the other man said, coming back to the table with one in his hand. He dropped into the chair, broke the seal on the bottle and had a long drink.

"That's good," he sighed, leaning back, eyes slitted, though if it was in pleasure or plain exhaustion Khat couldn't have said.

"What's the news, Uncle?" Seeli asked, quiet, like Grig had been. Feeling out trouble, Khat thought, considering the slump of Paitor's shoulders.

He sighed, and straightened, and got his eyes opened.

"Funny thing," he said, and it was Grig he was looking at. "You might find it so. Fella come by Terratrade today, asking for me by name. They sent him on up. Turns out he was in the market for fractins."

"The headcase," Seeli said, understanding, and reached for her brew. "I hope you sold him a warehouse full, and at a favorable price, too. Ship's General could use the cash."

He flicked a glance at her, then back to Grig. "I'd've done that, but it was special fractins he was after."

Grig shrugged, expressionless, and Khat felt something with lots of cold feet run down her spine.

"Seems what this fella was after, was Arin's fractins. Said he was willing to offer a handsome sum—he named it, and it was. Told him I couldn't oblige, that Arin's son had everything Arin had cared to leave behind, and the boy was 'prenticed to another ship."

There was a small pause, growing longer, as Paitor waited for Grig to say something.

Eventually, the lanky crewman shrugged again. "Should've been an end to it, then."

"Should've," Paitor agreed. "Wasn't. 'stead what he wants to know is if we got any other Befores on trade. Especially, he's interested in light-wands and duplicating units."

Grig laughed, sharp and ugly. "Man's a fool."

"Headcase," Seeli said again. "Told you."

"Close enough," Grig agreed, and reached for his brew.

"I'm asking," Paitor said, his hands folded 'round his own bottle and the knuckles showing, Khat saw, a shade or two pale.

Grig looked up and put the brew down. "Ask it, then."

"Was Arin dealing old tech?" The words came out kinda gritty and tight.

Grig lifted an eyebrow. "Dirt makin' you squeamish? Never took cash for a fractin, I guess."

Paitor took a hard breath, lifted his brew and had another long drink, thumping the bottle back to the table, empty. Khat got up and went to the cold-box, pulled four new bottles and brought them back to the table. She broke the seal on one and put it in front of Paitor, took another for herself and sat down. Across the table, Seeli was sitting tall, looking a frown between Paitor and Grig.

"Sure, I sold 'em—a piece of this, a part of that," Paitor said at last, his eyes pegged to Grig's. "Maybe a frame an' some fractins. Who knows what they were, or what they did?"

"I thought you wasn't a believer."

Paitor grinned, no humor in it at all.

"Don't need to be a believer when I got one across the table, asking for whole, working gadgets *by name*."

"Point." Grig lifted his brew and finished it off, put the bottle back soft on the table. "So you asked—yeah, Arin traded the underside in old tech. Far as I know, he was mostly buying—bought some few things, myself, now and then, like that weather maker Jeth adopted. Most of the stuff, it went—someplace else. And before you ask—no, I don't know where it is or how it went. Arin's business, first and finish. He didn't tell me everything." He reached to the middle of the table and snagged another brew; glanced back to Paitor's face. "You know how Arin was."

"This guy was buying," Paitor said, but Khat could see that he was finding Grig's story believable and in some part comforting.

Grig shrugged. "Man's running with old info," he suggested, breaking the seal on his brew. "Headcase, too." He flicked a quick smile at Seeli, who didn't let go of her frown. "You want me to talk to him?"

A pause, then a headshake. "No need. I told him we didn't have no fractins; told him we're fresh outta old tech. On planet for a refit, I told him. Got nothing worth trading at all." He lifted his bottle, but didn't quite drink. "Seemed satisfied with that. Though he left me a beam-code." Paitor's lips thinned. "In case I should come across something."

"Which won't happen, 'cause we ain't looking," Seeli said, firmly, reaching for the last bottle and breaking the seal with a vengeance. "We're well out of it." She favored Grig with a glare, and he dipped his head, agreeable-like.

"Sure, Seeli."

DAY 155

Standard Year 1118
Irikwae

"GOOD-DAY, JETHRI." Ren Lar looked up from his lab table, meter held delicately in one hand, blue eyes soft as ever. Somehow, he managed to look cool and elegant, though his apron was liberally painted with stains, and his sleeves rolled to his elbows.

Jethri, his own sleeves rolled up in anticipation of another long shift spent readying barrels to receive their next batch of wine, inclined his head, which he had found was considered respectful enough, in this circumstance.

"Good-day, sir. I hope I'm not late." He wasn't, just, which was no fault of the tailor who had been summoned to produce what Lady Maarilex was pleased to call "appropriate" clothes for himself. Not satisfied with the first set of readings, the tailor—one Sun Eli pen'Jerad—had measured him again—and yet again, muttering over his readings, and at last jerked his chin at Jethri, giving him leave to cover himself decently.

"I will bring samples, in six days," Mr. pen'Jerad said, gathering up his measuring devices and his notes. "Tarnia informs me that you are a trader-under-study, eh? What you wear now tells the world that you are a cargohand-for-hire. We will amend this." He patted his pockets, making sure of his notes and bowed farewell. "Six days."

Six days or never—it made no nevermind to Jethri, who cut out the door as soon as he was dressed and ran down the back halls to the winery, prudently pausing on the outside of the door until his breathing had returned to something like normal before entering and presenting himself to Ren Lar.

That gentleman looked dreamily amused. "My mother had warned me that you were with the tailor this morning. The pen'Jerad is a marvel with his needle. Would that he were as sure with his measure-tapes." A device on the table chimed, and he glanced down with a slight frown, and then back to Jethri.

"In any case, I had not hoped to see you so soon. Now that you are here, however . . ."

Jethri sighed to himself, knowing what he was going to hear.

"Ah." His face must've let something slip, 'cause Ren Lar smiled his slight, dreamy smile. "The barrels grow tedious, do they? Then you will rejoice to hear that the end of the racking approaches. The last of the blends will be assembled by the end of the twelve-day. Soon, we shall take to the vineyard and the pruning."

He said it like pruning was a high treat. On the other hand, he had shown Jethri the barrels, and explained the necessity of having them scrubbed spotless as if it were the most important job in the winery, which, Jethri thought now, having had some days to consider the matter, it might well be. Bacteria would grow in dirty barrels, and bacteria could spoil a whole batch of wine, so clean barrels was important, right enough.

'Course, cleaning a barrel wasn't anything so simple as shoving it into an ultraviolet box, because the UV broke down the wood too fast. No, cleaning a wine barrel involved gallons of hot water, scrub brushes, sodium carbonate and of all of things a length of plain chain. After the barrel was scrubbed down on the outside, and the inside filled with water, sodium carbonate and chain, then it was sealed up tight and rolled over to the agitator, locked in and shook up but good, while the faithful barrel-scrubber rolled another dirty over to his work space and started the process over again.

It was tiresome and tiring work, make no mistake. Empty barrels were heavy; full barrels heavier. Jethri figured he was earning gravity muscles, but that hardly made up for the ache in his arms and his shoulders and his back.

Halfway into his first shift, he'd come up with the conviction that chemical disinfection would be the surer—and easier—way to go, but he hadn't made the mistake of saying that to Ren Lar. After a session with the house library, he was glad he'd kept his mouth shut on the point, for it transpired that disinfectants turned the taste of the wine, which meant "spoiled" just as sure as if the bacteria'd got in.

"There are only a few barrels today," Ren Lar was saying. "When you have done with them, make yourself available to Graem, in the aging cellar. She will be able to put another pair of hands to good use."

"Yes, sir." Jethri inclined his head again, and went to see how many barrels was only a few.

DAY 158

Standard Year 1118
Irikwae

"TELL US ABOUT living on your ship," Miandra said, shuffling the cards with bewildering speed between nimble fingers.

Jethri blinked, and shifted in his chair, trying for a position that would ease his back. The three of them were alone in a little parlor situated closer to the kitchen than the front door. In theory, the twins were teaching him to play *piket*, which unlikely pastime had the full approval of Lady Maarilex.

"Indeed, a gentleman should know his cards and be able to play a polite game." She fixed the twins in her eye, one after the other. "Mark me, token wagers only. And all may practice the art of graceful loss."

"Yes, Aunt Stafeli," said Meicha.

"Yes, Aunt Stafeli," said Miandra.

"Yes, ma'am," said Jethri, though he'd been taught not to show temper for losing by kin years his elder in the subtle art of poker.

"What do you want to know?"

"Everything," said Meicha, comprehensively, while Miandra continued to shuffle, with a thoughtful look directed downward at the dancing cards.

"I would like to know how the kin groups sustain themselves," she said slowly.

"Sustain themselves? Well, there's ship life support, for air, temp and—"

Meicha laughed. Miandra didn't, though she did stop shuffling and raise her face to frown up at him.

"That was not at all funny," she said sternly.

"I—" he began, meaning to say he was sorry, though he didn't know, quite, what he should be sorry for, except that she was mad at him. His brain refused to pitch up the proper phrase, though, and after a moment's floundering he produced, "I am sad that you are angry with me."

"She's not so angry that you must be sad for it," Meicha said, matter-of-factly. "Only answer her question sensibly and she will be appeased."

"But you see, I don't understand why my previous answer was . . . annoying. We *do* sustain ourselves via ship's life support. If something else was meant by the question, then I don't know how to unravel it."

There was a small silence, then Meicha spoke again.

"He *is* a stranger to our tongue, sister. Recall Aunt Stafeli? We are only to speak to him in Liaden, and in proper mode and *melant'i*, to aid and speed his learning."

Miandra sighed and put the cards face down on the table. "Well enough. Then he must learn idiom." She raised her hand and pointed a finger at Jethri's nose, sharply enough that he pulled back.

"An inquiry into how the kin group sustains itself is an inquiry into genetics," she said, still tending toward the stern. "What I wish to know is how your kin group maintains its genetic health."

Maintains its . . . Oh. Jethri cleared his throat, thinking that his Liaden, improved as it was by constant use, might not be up to this. Good enough for Lady Maarilex to set rules on the twins for the betterment of his understanding, but nobody had drawn any lines for him about what was and wasn't considered proper topics of conversations between himself and two of the house's precious youngers.

"Is he shy?" Meicha inquired of her sister.

"Hush! Let him order his thoughts."

Right. Well, nothing for it but to tell the thing straight out and hope they took it for the strange custom of folk not their own—which, come to think, it would be.

"There are . . . arrangements between ships," he said slowly. "Sometimes, those. My older brother, Cris, came from an arrangement with *Perry's Promenade*. Seeli—my sister—she came out of a—a *shivary*, we call it. That's like a big party, when a lot of ships get together and there's parties and—and—" He couldn't put his tongue to a phrase that meant the polite of "sleeping around," but it turned out he didn't have to—Miandra knew exactly what he was on course for.

"Ah. Then your sister Seeli is as we are—Festival get and children of the house entire." She smiled, as if the translation comforted her, and looked over to Meicha. "See you, sister? It is not so different from the usual way of things. One child of contract and one from Festival—the genes mix nicely, I think."

"It would seem so," her sister agreed, unusually serious. "And you, Jethri? Were you contracted—or joyous accident?"

Well, *there* was the question that had formed his life, now, wasn't it? He shrugged and looked down at the table—real wood, and smooth under his palm, showing stains here and there, and the marks of glasses, set down wet.

"Unhappy accident, call it," he said to the table. "My parents were married, but my mother wasn't looking for any more children. Which is how I happened to be the extra, and available to 'prentice with Master ven'Deelin."

"The third child is produced from a lifemating," Miandra summed up. "It is well. And your cousins?"

He looked up. "My cousins? Well, see, the Gobelyn's are a wide family. We've got cousins on—I don't know how many ships. A couple dozen, I'd say, some small, none bigger than the *Market*, though. We're the mainline. Anyhow, we share around between us to keep the ships full. The extras—they take berths on other ships, and eventually they're . . ." he frowned after the word ". . . assimilated."

"So." Miandra smiled and put her hand over his. "We are not so brutal of our 'extras', but perhaps we have the luxury of room. Certainly, there are those who go off on the far-trade and return home once every dozen Standards—if so often. Your foster mother is one such, to hear Aunt Stafeli tell the tale. But, in all, it seems as if your customs match ours closely, and are not so strange at all." This was accompanied by a hard stare at Meicha, who moved her shoulders, to Jethri's eye, discomfited.

"But," he asked her, "what did you think?"

"Oh, she had some notion that the Terran ships used the old technology to keep their crews ever young," Miandra said. "Aunt Stafeli says she reads too many adventure stories."

"You read them, too!" Meicha cried, visibly stung.

"Well, but I'm not such a dolt as to *believe* them!"

Meicha pouted. "Terrans trade in old tech—Vandale said so."

"Yes, but the old tech mostly doesn't work," Jethri pointed out. "The curiosity trade gets it, and sometimes the scholars."

"Vandale said that, too," Miandra said.

"And Pan Dir said that there is still some old tech in the out-beyond that *does* work!" her twin snapped, with a fair sitting-down approximation of stamping her foot.

"If you want to know what I think," Jethri said, feeling like he'd better do his possible to finish the subject before the matter came to blows. "I think that Pan Dir likes to tell stories. My cousin Khat's exactly the same way."

There was a pause as Meicha and Miandra traded glances.

"There's that," Meicha said at last, and, "True," agreed Miandra.

Jethri sighed and reached for the cards, sitting forgotten by her hand.

"I thought you two were going to win my fortune from me."

That made them both laugh, and Meicha snatched the deck from him and began to shuffle with a will.

"I hear a challenge, sister!"

"As I do! Deal the cards!"

DAY 161

❀❀❀❀❀❀❀❀❀❀❀❀❀❀❀❀❀❀❀❀❀❀❀❀❀

Standard Year 1118
Irikwae

"OOF!"

The weight hit him right dead center, and Jethri jack-knifed from sound asleep to sitting up, staring blearily down into a pair of pale green eyes.

"You!" He gasped. Flinx blinked his eyes in acknowledgment.

"Might let a man get his rest," Jethri complained, easing back down to the pillows. Flinx stayed where he was, two-ton paws bearing Jethri's stomach right down onto his spine.

He yawned and turned his head to look at the clock. Not enough time to go back to sleep, even if the adrenaline would let him. Stupid cat had jumped on his stomach yesterday morning, at just this hour. And the morning before that. He was starting to wonder if the animal could tell time.

Down-body, Flinx began to purr, and shift his weight from one considerable front foot to the other—and repeat. He did *that* every morning, too. The twins swore that the purring and the foot-shifting—kneading, they called it—were signs of goodwill. Jethri just wondered why, if the cat liked him so much, he didn't let him sleep.

He sighed. The house crew tended to take Master ven'Deelin's view that he was fortunate to have fallen under Flinx' attention. What the cat got out of it, Jethri couldn't say, unless it was making notes for a paper on xenobiology.

Flinx had upped the volume on the purrs, and was pushing a little harder with his feet; the tips of his claws pierced skin and Jethri was off the pillows again with a yell.

"Hey!"

Startled, the cat kicked with his back feet, twisted and was gone, hitting the floor with a solid thump.

"Mud!" He flung to the edge of the bed, and peered over, half afraid he'd find the animal with a broken leg or—

Flinx was standing on four sturdy legs at the edge of the rug, his back to the bed. He looked over his shoulder—accusingly, to Jethri's eye.

"I'm sorry," he said, settling his head onto his crooked arm and letting the other arm dangle over the edge of the bed. "I don't like to be scratched, though."

There was a pause, as if Flinx was considering the merit of his apology. Then, he turned and ambled back to the bed, extending his head to stroke a whiskery cheek along Jethri's dangling fingers.

"Thanks." Carefully, he slipped his fingers under the cat's chin and moved them in the skritching pattern Meicha had shown him. Flinx immediately began to purr, loud and deep.

Jethri smiled and skritched some more. Flinx moved his head, obviously directing the finger action to his right cheek, and then to the top of his head, all the while purring.

Well, Jethri thought drowsily, fingers moving at a far distance, *what a relaxing sound.*

Across the room, the alarm chimed.

Flinx skittered out from under his hand a heartbeat before he snapped upright out of his doze.

Sighing, he rubbed his hand over his head, frowning at the lengthening strands, and swung out of bed.

Shower, breakfast, tailor—that was the first part of his day. Then an afternoon with Ren Lar. Pruning vines, it was today. After that, he was to join the twins with their dancing instructor, Lady Maarilex being of the opinion that a gentleman should show well on the floor, and then supper.

Supper done, he could retire to the library with the list of books the twins' tutor had produced for him—history books, mostly, and a bunch of marked-out sections of a three-volume set titled, *The Code of Proper Conduct*.

"Busy day," he said to the empty room, and headed for the shower.

COMPARE BANTH PORT to Kinaveral and Kinaveral came to look like the garden spot of the universe, Khat thought, throwing her duffle over one shoulder and heading across the wind-scoured tarmac. She had her goggles polarized, and her head down, much good it did. The constant hot wind was supersaturated with sand particles, stuff so fine it sifted through any join, clogged the nose, filled the mouth, and sank through the pores. Nose plugs helped some. So did keeping your mouth shut. Other than that, it was walk fast and hope the pilots' crash was climate controlled.

After a couple Standards of walking bent against the wind, she came to a service tunnel. Her body broke the sensor beam, the door irised open, and she ducked inside, barely ahead of the door closing.

Inside the tunnel, the light was dim and slightly pink. Khat pushed the goggles up onto her forehead, took a good, deep lungful of filtered air—and started to cough; deep, wracking spasms that left an acid taste in her mouth, overlaying the taste of the sand.

Eventually, she was coughed out and able to take some notice of her surroundings. A hatch closet built into the right wall of the tunnel said "drinking water" in Terran, which she could read fine, and, underneath, the written pidgin for the same—a stylized drawing of a jug—for them as couldn't read Terran.

The taste in her mouth wasn't getting much better. Khat stepped over and inserted her thumb into the latch. Inside the closet were a couple dozen sealed billy bottles carrying the same bilingual message. She snagged a bottle, slapped the door shut and popped the seal, taking a short, careful swallow, then another, and so on until the bottle was empty.

Feeling more or less human, she slid the billy into the wall recycler, and looked about her.

There were arrows painted in flourescent green on the floor, and the words, "Banth Port Admin," the Admin part repeated in pidgin, which was apparently her direction, whether she was going there or not. Though, as it happened, she was Admin bound.

She pulled the goggles off her forehead and snapped them onto her belt, taking another deliberately deep breath of filtered air. No coughing this time, which she took as a smile from the gods, even as she shook her head. She had some sympathy for the 'hands who would eventually be unloading her cargo, and shuddered with the memory of the constant dust storm, heat and battering white light of the world outside.

Granted, most Grounders're glitched in the think-box, she thought, setting her feet on the green arrow and walking on, *but a body'd think even a Grounder would know better than Banth.*

Khat sighed. Well, now she knew why Kinaveral Admin had put such a nice bonus on this job—and now she knew better than to take another flight to Banth.

"Live 'n learn," she said, and her voice sounded as gritty as her face felt, despite the water. "You live long enough, Khatelane, an' someday you might turn up smart."

"THERE! NOW WE SEE A SON of a High House in his proper estate!" Sun Eli pen'Jerad was pleased with himself and his handiwork, and Jethri supposed he had a right. Himself, he'd thought the trading coat and silk shirts provided by *Elthoria* plenty fancy enough and hadn't aspired to anything in the way of collar ruffles so high they tickled the tips of his ears, or belled sleeves that reached all the way to his fingertips. Then there were the trousers— tighter than his own skin and not near as comfortable—and over them both a long, and pocketless, black vest.

"Very good," Lady Maarilex said, from her chair, Flinx asleep on her lap. "Do you not think so, young Jethri?"

He sighed. "Ma'am, I think the work is fine, but the sleeves are too long and the trousers too tight."

Mr. pen'Jerad made an outraged noise. Lady Maarilex raised a hand.

"These things you mention are the current fashion, and not open to negotiation. We all bow to fashion and rush to do her bidding. How else should we show ourselves to be a people of worth?"

Jethri looked at her. "Is that a joke, ma'am?"

"Hah. Progress. Some bits, yes. Discover which bits and we shall have progress, indeed. In the meanwhile, we are pleased with Master pen'Jerad's efforts on behalf of evening clothes. Of your kindness, young Jethri, model for me the calling clothes."

Calling clothes weren't quite so confining, though they still showed a serious deficiency in the pocket department. The trousers were looser, the cream colored jacket roomy, the shirt dark blue, with an open collar and no ruffles anywhere. They were close enough to trading clothes to be manageable, and Jethri stepped out into the main room and made his bow to the seated matriarch.

"These please you, eh? And well they should. The jacket hangs well, despite what would seem to be too much breadth of shoulder. Well done, Sun Eli."

The tailor bowed. "That you find my work adequate is all that I desire," he murmured. "However, I must object—the shoulders are not too wide, but balance the rest of the form admirably. It is a balanced shape, and pleasing, taken on its own. It is when we measure it against the accepted standard of beauty that we must find the shoulders too wide, the legs too long, the chest too deep."

"Do you say so?" She raised a hand and motioned Jethri to turn, slowly, which he did, liking the feel of the silk against his skin and the way the jacket hugged his shoulders, too wide or not.

"No, I believe you are correct, Sun Eli. Taken in the context of himself alone, there is a certain pleasant symmetry." Jethri's turn brought him 'round to face her again and he stopped, hands deliberately loose at his sides.

"So tell me, young Jethri, shall you be a beauty?"

And that *had* to be a joke, given the general Gobelyn face and form. He bowed, very slightly.

"I expect that I will look much as my father did, ma'am, and I never did hear that he was above plain."

Surprisingly, she inclined her head. "Well said, and honest, too." She looked into his eyes and smiled, very slightly. "We must teach you better. However, there are still the day clothes to inspect, if you would do me the honor?"

THE TUNNEL WIDENED, and widened some more, and by the third widening it was a large round room, crowded with desks and chairs and people and equipment—and that was Banth Admin.

Khat stopped her steady forward slog and blinked, something bemused by all the activity, and scouting the room by eye, looking for her contact point.

The desks were on platforms a little higher than floor level, and each one had a sign on the front of it, spelling out its official station name in Terran and pidgin. Some of the signs weren't so easy to spot, on account of the people wandering around, apparently in search of *their* contact points. Lot of long-spacers in the mix, which she'd expected. Good number of Liadens, too, which surprised her. This close to the Edge, there was bound to be a couple working, looking for advantage, but to see so many . . .

"Edge is widenin' out again," Khat muttered. "Pretty soon, won't be nothing to edge."

She considered the crowd, rising up on her toes to count the Liadens, and filing that number away for Paitor's interest, on the far side of the trip. Might she'd head down to the Trade Bar, after a shower and a change, and scope out the ship names.

Right now, though, she was after Intake Station. Sooner she had her papers stamped and her cargo in line for off-load, the sooner she could hit the pilots' crash and have that shower.

After a time, it occurred to her that the only thing craning around the crowd was getting her was a cricked neck, and she settled the duffle and charted a course into the deeps of the room.

Up and down the rows she cruised, careful not to bump into anybody, Liaden or Terran, being not wishful of starting either a fistfight or a Balance. Admin crew was solidly Terran, sitting their stations calm enough, for all each one was busy.

Intake was on the third row, which made sense, Khat thought sarcastically. There were only two in line ahead of her—yellow-haired Liaden traders, looking enough alike to be mother and son. The boy was apparently determined on giving the clerk a difficult life experience. As Khat came to rest behind them, he was leaning over the desk, waving a sheaf of papers too close to the woman's face and talking, loud and non-stop, in Liaden, which was just stupid. Anybody who came to the Edge to trade ought to at least speak the pidgin.

And if the pidgin's too nasty for your mouth, Khat thought at the boy's expensively jacketed back, *you'd have done better to stay home and tend your knitting.*

In the meantime, his voice had risen and he was leaning closer over the desk, the wild-waving sheaf of papers now an active danger. Khat took a step forward, meaning to haul him back to a respectful distance, but the clerk had her own ideas.

"Security!" she yelled, and simultaneously hit a yellow button embedded in the plastic desktop.

The boy paused in his harangue, like he was puzzled by her reaction, the papers wilting in his hand.

"Peliche," Khat said helpfully, that being the pidgin for 'cop.'

He sent her an active glare over his shoulder, in the space of which time his mother stepped forward, hands moving in a pretty rippling motion, apparently meant to be soothing.

"Your pardon," she said to the clerk in heavily accented, but perfectly understandable pidgin. "We have cargo to be off-loaded. There is urgency. We must proceed with quickness."

The clerk's mouth thinned, but she answered civil enough. "I will need to see the manifests. As I said to this trader," a nod of the head indicated the boy, "since the manifests are written in Liaden, the cargo must be inventoried before it is off-loaded. Admin provides inventory-takers. There is a fee for this service."

The Liaden woman inclined her head. "What is the price of this fee?"

"Fifteen Combines the quarter-clock," the clerk said.

Now, that's steep, thought Khat, touching the zip-pocket where her own manifest rode, snug, safe, and printed out in plain, good Terran. *No wonder the boy's in a snit.*

His mam, though, she just bowed her head again and said, cool as if it weren't no money at all, "That is acceptable. Please produce these inventory-takers at once."

That cargo better be guaranteed profit, thought Khat, darkly.

The clerk reached for her keypad, and then looked up, annoyed for all to see, as a big guy in standard blues came striding toward her station.

"You call Security?" he demanded, hand on his stun-gun.

The clerk shrugged, eyes on her schedule screen. "Took your time."

His face, broad in all directions and unshaven on the south side, reddened. "I'm coverin' the whole floor by myself."

She glanced up at him, then back to the screen. The two Liadens were frankly staring.

"Sorry to bother you," the clerk said, in clear dismissal.

The cop stood for a couple heartbeats, giving a fair impression of a man who'd welcome a chance to put his fist authoritatively against somebody else's chin. He glared at the Liadens, daring them to start something. The woman touched the boy's arm and the two of them turned back to the clerk, the boy rolling his sheaf of papers into a tube, which Khat thought might have been nerves.

Finally, the cop turned and strode off into the crowd. The clerk slid a piece of paper out of her printer and handed it to the Liaden woman.

"The inspectors will be waiting for you at the security station in Access Tunnel Three. Give them this paper and follow their instructions. The red arrows are your guide to Access Tunnel Three."

"Yes," the woman said, folding the paper into her sleeve. She turned, her boy with her, and Khat was briefly caught in the cold stare of two pair of blue eyes, before they separated to walk around her—boy to the right, mam to the left.

Khat let go a breath she hadn't known she'd been holding and stepped up to the desk, pulling her papers out of the zip-pocket.

"Disaster shift?" she asked the clerk, crew-to-crew.

The clerk took the manifest. "Be nice if it was that calm," she said, unfolding the papers. "Let's take a look at what you got here . . ."

ESCAPED AT LAST into his own clothes from *Elthoria*, he slipped into the kitchen and wheedled an off-hours lunch from Mrs. tor'Beli, the cook.

"For the vines today, are you?" She asked, handing him a plate so full of eatables that he had to hold it in both hands for fear of losing some of the contents.

"Yes ma'am," he said politely, guiding his plate over to the table and setting it down.

"Be sure you have a hat and a pair of heavy gloves out of the locker before you go out," she said, placing a glass of grape juice on the table next to his plate. "Summer is still before us, but the sun is high enough to burn, and the vines not as weak as they might appear."

"Yes, ma'am," he said again. She returned to the counter where she was enthusiastically reducing a square of dough into a long, flat sheet, with the help of a wooden roller. Jethri nibbled from his plate as he looked around the kitchen, with its multiple prep tables, and its profusion of pots, pans and exotic gadgets. *Dyk would love this*, he thought, and gulped as tears rose up in his eyes.

C'mon, kid, what's up? He said to himself sharply. *You crying over Dyk?*

Well, in point of fact, he thought, surreptitiously using his napkin to blot his eyes, he *was* crying over Dyk—or at least crying over the fact that Dyk would never see this place, that would have given him so much pleasure . . .

"You had best hurry, young ven'Deelin," the cook called over her shoulder. "Ren Lar Maarilex puts the vines before his *own* lunch, much less yours."

He grinned, and sniffled, and put serious attention on his plate, which was very soon empty, and drained his glass. Pushing back from the table, he looked around for the dishwasher. . .

"Leave them," Mrs. tor'Beli said, "and betake yourself to the wine room—at a run, if you are wise."

"Yes, ma'am," he said for a third time, pushing in the chair. "Thank you, ma'am."

"Hurry!" she responded, and to please her he left at a pace, stretching his legs.

Outside of the kitchen, he kept moving, taking a right into the hall the twins had shown him, and arrived handily at the door to the wine room. It opened to his palm, and he clattered down the stairs, through the vestibule and tapped the code into the keypad set in the wall next to the ancient wooden door.

The lock *snicked*, and he worked the old metal latch. The door was slow on its metal hinges, and he put some shoulder into hurrying it along, stepping into the wine room proper only a little out of breath and scarcely mussed at all.

Ren Lar was not at his accustomed place at the lab table. Instead, there was Graem, busy with the drops and the calibrator. She glanced up as he entered, and frowned.

"The master's gone to the vineyard; he said that you're to find him on the north side."

Late, Jethri thought, and sighed, before remembering to incline his head. "Thank you, I will. Before I go, can you tell me where I might draw a hat and a pair of gloves?"

She jerked her head to the left, her attention already back with her calibrations. "Locker over there. Take shears, too."

"Thank you," he said again and moved to the locker indicated.

A few minutes later, wide brimmed hat jammed onto his head, too-small leather gloves on his hands as best he could get them, and shears gripped firmly in his right hand, he left the wineroom by the side doors and entered the vineyard.

No one was waiting for him, in the yard, and there were no signs to tell him which way to go. He considered, briefly, returning to the cellar and asking Graem for directions, but—no, blast it. He was tired of depending on the directions and help-outs of the various members of the household, like he was a younger—and a particularly backward younger, at that.

There had to be a way to figure out which way to go. If he put his thought on it, he ought to be able to locate north. He remembered reading a story once, where someone lost on a planet discovered his direction by observing which way a stream ran—not that there were any streams in his sight.

"And not that it would work, anyway," he grumbled to himself. "Meicha isn't the only one who reads too many stories, I guess."

He shifted his shears from his right hand to his left, pushed his hat up off his forehead and frowned around him. You'd think there'd *be* signs, he thought. What if somebody got turned around and didn't have a navigation device?

Navigation device.

He slapped his pockets, found what he wanted in the right leg and pulled it out. The mirrored black face grayed, displaying swirls, like clouds, or kicked-up dust, then cleared, showing the old, almost-forgotten icons along the top and bottom of a quartered screen.

Jethri frowned down into it, trying to put sense to symbols he hadn't seen for ten Standards—and suddenly, he *did* remember, the memory seating itself so hard that the inside of his head fair vibrated with the snap.

The icons at the top—those were detail buttons; the ones at the bottom indicated direction, while the quartered screen was meant to be read left-right/down-up, with the first square representing planetary north.

He touched a direction icon, and touched the north square. The screen changed, and now he was looking at a vid of the yard he was standing in, with a blue line superimposed over the image, shooting off to the left.

Making sure of his grip on the shears, he moved left, one eye on the screen and one eye on the treacherous dirt underfoot.

The next thing he'd do, Jethri thought some while later, would be to puzzle out if the device had a *distance* indicator. He'd walked a goodly distance, by his reckoning, along a dirt path crossing long corridors of wire fencing, against which bare wooden sticks leaned, dead vines like tentacles sprouting from their heads. It was an eerie landscape, and the vines just tall enough that he couldn't see around them, and sufficiently complicated to the eye that there was no need to look up at the unfettered sky. He did look the length of each corridor as he crossed it, and saw not one living thing. The birds, which sang outside his window, and in Meicha and Miandra's favorite garden, were silent, here in the vineyard—or maybe they preferred other circumstances.

Jethri had worked up a fair sweat and was reassessing how good an idea striking out on his own actually was, when he finally heard voices up ahead. Relief fetched up a sigh from approximately the soles of his boots, and he slipped the device back into his pocket before moving forward, quicker now. He turned right—and braked.

Ren Lar, hat on head, gloves tucked into his belt and looking just as comfortable as if he were standing in the coolness of the wine cellar, was talking with two men Jethri didn't know.

"This section here, today. If you finish while there is still sun, then begin tomorrow's section. We race the weather now, friends."

"Yes, sir," one of the men murmured. The other moved a hand, and Ren Lar acknowledged him with a slight nod of the head.

"Shall I call in my cousins, sir? They're able and willing for a day or three, while the warehouse refits."

Ren Lar tipped his head. "How many cousins?"

"Four, master. They tend our house vines and understand the pruning. If I call tonight, they can be here at first sun."

A small pause, then a decisive wave of a hand. "Yes, bring them up, of your kindness. It is, after all, a wind year—bitter beyond bearing last relumma, and now it grows warm too early. I do not wish the sap to surprise us."

The man inclined his head. "I will call them."

"Good. Then I leave you to your labors." He looked up. "Young Jethri. I trust you left Master pen'Jerad well?"

"Your honored mother was present, sir," Jethri said carefully, "so there was no hope of anything else."

Ren Lar's eyebrows rose. One of the strangers laughed.

"A stride, in fact. Well said. Now, walk with me and we will find you a section in need of your shears."

He moved a hand, beckoning, and turned left. At his feet a shadow moved, flowed, and gained shape.

"Flinx," Jethri said. "What are you doing out here?"

Ren Lar glanced down, and moved his shoulders. "He often comes to help in the vineyard. For which assistance we are, of course, grateful. Come with me, now."

Down the row they went, turned right down a cross-path—which would be north again, Jethri thought with pride.

"You will be tending to the needs of some of our elders," Ren Lar said, moving briskly down the pathway. "I will show you how to go on before I take up my own duty. But have no fear! I will be but one section over, and easily accessible to you."

That might have been a joke, though on consideration, Jethri didn't think so. He very likely *would* need a senior nearby. The wonder of it was that Ran Lar was apparently not going to be in the same row with him and keeping a close eye on the precious "elders."

"Here we are," the man said, and dodged left down a corridor, Jethri on his heels and Flinx flowing along in the shadows beside them.

The vines here were thick-bodied; some leaned so heavily into their support that the wires were bowed outward.

"Now, what we will wish you to do," Ren Lar said, pausing by a particularly bent specimen, its head-tentacles ropy and numerous. "Is to cut the thick vines, like this, you see?" He pulled a branch forward, and Jethri nodded.

"Yes, sir. I see."

"That is good. I must tell you that there is a reason to take much care, for *these*—" he carefully slipped his hand under a thin, smooth branchlet— "are what will give us this season's fruit, and next year's wine. So, a demonstration . . ."

He lifted his shears, positioned the blades on either side of the thick branch, and forced the handles together. The wood separated with a brittle snap, and before the severed twig had hit the ground,

Ren Lar had snipped another, and a third, the shears darting and biting without hesitation.

The old wood tumbled down into an untidy pile at the base of the vine. Ren Lar stepped back, kicked a few stray sticks into the larger heap, and inclined his head.

"At first, you will not be so quick," he said. "It is not expected, and there is no need for haste. The elders are patient. The cuttings will be gathered and taken to burn, later." He moved a hand, indicating the next vine down.

"Now, let us see you."

Teeth indenting lower lip, Jethri looked over the problem, taking note of the location of the new growth inside the woody tangle. When he had those locations in his head, he carefully lifted his shears, positioned the blades and brought the handles together.

The wood resisted, briefly, then broke clean, the severed branch tumbling down to the ground. Jethri deliberately moved on to his next target, and his next.

Finally, there was only new wood to be seen, and he stepped back from the vine, being careful not to tangle his feet in the grounded branches, and pushed his hat back up from his face.

"A careful workman," Ren Lar said, and inclined his head. "The elders are in good hands. You will work your way down this row, doing precisely what you have done here. When you reach an end of it, you will go one row up—" he pointed north— "and bring your shears to bear. I will be six rows down—" another point, back toward the house and the wine cellar— "should you have need of me."

"Yes, sir," Jethri said, still feeling none too good about being left alone to do his possible with what were seemingly valuable plants.

Ren Lar smiled and put his hand on Jethri's shoulder. "No reason for such a long face! Flinx will doubtless stay by to supervise."

That said, he turned and walked off, leaving Jethri alone with the "revered elders," his shears hanging loose in his right hand. Ren Lar reached the top of the corridor and turned right, back down toward the house, just like he'd said, without even a backward glance over his shoulder.

Jethri sighed and looked down at the ground. Flinx the cat was sitting three steps away, smack in the center of the dirt corridor, casually cleaning his whiskers.

Supervise. Sure.

Well, there was nothing for it but to step up and do his best. Jethri approached the next plant in line, located the fragile new growth, and set to snipping away the old. Eventually, he moved on to the next vine, and a little while after that, to the next. It was oddly comforting work; soothing. He didn't precisely *think*; it seemed like all his awareness was in his eyes and his arms, as he *snip, snip, snipped* the old wood, giving the new wood room to breathe.

It was the ache in his shoulders and his forearms that finally called him back to wider concerns. He lowered his shears and stepped away from his last vine. Standing in the middle of the dirt corridor, he looked back, and whistled appreciatively.

"Mud and stink," he said slowly, looking down the line of pruned vines, each with a snaggly pile of twigs at its base. He looked down at the base of his last victim, saw a twig 'way out in the corridor and swung his foot, meaning to kick it back into the general pile.

The twig—*moved*.

Jethri jerked back, overbalanced and fell, hard, on his ass, and the twig reared back, flame flicking from the rising end and a pattern of bronze and white scales on its underside, moving toward him and he was looking to see *how* it was moving, exactly, with neither feet nor legs, and suddenly there was Flinx the cat, with his feet on either side of the—the *snake*, it must be—and his muzzle dipped, teeth flashing.

The snake opened its mouth, displaying long white fangs, its twig-like body flailing in clear agony, and Flinx held on, teeth buried just behind the head.

"Hey!" Jethri yelled, but the cat never looked up, and he surely didn't let go.

"Hey!" he yelled again, and got his feet under him, surging upward. Flinx didn't flick an ear.

"Ren Lar!" He gave that yell everything he had and it worked, too. His panicked heart had only beat half-a-dozen times more before the master of the vine rounded the corner, running flat out.

But by the time, the snake was dead.

THE DOORMAN at the pilots' crash scanned her Kinaveral Port willfly card, and gave her a key to a sleeping room with its own sonic cleaner, which device Khat made immediate, grateful use of. She then hit the hammock for two solid clocks, arising from her nap refreshed and ravenous. Pulling on clean slacks and shirt, she remembered her idea of checking the Trade Bar for the names and numbers of Liaden ships at dock, for Paitor's eventual interest, and thought she'd combine that interest with the pleasure of a brew and a handwich.

The doorman provided a map, which she studied as she walked.

It seemed that most of Banth, with the notable exceptions of the shipyards and the mines, was under roof and underground. Ground level, that was the Port proper. Down one level was living quarters, townie shops, grab-a-bites, and rec centers. Khat thought about that—living *under* the dirt—and decided, fair mindedly, that it was a reasonable idea, given the state of the planet surface. Why somebody had taken the demented notion to colonize Banth at all remained a mystery that she finally shrugged away with a muttered, "Grounders."

The Port level, now, that was Admin, of course, and the pilots' crash, hostels for traders and crew, exhibit halls, Combine office, duty shops, eating places—and the Trade Bar.

Khat traced the tunnel route from her room to the bar, and checked the color of the floor arrows closely.

"Yellow arrow all the way," she said to herself, folding the map away into a pocket. Up ahead, her hall crossed another, and there was a tangle of color on the floor of the convergence. The yellow flowed to the right, and Khat did, too, lengthening her stride in response to her stomach's unsubtle urging.

Banth was close to Kinaveral-heavy, despite which Khat arrived at the Trade Bar barely winded.

Look at you, she thought smugly, swiping her card through the reader. There was a small hesitation, then the door swung open.

She'd expected a crowd, and she had one. Terrans outnumbered

Liadens, Liadens outnumbered the expectable, just like Admin, earlier. Noisy, like Trade Bars were always noisy—no difference if they was small, which this one was, or large—with everybody there trying to talk loud enough to be heard over everybody else.

Khat waded in, heading for the bar itself, and found it standing room only.

No problem. She got herself a place to stand, and swung an arm over her head, catching the eye of a bartender with spiked blue hair and a swirl of tattooed stars down one cheek.

"What'll it be, Long Space?" she bellowed

"Handwich an' a brew!" Khat yelled back.

"It's processed protein," warned the barkeep.

Khat sighed. "What flavor?"

"Package says chicken."

At least it wasn't beef. "Do it," Khat yelled, and the other woman gave her a thumbs-up and faded down-bar.

Khat fished a couple bills out of her public pocket, and eased forward, careful not to step on any toes. The bartender reappeared, and handed over a billy bottle of brew and a zip-bag. Khat tucked them in the crook of her arm, and handed over the bills in trade.

"Got change comin'," the woman said.

Khat waved a hand. "Keep it."

"You bet. Good flying, Long Space."

"Same," Khat said, which was only polite. The bartender laughed, and turned away, already tracking another patron.

Provisions firmly in hand, Khat squinched out of the crowd surrounding the bar, and looked around, hoping to find a ledge to rest her brew on. The booths and tables were full, of course, as was the available standing space—no, there was a guy coming off of his stool, his recyclables held loose in one hand. Khat moved, dancing between clusters of yelling, gesticulating patrons, and hit the stool almost before he left it.

Cheered by this minor bit of good luck, she popped the seal on the billy and had a long swallow of brew. Warm, dammit.

She had another swallow, then unzipped the food bag.

She's expected to find her flavored protein between flat rectangles of ship cracker, and was pleasantly surprised to find it served up on two fine slices of fresh bake bread, which was almost enough to make up for the warm brew.

A bite confirmed that the protein was no better than usual, with the bread contributing interest and texture. Khat made short work of it, and settled back on the stool, nursing what was left of her brew.

Good manners was that she should pretty soon surrender the stool and the little table, so someone else could have their use. Still, she had a couple minutes left before she hit the line for rudeness, and she wanted to study the floor a little closer before she went back to being part of the problem.

The Liadens traveled in teams—no less than two, no more than four—and all of the teams she could see from her stool were in conversation with Terrans. That struck her as funny, being as Liadens were always so stand-offish. On the other hand, shy never made no trades.

It did make a body pause and consider what it was that Banth had, that Liadens wanted.

She chewed on that while she finished her brew. The mines— what did they mine on this space-forsaken dustball? She made a mental note to find out, and slid off the stool, on-course for a view of the ship-board.

"AND NO ONE THOUGHT to tell our guest, before he was left alone among the vines, that kylabra snakes are poisonous?" Lady Maarilex inquired gently. Too gently, Jethri thought, sitting stiff in the chair she had pointed him to, Flinx tall and interested beside his knee.

Her son was standing, and his face had regained its normal golden color. He hadn't known that it was possible for a Liaden to pale, but Ren Lar had definitely lost color in the instant that he took in the snake, and whirled back to Jethri, snapping, "Are you bit?"

"Mother," he said now, voice quiet and firm. "You know that the kylabra do not usually wake so early."

"And you know, *Master Vintner*, that the weather in this wind year has been unseasonably warm. Why should the snakes sleep on?"

"Why, indeed?" murmured her son, and despite his level shoulders and expressionless face, Jethri was in receipt of the distinct idea that Ren Lar would have welcomed the ability to sink into and through the floor.

He cleared his throat and shifted a little in his chair.

"If you please, ma'am," he said slowly and felt like he wanted to sink through the floor on his own account when she turned her face to him—and took a breath. *Dammit*, he thought; *you took whatever Cap'n Iza was serving, you can sure take this.* He cleared his throat again.

"The fact is," he said, keeping his voice settled and easy, just like Cris would do, when their mutual mother was needing some sense talked to her, "that I wasn't left unguarded. Ren Lar left Flinx with me, to supervise, he said. I thought it was a joke—I've been studying on what is and isn't a joke, ma'am, as you'll remember—but it comes about that he was serious. Snakes—I read about snakes, but I've never seen one. And Flinx was there to do what was needful."

"I see." She inclined her head, maybe a bit sarcastic—he thought so. "You would argue, then, that the house provided adequate care to one who is perhaps naive in some of the . . . less pleasant aspects of planet-bound life."

"Yes, ma'am, I do," he said stoutly, and thought to add, "All's well that ends well, ma'am."

"An interesting philosophy." She turned to face her son. "You have an eloquent champion in the one whose life you endangered. Pray do not rest upon your good fortune."

Ren Lar bowed. "Mother."

She sighed, and moved an impatient hand. "Attend me a moment longer, if the vines can spare you. Jethri, you have had adventures enough for a day. Go and make yourself seemly for the dancing master."

"Yes, ma'am." He rose, made his bow and headed for the door, Flinx prancing at his side, tail high and ears forward.

THE SHIP-BOARD was hung along the backmost wall, the Combine-net computers lined up just below.

The computers was all taken, of course, not that Khat had need of a beam or a quote. She did want a clear view of the 'board, though, and that took some fancy dancing around various clustered jaw-fests.

Finally, she got herself situated behind a rare group—half-a-dozen Liadens, talking low and intense 'mong themselves and not minding anything else. No problem seeing over *those* heads, and there was the ship-board, plain as you please, showing the names of five Terran ships, including her own—and four Liaden ships, their names a garble of Terran letters and pidgin hieroglyphic.

Khat frowned at the listings, trying to work out the names and having a little less luck than none. Four Liaden ships at Banthport was *some* news and no doubt Paitor'd be glad of it. Nameless, though, that wasn't much good, especially as there was a Combine key graphic next to two of the four indecipherables, and Paitor would *really* want to know those names, so he could run a match through Terratrade's main database.

Some Liaden traders held Combine keys—it was 'specially found it 'mong those who worked the Edge. Banth being the Edge, it wasn't out of the question to find a Liaden-held key on-port. You might even stretch to two on a port the size of Banth, given the random nature of the universe. But *four* Liaden ships, two carrying keys?

Khat's coincidence bone was starting to ache.

She stared at the 'board, not really seeing it, trying to figure the odds of getting anything useful out of Admin and what plausible reason she might offer for her need-to-know. And how much it was likely to cost her.

". . . long time!" an exuberant male voice bellowed into her off-ear.

She started and blinked, coming around a thought too fast for such cramped quarters—and lowered her hand with a half-laugh.

"Keeson Trager, you near scared me outta my skin!"

"No more than you did me, thinking that strike was gonna land!" he retorted, blue eyes dancing in a merry round face. "Least I'd've been able to tell my captain it was Khat Gobelyn who decked me."

She cocked an eyebrow. "Your captain figure brawl fines by who takes you down?"

He pushed his chest out, pretending to be a tough guy. As Khat knew for certain, there wasn't no need to pretend, except for the joke of it. Keeson Trager was plenty tough.

"My captain says, anybody takes me down in a brawl, she'll waive the fine and give double to the one who done the deed." He let his chest deflate a little, and cast her a bogus look of worried concern.

"Not short on cash this trip, are you, Khati?"

She laughed and shook her head. "Even if I was, there's easier ways."

His relief was obvious—and ridiculous. "Well, I'm pleased to hear you're doing OK." He glanced over to the 'board.

"*Market* not with you?"

"*Market's* at Kinaveral for refit. Right now, I'm a hired wing." She waved a hand at the 'board. "Brought *Lantic* down today. The unloading goes timely, I'll lift out tomorrow."

"My luck," said Keeson with a sigh. "*Wager's* lifting inside the hour—I'm sweep. Of course."

Of course. "Who's missing?" Khat asked.

"Coraline."

Of course. Keeson's youngest sister had a restless urge to explore every station and port *Wager* put in to, roof beam to secret cellars, and she'd more than once been the cause of the *Wager* refiling a scheduled lift.

"Funny to look for her here," Khat commented. "You try the residences, down below?"

"Tried that first. Then all the tunnels and the crawlways. Figure she might be here on account she's takin' her approach from your Jeth and givin' some study to the Liaden side of things."

"What's with all the Liadens, anyway?" Khat asked, since Keeson would know, if anyone did. "Port the size of Banth, with hardly no trade . . ."

He shrugged. "Maybe they're looking to buy it for a resort."

Khat wrinkled her nose at him. "Seriously."

"Seriously—I don't know, nor neither does the captain. All Banth's got is the mines. Now, they're bringing high-quality gold up outta the ground, but it's still only gold. Ain't ever seen Liadens much interested in raw gold—even processed, it's a ho-hum, though they'll buy some, every once in a while, just to be polite."

This was true. "Something else comin' out of the mines, then?"

Keeson shrugged again. "Bound to be, but I don't know what it is, and my guess is Admin don't, too, though right about now they're prolly scrambling to find out."

"What about the ship names?" Khat asked abruptly, with a jerk of the head toward the 'board.

He grinned. "Bothered you, too, huh? Farli worked 'em out—I'll drop a beam under your name to the crash when I get back to the ship. Assuming." He shook his head. "Oughta leave her once, so she'd learn."

Khat could see where it might be tempting, given Coraline's rare ability to vanish, mud-side, but still— "Remember the Stars," she said, which family had done just that—left their wanderaway youngest and lifted, to teach him. When they set back down, couple hours later, the boy was dead.

He'd been up on one of those observation decks Grounders favored—nothing more than a platform and a rail. The Grounders who saw it, they said he panicked, but every spacer who heard the tale knew better'n that.

What more natural, after all, seeing your ship's running lights come up and knowing down to the heartbeat how much time you had to gain the hatch—what more natural than to calculate your angle and take off over that rail, all forgetful, until it was hideously too late, of planetside grav. . .

"I know," Keeson said. "But still."

Khat put her hand on his arm. "I'll help out. Let's take it to the back corners and sweep toward the door."

He looked around, firmed up his shoulders and nodded. "Good idea. Obliged."

"FLINX IS A HERO!" Meicha cried, swooping down to snatch the big cat into her arms. He flicked his ears and lifted his head to rub a cheek against her chin. She laughed, and spun away, her feet describing patterns that Jethri thought might be Liaden dancing.

"Are you well, Jethri?" Miandra had come forward to stand next to him, her eyes serious.

He grinned and shrugged, Terran-style. "Too ignorant to know my own danger. I shouted for Ren Lar, true enough, but because I didn't think it was right for Flinx to kill that thing. It turns out that it was a good job he didn't get bit, since I learn that the . . . kylabra . . . bite will leave you ill."

"The kylabra bite," she corrected, her eyes even more serious. "Will leave you dead, more often than not. If you have been bitten by a young snake, or one newly wakened, perhaps you will merely become ill, but it is wisest to assume that any snake you encounter is both mature and operating at full capacity."

He considered that, remembering how small the snake had been. But, then, he thought, a mouthful of anhydrous cyanide will kill you, sure as stars, no matter how big you are. If the kylabra carried concentrated poison . . .

He frowned.

"Why allow them to remain in the vineyard, then? Wouldn't it be better to simply kill them all and be sure that the workers are safe?"

"You would think so," Miandra agreed, her eyes on Meicha, who was bending so that Flinx might jump from her arms to the upholstered window ledge. "And, indeed, the winery logs show that there had at one time been a war waged upon the kylabra. However, the vines then fell victim to root-eaters and other pests, which are the natural prey of the snakes. The damage these pests gave to the vines was much greater than the danger kylabra posed to the staff, and so an uneasy truce was struck. The snakes are shy by nature and attack only when they feel that they have been attacked. And it is true that they do not usually wake so early."

"The weather has been unseasonable, Ren Lar said."

She glanced up at his face, her own unreadable. "Indeed, it has been. We pray that it remains so, and we have no sudden frosts, to undo what the early warmth has given us."

Jethri frowned. Frost was condensed water vapor, but— "I am afraid I do not understand weather as it occurs on-planet," he said slowly. "Is there not an orderly progression—?"

She laughed and Meicha smiled as she rejoined them. "Is Jethri telling jokes?"

"Not quite," her sister said. "He merely inquires into the progression of weather and wonders if it is orderly."

Meicha's smile widened to a grin. "Well, if it were, Ren Lar would be a deal more pleased, and the price of certain years of wine would plummet."

He worked it out. "The vines are vulnerable to the . . . frost. So, if there is a frost after a certain point, there are less grapes and the wine that is made from those grapes becomes more valuable, because less available."

Together, they turned to look at him, and as one brought their palms together in several light claps.

"Well reasoned," said Meicha and he shrugged a second time.

"Economic sense. Rare costs more."

"True," Miandra murmured. "But weather is random and there are some grapes of which we need to have no shortage. It is better, if rarity is desirable, to reserve the vintage to the house and sell it higher, later."

That made sense. The weather, though, you'd think something could be done.

"Do you watch the weather?"

"Certainly." That was Meicha. "Ren Lar has a portable station which he carries on his belt and listens to all his waking hours—and his sleeping hours, too, I'll wager! However and alas, the reports are not always—one might say, hardly ever—accurate, so that one must always expect that the weather will turn against you. Only think, Jethri! Before you is yet the experience of being awakened by the master in the still of night, in order that you might assist in tending the smudge pots, which will keep the frost from the buds."

There had to be a better way, he thought, vaguely thinking of domes, or the *Market's* hydroponics section, or—

"Good-day, good-day, Lady Meicha, Lady Miandra!" The voice was brisk and light and closely followed by an elderly gentlemen in evening clothes. He paused just inside the room, bright brown eyes on Jethri's face.

"And this—I find Jethri, the son of ven'Deelin?"

He made his bow, light and buoyant. "Jethri Gobelyn," he said in the mode of introduction. "Adopted of Norn ven'Deelin."

"Delightful!" The elderly gentleman rubbed his hands together in clear anticipation. "I am Zer Min pel'Oban. You may address me as Master pel'Oban. Now, tell me, young Jethri, have you been instructed in the basic forms and patterns?"

"I can dance a jig and a few line dances," he said, neither of which likely hit any of the basic forms and patterns, whatever they might be. Still, he was accounted spry on his feet, and at the shivary during which he came to sixteen, Jadey Winchester—mainline, right off the *Bullet*—had danced with him to the positive exclusion of the olders who were trying to court her—or, rather, to court the *Bullet*, since Jadey was in line for captain, as he found out later. But not 'til him and Mac Gold had come to blows over who had a right to dance and who was just a kid.

"A jig," Master pel'Oban murmured. "I regret, I am unfamiliar. Might you, of your goodness, produce a few steps? Perhaps I may recognize it."

Not likely, thought Jethri, but since he'd brought the subject up, there really wasn't any way he could ease out of a demo.

So— "I will attempt it, sir," he said, politely, and closed his eyes, trying to hear the music inside his head—flutes, spoons, banjo, drums, some 'lectric keys, maybe—*that* was shivary music. Loud, fast and jolly for a jig. Jethri smiled to himself, feeling his feet twitch as the remembered twang of Wilm Guthry's banjo echoed through his head. He closed his eyes, and there was Jadey, smiling a challenge and tossing her head, kicking high, once, twice—and on the third kick he joined her, then both feet down and hands on hips, look to the left and look to the right, and your feet moving quick through the weaving steps. . .

"Thank you!" he heard, and opened his eyes to the dancing

room with its wooden floor and blue-covered walls, and Master pel'Oban standing before him, his hands folded and a look on his face that Jethri thought might have been shock. The twins, at his right and left hands, were visibly trying not to smile.

He let his feet still, dropped his hands from his hips and inclined his head.

"A few steps only, sir. I hope it was—instructive."

Master pel'Oban eyed him. "Instructive. Indeed. You have grace, I see, and an athletic nature. Now, we will show you how the dance is done on Irikwae." He waggled his fingers at Miandra and Meicha.

"If the ladies will oblige me by producing a round dance?"

THE BAR WAS LESS FRENZIED NOW. In fact, the blue-haired bartender was leaning at her ease at the near end, in earnest conversation with a little girl wearing a ship's coverall, sitting cross-legged atop the bar.

"This one yours, Long Space?"

"Belongs to a friend," Khat said, sparing a hard frown for Coraline. "Her ship's going up in a quarter-clock and her brother's lookin' for her."

The 'keeper produced a frown of her own. "Bad business, worrying your brother," she said sternly.

Coraline bit her lip and stared down at the bar. "I'm sorry," she whispered.

"You tell him that," the barkeep recommended and tapped her on the knee. "Hey."

The girl looked up and the woman smiled. "It's been good talking to you. Next time you're here, stop by and give me the news, right, Cory?"

Coraline smiled. "Right."

"That's set, then. Go on now and find your brother."

"All right. Good flight." Coraline scooted to the edge of the bar and dropped to the floor, landing without a stagger.

Khat held out her hand. "Let's go." She said, and the two of them crossed the last bit of the bar and went out into the corridor.

✖ ✖ ✖

"YOU!" KEESON'S BELLOW got the frowning attention of a cluster of Liadens near the door. He ignored them and swept his sister up in his arms.

"I oughta break you in half," he snarled, giving her a hug that looked close to doing the job.

Coraline put her head next to his. "I'm sorry, Kee."

"You're *always* sorry," he said. "What you gotta be is *on time*. You keep up like this an' captain'll confine you to ship for sure." He set her on her feet, keeping a tight grip on her hand, and turned to give Khat a grin and an extravagant salute.

"Khat Gobelyn, you're my hero!"

She sputtered a laugh and shooed him down the tunnel. "Go on, or your captain'll leave both of you."

"And count herself ahead," Keeson agreed. He gave her another salute and tugged on Coraline's hand. "C'mon, Spark. Show me how fast you can run in grav."

"'bye, Khat," the little girl called and the two of them were gone, moving out with a will.

Khat shook her head and raised a hand to stifle a sudden yawn. *Time to get back to the crash*, she thought, and looked around for her guiding arrows.

"Gobelyn," a soft malicious voice said behind her. Khat spun, and met the cold blue eyes of the yellow-haired trader who'd been giving Intake so much grief.

"What about it?" she asked him in pidgin, not even trying to sound sociable.

He frowned. "Kin you are to *Jethri* Gobelyn?"

What was this? One of Jeth's new mates? "Yes," she allowed, slightly more sociable, trying to see Jethri having anything cordial to do with such a spoiled, pretty fellow, and having a tough go of it, even given that business was business . . .

"Your kin has damaged my kin," the Liaden was saying, and Khat felt her skin pebble with chill. "You owe Balance."

The Liadens standing all around were real quiet, watching them. A couple of Terrans slammed through the door, talking loudly, barged through the crowd without seeing it and disappeared down the tunnel.

"What did he do?" Khat asked the Liaden. "And who are you?"

"I am Bar Jan chel'Gaibin. Jethri Gobelyn by his actions has stolen from me a brother. He does not pay the lifeprice. You are his kin. Will I Balance the loss exactly? Or will you pay the lifeprice?"

What *was* this? Khat wondered wildly. Jethri had killed somebody—this man's brother? And now she was being threatened with—exact Balance—death? Or she could pay up? And Master ven'Deelin was allowing Jeth to dodge a legitimate debt? That seemed unlikely at the least.

Khat drew a careful breath, not cold now that her brain was engaged.

"How much?"

His eyes changed, though the rest of his face remained bland.

"For a gifted trader at the start of a profitable career—four hundred cantra."

She almost laughed—if he'd been Terran, she *would have* laughed. If he'd been Terran, they wouldn't be having this conversation.

She shrugged, indifferent. "Too much," she said and turned away, tracking the yellow arrows out of the side of her eye, moving firm but not so fast that he'd think she was running.

He *grabbed* her, the damned fool. Grabbed her arm, hard, and yanked her back around.

She came around, all right; she came around swinging, and caught him full across the face. The force of the blow lifted him off his feet and dropped him flat, backbone to deck, and there he laid, winded, at least, or maybe out cold.

A shout came out of the watching Liadens, and she figured it was time to show she was serious, so she kept on turning, until she was facing the lot of them, crouched low and the boot knife in her hand.

She let them see it, and when nobody seemed disposed to argue with it, eased out of the crouch.

"We can take it to Security, or we can leave it," she snarled. "We take it to Security, be sure I'll let them know that this man tried to rob me, and made threats against my cousin and myself—and that you stood by and watched."

There was a stir among the group of them, and another boy, not quite so pretty as the one on the floor, stepped forward.

"We leave it," he said. "No Security." He moved a hand so deliberately that the gesture must have meant something. "Safe passage."

Well, now, wasn't that sweet?

Khat bared her teeth at him, in no way a smile. "You bet," she said, and turned away, keeping the blade ready.

Nobody tried to stop her.

IT WAS EDGING onto the middle of the world-night, and he should have been well a-bed. Thoughts were buzzing loud inside his head, though, most notably thoughts regarding supply and demand and the unpredictability of weather.

So it was that Jethri was kneeling on the bench beneath the window in his bedroom, swearing at the latch, instead of sweet-dreaming in his bunk.

The latch came down all at once and the window swung out on well-oiled hinges. He damn near swung out with it, in the second before he remembered to let go and lean back, and then he just knelt there, waiting for his heart to slow down, breathing deep breaths of the cool mid-night air.

The breeze was slightly damp, and carried a confusion of odors. Tree-smells, he guessed, and flowers; rocks, grapes and snakes. The sky showed a ribbon of stars and two of Irikwae's three moons, riding the shoulders of the mountains.

The cushion he was kneeling on moved and he looked down to find Flinx. The cat looked at him, eye to eye, and blinked his, in what Miandra insisted was a cat-smile.

"Guess I owe you Balance," Jethri said, reaching down and tickling the underneath of the chin. Flinx purred and his eyes melted into mere slits of peridot. "Your life ever needs saving, you don't hesitate, take me?" Flinx purred even louder, and Jethri grinned again, gave the chin another couple skritches for good measure, then sat carefully back on his knees and pulled the weather device out of his pocket.

Sometime during the endless repetitions of the basic pattern of a round dance, it had come to him that the little machine might be well-used on behalf of Ren Lar's grapes. He frowned down into the screen, touched the icon which him and his father had figured out accessed the predictive program and knelt tall once more, elbows on the window ledge, the device held firmly between his two hands, slightly extended, allowing it to taste the night.

The screen displayed its characteristic transitional swirls, then cleared, showing a mosaic of symbols. Jethri frowned at them, then at the starry and brilliant night.

Rule of opposites, he thought, which was nothing more than whimsy, and touched the icon for "rain".

The screen swirled and cleared, showing him a duplicate image of the sky outside his window—and nothing else.

Well, that didn't exactly prove anything, did it?

Jethri tapped the upper right corner of the screen, and the icons reappeared. He touched another, at exact random. Nothing at all happened this time; the screen continued to display its mosaic of exotic icons, unblinking, unchanging.

He sighed, loud and frustrated. Beside him, the cat sputtered one of his rustier purrs and banged his head deliberately against Jethri's elbow.

"You're right," he said, reaching down and rubbing a sturdy ear. "The brain's on overdrive. Best to get some sleep, and think better tomorrow." He gave Flinx's ear one more tug, slid off the window seat and headed for the bed, taking a small detour to leave the weather gadget on the table with the rest of his pocket things.

He snapped the light off and climbed into bed, hitting a solid lump with his knee. Flinx grunted, but otherwise didn't move.

"Leave some room for me, why don't you?" Jethri muttered, pushing slightly.

The cat sighed and let himself be displaced sufficiently for Jethri to curl on his side under the covers, head on his favorite pillow, eyes drooping shut. He yawned, once. Flinx purred, briefly.

"GOT A PRINTOUT FOR YOU," the doorman said. "Come down from *Trager's Wager*."

It took a second, her mind still being on the problem back at the Trade Bar and thinking maybe Security'd be waiting for her at the crash, wanting to discuss the open showing of knives in a Combine port. But, no—Keeson had promised to send Farli's list, when he got back to the ship.

"Thanks," she said taking the gritty yellow sheet. She unfolded it, read the names—*Winhale, Tornfall, Skeen, Brass Cannon*—and tried to remember why she'd cared.

Right. Paitor would've been interested in the names, especially the ones that carried the keys. She glanced back at the paper and half-smiled. Never let it be said that Farli Trager was anything less than thorough. Both *Skeen* and *Brass Cannon* carried a key behind their names.

Well, Paitor would be happy, anyway. Assuming Khat managed to get off Port in one piece, and without acquiring a Liaden knife in her back. Which brought her back to wondering if Jethri *had* killed the blond Liaden's brother and if in that case he was all right. Or if, as she considered more likely, the boy had been trying to earn a little—a lot—of extra money by playing the stupid Terran for an idiot.

"You OK?" the doorman sounded genuinely concerned.

Khat shook herself and looked up at him.

"Had a little trouble at the Trade Bar. Heard some bad news about kin. You got a fastbeam I can use?"

He shrugged. "We got one. It'll cost you, though."

Well, what else were bonuses for? Khat nodded.

"I can cover it."

DYK'S BEEN MESSING *with the climate control again*, Jethri thought muzzily, pulling his blanket up around his chin. *Khat's gonna take his ear this ti—*

He sat up, clumsily, because of the heavy, hot boulder resting against his hip, blinked stupidly at the huge space, looming away into darkness—*Tarnia's house*, he remembered then, and shivered in a sudden flow of cool air, from, from—

"Mud!" He flung out of bed and went over to the open window, climbed up on the window seat, leaned out, got a grip on the cold, wet latch and hauled the window closed, pushing down on the lock with considerable energy.

"Ship kid," he muttered. "Think you'd know enough to be sure the hatches was sealed." He shook his head, and slid off the ledge, which was slightly damp where the rain had come in, and, yawning, went back to bed, shoved the cat out of his spot and snuggled back under the covers.

DAY 165

✺ ✺

Standard Year 1118
Irikwae

"WHAT IS THAT?" Miandra asked. Jethri started and looked up, fingers closing automatically around the gadget. "A mirror?" She settled onto the bench beside him, her arm pressing his as she craned to see.

"Not exactly." He held it out, displaying the screen in its transition phase. "It's a weather device."

She frowned down at it, extended a hand—and paused, sending a direct glance into his face. "May I?"

"Of course." He opened his fingers wide and she plucked the thing from his palm, eyes on the swirling screen, head cocked a little to one side. Jethri twisted around, so he could watch, too, without giving himself a crick in the neck.

Eventually, the swirls cleared and the icon dictionary appeared. Miandra's frown deepened.

"What does it do?"

"More than I know about," he said truthfully. "I'm trying to study it out, because one of the things it *does* do is show weather patterns. There should be a way to set it to watch for particular patterns in a specific area, and give a warning." He shrugged. "I haven't figured out quite how to do that, though."

"Perhaps if you consulted the instructions?" She murmured, her attention still on the screen.

"That would be a good idea," Jethri admitted, "if I had the instructions. There might be instructions on-board, but, if so, I've never found them—nor even my father."

"What a peculiar device." She extended a long forefinger and touched the screen, carefully between the rows of icons. "What do these symbols mean?"

"They represent kinds of weather." He put his finger under a sort of squiggle with dashes falling out of it. "That's rain. And this one—" a similar squiggle shape, but the stuff falling out of it was rounder and fuzzy looking— "that's snow. Snow is frozen rain."

Miandra looked up at him, still frowning. "I know what snow is. We have enough of it during the cold season."

He felt his ears heat and inclined his head. "Forgive me. Of course, you know more of these matters than a ship-born. Perhaps you might do me the favor of identifying those symbols that match weather you are familiar with."

She blinked, glanced down at the device and then back to his face.

"I think we do you no favor in teaching you to sharpen your words," she said. "What would you have said to me just then, if we had been speaking in your home-tongue."

"Eh?" He shrugged, feeling a brief sense of dislocation before the words slid into his mouth. "Figure it yourself, if you know so much."

Miandra blinked again. "I see—irritation sharpens your words, not our teaching."

"Well, see—" he began, and shook his head, hearing himself back in Terran. He raised a hand, signaling that he required a moment to himself, closed his eyes and took a deep breath, letting his mind just sort of go blank for a moment . . .

"Jethri, are you well?" Miandra's voice was worried, her words in Low Liaden. He felt something sort of twist inside his head, and opened his eyes.

"I am well," he said. "A momentary dislocation of language. To continue—my father wasn't able to break the puzzle of this device—nor was his cousin, and neither was a shy man with a puzzle. I've only been trying to work out how to operate it for last few days, but I am afraid my frustration—has the better of me. For something that seems so simple, it is remarkably difficult to understand!"

She laughed, and shifted closer to him, holding the device between them. "Well, let us see what we may deduce between us, then. Surely, *this*—" she ran her finger under a simple straight line, "is clear skies—no weather, as we say, though of course there is always weather . . ." Her voice trailed off, and she bent her head closer, reaching up absently to tuck a curl of reddish hair behind her ear. Jethri stared, then pulled his attention back to the problem at hand.

"This . . ." She tapped her finger on a crazy, swirly mess of lines. "Surely," she said, tapping again, "this is a wind-twist? No other weather pattern would be so—" She gasped to a stop, staring down at a screen gone smokey and opaque.

"What is happening?" She thrust the device at him, her eyes wide and panicked. "Jethri—what is it doing?"

Almost, he laughed at her. Almost. And then he remembered all the times neither she nor her sister had laughed at him, though he didn't doubt he was nothing less than comical.

So. Gently, he slid the little machine out of her hand. The transitional clouds were thinning on the screen, and he tipped it so she could see.

"It's only going to the next phase—see? Here is a picture of our day, here and now."

And so it was. Miandra gazed at it in silence, then looked back to him, her dark blue eyes showing unease.

"Now what does it do?"

"Nothing," he said, and smiled down at her. "We can go back to the icon screen—" he touched the go-back button; the screen swirled, then solidified. He held the device out to her. "Touch another icon. Any one."

She raised her hand, then slowly lowered it, her face troubled. "I—believe that I do not wish to do that."

"It's all right," he assured her. "Nothing else will happen at all. See?" He pressed the symbol for rain. The icons in place; the screen steady.

"I—see," she replied, but he got the idea she wasn't made easy by the demonstration.

"It's just an old weather predictor," he said, trying to jolly her, "and probably not very stable. I just thought it would be . . . convenient . . . if we had warning of—frost, or any other weather damaging to the vines."

"The weather net is in place," she pointed out.

"But you said it wasn't accurate," he countered.

She used her chin to point at the device in his hand. "That does not appear to be accurate, either."

He had to admit that she looked to be right there, and slipped the device into his sleeve.

"I suppose," he said, a trifle glumly.

Miandra laughed. "Come now, Jethri, do not be cast down! It is a most marvelous puzzle!"

Her laugh was infectious and he grinned in response. "I guess I like my puzzles to have answers."

"As who does not?" she said gaily, and bounced to her feet, the ruby pendant flashing in the brilliant day.

"It is nearly time for the gather-bell. Let us be at our places early and astonish Ren Lar!"

Since Ren Lar actually expected everyone to be in the yard the instant the shift-bell sounded, this was a remarkably sensible suggestion and Jethri got to his feet with alacrity, following her out of the small garden and toward the wine yard.

"What are wind-twists?" he asked as he came to her side. She glanced up at him, her face serious.

"Very destructive and unpredictable weather," she said. "A wind-twist might level a vineyard with a touch, or fling a house into the tops of the trees."

A breeze touched his face, moving off the side of the hill. "*Wind* can do that?" he asked, starting to believe that this was a joke.

"Oh, yes," she assured him. "Fortunately, they are very rare. And never in this season."

THE HYDRAULICS was up to spec for a wonder, and the yard boss wasn't available to talk. That was all right. Myra Goodin, his second, didn't talk much, but she did listen a treat, and tagged his specific concerns and problems in her clipboard, after which, she handed the 'board to him.

Grig read over what she'd input, nodded and thumbprinted it.

"Yard's doing good for us," he said, easy and companionable, as he handed the 'board back. "We appreciate the attention."

Myra looked him firm in the eye. Firm sort of woman, and not one to joke. Serious about her work in a way her boss didn't appear to emulate—or value. Which was too bad, so Grig thought, given that the reputation of the yard sat square on her shoulders.

She took the clipboard back, and counter-printed it, her eyes steady on his. "We got off to a rugged start," she said seriously. "I place the blame equal, there. Your captain shouldn't have popped off like she did and Roard shouldn't've egged her." She nodded. "We've been able to get back on a business-like footing since you and Seeli took over the inspections. I appreciate that you took the initiative, there. This is a joint project—we're all here to see that the refit's done right."

Which was true enough, but not something you'd hear comin' outta Boss Roard's mouth. Grig smiled at Myra.

"Joint project, right enough—and a pleasure to be working on it with you." He stood, and nodded at the 'board in her hand. "When d'you want me by to okay those?"

She frowned and touched the keypad, calling up her schedule.

"Three-day," she said after a moment. "I'll give you a pass."

Myra had been the one who had worked out the pass system that allowed them in the yard more often than Roard's so-called Official Inspection Schedule. It was best for all of them, if okays on inspection problems didn't have to wait 'til the next scheduled inspection, which you'd think a yard boss would understand. Well, Grig amended, a yard boss who wasn't thinking with his spite gland.

He reached out a long arm and snagged his jacket from where

he'd thrown it across the back of a chair. Myra went across the room, pulled a green plastic pass from its hook, set it in the 'coder and tapped a quick sequence in. The machine beeped, she slid the card free and held it out.

"We will speak again in three days," she said, which was dismissal, and right enough, busy as she was.

Grig took the card with smile and put it away in an inner pocket of the jacket. "Three days, it is," he said, gave her a nod for good-day, and let himself out of the office.

He cleared the gate and was maybe eight, nine steps on his way back toward the lodgings when he was joined by a long, soft-walking shadow. He sighed, and didn't bother to look, knowing full well what he'd see.

"Grigory," her voice was familiar. Well, of course it was.

"Raisy," he answered, still not looking, which maybe wasn't right, when a man hadn't seen his sister in so long, but *damn* it. . .

"Uncle wants to see you," she said, which he'd known she was going to, so it wasn't exactly surprise that spun him around, boot heels stamping the road.

'Well, now, there's welcome news!" he snapped, and watched Raisy's eyebrows go up on her long forehead.

"Trouble?" she asked, quiet enough to make him ashamed of showing temper.

"Not til you showed up."

She grinned. "Same could be said for yourself."

"'cept I'm where I was, doin' what I've been, and didn't go lookin' for relatives to complicate my life," Grig said. "And you know for a space cold fact that Uncle is more trouble than any of the rest of us, living or dead."

She appeared to consider that, head tipped to one side. "Exceptin' Arin."

He laughed, short and still sharp with temper.

"True enough. We'd none of us be anywhere, if it wasn't for Arin." He sighed. "What's Uncle want?"

His sister shrugged. "Wants to talk to you. Catch up. It's been—what?—twenty years?"

"Long as that?" He closed his eyes, not wanting it. Not wanting it down deep in his bones. Seeli—Seeli'd be after takin' his head, and she'd have nothing but the right of it on her side.

"Time flows," Raisy was saying, "when life is good."

He opened his eyes and looked at her, long and hard. "Life's *been* good," he said, sternly. "Don't laugh at me, Raisy."

She shook her head, and put a long hand on his sleeve. "No mocking here, brother," she said, serious as only Raisy could be. Her fingers tightened briefly, then withdrew.

"You know Uncle won't let it rest. Why not come along, get it over with? Be a shame to make him send an escort."

Uncle would, too, as Grig knew from bitter experience. Still— "What're you?" He asked Raisy.

She smiled. "Your older sister, here to show you the best course to not getting your arm broke. Or didja forget what happened the last time you turned stubborn?"

"I remember," he said and sighed, accepting it, because Uncle *wouldn't* let it go and there was some small advantage to showing meek and biddable in the first round.

"All right," he told Raisy. "You're persuadable; I'll come. They're expecting me back at the lodgings by a certain time. Lemme find a comm and file an amended course. Then Uncle can have me."

THE JOB TODAY was gathering up all the clippings they'd clipped over the last week and putting them in a cart parked at the end of each row. Filled carts were taken away, and an empty arrived to replace it.

Meicha was on cart duty, along with some youngers from the kitchen and maintenance staff. Jethri was on gather-up, and Miandra, too, him working the left hall off the main corridor, her working the right. Flinx was about, lazing under the vines, and amusing himself however cats did; Jethri'd see him out of the side of an eye when he'd bend down to pick up a bundle of sticks.

On one level, it was stupid, repetitive work—worse even than Stinks. But, where Stinks was a solitary aggravation that let a bad mood grow on you, the stick picking up was a group effort—and it was by large a merry group. The kitchen youngers sang when they pushed their carts, and laughter could be heard along the rows. The weather might have helped the spirit of the day, too—cool, with a light breeze to fan away the sweat of exertion, and some progressively denser clouds to cut the glare of the sun, as the day went on.

Jethri met Miandra at the cart. She threw her armful of sticks onto the growing pile, smiling. He placed his more carefully, because the cart was almost full and he didn't want to start a cascade of sticks to the ground.

"That's all for me!" the tender said cheerfully, reaching down to touch the power switch. She glanced up at the sky. "Hope it's not going to—Gods!"

Instinctively, Jethri looked along her line of sight, blinking up into a sky now almost entirely overcast with green-gray clouds, that seemed to be orbiting each other, picking up speed as he watched.

"Wind-twist!" the cart driver shouted, and shouted again, loud enough to hurt Jethri's ears. "Wind-twist! Everybody get to shelter!"

Apparently suiting her actions to her words, she snapped off the power switch, turned and ran down the hill, toward the house, and the cellar.

The green-gray clouds were moving faster, now, elongating, and there came a downward roar of ice-cold air, slapping the vines flat and abusing the ears, and he felt his arm grabbed and tore his attention away from the spectacle in the sky to Miandra's horrified face, her hair twisting and tangling in the wind.

"Jethri, quickly!" Close as she was, and shouting, too, he could barely hear her above the growing roar of the wind. "To the cellar!"

"You go!" He yelled back. "I'll get Flinx!"

"No!" She grabbed his arm. "Jethri, a wind-twist can pick you up and break you—"

"And you!" he yelled, and pushed her. "Run! I'm right behind you!" And he threw himself forward, away from the wagon, back down the row he'd been working. The vines were snapping like wild cable in the growing disturbance, and about halfway down the row, where he hadn't finished cleaning up yet, some loose twigs started to

stir, and dance above the ground, following a spiral path up into the
sky.

Just before that, crouched under a vine, all four feet under him,
tail twice its normal size and ears laid back, was Flinx.

Jethri jumped, grabbed the cat by the loose fur at the back of his
neck, hauled him up and got him against his chest, arms wrapped
tight. Flinx bucked, and he might have yowled, but the wind was
roaring too loud for Jethri to be certain. Cat crushed against him,
head down, so that none of the airborne sticks would hit his face, he
ran.

All around him, the wind roared, and there was the end of the
corridor, and the abandoned cart, and a slender figure in wind-torn
red hair, her ruby pendant flaring bright as a sun—

"Hurry!" she shouted, and he heard her, somewhere between the
inside of his head and the outside of his ears. "Hurry! It's slipping!"

He hurried, stretching his legs and the cat wrapped close, and
he was past the cart and Miandra was beside him and they were
running faster, *faster*, down the hill, and—

Behind them came a boom like a ship giving up all its energy at
once. Ahead of them, a meteor-shower of sticks and metal shred.
Jethri faltered, felt Flinx's claws in his flesh—

"Run!" screamed Miandra.

And he ran.

THE FAMILY had lodgings in an up-port hotel, which shouldn't
have surprised him any. Raisy's jumpsuit was a serviceable, sensible
garment, but it weren't spacer togs, no more than his good jacket and
respectful trading clothes could pass him as a credit-heavy grounder.

He did see some of those they passed in the lobby notice him,
then look back to Raisy and form certain opinions not particularly
generous of either of them.

"Should've stopped and bought me some dirt duds," he muttered,
and Raisy sent him a Look before pulling a key out of her pocket and
sliding it into a call box. Up on the lift board, a light glowed blue and
a second or two later a door opened, showing carpet, mirrors, and
soft lights.

"After you, brother," Raisy said, and he stepped in, boots sinking into the carpet.

Raisy settled herself beside him. The door slid closed, soundless, and the lift engaged with a subtle purr. Grig glanced to the side, catching their reflections in the mirror: Two long bottles of brew, craggy in the face and lean in the frame, both a little wilted with the heat. The man had his dark hair in a spacer's buzz; the woman kept hers long enough to cover her ears. Despite that, and given a change of clothes for either, they looked remarkably similar. Family resemblance, thought Grig, and laughed a little, under his breath.

"Something funny?" Raisy asked, but he shook his head and pointed at the numbers flicking by on the click-plate.

"Rent the rooftop?" He asked, not quite joking.

"Uncle likes the view," she answered, matching his tone precisely. "The equipment needs to be dry, though. So we compromise."

The numbers stopped flicking, settling on 30. The almost subliminal purr of the machinery stopped and the door slid open.

Raisy stepped out first, and turned to look back to where he stood, hesitating at the door, having fourth and fifth thoughts, and staring down a hall as deep in carpeting and showy with mirror as the lift.

"Come on, brother," she said, holding out a hand, like she was offering a tow. "Let's get you a brew, and a chance to clean up."

Grig shook his head and came into the hall under his own power, though he did give Raisy's hand a quick squeeze.

"Why not fast-forward?" he asked, with a lightness he didn't particularly feel. "I've always found Uncle went down better on an empty stomach."

Her smile flickered, and she shrugged, turning to lead the way. "Your call."

JETHRI SETTLED HIS SHOULDERS against the cool wall and closed his eyes. His chest hurt, inside and out, and multicolored stars were spinning around inside the dark behind his eyelids. Miandra had been appropriated by Meicha the second they cleared the winery door. He'd dropped Flinx about that same time and gone to find himself a nice, secluded piece of wall to lean up against.

It came to him, in painful bursts of thought uncomfortably timed to his gasps for air, that the weather device in his pocket was far more powerful—and far more dangerous—than he, or his father, had ever guessed. Definitely not a toy for a child. Possibly not a toy for a trader grown and canny. Certainly, the occasions that he mistily remembered, when Arin had used the device to "predict" rain, might just as easily been cases of rain being somehow produced by an action of the device. His father and Grig used to argue about it, he remembered, his breathing less labored now, and his brain taking advantage of the extra oxygen. His father and Grig used to argue about it, right. Arin had insisted that the little device was a predictor, Grig had thought otherwise—or said he thought otherwise. Jethri remembered thinking that Grig was just saying it, to tease, but what if—

"There he is!" A voice cried, 'way too loud, sending his overbusy brain into a stutter. He opened his eyes.

Meicha was standing close, Miandra a little behind her shoulder. Both were staring at his chest.

"Unfortunate," Meicha commented.

"Flinx was frightened," Miandra said, her voice slow and limp sounding. The other girl's mouth twisted into a shape that was neither smile nor grin.

"Flinx was not alone." She extended a thin hand, and brushed her palm down the front of Jethri's shirt.

"Hey!" He flinched, the contact waking long slices of pain.

"Hush," she said, stepping closer. "There's blood all over your shirt." She brushed his chest again—a long, unhurried stroke—and again, just the same, except now it didn't hurt.

"Much improved, I think." She stepped back. "Ren Lar wishes to speak with you."

Now there was an unwelcome piece of news, though not exactly unexpected. Ren Lar would have a duty to find out in what shape the foster son of his mother's foster child had survived his first encounter with wild weather. A duty he was probably more than a little nervous about, considering he had just lately almost lost that same foster son to a wild animal attack. Wild reptile. Whatever.

Still, Jethri thought, pushing away from the wall, he wished he could put the meeting off until he had sorted out his personal thoughts and feelings regarding the weather . . . device.

"Ren Lar," Meicha murmured, "is very anxious to see you, Jethri."

He sighed and gave the two of them the best smile he could pull up, though it felt unsteady on his mouth.

"I supposed you had better take me to him, then."

REN LAR WAS PERCHED on a stool behind the lab table, but the calibration equipment was dark. A screen over the table displayed an intricate and changing pattern of lines, swirls and colors that Jethri thought, uneasily, might be weather patterns, the depiction of which held Ren Lar's whole attention. Flinx the cat sat erect at his elbow, ears up and forward, tail wrapped neatly 'round his toes. He squinted his eyes in a cat smile as the three of them approached. Ren Lar didn't stir.

"Cousin?" Miandra said in her limp voice. "Here is Jethri, come to speak with you."

For a moment, nothing happened, then the man blinked, and turned, frowning into each of their faces in turn.

"Thank you," he said to the twins. "You may leave us."

They bowed, hastily, it seemed to Jethri, and melted away from his side. Flinx jumped down from the lab table and went after them. Jethri squared his shoulders and met Ren Lar's eyes, which weren't looking dreamy at all.

"Miandra tells me," the man said, with no polite inquiry into Jethri's health, or even an invitation to sit down on the stool opposite. "That you have in your possession a . . . device . . . which she believes, has the ability to influence weather. I have never seen nor heard of such a device, and I have made weather a lifelong study. Therefore, son of ven'Deelin, I ask that you show me this wonder."

Mud. He'd been hoping for time to think, to—but he couldn't, in justice, blame Miandra for bringing the business straight to her senior. Nor blame the senior for wanting a looksee.

Reluctant, he slipped the little machine out of his pocket and put it on the table. Ren Lar extended a hand—and then snatched it back like he'd been burned, a phrase Jethri didn't catch coming off of his tongue like a curse.

Ren Lar drew a hard breath and treated Jethri to a full-grown glare. "So. Put it away." He turned his head, calling out into the depths of the workroom. "Graem?

"Master?" Her voice came from somewhere deep within the shadow of the barrels.

"Call the Scouts."

"GRIGORY," the man who stood up from behind the desk was long, craggy and lean. His hair was hullplate gray, short, but not buzzed; his eyes dark and deep. He smiled, which was worth sixth thoughts. Uncle in an affable mood was never good news.

Well, there wasn't nothing for it, now. He was here. Just get it over with, like Raisy said.

Thinking that, he nodded, respectful-like, and made himself smile.

"Uncle Yuri," he said, soft-voiced. "You're lookin' well, sir."

The older man nodded, pleased with him. "I'm doing well," he allowed, "for an old fellow." He moved a hand, showing Grig a deep, soft chair at the corner of the desk.

"Sit, be comfortable! Raisana, your brother wants a brew."

Grig sat, though he wouldn't have owned to comfortable, and raised a hand. "No brew for me, thanks. Can't stop long."

Uncle didn't frown, but he did let his smile dim a bit. "What's this? You haven't seen your family—your own sister!—for twenty Standards and you can't stop for a couple hours, have a brew, catch us up on your news?"

Raisy had settled on the arm of a chair somewhat back from the desk; Grig dared a quick look at her out of the corner of his eye, much good it did him. She had on her card-playing face, and if there was only one thing certain in the universe as it was configured, it was that Grig would never be his sister's equal at cards. Sighing to himself, he put his attention back on Uncle Yuri.

"Raisy said you wanted to talk to me, Uncle. Made it sound urgent, or I wouldn't have come today. Ship's down for refit and there's only me and Seeli to do the needful, with part-time help from young Khat."

Uncle's smile had dimmed even more. He sat, carefully, and folded his hands on the desk. "I didn't realize you were doing the refit yourself," he said, only a little sarcastic. "I'd've thought even Iza Gobelyn would be smart enough to bring her ship to a yard."

Grig sighed, letting it be heard. "She did, but there's issues and the yard wants close watching. They started out shorting us on the shielding and when Iza called it, the boss pushed her into a fistfight and had her banned from the yard, on risk of losing the *Market*."

Uncle's face was a study in disinterest. Tough. Grig settled his shoulders against the back of the chair and made himself smile again.

"So, we got Iza bailed out and off-planet with a nice, safe pilot's berth, and the rest of the crew'd already done the same, excepting Khat, who signed on as a willfly for the port—and Seeli, who's Admin and hasn't got no choice but to stay. And me, backing up, just like I was born to do."

That last, it maybe wasn't smart; a sideways glance at Raisy's face certainly left him with that impression, but Uncle was still holding course on affable, despite the provocation—and that was bad.

"I'm glad to hear you're such a rich resource for your ship," Uncle said. "You do your family proud."

Uh-huh. Grig ducked his head. "Thank you, sir."

There was a small pause, during which Uncle traded stares with Raisy, which didn't do much for Grig's stomach. Raisy was his sister, but she advised Uncle—and handled him—that too. Another thing she'd always been better at than Grig.

"In fact," Uncle said, having gotten whatever advice Raisy had to give him, "it was about your ship that I wanted to talk. Word is that Arin's youngest brother is missing—and that *Gobelyn's Market* no longer trades in fractins."

Grig shrugged. "There's a wobble in your info, sir. For instance, the boy ain't 'missing'—he's 'prenticed. The fractins—what there was left of 'em, after certain experiments and explorations—he's got them, too."

Uncle's smile was back, full-force, mixed with no little measure of relief.

"The work continues, then. Excellent. And you are to be commended for your part in securing the position with the Liaden trader. Our studies indicate that there are many caches within Liaden-held space."

Old studies, those were. Extrapolations and wishful thinking. Gettin' wishfuller as the timonium ran down toward inertia.

"I didn't have no part in gettin' Jethri his 'prenticeship—he did that his own self," he said, into the teeth behind Uncle's smile. "And I don't exactly think he knows that there's any work he oughta be carrying on, for the good of the family, or otherwise."

Uncle *frowned*.

"Surely, you saw to his education, after Arin's death. Why else were you on that ship?"

Grig sat up straight, feeling his mouth forming a frown to match Uncle Yuri's. "I was there as Arin's back-up, and after he died, it fell on me to make sure the boy survived to adult. Which mostly came down to making sure Iza didn't shove him out an airlock or leave him grounded somewhere. It sure didn't have nothing to do with teaching him the family trade. If I'd tried, Iza'd've spaced *me*."

Uncle stared, not saying nothing—which was more natural. Out of the corner of his eye, he saw Raisy shake her head, just a mite, but the hell with that. Grig sat forward and gave Uncle his full attention.

"Arin shouldn't've played Iza Gobelyn for a fool. He knew it an' spent the rest of his life trying to amend it. If he'd lived, he might've reconciled her to the boy. If he'd lived, she might've been able to forget how she'd got him. Might've. So, anyhow, there's Iza, and she's got the cipher. Then *Toad* went down with the tilework overridin' ship's comps."

"*Toad* knew the risk." That was Raisy. Grig sent her a glance.

"They did. Some of us, though, we started asking if the risk was worth the prize."

"You're telling me that *Arin* thought of giving up on the project?" Grig could almost taste Uncle's disbelief.

Grig shook his head. "I'm tellin' you that the fractins are dying. They're dying, no matter what we do. It's inevitable. Irreversible. We need to give it up, Uncle."

"Give it up," Yuri repeated. "You're asking us to embrace death, Grigory."

"No, sir. I'm asking you to embrace life. We *know* what some of the Befores are capable of. We've made them the study of generations. Now—while the old ones still function and can serve as a baseline—now's the time for us to start trying to build our own, based in science that we understand."

"Grig," said Raisy, "some of that tech does stuff that is *no way* based in science we understand."

"That's right," he said, turning to face her. "That's right. And we been lucky—lucky that all we did was lose a ship every now an' then, or a couple arms and legs from somebody getting careless with a light-wand. Do you thank the ghosts of space that we never come across a planet-cracker? Do you, Raisy? I do."

"We don't know that they built planet-crackers."

"Do we know that they didn't?" he countered.

She said nothing.

"Grigory," Uncle said, talking soft, like maybe Grig needed calming down. "Where, exactly, is Arin's brother?"

"Arin's *son*," Grig snapped, and closed his eyes. "He's 'prenticed to Master Trader Norn ven'Deelin. Jethri's good at the trade—got a real flair for it. Wouldn't surprise me if Master Trader ven'Deelin sets him up as the first trader fully licensed by Terra and by Liad, both. It's sure how I'd work it, given what we're seeing at trade level."

"And where," Uncle continued, "are Arin's notes?"

Grig shrugged. "Jeth's got 'em, if anybody does. Understand, Iza went a little crazy when Arin died, spaced a lot stuff right off. Cris talked her into stowing the rest til she was cooler. That's what went after Jethri—the rest. His by right." He grinned. "Which you can't dispute."

"Of course not." Uncle put his hands flat on the desk and pushed down, though he didn't quite stand up.

"Grigory, it is time for you to return to the bosom of your family. We have need of your talents and your . . . particular . . . viewpoint."

"No."

Uncle blinked. "I beg your pardon?"

"I said," Grig explained, and not daring to look at Raisy. "No. I'm staying with the *Market*."

"Grig . . ." Raisy began, but he shook his head without looking at her yet, and rose to his full, gangly height.

"Sorry to leave so soon, sir," he said to Uncle, real polite. "But, like I said, I've got business elsewhere." At last he looked at his sister.

"Favor, Raisy."

"You got it," she answered, which he'd known she would.

"Keep that headcase you got working for you away from Seeli. He wants to talk to Paitor, that's your business, I guess. But you oughta know he was asking for duplicating units."

She nodded. "I'll take care of it."

"Good," he said and smiled, warmed, and feeling a little gone in the guts. Uncle allowed deviance, but there was always a price.

"Grigory, if you leave this room, you no longer have any call on us." Uncle's voice was cool, spelling exactly out how much this was gonna cost. Grig nodded.

"I can afford that, sir," he said, his own voice just as cool. "Good-bye, now."

He walked out and neither one stopped him, down the long hall, to where the lift stood, door open, waiting.

"HEALER HALL IS SENDING one of the masters," Miandra said, her voice a little stronger, and her hair neatly combed behind her ears. "I wonder who will arrive first?"

They were sitting in the parlor where Jethri had first met Lady Maarilex, in company with Norn ven'Deelin—and wouldn't he give a can full of canaries to see her walk through the door right now! Jethri had changed his sliced shirt for a whole one, taking a moment to marvel at the pale pink lines down his chest, each of which matched a cut in the ruined shirt. There hadn't been much time to wonder about it, though, and he'd hurried into the fresh shirt, hauled a brush over his hair, which mostly stayed flat, for a wonder, and run downstairs, to this very parlor, to find Miandra ahead of him, seated in the precise center of the white couch, one hand a fist around her ruby, and her face outright gloomy.

"Maybe," Jethri offered, deliberately trying to lighten her gloom, "the Healer and the Scout will arrive together and will entertain each other, leaving us free for other endeavors."

She didn't smile. He thought she clenched the ruby tighter.

The silence grew. Jethri shifted in his chair, looked around the room, and back at Miandra. She was staring, with great intensity, at a spot he calculated to be some ten feet beneath the vermillion floorboards.

Jethri cleared his throat. "An . . . unusual . . . thing," he said. "When I took my shirt off, there were these pink stripes—like brand-new scars—down my chest. I had expected, because there was blood, you know, to have found fresh cuts."

Miandra looked up. "Flinx was frightened," she said, as she had in the winery. "He is a very strong cat, and I am afraid he clawed you rather badly. The adrenaline masked the pain, but you would have felt it soon enough, so Meicha Healed you."

Sitting in the chair, he heard the words, blinked, listened to them again in his mind's ear, and then repeated the phrase, with the inflection that signaled a query: "Meicha Healed me?"

Miandra's mouth tightened. "Indeed. It is what we train to be— Healers. Meicha is—more skilled than I."

"Oh." He considered that, running his hand absently down his chest. No pain. He looked, tucking his chin in order to stare down his own front. No blood on the fresh shirt. Beyond dispute, he was patched, but—

"She—you—can make fresh wounds into new scars? In moments? How?"

Miandra moved her shoulders. "It is a talent, much like a talent for music, perhaps—or trade. For those of us with the particular talent to Heal, the . . . physics . . . and the methods are obvious. Intuitive." She smiled, very faintly. "Control is what must be taught, and . . . efficient use of one's energy."

Right. He had the idea she was simplifying things in order to save his feelings and almost laughed, considering what he carried around in his pocket.

"What else do Healers do?" he asked, to keep her talking, mostly. Talking, she seemed less gloom-filled, more like her usual self.

"Heal afflictions of the spirit. That is why a Healer is most often called. Someone is—sick at heart, or frightened. Perhaps they see things which are not there, or refuse to see those things which are directly before them. Those sorts of things. Physical Healing—there are not many Healers who can do that." Her face lightened a little— with pride, he thought. "Meicha will be a Healer to behold."

Well, that wasn't too unlikely, he allowed, given Meicha. But, wait—

"So it was—you or Meicha—who calmed me down that first day, when the curtains were open and I had the widespaces panic?"

"Yes," she said. "I calmed you and Meicha closed the curtains. It was not very difficult—you project a very solid . . . pattern, we call it. You are extremely easy to work with."

He didn't know as he particularly liked the sound of that, but before he could pursue the matter the door to the parlor opened and Lady Maarilex entered, leaning heavily on her cane and followed by a ginger-haired man whose thinness was accentuated by his black leather clothing.

"Scout Lieutenant Fel Dyn yo'Shomin," said the old woman. "Here is Jethri Gobelyn, foster son of ven'Deelin. Jethri, if you please, make your bow to the Lieutenant."

Cautiously, Jethri rose, and Lieutenant yo'Shomin's ginger-colored eyes followed his progress. There was something in the man's stance that irritated Jethri straight off. A little bit of a thrust in the shoulder, maybe, or an attitude with respect to the hips—a subtle something that said Scout Lieutenant yo'Shomin was the better of most men alive, and infinitely superior to grimy Terran 'prentice traders, no matter whose foster son they claimed to be.

That being his reading of the man, in between the time it took to start to rise and reach his full height, he made short shrift of the bow—crisp and brief, it was, and it could be that it would have given Master tel'Ondor pleasure. Certainly, its recipient took the point, and his sharp face got even sharper, the narrow mouth thinning 'til the lips all but disappeared.

The return bow was hardly more than a heavyish tip of the head, which was arrogant, but, then, Jethri thought, wasn't that what he had expected?

"It has been reported that you have in your possession a piece of forbidden technology," the lieutenant said, not even trying to sound polite. "You will surrender it at once."

"No." It had been his intention to hand the device over to the Scout. It was possible, after all, that the thing *had* somehow called the big wind, and if that was so, then it was better off in the keeping of folks who knew its treacheries. Too bad for him, the Scout had shown him reason to doubt. He'd rather take his own chances with the device than meekly hand it over to this . . . incompetent.

Jethri crossed his arms over his chest like Uncle Paitor did to show there was no joking going on, and added an out-and-out frown, for good measure.

The ginger-haired Scout drew himself up as tall as he could and delivered a respectable glare.

"The Scouts have jurisdiction in this. You will relinquish the dangerous device to me immediately."

Jethri kept the frown in place. "Prove it," he said.

The ginger eyebrows pulled together. "What?"

"Prove that the device is dangerous," Jethri said.

The Scout stared.

"Well," Lady Maarilex said, still leaning on her cane across next to the door. "I see that this may be amusing, after all. Miandra, child, help me to the chair, of your goodness. If you please, gentlemen—a moment."

"Yes, Aunt Stafeli." Miandra leapt up and moved to the old

lady's side, solicitously guiding her the first of the blue chairs, and seeing her seated.

"Yes—ah. A pillow for my back, child—my thanks." Lady Maarilex leaned back in the chair and put her cane by. Miandra took a step toward the couch— "Bide," Lady Maarilex murmured, and Miandra drifted back to stand at the side of the chair, hands folded demurely, her pendant—Jethri blinked. There was something odd about her pendant, like it was—

"Now," said Lady Maarilex, "the play may continue. The line is yours, Lieutenant. You have been challenged to prove that the device is dangerous. How will you answer?"

For a heartbeat, the Scout said nothing, then he bowed, very slightly, to the old woman in the chair, and glared up into Jethri's face.

"The device described by Lord Ren Lar Maarilex as being in the possession of the Terran Jethri Gobelyn is unquestionably of the forbidden technology. The form and appearance of such things are well known to the Scouts, and, indeed, to Lord Maarilex, who has attended several seminars offered by the Scouts on the subject of the Old War and its leavings."

"Adequate," commented Lady Maarilex, "but will it compel your opponent?"

Jethri shrugged. "I admit that the device is old technology," he told Lieutenant yo'Shomin. "You, sir, stated that it is *dangerous*, an assertion you have not yet proved."

The Scout smiled. "It called the wind-twist, did it not? I think we may all agree that wind-twists are dangerous."

"Undoubtedly, wind-twists are dangerous," Jethri said. "But you merely put yourself in the position of needing to prove that the device created the wind-twist—and I do not believe you can do that, sir."

"No?" The Scout's smiled widened. "The weather charts describe a most unusual wind pattern, spontaneously forming from conditions antithetical to those required to birth a wind-twist—and yet a wind-twist visited the Maarilex vineyard, a very short time after you were seen experimenting with the forbidden technology."

"I was the one," Miandra said, quietly, from the side of the chair, "who touched the icon for 'wind-twist'."

"And yet," Jethri countered, keeping his eyes on the Scout's face, "wind-twists do sometimes arrive out of season. I wonder if the same weather pattern anomaly was present on those past occasions, as well."

"Well played!" Lady Maarilex applauded from the blue chair. "Bravo!"

The Scout glowered. "Certainly, they would be," he snapped. "Out of season wind-twists must obey the same rule that forms all wind-twists."

"Then you agree," Jethri pursued, "that, unless it was proven in the case of all out-of-season wind-twists that they were every one created by grubby Terrans playing with old technology, it is as least just as likely—if not more likely—that the device which I own, and which was given me by a kinsman, is a *predictor*, rather than an agent to form weather."

Not bad, he congratulated himself, though, truth told, he didn't quite buy in to his own argument . . .

"This is a waste of my time," the Scout snarled. "You may well have possession of a device that cures blindness, restores lost youth, and everything else that is wholly beneficial—and *still* it would be forfeit! Forbidden technology is *forbidden*, in all its manifestations."

So much for that, Jethri thought. *You didn't really think this was gonna work, did you kid?*

Truth told, he hadn't. On the other hand, it was a poor trader who admitted defeat so easily. What was it Uncle Paitor had said? About keeping your opposite in a trade uncertain on his feet, to your best profit?

Jethri inclined his head and changed the ground.

"I am a Terran citizen," he said.

"Ah," Lady Maarilex murmured.

"As anyone can see," the Scout replied, nastily. "However, the point is unimportant. You are currently in Liaden space and are subject to Liaden law and regulations."

"Hah!" said Lady Maarilex.

Jethri raised a hand. "I am a Terran citizen and the device you wish to confiscate is a gift from a kinsman. Thus far, I have only your assertion that the confiscation of old technology falls into the duty of the Scouts. I will see the regulation in question before I relinquish what is mine." He lowered his hand. "Nor will I relinquish it to you, sir."

"You. . ." the lieutenant breathed and Jethri could see him tally up the insult and store it away for later Balancing. Much luck to him.

"I will relinquish the device—if it is proved that I must relinquish it at all—to Scout Captain Jan Rek ter'Astin."

There was a long moment of silence, strongly tinged with disbelief.

"Scout Captain ter'Astin is a field Scout," the lieutenant said, with a slight edge of distaste on the word *field*. "It will take some time to locate him, during which time the device will remain a danger to us all."

"Scout Captain ter'Astin was seen as soon as Day sixty-six at Kailipso Station, and I am persuaded that you will find him there still, for he had just recently been transferred," Jethri countered.

"Send for him," Miandra said, sharp and unexpected. "Jethri will swear not to use the device until the captain comes to claim it. And it will be better to give it over into the hands of a field Scout than a man who prefers the comforts of the regulations and his own bed—and who cares not to associate with *beastly Terrans*."

The Scout gaped at her.

"Do I have that correctly?" she asked, and there was a wild note to her voice that lifted the hairs up straight on Jethri's nape.

The Scout bowed, with precision, and straightened, his ginger-colored eyes like stone. "You have that most precisely," he said. "Dramliza."

Jethri shivered. Miandra had just made an enemy. A powerful enemy, with her stuck to the same ball of mud and not able to lift ship out of trouble . . .

"There are no dramliz in this house," Lady Maarilex snapped. "Merely two young Healers who are fond of parlor tricks."

"Of course," the Scout said cordially, and bowed once more.

"I will have the oath the *Healer* has promised for you," he said to Jethri. "And then I will go."

Jethri hesitated, wondering what this fellow might accept as a valid oath—and nearly laughed, despite the worry and upset in the air.

"I swear on my name—Jethri Gobelyn—that I will not use the old technological device and that I will hold it safe and harmless until such time as it is claimed by Scout Captain ter'Astin, bearing the regulation giving him the right."

"Witnessed," murmured Lady Maarilex.

Scout Lieutenant Fel Dyn yo'Shomin bowed. "On behalf of the Scouts, I accept your oath. Captain ter'Astin shall be summoned."

"Good," said Jethri. "I look forward to seeing him."

THE SCOUT WAS GONE, intercepted by a pale-faced Meicha at the hall door. Jethri let out a long, quiet sigh, and very carefully didn't think about what he had just done.

"Miandra," Lady Maarilex said, very quietly.

"Yes, aunt?"

"May I ask at what date and time you lost your wits?"

Silence.

Slowly, Jethri turned. Miandra was standing, rigid, eyes straight ahead, hands fisted at her sides. The ruby pendant swung in an arc at the end of its long silver chain.

"Your ruby," he said, seeing it now. "It's melted."

Miandra shot him a look from eloquent sapphire eyes, though what they were eloquent of he couldn't exactly have said. A bid for allies—it might be that, though what she thought he might do to divert one of Lady Maarilex's high octane scolds, he didn't know.

"Melted?" the old lady repeated, frowning up at Miandra. "Nonsense. Do you have idea how much heat is required to melt a—" Her voice died. Miandra closed her eyes, her mouth a white line of pinched-together lips.

"Give it to me," Lady Maarilex said, absolutely neutral.

Eyes closed, fists at her sides, Miandra stood like a life-size doll.

"Now," said Lady Maarilex.

Miandra wet her lips with her tongue. "If not this error, another," she said, speaking rapidly, raggedly, her eyes screwed tight. "I cannot—Aunt Stafeli. It is—too big. I drown in it. Let it be known, and done."

"Done it surely will be, witless child!" Lady Maarilex held out an imperious hand. "Give me the pendant!"

The last was said with enough force that Jethri felt his own muscles jerk in response, but still Miandra stood there, rigid, willfully disobedient, with tears starting to leak from beneath her long dark lashes.

It came to Jethri in that moment, that, for all she sat there stern and awful, Lady Maarilex was frightened.

"Miandra," she said, very softly. "Child."

Miandra turned her face away.

He had no business interfering in what he didn't understand—and no possible right to short circuit whatever decision Miandra had made for herself. But Lady Maarilex was afraid—and he thought that whatever could scare her was something no lesser mortals ever needed to meet.

Jethri took three steps forward, caught the chain in one hand and the misshapen ruby in the other and lifted them over the girl's head.

Miandra made a soft sound, and brought her hands up to hide her face, shoulders shaking. Jethri stepped back, feeling awkward and more than a little scared himself, and dropped the pendant into the old woman's waiting palm.

"My thanks, young Jethri," she said. He looked down into her eyes, but all he saw was bland politeness.

"What's amiss, ma'am?" He asked, knowing she wouldn't answer him, nor did she surprise him.

"Nothing more than an unseemly display by a willful child," she said, and the pendant was gone, vanished into pocket or sleeve. "I ask that you not regard it."

Right. He looked at Miandra, her face still hidden in her hands. No question, Stafeli Maarilex was fearless—Miandra was no hide-me-quick, neither. Despite which, both her and her sister managed to mostly keep within the law laid down by their seniors, and answer up clear and sharp when they were asked a question. In his experience, willful disobedience wasn't their style—though he didn't put covert operations out of their range—no more than just standing by, crying.

"Hey," he said, and reached out to touch her sleeve. "Miandra, are you well?"

She sniffed, shoulders tensing, then very slowly lowered her hands, her chin coming up as they went down.

"Thank you," she said, with the dignity of a ship's captain. "Your concern warms me."

"Yes," he replied. "But are you well?"

Her lips moved—he thought it might have been a smile. "As well as may be," she answered, and seemed about to say something more, but the door came open just then and there was Meicha making her bow and announcing—

"Healer Tilba sig'Harat."

Jethri turned and dropped back a couple steps as the Healer strode into the room: Long in the leg—relatively speaking—and gaunt, her hair done in a single pale braid, falling over her shoulder to her belt. She was dressed in regulation calling clothes, and looked a little rumpled, like she had started her shift early and was looking to end it late.

"Healer," Lady Maarilex said, and inclined her head in welcome. "You honor us."

Tilba sig'Harat paused just before the chair, her head to one side. "The message did say that the matter was urgent."

"One's son certainly believed it to be so," Lady Maarilex replied, evenly.

So, Jethri thought, Ren Lar had called the Healers off his own board and his mother thought he'd overreacted. That could explain the particular sharpness of her tongue so far.

But it didn't explain the fear.

"Just so," the Healer was saying, and looked beyond Lady Maarilex to Miandra, who was standing tall now, chin up and face defiantly bland. "Miandra, your cousin has said that you told him you had held the wind-twist back from the vineyard for a period of time before its strength overcame you. Is this correct?"

Miandra inclined her head. "It is."

"Ah. Would you care to explain this process of holding the wind back?"

Silence. Jethri, ignored, cast a quick glance aside and saw the girl lick her lips, her defiant chin losing a little altitude.

"Well?" asked the Healer, somewhat sharply. "Or is it that you cannot explain this process?"

Miandra's chin came back up.

"It is very simple," she said coolly. "I merely placed my will against the wind and—pushed."

"I—see." The Healer held up a hand. "Open for me, please."

The chin wavered; kept its position. Miandra closed her eyes and the Healer did the same. For the space of a dozen heartbeats, there was complete silence in the parlor, then Miandra sighed and the Healer opened her eyes and bowed to Lady Maarilex.

"I see that she believes what she has said, and that she has undergone a profound disturbance of the nerves. This is entirely commonplace; wind-twists unsettle many people. The hallucination—that she held back the winds until her friends reached her side—that is less common, but not unknown. In the immediacy of peril, knowing oneself helpless to aid those whom one holds dear, the mind creates a fantasy of power in which the wind is held back, the sea is parted, the avalanche turned aside. Sometimes, the mind remains convinced even after the peril has been survived. In its way, it is a kindly affliction, which is easily dispelled by a display of the facts—in this case, a recording of the path and pattern of the wind-twist."

Lady Maarilex inclined her head. "The child shall be shown the weather logs, Healer, I thank you." She moved a hand.

"Yes?" the Healer asked.

"You will see that Miandra has lost her apprentice's pendant in the wind. I would ask that the Hall send another."

A glance at Miandra showed her fingers curling into fists at her side, but no one was looking at Miandra except Jethri.

"Certainly," the Healer was saying to Lady Maarilex and Jethri cleared his throat.

"Well?" snapped Lady Maarilex, which Jethri chose, deliberately, to interpret as permission to speak.

He inclined his head. "If Healer sig'Harat pleases," he murmured, as polite as polite could be. "Isn't it possible that Miandra held the winds back? She and her sister do other things that seem just as impossible to myself, an ignorant Terran."

The Healer sent him a sharp glance.

"Jethri," Lady Maarilex murmured, "fostered of ven'Deelin."

"Ah." The Healer inclined her head.

"Certainly, Healers may work many marvels, young sir. But to do that which Miandra . . . believes herself to have done—that would require power and discipline as far from the abilities of a half-trained and erratic Healer as—as Liad is from Terra."

Well, and there was an answer that meant nothing at all, Jethri thought, though a quick glance at Miandra's rigid face suggested that maybe it meant something to her.

"Thank you, Healer," he said, politely. "I am grateful for the information."

"It is my pleasure to inform," she said, and bowed again to Lady Maarilex.

"My duty done, I depart," she said formally.

"Healer," the old lady replied. "We thank you for your care."

And so the Healer was hustled away by a pale-faced Meicha, the door closing behind both with a solid thump.

In the blue chair, Stafeli Maarilex stirred and reached for her cane.

"So, we survive this round," she said, using her cane as a lever, and struggling to ger her feet under her. Jethri stepped forward and caught her arm to help her rise. Miandra held her position, face frozen.

"My thanks," Lady Maarilex gasped, straightening to her full height. She looked from one to the other and used her chin to point at the door.

"Both of you, go to your apartments. You will be served dinner there. Study, rest and recruit yourselves. It has been a long and tiring day—for all of us."

"Yes, Aunt Stafeli," Miandra said tonelessly. She bowed, stiffly, and was on her way toward the door before Jethri could do more than gape and make his own hurried bow.

By the time he reached the hallway, she was gone.

"WHERE'VE YOU BEEN?" Seeli asked, sharper maybe than she needed to.

On the other hand, Grig thought, taking a deep breath, a talk with Uncle had a way of making the whole universe seem edgy, if not outright dangerous.

"I left a message," he said, trying to trump sharp with mild.

"He left a message, the man says." Seeli flung her hands out in a gesture of wide frustration, by which he knew she wouldn't be bought by a smile and a cuddle. He closed his eyes, briefly. Dammit, he didn't *need* a fight with Seeli. Regardless of which, it looked like he was going to get one.

"*Yes*, you left a message," she snapped. "You left a message *six hours* ago saying you'd met an old mate and was going to share a brew. Six hours later, you manage to get your sorry self back to your ship—and you ain't even drunk!"

Trust Seeli to grab the whole screen in a glance. He was in for it bad, now—Seeli had a temper to match her mam's, except it was worse when she'd been worried.

Grig took another breath, looking for center. Despite that his whole life had been one form of lie or another, he'd never been near as casual with the truth as Arin. Well, and he was light on most all the family talents, wasn't he?

"Grig?"

He met her eye—nothing otherwise with Seeli—and cleared his throat. He'd worked this out, in the hours between leaving Uncle and arriving back at the lodgings. His choice was his choice, and he'd made it, for good or for bad. Despite which, there was family considerations. He owed Raisy and the rest of his sibs and cousins— and Uncle, too, damn him—the right to their own free lives. Parsing out his truth from their safety—that was what kept him hours on the Port, walking 'til his legs shook. He'd found what he believed to be a course that would pass close enough to the truth to satisfy Seeli, without baring the others to danger. Assuming he could find the brass to fly it.

"I gotta ask you again?" she said, real quiet.

He spread his hands. "Sorry, Seeli. Truth is, I wasn't straight in that message, and I'm not feelin' good about that. What it was—you remember that headcase? Wantin' to buy fractins and Befores?"

He saw exasperation leach some of the mad out of her face, and took heart. Maybe he could pull this off, after all.

"Thought we agreed to leave that to Paitor."

"We did," he said. "We did—and I should've. No question, it was stupid. I figured, if I talked to the big man, I could show him there wasn't no sense promisin' to buy what we had none of, and tell him—" This was the approach to tricky. Grig kept his eyes straight on Seeli's. "Tell him that Arin's dead and the *Market* ain't in the business of sellin' Befores."

"Great," Seeli said, and shook her head. "So, what? The big man not at home?"

"He was home," Grig said, "and pleased to see me. Turns out, him, I knew—from the old days, when Arin was still Combine and we was dealing in the stuff pretty regular. Anyhow. He spent some considerable amount of persuasion, trying to get me to buy back in." He broke her gaze, then—it was that or die. "I'm not gonna hide it, Seeli—it was a mistake going to see this man."

She sighed. "If you'd called back, I'd've saved you the brain work. How much trouble you in?"

"Now, Seeli." He held up a hand and met her eyes, kinda half-shy. "I ain't in trouble. The man made me an offer—couple offers, as it happens. Didn't want to take 'no' for his final course, and it took some while to persuade him."

She frowned. "He likely to stay persuaded?" she asked, and trust Seeli to think of it. "Or might he want to talk to you again?"

"I—" Grig began.

The door to the hallway snapped open, spinning both of them around to stare as Paitor flung in, face flushed, and jacket rumpled.

Seeli started forward, hands out. "Uncle? What's gone wrong?"

He stopped and just stared down at her. Grig light-footed around him and pushed the door closed, resetting the lock.

"Got a beam from Khat," Paitor said as Grig made it back to Seeli's side. He put a hand inside his jacket and pulled out a piece of hardcopy—blue, with an orange stripe down the side. Grig felt his stomach clench. Priority beam—expensive, reserved for life and death or deals that paid out in fortunes. . .

"We got trouble," Paitor said, pushing the paper at Seeli. "Take a look."

HE SHOWERED, standing a long time under the pulsing rays of hot water, oblivious, for once, to the waste. By the time the water turned cool and he stepped out into the mirrored drying room, his fingertips were as wrinkled up as dried grapes, and he was feeling a little breathless from the steam.

Absently, he pulled the towel off its heated bar and applied it vigorously, first to his head and working methodically downward, where he noted that his toes were as wrinkled as his fingers.

Probably your face is wrinkled up, too, he thought, trying to josh himself out of a growing mood. *Bet your whole head's nothing but one big wrinkle.*

Nothing more than I traded for, he thought back at himself, in no state to be joshed, though he did, by habit, look into the mirror to see how bad his hair looked this time.

The hair was about as bad as he expected, but what made him frown was the smudge over his lip.

"Mud," he muttered. "All that time under water and your face isn't even clean?"

He used a corner of the towel to rub the smudge and looked again.

The smudge was still there, looking even darker against the pink rub mark.

"What the—" He leaned toward the mirror, frowning—and

then lifted his hand, fingertips stroking the first hopeful hairs of a mustache.

"Well." He smiled at his reflection, and stroked the soft smudge again, then turned to the supply cabinet, in search of depilatory cream.

Several minutes later, he was frowning again. The supply cabinet was more comprehensive than most ship's medical lockers, and included several ointments that were meant to be rubbed into the skin—but nothing like a depilatory.

SIGHING, JETHRI CLOSED the cabinet, and went to the bench where he had piled his fresh clothes. Tomorrow, he'd ask Mr. pel'Saba to provide the needed item. In the meantime, he had other rations to chew on.

Barefoot, shirt untucked, he walked into his sleeping room, and knelt next to the bench. Deliberately, he unsealed the B crate and pulled open the bit bottom hatch.

Deliberately, he removed the boxes of fractins, good and bad, the wire frame, and his old pretend trade journal and put them, one by one, on the rug by his knee.

Closing the crate, he settled down cross-legged and reached for the tattered little book, flipping through the laborious pages of lists—income, outgo, exchange rates and Combine discounts—

The door-chime sounded. Biting down on a curse, Jethri grabbed the box of true fractins—and then shook his head. No doubt fractins were old tech—and if Lady Maarilex or Ren Lar or the Scouts entire had decided that they was within their rights to search his room and belongings for old tech, then they'd find the fractins, whether they were on the rug or in the B crate.

The door-chime sounded again.

On the other hand, it was probably one of the kitchen crew, come to collect his untouched dinner tray.

Sighing, Jethri came to his feet and went to answer the door.

The twins tumbled over the threshold and skittered 'round to the far side of the door.

"Close it!"

"Quickly, close it!"

So much for wilful disobedience. Still, he did close the door, and locked it for good measure.

The twins stood in a tangle beside the wall, their reddish hair damp and curling wildly. As usual, they were dressed identically, this time in plain black jerseys and slacks, soft black boots on their feet. One wore a silver chain 'round her neck, supporting a big ruby.

"I thought the pair of you were confined to quarters," he said, hands on hips, trying for the stern-but-friendly look Cris had employed on similar past occasions, with Jethri on the wrong side of the captain's word.

"And so we are in quarters," snapped the twin with the ruby 'round her neck. "Your quarters."

"Come, Jethri," said the other, stepping away from her sister's side and looking gravely up into his face. "We are in need of companionship—and counsel."

Good line, Jethri thought. He'd never been smart enough to come up with something half so clever for Cris.

And, besides, he was glad to see them.

He let his hands fall from his hips and waved them into the parlor. "Come in, then, and welcome."

"Thank you," they murmured in unison and drifted deeper into the room, silent on their soft boots. Meicha wandered over to the table, where his untasted dinner sat under covers. Miandra went further, to the window, and stood gazing out at the sunset clouds crowding the shoulders of the mountains. High up, where the sky was already darkening, stars could be seen, shimmering in the atmosphere.

"The wide spaces do not frighten you now?" She asked, and Jethri moved across the room to join her, bare feet soundless on the carpet.

"I am—becoming accustomed," he said, pausing just behind her shoulder, and looking out. There were purple shadows down deep in the folds of the rockface. 'Way out, he could just see the Tower at the port, gleaming bright in the last of the sunlight.

"Mrs. tor'Beli sent delicacies," Meicha said from behind them. "Are you not hungry, Jethri?"

"Not much," he said, turning around to offer her a half-smile. "If you are hungry, have what you like."

She frowned, and put the lid back over the plate. "Perhaps later," she said, and sent an openly worried glance at Miandra's back.

"Sister?"

There was a pause, and a sigh. Miandra turned around and faced her twin.

"They are still arguing," she said.

"They are," Meicha replied. "And will be, I think, for some time. Aunt Stafeli will not yield the point. Nor yet will Ren Lar."

"Though surely it is his portion to yield to the word of the delm," said Miandra, "nadelm or no."

Meicha laughed. "Allow Ren Lar to tend the vines and he is complacent and calm. Invoke his *melant'i* as nadelm and remind him of his larger duty to the clan, and he is implacable." She paused, shrugged. "Aunt Stafeli trained him, after all."

Miandra actually smiled, though faintly. "True enough."

"What," asked Jethri, "are they arguing about? The old technology?"

Meicha and Miandra exchanged a glance.

"The old technology—that was the beginning," Meicha said, moving over to perch on the edge of one of his chairs, her ruby winking in the light. Miandra went forward and dropped to the rug at her twin's feet, legs crossed, face serious.

After a second, Jethri took the chair across, and leaned back, pretending he was comfortable.

"So," he said, "the argument started with the old technology."

"Just so," said Miandra. "Ren Lar, of course, wished the weather device to be away, *now*—the potential of harm to the vines distresses him, and rightly so. He *is* master of the vine, and it is his duty to protect and nourish them.

"Aunt Stafeli, however, felt that you had reckoned your *melant'i* correctly, that the Scout Lieutenant was well answered, and your oath rightly given. Ren Lar could scarcely argue with *that*."

Silence fell, stretched. Meicha was uncharacteristically quiet, sitting tense on the edge of the chair. Miandra—Miandra sat easily, her wrists resting on her knees, her fingers hanging loose, blue eyes considering a point just over his left shoulder.

Jethri cleared his throat; her eyes focused on his face.

"Yet, they are still arguing—your aunt and your cousin. About the two of you?"

"About *me*," Miandra said, with a depth of bitterness that startled him. Meicha reached down and put her hand on her sister's shoulder, but said nothing.

"It is well enough, to be a Healer," Miandra continued after a moment, her voice less bitter, though her eyes sparked anger. "But to be of the dramliz, here on Irikwae—that . . ." Her voice faded.

"Is untenable," Meicha finished quietly. "Irikwae was colonized by those clans who felt that the dramliz should be . . . should be . . ."

"Eradicated," Miandra said, and the bitterness was back in her voice. "It was believed that a mutation which allowed one such . . . abilities—that such a mutation endangered the entire gene pool. A purge was called for. The matter went to the Council of Clans, in very Solcintra, and debate raged for days, for who is truly easy in the presence of one who might hear your thoughts, or travel from port to center city in the blink of an eye? Korval Herself led the opposition, so the history texts tell us, and at last prevailed. The existing dramliz were allowed to live, unsterilized. The clans of the dramliz retained their rights of contract marriage, mixing their genes with the larger pool as they saw fit. And a guild was formed, much like the pilots guild, or traders guild, which gave the dramliz protection as a valuable commercial enterprise."

"The dissenting clans," Meicha said after a moment, "left the homeworld, and colonized Irikwae. At first, there was a ban on Healers, too. That was eventually lifted, as it became apparent that Healers worked for . . . social stability . . ."

Mentally breathless, Jethri held up a hand.

"Give me a little time," he said, and his voice sounded breathless, too. "Terrans do not commonly run to these mutations. You are the first Healer—and dramliza—I have encountered, and I am still not certain that I understand why one person who does things which are impossible is favored, while another, who does things which are just as impossible, is—feared."

Miandra actually grinned. "Prejudice is not necessarily responsive to cold reason—as you surely know."

He gaped at her, and Meicha laughed.

"Are all grounders stupid? Why else would they live among the mud and the smells and the weather?"

"Ouch," he said, but mildly, because they were right—or had been right. "I am—growing accustomed—on that front, as well. Learning takes time."

"So it—" Meicha began—and froze, head turning toward the door.

It came again, a scratching noise, as if a file were being applied, lightly, to the hall side face of the door.

Jethri rose and crossed the room. Hand on the latch, he sent a glance to the twins, sitting alert in their places. Miandra moved her hand, motioning him to open the door.

All right, then. He snapped the lock off and turned the latch, opening the door wide enough to look out into—

An empty hall.

Frowning, he looked down. Eyes the color of peridot gleamed up at him; and something else as well.

Jethri stepped back. Flinx pranced across the threshold, head high, silver chain held in his mouth, ruby dragging on the floor beneath his belly. As soon as he was inside, Jethri closed and locked the door. By the time he turned back to the room, Flinx had reached Miandra.

She sat perfectly still as the big cat put his front feet on her knee. Slowly, she extended a hand and Flinx bent his head, dropping the chain on her palm.

"My thanks," she said, softly, and held it high. The melted ruby spun slowly in the light, glittering.

"Flinx is proud of himself," Meicha said. "Aunt Stafeli had thrown it in the bin for the incinerator."

Jethri came forward and knelt on the carpet next to Miandra

and the cat. Flinx left the girl's knee and danced over to butt him in the thigh. Miandra looked up at him, blue eyes curious.

"May I see it?" he asked, and she put the chain in his hand without hesitation.

He sat back on his haunches and gave the thing some study. The fine silver links were neither deformed nor blackened. The ruby was—distorted, asymmetrical, the bottom bloated, as if it were an overfull water bulb, the force of the liquid within it distending the bulb nearly to the bursting point.

"So," he said, handing it back. "How did you do that?"

She moved her shoulders. "I—am not precisely certain. It—it may be that the gem, the facets, served as a focus for the power I expended but—I do not know!" she cried, sudden and shocking. "I need to be trained, before I—before . . . And all Aunt Stafeli will say is that I must be a Healer and a Healer only." She bent her head. "She does not know what it is like," she whispered. "I am—I am a danger."

He considered her. "Even if you cannot be trained on Irikwae, there are other places, isn't that so? Places where the guild of dramliz is recognized?"

"There are those a-plenty," Meicha said after Miandra had said nothing for half-a-dozen heartbeats. "The challenge lies in persuading Aunt Stafeli—and there we have been unsuccessful."

"What about Ren Lar?"

Meicha grimaced. "Worse and worse."

"Ren Lar," whispered Miandra, "sees the dramliz as no more nor less dangerous than the old technology." She laughed suddenly, and looked Jethri in the eye.

"Well, he is not so far in the wrong as that."

Despite himself, he grinned, then let it fade as he rocked off his knees and sat down on the carpet, crossing his legs in an awkward imitation of her pose.

"What about Master ven'Deelin?" he asked.

Two pair of sapphire blue eyes stared at him, blankly.

"What about her, I wonder?" asked Meicha.

"Well, she hails from Solcintra, on Liad, where the dramliz are allowed to go about their business unimpeded. She's your aunt's fosterling—who better to escort you?"

"Hear the lad," Miandra murmured, on a note of awe. "Sister—"

"We are still impeded," said Meicha. "Well to say that the ven'Deelin will escort you, yet it is empty hope unless Aunt Stafeli may be persuaded to let you go."

"Norn ven'Deelin is a master trader," Jethri commented, stroking Flinx's head while the big cat stood on his knee and purred.

"And master traders are all that is persuadable," Meicha concluded and inclined her head. "I take your point and raise another."

He moved his free hand in the gesture that meant "go on."

She took a deep breath. "It comes to me that Norn ven'Deelin— all honor to her!—may not love dramliz. Recall your first meal with us? And the ven'Deelin all a-wonder that there were dramliz in the house."

He had a particularly sharp memory of that meal, and he thought back on it now, looking for nuance he had been ill-able to detect, then . . .

"I think, perhaps," he said slowly, "that she was . . . joking. Earlier in the day—just before we met in the hall—I had understood that Lady Maarilex was about to read her a ringing scold for—for fostering a Terran and breaking with tradition. Seeing dramliz at the table, it might be that she merely remarked that she was not the only one who had broken with tradition."

"Hah," said Meicha, and bent her head to look at Miandra, who sat silent, running her chain through her fingers, eyes absent.

Jethri skritched Flinx under the chin.

"I judge that Jethri has the right of it," Miandra said abruptly. "Norn ven'Deelin has Aunt Stafeli's mark upon her. It is too much to hope that she would forgo her point, when the cards were delivered to her hand."

"True." Meicha slid back into her chair, looking relaxed for the first time since they had tumbled into his room. "The ven'Deelin is due back with us at the end of next relumma."

Jethri sent a glance to Miandra. "Can you hold so long?"

She moved her shoulders. "I will do what I might, though I must point out the possibility that the Scout Lieutenant will seek Balance."

"He would not dare!" Meicha declared stoutly. "Come against Aunt Stafeli in Balance? He is a fool if he attempts it."

"Jethri had already established him as a fool," Miandra pointed out. "And it was not Balance against the House that concerns me."

Meicha stared at her.

"He may try me, if he likes," Jethri said, the better part of his attention on Flinx.

"You are not concerned," Miandra murmured, and it was not a question. He looked up and met her eyes.

"Not overly, no. Though—I regret. He threatened you, and I did not understand that at the time. You need not be concerned, either."

Silence. Then Meicha spoke, teasing.

"You have a champion, sister."

"It was kindly meant," Miandra said placidly, and, deliberately, as if she had reached a firm decision, put the silver chain over her head. The deformed ruby swung once against her jersey, then stilled.

"I would like to hear more of this Scout captain you invoked over the head of the so-kind lieutenant," she said.

"I met him when I jumped off the edge of Kailipso Station," he began, and tipped his head, recalled of a sudden to his manners. "Would you like some tea?"

"Masterful!" Meicha crowed. "You have missed your trade, Jethri! You should 'prentice to a teller of tales."

He made his face serious, like he was considering it. "I don't think I'd care for that, really," he said, which earned him another crow of laughter.

"Wretch! Yes, tea, by all means—and hurry!"

Grinning, he put Flinx on the carpet and unwound, moving toward the galley. There, he filled the tea-maker, pulled the tray from its hanger and put cups on it. He added the tin of cookies Mrs. tor'Beli had given him a few days ago—it had been full, then; now it was about half-full. The tea-maker chimed at him; he put the pot on the tray and carried it out to the main room, being very careful of where he set his feet, in case Flinx should suddenly arrive to do his dance around Jethri's ankles.

He needn't have worried about that. The cat was sitting tall on the floor next to Miandra, tail wrapped tightly around his toes, intently observing the plates of goodies set out on the cloth from his table. The twins had set his neglected dinner out like party food. He grinned and went forward.

Meicha leapt to her feet and handed the cups, pot and tin down to Miandra, who placed them on the cloth. Jethri put the tray on the table and sat on the carpet between the two of them, accepting a cup of tea from Miandra with a grave inclination of his head.

"My thanks."

Meicha passed him a goody plate and he pinched one of the cheese roll-ups he was partial to and passed the plate around to Miandra. When they were all provided with food and tea, and each of them had taken a sip and a bite, Miandra looked up with a definite gleam in her eye.

"And, now, sir, you *will* tell us about your Scout captain and how it was you came to jump off the edge of a spacestation!"

He hid the grin behind another sip of tea. "Certainly," he murmured, as dignified as could be. "It happened this way . . ."

DAY 166

❀ ❀

Standard Year 1118
Elthoria

"MASTER TRADER, the captain bids me deliver this message to you." The first mate's voice was somber, and it was that which drew Norn ven'Deelin's attention away from the file she had under study. Gaenor tel'Dorbit was not a somber woman, and while she enjoyed a contract of pleasure with the librarian Norn had specifically instructed to deny her to all seekers, it could hardly be supposed that his *melant'i* was so lacking that he had let his paramour by on a mere whim.

Norn sighed. Somber first mates and disobedient, dutiful librarians. Surely, the universe grew too complex. She looked up.

Gaenor tel'Dorbit bowed and produced from her sleeve a folded piece of green priority paper.

The paper crackled as Norn received it and glanced at the routing line.

"Hah," she said, extending it. "Pray have communications forward this to my son at Irikwae."

The first mate bit her lip. "Master Trader," she said, more somberly, if possible, than previously, "the captain bids me deliver this message to you."

Oh, and indeed? Norn looked again at the routing: from Khatelane Gobelyn. The pilot cousin, was it not? And the same who had written before. That she sent now a priority message—that was notable. It was also notable that it had been some days in transit, for Khatelane had sent it to Avrix, where *Elthoria* would have been, had the schedule not been amended.

She glanced up at Gaenor tel'Dorbit, who was watching her with no small amount of anticipation. It came to her that Gaenor read Terran well and would certainly have been asked by the communications officer to vet a message written in Terran. She had also taken a liking to Jethri himself, saying that he reminded her pleasantly of the young brothers she left at home. Which handily explained, Norn thought, Kor Ith yo'Lanna's involvement in the proper disposition of a letter meant for a mere apprentice of trade.

"I expect," she said gently to Gaenor's tense face, "to read that Jethri's honored mother, Captain Iza Gobelyn, has passed from this to a more gentle plane, and that Jethri is called back to his kin, to mourn."

"Master Trader," the first mate inclined her head slightly. "To my knowledge, the health of Jethri's honored mother remains robust."

Well. Obviously, she was not going to be quit of Gaenor until she had read and made some disposition of Jethri's letter.

Leaning back in her chair, she flicked the page open and began, laboriously, to read.

Dear Jethri,

Never thought I'd be sending you a Priority, but I think I made a bad situation worse for you, so I'm sending a heads-up quick. I'm here on Banthport at the Trade Bar and run into Keeson Trager and Coraline.

Bunch of Liadens on the place, which don't figure, because you know as well as me, Jeth, Banth doesn't have nothing but the gold mines. But, anyhow, lots of Liadens, and one of them hears Kee name me. Pretty boy, in a skinny, sulky sort of way. Name of Barjohn Shelgaybin, near as I can make out. Said he knows you, that you lost him a brother, and you didn't settle up like you should've. Said, that being so, and me standing right there, he could take exact balance, or I could pay him four hundred cantra in compensation, which, if I could've done I wouldn't've been at Banth on Kinaveralport business, because I'd be captain-owner of a brand-new Cezna with nothing less than twelve pod-mounts.

So, it was stupid, and I figure it's best for all to leave, except he up and grabs me and—I decked him. Conked his head on the floor and went out cold. Another boy tells me I got safe passage—though he didn't tell me his name—so I left it and come back to the crash. I'm sending this to Elthoria, and a copy to Paitor.

For what it's worth, Farli Trager worked out the names of the Liaden ships on Banth: Winhale, Tornfall, Skeen, Brass Cannon. Don't know which your friend is off of, but you might, if he hasn't made the whole thing up out of spare parts. Skeen and Brass Cannon hold Combine keys.

I'm real sorry, Jeth, and I hope you're OK. If this is some kind of Liaden blood feud, let us know, will you? If that pretty boy's a head-case, let us know that, too—and tell us how you're getting on.

I'm gone by the time you get this—follow-ups to Paitor at Terratrade, Kinaveral.

Love,

Khat

Norn ven'Deelin folded the sheet and put it, carefully, atop the reader. She sat for a few heartbeats, eyes on the green paper, then looked up to Gaenor tel'Dorbit, standing patiently, her hands tucked into her belt, her face tense—worried. And she was right to worry, Norn thought. Indeed she was.

"So," she said softly. "I am informed. Of your goodness, First Mate, ask Arms Master sig'Kethra to join in my office for prime in—" she glanced at the clock—"one hour."

"Master Trader." Gaenor bowed, relief palpable, as if the problem—the problems—were now solved, with Jethri and his kin rendered impervious to chel'Gaibin spite. If only it were so.

The first mate removed herself from the study room. Norn ven'Deelin sat quietly for half-a-dozen heartbeats more, then slipped the green letter away into her sleeve, marked her place in the file, and went over to the wall unit to call the kitchen and alert the cook to her need for a working dinner for two to arrive in her office in an hour.

"SO," PEN REL SAID, putting the green paper down and reaching for his wine. "The chel'Gaibin heir aspires to the *melant'i* of a port tough. Are you surprised?"

"Alas, I am not—and we will not discuss what that might say about ven'Deelin's *melant'i*." She sipped her own wine, staring sightlessly at the meal neither had addressed with vigor.

"What I believe we have, old friend," she murmured, "is a play in two acts. I hope that you will lend me the benefit of your wisdom in crafting an appropriate answer to each."

"Now, I know a matter to be dire when ven'Deelin comes to me with sweet words of flattery in her mouth," he commented, irreverently. "All I have is yours to command. Has it ever been otherwise?"

"Surely, it must have been, at one time—but, stay! I will not insult you with more flattery. As I said, a play in two acts, their separate action linked by the chel'Gaibin heir. Indeed, if what I believe is true, I can only suppose Infreya chel'Gaibin to be in a goodly rage regarding the heir's impromptu freelancing—for I believe the approach upon young Khatelane to be nothing more nor less than a moment seized to determine what profit might be wrung from it. And why, you may wonder, would Infreya chel'Gaibin be quite so angry at her heir's attempt to terrorize a mere Terran?"

"The ships," Pen Rel murmured. "The transliterations are . . . challenging. However, if the name the pilot renders as *Brass Cannon* is, indeed, our own beloved *Bra'ezkinion*, then it's certain there's piracy afoot."

"And if *Tornfall* may be discovered to be *Therinfel*, we may add mayhem to the brew," Norn said, and fell silent for a long moment, her wineglass forgotten in her hand.

Pen Rel reached out and captured the letter, frowning at the Terran words.

"The pilot is right to wonder," he said eventually, "what interest

Banth holds for such a mixed flight of ships—" He looked up and made a rueful face. "Only hear me assume that *Wynhael* stands in association with *Bra'ezkinion* and *Therinfel*."

"Not invalid, I think," Norn said, absently. "Not invalid. I allow the pilot to be a clever child and her questions on-point. For, indeed, there *is* nothing to want at Banth that cannot be had elsewhere, with less cost and more convenience. And yet four Liaden ships—two of them known to us as rogues, in addition to the most excellent *Wynhael*, and the as-yet-undiscovered *Skeen*—simultaneously converge upon this port. Credulity strains to the breaking point, my friend."

"Past the breaking point, I would say. So, Master Trader, what is there to want at Banth, after all?"

She glanced at him, eyes gleaming. "How many times must I explain that the skills of a master trader are not those of the dramliz?"

"Until I lay down my last duty, I expect," he retorted. "I have seen you too often work magic."

"Pah! Now who flatters whom, sir? However, your question has merit, despite your deplorable manners. What, indeed, does Banth have which is desirable and has been overlooked, thus far, by all?" She moved her hand, discovered the wine glass and sipped.

"I do not know. And perhaps I may never know. However, the convergence of those four ships—two rejoicing in substantial guild misdemeanor files—allows me to call upon the masters of trade to interview the traders involved, immediately, to determine if there has been any breach of guild rule."

"Thereby infuriating Infreya chel'Gaibin and the so-honorable heir."

"Very possibly," Norn agreed, tranquilly. "But Infreya will not resist a guild investigation—she is, when all is counted, too canny a trader to bargain for her own downfall. It must be in her best interest to cooperate with the guild—and that is where we gain the small hope that we will, after all, learn what it is that Banth has of value."

"You will need to know for certain the names of those ships," Pen Rel said. "I will undertake that proof."

"I thank you," she smiled, briefly, and sipped her wine. "So, that act. The second, I own, may be knottier, for it involves dram-liz skills. One or both of us must look into the future and see whether chel'Gaibin will pursue its false Balance against Gobelyns, all and sundry, and, if they will, what measures we must take—in protection, I would say, preferring not to wait upon the necessity of retribution."

"I understand." He considered the matter for some time, frowning abstractedly at the table top. Norn sipped her wine and waited for him to return to himself.

"I believe that the larger population of Gobelyns need have no fear that the chel'Gaibin heir will attempt to pursue his Balance," he said after a considerable time had passed. "Like you, I consider that the attack upon Pilot Gobelyn was an opportunistic act, which it is unlikely he will repeat."

"Unlikely? Tell me why you say so."

He rattled the green paper. "The pilot states that she knocked him down for his impertinence in laying a hand upon her—and rightly so, may I say. You, yourself, know well that chel'Gaibins have no taste for being knocked down. I would consider that the encounter with the pilot will have provided a laudatory lesson to the heir." He raised his glass.

"And, too, when does *Wynhael* run so far out? Further opportunity to meet Gobelyns must be limited by the usual routes pursued by both."

"Fair enough," Norn murmured, "though I submit that *Wynhael* was at Banth as nearly as a few days ago."

"An isolated incidence, I believe," Pen Rel said stoutly. "I think we may assume that Gobelyns as a set reside at a safe distance from chel'Gaibins of any sort." He sipped his wine. "No, where we must focus our concern, I believe, is upon Jethri, who is at this moment well within Liaden space and, while more tutored regarding the rules of Balance than his most excellent kinswoman, is perhaps not as conversant with nuance as one might like."

"He has been living this while in the house of my foster mother," Norn said dryly. "Be assured that he will by this time be breathing and dreaming nuance. However, your point is taken. One does not leave an inexperienced player unshielded to danger. We know that Bar Jon chel'Gaibin has publicly proposed a grievance against Jethri Gobelyn—" she fluttered her fingers at the paper in his hand. "He must pursue satisfaction, or his *melant'i* suffers."

Pen Rel snorted. "As if it had not already. Shall we to Irikwae, then?"

She moved a shoulder. "Alas, we cannot. The cargo we have guaranteed for Lylan—"

"Ah," he murmured. "I had forgotten."

Norn sipped her wine. "Immediately, let us beam to Tarnia, with full particulars and a request to be vigilant. We have a little time, I calculate, purchased by the guild investigation. We will fulfill our contract, and transship what we may." She sighed. "Gar Sad will pin my ears to my head."

"Of course he will." Pen Rel put his glass and the letter on the table and came to his feet, not quite as lightly as was his wont. "You will have clear proof of the ships involved by the end of next shift."

She smiled at him. "Old friend. My thanks to you, on behalf of my student and son."

"My student, also, remember," he said bowing lightly. "By your leave, Norn."

She flicked a hand in bogus impatience. "Go then, if you are so eager for work."

He smiled, placed his hand briefly over his heart, and left her.

DAY 166

❀ ❀

Standard Year 1118
Irikwae

THE ALARM CHIMED, insistent. Jethri groaned and resisted the temptation to push his head under the bank of pillows to shut out the noise.

The chime grew louder. Manfully, Jethri flung the sheets back, got his feet on the floor. A few steps brought him to the alarm, which he disarmed, and then simply stood there, savoring the silence.

The clock displayed a time a few minutes later than his usual waking hour, which meant he was going to have to engage jets to get to breakfast on time. He yawned, the idea of engaging jets infinitely less attractive than collapsing back onto the bed and taking another half-shift of sleep.

Instead, he moved, at something less than his usual speed, on course for the 'fresher.

The twins had stayed late, trading stories of their own for his of Kailipso Station and Scout Captain ter'Astin, until Miandra looked out the window.

"The third moon has set," she said, whereupon Meicha pronounced the word Jethri considered to be the Liaden rendering of "mud!" and they both jumped up and took their leave, with smiles and wishes for his sweet dreaming, flitting like the ghosts of space down the dim-lit hall, Flinx the ghost of a cat, weaving 'round their silent feet.

Trouble was, he hadn't been at all sleepy and had spent some time more huddled over his old "trade journal," until he realized he had read the same entry three times, without making sense of it once, closed the old book and gone to bed.

Two hours ago.

He stepped into the shower and punched the button for *cold*, gasping when the blast hit him. Quickly, he soaped and rinsed, then jumped out, reaching for the towel. Drying briskly, he glanced in the mirror—and glanced again, moving closer and touching his upper lip, where last evening a hopeful mustache sprouted.

Gone now, stroked into oblivion by Meicha's magic fingers.

"I don't know how long that will last," she had said, half-scolding. "But you really *can*not, Jethri, go among polite people with hair on your face."

"I was going to ask Mr. pel'Saba for depilatory, tomorrow," he'd said, and Miandra had laughed, reaching over her twin's shoulder to put her palm against his cheek.

"He would not have had the least idea what you asked for," she said. "Leave it to Meicha until you may purchase some of this substance for yourself, perhaps at the port?"

"*Miandra* . . ." Meicha hissed, and her sister laughed again and withdrew her hand, leaving Jethri wishing that she hadn't.

In the bedroom, the alarm began again, signaling five minutes until breakfast.

Jethri swore and jumped for his closet.

THE BREAKFAST ROOM was empty, for all the food was laid out just like always on the long sideboard and the places were set at the table set in the tall windowed alcove overlooking the flower garden. Someone had thought it a mellow enough day to prop open the middle pane, and the smells of flowers and growing things danced into the room on the back of a dainty little breeze.

Jethri paused at the window, looking out over the banks of sweet smelling, prickle stemmed flowers that Lady Maarilex favored.

The garden appeared as always: pink and white blossoms crowding the stone pathways; the sunlight dappled with shade from the tall tree at the garden's center. Nothing seemed disturbed by yesterday's rogue wind.

"Good morning, Master Jethri," murmured a voice grown very familiar to him. Jethri turned and inclined his head.

"Mr. pel'Saba." He looked into the butler's bland, give-nothing face. "I fear I have overslept."

"If you did, it was not by many minutes," the old man said. "However, Master Ren Lar went early to the vines—and Mrs. tor'Beli has instructions to send a tray up to their ladyships." That would be Meicha and Miandra, Jethri thought with a start.

"For yourself . . ." Mr. pel'Saba continued, reaching into his sleeve and producing a creamy, square envelope, "there is a letter."

A letter. Jethri took the envelope with a small bow, fingertips tingling against the kiss of high-rag paper. "My thanks."

"It is my pleasure to serve," Mr. el'Saba assured him. "Please enjoy your breakfast. If anything is required, you have but to ring." He bowed and was gone, vanishing through the door at the back of the room.

Jethri turned his attention to the envelope. An irregular blob of purple wax glued the flap shut; pressed into the wax was a design. He brought the blob closer to the end of his nose, squinting—and recognized the sign of the traders guild.

Reverently, he flipped the creamy square over and stood staring at the name, written in purple ink the exact shade of the lump of sealing wax, the Liaden letters a thought too ornate: Jeth Ree ven'Deelin.

Now, he thought, *here's a message*. If only he knew how to read it.

Sighing, the envelope heavier in his hand than its weight accounted for, Jethri went to the sideboard, poured himself a cup of tea, and carried both to his usual place at the breakfast table. Only when he had seated himself and taken a sip of tea, did he slip his finger under the purple wax and break the seal.

Inside the envelope was a single sheet of paper, folded once in the middle. It crackled crisply when he unfolded it to find five precise lines, written in that over-ornate hand: *Jeth Ree ven'Deelin, apprentice to Master Trader Norn ven'Deelin, will present himself at Irikwae Guildhall on Standard Day 168 at sixth hour, local.*

In order to undertake testing for certification. The course will encompass one-half relumma. The candidate will be housed at the guildhall for the duration of the certification program.

That was it, the last line being a signature so over-written as to be nearly unreadable. Jethri sipped his tea, frowning at the thing until he finally puzzled out: *Therin yos'Arimyst, Hall Master, Irikwae Port.*

"Such a studious demeanor so early in the day!" Lady Maarilex remarked a few moments later, stumping to a halt on the threshold of the breakfast room. "Truly, Jethri, you are an example to us all."

He put the letter down next to his teacup and rose, crossing the room to offer her his arm.

"After yesterday, I wonder that you can say so, ma'am," he murmured, as he guided her to her usual place, and pulled back her chair.

She laughed. "Certainly, the portions of your yesterday which I was privileged to observe seemed to go very well, indeed. Your demeanor before the Scout Lieutenant—I live in the liveliest anticipation of sharing the tale with your foster mother."

Oh, really? "Do you think she will enjoy it, ma'am?" he asked.

She looked up at him, old eyes sparkling.

"Immensely, young Jethri. Immensely."

"Well, then," he said, with a lightness he didn't particularly feel, "I will judge that I have acquitted myself well, in the matter of the Scout." He paused. "May I bring you something, ma'am?" he asked, since neither Meicha nor Miandra was there to perform the service.

"Tea, if you will, child, and a bit of the custard."

He moved off to fulfill this modest commission, and returned to the table with tea and custard, and a sweet roll for himself.

"Ma'am, I wonder," he said, glancing at the letter as he took his place. "Does Hall Master Therin yos'Arimyst hold Master ven'Deelin in despite?"

She paused with her teacup halfway to her lips and shot him a sharp glance over the rim.

"Now, here's a bold start. What prompts it?"

Wordlessly, he passed her the letter and the envelope.

"Hah." She put her cup down, read the letter in a glance, considered the envelope briefly, and put both on the table between them.

"He gives you little enough time to arrive," she commented, reaching for her custard. "Today, you will pack—take what books you will from the library, too. I recall Norn telling us that there was precious little to read at the hall, saving manifests and regulations."

"Thank you, ma'am," he murmured, genuinely warmed.

A flick of her fingers dispensed with his thanks. "As to the other . . . Despite—perhaps not, though I would be surprised to learn that Therin yos'Arimyst counted Norn ven'Deelin among his favored companions." She spooned custard, contemplatively. Jethri broke his roll open and did his best to cultivate patience.

"It is, you understand," Lady Maarilex said eventually, "a difference in mode that separates Norn and the yos'Arimyst. In him, you will find a trader, oh, *most* conservative! Ring a rumor of change and be certain that Therin yos'Arimyst will be with the portmaster within the hour, speaking eloquently in defense of the proven ways. Norn, as I am certain you have yourself observed, is one to dance with risk and court change."

"I can see that the two of them might not have much to talk about," Jethri said, when a few moments had passed and she had said nothing else.

"Certainly, they would seem to be unlikely to agree on any topic of importance to either," she murmured, her eyes, and apparently her thoughts, on her custard.

Jethri sipped his tea, found it less than tepid and rose to warm his cup. When he returned, Lady Maarilex had finished her custard and was holding her cup between her two hands, eyes closed.

He slipped into his seat as quietly as he could, not wanting to disturb her if she was indulging in a nap. She opened her eyes before he was rightly settled, and extended a hand to tap the letter where it was between them on the table.

"I believe what you have here is politics, child. Mind you, I do not have the key to the yos'Arimyst's mind, but it comes to me that he *must* see you as a challenge to his beloved changelessness—indeed, you *are* just such a challenge—and never mind that change will come, no matter how he may abhor it, or speak against it, or forbid it within his hall. Norn ven'Deelin, who loves the trade more than any being alive, has taken a Terran apprentice. Surely, the foundations of the homeworld ring with the blow! And, yet, if not Norn, if not now—then another, later. Terrans exist. Not only do they exist, but they insist upon trading—and on expanding the field upon which they *can* trade. We ignore them—we deny them—at our very great peril."

Jethri leaned forward, watching her face. "You think that she was right, then, ma'am?"

"Oh, I believe she is correct," the old lady murmured. "Which is not to say—diverting and delightful as I find you!—that I would not have preferred another, and later. It is not comfortable, to be an agent of change." She shot him an especially sharp glance. "Nor is it comfortable, I imagine, to be change embodied."

He swallowed. "I—am not accustomed to thinking of myself so. An apprentice trader, set to learn from a . . . most astonishing master—that is how I think of myself."

She smiled. "That is very sensible of you, Jethri Gobelyn, fostered of ven'Deelin. Consider yourself so, and comport yourself so." She tapped the letter again, three times, and withdrew her hand.

"And do not forget that there are others abroad who find your existence threatens them, and who will do their all to see you fail."

Nothing new there, Jethri thought, retrieving his letter. *Just a description of trade-as-usual.* He folded the paper and slipped it into the pocket of his jacket.

"Anecha will drive you to the port and see you safe inside the hall," Lady Maarilex said. "If you require funds, pray speak to Mr. el'Saba—he will be able to rectify the matter for you."

He inclined his head. "I thank you, ma'am, but I believe I am well-funded."

"That is well, then," she said and pushed back from the table. He leapt to his feet—and was waved back to his chair.

"Please. I am not so frail as that—and you have eaten nothing. A custard may tide an old woman until nuncheon, but a lad of your years wants more than a shredded roll for his breakfast."

He looked down at his plate, feeling his ears warm. "Yes, ma'am," he murmured, and then looked back to her face. "Thank you for your care."

She smiled. "You are courteous child." She bowed, very slightly. "Until soon, young Jethri."

"Until soon, ma'am," he answered, and watched her stump down the room, leaning heavy on her cane, until she reached the hall and turned right, toward her office.

DAY 168

❊❊❊❊❊❊❊❊❊❊❊❊❊❊❊❊❊❊❊❊❊❊❊

Standard Year 1118
Irikwae Port

"I DON'T KNOW WHY he needs you here so early," Anecha muttered as she opened the big car's cargo compartment.

Jethri reached in, got hold of the strap and pulled his duffle out, slinging the strap over one shoulder.

"The port never closes," he said, softly. "Master yos'Arimyst has likely done me the courtesy of being sure that I arrive during his on-shift."

Anecha sent him one of her sharp, unreadable glances. "So, you interpret it as courtesy, do you? You've a more giving *melant'i* than some of us, then, Jethri Gobelyn." She swung the second bag out of the boot and got it up on a shoulder.

"I can carry that," he said mildly. She snorted and used her chin to point at the bag he already wore.

"Can isn't should," she said. "I'll have that one, too. Or do you think I will allow Norn ven'Deelin's son to walk into the guildhall dragging his own luggage, like a Low House roustabout?"

He blinked at her. "It can't be improper for an apprentice to carry his own bags—and his master's, too."

"Nothing more proper, if the master is present. However, when the apprentice is the representative of the master—"

Right. Then the honors that would properly go to the master were bestowed upon her 'prentice. Jethri sighed, quietly. Eventually— say, a couple years after he saw his eightieth birthday, he'd have *melant'i* thoroughly understood.

"So," said Anecha, with a great deal of restraint, really, "if the good apprentice will deign to give me his bag?"

The other option being a long stop in the street while they argued the point—which would earn neither his *melant'i* nor Master ven'Deelin's any profit. Jethri stifled a second sigh and handed over the duffle, settled his jacket over his shoulders and crossed the walk to the door of the Irikwae Port traders guild hall.

The door was locked, which didn't surprise him. He swiped his crew card from *Elthoria* through the lock-scanner, and then set his palm against the plate.

The status light blared red, accompanied by a particularly raucous buzzer—and the door remained locked.

"I see you are expected," Anecha commented drily from behind him, "and that every courtesy has been observed."

Thinking something closely along those lines himself, Jethri slipped his crew card into a pocket and put his hand against the plate, as might any general visitor to the hall.

The status light this time flared yellow, and there was an absence of rude noise, circumstances that Jethri tentatively considered hopeful. He dropped back two steps, head cocked attentively, waiting for the doorkeeper to open the door.

"*Every* courtesy observed," Anecha repeated some minutes later, voice edged.

Jethri moved forward to ring the bell again. His hand had scarcely touched the plate when it and the rest of the door was snatched away, and he found himself looking, bemusedly, down into the stern face of a man in full trade dress.

"What is the meaning of this?" The man snapped. "This is the traders' hall. The zoo is in the city."

Behind him, Jethri heard Anecha draw a sharp, outraged breath, which pretty much summarized his own feelings. Still, as Master tel'Ondor had taught him, it was best to answer rudeness with courtesy—and to remember the name of the offender.

Jethri bowed, gently, and not nearly so low as apprentice ought to a full trader. He straightened, taking his time about it, and met the man's hard gray eyes.

"I arrive at the hall at this day and hour in obedience to the word of Hall Master yos'Arimyst." He slipped the letter out of his pocket and offered it, gracefully, all the while meeting that hull-steel stare, daring him to compound his rudeness.

The man's fingers flicked—and stilled. He inclined his head, which was proper enough from trader to 'prentice, and stepped back from the door, motioning Jethri within.

The vestibule was small and stark, putting Jethri forcibly in mind of an airlock. Two halls branched out of it—one left, one right.

"'prentice!" the trader shouted. "'prentice, to the door!"

Jethri winced and heard Anecha mutter behind him, though not what she said. Which was probably just as well.

From the deeps of the hall came the sound of boots hitting the floor with a will, and shortly came from the left-most corridor a girl about, Jethri thought, the same age as the twins, her hair pale yellow and her pale blue eyes heavy with sleep.

"Yes, Trader?"

He flicked nearly dismissive fingers in Jethri's direction.

"A candidate arrives. See him to quarters."

She bowed, much too low, Jethri thought, catching the frown before it got to his face. "Yes, Trader. It shall be done."

"Good," he said, and turned toward the right hall, his hard glance scraping across Jethri's face with indifference.

Behind him, Anecha stated, dispassionately, "*Every* courtesy."

Jethri turned his head to give her a Look. She returned it with an expression of wide innocence Khat would have paid hard credit to possess.

"Your pardon, gentles," the girl who had been summoned to deal with them stammered. "It is—understand, it is very early in the day for candidates to arrive. Though of course!—the hall stands ready to receive . . . at any hour . . ."

Jethri raised a hand, stopping her before she tied her sentence into an irredeemable knot.

"I regret the inconvenience to the hall," he said, as gently as he could, and showed her the folded paper. "Master yos'Arimyst's own word was that I arrive at the hall no later than sixth hour today."

THE 'PRENTICE BLINKED. "But Master yos'Arimyst is scarcely ever at the hall so early in the day. Though, of course," she amended rapidly, her cheeks turning a darker gold with her blush, "I am only an apprentice, and cannot hope to understand the necessities of the hall master."

"Certainly not," Jethri said smoothly. "I wonder if Master yos'Arimyst is in the hall this morning?"

Her eyes widened. "Why, no, sir. Master yos'Arimyst left planet yesterday on guild business. He will return at the end of the relumma."

He heard Anecha draw a breath, and moved one shoulder, sharply. The crude signal got through; Anecha held her tongue.

"Certainly, guild business has precedent," he said to the waiting girl. "My name is Jethri Gobelyn. I may be in your lists as Jeth Ree ven'Deelin."

"Oh!" The girl bowed, not as deeply as she had for the irritable trader who had opened the door, but too deep, nonetheless. Briefly, Jethri wondered about the hall's protocol master.

"Parin tel'Ossa, at your word, sir." She said, eyes wide. "Please, if you will follow me, I will show you to your quarters."

"Certainly," Jethri said, and followed her down the left hall, pausing a moment to send a glance to Anecha, who managed not to meet his eyes.

THE QUARTERS WERE unexpectedly spacious, on the top level, with windows overlooking an enclosed garden. Having thanked and rid himself of both Parin and Anecha, Jethri worked the latch and pushed one of the windows wide, admitting the early breeze and the muffled sounds of the morning port.

It certainly seemed that Master yos'Arimyst intended deliberate insult to Norn ven'Deelin, through her apprentice and foster son. Or, thought Jethri, leaning his hands on the window still and sticking his nose out into the chilly air, did he?

After all, he, Jethri, was here for a certification—a test. What if this deliberate rudeness had a point *other than* insult? Suppose, for instance, that the masters and traders of the hall wanted a reading on just how well a beastly Terran understood civilized behavior?

He closed his eyes. Tough call. If the measuring stick for civilized was Liaden, then he ought to be making plans for a vendetta right about now—or ought he? A true Liaden would have the sense to know if he was being offered an insult or a test.

Jethri exhaled, with vigor, and turned from the window to inspect the rest of his quarters.

A worktable sat against the wall to the right of the window. A screen and keyboard sat ready before a too-short chair. Jethri leaned over to touch a key, and was gratified to see the screen come up, displaying an options menu.

He chose *map*, and was in moments engaged in a close study of the interior layout of the hall. Not nearly as complex as Tarnia's house, with its back stairs, back rooms and half-floors, but a nice mix of public, private and service rooms.

The quarters were in what appeared to be an older wing—perhaps the original hall—the public and meeting rooms were off the right-hand hall from the vestibule—and could also be accessed from the Trade Bar, which opened into the main port street.

Map committed to memory, Jethri recalled the menu—yes. There was an option called *check-in*. He chose it.

A box appeared on the screen, with instructions to enter his name. Fingers extended over the keypad, he paused, staring down at the Liaden characters. Slowly, he typed in the name under which he had been summoned for certification; the name that Parin had recognized.

Jeth Ree ven'Deelin.

The computer accepted his entry; another screen promised that his mentor would be informed of his arrival. Great.

He returned to the options menu, lifting a hand to cover a sudden yawn. Despite the fact that he'd been able to nap in the car coming down from Tarnia's house, he was feeling short on sleep, which was not a good way to start a test. He glanced at his watch. If he was still at Tarnia's house, he'd have just under six seconds to get to breakfast.

He blinked, eyes suddenly teary and throat tight. He *wanted* to be in Tarnia's house, running as hard as he could down the "secret" back stairs and sweating lest he be late for breakfast. He missed Miandra and Meicha, Mrs. tel'Bonti, Lady Maarilex, Mr. pel'Saba, Flinx and Ren Lar. And while he was listing those he missed, there was Norn ven'Deelin and Gaenor and Vil Tor, Pen Rel, Master tel'Ondor; Khat and Cris and Grig and Seeli. . .

He sniffed, and reached into his pocket for a handkerchief.

Put it in a can, he told himself, which is what Seeli'd tell him when he'd been a kid and got to blubbering over nothing. He unfolded the handkerchief and wiped his face with the square of silk, swallowing a couple times to loosen his throat.

Might as well unpack, he thought, putting the handkerchief away. *Get everything all shipshape and comfortable, and you'll feel more like the place belongs to you.*

Anecha had left his bags on the bare wooden floor against the opposite wall, under the control panel for the bed. That item of furniture at the moment formed part of the wall. When he wanted it down, according to Parin, all he had to do was slide the blue knob from left to right. To raise the bed, slide the knob from right to left, and up she went, freeing a considerable area of floor space.

Jethri opened the first bag—bright blue, with the Tarnia crest embroidered on it—and commenced unpacking, carrying his clothes over to the built-in dresser. He took his time, making sure everything went away neat; that his shirts were hung straight and his socks were matched up, but at last he was shaking out his second-best trading coat—the one Master ven'Deelin'd had made for him—out of the bottom of the bag, and hanging it with his shirts on the rod.

That done, he sealed the bag up, folded it and stowed it on the shelf over the rod.

The second duffle was dull green, *Gobelyn's Market* spelled out in stark white stenciling down one side. He unsealed it and pulled out the books he had borrowed from Tarnia's library. He'd taken mostly novels—some titles that he remembered from Gaenor's talks, and others at random—as well as a history of Irikwae, and another, of the Scouts, and a battered volume that appeared to be an account of the Old War.

He lined the books up on the worktable, and stood for a long moment, admiring them, before diving back into his duffle and emerging with the photocube showing his father, and Arin's metal box, with its etched stars, moons and comets.

He supposed he could've left his stuff in his room at Tarnia's house, but he'd got to thinking that maybe that wasn't a good idea, considering the fractins and the prevailing feeling against old tech—and he surely hadn't wanted to leave the weather gadget anywhere but secure in the inside pocket of his jacket, which was where it was right now. So, in the end, he'd tossed everything into his old duffle and left the empty B crate behind.

The photocube he placed with great care in the center of a low black wooden table in the corner by the windows. Arin's box, he put on top of the dresser. He stepped back to consider the room and found it . . . better, though still too much trader's hall and too little Jethri Gobelyn.

He returned to the duffle and pulled out the other photocube, with its record of strangers, and carried it over to the black table. The family cube, he placed near the keyboard on the table, where he could see it while he worked.

The remainder of the duffle's contents were best not displayed, he thought, those contents being fractins, true and false, the wire frame, and his pretend trade journal—though on second thought, there wasn't any reason that the old notebook couldn't be in with the rest of the books. Nobody who might visit him here was going to be interested in old kid stuff—even assuming that they could read Terran.

He resealed the duffle and put it on the shelf in the wardrobe next to the blue bag, closed the door and went back to the work table. He settled as well as he was able into the short chair and reached for the keyboard, meaning to explore the remainder of the options available to him.

A single line of tall red letters marched across the center of the computer screen. It seemed that his mentor, Trader Ena Tyl sig'Lorta would see him at the top of the hour, at meeting booth three, in the Irikwae Trade Bar.

Jethri looked at his watch. Not much time, but no need for a full-tilt run, either, if his understanding of the scale of the house was correct.

He tapped the 'received' key, slid out of the chair, brushed his hands down the front of his coat and went off to meet his mentor.

"GOT SOME NEWS," Seeli said, serious-like.

Grig looked up from his calcs. The yard had filed an amended, which they were required by contract to do, whenever section costs overran estimate by more than five percent. It was lookin' to be damn near five percent on the new galley module and Myra wanted to talk downgrade on some of the back up systems so as to make up the difference. He was doing the first pass over the numbers because Seeli'd been feeling not at the top of her form, and he'd finally this morning gotten her talked into going to the port clinic.

So, he looked up and got on a smile that the calcs made a little lopsided.

"Good news, I hope," he said, and even as he did felt his gut clench with the possibility of the news being bad.

"You might say." She sat down next to him, her arm companionably touching his. "Fact is, I hope you will say." She touched his hand. "I'm on the increase."

For a second he just sat there, heart in acceleration, mind blank—then all at once his brain caught up with his heart. He gave a shout of laughter and got his arms around her, and she was laughing, too, hugging him hard around the ribs, and for a while it was a mixup of kisses and hugs and more laughing, but finally they made it back to adult and sat there quiet, her head on his shoulder, their arms 'round each other still.

"How far along?" he asked, that being the first sensible sentence he'd made in the last half-hour.

"Couple Standard Months, the nurse said."

He felt his mouth pulling into another idiot grin. "The yard gets its promises in order, she'll be born in space, first newcrew on the refit."

Seeli snuggled a little closer against him. "We don't know what Mel might have cookin'. Come to it, Iza ain't beyond."

That took a little of the glow.

"Iza's done, beyond or not," he said, too seriously. "But I take your point about Mel. Girl's got the morals of a mink."

"What's a mink?" Seeli wanted to know, and it might've taken him the rest of the day to explain it to her, but the door come open and it was Paitor and Khat, each one looking as grim as Grig felt happy.

Seeli stirred, pushing against his chest to get upright. He let her go, and sighed gustily at the printout showing in the trader's hand.

"Paitor, I've been meaning to talk to you about this growing habit with the Priorities."

He shook his head. "Believe that I'd pay good cash never to get another." He tossed it on the table atop the printouts from the yard and headed into the galley.

"Who else wants a brew?" he called over his shoulder.

"I do," Khat said sitting in the chair across from Seeli, and rubbing a sleeve across her face. "Hot on the port."

"Brew'd be fine," Grig said, and looked over to Seeli, eyebrows up, asking.

"Juice for me," she called. "Thanks, Uncle."

Paitor could be heard clanking about in the cold box. Grig picked up the Priority, flicking a glance to Khat.

She shrugged. "I read it."

"All right, then," he said, unfolding the paper, with Seeli leaning close to read over his shoulder:

Honored Gobelyns:

Felicitations and fair profit to you and to your ship.

The priority message sent to the attention of Jethri from the esteemed Pilot Khatelane arrives at Elthoria. Your forbearance is requested, that I read this message, intended for the eyes of true kin only.

I commend Pilot Khatelane for the information she sends regarding certain Liaden vessels at dock on Port Banth. Several of these vessels are known to us adversely. A Guild inquiry has been called and you may repose faith that intentions of mischief or mayhem will quickly be learned.

Of the matter concerning the chel'Gaibin, I give you assurance that there lies no debt between himself and Jethri. The brother deprived was hale when we beheld him last, though deeply in the anger of his mother.

In the event, Jethri has been set down at Irikwae, at the house of Tarnia in the mountains of the moons. There, he is tutored in the ways of custom and of wine. Be assured that Tarnia values him high, as I do, and will stand as his shield and his dagger, should a false debt be called.

I am hopeful that these tidings will find you in good health, and I remain

Norn ven'Deelin Clan Ixin
Master at Trade

"Set *down*?" Seeli said, sounding every bit as horrified as Grig felt. "She left Jethri *alone*, on a Liaden world?"

"With a Liaden headcase after him for evenin' up a debt," Khat added, wearily, accepting a brew from Paitor. "Thanks."

"Welcome." He handed Seeli her drink, thumped Grig's down and folded into the chair next to Khat.

"Thing is," Grig said, glancing up from his second read. "She don't say the brother is alive now. She says he was OK the last time she saw him."

"Right." Khat nodded. "And the headcase, if you parse it right, never did say the boy *was* dead—though that's what I thought he must've meant. Thinking cold, though, it comes to me that there's more ways to 'deprive' somebody of a brother than by killing him.

If Jeth had—what? Called the proctors and got the boy put in the clink for a couple years—that'd deprive his family of him, wouldn't it? Or if Jeth had somehow gotten the brother's license pulled—"

"The point is," Seeli interrupted, sharp, but, there—she'd been Jethri's mother more'n Iza'd ever tried to be. "The *point* is that this master trader has gone off and left Jethri on a mudball, with no ship to call on, *and* there's a headcase lookin' for him, and she hasn't even told him!"

They blinked at her, in unison. Seeli snatched the Priority out of Grig's hand and snapped it at Paitor's face. He pulled back, impassive.

"Where does it say on this piece of paper that she's sending Khat's letter on to Jethri? Where does it say she's going back for him? Or that she's called—anybody at all!—to have the headcase taken under advisement, or, or whatever it is you do when somebody tries to collect on a 'false debt?'"

"We could send again," Khat said, making a long arm and tweaking the paper away.

"No beam code for Tarnia," Grig said quietly. "And no guarantees that this chel'Gaibin won't pursue his debt 'gainst the rest of us, like he tried with Khat." He looked at Seeli and his breath came short.

"One of us could go for him," Paitor said. "Not knowing the headcase's trajectory, that's tricky. For all we know, he's based outta Irikwae, wherever it is, and is on the route for home."

Grig took a breath, forcing it all the way down past tight chest muscles, to the very bottom of his lungs.

"I'll go," he said. "I owe."

Paitor frowned. "Owe? What can you possibly owe the boy?"

Grig looked him in the eye. "I'm still settlin' with Arin," he said evenly.

The other man studied him a long moment, then nodded, slow. "Can't argue with that."

"Grig." Seeli wasn't liking this. He turned to face her. "How're you goin'? Got a fastship in your back pocket?"

"Know a pilot-owner," he said, which was true enough. "Might be they're still settlin' with Arin, too."

"Back-up," Khat said, nodding. "Seeli, you know we all got

back-up. Grig's got it here, then he's the one to go. 'Less you can think of any other way to get Jethri the news, and an offer of his ship?"

Seeli hesitated; shook her head. "I can't. But we *offer him* ship, and if he wants it, we *give him* a ship—and Iza can deal with me! You hear it?" She rounded on Grig.

"I hear it, Seeli." He reached out and touched her cheek with his fingertip. "Khat."

"Sir?"

"My Seeli here's on the increase. I'd take it favorable, if you went off roster and devoted yourself to not letting any headcases inside her phase space."

"You got it," Khat said, sending a grin to Seeli, and pushing back from the table. "I'll file that change right now."

"Good." Khat had the right of it, Grig thought. No use putting it off.

Seeli reached out and grabbed his hand, pulling him with her as she stood up. She looked down at Paitor, ignoring his grin, and nodded her head, formal as a Liaden.

"Excuse us, Uncle. Grig and me got some business before he flies out."

IRIKWAE TRADE BAR was modest, and modestly busy—three of the six working public terminals were engaged, and four of the twelve meeting booths. A seventh terminal had been pushed into a corner—probably awaiting a repairman.

At the bar, a mixed cluster of traders, cargo masters and general crew sipped tea, or wine, or ate a quick-meal, while the status board over their heads showed a good dozen ships at port.

Goods on offer, portside, were heavily weighted toward agristuff—soybeans, rice, yams—with a smattering of handicrafts, textiles, and wine. The ships were offering metals—refined and unrefined—patterns, textiles, furniture, gemstones, books—a weird mix, Jethri thought, and then thought again. Irikwae was what Norn ven'Deelin was pleased to call an "outworld," far away from Liad's orbit. Ships bearing luxuries, small necessities, and information from the homeworld itself ought to do pretty well here.

"Are you lost, sir?" a voice asked at his elbow. He turned and looked down into the amused, wrinkled face of a woman. Her hair was gray, though still showing some faded strands of its original yellow color, and she had the trade guild's sign embroidered on the sleeve of her bright orange shirt.

"Only distractable, I fear," he answered, turning his palms up mock despair. "I am here for a meeting with a trader, but of course, the board caught my eye, and my interest . . ."

"Information is advantage," she said sagely. "Of course the board caught you—how not? At which booth were you to meet your trader?"

"Three."

"Ah. Just over here, then, sir, if you will follow me."

No choices there, Jethri thought wryly, and followed her to the back wall, where meeting booth three showed a bold blue numeral. The door was closed and the privacy light was lit.

His guide looked up at him. "Your name, sir?"

"Jethri—" he began, and caught himself. "Jeth Ree ven'Deelin."

Her eyebrows lifted, but she said nothing, only turned to put her hand on the door, which slid open, despite the privacy light, to reveal two traders, obviously interrupted in earnest conversation, and of two different minds of how to take it.

The woman seemed inclined toward amused resignation, the man—and wouldn't it just be the same stern-faced trader who'd been on door-duty?—was tending toward anger.

The staffer, unperturbed by either, bowed gently to the table, and murmured. "Jeth Ree ven'Deelin has a meeting with a trader in booth three."

The female trader sent a sharp glance to his face, and inclined her head slightly. Jethri received the impression that she was more amused and less resigned. The male trader frowned ferociously.

"Yes, Jeth Ree ven'Deelin is expected shortly, however—" he stopped, and favored Jethri with a hard stare.

In this moment of frozen disbelief, the staffer bowed once more to the table and went, soft-footed, away.

"*You* are Jeth Ree ven'Deelin?" the man demanded.

Not exactly encouraging, Jethri thought, and bowed—not low.

"In fact, I am Jethri Gobelyn, apprentice and foster son of Master Trader Norn ven'Deelin. The communication from the hall named me Jeth Ree ven'Deelin, and I felt it wise to continue under that construction until I was able to ask that the database be amended."

"ven'Deelin's Terran," the female trader murmured, and inclined her head when he looked at her. "Forgive me, sir. I am Alisa kor'Entec. Your fame precedes you, to the wonderment of us all."

"I had heard the ven'Deelin signed a Terran apprentice," the stern-faced trader said, looking to his mate. "I thought then that she had run mad. But—foster son?"

"Even so," she assured him, with relish. "Precisely so. Is it not diverting?"

"Dangerously demented, say rather," the other snapped, and Jethri felt himself warm to the man. Still, no matter his own doubts and feelings on the subject of his adoption, he couldn't—really couldn't—son or 'prentice, just stand by while Master ven'Deelin was made mock of.

He drew himself up stiffly where he stood and stared down his nose at the stern-faced trade, and then at the other.

"The *melant'i* of Master Trader Norn ven'Deelin is above reproach," he said, with all the dignity he could bring to it and hoping the phrase was on-point.

Alisa kor'Entec *smiled* at him. "It is, indeed. Which makes the matter infinitely more diverting."

"Perhaps for you," the man said irritably. He looked up at Jethri and moved a hand. "Of your goodness, Apprentice . . . Gobelyn. Trader kor'Entec and I must finish a small matter of business. Please, have a cup of tea and rest somewhat from your labors. I will be with you in a very short time."

A cup of tea would actually be welcome, Jethri thought, abruptly aware that the gone feeling in his middle wasn't all due to his upcoming testing, whatever it was. *And maybe a snack, too.* He inclined his head.

"Thank you, sir. I will await you at the bar." He looked to the lady. "Ma'am. Fair trading."

She gave him a slight, conspiratorial nod. "Good profit, Jethri Gobelyn."

"SORRY TO BE LATE," Raisy said, slipping onto the bench across.

"'preciate you comin' at all," Grig answered, pushing the second brew across to her.

She cocked him an eyebrow. "Thought that's Uncle you was peeved with."

"I'm not *peeved* with anybody." Grig snapped open the seal on his brew. "It's just—time's done, Raisy. We gotta move to something else. Thing's—aren't stable, and you know that for truth. You want to talk birth defects, for starters?"

Raisy opened her brew, took a long draught, leaned back, and sighed. "You bring me out on an Urgent for this?"

He glanced sideways, out over the rest of the bar—slow night, slim on customers—and back to his sister.

"No," he said, quiet. "Sorry." He had some brew, put the bottle back on the table and frowned at it.

"News, Raisy," he said, raising his eyes. "Seeli's increasing. I'm bound for dad duty."

She grinned, broad and honest, and leaned across the table to smack him upside the shoulder.

"News, he says! That's *great* news, brother! You give your Seeli my congrats, hear it? Tell her I said she couldn't have no finer man—nor her kid no finer dad."

He smiled, warmed. "I'll tell her that, Raisy. You ought to come by, meet her."

"Maybe I will," she said, but they both knew she wouldn't.

"So, that was the Urgent?" she said, after a small pause.

He shook his head, pulled the two Priorities out his pocket and passed them over.

"These're the Urgent."

She sent him a sharp look, took the papers and unfolded them with a snap.

Grig drank brew and watched her read.

She went through both twice, folded them together and passed them back. Grig slipped them away and sat waiting.

"So, we got a renegade Liaden, do we? Who depends on us not being able to check up on the rules?"

"Like that," Grig said.

"Right. And then we got this side issue of what's to have on Banth, which I'll second Khat on and say—nothing."

"How side an issue is that? If we got a buncha pirates lookin' to set up a base there?"

She stared at him. "Dammit—you think like Uncle."

Grig laughed.

"OK, let's look at where Banth is, ease-of-route speakin'." Raisy closed her eyes, accessing her pilot brain. Grig, who had pulled up star maps to study on Banth's location when Khat's letter had first arrived, sat back and waited.

She sighed. "I'd have to check the maps to be sure, but—first look, it's in a nice spot for someone wanting to do a little slip-trading from one Edge to the other." She reached for her brew. "Now, Banth's got tight admin."

"But what if they get used to these Liaden ships comin' in an' there always seems to be a problem, but it always turns out not to be, so the inspectors start thinkin' they got the pattern of it—"

"And then the Liadens change the pattern, and start ops for real, right under the clipboards of the inspectors?" Raisy shrugged. "Way I'd do it."

"OK," she said, briskly, counting off on her fingers. "Renegade Liaden. Smugglin' ring maybe settin' up on Banth. What else? Oh—Arin's boy on the ground in Liaden space with no warning going his way. You think the master trader is in with the renegade?"

No surprise that Raisy's thoughts went there—he'd considered the same thing himself. Still—he shook his head.

"I think she's square. This business about Jethri being safe with Tarnia on Irikwae? Strikes me she might've been giving us the Liaden for 'the kid has a ship to call on.' I'm leaning toward that."

"But you got something that's still bothering you."

"I do." He leaned his elbows on the table, reached out and put his hands loosely around the brew bottle.

"I'm thinking we need to let Jeth know that he's got trouble. Could be, he's got trouble enough for all of us, if you take me."

"You're thinking this chel'Gaibin boy might make a hobby out of hunting Gobelyns?"

"And Tomases," Grig said. "Yeah, I do."

Raisy finished off her brew and put the bottle down with a thump.

"What do you want, Grig?"

"Lend of a fastship," he said. "Last I knew, you owned one."

"If you think I'm gonna let you fly my ship, *you're* a headcase!" Raisy said and Grig felt his stomach sink as she pushed slid out of the booth and stood there, looking down at him.

"I'm coming with you," she said.

"I HAVE REVIEWED your file and I confess myself bewildered on several levels," Trader Ena Tyl sig'Lorta said, waving his hand at the screen on the table between them. "First, I find that there is no database error; you are correctly recorded as Jethri Gobelyn. A secondary entry was created for Jeth Ree ven'Deelin by the hall master's override. When it is accessed, however, the record it calls is precisely your own."

Jethri felt his stomach clench.

"Perhaps it was a test?" he offered, with as much delicacy as he could muster while cussing himself for plain and fancy mud-headedness.

Trader sig'Lorta stared at him, hard gray eyes wide with something near to shock. "You mean to suggest that the hall master had an interest in knowing how you would present yourself—as apprentice or as foster son?" His sharp face grew thoughtful. "That is possible. Indeed, now that I consider it—very possible. I see my task is not so simple as I had considered. Here . . ." He reached for the keypad, flicked open a log page and began, quickly, to type.

"I record in my mentor's notes—which will, you understand, be reviewed by a master at the end of your certification period—that your first request upon meeting your mentor was that the database be made to reflect your precise name." Another few lines, then a flick at the 'record' tab.

"So. That is well. We move on to lesser bewilderments." He touched a key, frowning down at the screen.

"I read here that the hall master at Modrid disallowed the trades you had completed at the word of your master trader—for which you utilized monies drawn on her accredited and known apprentice sub-account—and that he required the master trader to re-authorize each transaction recorded under that sub-account. Is this summation correct?"

Just a bit giddy with having escaped the name fiasco with his *melant'i* intact, Jethri inclined his head.

"Trader, it is."

"Hah." He touched another key, and sat frowning down at the screen.

"I also find that you are the holder of a ten-year Combine key, and have two trades of some small level of complexity attached to your name."

Jethri inclined his head once more. "Trader, that is so."

"Good. We have a Combine terminal here. When we have finished, you will use it to record your location, so that any trades you may make during the course of your certification will be appropriately recorded to your key, as well as entering your guild file."

Despite himself, Jethri blinked, which lapse went unnoticed by Trader sig'Lorta, who was still staring down at the screen.

Silence stretched, then Jethri cleared his throat.

"The hall master at Modrid said that no Terrans would be allowed into the guild."

His mentor shot him a hard, gray glance. "That is a matter for the masters, who—in all truth—could not have met and decided on any such question, as you are the first Terran who has sought entry into the guild. The rule as it is written—the rule which binds both the guild and yourself is: *Any candidate who has demonstrated mastery over the requirements put forth in the previous section may enter the guild as a trader. Those who once fail that demonstration may reapply after one Standard Year. Those who twice fail are banned from a third attempt.*

He tapped his finger sharply against the table top—click,click,click—and touched the forward key again.

"In your case, we have something of a conundrum. In the first wise, Modrid Hall had no authority to disallow a master trader's apprentice for any reason. That, however, is another matter for the masters, and I make no doubt that Norn ven'Deelin will see it discussed and decided ere long.

"In the second wise, a hopeful trader with two trades comparable to those recorded upon your key in his guild file would certainly rejoice in the *melant'i* of a junior trader, did he have no trader or master to whom he stood apprenticed." He gave the screen one more frowning glance and flicked the 'off' key.

"You and your master presented two claims to the hall master at Modrid—contracted association with a master trader, and the trades recorded on the key. Either should have assured you a place in the guild—as an apprentice, or as a junior trader. Since Modrid Hall allowed neither claim to be sufficient, you now are come to Irikwae Hall with a request from your master trader that you be independently certified, and given a formal ranking within the guild." He looked up, face serious.

"Understand, this is an unusual step. It has been done rarely in the past, most often when a dispute arose between traders regarding the talents or qualifications of a particular apprentice. In this instance, I would say that your master trader is wise to request independent certification—and doubly wise to ask it of Irikwae, where the hall master is known to be both conservative and stringent."

So, he was going to have to work his butt off, Jethri thought, and was surprised to find himself on his mettle, but not concerned. He was Norn ven'Deelin's apprentice, wasn't he? Hadn't he learned his basics from Arin and Paitor Gobelyn, neither one a slacker, if not precisely a master trader? Come to that, Trader sig'Lorta was shaping up to be the sort of mentor somebody might want for the upcoming tests—hard, and not exactly happy about Jethri *personally*, but a trader of virtue for all that, and upholding of the regs. He'd have to prove himself, right enough, but he didn't get the sense that his mentor would be changing the rules, if it got to looking like Jethri was about to win the game.

"May I know," he asked, "what the certification entails?"

"Surely, surely." Trader sig'Lorta flicked impatient fingers at the dark screen. "You will, I think, find it not at all unlike your apprenticeship. The hall will make an account available to you and you will be given various assignments of trade on the port. Those transactions will be recorded to your file, and at the end of the testing period, the file will be reviewed by a master trader, who will rule upon your precise level of skill. You will then be issued a card reflecting your standing within the guild. Of course, as you success-fully complete more, and more complex, trades, your standing will increase, and your guild card will reflect that, as well."

Jethri took a couple minutes to think about that.

"The purpose of this exercise," he said, slowly, "is to gain a guild card, so that I may not be denied the benefits and assistance of the guild."

"Say, so that it will be *less likely* that you will be denied those benefits," Trader sig'Lorta said, practically. "Certainly, there will be some who will risk the wrath of the masters over such niceties as whether Terrans may belong to the guild—but less, I think, than might, had you no certified standing."

"I see," Jethri said. He shot a straight look at his mentor's face and decided to risk it: "I wonder, Trader, if you might tell me where you personally stand on the issue of Terrans in the guild."

The hard gray eyes narrowed, with amusement or annoyance, Jethri couldn't have said.

"I believe that traders trade, Jethri Gobelyn. Show me that you are a trader, and I will accord you the respect due a guild brother."

Well enough. Jethri inclined his head. "Thank you, Trader. I will certainly endeavor to show you that I am a trader."

DAY 177

❀ ❀

Standard Year 1118
Irikwae Port

DURING HIS FIRST WEEK at the hall, Jethri shadowed Trader sig'Lorta, learning the general lay of the port. In the evening, he set himself to solving the trade problems that had been uploaded to his screen. All of which was better than bowing lessons, but wasn't exactly what he was craving.

Waking on the morning of the day that he had decided he would ask his mentor straight out when he could expect to start his own trading, his first assignment was on his work screen. The timing led Jethri to suspect that maybe the week-long set-up had been a test of his own, and he'd shaken his head a little as he shrugged into his good trading coat.

First day, it had been soybeans. Next, it had been ore. Today, it was something a little odd—toys.

Jethri's assignment was to assess the items on offer from the trader of the good ship *Nathlyr*, and, if he found the items to have value, to make an offer on no more than a dozen lots and no less than six. If he found the items wanting, he was to write up a report detailing their defects.

It was an interesting assignment on the face of it, and Jethri left the hall with a whistle on his lips, which gained him a frown from passersby, and recalled him to a sense of where he was and what was proper behavior for a trader on the street.

So far, he was liking his certification just fine. Soybeans were deadly dull—nothing more or less than trading the day-price off the board. Not quite enough to put a body right to sleep, but scarce enough to keep him full awake, either. Still, he'd moved his lot with precision, and added the extra tor to his drawing account.

The ore had been a bit more interesting. He'd needed to put some of his capital into trade goods. Soybeans, of course—that was sure—and an odd lot of blended wine from the Maarilex cellars—which wasn't so sure, but not a bad risk, either, especially not after he'd talked the co-op seller into taking another twelve percent off the lot on account it *was* odd and would have to be hand-sold, most likely one barrel at a time. Since that had been the precise problem the co-op had been having, the twelve percent came off pretty easy.

So, he'd had one barrel sent to the Irikwae trade hall to be placed in his trade space, and betook himself and his soybean ticket down to the tables, where he found a trader willing to talk ore.

The soybeans got some interest, which they had to, but the "short lot" of wine sweetened the deal to the tune of a side measure of rough cut turaline, which Jethri thought he might place with a port jeweler, to his profit.

He received the tickets with a bow and took himself off to the Street of Gems, where he was fortunate enough to locate a jeweler who was willing to take the turaline ticket off him for roughly double what he had paid for the short lot of wine.

He closed the deal, feeling some sharp—and found later that night, as he went over his comparisons, that he had let the gems go too cheap. Still, he consoled himself, he'd had a quick turnover, and doubled his money, too, which wasn't bad, even if not as good as could have been.

So, now, the toys, and he was looking forward to them, as he strode down the street to the exhibit halls.

He was early to the day hall, but not so early that there weren't traders there before him. The toy exhibit, in a choice center hall location, had not drawn a large crowd, which seemed strange—and then didn't as he got a closer look at what was on offer.

Exhibit hall protocol required a trader to show no less than three and no more than twelve pieces representative of that which he wished to sell. If *Nathlyr's* trader had followed the protocol, he stood in clear and present danger of going away with his hold still full of the things.

The examples set out were seemingly made of porcelain, badly shaped, with unexpected angles and rough-looking finish. Nothing about them invited the hand, or delighted the eye or engaged the mind, in the way that something billed as a *toy* ought.

Jethri picked up one of the pieces—in outline, it looked something like an old fin ship. It felt as gritty as it looked, and was slightly heavier than he had anticipated. Uncle Paitor had taught him that it sometimes helped to get a sense for a thing by holding it in the palm and getting comfortable with the shape and the weight of—

The thing in his hand was buzzing, slightly reminiscent of Flinx, setting up a nice fuzzy feeling between his ears. The buzzing grew louder and it was almost as if he could hear words inside of it— words in a language not quite Terran and not quite Liaden, but close—so close. He screwed his eyes shut, straining to hear—and gasped awake as pain flared, disrupting the trance.

Quickly, he replaced the toy among its fellows, and glanced down at his hand. There was a brand of red across the palm, already starting to blister. The . . . toy . . . had malfunctioned.

Or not.

He bit his lip, fingers curled over his burned palm. That the so-called toys were Befores of a type he had personally never seen was obvious. Befores being specifically disallowed on Irikwae at least, it seemed that his duty was to alert the Master of Exhibits to the problem.

And then, he thought, grimacing as he slipped his wounded hand into his pocket, he would go down to one of the philter shops on the main way and get a dressing for his burn.

As it happened, somebody else had been dutiful sooner. He

hadn't got half-way to the offices in the back of the big hall when he met a crowd heading in the opposite direction.

Two grim-faced port proctors, a woman in the leather clothing of a Scout, and the Master of Exhibits himself, walking arm in arm with a slightly wide-eyed trader not much older, Jethri thought, than he was. *Nathlyr* was fancy-stitched across the right breast of the trader's ship jacket.

Respectfully, Jethri stepped aside to let them pass, though he doubted any of the bunch saw him, except the Scout, then changed course for the exit. His hand was hurting bad.

"CERTAINLY! CERTAINLY!" The philterman took one look at the angry wound across Jethri's palm and ran to the back of the shop. By the time Jethri had arranged himself on the short stool and put his hand on the counter, the man was back, clutching a kit to his chest.

"First, we cleanse," he murmured, breaking the seal on an envelope bearing the symbol for "medical supply," and shaking out an antiseptic wipe.

Jethri braced himself, and it was well he did; the pressure of the wipe across his skin was painful, and the cleaning solution added another level of burn to his discomfort.

"Ow!" He clamped his mouth tight on the rest of it, ears hot with embarrassment. The philterman looked up, briefly.

"It is uncomfortable, I know, but with such a wound we must be certain that the area is clean. Now . . ." He pulled out a second envelope and snapped the seal, shaking out another wipe.

"This, I think, you will find a bit more pleasant."

The pressure still hurt—and then it didn't, as his skin cooled and the pain eased back to something merely annoying.

Jethri sighed, his relief so great that he forgot to be embarrassed.

"Yes, that is better, eh?" The philterman murmured, reaching again into his kit. "Now, we will dress it and you may continue your day, Trader. Remember to have the hall physician re-examine you this evening. Burns have a difficult nature and require close observation."

The dressing was an expandable fingerless glove that had a layer of all-purpose antibiotic against the skin. The largest in stock stretched to fit Jethri's hand.

"Else," the philterman said, "we should have had to wrap it in treated gauze, with an overwrap of sterile tape. So." He gathered up the spent wipes and broken envelopes and fed them into the countertop recycler.

"If I might suggest a portable kit, Trader?" he murmured. "It fits easily into a pocket, and includes three each of cleansing and pain alleviation wipes, and a small roll of antibiotic-treated gauze and wrapping tape. Two dex, only."

And cheap insurance at that, Jethri thought, glancing down at his gloved hand. Who expected toys to bite, anyway?

"An excellent suggestion," he said to the philterman. "I will have one of your kits. Also—" he said, suddenly remembering another item that might be found in such a shop. "I wonder if you have a sort of cream which is commonly sold to Terrans, which dissolves facial hair and keeps the face pleasing."

"Ah!" The man looked up at him interestedly. "Is there such a thing? I had no notion. We do not, you understand, much deal with Terrans at Irikwae. But hold. . ."

He bustled to the back and returned with a flat plastic pack prominently marked with the symbol for medical supplies. Slipping a finger under the seal, he unfolded the pack to display its contents—three each, cleaning wipes and painkiller wipes; one small roll of antibiotic gauze, one small roll of tape. Check.

"I thank you," Jethri murmured, slipping two dex from his public pocket and putting them on the counter.

"It is my pleasure to serve," the man said, folding the kit and resealing it. Jethri picked it up; it fit into one of the smaller of his jacket's numerous inner pockets, with room to spare.

"Of this other product," the philterman murmured. "There is a shop at the bottom of the street which does from time to time have specialty items on offer. It may be that you will find what you are seeking there. The shop is the last on the left side of the street. It has a green-striped awning."

"I thank you," Jethri said again and got himself disentangled from the stool and on his feet, heading for the door.

"DISSOLVES HAIR?" The woman behind the counter at the philtershop at the bottom of the street stared at him as if he'd taken leave of his senses. "Nothing like that here, young trader—nor likely to be! We offer oddities from time to time, but nothing—well. Perhaps you want the Ruby Club? The director has been known to keep . . . exotic items on hand."

"Perhaps I do," Jethri said, by no means certain. "My thanks to you." He departed the shop of the green awning, feeling the woman's eyes on his back as he paused, looking up and down the street for a public map.

The Ruby Club was somewhat behind and at a angle to the warehouse district, not quite adjacent to the salvage yards. Well. The toys having fallen through, he figured he had an hour or two at liberty and, while Meicha's handiwork had so far stood up, he didn't know how long that would be so, or if his first warning of its failure would be on the morning he woke up to find he'd overnight grown a beard down to his knees.

Prepared is better'n scared, he thought, which was something his father used to say, and Grig, too—and pushed the button on the bottom of the map to summon a taxi to him.

"YOU ARE CERTAIN that this is the location to which you were directed?" The taxi driver actually sounded worried, and Jethri didn't know as how he particularly blamed her.

The Ruby Club itself was kept up and lighted; with a red carpet extending from its carved red door right across the walkway to the curb. The surrounding buildings, though, were dark, not in repair, and in some cases overgrown with plants that Jethri's time in the vineyards had taught him were weeds.

"Is there another Ruby Club on the port?" he asked, half-hoping to hear that there was, and that it stood next to the Irikwae Trade Bar.

To his surprise, the driver leaned forward and tapped a

command into her on-board map. After a moment, he heard her sigh, lightly.

"There is only this one."

"Then this is my location," Jethri said, with more certainty than he felt. He wasn't liking the looks of this street, at all. On the other hand, he thought, given the general feeling that Terrans were pretty good zoo material, maybe it wasn't surprising that a place known for carrying exotic Terran items was situated well away from the main port. He pushed open the door.

"Wait for me," he said to the cabbie. She looked over the seat at him.

"How long?"

Good question. "I shouldn't be above twelve minutes," he said, hoping for less.

She inclined her head. "I will wait twelve minutes."

"My thanks."

He left the cab and walked briskly down the red carpeting. Seen close, the red door was carved; the carving showing a lot of naked people having sex with each other, and maybe some things that weren't exactly sex—or if so, not the kind that had been covered in either his hygiene courses or the bits of the Code the twins' tutor had marked out for him to read.

It did come to him that he was not prepared to deal with the consequences of that door, and he began to turn away, to go back to the cab and uptown and his quarters at the trade hall—

The door opened.

He glanced back, and down, into a pair of jade green eyes, slightly tip-tilted in a soft, oval face. Jade-colored flowers were painted along the ridge of . . . the person's . . . cheekbones, and their lips were also painted jade. They were dressed in a deep red tunic and matching trousers, beneath which red boots gleamed.

"Service, Trader," the doorkeeper said huskily, and the voice gave no clue to gender.

Jethri bowed, slightly. "I was sent here by a merchant uptown," he said, keeping his voice stringently in the mercantile mode. "It was thought that there might be depilatory for sale here."

"Why, perhaps there is," the doorkeeper said, standing back, and opening the door wide. "Please, honor our house by entering. I will summon the master to your aid."

It was either go in or cut and run. He didn't especially want to go in, but found his pride wouldn't support cut and run. Inclining his head, he stepped into the house.

THE DOORKEEPER INSTALLED him in a parlor just off the main entryway and left him. Jethri looked about him, eyes slightly narrowed in protest of the decorating. A deep napped crimson carpet covered the floor from crimson wall to crimson wall. A couch in crimson brocade and two crimson brocade chairs were grouped 'round a low table covered with a crimson cloth. A black wooden bookshelf along one short wall held volumes uniformly bound in red leather, titles outline in gilt.

Jethri was starting to feel a little uneasy in the stomach by the time the hall door opened and the master of the house joined him.

This was an older man, entirely bald, dressed in a lounging robe of simple white linen. His face was finely lined and unpainted, though a row of tiny golden hoops pierced the skin and followed the curve of his right cheekbone from the inner corner of his eye out to the ear.

Two paces into the room, he paused to bow, low, and to Jethri's eye, with irony.

"Trader. How may our humble house be of service?"

"House Master." Jethri inclined his head. "Pray forgive this unseemly disturbance of your peace. I had been told at a shop in the main port that perhaps I might find a certain cream here—it is often used by Terrans such as myself to remove hair and to condition the face."

"Ah." The man raised a hand and touched his shining bald head. "Yes, we sometimes have such a commodity in the house."

Jethri blinked. The amount of cream necessary to unhair a whole head would be considerable. Once the head in question was bald, it would take less cream to keep it that way, but the supply would need to be steady. The woman at the second philtershop had not sent him astray.

"I wonder," he said to the house master, "if I might purchase a small quantity of this cream from you. Perhaps, a vial—no more than two."

"Purchase? Let me consider . . ." The man ran his forefinger, slowly, along the line of tiny hoops, his eyes narrowed, as if it were pleasant to feel the gold slide against his cheek.

"No," he said softly. "I really do not think we can sell you any of our supply, Trader."

Well, there was a disappointment, Jethri thought. He took a breath, preparatory to thanking the man for his time . . .

"But we will trade for it," the house master said.

"Trade for it?" Jethri repeated, blankly.

"Indeed." Again, the slow slide of the forefinger along the row of piercings and the long look of narrow-eyed pleasure. "You are a trader, are you not?"

When I'm not busy being what Lady Maarilex calls a moonling, well yes, Jethri thought, *I am*. He inclined his head.

"I am a trader, sir, and willing undertake a trade for the item under discussion. However, it is so small a transaction that I am somewhat at a loss to know what might be fair value."

"There, I can provide guidance," the man said, turning his hand palm up in the gesture that meant, roughly, 'service'. "I understand, as you do, that the item under discussion is a rarity upon this port, as much as it might be commonplace upon other ports. We receive, as I am sure you have surmised, a small but steady supply, from a source that I am really not at liberty to share with you. This source also provides other . . . specialties . . . to the house. However, we have not been able to procure formal masks. In trade for two tubes of the cream, I will accept four half-face masks made from crimson leather, or two whole-face masks."

Red leather masks?

"Forgive me, sir, but the trade is uneven," Jethri said, which was sheer reflex, rather than any real knowledge of how costly red leather masks were likely to be. "Two half-masks for two tubes achieves symmetry."

The house master *blinked*—and bowed.

"Of course," he said smoothly, "you are correct, Trader. Two half-masks in red leather for two tubes of Terran depilatory cream. It is done." Straightening, he motioned to the door.

"When you acquire the masks, return, and we will make the exchange."

"Certainly, sir."

Jethri inclined his head, and took the hint. At the outside door, the person with the flower-painted face bowed him out.

"Fair profit, Trader. Come again."

"Joy to the house," he answered and went down the red carpet to the taxicab, waiting at the curb.

He settled into the back seat with an audible sigh.

"I thank you for waiting above the twelve minutes," he said to the cabbie.

She slammed the car into gear and pulled away from the curb more sharply than she should have.

"Are all Terrans fools?" she asked, sounding merely interested in his answer.

"Only the ones that apprentice to master traders and take certification at the Irikwae Trade Hall," he answered, feeling like she'd earned honesty from him—and a good sized tip, too.

"Hah," she said, and nothing more. Jethri leaned back as well as he could in the short seat and looked out the window at the unkempt streets.

The cab glided through an intersection, Jethri glanced down the cross-street—and jerked forward, hand on the door release.

"Stop the cab!" he shouted.

The driver braked and he was out, running back toward the scene he had glimpsed: four people, one on his knees, and all four showing fists.

Jethri had size and surprise, if not speed or sense. He grabbed a handful of jacket and yanked one of the attackers back from the victim, putting him down hard on his ass. The other two shouted, confused by the arrival of reinforcements, while the lone defender seized the opportunity and the room to leap to his feet and land a nice, solid punch on the jaw of the man nearest. In the meantime,

Jethri faced off with the third attacker, his body curling into the crouch Pen Rel had drilled him on, knees bent, hands ready.

The man yelled and swung, putting himself off-balance. Jethri ducked, grabbed the man's wrist and elbow, twisted—and shouted with joy as the attacker flew over his shoulder to land hard and flat on his back on the street.

His victory was short-lived. The first man was back on his feet, and moving in fast. This one had a cooler head—and maybe some training in Pen Rel's preferred style of brawl. Jethri dropped back, turning, caught sight of the yellow-haired victim, face cut and jacket torn, having heavy going with his man.

The guy stalking Jethri kicked. He sank back—but not quick enough. The edge of the man's boot caught his knee.

This time, the shout was pain, but he kept his feet, and there was a roaring in the street, growing louder, and then the blare of a klaxon, and it was the taxicab accelerating toward them, the cabbie's face implacable behind the windscreen.

The three attackers yelled and scrambled for the safety of the rotting sidewalk.

The taxi slammed to a halt, back door snapping open.

"In!" Jethri pushed the other man, and the two of them tumbled into the back seat, legs and arms tangled as the cab roared off, back door swinging. It slammed itself into place a few seconds later, when the cabbie took the next corner on two screaming wheels.

Fighting inertia, Jethri and the erstwhile victim slowly sorted out which legs and arms belonged to who and got themselves upright in the seats.

The yellow-haired man sank back on his seat with an audible sigh, and sat for a second, eyes closed. Jethri, blowing hard, leaned his head back, considering his rescue. It came to him that the man looked familiar, and he frowned, trying to bring the memory closer.

Across from him, the other opened his eyes a slit—and then considerably wider as he snapped straight upright.

"You! Jeth Ree Gobelyn, is it not?"

The voice rang the memory right up to the top of the brain. Jethri stared.

"Tan Sim?" he heard himself say, in a mode insultingly close to the one he used when talking with the twins. "What are you doing here?"

Tan Sim grinned, widely, then winced. "I could ask the same of you! Never tell me that the ven'Deelin sends you to the low port unguarded."

"That one," the taxi driver said over her shoulder, "should not be let to roam the high port alone. Where shall I have the extreme pleasure of dropping the two of you off?"

PATCHED AND WELL-SCOLDED by the hall physician, it occurred to them in a simultaneous way that they were hungry. Accordingly, they adjourned to the Trade Bar, where they were fortunate to find a booth open.

"Bread," Jethri said to the waiter. "And two of whatever the day meal is. Fresh fruit."

"Wine," Tan Sim added, and the waiter bowed.

"At once, traders."

Tan Sim sank into deep upholstery with a gusty sigh. "There's a day's work done and the afternoon still before us!"

Jethri grinned. "Now, tell me why you were walking alone on such streets."

"The short answer is—returning from inspecting a pod offered at salvage," Tan Sim retorted. "The longer answer is—longer."

"I have the time, if you have the tale," Jethri murmured, moving his hand in an expression of interest.

Tan Sim smiled. "Gods look upon the lad. Jeth Ree, you are more Liaden than I!"

"Surely not," he began, but a discreet knock upon the door heralded the arrival of the requested wine—a bottle of the house red, a comfortable blend, as Jethri knew—and two glasses.

"The meals are promised quickly, traders," the waiter said and left them, pulling the door closed behind him.

"Well." Tan Sim took charge of the bottle and poured for both of them. "If you will join me first in a sip to seal our friendship—"

Jethri put his glass down. Tan Sim paused, eyebrows up.

"What's amiss?"

Jethri tipped his head, considering the other. The physician had cleaned and taped the cut on Tan Sim's face, muttering that bruises would rise by nightfall, and suggesting, with a fair load of irony, that perhaps the trader might wish to cancel any engagements for the next few days.

Truth told, bruises were starting to rise already, but it wasn't that which took Jethri's notice. It was the face beneath the cut—thinner than he had remembered, the mouth tighter. The torn jacket hung loose, which bore out Jethri's impression that maybe Tan Sim had been eating short rations lately.

"I believe," he said delicately, wishing neither to offend nor expose a weakness, "that there is a matter of Balance unresolved between us."

"Which would—naturally!—constrain you from drinking with me. Very nice. If such an unresolved Balance sat between us, I would commend you for the precision of your *melant'i*."

Meaning that Tan Sim didn't think there was a debt, and that didn't jibe.

"I had considered you my most grievous error," Jethri said, making another pass at getting it out in the open where they both could look at it. "It has troubled me that, all unknowing, and wishing only to honor one who had shown me the greatest kindness, I brought to that one only grief, and separation from clan and kin."

"If you believe for one moment that separation from my honored mother or my so-beloved brother is a matter of *grief*, then I must allow you to be in your cups," Tan Sim retorted and paused, face arrested. "No, that cannot be. We've not yet had to drink." He leaned forward slightly, to look earnestly into Jethri's face.

"My sweet fool—does it occur to you that you have just now preserved my life for me? Even supposing that I held you to book for my mother's temper and my brother's spite—that small matter would put paid to all." He raised his glass.

"Come, do not be churlish! At least drink to the gallantry of a taxi driver."

Well, Jethri thought, 'round a mental grin, he could hardly refuse that. He raised his glass.

"To the gallant driver, who preserved both our lives—"

"And refused any tip, save a scold!" Tan Sim finished with a flourish of his glass.

They sipped, and again, the wine tasting more than usually pleasant.

"So, tell me then," Jethri said, putting his glass aside and relaxing into the cushions.

Tan Sim laughed lightly. "Demanding youth. Very well." He put his glass down and folded his elbows onto the table, leaning forward.

"Now, it happens that my mother was very angry indeed over the incident with the bow. She swore that I was a disgrace to her blood and that she would have no more of me. For some significant time, it did appear that she would simply cancel my contract and send me out to earn my own way. A not entirely unpleasing prospect, as you might imagine."

He extended a hand and picked up his glass, twirling it idly by the stem, his eyes on the wine swirling inside the bowl.

"Alas, it was then that my brother entered the negotiations, with a plea for leniency, which my mother was disposed to hear." He lifted the glass.

"Rather than cancel my contract, she sold it. I am now the trader of record aboard the good ship *Genchi*, which Captain sea'Kira allows me to know has never carried such a thing. Nor needs one."

A quick knock, and the door was opened by their waiter, bearing a tray well-loaded with eatables. He set it all out with noiseless efficiency, bowed and was gone, the door snicking shut behind him.

There was a pause in the tale, then, while the two of them took the day meal under consideration, Tan Sim eating with an elegant ferocity that confirmed Jethri's fears regarding short rations.

"Well," Tan Sim said at last, selecting a fruit from the basket between them. "Where did I leave the tale?"

"Your mother sold your contract to *Genchi*, though it had no need of a trader," Jethri said, around his last bit of bread.

"Ah. *Genchi*. Indeed. It happened that the ship owner had a desire to improve *Genchi's* fortunes and thought that a trader aboard might produce a rise in profit. Unfortunately, the owner is a person who has . . . limited funding available to him—and, very possibly, limited understanding as well. For I put it to you, friend Jethri: How does a ship on a fixed route raise profit?"

Jethri paused in the act of reaching for a fruit and looked over to him.

"By shipping more."

Tan Sim raised his fruit in an exuberant toast. "Precisely!"

"And *Genchi* is podded out," Jethri guessed, in case there were bonuses involved.

Tan Sim smiled upon him tenderly. "It's a dear, clever lad. But, no—there you are slightly out. It happens that *Genchi* can accept two additional pods. Which the trader is to purchase from the elevated profits his very presence upon the ship will produce."

Jethri stared at him. "Your mother signed that contract?" he demanded.

Tan Sim dipped his head modestly. "She was most wonderfully angry."

"How long?"

"Until I am in default? Or until the contract is done?"

"Both."

"Pah! You have a mind like a trader, Jeth Ree Gobelyn!" He bit into his fruit and chewed, meditatively.

"I will default at the end of the relumma. The contract has six years to run."

Jethri blinked. "She's trying to kill you."

Tan Sim moved a shoulder. "Break me only. Or so I believe. And, in truth, I am not without some blame. Were I less like my mother, I might send a beam, begging her grace, and asking for terms to come home."

Jethri snorted.

"Yes," Tan Sim said gently. "Exactly so."

Glumly, Jethri finished his fruit, wiped his fingers and reached for his glass.

"But you aren't going to default," he said. "You went down to the salvage yard this morning to look at a pod."

"Indeed I did. I found it to be a most excellent pod, of an older construction. Older, even, than *Genchi*. It is in extraordinarily good shape—sealed and unbreached—and the yardman's final price is . . . not beyond reach. However, it's all for naught, for it must have new clamps if it is to marry *Genchi*, and while I may afford those—I cannot afford those and the pod."

Jethri sipped wine, frowning slightly. "Still sealed, you say. What does it hold?"

"Now, that, I do not know. As old as the pod is, its contents are unlikely to have much value. Were matters otherwise, I might take the gamble, but—I do not scruple to tell you, cash is at present too dear."

Jethri finished his wine and set the glass aside. There was an idea, buzzing around in the back of his brain, slowly gaining clarity and insistence. He let it grow, while across the table Tan Sim wrestled silently with whatever thoughts engaged him.

"How much?" he asked softly, so as not to joggle the idea before it was set.

"The yard wants to see a cantra for the pod, entire. Clamps are four kais."

The idea had set firm, and he was liking it from all the angles he could see. He had a knack for salvage, Uncle Paitor'd always said so. . .

"I wonder," he said, looking up into Tan Sim's bruised and weary face, "if you might have time tomorrow to introduce me to the salvage yard?"

"Oh," said Tan Sim wisely, "do you think you might manage it? I wish you shall. Certainly. Meet me here at the opening of day port and I will show you where."

"And this time," Jethri said with a smile. "We will take a taxi."

IT LOOKED LIKE RED leather masks were going to be a problem, Jethri thought, leaning back in his chair and rubbing his eyes. He had written his report on the toys, and seen that his tomorrow's schedule had been amended to reflect the hall physician's orders that he "rest"—by which it was apparently meant that he not go on the port to trade, a concept that struck him as wrongheaded, at best. Still, it did give him a good piece of time to go to the salvage yards with Tan Sim and inspect the pod he had found.

But the masks, now. Never mind red leather—masks at all was a missing item along any of the lists open to the guild computer. He sighed and leaned way back in the chair, stretching—and grimacing, when the stretch woke muscles that had been pulled in the day's fisticuffs.

Nothing for it but to go back to the Trade Bar and use his key to find masks on the Combine net. Come to think of it, he might forget masks altogether and go for a pallet of depilatory, since there seemed to be a market.

He stood and reached for his second best jacket, his first being down at the laundry—and started badly when the door chime sounded.

Probably Trader sig'Lorta, come to read him Ship's General. Shrugging into his jacket, he walked over to the door and keyed it open.

"Why, look how the boy has grown!" Scout Captain ter'Astin said in cheery Terran. Miandra stood at his elbow, her face serious.

"Well met, Jethri," she said. "The captain came to the house and Aunt Stafeli said that I should bring him to you."

Captain ter'Astin bowed, lightly, hand over heart. "Summoned, I rush to obey."

Jethri felt his cheeks warm with the blush. "I have overstepped my *melant'i*, I fear," he admitted.

"Not a bit of it! The Scouts tend a wide business; it is our nature to answer summonses." He cocked his head. "Some, I do allow, with more alacrity than others."

Jethri smiled and stepped back, sweeping a bow. "Please, both, enter and be welcome."

The Scout entered first, Miandra trailing after, looking like a limp copy of herself.

Frowning, Jethri closed and locked the door, then turned to deal with his guests.

Miandra was already at the window, looking down into the garden. The Scout had paused to give the short row of books his consideration, and looked up as Jethri approached.

"I was asked to bring something besides myself to your side," he said, pulling a well-folded piece of paper from an inner jacket pocket. "Please, satisfy yourself. I have no other engagements to fulfill today."

"Thank you," Jethri said, receiving the paper with a bow. "May I call for tea? Wine?"

The Scout laughed. "You take polish well, Jethri Gobelyn. But, no, I thank you—I am not in need."

Jethri glanced over to the window, where his other guest still stared down into the garden.

"Miandra?" He asked, softly. "Would you like tea? Cookies?"

She flicked a distracted glance over her shoulder, tight lips moving in what she might have meant to be a smile.

"Thank you, but I am not—in need."

Which was as big a clunker as he'd ever heard, including the time Grig told Cap'n Iza that the odd lot of sweets he'd bought was a broker deal, and then shared them all out 'mong crew.

"What's amiss?" He asked, moving closer, the Scout's paper held close in his hand.

She turned her face away, and that—hurt. Weren't they friends, after all? He touched her sleeve.

"Hey," he said. "Miandra. Are you well?"

Her shoulders jerked, and a half-smothered sound escaped, sounding half laugh and half sob.

"You asked that—before," she said, and turned to face him squarely, chin up and looking more like herself, despite her wet cheeks. "Have we not taught you that strangers must keep a proper reserve?"

"Certainly, Lady Maarilex would not be behind in so basic a lesson," he allowed, inclining his head and putting on the gentleman. "However, such rules do not maintain between us, because we are kin."

Her eyes widened and the corner of her mouth twitched slightly upward. "Kin? How so?"

"What else would we be?" He held his hand up, fingers spread, and folded his thumb against the palm, counting. "I am Norn ven'Deelin's foster son." Forefinger down. "Stafeli Maarilex is Norn ven'Deelin's foster mother, my foster grandmother." Second finger joined thumb and forefinger. "You are a niece of Stafeli Maarilex." Third finger. "Therefore, we are foster cousins."

She laughed. "Well done! And the degree of consanguinity appropriate, too, I see!"

He grinned and reached again to touch her sleeve.

"So, cousin, if a cousin may ask it—are you well?"

She moved her shoulders and flicked a glance aside. He looked, as well, but the Scout was perched on the edge of the worktable, to all appearances immersed in one of the novels brought from Tarnia's library.

"I am . . . unwell in spirit," she said, lowering her voice. "Ren Lar—he treats me as if *I* were a piece of old technology. He forbids me the vines, the cellar, and the yards. I am scarcely allowed to come to the dining table at prime. At his insistence, Meicha and I must undergo—separately—intensive evaluation, by the Healers. Meicha completed hers last night; Anecha drove down to pick her up this morning. In the meanwhile, a car was made ready to take me to Healer Hall—so that we should not be able to speak together before I am evaluated, you know—but your Scout happened by and offered to save the house the trouble, as he was going back down to the port to find you."

He had no idea what an "intensive evaluation" might mean, but allowed as it sounded bad enough.

"Do you need to report in?" he asked.

"Testing does not begin until tomorrow morning," she said. "It was arranged that I should overnight at the hall." Her mouth got tight again. "I . . .would . . . that other arrangements had been made."

"If they don't need you until tomorrow morning," he said, moving his hand, to show her his quarters, "you're welcome to spend the night here. I am at liberty tomorrow and can escort you to Healer Hall."

"Perhaps it might be—less stressful of the relations of kin and foster kin," the Scout said, so suddenly that both of them spun to stare at him, sitting on the edge of the table, with the book opened over his knee. "If the lady would instead accept my invitation to guest with the Scouts this evening."

"You were listening," Jethri said, sounding like a younger, even to himself.

Captain ter'Astin inclined his head. "Scouts have very sharp ears. It is required."

Miandra took a step forward, frowning slightly. "And in addition to sharp ears, you are a Healer."

He moved a hand, deprecating. "A receiver only, I fear. Though I'm told I build a most impressive wall. Honor me with your opinion, do."

To Jethri's senses, nothing happened, except that the Scout's expression maybe took on an extra degree of bland, while Miandra stared intently at the thin air above his head.

She blinked. Captain ter'Astin tipped his head to one side.

"It is," Miandra said, slowly, "a very impressive wall. But you must not think it proof against attack."

"Ah, must I not? Tell me why."

She moved her hands in a gesture of—untangling, Jethri thought. Untangling her perception into words the two of them could understand.

"You have a—need. A very powerful need to be—acutely aware of surrounding conditions, at all times. Data is survival. So, you have left a—chink, very small—in your wall, that you may continue to be aware. It is through that chink that you are vulnerable. If I can see it, others may, as well."

The Scout slid to his feet, catching the book up neatly, and bowed. Acknowledging a debt, Jethri read, and looked at Miandra in close wonder. She bit her lip and half-raised a hand.

Captain ter'Astin raised the book. "Peace. The gratitude of a Scout is worth holding, and is not given lightly. Your observation may well have saved my life. Who can say? Certainly, I shall not leave Irikwae without consulting a Healer and learning the manner of sealing this—chink."

"And now," he said, lowering the book. "I believe Jethri has a paper to read, after which he and I have business. Shall we proceed?"

Miandra moved to the table and picked up one of the novels, carrying it back to the window with her. The Scout resettled himself on the edge of the table. Jethri went to the black corner table, pushed the photocube of strangers back, unfolded the paper and smoothed it flat with his palm.

Despite that by now he read Liaden as good or better than he'd ever read Terran, it was dense going. Stoically, he kept with it and finally arrived at the last word with the understanding that the Liaden Scouts were, indeed, specifically charged with the confiscation, evaluation and appropriate disposal of "Old War technology," such technology having been designated, by an action of the Council of Clans, meeting at Solcintra City, Liad, "perilous in manufacture and intent."

Sighing, he straightened, and turned.

Miandra was sitting in his desk chair, seriously involved with her novel. The Scout was reading Jethri's old pretend journal.

"I shouldn't think that would hold much interest for you, sir," he said, moving forward, and slipping a hand into his most secret pocket.

Captain ter'Astin glanced up, bounced to his feet, turning to put the book back in its place.

"The workings of mind and custom are always of interest to me," he said. "It is the reason I am a Scout—and a field Scout, at that."

Jethri looked at him sharply. The Scout inclined his head.

"So tell me, Jethri Gobelyn, are you satisfied that the disposal of Old War technology falls within the honor of the Scouts, and that such disposal is mandated by whole law?"

"Unfortunately, I am." He placed the weather machine, lingeringly, on the table, and stood there, feeling kind of dry and gone in the throat of a sudden, staring down into the unreflective black surface.

"Ah." Captain ter'Astin put a hand on Jethri's sleeve. "I regret your loss. I believe you had told Scout yo'Shomin that this device was given you by a kinsman?"

Jethri licked his lips.

"It was a gift from my father," he told the Scout. "After his death, I was without it for many years. It was only recently returned to me, with—" He waved a hand, enclosing the photocubes, Arin's box and the silly old journal— "other things of value."

"Accept my condolences," the Scout said softly. The pressure of his fingers increased briefly, then he withdrew his hand and picked up the weather machine, slipping it away somewhere inside his jacket.

Jethri cleared his throat. "I wonder if you might tell me if you will yourself be involved in the—evaluation—of this device. Whether it will be—will simply be destroyed, or if the work that my father did will be preserved."

The Scout's eyebrows rose. "Yes. I would say that you take polish very well, indeed." He paused, possibly gathering his thoughts, then inclined his head.

"I may possibly be asked for a preliminary evaluation; I do have some small expertise in the area. However, you must understand that there is a corps of Scout Experts, who have studied, built databases and cross-referenced their findings through the many dozens of Standards that this policy has been in force. If it is found that your machine, here, is unique, then it will undergo the most intense scrutiny possible by those who are entirely knowledgeable. Many of the old technology pieces that we have recovered are uniquities— that is, we have recovered only one."

Jethri bowed his gratitude. "I thank you, sir."

"Unnecessary, I assure you. A word in your ear, however, child."

"Yes?"

"It might be wisest not to state in public that such devices were part of your father's work."

Jethri frowned. "Old technology is not illegal, in Terran space," he said, evenly.

"Very true," the Scout said and it seemed to Jethri that he was about to say more.

"Is this your father?" Miandra asked from behind them.

Jethri turned, and saw her holding up the photocube, Arin's picture on the screen.

"Yes—that's him."

She turned it 'round to face her. "You resemble him extremely, Jethri. I had supposed him to be your elder brother."

"May I see?" The Scout extended a hand, and Miandra gave him the cube.

"Ah, yes, that is how I saw him, on the day of his dying. Strong, doubt free and worthy. A remarkable likeness, indeed." Bowing slightly, he handed the cube back.

"Now, children, I suggest that we adjourn to Scout Hall, where Jethri may sign the necessary paperwork and we may place this item—" He touched the breast of his jacket—"into safekeeping. We will also contact the Healers, to advise them of Lady Miandra's guesting arrangements, and to confirm the time of her arrival tomorrow. *After* which, I ask you both to lend me the pleasure of your companionship over prime. There is a restaurant on Irikwaeport which has long been a favorite of mine. I would be honored to share it with friends."

Jethri glanced to Miandra, saw her eyes shining and her face looking less pinched, and bowed to the Scout.

"We are more than pleased to bear you company, sir. Lead on."

DAY 178

❀ ❀

Standard Year 1118
Irikwae

IT WAS AN OLD POD, though he'd seen older; the seals were sound, the skin whole and undented. It rested on a cradle meant for a pod decades newer and massing twice as much; though its fittings could be said to be standard they were of an older and unfavored style. At some time in the past—perhaps not all that long ago—it had been underwater and a colony of hard-shells, now empty, still adhered to the hull. On the nose was a Liaden registry number, faint, but readable.

Jethri finished his circuit and paused, considering the thing as a whole.

"Well?" asked Tan Sim, who had been watching, one hip up on the wide windowsill, one booted foot braced against the rough crete floor. "Shall you take it for your own?"

Jethri turned. "You know what is in this pod," he said, not asking.

Tan Sim blinked, and then bowed slightly from his lean. "I know what was on the manifest," he said, "and the devil's own time I had finding it, too."

"So?" Jethri walked toward him. "What were they shipping?

Flegetets, dead and rotted, these sixty years? Cheeses, moldy and poisonous? Wine, now vinegar?"

Tan Sim moved a shoulder, grimacing. The bruises had risen with a will overnight, leaving his face a patchwork of yellow and purple.

"Mind you," he said, raising a hand. "I could only trace the registry number, which is in series with those ceded Clan Dartom, some sixty Standards gone. Indeed, Clan Dartom is itself fifty Standards gone, and nothing to say but that this pod was sold and sold again on the unregistered market."

"Clan Dartom is—gone?" Jethri asked, thinking epic scales of revenge, like in one of Khat's stories—or Gaenor's novels.

"Peace," Tan Sim said, as if he had read Jethri's thoughts—or was perhaps himself a reader of novels. "Dartom was based upon a young outworld; a plague destroyed them and the rest of the population, very speedily. Not even a kitten left alive. Medical analysis failed to produce anyone who might even be named a cousin." He waved a languid hand in the direction of the pod.

"So, Dartom's remaining uncontaminated assets fell to the Council of Clans, which took what it wanted, and distributed the remainder by lot. They then wrote Dartom out of the Book of Clans, and put paid to the matter."

"Anyone could have bought this pod at auction, then," Jethri said. "Or, as you say, on the unregistered market. And those who buy such things sometimes have unregistered business."

"In pursuit of which they would be foolish in the extreme to file a manifest," Tan Sim agreed.

Jethri turned back to the pod, and once again subjected the seals to the most minute scrutiny possible. Unbreached. Impossible to tell how long they had been sealed.

"You found a manifest," he said, turning back to Tan Sim. "How long ago?"

"Fifty-three years, which does put it in a . . . problematic time frame."

"The pod spent some time in the sea," Jethri pointed out.

"True, but we have no date there, either." Tan Sim turned his palms up, showing them empty. "Indeed, we have but one firm date: The salvage rig's log shows that it was brought into port two Standards back, when it was purchased by this yard, in lot with another dozen newer. This—" Tan Sim wiggled his fingers in the pod's general direction. "This was on the list for break-up, but the scrap market is over-subscribed and there is for the scrappers the considerable risk involved in taking possession of unknown goods."

"So they would just as soon sell it and shift the risk to other shoulders." Jethri sighed. "The manifest is public record?" he asked.

"My friend, public record?" Tan Sim bent upon him a look of gentle reproof. "The manifest had been sealed, then deep archived after the seal expired. Your average salvager, with his mind properly on scrap, is hardly busy mucking about in municipal archives, much less completing the rather daunting forms required by the Guild before one who is not a trader may request permission to pull and cross-reference ancient databases."

Jethri bowed acknowledgment, offering honor for a difficult task well-performed.

Tan Sim's bow of acceptance was nearly lost against the wall of Jethri's thought.

Jethri looked back to the pod. He *liked* it. He couldn't have put it otherwise, except that he had a good feeling about whatever might prove to be inside.

"What was on the manifest?"

"Ore, raw gem, artisan's metals."

Nonperishables. High-profit nonperishables, at that. If it was the right manifest. If it was the right pod, for that matter, it not being unknown for someone to borrow the legitimate registration number of a legitimate pod for illegitimate business.

"Buy the pod, sell the contents and realize more than enough profit to have the clamps refitted," he said. Again Tan Sim lifted a shoulder.

"A manifest, which may or may not be legitimate, for a pod which may or may not be this one? If I were plumper in the purse— perhaps. My present purse instructs me to assume that what is in that pod are dead flegetets, moldy cheese, and spoiled wine."

Jethri had done the math last night, worrying over his liquid. It were the Stinks money that made the difference—not quite enough to fund a ship, like Khat had joked, but close enough to fund this deal, after reserving an amount against the future. 'Course, there was more than enough money in his certification drawing account to cover the pod—and the clamps, too—but he didn't think the hall exactly wanted him to be using those funds for private deals.

"I will put four kais against the pod," he said to Tan Sim, "if we agree that the contents, whatever they are found to be, are mine, while the pod itself is yours."

Tan Sim raised his eyebrows, face thoughtful. Doing his own math, Jethri thought, and settled himself to wait.

"Four-six," Tan Sim said, eventually, which was about half the jump Jethri had been prepared to meet.

He inclined his head. "Done. Now, we shall need the pod moved to a less precarious position. What do you suggest?"

"As to that—nothing easier. The refit shop will send a hauler. They assured me that they have the means to unseal the pod without damaging the mechanisms, so the day after tomorrow should see an answer to your gamble. After which," he said, coming creakily out of his lean, "you may have free with whatever it is, and the shop will get on with the business of the clamps."

Jethri looked at him, and Tan Sim had the grace to look, just a little, discomfited.

"I thought you might do something like you have done," he said, softly. "So I made inquiries yesterday after we had parted." He sighed.

"I hope you will realize great profit, Jeth Ree."

"As to that," Jethri retorted. "I hope for a decent return."

Tan Sim grinned and offered his arm. "Spoken like a trader! Come, let us give the yardman his deposit and return to the hall to write the partnership papers."

THE PARTNERSHIP CONTRACT having been duly written, accepted and recorded by the hall scrivener, Jethri bounded up the stairs to his quarters, Tan Sim on his heels.

"Come and call the refit shop, so they may schedule an early pickup," he said as they moved down the hall. "For the salvage price—my part is in coin, which I will give to you, and you may transfer the balance to the yard."

Tan Sim smiled. "Such trusting ways. How if we both put our coin into the revolving account and authorize the hall to make the transfer in our names?"

Jethri paused in the act of unlocking the door to stare at him. "I had no idea such a thing was possible."

"Innocent. When we have sent the transfer, I will quiz you on the services a trader might expect a third-tier hall to provide."

The lock twittered and Jethri pushed the door open. "Is Irikwae in the third—" he began—and stopped, staring into his room.

All was neat and orderly, precisely as he had left it, with one addition.

Miandra sat cross-legged on his work table, reading a book.

Behind him, Tan Sim made a small noise, very much like a sneeze.

Miandra raised her head, showing them a face that was eerily serene.

"Cousin Jethri," she said clearly. "We need to talk."

Uh-oh.

"Certainly," Tan Sim said briskly, "the necessities of kin carry all before it. Jeth Ree, I will make that call from the Trade Bar and meet you there, when you have done here. Lady."

Jethri turned, but the door was already closing, with Tan Sim on the other side. He engaged the lock, then walked over to where Miandra sat, and stood looking down into her face.

She met his gaze without flinching, chin well up, an I-dare-you look in her eyes.

He sighed.

"How much trouble are you in?"

The chin might've quivered; the eyes never faltered.

"None, until they find me."

Well, that was the way it usually was, wasn't it? Jethri frowned.

"I thought you wanted my help."

She bit her lip. "I—indeed, Jethri, I am not certain what is that you might do. But I *will not* remain with the Healers, and I—fear—that I *cannot* go home . . ."

Jethri sighed again and made a long arm, hooking the desk chair to him. He sat down and looked up at her, showing her his hands, palm up, fingers spread, empty.

"I think you had better lay it out for me, one step at a time."

"Yes, I suppose I had better." She closed the book and put it on the table beside her, then leaned forward, elbow propped against a knee, chin nestled on her palm.

"As you know, I was to be evaluated by the Healers. Indeed, by the master healer himself. The evaluation—" she shot him a sharp glance. "You understand, Jethri, that when I say in this context that I was pushed, or prodded or that thus-and-so hurt me, I am not speaking of physical things, but rather use those words as an approximation of the exact . . . sensation . . . because there are no words precisely for those sensations."

He inclined his head. "But I may still understand that you found those things so described to be distressing and not at all what you could like, is that so?"

She smiled. "That is so, yes."

"Very well, then," Jethri said, starting to feel grim. "The master healer himself was assigned to your evaluation. What came next?"

"I was asked to—to take my shields down and to submit my will to the will of the master," she began, after a moment—and sent him another sharp glance. "This is not at all unusual and I did as I was bid. The master then began his examination, pushing here, prodding there—nothing terribly painful, but nothing pleasant either."

It sounded, Jethri owned, tiresome enough, something like a clinic check-up, with the medic pushing hard fingers here and there, trying to determine what was in line and what was out.

"Unpleasant, but hardly worth running away," he commented.

Miandra inclined her head. "I agree. After a time, the master began to concentrate on—say, a section of my will—and to—assault it. The first strike was so painful that I threw my shields up before I had even thought to do so. The master, of course, was very angry and had me lower them, whereupon he once again brought all of his scrutiny to bear on—on this anomaly in my—in my pattern." She sighed sharply. "By which I mean to convey that there are certain . . . constructions of intertwining ego, will, and intellect, which are intelligible to those who have Healer talent. While each pattern is unique, there are those which tend to be formed in a certain way—and which, more often than not, are indicative of Healer ability."

"So, the master healer was saying he thought your pattern was—shaped oddly," Jethri said, to show he was following this.

Miandra inclined her head. "Indeed, he went so far as to state that he felt it was this anomaly which was responsible for limiting my growth as a Healer, and he proposed to—restructure that portion, in order to allow my talent to flow more freely."

Jethri frowned. "He can do that?"

"That, easily," she assured him. "It is what Healers do."

Right. Jethri closed his eyes. Opened them.

"All right. So the master decided he would reshape you so you would look more like he thinks a Healer ought to. Then?"

She bit her lip.

"It—I told him that the process was . . . causing me pain. He assured me that it was not, and—pushed—harder." She glanced aside, took a hard breath and looked back to him, blue eyes swimming with tears.

"The pain was—immense. Truly, Jethri, I felt that I was afire, my flesh crisping off my bones as I stood there. I *pushed*, and threw my shields up."

"I see." He considered that, staring down at his hands where they rested on his knee, the one sporting a slightly grubby bandage. He looked up to find her watching him worriedly.

"Which moon did he fall onto?" he asked, mildly.

Miandra smiled, shakily. "You overestimate my poor abilities, cousin. I merely put him onto the top shelf of the bookcase." She took a breath. "Then I walked out, through the main reception hall. I willed that no one would see me, and no one did. And then I came here, and—overrode the lock and sat down to wait for you."

"Are they looking for you?"

"I suppose they must be, eventually." Another shaky smile appeared. "But as long as I keep my shields in place, they will not find me."

For however long that might be. He forbore from asking what happened to her shields when she slept. First order of business was to tell her what she'd done right. So—

"The rule on the ship I was born to was that one is allowed to defend oneself. Defense should be delivered as quickly and as decisively as possible, in order to prevent a second attack." He inclined his head, solemnly. "You have fulfilled ship rule admirably and I have no complaint to make regarding your actions to this point."

Relief washed her face.

"Our challenge now," Jethri continued, "is to be certain that our actions from this point on continue to be honorable and in the best interest of the ship." He tipped his head.

"That means you can't just hide on the port for the rest of your life."

Miandra outright laughed. "My shields aren't that good."

Jethri grinned, and let it fade into as serious a look as he could muster.

"You will need to let the house know where you are. Sooner or later, the Healers will have to call and admit that you've gone missing. That information is certain to distress your sister, your cousins and your delm, unless they know you are safe."

Miandra's look had turned stubborn.

"If I go home, Ren Lar will send me back. If I call, Aunt Stafeli will order me to return to Healer Hall."

Both probably true. But—

"If you explained to them what you have explained to me, that the examination was painful in the extreme and that you fear for your health if it continues?"

She considered it, chewing her lip. "That might bear weight with Aunt Stafeli, but Ren Lar—I do not believe that Ren Lar would be swayed, if I told him that the evaluation would, without doubt, murder me." She sighed. "Ren Lar is a badly frightened man. Old

Technology and wizard's get, *both* in his household! It is too much to bear."

"What if the evaluation proves that you are a dramliza?" Jethri asked.

She moved her shoulders. "I don't know."

This, Jethri thought, was 'way too snarly for a junior's simple brain. Clearly, Miandra needed help—and not just in this present mess. She needed schooling, whether or not Ren Lar or Stafeli Maarilex chose to believe in wizards. Jethri was pretty sure he didn't believe in wizards, himself. Still, there was no doubt Miandra had some very strange talents and that she needed to be trained in their proper use before she up and hurt somebody. If she hadn't already.

"Is the master healer harmed?" he asked.

She sighed. "No."

Jethri suppressed a grin.

"This is what I propose: That you come with me to the Trade Bar and be my guest for lunch. My friend and I have some business to discuss, which I hope you won't find too tedious. After, you and I will go together to the Scouts and ask Captain ter'Astin to advise us. For you know I'm a block, Miandra, and we are well past anything I can think of to assist you."

"Well, I don't know that you're a block," she retorted, and sat for a moment, contemplating the floor. Jethri sighed and stretched in his chair, careful of protesting muscles.

"I think that asking the captain's advice at this juncture is the wisest thing that I—that we—may do," she said, unfolding her legs and sliding to the floor. "It was very clever of you to have thought of it."

TAN SIM HAD ORDERED a cold platter of finger-nibbles, cheese, crackers, and tea—more than enough to feed two, Jethri thought—and possibly enough to cover three, if Miandra wasn't feeling particularly peckish.

He inclined his head. "I thank you. My cousin and I are needed elsewhere later in the day, and she has graciously said that she will allow us to conclude our business before hers."

"On condition," Miandra said, and Jethri could almost hear the glint in her eye, "that you feed me."

Jethri moved his hand. "You can see that Tan Sim has already thought of that."

"Indeed." She bowed, hand over heart. "Miandra Maarilex Clan Tarnia."

Seated, Tan Sim returned her bow. "Tan Sim pen'Akla Clan Rinork." He moved a hand, showing them both the laden table. "Please, join me."

Join him they did and there was a small pause in the proceedings while they each took the edge off.

"Well." Tan Sim sat back, teacup in hand. "While you and your cousin dealt kin to kin, Jeth Ree, I have performed wonders."

Jethri eyed him. "What, not marvels?"

Tan Sim waved an airy hand. "Tomorrow is soon enough for marvels. Behold my labors of today! Moon Mountain Refit Shop has been called. By the luck, the hauler was enroute to deliver scrap and other oddments at the very salvage yard where our pod awaited. They simply off-loaded their scrap, onloaded our pod and very soon now it should be in a bay at the shop. They say they will immediately perform a magnetic resonance scan. They do this to locate any hidden flaws or structural damage, so that they may adjust their entry protocol as necessary." He raised his cup and sipped, slowly, teasing, Jethri thought—and then thought of something else.

"How was it the salvager let the pod go before the transfer was made?" He asked.

Tan Sim lowered his cup, looking sheepish. "As it happens, I made the full transfer out of my account, knowing that you will place the coin for your portion in my hand."

"Such trusting ways," Jethri said, and Tan Sim sighed, holding up a hand.

"I knew you were going to say so, and I cannot but agree, that, in the normal way of things, it was an extremely foolhardy thing to do. However, I am adamant. My partner in this endeavor is a man of honor, who pays his just debts promptly."

"And so he is," Jethri said quietly, reaching into the depths of his jacket and extracting the purse containing four kais, six tor. He placed it on the table by Tan Sim's plate.

"My thanks," Tan Sim said softly, and lifted an eyebrow. "Now, may I tell you that the shop desires a call back in—" he glanced at the watch wrapped around his left wrist— "only a few minutes now. A side profit of the scanning is that it will give a rough image of the contents of the pod. When we call back, you will be able to know, with fair certainty, whether you have in fact taken an option on that reasonable return. Indeed, you may well be able to increase that reasonable return, with some judicious and well-placed announcements."

"You may tell me so," Jethri said. "But now you must tell me what you mean by it."

"I expect he means that you might upload the image to the tradenet, and invite advance bids," Miandra said, surprisingly.

Tan Sim raised his cup to her. "Precisely." He glanced at Jethri. "I can show you the way of it, if you like."

"I would very much like," Jethri assured him.

"Good." He put his teacup down and reached for the multipurpose screen. "Finish your meals, children. I will find if the shop has uploaded that image yet."

There wasn't that much to finish by then, but he and Miandra made quick work of what there was and by the time Jethri had drunk the last of his tea, Tan Sim said, "Ah!" and spun the screen around.

The image was a muddle of shape, shadow, hard edges, and glare, reminding Jethri of the relative densities screen on a piloting board. He looked up.

"Traders will bid on the strength of this image?"

"Traders," Tan Sim said, "will very often *buy* on the strength of such an image." He spun the screen so they all could see it, though Miandra had to scrunch against Jethri's side, and sort of lean her head against his chest, which was comforting and distracting at the same time.

"Attend me, now," Tan Sim said severely and Jethri obediently put his eyes on the screen, trying not to notice that Miandra's hair smelled like Lady Maarilex's favorite flowers.

"You see these, here, here, here—" He touched the screen over three of the glare spots. "Those are stasis boxes that have failed. These—" Quick finger touches on half-a-dozen bland blobs, "are stasis boxes that are still functioning as they should." He flicked a glance at Jethri.

"Already, your gains outnumber your losses."

"Depending on the contents of the boxes," Jethri pointed out. "The manifest listed ores, gems and metals. Not the sort of cargo that normally ships in stasis."

Tan Sim tipped his head. "I thought we had agreed that manifests do not always reflect cargo?"

Jethri smiled. "So we had. Please, continue."

"Very well, what else have we?" He turned his attention back to the screen, subjecting the image to frowning study. "Ah." A finger tap on a particularly muddy blur. "This, I believe, may be your ore. Were I interested in ore, I might well wish to be at hand when the pod is opened. For the rest . . ." He moved his hand, showing palm in a quick flip. "Who can tell? But there is enough possibility in the stasis boxes alone to warrant putting the image to the tradenet."

Jethri inclined his head. "I bow to the wisdom of an elder trader in this. May I impose further and ask that you teach me the way of putting an image to the tradenet?"

"Truly," Tan Sim said, round-eyed, "is this the lad I found practicing his bows in a back hallway, half-ill for fear of giving offense?"

"Who very shortly thereafter proceeded to give offense most spectacularly?" Jethri retorted.

The other trader grinned. "From which act springs both our fortunes."

"So you say." Jethri used his chin, Liaden style, to point at the screen. "How do I upload this image and invite bids?"

"Nothing simpler. First, feed your guild card to the unit."

"Already, we find difficulty. I have no guild card."

"*What?*" Tan Sim frankly stared. "Would the guild not grant you a card, after all?"

"I am at the hall in order to be certified, as apprentice, or junior trader—"

"Or master trader," Miandra put in, her head against his chest.

"Certified?" Tan Sim repeated. "But—"

"I was registered as Master ven'Deelin's apprentice," Jethri explained. "Despite that, the hall at Modrid declined to accept any of the purchases I had made on her account, because the hall master did not believe that Terrans belonged in the guild."

"Hah. The master of Modrid hall oversteps. As I am certain the ven'Deelin will demonstrate, in the fullness of time. So you tell me that you are on a hall account at the moment?"

"I have some liquid."

"Which you put into your speculation cargo, here. I see. However, matters become awkward if you lack a valid—"

"Will a Combine key do?" Jethri interrupted.

Tan Sim blinked at him. "Certainly," he said, adding delicately. "Have you a Combine key?"

"Yes." He reached inside his collar for the chain. Miandra ducked under his elbow and sat up, watching him pull the key up and then lift the chain over his head.

Tan Sim caught the key and held it in his palm, frowning at the inscription.

"A ten-year key?"

"With two trades on it—an acquisition and an assisting."

"And you are at the hall for certification?" Tan Sim raised a hasty palm. "No, do *not* tell me. I am merely a trader. The ways of the masters are too subtle for me. So." He released the key, and it swung gently at the end of the chain. "Well, then. If the young trader will do me the honor of using his key to access the Combine computer in the main bar, I will be pleased to guide him through the procedure for uploading an invitation to bid to the tradenet."

SCOUT CAPTAIN TER'ASTIN received them in Scout Hall's book cluttered common room. After tea had been called for and tasted, he inquired as to the purpose of their visit, and listened in attentive silence while Miandra recounted her tale.

"And I *cannot* go home, sir, though I know you will think me beyond the pale for saying it—and I *will not* go back to the Healers," she finished, heatedly, her hands folded tightly on her lap.

"A knotty situation," the Scout said seriously. "I am honored that you thought me worthy of advising you. Let me consider."

He picked up his teacup and sipped, Jethri and Miandra following suit, and sat for some few minutes, eyes not quite focused on the overladen bookshelf just behind Miandra's shoulder.

"I wonder," he said eventually, bringing his gaze to her face, "if you might consider going on with the evaluation, should a different master healer be found to conduct it."

Miandra's frowned, not liking the idea much—and the Scout held up a hand.

"I have in mind a particular master healer—in fact, a master healer attached to the scouts. I am able to vouch for her personally, having several times made use of her skill. I think you will find her a deft touch, with a proper respect for the perceptions of others. I have never known her to cause inadvertent suffering. As a Healer-in-training, I am sure you understand that it is not always possible to spare the patient all pain."

"I do understand that, yes," Miandra said, somewhat stiffly, to Jethri's ear. "The master healer at the hall believes that pain strengthens."

"Ah," said Captain ter'Astin. He put his hands flat on the arms of his chair and made a show of pushing himself to his feet.

"If you like," he said, extending a hand to Miandra. "I will introduce you to the lady I have in mind and the two of you may consult. Should you both agree to go forward, then Healer Hall will be notified of your whereabouts, and you may complete your evaluation while remaining here as a guest of the Scouts. Will that answer, do you think?"

Miandra hesitated and surprised Jethri by throwing him a look. He inclined his head.

"Truly, Miandra, it sounds as though the captain's solution answers all difficulties," he said, and of course right then what happened but that another possible problem jumped to the front of his brain. He looked to the scout, who inclined his head, black eyes amused.

"Healer Hall may take offense."

"No fear," Captain ter'Astin said. "I believe that my powers of diplomacy are equal to the task of explaining the matter to Healer Hall in such a way that they cannot possibly take offense."

DAY 180

Standard Year 1118
Irikwae

IT WAS A GOOD thing Raisy'd insisted on coming along, Grig thought, drinking off the last of his 'mite. A fastship was one thing, but pilots needed to sleep.

They'd done the run from Kinaveral to Irikwae straight through, manning the boards in shifts, six hours on, six hours off; 'mite and crackers at the station. He'd done many a run just that way, back when him and Arin was active on Uncle's business. 'Course, he'd been a couple hundred Standards younger then.

"Hull's cool," Raisy said. Grig sighed, spun the chair and came to his feet, pitching the cup at the wall recycler.

"Let's go, then." Raisy handed him his jacket, and he shrugged into it as he followed her down the cramped hallway. She unsealed the hatch and swung out down the ladder; Grig followed, feeling the solid thunk of the hatch resealing as a vibration in the rungs.

On the tarmac, Raisy was surveying things, hands on hips, eyes squinted.

"Nice little port," she said as Grig came up beside her. "You got an approach planned, brother?"

"Figured to check the exhibit halls and Trade Bar—boy's 'prenticed, after all. Guild oughta have a record of him and his location." He shrugged, pulling his jacket straight. "How's your Liaden, Raisy?"

"Better'n yours," she answered, which wasn't strictly true.

"Good." He paused, giving the port his own stare, and pointed. "Exhibition hall."

"Right," said Raisy. "Let's go."

HE'D FINALLY FOUND masks.

Red leather half-masks, with gilding around the eye, nose and mouth holes. Jethri accessed the detail screens and found an image. The red-and-gold reminded him of the books in the Ruby Club's public parlor, and he thought the house master might find them to be exactly what he wanted.

Trouble was, he'd have to buy at least a gross of the things, and they were dear at that level.

Grumbling to himself, he filed the information to his personal account, so he could access it from the computer in his quarters.

He'd also found depilatory, which was a far cheaper proposition at the gross level, but still more than he either wanted or needed. In fact, Meicha's work showed no signs of failing yet, so it could be that he was fixed good and proper and would never sprout another whisker. He made a mental note to ask Miandra if she could figure out what her sister'd done, the next time he saw her. Since she'd opted to have the Scout's master healer do the evaluation and report, that meant three days. They'd promised to share a meal with Captain ter'Astin on the evening of her last day of evaluation, and he was looking forward to it, anxious to hear what the tests showed—

He brought his mind ruthlessly back to the matter at hand.

It might be, he thought, pulling up the secondary detail screen, that the master of the Ruby Club *would* be willing to buy a skid, less two tubes, of depilatory. He had been interested in the masks, though, and now Jethri was interested in the masks, too, as an unexpected, and unexpectedly complex, exercise in trade.

He filed the depilatory info to his personal account, ended his session with the Combine computer and waited for his key to be returned to him.

"Ah, here is the earnest trader, in the midst of his labors," a distinctive voice said behind his shoulder. Jethri inclined his head without turning around.

"Trader sig'Lorta. How may I serve you?" The machine whirred and his key was extruded. He stood, slipping it into an inner pocket.

His mentor looked up at him. "Have you time to join me in a cup of tea, Jethri Gobelyn? I wish to discuss your progress with you."

Not that there had *been* much progress, Jethri thought, grumpily, with him on rest leave for two days. Still, when a man's mentor wanted tea and a chat, it was a good idea to have time for him.

So, he inclined his head again, murmured, "Certainly, sir," and followed the trader to a booth, where a pot and cups were already set out on the table.

"If you would do me the honor of pouring?" Trader sig'Lorta murmured, pulling the multi-use screen toward him.

Teapots were tricksy, the handles being just a bit too small to comfortably accept his hand. That aside, nobody could say that Lady Maarilex had neglected the niceties in her efforts to give him polish, no matter how many teapots it cost her.

He poured, with efficiency if not style, setting the first cup by his mentor's hand, taking the second for himself. Carefully, he replaced the pot on its warmer and composed himself to wait, cup simmering gently before him.

"Yes, here we are," murmured Trader sig'Lorta. He looked up from the screen, took his cup in hand and raised it to taste, Jethri doing the same.

Manners taken care of, the trader put his cup aside and folded his hands on the table.

"I hope," he said courteously, "that your injury no longer pains you."

"No, sir. The house doctor renewed the dressing this morning and is very pleased with the progress of healing."

"That is well, then." He moved a hand, showing Jethri the

multi-screen. "I find that you have been at trade on the days granted you to recover from your wound."

Uh-oh.

Jethri inclined his head. "Yes, sir."

"Ah." Trader sig'Lorta smiled. "You begin to demonstrate to me that you are, indeed, a trader, Jethri Gobelyn. I am further compelled by the . . . ambitiousness . . . of your offering on the tradenet. However, I am puzzled by something with regard to that, and I hope you may help me understand why I find no credit to your account, covering what I must believe to be a rather substantial cost."

"Sir, the merchandise under discussion was bought as a private speculation. Therefore, I used my own resources."

There was a small pause, then Trader sig'Lorta inclined his head.

"I see that I did not explain the process as well as I might have done," he said slowly. "In essence, any business that you conduct on port should be recorded to your file, so that the certification will reflect your actual skill level as nearly as possible. This includes private deals, side trades, and day-brokering. Have you any questions?"

So, he could have used the guild account to buy the speculation cargo, could he? Jethri sighed. Being as he had formed the intention to buy the pod's cargo to help Tan Sim out of defaulting on his contract in a way that wouldn't raise prideful Liaden hackles— maybe not.

"Thank you, sir. I had not understood that all my actions as a trader on port would be taken into balance by the master who will evaluate my file. The matter is now made plain."

"Good." Trader sig'Lorta sipped his tea, appreciatively. Setting the cup down, he reached again for the multi-use screen.

"I see that you have used your Combine key to record your offer—very good. I also see that the pod is scheduled to be opened this afternoon, so you should leave me very soon in order to be in good time. When you are returned this evening, I ask that you write a trade report of this particular transaction, and forward it to me. I will review it and enter it into your file."

Jethri inclined his head. "I will do so, sir." He hesitated. "Is there anything else I might do for you?"

"For today, I believe that will suffice." He raised his cup. "Drink your tea, Jethri Gobelyn, and may your speculation bring profit."

THE EXHIBIT HALL had a decent number of goods on display. Raisy, who'd never had any interest in that side of the business, strode right on past all the tables spread with tantalizing merchandise. Despite being wishful of locating Jethri, Grig's step slowed, his gaze darting from side to side, until Raisy retraced her steps, wrapped strong fingers around his wrist and pulled him along with her.

"I thought you wanted Jethri."

"Well, I do. But where's harm in seeing what's here and whether any of it could be had for a profit?"

She sighed gustily and dropped his arm. "Grigory, you are incorrigible."

"Maybe so—" He stopped, his eye drawn to one of the dozens of ceiling-suspended info screens. This one was only ten paces away, clearly visible over Raisy's left shoulder, and the phrase that had caught his eye—

Jethri Gobelyn.

"Raisy, turn around."

She caught the tone, and turned, cautious, checking for threats first, then put her attention on the screen, which had a resonance scan on display.

"Are you seeing what I'm seeing, brother?" Raisy breathed.

The screen changed to detail, all written out in plain Liaden, including the name of the trader-at-offer.

"*Just* like Arin!" Raisy shook her head, threw him a look over her shoulder. "I thought you said the boy didn't get his training."

"He didn't," Grig murmured, memorizing the address where the pod was due to be opened within the hour. "This has gotta be a fluke, Raisy. Boy likes salvage lots. Got a real touch with 'em. He's got a problem there, too, looks like to me."

"I saw it." She jerked her head at a sign bearing the Liaden for *Information*. "Get us a taxi?"

He nodded. "I've got the address."

WELL, THERE HADN'T BEEN any advance bidders, but there was a fair crowd waiting outside Bay Fourteen of the Moon Mountain Refit Shop—at least, according to Tan Sim it was a fair crowd. Jethri counted nine traders as they followed the shop technician to the bay door.

"An additional few moments, traders," the tech said to those gathered, as he unlocked the access hatch. "We treasure the gift of your patience."

Tan Sim ducked through the hatch, Jethri on his heels, the tech on *his* heels. Inside it was dim and a little too warm, as if the noisy air-moving unit wasn't up to the job. The pod took up most of the available floor space; half-a-dozen porta-spots took what was left. Tan Sim went against the wall to the left of the hatch, Jethri, wondering where nine more traders were going to fit in this space, to the right.

The tech kept straight on to the pod, and wrapped both hands around the emergency stick by the hatch.

"The mechanism operated correctly, if slowly, during initial testing, but it is always best to be certain in such cases that functionality has not failed." He hauled on the stick, putting his back into it.

For a heartbeat, nothing happened, then the door began, slowly, and with a long mechanical groan, to lift.

"So." The tech notched the lever down and the door sealed. "In case the internal lights are not currently operational, we have the portable spotlights available." He stood back, wiping his palms down the side of his coveralls, his eyes on the pod.

"If one of you gentlemen would admit the others, I believe we are ready."

Tan Sim waved Jethri toward the pod and pushed the access hatch wide.

"Please, traders! Enter and be welcome!"

Jethri scooped up one of the portables and stepped to the side of the hatch opposite the tech.

The bay was rapidly filling, with traders and the voices of traders—rather more traders, Jethri thought, than the nine he had counted only a few moments before. A pair of taller shadows at the back of the crowd drew his eye—

"Business of the Scouts!" the unmistakable voice of Scout Captain Jan Rek ter'Astin rang out—and there was the captain himself, flanked by two women in the uniform of the Irikwae Port Proctors, striding briskly forward. The attending traders scrunched close to the walls, giving them a clear course to Jethri. He caught a glimpse of Tan Sim, gridlocked by the now-silent crowd.

The Scout and his proctors settled into position to the left of Jethri, between the hatch and the attending traders. Jethri inclined his head.

"Have you come to arrest me, sir?" He asked, for the Scout's ears alone, not certain himself if he was joking.

Black eyes met his firmly. "That will depend on a number of things, young Jethri. And the sooner the hatch is opened, the sooner we will both know what duty demands."

Right. Jethri looked to the tech, who stood motionless, his hands around the emergency lever. He took a breath, held it, breathed, slowly, out.

"Technician," he said, loud enough to be heard to the back of the bay, "please open the hatch."

"Trader," the man murmured, and hauled down on the stick.

The hatch hesitated, and rose, moaning all the way to the top. Inside, lights flickered, and failed. Jethri pressed the switch on the porta-spot.

The beam flared, illuminating the inside of the pod with harsh blue light. Shapes leapt into being, sharply outlined. A busted stasis box, canted on its side, a large shape that reminded Jethri of the weather machine, built a hundred times bigger, another—

"Technician, close the hatch!" Captain ter'Astin ordered. "Proctors, clear the room."

The proctors turned as one and moved toward the crowd, hands making long, sweeping motions. Jethri pressed the switch on the porta-spot, killing the glare.

"Of your goodness," said the proctor on the right, "please leave the room. Business of the Scouts."

"Move along," said the one on the left, "there is nothing here for you to see. Business of the Scouts."

Inexorably, the traders were swept back toward the door. Tan Sim held his ground, creating an eddy in the flow of departing traders. The proctor on the right paused, and moved her hands sharply.

"Please, sir. We are clearing the area. There is no business here for you."

"There is business," Tan Sim said, sounding a bit breathless, but calm. "Yon trader is my partner in this matter—and that is my pod."

"That trader may remain, proctors," Captain ter'Astin said over his shoulder. He inclined his head to the technician. "Sir, you are required elsewhere."

The tech bowed, hastily— "Scout" —and was gone, not quite running, pushing past Tan Sim, who was striding forward. The tech darted between the proctors and vanished out the hatch. The proctors continued their sweep. Jethri bent to put the porta-spot down.

"Jethri!"

He snapped upright and spun, staring down the dim hall to find the proctors confronting two tall people and one of them was—

"Grig!" He spun back to the Scout.

"That man is my kin!"

The Scout's eyebrows rose. "Indeed. So we will be playing with the Liaden deck? You do trade bold, young Jethri." He raised his voice. "Proctors, those traders may remain, as well. Secure the door."

"Not a Liaden deck," Jethri said. "A human deck. In Terran, he's my shipmate."

The Scout tipped his head to one side. "I believe I begin to understand the scope of Norn's project. So—" He flicked his gaze to Tan Sim.

"Trader pen'Akla, I am Scout Captain Jan Rek ter'Astin."

"Sir," Tan Sim said stiffly. "I will be interested to learn what business Scouts have in interrupting the trading day."

Captain ter'Astin smoothed the air between them with a gentle palm. "Peace. Every matter in its time."

The confusion near the access hatch had sorted itself out and Grig was taking long strides forward, followed by a woman who looked familiar, though Jethri was sure he'd never seen her before.

"You OK, Jeth?" Grig reached out and grabbed his shoulder, squeezing, hard and comforting.

"I'm fine," Jethri said, though it took him a stupidly long time to get the Terran to his mouth. He glanced over Grig's shoulder at the woman. She smiled at him and nodded, agreeable-like. Grig turned, letting go of Jethri's shoulder.

"Don't tell me you're shy, now," he said to her. "Come up here and tell Jethri 'hey'."

She took a couple steps and came even with Grig. "Hey, Jethri," she said, her voice deep and pleasant. "I'm Grig's sister, Raisana." She held out a hand. "Call me Raisy."

He took her hand and squeezed her fingers lightly. "Raisy. I'm glad to meet you," he said, thinking that he'd never heard Grig mention a sister, but for all of that, they sure did—

"That's it," he said, the Terran coming a little *too* quick, now. "Couldn't place why you seemed familiar. You look like Grig, is why."

"Indeed," Scout Captain ter'Astin said, in his mud-based Terran. "It is a remarkable likeness, even for fraternal twins." He paused, head tipped to a side. "You *are* twins, are you not?"

Grig shrugged. "Raisy's older'n me," he said, eyeing the Scout's leathers. "Field Scout, are you?"

Captain ter'Astin bowed, hand over heart.

"Grig," Jethri said, quick, before his cousin thought of another way to provoke sarcasm out of the Scout. "What're you doin' here? Where's Seeli? How's Khat? Uncle Paitor—"

Grig held up a hand, showing palm. "Easy. Easy. Everybody's fine. You'll want to know that Seeli's increasing. She sends her love. Khat sends hers, too. Paitor tells me to tell you stay outta trouble, but I got a feeling he's too late with that one."

"I think he might be," Jethri said, suddenly and grimly recalled to the looming loss of six kais-six. He turned to glare at Captain ter'Astin, who raised an eyebrow and made a show of displaying empty palms.

"Tell me you did not know that this pod was filled with Old Technology, Jethri Gobelyn."

"He did not," said Tan Sim, speaking Terran as if it were Liaden, only much slower. He used his chin to point at the pod. "I find pod. I find manifest. Ore. Art metal. Jewels." He paused, bruised face showing grim. "I buy pod. Jeth Ree buys contents. Partners, we are."

"I see," said the Scout. "And neither one of you had the skill to read the image and deduce the presence of Old Technology?"

"Prolly neither one did," Grig said, matter of factly. "If the paper said ore, they'd've naturally thought the spot that caught my attention—and Raisy's—was ore. 'Course, I expect us three," he continued to the Scout's speculative eyes, "seen a lot more Old Tech than either of the youngers, there. You gonna get a blanket over that, by the way? 'Cause, if you're not, I'll beg your pardon, but me, my sister, our cousin and our cousin's partner have an urgent need to lift ship."

"As unstable as that?" Captain ter'Astin pulled a comm from his belt and thumbed it on. "ter'Astin. Dispatch a team and a containment field to Moon Mountain Refit Shop. Level three." He thumbed the device off and slipped it away.

"'preciate it," Grig said, giving him a nod. He looked to Jethri. "You seen them distortions in the scan you uploaded—kinda cloudy and diffuse?"

"Yes," Jethri and Tan Sim said in unison.

"Right. That's fractin sign. Non-industrial quantities of timonium being released as the tech degrades. Now, that blob—it does look convincing for ore, and the ghosts of space know I'd've been tempted to read it that way myself, if I was holding a paper that said ore. But what it is—it's one of the bigger pieces going unstable, releasing more timonium—and then more. That's why we gotta get a blanket over it right now. If it goes without being contained, it could leave a sizeable hole in this planet."

"Is that fact or fancy?" asked the Scout.

Grig looked at him. "Well, now, I'd say fact. My sister, there, she'd argue the point. You want to open the hatch, and we'll take a look at what else you got in there?"

"An interesting proposition," said Captain ter'Astin. "I wonder why I should."

"Grig an' me're the closest you're going to find to experts on the Old Tech," Raisy said, surprisingly. "There's better, mind you, but I don't think Uncle'd be much interested in talking with you—no offense intended.

"Now, me, I'd ask day rate, if we was gonna do the thing right and clear the stuff for you. But a quick looksee—" She shrugged. "I'm curious. Grig's curious. The boys here are curious—and you're curious. Where's the harm?"

"A compelling argument, I allow." The Scout stepped forward, grabbed the emergency stick with one hand and hauled it down.

The hatch rose, screaming in agony. Tan Sim swept forward and came up with Jethri's portable, blue-white beam aimed inside.

"All right." The five of them stepped close, staring into the depths of the pod.

"That big one over against the far wall," Raisy said. "That'll be your unstable. Look at all the busted stasis boxes around it." She shook her head.

"Now, *that* one," Grig said, pointing to a device that looked peculiarly coffin-like. "That one I'd recommend you hold for study. I don't say it ain't treacherous. All Befores are treacherous. But that particular one can heal terrible wounds."

The Scout looked at him. "How do you know that?"

"Well, now, that's a story. Happens our point man had made a lucky guess or he really *could* read some of them pages from 'way back, like he claimed. No matter the how of it, we had the location of a significant cache. Biggest any of us, 'cept Arin an' maybe Uncle, had ever seen. Trouble is, we was about a half-Jump ahead of a couple field Scouts who'd taken it into their heads that this particular world I'm talking about was interdicted an' so we needed to work fast." He shook his head.

"That meant we had to use every pair of hands we could get,

whether they was attached to a trained brain or not. Which is how we happened to have the kid doing his own packing. Now, he'd been told over and over not to just turn the Befores on, or ask them to do things, or think about them doing things, or listen to them, if they started to talk in the space between his ears where his brain ought've been. He'd *been* told, but he was a kid, and a slow learner, besides."

"So he picked up a piece of the Old Tech and it killed him," the Scout said, softly.

"Good guess," Raisy said. "But it didn't kill him—though no question he'd've died of the damage. Chewed his left hand to bits, fingertips to elbow. Happened so fast, he didn't have time to scream, did so much damage, he dropped into shock. It was Arin who shoved him in the—we call 'em duplicating units. Don't know what gave him the idea it'd do a bit of good, but as it turned out, it was the best thing he could've done.

"By the time we'd gotten everything else loaded, the machine chimed, lid popped and there was the kid, a little groggy, with two good hands on him and not a drop of blood on his coveralls."

Scout Captain ter'Astin frankly stared. "It regenerated the hand and arm?"

"Good as new," Grig said. "Never given me a day's worth o'trouble. Though here's a funny thing." He held his hands up, palms out toward the Scout. "The fingerprints on the left hand're the same as the fingerprints on the right, just reversed." He flexed his fingers and let both hands drop to his side. "Works fine, though."

"So I see. A most fortunate circumstance."

"Nothing fortunate about it. Arin told us later he'd read that the duplicating machines could do more than what we'd been using them for. He really could read them old pages—you ever seen any? Metal, but soft and flexible, like paper, with the characters etched in, permanent."

"There are one or two specimens at Headquarters," the Scout said. "Though I admit that deciphering them has thus far proven beyond our ability. Arin Gobelyn was an exceptional man."

"Well, he'd been at it a long time," Grig said, with the air of one being fair. "He'd had a key, but I'm thinking that got spaced early, right after Iza come back from identifying the body."

"Or he may have left an abbreviated form of it in the book he had made for his heir."

"What!" Jethri squawked, shaken out of a state of blank amazement. "My journal?"

Scout Captain ter'Astin turned stern black eyes upon him. "Indeed. Your journal. You say you did not know it?"

"There were some odd—" He stopped, seeing the pages in memory; his kid notes and next to them, the various weird squiggles of his father's doodling . . .

"Not until this minute did I realize, sir," he said, unconsciously dropping into Liaden. "Truly, as I had told you, I had been without the book and other remembrances of my father for many years, having only recently been reunited with them."

"Boy didn't get his training," Grig said softly. "Arin died too soon."

"You didn't train him?" the Scout asked. Grig shook his head.

"If Iza—his mam, you understand—had even thought I was, the boy was forfeit—me, too, more than sure, though Raisy'll tell you that's no loss."

"No such thing," she said, stoutly.

"Ah," said the Scout. "I wonder, this planet where you were a half-Jump ahead of a pair of field Scouts intent upon enforcing the interdiction—would that have been in the Nafrey Sector?"

Grig and Raisy exchanged a glance.

"Stuff's long gone," Grig said.

"True," Raisy answered. She nodded to the Scout. "You got a good mind for detail."

"I thank you. And you, if I may say so, are a great deal older than you look."

"That's because we got hold of some duplicating machines early," Raisy said, "and kept on reproducing the pure stock. We breed, like Grig here gone and done, the very next generation goes back to default."

"That's what was driving Arin to find out how to manufacture good fractins," Grig said. "The machines are going unstable, and he wanted his boy to be able to continue the line."

The Scout inclined his head. "I understand. However, the Old Technology is forbidden."

Jethri cleared his throat. Four pair of eyes turned to him, Tan Sim's looking more bewildered than anything else.

"I'm a—clone?" he asked, very calmly. He used his chin to point at the machine Grig had recommended for study. "I was born from one of those?"

"Almost," said Grig. "I'm sorry to tell you that Arin wasn't entirely straight with Iza, Jeth. I'll give you the details when we're private." He looked at the Scout. "Family business."

The Scout bowed.

"Captain ter'Astin?" A voice inquired. They all turned.

Four Scouts stood in the cramped bay behind them, equipment packs on their backs. The lead Scout saluted. "Containment Unit reporting, sir."

"Good." The Scout waved his hand at the big piece Raisy had identified as unstable. "There is your target. We will remove ourselves until the containment is complete. After . . ." He considered Grig and Raisy thoughtfully.

"After, I believe I would like to pay the pair of you day-rate, and sit at your feet while you *clear* the Old Technology in this pod."

Raisy shrugged. "All right by me." She sent a look and a grin to Jethri, who couldn't help but grin back. "We're fast, cousin. Couple days from now, the only thing you'll have to worry you is how to profitably place what's left."

DAY 185

※ ※

Standard Year 1118
Irikwae

AFTER THE BEFORES were cleared and cleared out, and the broken stasis boxes sold for scrap, there'd been enough in the contents of the good boxes to return the initial investment, and one kais, three for profit.

"Not a large profit," Trader sig'Lorta commented, appending the information to Jethri's file.

"True," he'd replied. "However, if the coin had stayed in my pocket, I would have realized no profit at all."

His mentor glanced up, gray eyes amused. "The trade is in your bones, Jethri Gobelyn."

In between his assignments for the hall, and their work with the Scout, he spent time with Grig, sometimes with Raisy, though most often not. Family business, family secrets—he was clear he wasn't gettin' it all. Not even close to it all. No need, really.

As Grig said, "You ain't Arin. No need for an Arin now, if there ever was, with the machines going into unstable—but you're worried about the other. And you *ain't* Arin, Jeth, no more'n I'm Raisy. We're each our own self, give or take a shared gene-set. Like identical twins, if you know any.

"I will say Arin'd be proud of the way you're going about setting yourself up, building your credentials and associations. He *would* be proud if he was here for it—just like I'm proud. But—here's another secret for you—he'd've never gone at it like you done. Arin was smart about lots of things, but human hearts wasn't among 'em. I'm thinkin' it'll prove that your way's the better one."

"What was he trying to do with the fractins?" Jethri'd asked. "Remember how we built the patterns, an'—"

"Right." Grig nodded. "Remember what I told you? How all the fractins was dying at once? Duplicating units are powered by fractins, same as your weather maker, and that tutoring stick went bad on you in the exhibit hall. Arin, he had this theory, that if you put fractins together in certain ways—certain patterns—they'd know—and could do—some interesting things. So, he—"

"*WildeToad*," Jethri whispered, and Grig shot him a Look.

"What do you think you know about *Toad*, Jeth?"

"Nothing more than what's on the sheet of printout my father used to shim my nameplate," he said. "*Breaking clay*, it said. *Arming* and *going down*. If the clay was fractins, arranged in a certain pattern . . ."

"Then you got most of it," Grig interrupted. "Arin'd worked out what he figured to be an auxiliary piloting computer. *Toad's* captain agreed to give it a test run. Looked good, at first, the fractin-brain merged in with ship's comp. What they didn't figure on was ship's comp getting overridden by the fractins. Suddenly *Toad* was out of the control of her crew. Captain's key was worse than useless. The fractin-brain, it locked in a set of coordinates nobody'd ever seen, and started the sequence to arm the cannons . . ."

"They broke the fractins, but they still didn't get the ship back," Jethri said, guessing. "So, they crashed it, rather than risk whatever had their comp getting loose."

Grig sighed. "Near enough." He paused, then said, real quiet.

"It was a bad business. So bad Arin stopped trying to figure out the thinking patterns—for awhile. But he had to go back to it, Jeth. See, he was trying to find the pattern that would produce the fractin-brain that would tell him how to make more fractins."

He leaned forward to put his hand on Jethri's arm.

"You listen to me, Jethri, if you forget everything else I ever told you. Befores, Old Tech, whatever you want to call it—*you can't trust it.* Nobody knows what they'll do—and sometimes it's worth your life to find out." He sat back with a tired grin. "And that was *before* they started to go unstable."

Jethri glanced down at his palm, the burn nothing more now than a broad red scar.

"I'll remember," he promised.

Eventually, they come around to the reason Grig and Raisy were on Irikwae at all.

"He said *what*?" Jethri demanded. "The trader who bought the pod—my partner?"

They nodded.

"That trader," Jethri said, "is the brother chel'Gaibin claims to be *deprived of.* He's pushing a false claim against people who aren't tied by the, the Code." He took a hard breath, and inclined his head. "Thank you," he said, dropping into Liaden for the proper phrasing. "Please be assured that this matter will be brought into proper Balance."

"All right. Now, I gotta ask you, for Seeli: You sure you're OK? 'Cause if you need a ship, Seeli says you got the *Market* to call on— and she'll deal with Iza."

Jethri felt tears rise up and blinked them away. "Tell her—the offer means a lot to me, but I've got a ship, and a crew, and a— course that I'm wanting to see the end of."

Grig smiled, and sent a glance to his sister. "Boy's got it under control, Raisy. We can lift on that news."

And by the next morning, they had.

"WHAT ARE THOSE?" Miandra asked, as he placed the wire frame and the boxes of fractins, true and false, before Scout Captain ter'Astin. They were once again in the common room of the Scout hall, sharing a pre-dinner glass of wine to celebrate Miandra's completion of her evaluation.

"Fractins," Jethri said, and, when she gave him a perfectly blank stare. "Old Technology. Put enough fractins together in the right order and you have—a computer. Only different."

"And dangerous," she added.

"Sometimes," he said, thinking of the healing unit. He met Captain ter'Astin's eyes, and moved his shoulders. "Usually." He reached into one of his inner pockets, his fingers touched the familiar, comforting shape. His lucky fractin. With a sigh, he brought it out and placed it on the table.

"Ah," the Scout said. "I do thank you for these, young Jethri, and appreciate your display of goodwill. I wonder, however, about the journal."

Jethri bowed, slightly. "The journal is not Old Technology, sir. The contents of the journal are of no use to the Scouts and of much sentimental value to me."

"I see." The Scout glanced down at the table and its burden. "I suggest a compromise. You will place the book in my custody. I will cause it to be copied, whereupon the original will be returned to you. I give you my word that all will be accomplished within the space of one day." He looked up, black eyes bright. "Is this acceptable?"

"Sir, it is."

"Spoken like a true son of a High House! Come now, let us put business and duty both behind us and drink to Lady Miandra's very good health!"

The wine being poured, they did that, and Jethri turned to Miandra.

"What was the outcome?" he asked. "Are you dramliza, or Healer?"

She sipped her wine. "Dramliza, though untrained in the extreme. I am offered a teacher upon Liad itself. If Aunt Stafeli agrees, the thing is done."

"Oh." Jethri lowered his glass.

"What's amiss?"

He moved his shoulders. "Truly—it is all that you hoped for—and I share your joy. It is just that—I will miss you."

Miandra stared—and then her laugh pealed.

"I have missed the joke, I fear," he said, a little hurt. She leaned forward to put her hand on his sleeve.

"Jethri—cousin. You are to leave very soon, yourself. Do you recall it? Norn ven'Deelin? *Elthoria*? The wide star trade?"

He blinked, and blushed, and laughed a little himself. "I had forgotten," he admitted. "But I will still miss you."

Miandra had recourse to her wine, eyes dancing.

"Never fear! I will certainly remain long enough to dance at your age-coming ball!"

"When does Norn come to port?" the Scout asked, sipping his own wine.

It took a moment to remember the date. "Day three-three-one."

"Ah," the Scout moved his shoulders. "A pity. I will have gone by then."

"Back to Kailipso, sir?"

"No, thank the gods. I have been given a new assignment, which may prove . . . interesting." He put his glass next to Jethri's lucky fractin.

"I have reserved our table for the top of the hour. We will stop at the desk to ask that someone from the proper unit come to collect those. Then, if you will accompany me, we may proceed to the restaurant. I believe it is a lovely evening for a stroll."

DAY 189

Standard Year 1118
Irikwae

THE ALARM RANG 'way too early. Jethri pitched out of bed and headed for the shower before his eyes were properly open, emerging some few minutes later, eyes open, hair damp. He pulled on trousers, boots and shirt and, still sealing that last garment, walked over to the computer to discover the instructions that would shape his day.

He was to meet Tam Sin for luncheon—a last agreeable meal before aged *Genchi*, now embracing a third pod, lifted. Besides that, there was a certain odd lot he wanted to have a look at, over—

Red letters blinked urgently on his screen, alerting him to a serious scheduling change. He touched a key and the day-sheet snapped into being, the new item limned in red.

Jethri swallowed a curse. He was to meet with the master trader in charge of evaluating his file in the hall master's office in—he threw a glance at the clock—now.

"Blast!"

He snatched his best trading coat off the hook and ran.

OUTSIDE THE HALL master's office, he did take a moment to catch his breath, pull his jacket straight, and run quick, combing fingers through his hair. One more deep breath, and he leaned to the annunciator.

"Jethri Gobelyn," he said, clearly.

The door chimed. He put his hand on the latch and let himself in.

The office had the too-tidy look of a place that had been out of use for a time. The desk top was bare, and slightly dusty; the books lined up, all orderly, in their shelves. Two chairs and a low table made a pleasant grouping by the window. A portable comp and a tray holding two glasses and a bottle of wine bearing the Maarilex Reserve label sat at the center of the table.

But for himself, the room was empty, though the wine and the comp indicated that he could expect the master trader soon.

Taking a deep breath to center himself, Jethri moved to the bookshelves, and brought his attention to the titles.

He had just discovered that Hall Master yos'Arimyst had an interesting half-a-dozen novels shelved among his volumes of Guild rule and trade regs, when the door chimed and opened.

Turning, he began his bow—and checked.

"Master ven'Deelin?"

She raised her eyebrows, black eyes amused. "Such astonishment. Do I not wear the amethyst?"

"Indeed you do, ma'am," he said, bowing the bow of affectionate esteem. "It is only that one's mentor has been at pains to let me know that my file will be evaluated by an impartial master."

"As if there were ever such a thing—or could be." She paused and looked him up and down, her hands tucked into her belt.

"You look well, my son. Irikwae suits you, I think."

"I have learned much here, mother."

"Hah." Her eyes gleamed. "So it seems." She moved a hand, inviting him to walk with her to the pleasant grouping of chairs and table. "Come, let us sit and be comfortable. Open and pour for us, if you will, while I consult the notes left by the evaluating master."

He opened and poured, and settled into the chair across from her. She sat for a moment or two longer, perusing her screen, then sat back with a sigh.

"Yes, precisely did he say, when I met him just now in the Trade Bar," she murmured, and reached for her glass, lifting it in a toast, Jethri following.

"To Jethri Gobelyn, junior trader."

He sipped—a small sip, since his stomach suddenly felt like it didn't know how to behave.

"Truly, ma'am?"

"What question is this?" She slipped a card out of her sleeve. "Honor me with your opinion of this."

He received it, fingers tracing the Guild sigil on the obverse. On the front, there was his name, and *junior trader*, right enough, and the silver gleam of the datastrip that held the records of his transactions thus far.

"I find it a handsome card, ma'am."

"Then there is no more to be said—it is yours."

One more long look and then he slipped it away, into the same inner pocket that held his Combine key.

"You do well, my child. I am pleased. We will need to talk, you and I, to discover whether you wish to continue an association with *Elthoria*, now that you are a trader in your own name. First, however, I must bring you news of chel'Gaibin, which I fear and trust will not delight you."

He held up a hand. "If this has to do with Trader chel'Gaibin's attack upon my kinswoman on Banthport, ma'am, I have had that tale already."

"Have you indeed? May one ask?"

"My cousins Grig and Raisy found the incident so alarming that they came to me here on Irikwae, to inform me of my need for vigilance."

"All honor to them." Master ven'Deelin sipped her wine. "I have invoked a Guild inquiry, which will hold chel'Gaibin this next while. That he claims false Balance—that is a matter for the Council, and is not a matter that you must or may take under your own *melant'i*. Am I understood in this?"

"Ma'am, you are." He inclined his head. "Grig asked me to tell you, ma'am, that you should consider, not what Banth has, but where it is."

She paused with her glass half-way to her lips. "So. You have remarkable kin, young Jethri. I know nothing but admiration for them. I will consider, as he has suggested."

She flicked her fingers toward the comp. "I learn here that you partnered with young pen'Akla in the pod deal. How did you find that?"

"Well enough," Jethri said carefully. He put his glass down and sat forward, elbows on knees. "Ma'am, might you buy his contract?"

"Ixin, buy the contract of one of Rinork? chel'Gaibin will cry Balance in truth!"

Right.

"I had not considered," he confessed. "Then I—wonder if you will advise me."

She considered him. "Now, this has the promise of a diversion. Of course I will advise you, my son. Only tell me what troubles you."

"I find myself plumper in purse than I had anticipated," he said, slowly. "And it came to me that a good use of my resources might be to invest in—a trader."

Master ven'Deelin tipped her head to one side. "Invest in a trader, young Jethri?"

"Indeed, ma'am. Suppose I were to buy the contract of a full trader. Not only would I, a junior, have the opportunity to learn from him, my elder in trade, but as owner of his contract, a percentage of each trade he made would be credited to—"

"Your guild card." She raised her hand. "Enough."

Jethri sat back, watching her as she sipped her wine, eyes closed.

"It only amazes me," she said eventually, "that no one has thought of this before. Truly, young Jethri, you have a gift." She opened her eyes.

"You will now tell me if this notion of yours was serious, or merely brought forward to plague me."

"Ma'am, you know I would never deliberately plague you—"

"Pah!"

"But, I *had* considered buying Trader pen'Akla's contract, so that he might find a ship and a route that will value him, to their mutual profit." He opened his hands, palm up, showing empty.

"I do quite see that such an arrangement would be—questionable, at best. But, if *Elthoria* bought his contract—" He leaned forward again, hands cupped, as if he held a rare treasure.

"Ma'am, allow me to present Tan Sim pen'Akla to you as a young trader of heart, imagination and energy. His *melant'i* is unimpeachable. He speaks Terran, he honors guild rule, and—" He swallowed, keeping his eyes on hers. "And if he continues on that route, ma'am, it will break his heart and suck his spirit dry."

Silence. Jethri forced himself to sit back, to pick up his wine glass—

"You make a compelling case," Master ven'Deelin said softly. "I will speak to young pen'Akla."

Seated, he bowed, as deeply as he was able. "Thank you, ma'am."

"Such drama. So, while we are making dispositions of traders and contracts—what is your wish, Junior Trader Gobelyn? Shall you write contract with *Elthoria*, or has another ship caught your eye?"

Another ship? Jethri inclined his head.

"Ma'am, of course I wish to stay with *Elthoria*, and sit at the feet of her master trader. I have—much yet to learn."

"Yes," said Master ven'Deelin, smiling. "And so have I."

LIADEN/TERRAN
DICTIONARY

Liaden/Terran Dictionary

Aelantaza: A specially bred human

Aetherium: A folded-space confinement area

A'nadelm: Heir to the nadelm

A'thodelm: Head-of-Line-to-Be

A'trezla: Lifemates

Al'bresh venat'i: Formal phrase of sorrow for another Clan's loss, as when someone dies

Al'kin Chernard'i: The Day Without Delight

Balent'i Kalandon: Our local galaxy

Balent'i tru'vad: The starweb of all creation

Batch: Humans made to order

Batcher: An individual grown as part of a Batch

Bounty hunters: Hunters, also charity agents

Candesa: A vapor which, enclosed and compressed, emits a cloudy white light, at once too bright and hard to see by

Carolis: Next coin down from qwint

Cha'leket: Heartkin (heartbrother, heartsister)

Cha'trez: Heartsong

Chernubia: Confected delicacy

Chiat'a bei kruzon: Dream sweetly

Ckrakec: (derived from the Yxtrang) Approx. "Master Hunter"

Coab minshak'a: "Necessity exists"

Coderoy: Tough fabric from which soldier kit packs are constructed

Confusion: A card game

Conselem: An absurdity

Delm: Head of Clan (Delm Korval, Korval Himself/Herself)

Delmae: Lifemate to the Delm

Demi-qwint: Small change

Denubia: Darling

Dramliza: A wizard; PLURAL: dramliz

Dri'at: Left

Dueling stick: A cross between a cattle prod and a stave

Edonai: Roughly, "My Lord" when speaking to an Iloheen

Eklykt'i: Unreturned

Eldema: First Speaker (most times, the delm)

Eldema-pernard'i: First-Speaker-In-Trust

Entranzia volecta: Good greetings (High Liaden)

Fastflame: Chemical fire that dies out after it consumes its own fuel

Fa'vya: An aphrodisiac-laced wine sold at Festival

Flan: Next coin up from qwint

Flaran Cha'menthi: "I(/We) Dare"

Galandaria: Confederate? Countryperson?

Ge'shada: Mazel tov, congratulations

Galunus, two-headed: A mythic creature of loathsome aspect and third-rate thought process

Glavda Empri: yo'Lanna's house

I'ganin brath'a, vyan se'untor: Play with the body, rest the mind

I'lanta: Right

Ilania frrogudon palon dox: Approx. young ladies should speak more gently

Illanga kilachi: (no translation available)

Iloheen: Sheriekes

Iloheen-bailed: Roughly, "Lord of Space and Matter"

Indra: Uncle

Jelaza Kazone: The Tree, also Korval's Own House. Approx. "Jela's Fulfillment"

Lazenia spandok: Son of a bitch (REAL approximate)

Lisamia keshoc: Thank you (Low Liaden)

Jumping-jack(s), also 'jack(s): Cheap rooms for rent

Kalfer Shimni: Really expensive wiskey

Kenake: Roughly, "Foreigner," "person without couth or shoes," "Flatlander"

Level One shielding: Lowest level energy shield

Logic tile: The smallest component of a computational device

Lumenpaint: Paint that lights itself up

Master of Unmaking: The Iloheen

Megelaar: The Dragon on Korval's shield

Melant'i: Who one is in relation to current circumstances; also who one is in sum, encompassing all possible persons one might be

Menfri'at: Liaden karate

Mirada: Father

Misravot: Altanian wine; blue in color

Nadelm: Delm-to-Be

Nubiath'a: Gift given to end an affair of pleasure

OS-633: Overhead Shields Series 633

Palesci modassa: Thank you (High Liaden)

Prena'ma: Storyteller

Prethliu: Rumorbroker

Phantom lover: A punishment device

Pilot's Undernet: Pilot information network

Pin-laser: Sneak weapon

Pod: A Batch

Qe'andra: Man of business

Qua'lechi: Exclamation of horror

Qwint: Coin

Relumma: Division of a Liaden year, equaling 96 Standard days
Four relumma equal one year

Sadiline: A gemstone

SATA: Spiral Arm Trade Association

Ser: "Sir", "Mr."

Sheriekas: The Enemy

Skileti: Naturally occurring lycra

'Skins: protective suit for pilot wear on-planet

Smaly Tube: Used to move pallets from the port
to wharehouses within the city

Smartstrands: Computational media

Smartwire: Binding wire

Starsilk: Expensive fabric

Tanjalyre Institute: A school for aelantaza

Telomite: Rock, for carving

Tempo: A drug that increases mental acuity and reduces
the need to sleep, for a while.

Thawla: Mother (Low Liaden; approx. Mommy)

Thawlana: Grandmother

Thodelm: Head of Line

Tra'sia volecta: Good morning (Low Liaden)

Trealla Fantrol: The yos'Galan house

Truth-blade: A scholar's instrument of proof

Undertrade: black market, specifically trade with the sheriekas

Valcon Berant'a: Dragon's Price or Dragon Hoard, the name of Korval's valley

Valcon Melad'a: Dragon's Way, the Delm's Own ship

van'chela: beloved friend

va'netra: charity case, lame puppy

Viezy hide: Tanned hide of an extremely rare and poisonous reptile

World-eaters: Sheriekas doomsday machines

Zaliata: Energy creatures

zerlam'ka: kinslayer